BARBARA TAYLOR BRADFORD

THREE COMPLETE NOVELS

Hold the Dream
To Be the Best
Act of Will

BARBARA TAYLOR BRADFORD

THREE COMPLETE NOVELS

Hold the Dream
To Be the Best
Act of Will

WINGS BOOKS

New York · Avenel, New Jersey

This 1992 edition is published by Wings Books, distributed by Outlet Book Company, a Random House Company, 40 Engelhard Avenue, Avenel, New Jersey, 07001, by arrangement with Bantam Doubleday Dell Publishing Group.

Printed and bound in the United States of America

Library of Congress Cataloging-in-Publication Data

Bradford, Barbara Taylor, 1933–
   [Novels.   Selections]
   Barbara Taylor Bradford : three complete novels.
      p.   cm.
   Contents: Hold the dream — To be the best — Act of will.
   ISBN 0-517-08470-8
   I. Title. II. Title: Three complete novels.
PS3552.R2147B3   1992
813′.54—dc20   92-19641
                                     CIP

8 7 6 5 4 3 2 1

New York · Toronto · London · Sydney · Auckland

CONTENTS

Hold the Dream
1

To Be the Best
473

Act of Will
763

Hold
the
Dream

For Bob—who makes everything possible
for me, with my love.

CONTENTS

———— ✑ ————

Book One   *Matriarch*   11

Book Two   *Heiress*   197

Book Three   *Tycoon*   395

FAMILY

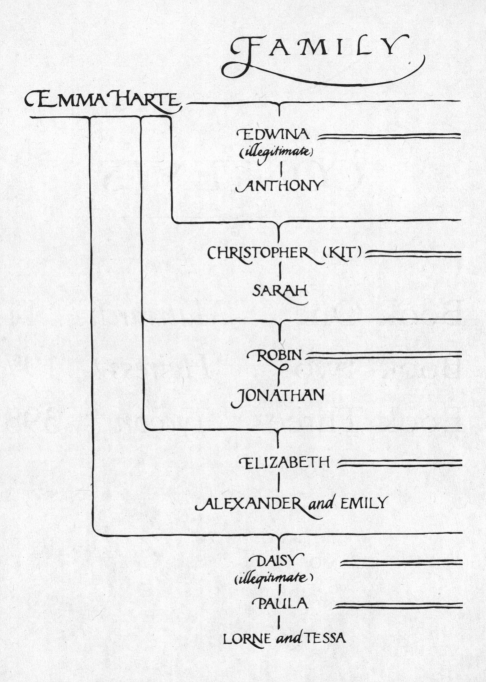

EMMA HARTE

EDWINA
(illegitimate)

ANTHONY

CHRISTOPHER (KIT)

SARAH

ROBIN

JONATHAN

ELIZABETH

ALEXANDER *and* EMILY

DAISY
(illegitimate)

PAULA

LORNE *and* TESSA

TREE

EDWIN FAIRLEY

JEREMY, *EARL* OF DUNVALE

JOE LOWTHER
(first husband)

JUNE ROWE

ARTHUR AINSLEY
(second husband)

VALERIE LUDDEN

TONY BARKSTONE ═══ DEREK LINDE

AMANDA *and* FRANCESCA

PAUL McGILL

DAVID AMORY

JAMES ARTHUR FAIRLEY   PHILIP

She possessed, in the highest degree, all the qualities
which were required in a great Prince.
                    Giovanni Scaramelli,
                    Venetian Ambassador
                    to the Court of Elizabeth Tudor,
                    Queen of England

I would have you know that this kingdom of mine
is not so scant of men but there be a rogue or two
among them.

                              Elizabeth Tudor,
                              Queen of England

BOOK ONE

Matriarch

I speak the truth, not so much as I would, but as much as I dare; and I dare a little more, as I grow older.

Montaigne

One

Emma Harte was almost eighty years old.

She did not look it, for she had always carried her years lightly. Certainly Emma felt like a much younger woman as she sat at her desk in the upstairs parlor of Pennistone Royal on this bright April morning of 1969.

Her posture was erect in the chair, and her alert green eyes, wise and shrewd under the wrinkled lids, missed nothing. The burnished red-gold hair had turned to shining silver long ago, but it was impeccably coiffed in the latest style, and the widow's peak was as dramatic as ever above her oval face. If this was now lined and scored by the years, her excellent bone structure had retained its clarity and her skin held the translucency of her youth. And so, though her great beauty had been blurred by the passage of time, she was still arresting, and her appearance, as always, was stylish.

For the busy working day stretching ahead of her, she had chosen to wear a wool dress of tailored simplicity in the powder-blue shade she so often favored, which was so flattering to her. A frothy white lace collar added just the right touch of softness and femininity at her throat, and there were discreet diamond studs on her ears. Otherwise she wore no jewelry except for a gold watch and her rings.

After her bout with bronchial pneumonia the previous year, she was in blooming health, had no infirmities to speak of, and was filled with the restless vigor and drive that had marked her younger days.

That's my problem, not knowing where to direct all this damned energy, she mused, putting down her pen, leaning back in the chair. She smiled and thought: The devil usually finds work for idle hands, so I'd *better* come up with a new project soon before I get into mischief. Her smile widened. Most people thought she had more than enough to keep her fully occupied, since she continued to control her vast business enterprises which stretched halfway around the world. Indeed they did need her constant supervision; yet for the most part they offered her little challenge these days. Emma had always thrived on challenge, and it was this she sorely missed. Playing watchdog was not particularly exciting to her way of thinking. It did not fire her imagination, bring a tingle to her blood, or get her adrenaline flowing in the same way that wheeling and dealing did. Pitting her wits against business adversaries and striving for power and supremacy in the international market place had become such second nature to her over the years that they were now essential to her well-being.

Restlessly she rose, crossed the floor in swift light steps, and opened one of the soaring leaded windows. She took a deep breath, peered out. The sky was a faultless blue, without a single cloud, and radiant with spring sunshine. New buds, tenderly green, sprouted on the skeletal branches, and under the great oak at the edge of the lawn a mass of daffodils, randomly planted, tossed yellow-bright heads under the fluttering breeze.

"I wandered lonely as a cloud that floats on high o'er vales and hills, when all at once I saw a crowd, a host, of golden daffodils," she recited aloud, then thought: Good heavens, I learned that Wordsworth poem at the village school in Fairley. So long ago, and to think that I've remembered it all these years.

Raising her hand, she closed the window, and the great McGill emerald on the third finger of her left hand flashed as the clear northern light struck the stone. Its brilliance caught her attention. She had worn this ring for forty-four years, ever since that day in May of 1925 when Paul McGill had placed it on her finger. He had thrown away her wedding ring, symbol of her disastrous marriage to Arthur Ainsley, then slipped on the massive square-cut emerald. "We might not have had the benefit of clergy," Paul had said that memorable day, "but as far as I'm concerned, you are my wife. From this day forward until death do us part."

The previous morning their child had been born. Their adored Daisy, conceived in love and raised with love. Her favorite of all her children, just as Paula, Daisy's daughter, was her favorite grandchild, heiress to her enormous retailing empire and half of the colossal McGill fortune which Emma had inherited after Paul's death in 1939. And Paula had given birth to twins four weeks ago, had presented her with her first great-grandchildren, who tomorrow would be christened at the ancient church in Fairley village.

Emma pursed her lips, suddenly wondering if she had made a mistake in acquiescing to this wish of Paula's husband, Jim Fairley. Jim was a traditionalist and thus wanted his children to be christened at the font where all of the Fairleys had been baptized—and all of the Hartes, for that matter, herself included.

Oh well, she thought, I can't very well renege at this late date, and perhaps it *is* only fitting. She had wreaked her revenge on the Fairleys. The vendetta she had waged against them for most of her life was finally at an end, and the two families had been united through Paula's marriage with James Arthur Fairley, the last of the old line. It was a new beginning.

But when Blackie O'Neill had heard of the choice of church, he had raised a snowy brow and chuckled and made a remark about the cynic turning into a sentimentalist in her old age, an accusation he was frequently leveling at her of late. Maybe Blackie was right in this assumption. On the other hand the past no longer troubled her as it once had. The past had been buried with the dead. Only the future concerned her now. And Paula and Jim and their children were that future.

Emma's thoughts centered on Fairley village as she returned to her desk, put on her glasses, and stared at the memorandum in front of her. It was from her grandson Alexander, who, with her son Kit, ran her mills, and it was bluntly to the point, in Alexander's inimitable fashion. The Fairley mill was in serious trouble. It had been failing to break even for the longest time and was now deeply in the red. A crucial decision hovered over her head . . . to close the mill or keep it running at a considerable loss. Emma, ever the pragmatist, knew deep in her bones that the wisest move would be to close down the Fairley operation, yet she balked at this drastic measure, not wanting to bring hardship to the village of her birth. She had asked Alexander to find an alternative, a workable solution, and hoped he had done so. She would soon know. He was due to arrive for a meeting with her imminently.

One possibility which might enable them to resolve the situation at the Fairley mill had occurred to Emma, but she wanted to give Alexander his head, an opportunity to handle this problem himself. Testing him, she admitted, as I'm constantly testing all of my grandchildren. And why not? That was her prerogative, wasn't it? Everything she owned had been hard-won, built on a life rooted in single-mindedness of purpose, the most grueling work and dogged determination and relentlessness and terrible sacrifice. Nothing had ever been handed to her on a plate. Her mighty empire was entirely of her own making, and since it was hers and hers alone, she could dispose of it as she wished.

And so with calm deliberation and judiciousness and selectivity she had chosen her heirs one year ago, bypassing four of her five children in favor of her grandchildren in the new will she had drawn; yet she continued to scrutinize the third generation through wise old eyes, forever evaluating their worth, seeking weaknesses in them whilst inwardly praying to find none.

They have lived up to my expectations, she reassured herself, then thought with a swift stab of dismay: No, that's not strictly true. There is *one* of whom I am not really sure, *one* whom I don't think I can trust.

Emma unlocked the top drawer of her desk, took out a sheet of paper, and studied the names of her grandchildren, which she had listed only last night when she had experienced her first feelings of uneasiness. Is there a joker in this pack, as I suspect? she asked herself worriedly, squinting at the names. And if there really is, how on earth will I handle it?

Her eyes remained riveted to one name. She shook her head with sadness, pondering.

Treachery had ceased to surprise Emma long ago, for her natural astuteness and psychological insight had been sharply honed during a long, frequently hard, and always extraordinary life. In fact relatively few things surprised her anymore, and, with her special brand of cynicism, she had come to expect the worst from people, including family. Yet withal she *had* been taken aback last year when she had discovered through Gaye Sloane, her secretary, that her four eldest children were willfully plotting against her. Spurred on by their avariciousness and vaunting ambition, they had endeavored to wrest her empire away from her in the most underhanded way, seriously underestimating her in the process. Her initial shock and the pain of betrayal had been swiftly replaced by an anger of icy ferocity, and she had made her moves with speed and consummate skill and resourcefulness, which was her way when facing any opponent. And she had pushed sentiment and emotions aside, had not allowed feelings to obscure intelligence, for it was her superior intelligence which had inevitably saved her in disastrous situations in the past.

If she had outwitted the inept plotters, had left them floundering stupidly in disarray, she had also finally come to the bitter, and chilling, realization that blood was not thicker than water. It had struck her, and most forcibly, that ties of the blood and of the flesh did not come into play when vast amounts of money and, more importantly, great power were at stake. People thought nothing of killing to attain even the smallest portions of both. Despite her overriding disgust and disillusionment with her children, she had been very sure of *their* children, *their* devotion to her. Now one of them was causing her to re-evaluate her judgment and question her trust.

She turned the name over in her mind . . . Perhaps she was wrong; she hoped she was wrong. She had nothing to go on really—except gut instinct and her prescience. But, like her intelligence, both had served her well throughout her life.

Always when she faced this kind of dilemma, Emma's instinctive attitude was to wait—and watch. Once again she decided to play for time. By doing thus she could conceal her real feelings, whilst gambling that things would sort themselves out to her advantage, thereby dispensing with the need for harsh action. But I will dole out the rope, she added inwardly. Experience had taught her that when lots of freely proffered rope fell into unwitting hands, it invariably formed a noose.

Emma considered the manifold possibilities if this should happen, and a hard grimness settled over her face, and her eyes darkened. She did not relish picking up the sword again, to defend herself and her interests, not to mention her other heirs.

History does have a way of repeating itself, she thought wearily, especially in my life. But I refuse to anticipate. That's surely borrowing trouble. Purposefully she put the list back in the drawer, locked it, and pocketed the key.

Emma Harte had the enviable knack of shelving unsolvable problems in order to concentrate on priorities, and so she was enabled to subdue the nagging—and disturbing—suspicion that a grandchild of hers was untrustworthy and therefore a potential adversary. Current business was the immediate imperative, and she gave her attention to her appointments for the rest of the day, each of which was with three of the six grandchildren who worked for her.

Alexander would come first.

Emma glanced at her watch. He was due to arrive in fifteen minutes, at ten-thirty. He would be on time, if not indeed early. Her lips twitched in amusement. Alexander had become something of a demon about punctuality; he had even chided *her* last week when she had kept him waiting, and he was forever at odds with his mother, who suffered from a chronic disregard for the clock. Her amused smile fled, was replaced by a cold and disapproving tightness around her mouth as she contemplated her second daughter.

Elizabeth was beginning to push her patience to the limits—galavanting around the world in the most scandalous manner, marrying and divorcing haphazardly and with such increasing frequency it was appalling. Her daughter's inconsistency and instability had ceased to baffle her, for she had long understood that Elizabeth had inherited most of her father's worst traits. Arthur Ainsley had been a weak, selfish, and self-indulgent man; these unfortunate flaws were paramount in his daughter, and following his pattern, the beautiful, wild, and willful Elizabeth flouted all the rules and had remained untamed. And dreadfully unhappy, Emma acknowledged to herself. The woman has become a tragic spectacle, to be pitied perhaps rather than condemned.

She wondered where her daughter was at the moment, then instantly dropped the thought. It was of no consequence, she supposed, since they were barely on speaking terms after the matter of the will. Surprisingly even Alexander had been treated to a degree of cold-shouldering by his adoring mother because he had been favored in her place. But Elizabeth had not been able to cope with Alexander's cool indifference to her feelings, and her hysterical tantrums and the rivers of tears had abruptly ceased when she realized she was wasting her time. She had capitulated in the face of his aloofness, disapproval, and thinly veiled contempt. Her son's good opinion of her and his love were vital, apparently, and she had made her peace with him, had mended her ways. But not for long, Emma thought acidly. *She* soon fell back into her bad habits. And it's certainly no thanks to that foolish and skittish woman that Alexander has turned out so well.

Emma experienced a little rush of warmth mingled with gratification as she contemplated her grandson. Alexander had become the man he was because of his strength of character and his integrity. He was solid, hardworking, dependable. If he did not have his cousin Paula's brilliance and lacked her unique vision in business, he was nonetheless sound of judgment. His conservative streak was balanced by a degree of flexibility, and he displayed a genuine willingness to weigh the pros and cons of any given situation and, when necessary, to make compromises. Alexander had the ability to keep everything in its proper perspective, and this was reassuring to Emma, who was a born realist herself.

This past year Alexander had proved himself deserving of her faith in him, and she had no regrets about making him the chief heir to Harte Enterprises by leaving him fifty-two percent of her shares in this privately held company. Whilst he continued to supervise the mills, she deemed it essential for him to have a true understanding of every aspect of the holding corporation, and she had been training him assiduously, preparing him for the day when he took over the reins from her.

Harte Enterprises controlled her woolen mills, clothing factories, real estate, the General Retail Trading Company, and the Yorkshire Consolidated Newspaper Company, and it was worth many millions of pounds. She had long recognized that Alexander might never increase its worth by much because of his tendency to be cautious, but for the same reason neither would he ruin it through rash decisions and reckless speculation. He would keep it on the steady course she had so carefully charted, following the guidelines and principles she had set down years ago. This was the way she wanted it, had planned it in fact.

Emma drew her appointment book toward her and checked the time of her lunch with Emily, Alexander's sister.

Emily was due to arrive at one o'clock.

When she had phoned earlier in the week, Emily had sounded somewhat enigmatic when she had said she had a serious problem to discuss. There was no mystery as far as Emma was concerned. She knew what Emily's problem was, had known about it for a long time. She was only surprised that her granddaughter had not asked to discuss it before now. She lifted her head and stared into space reflectively, turning the matter over in her mind, and then she frowned. Two weeks ago she had come to a decision about Emily, and she was convinced it was the right one. But would Emily agree? Yes, she answered herself. The girl will see the sense in it, I'm positive of that. Emma brought her eyes back to the open page of the diary.

Paula would stop by at the end of the afternoon.

She and Paula were to discuss the Cross project. Now if that is skillfully handled by Paula and she brings the negotiations to a favorable conclusion, then I'll have that challenge I'm looking for, Emma thought. Her mouth settled into its familiar resolute lines as she turned her attention to the balance sheets of the Aire Communications Company, owned by the Crosses. The figures were disastrous—and damning. But its financial problems aside, the company was weighted down with serious afflictions of such enormity that they boggled the mind. According to Paula, these could be surmounted and solved, and she had evolved a plan so simple yet so masterful in its premise that Emma had been both intrigued and impressed.

"Let's buy the company, Grandy," Paula had said to her a few weeks ago. "I realize Aire looks like a catastrophe, and actually it is, but only because of its bad management and its present structure. It's a hodgepodge. Too diversified. And it has too many divisions. Those that make a good profit can never get properly ahead and really flourish because they're burdened down by the divisions which are in the red and which they have to support." Paula had then walked her through the plan, step by step, and Emma had instantly understood how Aire Communications could be turned around and in no time at all. She had instructed her granddaughter to start negotiating immediately.

How she would love to get her hands on that little enterprise. And perhaps she would and very soon too, if her reading of the situation was as accurate as she thought. Emma was convinced that no one was better equipped to deal with John Cross and his son, Sebastian, than Paula, who had developed into a tough and shrewd negotiator. She no longer equivocated when Emma hurled her into touchy business situations that required nimble thinking and business acumen, which she possessed in good measure. And of late her self-confidence had grown.

Emma glanced at her watch again, then curbed the impulse to telephone Paula at the store in Leeds, to give her a few last-minute tips about John Cross and how to deal with him effectively. Paula had proved she had come into her own, and Emma did not want her to think she was forever breathing down her neck.

The telephone rang. Emma reached for it. "Hello?"

"It's me, Aunt Emma. Shane. How are you?"

"Why Shane, how lovely to hear your voice. And I'm fine, thanks. You sound pretty good yourself. I'm looking forward to seeing you tomorrow, at the christening." As she spoke, she took off her glasses and laid them on the desk, relaxed in the chair.

"I was hoping to see you before then, Aunt Emma. How would you like to go out on the town tonight with two fun-loving bachelors?"

Emma laughed gaily. "And who's the *other* fun-loving bachelor?"

"Grandfather, of course, who else?"

"Fun-loving! He's getting to be an old stick-in-the-mud, if you ask me."

"I wouldn't be saying that, mavourneen," Blackie boomed into the phone, having taken it away from his grandson. "I bet I could still give *you* a run for your money, if I got half the chance."

"I'm sure you could, darling." Emma smiled into the phone, her heart warming to him. "However, I'm afraid you won't get that chance tonight. I can't accept your invitation, Blackie dear. Some of the family are arriving later, and I ought to be here."

"No," Blackie interjected peremptorily, "you can see *them* tomorrow. Ah now, don't be refusin' me, darlin'," he cajoled. "Apart from wanting the pleasure of your lovely company, I need your advice on an important business matter."

"Oh." Emma was mildly taken aback by this statement. Blackie had retired and left the running of his companies to his son Bryan and to Shane.

Not unnaturally her curiosity was piqued, and she said, "What kind of business?"

"I don't want to be discussing it on the telephone, Emma," Blackie said in a softly chiding tone. "It's not something that's so cut and dried it can be settled in the matter of a few minutes. We have to be going back and forth, you know, dissecting it a bit, and I think we should be doing it over a nice drop of Irish and a fine meal."

Emma laughed under her breath, wondering how important this so-called business matter really was, but found herself conceding, "I suppose I can let them fend for themselves. To tell you the truth, I wasn't much looking forward to tonight. Even though Daisy and David will be here, the prospect of a family gathering isn't particularly exciting. So I accept. And where are you and your dashing grandson planning to take me? Out on the town in Leeds isn't too exciting."

Laughingly Blackie concurred and said, "But don't worry, we'll cook up something, and I promise you won't be bored."

"What time then?"

"Shane will pick you up around six. Is that all right, me darlin' girl?"

"It's perfect."

"Good. Good. Until later then. Oh and Emma?"

"Yes, Blackie?"

"Have you given any more thought to me little proposition?"

"Yes, and I have serious doubts about it working."

"Oh, so you're still me Doubting Emma after all these years, I can see. Well, we'll discuss that tonight, too, and maybe I can be convincing you yet."

"Perhaps," she murmured softly as he hung up.

Emma sat back, contemplating Blackie O'Neill. *Doubting Emma.* A faint smile flickered in her eyes. When had he first called her that? Was it 1904 or 1905? She was no longer sure, but it had been thereabouts, and Blackie had been her dearest, closest friend for all those sixty-five years. For a whole lifetime. Always there when she needed him, loyal, devoted, supportive, and loving. They had been through most of life's exigencies together, had shared each other's terrible losses and defeats, pain and anguish; had celebrated each other's triumphs and joys. Of their contemporaries there were only the two of them left, and they were closer than ever, inseparable really. She did not know what she would do if anything happened to him. She resolutely squashed this unacceptable thought before it took hold. Blackie was an old war horse, just as she herself was an old war horse, and even though he was eighty-three there was a great deal of surging life and vitality left in him. But no one lasts indefinitely, she thought, experiencing a twinge of anxiousness whilst acknowledging the inevitable. At their grand ages mortality was a given, one which could not be argued with, and impending death was an old if unwelcome familiar.

There was a knock on the door.

Emma glanced at it, adopted her normal expression of cool inscrutability, and called, "Come in."

The door swung open and Alexander entered. He was tall, lean, and trim in build, with his mother's dark good looks, her large, light blue eyes; but his somewhat serious, saturnine face made him appear older than his twenty-five years, gave him a dignified air. He wore a well-cut dark gray worsted suit, a white shirt, and a burgundy silk tie—all of which reflected and reinforced his rather sober personality.

"Good morning, Grandmother," he said, striding toward her. Reaching the desk, he added, "I must say, you're looking pretty nifty today."

"Morning, Alexander, and thank you for the compliment. Mind you, flattery's not going to get you anywhere with me," she responded crisply. Nonetheless her eyes danced and she regarded her grandson fondly.

Alexander kissed her on the cheek, seated himself opposite, and protested, "I'm not trying to flatter you, Grandy, honestly I'm not. You do look absolutely spiffing. That color really suits you, and the dress is very chic."

Emma nodded impatiently, waved her hand in airy dismissal, and fixed her grandson with a keen and penetrating stare. "What have you come up with?"

"The *only* solution to the Fairley problem," Alexander began, understanding she wanted to curtail the small talk and plunge into business. His grandmother loathed procrastination, unless it suited her own ends; then she could elevate procrastination to an art. But she scarcely tolerated it in others, so he rushed on, "We have to change our product. By that I mean we have to stop manufacturing the expensive woolens and worsted cloths that hardly anybody is buying, and start weaving blends. Man-made fibers, such as nylon and polyester, blended with wool. Those are our best bets."

"And you think this move will get us out of the red and into the black?" Emma asked, her stare intensifying.

"Yes, I do, Grandy," he replied, sounding sure of himself. "One of our chief problems at Fairley has been trying to compete with the man-made fiber goods on the market today. Nobody wants pure wool anymore, except the Savile Row boys, and they're not a big enough market for the Fairley output. Look, either we produce the blends or shut up shop—which you don't want to do. It's as simple as that."

"Can we make the changeover easily?"

Alexander nodded emphatically. "We can. By manufacturing cheaper goods we can capture the more popular-priced markets here and abroad and do volume sales. Of course, it *is* a question of sales and getting a real foothold in those new markets. But I'm sure we can pull it off." He reached into his inside breast pocket, pulled out a sheet of paper. "I've analyzed every aspect of the plan, and I'm certain I've not overlooked one thing. Here it is."

Emma took it from him, reached for her glasses, studied the closely typed sheet. She recognized immediately that he had done his homework with his usual diligence. He had refined the idea she herself had toyed with, although she had no intention of revealing this, not wishing to undermine him or diminish his efforts. She looked up, removed her spectacles, and gave him the benefit of a warm congratulatory smile.

"Well done, Sandy!" she exclaimed, reverting to the affectionate diminutive of his childhood. "You've put a lot of sound thinking into this, and I'm delighted, really delighted."

"That's a relief," he said, a smile breaking through. Reserved of nature though he was, Alexander was always completely relaxed and outgoing with Emma, who was the one person he truly loved, and now he confessed, "I've really bashed my brains out on this one, Grandy, played around with all manner of convoluted ideas, I don't mind telling you. Still, I kept coming back to my original plan for creating the new blends." He leaned closer to the desk and gave her one of her own penetrating stares. "But knowing you, I have a feeling you'd already thought of the solution before you threw the problem at me."

Emma was tickled at his perceptiveness, but she stifled the laugh that bubbled in her throat. She looked into his candid blue eyes and slowly shook her head. "No, I didn't," she lied. Then, observing his disbelief, she added, "But I suppose I would have. Eventually."

"You're damned right you would," he acknowledged. He shifted slightly in the chair and crossed his legs, wondering how to break the bit of bad news to her. He decided to jump in with both feet. "There is one other thing, though, Grandmother." He hesitated, worry suddenly clouding his face. "I'm afraid we'll have to cut down on our running costs at the mill. Really tighten our belts out there at Fairley, if we want to operate more efficiently—and profitably. I hate to tell you this, but a number of men will have to be laid off." There was a slight pause, before he finished gloomily, "Permanently laid off."

Emma's face tightened in aggravation. *"Oh dear."* She nodded slowly, as if confirming something to herself. "Well, I sort of expected that, Alexander. If you have to do it, you have to do it. I presume you'll be letting the older men go, those who are near retirement age?" she asked, one brow lifting questioningly.

"Yes. I think that's the fairest thing."

"See to it that they get a special bonus, severance pay, whatever you want to call it. And naturally their pensions will become effective immediately. No penny-pinching and waiting it out until they actually reach retirement age. I won't have any of that nonsense, Sandy."

"Yes, of course. I second-guessed you on that one. I'm preparing a list of names and details of our financial obligations to the men. I'll get it to you next week, if that's all right with you." He sat back, waiting.

Emma made no response. She pushed herself up and walked slowly to the oriel window, where she stood looking down into the magnificent gardens of Pennistone Royal. Concern edged onto her wrinkled face as she ruminated on the mill at Fairley. Her life had been bound up with it in so many different ways. Her father had worked there, and her brother, Frank, when he was only a small boy and should have been at school. Frank had been a bobbin ligger, slaving from early morning until nightfall, hardly able to drag his weary little legs home at the end of the long day, sickly pale from exhaustion and a lack of fresh air and sunshine.

Adam Fairley, Jim's great-grandfather and the Squire of Fairley, had been the owner of the mill then. How she had hated him as a girl—for the best part of her life, really. With the wisdom of great age, she knew Adam had not been the tyrant she had believed him to be. But he had been negligent, and that in itself was a crime in her eyes. His monumental negligence and his selfish preoccupation with his personal problems and his all-consuming love for Olivia Wainright had caused grievous trouble for others less fortunate. Yes, Adam Fairley had been guilty of abdicating his duties in the most careless and callous fashion and without so much as a glance at those poor souls who toiled in his mills: The workers who made his cushioned life of ease and privilege possible, who were dependent on him, and were, in a very real sense, his responsibility. Half a century ago, she commented silently. I may understand something of the man now, but I'll never forget what he did. Never.

She glanced down at her small but strong hands, soft and well cared for, the nails manicured to expensive perfection. But once those hands had been red and chapped and sore from scrubbing and polishing and washing and cooking for the Fairleys, when she had been bound in service to them as a child. Lifting one hand, she touched her face and remembered with stunning clarity Murgatroyd's sharp blows on her cheek. The detestable Murgatroyd, Adam Fairley's butler, who had been permitted by the squire to rule that pernicious and secretive doomed house with a cruelty that bordered on savagery. Despite his harshness and his unremitting persecution of her, Murgatroyd had never frightened her. It was that monstrous house which had filled her with a nameless terror and from which she had wanted always to flee.

Then, one day, *she* had owned that great mausoleum of a place—Fairley's Folly, the villagers had called it—and she had known at once that she would never live in it, would never play the role of the grand lady of the manor. And with a flash of sudden and intense vision she had understood exactly what she must do. She must obliterate it from the face of the earth as if it had never existed. And so she had torn it down, brick by brick by brick, until not a trace of it was left, and she could still recall to this very day the grim satisfaction she had experienced when she had finally razed it to the ground.

Now, across the span of four decades, she heard an echo of her own voice saying to Blackie, "And destroy this garden. Demolish it completely. I don't want a rosebud, one single leaf left growing." Blackie had done exactly as she had instructed, uprooting that walled rose garden where Edwin Fairley had so inhumanly and shamefully repudiated her and their child, which she had been carrying. Miraculously, in the space of a few hours, the garden, too, had disappeared as if it had never been there at all, and only then had she felt free of the Fairleys at last.

At this time in her life, Emma had acquired the mill. She had done her utmost to give the men proper living wages and overtime and all manner of fringe benefits, and she had kept the village going for years, often at great financial cost to herself. The workers were part of her in a way, for it was from their class that she herself came, and they held a favored and unique place in her affections. The thought of letting a single one of them go distressed her, yet she had no choice, it seemed. Better surely to operate at half her work capacity and keep the mill rolling than to close it down completely.

Half turning she said, "By the way, Alexander, have you discussed any of this with Kit?"

"Uncle Kit," Alexander exclaimed, his startled tone reflecting the expression flicking onto his face. "No, I haven't," he admitted. "For one thing, he hasn't been around. And for another, he doesn't seem interested in any of the mills, Fairley least of all. He hasn't appeared to give a damn since you dumped him out of your will."

"That's a crude way of putting it, I must say!" Emma snapped and returned to her desk with a show of briskness. "I didn't *dump* him, as you call it. I passed him over. For his daughter, remember. As I did your mother for you and Emily, and your Uncle Robin for Jonathan. And you know the reasons why, so I won't bother elucidating on them again. Also let's not forget that my will doesn't come into effect until I die. Which won't be for a long time if I have anything to do with it."

"Or me either," Alexander cried swiftly, as always dismayed by her talk of dying.

Emma smiled at him, fully aware of his devotion to her, his genuine concern for her well-being. She continued in that businesslike tone, "Well, so much for Kit. *Mmmm.* Of course, I realized he was being a bit derelict in his duties. On the other hand, I did think he made an *occasional* visit, if only for appearances' sake."

"Oh yes, he does do that. But he's so morose and uncommunicative he might as well not be there," Alexander explained, adding as an afterthought, "I can't begin to guess what he does with his time these days."

"Not much, if I know my eldest son. He never was blessed with much imagination," Emma shot back sardonically, the suggestion of a disdainful smirk playing on her mouth. She made a mental note to talk to Kit's daughter, Sarah, about her father's present mood. Morose indeed, Emma thought, with disgust. He brought his troubles on entirely by himself. No, not true. Robin gave him a helping hand, and Elizabeth and Edwina, his cohorts in the plot against me. Aware that Alexander was waiting expectantly, Emma finished, "Anyway, since Kit's not around, he's not going to hamper you—as he has so often in the past. Your way is clear. Put this plan into operation immediately. You have my blessing."

"Thanks, Grandy." He leaned forward, said with earnestness, "We *are* doing the right thing."

"Yes, I know that."

"And don't worry about the men who are to be retired. They will be all right, really they will."

She glanced at him quickly, her eyes narrowed under the hooded lids. She thought: I am so glad it's not Alexander whom I suspect of treachery and duplicity. That I could not bear. It would kill me. She said, "It pleases me that you've always been so involved with the Fairley mill and on such a personal basis, Sandy. You *care,* and that's important to me. And I appreciate your understanding . . . I mean of my involvement with that particular mill." She smiled wryly and shook her head. "The past, you know, is always with us, always reaching out to claim part of us, and I learned a very long time ago that we cannot escape it."

"Yes," he said laconically, but the look in his eyes expressed so much more.

Emma said, "I've decided to go to the Fairley mill next week. I'll be the one to explain the changes we're going to make. Tell them about the retirements myself, in my own words. It's only proper."

"Yes, it is, Grandy. And they'll be thrilled to see you. They all worship you, but then you know that."

"Humph!" she snorted. "Don't be so foolish, Alexander. And don't exaggerate. You know I can't abide exaggeration."

Alexander swallowed a smile, remained silent, watching her closely as she sorted through some of the papers on the desk, her head bent. She had spoken swiftly, crossly even, but there had been a curious gruffness in her voice, and he knew that she had been touched by his words. He was amused by her mild chastisement. It was a hoot. Her whole life had been an extraordinary exaggeration, for God's sake. Why, she was *larger* than life.

"Are you still here?" Emma said, glancing up, frowning and feigning annoyance. "I thought you'd be halfway to the office by now, with all you've got to do today. Get along with you!"

Alexander laughed, jumped up, and went around the desk. He hugged her to him and kissed the crown of her silvery head. "There's nobody like you in this entire world, Emma Harte," he said gently. "Nobody like you at all."

Two

"Nobody in this world but Emma Harte would have come up with such a preposterous proposition," Sebastian Cross cried indignantly, glaring, his face turning choleric.

"She didn't come up with it, I did," Paula replied in her coldest voice, returning his angry look with a steady unblinking gaze.

"Tommyrot! It's your grandmother talking, not you!"

Paula felt herself stiffening in the chair, and she suppressed the swift denial that sprang to her lips. Self-control was essential in all business dealings and particularly with this odious man. She would not permit him to put her down, nor bait her with his inference that her grandmother was manipulating this negotiation from afar.

"Think what you will," she said after a slight pause, "but regardless of whomever formulated the deal, that's it, as I've outlined it. It's a take it or leave it situation."

"Then we'll leave it, thank you very much," Sebastian shot back, filled with rancorous hatred for her, for her strange yet compelling beauty, and her money, and her power. His dark eyes blazed as he added, "Who the hell needs you or your grandmother."

"Now, now, Sebastian, let's not be too hasty," John Cross said soothingly. "And please, do calm down." He threw his son a cautionary look, then turned to Paula, his whole manner unexpectedly conciliatory. "You must make allowances for my son. Naturally he's rather upset. After all, your proposal came as something of a shock to him. He is very committed to Aire Communications, as I have always been, and he has no desire to leave the company. Neither do I. In short, we both expect, indeed fully intend, to continue in our present positions. I as chairman of the board, and Sebastian as managing director. Harte Enterprises would have to agree to that."

"I don't believe that is possible, Mr. Cross," Paula said.

"Forget it, Dad," Sebastian almost shouted, "we'll go elsewhere for the money."

"You've nowhere else to go," Paula could not help retorting icily, reaching for her briefcase on the conference room table. She stood up, announced with finality, "Since we seem to have reached an impasse, there's obviously nothing more to say. I think I'd better leave."

John Cross sprang to his feet, took her arm. "Please," he said quietly, "please sit down. Let's talk a little more about this."

Paula hesitated, staring at him. Throughout their relatively short meeting, whilst his son had blustered and snarled, John Cross had adopted a stance of inflexibility, displayed a quiet but firm resoluteness to make the deal on *his* terms, despite their original understanding. Now, for the first time, she detected a sign of wavering on his part. And whether he was aware of it or not, the preceding months of tension and anxiety had taken their toll. The troubles of his floundering company were much in evidence, clearly imprinted on his gaunt and weary face, and there was a quiet desperation behind the bloodshot eyes which held a hint of new panic. He knows I'm right about everything, she thought, carefully assessing him yet again, but he just won't admit it. The fool. She instantly corrected herself. The man standing before her had built up Aire Communications from nothing, so she could hardly characterize him as a fool. Misguided, yes—and regrettably he suffered from the serious malady of paternal blindness. He had long invested his son with qualities Sebastian did not possess nor was ever likely to possess, and therein lay his downfall.

"All right," she said at last, seating herself tentatively on the edge of the chair. "I'll stay for a few minutes to hear what you have to say. But very frankly, I meant it when I said we'd reached an impasse."

"That's not strictly true in my opinion," he responded, smiling faintly, and his relief at her continuing presence in his board room was barely concealed as he took a cigarette and lit it. "Your proposition *is* a bit preposterous, you know. We want new financing. We don't want to be taken over and thrown out of our own company. No, no, that's not what we had in mind when we came to you," he finished, shaking his head several times for added emphasis.

Paula gazed at him in amazement. She gave him a curious smile. "You've just pin-pointed the crux of the matter. *You* came to *us,* remember. We didn't seek you out. And you certainly knew enough about Harte Enterprises and how we operate, to understand that we never invest in companies that are in trouble. We take those over, reorganize them, and put them under new management. Our management. In other words, we get them running smoothly, efficiently, and on a profitable basis. We're not interested in financing other people's continuing disasters. It doesn't pay."

John Cross winced at this unmistakable thrust, but resisted the parry. Instead he said, "Quite so, quite so. I've been thinking . . . Maybe we can arrive at a workable compromise—"

"*Dad!* Don't!" Sebastian exploded irately, moving violently in his chair.

His father held up one hand and frowned at him. "Hear me out, Sebastian. Now, Paula, here's what I think we might do, how we might make a deal after all. Harte Enterprises could buy fifty-two percent of Aire Communications' shares. That gives you the control you insist you must have. You put in your management, reorganize as you wish, but you must let us stay with—"

"Dad! What are you saying? Are you crazy?" Sebastian bellowed, his flushed face darkening considerably. "Where would that leave *us?* I'll tell you where. Out in the bloody cold, for Christ's sake."

"Sebastian! *Please,*" John Cross shouted back, finally losing his composure, his exasperation running high. "Let me finish for once in my life."

"Just a minute, Mr. Cross," Paula cut in rapidly, her irritation echoing in her voice. "Before you go any further, I must point out, *yet again,* that we wouldn't be interested. It must be a *full* buy out. One hundred percent or nothing. And I told you this right from the—"

"That's the old monster talking again, Dad," Sebastian interrupted derisively, his mouth contorted into an ugly line. "Emma Harte! Jesus Christ, the only heart she's got is in her name. Don't deal with them, Dad. They're vultures, both of them, and this one learned well at the knee of the master, that's patently bloody obvious. She wants to swallow us up in the same way her grandmother has swallowed up companies over the years. I told you, we don't need *them*."

Paula chose to ignore this unruly and vindictive outburst, deeming it unworthy of a response. She focused all of her attention on John Cross. She was appalled at his deviousness and enraged, but controlling herself, she said as evenly as possible, "I started to say that I quite clearly recall mentioning the full buy out to you, Mr. Cross, long before today's meeting. I find it hard to believe you've forgotten the protracted conversations we've had about that very matter." She gave him a hard stare, wondering if he thought she was stupid.

John Cross colored under her sharp scrutiny. He remembered her initial statements only too well. But he had hoped to get Harte Enterprises interested in the company, whet Emma Harte's appetite, then structure the deal to suit himself. He had been elated when he had realized it was Paula who would do the negotiating. He had believed he could manipulate her and the situation to his advantage. His plan had somehow misfired. Maybe Sebastian was right. Yes, Emma Harte was undoubtedly working behind the scenes; all of this had her unmistakable stamp to it. An unreasonable anger surged through him, and he exclaimed heatedly, "Look here, you're not being fair."

"Fair," Paula repeated. She smiled thinly, added in a clipped tone, "The issues of fair or unfair just won't play in this instance." She held him with her startlingly blue eyes. "I'm surprised to hear *you* use that word. I told you at the outset of today's meeting that Harte Enterprises is prepared to pay you two million pounds for Aire Communications. That's more than *fair*. It's downright generous. Your company is in an unholy mess. It could go belly-up at any moment." She shrugged. "Well, I suppose that's your affair, Mr. Cross, not mine." She leaned forward, grasped the handle of her briefcase. "We seem to have nothing further to say to each other."

The senior Cross said, "If, and I am saying *if,* we do decide to accept your offer, can my son and I remain with the company?"

She shook her head.

John Cross thought rapidly, came to an unpalatable but necessary decision. "I would be willing to step aside. After all, I am near retirement age." He stubbed out his cigarette, fixed his pale eyes on her. "However," he went on firmly, "you must reconsider your decision regarding Sebastian. No one knows this company like my son. Why, he would be invaluable to you. I must insist that he be appointed to the new board of directors and that he be given a contract for five years as special consultant. I would have to have your guarantee on that and in writing before we can proceed any further."

"No," she said. "There is no place in Aire Communications for your son if we take the company over."

The older man was silent.

Sebastian looked pointedly at his father, his expression at once both baleful and condemning. John Cross dropped his eyes, unable to meet that accusatory gaze, toyed with his gold pen, said nothing at all. Sebastian leaped up angrily, seething, and strode across the board room. He stood looking out of the window, his body rigid, and he cursed Paula Fairley under his breath.

Paula's glance followed Sebastian. She felt the malignancy and alertness in him, but intuitively so, for she could not see his face. It was turned into the shadows cast by the window and the buildings outside. Involuntarily she shivered and brought her eyes back to his father. They regarded each other alertly, each wondering which of them would make the next move. Neither did.

Paula saw a thin, gray-haired man in his early sixties, a self-made man who had pulled himself up by his bootstraps, and who in the process had acquired a distinguished air and a degree of superficial polish. He was also a frightened man. His company was sinking like a torpedoed battleship with a gaping hole in its bow, yet seemingly he was prepared to spurn the life belt she had thrown him because of his love for his son. The son who had so badly mismanaged Aire Communications he had brought it to its present weakened and crippled state. She noticed a muscle twitching in the elder Cross's face and glanced away.

John Cross, for his part, sat facing a young woman of great elegance in her grooming and dress. She wore a magenta wool suit, magnificently cut and tailored, obviously a pricey piece of *haute couture,* with a man-tailored shirt of white silk. There was an absence of jewelry, except for a simple watch and a plain gold wedding band. He knew that Paula McGill Amory Fairley was only in her mid-twenties, yet she gave the impression of being so much older with her inbred caution, her cool authoritative manner. She reminded him of her famous grandmother, even though her coloring was so different. The glossy black hair, cut in a straight bob that grazed her jawline, the blue eyes flecked with violet, and the ivory complexion were unquestionably striking; but whereas Emma's fabled russet-golden tints had always suggested softness and beguiling femininity, Paula's beauty was somewhat austere, at least to suit his taste in women. Neither were her features quite as perfect as Emma's had once been. Still they did share the same aura of presence, and she had apparently inherited the old lady's steely toughness as well as that uncommon widow's peak, those sharp eyes that penetrated with a keen intelligence. His heart sank as he continued to study that palely beautiful but obdurate face.

He would never win with her. As this unpleasant realization sank in he did another volte-face, made yet another decision, and this one was final. He would seek financing from another source and insist that the deal include Sebastian. He must ensure his boy's future with the company—one which had been built up expressly for him. That was the only thing he could do, the right and proper thing to do. Yes, he must protect his son above all else—otherwise what had his life been about?

John Cross was the one who broke the prolonged silence. "We are dead-locked, Paula. I have to pass." He lifted his hands in a helpless gesture, then let them fall onto the conference table limply. "Thank you for your time. And please tell your grandmother that her terms are too harsh for my palate."

Paula laughed softly as they both rose. "They're my terms, Mr. Cross, but I won't belabor the point." Being a courteous young woman she thrust out her hand. "I wish you lots of luck," she said with studied politeness.

"Thank you," he said, his voice equally as civil as hers but not quite as steady. "Let me escort you to the lift."

As they passed the window, Paula said, "Goodbye, Sebastian."

He swiveled his dark head, nodded curtly, and she was so startled by the naked hatred etched on his cold and bitter face she hardly heard his muttered response. She had recognized a most dangerous enemy.

Three

Paula was blazing mad.

Walking rapidly down the Headrow, one of the main thoroughfares in Leeds, she soon put distance between herself and the Aire Communications building. Her mind was racing. Although she had felt the sharp thrust of Sebastian Cross's vindictive and combative personality, had readily acknowledged that he detested her and had become her arch enemy, her thoughts now centered on his father and with good reason. Having more or less agreed to her terms right from the start, John Cross had ultimately reneged and, moreover, in the most treacherous and despicable way.

It did not require much analysis on her part to understand why he had done so. It was apparent that he did not want to lose face in front of his domineering son, whose presence had unnerved him, made him defensive and, very possibly, more reckless than he had ever been in his entire life. Yet surely his honor and integrity were important to him too, took precedence over everything else. And what about retaining his son's respect? She laughed hollowly at herself for entertaining such ridiculous thoughts. A young man of Sebastian's perfidious nature had never made the acquaintance of those particular qualities. During the meeting, when she had understood that John Cross was not to be trusted, she had been momentarily astonished. He enjoyed a good reputation in Yorkshire's business community, had always been considered honorable if not necessarily the wisest of men. That he would go back on his word was inconceivable to her.

Her pace accelerated, and so did her anger, as she recalled the energy and thought and time she had expended on Aire Communications. Her grandmother was going to be as infuriated as she was. Emma Harte would not tolerate being played for a fool; neither could she abide anyone who did not deal from a straight deck. Grandy would handle the situation in one of two ways. She would either shrug disdainfully and turn away in disgust, or she would treat Mr. Cross to a tongue lashing the likes of which he had never heard before. Her grandmother had an intractable sense of honor, never went back on her handshake or her word, both of which were as good as a written contract, as the whole world knew.

The thought of Emma Harte putting the duplicitous John Cross firmly in his place brought a flicker of a smile to Paula's violet-blue eyes. He deserved that if nothing else. But in reality he was facing much worse than Emma's acid tongue and her virulent condemnation. He was looking disaster right in the eye. Bankruptcy. Total ruin. Obliteration. She knew he was convinced that he could easily find another conglomerate or company to refinance Aire. She also knew he was absolutely wrong in this foolish belief. She had her ear to the ground, and the word was out. Nobody wanted to touch Aire Communications. Not even those ruthless and rapacious asset strippers who bought companies, plundered them, and then tossed to one side the empty shells which were left.

It suddenly occurred to Paula, as she cut down Albion Street, that, unbelievable though it was, John Cross had no real conception of what was about to happen to him or his company. She thought then of those he would take down with him and of the many employees at Aire who would be thrown out of work. We could have saved him, more importantly saved *them,* she muttered under her breath. The man is unconscionable. Ever since she could remember, her grandmother had instilled a sense of responsibility in her, and this was one of the mandatory rules in Emma's special code of ethics.

"Great wealth and power bring enormous responsibilities, and don't you ever forget that," Grandy had told her time and time again. "We must always look after those who work for us, and with us, because they help to make all this possible. And they rely on us, just as we rely on them in other ways," she had constantly pointed out. Paula was well aware that there were those magnates and industrialists who were jealous of Emma Harte, and who, as adversaries, misguidedly saw her as a hard, ruthless, driven, and power-hungry woman. Yet even they did not have the temerity to deny that she was eminently fair. That was something every Harte employee knew from first-hand experience— hence their extraordinary loyalty and devotion to her grandmother and their love for her.

Paula stopped abruptly and took several deep breaths. She must get rid of the anger boiling inside her. It was exhausting, took too much of her precious energy—energy which could be directed elsewhere and to much better purpose. And besides, rage blocked reasonable and intelligent thought. She started to walk again, but now her step was slower and more regulated, and by the time she reached Commerical Street she had managed to calm herself considerably. She dawdled a little bit, stopping to glance in shop windows until finally she was drawing to a standstill in front of E. Harte, her grandmother's huge department store at the end of the street. She smiled at the uniformed doorman whom she had known since childhood. "Hello, Alfred," she said, smiling.

" 'Ello, Miss Paula," he responded with a benevolent grin, touching his cap. "It's a right beautiful day. Yes, luvely, it is that, Miss Paula. Let's 'ope t' weather 'olds til termorrer, for yer bairns' baptisms."

"Yes, let's hope so, Alfred."

He grinned again and pushed open the door for her. She thanked him, hurried through the perfume department and took the lift to her office on the fourth floor. Her secretary, Agnes, looked up as she walked in and exclaimed with a small frown, "Oh dear, Mrs. Fairley, you've just missed Mr. O'Neill. Shane O'Neill, that is, and only by a few minutes too. What a shame. He waited for quite a while, then had to rush off to an appointment."

"Oh." Paula stopped dead in her tracks, taken aback, but she recovered herself and asked quickly, "Did he say why he dropped in? Or leave a message?"

"I gathered he was passing the store and decided to say hello on the spur of the moment. No message though, other than to tell you he would be coming to the christening."

"I see. Anything else, Agnes?"

"Mr. Fairley phoned from London. You can't call him back—he was on his way to a luncheon at the Savoy Hotel. He'll be arriving on schedule at six with your parents. The other messages are on your desk. Nothing vital." Agnes hesitated, then asked, "How did your meeting go at Aire?"

Paula made a sour face. "Not good, Agnes. In fact I'd venture to say that it went extremely badly."

"I am sorry, Mrs. Fairley. I know the amount of work you put in on those dreadful balance sheets and then the hours you devoted to the contracts." Agnes Fuller, prematurely gray at thirty-eight, plain of feature and with a severe expression that actually betrayed the kindest of hearts, had worked her way up through the ranks of the Leeds store. She had been flattered yet apprehensive when Paula had promoted her to private secretary. After all, Paula was the heiress apparent, and Emma Harte's favorite; also there were those in the store who thought she was cold, remote, unyielding, and something of a snob who lacked Emma's extraordinary common touch. But Agnes had soon discovered that Paula had none of the characteristics so unkindly attributed to her by detractors. She was reserved of nature—even a little shy—cautious and prudent, and a veritable work horse, and these traits had very simply been misconstrued. Over the past three years Agnes had come to love the younger woman, was admiring of her, and considered her to be a brilliant executive who was a warm and caring person and a considerate employer.

As she peered at her young boss through her bifocals, Agnes noticed that Paula was paler than usual and drawn. She gave her a look of sympathy mingled with regret. "It's all very annoying," she clucked in commiseration, shaking her head. "And I hope you're not going to let it bother you, particularly this weekend."

"No, I won't, I promise you that," Paula reassured. "As my grandmother always says, you win a few, lose a few. We lost this one—" She did not finish, and a reflective expression settled on her face. "But, come to think of it, perhaps that's just as well." There was a thoughtful pause before she finished. "Excuse me, Agnes, I'll see you shortly."

Paula went into her office and sat down at the huge antique partners' desk which dominated the room. After taking the Aire Communications papers out of her briefcase, she picked up a red pen and wrote *dead* in capitals across the front of the bulging folder. She rose, went to the filing cabinet, and slipped it inside, then returned to her desk. The deal *was* dead as far as she was concerned. The negotiations had ended in a fiasco, and in consequence she had lost all interest in Aire Communications.

More than any other of the Harte offspring, Paula had inherited an unusual number of Emma's characteristics, and those she had not been born with she had acquired by osmosis from years of working at Emma's side. Chief amongst these was the ability to admit any kind of mistake with openness and candor and then put it behind her philosophically. Like Emma, she would invariably say: It didn't work. Perhaps my judgment was flawed. But let's go on from here. We mustn't look back.

And this was exactly what she said to herself now. In her mind Aire Communications was already a thing of the past. If she had gravely misjudged John Cross and wasted a great deal of time and effort on him, she had no intention of compounding these errors by dwelling on them unnecessarily. She wondered whether she ought to give her grandmother a ring to explain what had happened, then decided against it. Grandy was seeing both Alexander and Emily this morning and was bound to be busy. Later she would drive out to Pennistone Royal as arranged and apprise her of the situation. Grandy is going to be disappointed, of course, she thought, sorting through the sheaf of messages. But that won't last long, and I'll soon find another project for her.

Picking up the telephone, Paula returned all of her business calls, signed the stack of letters Agnes had typed, and then sat back in the chair, glancing at her personal messages.

Her mother had called. *Nothing important. Don't bother to call back. Will see you tonight,* Agnes had scribbled, then added one of her inimitable postscripts: *Mrs. Amory sounded marvelous, elated about tomorrow. We had a lovely chat. She's got a new hairstyle and is wearing a gray Christian Dior suit for the event.*

Paula smiled at Agnes's comments, then scanned the message from her cousin, Sarah Lowther. Apparently she was fighting a cold and might not be well enough to attend the christening. *But she didn't sound at all sick,* Agnes had written cryptically. How strange, Paula thought, frowning and rereading the slip of paper. Sarah obviously doesn't want to come. I wonder why? Since she could not hazard a guess, she turned to the last message. Miranda O'Neill was at the Leeds office of O'Neill Hotels International. *Please call her back before lunch,* Agnes had instructed.

Paula immediately dialed Miranda's private number. The line was busy, as it usually was when she was in the city. Like her grandfather, Miranda had what the poet Dylan Thomas had called, "the beautiful gift of the gab." She could easily be talking for the next hour. Automatically Paula's thoughts turned to Miranda's brother, Shane, and instantly she saw his vivid laughing face in her mind's eye. She was terribly disappointed she had missed him earlier. Such a visit had become a rarity. For years he had made it a habit to drop in on her, both in Leeds and London, and when these unexpected visits had ceased abruptly, she had been hurt and baffled.

Shane O'Neill, son of Bryan, grandson of Blackie, had been Paula's closest friend since childhood. They had grown up with each other, had spent all of their school holidays together, and had been inseparable for most of their lives —so much so that Emma had nicknamed Paula the Shadow. As her mind lingered on Shane, she realized she had not set eyes on him for many, many months. He was constantly traveling these days, dashing off to Spain and the Caribbean, where a number of the O'Neill hotels were located; when he was in England and if she chanced to run into him, he had a preoccupied air and a distant manner. She exhaled softly, slowly. How odd it was that their closeness should end with such finality, as it had a year ago. This still puzzled her. When she had eventually tackled Shane, had asked him what had happened between them, he had looked at her in the most peculiar way and denied that anything had. He had blamed business and his time-consuming schedule for his absence from her life. Perhaps he had simply outgrown her. Childhood friendships often did change radically; very frequently they deteriorated to such an extent they could never be reinstated. Regrettably, she thought. And I do miss him. I wish I'd been here this morning.

The buzz of the telephone cut into her thoughts. She reached for it. Agnes said, "It's Miss O'Neill, Mrs. Fairley."

"Thanks, Agnes, put her through, please."

A split second later Miranda's lilting voice flowed over the wire. "Hello, Paula. I thought I'd better call you again, since my phone's been busy for ages."

"That's par for the course," Paula said with an affectionate laugh. "When did you get in from London?"

"Last night. I drove up with Shane. And for the last time, I don't mind telling you. He's a maniac in a car. The tires sizzled the roads. I thought we'd end up in a ditch. I'll never know how I got here safe and sound. I was so shaken up and white when we arrived at the house, Mummy knew immediately what had happened. She's forbidden me to drive with him again. She gave him quite a piece of her mind, and—"

"I'll bet," Paula broke in with another laugh. "Your mother thinks the sun shines out of Shane. He can't do anything wrong in her eyes."

"Well, he's in the doghouse at the moment, my dear. She really told him off, and so did Dad."

"Shane came to see me today, Miranda."

"Hey, that's good news. Like you, I can't understand why he's so aloof with you these days, but then he's a strange one, that big brother of mine. Too much of the Celt in him, perhaps. Anyway what did he have to say?"

"Nothing, Miranda, since I wasn't here. I was out at a meeting."

"Too bad. Still he's coming to the christening. I know *you* had your doubts, but he told me he was definitely going to go. He even offered to drive me." Miranda groaned in mock horror at this idea. "I declined. I was going to go with Grandpops, but naturally he's escorting Aunt Emma. So I'll toddle over by myself. Listen, Paula, apart from wanting to say hello, I was wondering if you'd like to have lunch? I've got to come over to the store to pick up a package for my mother. I could meet you in the Bird Cage in half an hour. What do you think?"

"That's a nice suggestion, Merry. I'll see you there at noon."

"It's a date," Miranda said. "Bye."

"Bye." As she began clearing her desk of papers, Paula was suddenly glad Miranda had suggested lunch. Her friend was a delight to be with and a very special girl, with her naturalness, her sweetness, her gaiety and effervescence. She had a joyous, carefree disposition, and laughter sprang readily to her lips, undoubtedly the reason why her nickname *Mirry* had soon turned into *Merry* when she was small.

Paula smiled to herself, wondering what Miranda was wearing today, what surprise was in store for her. The twenty-three-year-old girl had a penchant for creating the most outlandish outfits—costumes really—but they were put together with imagination and style, and she certainly carried them off with élan. They would have looked perfectly ridiculous on anyone else, but somehow they were exactly right on Miranda O'Neill. Apart from suiting her tall, somewhat boyish figure, they were an adjunct to her fey and whimsical personality. Or so it seemed to Paula, who considered Merry to be an original, the one genuine free spirit she knew. Her grandmother was equally as fond of Miranda and said that Blackie's granddaughter was the best tonic in the world for all of them because she chased their blues away. "There's not a bad bone in that girl's body," Emma had remarked to Paula recently. "And now that she's grown up, she reminds me a lot of her grandmother. There's a good deal of Laura Spencer in Merry—Laura's true goodness for one thing. Also there's a wise head on those young shoulders, and I'm pleased you two have become such good friends. Every woman needs a close and trusted friend of the same sex. I should know. I never really had one after Laura died."

Remembering these words of Emma's, Paula thought: But she always had Blackie, and she still has him; whereas I've lost Shane. Funny, though, that Miranda and I drew closer together once Shane had dropped out . . .

There was a knock, and Agnes poked her head around the door. "These proofs just came up from the advertising department. Can you give them your okay?"

"Yes, come in, Agnes."

"They're the advertisements for the spring fashion sales," Agnes explained, handing them to her.

After studying the newspaper advertisements for a few seconds, Paula initialed the proofs, gave them back to her secretary, and stood up. "I'm going out onto the floor for a while. Could you phone the Bird Cage, Agnes, and tell them I'll need my usual table, please. At noon."

"Right away," Agnes said as they went out together.

When Emma Harte had first opened the café on the second floor of the Leeds store, she had called it the Elizabethan Gazebo and had decorated it in the style of an English country garden. Such things as handpainted wallpaper depicting pastoral scenes, panels of white trellis, artificial topiary animals, and antique bird cages combined to create a most enchanting little setting.

Over the years, as she refurbished the café, the name changed to match the theme, or vice versa. But always a garden or outdoor motif prevailed, often with an international flavor, as Emma had given rein to her imagination and fantasies with flair and not a little wit. After a trip to the Bosphorus with Paul McGill, she had been inspired to create the effect of a courtyard in a seraglio. Mosaic tiles, silver wallpaper painted with peacocks, potted palms, and a splashing fountain were combined in the new design. She had called the café Turkish Delight and had been delighted herself to witness its instantaneous popularity as a smart gathering place, not only for women shoppers but local businessmen who came in for lunch. Several years later Emma decided a more homespun motif was in order. Highland Fling was the name she chose, and the setting took on the appearance of a Scottish castle yard, featuring rustic furniture and colorful tartans. Eventually this ambiance gave way to one which suggested an oriental teahouse and drew its inspiration from the elegant decorative elements of the Far East. The café was renamed the China Doll. Then came the Balalaika, redolent of nineteenth-century Russia; after that it was transformed into Riviera Terrace, and in 1960 Emma redid the café yet again. This time she used a sophisticated theme based on the skyline of New York City, lining the walls with giant-sized photographic murals of Manhattan. The decor suggested a big-city roof garden, and she called it Skyscrapers. But by the late summer of 1968 Emma had grown tired of this decorative mood; and as the café needed a complete overhaul at this time, she gave the project to Paula, asking her to create something different.

Paula knew everything there was to know about all of the stores in the Harte chain, and she remembered the photographs she had seen of the original Elizabethan Gazebo. She went into the archives, dug out the original plans and sketches, and was instantly struck by the uniqueness and beauty of the antique bird cages. Since she was aware they were stored in packing cases in the basement, she had them brought up and unwrapped. And so the current theme and the latest name were born.

Paula had the wooden and brass bird cages repainted or repolished and, after finding more to add to the collection, she featured them throughout the restaurant. They stood out beautifully against a background of lime-green wallpaper overpatterned with a sharp white trellis design; white wicker chairs and matching tables with glass tops reiterated the outdoor mood. Paula loved all growing things, was in fact a gifted gardener, and so her final, masterful touch was a lush assortment of small trees, flowering shrubs, and plants. It was the many pots of hydrangeas and azaleas that gave the Bird Cage its cachet, and this real garden within the heart of the store bloomed in all seasons under her personal supervision. Emma had recognized at once that it was an evocation of her own first design and as such a little tribute to her, and she was flattered.

A few minutes after twelve on this Friday morning, Paula hurried into the Bird Cage, and as always she was struck by the refreshing sight of the flowers and foliage, one which appeared to cheer everyone up. Moving between the tables, where morning shoppers were settling down to lunch, Paula saw that Miranda O'Neill had already arrived. Her burnished copper hair, cascading in a glorious mass of waves and curls around her heart-shaped face, seemed to catch and hold all the light, was like a shining beacon at the far side of the room. Miranda glanced up from the menu she was perusing, saw Paula, and waved.

"Sorry I kept you waiting," Paula apologized when she reached the table. "I was delayed in the Designer Salon. We've been having the most awful trouble with the new lighting, and I wanted to check on it again. It's still not right, I'm afraid." She bent down and kissed her friend, slipped into the next chair.

Miranda grinned a little impishly, and said, "Oh dear, the trials and tribulations of running a store! I'll swap jobs with you any day. Doing public relations for a chain of hotels can be the pits at times."

"If I remember correctly, you really badgered your father for that job."

"That's true. But I wouldn't have if I'd known what I was letting myself in for," Miranda grumbled, making a long face. But she then had the good grace to laugh and admitted, "I suppose I enjoy it, really. It's only occasionally that I feel the pressure. But right now I'm in Dad's good books. He's very happy with my latest campaign, and he even went so far as to say I'd been innovative the other day. That's praise indeed from him. He's not given to paying me compliments, as you know. He even said that if I behave myself, he's going to send me to Barbados in a few weeks, to look over the hotel we've just bought there. By the time we've remodeled it and redecorated, it'll be super deluxe and as elegant as the Sandy Lane. We all believe it's going to be an important addition to our chain."

"That's marvelous, Merry. Really exciting for you. Now, shall we order? I don't want to rush you, but I have to leave the store early today."

"No problem, I'm a bit pushed myself." Miranda glanced at the menu again and said, "I'll have the plaice and chips, I think."

"Good idea. I'll join you." Paula caught the attention of the waitress, ordered, and then turned to Miranda, looking her over quickly, at once captivated by her outfit. Today she was wearing a rather theatrically styled jerkin with a wide, flaring collar and three-quarter sleeves, and it was laced up the front over a white silk shirt with longer sleeves. There was a twinkle in Paula's eyes as she said, "You look like a female Robin Hood in all that Sherwood Green suede, Merry. The only things that are missing are a quiver of arrows and a perkly little felt hat with a sweeping feather."

Miranda broke into laughter. "Don't think I don't have the hat! I *do*. But I didn't dare wear it to lunch, in case you'd think I was bonkers. Everyone else does." She swiveled in the chair to reveal her legs, which were encased in tight green-suede pants and matching boots that came up above her knees. "When Shane saw me this morning, he said I looked like the Principal Boy in a pantomime. I went the whole hog with this outfit, I'm afraid. *Is* it too theatrical?"

"Not really. And you could have worn the hat. I for one happen to like you in your fanciful costumes."

Miranda looked pleased. "Coming from the elegant you that's a real compliment." Leaning closer, she hurried on, "Are you and Jim busy tonight? I was wondering if I could invite you out to dinner?"

"I'd love *you* to join us tonight, if you won't be bored. Grandy's having a family dinner at Pennistone Royal."

"I'm not sure that that's still on, Paula. *Your* grandmamma has a hot date with *my* grandfather." Miranda's laugh held a hint of mischief, which was reflected in her eyes, as she said, "Can you imagine, and at their ages!"

Paula was thrown by this statement. "Oh you must be mistaken. I'm certain Grandy intends to be there."

"I'm not wrong, honestly I'm not. I heard Shane talking to my father a little while ago. Grandfather *is* taking Aunt Emma out to dinner. But I was only teasing when I said they had a hot date, since Shane's going with them."

"Then Grandy must have changed her plans," Paula said, dreading the thought of the dinner without her grandmother's presence. "I expect my mother will play hostess in her place, since I can't imagine Grandy actually canceling it without talking to me first."

"No, I don't think she would do that." Leaning forward again, her manner still teasing, Miranda said, "When my grandfather and your grandmother get together, they're incorrigible. I told him the other day that it was about time he made an honest woman out of Aunt Emma and married her."

"If anyone's incorrigible, it's you, Merry! And what did Uncle Blackie say to that?"

"He chuckled and told me he'd only been waiting for my approval, and now that he had it, he was going to pop the question. 'Course, I knew he was only kidding me in return. But to tell you the truth, I don't think it's such a bad idea, do you?"

Paula merely smiled. She said, "Anyway, getting back to the family dinner, you're very welcome. Come around seven-thirty for drinks. Dinner's at eight-thirty."

"You are a darling, Paula. Thank you. You've just rescued me from a boring evening with Ma and Pa. All they do these days is talk about the baby."

"I'm not sure your evening with us will be much more stimulating. My mother has become something of a doting grandma. All *she* does is rave about the twins. I can't seem to shut her up."

"But I adore Aunt Daisy. She's such a lovely woman and not a bit like the rest of you—" Miranda stopped, horrified at her words. Her pale, freckled face flamed to scarlet.

"And what's that supposed to mean?" Paula demanded, a dark brow arching as she pretended to be insulted, but the amusement touching her mouth betrayed her.

"I didn't mean it the way it came out," Miranda exclaimed in embarrassment. "I wasn't referring to you or Aunt Emma or your cousins, but to your aunts and uncles actually. I am sorry, though. It was rather rude of me."

"Don't apologize, I happen to agree with you." Paula fell silent, thinking specifically of her Aunt Edwina, the Dowager Countess of Dunvale, who was due to arrive from Ireland later that day. It was because of Edwina that she and Jim had had their first truly serious quarrel. Some weeks ago, to her utter astonishment and disbelief, Jim had decided that Edwina must be invited to the christening. When Paula had objected strenuously and had reminded him that Edwina was no favorite of Grandy's, he had brushed aside her protestations and told her she was being silly. And then *he* had reminded *her* that Emma wanted bygones to be bygones, sought peace within the family. "Well, you'd better not invite Edwina until I've mentioned it to Grandy," Paula cautioned, and he had acquiesced to this suggestion at least. When she had told her grandmother about it, Emma had appeared off-hand, indifferent even, and had told her to accept the situation gracefully, to let him invite Edwina, and to put a good face on it if she accepted. But there had been a strange look in Grandy's eyes, and Paula suspected that Emma had been disappointed in Jim. As she had herself, but she had overcome this feeling, loving him as much as she did; and she had excused Jim, too, because he had no family of his own to invite to his children's christening, and Edwina *was* half Fairley. If only Edwina weren't so hostile to Emma and to her.

Miranda, studying her friend, saw that she looked troubled, and ventured, "You're awfully pensive all of a sudden, Paula. Is something wrong?"

"No, no, of course not." Paula forced a smile and, changing the subject, asked, "How's your mother?"

"Her health's much better, thanks. Also I think she's finally recovered from the shock of getting pregnant at forty-five and giving birth to a change-of-life baby. And little Laura is simply adorable. I love to watch Grandfather playing with her. He's quite infatuated, and of course he's thrilled they called her Laura after my grandmother. They almost gave *me* that name, you know."

"No, I didn't, Merry."

"Yes. Then they changed their minds, I suppose. But I wouldn't have minded being named for my grandmother, and I certainly wish I'd known her. She must have been a remarkable woman. Everyone loved her so, especially Aunt Emma."

"Yes, and Grandy told me only the other day that she's never stopped missing Laura since the day she died."

"We're all muddled up, aren't we, Paula?"

"What do you mean?"

"The Hartes and the O'Neills. And the Fairleys, for that matter. Our lives are inextricably linked . . . we can't really escape each other, can we?"

"No, I don't suppose we can."

Miranda reached over and squeezed Paula's hand. "I'm glad we can't. I think it's rather nice to have you and Aunt Emma and Aunt Daisy for a second family." Her huge hazel eyes, sparkling with tiny prisms of gold, overflowed with warmth and affection.

Paula returned the pressure of her hand. "And it's nice for me to have the O'Neills."

The arrival of the waitress with the tray of food interrupted this exchange, and for the next fifteen minutes or so the two young women talked mostly about Paula's babies, the christening the next day, and the reception Emma was giving after the church ceremony. But then Miranda quite suddenly adopted a serious tone when she said, "There's something very important I'd like to discuss with you."

Paula, at once noticing the change in her friend's demeanor, asked swiftly, "Do you have problems?"

"Not at all. But I do have an idea I'd like to throw at you, to get your reaction."

"What kind of idea, Merry?" she asked curiously.

"You and I doing business together."

"Oh." This was the last thing Paula expected, and after her initial exclamation she was startled into momentary silence.

Miranda grinned and, not giving her a chance to comment further or brush the idea to one side, rushed on, "I had a flash of inspiration last week when I was going over the blueprints for the new hotel we're building in Marbella. The architect has planned a galleria of shops, and it struck me immediately that we must include a boutique. Naturally I thought of Harte's; then I realized one boutique wouldn't interest you. So I took the idea a step further . . . Harte boutiques in all of our hotels. There's the new one we're doing over in Barbados, we're about to remodel the Torremollinos hotel, and eventually the entire chain will get a revamp. We could have a boutique in each one, and Harte's could run them." Miranda sat back and searched Paula's face for a clue to her feelings, but it was unreadable. She asked eagerly, "Well, what do you think?"

"I'm not sure," Paula said noncommittally. "Have you discussed this with Uncle Bryan?"

"Yes, and Dad liked the idea. He was very gung ho actually and told me to talk to you." Miranda gazed at her friend expectantly and crossed her fingers. *"Would* you be willing to go into the venture with us?"

"I think we might be. I'd have to talk to my grandmother, of course." This was uttered with Paula's usual caution, but she could not conceal the interest quickening on her face. With a small rush of excitement, she thought: It could be the perfect project for Grandy. The one I've been looking for, and it would certainly take the sting out of the Cross fiasco. Straightening up, Paula said in a more positive voice, "Give me some additional details, Merry," and she listened attentively as the other girl talked. Within minutes she began to recognize the endless possibilities and advantages inherent in Miranda O'Neill's idea.

Four

Emma sat up with an abrupt jolt.

I don't believe it, I almost dozed off, she thought with exasperation. Only old ladies do that in the middle of the day. She began to laugh. Well, she was an old lady, wasn't she, even though she was loathe to admit that to anyone, least of all herself.

Shifting her position on the sofa, she stretched, then straightened her skirt, and immediately became aware of the heat from the blazing fire. The room was stifling even for her—she, who had always suffered from the cold and rarely ever felt warm enough. No wonder she had become so drowsy.

With a burst of energy she propelled herself up and off the sofa and hurried to the windows. She opened one of them and took several deep breaths, fanning herself with her hand. The crisp air felt good, and the breeze brushing against her face soon refreshed her, and she stood there for a moment or two until she was cooler before turning away and retracing her steps.

Her pace was slower, and she looked around as she skirted the two large plump sofas in the center of the floor. She nodded with pleasure, thinking how lovely the room appeared at this moment, washed as it was in the golden sunlight now streaming in through the many windows. But then it always did look beautiful to her, and she would rather be here than anywhere else on this earth.

Is it age, I wonder, that makes us cleave to the best-known spaces in our lives, to the well-loved and familiar things? Is it the memories of the years gone by and of those we cared so much about, which bind us to those places and make them so special in our deepest hearts? She believed that this was true—at least for her. She felt safe, and comforted, when she was in surroundings where so many episodes of her long and colorful life had been played out.

Such a place was Pennistone Royal, this ancient, historic and rambling house on the outskirts of Ripon, which she had purchased in 1932. In particular she favored this room—the upstairs parlor—where she had spent so many endless happy hours over the years. She had often wondered how it had come to be called the upstairs parlor, for there was nothing parlorlike about it at all. This struck her once again as her glance took in the impressive architectural details and the splendid furnishings.

By the very nature of its dimensions, the room had a singular grandeur, with its high, Jacobean ceiling decorated with elaborate plasterwork, its tall leaded windows flanking the unique oriel window, and the carved fireplace of bleached oak. Yet for all its imposing detail and despite its size, Emma had introduced a mellow charm and great comfort, plus a subtle understated elegance that had taken time, much patience, superb taste, and a vast amount of money to create.

Being confident of her original choices, Emma had never felt it necessary to change anything, so the room had remained the same for over thirty years. She knew for instance that no other paintings could ever surpass the fine portraits of a young nobleman and his wife by Sir Joshua Reynolds, or the priceless Turner landscape. The three oils were in perfect harmony with her graceful Georgian antiques, collected so lovingly and with infinite care. And such things as the Savonnerie carpet, faded now to a delicate beauty, and her Rose Medallion china in the Chippendale cabinet, were matchless touches that added to the room's graciousness and style. Even the walls were always repainted in their original primrose, for to her discerning eye this pale and delicate color made the most restful backdrop for the art and the rich patinas of the dark woods, and it introduced the cheerful sunny aspect she preferred.

This morning the springlike mood of the setting, created by the airy color scheme and the brightly patterned chintz on the sofas, was reinforced by porcelain bowls brimming with jonquils, tulips, and hyacinths, which spilled their lively yellows, reds, pinks, and mauves onto some of the darkly gleaming surfaces, and their fragrant scents were aromatic on the still and gentle air.

Emma moved forward, then paused again in front of the fireplace. She never tired of looking at the Turner which hung above the mantelpiece, dominating the soaring chimney wall with its misty greens and blues. The landscape was bucolic, evocative, and a superb example of Turner's poetic and visionary interpretations of the pastoral scene.

It's definitely the light, she decided for the hundredth time, as always fascinated by the luminous sky in the painting. In Emma's opinion no one had ever been able to capture light on canvas in quite the same manner as Turner. The clear cool light in this masterpiece was forever associated in her mind with the northern skies under which she had grown up and had lived for most of her life, and which she would love always. She believed them to be unique because of their clarity and a radiance that seemed unearthly at times.

Her eye now caught the carriage clock, reposing on the mantelpiece. It was almost one. She had better pull herself together and very smartly, since Emily was due momentarily, and everyone had to be on their toes when the volatile, whirlwind Emily was around. Most especially old ladies, she added, chuckling softly again.

Hurrying briskly into the adjoining bedroom, she sat down at her dressing table. After dabbing her nose with powder, she renewed her pink lipstick and ran a comb through her hair. There, that does it. Passable, she added under her breath, peering into the glass. No, more than passable. I really do look pretty nifty today, as Alexander said I did.

She swung her head and stared at Paul's photograph standing on one corner of the dressing table, and she began to speak to him in her mind. This was an old habit of hers and one which had become something of a ritual.

I wonder what you would think of me if you could see me now? Would you recognize your glorious Emma, as you used to call me? Would you think that I have grown old gracefully, as I believe I have?

Picking up the photograph, she sat holding it with both hands, gazing down into his face. After all these years she still remembered every facet of him and with a poignant vividness, as if she had seen him only yesterday. She blew a mote of dust off the glass. How handsome he looked in his white tie and tails. This was the last picture taken of him. In New York on February the third of 1939. She recalled the date so easily. It had been his fifty-ninth birthday, and she had invited a group of their friends for drinks at their lavish Fifth Avenue apartment, and then they had gone to the Metropolitan Opera to hear Risë Stevens and Ezio Pinza sing *Mignon*. Afterward Paul had taken them to Delmonico's for his birthday dinner, and it had been a wonderful evening, marred only at its outset by Daniel Nelson's talk of impending war, and Paul's equally bleak assessment of the world situation. Paul's mood had been gay later at dinner. But it was the last carefree evening they ever spent together.

She touched the white wings of his hair with a fingertip, and half smiled to herself. The twins who were being baptized tomorrow were *his* first great-grandchildren too, a continuation of his bloodline. Upon his death, the McGill dynasty had passed into her hands for safekeeping, and she had guarded it well and faithfully, just as she had preserved and multiplied his great fortune, which she had solemnly vowed she would.

Sixteen years, she thought. We only had sixteen years together. Not very much time really, in the span of a life . . . particularly a long life like mine.

Without thinking, she spoke aloud, "If only you had lived longer. If only we could have shared our later years, grown old together. How wonderful that would have been." Unexpectedly her eyes misted over and she felt a tightening in her throat. Why you foolish, foolish old woman, she admonished herself silently. Weeping now for something gone so far beyond tears. With a swift and darting movement she returned the photograph to its given place.

"Grandma . . . are you alone?" Emily asked in a tentative voice from the doorway.

Startled, Emma jumped and turned in the chair. Her face lit up. "Oh hello, Emily dear. I didn't hear you come through the parlor. And of course I'm alone."

Emily ran to her, gave her a resounding kiss, and then looked down at her curiously. She said, with a funny little smile, "I could have sworn I heard you talking to someone, Gran."

"I was. I was talking to him." She inclined her head at the photograph and added dryly, "And if you think I'm getting senile, you can forget it. I've talked to that photograph for thirty years."

"Gosh, Grandy, you're the last person I'd ever think of as being senile!" Emily was quick to reassure, meaning every word. "Mummy maybe, but never you."

Emma fixed her coolly probing eyes on her granddaughter. "Where is your mother, Emily? Do you know?"

"Haiti. Basking in the sun. At least I *think* that's where she's gone."

"Haiti." Emma sat up in the chair, surprise registering, and then she let out a small whoop of a laugh. "Isn't that the place they practice voodoo. I hope she isn't having a wax doll made called Emma Harte, into which she can stick pins and wish me ill as she does."

Emily also laughed, shaking her head. "Honestly, Gran, you are a card. Mummy wouldn't think of anything like *that*. I doubt she's ever heard of voodoo. Besides, I'm sure she's far too preoccupied. With the Frenchman."

"Oh. So, she's done another bolt, has she? And with a Frenchman this time. Well, I must say, your mother is getting to be a regular United Nations."

"Yes, she does seem to have developed a fondness for foreign gentlemen, Grandy." Emily's green eyes brimmed with laughter as she stood rocking on her heels, regarding her grandmother with delight, enjoying their bit of repartee. There was no one like her Gran when it came to the caustic jab which got right to the heart of the matter.

Emma said, "Knowing your mother, he undoubtedly has an uncertain character, not to mention a dubious title. What's this one's name?"

"Marc Deboyne. You might have read about him. He's always in the gossip columns. And you're right on target regarding his character. But he doesn't have a title, dubious or otherwise."

"That's a relief. I'm sick to death of all these counts and princes and barons with unpronounceable names, grandiose ideas, and empty wallets, whom your mother unfailingly collects. *And* invariably marries. Deboyne *is* a playboy though, isn't he?"

"I'd categorize him as IWT, Gran."

"What on earth does that mean, dear?" Emma asked, her brows lifting, expressing her puzzlement.

"International White Trash."

Emma guffawed. "That's a new one on me. And whilst I get the implication, explain further, please, Emily."

"It's a term for men with murky backgrounds, even questionable backgrounds, who have social aspirations which they can only hope to fulfill in another country. I mean a country not their own. You know, where inconsistencies won't be spotted. It could be an Englishman in Paris, a Russian in New York, or, as in this instance, a frog in London." Emily made a disagreeable face. "Marc Deboyne has been flitting around Mayfair's fashionable drawing rooms for years, and I'm surprised Mummy got involved with him. He's so *transparent*. He must have managed to dupe her somehow. Personally, I think he stinks, Gran."

Emma frowned. "Have you met him then?"

"Yes and before Mummy too." She stopped short, deciding not to mention that Deboyne had made a pass at her first. That would really be inflammatory to her Gran. She finished, "He's quite ghastly."

Emma sighed and wondered how much this one was going to cost her daughter. For cost her he would. That type of man always came expensive— frequently emotionally, but *always* financially. Dismally she thought of the million pounds she had given Elizabeth last year. Cold cash too. Most of it had probably been frittered away by now. Still, what that foolish woman did with the money was no concern of hers. She had only been interested in buying Elizabeth off, and in so doing, protecting Alexander, Emily, and the fifteen-year-old twin girls. Emma said with some asperity, "Your mother is impossible. *Impossible*. Where are her brains, for God's sake? Don't bother to answer that, Emily. In the meantime, out of curiosity, whatever happened to the current husband? That lovely Italian."

Emily stared at her in disbelief. "Grandy!" she shrieked. "What a switch! You always said you thought he was a gigolo. In fact you were usually quite unkind about him, and I was certain you detested him."

"I changed my mind," Emma replied loftily. "As it turned out he wasn't a fortune hunter, and he was nice to the twins." She stood up. "Let's go into the parlor and have a drink before lunch." She tucked her arm through Emily's companionably and steered her across the floor. She asked again, "So where is Gianni what's-his-name?"

"He's around. He's moved out of Mummy's flat, of course. But he's still in London. He's got himself a job with some Italian importing company—antiques, I believe. He often telephones me to ask about Amanda and Francesca. He's rather attached to them, I think."

"I see." Emma disentangled her arm and lowered herself onto one of the sofas. "I'd like a gin and tonic, Emily, instead of the usual sherry. Do the honors, please dear."

"Yes, Grandy. I think I'll have one myself." Always in a tearing hurry, Emily dashed across the room to the Georgian table which held a silver tray of bottles and Baccarat crystal glasses. Emma's eyes followed her. In the red wool suit and frilly lilac blouse, Emily reminded her of an iridescent hummingbird, so small, so swift, so brilliantly plumed, and so full of life. She's a good girl, Emma thought. Thank God she hasn't turned out like her mother.

Mixing the drinks deftly, Emily said, over her shoulder, "Talking of my baby half-sisters, Gran, are you going to let them stay at Harrogate College?"

"For the moment. But I fully intend to pack them off to finishing school in Switzerland this September. In the meantime they seem to be happy at the college. Of course I realize that's because of my proximity. I suppose I spoil them, letting them come home so much." Emma paused, remembering the fuss and bother and upset the previous year, when her two youngest grandchildren had tearfully begged to come and live with her. Emma had finally succumbed under their constant pressuring, although her acquiescence had been conditional. For their part, they had had to agree to attend the nearby boarding school Emma had selected. The girls had been thrilled, their mother delighted to be rid of them, Emma relieved that she had averted a nasty family contretemps from developing further.

Leaning back against the cushions, she let out a tiny sigh. "Anyway, spoil them or not, I do feel those two need mothering and a chance to lead a normal family life. They've had little enough of either with your mother."

"That's true," Emily agreed, carrying the drinks over to the seating arrangement in front of the fire. "I feel a bit sorry for them myself. I suppose Alexander and I got the best of Mummy—I mean, her better years. The girls have had a rough time of it . . . all those husbands. It seems to me that ever since she left their father, our mother has been on a downward slide. Oh well, what can you do? . . ." Emily's young breathy voice petered out sadly. She shrugged in resignation, and her whole demeanor reflected her disenchantment. "There's not much you or I *can* do about *your* daughter, *my* mother, Grandy. She's not likely to change."

Emily now looked across at her grandmother, her blond brows meeting in a frown. She said in a fretful tone, "The trouble with poor Mummy is that she suffers from the most terrible insecurity about herself, her looks, her figure, her personality . . . well, just about everything."

"Oh, do you think so?" Emma exclaimed in astonishment at this remark. Her face changed, and there was a glint of malice in her flinty green eyes as she remarked, with immense coldness, "I can't *imagine* why." She lifted her glass. "Cheers."

"Cheers, Gran darling."

Emma settled into a corner of the vast sofa, and, squinting in the sunlight, she focused on the attractive twenty-two-year-old Emily. The girl had a special place in her affections, for apart from being open and uncomplicated, she had a very lovable personality, one that was sunny, cheerful, and perennially optimistic, and she was a dynamic girl, filled with enthusiasm for life and her work. If Emily's pink-and-cream blond prettiness had the porcelain fragility of a Dresden shepherdess, it was nevertheless deceptive, belying an extraordinary drive that had the velocity and power of an express train running at full speed. Emma knew there were those in the family, specifically her sons, who thought Emily was scatterbrained and flippant. This secretly amused Emma, since she was fully aware that Emily purposely chose to give this fraudulent impression. In no way did it reflect her basic seriousness and diligence. Emma had long ago decided that her sons really disliked their niece because she was far too blunt and opinionated—and truthful—for their comfort. Emma had been witness to more than one scene when the intrepid Emily had made Kit and Robin squirm.

Emma looked into the clear green eyes, a reflection of her own as they had once been, saw the expectancy flickering in them, then noted the confident smile etched on Emily's mouth. Emily had obviously convinced herself she was going to get her own way. *Oh dear.* Taking a deep breath, Emma said with a faint laugh, "For someone with a serious problem, you certainly don't look very troubled, dear. You're positively glowing this morning."

Emily nodded and admitted, "I don't think my problem's all that serious, Grandy. I mean, it doesn't seem to be today."

"I'm glad to hear that. You sounded as if you had the burdens of the world on your shoulders, when you spoke to me on Tuesday morning."

"Did I really?" Emily laughed. "I suppose things seem so much brighter when I'm with you. Perhaps that's because I know you can always solve any problem, and I just know you'll—" She broke off when Emma held up a silencing hand.

Emma said, "I've known for some time that you want to go back to Paris, to work in the store there. That *is* what you want to discuss, isn't it? That is your *problem?*"

"Yes, Gran," Emily said, her eyes shining with eagerness.

Emma put down her drink on the butler's tray table and leaned forward, her expression suddenly serious. She said carefully, "I'm afraid I can't let you go to Paris. I'm very sorry to disappoint you, Emily, but you will have to stay here."

The happy smile vanished, and Emily's face dropped. "But why, Grandy?" she asked in a crushed voice. "I thought you were pleased with the way I handled things in Paris all last summer and through the autumn."

"I was. Very pleased in fact and proud of you. Your performance has nothing to do with my decision. No, that's not strictly true. One of the reasons I've formulated new plans for you is because of the way you performed over there." Emma's eyes did not leave her granddaughter's face as she explained carefully, "Plans for your future. Which, in my considered opinion, is with Harte Enterprises."

"Harte Enterprises!" Emily cried, her voice rising incredulously.

She froze on the sofa, staring at her grandmother dumbfounded. "Where would I fit in *there?* Alexander, Sarah, and Jonathan are working in that company, and I'd just be a spare wheel! A dog's body, with nothing to do. Anyway, I've always worked for *you.* In the stores. I love retailing, and you know that, Gran. I'd just hate, positively hate and detest, being pushed into that organization," Emily protested with uncommon fierceness, flushing bright pink. Breathlessly she rushed on, "I really mean it. You've always said it's important to enjoy one's work. Well, I certainly wouldn't enjoy working at Harte Enterprises. Oh please let me go to Paris. I really love that store, and I want to continue to help you get it properly on its feet. Please change your mind. Please, oh *please,* Gran darling. I'll just be miserable if you don't," she wailed, and her face was as woebegotten as her voice as she clenched her hands together in her lap.

Emma made an irritated clucking noise and shook her head reprovingly. "Now, now, Emily, don't be so dramatic," she exclaimed with unusual sharpness. "And do stop trying to cajole me. I know all about your wheedling. Sometimes it works; other times, like right now, I am quite impervious to it. And incidentally, the Paris store *is* on its feet, thanks in no small measure to you. So you're not needed there anymore. Very frankly, I need you here."

This remark, although uttered mildly, caused Emily to sit up swiftly, and she frowned, further taken aback. *"You* need me, Grandy. What for? What do you mean?" Emily's eyes widened and filled with worry. She wondered if her grandmother had a serious problem within Harte Enterprises. Hardly. Her health? That seemed unlikely too. But obviously something was amiss.

"What's wrong, Grandma?" she asked, giving words to her spiraling anxiety, all ideas about Paris swept completely out of her head.

"There is nothing *wrong,* dear," Emma said with a bright smile, detecting the girl's concern. "Before I explain my reasons for wanting you here, I would like to clarify my remark about your future. Naturally I realize you like working at the stores, but you can't get much further at Harte's. Paula and your Uncle David have the real power there these days, and Paula will inherit all of my shares one day. Paula respects your ability, and she would love to keep you by her side, but Emily, you'd always be a salaried employee, with no financial interest whatsoever. I do—"

"I know that," Emily interjected. "But—"

"Don't interrupt me," Emma snapped, cutting her off. "As you learned last spring, I have left you sixteen percent of Harte Enterprises, and that's a huge interest, since the company is so very rich. And solid. As solid as the Bank of England, in my opinion. Your wealth, your future security will come from your shares in Harte Enterprises, and I have felt for the longest time that you must have a hand in running it. After all, it will belong in part to you one day."

Emma could not fail to miss the worried expression now settling on Emily's face, and she reached across the table and squeezed her arm affectionately. "Don't look so distressed. I'm not implying that I lack confidence in your brother. You must know that I don't. Alexander will guide and guard Harte Enterprises with all of his strength and ability, and with great devotion, I've no fear. Nevertheless I want *you* to be active there, along with Sandy and your cousins. I really believe that you must direct that considerable energy of yours, and your many talents into the company in which you have such a major stake, and from which you will reap so many benefits."

Emily was quiet, mulling over her grandmother's words, and after a longish pause, she said slowly, "Yes, I see what you mean, and I know you have my interests at heart, but there's nothing about the company that appeals to me. Anyway, Sarah has always enjoyed running the clothing end, and she'd resent it if you shoved me in there with her. As for Jonathan, he'd really get on that high horse of his, if you foist me on *him.* He considers the real estate division to be his little kingdom and his alone. He'd be in revolt if I started poking around there. So what would I do at H.E.? The only thing I understand is retailing." Her voice faltered, for she was on the verge of tears, and she looked away swiftly, staring out of the window, her expression exceedingly glum.

The prospect of leaving the Harte chain of stores and Paula, whom she worshiped, was depressing and distressing to Emily. And she *would* have to leave. That had already been decided, she had the good sense to recognize. Her opinion wasn't being sought. She was being *told* what to do, told what was expected of her, and her grandmother's authority was unassailable. Besides that cold and stubborn look was now engraved on her grandmother's face, and it was a look they were all familiar with, one which left nothing to the imagination. It said in no uncertain language that Emma Harte would have her own way no matter what. Emily felt the prick of tears behind her eyes as she contemplated her miserable future. Mortified, she blinked them back and swallowed, endeavoring to hold on to her diminishing composure. Tears, emotion, and any other sign of weakness in business were anathema to her grandmother.

Emma, observing the girl closely, saw how troubled and upset she was growing, and realized immediately that she must allay Emily's worries. Adopting her most sympathetic manner, Emma said, "Don't take this so hard, dear. It's not half as bad as you imagine. And I certainly had no intention of putting you in either of the divisions run by your cousins. That wouldn't be fair to any of you. Nor am I considering making you Sandy's assistant—if that idea has entered your agile little brain. No, no, nothing like that. When I said I needed you here, I did mean *here*. In Yorkshire. I would like you to work at General Retail Trading and learn everything there is to know about that division of Harte Enterprises. You see, Emily, I want you to run it for me eventually."

For a moment Emily thought she had misheard. She was so surprised she was speechless. She gaped at her grandmother and then finally managed to ask, "Are you serious?"

"Really, Emily, that's a stupid question. Do you honestly think *I* would joke about my *business?*"

"No, Grandy." Emily bit her lip, trying to digest her grandmother's words. The General Retail Trading Company, known within the family as Genret, was one of Harte Enterprises' most important assets and an enormous money maker. As the implications behind her grandmother's announcement began to sink in, she was assaulted by a mixture of emotions: She was flattered, overwhelmed, worried, and scared all at once. But these feelings were almost instantaneously overshadowed by genuine bafflement.

Sitting forward with a jerk, she asked in a puzzled voice, "But why do you suddenly need *me?* You have Leonard Harvey. He's been running Genret for years and brilliantly. Or so you've always said."

"And I meant what I said." Emma picked up her drink, took a sip, sat nursing it in her hands. "However, Len reminded me several weeks ago that he will be retiring in three years. I'd hoped he would stay on, but he insists on going when it's time. He wants a chance to enjoy life, do a few of the things he's always wanted to do, like take a trip around the world, for one thing." Emma laughed softly. "I can certainly understand his point of view. That man's worked for me for over thirty-five years, and I don't remember him ever taking a day off, except for his annual summer holidays in August. Naturally, I'd no option but to agree, albeit reluctantly."

Emma put down her drink, rose, and went to stand with her back to the fireplace. She stared down at Emily and continued matter-of-factly, "Len brought up his retirement because he thought it was high time I started to think about his successor. It occurred to me at once that here was the perfect opening for you. I've been wracking my brains for months, wondering how to get you situated within Harte Enterprises in a division you would enjoy. I believe I've found it, Emily, and I'm also convinced Genret could well use your special talents."

Emily said nothing. She, who had an opinion about everything which she usually had no qualms expressing, was now oddly at a loss for words.

Emma stood waiting, giving Emily a chance to catch her breath and marshal her thoughts. She understood perfectly the girl's unprecedented reticence. She had just dropped a bombshell on her. But as the silence grew, Emma, always in a hurry to settle matters and move on, announced peremptorily, "I need you to start working at Genret immediately. Len wants to begin his training program at once. Three years may seem like a long time to you, but it isn't really. Genret is a large company, and you will have a great deal to absorb and understand. So what do you say?"

Still Emily was mute, and Emma threw her a sharper look. Then she scowled at her. "Come along, dear, you must have some comment to make. I can't believe that the cat's got *your* tongue permanently."

Pulling herself together, Emily gave her grandmother an uncertain smile. "Are you sure? Really sure about me going into Genret?"

"I wouldn't have suggested it, if I'd had any doubts," Emma retorted crossly.

"But what about the group at Genret?" Emily asked quickly. "I mean, will they sit still for it? For me?"

"I *am* Genret, Emily. Or had you forgotten that?"

"No, no, of course I hadn't, Grandmother. What I meant was, will Len and the top management team accept me? I know you can appoint anybody you want, since it's your company, but surely Len must have a protégé, somebody he would like to follow in his footsteps, who knows the inner workings of Genret."

"He doesn't. Furthermore he thinks you're the ideal choice. And he's not just pandering to me. Len's too shrewd and outspoken to fall into that trap. And, while he realizes I would *like* a member of the family inside Genret once he goes, he would tell me point-blank if there was no suitable candidate. He would insist we look outside the family. It just so happens that he thinks you're ideally suited to head up a wholesale supply company. For several reasons, all of them excellent. Your experience with the stores, your considerable knowledge of retailing, not to mention merchandise, plus your natural business abilities. That you also happen to be my granddaughter is simply fortuitous. It didn't influence him one iota, I can assure you of that. Besides, you're a quick study, Emily, and you've learned a lot in the last five years."

"I'm glad to have Len's vote of confidence as well as yours, Grandy." Emily started to relax, and as her depression also began to lift, she discovered she was excited about the sudden turn of events. She asked, "And Alexander? Have you discussed it with him?"

"Naturally. He thinks you'll be marvelous."

"What does Paula say?"

"She's delighted too. She's going to miss you at the stores, but she recognizes the good sense behind my plans for you."

"Then it's settled!" Emily beamed and allowed her natural enthusiasm to surface. "Genret is a big responsibility, but now that I've recovered from my initial surprise, I'm looking forward to it, I really am. I'll try very hard, and I'll do my best not to let you down."

"I know you will, dear." Emma returned her smile, delighted to finally witness Emily's eagerness and her excitement. Not that she had had any doubts about her offer being accepted. Emily was far too clever to thwart her, *or* to pass up the opportunity to head a division. Besides Emily loved a challenge. This last thought prompted Emma to add, "I'm quite certain you'll enjoy this new venture as much as you did your sojourn in Paris last year. It's going to be equally as challenging and ultimately very rewarding."

"Yes, I know it will be." With a sudden flush of embarrassment, Emily recalled her outburst of earlier. Looking extremely shamefaced, she apologized, "I'm sorry I behaved in such a childish way, when you said I couldn't go back to Paris, Grandy. It was ridiculous of me to act like that."

"I understand. You were disappointed. In any case, you'll be going to Paris quite a lot for Genret and traveling all over the world on your buying trips. That's certainly something to look forward to, Emily."

"Oh it is, Grandy. And thank you for your faith in me and for this wonderful opportunity." Emily jumped up and hugged Emma tightly. With a happy little laugh, she said, "Oh Grandy, you're such an inspiration! You make everything seem possible—and attainable. And exciting as well. Do you know what? I feel like rushing down to the Genret offices in Leeds right now and getting stuck into the work with Len immediately."

"Len and Genret have managed to exist without you until now, Emily, so I think they'll survive for another few days," Emma replied, her mouth twitching with hidden laughter. "In the meantime I have a much better idea. I think you should come downstairs with me and have lunch instead. I don't know about you, but I'm famished."

Five

Emma sat at the table in her splendidly appointed Adam dining room, sipping a cup of coffee after lunch, smiling and nodding occasionally, enjoying Emily's natural *joie de vivre* and bubbling enthusiasm for everything. Earlier, when they had been eating, Emily had bombarded her with questions about Genret. Each one had been probing and not without a certain shrewdness, and this had pleased Emma.

Now, the twenty-two-year-old was entertaining her with tidbits of gossip about the family, and as usual Emma found her pithy comments hilarious. Robin and Kit were most often the butts of her barbed wit, and she had already managed to get in a few sharp digs about her uncles.

But here her sarcasm stopped, for she never made astringent or unkind remarks about anyone else. Although Emily tended to be something of a chatterbox, she was not malicious, nor was she a talebearer intent on stirring up trouble. In point of fact, she was anything but this, and Emma was well aware that her granddaughter's predilection for chattering was harmless enough, especially since she knew herself to be the girl's only confidante. To Emma's considerable relief, Emily was not only discreet but extremely close-mouthed with everyone else in the family, and even Paula and Alexander, with whom she was on very intimate terms, were no exceptions to this rule.

Unexpectedly Emily veered away from her discourse on the family and launched into glowing descriptions of the outfits she had chosen for the fifteen-year-old twins to wear the next day. Recently Emily had elected to play a motherly big-sister role with Amanda and Francesca, and Emma had assigned to her the task of selecting their clothes and looking after similar details.

But it was not very long before Emma found her attention straying, her mind forever preoccupied with business, and specifically Paula's meeting with the Crosses. She could not help speculating on the outcome, wondering how Paula had fared. If the negotiations had gone well, she was facing a fair amount of work. Not that this troubled Emma unduly. She had always thrived on honest-to-goodness toil and still did, and Paula had laid out foolproof plans for the takeover.

Emma and Paula wanted Aire Communications for its three most impor-

tant assets: its magazine division, its local radio stations, its huge, modern building in the Headrow. Following Paula's advice, she fully intended to make Aire
Communications a subsidiary of the Yorkshire Consolidated Newspaper Company. Once she had relocated the entire staff of Aire in the offices of the
Yorkshire *Morning Gazette,* her newspaper headquartered in Leeds, she would
sell the Aire Communications building. This would enable her to cut down on
Aire's staggering overhead, and at the same time she would cleverly recoup part
of the purchase price, possibly a good half of her two-million-pound investment. Yes, that building's worth at least a million, Emma reflected, whatever
Jonathan says to the contrary. She would have to have a little talk with her
grandson tomorrow, a very serious talk. He was dragging his feet with his
second evaluation of Aire's prime bit of real estate. She had asked him for it
days ago, and he had not yet responded. Once again she wondered why, and
her mouth tightened.

"Grandy, you're not listening to me!" Emily shook her arm impatiently.

"Oh sorry, dear. You were saying you'd chosen navy blue dresses and
coats for the twins. I'm sure they're very smart, you have such good—"

"Goodness, Gran, that was five minutes ago," Emily interjected. "I was
already onto another subject. Aunt Edwina to be precise."

"Now why on earth is *she* suddenly so interesting to *you?*"

"She's not really. I think she's an old sourpuss and a crashing bore," Emily
said in her typical blunt fashion. "However, I'm positive we're going to be in
for a rocky ride with her this weekend. I bet she's going to give us all an
earful."

"What about?" Emma asked, sounding slightly baffled.

"The divorce," Emily said succinctly.

This reply brought Emma upright in her chair, and she stared hard at
Emily. "So, you've heard about *that,* have you?" Surprise immediately gave way
to humor, and Emma chuckled and shook her head. "Is there anything you
don't know about this family of ours?"

"Not much," said Emily, grinning at her. "But I don't pry, Gran. You
know that. Everyone just tells me things automatically. It must be my sympathetic nature." Her grin widened. "And then I tell you. Never secrets, though.
I don't break a confidence. Ever."

"I should hope not, dear. Remember what I've always said . . . a still
tongue and a wise head. Anyway, who mentioned Anthony's divorce?"

"Jim. He came to see me last weekend. He wanted my opinion about
something, my advice really. He brought up the divorce in passing. It was Aunt
Edwina who told him. Apparently she's terribly upset . . . scandal touching
the sacred name of the Dunvales and all that silly nonsense. As if anybody *cares*
about divorce these days. But she'll harp on about it for the next few days, you
mark my words."

"I doubt it, since Anthony will be here himself. In fact, he's already here."

"In this house?" It was Emily's turn to be astonished.

"No. He's staying with your Uncle Randolph up at Middleham. Actually,
he's going to be there for the next week." A wicked gleam entered Emma's
eyes, and she could not resist teasing, "Obviously there are *some* things you
don't know, Emily. Our young earl is staying with the Hartes because he's
courting Sally. Very seriously courting her." Emma was unable to hold back a
laugh as she observed the expression on Emily's face.

Emily was so dumbfounded by this piece of news that her jaw dropped. But it took less than a second for her to recover, and she retorted, "And I bet Aunt Edwina doesn't know either! Otherwise she would have scuttled that relationship ages ago. And she'll still try."

"She can do nothing," Emma snapped, her face hardening. "Anthony is not only of age, he's thirty-three. He doesn't have to answer to his mother, or anyone else for that matter, and I told him so last night. He has my blessing. Frankly, I'm glad he's going to marry Sally. She's a fine girl and quite lovely, and it's a perfect match in my opinion."

"I second that about Sally being a lovely person. But then I'm prejudiced. So are you—even more so, because she looks so much like your mother. And Edwina's going to be prejudiced too, in the other direction." Emily stopped, thinking of her aunt's reaction, which would be violent, and she cried excitedly, "Oh my God! I can't wait to see Aunt Edwina's face when she finds out he's involved with Sally Harte. She's going to be absolutely furious, Grandma. She has such grand ideas about everything. And after all, Sally's only a generation removed from the working class."

"And what do you think Edwina is?"

"A countess," Emily giggled gleefully, "and a Fairley to boot! She's never been the same since she discovered her father was Sir Edwin Fairley, and a K.C., no less. She's an even bigger snob now than she was before. It's a pity you ever told her the truth about you and old Edwin, Gran."

"I'm inclined to agree with you."

Emma averted her face, looked out of the window, focused her thoughts on her eldest grandchild, son of her own first-born child. Anthony Standish was the only offspring of Edwina's marriage with the Earl of Dunvale, and as such he was her whole life. Because Emma had been estranged from Edwina for years, she had not really come to know Anthony until he was eighteen. That was in 1954, when her brother Winston had affected a reconciliation between her and her daughter. More like an armed truce, Emma said inwardly, but at least the boy and I took to each other immediately, and thankfully we have continued to be close. She was extremely fond of Anthony, who, despite his reserved nature and gentle manner, had an inner strength and a toughness of mind that Emma had recognized instantly and privately applauded. Upon his father's death, he had inherited the latter's title and lands in Ireland. For the most part Anthony lived at Clonloughlin, his estate in County Cork, but whenever he had the occasion to be in England, he never failed to visit her. It was on one of these trips to Yorkshire six months ago that he had become reacquainted with Sally, Winston's granddaughter, who was his cousin. According to Anthony they had fallen in love at once. "It was a *coup de foudre,* Grandmother," he had confided shyly last night. "And as soon as my divorce from Min is final, I intend to marry Sally." Emma, delighted at this news, had indicated her pleasure and assured him of her full support.

Shifting in the chair, Emma glanced at Emily and said, "I wouldn't worry your head about Anthony. He can take care of himself. I told him not to hide his relationship with Sally anymore—from his mother, that is—and to behave naturally at the christening. We might as well get this out in the open once and for all."

"Edwina will make trouble, Grandma. Big, big trouble," Emily warned, rolling her eyes at the ceiling.

"If she knows what's good for her, she won't," Emma replied, her voice murderously soft. "Now, on to other things. You said Jim wanted your advice. What about, Emily?"

"The gift he's bought for Paula. It's a strand of pearls, and he wasn't sure she'd like them. But they're beautiful, and I told him she'd be thrilled."

"That's nice." Emma glanced at her watch, feeling restless. "I'll have another quick cup of coffee, and then I'd better go up and do a little paperwork until Paula arrives."

"I'll get the coffee for you," Emily volunteered, taking Emma's cup to the sideboard. Returning with it, she said, "I had dinner with T.B. when I was in London on Tuesday. He sends his love."

Emma's face softened considerably. She had always cared for Tony Barkstone, Elizabeth's first husband and father of Emily and Alexander. They had remained good friends over the years, and she asked, with a warm smile, "How is he?"

"In good form. He's as sweet as always, and he seems happy. No, *content* might be a better word. Or perhaps *accepting* is even better. Yes, that's it. He's accepting." Emily sighed heavily.

And a little too dramatically, in Emma's opinion. But then Emily was a romantic girl and Emma knew that she had long harbored the desire for her parents to be reunited. A most unlikely event, as far as Emma was concerned. Looking at Emily thoughtfully, Emma's brow lifted quizzically, and she murmured, *"Accepting* is a peculiar word to use about your father's life, isn't it, dear?"

"Not really. I think T.B. *is* accepting—of his new family. But I don't believe my father has been really happy since he split with Mummy. To tell you the truth, Gran, I think he's still in love with her." She confided this in an intense tone, giving Emma a long and knowing look.

"Oh phooey!"

"Well, she *was* his grand passion, that I know for a fact—because he once told me so. I believe he's carrying a torch for her."

"That's a bit farfetched, Emily. They've been divorced for donkey's years."

"Even so, he could have remained shackled to her emotionally." Emily tilted her blond head to one side and wrinkled her nose. "Unrequited love and all that. Why are you looking so skeptical, Grandma? Don't you believe that's possible?"

"Possible. Not very practical. And I'm quite certain your father has more common sense than to yearn after Elizabeth. He had *her* pegged years ago."

"I hope you're right. I'm sure that being in love with someone who doesn't care in return is most unsatisfactory, not to mention painful. Very impractical in the long run, as you just said." A faraway expression flickered in Emily's wide green eyes, and she said, almost inaudibly, "If only Sarah would recognize that."

As quiet as her voice had been, Emma had heard her. She put down her coffee cup with a loud clatter and gaped at Emily, frowning. *"Our Sarah.* Is she in love with someone who doesn't love her?"

"Oh gosh, Gran, I shouldn't have mentioned Sarah. It's really none of my business," Emily muttered, her face flushing and filling with chagrin. "Please don't say anything to her, will you? She'd be ever so upset."

"Of course I won't say anything. I never do, do I? Who's she carrying a torch for? That's what you implied, you know."

Emily hesitated. She was suddenly tempted to fib. But she had never lied to her grandmother in her whole life. Still, perhaps in this instance she ought to resort to a white lie.

Emma pressed, "Who is it?"

There was a moment of silence. Emily swallowed, and, knowing herself to be trapped, she mumbled, "Shane."

"I'll be damned." Emma leaned back and focused her keen old eyes on her granddaughter, "Well, well, well," she said, and a slow smile spread across her face.

Emily shot up in her chair, her eyes flaring open, and she cried, "Oh Grandy, don't look like that! *Please* don't look like that!"

"And how am I looking?"

"Gratified. And ever so conspiratorial. I know you and Uncle Blackie have long had hopes that one of us, or one of the Harte girls, would marry Shane O'Neill and unite our families. But he's not interested in any of us, except for—" Emily bit off the rest of her sentence abruptly, instantly wishing she could also bite off her tongue. This time she really had said far too much. She jumped up and went to the Hepplewhite sideboard, where she hovered over the silver bowl of fruit. "I think I'll have a banana," she said, attempting nonchalance. "Would you like one too, Gran dear?"

"I certainly wouldn't, thank you very much." Emma swung her head and studied her granddaughter's back. "Except for *whom,* Emily?"

"No one, Gran." Emily wondered how to extricate herself adroitly, without arousing her grandmother's suspicions further. She sauntered back to her chair, flopped down, and attacked the banana with her dessert knife and fork, her head studiously bent.

Emma watched her, knowing that Emily was avoiding her eyes. And avoiding answering.

"I know you were about to tell me who Shane *is* interested in, Emily. If anyone knows, it's you." She laughed lightly, endeavoring to be casual. "You've always been my conduit for information about everyone in the family. And *out* of it for that matter. So come along, finish your sentence."

Emily, who was still cutting the skin off the banana with painstaking care, finally lifted her head. Her face was a picture of innocence as she said, "I wasn't about to reveal a thing, really I wasn't. I'm not in Shane's confidence—I don't know anything about his love life. What I was going to say, before, is that he isn't interested in any of us except for a one-night stand."

"Really, Emily!"

"Sorry." Emily dropped her eyes, then coyly looked up at Emma through her long lashes. "Have I shocked you, Grandma?"

"At my age I'm shock-resistant, my girl," Emma replied tartly. "But I am rather surprised by your remark about Shane. It wasn't very nice. Extremely unkind in fact." A new thought struck Emma, and she gave her granddaughter a fierce stare. "Has he ever suggested anything of the sort—"

"No, no, of course not," Emily burst out peremptorily before Emma could finish. And then she was swift to qualify her previous statement about Shane. "It's just a *feeling* I have about him," she mumbled, hating herself for maligning Shane, who was the nicest person imaginable. "I didn't mean any harm, Grandy, honestly I didn't. Besides, who can blame him for being a bit of a lady killer, when women fall at his feet like ninepins? That's hardly his fault."

"True," Emma acknowledged. "But getting back to Sarah, I hope this crush she has on him is going to pass soon. I can't bear to think that she's miserable. How does she *really* feel, dear?"

"I don't know, Gran," Emily replied in all truthfulness. "She's only discussed Shane with me once, ages ago, and I think she's regretted mentioning him ever since. But I know she's smitten with him, just through my own observation. She always blushes furiously whenever his name comes up, and she gets all self-conscious and sort of dopey when he's around." Emily leveled her gaze at Emma, and it was direct and candid as she added, "No, she'll never say anything to anyone about her feelings. Sarah's basically much too secretive to confide."

This last comment further surprised Emma, but she decided not to pursue it for the moment. Conscious of the girl's stricken expression, she hastened to say, "You don't have to be apprehensive about me, darling. Have no fear, I won't mention Shane to Sarah . . . I wouldn't dream of embarrassing her. And she'll come to her senses if she hasn't already." Emma's eyes rested on the bowl of spring hyacinths in the center of the table, and she ruminated briefly on all that had been said. When she raised her head, she smiled kindly at Emily. "I don't want you to think I'm questioning your powers of observation or your judgment, but you do have a tendency to be overly imaginative at times. You could be wrong about Sarah. Perhaps she has forgotten Shane by now in view of his lack of interest in her. She *does* have her feet on the ground, you know."

"Yes, Gran," Emily said, although she did not agree with her grandmother's assessment of her cousin. Sarah might look as if her feet were firmly planted on the ground, but her head was most definitely in the clouds. Emily bit her lip, and she wished more fervently than before that she had never mentioned Sarah in the first place. Embarking on this kind of conversation with her canny grandmother had been a horrible mistake. The trouble was she was constantly doing it. Emma had always been the most dominant and important person in her young life, and confiding everything in her was a childhood habit which was difficult if not impossible to break. But Emily was thankful for one thing—she had caught herself in the nick of time, had managed not to reveal the truth about Shane to Grandy, who doted on him as if he were one of her own.

The realization that she had protected him made Emily feel better, for she liked and admired Blackie's grandson. She smiled to herself as she toyed with the banana in front of her, filled with sudden self-congratulation. For once she had been rather clever, side-stepping Grandy's probing so skillfully. And thankfully Shane O'Neill's secret was still safe. It would always be safe with her. Poor Shane, she thought with a twinge of sadness, what a terrible burden he has to carry. Stifling a sigh, Emily finally said, "I don't think I want any more of this," and she pushed her dessert plate away, making a face.

Emma, anxious to bring the lunch to an end, nodded quickly and said, "I'd better get back to my desk. What are your plans for this afternoon? You've finished at the Harrogate store, haven't you?"

"Yes, Grandy. I completed the stock inventories you wanted and selected the clothing for the sales," Emily explained, relieved that Emma had apparently now dismissed Shane and Sarah Lowther from her mind. "I'm going to potter around in my room. Hilda asked one of the maids to unpack my suitcases when I arrived, but I prefer to arrange my things myself."

"Suitcases in the plural, Emily? How many did you bring?"

"Ten, Gran."

"For the *weekend?*"

Emily cleared her throat and gave her grandmother one of her most engaging and persuasive smiles. "Not exactly. I thought I'd stay with you for a while, if that's all right with you. It is, isn't it?"

"Well, yes, I suppose so," Emma answered slowly, wondering what this unexpected move on Emily's part was all about. "But what about your flat in Headingley?" she thought to ask with a small frown.

"I want to get rid of it. I have for some time, actually. I decided to sell it, or rather that you should ask Jonathan to do so. Anyway, last night I packed a lot of my clothes and other things, because I'd convinced myself you'd be sending me to Paris next week. Now that I'm not going, I might as well stay here at Pennistone Royal. I'll be company for you, Gran. You won't be so lonely."

I'm not lonely, Emma thought but said, "I'm probably being dense, but you seemed awfully taken with that flat when I bought it for you last November. Don't you like it anymore, Emily?"

"It's a very nice flat, really it is, but— Well, to be honest, Gran darling, I have felt rather isolated there by myself. I'd much rather be *here*. With you." Emily flashed her beguiling smile again. "For one thing, it's a lot more fun. And exciting."

"Personally I find it pretty dull here. Pretty dull indeed," Emma muttered and stood up, headed for the dining room door. Over her shoulder she said, "But you're quite welcome, Emily," and she hoped she had not sounded too grudging. First the twins and now Emily, she sighed under her breath. Suddenly they're all moving in on me. And just when I thought I was going to get some peace and quiet for once in my life.

As she walked briskly across the vast Stone Hall and mounted the staircase, with Emily trailing in her wake, Emma had another thought: Maybe she would take Blackie up on his little proposition after all.

Paula talked and Emma listened.

They sat together in the upstairs parlor, facing each other across the Georgian silver tea service which Hilda had brought up a few minutes after Paul had arrived.

Emma had poured tea for them both, but she had hardly touched her own cup. She sat so still on the sofa she might have turned to stone, and the familiar mask of inscrutability had dropped down over her face as she concentrated on Paula's words, absorbing each one.

Paula spoke well, recounting the meeting at Aire Communications with precision and careful attention to the smallest detail, and her narration was so graphically descriptive Emma felt as though she had been present herself. Several times she experienced a spurt of anger or annoyance, but not an eyelash flickered, not a muscle moved in her blank, impenetrable face, and not once did she interrupt the flow of words.

Long before Paula came to the retelling of the final scene in the boardroom, Emma's mind, so agile and astute, leaped ahead. She knew without having to be told that John Cross had reneged on the deal. For a moment she was as startled as Paula had been earlier in the day, but when this initial reaction passed with some swiftness she realized she was not so surprised after all. And she came to the conclusion that she knew John Cross better than she had believed. Years ago she had spotted him for what he was—an egotist, puffed up with his own self-importance, a foolish man with immeasurable weaknesses. At this time in his life he was between a rock and a hard place, dealing from fear and desperation and propelled by increasing panic, and it was patently clear that he would be capable of just about anything. Even a dishonorable action, for apparently he was a man without scruples. And then there was that disreputable son of his, goading him on. A pretty pair indeed, she thought disdainfully.

Paula came to the end of her story at last and finished with a tiny regretful sigh, "And there you have it, Grandy. I'm sorry it ended in a debacle. I did my best. More than my best."

"You certainly did," Emma said, looking her fully in the face, proud of her, thinking how she had progressed. A year ago Paula would have blamed herself for the breakdown in the talks. "You've nothing to reproach yourself for, and just chalk this one up to experience and learn from it."

"Yes, Grandy, I will." Paula regarded her closely. "What are you going to do now?" she asked, continuing to study that impassive face in an effort to gauge her grandmother's feelings about the Cross situation.

"Why nothing. Nothing at all."

Although she was not altogether surprised by this statement, Paula nevertheless felt bound to say, a bit heatedly, "I thought that might be your attitude, but I can't help wishing you'd give John Cross a piece of your mind, tell him what you think of him. Look at all the effort we put into this deal. He's not only wasted our valuable time but played us for a couple of fools."

"Played himself for a fool," Emma corrected, her voice low and without a trace of emotion. "Very frankly, I wouldn't waste my breath or the tuppence on a phone call to him. There's not much to be gained from flogging a dead horse. Besides, I wouldn't give him the satisfaction of knowing I'm put out. There's another thing . . . indifference is a mighty powerful weapon, and so I prefer to ignore Mr. Cross. I don't know what his game is, but I won't be a party to it." The look Emma gave Paula was full of shrewdness and her eyes narrowed. "It strikes me that he might be using our offer to jack up the price with another company. He won't succeed, he won't have any takers." A cynical smile glanced across her face, and she laughed quietly to herself. "He'll come crawling back to you, of course. On his hands and knees. And very soon. Then what will *you* do, Paula? That's more to the point." Settling back against the cushions, she let her eyes rest with intentness on her granddaughter.

Paula opened her mouth to speak, then closed it swiftly. For a split second she hesitated over her answer. She asked herself how Grandy would act in these particular circumstances and then dismissed the question. She knew exactly what *her* course of action was going to be.

In a resolute tone, Paula said, "I shall tell him to go to hell. Politely. I know I could hammer him down, get Aire Communications at a much lower figure, because when he does come back to us, and I agree that he will, he'll be choking. He'll accept any terms I offer. However, I don't want to do business with that man. I don't trust him."

"Good girl!" Emma was pleased with this reply and showed it, then went on, "My sentiments exactly. I've told you many times that it's not particularly important to like those with whom we do business. But there should always be an element of trust between both parties in any transaction; otherwise it's begging for problems. I concur with what you think about Cross and that son of his. Their behavior was appalling, unconscionable. I wouldn't touch them with a ten-foot barge pole myself."

Despite these condemning words and the stern expression lingering on Emma's face, her overall reaction had been so understated, so mild that Paula was still a trifle puzzled. "I thought you'd be much more annoyed than you are, Grandy, unless you're not showing it. And you don't seem very disappointed either," she said.

"My initial anger soon changed to disgust. As for being disappointed, well, of course I am in some ways. But even that is being replaced by an enormous sense of relief. As much as I wanted Aire Communications, now, quite suddenly, I'm glad things turned out the way they did."

"I am too." There was the slightest hesitation on Paula's part before she remarked quietly, "Sebastian Cross has become my enemy, Grandmother."

"So what!" Emma exclaimed in a dismissive tone. "If he's your first, he's surely not going to be your last." As she spoke, Emma became aware of the concern reflected in the lovely, deep violet eyes fastened on hers, and she sucked in her breath quickly. Making an enemy troubles Paula, she thought, and she reached out and squeezed the girl's arm, adopted a gentler tone. "As unpleasant as it may be, you're bound to make enemies, as I myself did. Very frequently it happens through no fault of ours—that's the sad part." Emma let out a tiny sigh. "So many people are jealous and envious by nature, and *you* will always be vulnerable to that kind and a target, because you have so much. Wealth and power through me, not to mention your looks, your brains, and your immense capacity for work. All very enviable attributes. You must learn to ignore the back biting, darling, rise above it. As I have always done. And forget Sebastian Cross. He's the least of your worries."

"Yes, you're right on all counts, as usual, Grandmother," Paula said and pushed away the dismaying memory of those hard eyes which had filled with loathing for her that morning. She felt a shiver trickle through her. Sebastian Cross would do her harm if he could. This unexpected thought immediately seemed silly, farfetched, and overly imaginative. Paula laughed silently at herself and dismissed such an idea.

Rising, she crossed to the fireplace and stood warming her back for a moment or two. Her eyes swept around the lovely old room. It looked so peaceful, so gentle in the late afternoon sunlight filtering in through the many windows, with every beautiful object in its given place, the fire crackling merrily in the huge grate, the old carriage clock ticking away on the mantelpiece as it had for as long as she could remember. She had loved the upstairs parlor all her life, had found comfort and tranquility here. It was a room abundant with graciousness and harmony, where nothing ever changed, and it was this timelessness which made it seem so far removed from the outside world and all its ugliness. It's a very civilized room, she said to herself, created by a very civilized and extraordinary woman. She looked across at Emma, relaxed on the sofa and so pretty in the pale blue dress, and her eyes became tender. Paula thought: She is an old woman now, in her eightieth year, yet she never seems old to me. She could easily be my age with her vigor and strength and zest and enthusiasm. And she is my best friend.

For the first time since she had arrived, Paula smiled. "So much for my wheeling and dealing . . . skirmishing might be a better way to describe it, Grandy."

"And so much for my new project. Now that that's flown out of the window, I'll have to find another one or take up knitting."

Paula could not help grinning. "That'll be the day," she retorted, merriment swamping her face. Stepping back to the sofa, she sat down, lifted her cup, and took a sip of tea, then remarked casually, "I had lunch with Miranda O'Neill today, and—"

"Oh dear, that reminds me, I'm afraid I won't be here for dinner this evening. I'm going out with Blackie and Shane."

"Yes, so Merry told me."

"My God, can't I take a breath around here without everyone knowing!" Emma paused, scanned Paula's face. "Well, you don't seem too upset, so I presume you don't mind that I'm trotting off and leaving you to cope with Edwina. Don't worry, she'll behave."

"I'm not concerned. I was at first, but I decided she's Jim's problem. He invited her, so he can entertain her. In any case, Mummy's always pretty good with Edwina. She knows how to appropriately squelch her, in the nicest possible way too." Paula put down her cup and saucer, leaned closer. "Listen, Grandy dear, Merry has had an idea, one that might appeal to you. It could be just the project you're looking for."

"Oh, has she. Well then, tell me about it."

Paula did so, but as she came to the end of her little recital, she made a small moue with her mouth and finished lamely, "I can tell you're not enthusiastic. Don't you think it's a good idea?"

Emma laughed at her crestfallen expression. "Yes, I do. However I'm not interested in taking it on as a *personal* project. Still, that doesn't mean you shouldn't pursue the idea and develop it further with Merry. It could be good for the stores. Come back to me when you have it refined. Perhaps we *will* open the boutiques."

"I'll set up a meeting with her for next week—" Paula stopped, peered at Emma. "Out of curiosity, *why* don't you think it's a project for you?"

"There's no challenge to it. I like tougher nuts to crack."

"Oh Lord! And where on earth am I going to find such a thing for you?"

"I might find my own project, you know." Emma's green eyes twinkled, and she shook her head. "You're constantly trying to mother me these days. I do wish you'd stop."

Paula joined in Emma's laughter and admitted, "Yes, I am doing that lately, aren't I. Sorry, Gran." She glanced at the clock, swung her eyes back to Emma, and said, "I think I'd be much better off going home and mothering my babies. If I hurry, I'll get back in time to help the nurse bathe them."

"Yes, why don't you do that, darling. These early years are the most precious, the best really. Don't sacrifice them."

Paula stood up and slipped into the magenta jacket, found her handbag, came to kiss Emma. "Have a lovely time tonight, and give Uncle Blackie and Shane my love."

"I will. And if I don't see you later, I'll talk to you in the morning."

Paula was halfway across the room when Emma called, "Oh, Paula, what time do you expect Jim and your parents?"

"Around six. Jim said he'd be landing at Leeds-Bradford airport at five."

"So he's flying them up in that dreadful little plane of his, is he?" Emma pursed her lips in annoyance and gave Paula the benefit of a reproving stare. "I thought I'd told the two of you I don't like you flitting around in that pile of junk."

"You did indeed, but Jim has a mind of his own, as you well know. And flying is one of his main hobbies. But perhaps you'd better mention it to him again."

"I certainly will," Emma said and waved her out of the room.

Six

They all said that he was a true Celt.

And Shane Desmond Ingham O'Neill had himself come to believe that the heritage of his ancestors was buried deep in his bones, that their ancient blood flowed through his veins, and this filled him with an immense satisfaction and the most profound pride. When he was accused by some members of his family of being extravagant, impetuous, talkative, and vain, he would simply nod, as if relishing their criticisms as compliments. But Shane often wanted to retort that he was also energetic, intelligent, and creative; to point out that these, too, had been traits of those early Britons.

It was as a very small boy that Shane O'Neill had been made aware of his exceptional nature. At first he had been self-conscious, then confused, puzzled, and hurt. He saw himself as being different, set apart from others, and this had disturbed him. He wanted to be ordinary; they made him feel freakish. He had detested it when he had overheard adults describe him as *fey* and *overly emotional* and *mystical*.

Then, when he was sixteen and had more of an understanding of the things they said about him, he sought further illumination in the only way he knew—through books. If he *was* "a curious throwback to the Celts," as they said he was, then he must educate himself about these ancient people whom he apparently so resembled. He had turned to the volumes of history which depicted the early Britons in all their splendor and glory, and the time of the great High Kings and the legendary Arthur of Camelot had become as real to him and as alive as the present.

In the years that followed his interest in history had never waned, and it was a continuing hobby. Like his Celtic forebears he venerated words and their power, for filled with a recklessness and gaiety though he was, he was also a man of intellectual vigor. And perhaps it was this extraordinary mingling of contrasts—his mass of contradictions—that made him so unusual. If his angers and enmities were deep-rooted, so his loves and loyalties were immovable and everlasting. And that theatricality, constantly attributed to the Celt in him, existed easily alongside his introspection and his rare, almost tender understanding of nature and its beauty.

At twenty-seven there was a dazzle to Shane O'Neill, an intense glamour that sprang not so much from his remarkable looks as from his character and

personality. He could devastate any woman in a room; equally, he could capti-
vate his male friends with an incisive discussion on politics, a ribald joke, a
humorous story filled with wit and self-mockery. He could entertain with a
song in his splendid baritone, whether he was rendering a rollicking sea shanty
or a sentimental ballad, and poetry flew with swiftness from his tongue. Yet he
could be hard-headed, objective, outspoken, and honest almost to the point of
cruelty, and he was ambitious and driven, by his own admission. Greatness, and
greatness for its own sake in particular, appealed strongly to him. And *he* appealed to everyone who crossed his path. Not that Shane was without enemies,
but even they never denied the existence of his potent charm. Some of these
traits had been passed on from his paternal Irish grandfather, that other larger-
than-life Celt, whose physique and physical presence he had inherited. Yet
there was also much of his mother's ancestry in him.

Now on this crisp Friday afternoon, Shane O'Neill stood with his horse,
War Lord, high on the moors overlooking the town of Middleham and the
ruined castle below. It was still proud and stately despite its shattered battlements, roofless halls, and ghostly chambers, all deserted now except for the
numerous small birds nesting in the folds of the ancient stone among the daffodils, snowdrops, and celandines blooming in the crannies at this time of year.

With his vivid imagination, it was never hard for Shane to visualize how it
had once been centuries ago when Warwick and Gareth Ingham, an ancestor
on his mother's side, had lived within that stout fortress, spinning their convoluted schemes. Instantly in his mind's eye, he saw the panoply unfolding as it
had in a bygone age . . . glittering occasions of state, princely banquets, other
scenes of royal magnificence, of pomp and ceremony, and for a few seconds he
was transported into the historical past.

Then he blinked, expunging those images, and lifted his head, tore his eyes
away from the ruined battlements, and gazed out at the spectacular vista spread
before him. He always felt the same thrill when he stood on this spot. To Shane
there was an austerity and an aloofness to the vast and empty moors, and a most
singular majesty dwelled within this landscape. The rolling moors swept up and
away like a great unfurled banner of green and gold and umber and ochre,
flaring out to meet the rim of the endless sky, that incredible blaze of blue
shimmering with silvered sunlight at this hour. It was a beauty of such magnitude and stunning clarity that Shane found it almost unendurable to look at,
and his response, as always, was intensely emotional. Here was the one spot on
this earth where he felt he truly belonged, and when he was away from it, he
was filled with a sense of deprivation, yearned to return. Once again he was
about to exile himself, but like all of his other exiles, this too was self-imposed.

Shane O'Neill sighed heavily as he felt the old sadness, the melancholy,
trickling through him. He leaned his head against the stallion's neck and
squeezed his eyes shut, and he willed the pain of longing for her to pass. How
could he live here, under the same sky, knowing she was so close yet so far
beyond his reach. So he must go . . . go far away and leave this place he
loved, leave the woman he loved beyond reason because she could never be his.
It was the only way he could survive as a man.

Abruptly he turned and swung himself into the saddle, determined to pull
himself out of the black mood which had so unexpectedly engulfed him. He
spurred War Lord forward, taking the wild moorland at a flat-out gallop.

Halfway along the road he passed a couple of stable lads out exercising two magnificent thoroughbreds, and he returned their cheery greetings with a friendly nod, then branched off at the Swine Cross, making for Allington Hall, Randolph Harte's house. In Middleham, a town famous for a dozen or more of the greatest racing stables in England, Allington Hall was considered to be one of the finest and Randolph a trainer of some renown. Randolph was Blackie O'Neill's trainer and permitted Shane to stable War Lord, Feudal Baron, and his filly, Celtic Maiden, at Allington alongside his grandfather's string of race horses.

By the time he reached the huge iron gates of Allington Hall, Shane had managed to partially subdue his nagging heartache and lift himself out of his depression. He took several deep breaths and brought a neutral expression to his face as he turned at the end of the gravel driveway and headed in the direction of the stables at the back of the house. To Shane's surprise, the yard was deserted, but as he clattered across the cobblestones, a stable lad appeared, and a moment later Randolph Harte walked out of the stalls and waved to him.

Tall, heavyset, and bluff in manner, Randolph had a voice to match his build, and he boomed, "Hello, Shane. I was hoping to see you. I'd like to talk to you if you can spare me a minute."

Dismounting, Shane called back, "It *will* have to be a minute, Randolph. I have an important dinner date tonight and I'm running late." He handed the reins of War Lord to the lad, who led the horse off to the Rubbing House to be rubbed down. Shane strode over to Randolph, grasped his outstretched hand, and said, "Nothing wrong, I hope?"

"No, no," Randolph said quickly, steering him across the yard to the back entrance of the house. "But let's go inside for a few minutes." He looked up at Shane, who at six feet four was several inches taller, and grinned. "Surely you can make it *five* minutes, old chap? The lady, whoever she is, will no doubt be perfectly happy to wait for *you.*"

Shane also grinned. "The lady in question is Aunt Emma, and we both know *she* doesn't like to be kept waiting."

"Only too true," Randolph said, opening the door and ushering Shane inside. "Now, have you time for a cup of tea or would you prefer a drink?"

"Scotch, thanks, Randolph." Shane walked over to the fireplace and stood with his back to it, glancing around the room, feeling suddenly relaxed and at ease for the first time that afternoon. He had known and loved this study all his life, and it was his favorite room at the Hall. Its ambiance was wholly masculine, this mood reflected in the huge Georgian desk in front of the window, the Chippendale cabinet, the dark wine-colored leather chesterfield and armchairs, the circular rent table littered with such magazines as *Country Life* and *Horse and Hounds,* along with racing sheets from the daily papers. A stranger entering this room would have no trouble guessing the chief interest and occupation of the owner. It was redolent of the Turf and the Sport of Kings. The dark green walls were hung with eighteenth-century sporting prints by Stubbs. Framed photographs of the winning race horses Randolph had trained graced a dark mahogany chest, and cups and trophies abounded. There was the gleam of brass around the fireplace, in the horse brasses hanging there, and in the Victorian fender. On the mantelpiece, Randolph's pipe rack and tobacco jar nestled between small bronzes of two thoroughbreds and a pair of silver candlesticks. The study had a comfortable lived-in look, was even a bit shabby in spots, but to Shane the scuffed carpet and the cracked leather on the chairs only added to the mellow feeling of warmth and friendliness.

Randolph brought their drinks, the two men clinked glasses, and Shane turned to sit in one of the leather armchairs.

"Whoah! Not there. The spring's going," Randolph exclaimed.

"It's been going for years," Shane laughed but seated himself in the other chair.

"Well, it's finally gone. I keep meaning to have the damn thing sent to the upholsterers, but I always forget."

Shane put his glass on the edge of the brass fender and searched his pockets for his cigarettes. He lit one and said, "What did you want to talk to me about?"

"Emerald Bow. What do you think Blackie would say if I entered her in the Grand National next year?"

A surprised look flashed across Shane's face, and he sat up straighter. "He'd be thrilled, surely you know that. But would she have a chance? I know she's a fine mare, but the Aintree course . . . Jaysus! as Blackie would say."

Randolph nodded, stood up, took a pipe, and began to pack it with tobacco. "Yes, it *is* a demanding course, the supreme test for a man and his horse. But I really do think Emerald Bow has a chance of winning the greatest steeplechase in the world. The breeding is there, and the stamina. She's done extremely well lately, won a few point-to-points and most impressively." Randolph paused to light his pipe, then remarked with a twinkle, "I believe that *that* lady has hidden charms. But seriously she is turning out to be one of the best jumpers I've ever trained."

"Oh my God, this is wonderful news!" Shane cried, excitement running through him. "It's always been Grandfather's dream to win the National. Which jockey, Randolph?"

"Steve Larner. He's a tough sod, just what we need to take Emerald Bow around Aintree. If anyone can negotiate her over Becher's Brook *twice,* it's Steve. He's a brilliant horseman."

"Why haven't you mentioned it to Grandfather?"

"I wanted to get your reaction first. You're the closest to him."

"You know he always takes your advice. You're his trusted trainer and the best in the business, as far as we're concerned."

"Thanks, Shane. Appreciate the confidence. But to be honest, old chap, I've never seen Blackie fuss over any of his horses the way he does that mare. He'd like to keep her wrapped in cotton wool, if you ask me. He was out here last week, and he was treating her as if she was his great lady love."

A grin tugged at Shane's mouth. "Don't forget, she *was* a gift from his favorite lady. And talking of Emma, did I hear a hint of annoyance when you mentioned her earlier?"

"Not really. I was a bit irritated with her last night, but . . ." Randolph broke off and smiled genially. "Well, I never harbor a grudge where she's concerned, and she *is* the matriarch of our clan, and she's so good to us all. It's just that she can be so bloody bossy. She makes me feel this high." He held his hand six inches off the ground and grinned. "Anyway, getting back to Emerald Bow, I'd intended to mentior. it to Blackie tomorrow. What do you think about my timing? Should I wait until next week perhaps?"

"No, tell him tomorrow, Randolph. It'll make his day, and Aunt Emma will be delighted." Shane finished his drink and stood up. "I don't mind telling you, I for one am thrilled about this decision of yours. Now, I'm afraid I really have to leave. I want to stop by the stables for a second, to say goodbye to my horses." Shane smiled a trifle ruefully. "I'm going away again, Randolph. I'm leaving Monday morning."

"But you just got back!" Randolph exclaimed. "Where are you off to this time?"

"Jamaica, then Barbados, where we've recently bought a new hotel," Shane explained as they left the study together. "I've a great deal of work there, and I'll be gone for quite a few months." He fell silent as they crossed the stable yard, and Randolph made no further comment either.

Shane went into the stalls, where he spent a few moments with each of his horses, fondling them, murmuring to them affectionately.

Randolph hung back, watching him intently, and suddenly he experienced a stab of pity for the younger man, although he was not certain what had engendered this feeling in him. Unless it was something to do with Shane's demeanor at this moment, the look of infinite sadness in his black eyes. Randolph had retained a soft spot for Shane O'Neill since he had been a child and had once even hoped that he might take a fancy to Sally or Vivienne. But the boy had always been patently uninterested in his two daughters, had remained slightly aloof from them. It was his son, Winston, who was Shane's closest friend and boon companion. A few eyebrows had been raised two years ago when Winston and Shane had bought a broken-down old manor, Beck House, in nearby West Tanfield, remodeled it, and moved in together. But Randolph had never questioned the sexual predilections of his son or Shane. He had no need to do so. He knew them both to be the most notorious womanizers, forever chasing skirts up and down the countryside. When his wife, Georgina, had been alive, she had often had to comfort more than one broken-hearted young woman, who showed up at the Hall in search of Winston or Shane. Thankfully this no longer happened. *He* wouldn't have known how to cope with such situations. He presumed that if there were any disgruntled young ladies, they beat a track directly to Beck House. Randolph smiled inwardly. Those two were a couple of scallawags, but he did love them both very dearly.

Shane finally took leave of his horses and walked slowly back to Randolph standing at the entrance to the stalls. As always, and especially when he had not seen him for a while, Randolph was struck by Shane's unique good looks. He's a handsome son of a gun, Randolph commented silently. Blackie must have looked exactly like Shane fifty years ago.

Putting his arm around the older man's shoulder, Shane said, "Thanks for everything, Randolph."

"Oh lad, it's my pleasure. And don't worry about the horses. They'll be well cared for, but then you should know that by now. Oh and Shane, please ask Winston to call me later."

"I will."

Randolph's eyes followed Shane O'Neill as he strode off to his car, and there was a thoughtful look on his face. There goes one unhappy young man, he muttered under his breath, shaking his head in bafflement. He has everything anybody could ever want. Health, looks, position, great wealth. He tries to conceal it, but I'm convinced he's miserable inside. And I'm damned if I know the reason why.

•••

Beck House, so called because a pretty little stream ran through the grounds, stood at the bottom of a small hill, at the edge of the village of West Tanfield, about halfway between Allington Hall and Pennistone Royal.

Situated in a dell, shaded at the rear by a number of huge old oaks and sycamores, the manor dated back to the late Elizabethan period. It was a charming house, low and rambling, made of local stone supposedly from Fountains Abbey, and it had a half-timbered front facade, tall chimneys, and many leaded windows.

Winston and Shane had originally bought the old manor with the intention of selling it once they had rebuilt the ruined parts, remodeled the old-fashioned kitchen and bathrooms, added garages, and cleared away the wilderness which covered the neglected grounds. However, they had devoted so much time and energy and loving care on the house, had become so attached to the manor during the renovations, they had finally decided to keep it for themselves. They were the same age, had been at Oxford together, and had been close since their salad days. They enjoyed sharing the house, which they used mainly on weekends, since they both maintained flats in the Leeds area to be near their respective offices.

Winston Harte was the only grandson of Emma's brother Winston, and her great-nephew, and he had worked for the Yorkshire Consolidated Newspaper Company since he had come down from Oxford. He did not have a specific job or a title. Emma called him her "minister without portfolio," which, translated, meant troubleshooter to most people. He was in a sense her ambassador-at-large within the company, her eyes and ears and very frequently her voice as well. His word on most things was the final word, and he answered only to Emma. Behind his back the other executives called him "God," and Winston knew this and generally smiled to himself knowingly. *He* was well aware who "God" was at Consolidated. It was his Aunt Emma. She was the law, and he respected and honored her, and she had his complete devotion.

Young Winston, as he was still sometimes called in the family, had always been close to his namesake, and his grandfather had instilled in him a great sense of loyalty and duty to Emma, to whom the Hartes owed everything they had. His grandfather had worshiped her until the day he had died at the beginning of the sixties, and it was from him that Winston had learned so much about his aunt's early life, the hard times she had had, the struggles she had experienced as she had climbed the ladder to success. He knew only too well that her brilliant career had been hard won, built on tremendous sacrifices. Because he had been reared on so many fantastic and often moving stories about the now legendary Emma, Winston believed that in certain ways he understood her far better than her own children. And there was nothing he would not do for her.

Winston's grandfather had left him all of his shares in the newspaper company, while his Uncle Frank, Emma's younger brother, had left his interest to his widow, Natalie. But it was Emma, with her fifty-two percent, who controlled the company as she always had. These days, however, she ran it with Winston's help. She consulted with him on every facet of management and policy, frequently deferred to his wishes if they were sound, and constantly took his advice. They had a tranquil working relationship and a most special and loving friendship which gave them both a great deal of satisfaction and pleasure.

The newspaper company was very actively on Winston's mind as he drove slowly into the grounds of Beck House. Even so, as preoccupied as he was, he noticed that the little beck was swollen from the heavy rains which had fallen earlier that week. He made a mental note to mention this to Shane. The banks would probably need reinforcing again; otherwise the lawns would be flooded in no time at all, as they had been the previous spring. O'Neill Construction will definitely have to come out here next week, Winston decided, as he pulled the Jaguar up to the front door, parked, took his briefcase, and alighted. He went around to the trunk of the car to get his suitcase.

Winston was slender, light in build, and about five foot nine, and it was easy to see at a glance that he was a Harte. In fact, Winston bore a strong look of Emma. He had her fine, chiseled features and her coloring, which was reflected in his russet-gold hair and vivid green eyes. He was the only member of the family, other than Paula, who had Emma's dramatic widow's peak, which, his grandfather had once told him, they had all inherited from Big Jack Harte's mother, Esther Harte.

Winston glanced up, squinting at the sky as he approached the short flight of steps leading into the house. Dark clouds had rumbled in from the east coast, and they presaged rain. There was a hint of thunder in the air since the wind had dropped, and a sudden bolt of lightning streaked the tops of the leafy spring trees with a flash of searing white. As he inserted the key, large drops of rain splashed onto his hand. Damn, he muttered, thinking of the beck. If there's a storm, we're going to be in serious trouble.

Dimly from behind the huge carved door, he heard the telephone ringing, but by the time he had let himself inside the house, it had stopped. Winston stared at it, fully expecting it to ring again, but when it didn't he shrugged, deposited his suitcase at the foot of the staircase, and walked rapidly through the hall. He went into his study at the back of the manor, sat down at his desk, and read the note from Shane telling him to call his father. He threw the note into the wastepaper basket and glanced vaguely at his mail—mostly bills from the village shops and a number of invitations for cocktail parties and dinners from his country neighbors. Putting these on one side, he leaned back in his chair, propped his feet on the desk, and closed his eyes, bringing all of his concentration to bear on the matter at hand.

Winston had a problem, and it gave him cause for serious reflection at this moment. Yesterday, during a meeting with Jim Fairley at the London office, he had detected a real and genuine discontent in the other man. Oddly enough, Winston discovered he was not terribly surprised. Months ago he had begun to realize that Jim loathed administration, and in the last few hours, driving back from London, he had come to the conclusion that Jim wanted to be relieved of his position as managing director. Intuitively Winston felt that Jim was floundering and was truly out of his depth. Jim was very much a working newspaperman, who loved the hurly-burly of the newsroom, the excitement of being at the center of world events, the challenge of putting out two daily papers. After Emma had promoted him a year ago, upon his engagement to Paula, Jim had continued to act as managing editor of the Yorkshire *Morning Gazette* and the Yorkshire *Evening Standard*. Essentially, by holding down the old job along with the new one, Jim was wearing two hats. Only that of the newspaperman fitted him, in Winston's opinion.

Maybe he ought to resign, Winston thought. It's better that Jim does one job brilliantly, rather than screw up on two. He snapped his eyes open, swung his legs to the floor purposefully, and pulled the chair up to the desk. He sat staring into space, thinking about Jim. He admired Fairley's extraordinary ability as a journalist, and he liked the man personally, even though he knew Jim was weak in many respects. He wanted to please everybody, and that was hardly possible. And one thing was certain: Winston had never been able to comprehend Paula's fascination with Fairley. They were as different as chalk and cheese. She was far too strong for a man like Jim, but then that relationship was none of his business really, and anyway perhaps he was prejudiced, considering the circumstances. She was a blind fool. He scowled, chastising himself for thinking badly of her, for he did care for Paula and they were good friends.

Winston now reached for the phone to ring Emma and confide his problem in her, then changed his mind at once. There was no point worrying her at the beginning of her very busy weekend of social activities which had been planned for weeks. Far better to wait until Monday morning and consult with her then.

All of a sudden he felt like kicking himself. How stupid he had been. He should have challenged Jim yesterday, asked him point-blank if he wanted to step down. And if he did, who would they appoint in his place? There was no one qualified to take on such heavy responsibilities, at least not inside the company. That was the crux of the problem, his chief concern. At the bottom of him, Winston had the most awful feeling that his aunt might lumber him with the job. He did not want it. He liked things exactly the way they were.

It so happened that Winston Harte, unlike other members of Emma's family, was not particularly ambitious. He did not crave power. He was not crippled by avarice. In fact he had more money than he knew what to do with. Grandfather Winston, with Emma's guidance, advice, and help, had acquired an immense fortune, had thus ensured that neither his widow, Charlotte, nor his offspring would ever want for anything.

Young Winston was dedicated, hardworking, and he thrived in the world of newspapers where he was in his element. But he also enjoyed living. Long ago he had made a decision, and it was one he had never veered away from: *He* was not going to sacrifice personal happiness and a tranquil private life for a big-business career. Treadmills were decidedly not for him. He would always work diligently at his job, for he was not a parasite, but he also wanted a wife, a family, and a gracious style of living. Like his father, Randolph, Winston was very much at ease in the role of country gentleman. The pastoral scene held a special appeal for him, gave him a sense of renewal. His weekends away from the city were precious and recharged his batteries. He found horse riding, point-to-point meetings, village cricket, antiquing, and pottering around in the grounds of Beck House therapeutic and immensely satisfying. In short Winston Harte preferred a quiet, leisurely existence and he was determined to have it. Battles in boardrooms made him irritable, and he found them endlessly boring. That was why Paula continued to surprise him. And it was becoming increasingly apparent to Winston that she was indeed cast in the same mold as her grandmother. Both women relished corporate skirmishing. It seemed to him that business, power, and winning hands down over a business adversary were narcotics to them. When Emma had wanted him to be Paula's backup in negotiations with Aire, he had swiftly demurred and suggested that she send Paula in alone. His aunt had readily agreed, to his considerable relief.

Oh what the hell, he thought, becoming impatient with himself. I'm not going to spend the entire weekend worrying about Jim Fairley's intentions. I'll thrash it out with him next week, once the plans for taking over Aire Communications have been put into operation. Pushing business matters to the back of his mind, he rang his father at Allington Hall and chatted with him for a good twenty minutes. He then dialed Allison Ridley, his current girlfriend. He felt a rush of warmth when he heard her voice, and she sounded equally pleased to hear his. He confirmed that he and Shane would be at her dinner party the following evening, made plans with her for Sunday, and finally dashed upstairs to change.

Ten minutes later, wearing comfortable corduroys, a heavy wool sweater, Wellington boots, and an old raincoat, Winston meandered through the dining room and out onto the flagged terrace overlooking the fish pond. The sky had brightened after the brief shower. The trees and shrubs and lawns appeared to shimmer with dewy greenness in the lovely late afternoon light which brought a soft incandescent glow to the fading blue of the sky. The scent of rain and damp grass and wet earth and growing things pervaded the air, and it was a smell Winston loved. He stood on the terrace for a moment, inhaling and exhaling, relaxing and shedding the rest of his business worries; then he ran lightly down the steps into the gardens. He hurried in the direction of the beck, wanting to satisfy himself that the condition of the banks had not deteriorated after the recent shower.

Seven

Edwina had arrived.

Emma was aware that her eldest daughter was sitting downstairs in the library, having a drink and recovering from her journey from Manchester Airport. In the last few minutes, first Hilda then Emily had been up to see her, to pass on this news.

Well, there's no time like the present, Emma murmured as she finished dressing in readiness for her dinner date with Blackie and Shane. Putting off the inevitable is not only foolish, it frays the nerves. There's a time bomb ticking inside Edwina, and I'd better diffuse it before the weekend begins.

Nodding to herself, glad she had stopped wavering, Emma fastened a pearl choker around her throat, glanced at herself in the mirror, picked up her evening bag and sable jacket, and hurried out.

She descended the long winding staircase at a slower pace, thinking about the things she would say, how she would handle Edwina. Emma had an aversion to confrontation and conflict, preferred to move in roundabout ways and often with stealth to accomplish her ends. Accommodation and compromise had been, and still were, her strong suits, both in business and personal matters. But now, as she approached the library, she recognized there was only one thing she could do: tackle Edwina head on.

Her quick, light step faltered as she walked through the vast Stone Hall, and dismay flew to the surface as she thought of doing battle. But Anthony's happiness was at stake, and therefore Edwina had to be dealt with before she made serious trouble for him, for everyone in fact. Emma took a deep breath, then continued across the hall, her step now ringing with new determination, her manner resolute.

The library door was partially open, and Emma paused for a moment before going in, one hand resting on the door jamb as she observed Edwina sitting in the wing chair in front of the fire. Only one lamp had been turned on, and the light in the rest of the room was gloomy. Suddenly a log spurted and flared up the chimney, the lambent flames illuminating the shadowed face, bringing it into sharper focus. Emma blinked, momentarily startled. From this distance her daughter was the spitting image of Adele Fairley . . . the same silvery blond hair, the delicate yet clearly defined profile, the shoulders hunched in concentration. How often had she seen Adele sitting like that beside the fire in her bedroom at Fairley Hall, staring into the distance, lost in her thoughts. But whereas Adele had not lived to see her thirty-eighth year, Edwina was sixty-three and her beauty had never been as ethereal and as heart stopping as Adele's once was. So Emma knew this image was part illusion; still the resemblance was there, had been there since Edwina's birth, and she had always been more of a Fairley than a Harte in many respects.

Clearing her throat, Emma said, "Good evening, Edwina," and bustled forward with briskness, not wanting her to know she had been watching her from the doorway.

Her daughter started in surprise and swung her head, straightening up in the chair as she did. "Hello, Mother," she replied in a formal voice that rang with coldness.

Emma paid no attention to the tone, accustomed to it by now. It had not changed much over the years. She deposited her jacket and bag on a chair, then proceeded to the fireplace, turning on several lamps as she walked past them. "I see you have a drink," she began, seating herself in the other wing chair. "Does it need refreshing?"

"Not at the moment, thank you."

"How are you?" Emma asked pleasantly.

"I'm all right, I suppose." Edwina eyed her mother. "There's no need to ask how you are. You're positively blooming."

Emma smiled faintly. Sitting back, she crossed her legs, and said, "I'm afraid I won't be here for dinner after all. I have to go out. A last minute—"

"Business as usual, I've no doubt," Edwina sniffed scornfully, giving her an unfriendly look.

Emma winced but suppressed her annoyance. Edwina's rudeness and sneering manner were generally inflammatory to Emma, but tonight she was determined to overlook her daughter's unwarranted attitude toward her. You don't catch flies with vinegar, she thought dryly, and so she would continue to be pleasant and diplomatic, no matter what. Studying Edwina's face, she at once noticed the tiredness of the drooping mouth, the weary lines around her silver-gray eyes which swam with sadness. Edwina had lost weight, and she seemed nervous, anxious even; and certainly the Dowager Countess of Dunvale, usually filled with her own importance, was not quite so smug this evening. It was apparent she was besieged by troubles.

Emma felt a stab of pity for her, and this was such an unprecedented feeling and so unexpected that she was a little amazed at herself. Poor Edwina. She is truly miserable and frightened, but she does bring it on herself, I'm afraid, Emma thought. If only I could make her see this, get her to change her ways. Then, becoming aware that she was being looked over as carefully as she was scrutinizing, Emma said, "You're staring at me, Edwina. Is there something wrong with my appearance?"

"The frock, Mother," Edwina replied without a moment's hesitation. "It's a little young for you, isn't it?"

Emma stiffened and wondered if her charitable feelings had been misplaced. Edwina was intent on being obnoxious. Then she relaxed her muscles and laughed a gay, dismissive laugh, resolved not to let Edwina get her goat. When she spoke, her voice was even. "I like red," she said. "It's lively. What color would you like me to wear? *Black?* I'm not dead yet, you know, and while we're on the subject of clothes, why do you insist on wearing those awful lumpy tweeds?" Not waiting for a reply, she added, "You have a lovely figure, Edwina. You should show it off more."

Edwina let this small compliment slide by her. She asked herself why she had ever accepted Jim Fairley's invitation or agreed to stay here at Pennistone Royal. She must be insane to expose herself to her mother in this way.

Emma compressed her lips, her eyes narrowing as they weighed Edwina speculatively. She said with the utmost care, "I'd like to talk to you about Anthony."

This statement jolted Edwina out of her introspection; swinging to face Emma, she exclaimed, "Oh no, Mother! When Emily said you'd be coming down to see me, I suspected as much. However, I refuse to discuss my son with *you*. You're manipulative and controlling."

"And you, Edwina, are beginning to sound like a broken record," Emma remarked. "I'm tired of hearing that accusation from you. I'm also fed up with your continual sniping. It's impossible to have a decent conversation with you about anything. You're defensive and hostile."

Strong as these words were, Emma's tone had been mild, and her face was devoid of emotion as she pushed herself up and out of the chair. She went to the William and Mary chest in the corner, poured herself a small glass of sherry, then resumed her position in front of the fire. She sat holding her drink, a reflective light in her eyes. After a long moment, she said, "I am an old woman. A very old woman, really. Although I realize there will never be total peace in this family of mine, I would like a bit of tranquility for the rest of my life if that's possible. And so I'm prepared to forget a lot of the things you've said and done, Edwina, because I've come to the conclusion it's about time you and I buried the hatchet. I think we should try to be friends."

Edwina gaped at her in astonishment, wondering if she was dreaming. She had hardly expected to hear these words from her mother. She finally managed, "Why *me?* Why not any of the others? Or are you planning to give the same little speech to *them* this weekend?"

"I don't believe they've been invited. And if they had, I would hope they'd have enough sense not to come. I don't have much time for any of them."

"And you do for me?" Edwina asked incredulously, mentally thrown off balance by her mother's conciliatory gesture.

"Let's put it this way, I think you were the least guilty in that ridiculous plot against me last year. I know now that you were coerced to a certain extent. You never were very devious, avaricious, or venal, Edwina. Also I *do* regret our estrangement over the years. We should have made up long ago, I see that now." Emma genuinely meant this, but she was also motivated by another factor: *Anthony.* Emma was convinced that only by winning Edwina over to her side could she hope to influence her, get her to adopt a more reasonable attitude toward her son. So she said again, "I do think we should give it a try. What do we have to lose? And if we can't be real friends, perhaps we can have an amicable relationship at the very least."

"I don't think so, Mother."

Emma exhaled wearily. "I am saddened for you, Edwina, I really am. You threw away one of the most important things in your life, but—"

"What was that?"

"My love for you."

"Oh come off it, Mother," Edwina said with a sneer, looking down her nose at Emma. "You never loved me."

"Yes, I did."

"I don't believe this conversation!" Edwina exclaimed, shifting in her chair. She took a gulp of her Scotch, then brought the glass down on the Georgian side table with a bang. "You're incredible, Mother. You sit there making these extraordinary statements and expecting me to swallow them whole. That's the joke of the century. I might be stupid, but I'm not that stupid." She leaned forward, staring hard at Emma, her eyes like chips of gray ice. "What about you? My God, it was *you* who threw *me* away when I was a baby."

Emma brought herself up in the chair with enormous dignity and her face was formidable, her eyes steely as she said, *"I did not.* And don't you ever dare say that to me again. *Ever,* do you hear? You know that I put you in your Aunt Freda's care because I had to work like a drudge to support you. But we've gone through this enough times in the past, and you'll think what you want, I suppose. In the meantime I have no intention of being sidetracked from what I have to say to you, just because you have the need to dredge up all your old grudges against me."

Edwina opened her mouth, but Emma shook her head. "No, let me finish," she insisted, her green eyes holding Edwina's sharply. "I don't want you to make the same mistake twice in your life. I don't want you to throw Anthony's love away as you did mine. And you're in grave danger of doing so." She sat back, hoping her words would sink in, would have some effect.

"I have never heard anything quite so ridiculous," Edwina snorted, assuming a haughty expression.

"It's the truth nevertheless."

"What do you know about my relationship with my son!"

"A great deal. But despite his love for you, which is considerable, you are hell-bent on driving a wedge between the two of you. Why only last night he told me how concerned he is about your relationship, and he looked pretty damn worried to me."

Edwina lifted her head swiftly. "So he *is* here. When I phoned him at his London club last night, they said he'd already left. I couldn't imagine where he was. I had no idea he was coming to the christening. Is he here?"

This was asked with anxiousness, and Emma saw the eager light flickering in her daughter's eyes. She said, "No, he's not."

"Where is he staying?"

Emma chose to ignore this question for the moment. She said, "Anthony can't understand why you're so opposed to his divorce. It seems you're making his life miserable, badgering him night and day to reconcile with Min. He is baffled and distressed, Edwina."

"So is poor Min! She's heartbroken, and she can't comprehend *him* or his behavior. Neither can I. He's upsetting our lives in the most disturbing way, creating havoc. I'm almost as distraught as she is."

"Well, that's understandable. No one likes divorce, nor the pain it involves. However, you must think of Anthony before anyone else. From what he tells me, he's been very unhappy for—"

"Not *that* unhappy, Mother," Edwina interrupted, her voice snippy and high-pitched with tension. "He and Min do have a *lot* in common, whatever he might have told *you*. Naturally, he's disappointed she hasn't had a child. On the other hand, they've only been married six years. She could still get pregnant. Min is perfect for him. And don't look at me like that, Mother, so very superior and knowing. It just so happens that I *know* my son better than you do. Anthony might have strength of character, as you're so fond of pointing out to me whenever you get the opportunity. Nonetheless he does have certain weaknesses."

Edwina stopped, uncertain about continuing, then decided her mother might as well know the truth. "Sex, for one thing," she announced flatly, staring Emma down with a show of defiance. "He'll go for a pretty face every time. He got himself into the most awful scrapes with women before he married Min." Edwina shook her head and bit her lip, muttering in a low voice, "I don't know how much Min actually knows, but *I'm* aware that in the last couple of years Anthony has had several affairs and as usual with the wrong sort of women."

Emma was not unduly surprised by this bit of information, nor was she particularly interested, and she did not rise to the bait. Instead she gave Edwina a curious look and asked, "What exactly do you *mean* by the wrong sort of women?"

"You know very well what I mean, Mother. Unsuitable females with no background or breeding. A man in Anthony's position, a peer of the realm with enormous responsibilities, should have a wife who comes from the aristocracy, his own class, who understands his way of life."

Stifling her amusement at Edwina's hidebound snobbery, Emma said, "Oh for God's sake, stop talking like a Victorian dowager. We're living in the twenty-first century—well almost. Your views are outdated, my dear."

"I might have known *you'd* say something like that," Edwina replied in a snooty voice. "I must admit, you constantly surprise me, Mother. For a woman of your immense wealth and power, you are awfully careless about certain things. Background is one of them."

Emma chuckled and sipped her sherry, and her eyes twinkled over the rim of the glass. "People who live in glass houses shouldn't throw stones," she said and chuckled again.

Edwina's face colored, and then, wrinkling her nose in a gesture of distaste, she said, "I dread to think of who he'll end up with if this divorce ever goes through."

"Oh, it's going through all right," Emma said in her softest tone. "I think you would be wise to accept that. *Immediately*. It's a fact of life you cannot change."

"We'll see about that. Min has to agree before he can do anything."

"But, my dear Edwina, she has agreed."

Edwina was shocked, and she stared at her mother through horrified eyes, trying to grasp these words. For a split second she was disbelieving, and then with a sinking heart she acknowledged that her mother spoke the truth. Whatever else she was, Emma Harte was not a liar. Furthermore her information was always reliable, deadly accurate. Edwina finally stammered, "But . . . but . . ." Her voice let her down, and she was unable to continue. She reached for her glass with a shaking hand and then put it back on the table without drinking from it. Slowly she said, "But Min didn't say anything to me last night when we had dinner. How very strange. We've always been close. Why, she's been like a daughter to me. I wonder why she didn't confide in me. She always has in the past." Edwina's face was a picture of dismay as she pondered Min's extraordinary behavior and her very perplexing reticence.

For the first time, with a sudden flash of insight, Emma understood why her daughter was so frantic. She was obviously on intimate terms with Min, happy in the relationship. Yes, she was comfortable, secure, and safe with her daughter-in-law. Anthony, in upsetting the matrimonial applecart, had put his mother's world in jeopardy, or at least so Edwina believed. She was petrified at the thought of change, of a new woman in her son's life, who might not accept her quite as readily as Min had, who might even alienate her son from her.

Leaning toward Edwina, Emma said with more gentleness than usual, "Perhaps Min was afraid to tell you, afraid of distressing you further. Look here, you mustn't feel threatened by this divorce. It's not going to change your life that much, and I'm sure Anthony won't object if you remain friendly with Min." She attempted a light laugh. "And after all, Anthony is getting a divorce from Min, not from you, Edwina. He would never do anything to hurt you," she placated.

"He already has. His behavior is unforgivable." Edwina's voice was harsh and unrelenting, and her face flooded with bitterness.

Emma drew back, and the irritation she had been suppressing suddenly rose up in her. Her mouth curved down in a tight line, and her eyes turned cold. "You're a selfish woman, Edwina," she admonished. "You're not thinking of Anthony; you're only concerned with yourself. You claim your son is the center of your life—well, if he is, you have a damn poor way of showing it. He needs your love and support at a difficult time like this, not your animosity." Emma threw her a condemning stare. "I don't understand you. There's far too much resentment and hostility in you, for everyone, not only me. I can't imagine why. You've had a good life, your marriage was happy—at least I presume it was. I know Jeremy adored you, and I always thought you loved him." Her glance remained fixed on Edwina. "I hope to God you *did* love him, for your own sake. Yet despite all the wonderful things life has given you, you are filled with an all-consuming anger. Please turn away from it, put this bitterness out of your heart once and for all."

Edwina remained engulfed in silence, her expression as obdurate as ever, and Emma went on, "Trust your son, trust his judgment. I certainly do. You're knocking your head against a brick wall fighting this divorce. You can't possibly win. In fact you'll end up the loser. You'll drive Anthony away forever." She searched her daughter's face, seeking a sign of softening on her part, but it was still closed and unyielding.

Sighing to herself, Emma thought: I give up. I'll never get through to her. And then she felt compelled to make one last stab at convincing her to change her views. She cautioned gravely, "You'll end up a lonely old woman. I can't believe you would want that to happen. And if you think I have an axe to grind, remember I have nothing to gain. Very genuinely, Edwina, I simply want to prevent you from making the most terrible mistake."

Although Edwina was unresponsive, sat huddled in the chair, avoiding her mother's penetrating eyes, she had been listening attentively for the last few minutes and digesting Emma's words. They had struck home, Emma's belief to the contrary. Now, in the inner recesses of Edwina's mind, something stirred. It was a dim awareness that she had been wrong. Suddenly, discomfort with herself overwhelmed her, and she felt guilty about Anthony. She *had* been selfish, more selfish than she had realized until this moment. It was true that she loved Min like the daughter she had never had, and she dreaded the thought of losing her. But she dreaded losing her son more. And that had already begun to happen.

Edwina did not have much insight, nor was she a clever woman, but she was not without a certain intelligence, and this now told her that Anthony had turned to his grandmother in desperation, had confided in Emma instead of her. Resentment and jealousy, her worst traits, flared within her at the thought of this betrayal on her son's part. And then, with a wisdom uncommon for her, she put aside these feelings. Anthony had not really been treacherous or disloyal. *It was all her fault.* She was driving him away from her, as her mother had pointed out. Emma was being sincere in trying to bridge the rift rapidly developing between herself and her son. Emma did want them to remain close—that seemed obvious if she considered her words dispassionately and with fairness. This admission astonished Edwina, and against her volition she experienced a feeling of gratitude to her mother for making this effort on her behalf.

Edwina spoke slowly in a muted voice. "It's been a shock—the divorce, I mean. But you're right, Mother. I must think of Anthony first. Yes, it's *his* happiness that counts."

For the first time in her life, Edwina found herself turning to Emma for help. Her anger and bitterness now somewhat diffused, she asked softly, "What do you think I should do, Mother? He must be very angry with me."

Believing that her attempts to drill some common sense into Edwina had had no effect whatsoever, Emma was a bit taken aback by this unanticipated reversal. Rapidly regrouping her thoughts, she said, "No, he's not angry. Hurt perhaps, worried even. He loves you very much, you know, and the last thing he wants is a permanent split between you." Emma half smiled. "You asked me what you should do. Why, Edwina, I think you should tell him exactly what you've just told me . . . that his happiness is the most important thing to you and that he has your blessing, whatever he plans to do with his life."

"I will." Edwina cried. "I must." She gazed at Emma, for once without rancor, and added, "There's something else." She swallowed, finished in a strangled voice, "Thank you, Mother. Thank you for trying to help."

Emma nodded and glanced away. Her face was calm, but she was filling with uneasiness. I have to tell her about Sally, she thought. If I avoid revealing his involvement with the girl, holy hell will break loose tomorrow. Everything I've accomplished in the last half hour will be swept away by Edwina's wrath when she sees them together. This way, she'll have time to sleep on her rage, perhaps put it behind her. When she's calm, she'll surely recognize she cannot live her son's life for him.

Gathering her strength, Emma said, "I have something further to say to you, Edwina, and I want you to hear me out before you make any comment."

Edwina frowned. "What is it?" she asked nervously, clasping her hands together in her lap. Emma was silent, but her face was readable for a change. It telegraphed trouble to Edwina. Steeling herself for what she somehow knew would be a body blow, she nodded for her mother to proceed.

Emma said, "Anthony is in love with another woman. It's Sally . . . Sally Harte. Now, Edwina, I—"

"Oh no!" Edwina cried, aghast. Her face had paled, and she gripped the arms of the chair to steady herself.

"I asked you to hear me out. You just said your son's happiness was the only thing that matters. I trust you really meant that. He intends to marry Sally when he is free to do so, and you are—"

Again Edwina interrupted. "And you said you had no axe to grind!"

"I don't," Emma declared. "And if you think I've encouraged them, you're mistaken. I *was* aware he'd taken her out several times, when he'd been in Yorkshire. I don't deny that. But I hadn't paid much attention. Anyway, it seems they are seriously involved. Also, Anthony came to *announce* his plans to me, not to ask my permission to marry my great-niece. Furthermore I gather he took the same stance with Randolph, told him he was going to marry his daughter, and without so much as a 'by your leave.' Randolph can be old-fashioned at times, and his nose was considerably out of joint when we spoke late last night. But I soon put *him* straight."

Moving to the edge of the chair, the fuming Edwina let her furious glance roam over Emma. She examined that old and wrinkled face minutely, looking for signs of duplicity and cunning. But they were absent, and the hooded green eyes were clear, guileless. Then without warning, a vivid picture of Sally Harte flew into Edwina's twisting mind. They had run into each other nine months ago, at the exhibition of Sally's paintings at the Royal Academy. She had sought Edwina out actually and had been charming, very friendly. At the time Edwina had thought that Sally had grown up to become one of the most beautiful women she had ever laid eyes on. A Harte though, through and through, with her grandfather Winston's arresting looks, his carefree blue eyes, his dark wind-blown hair.

Edwina snuffed out the beautiful yet nevertheless disturbing image of Sally Harte and concentrated her attention on the old woman sitting opposite her, who in turn was observing her acutely and with sternness. Always ready and willing to brand her mother a manipulator, a schemer who contrived to control them and run all of their lives, Edwina decided that in this instance Emma Harte had indeed been an innocent bystander. As much as she wanted to blame her for this . . . this disaster, she could not. She had the most dreadful conviction that it was her son's doing and his alone. Anthony would be unable to resist that lovely, laughing, bewitching face, which she had been so struck by herself. It was his pattern, after all . . . falling for lovely features and a shapely figure. Yes, once again Anthony had managed to get himself involved with the wrong sort of woman and all because of sex.

With a little shiver, Edwina drew herself up and said in a clipped voice, "Well, Mother, I must admit you've convinced me that you've not been a party to this unfortunate relationship. I give you the benefit of the doubt."

"Thanks a lot," Emma said.

"Nonetheless," Edwina continued purposefully, her face set, "I must voice my disapproval of this match, or I should say mismatch, to my son. Sally is not cut out to be his wife. She is most *unsuitable*. For one thing, she is dedicated to her career. Her painting will always come first with her. Consequently she most certainly won't fit into his life at Clonloughlin, a life that revolves around the estate, the local gentry, and their country pursuits. He is making a terrible mistake, one he will live to regret for the rest of his life. So, therefore, I intend to put a stop to this *affair* at once."

How could I have ever given birth to such a pig-headed fool? Emma asked herself. She stood up and said, with great firmness, her manner conclusive, "I must leave. Shane will be here any minute. But before I go, I have two statements to make, and I want you to listen most carefully. The first concerns Sally. You cannot point a finger at her, since she is beyond reproach and her reputation is impeccable in every sense. As for her career, well, she can just as easily paint at Clonloughlin as she can here. I might also remind you, silly snob that you are, that she is not only accepted by those ridiculous nitwits in so-called high society, whom you have the desire to kowtow to constantly, but is assiduously courted by them. Thank God *she* has more sense than you and hasn't fallen for all that worthless, highfalutin claptrap."

"As usual, you're being insulting, Mother," Edwina snapped.

Emma shook her silvered head disbelievingly, her lips pursing. Trust Edwina to interrupt a serious conversation because her sensibilities were offended. She said with a small, very cold smile, "Old people believe that age gives them the license to say exactly what they think, without being concerned that they may be giving offense. I *don't* mince my words these days, Edwina, I speak the truth. And I will continue to do so until the day I die. Anything else is a waste of time. But getting back to Sally, I would like to remind you that she is an artist of some repute. Also, in case you'd forgotten, she is an heiress in her own right, since my brother Winston left his grandchildren a great fortune. Mind you, I'll give you your due; I know money isn't particularly interesting to you or Anthony, for that matter. Still that doesn't change the facts, and you're making yourself look ridiculous by saying she is unsuitable. Poppycock! Sally is ideal for him. And let's not dismiss their feelings for each other. They are in love, Edwina, and that's the most important consideration of all."

"Love? Sex, you mean," Edwina began and then stopped, seeing the look of disapproval in Emma's eyes. "Well, you are correct about one thing, Mother, money doesn't matter to the Dunvale family," Edwina finished, looking as if she had just smelled something rotten.

Emma said with cool authority, "Anthony is his own man, and for that I will be eternally grateful. *He will do as he wishes.* And if this relationship is a mistake, then it will be his own mistake to make. Not yours, not mine. Anthony is a man of thirty-three, not a snot-nosed boy in short pants. It would behoove you to stop treating him as such."

Abruptly Emma swung away from Edwina and crossed to the desk in front of the window. She stood behind it, regarding her daughter intently. "And so, my dear Edwina, if you do speak to Anthony, I suggest you restrict your conversation to motherly words of love and concern for his well-being. And I want you to restrain yourself when he mentions Sally, as no doubt he will. I don't believe he will tolerate any criticism of her or his future plans."

A horn hooted outside the window, startling both women. Emma glanced over her shoulder, saw Shane getting out of his bright red Ferrari. Turning back to Edwina, she lifted the address book off the desk and waved it at her. "You will find Randolph's number in here. Anthony is staying at Allington Hall. Take my advice, call your son and make up with him." Emma paused and added with finality, "Before it is too late."

Edwina sat rigidly in the chair, and not one word passed her white and trembling mouth.

Emma gave her only a cursory glance as she passed the chair, picked up the jacket and evening bag, and left the library. Closing the door quietly behind her, she reassured herself she had tried her very best to solve this troublesome family problem and make friends with Edwina at the same time. But she and Edwina did not matter. They would live with their armed truce as they had always done. Only Anthony and Sally were important in the scheme of things.

Emma threw back her shoulders and drew herself to her full height, striking out across the Stone Hall to the front door. And she hoped against hope that Edwina would come to her senses about her son and give him her blessing.

Eight

Blackie O'Neill had a plan.

Now this plan vastly entertained him whenever he thought about it, which had been frequently in the last few days. He was mostly amused because he had never come up with a plan in his entire life.

It had always been Emma who had had a plan. When she had been a little snippet of a girl in patched clothes and worn-out button boots, there had been her Plan with a capital P. That had been a plan so grand it had left no room for doubt, and when she had set it finally in motion, it had carried her away from Fairley and out into the wide world to seek her fame and fortune. Later she had devised innumerable other plans—for her first shop, her second, and her third; then she had created plans to acquire the Gregson Warehouse, the Fairley mills, and yet another for the creation of the Lady Hamilton line of fashions with David Kallinski. And of course there had been her Building Plan, which she tended to pronounce as if this, too, were capitalized. He had been very much a part of that most grandiose plan of all, drawing the architectural blueprints and building her enormous store in Knightsbridge. And this great edifice still stood, a proud testament to her most extraordinary achievements.

Yes, his Emma had lived with one kind of plan or another for as long as he had known her, and each one had been put into operation with determination and carried through with consummate skill in her inimitable way. And with every success she would give him a tiny smile of cold triumph and say, "You see, I told you it would work." He would throw back his head and roar and congratulate her and insist they celebrate, and her face would soften, and he knew that she was giddy with excitement inside, even if she did not really want to show it.

But *he* had never made a plan before.

In fact almost everything that had happened to Blackie O'Neill in his long life had been by sheer happenstance.

When he had first come over from Ireland as a young spalpeen, to work on the Leeds canals with his Uncle Pat, he had never imagined in his wildest fantasies that he would become a millionaire many times over. Oh, he had boasted that he was going to be a rich "toff" to young Emma when she had been a servant at Fairley Hall, but at that time it had seemed unlikely ever to come true. It had been something of an idle boast, and he had laughed at himself in secret. His boasting had proved not to be so idle after all.

Over the years Emma had often teased him and said that he had the luck of the Irish, and this was true in many respects. He had had to work hard; on the other hand he had also carried Lady Luck in his breast pocket, and great and good fortune had continually blessed him. There had been times of terrible sadness in his personal life and sorrow too. For one thing he had lost his lovely Laura far too young, but she had given him his son, and he considered Bryan to be his best bit of luck of all. As a child Bryan had been warm and loving, and they had stayed close, enjoyed a unique relationship to this day. Bryan had a shrewd, sharp brain, was inspired and fearless in business, a genius really, and together they had parlayed O'Neill Construction into one of the biggest and most important building companies in Europe. When Bryan's wife, Geraldine, had inherited two hotels from her father, Leonard Ingham, it was Bryan who had had the foresight and brains to hang onto them. Those little hotels in Scarborough and Bridlington, catering to family holidaymakers, had become the nucleus for the great O'Neill chain, which was now an international concern and a public company trading on the London Stock Exchange.

But had Blackie planned all this? No, never. It had simply come about by chance, through the most marvelous serendipity. Of course he had been smart enough to recognize *his* train when it had come rolling through *his* station, and he had jumped on it with alacrity, and he had used every opportunity that presented itself to his advantage. In so doing he had, like Emma, created an empire and founded a dynasty of his own.

These thoughts ran through Blackie's head as he dressed for dinner, and he chuckled to himself from time to time as he contemplated *his* first Plan, also with a capital P. Not unnaturally it involved Emma, with whom he spent a great deal of time these days. *He had decided to take her on a trip around the world.* When he had first suggested this a few weeks ago, she had looked at him askance, scoffed at the idea, and told him *she* was far too busy and preoccupied with her affairs to go galavanting off on a holiday in foreign parts. His smooth Irish tongue and persuasive manner had seemingly had no effect. Nevertheless he had made up his mind to get his own way. After a great deal of thought and pacing of the floor wracking his brains, he had devised a plan—and the key to it was Australia. Blackie knew that Emma secretly itched to go to Sydney, to see her grandson Philip McGill Amory, who was being trained to take over the vast McGill holdings. He was also aware that Emma had balked at the thought of the long and exhausting trip to the other side of the world, and she was still vacillating about going.

So he would take her, and they would travel in style.

Naturally she would be unable to resist his invitation when he explained how comfortable, luxurious, leisurely, and effortless their journey would be. First they would fly to New York and spend a week there before going to San Francisco for another week. Once they were rested and refreshed, they would hop over to Hong Kong and the Far East and slowly head to their final destination in easy stages.

And he fully intended to make sure she had a little fun on their peregrinations. Blackie could no longer count the times he had asked himself if Emma had ever really had any honest-to-goodness fun in her life. Perhaps becoming one of the richest women in the world had been her way of enjoying herself. On the other hand he was not sure how much pleasure she had derived from this consuming, backbreaking endeavor. In any event he was planning all sorts of entertaining diversions, and young Philip was the tempting morsel he would dangle in front of her nose; if he was not mistaken, the trip would prove to be irresistible to her.

Blackie knotted his blue silk tie and stood away from the mirror, eyeing it critically.

It's sober enough, I am thinking, he muttered, knowing Emma would make a sarcastic remark if he wore one of his gaudier numbers. Long, long ago Laura had curbed, at least to some extent, his exotic taste for colorful brocade waistcoats, elaborately tailored suits, and flashy jewelry; Emma had cured him completely. Well, almost. Occasionally Blackie could not resist the temptation to indulge himself in a few jazzy silk ties and handkerchiefs and ascots in florid patterns and brilliant colors, but he made certain never to wear them when he was seeing Emma. He reached for his dark blue jacket and put it on, smoothed the edge of his pristine white collar, and nodded at his reflection. I might be an old codger, but sure an' I feel like a young spalpeen tonight, he thought with another chuckle.

Snowy-haired though he was, Blackie's bright black eyes were still as merry and mischievous as they had been when he was a young man in his prime, and his bulk and size were undiminished by age. He was in remarkable health and looked more like a man in his seventies than one who was eighty-three. His mind was alert, agile, and unimpaired, and senility was a foreign word to him in much the same way as it was to Emma.

Pausing in the middle of the bedroom, he dwelled momentarily on the evening ahead, the business matter he would discuss with Emma. He was glad Shane and he had decided to broach the subject to her. Once that was out of the way and when they were alone, he would move gently into the conversation about the trip. It won't be easy, he told himself. You know she's the stubborn one. When he had first met Emma, he had recognized at once that she had the most pertinacious will it had ever been his misfortune to encounter, and it had only grown more inflexible over the years.

A scene flashed, transporting him back to the past: 1906. A bitter cold January day. Emma sitting next to him on the tramcar going to Armley, looking impossibly beautiful in a new black wool coat and the green-and-black scarf and tam-o'-shanter he had given her for Christmas. The green tones in the tartan bringing out the green depths in her eyes, the black showing off the flawlessness of her alabaster skin.

What a pallor her face had held that Sunday. Nonetheless it had not

marred her loveliness, he ruminated, remembering every detail of that afternoon so clearly. She had been sixteen and carrying Edwina, and oh how rigid
she had been in her obstinacy. It had taken all of his powers of persuasion to
maneuver her onto that tram. She had not wanted to go to Armley, nor to
make the acquaintance of his dear friend, Laura Spencer. Still when the two
girls had met, they had taken to each other instantly and were the closest of
loving friends until the day poor Laura died. Yes, Emma's terrible burdens had
eased once she had moved into Laura's snug little house, and he had experienced an enormous sense of relief knowing that Laura would mother her,
watch over her. And he had won that day, as he fully intended to win with her
now, sixty-three years later.

Opening the top drawer of the bureau at the other side of the room, he
took out a small black leather jewel box, stared at it thoughtfully, and then
slipped it in his pocket. Humming to himself, he strode out and went downstairs.

Blackie O'Neill still lived in the grand Georgian mansion he had built for
himself at Harrogate in 1919. A handsome wide staircase, so beautifully designed it appeared to float, curved down into a charming circular entrance hall
of lovely dimensions, where walls painted a rich apricot acted as a counterpoint
to the crisp black-and-white marble floor. The square marble slabs had been set
down at an angle so that they became diamond shapes, and they led the eye to
the niches on either side of the front door. White marble statues of the Greek
goddesses Artemis and Hecate graced these niches and were highlighted by
hidden spots. An elegant Sheraton console, inlaid with exotic fruitwoods, stood
against one wall underneath a gilt Georgian mirror, and was flanked on either
side by Sheraton chairs upholstered in apricot velvet. Illuminating the hall was a
huge antique crystal-and-bronze-doré chandelier which dropped down from
the domed ceiling, and the setting had elegance without the slightest hint of
ostentation.

Crossing the hall, Blackie went into the drawing room. Here a log fire
burned cheerily in the Adam fireplace, and the silk-shaded lamps cast rafts of
warming light onto the cool green walls, on the sofas and chairs covered in
darker green silk. Splendid paintings and Sheraton and Hepplewhite antiques
added to the graciousness of the room, which exemplified Blackie's sense of
style, color, and perspective in furniture and design.

He fussed with the bottle of champagne in the silver wine cooler, turning
it several times, shifting the ice around; then he took a cigar from the humidor
and went over to his favorite chair to wait. He had no sooner trimmed the cigar
and lit it than he heard them in the hall. He put the cigar in the ashtray and
rose.

"There you are, mavourneen," he cried, hurrying to meet Emma as she
came into the room. There was a wide smile on his ruddy face as he exclaimed,
"You're a sight for sore eyes." He hugged her tightly to his broad chest, held
her away, and looked down at her. He smiled again, admiration shining in his
eyes. "And aren't you my bonny colleen tonight."

Emma smiled back at him, love and warmth overflowing in her. "Thank
you, Blackie dear. And I must admit, you don't look so bad yourself. That's a
beautiful suit." Her eyes twinkled merrily as she ran a hand down his arm
expertly. "Mmmm. Very nice cloth. It feels like a bit of my best worsted."

"It is, it is," Blackie said and winked at Shane, who was standing behind

Emma. "Would I be wearing anything else now. But come, me darlin', and sit here and let me get you a glass of champagne."

Emma allowed him to guide her across the room to the sofa. She sat down, and a brow lifted. "Are we celebrating something?"

"No, no, not really. Unless it's reaching our grand old ages and being in such good health." He squeezed her shoulder affectionately and added, "Also I know you prefer wine to the stronger stuff." He glanced at Shane. "Would you do the honors, me boy? And make mine a drop of me good Irish."

"Right you are, Grandfather."

Blackie seated himself in the chair facing Emma, picked up his cigar, and puffed on it reflectively for a moment, then said to her, "And I expect you've had a busy day as usual. I'm beginning to wonder if you'll ever retire . . . as you're constantly threatening to do."

"I don't suppose I ever will," Emma laughed. "You know very well I plan to go with my boots on."

Blackie shot her a chastising look. "Don't talk to *me* about dying. I've no intention of doing that for a long time." He chuckled softly. "I've a lot more damage to do yet."

Emma laughed with him, and so did Shane, who carried their drinks over to them. He fetched his own, and they clinked glasses and toasted each other. Shane took a swallow of his Scotch and said, "Would you both excuse me for a few minutes. I have to phone Winston."

Emma said, "I hope you have better luck than I did. I was trying to get him for ages earlier. First the line was busy; then there was no answer."

Shane frowned. "Perhaps he'd slipped down to the village. Any message, Aunt Emma?"

"Tell him that we didn't—" Changing her mind, she broke off and shook her head. "Never mind, Shane. It's not important. I'll be seeing him tomorrow, and I'm sure we'll have a chance to chat at some point then."

When they were alone, Blackie reached across and took Emma's hand in his and stared deeply into her face. "It's grand to see you, me darlin'. I've missed you."

Emma's eyes danced. "Get along with you, you silly old thing. You just saw me the day before yesterday," she exclaimed, amusement surfacing. "Don't tell me you've forgotten our dinner at Pennistone."

"Of course I haven't. But it seems like a long time to me, caring about you the way I do." He patted her hand affectionately and sat back in his chair, giving her the fondest of looks. "And I meant it when I said you looked bonny, Emma. You're a real bobby dazzler in that dress; it's very flattering on you, me darlin' girl."

"Some girl! But thank you, I'm glad you like it," she answered with a smile of real pleasure. "My friend Ginette Spanier, at Balmain's, picked it out for me and had it shipped over from Paris last week. Mind you, Edwina was rather scathing earlier. She told me it was too young for me—the color, you know."

Blackie's expression altered radically. "She was just being catty, Emma. Edwina's got a chip on her shoulder the size of that old oak tree out yonder in my garden. *She'll* never change." He noticed the look of pain flit across Emma's face, and he frowned with concern for her, cursing her daughter under his breath. Edwina had always been troublesome. But then so had most of the others, and there were a couple of Emma's children whom he could quite cheerfully strangle with his bare hands. He cried heatedly, "I hope she's not been giving you a hard time!"

"No, not really."

She sounded unusually hesitant, and Blackie spotted this immediately, shook his marvelous white, leonine head, and exhaled in exasperation. "I'll never understand Jim. I don't know what prompted him to invite her. It was stupid on his part, if you ask me."

"Yes, and Paula was upset too, but I decided not to intervene. I thought it would look petty. But . . ." Emma shrugged, and, since she confided most things in Blackie these days, she told him about her conversation with Edwina, her attempts to reason with her daughter.

Blackie listened carefully, occasionally nodding, and when she had finished, he said in a low voice, "Well, I'm happy for Sally if this is what she wants. She's a lovely lass, and Anthony is a nice chap. Down-to-earth and not a bit stuck-up, which is more than I can say for that mother of his." He paused. Recollections swamped him. Slowly, he added, "She was most peculiar when she was growing up and never very nice to you, Emma. Always slighting you if I remember correctly, and believe me I do. I haven't forgotten how she used to show her preference for Joe Lowther, making it so bloody obvious, too. She was a little bitch, and she hasn't changed. Please promise me you'll let this matter about Anthony rest. I don't want you getting agitated because of Edwina. She's not worth it."

"Yes, you're right, and I promise." She smiled faintly. "Let's forget about Edwina. Where are you taking me to dinner? Shane was most mysterious when we were driving over here."

"Was he now, mavourneen." Blackie grinned from ear to ear. "To tell you the truth, Emma, I couldn't think of a nice enough place, so I told Mrs. Padgett to prepare dinner for us here. I know you like her home cooking, and she's rustled up a lovely bit of spring lamb. I told her to make new potatoes, Brussels sprouts and Yorkshire pudding—all your favorites. Now, me darlin', how does that sound to you?"

"Delicious, and I'm glad we're not going out. It's much cozier here, and I do feel a bit tired."

His black eyes narrowed under his bushy brows as he examined her alertly. "Ah," he said softly, "so you're finally admitting it. I do wish you wouldn't push yourself so hard. There's no need for it anymore, you know."

Dismissing this comment with an easy smile, Emma leaned closer to him. No longer able to suppress her curiosity, she asked eagerly, "What do you want my advice about? You sounded cagey on the phone this morning."

"I didn't mean to, darlin'." He sipped his whiskey, puffed away for a moment, and continued, "But I'd prefer to wait until Shane comes back if you don't mind, since it concerns him."

"What concerns me?" Shane asked from the doorway. He strolled into the room, his drink in his hand.

"The business matter I want to discuss with Emma."

"I'll say it concerns me!" Shane exclaimed rather forcefully. "It was my idea in the first place." Seating himself on the sofa next to Emma, he settled against the cushions, crossed his legs, and turned to her. "Winston's sorry he missed your calls. He was out in the garden earlier, worrying about the beck flooding. It's dangerously near to it apparently." His eyes swiveled to his grandfather. "I just rang Derek and asked him to get a couple of our men over to Beck House tomorrow, to check things out."

"Aye, that's a good idea. But they'll have to shore up those banks a lot better than they did last year," Blackie remarked pointedly. "Now, if you'd both listened to me, it would have been done right in the first place. Let me explain a couple of things." He commenced to do so, not giving Shane a chance to respond. And then for the next couple of minutes they discussed various methods of reinforcement. They sounded for all the world like a couple of builders about to embark on a major construction project, and Blackie was most vociferous in his opinions, which tickled Emma. He was still a bricklayer at heart.

But she soon lost interest in their somewhat technical conversation. She had become extremely conscious of Shane's presence next to her. His bulk did more than fill the sofa, it commandeered it. For the first time in years she began to regard him through newly perceptive and objective eyes, not as an old family friend, but as a younger woman—a stranger—might. How marvelous looking he was tonight, dressed in an impeccably tailored gray suit and a pale-blue voile shirt with a silver-gray silk tie. He had inherited his grandfather's large frame, his broad sweeping back and powerful shoulders, along with Blackie's wavy black hair and those sparkling eyes so like jet. His complexion was dark too, but *his* light mahogany tan came from sun, garnered on the ski slopes of Switzerland or a lazy Caribbean beach, not from toiling long hours as a navvy out in the open, as his grandfather had once done.

His appearance was much like Blackie's had been at his age. The face is different, though, she thought, sneaking another surreptitious look at him, but he does have Blackie's distinctive cleft in his chin, the same dimples when he smiles. And that long upper lip betrays his Celtic origins. I bet he's broken many a heart already, she added silently with an inward smile of amusement. Then she experienced a tiny pang of sadness for Sarah. Easy to understand why the girl had a crush on him. He was a splendid young man who exuded virility and manliness, and there was a unique warmth and gentleness in him. That was the most devastating of combinations, and she knew only too well about men like Shane O'Neill. She had loved such a man herself, had had her heart broken by him once when she had been young and vulnerable and very much in love. But *he* had repaired *her* broken heart, had given her immeasurable happiness and fulfillment in the end. Yes, Paul McGill had had the same kind of potency and fatal charm that Shane O'Neill possessed in some abundance.

Blackie said, "Daydreaming, Emma darlin'."

She shifted her position on the sofa and smiled lightly. "No, I'm patiently waiting for you two to finish discussing that damn beck, so we can get down to brass tacks about the business you want my advice on."

"Why yes, of course, it's wasting time we are," he admitted, his manner more genial than ever. In fact conviviality seemed to spill out of Blackie tonight, and he beamed first at Emma, then at Shane. "Now, me boy," he said, "please top up Emma's glass with a drop more of that bubbly, and give me a refill, and we'll settle in for a nice little chat."

And this they did after Shane had attended to their drinks.

It was Shane who began, concentrating his attention entirely on Emma, his tone as sober as his face had become. He spoke rapidly but clearly, as he generally did in business, plunging in without preamble. Emma appreciated his directness, and she in turn gave him all of her attention.

Shane said, "We've been wanting to build or acquire a hotel in New York for several years. Dad and I have both spent a great deal of time scouting out possibilities. Recently we found the ideal place. It's a residential hotel in the East Sixties. Old-fashioned, of course, and the interiors are in need of considerable remodeling, rebuilding actually. That's what we'll do—most likely. You see, we tendered a bid, it has been accepted, and we're buying the hotel. The papers are currently being drawn up."

"Congratulations, Shane, and you too, Blackie!" Emma looked from one to the other, her face bathed in genuine delight. "But how can I be of help to you? Why do you need to talk to me? I don't know a blessed thing about hotels, except whether or not they're comfortable and efficient."

"But you do know New York City, Emma," Blackie countered, leaning forward with intentness. "That's *why* we need you."

"I'm not sure that I follow you—"

"We need you to steer us in the right direction to the best people," Shane cut in, wanting to get to the crux of the matter. He pinned her with his bright black eyes. "It seems to me that you've made that city your own in so many different ways, so you must know what makes it tick. Or rather what makes its business and commerce tick." His generous mouth curved up into the cheekiest of grins. "We want to pick your brains and use your connections," he finished, regarding her carefully, his cheekiness still very much in evidence.

Amusement flickered in Emma's eyes. She had always liked Shane's style, his directness, his boyish impudence. She stifled a laugh and said, "I see. Do continue."

"Right," Shane replied, all seriousness again. "Look, we're a foreign corporation, and in my opinion that city's as tight as a drum. We can't go in cold . . . well, we could, but we'd have a tough time. I'm sure we'd be resented. We need advisers—the proper advisers—and some good connections. Political connections for one thing. And we'll need help with the unions, with any number of things. I'm sure you of all people understand what I'm talking about, Aunt Emma. So where do we go? Who do we go to?"

Emma's mind had been working with its usual swiftness and acuity, and she saw the sense in Shane's words. He had analyzed the situation most shrewdly. She told him this, went on without hesitation, "It *would* be unwise of you to start operating in New York without the most influential backing and support. You'll need everybody in your corner, and the only way you'll get them in it is through friends. Good friends with clout. I think I can help."

"I knew if anybody could, it would be you. Thanks, Aunt Emma," Shane said, and she saw him visibly relaxing.

"Yes, we're very grateful, me darlin'," Blackie added, pushing himself up out of the chair. He took his drink to the console behind the sofa, plopped in extra ice, added more water to his whiskey, and said, "Well, go on, Shane, as Emma asked." He touched her shoulder lightly, lovingly. Emma glanced behind her, questions on her face. Blackie chuckled. "Oh yes, there's more," he said and ambled back to his chair by the fireside.

Shane said, "We have a solid, well-established law firm representing us in the purchase of the hotel—they're specialists in real estate. However, I feel we are going to need additional representation for other business matters. I'd like to find a really prestigious law firm that has political savvy and a few gilt-edged connections. Any suggestions about that?"

There was a moment of thoughtfulness before Emma said, "Yes, of course. I could send you to my lawyers and to any number of people who would be of use to you. But I've been thinking hard whilst I've been listening, and I believe there is one person who would be of more assistance to you than me and my lawyers and my friends put together. His name is Ross Nelson. He's a banker—head of a private bank in fact. He has the very best connections in New York, throughout the States for that matter. I'm sure he'll be able to recommend the law firm most qualified for your purposes and assist you in a variety of other ways."

"But will he do it?" Shane asked, doubt echoing.

"He will if *I* ask him," she said, giving Shane the benefit of a reassuring smile. "I can telephone him on Monday and explain everything. I hope I'll be able to enlist his help immediately. Would you like me to do that?"

"Yes, I would. *We* would." He swung his head to Blackie. "Wouldn't we, Grandfather?"

"Anything you say, my boy. This is your deal." Blackie tapped ash from his cigar, looked across at Emma. "That name Nelson rings a bell. Have I met him?"

"Why yes, I think you did once. It was some years ago, Blackie. Ross was over in England with his great-uncle, Daniel P. Nelson. Dan was a close friend and associate of Paul's, if you recall. He's the fellow who wanted me to send Daisy over to the States during the war, to stay with him and his wife, Alicia. But as you know, I never wanted Daisy to be evacuated. Anyway, the Nelsons only had one child, Richard. The boy was killed in the Pacific. Dan was never quite the same after that. He made Ross his heir, after his wife of course. Ross inherited controlling interest in the bank on Wall Street when Dan died, and God knows what else. Not millions. *Zillions,* I think. Daniel P. Nelson was one of the richest men in America, had tremendous power."

Shane was impressed, and this showed in his face. He asked quickly, "How old a man is Ross Nelson?"

"Oh he must be in his late thirties, early forties, not much more."

"Are you sure he won't mind helping us? I'd hate to think he would regard your request as an imposition. That kind of situation can create difficulties," Shane remarked. He was intrigued with Nelson, wanted to know more about him. He reached for his drink and took a swallow, observing Emma out of the corner of his eye.

Emma laughed quietly. "He owes me a few favors. And he won't think I'm imposing, I can assure you of that." She gave Shane a shrewd look through her narrowed green eyes. "Mind you, I know Ross, and he's going to expect something in return. Business, I'm sure, in one form or another. Actually, you might consider doing some of your investment banking with him and let his bank handle your affairs on that side of the Atlantic. You could do worse." There was a cynical edge to her voice as she finished, "There are two things you must remember, Shane . . . one hand always washes the other, and there's never anything free in this world. Especially in business."

Shane met her cool, concentrated gaze steadily. "I understand," he said softly. "And I learned long ago that anything for nothing is usually not worth having. As for Ross Nelson, I'll know how to show my appreciation—you have no worries there."

Blackie, who had been following this exchange with considerable interest, slapped his knee and laughed uproariously. "Ah, Emma, it's a spry one I've got me here." He shook his head, and his benevolent smile expressed his love and pride. "There are no flies on you, my boy, I'm glad to see, and it won't be the same without you." A hint of sadness crept onto his face, wiping away the laughter. "I know it's important and necessary, but I hate to see you go away again and so quickly. It pains me, it truly does."

Emma put down her glass and stared at Shane. "When *are* you leaving, Shane?"

"I fly to New York on Monday morning. I'll be staying there for a good six months, maybe longer. I'll be supervising the rebuilding of the hotel in Manhattan and trotting down to the Caribbean every few weeks to check on our hotels in the islands."

"Six months," she repeated in surprise. "That *is* a long time. We shall miss you." But perhaps it's just as well he won't be around for a while, she added under her breath, thinking of her granddaughter Sarah Lowther. Out of sight, out of mind. Or so she hoped.

Shane cut into her thoughts when he said, "I shall miss you too, Aunt Emma, and Grandfather, everyone in fact. But I'll be back almost before you can say Jack Robinson." He leaned into Emma and squeezed her arm. "And keep an eye on this lovable old scoundrel here. He's very dear to me."

"And to me too, Shane. Of course I'll look after him."

"Ah, and won't we be taking care of each other now," Blackie announced, sounding extremely pleased with himself all of a sudden, thinking of his Plan with a capital P. "But then we've been doing that for half a century or more, and it's a difficult habit to break, sure an' it is."

"I can imagine." Shane laughed, marveling at the two of them. What an extraordinary pair they were, and the love and friendship they felt for each other was a most enviable thing. Sighing under his breath, he reached for his Scotch, peered into the amber liquid, reflecting. After a swallow he turned to Emma. "But getting back to Ross Nelson, what kind of a chap is he?"

"Unusual in many ways," Emma said slowly, staring into space, as if visualizing Ross Nelson in her mind's eye. "Ross is deceptive. He has a certain charm, and he appears to be very friendly. On the surface. I've always thought there was an innate coldness in him and a curious kind of calculation, as if he stands apart from himself, watching the effect he has on people. There's a terrific ego there, especially when it comes to women. He's something of a ladies' man and has just been divorced for the second time. Not that this is significant. On the other hand it's frequently struck me that he might be unscrupulous . . . in his private life."

She paused, brought her eyes to meet Shane's, and added, "But that has nothing to do with you or me. As far as business is concerned, I deem Ross to be trustworthy. You have no cause to worry in that respect. But be warned, he's clever, razor sharp, and he has the *need* to get his own way—that monumental ego rears up constantly."

"Quite a picture you've painted, Aunt Emma. Obviously I'll have to have my wits about me."

"That's always wise, Shane, whomever you're dealing with." She smiled faintly. "On the other hand you're going to Ross for advice, not pitting your-self against him in a business deal. You'll be able to handle Ross Nelson very nicely. In fact I think you'll get along with him just fine. Don't forget, he owes me a few favors, so he'll bend over backward to be cooperative and helpful."

"I know your judgment is never flawed," Shane replied. He rose, walked around the sofa to fix himself another drink, thinking of the characterization she had drawn in her precise, thumbnail sketch. He was anxious to meet the man. It was obvious that Nelson was going to be invaluable. And he was impatient to get the ball rolling with the New York hotel. He needed to submerge himself in business, to take his mind off troubling personal matters. Ross Nelson might possibly be a pain in the neck in his private life, but who cared about his philandering. As long as he was smart, shrewd, trustworthy, and willing to help, that was all that mattered.

Blackie's eyes flicked briefly to his grandson, and then settled on Emma. "I'm not so sure I like the sound of this Ross Nelson fellow," he began.

Emma cut him off with a laugh. "My money's on Shane. He's a grown lad who knows how to take care of himself very well. Very well indeed, Blackie. I'll even go as far as to say that Ross Nelson might have met his match in Shane." This observation seemed to entertain her, and she continued to laugh.

Shane grinned but made no comment.

He was looking forward to meeting Mr. Ross Nelson more than ever. The banker would add spice to the New York venture.

Nine

They sat in front of the blazing fire in the library—just the two of them.

Blackie nursed a snifter of aged Napoléon cognac, and Emma sipped a cup of tea with lemon. He had poured her a small glass of Bonnie Prince Charlie, her favorite Drambuie liqueur, but it remained untouched on the Sheraton side table next to her chair.

They were quiet, lost in their diverse thoughts, relaxing after Mrs. Padg-ett's fine dinner. Shane had left, and, as much as they both loved him in their individual ways, they were content to have this time alone together.

The firelight flickered and danced across the bleached-pine-paneled walls, which had taken on a mellow amber cast in the warm roseate glow emanating from the hearth. In the garden beyond the French doors, the towering old oak creaked and rustled and swayed under the force of the wind that had turned into a roaring gale in the last hour. The door and the windows rattled, and the rain was flung against the glass in an unrelenting stream, beating a steady stac-cato rhythm, and it was difficult to see out through this curtain of falling water. But in the fine old room all was warmth, coziness and comfort. The logs crackled and hissed and spurted from time to time, and the grandfather clock, an ancient sentinel in the corner, ticked away in accompaniment.

His eyes had been focused on her for a while.

In repose, as it was now, Emma's face was gentle, the firm jaw and deter-mined chin and stern mouth softer, less forbidding in the flattering light. Her hair held the luster of the purest silver, and she seemed to him to be a lovely dainty doll, sitting there so sedately, perfectly groomed and dressed as always, elegance and refinement apparent in every line of her slender body.

She had not changed really.

Oh he was aware that when the flames blazed more brightly, he would notice the wrinkles and the hooded lids and the faint brown spreckles of age on her hands. But he knew, deep in his soul, that she was still the same girl inside.

She would always be his wild young colleen of the moors, that little starveling creature he had come across early one morning in 1904 when she had been tramping so bravely to Fairley Hall to scrub and clean in order to earn a few miserable coppers to help her impoverished family. His destination had been the same place, for Squire Adam Fairley had hired him to do bricklaying at the Hall, and then he had stupidly gone and lost himself in the mist on those bleak and empty godforsaken hills . . . so long ago . . . but not so long to him. He had never forgotten that day.

Blackie's gaze lingered on Emma.

He had loved this woman from the first moment he had met her and all the days of his life thereafter. He had been eighteen that day on the lonely moors, and she had been a fourteen-year-old waif, all skin and bones and huge emerald eyes, and she had touched his heart like no one else before or after and bound him to her forever without even trying.

Once he had asked her to marry him.

She, believing it was out of kindness and friendship and the goodness of his heart, had refused him. She had thanked him sweetly, her face wet with tears, and explained that she and the child she was carrying, by another man, would only be burdens to him. And she would not inflict such a terrible load on her dearest friend Blackie, she had said.

Eventually he had married Laura Spencer, and he had loved her well and true. And yet he had never stopped loving his bonny mavourneen, even though at times he was hard-pressed to explain that unique love to himself, or to articulate it to her or anyone else for that matter.

There was a time when he had half expected Emma to marry David Kallinski, but once again she had turned down a splendid, upright young man. Later she had confided the reason to him. She had not wanted to create trouble between David and his family, who were Jewish. Although Mrs. Kallinski was motherly toward her, Emma said she had long realized that as a gentile she would not be considered appropriate as a daughter-in-law by Janessa Kallinski, who was Orthodox and expected her son to marry in the faith.

Then one day Joe Lowther had come riding by, metaphorically speaking, and to Blackie's astonishment—and not inconsiderable bewilderment—Emma had plunged into holy matrimony with Joe. He had never been able to fully comprehend their union. In his opinion it was difficult, if not downright impossible, to hitch a racehorse and a cart horse to the same wagon. But Joe had been a kindly man, if plodding and dull and not particularly brilliant or engaging. Still he and Blackie had liked each other well enough and had gone off to fight a war together. And he had seen Joe Lowther killed in the muddy trenches of the bloody, battle-torn Somme and had wept real tears for him, for Joe had been too young a man to die. And he had never been able to talk about Joe's ghastly death, to tell her that he had seen Joe blown to smithereens. Only years later did he learn from Emma that she had married Joe, who adored her, to protect herself and her baby daughter Edwina from the Fairleys, after Gerald

Fairley had attempted to rape her one night at her little shop in Armley. "It wasn't as calculating as it sounds," she had gone on, "I liked Joe, cared for him, and because he was a good man, I felt honor-bound to be a good wife." And she *had* been devoted, *he* knew that.

The second time he had wanted to marry Emma he had truly believed his timing was perfect, that he had every chance of being accepted, and he was buoyed up with soaring hopes and anticipation. It was a short while after the First World War when they were both widowed. In the end, though, uncertain of her true feelings for him, and filled with sudden nervousness about Emma's astonishing achievements in comparison to his own, he had lost his nerve and his tongue, and so he had not spoken up. Regrettably. And she had unexpectedly gone off and married Arthur Ainsley, a man not good enough to lick her boots, and had suffered all kinds of pain and humiliation at Ainsley's hands. Finally, in the 1920s, as he was biding his time and waiting for the propitious moment, Paul McGill had come back to England to claim her at last for himself.

And he had lost his chance again.

Now it was too late for them to marry. Yet in a sense they had something akin to marriage and just as good to his way of thinking . . . this friendship, this closeness, this total understanding. Yes, all were of immense and incalculable value. And Emma and he were perfectly attuned to each other in the twilight of their days, and what did the rest mean or matter at this stage in the game of life?

But he still had that ring . . .

Much to his own surprise, Blackie had kept the engagement ring he had bought for Emma so long ago. There had never been another woman to give it to, at least not one he cared enough about; and for a reason he could not fathom, he had never wanted to sell it.

Tonight the ring had burned a hole in his pocket all through drinks and dinner, in much the same way his Plan with a capital P burned a hole in his head. Putting down his drink, he leaned closer to the hearth, lifted the poker, and shoved the logs around in the grate, wondering if it was finally the right time to give it to her. Why not?

He heard the rustle of silk and a sigh that was hardly audible.

"Did I startle you, Emma?"

"No, Blackie."

"I have something for you."

"You *do*. What is it?"

He reached into his pocket and brought out the box, sat holding it in his large hands.

Emma asked curiously, "Is it my birthday present?" and she gave him a warm little smile of obvious pleasure, laughter sparkling in her eyes.

"Oh no, indeed it's not. I intend to give you *that* on your birthday at the—" He curbed himself. The elaborate party he and Daisy were planning was very hush-hush and meant to be a big surprise for Emma. "You'll get your birthday gift at the end of the month, on the very day you're eighty," he improvised adroitly. "No, this is something I bought for you—" He had to laugh as he added, "Fifty years ago, believe it or not."

She threw him a startled look. "Fifty years! But why didn't you give it to me before now?"

"Ah, Emma, thereby hangs a long tale," he said and fell silent as memories came unbidden.

How beautiful she had looked that night, with her red hair piled high on her head in an elaborate plaited coil, wearing a superb white velvet gown, cut low and off the shoulders. Pinned to one of the small sleeves was the emerald bow he had had made for her thirtieth birthday, an exquisite replica of the cheap little green glass brooch he had given her when she was fifteen. She had been touched and delighted that he had not forgotten his old promise, made to her in the kitchen of Fairley Hall. But on that particular Christmas night, in all her elegant finery, with McGill's magnificent emeralds blazing on her ears, he had thought his emerald bow, costly though it had been, looked like a trumpery bauble in comparison to those earrings . . .

Growing impatient, Emma frowned and exclaimed, "Well, are you going to tell me the tale or not?"

He pushed the past to one side, flashed her a smile. "Do you remember that first party I gave here? It was Christmas—"

"Boxing Day night!" Emma cried, her face lighting up. "You had just completed this house, finished furnishing it with all the lovely Sheraton and Hepplewhite pieces you'd scoured the country to find. And you were so proud of what you'd created all by yourself. Of course I remember the party and very clearly. It was the year 1919."

Blackie nodded, glanced down at the box, continuing to finger it. He raised his head. Unabashed love shone on his craggy, wrinkled face, giving it a more youthful appearance. "I'd bought this for you earlier that week. I'd traveled down to London to choose it, gone to the finest jeweler, too. It was in the pocket of my tuxedo. I'd intended to give it to you at the party."

"But you never did . . . why not? What ever made you change your mind, Blackie?" She looked at him oddly, through eyes awash with perplexity.

"I'd decided to have a talk first—with Winston. Why, it was here, in this very room, as a matter of fact." He looked about him as if seeing that ancient scene being re-enacted in the shadows, seeing the ghost of Winston as he had been as a young man, lurking there. He cleared his throat. "Your brother and I talked about you, and—"

"What *about* me?"

"We discussed you and your business ventures. I was worried to death about you, Emma, distressed because of the way you had plunged into the commodities market and recklessly, or so I thought. I was concerned about your rapid expansion of the stores in the north, your determination to keep on building, acquiring other holdings. I believed you were overextending yourself, gambling—"

"I've always been a gambler," she murmured softly. "In a way that's the secret of my success . . . being willing to take chances . . ." She left the rest unsaid. He surely knew it all by now.

"Aye," he agreed, "maybe it is. Anyway Winston explained that you'd stopped the commodities lark after making a fortune speculating, and he told me you were not in over your head. Just the opposite. He told me you were a millionairess. And as he talked and ever so proudly, I began to realize that you were a far, far bigger success than I'd ever dreamed, that you'd surpassed me, outstripped David Kallinski, left us both behind in business. It suddenly seemed to me that you were quite beyond my reach. That's why I never gave you this ring . . . You see Emma, I was going to ask you to marry me that night."

"Oh, Blackie, Blackie darling" was all she could manage to say, so stupe-fied was she. Tears pricked the back of Emma's eyes as a variety of emotions seized her with some force. Her love and friendship for him rose up in her to mingle with a terrible sadness and a sense of regret for Blackie, as she envi-sioned the pain he must have suffered then and afterward, perhaps. He had wanted her, and he had not said a word. That was his tragedy. At the party in 1919 she had believed Paul McGill was lost to her forever. How vulnerable and susceptible she would have been to her one true friend Blackie in her heart-break, loneliness, and despair. And if he had been more courageous, how different their lives would have turned out. Her thoughts ran on endlessly. Why had she never suspected that he cared for her in that way . . . that he had marriage on his mind? She must have been blind or dense or too involved with business.

The silence between them drifted.

Blackie sat unmoving in the chair, staring into the fire, saying not a word, remembering so much himself. It's odd, he thought suddenly, how things which happened to me when I was a young man have an extraordinary vivid-ness these days. More so than events of last week or even yesterday. I suspect that's part of growing old.

Emma was the first to rouse herself.

She said in a small, pained voice, "Were you trying to tell me a few minutes ago that my *success* put you *off*? Prevented you from proposing?" She studied that dear familiar face with infinite compassion, thinking of the years he had wasted, the happiness he had let slip through his fingers, and all because of his love for her. A love unuttered.

Blackie nodded. "Aye, I suppose I am, mavourneen. I decided, there and then, that you could never be weaned away from your business because it was very much a part of you, *was* you, really. In any event I lost my confidence. After all I wasn't half as rich and successful as you in those days. I didn't think you'd have me. My nerve failed me. Yes, that's precisely what happened."

A deep sigh trickled out of Emma, and slowly she shook her head. "How foolish you were, my dearest, dearest friend."

Blackie gaped at her, his jaw slack with astonishment. "Are you saying that you would have married me, Emma Harte?" he asked, unable to keep the shock and incredulity out of his voice.

"Yes, I believe I would, Blackie O'Neill."

Now it was Blackie who began to shake his head, and he did so in wonderment, trying to absorb her words. For a few minutes he could not speak as old emotions took hold of him, surprising him with the strength of their impact.

At last he said, "It does me good to hear that, even so long afterward." His voice took on a quavering treble, as he added, "Perhaps it's just as well we didn't marry, Emma. I'd have been left high and dry, not to mention broken-hearted, when Paul swept you off your feet again."

"How can you say such a thing! What kind of woman do you think I am!" she cried, her indignation flaring as she jerked herself up in the chair and glared at him with such unprecedented ferocity he flinched. "I would never have hurt *you!* I've always loved you, cared about your well-being, and you know it.

Apologize at once," she spluttered angrily and added as an afterthought, "or I'll never speak to you again!"

He was so startled by her vehemence that he was speechless for a few seconds. Slowly a shamefaced look crept onto his face. He said in a most tender and placating voice, "It's sorry I am, Emma. I take back those words. I believe you. I don't think you would have left me for Paul. And that's not my ego talking. I know you . . . better than anyone does. No, you wouldn't have betrayed me, you wouldn't have given him the time of day if you'd been married to me. It's not in you to be cruel to someone you love, and then there's your morality and your loyalty and goodness and sense of responsibility. Those would have worked in my favor. Besides—" He gave her a boyish grin that brought his dimples out. "*I* would have made you happy."

"Yes, Blackie, I believe you would."

This was said rapidly, and there was a sudden urgency in her manner as she leaned forward anxiously, needing to clarify the past, to make him understand the reasons which had motivated her and Paul, quite aside from their great love. "Don't forget," she began, intent on jogging his memory, "my marriage to Arthur Ainsley was on the rocks long before Paul McGill returned to this country. I was on the verge of divorce when Paul showed up. Besides, and this is most important, Blackie, Paul wouldn't have intruded, wouldn't have sought me out if I'd been happily married. It was only because Frank had told him I was miserable and separated from Ainsley that he arrived on my doorstep."

She paused, settled back in the chair, and clasped her hands tightly in her lap. "I *know* I would not have seen hide nor hair of Paul ever again *if* my life had been on an even keel. He told me that himself. He came searching for me because he was aware I was unhappy—and also available. He most certainly wouldn't have done that if I'd been married to *you*. Have you forgotten how much he liked and respected you?"

"No, I haven't. And you're correct in what you say . . . Yes, Paul was a fine and honorable man. I always had a lot of time for him."

Blackie now rose.

"Well," he said, "that's all water under an old and decrepit bridge, my girl. There's no point rehashing our troubles of half a century ago. And maybe it was meant to be . . ." He lifted his hands and shoulders in a brief shrug. ". . . exactly the way it is. But I would like you to have the ring. It's always been yours, you know."

He bent over her. She looked up at him and then at the black leather box in his hands. He lifted the lid, turned the box to her.

Emma gasped.

The ring was exquisite, throwing off the most brilliant prisms of light and sparkling with life and fire against the black velvet. The central diamond was round, multifaceted, and very large, at least twenty carats, and it was surrounded by smaller stones which were equally as lovely and superbly cut, and these formed a circle at the base of the mounting.

Even Emma, accustomed to magnificent jewelry, was awestruck, and she found herself blinking, truly taken aback by its size and beauty. "It's stunning, Blackie," she said a bit breathlessly, "and one of the most beautiful rings I've ever seen."

His joy at her words was evident. "It's an old setting, of course, the original, and perhaps it's even a bit outdated. But I didn't want to have it reset. Here, slip it on, mavourneen."

She shook her head. "No, you do it, my fine black Irishman." She offered him her left hand. "Put it on the third finger, next to my wedding ring."

He did so.

Emma held out her small, strong hand, her head on one side, admiring the ring glittering so brightly in the fire's glow. And then she glanced up at him, her expression unmistakably mischievous. "Are we finally engaged to be married then?" she teased in a flirtatious voice and offered him a smile that was decidedly coy.

Blackie laughed with delight, hugely amused. He'd always enjoyed her sense of humor.

Bending closer to her, he kissed her cheek. "Let's just say we're engaged to be—to be the dearest and closest friends and companions for the rest of the time we have on this earth."

"Oh, Blackie, that's such a lovely thing to say, and thank you for my beautiful ring." She caught his hand and held on to it and pressed it tightly and looked up at him again; then she smiled that incomparable smile that filled her face with radiance. "My dear old friend, you're so very, very special to me," she said.

"As you are to me, my Emma."

He stepped away from her chair as if heading to his own, and then he paused and swung his white head. "I hope you're going to wear the ring," he remarked offhandedly, but his glance remained riveted intently on hers. "I sincerely hope you're not going to put it away in that safe of yours."

"Certainly *not*. How could you think such a thing. I'm never going to take it off . . . ever again."

He touched her shoulder and returned to his seat, smiling to himself. "I'm glad I gave you your ring, me darlin'. I've thought about doing so many times, and I've often wondered what you'd say. I know I'm always accusing *you* of being a sentimentalist in your old age, but I do believe *I've* become a sentimental old man myself."

"And tell me, Blackie O'Neill, what's wrong with sentiment? It's a pity there isn't more of it in this world," she said, her eyes unexpectedly moist. "It might be a better place to live in, for one thing."

"Aye," was all he said.

After a short while Blackie cleared his throat and remarked, "Now, what about that little proposition of mine, Emma? This morning you said you were doubtful that it would work, but I can't agree."

"Do you know," she exclaimed brightly in an enthusiastic voice, "I was thinking about it again this afternoon. Emily's moved in with me, and it suddenly struck me that the only way I'll get a bit of peace and quiet is to accept your generous invitation."

"Then you'll come with me! Ah, me darlin', this news warms the cockles of me heart, sure an' it does." He beamed at her, happiness and excitement welling inside him. He lifted his brandy balloon high. "Come along, take a sip of your Bonnie Prince Charlie, Emma. This calls for a toast, it does indeed."

She held up her hand instead. "Wait a minute! I didn't actually say *yes*. I can't accept—at least not just yet. I *am* seriously thinking about the trip, but you'll have to give me a few more weeks to settle things, to adjust to the idea of being absent for several months.''

Biting down on his disappointment, he said, "All right, I'll be patient. However, I will have to start making the arrangements soon, so please don't delay your answer for too long.''

"I'll let you know as quickly as possible. I promise.''

He sipped his cognac, savoring it, and slowly a sly gleam entered his eyes. He was wrapped in thought for a minute or two longer and said finally, "By the way, Emma, I've recently made a plan, as no doubt *you'll* be surprised to hear. I think of it as my Plan with a capital P, since it happens to be the first plan *I've* ever made.'' He was unable to contain himself and let out a throaty chortle, and his eyes became merry and teasing. "Do you remember that first plan of *yours?''*

"Goodness me, I'd forgotten all about *that.''*

"I never did. And I even recall the day you confided it in me. Such a small slip of a thing you were, too, and I was most impressed. Anyway, if you've got a few minutes, I'd like to tell you about mine. It's a most marvelous plan, me darlin', even though I say so myself. And I'll bet my last quid it's going to intrigue you, sure an' I know it will.''

Amusement touched her mouth. "I'd love to hear about your plan, Blackie dear.''

He sat back expansively, nodding to himself, and began, "Well, it's like this. There is this woman I know, and she's the most stubborn creature I've met in all my born days. It just so happens that this stubborn, contrary, maddening, but quite adorable woman has a grandson living in Australia. I know she wants to go and see him, and I thought it would be a wonderful treat for her if I took her out there to see him myself. And so I've made a very *special* plan, and this is how it goes . . .''

Emily had fallen asleep on one of the huge sofas in the upstairs parlor.

To Emma, standing over her, she looked small and defenseless and innocent, wrapped in a white toweling robe and curled up in a ball against the pile of cushions. A feeling of infinite tenderness swept through Emma. She bent down and gently moved a strand of pale blond hair away from Emily's eyes and brushed her lips against the girl's smooth young cheek. She straightened up, wondering whether to awaken her or not, decided to get ready for bed herself first, and tiptoed into the adjoining bedroom.

Emma hung up her sable jacket, took off her pearl choker and matching earrings, and placed them on the dressing table. After removing her watch and the McGill emerald, she started to pull on Blackie's ring, then stopped and looked down at it. This ring had lain in a vault waiting for her for fifty years, and she had promised Blackie she would never take it off. She pushed the ring back on her finger, next to Paul's platinum wedding band, and finished undressing. She had just put on her nightgown when there was a tap on the door and Emily's smiling face appeared around it.

"There you are, Grandy. I waited up for you.''

"So I noticed, darling. But you didn't have to, you know.''

"I wanted to, Gran. But to be honest, I didn't think you'd be as late as this. It's turned *twelve-thirty!''*

"I'm well aware of the time, Emily. And look here, if you're going to live with me, you mustn't start monitoring my comings and goings. And I don't need mothering either. I get enough of that from Paula at the store," Emma remarked evenly, putting on her silk dressing gown and knotting the belt.

Emily giggled and skipped into the room, obviously wide awake and full of her usual *joie de vivre*. "It's not role reversal, if that's what you're thinking. I'm *not* trying to mother you. I was merely commenting on the time."

"Just bear in mind what I said."

"I will, Grandma." Emily hovered near the dressing table. She saw the jewelry strewn across it and her eyes darted to Emma's hand. She noticed the diamond at once, which shone with brilliance in the bright light from the lamps. "Aren't you going to show me Blackie's ring?" she asked.

Emma's brows shot up. "And how did *you* know about the ring?" The words had no sooner left her mouth than she wondered why she had even bothered to ask Emily, of all people, such a question.

"Merry and I were Blackie's conspirators," Emily explained. "About two weeks ago he asked *her* to ask *me* to check your ring size. He thought your fingers might have shrunk."

"Did he indeed! I'll have to have a few strong words with him tomorrow. Does he think I've turned into a shriveled-up old crone," Emma exclaimed pithily.

Emily could not keep the laughter out of her voice as she said, "Nobody would think that about you, Gran, least of all Blackie. You're still beautiful."

"No, I'm not. I *am* an old woman," Emma stated flatly. "But thank you for being nice, Emily. Of course," she added with a laugh, "everyone knows *you're* prejudiced." She held out her left hand. "Well, how do you like it?"

Emily took hold of Emma's hand, her bright green eyes huge and as round as saucers, her excitement apparent on her expressive, mobile face. "Gosh, Gran, I'd no idea it was going to be so big and such a beauty! It's fabulous!" She scrutinized the ring more closely and, with an expert's eye, lifted her head and nodded knowingly. "It's a perfect diamond, Gran. I bet it cost a fortune . . ." Her voice trailed off and she hesitated, then asked in an uncertain tone, "Does this mean you and Blackie are going to get married?"

Emma burst out laughing and extracted her hand. "Of course not, you silly goose. Whatever will you think of next." She touched Emily's face lovingly, "You're such a romantic girl," she murmured, sighing softly. "No, it wouldn't be appropriate. Not at our ages. As Blackie said, we're engaged to be the best of friends for the rest of our lives." Emma now became aware of the undisguised curiosity and interest lingering on Emily's face, and before she could stop herself, she said, "I'll tell you the story about the ring, if you like."

"Oh yes, I'd love to hear it, Grandy. Let's go to the parlor, though. I have a thermos of hot chocolate waiting for you. Come along." She took hold of her grandmother's arm possessively and shepherded her next door, not realizing she was fussing and bustling like a mother hen. Emma merely smiled and allowed herself to be bullied, secretly amused.

After filling two mugs with chocolate and giving one to Emma, Emily curled up on the sofa she had so recently vacated, tucked her feet under her, and gleefully snuggled down into the cushions. Lifting her mug, she took a sip and cried with delight, "This is such fun, it's like being back at boarding school and having midnight feasts."

Emma's mouth twitched. "Don't get carried away, Emily," she laughed. "We won't be doing this every night. I'm usually in bed by this time. And talking of bed, it's getting *very* late. I'd better tell you the story quickly so that we can go to sleep. We have a hectic day tomorrow."

"Yes, Gran." Emily gave her grandmother her rapt attention.

When the old story was finally told, Emily said, "Oh Grandma, that's so lovely and touching and a little sad in a way. And imagine him keeping the ring all these years. Gosh, that's real devotion." A wistful look swept across her delicately pretty face and she shook her head. "And you're *skeptical* about unrequited love! This should prove you're absolutely wrong."

Emma smiled indulgently, made no comment.

Brightening, Emily rushed on in her breathy voice, "Just think, if you'd married Blackie instead of Awful Arthur all those years ago, your children would have been very different—it's all a matter of genes, you know. I wonder if the oldies would have been any nicer?" Emily tilted her head and pursed her lips, lost in thought, her mind racing. Several things occurred to her all at once, and she burst out, "What about your grandchildren? Paula, for instance. And *me*. Goodness, Grandy, I might not have been *me* at all. I could have been someone altogether different—"

Emma cut in, "But I would have loved you just as much, Emily, and Paula too."

"Oh yes, of course you would, I know that. But your family would have been very—"

"Now you're speculating about things we'll never know. And it's all *much* too complicated for me, especially at this hour," Emma said with a dismissive yet kindly smile. "But speaking of my family, what happened here this evening? How was the dinner party?"

Instantly Emily's face underwent a change, became serious as she sat up abruptly, swung her feet to the floor, and leaned closer to Emma. Her manner was confiding as she said, "You're not going to believe this, but Edwina's behavior was quite extraordinary—"

"In what way?" Emma asked sharply, dreading the worst.

Seeing the apprehensive expression settling on her grandmother's face, Emily shook her head with some vehemence. "Don't look like that. It was *all right*. Edwina was nice . . . so nice I couldn't get over it, and neither could Paula. The Dowager Countess was charm personified. Well, that's not strictly true." Emily made a moue. "You know I have a tendency to exaggerate." Emily wrinkled her nose, went on, "She was sort of . . . *cautious* with Paula and me. She doesn't really like us. She was polite, though, and pleasant to everyone else. I can't imagine what you said to her earlier, Grandma, but it certainly had a drastic effect on her." Emily searched Emma's face and probed, "You must have given her an awful lecture. You *did*, didn't you?" A blond brow lifted quizzically.

Emma said nothing.

Emily volunteered, "I think Aunt Edwina had been crying before she came down for drinks. Her eyes were puffy and red, and so was her nose. She didn't want a drink. She asked me for aspirins and a glass of water. We'd only been alone together for a couple of minutes when Paula and Jim arrived with Aunt Daisy and Uncle David. Edwina attached herself to Daisy immediately—it's funny, she seems to have a thing about Daisy. Anyway she didn't say much to anyone else, not even Jim, during cocktails." Emily's shoulders hunched in a small offhanded shrug. "I thought she seemed ever so subdued, and she was certainly abstemious. You know how incorrigible she and Mummy are, always tippling. They never know when they've had enough. Edwina didn't touch a drop all night though, not even wine with dinner.'' Flopping back against the cushions, regarding Emma more closely, she pressed, "What actually *did* you say to her, Gran?''

"Now, Emily, don't be so nosy. That's a private matter between Edwina and me. Anyway it's not important. What matters is that my words penetrated. Perhaps I drilled some sense into her after all.''

"Oh I'm sure that's true,'' Emily agreed. "And there's something else— you'll never guess what she did before we went in to dinner.''

"No, I'm certain I won't. So you might as well tell me, Emily.''

"She asked Aunt Daisy if she could invite Anthony over for coffee later and then went to telephone him at Uncle Randolph's.''

Emma stiffened and asked with a frown, "Did he come?''

"Oh yes.'' Emily grinned. "With cousin Sally. Oh, Gran, they're so much in love and super together.''

"Sally came with him! How did Edwina treat her?''

"With cordiality. *My* eyes were popping, I can tell you that, and I wouldn't have missed that little scene for all the tea in China. 'Course Edwina was falling all over Anthony. She was a bit *too* obsequious, if you ask me—you know, Uriah Heepish—but then she's always fawned over her son.'' She gave Emma a huge smile and finished, "In a nutshell, Grandma, the dinner was a roaring success.''

Emma was flabbergasted and temporarily rendered speechless. "Well,'' she said at last, "this is one for the books. I never expected Edwina to do such a volte-face.'' Privately she congratulated herself. Her dire warnings had frightened Edwina into behaving like a normal person seemingly. This is a major victory, she thought, and hoped that her daughter would not have a change of heart. Edwina *was* unpredictable. There was no telling what she might do in a moment of pique. Now, don't go begging for trouble, Emma cautioned herself. Relax.

Smiling brightly, filled with an enormous sense of relief, Emma propelled herself to her feet. "On that rather surprising but pleasant note, I think I'll get off to bed, darling girl.'' She leaned over and kissed Emily. "It looks as if everyone is going to behave with decorum tomorrow. Well, let's hope so. Goodnight, Emily.''

Emily rose and hugged her tightly. "I do love you so much, Gran. And goodnight, sleep tight.'' She picked up the tray. "I suppose I'd better do the same. I've got to collect the twins from Harrogate College tomorrow, and I've *thousands* of other chores.'' She sucked in her breath. *'Phew!''* she exhaled, "I never seem to have a minute to spare.''

Emma swallowed a smile and disappeared into her bedroom before Emily decided to regale her with those chores she had planned for the following morning.

"Oh, Grandy,'' Emily called after her, "I'm glad you're not upset about the Aire Communications deal collapsing.''

Emma came back to the doorway. "I'd venture to say that it's their loss, our gain.''

"Yes, so Paula indicated when she mentioned it earlier.'' Emily glided to the door and muttered with a degree of terseness, "Sebastian Cross is simply dreadful. I thought Jonathan might make headway with him. Apparently he didn't, and if Jonathan couldn't succeed, then nobody could."

Emma stood perfectly still and said with the utmost care, "What are you chattering on about, Emily?"

Emily stopped in her tracks, swung to face Emma. "The Aire deal. You asked Jonathan to talk to Sebastian, didn't you?"

"No," Emma replied in the quietest of voices.

"Oh," Emily said, looking confused.

"What makes you think I propelled Jonathan into those particular negotiations?" As she spoke, Emma steadied herself against the door jamb, her astute eyes glinting darkly as they rested with fixity on her grandchild. All of her senses were alerted, and she remarked tersely, "Obviously *something* did."

"Well, yes," Emily began and scowled. "On Tuesday, when I had dinner with Daddy in London, I saw the two of them in the bar of Les Ambassadeurs when we were leaving. We'd had an early dinner, you see, and Daddy was in a frightful stew about being late for a business meeting. He was in such a hurry I didn't get a chance to go over and speak to Jonathan."

"I see." Emma was thoughtful for a moment, asked, "Why did you suggest Jonathan would be able to influence young Cross?"

"Because of their old friendship . . . they were at Eton together. But then you know that, Gran. You once took me there with you when you went to visit Jonathan at half-term. Don't you remember?"

"Yes. Naturally I also remember that Jonathan went to Eton. What I hadn't realized was that Cross was a pupil there as well or that Jonathan and he had been friends in those days. I had—"

"I think they're still friends actually," Emily interrupted.

This bit of information chilled Emma to the bone, but she attempted a smile. "He probably wanted to surprise me. He might have realized the negotiations were going to be touchy and was endeavoring to smooth the way for Paula," she said, trying to convince herself this was the truth. But her intuition told her it was not. Emma gripped the door jamb more tightly, and, adopting a meticulously casual tone, asked, "Did Jonathan see you in Les Ambassadeurs, Emily?"

Emily shook her head. "He was in deep conversation with Cross." She pondered, asked swiftly, "Why? Is it important?"

"Not really. Did you mention this to Paula?"

"I didn't get an opportunity. She had just started to tell me about the Aire fiasco, as she called it, and Cross being horrid to her, when Hilda announced dinner." Emily bit her inner lip, frowning, beginning to wonder precisely what her grandmother was leading up to with her questions.

Emma nodded as though to herself, then remarked in that same lightly casual voice, "I'd prefer you not to say anything about this to Paula. I wouldn't want her to think he was interfering, queering her pitch. Unintentionally of course. And don't bother to bring it up with Jonathan either. I'll talk to him, find out what his aim was, if indeed he had an aim. It might have been a strictly social evening, you know, in view of their friendship."

"Yes, Grandy, whatever you say."

Emily stood rooted to the spot, studying her grandmother closely, filling with alarm. Emma's face had paled as they had been talking, and she noticed that the happy light in her eyes had fled. They were uncommonly dull, lifeless for once. Emily put down the tray hurriedly and flew across the room. She grasped Emma's arm, exclaimed with concern, "Are you all right, Gran darling?"

Emma made no response. Her mind was working with that razor-sharp precision and vivid intelligence which were so integral to her great genius. Assessing and analyzing with her rare brand of shrewdness and perception, she suddenly saw things with a clarity that shocked. For a split second she recoiled from the truth. I'm making assumptions, she thought, but then her ingrained pragmatism reminded her that she was rarely wrong. The truth was staring her in the face.

Becoming conscious of Emily's hand clutching her arm, her worry and anxiousness apparent, Emma dragged herself out of her disturbing thoughts. She patted the girl's hand, brought a smile to her face that was convincing, reassuring in its certitude.

"I'm just tired," Emma said in a contained voice and smiled again. But she felt as though something cold had touched her heart.

Ten

The medieval church at the top of the hill in Fairley village was filled to capacity, almost bursting at the seams.

Family and friends occupied the front pews, and the villagers were crowded in closely behind, for they had turned out in full force to honor Emma Harte at the baptism of her great-grandchildren. And after the ceremony they would troop across the road to the parish hall to partake of the special celebration tea, which Emma had instructed Alexander to arrange.

All was peace and serenity within the ancient gray stone walls. Sunshine pouring in through the stained glass windows threw rainbow arcs of dancing, jeweled light across the somber stone floor and the dark wood pews. Masses of spring flowers were banked around the altar and on the altar steps. The mingled scents of hyacinths, narcissus, freesia, imported mimosa, and lilac filled the air, diminishing the peculiar musty smell of mildew and dust and old wood that was so prevalent in the church. It was the odor of antiquity, one that Emma had detested since childhood, and she had automatically chosen the most fragrant of flowers for this occasion in an attempt to counteract it.

She sat in the front pew, proud and dignified, wearing a midnight-blue wool-crepe dress and loose matching coat. A small velvet beret of the same deep blue was perched at a jaunty angle on her immaculate silver hair, and she wore the McGill emeralds and a long rope of matchless pearls. Blackie was seated to her left, handsome in a dark suit, whilst Daisy sat with her husband, David Amory, to Emma's right. Edwina was wedged in between David and Sarah Lowther, her posture rigid, her expression rather prim, as usual.

Emma had been somewhat taken aback to find Sarah standing on the porch steps when they had arrived. No one had expected to see her, since she was supposed to have a bad cold. They had spoken briefly at the back of the church before taking their seats, and Emma had been immediately struck by her granddaughter's healthy appearance. In her opinion Sarah had either made a miraculous recovery overnight or had not been sick in the first place. It was more than likely she had toyed with the idea of not coming in order to avoid Shane. Emma could not hold that against her. She understood, had a good idea how Sarah probably felt. But, she thought, I'll say this for Sarah. She's a cool customer. Sarah had not blinked an eyelash nor displayed the slightest sign of self-consciousness when Shane had greeted them earlier.

Now Emma sneaked a look at him.

He was sitting with his parents in a pew across the nave, his face in profile. Suddenly, as if he knew he was being observed, he turned his head slightly to the right and caught Emma's eye, half smiled, and then gave her a conspiratorial wink. Emma returned his smile, swung her eyes back to the altar.

Paula and Jim were standing at the carved stone font which dated back to 1574, surrounded by the godparents of their children, totaling six in all. The vicar, the Reverend Geoffrey Huntley, having christened the boy Lorne McGill Harte Fairley, was now preparing to baptize the girl, who was to be named, Tessa. Like her twin, she would bear the same additional middle names.

Emily, one of Tessa's godmothers, was holding the baby in her arms, and standing on Emma's left were Anthony and Vivienne Harte, who were the other godparents. Vivienne's elder sister, Sally, was godmother to Lorne and cradled him, flanked on either side by his godfathers, Alexander and Winston.

What an attractive group of young people they are, Emma said inwardly, her eyes lighting up with pleasure, and she saw in her mind for a brief instant their antecedents . . . her own parents, her brother Winston, Arthur Ainsley, Paul McGill, Adele and Adam Fairley. How miraculous it was that she and Blackie were still alive and were able to be here today to witness this event, to share in the joyfulness of the occasion.

She shifted her eyes to Paula and Jim.

They do look well together, she thought. He, so tall and broad and fair, the living embodiment of his great-grandfather Adam; Paula, so slender and willowy and dark, so dramatic-looking with her vivid McGill coloring. And Paula's inbred elegance was most apparent in the way she held herself and in her clothes. She had chosen a tailored wool suit of a deep violet tone and wore it with a lighter-colored violet satin blouse and a satin pillbox of the same tone. The violet echoed her eyes. She's still too thin, Emma thought, but she has such an extraordinary radiance this afternoon.

Her love for her granddaughter and her pride in the girl, were emotions most paramount in Emma at this moment, and her face relaxed into softer lines as she continued to regard Paula. The young woman standing up there at the font had given her nothing but happiness and comfort since the day she had been born, in much the same way that her mother, Daisy, had done and continued to do.

Emma closed her eyes. Paul would have been as proud of Paula as she was, for the girl had all the qualities he had most admired: honor, integrity, honesty, fairness, and an intelligence that frequently startled with its brilliance. Although she had gentle manners and was inclined to shyness, Paula possessed a certain cool poise, and she had inherited her grandfather's great sense of fun, as had Daisy. Yes, she's a McGill all right, Emma remarked under her breath. But she's a Harte as well. Thank God she has my toughness and astuteness, my indomitability and stamina. She's going to need all of those in the years to come, with what I'm leaving her, with what she has inherited from her grandfather. I hope she never thinks of her inheritance as a terrible burden. It *is* an enormous responsibility, of course . . .

Baby Tessa started to shriek, her piercing wails echoing throughout the church. Emma opened her eyes and blinked. She leaned forward, peered at the scene at the font. Everyone wore expressions of concern. The vicar was holding the baby, sprinkling the holy water on her forehead, christening her now in the name of the Father, the Son, and the Holy Ghost. When he had finished, he handed the child back to Emily, obviously with some relief. Emily began to rock her, trying to calm and soothe the infant to no avail.

Emma chuckled quietly, knowing it was the shock of the cold water on her forehead which had made Tessa cry. The child was protesting—and most vociferously. I can see it already, she thought, little Tessa McGill Harte Fairley is going to be the rebellious one in *that* family.

Daisy, also smiling, took hold of her mother's arm and squeezed it. She whispered, "It sounds to me as if Tessa is a chip off the old block, Mummy."

Emma turned her head to look into her favorite daughter's wide clear blue eyes. "Yes," Emma whispered back, "she's always been the livelier of the two. Another maverick in the brood?" She arched a silver brow most eloquently. Daisy simply nodded in answer, her fine eyes dancing with happiness and some amusement.

Within minutes the ceremony was over and they were slowly filing up the aisle. Emma, her arm tucked through Blackie's, smiled and nodded graciously, but she did not pause to speak to anyone.

Before long the entire family, their friends, and the villagers were assembled on the porch, congratulating the parents and chatting among themselves.

Several of the local residents came up to Emma, stood talking to her for a few minutes, but very shortly she excused herself and drew Blackie away from the crowd. She said, "I'll slip away now, and I'll be back before anyone notices my absence. Then we can get off to Pennistone Royal."

"All right, Emma. Are you sure I can't go with you?"

"No. But thanks anyway, Blackie. I won't be a minute."

As Emma edged away from the busy porch, Milson, Blackie's chauffeur, hurried toward her carrying a basket of flowers. She took it from him, smiled, and murmured her thanks.

She went through the lych-gate leading into the graveyard adjoining the church.

Her feet knew the way by heart, and they led her down the flagged path to the far corner, a bit secluded and bosky and shaded by an old elm tree growing by the side of the moss-covered stone wall. Lying in that corner, beneath the headstones she herself had chosen years before, were her parents, John and Elizabeth Harte. Next to them were her two brothers, Winston and Frank. She took bunches of flowers from the basket and placed one on each of the four graves. Straightening up, she rested her hand on her mother's headstone and stared out toward the bleak moors, a smudged dark line against the periwinkle blue sky filled with scudding white clouds and intermittent sunshine. It was a lovely day, surprisingly warm, balmy even, after the thunderstorms of yesterday. A perfect day to go climbing to the Top of the World. She strained her eyes, but that spot was too far away in the distance to see and was obscured by the soaring fells. She sighed, remembering. Her eyes swept from headstone to headstone, name to name. I've carried each one of you in my heart all the days of my life, she said silently. I've never forgotten any of you. Then unexpectedly the queerest thought entered her mind—she would not be coming back here again to visit these graves.

Emma turned away at last.

Her steps carried her along the same flagged path that curved through the cemetery, and she did not stop until she reached a wide plot of ground at the other side, in the gloomy shadows of the church. This large private plot was encircled by iron railings which set it apart, told everyone that it was special and exclusive. She pushed open the small gate and found herself amongst generations of Fairleys. She glanced at the graves, and finally her eyes came to rest on Adam Fairley's headstone made of white marble. On either side of him were his two wives—Adele, the first; and Olivia, the second. Those two beautiful sisters who had loved and married the same man, and who had in their own ways been good to her when she had been a young girl. She had never forgotten their kindness to her, but it was on the middle grave that her gaze lingered for a moment longer.

Well, Adam Fairley, she thought, I won. In the end it was I who triumphed. There is nothing left that your family owns in the village, except this plot of land where you are buried. Everything else belongs to me, and even the church operates mostly through my largesse. Your great-great-grandchildren have just been christened, and they bear both of our names, but it is from *me* that they will inherit great wealth and power and position. These thoughts were not rancorous but ran through her mind in a matter-of-fact way, for she had lost all hatred for the Fairleys, and it was not in her nature to gloat, especially when standing next to a man's last resting place.

Slowly she walked back to the church, and the smile on her serene face was one of gentleness and peace.

Coming through the lych-gate, Emma saw Blackie standing to one side, away from the large group of people, talking to her two youngest grandchildren, Amanda and Francesca.

Blackie chuckled as she came to a standstill by his side. "You might know *these* two would see you do your disappearing act! I had to forcibly restrain them from running after you. Well, almost."

"We wanted to look at the graves, too, Grandy," Amanda explained, "we love cemeteries."

Emma gave her a look of mock horror. "How morbid."

"No, it isn't, it's interesting," Francesca chirped up. "We like to read the tombstones, and we try to guess what the people were like, what kind of lives they led. It's like reading a book."

"Is it now." Emma laughed, and the look she gave the fifteen-year-old was affectionate. "I think we should go back to the house," Emma continued, "Did Emily tell you we're having a champagne tea this afternoon?"

"Yes, but she said we couldn't have any champagne. We can, though, can't we, Gran?" Amanda asked.

"Just one glass each, I don't want you both getting tiddly."

"Oh thank you, Gran," Amanda said, and Francesca linked her arm in Emma's and announced, "We'll come with you. Uncle Blackie's car is much nicer than Emily's old Jag."

"That's not a very nice attitude, Francesca. You came with Emily, and you will drive back with her. Besides, Uncle Blackie and I have things to discuss."

• • •

But they did not really have anything very special or important to talk about. Emma simply wanted to be alone with her dear old friend, to relax before the reception, to catch her breath before she was engulfed by her large and unorthodox clan.

At one point as they were driving along, Blackie looked at her and said, "It was a grand christening, Emma. Very beautiful. But you had such a strange look on your face when the vicar was baptizing Lorne, I couldn't help wondering what was going through your mind."

Emma half turned to face him. "I was thinking about another christening . . . the one you performed when you baptized Edwina with Armley tap water in Laura's kitchen sink." Her eyes held his for the longest moment. "I couldn't help dwelling on the past. You know, Edwin Fairley wouldn't have been permitted to marry me when I was pregnant, even if he had wanted to, and so Edwina could never have been christened here at Fairley. That really struck home today."

"Yes," he said in agreement, "it would have been denied her, no matter what."

Emma nodded. "And so, as I thought of everything that has gone before in my long life, it suddenly occurred to me that this occasion today was a most compelling example of ironic reversal. And that Adam Fairley, more than anyone else, would have appreciated the poetic justice of it all."

She paused, smiled faintly. "The wheel of fortune truly has come full circle."

Eleven

Jim Fairley, orphaned at the age of ten and raised by his widowed grandfather, had always been lonely as a child.

In consequence he thoroughly enjoyed being a part of Emma Harte's huge family, one which had become his own when he married Paula in 1968. In a way, being flung headfirst into this extraordinary clan was something of a novelty to him; also, as yet he remained unscathed by them and thus had kept an open mind about their individual characters, had not attempted to do a tally of their attributes or their faults. And he had held himself apart from the complex animosities and alliances, feuds and friendships that flourished around Emma.

Because Jim rarely thought ill of anyone, he was frequently startled when Paula came down hard on one of her aunts or uncles, and at times he even wondered if she exaggerated when she listed their imperfections, the terrible wrongs they had done her grandmother. But then she was fiercely protective of her beloved Grandy, whom she doted on. Jim was secretly amused by his wife's attitude, since he believed no one was better equipped to take care of herself than Emma Harte.

A short while ago Jim had decided that Paula's warnings about the Countess of Dunvale were written in water. So far this weekend Edwina had behaved impeccably—as he had fully expected she would. If she was somewhat reserved with Paula, she was at least civil, and he had even managed to make Edwina laugh on their way back from the church. She was still in an amiable mood, as he could now see.

His aunt was chatting with her son Anthony and Sally Harte near the fireplace, and her usually stiff, tight-lipped expression had all but vanished. For once she appeared to be relatively at ease. Poor old thing, she's not so bad, he thought, as always charitable about others, and swung his eyes to the painting to Edwina's left. This hung over the white marble fireplace; and it was one of his favorites.

Jim stood at the entrance to the Peach Drawing Room. Pennistone Royal, that lovely mixture of Renaissance and Jacobean design, boasted two formal reception rooms. Paula had chosen this one for the christening party.

He was glad that she had.

He thought it was the loveliest spot in the entire house, with its cream and peach color scheme and exquisite paintings. Although Emma had depleted her renowned collection of Impressionists by selling some of them off last year, she had retained the two Monets and the three Sisleys that graced these walls. In his opinion it was the works of art that gave the tranquil and elegant Regency room its great beauty.

Jim gazed at the Sisley for a second or two longer, admiring it from this vantage point. He had never coveted anything material in his whole life, but he longed to own this painting. Of course he never would. It would always hang in this house, as Emma had decreed in her will. One day it would be Paula's property, and therefore he would never be deprived of it, could gaze at the landscape whenever he wished. That was why his intense desire for personal possession of it constantly startled him. He had never felt so strongly about anything, except perhaps his wife. His eyes sought Paula without success. The room had filled up during the ten minutes he had been absent with the photographer, who was setting up his equipment in the Gray Drawing Room. It was just possible she was hidden from view.

He went in rapidly.

At six-foot-one, well built but trim of figure and with long legs, James Arthur Fairley cut quite a swathe, especially since he was something of a clotheshorse, was never anything but faultlessly dressed right down to his hand-made shoes. Like his great-grandfather before him, he had a weakness for elegant clothes and a penchant for wearing them with a bit of a dash. Fair of coloring with light brown hair, he had a pleasant, rather sensitive face and soulful grayish blue eyes. Born and bred a gentleman, he had a natural self-confidence and handled himself easily and with aplomb in any given situation. He had a certain quiet charm and a ready smile for everyone.

This flashed as he strode into the center of the room and glanced about, looking for Paula.

Since he could not find her, he took a glass of champagne from a passing waiter and made a move in his father-in-law's direction. Edwina spotted him and hurried over, cutting him off before he reached David Amory. She at once launched into a rave about the church ceremony and then engaged him in a conversation that centered on Fairley village. As he listened patiently, Jim realized yet again, with a recurrence of his initial surprise, that being a Fairley was of tremendous importance to her. Ever since their first meeting, she had continued to ply him with questions about his grandfather, his grandmother, and her father, the long-dead Earl of Carlesmoor, and was inquisitive about his own parents, who had been tragically killed in a plane crash in 1948.

On the various occasions he had been with his half great-aunt, for that was what she actually was, he had detected a sense of embarrassment in her because of her illegitimacy, and he had always felt slightly sorry for her. This was one of the reasons he tried to be kind, to include her in those family celebrations about which he had something to say. His mother-in-law had a nice way with Edwina, but apart from this, Jim recognized that Edwina was drawn to Daisy because they had both been born on the wrong side of the blanket. Emma's first child strongly identified with her youngest because of this similarity in their births. But their illegitimacy was the only thing they had in common. The two women were the antithesis of each other. His mother-in-law had the sweetest nature, was a compassionate and considerate woman and a lady in the truest sense of that word. There was no "side" to Daisy Amory, and he liked her for her relaxed attitude toward life, her gaiety, and her sense of humor. Sadly his Aunt Edwina was inflexible and sour, tense and standoffish, a dyed-in-the-wool snob whose basic values were quite alien to him. Yet there was something indefinable in her that touched him, filled him with a curious sympathy for her. Perhaps this was because they shared the same blood. Paula constantly said that blood was *not* thicker than water, but he tended to disagree. He was sure of one thing. His relationship with Edwina, slender and tenuous though it was, annoyed Paula to the point of anger. He found this to be most unreasonable on her part, and he fervently wished she could be less emotional about his aunt. In his opinion Edwina was a harmless old lady.

"I'm so sorry, Aunt Edwina, I missed that," Jim said with an apologetic smile, giving her his undivided attention again.

"I was saying that it was a pity my mother had Fairley Hall torn down." Edwina gave him a long and careful look through her narrowed silvery eyes. "The house was very old, and by rights it really ought to have been preserved as a landmark in Yorkshire. And just think, if it were still standing, you could have lived there with Paula."

Jim missed the inherent criticism of her mother in these words. He laughed and shook his head. "I don't think so. I didn't like the look of Fairley Hall from the photographs I've seen. According to Grandfather it was a hodgepodge of architectural styles and a bit of a monstrosity. He never liked it himself, and personally I think Grandy did the right thing."

Daisy, who had been hovering close by, caught the tail end of their conversation and exclaimed, "I second that, Jim. Besides, Mother put the land it stood on to very good use by turning it into a park for the villagers. It's a charming spot for them during the warm weather. It was very generous of her." She glanced across at the Vicar of Fairley, who was talking to her husband, and explained, "And the reason Reverend Huntley is beaming right now is because Mother has just given him a large check for the church restoration fund. She keeps that village going in more ways than one." Having rebutted Edwina, squelched her in the pleasantest way, Daisy gave her half sister a warm smile. "I haven't complimented you, Edwina dear. You look lovely, and that's a very smart suit you're wearing."

"Oh," Edwina said, startled by these kind words. She hardly ever received compliments. She preened a little, a sparkle entered her pale eyes, and she automatically reached up and patted her hair. Then, remembering her manners, she rushed on, "Thank you very much, Daisy. You look beautiful yourself, but then you always do. As for my suit, it's by Hardy Amies. I wasn't sure it was right for me, but he persuaded me it was."

The two women discussed clothes for a few seconds; then Daisy exclaimed, "You'll have to excuse me, I'm afraid. I can see Mother trying to catch my eye."

Left alone with Jim again, Edwina began to enumerate the delights of her home in Ireland. "I do wish you could see Clonloughlin at this time of year, Jim. It's perfectly beautiful. Everything's so green. Why don't you and Paula make plans to come over for a weekend soon? You've never seen it, and we'd love to have you. It's only a hop, skip, and a jump in that plane of yours."

"Thank you, Edwina, perhaps we will." As he spoke, Jim knew Paula would never agree. He decided to cover himself and added, "However, I don't think I'll be able to drag her away from the babies for some time yet."

"Yes, I do understand," Edwina murmured, wondering if she had been rebuffed, and to cover her confusion she went on talking nonstop.

Jim, listening politely and trying to be attentive, wished he could make his escape. Because of his height he towered above Edwina, who was quite small, and now he glanced over her silvery blond head, looking around, wondering what had happened to Paula. Most of their guests had arrived. *She* was noticeably absent.

Sarah Lowther had just walked in on the arm of her cousin, Jonathan Ainsley. Bryan and Geraldine O'Neill were talking to Alexander Barkstone and his girlfriend. Blackie was standing by the window, engaged in an animated conversation with Randolph Harte, and he appeared to be excited about something, was beckoning to his granddaughter. Miranda floated over to join them, a vision in one of her crazy costumes, her freckled face brimming with laughter, her bright auburn hair gleaming like a copper helmet in the sunshine pouring through the tall windows.

Jim shifted slightly on his feet, surveying the room at large. Emma was perched on the arm of a sofa, being attentive to her brothers' widows, Charlotte and Natalie. These two genteel-looking ladies gave the impression of frailty and great age in comparison to Emma, who exuded vitality and happiness this afternoon. He studied her face for a moment. He had revered and respected this remarkable woman all the years he had worked for her; since his marriage to her granddaughter, he had come to know a different side of her, had grown to love her. Emma had such an understanding heart, was kind and generous, the most fair-minded person he had ever met. What a fool his grandfather had been to let her escape. But he supposed things were difficult in those days. Stupid class differences, he thought and sighed under his breath. Then, quite suddenly, he wished that Edwin Fairley had lived long enough to witness this day . . . to see the Fairleys and the Hartes united at last through matrimony. Their blood was mingled now. He and Paula had started a new bloodline.

He became aware that Edwina had stopped her ceaseless chattering and was staring up at him. He said quickly, "Let me get you a refill, Aunt Edwina; then I think I'd better go and look for Paula. I can't imagine what's happened to her."

"No more champagne at the moment, thank you, Jim," Edwina said with the faintest of smiles. She was determined to remain cool and collected and keep a clear head this afternoon. Too much wine would have an adverse effect on her, make her lose her self-possession. That she could not afford. She said, "Before you disappear there is one thing I'd like to ask of you. I've been wondering if you would be kind enough to invite me to your house in Harrogate. I know it belonged to your grandfather." She hesitated, nervously cleared her throat, and finished, "I'd love to see where he . . . where my father lived for so many years of his life."

"Of course you must come over for drinks," Jim said, understanding this need in her. He hoped Paula would not fly into one of her tempers when he told her he had acquiesced to his aunt's request. He began to edge away when Emily, with Amanda and Francesca in tow, breezed up to them, cutting off his escape route.

Smiling brightly, Emily grabbed his arm, glanced at Edwina, and cried, "Hello, you two. Isn't this the most amazing bun fight. I think it's going to be a super party."

Jim smiled at her indulgently. He was extremely fond of young Emily. "Have you seen my wife anywhere?" he asked.

"She went upstairs with the nursemaids and the babies, muttering something about changing them. I guess they wet themselves rather thoroughly." Emily giggled and rolled her eyes in an exaggerated fashion. "Just be glad they didn't get that elegant Kilgour and French suit of yours drenched with their wee-w—"

"Really, Emily," Edwina sniffed reprovingly, "don't be so vulgar." She gave her niece a cold and disapproving look.

Emily, blithely unconcerned, giggled again. "Babies do do that, you know. They're like puppies. They can't control their bladders. And I *wasn't* being vulgar, Aunt Edwina, merely stating a fact of life."

Jim could not resist laughing, recognizing that Emily was purposely being provocative. He threw her a warning frown, glanced at his aunt, praying she would not pounce on Emily.

Edwina was obviously annoyed. Fortunately, before she could think of a suitably chilly response, Winston hove in view, made a beeline for them, greeted everyone, and positioned himself between Emily and Amanda.

He turned to Jim and said, "Sorry to bring up business on such a festive occasion, but I'm afraid I have no alternative. I'd like to get together with you first thing on Monday to discuss a couple of matters. Will you have time to see me?"

"Of course," Jim said, giving Winston a puzzled look. Concern edged into his eyes, and he frowned. "Anything serious?"

"No, no, and the only reason I mentioned it now was to make sure you'd keep an hour free for me. I have to go to Doncaster and Sheffield that day, and the rest of the week is impossible. I'm really jammed."

"Then let's make a definite date, Winston. Say about ten-thirty? I'll have the first edition out on the streets by then."

"That's fine," said Winston.

With this matter settled, Jim said, "Your father seems very pleased with himself, and so does Blackie. Look at them both. They're behaving like a couple of kids with a new toy. What's all the excitement about?"

Winston glanced over his shoulder and laughed. "My father wants to run

Emerald Bow in the National next year, and Blackie's tickled to death about it. I think Aunt Emma's just as thrilled."

"Gosh, what marvelous news, Winston," Emily exclaimed. "I hope Grandma invites us all to go to Aintree next March." The conversation now centered around the Grand National and the possibility of Emerald Bow winning the steeplechase. All kinds of opinions were voiced, and even the fifteen-year-old twins had something to say.

But not Edwina. She was silent.

She sipped the last drop of champagne in her glass, eyed Winston with an oblique surreptitiousness. She did not particularly like him. But then she had never had much time for the Hartes. All they had were pots and pots of money. And looks. She could not deny that they were a good-looking family—each and every one of them. Suddenly with a small start of surprise, she saw how closely Winston resembled her mother. She had always been aware that they shared certain physical characteristics, yet had never realized how pointed and strong these were. Why, Winston Harte is a younger, male replica of *her,* Edwina muttered to herself. More so than any of her children or grandchildren. The same features, so clearly defined they might have been cut by a chisel; that red hair shot through with gold; those quick intelligent eyes of an unnatural green. Even his small hands holding the glass are like *hers.* My God, it's uncanny, Edwina thought and looked away quickly, wondering why this revelation disturbed her.

Jim, who had been listening with interest to Winston talking about Steve Larner, the jockey, interrupted him when he exclaimed, "There's Paula at last." His face filled with pleasure, and he waved to her. "I'll see you all a little later." He squeezed Edwina's arm reassuringly and dashed across the room.

Paula watched him hurrying to her, a happy expectant smile playing around her mouth. Her heart tightened. She loved Jim very much, and she was so lucky to have found him. He was the dearest, sweetest man, and fine and honorable and good. She would have to try harder with Edwina . . . she wanted so much to please her husband.

Jim caught Paula's hands in his as he came to a standstill by her side. He smiled down into her face. "You were gone such a long time," he said. "I missed you."

"The babies, darling, they needed me." Her sparkling bright eyes rested on him lovingly. "I hope you're not going to turn out to be one of those jealous fathers I keep hearing about."

"Not on your life. I adore those little moppets." He leaned into her, pulled her closer, and lowered his voice to a hoarse whisper. "But I also adore *you.* Listen, darling, let's sneak away tonight and have a quiet dinner. Just the two of us. Your parents won't mind. They can have dinner with Emma."

"Well—"

"I won't take no for an answer, my pet." He bent over her and whispered in her ear, gripped her hands all that more tightly as he did so.

Paula blushed at his words, then laughed a light sweet laugh. "You're positively wicked. A regular devil." Looking at him archly, she teased flirtatiously, "I'll have you know I'm a married woman, sir. What you propose is most indecent. Quite improper, I'd say."

"Do you really think so?" He laughed and then he winked, *"I think my ideas are very exciting."*

"Mummy's heading this way," Paula said, laughing and adroitly changing the subject. "And she's looking very determined about something."

"Say yes," Jim demanded. "To everything."

"Yes. Yes. Yes."

Daisy looked from one to the other fondly and shook her head. "Sorry to break up you two lovebirds, but Mother is champing at the bit. She wants to get the photography out of the way as soon as possible now. I'm rounding everyone up. So come along, let's start assembling in the Gray Drawing Room. Oh and by the way, Jim dear, I've suggested that Edwina be included in one of the family group portraits, and my mother has agreed."

"How very nice of you, Daisy," Jim exclaimed with warmth and sincerity, thinking how typical it was of her to be thoughtful and caring about another person's feelings. That Daisy had shown such consideration for Edwina was doubly commendable.

Emma Harte had never missed a trick in her entire life.

This afternoon was no exception. Her eyes were everywhere, and from her position near the fireplace, she had an overall view of the room and everyone in it. In much the same way that Jim Fairley held himself apart and took in everything, so Emma herself played the observer much of the time these days.

However, unlike Jim, who only saw things on the surface and moreover believed exactly what he saw, Emma had an almost frightening perceptiveness, one that pierced any facade to comprehend what actually lay behind it. She understood that nothing was ever the way it seemed, and so she was acutely conscious of the undercurrents in the room—the rivalries, the conflicts, the bad blood that existed between some of those present.

A sardonic smile touched her lips. As usual, cliques had formed. It was easy to see who was allied to whom. And she could read them all like an open book.

Edwina was the one who had surprised her the most, in that she had obviously had the intelligence to accept the inevitable. Her eldest daughter was giving off an aura of cordiality, sitting on the sofa near the window, chatting with Sally. On the other hand, Emma had noticed that she was assiduously avoiding any real contact with the other Hartes in the drawing room.

Randolph, Sally's father, and his two other children, Vivienne and Winston, were most decidedly *persona non grata* with Edwina, and her intense dislike of them was barely concealed behind the stiff and chilly smiles she had given them earlier. Edwina was also cold-shouldering Blackie, although there was nothing new about that. Once last year Edwina had referred to him as the grand seigneur, meaning it disparagingly, her voice ringing with sarcasm.

Emma smiled inwardly. She had rather liked the description then, she did so now. It was apt.

Blackie was indeed behaving like the grand patrician gentleman, strolling around as if he had territorial rights, his manner distinctly proprietary, being gracious and charming, playing the genial host to the limit. And why not? He was her greatest friend and her escort after all; this was her house, and she was the hostess at this gathering. He had stood at her side during the toasts and the cutting of the christening cake, and after Randolph had finished speaking, he had made a toast himself. To her. He had called her the youngest and most beautiful great-grandmother in the world. Now he had paused, was hovering over Paula, who in turn hovered over her babies. Daisy joined them, her serenity and sincerity and goodness a beacon in this room.

Emma shifted her eyes to the far corner, where they settled on her grandson, Alexander.

Always reserved, Alexander seemed particularly so with Jonathan and Sarah, whom he had briefly acknowledged when he had arrived. Since then he had consistently and carefully ignored them. He had attached himself to Bryan and Geraldine O'Neill at the commencement of the reception and returned to sit with them after the photographs had been taken. She did not understand why he was being cool and distant with Sarah and Jonathan. Could they have had a disagreement? Even a falling-out? Or was he simply bored by the company of his cousins with whom he worked at Harte Enterprises? She turned these possibilities over and then let them go. She would know soon enough if there were any real problems amongst these three. She wished Alexander would make up his mind about that nice Marguerite Reynolds. He had kept that poor girl dangling for too long. Now where was *she* hiding herself?

Emma scanned the room. Ah yes, there she was near the door, laughing with Merry O'Neill and Amanda. Good God, was that child drinking another glass of champagne. Her *third?* Emily is supposed to be looking after those sisters of hers, and she's not even in the room, Emma thought and took a step forward, making for Amanda, then stopped in her tracks. Emily had just returned with Winston and Shane, had spotted Amanda, and was about to chastize her little sister, who wore a guilty expression. Emma nodded to herself, amused at the little scene being enacted. Emily, for all her youth and gay disposition, could be very tough when she wanted to be.

Shane had detached himself from Winston and Emily and was prowling across the floor. Her eyes followed him. He came to a stop next to David, drew Paula's father to one side, began speaking to him intently. Shane is not himself today, Emma decided. He has a remote air. It occurred to her that he might be suffering from ennui at this family function of hers, not to mention preoccupation with his impending trip to New York.

As for Sarah, her auburn-haired granddaughter appeared to be patently uninterested in Shane. Did Emily exaggerate? No, definitely not. Sarah, clinging to Jonathan like a barnacle to a hull, was by her very actions proving to Emma that she did indeed care greatly. If Shane no longer mattered to her, she would not be huddled in a corner staying out of his way. Was Jonathan a handy convenience? Or had he and Sarah formed some kind of special alliance lately? If so, why? They had never been particularly close in the past.

Emma gave Jonathan a long hard stare, studying that bland and smiling face, noting his insouciant manner. How disarming he could be. He's clever, she thought, but not quite as clever as he believes he is. He has acquired the knack of dissembling, most likely from me. And because I'm better at dissimulation than he is, he doesn't deceive me one little bit. I have no hard evidence of his treachery, nothing concrete with which I can nail him, and yet I know he's up to no good.

When Emma had first arrived at the Fairley church, Jonathan had rushed over to her and told her he would see her on Monday morning, would bring her his new evaluation of the Aire Communications building. She had merely nodded, kept her face inscrutable. But she had immediately wondered why he suddenly thought the evaluation of the building's worth was no longer urgent, that it could now wait until Monday. She had been stressing its urgency to him for some time. Emma had not had to think very hard to come up with the answer. Jonathan knew the evaluation was no longer pressing because he was aware that the Aire deal had collapsed. Neither she nor Paula had mentioned the failure of those negotiations, so he could only have acquired his information from Sebastian Cross and in the last twenty-four hours.

This conversation at the church, coupled with Emily's revelation of the night before, had convinced Emma that Jonathan was somehow involved with the Crosses, in cahoots with them. But to what purpose?

She did not know. But she would soon find out. She had no intention of confronting Jonathan on Monday morning. It was not her way to show her hand when that hand could be doling out rope, forming a noose. Instead she would go to London next week and start digging. Discreetly. Jonathan's behavior today had only served to underscore the nagging suspicion that he was not trustworthy, a feeling that she had harbored for weeks. Without realizing it, he had alerted her further. If he were really smart he would have acted as though the Aire deal were still alive. He had made a small slip—but it was a fatal one in her eyes.

Jonathan happened to turn around at this moment. His glance met hers. He smiled broadly and loped across the room to her.

"Goodness, Grandy, why are you standing here all alone?" he asked, showing concern for her. Not waiting for a reply, he went on, "Do you want anything? A glass of champagne or a cup of tea maybe? And do come and sit down. You must be tired." He took hold of her arm affectionately, and his posture was loving.

"I don't want anything, thank you," Emma said. "And I'm not a bit tired. In fact I never felt better." She gave him a smile as fraudulently sweet as his had been. Extracting her arm ever so gently, she remarked, "I've been enjoying myself, standing here watching everyone. You'd be surprised what people reveal about themselves when they believe they're unobserved." Her eyes were riveted to his face.

She waited.

He squirmed under her unflinching gaze, returned it, managed to keep his expression open and candid. But he laughed too quickly and too loudly as he said, "You are a card, Grandy."

And possibly you're the joker in the pack, Emma thought coldly. She said, "What's wrong with Sarah? She's being rather aloof with everyone, apart from you of course."

"She's not feeling well," he answered with swiftness. "Fighting a bad cold."

"She looks as fit as a fiddle to me," Emma observed dryly, throwing a rapid glance in Sarah's direction.

Emma suddenly stepped back, moved away from Jonathan, and leveled her direct stare on him again. "Did you come up here together? And when did you arrive in Yorkshire?"

"No, we came separately. Sarah by train last night. I drove up this morning." This was said steadily enough, and he smiled down at her.

Emma saw the faintest flicker of deceit in his light eyes. She studied his face briefly. Arthur Ainsley's weak mouth, she thought. She said, "I'm glad Sarah has you to look after her today, Jonathan. It's most kind of you."

He said nothing, changed the subject by remarking, "Are you sure you don't want to sit down, Grandmother?"

"I suppose I might as well."

He steered her across the room toward Charlotte and Natalie, and Emma smothered a laugh. So that's where he thinks I belong, with the old ladies, she thought with some acerbity.

He saw her settled on the sofa, spoke briefly to his great-aunts, and disappeared, heading back to Sarah.

Emma watched him go, filled with sadness and disappointment. Too bad about Jonathan, she thought with resignation. He surely doesn't realize it, but he's as transparent as water. Just like his father. She had always seen right through Robin and had been several jumps ahead of *him* all of his life, usually to his perpetual irritation and discomfort. Sighing, Emma pushed herself into the cushions and accepted a cup of tea offered by one of the waiters, then turned to her sisters-in-law. Natalie, Frank's widow, was unusually garrulous this afternoon, and she soon dominated the conversation, caught up in an endless recital about her only child, Rosamund, who lived in Italy with her diplomat husband. Charlotte and Emma listened, eyeing each other with amusement from time to time, but Emma's interest rapidly waned. She soon fell into her myriad thoughts.

Emma would never know what prompted her to suddenly put down her cup of tea, stand up, and swing around at the precise moment that she did. And later, when she thought about it in private, she was to wish she had remained seated.

But she did go through these motions and found Shane O'Neill in her direct line of vision. He did not see her. He stood alone, leaning against the wall in the shadow of a tall Regency cabinet. There was an expression of such unadulterated love and aching yearning on his handsome face that Emma had to stifle a gasp of surprise. His face was naked, utterly vulnerable, and it revealed the strongest and most powerful emotions a man could feel for a woman.

And it was Paula whom Shane was staring at with such concentrated intensity and longing.

Oh my God, Emma thought, dismay flooding through her. Her heart missed a beat. How well she knew that look on a man's face. It signified passion and desire, the overwhelming urgency to possess absolutely. And forever.

But her granddaughter was oblivious to him. She was bending over the nursemaid who sat cradling Tessa, adjusting the child's christening robe, cooing to her. Paula's face was tender with a mother's love, and she was completely absorbed in the baby.

Emma was so shocked by what she saw that she could not move. She was rooted to the spot, staring at him transfixed, unable to tear her eyes away from Shane, who undoubtedly believed he was safe from prying eyes. Emma reached out blindly and gripped the back of the sofa, filled with a terrible shaking sensation.

To her immense relief the expression on Shane's face was fleeting. In a flash it vanished, was replaced by a studied expression of assumed nonchalance, one she knew so well. He moved out of the shadows without noticing her and mingled with the crowd again. Distantly she heard his vibrant, throaty laugh and then Randolph's voice in response to something he had said.

Endeavoring to marshal her thoughts, Emma shifted her stance, turned to face the room. Had anyone else witnessed this intensely private moment of Shane's when his guard was down? Where was Jim? Emma's quick alert eyes darted from side to side, came to rest on Emily, who stood motionless a few yards away, staring back at her appalled, anxiety clouding her pretty young face.

Emma frowned. She pinned Emily with a knowing look, then motioned to the door with a brief nod of her head. Emma went out of the drawing room slowly. She was filled with sorrow, and her heart ached for Shane O'Neill. And as she crossed the Stone Hall, everything became crystal clear to her, and her sorrow deepened immeasurably.

Upon entering the library, Emma sat down heavily on the nearest chair. She was surprised her legs had carried her this far. She felt weak at the knees.

Emily came in a split second later, closed the door firmly behind her, and leaned against it speechlessly.

To Emma she looked as if she had seen a ghost. She was unnaturally pale, and her face was tight, very strained.

Emma said, "You saw it then? The way Shane was gazing at Paula?"

"Yes," Emily whispered.

"He's very much in love with her," Emma said, her voice husky. Her throat tightened. She paused, got a grip on herself. "But then you knew that *before* today, Emily. In fact you almost let it slip out yesterday. But you managed to stop yourself just in time. That is correct, isn't it?"

"Yes, Gran."

"Don't look so scared, Emily. And come here and sit with me. I must talk to you about this. It's most disturbing."

Emily ran across the room and took the adjoining chair. She gazed deeply into Emma's troubled face, which looked oddly fatigued and weary all of a sudden. She said, "I'm truly sorry you had to find out. I never wanted you to know, Grandma. I knew it would pain you."

"Yes, that's true, it does. But now that I do know, I've a couple of questions. First of all, how did you find out that Shane was in love with Paula in the first place?"

"Because I've seen that look on his face before. It was at Paula's wedding in London last year . . . when he thought no one was watching him. Much the same kind of situation as today. He was tucked away in a corner, at the reception at Claridge's, and his eyes never left her. And then there's his behavior . . . let's face it, Grandy, he's been distant and peculiar with her for the longest time. Actually to be honest he's dropped her like a ton of bricks. Obviously he can't bear to be around her, knowing she's married to someone else."

Emily bit her lip nervously. "I suspect that's also one of the reasons he spends so much time abroad. I know he has to travel because of their hotel chain, but Merry recently said something to me about Shane constantly jumping on planes at the slightest excuse. She said he seemed to have ants in his pants these days."

"I see," Emma said. "So Shane has never confided in you?"

"God no! He *wouldn't*. He's too proud."

"Yes," Emma said, "I know what you mean." She was reflective for a moment, then said almost to herself, "That seems to be a family characteristic. And it's false pride, too. What a waste of time *that* is. So very foolish in the long run. It serves no good purpose." She looked away, staring into the distance absently, seeing so much, understanding.

Emily patted her hand in her old-fashioned, motherly way, and urged, "Try not to worry, Gran. I know you love Shane like one of your own grandchildren, but there's nothing you can do about this."

"I'm aware of that, darling. But getting back to the incident in the drawing room, do you think anyone else saw what we saw? Jim for instance?"

"Jim had gone outside a few minutes before, Gran. I spoke to him as he followed Anthony and Sally out onto the terrace. Then Miranda joined them and the twins." Emily chewed her inner lip again. *"Sarah.* She has been sneaking looks at Shane all afternoon. She might have caught it; I'm just not sure."

"I certainly hope she didn't!" Emma exclaimed worriedly.

"So do I." Emily took a deep breath, volunteered in a low voice, "There was one person who noticed—"

"Who?" Emma demanded, looking at her swiftly.

"Winston."

"Well, thank God for small mercies. I'm glad it wasn't anyone else. Go and fetch him to me, Emily, and don't discuss a thing. Not in there. Too many nosey Parkers around."

"Yes, Grandmother." Emily flew out of the room.

Emma rose and went to the windows, staring out at her beautiful gardens. How peaceful they look in the radiant sunlight . . . next door in the drawing room there is a young man who has everything except the woman he loves and who may never know genuine peace in his whole life because of that. Unless his love for Paula ceases to exist. Emma doubted this would happen. The kind of love she had seen etched on his face was everlasting. Its depth and intensity chilled her to the bone. She was absolutely convinced that a man like Shane O'Neill would not be content to worship from afar. His emotions could easily propel him to take more overt action in time. He might try to fight for Paula one day in the future. And even if Paula was not interested in Shane, the situation still spelled trouble, in Emma's opinion. Triangles were not only uncomfortable, they were explosive.

Emma let out a tiny sigh. She had no answers, no solutions, and speculating was surely a big waste of time.

Her thoughts settled on Paula. She prayed her granddaughter would be happy with Jim Fairley for the rest of her life. If she was not, Shane might indeed make headway with her. Yet this first year of the marriage had been idyllic. On the other hand there were things she herself had noticed and which had given her food for thought and cause to wonder about Jim. Instinctively she knew that he was no match for Paula when it came to inherent strength of character. Paula was inordinately stubborn, and she had a will of iron. And she was so much cleverer than Jim—on every level.

Emma admired Jim professionally—he was a brilliant newspaperman. Also she was fond of him personally. It was difficult not to be. On the other hand, Emma had recognized for some time that his judgment was flawed in many areas, most especially when it came to his assessment of people. He was not terribly discriminating. He liked everyone; furthermore he wanted everyone to be happy and all of the time, no less. He hated controversy and upset, bent over backward to keep the peace—and very often that was to his own detriment. In Emma's mind one of Jim's main problems was his overwhelming need to be liked in return, to be popular with every member of the family, his friends, and those in his employment. This trait in him both dismayed and irritated Emma. It was lonely at the top. And it was generally not very wise to be overly familiar with employees. That quickly led to trouble. Loath though she was to admit it, Jim was simply not of the same caliber as Paula. Would he hold up over the years? Every marriage had its problems, its stresses, its emotional upheavals. If Jim caved in because of his lack of stamina and endurance under pressure, what would happen to that marriage? To Paula? To their children? She hated to contemplate the future in this dismal way and instantly pushed all negative thoughts out of her mind. They did love each other very much, and perhaps their love would overcome any differences they may have.

Winston said, "You wanted to see me, Aunt Emma?" He sounded both nervous and concerned.

"Yes," Emma said, pivoting. She walked over to a grouping of chairs, motioned Winston and Emily to join her.

They sat down opposite her, waiting.

Winston had been mystified when Emily had dragged him out of the drawing room, whispering that Emma had sent her to get him. He knew at once, from the girl's anxious demeanor, that something was wrong. Now his worried air intensified as he puffed rapidly on his cigarette. Out of the corner of his eye he saw that Emily's face was stark above her yellow suit, its bony pallor more pronounced.

Getting right to the point, Emma said, "A few minutes ago I saw Shane looking at Paula in such a way that it left no doubt in my mind about his feelings for her. Emily tells me you also noticed."

"Yes, I did," Winston said at once, realizing there was no point in denying it or lying. He braced himself, wondering what she would say next. He studied her face, which was severe and grave.

"Shane is in love with Paula," Emma announced in a clipped tone.

"Yes. And desperately so," Winston replied, shaking his head. He had wondered for a long time when this would come out in the open, and now that it had, he decided it was wisest to be completely candid with Emma. In a way he felt relieved that she finally knew. It had been a heavy burden for him to carry alone.

Desperately Emma repeated under her breath. And her heart sank. Winston was underscoring her own suspicions, confirming her conclusions. She said slowly, "Has Shane discussed his feelings for her with you, Winston?"

"No, Aunt Emma, he hasn't. He's a very private man and discreet. But I've picked up a few things lately, and I've known about his emotional involvement with Paula for a while now . . . through my own observations. After all we do share the same house at weekends. To be honest I have a feeling Shane *thinks* I know, but he's never brought the matter up. As I said, he's extremely discreet."

Emma sat back, pursing her lips, her eyes more reflective than before. After a short silence, she said, "They've been as close as two peas in a pod all of their lives, Winston. How could he have let her slip through his fingers?"

"I can only hazard a guess," Winston muttered, eyeing her closely. He stubbed out his cigarette, the gesture filled with sudden anger. "It's because they grew up together . . . I mean, I don't think he could see the wood for the trees, see what was under his nose. I'm positive Shane only realized the depth of his feelings for her when she became engaged to Jim. And they got married so quickly after their engagement was announced, Shane hardly had time to catch his breath. Or act. It all went very fast, as you know."

Winston now lifted his shoulders in a weary shrug and glanced away, thinking of Shane's abject misery. It had grown more intense and acute—and more noticeable—lately. He was glad Shane was going to the States—for Shane's own sake. He turned back to Emma and finished, "That's my analysis of what happened, for what it's worth, Aunt Emma. I truly believe that it took another man in the picture to make Shane understand how much he loved Paula."

"Yes, I think you're correct, Winston," Emma said.

"Do you think Paula ever knew or knows that he cares about her in that way?" Emily asked Winston in a hushed voice, touching his arm lightly, looking up at him.

"I honestly can't answer that, Emily. But I—"

Emma interrupted with great firmness, "I'm sure she didn't and doesn't have an inkling, dear." She cleared her throat and continued in that same clear strong tone, "This is a most tragic state of affairs for Shane, but there's nothing anyone can do, least of all me. Not anymore. Also it's really none of my business. Nor is it anyone else's, for that matter. The last thing I want is for Shane or Paula to become topics for the gossip mongers in this family, and we all know there are a few who would love to tittle-tattle, perhaps blow this matter out of proportion. I have implicit faith in the both of you and in your discretion and loyalty. However, I must ask you both to promise me faithfully that you will never mention what you saw this afternoon to anyone ever. Is that clearly understood?"

"Of course I promise, Grandma," Emily cried in a shocked voice, looking at Emma aghast. "You must know I would never talk about Paula or do anything to hurt her. I feel the same way about Shane."

"I wasn't doubting you, Emily. I simply felt compelled to stress the importance of your absolute silence on this matter." She directed her attention at Winston.

He said, "I promise, Aunt Emma. I care about Paula and Shane as much as Emily does. And I tend to agree with you about the gossips in our family. There's also a lot of free-floating jealousy about Paula. Shane too, in many ways. They're very special people, so obviously they'll always be targets. My lips are sealed, Aunt Emma. Please don't worry about *me*."

"Thank you," Emma said and made a mental note of Winston's astute comments. She smiled thinly. "I would prefer it if we ourselves never referred to this matter again. I believe it would be best forgotten by the three of us. Shane is going away for six months. Let's hope he will forget Paula—"

"He'll never let go of her!" Winston cut in fiercely, heatedly. "It's not in his nature to—" Angrily he clamped his mouth shut, regretting that he had opened it in the first place.

But he had said enough for Emma to get a clear picture. Yes, she thought, that's what I'm afraid of, too. She said, as steadily as possible, "Perhaps he *will* always care for her, Winston. But he's a young man and virile. He has normal appetites and desires, I've no doubt. Let us hope that he'll eventually find someone who'll meet his needs and come up to his standards, a woman who can help him to forget Paula. I sincerely hope he makes a rewarding life for himself, finds fulfillment and happiness.''

"I don't know about that,'' Winston muttered, changing his mind yet again. He ought to be truthful with Emma. He owed her that, after all. He threw his aunt a gloom-filled glance. And then, because he had always been able to say anything to her without a shred of embarrassment, he added bluntly, "I'm sure he'll continue to have his brief, hit-and-run affairs, his sexual entanglements. He couldn't avoid them, not the way women throw themselves at him. Shane's no saint, you know. And he's hardly the type to lead a celibate life. After all, Aunt Emma, you don't have to be in love with a woman to sleep with her.''

"Quite,'' Emma said, lifting a brow, glancing at Emily.

Winston noticed this, but Emily was a big girl. She knew what was what. Undeterred, he plunged on, "I suppose you won't want to hear this, but I'm going to say it anyway. In my opinion, Shane O'Neill will never love anyone but Paula. You said a few minutes ago that this was a tragic thing for Shane. And it is. But it's also tragic for Paula, *I* think. She'd have been far better off and happier with a man like Shane than with Jim Fairley.''

Winston's harsh tone, not to mention his condemning words, brought Emma up with a start. She looked at him swiftly in astonishment, noticing the grim expression ringing his mouth, the angry glint in his eyes. Why, he bears a grudge against Jim, she thought, that's what his suppressed rage and resentment are all about. Winston is against Jim Fairley because he won Paula, cut Shane out.

Emma nodded, made no comment whatsoever.

Emily, her face puckering up, said quietly, "Poor Shane, life's so unfair.''

"Come now, darling, you're only seeing Shane's side of this situation,'' Emma clucked gently, reprovingly. "Perhaps Paula doesn't think life is unfair. I'm sure she's happy with Jim. I know she loves him. And besides, Emily, whoever told you life is fair? It's most *unfair,* and it has always been damned hard in my experience. How we cope with life, react to our hardships and suffering, and overcome them—that's what really counts in the end. We must all be strong, learn from our troubles, grow in stature and character. We can't ever let adversity get us down, Emily. Now, let us end this discussion. Run along, the two of you. I want to be alone for a few minutes.''

Winston went over and kissed her. So did Emily. They left together in silence.

Emma sat by herself for a while.

She felt weary, bone-tired. It seemed to her that she solved one problem only to encounter another. But then her life had never been any different. Dear, dear Shane, she murmured under her breath. My heart goes out to you. Life has dealt you a bad hand in this particular instance. But you'll survive. We all do.

Quite unexpectedly tears came into her eyes and trickled down her cheeks. She searched her pockets for a handkerchief and dabbed at her wrinkled old face. She felt like weeping buckets of tears. But that was not her way, giving in like that. And tears solved nothing. She blew her nose, pocketed her handkerchief, and stood up, smoothing down her dress as she did.

Emma walked over to the windows again, taking a few deep breaths, drawing on her great strength, her willpower. And slowly she pulled herself together. Her thoughts came back to Shane. Perhaps Winston was right in his assessment. Maybe Shane hadn't realized how he truly felt about Paula until it was too late. Then again, maybe he had believed he had all the time in the world to claim her for his own. We all think that time is endless when we're young, she sighed to herself. The years ahead seem to stretch out forever and indefinitely. But they don't . . . they disappear in a flash, in the wink of an eye. Blackie edged into her mind. She wondered what he would have to say about this situation. She decided at once not to tell him. It would upset him, cause him too much grief.

Last night Blackie had said that life was too damned short for dilly-dallying. There was a great deal of truth and wisdom in his words, especially when it came to a couple of old warriors like themselves. Emma made another sudden decision. She was going to accept Blackie's invitation to go on that trip around the world after all. No more dilly-dallying for her.

Turning away from the window, Emma walked briskly across the floor and left the library. She went into the drawing room purposefully, seeking Blackie, picturing his expression when she told him to put his Plan with a capital P into operation immediately. And this she fully intended to do the minute she found him in the crowded room.

Twelve

"Do you think all families are like ours?"

"What do you mean—*exactly?*" Winston asked, turning to face Emily.

"We've always got a drama of one kind or another erupting. It seems to me there's never been a minute's peace for as long as I can remember. If it's not the awful aunts and uncles being beastly and scratching everyone's eyes out, it's our generation quarreling and creating the most dreadful upsets. To tell you the truth, I feel as though I'm on a battlefield half the time, and I don't think I'm a very good combatant."

Winston chuckled at her mournful tone, which reflected her dire expression. "You manage all right, Emily. You're a good little scrapper—so I've noticed."

The two of them sat together on an old stone garden seat at the bottom of the rolling lawns that sloped away from the wide terrace which fronted the Peach Drawing Room. Behind them, Pennistone Royal soared up into a sky of deepening blue, awesome in its grandeur and majestic beauty, the many windows glittering in the sunshine of late afternoon.

Now Winston said more thoughtfully, "But to answer your question, I don't suppose other families are *quite* like ours. After all, how many have an Emma Harte as the matriarch."

Emily drew away, looking up at him, a small frown wrinkling her smooth brow. Her eyes held his gravely as she said, "Don't blame Grandma for the dramatics that are being endlessly enacted. I think she's an innocent bystander, poor thing. I really get angry when I think of the heartache some members of this family cause her."

Winston exclaimed, "I wasn't being critical of her, if that's what you think. Or suggesting for one minute that she's responsible for these situations,

Emily. I agree with you—she's not at fault. I was merely pointing out that as the most remarkable woman of our time and an original, there's bound to be controversy surrounding her. Look, she's had a very complex and complicated life, and one she's certainly lived to the fullest. She has shoals of children and grandchildren, and if you include all of us Hartes, which you must, her family is *huge*. Bigger than most. And don't forget her other close attachments—the O'Neill and Kallinski clans. Add up the numbers—and you've got an army, more or less."

"Everything you say is true, Winston. Still I do get awfully fed up with the infighting and bickering. I just wish we could all live peacefully together and get *on* with it, for God's sake."

"Yes . . . but there's another thing you must take into consideration, Emily. Immense wealth and power are vested in her and in this family, so obviously there are going to be jealousies and competitiveness and all kinds of machinations. It strikes me that intrigues are inescapable, given the nature of people . . . they *can* be rotten, Emily. Selfish, greedy, self-serving, and ruthless. I've discovered that some people will stop at nothing when their own interests are at stake."

"Don't I know it!" Emily stared down into the murky depths of the pond, looking troubled. Finally she lifted her head and swung her eyes to Winston. "When I mentioned dramas a few minutes ago, naturally I was referring to Shane. But, I must admit, I sensed things this afternoon—you know, *undercurrents*. As usual the room was divided into camps. There was a lot of maneuvering going on."

"And who was doing what to whom?" Winston asked with some alertness, his curiosity aroused.

"Jonathan and Sarah are as thick as thieves, for one thing. That's very strange, because I know she never used to like him. I can't put my finger on it, yet I can't help feeling they're concocting something. Alexander is probably suspicious of that new liaison. Didn't you notice how he's steered clear of them today?"

"Now that you mention it, yes. Personally I've never had much time for Jonathan Ainsley. He was a bully as a child, and like all bullies he's basically a coward. He projects a lot of charm these days, but I don't expect he's changed much over the years, not *inside*. I haven't forgotten the time he hit me over the head with a cricket bat. The nasty little bugger. He could have done me real damage."

"I know he could, and he was always horrid to me when we were growing up. I still believe it was Master Jonathan who cut the tires on that bicycle Grandy gave me when I was ten, even though he denied it when she challenged him. He came up with some sort of plausible alibi about his whereabouts that day, but I just *know* it was a total fib." Emily scowled. "As for Sarah, well, she's been a loner and secretive all of her life."

"You know what they say—still waters run deep and the devil's at the bottom," Winston remarked.

He bent down, picked up a pebble, and idly threw it into the pond, watching the ripples eddying out from the pool's center. "There have been occasions when I've thought that Sarah has the hots for Shane."

Emily started in surprise. "You're not the only one," she admitted quietly. "Well, fat chance she's got—" She stopped, added swiftly, "That sounded mean, and I didn't intend to be catty, Winston. I don't dislike Sarah. She can be very sweet, and I feel sorry for her really. Carrying a torch for a man like Shane O'Neill must be positively awful. Even heartbreaking perhaps. She and I have never been all that close, but . . . well, I always thought she was true-blue—until today. Now I'm not sure anymore."

"She might have been using Jonathan as a shield, and that's all. It was pretty obvious she was trying to disappear into the woodwork because of Shane's presence, I've no doubt."

"Maybe you're right." Changing the subject, Emily remarked, "Jim's very taken with Edwina and with Anthony by the look of it. He's been glued to our young earl for the last hour or so. Maybe titles impress him. Anyway, what do you think about Anthony and Sally getting together?"

"Anthony's decent enough, but my father's not so happy about Sally's involvement with him, mostly because of Edwina. If Sally does marry him, we're going to have that old battleaxe slap bang in our midst. Not a very pleasing prospect. She hates the Hartes for some reason."

"It's because Grandma is a Harte!" Emily exclaimed. "Edwina has always looked down her nose at her mother. What a stupid woman she is. I really can't bear her." Emily looked away, pondering. After a short silence, she said in a casual tone, "You don't like Jim Fairley, do you?"

Winston shook his head vehemently. "No, no, you're wrong there. I *do* like him, and I certainly have a high regard for his professional abilities. It's just that—" Winston shrugged, made a face. "Well, I know Paula better than most people. Despite that quiet facade she's very strong, as *you* know. She's also ambitious, driven, a workhorse, and a brilliant businesswoman to boot. She's quite extraordinary for her age, and the older she gets, the more like Emma she'll become, you mark my words. Actually she's been brought up and groomed to be exactly that—the next Emma Harte. By Emma Harte herself. So because of this and the differences in their personalities, I can't help thinking she and Jim are ill-suited. But then I'm prejudiced, I suppose . . . in Shane's favor. He's my best friend and one hell of a man. But then—"

Emily broke in peremptorily, "There's something I want to tell you about Jim, Winston. I believe he's got a lot more depth and strength than some people realize. Paula told me that he used to have the most terrible and agonizing fear of flying because his parents were killed in a plane crash when he was a small boy. And that's why he took up flying and bought his own plane. He became a pilot to conquer his fear. I know Gran hates him tootling around in his little tin bird, as she calls it, but it's obviously important for him to do so, perhaps even essential to his well-being."

Winston looked surprised. He said, "Then I've got to hand it to him, it takes guts and courage to overcome that kind of paralyzing fear. I'm glad you told me, Emily. Anyway, I was about to say that I could be wrong about Paula and Jim. I'm not infallible. Maybe those two will make it together. I certainly don't wish any unhappiness on Paula, of whom I'm very fond. Or on Jim for that matter."

He paused, gave Emily a cheeky grin, and finished, "Besides, nobody knows what really goes on between two people, or what happens in the privacy of the bedroom. Jim could have hidden charms, you know." He winked at her suggestively.

Emily could not help laughing. "You are wicked, Winston." Her eyes filled with mischief. "You should have seen Grandy's face when you were rattling on about Shane and his hit-and-run affairs and sexual entanglements. It was a picture. And she kept giving me the most surreptitious and concerned glances, as if I wasn't supposed to know about sex."

"And of course you *are* the lady of great experience, eh, Tiddler?"

Emily adopted a haughty expression and drew herself up on the bench. "Have you forgotten that I'm now twenty-two years of age? *I* know exactly how many beans make five."

They grinned at each other. She saw that Winston was highly amused.

Emily went on, "Do you know, you haven't called me Tiddler since I was just that—a very little girl."

"And you were, too. The tiniest of little tots for your age."

"But I did sprout suddenly. I'll have you know I'm now five-feet, five-inches tall, Winston Harte!"

"And a very grown-up young woman, I'll wager," he teased. "We had fun as kids, though, didn't we, Tiddler? Do you remember that day we decided to play at being early Britons, and I dubbed you Queen Boadicea?"

"How could I forget!" Emily shrieked. Her face flooded with merriment. "You painted me blue. *All over.*"

"Not quite, since you insisted on keeping your knickers on, and your liberty bodice. You *were* a modest little thing, as I recall."

"No, I wasn't! It was the dead of winter and freezing in Grandy's garage. Besides, why would I be bashful *then?* I didn't have anything to show off when I was five years old."

Winston gave her an appraising look, one full of speculation, seeing her through the eyes of a grown man. "But you do now—" He left the rest of his sentence unfinished, feeling self-conscious all of a sudden. Then he became intensely aware of her close proximity as he breathed in the scent of her floral perfume, the lemony tang of her newly washed hair. Her face, at this moment upturned to his, was trusting, and it had lost its earlier pallor. She looked more like herself, so very pretty and delicate and as sweet as a summer rose, dewy and fresh and innocent.

Winston cleared his throat and could not resist drawing her closer to him, wanting and needing that closeness. He said tenderly, in a newly gentle voice, "It's a good thing you were a modest child, Emily. If you hadn't kept some of your clothes on, I *would* have painted you all over and probably killed you in the process."

"How were we to know at our ages that skin can't breathe through paint. It wasn't really your fault, Winston. I was just as bad, and after all I painted parts of you." Emily relaxed against him. She was as conscious of Winston as he was of her, and she longed to prolong this unanticipated and unexpected moment of real physical contact.

He let out a deep chuckle. "I'll never forget Aunt Emma's terrible fury when she found us in the garage. I thought she was going to give me the whipping of my life. Do you know, every time I smell turpentine I think of that day, of those gruesome turpentine baths she and Hilda gave us. I swear to God she scrubbed me twice as hard as she did you. Extra punishment for me, of course, the irresponsible ten-year-old boy, who should have known better. I was raw for days."

Emily squeezed his arm. "We were always getting into trouble, weren't we? You were the ring leader, I the devoted follower, faithfully trailing after you, doing your bidding. I did adore you so, Winston."

He nodded, looked down into a pair of sparkling eyes that were extraordinary reflections of his own.

Winston caught his breath. He saw something flashing in those green depths, an intensity of feeling, the self-same adoration she had had for him when she had been a child. Unexpectedly his heart began to clatter, and before he could stop himself he bent forward and kissed her on the mouth.

Instantly Emily's arms went around his neck, and she returned his kiss so fervently he was momentarily taken aback. He gripped her tighter and kissed her again and then again, with increasing passion. He felt an overwhelming desire for her flowing through him, rising in him. My God, he was suddenly as hard as a rock. He wanted Emily and with every part of himself. His whole body was throbbing for her, and he was stunned, thrown off-balance by this discovery.

Eventually they loosened their grip on each other and pulled apart breathlessly.

They stared at each other in amazement.

Emily's face was flushed, her eyes startlingly bright, and he saw with sudden clarity the love burning in them. Love for him. He touched her cheek and found it was red-hot under his caress, burning like her eyes burned. Impatiently he dragged her into his arms again, and his mouth sought hers roughly. They kissed with mounting passion. Their tongues met tantalizingly. He probed her mouth, devoured it. They pressed closer, their bodies cleaving.

Vaguely, dimly, at the back of his swimming mind, Winston remembered how he had always had the urge to undress her when they had been children. In a rush he recalled the long-forgotten games they had played in the attics here . . . secret, intimate, exciting games when he had experienced his first arousals. He thought of how his clumsy boy's hands had explored her little girl's body . . . he wanted to explore it again with the sure hands of the experienced man he now was, to touch every part of her, woman that she now was, to plunge into her, to possess her completely. His erection was enormous, and he thought he was going to explode. He struggled for control, knowing he ought to curtail their lovemaking at once, but he found he was unwilling to release her from his arms. He gave in to his feeling, kissing her face, her neck, her hair, touching her breasts, taut under the flimsy silk blouse.

It was Emily who finally broke the spell which held them enraptured with each other. She extricated herself from his forceful embrace, but ever so gently and with reluctance. She gazed up at him. Her expression was one of stupefaction.

"Oh, Winston," she whispered and reached out to touch his sensual, trembling mouth with two fingers. She let them rest there for a moment, as if gentling him.

Winston was speechless.

He sat rigidly on the bench, waiting for his excitement to subside. Emily was motionless at his side, looking up into his face. His eyes bored into her, telegraphing so much to her.

At last he managed, in a strangled voice thick with emotion, "Emily, I—"

"Please," she whispered quaveringly, "don't say anything. At least not now." She glanced away, biting her inner lip, giving him a few moments to steady himself, to regain his composure. Then she stood up, held out her hand. "Come on," she said, "we'd better go inside. It's getting ever so late."

He said nothing but simply rose; and they walked up the steps in silence, holding hands tightly, each conscious of the other, while lost within themselves.

Emily was filled with euphoria.

He has noticed me again, she thought, her heart soaring. At last. Since I was sixteen, I've been waiting for him to see me as a woman. I want him. I've never stopped wanting him since we were children. Oh, Winston, please feel the same way as I do. Take me for yourself. I've always belonged to you. You made sure of that when I was a child.

Winston for his part was awash with all manner of conflicting emotions and turbulent feelings.

He was not only astonished at himself, but at Emily as well—staggered really. They had fallen into each other's arms a moment ago with such ardor and passion he knew that if they had been in more suitable surroundings, they would have made love. Nothing would have stopped them. And they had come together without premeditation.

Self-analysis and self-appraisal now edged into his whirling thoughts, cooling him down considerably. He came to his senses, asked himself how this could have happened. She was his cousin, after all. Well, his third cousin. And he had known her for his entire life, although he had paid little attention to her over the past ten years. And inevitably he asked himself finally how he could feel so strongly about Emily when he was in love with Allison Ridley.

This thought nagged at him and maddeningly so as they mounted the long flight of steps. But when they stepped out onto the circular driveway, he let the thought go free as he saw Shane's red Ferrari hurtling around the corner. It slowed to a standstill with a screeching of brakes.

Shane rolled down the window and poked his head out, grinning at them. "Where have you two been?" he asked. "I've been looking all over for you, to say goodbye."

"Emily was feeling a bit bilious in that packed room, so we came out for a breath of fresh air," Winston ad-libbed quickly. "Where are you off to in such a tearing hurry and at this early hour?"

"Like Emily, I was beginning to feel oppressed indoors. I thought I'd take a drive. To Harrogate. I have to say a few farewells . . . to a couple of chums."

Winston's eyes narrowed imperceptibly. He's going to see Dorothea Mallet, he thought. Some good that'll do him. He said, "Don't be late for Allison's dinner party. Eight sharp."

"I'll be there on time, don't worry."

Emily asked, "Will you be around tomorrow, Shane?"

"I don't think so, Emily." He opened the car door and got out. He took hold of her, hugged her tightly. "I'll see you in six months or so. Unless you come to New York first." He smiled at her fondly. "Aunt Emma just told me you're going to work for Genret. Congratulations, little one."

"Thank you, Shane, I'm excited about it." She stood on tiptoe and kissed his cheek. "And perhaps I will get over to the States on my travels for Genret. You'll have to show me the town, you know!"

"That's a date," he laughed. "Take care of yourself, Emily."

"And you too, Shane."

"See you later, Winston," Shane said and got back into the car.

"Yes," Winston answered laconically. He looked at Emily oddly as Shane drove off. "You didn't tell me about Genret." This was said fretfully, and he felt so unexpectedly gloomy, he was surprised at himself.

She said, "I haven't had a chance, Winston."

"Does it mean you'll be doing a great deal of traveling?" he probed, scowling at her.

"Eventually. Why?" Emily lifted a brow quizzically, secretly delighted by his reaction.

"Oh, I just wondered," he muttered. He realized, with a small shock, that he did not relish the idea of her roaming the world by herself, trotting off on buying trips for Genret.

They fell silent again as they continued up the drive to the house, but just before they went inside, Emily ventured in a hesitant tone, "Is it serious? With you and Allison, I mean?"

"No, of course not," Winston exclaimed swiftly, then asked himself why he had told such a bare-faced lie. He was on the verge of proposing to Allison.

Emily's face brightened. She said, "I'm sorry you're busy tonight. I'd hoped you'd stay and have dinner with us."

"I'm afraid I'm stuck." Winston grimaced to himself, discovering to his further astonishment that he was no longer looking forward to the dinner party. He smiled with some wryness, then took hold of Emily's arm as she pushed open the back door, and swung her to face him. "What are you doing tomorrow?"

"I have to take the girls back to Harrogate College after Sunday lunch here. I'm free in the evening," she volunteered and returned his steady gaze unblinkingly. Expectancy illuminated her face.

"How would you like to cook supper for a lonely bachelor? I could come over to your flat in Headingley, Emily," he suggested.

The smile slipped off her face, and she shook her head. "It's not possible, Winston. I've just moved in here with Grandy. Yesterday, actually. I'm getting rid of the flat. Otherwise I'd have loved to cook for you."

Winston stood staring down at her, his hands resting on her shoulders. He was swamped with mixed emotions. He was positive she wanted him. He certainly wanted her. Urgently. Allison loomed up between them. Oh what the hell, he thought, making a decision he hoped he would have no reason to regret later.

Tilting her chin, he kissed her quickly on the mouth. He said with a wide grin, "Then we're neighbors. Come over to Beck House tomorrow night, and *I'll* cook for *you*. We'll have a nice evening, I promise. What do you say?"

"I think it's a super idea, Winston," she said filling with happiness and excitement. "What time shall I come over?"

"As soon as you possibly can, darling."

—— *Thirteen* ——

The room was in total darkness.

Not even the merest sliver of light penetrated the tightly drawn curtains, and the lamps had been doused. He craved the darkness. It was like a balm to him. The darkness brought anonymity. He liked it that way. He could not bear to make love in the light anymore.

He lay absolutely still, with his eyes closed, flat on his back, his long legs stretched out in front of him, his arms resting by his sides inertly. His shoulder barely touched hers. He could hear her breathing softly in unison with himself.

It was not working between the two of them.

And it would not work—he knew that and wondered why he was here at all. He really ought to leave. Make a graceful exit. Immediately. He swallowed, fighting back the nausea, wishing he had not downed two glasses of whiskey on top of all that champagne. His head was swimming and he was dizzy, but he was not drunk. In a way he regretted he was not.

She murmured his name, meltingly, pleadingly, repeating it several times, her fingers brushing up and down his arm.

He was motionless, saying nothing, endeavoring to find the energy to get up and dress and leave. He felt enervated, lethargic. The ghastly afternoon, with its extreme tensions and painful moments, plus the effort he had exerted to conceal his raw emotions, had vitiated him, undermined his stamina.

Now he felt an imperceptible movement close to him, but still he did not open his eyes.

She touched one of his nipples, tentatively at first, then more insistently, pinching it between her fingertips. Absently he moved her hand away, without bothering to explain that his nipples were not as sensitive as she obviously believed they were. But he had told her that before, hadn't he? Her hand rested on his chest for a moment, then fluttered onto his stomach, making gentle circular movements, creeping down in the direction of his crotch. He knew what she had in mind, what she was about to do next, but he lacked the will to stop her or to tell her he was leaving in a moment.

She began to stroke him. He hardly paid attention, drifting off into his thoughts. Vaguely he heard the rustle of sheets. She had slithered down the bed and was crouched over him. Her long hair brushed his thighs, and then her warm lips encircled him, enclosed him fully. She was a versatile lover. Despite his buzzing head, his queasy stomach, and his lack of interest in her, slowly, steadily, with infinite care, and painstaking deliberation, she managed to arouse him. And in doing so she took him by surprise. When finally she lifted her head and moved her lips higher onto his stomach, trailed them up over his chest to settle on his mouth, he found himself responding automatically. He returned her fervent kisses, his excitement mounting.

With suddenness, abruptness, he moved rapidly, holding her tightly against him, rolling them both over so that he was lying on top of her. His hands went into the cloud of dark hair, and he held her head in his hands, kissing her more deeply and thoroughly, their tongues grazing. He squeezed his eyes tightly shut, not wanting to look into her face pressed so close to his. His fingers left her hair, moved down to fondle her full, voluptuous breasts, her hardening nipples; he pushed his hands under her shoulder blades, then her buttocks, lifting her body, fitting it into the curve of his. He was hard enough to slide into her swiftly, easily, expertly. Together they found a rhythm, rising and falling, their movements growing swifter, more frenzied, gaining in momentum. Her legs went high around his back so that he could shaft deeper and deeper into the warmth of her.

The darkness . . . the blackness . . . welcoming him . . . enveloping him. He was falling . . . falling into that endless, bottomless, velvet pit. Paula. Paula. Paula. I love you. Take me. Take all of me. All of my essence. Brilliantly clear images of her exquisite face flashed behind his eyes, were trapped beneath his lids. Paula, my darling, he cried silently, oh Paula . . .

"Shane! You're hurting me."

He heard the voice as if from a long distance, and it was like a knife slashing at his viscera.

It brought him down. Brought him back to this room. And back to her. And it killed the mood he had so carefully created for himself and only for himself. His fantasy shattered around him.

He fell against her body and lay perfectly still. He was deflated, flaccid, all of his vitality draining away.

At last he said in a low mumble, "I'm sorry if I hurt you, Dorothea. It seems I don't know my own strength." Perhaps you do, he added sardonically under his breath. Or rather your want of it. Instantly he was embarrassed by his lack of staying power, his inability to bring the act of love to its proper culmination for them both. Act of sex, you mean, he thought, and he shuddered. Revulsion trickled through him, for himself, for her, although she was hardly to blame.

Dorothea said, "Your watch strap was cutting into my back. But I suppose I shouldn't have said anything just then. You were on the edge, the verge of—"

He covered her mouth with his hand, gently but firmly, in order to stop the flow of words. He did not want to hear her apology. He did not say one single word, but just lay against her for the longest moment, his heart slamming against his rib cage, his throat tight with a strangling sensation. Thankfully she too was silent. Finally he lifted himself off her body, touched her shoulder lightly, and left the rumpled bed.

Shane went into the bathroom, locked the door, and leaned against it, filled with considerable relief. He fumbled for the switch, snapped on the light, blinked rapidly in the sudden intense glare. The room swam in front of him, and the white-tiled floor appeared to tilt upward to hit him between the eyes. The vertigo and the nausea returned.

He stumbled to the wash basin, leaned over it, and vomited. Blindly he searched for the tap with one hand and turned it on so that the sound of running water would drown out his retching. He retched and retched until he thought he had nothing left in his insides. When the nausea mercifully subsided, he wiped his mouth with the washcloth and drank several glasses of cold water, braced himself against the sink, staring down, his eyes closed.

Eventually Shane lifted his head and saw himself in the mirror, and he did not like what he saw. His eyes were red-rimmed and bloodshot, his face puffy and congested, and his tousled black hair stood on end. He noticed a smudge of bright red lipstick on the side of his mouth and took the damp washcloth and scrubbed at it furiously, angrily. But his anger was directed solely at himself. It had nothing to do with Dorothea. This was not her fault. He was entirely to blame.

He could no longer make love to her successfully, or to any other woman for that matter. Something always happened to bring him back to reality, and when he realized it was not Paula in his arms, as he had fantasized, he fell apart, could not reach fulfillment. Sometimes, stupefied by drink, his vision and his senses blurred, he could somehow manage, but even these rare occasions were becoming rarer.

He stared at his face in the mirror, and without warning he was struck by panic and fear.

Was it always going to be like this? For the rest of his life? Would he never have a happy sexual relationship again? Was he doomed to lead an arid existence without a woman? Would he have to resort to celibacy to save face? To stave off that dreadful moment of embarrassment, such as the one which had just occurred in Dorothea's bed?

He was not impotent. He knew he was not afflicted in that way. It was a simple matter really—if his partner intruded into his thoughts, made her presence felt, no longer remained anonymous, then he lost his erection. Try though he did, he could not hold it long enough to satisfy her or himself. The woman he idolized impinged, edged in between them, rendering him weak and ineffectual, he who had always been considered a good lover. What would he *do,* for Christ's sake? *How* would he cure himself? *Was* there a cure? Did he *need* to see a doctor?

The silence in the room pressed in on him. He had no ready answers for himself in his awful predicament.

His anguish flared. God damn it! God damn it to hell! he blasphemed silently, and unexpectedly his eyes filled with tears of helplessness, frustration, and rage, startling him. And then instantaneously he was shocked and mortified by this shameful loss of control. For a split second he wanted to smash his fist into the mirror, to shatter that tearful image of himself staring out to mock him. He wanted to smash those finely tuned, crystalline images of Paula. Damn *her.* Destroy those indelible imprints of her that were stamped so strongly on his tormented, aching brain they seemed to control his life, affected everything he did. At times he felt hopelessly victimized by the vibrant inner vision of her face, the sound of her laughter, and her gentle voice that echoed endlessly in his head. But all were locked so securely in his imagination he could not eradicate them, no matter how hard he tried.

But he did not move. He kept his hand clenched at his side, the knuckles white, protruding sharply. Then he closed his eyes convulsively, no longer able to look at himself in this moment of weakness. He leaned against the wall to steady himself, was immobilized like this until he grew calmer, got a grip on himself. Swinging around, he stepped into the shower stall, turned on the taps, let the water sluice down over him. And slowly but with an iron-clad determination, he emptied his heart and his mind, threw out every vestige of emotion, all feeling.

Minutes later he emerged from the steaming shower, took a bath sheet, and dried himself vigorously. He found a fresh towel, tied it around his waist, then searched the cupboard under the sink for the toilet kit he had left there weeks ago. He cleaned his teeth, ran the electric razor over his chin to remove his faint five o'clock shadow, splashed cologne on his face, and combed his damp hair.

He was refreshed, looked more like himself . . . coolly contained, smoothly in control once more. He stared at his reflection a fraction longer, wondering about himself. He was a strapping, healthy young man of twenty-seven, stood six-foot-three, and had a muscular body that was strong and powerful. He had an equally powerful brain to go with his splendid physique. And yet . . . he was so fragile really. The mind is a peculiar thing, he thought, it has such a delicate balance. And who can explain the logic of the heart?

Turning away, he took a deep breath, prepared himself for the inevitable scene with Dorothea. Today he had come to her against his own volition—he could not wait to leave her.

He opened the bathroom door, blinked as he walked back into the shadow-filled bedroom, adjusting his eyes to the darkness. The room was silent, and he wondered if she had fallen asleep, prayed that she had. He groped around for his clothes on the chair where he had discarded them earlier, pulled on his underpants and socks, dispensed with the towel. He slipped on his shirt, buttoned it quickly, dragged his trousers up over his legs, and zipped them.

At this moment the bedside lamp flared into life, flooding the room with chilly brightness.

"You're not leaving!" Dorothea exploded. She sounded aghast, furious.

He pivoted.

He could not look at her. Unable to meet her gaze, which he knew would be hurt and condemning, he stared at the far wall.

"I have to go," he said after a short pause. He sat down on the chair and began to put on his shoes. He could feel her eyes on him.

"You've got a nerve!" she cried, sitting up violently, rattling the headboard as she did. She pulled the sheet around her body with an angry gesture. "You stroll in here unannounced, help yourself to my booze, bed me, fumble *that,* and leave me high and dry while you disappear into the bathroom for half an hour." She glared at him, added in the same harsh, accusatory tone, "Then you creep back in here and calmly proceed to dress in the dark as if you owe me nothing. You were obviously going to *sneak off* to your blasted dinner party!"

He winced. Sighing under his breath, he stood up and walked over to the bed. He sat down on the edge, took hold of her hand, wanting to be nice, to part with her in a friendly manner. She snatched her hand away and pressed it to her trembling mouth, attempting to quell the tears glittering in her dark eyes.

Shane said in his gentlest voice, "Come on, don't get upset. I told you last week about the dinner tonight. And I reminded you about it when I first arrived this afternoon. It didn't seem to bother you a few hours ago; you were very welcoming."

"Well, it bothers me now," she gasped, choking on her words. "I didn't think you'd leave me, not on your last evening in Yorkshire. Especially after we'd spent several hours in bed together. I thought we'd be having supper—we usually do—and that you would be sleeping here tonight, Shane."

He was silent. He glanced away uncomfortably.

She misconstrued his reticence. "I'm sorry I spoiled it for you, Shane. At the last minute, I mean," she whispered, her voice softer, more cajoling. She adopted a most winning and conciliatory demeanor. "Please say you forgive me. I love you so much. I can't bear it when you're angry."

"I'm not angry, and there's nothing to forgive," he muttered, striving for patience whilst longing to be gone. "Don't start flagellating yourself or donning a hair shirt. Look, it doesn't matter, honestly it doesn't, Dorothea."

She caught something strange in his voice. She was not sure what it was exactly, but it riled her nevertheless. "It matters to me," she snapped, her sweetness immediately evaporating. When there was no response from him, she cried heatedly, "This afternoon finally *proves* it to me."

"Proves what?" he asked, sounding bored.

"That you can't make it with *me*—because there's another woman. You're in love with someone else, Shane, and I think you're a bastard for using me the way you have."

Stunned that she had unwittingly stumbled on the truth but trying to hide this, he stood up at once, his movements jerky. He edged away from the bed. "I haven't used you," he protested, his mouth tightening. He glanced at the door.

"I haven't used you," she mimicked, her tone mocking, hard, her lip curling down with derision. "Of course you have. *And,* by the way, I think your friend Winston Harte is as big a bastard as you are for not inviting me to the dinner party tonight."

"He's not giving it—Allison Ridley is, and she doesn't know you or know about our relationship. You and I always agreed we would lead our own lives, with our own friends, and not become a special twosome," he exclaimed, his voice rising. "There've never been any strings attached to our relationship . . . that's the way *you* wanted it if I'm not mistaken."

Shane took a breath, curbed his increasing annoyance. "Besides you've never been interested in my chums before today," he reminded her with a cool indifference now, wishing she would not color everything with emotion.

"I've changed my mind. Please take me with you, Shane. I want to come. I really do. This *is* your last night. Please, darling," she begged, offering him a wistfully sweet smile, but it faltered in the face of his chilly expression, his rigid stance.

"You know that's not possible, not at this late hour. Anyway, it's a seated dinner. Look, don't try to make *me* wear a hair shirt—" He moved wearily toward the door.

"I know *I'm* not welcome in *your* precious little clique!" she yelled, further losing her control. "My God, you all make me want to puke! The O'Neills, the Hartes, the Kallinskis . . . what a tight, toffy-nosed group you are. No outsiders permitted to join *your* exclusive club, to become part of *your* charmed circle. No room for us common folk among your snooty lot. Anybody would think you're royalty the way you all behave, what with your airs and graces and pretensions. And your stinking money," she scoffed irately, her face ringed with bitterness. "You're just a bunch of rotten snobs—the lot of you. And bloody incestuous if you ask me, huddling together in the rarified air of your posh compounds, shutting out the rest of the world. It's sick!"

Flabbergasted at her violence, he looked at her icily and with spiralling disdain. He was appalled at her words, her venom, but immediately held himself in check, deciding not to be provoked into retaliating.

There was an unpleasant silence.

"I've got to go. I'm extremely late." This was said evenly enough, but

Shane was seething inside. He strode across the room, his blood boiling at her insults, threw his tie around his neck, picked up his jacket, and slung it over his shoulder.

"I'm sorry we're parting on such a bad note," he said, giving her a glance of condemnation, "but there seems to be nothing more to say." He shrugged. "I had hoped we could remain friends, at the very least."

"*Friends!*" she repeated shrilly, her temper blazing. "You must be crazy. Go on, get out! Go to your lady love. No doubt *she'll* be at your precious dinner!" She laughed hysterically through her blinding tears, then brushed her eyes, made an effort to cling to her last ounce of composure, without success. She swallowed a sob, cried, "I must admit, I'm curious about one thing! What makes you come crawling back into *my* bed all the time, hot and bothered and raring to go, when someone else has a claim on your heart? Is she a crown princess from one of the clans? A young lady of such refinement—so chaste and virginal—you wouldn't dream of sullying her? What's wrong, Shane, don't you have the guts to sleep with *her* until you're well and truly married and have the blessings of your families? Or could it be that *she's* not interested in *you?* Don't your fatal charms have any effect on *her?* Are you less than irresistible—" She bit off the end of her sentence when she saw the look of intense pain fly across his face, understanding that somehow she had struck the mark, albeit inadvertently.

"Shane, I'm sorry," she apologized at once, instantly contrite. She was genuinely concerned, afraid she had gone too far this time.

She leaped out of bed, struggled into her robe. "Shane, forgive me! I didn't mean it, didn't mean to be cruel, to hurt you. I love you, Shane. I have since the first day we met. Please, please forgive me. And forget what I just said." She started to weep.

He did not answer. Nor did he look at her again.

He left. The door slammed with finality behind him.

Shane hurried across the hall, let himself out of her flat, and ran down the stairs at breakneck speed. His head was pounding, and his stomach lurched as the nausea rose in him again.

He sprinted across the lawn, wrenched open the door of his car, and jumped in with agility. He drove off with a roar, his hands tightly gripping the wheel, his face set in angry lines, a muscle throbbing on his temple.

When he reached the Stray, the stretch of breezy open common ground in the center of Harrogate, he slowed down and parked.

Shane sat smoking for a few minutes, pulling himself together, calming his frazzled nerves, a remote look in his troubled black eyes. He stubbed out the cigarette impatiently, suddenly hating the taste of the nicotine. His head ached, reverberated with Dorothea Mallet's vituperative words. Her attitude had been extreme, uncalled for under the circumstances, but then that was her usual pattern. She had displayed her jealousy before, and by now he ought to be accustomed to her tantrums, her temperamental outbursts.

Quite unexpectedly it struck him that he had no reason whatsoever to chastise himself about his behavior toward her. He had always been considerate and kind to Dorothea. He was a decent man, and he had integrity and honor; furthermore he would never willingly hurt her or any woman.

He considered the lousy things she had said. In particular her comment about another woman in his life had been like a punch in his stomach. But she was obviously stabbing in the dark, conjecturing, since she could not possibly know he loved Paula. No one knew. It was his secret.

Shane's heart tightened as reality hit him in the face with some force. There was no chance that Paula would ever be his. She was most obviously very much in love with Jim Fairley. He had seen it written all over her face earlier in the day. Not only that, she was a mother now . . . *they were a family*. She had been transparently delighted to see him at the christening, yet despite her loving warmth, she had been preoccupied with her husband and her babies.

He squeezed his eyes tightly shut, his face twisting in a grimace of mental anguish. His love for her was a hopeless love without a future. It had nowhere to go. He had known this for the longest time, and yet a faint hope that something might happen to change things had lingered in his mind. Of course it would not. He must put Paula Fairley out of his heart, obliterate her from his consciousness, as he had decided on the moors yesterday. It was not going to be easy, he was well aware. On the other hand it was imperative that he make the effort, draw on his inner reserves for strength. He had to make his sojourn in New York a new beginning . . . it was his chance to make some sort of worthwhile life for himself. His resolve intensified.

At last Shane opened his eyes, swung his head, and gazed out of the window, shaking off the memories of Paula . . . his dearest love. And a married woman, a mother, he reminded himself.

Blinking, he became conscious of his surroundings.

He noticed the daffodils blowing in the breeze that had lately sprung up—rafts of stinging yellow against the verdant green of the grass. I ought to have bought flowers for Allison, he thought absently, remembering the dinner party. He glanced at the clock on the dashboard. It read seven-thirty. The shops were closed . . . and he was going to be late. But if he kept his foot down on the accelerator, he would make it in half an hour.

He switched on the radio, twiddled the knob to the BBC's classical station. The strains of the Pachelbel *Canon* filled the car as he swung it out onto the main road.

Within minutes the Ferrari was hurtling in the direction of the ancient cathedral town of Ripon where Allison Ridley lived. He gunned the engine forward, concentrating on the road ahead.

Fourteen

There was something of the actor in Shane O'Neill.

It was a talent inherited from Blackie, and he was able to fall back on that skill whenever it suited him. It did now.

He pushed open the front door of Holly Tree Cottage, took several deep breaths, donned a mask of geniality, and headed down the stone-flagged passageway.

He paused at the entrance to the living room, drew his inbred self-assurance around him, and stepped over the threshold.

At this instant he became what they expected him to be—a man without the slightest care, one who held the world in his arms.

Laughter sprang readily to his lips, a sparkle entered his brilliant eyes, and he exuded ebullience and bonhomie, strolling forward at a leisurely pace to join his closest male friends—Winston Harte, Alexander Barkstone, and Michael Kallinski. Allison and her women guests were nowhere in sight, and these three stood huddled in front of the window next to the refectory table set up as a bar for the evening.

Meandering across the floor, Shane glanced about with interest, struck at once by the beauty of this main room in the cottage, which was really two dwellings knocked into one. He remembered that Allison had recently finished decorating it, and she had done wonders with the place. The low, beamed ceiling and wide stone fireplace—both Tudor—gave the setting its real character, but the colorful cretonnes covering the sofas and chairs, the old pine furniture, and Sally Harte's dreamlike watercolors on the white-washed walls contributed much to its intrinsic charm. It was a rustic country room, free of pretensions and fussiness, yet eminently comfortable and cozy, the kind he liked. He made a mental note to congratulate Allison the minute he saw her.

As soon as Shane drew to a standstill in front of his friends, the banter started.

They joshed him unmercifully about being late and made innumerable innuendos about the real reason behind his tardiness. He took it all with good humor, laughed good-naturedly, and shot back a few missiles of his own. The strain and tension eased out of his aching muscles, and he started to relax at last, feeling comfortable and at home with the three men. And within minutes he was responding fully to their warmth, affection, and friendship, and to the carefree mood, the jollity that prevailed here this evening.

At one moment he took a cigarette, brought his lighter to its tip, and as he did he thought fleetingly of Dorothea's virulent condemnation of his set, their world. Well, she had been correct in one sense—they were extremely clannish, he had to admit that. If they clung together, it was because they had been brought up with each other, had always been close and intimately involved on every level. Blackie, Emma, and David Kallinski, Michael's grandfather, had seen to that. *They* had been through a lot together in the early days at the turn of the century, sharing their terrible struggles and later triumphs, and it was from them that the unbreakable bonds of friendship sprang. That extraordinary trio, founders of three powerful Yorkshire dynasties, had been tight most of their lives, from the day they had met in fact, and devoted thereafter, right up to David's untimely death in the early sixties. Because their children and grandchildren had been thrown together since birth and in the ensuing years, it was only natural that a large number of them remained staunchly loyal, the dearest of friends, and constant companions.

What the hell, Shane thought, filling with a spurt of impatience with himself. Why do I worry about *her* opinions of *us?* This is the way we are, the way we live; and what's more we genuinely care about each other, deeply so. And we've always been there for each other in times of trouble and grief—just as our grandparents were before we were born.

Winston, misunderstanding Shane's sudden silence, said to the others, "Okay, chaps, let's give him a breather. What would you like, Shane? A Scotch?"

"No thanks. Just soda water, please."

"What's the matter with you tonight?" Winston asked as he filled the glass. "It's not like an Irishman to be imbibing this innocuous stuff."

Shane grinned as he took the drink. "Too much champagne earlier. But I must say, none of you seem the worse for wear, and you were *all* knocking it back like sailors on shore leave." Looking at Michael, he went on, "I assume your parents are still in Hong Kong, since they weren't with you at the christening."

"Yes. They get back in two weeks, and then I leave for New York. I hope we can get together, Shane. Where will you be staying?"

"At Aunt Emma's Fifth Avenue flat until I find a place of my own. And I'll be bloody furious if you don't phone me." Shane now glanced past Winston. Valentine Stone, Michael's girlfriend, was coming back into the room from the garden, followed by Marguerite Reynolds and a blond girl. He guessed she was Allison's American friend and the reason for the dinner party. He waved to them, then took Michael's arm. "Do I notice a ring on Valentine's finger?"

"Yes, but it's on her right hand, not her left, you idiot!" Michael Kallinski made a face, chuckled. "You'll be the first to know when I decide to take that ghastly step, Shane."

Alexander cut in, "Just listen to the man . . . we all know she's got you where she wants you, Mike."

"You've got room to talk," Michael shot back. "Marguerite has you pinioned down in the same position, flat on your back in a stranglehold, gasping for air."

They all laughed.

Alexander flushed and retorted, "Don't be too sure." He hesitated, then volunteered, "One thing is certain though, Grandmother likes Maggie, approves of her. *She* thinks I should pop the question now before some other fellow steals her áway from under my nose. Some confidence Emma Harte has in her grandson, I must say." Alexander shook his head, took refuge in his usual reserved shell, observing Maggie out of the corner of his eye. She looked stunning tonight in a scarlet pants suit, her light brown hair swept up in an old-fashioned pompadour. Perhaps he *should* take his grandmother's advice.

Shane, who had flinched inside at Alexander's words, said in a low voice, "Don't let her escape. Aunt Emma's right, she's quite a catch, Sandy, and such a nice girl."

Michael added, "And the world *is* full of predatory males, as we all know, Alexander. You'd better do what E.H. says before it's too late."

Shane swung to Winston. "And where's *your* lady love hiding herself."

"What?" Winston asked, pulling himself away from thoughts of Emily. He frowned. "What are you talking about?"

"*Allison.* Where is she?" Shane stared at him and went on, "I haven't said hello to my hostess yet."

"Oh! Yes, Allison. She dashed off to the kitchen just before you arrived," Winston said quickly, trying to cover his lápse. "She'll be back in a second. She went to see if the two local girls she hired for the evening are coping. In the meantime I'd better take you over to the guest of honor and introduce you; otherwise Allison'll have my guts for garters." Winston gave Shane a knowing wink. "Allison's friend lives in New York. If you behave yourself tonight, she might even agree to go out with you."

"I won't have time for women. I'll be far too busy with the hotel. Stop trying to fix me up, Winston," Shane remonstrated, then thought to ask, "Anyway, what makes you think I'd be interested?"

"Because she's rather nice," Winston replied.

Shane made no comment, followed his friend down the long room to the fireplace where the three women stood chatting.

The tall, slender blonde watched them approaching, trying not to give the appearance of doing so, instantly struck by Shane O'Neill's undeniable presence even from this distance. In fact she had been aware of him the minute she had returned to the living room. Allison had told her who and what he was . . . the young scion of a famous Yorkshire family, the most eligible of bachelors, and one who had been born with a golden spoon in his mouth, the money to buy himself the world if he wanted. He also had the looks to take him wherever he wanted. And right into *any* woman's bed, if he so wished, she decided. Allison had not exaggerated.

Shane kissed Valentine and Marguerite, and Winston said, "Skye, I'd like you to meet Shane O'Neill. Shane, this is Skye Smith from New York."

They shook hands, exchanged greetings.

Shane said pleasantly with a friendly smile, "I hear this is your first trip to Yorkshire. Are you enjoying it?"

"I'm loving every minute. It's so beautiful . . . the Dales are breathtaking. Allison's whizzed me all over this past week, buying antiques, so I've seen a lot of your glorious countryside."

"Allison's the expert, so I'm sure she helped you find some really interesting things. You're in the same business, Winston tells me," Shane remarked.

"Yes, I have a small antique shop on Lexington Avenue, in the Sixties. And fortunately a lot of good customers who are hungry for English antiques and silver." She laughed lightly. "I've bought up half of Yorkshire, and now I'm worrying about storing everything I'm having shipped home next week. My shop's going to be bursting at the seams."

Valentine said, "Allison told me you came across some beautiful old Victorian silver in Richmond. Surely you won't have a problem selling those pieces. And immediately."

"No, I won't," Skye said and gave them a detailed description of every item of silver now in her possession. Winston excused himself and ambled off. Shane lolled against the fireplace, bored with the subject of antiques and only vaguely listening to the women's chatter. He studied the American girl. She was charming; certainly she was good-looking, personable, and obviously very bright. Still he had known at once that she was not his type. Cool, pristine blondes who looked like Scandinavian ice maidens had never appealed to him much. He preferred dark exotic women. Like Paula. He crushed the thought of her.

After a polite interval had elapsed, he said, "I really ought to go and find Allison. Please excuse me." With a brief nod he disappeared, went down the narrow hall, making for the kitchen. But as he passed the small intimate dining room, he spotted Allison through the open door. She was surveying the table intently.

"There you are, Mrs. Ridley!" he exclaimed, striding inside, pulling her to him, enveloping her in a bear hug. "Congratulations! The cottage looks lovely. Now, why are you hiding from me? I've begun to think you're punishing me for being so late."

"Not you, Shane darling. You can do anything—I'd never be angry with you."

"You'd better not let Winston hear you say things like that. You'll make him jealous."

The merriment left Allison's face, and she said in a tight voice, "I'm not so sure . . ."

Shane threw her a questioning look. "What's that supposed to mean?"

Allison shrugged, bent over the table, and moved a small silver bird closer to its companion, averting her head.

Shane's face was a study in perplexity as he waited for her to finish fiddling with the table decorations, to respond to his question. When she did not, he took her arm gently, turned her to him. He immediately perceived she was upset.

"Hey, what's wrong?" he murmured softly, staring down into her bleak face.

"Nothing. Really and truly—" she began and broke off, wavering. Finally she said in a great rush of words, "Oh, I'm not going to lie to *you*, Shane. Winston's been funny with me since he arrived tonight. Not himself. Distracted." Her light gray eyes searched his face. "Did something happen this afternoon . . . something that might have upset him?"

Shane shook his head. "Not that I know of, Allison."

"I think it must have. If it didn't, then his odd behavior must have something to do with me, with us. Perhaps he's lost interest in me."

"I'm sure you're wrong."

"I'm *not*, Shane. I know Winston almost as well as you do. Generally he is sunny-tempered, and he's warm and affectionate. We've been getting on wonderfully these last few months. So much so, I had the feeling he might propose soon. He's been sending out signals . . . he told me how much his father liked me and, perhaps more importantly, Emma Harte. When he arrived earlier, I noticed a chance in him . . . he was different, preoccupied. He got here late, when he'd promised to come before the other guests to help me move the refectory table and do a few other things—and you know he's never late. That didn't matter of course. But he was cool, even a bit brusque, and naturally I was taken aback. He did soften during drinks, after Alexander and Maggie had arrived, but frankly he *is* distant. It's not like him in the least—being so moody, I mean."

Shane was more baffled than ever. He ran the events of the afternoon through his head, wondering if something had occurred which had disturbed Winston. But nothing untoward had happened to his knowledge, and Winston had seemed untroubled to him.

He said, "Listen, maybe it *is* something to do with business. That seems to be the most plausible explanation to me. Yes, it must be a business worry." He offered her a reassuring smile. "I'm convinced his attitude has nothing to do with your relationship. And he's certainly not lost interest in *you*. How could you think that?"

She looked at him for the longest moment and smiled regretfully. "A woman senses these things."

Shane exclaimed, "You're reading this the wrong way, imagining the worst." He took her hand, tucked it through his arm, and walked her to the door. "Come on, let's go back to the sitting room and I'll buy you a good stiff drink. I could use one myself." His eyes were warm with affection. "You'll see, Winston will be his old self with you."

"You sound more certain of that than I feel," she replied softly. But she brought a carefree expression to her face as she returned to her guests, clinging to Shane's arm, thankful to have his moral support.

Later in the evening, when they were at dinner, Shane decided that Allison had been right in one respect: Winston was not entirely himself.

He sat at the head of the table, and although he was pleasant and charming, played the good host to the hilt, Shane detected an abstracted look flickering behind his eyes, recognized the forced note in his laughter, the falseness behind his joviality.

To distract everyone's attention and to give Winston breathing space, Shane became the life and soul of the dinner party. He was gregarious, outgoing, witty, and amusing. He was particularly attentive to Allison, on whose right he sat, was pleased that she responded in a positive way, and appeared to be more relaxed and at ease as the evening progressed.

But it was she who brought the meal finally to an end when after dessert she said, "Let's have coffee and liqueurs in the sitting room, shall we?"

"That's a splendid idea," Winston exclaimed, smiling at her more warmly than he had since his arrival. He was the first to rise and ushered Allison and the other women out of the dining room. Shane followed with Michael and Alexander at his heels.

Winston went immediately to the refectory table, where he began to pour different liqueurs for the women guests. Shane strolled over to him and, striving to be casual, said, "Make mine a Bonnie Prince Charlie, please."

"Since when have you been drinking that awful stuff?" Winston asked, looking up. He grinned, turned back to his task of pouring white *crème de menthe* over the crushed ice he had spooned into a goblet.

"Don't sound so disapproving. You used to like it as much as I did when we were kids, gulping it down wholesale when Aunt Emma wasn't looking."

"Yes, and if I remember correctly, we both used to get bloody sick on it. But okay, if that's what you want." Winston filled a glass with the liqueur, handed it to Shane with another grin, and finished pouring cognacs for Michael, Alexander, and himself.

Shane stood watching him. At last he asked in a low voice, "Are you okay?"

Winston lifted his head sharply. "Of course I am. Why do you ask?"

"You've seemed a bit out of it tonight."

"It's been a long day, hectic. I am a bit weary, I'm afraid. Do me a favor, toddle over to Skye and ask her if she's changed her mind about an after-dinner drink, whilst I dutifully dispense these to the others. Allison will be back in a minute with the coffee." Winston picked up the tray and walked across the room, whistling under his breath.

Shane's eyes followed him, narrowing thoughtfully. Winston seemed normal enough now, and perhaps he had spoken the truth when he had claimed fatigue. Shane sauntered over to Skye Smith, who sat on the wide stone hearth by herself. "You're not drinking. Try this," he said in a commanding tone, handing her the glass.

She took it, sniffed it delicately, and looked up at him questioningly.

"It's a Bonnie Prince Charlie," Shane explained.

"What's that?"

He laughed. "Drambuie. Go on, take a sip; it won't poison you."

She did as he said and nodded her approval. "It has an unusual taste. I like it. Thank you, Shane."

"Don't move. I'll be right back." He returned a moment later with a Drambuie for himself, sat down next to her, and clinked her glass with his. "Cheers."

"Cheers." Skye glanced at him out of the corner of her eye. He *was* handsome. Perhaps too handsome. Men who looked like Shane O'Neill terrified her. They were usually untrustworthy . . . too much temptation fell into their paths.

Shane savored his drink for a minute, then put his glass on the hearth and asked, "Do you mind if I smoke a cigar?"

"No, not at all. And tell me something—why is Drambuie called Bonnie Prince Charlie?"

"Because when Bonnie Prince Charlie went to Scotland in 1745, trying to regain the throne of his ancestors, he was aided by a Mackinnon of Skye. In gratitude Prince Charlie gave the man his own recipe for his personal liqueur. Ever since then, the secret for its preparation has remained with the Mackinnons, and Drambuie gets its nickname from the legend. And speaking of the Isle of Skye, is that how you spell your name . . . sky with an *e* at the end?"

"Yes, but my name is really Schuyler. It's Dutch. A family name. I have a feeling my Mom thought plain old Smith needed jazzing up a bit." She smiled at him slowly.

"It's a very pretty name. It suits you," he said with a show of gallantry.

"Why thank you kindly, sir."

They fell silent.

Skye Smith was trying to decide whether she could suggest he call her in New York without appearing forward. She was not interested in him as a lover; on the other hand she had found herself drawn to him during dinner, almost against her will. He was entertaining, good company, and a delightful man, if a little vain and too sure of himself. But perhaps they could be friends.

Shane was still dwelling on Winston, discreetly observing him. He lounged on a sofa at the other side of the room, nursing his brandy, looking relaxed. Whatever problem had been bothering him earlier had apparently been resolved or dismissed as unimportant. He was laughing suddenly in a natural manner and teasing Allison. Shane noticed that her face was radiant. So much for all that, he thought, it was a storm about nothing. He filled with relief. He was going away tomorrow, and he did not like to think he was leaving when his dearest friend had troubles.

Skye finally spoke, interrupting Shane's contemplations. She said, "I hope this doesn't sound pushy or anything like that, but if I can be of help in New York, do feel free to call me." She added quickly, wanting to sound more businesslike, "The shop is listed under Brandt-Smith Antiques."

"That's very kind of you. I will," Shane said and startled himself with his ready acquiescence to her suggestion. He puffed on his cigar for a second; then, feeling the need to explain, he went on, "I don't know many people in New York. Just a couple of lawyers who work for our company. Oh, and I have an introduction to a man called Ross Nelson. A banker."

"Oh," she exclaimed.

Shane glanced at her, saw the surprise in her eyes. Or was it shock that had registered? "So you know Ross," he said, his curiosity flaring.

"No. No, I don't," she replied too swiftly. "I've heard of him, read about him in the newspapers, but that's all."

Shane nodded, and for a reason he could not fathom, he immediately changed the subject. But as they talked about other things, he could not help thinking that Skye Smith was much better acquainted with the notorious Mr. Nelson than she wanted him to believe. And he asked himself why she had felt the need to lie about this.

Shane O'Neill left Yorkshire the following morning.

It was dawn. The mist had rolled down from the moors and the higher fells to spread across the meadows like a mantle of gray lace, partially obscuring the trees and the drystone walls and the cottages nestling in the folds of the fields. And all were inchoate images, spectral and illusory under the remote and bitter sky. Dew dripped from the overhanging branches, glistened on the white wildflowers gleaming in the hedgerows, ran in little rivulets down the grassy banks at the sides of the lane. Nothing stirred in the drifting vaporous mists, and there was an unearthly quiescence, an unmoving stillness lying over the whole of the countryside, and it was a dreamlike landscape . . . the landscape of his childhood dreams.

Gradually, from behind the rim of the dim horizon, the early sun began to rise, its streaming corridors of slanting light piercing outward to illuminate the bowl of that cold and fading sky with a sudden breathtaking radiance. And through the tops of the leafy domes of trees, caught in the distant shimmer of sunlight like a mirage, glittered the chimneys of Pennistone Royal. House of his childhood dreams. But there was another house in his childhood dreams . . . a villa by the sea where they had laughed and played and dreamed away the careless carefree days of their childhood summers, where nothing had ever changed and time had been an eternity.

And she was always there with him . . . at that villa high on the cliffs above the sunlit sea, laughter in her eyes the color of the summer sky and gentleness in her smile that had truly been only for him. Dreamlike landscapes . . . dreamlike houses . . . dreamlike child of his childhood dreams . . . locked in his heart and mind for all of time . . . haunting him always, dim shadows on his Celtic soul.

He was going away now . . . so far away . . . leaving them behind. But he never left them behind. He carried them with him wherever he went . . . and they would never change . . . they were his childhood dreams . . . Paula and Pennistone Royal and the villa by the sunlit sea . . . .

The car sped on down the narrow winding country lanes, past the great iron gates of Pennistone Royal, on through the village of the same name, out now onto the main road. Shane glimpsed the familiar signs flying by . . . South Stainley, Ripley, Harrogate, Alwoodley.

He slowed down as he roared into Leeds, although there was no traffic, no one abroad, deserted as it was at this hour and without a sign of life. Gray, grimy, vital Leeds, great industrial city of the north, the seat of Emma's power and his grandfather's and David Kallinski's family.

Circling City Square, where the statue of the Black Prince dominated, he passed the post office and the Queen's Hotel and plunged on, down the short hill near City Station, heading toward the M1, the road leading south to London. Shane picked up speed the moment he rolled onto the motorway, and he did not reduce it until he was nosing the car over the county boundary . . . leaving Yorkshire behind.

Fifteen

The garden was her magical place.

It never failed to give Paula a sense of accomplishment and satisfaction, and it was therapeutic when she was frustrated or needed a release from the stresses and tensions of business. Whenever she began to plan a garden, whether large or small, she gave free rein to her imagination, and every plot of ground that fell into her sure and talented hands was miraculously transformed, became a breathtaking testament to her instinctive understanding of nature.

In fact she was an inspired gardener. Flowers, plants, trees, and shrubs were woven into a tapestry of living color and design by her, one that stunned the eye with its compelling beauty. Yet despite her careful planning, none of her gardens ever looked in the least contrived.

Indeed there was a genuine old-world air about them, for she planted them with an abundance of old-fashioned flowers and shrubs that were typically English in character. The garden, which she now called her own and which she had been working on for almost a year, was beginning to take on this particular look.

But for once she was hardly aware of the garden.

She stood poised at the edge of the terrace, gazing down the long green stretch of lawn, yet not really seeing it, an abstracted expression on her face. She was thinking of Jim. Their quarrel of last night had been dreadful, and although they had eventually made up—in bed, where they usually managed to put aside their mutual anger—she was still shaken. They had quarreled about Edwina. Again. And in the end he had won, since she was hopelessly weak where he was concerned, loving him the way she did. And so she had finally agreed to entertain Edwina tonight, to show her the house and the grounds, to offer her cocktails before they went out to dinner. But Paula wished now that she had been more resolute with him. In the early hours of the morning, after he had made love to her, he had cajoled, teased, and laughed her into agreeing to do as he wished. He had cleverly twisted her around his little finger, and she resented it suddenly.

Sighing, she walked purposefully over to the rockery she was creating, trying to shake off the remnants of the violent quarrel. I refuse to harbor a grudge, she told herself firmly. I've got to let go of my anger before he comes home tonight. She knelt down, continuing the work that she had started earlier that day, hell-bent on bringing order to that intractable pile of stone, filled with the intense desire to make this rockery as beautiful as the one at Grandy's seaside house.

As usually happened, Paula soon lost herself entirely in gardening, concentrating totally on the work, allowing the tranquility of nature to lap over her until she was enfolded by its soothing gentleness, at peace within herself.

•••

It was as a child that Paula had discovered her love of the earth and all growing things. She had been eight years old.

That same year Emma had bought a house to use during her grandchildren's spring and summer holidays from school. It was called Heron's Nest, and it stood on the high cliffs at Scarborough, overlooking the pale sands and the lead-colored bay beyond, a piece of Victorian gingerbread with its intricately wrought wood portico, wide porch, large sunny rooms, and a sprawling garden that was a veritable wilderness when Emma had first taken title to the property.

Aside from wanting a place where she could spend the holidays with her young brood and enjoy their company, Emma had had another valid reason for purchasing Heron's Nest. She had long felt the urgent need to have her grandchildren under her complete control and influence for uninterrupted periods. Her objective was simple. She wanted to teach them a few of the essentials of life, the practicalities of everyday living, and to make sure that they understood the true value of money. Emma had for years found it intolerable that most of her children had grown accustomed to living in luxury without giving one thought to the cost of their pampered existences and that they were overly dependent on armies of servants to take care of even their simplest needs.

And so, in her inimitable way, she had devised a scheme when she had decided that her grandchildren must be brought up to be less spoiled, more self-reliant, and certainly down-to-earth where matters of money were concerned. "There's an old Yorkshire saying, and it goes like this—" she had remarked to her investment banker, Henry Rossiter, one day, "from clogs to clogs in three generations. Well, you can be damned sure that that's not going to hold true for my lot!" Immediately afterward she had signed the check for the house.

Heron's Nest was the answer to many things in her mind. And it would become her school. To this end Emma had seen fit to engage only one maid, a local woman from the town who would come every day. And she had told the rather jolly, plump Mrs. Bonnyface that her main task would be to take care of the seaside villa when the family was not in residence. Emma had gone on to outline her rather unorthodox plans, had explained how she fully intended to run the house herself—with the help of her numerous grandchildren. Whatever Mrs. Bonnyface had thought of this unusual state of affairs, she had never said. She had accepted Emma's scheme with enthusiasm and had obviously felt privileged to work for the famous Mrs. Harte, if her general demeanor was anything to judge by.

Being clever and a dissembler of the highest order, Emma had not confided her intentions or motives in anyone else, least of all her grandchildren. Only after she had made the acquisition and hired Mrs. Bonnyface had she told them about Heron's Nest, but she had given glowing details, cloaked it with such an aura of glamor they had been agog with excitement. They regarded the whole idea of a house by the sea as a great adventure, since they would be alone with Emma and faraway from their parents.

Emma had realized almost immediately that the regime she had instituted had come as something as a shock, and she had smiled inwardly as she had watched them floundering around with mops and buckets, carpet sweepers and brooms, furniture polish and dusters, and unmanageable ironing boards. There had been huge disasters in the kitchen . . . demolished frying pans, pots charred to cinders, and vile, unpalatable meals. They had grumbled about burned fingers, blisters, headaches, housemaid's knee, and other minor ailments, real and imaginary, some of which had sounded extremely farfetched to Emma.

But it was Jonathan who had come up with the most inventive and imaginative excuse for wriggling out of his allocated chores, on the day he had told her that he had strained his Achilles tendons mowing the lawn, and was far too crippled to do any more work for days. Emma had been both startled and impressed by his cleverness. She had nodded most sympathetically. And to prove to this canny little boy that she was so much smarter than he believed she was, she had explained to him in diabolically graphic terms exactly how strained Achilles tendons were treated. "And so, since you're in such dreadful agony, I'd better drive you down to the doctor's office so that he can get to work on you immediately," she had said, reaching for her handbag and the car keys. Jonathan had swiftly suggested that they wait for a few hours, just in case the pain went away. Seemingly it did. He had made a stunningly rapid recovery, apparently not relishing the prospect of spending the remainder of the spring uncomfortably encased in a plaster of Paris cast reaching from the tip of his toes to his waist—or of being left behind with Mrs. Bonnyface when his cousins returned to their respective schools and his grandmother returned to Pennistone Royal.

During those first few weeks at the holiday house in Scarborough, they soon settled down to a steady routine. The girls quickly began to show a certain proficiency in their housework and cooking, and the boys readily learned to cope with the heavier household work, weeding the garden and mowing the lawns. Not one of them was ever permitted to shirk his or her duties. Emma was not the type to stand any nonsense for long, and she was relatively strict, showed no favoritism whatsoever.

"I've never heard of anyone dying from scrubbing a floor or polishing the silver," she was fond of saying if one of them dared to complain or invent an imaginary illness as Jonathan had done. The recalcitrant child who had screwed up enough nerve to protest or fib would instantly blanch under her steely green gaze, remembering Jonathan's narrow escape.

And when the time came for them all to pack up and leave the seaside house, Emma had congratulated herself, had admitted that they had been real troopers indeed. They had put on good faces and had truly pulled together to please her. As far as she was concerned, the experiment had proved to be an unconditional success. Every year thereafter, when the harsh Yorkshire winters gave way to the warmer weather, she had gathered them up and carted them off to Scarborough.

Eventually the Harte cousins and the O'Neill and Kallinski grandchildren became regular visitors. Even they were given their fair share of chores, and they had had no choice but to pitch in cheerfully when they arrived to spend July and August by the sea. They quickly came to understand that they would not be invited back if they did not comply with Emma's wishes and pull their weight.

The children had called Emma "The General" behind her back, and indeed they had often felt as though they were living in an army camp because of her stringent rules and regulations. On the other hand they had truly enjoyed themselves during those happy, carefree years, and they had ended up having such enormous fun together that even the chores were regarded as games.

Much to their parents' astonishment and Emma's immense satisfaction, each one had come to so look forward to those sojourns in the little seaside town that they vociferously declined any other holiday invitations. They had insisted on returning to Heron's Nest the minute Emma opened up the house.

Despite her own terrible addiction to work and little else, Emma had been shrewd enough to recognize that her "small band of brigands," as she called them, needed plenty of opportunities to let off steam and lots of pleasurable pursuits to fill the long summer days. "All work and no play makes Jack a dull boy, you know," she would constantly repeat to Mrs. Bonnyface and then proceed to invent exciting projects in which she and the children could participate together.

She took them on interesting expeditions up and down the coast, to Whitby, Robin Hood's Bay, and Flamborough Head, and gave them numerous other rewards for their strenuous endeavors. There were visits to the local picture house and the town's little theater; they went for leisurely picnics on the cliffs, sailed in the bay, and had swimming parties on the beach. Frequently they went fishing with the local fishermen and were thrilled when they were allowed to keep some of the catch. On those propitious days they would return in triumph to Heron's Nest, where they would cook their small and meager fish for Emma's supper, and she had eaten them as if they had been prepared by the French chef at the Ritz. When the weather was overcast and the seas rough, Emma had organized egg-and-spoon races and treasure hunts in the garden; and, since she truly understood the acquisitive nature of children, she made certain that the treasure was extra special and worth finding. And she had always provided more than enough items for each child, had usually dropped blatant clues to those who were coming up empty-handed and wearing tearful or disappointed expressions. On rainy days when they had to stay indoors, they had played charades or put on their own plays.

One year the boys formed their own band.

They called themselves the Herons, and Shane and Winston were the chief instigators and organizers. Shane appointed himself the band leader. He was also the piano player and the vocalist. Alexander played the drums and cymbals, Philip blew the flute, Jonathan scraped the violin, and Michael Kallinski warbled the harmonica. But it was Winston who thought he was the most important and talented member of the ensemble. He adopted the trumpet as his own and fervently insisted he was the new Bix Beiderbecke, inspired no doubt by a film Emma had taken them to see called *Young Man with a Horn*. Sarah wondered out loud where he had learned to play, and Emma smiled thinly and said that he hadn't, and that was the trouble. And at times she thought her eardrums would burst when the cacaphony of sound filled the house during practice times, which seemed never ending to her.

Eventually, when they believed themselves to be polished enough to perform before a live audience, the Herons invited Emma and the girls to a concert in the garden. Emma watched them in amazement, secretly amused by their elaborate and endless preparations. They put out deck chairs, set up a small stage made of planks balanced on bricks, and rolled out the piano to stand next to it. And they took great pains dressing themselves in what they called their "rig-outs"—their new white cricket flannels worn with brilliant scarlet satin shirts, made no doubt at one of the Kallinski factories, Emma decided.

Purple satin kerchiefs were tied around their necks and debonair straw boaters were rakishly angled on top of their heads.

Having caught a glimpse of them assembling on the stage, from her bedroom window, Emma immediately changed into a silk afternoon dress and hurried down the corridor to the girls' rooms. She insisted they wear their best cotton frocks in honor of the auspicious occasion, and they had all trooped out just after four o'clock dressed in their finery, curiosity and expectancy written on their pretty young faces.

As Emma listened to the Herons give their renditions of current popular songs and a couple of old ballads, she found herself enjoying the concert and was rather surprised to discover that they really weren't such bad musicians after all. At the end of their recital, she praised the boys, laughing with merriment as she showed her delight in them. The boys laughed too, and taking her lavish accolades to heart, they had gone on playing relentlessly all that summer, much to the horror of the girls. Whenever they heard them rehearsing, they made snide remarks, sniggered loudly, and declared that the Herons stank to high heaven.

Shane like Winston was exceptionally vain about his musical accomplishments and most especially his voice. He soon made certain that the critical young females were suitably intimidated. One night all of them found a foul-smelling object in their beds, ranging from frogs and dead fish with glassy eyes, to raw onions and bags of sulphur. Shane's retaliatory measure worked. After that dreadful night of changing sheets, opening the windows wide, and shaking Emma's good perfumes all over their rooms, none of the girls dared to use the word stinking for the rest of the holidays. At least certainly not in reference to the Herons.

And slowly but very deliberately over these years, Emma had strived to instill in every child the importance of the team spirit, playing the game, being a good sport, and abiding by the rules. Duty and responsibility were words forever on her lips, for she was resolute in her determination to arm each and every one of them with sound principles and the proper precepts for the future when they became adults. She taught them the meaning of honor, integrity, honesty, and truthfulness, amongst so many other things. But her frequently strong and tough pronouncements were always spoken with an underlying kindness, and she gave them a great deal of love and understanding, not to mention genuine friendship. And it was a friendship most of them were never to forget for the rest of their lives. Deep in her heart Emma regretted that she had neglected her own children at certain times in her life, when they were in their formative years and growing up. She wanted her grandchildren to benefit from the mistakes she had made in the past, and if some of this washed off on her great-nephews and nieces and on the grandchildren of her closest friends, then so much the better.

But of all the years they had spent in the tall old villa on the cliffs, that very first spring of 1952 had been the most meaningful to Paula, and it would live in her heart and mind always. That particular year she became aware of her affinity with nature and her overwhelming desire—the need in her really—to make things grow.

One blustery Saturday in April she wandered out into the garden with little Emily, whom Emma had put in her charge that day. Paula glanced around, her eager young eyes keenly observing, newly perceptive. The undergrowth had been cut away, the hedges neatly trimmed, and the lawns mowed to such perfection by the boys that they resembled bolts of smooth emerald velvet rolled out to touch the perimeters of the high stone walls. The piece of land behind the house was now uncommonly immaculate—and totally lacking in character.

She was amazed at herself when she unexpectedly realized how the garden *could* look if it was correctly planted. The eight-year-old girl had a vision, saw reflected in her child's imagination an array of textures and shapes and great bursts of color . . . luscious pinks and mauves, blazing reds and blues, brilliant yellows, warm ambers, oranges, and golds, and cool clear whites. She instantly envisioned dazzling mixtures of flowers and shrubs . . . plump bushes of rhododendrons with their delicately formed petals and dark polished leaves . . . pale peonies, waxlike in their perfection . . . splayed branches of azaleas laden down with heavy bright blossoms . . . masses of stately foxgloves brushing up against merry tulips and daffodils . . . and hugging cozily to the ground, dainty beds of pansies, primroses, and violets, and the icy little snowdrop scattered randomly under the trees.

And as she saw all this in her mind's eye, she knew what she must do. She must create the most beautiful garden—a garden for her Grandy. And it would be filled with every flower imaginable, except roses of course. For some unknown reason her grandmother hated roses, detested the smell of them, said they made her feel nauseous and she could not stand to have them in her houses or her gardens. She rushed into the house, bursting with excitement, her young face flushed, her eyes sparkling. Paula raided her money box, hurriedly breaking it open with her embroidery scissors.

As the pennies and threepenny bits and half crowns and shillings came tumbling out, Emily cried fretfully, "You'll get into trouble when Grandma finds out you've smashed your new money box and stolen the money."

Paula shook her head. "No, I won't. And I'm not stealing it. All this is mine. I saved it from my weekly pocket money." Armed with her precious hoard and with Emily trotting faithfully after her, she walked purposefully into the town.

As it turned out, Emily became something of a nuisance in Scarborough, and Paula soon began to regret bringing her along. Emily wanted to stop for mussels and winkles at the shellfish stand, then for lemonade at a nearby café, claiming she was hungry and thirsty, and in a burst of willfulness she stamped her foot.

Paula gave her a stern look. "How can you be hungry? We've just had lunch. And you ate more than anybody. You're growing more like a fat little porky pig every day." She hurried on, leaving Emily trailing behind, pouting.

"You're mean!" Emily yelled, and she increased her pace, endeavoring to keep up with her cousin's longer strides.

Paula glanced back over her shoulder and said, "I think you must have a tapeworm."

This was announced so suddenly and so fiercely that Emily stopped dead in her tracks. After a moment's shocked silence, she began to run after Paula as fast as her little legs would carry her. "What a horrid thing to say!" Emily shouted at the top of her lungs. She was terrified by Paula's words, and the mere thought of some huge worm growing inside her propelled her forward with urgency. "I don't have a worm! I don't!" She caught her breath and gasped, *"Do* I, Paula? Oh please, please tell me I don't. Can Grandma fish it out of me?"

"Oh, don't be so silly!" Paula snapped with growing irritation, intent on her purpose, anxious to find a flower shop selling bulbs and plants.

"I don't feel well, Paula. I'm going to be sick!"

"It's all that bread-and-butter pudding."

"No, it isn't," Emily wailed. "It's thinking about my worm. I feel awful. I'm going to throw up," the child threatened. Emily turned ashen, and her huge eyes swam with tears.

Paula was instantly filled with chagrin. She did love little Emily, and she was rarely unkind to her. She put her arm around the five-year-old's heaving shoulders and stroked her soft blond hair. "There, there, don't cry, Emily. I'm sure you don't have a tapeworm, really I am. Cross my heart and hope to die."

Eventually Emily stopped crying and searched the pocket of her cardigan for a handkerchief. She blew her nose loudly, then put her hand trustingly in Paula's and trotted along next to her quietly, tamed and subdued as they walked along the sea front past the many quaint old shops. At last she plucked up her courage and ventured timidly in a whisper, "But just suppose I do have it? What will I do about my—"

"I forbid you to discuss your nasty worm, you horrid little girl!" Paula exclaimed, her impatience returning. "You know what, Emily Barkstone, you're a pest. A *terrible* pest. I may send you to Coventry if you don't shut up."

Emily was crushed. "But you always say I'm your *favorite*. Do you mean I'm your favorite pest?" Emily asked, hurrying to stay in step, gazing longingly at her older cousin, whom she worshiped.

Paula started to laugh. She pulled Emily into her arms and hugged the small round child. "Yes, you're my favorite pest, Apple Dumpling. And because I know you're going to be a good girl and stop behaving like a spoiled baby, I'm going to tell you a very, very special secret."

Emily was so flattered that her tears ceased and her green eyes widened. "What kind of secret?"

"I'm going to make a garden for Grandy, a most beautiful garden. That's why we came to Scarborough, to buy the seeds and the things I need. But you mustn't say anything to her. It's a big, big secret."

"I promise, I promise!" Emily was excited.

For the next half hour, as the two little girls roamed from florist to florist, Paula kept Emily completely enthralled. She was articulate as she spoke about the wonderful things she was going to plant in her garden. She described the colors and the petals and the leaves and the scents of the flowers in detail, and Emily was so utterly enchanted and delighted to be part of such a grown-up enterprise she soon forgot about the tapeworm. Slowly, with painstaking care, Paula finally settled on her grandmother's favorite flowers and made her purchases. They left the last flower shop with a bag brimming with bulbs and packets of seeds and gardening catalogs.

When they reached the top of the street, Emily looked up at Paula and smiled with great sweetness, her round little face dimpling. "Can we go to the winkle stand now then?"

"Emily! You're being a pest again! You'd better behave yourself."

Emily paid no attention to this remonstration. "I've got a better idea. Let's go to the Grand for tea. I'd like that. We can have cream puffs and cucumber sandwiches and scones with strawberry jam and clotted cream and—"

"I don't have any money left," Paula announced with firmness, hoping to demolish this idea immediately.

"Scribble on the bill like Grandma does," Emily suggested.

"We're not going to the Grand, and that's final. So shut up. And look, Emily, stop dawdling . . . it's getting late. We'd better hurry now."

By the time the two little girls arrived at Heron's Nest, they had become firm friends again. Emily immediately volunteered to help, wishing to ingratiate herself with her cousin, as always seeking Paula's approbation and her love. She crouched on the ground, offering unsolicited advice in her piping child's voice. After watching Paula for a while, Emily said, "I bet you've got green fingers, if anybody does, Paula."

"It's a green thumb," Paula corrected without looking up, intent on her work. And she continued digging into the rich soil, planting her first flowers with supreme self-confidence, never doubting for a moment that they would flourish and grow. She was gathering up the garden tools when Emily startled her as she leaped up and let out a wild scream of terror.

"Oh! Oh!" Emily screeched, jumping up and down and brushing her skirt in a frantic fashion. "Oh! Oh!"

"What's wrong with you, you silly thing? You'll have Grandy out here in a minute, and then the garden won't be a surprise."

"It was a worm! Look, there near your foot! It was crawling on my skirt. Ugh! All slimy and wriggly." Emily had gone as white as chalk and she was trembling.

Paula was struck by her second inspired idea that day, and she cleverly seized the opportunity. She grabbed the trowel and jabbed at the worm, cutting it in half. She piled soil over it and gave Emily a cheerful and triumphant grin. "It must have been your tapeworm. I expect it left you of its own accord. And I've killed it, so now everything's all right."

Paula picked up the small box of tools and beckoning Emily to follow, she hurried up the garden path to the potting shed. She stopped suddenly and, after a minute's rapid thought, said, "But you'd better not mention anything about it to Grandy, or she might make you take some medicine just to be sure you don't get another."

Emily shuddered at the very idea.

Later that same summer, when Paula and Emily came back to the villa by the sea, they could hardly contain themselves when they saw the garden in full bloom. A profusion of flowers had sprouted up during their absence, and the many different species Paula had selected splashed the dark earth with their brilliant paintbox hues.

Emma was touched when, on their first day at Heron's Nest, the two girls led her through the garden, showing her everything that Paula had planted, looking up at her expectantly, watching her face for her reactions. Emily told her all about their trip into Scarborough, although she was careful to omit any mention of worms. Emma had been aware of their little expedition on that Saturday in the spring, but she pretended to be surprised. She praised them both for being so clever, and, recognizing Paula's potential as a budding horticulturist, she had encouraged her to pursue her hobby.

And so Paula's long and passionate love affair with gardening began that year. She had not stopped planting, weeding, pruning, and hoeing since then.

With Emma's approval, she had cultivated vegetable and herb gardens on her grandmother's Yorkshire estate, and eventually she had created the now famous Rhododendron Walk. The Walk took her years to plan, plant, and grow, and it was another example of her determination to excel at whatever she did, and in this instance it was a rather spectacular example of that.

But of all the gardens Paula had created, the one at Heron's Nest remained the dearest.

She was reminded of it this afternoon, seventeen years after she had started it, as she stood up and stretched. She pulled off her gardening gloves, placed them on the wheelbarrow, and stepped back to regard the rockery.

Finally it's beginning to take shape, she thought. Making Edwin Fairley's garden beautiful was giving her as much pleasure as her first garden had done.

After Edwin Fairley's death, Jim had inherited his house in Harrogate called Long Meadow. It was here that Paula had come to live as a bride almost a year ago. Although the house was sound and in good repair, it was badly in need of remodeling as well as redecorating. Conversely Edwin Fairley had seen to it that his gardener had tended the grounds religiously. Nevertheless they were bereft of color since little replenishing had been done as flowers and flowering shrubs had died. Paula had seen these deficiencies the moment it became hers and had itched to start working on it. However, the house took precedence; yet somehow she managed to cope with both at the same time, bringing wholly new aspects and fresh dimensions to both.

Glancing at the herbaceous borders, she decided that her dogged toil over the last eleven months *had* been worthwhile. The garden was her private world, and here she found escape and emotional enrichment as her business and personal problems fled.

Well, for a short while. For the last hour or so she had not given one thought to their quarrel of the night before. Now the memory of their heated words edged back. The problem was that Jim could be so stubborn. But then so could she and very often to her own annoyance. We both have to be more flexible, she thought; otherwise we're always going to be at loggerheads about certain matters. The funny thing was they hadn't really had any disagreements before their marriage and no serious quarrels until the problem of Edwina had arisen. They had certainly locked horns about her. She loathed her aunt; Jim was much taken with her. Therein lay the problem.

Quite unexpectedly Paula remembered something her grandmother had said to her last year, words spoken with love immediately prior to her wedding. They echoed with great clarity in her mind.

"Love is a handful of seeds, marriage the garden," Emma had said softly. "And like your gardens, Paula, marriage requires total commitment, hard work, and a great deal of love and care. Be ruthless with the weeds. Pull them out before they take hold. Bring the same dedication to your marriage that you do to your gardens, and everything will be all right. Remember that a marriage has to be constantly replenished too, if you want it to flourish . . ."

Such wise words, Paula thought, turning them over in her mind. She closed her eyes. Their quarrel was a weed, wasn't it? So she must uproot it. At once. Yes, she must toss it aside before it took hold. The only way to do that was to dismiss their differences about Edwina.

Paula opened her eyes and smiled to herself. She felt better all of a sudden. She pulled off her muddy Wellington boots, put on her shoes, and went into the house. She loved Jim. He loved her. Surely that was all that really mattered. Her heart felt lighter as she flew up the stairs to the nursery and their children.

Sixteen

Nora, the nursemaid who looked after the Fairley twins, sat sewing in a rocking chair in the nursery. As Paula's smiling face appeared around the door, she brought her finger to her lips and made a soft shushing sound.

Paula immediately nodded her understanding, mouthed silently, "I'll be back in a while. I'm going to take a bath."

After luxuriating in a hot tub for fifteen minutes, Paula felt rejuvenated. But as she dried herself vigorously, she had to admit that although the warm water had eased her tired body, this lovely sense of well-being sprang from the decision she had just made in the garden to be more understanding about Jim's feelings for Edwina. Yes, it was the only attitude she could take; she saw that clearer than ever. To adopt any other stance would be utterly self-defeating. She would simply rise above it all, as Grandy would do in similar circumstances. Her grandmother was too big a woman to succumb to pettiness, and she would try her level best to act exactly in the same way.

Paula put on a toweling robe and went back into the bedroom. This was spacious, with a high ceiling and a bay window overlooking the gardens, and it bore no resemblance to the way it had looked when Edwin Fairley had been alive. The first day Paula had seen the room, her heart sank as she had stood staring in horror at the dark blue-flocked wallpaper and the heavy, ponderous mahogany furniture crammed into the space. The bedroom had reflected the rest of the Victorian house, which was a dubious monument to a bygone age. All of the rooms had been old-fashioned, dark, lifeless, and depressing. The house had oppressed her with its gloomy, shadow-filled rooms and antiquated furniture and ornate festooned draperies and ugly lamps. She had wondered dismally how she could ever live at Long Meadow with any degree of comfort or happiness, or bring up children in such a bleak and dreary ambiance.

But Jim had insisted they move in, and he had refused point-blank even to take one look at the lovely old farmhouse which Winston had found for her at West Tanfield. And so she had been obliged to acquiesce to keep the peace, but only with the understanding that Jim allowed her *carte blanche* to renovate and redecorate the entire house. Fortunately he had agreed, and this she had done immediately before he had a chance to change his mind or tried to persuade her to live in the midst of the hopeless muddle of nondescript furnishings which his grandfather had so assiduously accumulated during his lifetime. The refurbishing of the house had been her parents' wedding gift to them. Her mother had helped her create a totally new look with such efficiency, boldness, and speed that even Emma had been surprised and somewhat amused by their ruthlessness. They threw out everything except a few good pieces of furniture, including Edwin's desk, a Venetian mirror, and a French Provincial armoire of light oak, as well as several relatively valuable oil paintings. The pale pastel colors she and Daisy had selected for the rooms instantly brought an airy lightness to the house and opened it up to introduce a feeling of great spaciousness and freedom. Pretty fabrics, porcelain and jade lamps, and the charming country antiques her mother had found added charm, liveliness, understated elegance, and comfort.

The dark blue bedroom was transformed into a bower of yellow, white, peach, and pale green, with these clear colors repeated throughout in the floral wallpaper and matching fabrics and in the Chinese lamps. Although Jim had voiced the opinion that the white carpeting was rather impractical, he had afterward acknowledged that the room was lovely and in perfect taste. And to Paula's relief he had liked the rest of the house.

Their bedroom looked sunny and restful this afternoon as she padded across the floor to the dressing table which took pride of place in the wide and curving bay window. She sat down and, after brushing her hair, applied her makeup in readiness for the evening ahead. Her thoughts lingered on her grandmother. How lovely she had looked at the christening; she had been so charming and gracious, so alive with energy and spirit that everyone else had paled in comparison. Jim had said the same things about her grandmother over dinner on Saturday night at the Red Lion in South Stainley, where they had gone to dine alone. Then he had lapsed into one of his strange silences for a few minutes, and she had known he was thinking of his grandfather.

Paula put down her lipstick, swiveled in the chair, and sat staring into space, remembering the night Jim had first brought her to this house to meet Sir Edwin Fairley K.C.

The scene played for her again, vividly alive in her mind.

He had been dozing in front of the fire in the small, pine-paneled library, and he had roused himself when they arrived, had walked across the floor, smiling warmly, his hand outstretched, a frail, white-haired old man, lovely in his gentleness and courtesy. When he had been only a few feet away from her, his step had faltered as he had seen her more clearly in the dimming light. Shock struck his face, and he had looked as if he had seen a ghost as Jim had introduced them. And of course he had. He had seen a reflection of Emma Harte in *her,* although she and Jim had not understood this at that time. But he must have dismissed the resemblance as mere coincidence because he had recovered himself almost immediately. And then during drinks he had asked her what she did, and she had said she worked for her grandmother, Emma Harte, as Jim did, but that she was employed at the stores. He had started violently in the chair, stifled a gasp, and stared at her more intently. His eyes were suddenly alive with burgeoning interest and an unveiled, avid curiosity. He had asked her about her parents and her life, and she had answered him frankly. He had smiled and nodded and patted her hand and told her she was a lovely young woman, that he approved of this match. She had met him several times after that first occasion, and he had never been anything but welcoming, obviously overjoyed to see her. After she and Jim had broken up, he had apparently been disconsolate and extremely distressed as their rift had widened, Jim had told her.

Sir Edwin had died before they had reconciled and then married, with Emma's blessing.

She had asked her grandmother innumerable questions about Edwin, once *their* old story was out in the open and no longer relegated to the closet along with the other skeletons Emma had hidden there.

Emma, who had hitherto glossed over certain aspects of her early life, had suddenly been quite willing to talk, and she had been surprisingly candid. She had told Paula how she had become involved with Edwin when she had been a servant at Fairley Hall, how they had drawn together after both of their mothers had died. She spoke of the moors and the Top of the World and the cave where they had sheltered from the raging storm and where Edwin had seduced her. "Oh, but Edwin Fairley wasn't a bad person," Grandy had said to her only a few weeks ago, when they had been discussing things again. "Just terribly, *terribly* weak, and afraid of his father, and hidebound to his class. Naturally. That was the way it was in those days. We're going back over sixty years, you know. Still, I've often wished that he hadn't been so cowardly, that he had made some sort of effort to help me when I was carrying his child. Then perhaps I wouldn't have hated him so much."

Emma had shrugged. "But there you are, that's the way it happened. I survived, didn't I? I was sixteen and about to have an illegitimate child, and because I didn't want to bring shame to my father, I ran away to Leeds. To Blackie. He was my only friend in my dreadful predicament. And Laura, of course, though Blackie wasn't married to my lovely Laura at the time. I had the baby, obviously. You know the rest."

Paula had asked her why she had called the child Edwina. "A peculiar, rather unfortunate slip of the tongue," Emma had replied with a dry laugh. "When I wasn't thinking. Or rather, perhaps I should say when I was thinking about Edwin."

"But how on earth did you manage, Grandma?" Paula had next asked, her eyes full and her heart aching as she had pictured the young Emma's awful ordeal, one she had had to face alone and penniless and without her family.

"Ah well, I had a couple of things going for me," Emma had remarked with an odd smile, "and they pulled me through." Paula had quietly insisted that she elaborate further, and Emma had said, "Well, let's see. I had my strength of character, my physical stamina, a few brains, not such bad looks, and most importantly an implacable will to succeed. Plus a hell of a lot of courage, now that I think about it. But that's enough of my life story today." And at this point Emma had brought the conversation to an abrupt halt.

Now Paula thought: Edwin Fairley was not only weak, he was unconscionable in the way he treated her. She shifted her thoughts to her grandmother and was overwhelmed with pride and enormous love for her. Emma Harte had been strong, and because of her great strength and her immense courage, she had conquered the whole damned world. She had stood tall and still stood tall. Edwina suddenly flashed through her mind. That child born a Fairley had caused Emma nothing but heartache from the day she had been born. And that's one of the reasons I can't bear being near her, Paula muttered. Why doesn't Jim understand? she asked herself and squashed this question instantly. Edwina had caused *her* problems recently, but only because she herself had allowed that to happen. Edwina is insignificant in the scheme of things. Grandy said so weeks ago, and as usual she is absolutely right.

The clock struck the half-hour. Paula glanced at it, saw that it was four-thirty. She had no more time to waste, she realized, pulling herself away from her reflections. Jumping up, she went to her clothes closet, found a pair of gray flannel pants and a white silk shirt, dressed in them swiftly. Her step had a ring of decisiveness as she walked across the upstairs hall and into the nursery.

Nora peered out of the tiny kitchen, once a large cupboard that Paula had had remodeled into a nursery pantry. She was holding a baby's milk bottle and said, "I was about to feed them, Mrs. Fairley."

"Then I'm just in time to help you, Nora." Paula bent over the cot nearest to her. Tessa was now wide awake, gazing up at her through eyes as stunningly green as her great-grandmother's, and she suddenly began to gurgle and kick her little fat legs in the air. Paula picked up her daughter, holding her tightly, kissing the child's fuzzy head and soft downy cheek, her heart clenching with love. She held Tessa for a second longer before returning her to the cot. Immediately the baby girl began to cry.

Paula glanced down at Tessa, and there was joyful laughter in her voice as she said, "Well, my goodness, aren't you the rambunctious little one, Miss Fairley. But we don't play favorites in this family. I have to give your brother a few kisses too, you know, and a little bit of attention as well."

Almost as if she had understood, the baby girl stopped her wailing.

Paula stepped over to the other cot to see Lorne staring at her solemnly. She lifted him out, hugging him as fiercely as she had his sister, experiencing the same profound emotions of protectiveness and tender love.

"Oh, you darling," she whispered against his cheek, so warm and wet with slaver. "Your father is right, you're a little poppet." She kissed Lorne, held him away from her, and shook her head, grinning broadly at him. "But you're always so serious, Lorne. You remind me of a little old man. Goodness me, you have such ancient worldly eyes, and you gaze at me as if there's nothing you don't know."

Paula walked over to the small loveseat in front of the windows and sat down. She bounced Lorne up and down on her knees and the baby seemed to enjoy this, since he at once started to chortle and slaver, and he waved his clenched fists as if he was happy and glad to be alive.

"I'll feed Lorne since I have him, Nora, and you can take care of his more vocal sister," Paula said.

"Yes, Mrs. Fairley." Nora smiled at her, glanced over at Tessa's cot. "She is a little minx, I must admit. She certainly wants to make sure we all know she's here."

Paula and Nora chatted desultorily about the babies and matters pertaining to their care as they fed the twins. At one moment Paula explained that she had adjusted her timetable and office hours again so that she could fit in with the schedule the twins were currently following. Then she went on, "So I'll be home early every day to help you feed and bathe them. But I won't be able to spend bath time with you tonight, I'm afraid, Nora. We're having guests for drinks before we go out to dinner."

"Yes, I understand, Mrs. Fairley." Nora brought Tessa upright in her arms. She laid the baby against her shoulder and patted her back. The little girl burped loudly several times.

This brought a smile to Paula's face.

Nora said, "Isn't she a pickle! She'll find a way to make herself heard, no matter what. But she's a good baby; so is Lorne."

Paula nodded. "Let's be thankful for that. But, you know, both my mother and my grandmother seem to think that Tessa's going to be the maverick in the family." She smiled to herself, mulling this over, and leaned back against the cushions, concentrating on Lorne.

Paula cherished these quiet times with her children, away from the bustle and frantic pace of her hectic working life. All was peace and gentleness in the large yet cozy nursery, with its white-painted walls and furniture, with blue and pink accents, and nursery-rhyme paintings hanging on the walls. Golden sunlight filtered in through the filmy curtains blowing gently in the light breeze, and there were the mingled smells of babies, talcum powder, boiled milk, freshly ironed clothes permeating the air. She looked down at her son, so contentedly sucking on his bottle, and stroked his small fair head. How lucky I am, she mused. I have so much to be thankful for—these adorable healthy beautiful babies . . . Grandy and my parents . . . a job that excites me, and most important of all the most wonderful husband. Quite suddenly she couldn't wait for Jim to get home from the newspaper so that she could tell him how much she loved him and how much she regretted their ridiculous quarrels about their aunt.

"I'm glad everything's gone well on your first day, Emily, but don't overdo it this week. You sound awfully tired," Paula said. "Please try and pace yourself properly." She sat back in the chair, dragging the telephone across the white wicker desk as she did.

"Oh yes, I will, don't worry," Emily exclaimed, her voice rising slightly as it came over the wire. "Grandy's already told me to keep regular office hours, not to try and gulp everything down all at once. But it's so exciting here at Genret, Paula, and I've so much to absorb and learn. Len Harvey is a super person, we're going to get on fine together. He says we'll probably go to Hong Kong next month. On a buying trip. We may even go into mainland China. Something to do with purchasing pigs' bristles or whiskers."

Paula's laugh rang out. "What on earth are you talking about?"

"*Brushes.* Made of pig's bristles. They're the best, so I understand. Paula . . . it's quite amazing here. I hadn't realized how much merchandise we bought abroad. Genret is the biggest importing company in England. Well, *one* of the biggest. We stock everything . . . false eyelashes, wigs, cosmetics, silks and satins, pots and pans—"

"Not to mention pigs' whiskers," Paula teased. "Yes, I knew that, Emily, and I think this job is going to be marvelous for you. A lot of responsibility— but I know you can handle it. To tell you the truth, Apple Dumpling, I miss you already, and this is only your first day over there."

"I feel the same way. I shall miss working with you, too. Still, it's not as if we're disappearing from each other's lives. What made you call me Apple Dumpling just then? You haven't for years."

Paula smiled into the phone. "I've been gardening today, making a rockery, and I kept thinking about the first garden I planted . . . at Heron's Nest. Do you remember that day I took you into Scarborough—"

"How could I ever forget it. I've been terrified of worms ever since," Emily cut in with a light laugh. "And I *was* an apple dumpling then, wasn't I? More like a roly-poly butterball."

"But not anymore, little one. Listen, would you like to join us for dinner tonight? We're going to the Granby . . . at least I think that's where Jim's decided to take us."

"I'd love to, but I can't, I'm afraid. Anyway, who's *us?*"

"Sally, Anthony, and Aunt Edwina."

"Oh God, I don't envy you, Paula," Emily groaned. "I would come if I could, just to give *you* moral support. However—" She broke off and giggled. "I have a rather special date."

"Oh! Who with?"

"My secret lover."

"And who's that?" Paula asked quickly, her curiosity aroused.

"If I told you, he'd no longer be my secret lover, now would he?" Emily replied mysteriously. "He's someone extra special and gorgeous, and when the time comes—if it comes, that is—you'll be the first to know." Laughter shaded her voice.

"Have I met him?" Paula probed, as usual feeling protective of Emily.

"I refuse to say one more word about him." Wanting to change the subject, Emily asked in a more sober tone, "By the way, why did Grandy go to London this afternoon?"

"She said something about pulling a new wardrobe together, for her trip with Blackie to far-flung places. Why do you ask?"

"That's what she said to me, but I just wondered if there was another reason. She always tells *you* everything."

"What other reason *could* there be?" Paula asked, sounding baffled.

"Well . . . she popped in to see me a little while ago, and she looked as if she was on the war path. You know that expression she gets on her face when she's about to do battle. *Implacable* is the best way to describe it, I suppose."

Paula was thoughtful at the other end of the phone. She stared out at the garden, a frown marring her smooth brow. "I'm sure she doesn't have any business in London, Emily," she said after a short pause and laughed dismissively. "Besides, you ought to know by now that Grandy always looks implacable. It's become her normal expression. Also, she was probably in a hurry when you saw her. Mummy and Daddy were driving back with her, and she wouldn't have wanted to keep them waiting in the car. I know the clothes are preoccupying her. She told me yesterday that they're going to be hitting a lot of different climates and that they'll be gone for three months. Let's face it, Emily, she has quite a task ahead of her selecting the appropriate things."

"Perhaps you're right," Emily conceded slowly, not entirely convinced. "She's very excited by the trip, Paula. She's done nothing but talk about it to me all weekend."

"It'll do her good, since it's the first real holiday she's had in years. And she can't wait to see Philip and visit Dunoon. She always had such wonderful times there with my grandfather. And listen, Dumpling darling, talking of my baby brother, I'm going to have to hang up. When he telephoned from Sydney yesterday, I promised I'd write to him today and tell him all about the christening. I must get the letter out of the way before Jim gets home."

"I understand. Thanks for ringing, Paula, and I'll see you later in the week. Give Philip my love. Bye."

Paula murmured her goodbye, replaced the receiver, and immediately started her letter to Philip. Her young brother was recuperating from a bout of pneumonia, and she and her parents and her grandmother had all agreed it was unfair and unnecessary to drag him from Australia just for one day. As she wrote, Paula relived the weekend, filling the letter with details about the church ceremony, the reception afterward, along with news of the entire family and their mutual friends, especially the O'Neills and the Kallinskis.

She stopped after three pages in her small neat script and looked up, thinking about Philip. They had always been close and were good friends, and she missed him. She was aware that Philip missed her too, and their parents and Grandy, and that he was sometimes awfully homesick for England. On the other hand, Dunoon, their sheep station at Coonamble in New South Wales, had fired his imagination since his childhood, and she believed it now held his complete affection. Also, running their vast Australian holdings, which their grandfather, Paul McGill, had left Emma, was a tremendous challenge. She knew Philip more than relished his job. He had settled down at last in this past year and had started to make a full and complete life for himself out there, and she was glad of that. She finished the letter, addressed and sealed the envelope, then stood up, walked to the far end of the room. She bent down and picked up several blossoms which had dropped off a bright pink azalea, laid them in an ashtray on a ceramic drum table, and then glanced around, wondering whether to serve drinks in here or in the drawing room.

Although Paula thought of this favorite room as her very own private spot in the house, it had fallen into general use lately. She often found Jim reading here, and most of their guests automatically gravitated to it. In actuality the room was a conservatory, typical of those built onto Victorian mansions in the second half of the nineteenth century, after Joseph Paxton had pioneered the use of iron girders as support for glass houses. Paula considered the large conservatory, like the garden, one of the few real assets at Long Meadow. It was Gothic in design, and she had filled it with tropical green plants, small trees, and exotic orchids, plus a lovely array of small and colorful flowering shrubs. The fir-green carpeting, and the green and white ivy print she had chosen for the wicker furniture and skirted tables produced a cool restful ambiance, and the conservatory appeared to flow out into the grounds beyond the glass walls. Since Paula's redecoration, it provided an extra sitting room as well as a study for her in the refreshing environment of a garden that grew the year round.

As she turned around, her eyes fell on one of her prized hydrangeas; she was concerned to see that it had developed discolored edges. She continued to examine it thoughtfully until the shrilling telephone forced her to return to her desk. She answered it with a bright "Hello?"

"And how's the little mother?" Miranda O'Neill asked in her lovely, lilting voice.

"I'm fine, Merry. How're you, lovey?"

"Exhausted if you want to know the truth. I've had my nose to the grindstone all day, and I was in the office most of yesterday, developing my idea for the Harte boutiques in our hotels. I believe I've formulated some really workable plans. I want to show them to my father tomorrow, and then I thought we might get together later in the week if you have time."

"Of course I do, and I must say you've been awfully fast and extremely diligent."

"Thanks. Aunt Emma was most enthusiastic when I spoke to her on Saturday, and I didn't want to lose any time. As your grandmother always says, time is money. Besides, if we're going to do it, the areas for the boutiques must be included in the new architectural blueprints, and those will be on the drawing board soon."

"I realize there's a time element involved here because of your building and remodeling program, Merry. So let's meet on Wednesday. About two o'clock?"

"That's perfect for me, and let's do it in my office." Miranda chuckled and said, "Isn't it fabulous news about Aunt Emma going off on a world tour with Grandpops? We're all thrilled at home."

"So are we . . . it'll do them both good."

Merry said, "You should have seen him this morning. I couldn't believe it when he showed up at the office bright and early. There he was behind his desk, where he hasn't been for months, making phone calls, hustling and bustling, and driving that poor old secretary of his crazy. He kept saying to her, 'First class, *first class,* and all the way, Gertie! This has to be a deluxe trip.' Aunt Emma's agreeing to go with him has given him a new lease on life—not that he really needed one, actually, since he's always so *up* and bubbly. But do you know, he got quite miffed with me when I mentioned my idea about the boutiques. He actually bellowed at me to keep Emma out of it, said that he didn't want my piddling bit of business interfering with his Plan with a capital P. It took me ages to calm him down."

"How did you manage to do that?" Paula asked, laughing under her breath, trying to envision Blackie in a rage, which was rather difficult to do.

"When I finally got a word in edgewise, I said Aunt Emma wasn't involved, that you were and that *we* could cope very well without *either* of them. Then he beamed and said I was his clever darling girl but just to be sure to keep out of his way for the next few days because he was very preoccupied and extremely busy. Anybody would think they were going off on a honeymoon."

"Well, he did give her the ring, you know, Merry."

"Isn't it *sweet.* They're a couple of lovely old dears, aren't they?"

Paula burst out laughing. "I'd hardly characterize *my* grandmother and *your* grandfather as a couple of *old dears.* Blackie and Emma are more like firecrackers, in my opinion. And weren't you the one who told me only the other day that they were incorrigible when they got together?" Paula reminded Miranda.

Merry had the good grace to laugh with Paula, and she admitted, "That's true, I did, and you're right. And by the way, talking of Aunt Emma, I don't know what to buy her for her eightieth birthday. I've been wracking my brains for days. Any suggestions?"

"You've got to be joking! We all have the same problem. Mummy and Daddy were discussing it with me over lunch today. And Emily's been nagging me to think of something she can get. Frankly, I'm at a loss, like you and everyone else."

"Well, let's compare notes again on Wednesday," Merry said. "I'd better go, Paula. My father's waiting for me. We have to go over some of my rough drafts for the press release—about the acquisition of the hotel in New York. I hope to God he likes *one* of the versions; otherwise I'm going to be at my desk until midnight. Not that that would be anything unusual," Miranda grumbled. "I seem to have become a workhorse lately. No wonder I don't have any private life these days."

"I just told Emily to take it easy at Genret. And you'd better do the same, Merry," Paula cautioned.

"Listen who's talking!" Miranda said and laughed hollowly.

Seventeen

Since the conservatory opened directly off the marble-floored entrance hall, Paula heard Jim's footsteps the moment he entered the house. She was standing near the fading hydrangea plant, holding the discolored leaf in her hand, and she turned, expectancy and warmth filling her face.

"Hello, darling," she said, as he came down the two steps, and moved swiftly toward him, her eagerness to see him most apparent.

"Hello," he replied.

They met in the center of the room. He gave her a light kiss, then lowered himself into a chair without saying another word.

Paula stood staring down at him, puzzlement in her eyes. He had sounded so apathetic, and the kiss was so perfunctory she knew he was not himself. She said instantly, "Is there something the matter, Jim?"

He shook his head. "Just tired," he said, smiling that bland, dismissive smile she had come to know so well. "There was an accident on the Harrogate road, quite a pileup of cars because of it, and it slowed the traffic. We crawled along for miles. Frustrating . . . exhausting, actually."

"How awful. I'm sorry. That's all you needed. Let me fix you a drink," she suggested, not entirely satisfied with this explanation but making up her mind not to press too hard for the moment.

"That's a good idea," he exclaimed in a stronger tone. "Thanks, a gin and tonic should hit the spot."

"I'll just go for some ice," she said and made to leave the conservatory.

"Ring for Meg. She can bring it." He frowned. "The bell's not broken again, is it?"

"No, but it'll be quicker if I go," Paula said, pausing with one foot on the step, glancing over her shoulder.

"I wonder sometimes why we have a maid," he said with a hint of irritation, looking up, leveling his pale grayish blue eyes on her.

She stared back at him, detecting criticism in his tone and manner, but she remarked with evenness, "She's awfully busy right now, and anyway Grandy brought us up not to be overly dependent on servants, as I've told you so many times." Not waiting for a response, she hurried out, but she heard his pained sigh as she went into the hall. Maybe it *is* only weariness, a hard day at the paper, the difficult drive home, plus the hectic weekend, Paula thought, endeavoring to persuade herself that these were the real reasons for his peculiar mood. He wasn't often moody, at least not exactly like this. As she pushed open the kitchen door, she noticed she was still holding the leaf. It was mangled in her hand. Relax, she instructed herself, his moodiness means nothing. He'll be more like himself after a drink.

Meg said, "Do you think I've made enough canapés, Mrs. Fairley?" She indicated the silver tray, pausing in her work.

"Yes, that's plenty, Meg, and they look delicious. Thank you. Could you fill the ice bucket, please?" Whilst the maid busied herself at the refrigerator, Paula threw the leaf in the rubbish bin and washed her hands at the kitchen sink.

Jim had risen in her absence, and he was standing looking out into the garden when Paula went back to the conservatory with the ice. His face was in profile; nonetheless she could not fail to miss the morose curve of his mouth, and when he swung around, his eyes were vague.

Questions flew to her tongue, but she bit them back and hurried to the skirted table, which held bottles and a tray of glasses. Pouring his gin and tonic, she said without turning around, "I thought we'd have drinks in here later, or do you prefer the drawing room?"

"Wherever you wish," he replied in a disinterested voice.

Striving for a normal manner, she continued steadily, "Did you book at the Granby after all, Jim?"

"Yes. We have a table reserved for eight-thirty. Anthony called earlier today and said they wouldn't be able to get here until seven-fifteen. That gives us an hour to relax."

"Yes." Anxiety was rising in her. He *was* strange, there were no two ways about it, and she wondered if their quarrel of the previous evening still lingered in the back of his mind, rankled perhaps. But why would it? He had won, and anyway he had been chatty and pleasant at breakfast. But she resolved to get to the root of whatever was bothering him. She also decided to have a vodka and tonic, even though she hardly ever drank hard liquor.

Jim seemed to visibly cheer up as he sipped his drink. He lit a cigarette and asked casually, "Heard from anybody today?"

"Emily, Merry O'Neill. And Grandy, of course. She rang me just after you left this morning to let me know she was going to London for a few days." Paula now looked directly at him, took a deep breath. "Why are we making small talk, Jim, when you're troubled? I know something's wrong. Please tell me what it is, darling."

He was silent.

She leaned forward intently, her unwavering eyes holding his. "Look, I want to know what's bothering you," she insisted.

Jim sighed heavily. "I suppose there's no point putting it off . . . I had a bit of a set-to with Winston today, and—"

Paula laughed with relief. "Is that all! Well, you've had clashes with him before, and they always blow over. So will this—"

"I've resigned," Jim announced flatly.

She looked at him uncomprehendingly, totally at a loss for words. Slowly she put down her drink. Her dark brows drew together in a frown. *"Resigned?"*

"As managing director of the company, that is," he added quickly. "Effective immediately."

Thunderstruck, she continued to gape at him. She found her voice and it rose slightly as she asked, "But *why?* And why didn't you mention it to me, tell me what was on your mind? I simply don't understand . . ." She did not finish her sentence, sat tensely in the chair.

"There was nothing to discuss. You see, I didn't know I was going to resign—until I did."

"Jim, this is perfectly ridiculous," she said, attempting a laugh. "Just because you had a little row with Winston doesn't mean you have to do something as drastic as this . . . after all, Grandy has the final word, you know that. She appointed you; she'll reinstate you at once. She'll put Winston straight, deal with him. Look, I'll speak to her tomorrow, ring her first thing in the morning." She gave him an encouraging smile, but it faltered as he held up his hand with an abrupt movement that was uncharacteristic.

"I'm afraid you're misunderstanding me. Winston didn't force me to resign or anything like that, if that's what you're thinking. I did so of my own accord. I wanted to, and rather badly, although I must admit in all truthfulness that I didn't realize this until the opportunity presented itself. So I certainly don't want to be reinstated."

"But why not, for heaven's sake?" she cried, her perplexity and concern mounting, rising to the surface to cloud her face.

"Because I don't like the job. Never have. When Winston came to see me this morning, he asked me point-blank if I wished to continue as managing director; and as he was speaking, I knew—really *knew*, Paula—that I didn't. I've never been particularly good at administrative work or interested in it, and I told Winston so, and he said he'd sensed this for some time. He pointed out that perhaps it would be better if I stuck to journalism, ran the papers but not the company. I thoroughly agree with him, so I stepped down. That's all there is to it, actually," he shrugged, smiled faintly.

"All there is to it," she echoed incredulously. She was aghast at what he had done and at his attitude. "I don't believe I'm hearing *you* say these things. You're acting as if it didn't matter, as if this wasn't serious, when it's terribly serious. And you're being so cavalier, so dismissive, I'm absolutely staggered."

"Don't get so het up. Frankly, *I'm* filled with relief."

"Relief should be the last thing on your mind," she said in a small dismayed voice. "What about duty? Responsibility? Grandy showed a great deal of faith in you, put her trust in you when she appointed you managing director last year. *I* think you've let her down and rather badly."

"I'm sorry you feel that way, Paula, because I must disagree with you. I haven't let Grandy down," he protested. "I'm still going to be managing editor in charge of two of the most important newspapers in the Consolidated group. I'll be doing what I do best, being a newspaperman and a damned good one at that." He sat back, crossed his legs, and returned her penetrating stare with an unblinking gaze. His expression was adamant.

"And who's going to run the company, now that you've stepped down?"

"Winston, of course."

"You know very well he doesn't want that job."

"Neither do I."

Paula's lips drew together in aggravation. Another thought struck her, and she exclaimed fiercely, "I hope this sudden and rather extraordinary decision of yours doesn't mean that Grandy will have to cancel her trip with Blackie. She really needs that holiday. What did she say? I presume you've told her."

"Naturally I've told her. Winston and I walked over to the store at lunch time for a meeting with her. Your grandmother accepted my resignation, Winston's agreed to take the job, and he didn't seem very perturbed about the idea either. Grandy isn't going to cancel her holiday—rest assured of that." He leaned forward and clasped her hand in his. "Come on, relax. You're the one who's more upset than anyone. Grandy and Winston respect my decision. They didn't quibble. In fact there was very little discussion . . . it was rather cut and dried, actually."

"You've simply misunderstood their reactions," she murmured, filled with misery.

Jim laughed. "Now *you're* being ridiculous, Paula. I know them both very well, and I can assure you that everything is all right."

Paula could think of no easy reply to this statement. She was astonished at his lack of insight, and his assumption that things were on an even keel showed extremely flawed judgment on his part. Jim obviously had no conception of what made her grandmother and Winston tick. *She* didn't have to think twice to know that they had accepted the situation because they had had no alternative. They would pull together to keep the company running smoothly. That's *our* way, she thought. We do our duty and accept responsibility, no matter how difficult that is. Things were far from *all right,* as he so glibly put it.

Jim was watching her, trying to ascertain what she was thinking, but her violet eyes were veiled, unreadable. He said anxiously, "Please try to see my point of view, understand my feelings about the situation. Your grandmother and Winston do. And don't let's argue about my resignation. Since it's a *fait accompli,* this is all rather silly, wouldn't you say?"

Paula said nothing. She leaned back in her chair, extracted her hand quietly, and reached for her drink. She took a quick sip. There was a protracted silence before she said, "Jim, I do wish you'd reconsider . . . there are other things involved here. Grandy was going to tell you this herself later in the week, but I know she won't mind if *I* tell you *now*. She's going to change her will. At the moment her shares in the newspaper company are part of the assets of Harte Enterprises, which as you know my cousins are to inherit. But she's decided to leave the newspaper shares to the twins—our children—so I know it's important to her that you're totally involved with the newspaper company and on every level. I don't care what she said to you this morning, I'm absolutely convinced she's terribly disappointed deep down because you've chosen to step away from the managerial side—"

Jim's brief laugh stopped her short. She looked at him, searched his face, wondering if she had imagined the edge to that laugh.

He said patiently in a soft, smooth voice, "Paula, whether I'm managing director, managing editor, or both, or neither, for that matter, your grandmother will still change her will. She'll leave those shares to our children no matter what and for several good reasons."

"What reasons?"

"They're Fairleys for one thing, and then there's her guilt."

Paula blinked, for a second not understanding what he was getting at; then quite suddenly she had a flash of insight, and she stared at him intently. She hoped she had misunderstood the implication behind his words. She took a deep breath to steady herself and asked very slowly, "Her guilt about *what* exactly?"

"Wresting the Yorkshire *Morning Gazette* away from my grandfather, grabbing control of the company," he said off-handedly, lighting a cigarette.

"You make it sound as if she stole it!" Paula tersely exclaimed. "You know very well that your grandfather ran that newspaper into the ground, and that certainly had nothing to do with Grandy. You've said often enough that he was a brilliant barrister but a lousy businessman. Surely I don't have to remind you that the other shareholders begged Grandy to take over. She bailed them out—and your grandfather, for that matter. He made a lot of money on his shares."

"Yes, you're correct—especially about him mismanaging the paper—but I suppose he would have muddled through, limped along somehow, and retained control, if your grandmother hadn't swooped down and scooped it up." He gulped some of his drink, drew on his cigarette.

"The paper would have gone bankrupt! Then where would your grandfather have been?" She glared at him. "In a mess—that's where!"

"Look here, Paula, don't sound so shocked. I'm only reminding you of the facts. We both know that Grandy ruined the Fairleys." He gave her an easy lopsided smile. "We're both adults, so we'd be rather silly if we tried to sweep all that under the rug, just because you and I are married. What happened did *actually* happen, you know. You and I are not going to change it, and it's certainly nonsensical for us to quarrel about it now, so long after the event."

Paula recoiled, gaping at him. Dismay had lodged like a rock in the pit of her stomach, and she was shaking inside. As his words echoed in her head, her patience evaporated, the tension of the last few weeks rose up in her, and something snapped all of a sudden. "She no more ruined the Fairleys than I did! It just so happens that Adam Fairley and that eldest son of his, Gerald, did it all by themselves. Whether you want to believe it or not, your great-grandfather and great-uncle were negligent, stupid, self-indulgent, and very poor businessmen. And besides, even if she had ruined them, I for one wouldn't blame her. I'd applaud her for settling the score. The Fairleys treated my grandmother abominably. And as for your sainted grandfather, what he did to her was . . . was unspeakable!" she gasped. "Unconscionable, do you hear! Fine upstanding young man Edwin was, wasn't he? Getting her pregnant at sixteen and then leaving her to fend for herself. He didn't even lift a finger to help her. As for—"

"I know all that—" Jim began, wondering how to placate her and stop this flow of angry words.

She cut him off peremptorily. "What you don't know perhaps is that your great-uncle Gerald tried to rape her, and believe you me, no woman ever forgets the man who has attempted *rape* on her! So don't start presenting a case for the Fairleys to me. And how dare you point a finger at my grandmother, after all she's done for you! Could it be that you're trying to gloss over your abdication of your duty to her—" Paula stopped herself from saying any more. Her emotions were running high, and she was so furious she was shaking like a leaf.

A sudden chill settled in the room.

They stared at each other. Both of them were appalled. Paula's face was so white her deep blue eyes seemed more startling than ever, and Jim's face was taut with shock.

His distress prevented him from speaking for a few seconds. He was stunned by her outburst and dismayed that she had chosen to totally misconstrue his words—uttered idly and rather carelessly, he now had to admit.

He finally exclaimed with great fervency, "Paula, please believe me, I wasn't making a case for the Fairleys or pointing a finger at Emma. How can you possibly think I would do anything like that? I've always respected and honored her, since the first day I worked for her. And I've grown to love her since we've been married. She's a wonderful woman, and I'm the first to appreciate everything she's done for me."

"That's nice to know."

Jim caught his breath, cringed at her sarcastic tone. "Please, Paula, don't look at me like that. You've misunderstood me completely."

She did not reply, averted her face, and stared at the mass of plants lining the glass walls of the conservatory.

Jim jumped up. He grabbed her hands and pulled her out of the chair, took her in his arms. "Darling, please listen to me. I love you. The past doesn't matter; Grandy's the first person to say so. I was wrong to even bring it up. What *they* all did to each other half a century ago has nothing to do with *us*. Somehow we've gone off the rails because of this . . . this discussion about my resignation. Everything has been blown out of proportion. You're overly upset about nothing. Please, please calm yourself." As he spoke, he led her to a loveseat and pressed her down, seated himself next to her, and took her hand, looked deeply into her face.

He said, "Look, I agree with you, Paula—what my grandfather did *was* unspeakable. And he knew that himself. He lived with a guilty conscience for the rest of his life. In fact his actions as a young man *ruined* his life in many ways. He confided that in me before he died. He never stopped regretting losing Emma and their child, nor did he stop loving her, and at the end all he wanted was your grandmother's forgiveness. When he was dying, he implored me to go to Emma and beg her forgiveness for everything the Fairleys had done to her, himself most of all. Don't you remember? I told you this, I spoke to Grandy about it the night she announced our engagement."

"Yes," Paula said.

"I repeated everything to Grandy—his last words just before he slipped away. He said, 'Jim, it will be an unquiet grave I lie in if Emma does not forgive me. Implore her to do so, Jim, so that my tortured soul can rest in peace.' And when I told Emma, she wept a little, and she said, 'I think perhaps your grandfather suffered more than I did, after all.' And Paula, Emma forgave him. She forgave all of the Fairleys. Why can't you?"

She lifted her head sharply, startled by the question. "Oh, Jim, I—" There was a short pause before she finished, "There's nothing for *me* to forgive. I think *you've* misunderstood *me?*"

"Perhaps. But you were so angry, shouting at me, going on about the Fairleys . . ."

"Yes, I did lose my temper, but you riled me when you said Grandy had guilt feelings. I know her, and far better than you, Jim, and I'm convinced she doesn't feel guilty about anything."

"Then I was wrong," he said with a weak smile. "I apologize." He was relieved she sounded more normal.

"You're wrong about something else too."

"What's that?"

"The past. You just said that the past doesn't matter, but I can't agree with you. The past is always coming back to haunt us, and we can never escape it. It makes prisoners of us all. Grandy might give lip service to the idea that the past is no longer important, but she doesn't really believe this. She's often said to me that the past is immutable, and it most certainly is in my opinion."

"The sins of the fathers and all that—is that what you mean?" he asked quietly.

"Yes."

Jim exhaled, shook his head.

Paula looked at him carefully. "I have a question. You might not like it, but I feel compelled to ask it." She waited, watching him closely.

He stared back at her. "Paula, I'm your husband, and I love you, and there should never be anything but complete honesty and directness between us. Obviously you can ask me anything. What's the question?"

She took a breath, plunged. "Do you resent Grandy? I mean because she's the owner of the *Gazette* and not you? If your grandfather had managed to retain control, you would have inherited the paper."

Jim's jaw dropped in astonishment, and he gaped at her; then he laughed. "If I had any resentment—or bitterness or jealousy—I'd hardly be resigning as managing director. I'd be scheming to get the paper for myself—at least, to get as much power as I possibly could. And I'd have been dropping hints to you long ago to influence Grandy to leave the newspaper shares to our children . . . so that I could get absolute control through their holdings. With that kind of clout at my fingertips, I would be kingpin in the company after Emma was dead. Actually, it would be mine in a manner of speaking, since I would be handling their business affairs until they came of age." He shook his head, still laughing. "Now wouldn't I have done that?"

"Yes, I suppose so," Paula admitted in a drained voice, feeling suddenly debilitated.

Jim said, "Paula, surely you realize by now that I'm not money hungry, nor particularly ambitious for power. I like running the papers, being managing editor—I admit that—but I don't want to be involved in business and administration."

"Not even when you know that the newspaper company will be your children's one day?"

"I trust Winston. He'll do a good job. After all, he does have rather a big stake in the Consolidated group when you consider that he and the Hartes own half the company. He controls forty-eight percent of the shares, don't forget."

Paula knew there was no point arguing with Jim any further about his resignation, at least not now. She stood up. "I think I've got to go outside . . . I need some fresh air."

Jim also rose, looking at her with concern. "Are you all right? You're awfully pale."

"Yes, really. Why don't you spend a few minutes with the babies before you change? I'll be up in a short while—I just need to take a stroll around the garden."

He caught her arm as she moved toward the door and swung her to face him. "Friends again, darling?" he asked softly.

"Yes, of course," she reassured him, conscious of the anxiety reflected in his eyes and recognizing the plea in his voice.

Paula walked slowly through the garden, circumvented the plantation of trees, and took the narrow path leading to the second lawn that sloped down toward the grove of laburnum trees and the pond.

She was considerably shaken by their quarrel, and her senses were swimming. She sat down on the steps of the white-painted summerhouse, relieved to be alone, to regain her equilibrium. She deplored the fact that she had lost control, flown into a temper, and her only excuse was the extreme provocation. Jim's remark that her grandmother was guilt-ridden about the Fairleys had been so inflammatory it had made her blood boil. The suggestion was ridiculous. Just as his resignation was ludicrous.

Although she was desperately troubled by that impulsive and irresponsible move on his part, her dismay about it had been jostled to one side by the impact of their collision. This last row was a lot more serious than one of their quarrels about Edwina. It had struck at an important fundamental in any marriage—trust. And it raised questions in her mind about Jim, his innermost feelings for her grandmother, and his loyalty to Emma. Her head was teeming with questions. Did he bear a grudge against Emma Harte because she now owned everything the Fairleys had once owned? Perhaps subconsciously, without really understanding that he did? It struck her and very sharply that this was not beyond the realms of possibility. After all, he had been the one to launch into the past, not she; and if the past didn't matter, as he had claimed, then why had he brought it up in the first place?

Were resentment and bitterness at the root of his statement after all? She trembled at this thought. Those were the most dangerous emotions in the world, for like cancer they gnawed away at a person's insides; they were destructive and colored everything a person did. Yet when she had asked Jim bluntly if he resented Grandy, he had obviously been flabbergasted by the idea, and his answer had been immediate, direct, and totally without guile. He had been genuine—she had seen that instantly. She had always found Jim relatively easy to read. He was not a devious man but was quite the reverse really, in that he was not constitutionally cut out to dissemble.

Paula leaned against the railings and closed her eyes, her mind working at its rapid and most intelligent best, assessing and analyzing. She had always believed she knew Jim inside out, but did she really? Perhaps it was arrogant of her to think she had such great insight into him. After all, how well did anyone know another person when one got right down to it? There had been times when she had found those who were closest to her, with whom she had grown up, difficult and even impossible to comprehend on occasions. If members of her immediate family and her oldest friends were frequently baffling, how could she possibly understand a man she had known for a brief two years, a man who might easily be termed a stranger even though he was her husband? She had come to realize that people could not always be taken on face value . . . most people were highly complex. Sometimes they themselves did not recognize what motivated them to do the things they did. How well did James Arthur Fairley actually know himself? And, come to think of it, how well did he know *her?*

These nagging questions hung in the air, and she finally let go of them, sighing, understanding that she had no ready answers for herself. She opened her eyes and looked down at her hands, so relaxed, curled in her lap. The tension had gone, and now that her anger had all but dissipated entirely, she was able to think objectively and with a cool head. She acknowledged that she had leaped down Jim's throat. Of course he had been awfully provocative, but that was no doubt unintentional on his part. They were both at fault, and if he had a few imperfections, then most assuredly so did she. They were both human. As he had defended himself against her strong verbal onslaught, she had heard the ring of truth and sincerity in his voice, had noted the genuine love written all over his face. It suddenly seemed inconceivable to her that Jim could harbor ill feelings for her grandmother. Furthermore she owed it to her husband to believe that he did not. Yes, she must trust him, must give him the benefit of the doubt. If she was not capable of doing that, then their relationship would be threatened. Besides, he had made a very salient point, one she could not now ignore. He had said he would hardly be resigning as managing director if he was embittered and felt that the *Gazette* was his by rights, that instead he would be making sure he grabbed all the power for himself. She could not deny that his words made sense. Anybody who was goaded on by resentment to get even, to win, would hardly be quitting the arena. He would be planning the *coup-de-grâce*.

Thoughts of his resignation intruded more sharply, but she clamped down on them with resoluteness. Wisely she decided she had better shelve that sensitive issue for the time being. It was hardly the time to start tackling him about that again when their guests were due to arrive shortly. And especially since Edwina was one of those guests. She most certainly wasn't going to let *her* see a chink in the armor.

Jim stood at the window where, from this angle, he could see Paula sitting on the steps of the summerhouse. His eyes remained riveted on her, and he wished she would come back inside. It was imperative that he smooth things over between them.

He had not meant any harm when he had mentioned that old worn-out story about Emma Harte ruining the Fairleys. But he had been tactless, no use denying it, and a bloody fool for not realizing that Paula would react fiercely. Jim exhaled wearily. She had overreacted in his opinion; after all facts were facts and quite inescapable. But then his wife was irrational about her grandmother, worshiping her the way she did. She wielded a club on anyone who dared to even hint that Emma was less than perfect. Not that he ever said a wrong word about her . . . he had no reason to criticize or condemn Emma Harte. Just the opposite, actually.

Paula's revelation about Gerald Fairley attempting to rape the young Emma edged to the front of his mind. It was undoubtedly true, and the very idea of it was so repellent to him that he shivered involuntarily. On the rare occasions Gerald's name had cropped up in conversation, he had divined a look of immense distaste and contempt on his grandfather's face, and now he understood why. Jim shook his head wonderingly, thinking how entangled the lives of the Fairleys and the Hartes had been at the turn of the century; still the actions of his antecedents were hardly his fault or his responsibility. He had not known any of them, except for his grandfather, so they were shadowy figures at best; anyway, the present was the only thing that mattered, that counted for anything.

This thought brought his eyes back to the window. He moved the curtain slightly. Paula was a motionless figure on the steps of the old summerhouse, lost in her contemplations. Once she had returned to the bedroom to change her clothes, he would sit her down, talk to her, do his damnedest to make up to her, apologize again if necessary. He was beginning to loathe these quarrels, which had become so frequent of late.

He ran his hand through his fair hair absently, a meditative look settling on his finely drawn, rather sensitive face. Paula could be right—maybe Emma was not in the least troubled by her past deeds. Now that he considered it objectively, in a rational manner, it suddenly struck him that she was far too pragmatic a woman to worry about matters that could not be altered. And yet he could not dismiss the sense of guilt he had detected in her from time to time.

Perhaps her guilt was centered solely on him, had nothing to do with those long-dead Fairleys. There was no question in his mind that Emma worried about him. This was the reason he had not been in the least surprised when Paula had mentioned the will, since he had always expected Emma to change it, to favor his children. He did not crave the shares for himself; nor could Emma leave him her interest in the papers without causing a stink in the family. And so Emma, being fair-minded and scrupulous, was doing her level best to make amends, to make things right and proper in the only way she knew how. She was giving Lorne and Tessa their birthright . . . the inheritance he himself would have willed to his children if his family had retained control of the newspaper.

Jim was completely convinced that genuine emotion motivated Emma. She had once loved his grandfather, and in consequence she cared deeply about him. There was not the slightest doubt in his mind about that. He might even have been her grandson if circumstances had been slightly different.

Yes, Grandy had shown her true feelings for him in an infinite variety of ways—he had hard evidence. He ran all of the instances through his head . . . she had given him the job as managing editor when there had been other candidates just as well qualified; she had ended her vendetta against the Fairleys because of him; she had blessed his marriage to her favorite grandchild. In fact Emma Harte was always bending over backward to please him, and she was on his side—her actions more than proved this. Grandy had persuaded Paula to live here at Long Meadow because he so wished it. She had acknowledged that the twins must be christened at Fairley church, and moreover, she had not objected when he had invited Edwina. It was only Paula who ever made a fuss about that unfortunate woman who had never done anybody any harm.

Jim shifted his stance impatiently, wondering how long Paula intended to sit out there. He glanced at his watch with irritation. If she did not come in within the next few minutes, he would go out and talk to her in the garden. He did want to make sure she understood one thing . . . Emma was not disappointed in him. That morning, when he had told her he wanted to resign, Grandy had agreed and said that she appreciated his honesty. "If that's what you want, then that's what you must do," Emma had said with a little smile. "I'd be the last person to stop you." Emma was compassionate and full of humanity, and she loved him in her own way. And he was loyal to her, devoted. There was a special bond between them. It was never mentioned, but it existed nevertheless.

Much to his relief Jim now saw Paula walking up the path. Thank God she was coming back to the house. His tension lessened, even though it was impossible from this distance to gauge her state of mind or to ascertain what her attitude would be. But then he always had trouble doing that. It seemed to him that she constantly had him on the edge, kept him guessing. She was tempermental, even difficult at times, but no woman had captivated him, ensnared him as she had. And she had done so without even trying. There was enormous chemistry between them, and their sexual attraction for each other was so strong it was overpowering. Paula was so intense, so serious, so complex she often left him floundering and baffled. Yet he found her depth and sincerity gratifying; equally he was thrilled by her passion, her desire for him in bed. The women he had been involved with before her had often complained about his sex drive. They seemed to think it was abnormal, were unable to cope, balked at his staying power. But not Paula . . . she never complained, always welcomed him with open arms, as ready as he to abandon herself to their lovemaking, and he could never get enough of her. He knew she felt the same.

Paula was the best thing in the world that had ever happened to him, and he was struck by this realization more and more every day. How lucky he had been to meet her on that plane journey from Paris.

He thought back to it now, remembering clearly every little detail of their first meeting. Her name had sounded familiar, and her lovely face had touched a chord in his memory, but he had not been able to place her. But later that night, restless, unable to sleep, haunted by her, everything had suddenly clicked into place. It had dawned on him that she was the daughter of David Amory, who ran the Harte stores, and that she was therefore the granddaughter of Emma Harte, his employer. He had been at once intimidated and dismayed, had not closed his eyes all night, worrying about the situation and the ramifications it involved.

The following morning, confused, disturbed, and ambivalent, he had wavered and wondered whether to cancel their dinner date planned for that evening. In the end he had been unable to resist seeing her again, had gone to the Mirabelle in a troubled state. He had been keyed up, anxious, and his heart had been in his mouth. After one of the waiters had made a remark about her grandmother, he had seen his chance. He had the perfect opening gambit, had asked her who her prestigious grandparent was, and Paula had told him without hesitation. She had made light of this, had made it easy for him, and surprisingly her relationship to Emma Harte had suddenly not mattered. His extraordinary feelings for Paula swept everything to one side, and he had fallen in love with her over dinner at the Mirabelle, had made up his mind to marry her—even if Emma sacked him and disinherited her heiress.

Jim recalled the night, a month after their first date, when he had finally succeeded in getting Paula into bed. Unexpectedly, erotic images of them together began to dance around in his head, made the heat rush through him. He knew what he was going to do the minute she walked in, knew how to put everything right between them. Words and long explanations were meaningless, inconsequential, now that he thought about it. Actions counted. Yes, his was the best way, the only way, to demolish the residue of their quarrel completely.

As Paula entered the bedroom, Jim saw that she was calmer, that her color was perfectly normal. He went to her, took her hands in his. "I can't bear these awful rows," he said.

"Neither can I."

Without saying anything else, he took her face between his hands and kissed her, his mouth working sensually on hers. His passion soared. He was at full arousal. His arms went around her, and he brought her closer so that she was positioned into the curve of his body. His hands slid down her back onto her buttocks, and he pressed her into him with impatience. She must understand the extent of his excitement, understand that he intended to possess her immediately.

Paula accepted his kisses and then quickly but gently pushed him away. "Jim, please. They'll be here in a few minutes. We don't have time—"

He silenced her with another kiss; then, breaking away from her, he led her to the bed. He pushed her down onto it purposefully, lay next to her, wrapped his long legs around her. In a voice thickened by desire, he said against her neck, "I must have you. *Now*. Quickly, before they arrive. We do have time. And you know we always make up, once we've made love. Come on, take your clothes off for me, darling."

Paula started to protest, not wanting this, wary of him, sensing she was being manipulated again. But he was already fumbling with the buttons on her shirt, and so she swallowed her words. It was far easier if she was compliant, as she had so quickly come to realize in the last year. Jim believed that sex solved every one of their problems. But of course it did not.

Eighteen

At six-thirty the following morning Paula left Long Meadow for the office, looking coolly elegant in a smartly tailored black linen suit and a crisp white silk shirt.

After a restless night of tossing and turning and worrying, she had risen earlier than usual. Only Nora had been astir at that hour, preparing the babies' bottles, and after she had showered and dressed, Paula had spent fifteen tranquil minutes with her and the twins in the nursery before going downstairs to the kitchen. As she had drunk a quick cup of tea, she had scribbled a note to Jim, explaining that she was facing a hectic day at the store and wanted to get a head start.

This was only partially true. Paula had the most urgent need to unscramble her jumbled thoughts and take stock of the situation. She could only do that when she was alone—and the only time she was not surrounded by people was either when she was gardening or driving.

As she pointed the car down the gravel driveway, she realized she was relieved to be escaping from the house. It seemed more suffocating than ever to her today. Although she enjoyed the grounds and the conservatory, Long Meadow would never really be her favorite place, despite the more attractive ambience she and her mother had created. As Grandy had said, "You've both done your best, but you can't make a silk purse out of a sow's ear."

And whatever Jim believed, the house *was* oppressive. Her grandmother felt the same way as she did and rarely came, preferring instead to have them over to Pennistone Royal. This aside, it was extremely difficult to run efficiently. It was poorly designed, had endless staircases, winding corridors, and dark landings. Meg and the daily char, Mrs. Coe, were constantly complaining, and even Nora, who was younger than they, had taken to grumbling about her aching legs lately. Jim made light of their complaints. He loved Long Meadow, and she knew he would not consider moving, so there was no point in dreaming about another house, one which was more practical and suitable for their needs.

He was selfish.

So jolted was Paula by this unexpected thought that she stiffened and gripped the steering wheel tighter. She stared ahead at the road, her eyes momentarily glazed by her troubles. What an unkind and disloyal thing to think, she chided herself. But try though she did to convince herself she was wrong about Jim, she did not succeed. It was the truth. For months she had tried to ignore this unfortunate and dismaying characteristic in him, had made perpetual excuses for him. Suddenly this was no longer possible. She had to stop deluding herself about Jim, look at the facts unflinchingly, accept that he only ever did what he *wanted* to do. He was deceptive in that he gave the impression of trying to please, especially with colleagues and friends and when small irrelevant matters were involved. Then he bent over backward to be obliging. When it came to major issues, he dug his feet in and always strove to get his own way, regardless of anyone else's wishes. That was the dichotomy in his nature, and it had begun to worry her.

Paula sighed to herself. They were both stubborn, but at least she was not inflexible. With a start, Paula recognized that Jim was absolutely rigid. This trait had been staring her glaringly in the face for months, yet she had been reluctant, perhaps even afraid, to acknowledge it.

She began to scrutinize the pattern of their life together for the past year, and now discovered that she could remember innumerable examples of that ingrained rigidity. There had been his refusal point-blank to accept a new plane from Grandy, not to mention the fuss about their wedding plans. He had been adamant when her grandmother had asked him to get rid of his rickety old four-seater plane, and suggested he buy a more up-to-date jet at her expense. Being conscious of his pride, Grandy had handled it diplomatically, had pointed out that she felt she should have a company plane at her immediate disposal, and who better to select the best piece of equipment and make the purchase than he. But he would not budge from his position, and Emma had thrown up her hands in exasperation at his intractability.

Almost immediately afterward he had told her parents and Grandy that he wanted to have their marriage ceremony at Fairley Church. They had all three been staggered by this suggestion, and so had she. Apart from the fact that the village church was far too small to accommodate some three hundred guests, her parents and Emma had wanted the wedding to be held in London, to be followed by a reception at Claridge's Hotel. It had been especially important to her grandmother that she have a lovely, elegant, and glamorous wedding. It was her mother who had scotched Jim's idea. Daisy had told him that the marriage arrangements were hardly his concern, since they were always the prerogative of the bride's parents. Clever, clever Daisy. She had won by simply pointing out the correct etiquette, the proper form. In this instance he had had no option but to back down.

But he had made a swift recovery, and the next battle had been about Long Meadow. Jim had been the winner that time but in a sense by default. She had only agreed to live there to keep the peace and also because her grandmother had told her to be accommodating. "Jim's ego and his masculinity are on the line," her grandmother had remarked. "I agree the house is a monstrosity, but he has a genuine need to be the provider, to give you a home on his own terms. You'd better accept the situation for now."

For this same reason she and Grandy had gone along with his wish to have the twins christened at Fairley Church, even though Emma had initially balked at this idea, had hardly been overjoyed to trek all the way to Fairley, of all places. She rarely went *there* these days.

Paula slowed down and stopped at a traffic light, mulling over this first year of marriage. People said it was the most difficult year, and perhaps it *was* inevitable that there would be a few unpleasant revelations. Whizzing up the short hill, she cruised past the Stray and turned onto the main road to Leeds. I suppose I might as well accept that the honeymoon is now definitely *over,* she muttered under her breath, then laughed ironically. He had even been contrary about their actual honeymoon, had whisked her off to the Lake District instead of to the sunny south of France. Wanting to please him, in love and feeling euphoric, she had accepted his decision, even though France had been more appealing to her. They had been greeted by inclement weather and thunderstorms when they had reached Windermere, and had spent the week shivering in front of the fire in their hotel suite, or in bed making love.

Her thoughts automatically settled on their sex life. She was in love with Jim and wanted him physically, had normal desires and a healthy attitude about sex. But lately it was growing more and more apparent to her that Jim was abnormally driven. His marathons were becoming tiring, even tedious. There were other things in a marriage as well as sex. He was insatiable, and endless, mindless sex was not particularly fulfilling to her. Sometimes she found herself wishing he had more finesse, a better understanding of a woman's body—*her* body, *her* needs. Loathe though she was to admit it, she knew deep within herself that Jim was just as selfish in bed as he was out of it, always pleasing himself, never giving a thought to her. It was growing harder and harder for her to cope with his need to make love all the time. Her work was demanding, and she craved sleep, but he was seemingly tireless.

Sudden anger flared in Paula as she considered the way he used sex as an antidote for their rows. Her resentment was increasing, because it was manipulative. It seemed incredible to her that he believed their problems evaporated into thin air once they were locked in a tight embrace. Of course that didn't happen; their difficulties were still there afterward. And naturally they remained unsolved.

Oh God, if only he would *talk* to me, Paula thought. He should communicate. Instead he retreats behind his charm and his jokes, and whenever I try to explain my feelings, he laughs me off. Yes, Jim had a childish tendency to pretend their differences did not exist. She could never get him to open up, try though she did. It occurred to her that she had reached an impasse. She had come to a turning point in her marriage. And after only one year, she said to herself wonderingly. Had she made a terrible mistake? Was divorce the only solution?

Horror trickled through her at the mere idea of breaking up and was quickly replaced by a rush of panic. Beads of sweat broke out on her forehead, and she began to tremble inside. Slowing the car to a crawl, she pulled onto the first side road she saw and parked. Leaning forward, she rested her head on the steering wheel and closed her eyes. Divorce was unthinkable. She was stunned that it had even crossed her mind a moment ago. She loved him . . . truly, truly loved him. And in spite of their problems they were compatible in so many important ways. And there were the twins . . . Lorne and Tessa needed a father, needed Jim as much as she needed him.

Instantly it struck her that she had been unfair to her husband, adding up his faults, mentally compiling lists of grudges against him when he was not present to defend himself. He was a nice man, a good man, and he had so many lovely qualities. She owed it to him to be scrupulously honest with herself about his manifold attributes.

Silently she began to tick them off in her head. He understood about her work. He appreciated her desire to be out there in the marketplace. Certainly he never interfered with her career; he did not grumble about her preoccupation with the stores, the late hours she kept. At least he's an enlightened man in that respect, she acknowledged swiftly, and he allows me to be myself. He's not threatened by me either. Furthermore he was obviously cut out to be a marvelous father; that was already evident. There was no question that he adored her, was devoted to her. Jim would never be a philanderer who played around with other women. He was strictly a one-woman man and totally geared to his family and family life, and she was thankful of that.

Straightening up, Paula smoothed her hair into place. I've got to make a go of this relationship, she told herself. It's vitally important to me, and I know it's essential to Jim. She remembered something her grandmother had once said . . . that it was always the woman who made a marriage work. Paula believed this. Her grandmother was wise and experienced; she had lived it all, seen it all. No one knew better about marriage than Emma Harte.

Paula resolved to be as understanding of Jim as she possibly could. She would put extra effort and time into their relationship. She would be loving and tolerant. It would be immature of her if she did not. After all, everybody had faults, and you didn't stop loving a man simply because he had a few imperfections. You loved him in spite of them.

Turning the ignition key, Paula started the car and backed out of the side road. Her mind began to revolve around her grandmother and Jim's resignation as she sped down the road heading in the direction of Alwoodley. Convinced though she was that Jim had totally misjudged Emma's reaction to his decision, she nevertheless hoped that her grandmother was not angry with him. She did not want Grandy to think badly of Jim.

Less than half an hour later, Paula sat behind her desk in her office at the Harte store in Leeds, talking to her grandmother, whom she had reached at the flat in Belgrave Square.

"I'm sorry to wake you up," Paula apologized, although she strongly suspected she had not done so.

Emma's warm and vibrant voice flowed over the wire and confirmed this as she said, "I was having my morning tea and waiting for your call. You want to talk to me about Jim, his resignation, don't you?"

"Yes, Gran. I was a bit floored last night when he told me what he'd done and naturally rather upset. I feel he's let you down and at the worst time, when you're about to go away. I can't help thinking that you must be disappointed in him."

"A little," Emma said. "However, I decided not to persuade Jim to retain the managing directorship . . . not under the circumstances. His heart's not in the job, Paula, and that's not good. It's better he steps down."

"Yes," Paula agreed quietly. "What about Winston? Is he frightfully annoyed?"

"Well, he was at first, and I thought for a moment he was going to explode when I told him he would have to take on the job. But he agreed almost at once. There's no one else, as you well know."

"I feel awful about this situation, Grandy. There's not much I can say except that I'm sorry. Jim shouldn't have done this in my opinion. I think it was irresponsible. *He* doesn't agree with me, of course." There was a fractional pause, and then Paula added, "I'm not trying to make excuses for him, Gran, but I've come to realize that Jim isn't like *us,* you know, as far as duty is concerned. We've all done jobs we haven't really liked during the years we've all worked for you. Those jobs never killed us, and we learned a lot from the experience. I know I shouldn't make comparisons, but last night when Jim was talking I kept thinking of little Emily—her example. She's been a brick, the way she's gone into Genret and with the best will in the world."

"That's true," Emma agreed, then added swiftly in a kinder tone, "You mustn't be too hard on Jim, Paula dear. People do have their limitations, and remember, he wasn't brought up in the same way as you and your cousins. Anyway, let's be grateful for his talent as a managing editor. He's brilliant, the best in the business, and that's why I gave him the job years ago. Now, if he'd resigned from that position, we *would* have a major tragedy on our hands."

"I realize that. He does love the newspaper business, and that's why he's so successful as a journalist." Paula was beginning to feel easier in her mind, and she went on, "I have to defend Jim in one respect . . . he's been honest with you, and we must give him credit for that. He's as straight as a die, Grandy."

"You don't have to tell me, Paula. Jim's not duplicitous, far from it, and I told him yesterday morning that I appreciated his truthfulness. Half-hearted, unenthusiastic executives spell disaster to me."

"Then you're not too angry with him?" Paula asked, clutching the phone tensely, holding her breath.

"That was only a passing feeling yesterday. It quickly dissipated," Emma said. "We can't let emotions take charge of us in business, we must always deal from intelligence; but then I've told you that all of your life. Sorry to keep repeating myself."

"That's all right, and I must admit I'm relieved you're taking this so well, Grandma. He'd never *intentionally* do anything to hurt or upset you."

Brushing this remark aside, considering it unimportant, Emma said, "I want you to relax, Paula. This is not really your problem. Anyway, we do have everything under control. Actually, when I was talking to Winston after Jim had left, it occurred to me—and rather forcibly—that things are not going to be much *different* at Consolidated. Winston was sitting there, grousing away, going on and on *ad infinitum* about being overworked, listing his present duties, demanding to know how I expected him to cope with everything. And as he talked his head off, I began to realize that he's actually been carrying the administrative and business load at Consolidated for the longest time. He's been functioning as managing director without knowing it. I told him so, told him he was now getting the title to go with his tremendous responsibilities, plus a large raise in salary. You know Winston has a great sense of humor, and he began to laugh. He said, 'Damn it, Aunt Emma, we both think we're so smart, so why haven't we realized before today how brilliant *I* am.' So, darling, you don't have to be concerned about me, Consolidated, or Winston either."

"I'm glad to hear that, Grandy. Look, can I ask you something? It's about the shares in Consolidated. Why are you changing your will and leaving your interest to the twins?"

"What a funny question. I thought I'd made it clear, thought that you'd understood me. Surely it's obvious—I'm leaving my shares in the newspaper company to the twins because they are *your* children, Paula. What other reason could there be?" Emma murmured, sounding extremely perplexed.

"None—I just wondered, that's all," Paula answered. "However, it struck me the other day that your decision might have something to do with Jim. You know, because he's a Fairley. I mean, if his grandfather had hung onto the *Gazette,* it would have been his today, wouldn't it?"

Emma burst into peals of laughter. "I very much doubt that," she gasped. Immediately recovering herself, she said, "Edwin Fairley would have lost the paper eventually, as I've told you before. Besides, the Fairleys owned only the Yorkshire *Morning Gazette,* none of the other papers in the Consolidated chain. You know I acquired those myself and with the help of my brothers." Her incredulous laughter reverberated down the wire again. "You can't possibly think that I feel *guilty* about the Fairleys," she spluttered, obviously highly entertained by this idea.

"Of course I don't," Paula exclaimed heatedly, wishing she had never brought the subject up, realizing that she had been right and Jim wrong all along.

"I should hope not, my darling girl," Emma said, stifling her merriment. "I've always admitted that I gave the Fairleys a few nudges and very sharp ones at that, as they waltzed down the path to folly which they had chosen for themselves. But I can assure you that I never once lost a wink of sleep about any of my actions. I was delighted I was able to turn the tables on them, come out the big winner. So don't think for one minute that I'm troubled by any guilty feelings about a lot of dead Fairleys or Jim for that matter. And if he has suggested such a thing to you, you can tell him from me that he's wrong, quite wrong."

"Oh no, he didn't bring it up," Paula lied smoothly, knowing such an admission would annoy her grandmother. "It was merely a thought that flitted through my active brain."

Emma chuckled under her breath at Paula's hurried response, uncertain of its veracity. She said, "I hope you feel better now that we've cleared the air about Jim's resignation."

"Yes, Gran, you always help me to get everything in its right perspective."

Nineteen

Ten days later Emma could not conceive how she had managed to do all that she had since she had been in London. But she had worked miracles, accomplished more in that brief span of time than in the last six months. Or so it seemed to her this afternoon as she glanced at her checklist on the yellow legal pad.

She had reviewed her various business enterprises to be certain that everything was in perfect order and to reassure herself that there would be no snags during her long absence. She had met with her solicitors several times and with her banker Henry Rossiter; she and Henry had even been able to spend a couple of pleasant social evenings together. There had been long sessions with Winston and Alexander respectively; she had conferred with Sarah, approved all the designs for the 1970 Spring Collection of Lady Hamilton clothes, and had gone over the new advertising campaign with her. And as she had worked late at the store, rushed hither and yon, switching mental gears as she went from one meeting to the next, she had found time to pull together that all-important wardrobe for her round-the-world trip with Blackie.

Emma felt settled in her mind about everything—except Jonathan. He was her enemy. She did not know the reason why; nor could she prove it. Nonetheless Emma was filled with the growing conviction that he was the one grandchild she could not trust.

Opening the folder on her desk, her shrewd eyes scanned the report from private investigators she had engaged to check on Jonathan's activities in his business and personal life. They had turned up nothing untoward, but this did not convince her that he was innocent of any wrongdoing. The firm of Graves and Saunderson would have to dig deeper, look farther afield. She was positive there was something—somewhere.

All her life Emma Harte had been able to see through everyone, had the gift of second-guessing her family and friends and adversaries alike. It was almost as if she had a demon telling her things. She also possessed that highly sensitive built-in antenna which born survivors are usually blessed with, a sort of sixth sense that enabled her to pick up vibrations—both good and bad, but especially bad. And then of course there was her gut instinct which she had come to trust, to rely on without questioning it, knowing it would never mislead her. For some time now, all of her faculties of acute perception had combined to alert her to trouble brewing, yet so far she had not put her hand on anything concrete. Still it was there, as if hovering in the dark and just beyond her reach.

Her gaze now settled on the few brief paragraphs about Sebastian Cross. They were good friends, he and Jonathan, real intimates in fact, but that was the extent of it. When she had first learned of their close relationship, which dated back to their school days at Eton, she had wondered whether or not there was a homosexual involvement here, but apparently not—quite to the contrary, according to Mr. Graves. She closed the folder with a decisive slap. There was no point in reading it over and over again. That was a waste of time. Besides, she had gone through it with a small-tooth comb already, searching for one single clue, a small lead, and had come up empty-handed. Emma slipped the folder in the desk and locked the drawer, not wanting to dwell any longer on the possibility of treachery.

A dismal feeling trickled through her. It had been painful and sad for her to resort to these awful and chilling measures—to put detectives on one of her own kin. But she had not known what else to do. And she had only ever taken such a dreadful step—spied on someone—once in her life before; and then, like now, it had been repugnant, had gone against her nature. Some forty years ago she had seen fit to have the activities of her second husband monitored . . . to protect herself and her children. She was suddenly struck by the bitter irony of the present situation. Her second husband, Arthur Ainsley, had been Jonathan's grandfather.

Sitting back in the chair, Emma wrestled with another pressing problem— whether or not to discuss her suspicions about Jonathan with Alexander and Paula. Maybe it would be wisest to confide in them. What if something happened to her when she was abroad? What if she fell sick? Or dropped dead? She did not think there was much chance of either. She was in good health, and she felt strong and vital, and certainly she was more energetic than ever. On the other hand she *would* be eighty years old in a couple of days. Perhaps, to be on the safe side, she ought to tell them. They were her chief heirs. Her empire would be under their control one day in the future . . .

There was a knock on the door, and as she said, "Come in," Gaye Sloane's face appeared around it. "Do you need anything else, Mrs. Harte?" her private secretary asked.

Emma shook her head. "No, Gaye, thanks very much. I'm waiting for Paula. We're going out to dinner. But there's no need for you to hang around. You might as well get off."

"Thanks, Mrs. Harte, I will. See you tomorrow, and good night."

"Good night, Gaye dear."

Ten minutes later Paula walked in, and Emma looked up from the papers on her desk, her face softening, and then instantly her eyes narrowed. "Paula, you look awfully tired!" she exclaimed, her worry resounding audibly. "You've got dark shadows, and you're very pale. Are you sure you're all right?"

"Yes," Paula reassured her and gave her a small rueful smile as she flopped down into the chair opposite the desk. "It's been one of those beastly days. Interminable problems with the French Week planned for July."

"What kind of problems?" Emma asked, straightening up and then leaning over the desk, resting her chin in her hands.

"People problems mostly. You know—temperaments, ruffled feathers, noses out of joint. But I've managed to get things moving smoothly again. I really miss Emily, though, Grandy. She was always so good at pulling our special events together, and she was certainly a soothing influence on everybody."

"That's part of Emily's talent, I've always thought. I know she used to make the store managers tremble in their boots, but she usually had them eating out of her hand in the long run, charming them all the way. Perhaps you ought to consider getting an assistant—someone to replace Emily." Emma's brows lifted. "Why not?"

"Oh, I don't know—" Paula shrugged. "I think I can cope; anyway, let's not worry about that now. The French Week is finally under control, and I don't foresee any more major difficulties cropping up. God forbid! In the meantime did you get a chance to look at the boutique plans? And did you speak to Merry?"

"Yes, I did. This afternoon. I spent an hour poring over the plans, and then I phoned her, told you both had my blessing. You were right, Paula, the scheme is excellent, and we should do very well with the boutiques."

"Oh, I'm so glad you agree, Grandy." Paula looked pleased as she added, "Merry worked so hard, and *she* deserves all the credit, not I. Incidentally, I mentioned our new venture to Emily yesterday. Since she's going to Hong Kong early next month, I thought she might keep her eyes open for special merchandise for the boutiques. You know, straw hats and bags, sandals, pretty shawls, summer jewelry, *anything* really that would be suitable for holiday and resort wear."

Emma nodded her approval. "Very good thought, and Emily does have a penchant for spotting fashionable goods." She paused, placed a pile of papers in a blue folder, then glanced up, gave her granddaughter a careful look. "Did Emily tell you anything special? I mean, confide anything in you?"

Paula began to laugh. "I suppose you're referring to her new boyfriend. I must admit, she's being awfully cagey with me, and that's not like Emily. We've always shared our secrets, as you well know. However, she hasn't shared a thing about her new love, other than to drop hints that he's gorgeous and special. She calls him her mysterious lover, no, *secret* lover. Mind you, I'm sure he's not *actually* her *lover,*" Paula suddenly thought to add, being protective of Emily, not wanting her grandmother to get the wrong impression about the younger girl's morals. "You know how she tends to exaggerate."

Emma bit back a smile, filling with understanding. "You don't have to defend Emily to me, Paula dear. I know she's not promiscuous . . . she hasn't followed in her mother's footsteps, that's one thing I'm absolutely certain of. However, he *is* her lover."

Paula, very startled, said, "How do you know that?"

"Why, I got it from the horse's mouth," Emma announced, mischief sparking her tired eyes with sudden life. She sat back and grinned at Paula.

"You're looking like the cat that's swallowed the canary, Grandy," Paula laughed. "Which horse?"

"Emily. She told me all about him herself. And the so-called secret lover is no longer a *secret;* neither is he very mysterious." Emma's mouth twitched with amusement as she watched Paula, noted the surprised expression settling on her face.

"Oh," was all Paula could manage.

Emma's light laugh rang out. "Emily came to see me the night before last, and she was rather blunt—in her usual fashion. She said, 'Gran, I'm terribly in love, and it's very serious. I'm sleeping with him, but I don't want you to worry. I won't get pregnant. I'm taking birth control pills.' That didn't surprise me, after all she was always a rather practical girl . . . Emily does have her head screwed on the right way, like you. In fact, Elizabeth could take a few lessons from the two of you. Well, I *was* taken aback—I don't mind admitting *that*—but not shocked, though I suspect Emily had anticipated that I would be. I wonder occasionally if that girl thinks I'm the Virgin Mary. Anyway, she was very honest, endearingly so." Emma paused, then smiled her very special smile that filled her face with radiance. "Our little Emily has stars in her eyes right now, darling. She's genuinely in love. Very much so."

"But who *is* he?" Paula pressed. "You said he's not mysterious, so it must be somebody I know."

"Oh yes, it is." Emma chuckled, and her eyes twinkled brightly. She was suddenly enjoying herself, enjoying teasing Paula, glad to turn away from the unpleasantness surrounding Jonathan, which she found so appalling.

"Come on, don't be so mean," Paula admonished, smiling herself, picking up on her grandmother's gaiety which was infectious. "Tell me his *name,* for heaven's sake! I'm dying to know."

"Winston."

"Winston," Paula gasped, and her violet eyes widened. "I don't be-lieve it!"

"Oh, but you must, because it's absolutely true. Don't look so shocked, darling. Winston's very eligible, and let's face it, he has lots of charm, a lot going for him. He's also rather good-looking. He's a lot like me, you know."

Paula hooted with laughter, tickled by this small show of personal vanity on her grandmother's part. She said, "Yes, Grandma, I have noticed the resem-blance from time to time." She then continued, "The *only* reason I'm thunder-struck is because this news is so unexpected. And rather startling—I mean,

Winston and Emily . . . goodness me, when did they become romantically entangled? When did all this start?" Paula's black brows drew together in a sudden frown. "Oh dear, what about nice Allison Ridley?"

"Yes, nice Allison indeed. That part is sad—I always rather liked that young woman. But I'm afraid it's off with her. Winston spoke to me yesterday about Allison, explained that he went to see her, told her as kindly and as gently as possible that it's over between them. As to the first part of your question, I believe Emily and Winston realized the depth of their feelings for each other on the day of the christening. Winston asked me if I minded about his involvement with Emily, and I told him I didn't, that I was delighted." Emma once again leaned across the desk, the expression of deeply felt happiness flashing on her face. She confided, "I had a business meeting with Winston this morning, and after we'd finished, he brought out the ring he's bought for Emily. It's an emerald." Emma paused, then announced, "Winston asked my permission to marry Emily. I gave it, and they're going to announce their engagement this week, before I leave for New York."

"Oh, Gran, this is going a bit fast, isn't it?" Paula asked softly, with a hint of concern, staring at Emma.

"I wouldn't say that, dear," Emma remarked. "They're hardly strangers, Paula. They grew up together, and I should think they know each other pretty well by now. They won't have any unpleasant surprises about each other after they're married. Of course, the wedding can't take place until *next* summer, what with my trip to Australia and their traveling. But frankly, I'm relieved to know Emily has someone to look after her . . . I won't be around forever, you know. Yes, I find it most satisfying that those two are settling down together, most satisfying indeed. It gives me a lovely warm feeling here." She patted her chest, continuing to smile.

"If you're happy and Emily is happy, then I am too," Paula said. "And come to think of it, she and Winston were extremely close when they were little . . . they're admirably suited. Shouldn't I call her, Gran, to congratulate her?" Paula half rose, made to reach for the telephone on Emma's desk.

Emma said, "I don't think you'll find her at Belgrave Square. She was going to the theater with Winston, and she's probably left the flat by now." Glancing at her watch, Emma nodded. "Yes, it's already turned seven. You'll have to ring her late tonight. In the meantime I really think I've got to get out of this place; I've been here since eight this morning. I've had it—and you look as if you have too." Emma stood up, frowning at Paula as she did. "Are you sure you're quite well?"

Paula summoned a smile. "Never better, Gran," she fibbed, not wanting to worry her grandmother.

Privately Emma thought that Paula looked completely exhausted, worn down. She had never seen the girl like this, and it concerned her. But she made no further comment, and turning away she picked up her handbag. Her mouth tightened imperceptibly. She had a sneaking suspicion that for all his easy grace and lighthearted charm and boyish manner, Jim Fairley was a difficult man. But she would not pry; nor would she try to live her granddaughter's life for her.

As they left the office, Emma said, "I've booked a table at Cunningham's —I hope you fancy fish."

"Yes, and I'm not very hungry anyway, Gran."

Later, over dinner at the Mayfair oyster bar and fish restaurant, Paula's appearance underwent a change, one which pleased Emma. Her alabaster complexion took on a soft shell-pink cast, and her eyes lost their haunted expression as she visibly relaxed. By the time coffee was served, Paula seemed so much more like her normal self that Emma made a decision: She would take Paula into her confidence. Before they left Cunningham's this evening, she would make brief mention of her suspicions about Jonathan, but casually so and in passing. She felt it was necessary to warn Paula; on the other hand she did not wish to alarm her unduly. And tomorrow, when she had dinner with Alexander, she would apprise *him* of the situation. In one sense it was more important that he was alerted, put on his guard, since Jonathan Ainsley worked for Harte Enterprises.

Twenty

It was the thirtieth of April, and today she was eighty years old.

She awakened early, as was usual, and as she lay in her bed, shaking off the residue of sleep, she thought: Today is a special day, isn't it? And then instantly she remembered why this day was different from others. *It was her birthday.*

Emma had an aversion to lying in bed once she was awake, and she pushed herself up and brought her feet to the floor, half smiling to herself as she padded across the carpet to the windows. *She had made it.* She had never imagined she would live so long. Why, she was eleven years older than this century. In 1889, in that small cottage in Top Fold in Fairley village, her mother Elizabeth Harte had brought her into the world.

Drawing the draperies, she peered out. Her smile widened. It was a gorgeous day, full of sunshine and a startling brilliance. The sky was a crystalline blue and cloudless, and the trees below her in Belgrave Square were full blown and brightly green, their heavily laden branches undulating with shimmering light under the breeze. She had been born on such a day as this, a balmy spring day, her mother had once told her, a day that was unusually warm for this time of year, especially in the cool northern climes of Yorkshire.

Emma stretched. She felt alert and refreshed after a good night's rest, and as vigorous as she had ever been. Full of piss and vinegar, she thought, and immediately an image of her brother Winston flashed into her mind. That had been his favorite expression to describe her, when she had been revved up and bubbling over with enthusiasm, energy, and drive. She wished he were still alive, and her younger brother Frank, too. Sudden sadness streamed through her, but it was fleeting. Today was not a day for feeling sorry for herself, for missing those whom she had so dearly loved and who had departed this world. Today was a day for positive thoughts. A day for celebration. A day for looking to the future, concentrating on the younger generation . . . her grandchildren.

If all of her children except Daisy were lost to her, at least she had the immense satisfaction of knowing that their offspring would carry her bright banner forward, continue the great dynasty she had created, preserve her mighty business empire.

She stopped abruptly, paused in her progress across the room, and asked herself if it was a ferocious personal vanity that had fostered the dynastic impulse in her. *A desire for immortality perhaps?* She was not certain. But she did comprehend one thing—to produce a dynasty such as she had done, it was absolutely necessary to view ambition on the grandest of scales, to imbue it in others.

Emma laughed out loud. It was just conceivable that she had always envisioned herself as being larger than life, different, and so truly indomitable that she was not mortal at all. Egotism, she thought, and once more her rippling laughter filled the silent bedroom. Her enemies had frequently labeled her the total and supreme egotist. But why not? It was the truth, indeed it was. And without her enormous ego, surely she would never have done the things she had done, accomplished all that she had. That ego, that belief in herself, had given her courage and self-confidence, had propelled her forward and upward, right to the top. To the glittering pinnacle of success.

Well, she didn't have time to waste this morning, contemplating her motives, analyzing the internal forces that had driven her all the days of her life. She had done what she felt had to be done, and very simply that was that. She walked purposefully into the bathroom to prepare herself for the day facing her, shoving to one side these thoughts, deeming them unimportant.

An hour later, after she had bathed, dressed, and breakfasted, Emma hurried downstairs to the second floor of her maisonette. She looked fresh and vitally alive, dressed in a crisply tailored light-wool dress in a shade of delphinium blue. She wore splendid jewelry with it—sapphire earrings and a matching broach pinned onto one shoulder, a double strand of pearls, Paul's wedding ring, and Blackie's large diamond. Not one hair of her immaculate, gleaming silver head was out of place, her makeup was perfect, and the bounce in her step belied her great age.

Emma still lived in Belgrave Square, in the elegant, beautifully appointed mansion which Paul McGill had purchased for them in the late summer of 1925, soon after the birth of their daughter Daisy. At the time, catering to Emma's fear of vicious gossip, her reluctance to flaunt their relationship, and her overwhelming need to be discreet and circumspect, he had had the house remodeled into two flats. And he had spared no expense in the process. The noted architect he had engaged had designed small bachelor quarters on the ground floor for Paul; the three floors which soared above were transformed into the luxurious triplex flat for Emma, Daisy, the nanny, and the rest of the staff. To the outside observer, the bachelor apartment and the large airy flat spanning three floors were entirely separate, were two distinct, self-contained dwellings, each having its own entrance. However, the two were ingeniously linked by a private interior elevator, which ran between the small hall in Paul's bachelor quarters to the larger and more elegant foyer in Emma's flat on the next floor. Because of this lift, the dwellings operated efficiently as one house.

During the war years, immediately following Paul's crippling accident and tragic suicide in Australia in 1939, Emma had closed up his bachelor flat. Unable to enter it without breaking down with uncontrollable grief and searing despair, she had turned her back on these rooms, ignoring them except for having them regularly cleaned. In 1948, when she was finally able to confront his possessions, she had had some of the rooms modernized and redecorated. Since then, she had utilized the smaller downstairs flat as guest quarters for visiting friends or her grandchildren.

Parker, her butler, was busy sorting the morning mail when Emma walked into her study. This was a pleasant, airy room of medium size, comfortably furnished with country antiques.

"Happy birthday, Mrs. Harte," said Parker, looking up and smiling. "Quite a heavy post this morning, madam."

"Oh my goodness, I see what you mean!" Emma exclaimed. The butler had stacked a staggering amount of mail on the chintz-covered sofa and was methodically opening envelopes with a paper knife, removing the birthday cards, and throwing the envelopes into the wastepaper basket.

Emma joined him in this task, but soon she had to keep breaking off to answer the phone, and then, not long afterward, the door bell began ringing as flowers and gifts arrived in a steady and continuing stream. Parker and Mrs. Ramsey, the housekeeper, had their hands full, and Emma was left alone to cope with the mail.

At about eleven-thirty, when the activity was at its height, Daisy McGill Amory walked in, unexpected and unannounced.

Emma's youngest daughter would be forty-four in May, but she did not look her age. She had a slender figure, softly curling black hair that framed her tranquil, unlined face, and luminous blue eyes that mirrored her lovely disposition and gentle nature. Unlike her daughter Paula, who favored a hard-edged chic and was extremely fashion-conscious, Daisy was more like Emma in her taste in clothes. She always chose soft, rather feminine outfits, and this morning she wore a simple lilac wool suit and a matching blouse with a frilly jabot which fell down the front, gold jewelry, and black patent pumps and handbag.

"Happy happy birthday, Mother," Daisy said from the doorway, her expression loving, her eyes awash with tenderness.

Emma looked up from the pile of envelopes and broke into smiles. She was delighted to see Daisy and welcomed her calm presence. Springing up from behind the desk, Emma went to greet her with affection and warmth.

"This is from us . . . David and I do hope you like it, Mummy." She laughed. "You're awfully hard to buy for, you know. You *do* have everything." She thrust a package at Emma.

"Thank you, Daisy, and since you have the best taste in the world, I'm sure it's going to be something quite lovely."

Sinking onto the sofa, Emma began to unwrap Daisy's gift. "All this fuss! And at my age!"

Daisy knew that her mother was enjoying every minute despite her protestations. She joined her on the sofa and said, "But Mummy, that's just the point. This is an important day . . . you must sit back, relax, and savor every minute of it."

"Perhaps you're right. But it certainly looks as if I'll never get to the store this morning."

Daisy stared at her, her bright blue eyes aghast. "You can't go to work this morning, darling, it—"

"Why ever not?" Emma interrupted. "I *always* go to work."

"Not today you're not! It wouldn't be appropriate." Daisy shook her head vigorously. "Besides," she paused, glanced at her watch, and went on, "In a short while I'm going to take you off to lunch."

"But I—"

"No buts, my darling Mummy," Daisy said, her tone amused yet firm. "I'm not your daughter, *and* Paul McGill's, for nothing. I can be just as tough as he *was* and as you *are,* when I want to be. And this is one of those days when I'm putting my foot down. *Hard.* We haven't had lunch together for the longest time, and in a few days you'll be leaving with Uncle Blackie—and you'll be gone for months, from what *I* hear. Please don't disappoint me; I've been so looking forward to it, and I've already reserved a table at the Mirabelle."

Emma smiled at Daisy, who was her favorite, her best-loved child. She had always found it hard to refuse her anything. "All right," she said, relenting. "We'll have lunch together, and then I'll go to the store this afternoon. Oh, Daisy, this is lovely!" Emma now exclaimed, staring at the solid gold, hand-made evening bag she held in her hands. "Why, darling, it's simply beautiful." Her pleasure was apparent as she turned the bag around, opened it, looked inside, closed it. After examining it for a few seconds longer, she returned it to its protective black leather case, leaned over, and kissed her daughter. "Thank you, Daisy, this is stunning. And perfect for my trip, since it'll go with all my evening clothes."

Daisy nodded, pleased and relieved that the gift was a success. "That's what David and I thought, and we really racked our brains to come up with an unusual present. Are you sure you like the style? If you don't, Asprey's will be happy to send a salesperson over with two or three others for you to look at."

"No, no, I don't want to see anything else. I like this one," Emma assured her. "Actually, I shall carry it tonight."

The phone rang. "Shall I get that for you, Mummy?"

"Would you, darling, please?"

Daisy took the phone, answered crisply. There was a brief exchange of pleasantries and after a moment, Daisy said, "I'll see if she can come to the phone. It's a little hectic here this morning. Just a minute, please." Depressing the hold button, Daisy glanced at her mother. "It's Elizabeth. She's back in London. Do you want to speak to her? I think perhaps you should."

"Of course I'll speak to her." Emma crossed to the desk. If she was surprised, she did not show it and said steadily, "Hello, Elizabeth." Sitting down, she leaned back in the chair and cradled the receiver on her shoulder, toying with the pen in the onyx inkstand.

"Thank you," she responded shortly, "yes, it *is* a grand age, but I don't feel eighty. More like fifty-eight! And I'm as fit as a fiddle." There was another pause. Emma focused her eyes on the wall opposite. They narrowed slightly, and suddenly she cut in peremptorily, "I think Winston was simply being courteous when he asked my permission. It wasn't really necessary. I don't think I have to remind you that Emily is of age. She can do anything she wants. And *no,* I didn't speak to Tony. I thought it was up to Emily to break the news to her father."

Emma fell silent as her middle daughter talked incessantly at the other end of the phone. She looked across at Daisy, and made a face, rolled her eyes heavenward. Her patience began to dwindle, and she interrupted again. "I thought you phoned to wish me a happy birthday, Elizabeth, not to complain about Emily's engagement."

An ironic smile flitted across Emma's face as she listened to Elizabeth's protests that she was not complaining.

"I'm glad to hear you say so," Emma said into the receiver, "because that would be a waste of breath. Now, how was your trip to Haiti? And how's your new boyfriend—Marc Deboyne?"

Elizabeth gurgled ecstatically into Emma's ear for a few more minutes, and finally Emma brought their conversation to a close with a brisk, "Well, I'm glad you're happy, and thank you for calling and for the birthday present. I'm sure it will arrive here any minute. Goodbye, Elizabeth." She hung up.

Daisy asked, "Is she upset about Emily and Winston?"

Emma laughed with some acerbity. "Of course not. She's just making appropriate noises because she wasn't informed first, before me. You know Elizabeth as well as I do, she's very self-involved. But it was nice of her to ring up for my birthday." Emma walked back to the couch and sat down. She gave Daisy an odd look and half shrugged. "Edwina phoned earlier, and so did Robin and Kit . . . I must say, I was very surprised to hear from my sons. I haven't heard a peep out of them since that debacle over the will last year. Then today, they're as nice as pie and tell me they've sent me gifts too. Can you believe it?"

"Perhaps they're sorry, Mother, and regret their plotting—"

"I doubt it!" Emma exclaimed softly. "I'm far too cynical to think that either of *them* would have a change of heart. No, I'm sure their wives were behind the calls. June and Valerie have always been decent women. I can't imagine how they've managed to put up with my sons all these years. Kit plots. Robin schemes. Oh well—" Emma reached out now and took Daisy's hand in hers. "There's something I've been meaning to ask you, darling. It's about this house . . . are you sure you don't want it?"

Daisy was startled, and she said in a surprised voice, "But you've left this house to Sarah, haven't you?"

"Yes. However, I only bequeathed it to her because you indicated that you weren't interested in owning it when we discussed the matter last year. But it should be yours or your children's. After all, your father did buy it for us."

"I know, and I've always adored this house. It holds so many special memories for me . . . of my years growing up, of Daddy and you, and the lovely times the three of us had here. It is a little big, though, and—"

Emma held up a silencing hand. "Not if you think of it as two flats rather than one house. He did that for me, as you know. I did so want to keep up appearances . . ." Emma broke off and started to laugh. "Goodness, Daisy, how times have *changed*. People think nothing of living together quite openly these days. Anyway, getting back to the disposition of this house, I thought you might want to reconsider. You have grandchildren now. Philip's bound to marry one day and in the not too distant future, I expect. He'll have children; he may even want to send them to school in England. Two self-contained flats under one unifying roof is awfully useful."

"I'm not sure what to say, Mother. Your points are well taken, though."

"Think about it. I can always change my will."

"But you've left me so much . . . more than I'll ever need. It seems greedy, accepting this house."

"That's a load of cod's wallop, Daisy. By rights it should be yours. If you decline, then I think that perhaps I'd better leave it to Paula or Philip."

"But what about Sarah?"

"She's not a McGill."

Daisy pursed her lips thoughtfully. "All right, I'll do as you say—think about it. Look here, Mother, I know a woman of your immense wealth has to have her affairs in proper order at all times, but to tell you the truth, I do hate these discussions about your will and your death. They really make my stomach churn. Your death is certainly something I can't bear to think about, never mind discuss in this offhanded way. I get very upset."

Emma looked at Daisy and said nothing. She squeezed her hand, sat back, continuing to stare at her intently.

Daisy took a deep breath, exhaled, and forced a weak smile. "Sorry, I didn't mean to speak to you so harshly. However, I do especially dislike talking about such things today of *all* days. It's your birthday, remember."

"I understand." There was a tiny silence, and eventually Emma said in the quietest voice, "I have been a good mother to you, haven't I, Daisy darling?"

"How could you ever think otherwise!" Daisy cried, her face ringed with concern. Her large and brilliant eyes of the deepest cornflower blue widened considerably, unexpectedly filled. "You've been the most wonderful mother anyone could ever have wished for, always so loving and understanding." Daisy returned Emma's stead-fast gaze unblinkingly, and as she looked deeply into that wrinkled face, her heart clenched with the most profound love for this remarkable woman who had borne her. She knew that the forbidding demeanor and the permanently stern expression were only surface characteristics, camouflage for a vast reservoir of emotion and compassion. Emma Harte was a complex, many-faceted person, and contrary to what some believed, she was much more vulnerable and sensitive than most.

Daisy's gentle face underwent another change as her adoration and loyalty to her mother rose up in her. "You're so very special, Mummy." Daisy stopped, searched Emma's face, and shook her head wonderingly. "You're the most honorable and loving person I've ever known. I've been so very lucky to have you all these years. Really blessed."

Emma was deeply moved. "Thank you, Daisy, for saying those beautiful things." She looked into the distance, then murmured in a saddened voice, "I've failed miserably with your half brothers and half sisters. I couldn't bear to think that I'd also failed with you or that I'd ever let you down in any way and not given you my best and dearest love."

"You've given me everything . . . why I couldn't begin to tell you what I owe you. And I don't believe you've failed the others. Not in the slightest. Didn't my father say once that each of us is the author of our own lives? That we are responsible for what we are? For the deeds, both good and bad, that we do?"

"He did."

"Then *believe* it, Mother. It's true!"

"If you say so, darling."

Emma fell into momentary silence, reflecting on her daughter's words. She was proud of Daisy, of the woman she had become. For all her sweetness, her soft manners, and her intrinsic charm, Daisy had a strong, even tough inner core, and immense resilience and fortitude. Emma knew that when she chose to be, her Daisy was as immovable as a mountain and unwavering in her resoluteness. This was especially true if her convictions and principles were involved. Daisy, so young-looking, was also inordinately youthful in her attitudes. She had a gaiety, a joyousness about life that was infectious, and she was of that rare breed of women who are liked by their own sex as well as by men. In fact Emma was well aware that most people found it difficult, if not indeed impossible, to dislike Daisy. She was so full of integrity, so honorable, so beyond reproach, yet so truly human and caring that she towered above every-one. If her half brothers and half sisters were jealous of her, even resented her slightly, they were nevertheless rendered helpless under the force of her warm personality and extraordinary sincerity. It was her goodness, purity, and sense of fair play that also kept them off balance and at bay. She was the conscience of the family.

"You've got a faraway look on your face, Mother. Are you daydreaming? You seem so intense all of a sudden, what are you thinking about?" Daisy leaned closer to Emma, searching her face and touching her cheek lightly.

"Oh, nothing much." Emma shook off her introspection, gave Daisy's clothes an appraising glance. "Perhaps I ought to go and change, since we're going to the Mirabelle for lunch."

"You don't have to, darling. Don't bother struggling into something else."

"All right, I won't. But what about tonight? Blackie tells me he's wearing a dinner jacket. You don't think he actually wants me to wear a *long* frock, do you? I mean, after all, we're only going to be eight."

Oh my God, Daisy thought, wait until she finds out it's closer to sixty. She wondered if her mother would be annoyed with them for giving the surprise party. Clearing her throat, praying that she sounded offhand, Daisy remarked, "But Uncle Blackie wants this to be a festive evening, extra special. As he said to me the other day, 'How often is your mother going to be eighty?' So naturally I agreed with him that we should dress. Still, you don't have to be that grand, wearing a long frock, I mean. I've decided on a peacock-blue faille cocktail dress myself. Look, I'd wear one of those lovely chiffons of yours, if I were you."

"That's a relief. I have the green chiffon, it'll do quite nicely. Oh dear, there's the door bell *again!* I do hope it's not more flowers. This place is beginning to resemble a funeral parlor."

"Mother! What an awful analogy!"

Daisy sprang up, moved swiftly across the floor, said over her shoulder, "Perhaps it's the gift Elizabeth sent or the ones from Kit and Robin. I'll go and ask Parker."

Before Emma had a chance to blink, Daisy returned. "It *is* a gift, Mother." She glanced into the foyer, nodded, then took up a position near the fireplace, standing under the portrait in oils of Paul McGill.

Emma, acute as ever, peered at her suspiciously. "What's going on? You look exactly like your father did when he had something up his sleeve." Her eyes strayed to Paul's portrait and then back to Daisy. There was no doubt whose daughter she was. Her likeness to him was more pronounced than ever today . . . the same bright blue eyes, the black hair, the cleft in the chin. "Come on, what are you hiding?"

Daisy looked expectantly at the door and beckoned. On cue Amanda and Francesca walked in, doing their level best to be sedate and grown-up. They came to a halt in the center of the floor, focused on Emma.

"Happy birthday to you, dear Grandma, happy birthday to you," they chorused, sounding enthusiastic if slightly off-key.

Sarah, Emily, and Paula had followed them into the study, stood behind their young cousins. They echoed, "Happy birthday, Grandma," gazing at her lovingly.

"Good heavens, what's all this!" Emma cried, truly taken by surprise. She gaped at her granddaughters; then, addressing the twins, asked, "And what are you *two* doing here? It's not half-term, is it?"

Daisy cut in, *"I* took them out of school for a couple of days, Mother. They're staying with me and David. After all, it *is* your birthday."

"I knew somebody was cooking up *something,"* Emma said, giving Daisy a sharp penetrating look. "To tell you the truth, I thought you and Blackie were conniving together, Daisy. I suspected that you'd planned some sort of celebration for tonight."

Daisy managed to keep her face neutral. But before she got the opportunity to say anything, Emily came forward purposefully. She handed a beautifully wrapped package to Francesca and touched Amanda's shoulder lightly. "You haven't forgotten your speech, have you?"

"Course not," Amanda hissed back indignantly, reached for Francesca's hand, and gave her twin a little tug, drew them both nearer to Emma.

Taking a deep breath, the fifteen-year-old said carefully, enunciating each word clearly, "Grandy, this gift is from all of your grandchildren—from Philip, Anthony, Alexander, Jonathan, Paula, Sarah, Emily, Francesca, and me. Each one of us has contributed to it, so that we could present you with something special on this, your eightieth birthday. We give it to you with our very dearest love always."

Amanda went to Emma, bent down, and kissed her; Francesca followed suit, then handed her the present.

"Thank you, girls," Emma said to the twins. "And your little speech was very nicely rendered, Amanda. Well done." She looked over at their sister and cousins. "My thanks to *all* of you."

Emma sat for a moment without moving, holding the present on her lap. She let her eyes rest on each one of her elder granddaughters who were grouped together, and she smiled at them individually, nodding to herself, thinking how pretty and charming they looked. Tears welled unexpectedly, and she blinked them back, glanced down at the package, endeavoring to conceal her emotional reaction to this unexpected family scene. To her astonishment her hands shook as she untied the purple ribbon and lifted the object from its box.

The gift was a clock in the shape of an egg, made of the most translucent blue enamel she had ever set eyes on. A miniature cockerel, enameled and delicately worked, was mounted on top of the egg, heavily bejeweled with diamonds, rubies, and sapphires. Emma marveled at the design and craftsmanship, which were exquisite, and she recognized the clock for the precious work of art it truly was.

"It's by Fabergé, isn't it?" she managed at last, her voice hardly audible.

"Yes," Emily said. "Actually, Gran, it's an Imperial Easter egg which Fabergé made for the Empress Marie Fedorovna of Russia. Her son, Nicholas II, the last Tsar, ordered it for her."

"How on earth did you manage to find something as rare and valuable as this?" Emma asked, awed. As an art collector of discernment, she was aware that such pieces by Fabergé were becoming increasingly scarce.

"Paula heard about the clock through Henry Rossiter," Emily volunteered. "He had learned it was going to be auctioned last week at Sotheby's."

"And Henry went to the auction for you?"

"No, Grandy. We all went *en masse,* except for the twins, who were at school, of course. Henry did come with us, though. Paula had called us, and we got together for a confab. We each agreed at once that we should try to buy the clock for you—as a collective gift from us. It was terribly exciting! We almost lost it several times, but we just kept on going, topping other bids. And suddenly we had it. We were so thrilled, Grandma!"

"And so am I, my darlings." Her eyes encompassed them all.

Parker suddenly appeared, also on cue from Daisy, bringing in a tray of glasses brimming with sparkling champagne. When each of them had a drink, they clustered around Emma, wished her a happy birthday again, and toasted her health.

Once things had calmed down, Emma turned to Daisy and said, "Are we really going to lunch at the Mirabelle? Or was that a ruse to prevent me from going to the store?"

Daisy grinned. "Of course we're going to lunch—all of us who are present, in fact. Anthony, Alexander, Jonathan, and David will be joining us. So you can forget about going to work today, Mother."

Emma was about to assert herself on this point, but she recognized the look on Daisy's face. Since it forbade argument, she held her tongue.

It was dusk.

Emma walked across the entrance foyer, so bosky and still at this hour, her step light as she entered her study.

She was dressed for the dinner party Blackie was giving at the Ritz, wearing a short dress made of layers and layers of pale and dark green chiffon, simply cut with long floating Mandarin sleeves. The magnificent McGill emeralds, blazing at her throat, on her ears, arms, and hand, looked stunning against the mingled greens of the delicate fabric, the fire, depth, and brilliance of the gems intensified by the repetition of their color.

Yes, it was a good choice, Emma decided as she passed the one mirror in the room and caught a fleeting glimpse of herself. She did not stop but continued across the floor, the only sound the swishing of her dress as she moved with her usual briskness.

When she reached the console where some of her many birthday presents were stacked, she picked up the Imperial Easter egg and carried it back to the drawing room.

Placing it on an antique occasional table near the fireplace, she stood back, admiring it again. It was undoubtedly one of the loveliest things she had ever been given, and she could not wait to show it to Blackie.

The sharp trilling of the bell made her start, and in rapid succession she heard Parker's footsteps resounding in the foyer, the front door banging, and muffled voices.

A moment later Blackie was striding into the room, splendidly attired in a superbly cut tuxedo, the wide grin on his face competing with the sparkle in his black eyes, and he was obviously buoyed up with excitement.

"Happy birthday, me darlin'," he boomed, and drawing to a standstill he swept her up into his arms. Then he released his grip, stepped away, and caught her hands in his, looked down into her face, repeating the gestures practiced on her for years. "You look bonnier than ever tonight, Emma," he said beaming and bent to kiss her.

"Thank you, Blackie." Emma returned his smile and moved toward the sofa. "Did you tell Parker what you wanted to drink?"

"Sure and I did. My usual." He lowered himself into the chair opposite her, his large frame filling it completely. "I don't want you to think I've come empty-handed—your birthday present is outside. I'll go and get it—"

The butler's discreet knock interrupted him, and Parker came in with a tumbler of neat Irish whiskey for Blackie and a goblet of white wine for Emma.

As soon as they were alone, Blackie raised his glass. "Here's to you, mavourneen. And may we celebrate many, many more of our birthdays together."

"I know we will," Emma laughed. "And here's to our trip, Blackie dear."

"To the trip." After only one sip, Blackie sprang up. "Don't move," he instructed, "and when I tell you to close your eyes, I want you to do just that, and no cheating, mind you."

She sat waiting for him to come back, guessed he had enlisted Parker's help when she heard the low murmur of the butler's voice, Blackie's response, then the sound of paper being ripped.

"Close your eyes," Blackie ordered from the doorway several seconds later. "Remember what I said, no peeking, Emma!"

"I won't," she reassured him, laughter bringing a lilt to her voice. She sat perfectly still, her hands clasped in her lap, and she suddenly felt like a young girl again, like the little starveling girl who had received her first real present wrapped in silver paper and tied with silver ribbon. It had been from him—had been that cheap little green glass brooch which she had cherished all of her life. She still had it tucked away in her jewel case, alongside the fine replica he had eventually had made in emeralds. And once, long ago, that bit of green glass had been her most treasured and valuable possession.

"Now!" Blackie cried.

Slowly Emma opened her eyes, and as she looked at the painting he was holding in front of her she instantly recognized the work of her great-niece, Sally Harte. Emma gasped in astonished delight, and then she filled with a swift and piercing pain of poignant nostalgia as haunting memories rippled through her. Her throat tightened. She focused her eyes, took in every detail, every brushstroke, and she could only gaze at the painting's evocative beauty, unable to say a word.

"Oh, Blackie," she said at last, "it's perfectly lovely . . . the moors above Fairley. My moors, where we first met."

"Look a bit closer, me darlin'."

"I don't have to, I can see it's the Top of the World." She raised her eyes and shook her head in wonderment. "What a truly meaningful gift this is, my dear old friend. The painting is extraordinary. Why, I feel as though I can reach out and pick a bunch of that heather, as I used to do for my mother." She let one finger rest lightly against the canvas, barely touching it. "I can hear the tinkle of this little beck, here in the corner, and the sound of its crystal water tumbling down over the polished stones. It's so . . . so real, I can even smell the scent of bilberry and bracken and the heather. Oh, Blackie darling . . ."

Emma looked up at him and smiled her incomparable smile, then swiftly brought her gaze back to the painting. "It's a real Yorkshire sky, isn't it? So full of clarity and shimmering radiance. What immense talent that girl has, and only Turner and Van Gogh have ever been able to capture the true quality of light on canvas in such a way. Yes, Sally has surpassed herself with this."

Gratification and pleasure shone on his craggy, expressive face. "I took Sally over there myself, showed her the exact spot. And she kept going back, time and time again. She wanted perfection for you, Emma, as I did, and I think she got the painting just right in the end."

"She most certainly did. Thank you, thank you so much for thinking of such an unusual present."

Blackie said softly, "I had her write this on the back. In paint." He turned the painting around, indicated the neat lettering. "You won't be able to read what it says without your glasses, so I shall tell you what I asked her to put. It says, 'To Emma Harte on reaching her eightieth birthday with love from her life-long friend, Blackie O'Neill.' Then there's the date underneath."

For the second time that day, Emma was greatly moved. She could not speak, and she turned away quickly so that he would not see her misty eyes. She sat down, took a sip of her drink, composed herself, and finally murmured, "That's lovely, just lovely, darling."

After propping the painting against a console table and making sure it was in her direct line of vision, he returned to his seat and lifted his own glass. "And it *is* a lifetime, too, Emma. Sixty-six years to be precise." He nodded at the painting. "Aye, the Top of the World—your mother's name for Ramsden Crags. I'll never forget the day you found me lost on the moors, and we came up out of the Ghyll, and I saw the Crags for the first time."

Emma followed the direction of his eyes. Over six decades dropped away, and she saw herself as she had been at fourteen. A poor little servant girl . . . trudging across the moors at dawn in her broken-down button boots and the old patched coat Cook had given her. That coat had been a treasured item too, even though it had been small and tight and threadbare. It had hardly protected her from the rain and snow and bitter north wind.

Now she stared fully at Blackie, seeing him as he was tonight but remembering how he had looked in his rough, drab workman's clothes and his cheap cloth cap worn at such a cheeky angle, carrying his sack of tools slung over his broad shoulder. *Disreputable,* Cook had called the dirty old burlap bag that contained *his* most treasured possessions—his hammers and trowels and mortar board.

Emma said slowly, "Who would have thought that we would both live to such great ages . . . that we would acquire so much in our lifetimes . . . immense power, immeasurable wealth . . . that we would become what we are today."

Blackie gave her an odd look, then chuckled at the amazement ringing in her voice. "I for one never doubted our rosy futures," he announced, his voice underscored by a bubbling merriment. "I told you I was going to be a toff, a real millionaire, and that you would be a grand lady. Mind you, me darlin', I'll be confessing to you now that I never suspected you'd be quite as *grand* as you are."

They both smiled, their wise old eyes holding, secure in their love and friendship, revelling in the knowledge that they truly understood each other as no other person alive did. So many years . . . so many experiences shared welded them. The bonds between them were like steel and so strong they were unbreakable.

The silence drifted along for a while.

Eventually Blackie roused himself. "Now, mavourneen mine, tell me about your busy day."

"One thing surprised me, Blackie. *They* called. *The plotters.* I was startled to hear from my sons and Elizabeth, I don't mind telling you. She's back in London of course. No doubt with the French boyfriend. Edwina gave me a ring this morning, and she was pleasant, believe it or not. Perhaps *she's* mended her ways finally. And I had two other most wonderful calls . . . they really touched me." Her eyes lit up. "Philip rang from Sydney, and your Shane from New York. Wasn't that nice?" He nodded, smiling, and she continued, "It seems that your grandson and mine are planning birthday parties for me when we arrive in their cities, so be prepared. As for my day, well, you can see for yourself what it's brought." Emma waved her hand around, her eyes sweeping the room. "Flowers, cards, and so many gifts. And I had lunch with Daisy, David, and my grandchildren at the Mirabelle."

She proceeded to recount every detail of the luncheon party, then told him how they had whisked her away from the restaurant at three-thirty and taken her to her store in Knightsbridge. Marched by her grandchildren into her boardroom, she had been greeted by her top executives, who were awaiting her arrival at the special reception they had arranged for her.

When she had finished this somewhat breathless recital, Emma rose and picked up the Imperial Easter egg, said confidingly, "This is what my grandchildren gave me, and like your painting it is a most meaningful gift. I shall treasure them both always."

"So you had a lovely day—I'm glad. That's the way it should always be." Blackie stood up. "Come along, I think we'd better be on our way. We're meeting in Bryan's suite at the Ritz for a drop of bubbly before we go down to dinner."

Ten minutes later, when they arrived at the Ritz Hotel in Piccadilly, Blackie ushered Emma up the steps. He paused briefly at the reception desk, asked the young man behind it to announce his arrival to his son, Mr. Bryan O'Neill, and gave the number of the suite.

"Of course, Mr. O'Neill." The young assistant manager smiled at Emma. "Good evening, Mrs. Harte."

Emma acknowledged his greeting pleasantly, and after Blackie had expressed his thanks they proceeded through the lobby, unaware of how striking they looked and of the heads turned to watch them.

Emma remained silent as they rode up in the lift, and Blackie stole several surreptitious looks at her, wondering if she had any inkling about the party which had been planned with such secrecy. He could not hazard a guess. Her face, as always, was inscrutable. He believed Emma would not be angry, despite Daisy's prediction that her mother might easily react adversely. He knew his Emma, understood that she was like a child at times. She enjoyed surprises and gifts and special occasions, particularly when those occasions revolved around her.

That's because of the deprivations of her youth, he said to himself. In those days she had had nothing, nothing of any real value. No, that wasn't strictly true. She had had her startling looks, her brains, her stamina, her extraordinary health, and her enormous courage. Not to mention that terrible pride of hers. Oh that pride and oh the shame she had experienced because of that pride and because she was poor. "But poverty's not a crime, even though people who're better off always try to make you feel like a criminal," she had once cried to him, her anger bringing a fierce dark gleam to her young eyes. Ah yes, he remembered everything . . . Emma had had more than her fair share of pain and sorrow and grief in her life. But she would not suffer again, nor ever be deprived again, and there would be no more pain. They were both far too old for tragedies . . . tragedies were for the young.

Finally they drew to a stop in front of the door to the suite. Blackie smiled inwardly. The phone call from reception had been the alert signal for Bryan and Daisy to keep the guests absolutely quiet. Obviously they had succeeded admirably. A pin dropping would have sounded like a gun going off in the silence permeating the corridor.

Giving Emma a final rapid glance, Blackie raised his hand and rapped. The door was opened almost at once by Daisy. "There you are, Mother, Uncle Blackie. We've been waiting for you. Do come in."

Blackie propelled Emma forward and stepped inside after her.

"Happy birthday!" fifty-eight people shrieked in unison.

That Emma was thunderstruck was immediately evident to everyone present. She stared at the crowd made up of relatives and friends who had gathered together to celebrate her birthday, her expression startled, and she colored slightly, the blush rising from her neck to suffuse her face. Her eyes immediately swiveled to Blackie's, and she whispered, "You devil! Why didn't you give me a hint, some warning at least?"

He grinned, gratified that the secret had obviously been well and truly kept. "I didn't dare. Daisy said she'd kill me. And don't start telling me you're annoyed, because I can see from your face that you're not!"

"That's true," she admitted and finally permitted herself to smile.

She swung her head, faced the packed room, and was momentarily rooted to the spot. The lingering smile slowly grew wider and wider as she noted the familiar faces smiling back at her in welcome.

Her two sons, Kit Lowther and Robin Ainsley, were there with their wives, June and Valerie; her daughters Edwina and Elizabeth flanked a distinguished-looking man who was outrageously handsome. She supposed this was the notorious Marc Deboyne—International White Trash, Emily had so succinctly labeled him. Still, he did have a rather fascinating smile and a glamorous aura. Elizabeth always went for the pretty ones, of course. Well, *she* was hardly the one to criticize. The men who had tenanted her life had had their fair share of good looks.

Daisy had slipped across the room, stood with her arm linked through David's, and he in turn was positioned next to her sisters-in-law, the two old ladies Charlotte and Natalie, who were dressed to the nines and dripping with jewels. Paula and Jim hovered next to them; Winston was shepherding Emily, Amanda, and Francesca, and was apparently enjoying his role of protector. Emma's eyes automatically dropped to Emily's left hand, and she winked at her granddaughter when she spotted the glittering emerald engagement ring.

She stared beyond them into the adjoining suite, saw Sarah, Jonathan, Alexander, and his girlfriend Maggie Reynolds crowded together in the entrance. On their left was the entire Kallinski family, and edging up to them were Bryan, Geraldine, and Merry O'Neill. Positioned next to the latter were the rest of the Hartes. Randolph's beaming face peered out at her, just visible above the shoulders of his two daughters, Vivienne and Sally. Anthony, her grandson, smiled back at her from Sally's side.

Henry Rossiter was leaning against the fireplace at the far end of the second suite. He looks better than ever, Emma thought, and eyed his current girlfriend, the noted model Jennifer Glenn. She was at least forty years younger. That's one way to ensure a heart attack, dear Henry, Emma thought to herself, her eyes amused. Gaye Sloane, her private secretary, graced Henry's right, and the remainder of the guests were made up of old friends as well as close business associates such as Len Harvey, who ran Genret, and his wife Monica.

Emma's initial stunned surprise had completely dissipated in the few minutes she had stood motionless surveying the gathering. Now she was again totally in command of herself, all those present, and this occasion. Looking autocratic, proud, dignified, and supremely elegant, she took a step forward and inclined her head.

"Well," she exclaimed, her strong clear voice ringing out as she broke the silence at last, "I never realized I knew so many people who were capable of keeping a secret. At least from *me*." Their laughter rippled around her as she glided forward into their midst, accepting their affectionate greetings and good wishes with a graciousness that few could match.

Blackie edged over to Daisy, stood watching Emma circulating, dispensing her inimitable charm. And by the ladleful, he muttered under his breath. A huge grin suddenly illuminated his face, and his eyes crinkled with humor. He exclaimed to Daisy, "And you worried yourself to death, thinking she was going to be upset! Just *look* at her . . . she's in her element, handling them all with aplomb and behaving as if she's royalty."

Twenty-One

An hour later, at eight o'clock, Blackie escorted Emma into the private dining room farther along the corridor where the birthday celebration dinner was to be held.

Bending toward her, he whispered, "Daisy didn't want anybody's feelings to be hurt, nor did she wish to be accused of favoritism, so none of your children or grandchildren will be sitting at our table."

"That was smart of her," Emma murmured, her mouth twitching with hidden laughter. Well, Daisy *was* the one true diplomat in the family; on the other hand she knew her sons would not exactly be clamoring to sit with her. Emma was still astonished that they had deigned to come at all. Elizabeth's presence did not surprise her. It was just conceivable that her daughter wanted to make friends again, since she always had her eye on the main chance. No doubt she thought she could ingratiate herself, probably with the hopes of extracting more money. Her other motivations would be a desire to see her children and show off her new boyfriend. As for Edwina, she was currying favor with Anthony, who would have disapproved if his mother had declined the invitation.

Slowly she and Blackie crossed to the main table, which was flanked on either side by two other tables. All were arranged in a semicircle around the small dance floor, and at the opposite side of this square of polished parquet a band was already playing a selection of popular music.

Emma's all-encompassing glance took in everything. In the flickering candlelight emanating from the five round tables, the room resembled a charming summer garden, with masses of flowers banked on every side and small colorful bouquets decorating the tables. The latter were covered in shell-pink tablecloths and gleamed brightly with the sparkle of crystal, silver, and fine china.

Nodding with pleasure and smiling with approval, Emma turned to Blackie as they came to a standstill and said, "What a lovely setting Daisy has created . . . it's so very festive."

Blackie beamed. "Yes, she worked hard with the banqueting manager and supervised everything herself." He pulled out a chair for her but remained standing himself.

Once she was seated, Emma squinted at the place cards on either side of her and said, "I see you're on my right, Henry on my left, but who else will be joining us?"

"Charlotte and Natalie of course, Len and Monica Harvey, and Henry's girlfriend Jennifer. We've also got Mark and Ronnie Kallinski and their wives with us, which makes twelve altogether."

"Oh, I *am* glad some of the Kallinskis will be sitting with us. I couldn't help thinking of David tonight, wishing he were here. Although Ronnie doesn't look as much like David as Mark, he does remind me of his father. He has many of his mannerisms. Don't you agree?"

"I do indeed, me darlin'. Ah, here comes Randolph with his mother and his aunt."

Emma half turned, welcomed Charlotte and Natalie, and with his usual flourish and show of old-world gallantry, Blackie ushered Emma's sisters-in-law to their seats.

Randolph, bluff and hearty as always, squeezed Emma's shoulder and boomed, "I'm sitting at Bryan's table, over there. But I'll be back, Aunt Emma." He winked at her. "I intend to claim at least one dance."

Laughing, Emma said, "A foxtrot, Randolph, nothing more energetic than that."

"You're on."

His mother leaned over to Emma and confided, "Emily's the best thing that has happened to that grandson of mine. I couldn't be more delighted about the engagement."

"Oh so am I, Charlotte, and that was a sweet gesture of yours, giving Emily the strand of pearls as an engagement present. I remember when Winston gave them to you."

Charlotte beamed. "Yes, when we became engaged in 1919. Now about the wedding, I do hope they'll get married in Yorkshire, Emma. Elizabeth was talking to me earlier, and she seems to think the wedding should be in London."

"Does she now," Emma said with dryness. "I wouldn't worry about it for one moment. Elizabeth's always had grand ideas, and usually they're self-serving. Under the circumstances, I think it's for Emily and Winston to decide, and they've indicated to me that they want to get married in Ripon Cathedral. I think that's a lovely idea, and then we can have the reception at the house."

The three women talked about Emily's wedding, planned for the following summer for a few minutes longer, and then Emma started to tell them about her impending trip with Blackie and the places they would visit on their journey to Australia.

Blackie continued to direct traffic, and within a few minutes the room had filled up, everyone was seated, and the waiters were gliding between the five tables, filling glasses with white wine. There was a feeling of conviviality, gaiety in the air. Laughter reverberated, the cacophony of voices rose to a crescendo, the hubbub of noise balanced by the strains of the light music playing in the background.

Emma, her mind as razor-sharp as always, her eyes everywhere, soon discerned that her family and friends were enjoying themselves wholeheartedly, appeared to be having the best of times. After the first course of smoked salmon had been served, some of the younger guests immediately took to the dance floor, and Emma watched them, filled with pride, thinking how attractive they looked . . . the girls in their pretty dresses, the young men in their smart dinner jackets. They whirled around the dance floor, their clear young faces shining with happiness, their eyes bright with hope and limitless expectations for the future, their lives ahead of them, offering so much.

Jonathan's bland and smiling face came into her line of vision as he guided young Amanda around the perimeters of the floor, and for a split second she wondered if she had been wrong about him. She clamped down on this thought, not wanting to dwell on problems tonight, and swung her eyes to his father. Robin was dancing with his half sister, Daisy, and oozing charm. Dark, exotic-looking Robin, once her favorite son, the dashing Member of Parliament, currently politically secure after a few rocky rides. Well, he *was* shrewd and smart when it came to his own career. He had always been the dyed-in-the-wool politician, the consummate deal maker, and, she had to admit, popular in the Labor Party, not to mention with his constituents in Leeds.

Blackie cut into her thoughts when he touched her arm lightly, pushed back his chair, and said, "Come on, Emma, you owe me the first dance."

He led her proudly onto the floor, took her in his arms, and they glided away, smoothly in step to the strains of the Cole Porter medley the band had begun to play.

Blackie was well aware that they cut quite a swath together, and towering above Emma as he did, he was conscious that they were the center of attraction, knew that all eyes were on them. He caught sight of Kit scrutinizing them, and he inclined his head, smiled, and peered around, seeking Robin. There he was, swinging Daisy across the floor, so smooth, so sleek . . . and so slippery. Blackie despised her sons for their treachery toward Emma, and now he wondered if either of them had enough sense to realize how foolish they had been, pitting themselves against this brilliant woman, trying to outsmart her. They had had as much chance as a snowball in hell. Of course she had won hands down. She always won.

Emma whispered against his chest, "Everybody's looking at us, talking about us, Blackie."

"Nothing's changed much then."

Emma simply smiled, and they finished their dance in silence.

The evening continued to progress without a hitch. Everyone ate the delicious food, partook of the excellent wines, talked, joked, laughed, and danced, with a carefreeness that surprised Emma. It seemed to her that for once there were no undercurrents. It was as if an unspoken truce had been automatically declared between the various factions, as if animosities, rivalries, hatreds, and jealousies had been temporarily buried. Tomorrow they might well be at each other's throats, but tonight they were friendly and apparently at ease with each other. Perhaps this was only on the surface, but nonetheless it pleased her to see them behaving with a decorum that befitted the occasion.

Emma, too, was enjoying herself, but as the hours sped by, she realized the evening was inducing mixed emotions in her. Memories came unbidden . . . memories that were both joyous and heartrending. Bits of her life kept rushing back to her, and even the location had a profound effect on her at one moment. The Ritz Hotel was so bound up with Paul and their early years together, for here they had snatched shreds of happiness during the First World War before he had gone back to the trenches in France. For a second or two Paul McGill dominated her mind, and she sank back into herself, looking inward, her eyes momentarily glazed as she drifted into the past. But then she heard Daisy's vivid laughter at the next table and looked up sharply as the present intruded forcefully. She shook off the wistfulness that had briefly enveloped her, sternly reminded herself that she had recently resolved to look only to the future.

Blackie, who had become conscious of her periodic lapses into silence, drew her into conversation, and had her laughing in a matter of minutes. Suddenly, he interrupted himself in the middle of a story he was recounting and exclaimed, "Brace yourself, me love, here comes Randolph to claim his dance."

"Then dance I shall," Emma said and allowed herself to be swept off by her beaming nephew. They had circled the floor once when Jonathan cut in, who in turn had to give way to Winston after only a few minutes. Anthony was the next to steal his grandmother away, and soon Alexander was tapping his cousin on the shoulder so that he could complete the waltz with her.

When the music stopped, Alexander did not release her but stood looking down at her as they lingered in the middle of the floor, an unreadable expression in his eyes.

Emma searched his face inquiringly. "What is it, Sandy? You look as if you're about to say something important."

"I am, Grandy." He bent closer and whispered.

"Of course," Emma said, smiling. She whispered something back to him as he escorted her to her table.

Sitting down, Emma turned to Blackie, fanned herself with her hand. "Phew! That was a *marathon*. To tell you the truth, I think I'm getting too old to be galavanting around dance floors."

"What, a spring chicken like you. *Never*. Anyway, you seem to be thoroughly enjoying yourself," Blackie laughed.

"I am, darling. It's a lovely party, and everyone's so very friendly with each other." When he did not answer, she stared hard at him. "They really are, you know."

"Aye," he said at last, laconic, very noncommittal, "perhaps you're right." But Blackie was not so certain she *was* right, found her children's unexpected chumminess suspect. On the other hand, they were behaving themselves, and that was all that mattered to him. In a few days the two of them would be winging their way to New York, and when Emma was gone from their midst, her family could start murdering each other for all he cared.

Suddenly the din ceased, and everyone glanced at each other as the wall candelabras and ceiling chandelier were dimmed. There was a deafening drum roll. A waiter came forward pushing a trolley on which there reposed an enormous birthday cake topped with eighty candles flickering brightly in the muted light. The moment the waiter came to a halt in the middle of the dance floor, the band struck up the "Happy Birthday" refrain, and the majority of the guests followed Blackie's lead as he began to sing, joining in exuberantly. When the music finished, Blackie assisted Emma to her feet and walked her over to the cake, and together they blew out the candles. Emma picked up the knife and cut the first slice, and smiling and nodding to the guests, she returned with Blackie to their table.

Champagne was poured, the cake passed around by the waiters, and once each person had been served, Daisy rose and tapped her glass with a spoon. "Can I have your attention! *Please!*" Conversation ceased, and all eyes settled on her.

"Thank you," Daisy said, "and thank you very much for coming tonight to celebrate my mother's birthday. Blackie and I are delighted you managed to keep our secret. We knew from Mother's face when she arrived that she was truly surprised."

Daisy gave them her warmest smile and continued, "In the past few weeks Blackie and I have been approached by various members of the family, and friends, who wanted to say a few words, to pay tribute to Emma Harte this evening. It was quite a dilemma for us—knowing who to choose, and inevitably we realized that the great lady we are honoring would soon become impatient if she had to sit through a lot of speeches. Especially since she herself would be the subject of those speeches. It was Blackie who came up with the best solution, but before I announce the first speaker, I would like my mother and all of you to know that we had requests from the following."

Daisy picked up a piece of paper, glanced at it, lifted her head and focused her eyes on Emma. "All of your grandchildren wanted to propose a toast to you, Mother, to be the representative of the third generation. Robin and Elizabeth both wished to say something on behalf of us, your children. Henry, Jim, Len, and Bryan all asked to be the one to offer you the very best wishes of your many friends and business associates."

Emma inclined her head graciously, looking first to her right, then to her left, acknowledging those whom Daisy had mentioned.

Daisy proceeded, "As I told you, Blackie solved our little problem and most appropriately, in my opinion. Now I would like to introduce our first speaker—Mr. Ronald Kallinski."

Ronnie rose. He was a man of dominating presence, tall, slender, with a saturnine face and black wavy hair tinged with gray. He had inherited the eyes of his father and his grandmother Janessa Kallinski. These were of the brightest blue and seemed all the more startling because he had a weatherbeaten complexion.

"Daisy, Emma, Blackie, ladies and gentlemen," he began, his generous smile revealing flashing white teeth. Ronnie had a considerable amount of charm and *savoir faire,* and as chairman of the board of Kallinski Industries, he was used to public speaking. "There are many of Emma's friends and business associates present; however, I feel certain that they will not be offended if I term this evening a gathering of the clans. Three clans to be precise . . . the

Hartes, the O'Neills, and the Kallinskis. Well over half a century ago three young people became bosom friends—Emma, Blackie, and David, my father. From what I've been told, this friendship apparently seemed startling, even peculiar to many people, who could not understand what a Gentile, an Irish Catholic, and a Jew could possibly have in common. But those three young people knew. They recognized their own likeness in each other, saw qualities that were common denominators. They were warm, loving, outgoing, and filled with hope. They shared ambition, drive, a determination to succeed at all costs, yet without sacrificing honor, honesty, or integrity. And they believed in charity to others. The trio was soon bound together by bonds of love and respect, and they remained loyal and devoted throughout their lives, until my father's death a few years ago."

Ronnie shifted his stance slightly as he paused for breath. "Some of you may not know this," he remarked after a moment, "but the trio dubbed themselves the Three Musketeers, and when Blackie asked me to speak to you tonight, to pay homage to Emma, he said I would be standing in for that third musketeer who is no longer with us. *My father.*"

After a quick sip of water, Ronnie leveled his eyes at the main table. "Emma Harte is the most remarkable of women, and her attributes are manifold. So it is hard, if not downright impossible, to know which one to single out as being extra special. However, if David Kallinski were present tonight, I know that he would choose to speak to you about the immense and extraordinary *courage* of Emma Harte. This quality first manifested itself to the Kallinski family in 1905 when Emma was sixteen. Let me tell you about this. One day, as she wandered in the North Street area of Leeds seeking work, she came across a group of ruffians attacking a middle-aged man. He was in need of help, since he had fallen to the ground and lay huddled near a wall trying to protect himself as they continued to stone him. Without giving a thought to her condition— Emma was pregnant at the time—this young girl on the deserted street instantly rushed to his aid. She was fearless as she drove the attackers away. After helping the man to his feet and checking his injuries, she retrieved his scattered packages and insisted on escorting him to his home in the Leylands. The name of that man was Abraham Kallinski. He was my grandfather. As Emma guided him to the safety of his simple abode, she asked Abraham why the ruffians had been stoning him. Abraham told her: *Because I am a Jew.* The young Emma was baffled by this statement, and Abraham went on to explain to her that the Jews in Leeds were persecuted because their religion, dietary laws, and customs appeared foreign to the local people. He told her of the terrible brutalities the Jews suffered at the hands of marauding bands of hooligans who entered the Leylands, which was a ghetto, and attacked them and their homes. Emma was disgusted and outraged to hear such things. And she at once condemned these persecutors as cruel, stupid, and ignorant."

Ronnie Kallinski nodded to himself, then looked directly at Emma, his face reflecting his love and admiration for her. He said slowly, "From that day to the present, this most extraordinary woman has fought stupidity, ignorance, and every kind of inequity, has always condemned the wicked traits she recognized in some at such a tender age. She has continued to loathe religious and ethnic prejudice—any kind of prejudice, in fact. Her courage has never diminished. It has only grown in strength. She has remained consistent in her belief in justice, truth, and fair play."

Henry Rossiter began to clap, and others followed suit, and Ronnie eventually had to call out for them to be quiet. "My father once told me that
Emma, Blackie, and he had helped to create a city's greatness as they had lifted
themselves out of the grinding poverty of their youth but that it was Emma
most of all who had put her indelible stamp on the city of Leeds. Indeed he
spoke the truth, and her contributions to industry and her philanthropies are
renowned. However, I would like to add a comment of my own, and it is this:
Emma has also put her inimitable imprimatur on each one of us present . . .
not only on every member of the three closely knit clans, but on her friends
and business associates. We must be proud of that, for we are better people for
knowing her, for being part of her circle. Emma Harte honors us with her
devoted friendship, her love, and depth of understanding. And she does us the
greatest honor by her presence tonight. And so in my late father's name and in
the name of all the Kallinskis absent and present, I ask you to raise your glasses
to Emma Harte. A woman of outstanding courage and indomitability who has
never been defeated and who has always stood tall . . . so tall she towers above
all of us."

Ronnie raised his glass. "To Emma Harte."

After the toast had been repeated, Ronnie said, "And now Blackie will say
a few words."

Blackie pushed himself to his feet. "Thank you, Ronnie. David could not
have said it better, and your own tribute to Emma was fitting and most moving.
As Daisy told you, we knew Emma would not sit still for a lot of laudatory talk.
Also, since I'm aware she regards the shortest of speeches a humbug, I'm going
to be brief." Blackie chuckled. "Well, as brief as I can be. Obviously on this
special occasion of Emma's eightieth birthday, I do feel the need to say a few
kind words about her."

As Blackie launched himself into a recital about her strength of character,
her ability to conquer against all odds, and her great business achievements,
Emma sat back. She was only partially listening. During Ronnie's speech, she
had begun to ruminate on her early beginnings. She thought of the place she
had started out from, the great distance she had traveled, and she marveled at
herself, wondering how she had accomplished all that she had, and for the most
part entirely by herself.

But after a short while she became aware that many pairs of eyes were on
her as well as on Blackie, and she roused herself from her reflections. Her old
friend was moving away from bygone eras, talking of the present. And Emma's
thoughts instantly settled on her life as it was today.

Well, she thought, whatever my life has been about, my grandchildren are
proof positive to me that it has been worthwhile. Quite unexpectedly, in a
sudden flash, everything became clear to Emma. So clear that she was startled
for a moment. And she knew what she must do tonight, what her course of
action must be.

Blackie was drawing to a close. "It has been the greatest privilege of my
life to be her friend. So please join in my toast to Emma, which comes from my
heart." Blackie leaned forward, grasped hold of his glass.

Lifting it high, Blackie smiled down at her. "Emma, you truly are a
woman of substance in the finest sense of that phrase. May you long be with us.
To you, Emma."

Emma felt the heat rush to her face as the roomful of smiling friends and relatives toasted her and her throat tightened with sudden emotion.

Once everyone was seated, Blackie, who had continued to stand, said, "I give you our guest of honor, Emma Harte."

Emma rose, stepped around her chair, and pushed it under the table. She stood with her hands resting on its back, her eyes slowly roving around the room, her glance touching each of them briefly.

Finally she said, "Thank you for joining me on my birthday and for the lovely gifts and flowers you sent me today. I was very touched. I must also express my thanks to Blackie and Daisy for giving this party and for being such wonderful hosts."

She let her gaze linger on Ronnie Kallinski, her eyes very bright, glittering with moisture under the wrinkled lids. "I am so glad you and your family are here with me tonight, Ronnie. And I thank you for your eloquent words, for standing in for your father. David is sorely missed." She turned her attention to Blackie. "You said some beautiful things about me too . . . thank you, Blackie."

Then, in a crisper tone, Emma said, "As many of you know, Emily and Winston are to be married next year. However, they did want me to formally announce their engagement to you all this evening. It seems that romance is in the air in the Harte clan. Alexander also asked me to announce his engagement to Marguerite Reynolds. So let us drink to the future happiness of these four young people."

The toast was given amidst a ripple of excited whispers, exclamations. Emma stood waiting, gripping the back of the chair more tightly than ever. Her expression was benign, but her narrowed green eyes were watchful. She knew exactly what she would say, even though she had decided to make this announcement only ten minutes before.

Paula, scrutinizing Emma, took note of the friendly expression on her face. But her grandmother did not fool her for one moment. She recognized that implacable glint in her eyes. It signaled something . . . Emma was about to drop one of her bombshells. Paula instantly tensed, wondering what this could be. She could not hazard a guess. Her eyes remained riveted on Emma. How imperious Grandy looks at this moment, she thought, standing there so erect and proud, totally in command of herself and this audience.

Emma moved slightly, and in the soft light emanating from the many candles the emeralds blazed more brilliantly, and there was a shimmer, a luminosity about Emma at this moment. Power, Paula thought, my grandmother exudes immense power.

A hush had fallen over everyone. Like Paula, they stared at Emma, filled with unexpected anticipation.

Finally Emma spoke. Her voice rang out clear and strong, dominating the room. "In everybody's life there comes a time when it is appropriate to step aside, to permit younger voices to be heard, greater visions to be perceived. *Tonight is that time for me.*" Emma paused, letting her words sink in.

There was a collective gasp.

"*I am going.* And going willingly. It struck me tonight that I've earned the right to rest these tired old bones at last, to relax for the first time in my life; and who knows, I might even get around to having a little fun."

Her light laugh reverberated as she scanned their faces. Their shock was unconcealed. "How surprised you're looking," she remarked, almost offhand-edly. "Well, perhaps I've even surprised myself. But I came to a decision during the speeches. As I sat there listening to my life being recounted, it suddenly occurred to me that now is the right time for me to retire. And to retire gracefully. Everyone knows that Blackie and I are about to leave on a trip around the world. I am happy to announce to you that I've decided to spend the rest of the days left to me on this earth with my oldest, dearest, and most trusted friend."

Half turning, Emma lifted one hand and let it rest easily on Blackie's broad shoulder. She said, in a more confiding tone, "Blackie said to me the other day, 'Grow old with me, the best is yet to be,' and you know, he might just be right."

No one moved or spoke. Each guest continued to regard her intently, understanding that this slender, silver-haired woman who wielded enormous power had something more to say to them.

Emma stepped away from her chair and walked with swiftness to one of the other tables. She came to a halt next to Alexander, who jumped up imme-diately. His eyes were brilliant in his white face. Recognizing that he too was reeling from shock, she touched his arm lightly as if to reassure him.

Glancing around at the expectant faces, Emma said briskly, "My grandson Alexander has just become the head of Harte Enterprises." She thrust out her hand. He took it, staring at her speechlessly. "Congratulations, Alexander." He stammered his thanks.

Moving at a dignified pace to the table diagonally opposite, Emma was aware of the tension and the sheathed excitement permeating the air. She drew to a standstill next to Paula. Pushing back her chair, Paula was on her feet as speedily as Alexander had been.

Taking the young woman's hand in hers, Emma held onto it tightly. How icy it is, she thought absently and squeezed it, endeavoring to impart some of her own great strength to Paula, who had begun to tremble.

Once again Emma's piercing green gaze swept the entire room. "The Harte department store chain will, as of tonight, be run by my granddaughter, Paula McGill Amory Fairley."

She pivoted to face Paula and gazed long and hard into her violet eyes. And then Emma smiled her incomparable smile that filled her face with radi-ance.

"I charge you to hold my dream," Emma said.

BOOK TWO

Heiress

Passions spin the plot: We are betrayed by what is false within.

George Meredith

I am not made or unmade by the things which happen to me but by my reactions to them. That is all God cares about.

St. John of the Cross

Twenty-Two

She had been alone for two weeks and had drawn strength and a sense of renewal from her solitude.

But now on this warm and pleasant Sunday Paula suddenly experienced a little spurt of pleasure at the thought of seeing Emily. Her cousin was driving over from Pennistone Royal for tea, and she was really looking forward to her company.

After she had finished setting the wrought-iron table on the terrace, Paula hurried down the steps and onto the lawn, to check on the twins. Lorne and Tessa lay in the double pram, sleeping peacefully in the shade. They looked so contented she could not help smiling before turning away and going back to the terrace to wait for Emily.

It was one of those afternoons in the middle of September which frequently occur in Yorkshire and rival the most beautiful days of midsummer. The arc of the sky was a light periwinkle blue, clear and radiant, with a few scattered cotton-ball clouds scudding intermittently across the sun which had blazed down since the late morning. The gardens at Long Meadow were riotous with color and the warm air was filled with the pervasive scents of the flowers and shrubs.

Paula stretched out on the garden chaise, basking in the golden light, thinking of nothing very special as she relaxed. The tranquility soothed her, was like a balm after her particularly hectic week, during which she had been on the go nonstop. They had been holding their annual Autumn Fashion Fair for five days; models had paraded through the Bird Cage at lunchtime wearing the latest ready-to-wear winter styles; every afternoon at three o'clock there had been a fashion show of designer clothes in the couture salon. Fashion aside, Harte's had had other special events during the past week, including the opening of a cooking school in the basement; daily appearances by a famous makeup artist in the cosmetics department; on Thursday evening there had been a cocktail party for the unveiling of the new art gallery in the store and the exhibition of oils and watercolors by Sally Harte. The *vernissage* had been a huge success and most of Sally's paintings of the Yorkshire Dales and the Lake District had already been sold. Whilst coping with these in-store promotions, Paula had had to handle her normal work load and it seemed to her now that every department had needed her complete attention. Much to her dismay, two buyers had resigned on Tuesday and she had had to start interviewing replacements immediately; she had also found it necessary to dismiss the jewelry buyer for incompetence late on Friday and this had proved to be a most unpleasant scene. But continuing daily problems and constant activity of this nature were par for the course, part of the daily routine of a large and successful department store such as theirs. Still, Paula knew she had been pushing herself harder than ever since Jim had been abroad, rising at five in the morning to get to the store by six-thirty so that she could leave early on most days in order to arrive home in time to bathe the twins.

She had eaten dinner alone every night, had not done any socializing whatsoever, and, apart from Sally Harte, the only other people she had seen were her staff at the house, her business colleagues, the few friends who had attended the art gallery opening. During these two weeks of solitariness in her private life Paula had come to realize more fully how vital it was for her to have these stretches of absolute peace and rest at the end of each frantic day. Working as intensely as she did, in a job that required her total concentration, frequently left her frazzled. It was essential for her well-being to have periods entirely alone so that she could recoup her sapped strength. She had the need to think, to review her schedule, to plan ahead as she pottered around in the garden, played with the babies, read or simply listened to classical music in the cool greenness of the conservatory.

With a wry smile Paula had to admit that even if she had wanted to gad about, lead a gay life during Jim's absence in Canada, there was no one available to play with. Winston had flown off a week ago to join Jim in Toronto where they were attending a world conference of newspaper editors, publishers, and proprietors. But the real reason for Winston's trip was to start negotiations with a Canadian paper mill which was up for sale. He hoped to acquire it for the Yorkshire Consolidated Newspaper Company. Miranda O'Neill was in Barbados for the opening of their new hotel and the launching of the Harte boutique. Sarah was with her, acting as fashion adviser, supervising the interior displays and the dressing of the windows. Alexander was taking a holiday in the South of France with Maggie Reynolds, and they were staying at Emma's house in Cap Martin. Until last night Emily had been in Paris on a buying trip for Genret.

Jonathan was the only member of the family who was not traveling somewhere, but *their* paths rarely crossed. This was the chief reason Paula had been surprised when he had dropped in to see her at the store on Wednesday. Before she had even asked what he was doing in Yorkshire, he had volunteered, and rather defensively she had thought, that he was in Leeds on real estate business for Harte Enterprises. He had wasted an hour of her precious time chatting about absolutely nothing, although he had asked her, and several times during the course of their aimless conversation, when Grandy was returning from Australia. She had said she had no idea, which was the truth, and had been noncommittal about matters in general. Cautious by nature, Paula had never been overly fond of Jonathan Ainsley, always wary of him. This feeling had only intensified since Emma had alerted her to him, confided her worries about his loyalty.

After her grandmother's unexpected retirement and her departure on her world tour—almost five months ago—she and Alexander had met in London to discuss the situation in general. They had agreed they should continue to confer regularly once a month, in order to review matters pertaining to the business empires they were running, had even acknowledged they might well need each other as a sounding board.

At their first get-together they had come to the conclusion that Emily should be told about Emma's suspicions regarding Jonathan. They had invited her to lunch the following day, and had taken her into their confidence, had suggested that she attend their monthly brainstorming sessions. All three had concurred that they must watch Jonathan like a hawk. By mutual agreement they had also made the decision to exclude Sarah from their confabs, feeling that her sudden closeness to Jonathan was suspicious. Paula, Emily, and Alexander had thus become the self-appointed triumvirate who were resolved in their determination to run Emma's companies in the way she wanted, whilst guarding her great legacy.

The French doors leading to the drawing room were open and dimly, in the background, Paula heard the grandfather clock in the hall striking four. She roused herself and went inside, hurrying through into the kitchen. She put the babies' bottles in a pan of water to be warmed up later, loaded the tray with tea sandwiches, scones, strawberry jam, and a cream cake, then went to the cupboard for the tea caddy. Ten minutes later, as she completed her tasks, she heard a car in the driveway and looked out of the window to see Emily alighting from her battered white Jaguar.

Emily bounced into the kitchen with her usual *joie de vivre,* wearing a happy grin. She ran to Paula and hugged her. "Sorry I'm late," Emily said as they drew apart, "but that pile of old junk has been acting up all the way from Pennistone Royal. I really think I'll have to splurge and buy myself a new car."

Paula laughed. "You're not late, and I think you're right about the Jag, it has seen better days. Anyway, welcome back, Emily."

"It's good to be home, although I did enjoy Paris. It's still my favorite city." Emily perched on the edge of a kitchen chair as Paula hovered near the stove. "Have you heard from anybody? Grandy, to be specific?"

"Yes." Paula swung around, the kettle in her hand. "She rang me up at midnight on Thursday. She wanted to hear about the *vernissage* and how the opening of the art gallery went—you know that's been her pet project for the last year. She said she and Blackie were going to Coonamble with Philip for four or five days. She sends you her love."

"I'm beginning to think she'll never come back. Did Gran indicate what their plans were?"

"Yes she did, as a matter of fact. She and Blackie intend to leave Sydney in the middle of October, wend their way back to New York before returning here sometime in late November. She promised to be home in time for Christmas at Pennistone Royal."

"My God, that's a long way off! I can't wait to see her. It's not the same without Grandma is it?"

"No." Paula stared at Emily, scowled. "You've got a face like a wet week, Emily. Do you have problems with Genret?"

Emily shook her head. "No, no, everything's fine. I miss Gran, that's all, and even though she *has* retired, it's awfully reassuring to know she's in the background. And right now she seems so far away, sitting over there at the other side of the world."

"I know what you mean," Paula said slowly, having sorely missed Emma's presence herself. She dreaded to think what it would be like, how they would manage, when her grandmother was gone from them forever. She instantly squashed this morbid and distressing thought, and forced a bright smile. "Come on, Emily, let's go out to the terrace. I thought we'd have tea in the garden, it's such a gorgeous day. But we have to feed the babies first. Nora asked to change her day off this week, and Meg is never here on Sundays, so I've been coping alone today. I've enjoyed it, actually."

Emily followed her outside to the terrace. She ran down the steps to the pram. "They're both wide awake," she called over her shoulder, and began making cooing noises to the twins, leaning into the pram and touching their downy cheeks.

"Upsy-daisy," Paula murmured, lifting Lorne into her arms, "time for your bottle, little boy."

Emily scooped up Tessa and the two young women returned to sit at the table on the terrace. Half an hour later, after the children had been slowly fed, dutifully burped, and then returned to their perambulator, Paula went inside. Not long after, she came back carrying the tea tray.

As she poured, she said, "Any news from Winston?"

"Yes, he phoned me last night. He's gone up to Vancouver. He's already in negotiations with the directors of that paper mill, and he thinks he's going to make the deal. There are a few more details to iron out, but he says they'll be able to conclude everything in a matter of days. He was very optimistic, and the mill will be a wonderful acquisition for Consolidated. Anyway, he's going to stop off in New York to spend a few days with Shane. Apparently *he's* in Barbados for the opening of the hotel, and won't be in New York until the middle of this coming week."

"I'm glad to hear the deal is going through!" Paula exclaimed. "When I spoke to Jim a few days ago he sounded uncertain about its outcome, and said Winston was down in the dumps. Obviously he was wrong, or things have changed radically overnight." She sipped her tea and continued, "Talking of Barbados . . . Sarah flew out there ten days ago to help Merry supervise the unpacking of the Lady Hamilton clothes and get the merchandise on the racks. I expect they're all having a whale of a time—"

Emily exclaimed, "Sarah went to Barbados! Why ever was that necessary?" She banged the cup down with such an angry clatter Paula was taken aback.

She threw Emily a baffled look. "Goodness, you *do* sound fierce. Sarah seemed to think it was her *duty* to go out there. In fact, she was hell-bent on going. Since she *is* running our fashion division, and since the boutiques are mostly stocking Lady Hamilton beach clothes and resort wear I suppose she has a point. Besides, I couldn't very well interfere. She doesn't have to answer to me . . . only to your brother. You know Sarah, she considers herself her own boss."

"Oh well." Emily shrugged, trying to act as if Sarah was of no consequence. But her fertile brain whirled and two and two suddenly made more than four. She was convinced the only interest Sarah Lowther had in Barbados and the Harte boutique was Shane O'Neill. Sarah must have found out from Miranda that he was going to be in the Caribbean for the opening of the hotel. Sarah was probably making a fool of herself at this very moment—throwing herself at Shane.

Emily, changing the subject, said with a rueful smile, "Poor Alexander. I called him yesterday before I left Paris and found out that Mummy's descended on him with Marc Deboyne in tow. She's installed them at Grandy's villa, claims she has a right to be there and to visit with her darling daughters. Sandy says she's being a pain in the neck. Very bossy. I think Amanda and Francesca are anxious to fly home immediately. They haven't had much time for Mummy, not for ages."

"Oh what a shame he's having to cope with problems on holiday—he was so looking forward to going away. Won't your little sisters have to be back here very soon anyway?"

"Yes. They're due at Harrogate College on the last day of this month. I'm glad Gran agreed to let them stay there for another term before packing them off to Switzerland. I don't think those two relish the idea of being far away from her, and—" Emily stopped, cocked her bright blond head, listening. "Isn't that the phone?"

"Yes. I'll be back in a second." Paula dashed through the drawing room into the hall to answer it, snatching at the receiver.

Before she had a chance to say a word, the caller was exclaiming, *"Jim?* Is that you?"

"Oh hello, Aunt Edwina," she said, surprised. "It's Paula. Jim's not here. He's in Canada on business."

"Canada. Oh my God!"

Instantly recognizing the anxiety in the high-pitched voice, Paula asked, "Is there something wrong?"

Edwina began to babble so hysterically Paula was unable to make sense of her aunt's words. She was incoherent, obviously distraught. Paula listened for a few seconds longer, filling with increasing alarm. Finally she cut in. "Aunt Edwina, I can't understand a thing you're saying. Please speak a little more clearly, and slower."

Paula heard Edwina sucking in her breath. There was a drawn-out moment of silence.

"It's poor Min," Edwina gasped at last. "Anthony's wife . . . she's . . . she's . . . *dead.* She's been found . . . drowned . . ." Though she had choked on these words, Edwina managed to add, "In the lake at Clonloughlin. And . . . and . . ." Edwina was unable to continue and began to weep.

Paula went cold from head to toe. Innumerable questions leapt into her mind. How had she drowned? Accident? Suicide? And why had Min been at Clonloughlin in the first place when she and Anthony were estranged? Aware suddenly that her aunt's sobbing had lessened, if only a fraction, Paula said sympathetically, "I'm so sorry, so very sorry. This must be a terrible shock for you."

Edwina gasped, "It's not only Min. It's poor Anthony. Paula—the police are here. They're questioning Anthony again. Oh my poor boy! I don't know what to do! I wish I could talk to Jim. It's also a pity Mother isn't in England. She'd know how to handle this ghastly mess. Oh dear God, what am I going to do?"

Paula stiffened. Her mind worked swiftly, striving to comprehend what Edwina was intimating. "What do you mean about the police? You're not trying to tell me they think Anthony is somehow involved in Min's death are you?"

There was an awful stillness at Edwina's end. Her voice was a terrified whisper when she spoke. *"Yes,"* she said.

Paula sat down heavily on the hall chair. She felt prickles of gooseflesh on her arms and her heartbeat accelerated against her rib cage. Horror was trickling through her but instantly this gave way to a burst of anger. "How ridiculous! Your local police force must be bonkers. Anthony under suspicion of murd—" Paula bit off the remainder of the word, reluctant to say it. Again she exclaimed, "This is *preposterous!"*

"They think he ki—" Edwina faltered, for like Paula she was unable to voice the unthinkable.

Striving to take hold of herself, Paula said in her firmest manner, "Aunt Edwina, please start at the beginning and tell me everything. Grandy and Jim may not be here, but I am, and I will do everything I can to help, but you must be absolutely honest with me so that I can make the proper decisions."

"Yes. Yes. All right." Edwina sounded slightly calmer, and although she stumbled a few times she was able to give Paula the essential details about the discovery of Min's body early that morning, the arrival of the police, who had been summoned by Anthony, their departure and their subsequent return two hours ago. After poking around the estate they had ensconced themselves with Anthony in the library at Clonloughlin and were still with him.

When Edwina finished, Paula said, "It sounds very cut-and-dried to me. Min obviously had an accident." She hesitated. "Look," she went on, "I think this is merely routine . . . I mean, the police coming back this afternoon."

"No! No!" Edwina cried. "It isn't routine. Min's been creating problems lately. She changed her mind several weeks ago—about the divorce. She refused to go ahead with it. Other things have been happening. Dreadful things." Then Edwina added rapidly, in a voice so quiet Paula had to strain to hear, "That's why the police are here."

"You'd better tell me everything," Paula said as steadily as she could, even though her sense of dread was mounting by the second.

Edwina gulped. "Yes, I think I must. The trouble started a month ago, actually. Min came down here—she's been living in Waterford—and started to make a nuisance of herself, caused the most horrendous scenes. Sometimes she was really sloshed, reeling from drink. She and Anthony had fierce quarrels and there were some unfortunate scenes in front of the staff, the estate workers, and even a nasty confrontation one afternoon in the village, when she accosted Anthony. All of the rows, the violence, have inevitably caused gossip, and Sally Harte's presence here earlier this summer hasn't done anything to help the situation. You know what people are like in a small place, Paula. Gossip is their way of life. There's been an awful lot of talk—distressing talk—about *the other woman."*

Paula groaned inwardly. "Let's go back for a moment. What did you mean when you referred to *violence?"*

"Oh, violent words mostly. Shouting and screaming on Min's part, but Anthony did become enraged last weekend when she showed up on Saturday. At dinnertime. He had guests. I was there. They had a fight, a verbal fight that is, and she hit Anthony with a golf club. He pushed her away from him, a natural reaction, I suppose. She fell, though, in the hall. Min wasn't really hurt, but she pretended she was. She was overly dramatic about it, screamed something about Anthony wanting her—"

"Yes, Aunt Edwina, go on," Paula gently encouraged as the silence lengthened.

There was a sound of harsh breathing before Edwina told Paula, with a sob, "Min shouted something about Anthony wanting her dead and buried and that she wouldn't be surprised if she was found murdered. And very soon. Several people heard her say this. I did myself."

"Oh my God!" Paula's heart sank and her apprehension spiraled into genuine fear. She did not think for a single moment that her cousin had killed his wife, but it was suddenly apparent to her why the police harbored suspicions about Anthony. Her mind momentarily floundered, then rallied, as she told herself she had to come to grips with this dilemma. But where to begin? Who to enlist?

Paula said in a strong, calm voice that belied her inner nervousness, "All the gossip, the scenes are meaningless in the long run. The police need hard evidence before they can do anything—arrest Anthony, accuse him of killing her. When did she drown? What about an alibi? Surely Anthony has one."

"They're not sure about the time of death . . . at least that's what they say. I think they're doing an autopsy," Edwina went on miserably. "Alibi? No, that's the terrible part, Anthony doesn't have one."

"Where was he yesterday? *Last night?* Those must be the crucial hours."

"Last night," Edwina repeated as if she was confused. Then she said quickly, "Yes, yes, I see what you mean. Min arrived at Clonloughlin at about five o'clock yesterday. I saw her driving up—from my bedroom window in the Dower House. I phoned Anthony to warn him. He was annoyed. He told me he was going to hop into his old Land-Rover and drive out to the lake—in the hopes of avoiding her."

"And he did that? Went out to the lake?" Paula asked.

"Yes. But she must have seen him driving off in that direction, or she simply second-guessed where he had gone. It was one of his favorite spots. She followed him out there, and—"

"They had a quarrel at the lake?" Paula cut in.

"Oh no. He never even spoke to her!" Edwina cried. "You see, he saw her mini in the distance—the land is flat around the far side of the lake. He simply got back into the Land-Rover and was going to return to the house the long way round. But he hadn't driven very far when the Land-Rover conked out. Anthony left it parked and started to walk home. He wanted to avoid Min . . . don't you understand?"

"Yes. And he left the Land-Rover near the lake, is that what you're saying?" Paula demanded, wondering if this was incriminating or not.

"Of course he left it there. It wouldn't start . . ." Edwina was saying, her high-pitched voice trembling again.

"Please don't cry, Aunt Edwina," Paula pleaded. "It's essential that you control yourself. *Please.*"

"Yes. Yes. I'll try," she sniffed.

Paula heard her blowing her nose and then her aunt resumed, "You don't know Clonloughlin, Paula, it's vast. It took Anthony an hour to walk back. He had to go up the hill, through the wood and several fields to get to the road that cuts across the estate and leads to the village. He—"

"Road!" Paula exclaimed, seizing on this fact immediately. "Didn't he see anyone?"

"No, he didn't. At least he never mentioned that. Anyway, Anthony got back to the house around six-thirty. He phoned me, told me about the Land-Rover breaking down. Then he said he would change for dinner, see me later. I went up to the house around seven. We had drinks and ate, but Anthony was very nervous, not himself. You see, he thought Min would show up and start behaving offensively again."

"But she didn't, did she?"

"No, we were alone all evening. As I said, Anthony was out of sorts and he walked me back to the Dower House around nine-thirty, perhaps nine forty-five, then he returned to Clonloughlin."

"And who found Min's body?"

"The estate manager. He was driving past the lake very early this morning and saw the Land-Rover, also the mini. Then he found—" Edwina broke down, sobbing as if her heart would break.

Paula tried to soothe her aunt, reassure her, and said, "Please, Aunt Edwina, be brave. I'm sure everything is going to be all right." She prayed she was right.

"But I'm frightened for him," Edwina mumbled in a tear-filled tone, "truly frightened—"

"Now listen to me and please do as I tell you," Paula instructed peremptorily, taking charge. "Don't make any more phone calls, and if you receive any, hang up as quickly as possible. I want you to keep this line open. I shall ring you back very shortly. I presume you're calling from the Dower House?"

"Yes." Edwina hesitated, asked, "But what are you going to do?"

"I think I'd better get my mother over there to stay with you for the next few days. You shouldn't be alone at a time like this. I assume there's going to be an inquest. The main thing is, I don't want you to worry. Fretting won't help anyone. I know it won't be easy, but you *must* try. I'll ring you back within the hour."

"Th-th-th-thank you, P-P-Paula," Edwina stammered.

They said good-bye and hung up. Paula immediately lifted the phone and dialed her parents' flat in London. The line was busy. She flung the receiver back into the cradle with impatience and leapt up, realizing she had better go and talk to Emily.

As Paula raced through the drawing room, she almost fell over an occasional table. She righted it and stumbled out onto the terrace, blinking as she came out in the bright sunlight.

Having heard the crash, Emily swung her head and grinned. "You are a clumsy clot—" She stopped, her eyes opening wide. "What's happened?" Emily asked worriedly. "You're as white as a sheet."

Paula leaned against a chair. "We have some trouble, really *serious* trouble, Emily. I'm going to have to deal with it—and you'll have to help me. Please come inside. I must reach my mother. It'll save time if you listen whilst I explain everything to her."

Twenty-Three

"You don't think he could have done it, do you?"

Paula lifted her head sharply. "Of course not!" She stared at Emily, who sat opposite her on the sofa in the conservatory. Her stare intensified and she frowned, "Why, do you?"

Without hesitation, Emily exclaimed, "No. I don't think he would be capable of it." There was a pause, and Emily bit her lip. She said in a rush, "On the other hand, you said something . . ."

"*I* did? What do you mean? When?"

"Oh, not today, Paula, months ago, when you and Alexander took me to lunch just after Gran left. You know, the day we discussed Jonathan. We also spoke about Sarah. You made an interesting remark and it's stuck in my mind ever since. You said we never *really* know about other people, not even those who are closest to us, and that we know very little about what goes on in people's private lives. I was struck by the essential truth in your words at the time, and, let's face it, we don't know Anthony all that well. We've never spent a lot of time with him."

"You're right. But I've got to go with my gut instinct on this, Emily. I just know he didn't have anything to do with Min's death. Admittedly, the circumstances *sound* peculiar, but no"—Paula shook her head vehemently—"I don't believe he killed her. I'm convinced it was an accident. Or suicide. Look here, Emily, Grandy is the shrewdest person we know, and she is brilliant at reading people, spotting character flaws. She thinks the world of Anthony and—"

"Even the nicest people can commit murder," Emily interrupted quietly. "If they're under pressure, pushed hard enough. What about crimes of passion, for instance?"

"We must presume Anthony's innocence! That is British law, after all—innocent until proven guilty."

"Please don't think I was implying that he *did* kill her, because I wasn't. I was just speculating, that's all. To be honest, I'm inclined to go along with you on the suicide theory. Still, I hope she didn't kill herself. Think how hard that would be on Sally and Anthony—having to live with the knowledge that Min took her own life because of them."

"Yes, that had crossed my mind earlier. It would affect them in the worst way," Paula said, her eyes darkening with worry. She glanced at her watch. "I wish my mother would call back. I hope she's not having a problem getting a plane to Ireland."

Emily also checked her watch. "She's only had fifteen minutes, Paula. Give her a chance. In the meantime, let's go over your list again, check your plan."

"Right," Paula replied, aware positive action would help to subdue her nagging anxiety. Lifting the pad, she scanned it, said, *"One:* We get Mummy over to Ireland as soon as possible, so that she can hold the fort. She's already working on that, so—" Paula picked up her pen, ticked it off. *"Two:* My father has to put a call through to Philip at Coonamble between nine and ten tonight, to alert Philip. God forbid Grandy reads about this trouble in the papers first. Daddy understands he must do this once Mother is on the plane." Again this item was checked off, and she went on reading aloud. *"Three:* Put a lid on this mess as far as the newspapers are concerned. I'll call Sam Fellowes at the Yorkshire *Morning Gazette* and Pete Smythe on our evening paper. Actually, I'll have to call all of the papers in our chain. I can't control the national press but I can certainly make sure those we own don't carry a single line. *Four:* Talk to Henry Rossiter about legal advice. We might have to send John Crawford. As the family solicitor, he could represent Anthony, if necessary. *Five:* Get hold of Winston, Jim, or both, to let them know what's happened." She lifted her eyes. "Maybe you can make *that* phone call, Emily, but not until *we* have everything under control. I don't want either of them flying back here. *Six:* Ring Edwina to reassure her, and talk to Anthony, tell him what we've done. *Seven:* Locate Sally Harte. You can do that as well."

"Okay." Emily peered through the door of the conservatory and out into the hall. The telephone was in her direct line of vision. "I think you should work at your desk here, and I'll use the phone in the hall. That way we can see each other, talk easily between calls."

"Good idea. Look, I had better speak to Fellowes and get that out of the way."

"Yes, and I'll start trying to find Sally. Did she tell you on Thursday where exactly she was going in the Lake District?"

"No, and I didn't think to ask, but Uncle Randolph will know. Don't mention a thing about this—not yet," Paula warned.

"Not on your life. He'd go into a flat spin." Emily jumped up. "If the other line rings while you're talking to Fellowes, I'll pick it up. It'll probably be your mother."

As Emily ran out, Paula lifted the receiver and dialed the editor's private line at the Yorkshire *Morning Gazette*. He answered on the second ring, and Paula quickly cut through the usual pleasantries. "Sam, I'm calling about a family matter. My cousin, the Earl of Dunvale, has had a terrible tragedy. His wife has been drowned in the lake on his estate in Ireland."

"That is indeed tragic," Fellowes said. "I'll get one of my top writers onto the obituary immediately."

"No, no, Sam. The reason I'm calling is to let you know I don't want anything in the paper. I'm pretty sure the wire services will be carrying something later tonight or tomorrow. In any event, I want the story killed. No obituary, either."

"But why not?" he demanded. "If the story's on the wires, the national press will be running it. We'll look ridiculous if we don't mention—"

"Sam," Paula cut in quietly, "you should know by now that Emma Harte does not wish to read anything—*anything at all*—about *her* family in *her* newspapers."

"I know that," he snapped, "but surely this is different. How's it going to look if every paper in the country but ours has it? What kind of newspaper are we, anyway? I definitely do not like suppressing news."

"Then perhaps you're working on the wrong newspaper, Sam. Because, believe you me, Emma Harte makes the rules around here, and you'd better respect them."

"I'm going to call Jim and Winston in Canada. *They* run the papers and it seems to me that it's their decision—about what we print and what we don't print."

"In their absence, and in the absence of my grandmother, it is my decision and mine alone. *I* have told you what to do. *No* story. *No* obituary."

"If you say so," he said, his anger ill-concealed.

"I *do* say so. Thank you, Sam, and good-bye."

Paula hung up, bristling. She pulled her address book toward her, looking up Pete Smythe's home number, since the evening paper was closed on Sundays. She hoped she would not get the same argument from Smythe. She was about to dial when Emily flew down the steps, and she swung around in the chair. "Was that my mother?"

"Yes, or rather, Uncle David. Aer Lingus has a flight out early this evening, but he doesn't think Auntie Daisy will make the airport in time. So he's arranged for your mother to be flown over by private plane. Uncle David's going to phone Edwina right now to let her know Auntie Daisy's virtually on her way. Your mother's packing. She'll call before she leaves the flat."

"That's a relief. Did you speak to Uncle Randolph?"

"No, he was out. But Vivienne told me Sally's due back in Middleham shortly. It's been raining in the Lake District, so she packed her painting gear and is driving home. I told Vivienne to have her call here the minute she arrives."

"Was she curious?"

"Not really. I said you wanted to speak to Sally, and got off the phone quickly."

"I dread having to tell her about this—" Paula murmured, her face grim, her eyes reflecting her deep concern.

"Yes, it's going to be awful for her, but she'll *have* to be told. In person, I think, don't you?"

"*Absolutely.* Well, let's not waste time. We'd better get on, Emily."

"What shall I do next?"

"Could you bring the babies into the house, please? You can park the pram in here for a while. I must call those other editors."

"Yes, do it, and I'll be back in a jiffy."

Paula reached Pete Smythe, editor of the Yorkshire *Evening Standard,* at his home in Knaresborough. She repeated the story she had told Sam Fellowes. After sympathizing with her about the accident, Pete concurred with her decision and gave her no arguments.

"I wouldn't have run anything anyway, Paula," Pete told her. "I know how Mrs. Harte feels. She'd skin me alive if a single line appeared about any of you, regardless of the circumstances."

"Sam Fellowes was a bit difficult," Paula volunteered. "I hope I'm not going to meet any similar resistance from our other editors."

"You won't. Sam's a special case. Not the easiest person to deal with. If you want, I'll make the calls to our Doncaster, Sheffield, Bradford, and Darlington papers."

"Oh, would you, Pete? That'd be marvelous. I really appreciate your help. Thanks a lot."

The phone shrilled the moment Paula put it down. It was her mother.

"Hello, darling," Daisy said with her usual calm control. "I'm about to leave. I'm taking a cab to the airport so that your father can be here at the flat, just in case you need him. He spoke to Edwina a few minutes ago. She's relieved I'm on my way. He said she sounded less agitated. The police have left. Anthony's with her. They're waiting for your call."

"I know. I'll ring them when we hang up. Thanks for going over to Ireland, Mother. You're the only one who can handle this. Edwina does trust you, and you'll deal with everyone diplomatically, which is more than she could manage."

"Heavens, Paula, I don't mind. We are a family and we must stick together. But what an appalling situation! I can't understand the police over there . . . it seems very straightforward to me. Your father agrees. Anyway, talking about it endlessly won't solve a thing. I must rush. Good-bye, dear."

"Bye, Mummy, and have a safe journey. We'll speak tomorrow."

Emily was pushing the pram down the two low steps into the conservatory when Paula glanced up from her pad. "I'm going to make a fast call to Henry, and then I'll talk to Ireland." As she dialed Henry's number, Paula quickly gave Emily details about her conversations with Pete Smythe and her mother.

It was Henry Rossiter's housekeeper who answered at his Gloucestershire house. Paula spoke to her briefly, replaced the receiver, said to Emily, "I just missed him. He's driving back to London. Apparently he should be arriving around eight-thirty. Do you think I should call Gran's solicitors or wait to speak to Henry?"

"I'm not sure . . . What do you think Grandy would *do?*" She answered herself instantly. "She'd talk to Henry first."

"That's my feeling," Paula agreed, her hand resting on the telephone. She took a deep breath, preparing herself to make the call to Edwina at Clonloughlin. After picking up the receiver, she instantly put it back in the cradle, swung around. "Sally may be in touch any minute. You'll have to talk to her, Emily, so let's decide what you'll say."

The two young women stared at each other worriedly for the longest moment.

Finally Paula said, "It seems to me that the wisest thing would be to tell her that *I* have a problem, that I want to see her, talk to her, and will she please drive over immediately."

"She'll want to know what's wrong on the phone!" Emily cried, her eyes flaring. "I know I said we should tell her face to face, but now I'm wondering what explanation to give."

"You'll manage. Wriggle out of it, don't say anything concrete. You're very good at being evasive, Emily."

"I *am?*" Emily gave Paula a doubtful stare. "If you say so." She shrugged, then ran over to the pram, where Tessa was wailing.

Paula sprang up and followed her cousin. "They're probably *both* damp and need changing. Let's take them upstairs anyway, and maybe you could then start preparing their bottles."

"Nora would be off today, wouldn't she?" Emily moaned.

"It's always the way," Paula murmured, rocking her baby daughter in her arms, making soft, hushing sounds.

"Dower House, Clonloughlin," a quiet male voice announced when Paula got through to Ireland fifteen minutes later.

She gave her name, asked to speak to the Earl, and a split second later Anthony was on the line.

"Paula . . . hello. Thanks for everything, for taking charge the way you have. I'm very grateful. My mother was panicked earlier, quite at her wits' end, and she fell apart when the police came back."

"I realize that, and it was nothing, really. I'm glad to help in any way I can. How are you feeling?"

"Fine. Very fine," he asserted. "I'm holding up pretty well under the circumstances. This is extremely unpleasant, of course, but I know it's going to be all right."

"Yes," Paula said, thinking he did not sound fine. Not in the least. His voice was weary, drained. Hoping she sounded more positive than she felt, she added, "Everything will be over and done with in the next twenty-four hours. You'll see. Try not to worry in the meantime. I'd like to know what's been happening, but first I must tell you that Emily spoke to Sally a few minutes ago. She's coming over here. She thinks *I* have some sort of crisis. We thought it was wiser not to tell her about this on the telephone."

"I'm relieved to hear you've contacted her, Paula. I've been worried about Sally. I didn't know where to reach her in the Lake District. When we spoke on Friday, Sally said she'd call me on Monday or Tuesday. Perhaps you would ask her to ring me, once you've explained this dreadful situation."

"Of course. What are the latest developments? I know from my mother that the police have left . . . Obviously they haven't charged you—"

"How could they!" he interrupted heatedly. "I haven't done anything *wrong,* Paula! I wasn't involved in Min's death—" His voice cracked and there was a pause as he struggled for control. After a moment he spoke more steadily, apologized, "Sorry for breaking down. It's been such a terrible shock. Min and I have been having bitter quarrels, and she *was* being impossible, but I didn't wish anything like this to happen." He lapsed into silence.

Paula heard his harsh breathing as he tried to compose himself. She said gently, "You must be strong. We'll get you through this safely, Anthony, I promise."

Eventually he said, "You've been awfully good, Paula, awfully helpful. Well," he sighed, added wearily, "they've established the time of death. The local doctor did an examination. He thinks it was between ten-thirty and midnight."

Paula's mouth went dry. From what Edwina had said, Anthony had taken her back to the Dower House around nine forty-five, then returned home. To go to bed? If so, it was most unlikely that he had an alibi for his whereabouts during those key hours. But she made no comment, not wanting to alarm him further. "Your mother said something about an autopsy."

"Oh yes. I hope that'll be tomorrow. The inquest and coroner's court will be on Wednesday or Thursday. Everything's so tediously slow here." There was another heavy sigh, then dropping his voice, Anthony confided, "It's that damnable Land-Rover. I'm not certain the police believe me—about its breaking down in the afternoon."

"Yes," Paula acknowledged. "But are you sure no one saw the Land-Rover out there in the late afternoon, when it really *did* break down? Perhaps one of the estate workers? That would prove to the police that you're speaking the truth."

"No one has come forward, and it's very deserted in that area of the estate —miles away from the house. I doubt anyone was around. However, there has been *one* positive development. A bit of good news. The police have information that should exonerate me. They've been interviewing everyone here for the past few hours . . . the staff, the estate workers . . . Bridget, my housekeeper, told them that she saw me in the house between eleven and midnight."

"Why didn't you tell me this before! Then you have an alibi!" Paula was flooded with relief.

"Yes, I do. I only hope the police believe her story."

"Why wouldn't they?" she demanded, tensing.

"Don't misunderstand me, Paula. I've no reason to think they don't believe her, but Bridget has worked at Clonloughlin all of her life. Her mother was the housekeeper here before her, and she and I—well, we sort of grew up together. I'm praying the police don't get the idea she's lying to protect me. Mind you, she's unshakable in her story."

Puzzled, Paula asked nervously, "Why didn't *you* mention this to the police before? If you were with her last night after your mother left, surely—"

"I wasn't with her," Anthony interjected. "Actually, I didn't even see her. Bridget suffers from migraines, and apparently she had one all last evening. She was cleaning the kitchen after dinner when the migraine became unbearable. She passed the library on her way upstairs to her room. The light was on, the door was open, and she glanced in, saw me reading. However, she didn't call out to me because of her blinding pain. She ran upstairs, found her pills, and returned to the kitchen. She made herself a pot of tea, rested in the chair for half an hour, finished her work, set the dining room table for breakfast, and just after midnight she went to bed. Again she glanced through the open library door. I was by then working on the estate books, doing the accounting, and, not wishing to disturb me, she simply went on up to bed without even saying good night. It was her day off today and she wasn't here when the police first came."

"Oh Anthony, this is the best news I've heard today!"

"I think it is. Still, she is the only person who saw me during those crucial hours. The two maids who work here had already gone home to the village—they come in daily. So . . . there's no one to corroborate her story, and it's well known around these parts that she's devoted to me and is extraordinarily loyal to our family. The police might—and remember I'm only saying *might*—doubt her word, think she and I concocted the alibi."

Paula's heart plummeted, her relief of a moment ago evaporating entirely. "Oh God, don't say that."

"I have to look at the worst, view this situation objectively," Anthony said. "On the other hand, I don't see how the police can dismiss her, say she's lying without being absolutely certain that she *is* making it up, and I know she'll stick to her guns."

Pulling herself upright in the chair, Paula said slowly, "Yes, that's true. However, when I talk to Henry Rossiter later, about getting legal advice, I'm also going to suggest we retain a criminal lawyer."

"Hang on a minute!" Anthony exclaimed. "That's jumping the gun, isn't it?" He sounded aghast at this idea. "I haven't done anything *wrong,* I've told you that, Paula. *A criminal lawyer.* Christ, that's going to make me look as guilty as hell."

"Of course it isn't," Paula shot back sternly, determined to stand her ground. "And let's wait to hear what Henry has to say. I trust his judgment, as Grandy has for many years. He won't steer us in the wrong direction. Please, Anthony, don't make swift decisions out of hand."

"Very well, get Henry's opinion," he agreed, although somewhat grudgingly.

After they had concluded their conversation, Paula sat at her desk in the conservatory. She ran a hand through her hair, rubbed her eyes, stretched. Then eyeing the pad in front of her on the desk, she dragged her thoughts back to her list. Three people still had to be called—Jim, Winston, Henry Rossiter. Looking at her watch she saw that it was now seven-thirty. Henry would not be available for another hour at least, and obviously Emily had not had a chance to reach Jim or Winston in Canada, since she was preparing the babies' bottles in the nursery. Paula went to join her there.

Once they were settled comfortably, each cradling a child, Paula recounted her conversation with Anthony.

Emily listened carefully as she adjusted the feeding bottle, glancing at Paula several times, nodding her understanding.

"That's the gist of it then . . . Bridget has given Anthony an alibi."

A silence fell between them as they concentrated on the babies. Then very quietly, but in a voice of steel, Paula said, "No grandson of Emma Harte's is going to be in the dock standing trial for murder. *I promise you that.*"

——— *Twenty-Four* ———

"I hope you really *do* understand why we had to lie to you, Sally," Paula said gently.

"Yes. And it's just as well that you did." Sally Harte swallowed and cleared her throat nervously. Her voice shook as she added, "I don't think I could have driven over here without having an accident if Emily had told me the truth on the phone."

Paula nodded, continued to survey her cousin intently, filled with anxiousness for her.

For the last fifteen minutes, all through Paula's account of the events in Ireland, Sally had managed to cling to her self-control. Paula admired her for taking the terrible news without flinching. I ought to have known she would be brave, Paula thought. She always was stoical, even as a child. The Harte backbone, her grandmother called it. Yes, despite this extraordinary show of strength, Paula knew Sally was shattered. It showed in her cornflower-blue eyes, now so devastated, and in her lovely face, which was stark with shock.

Sally was holding herself so rigidly in the chair she looked as if she had been paralyzed by Paula's recital, and leaning forward Paula took hold of Sally's hand. She was alarmed at its deathly coldness, said, "Sally, you're frozen! Let me get you a brandy, or make you a cup of tea. You need something to warm you up."

"No, no, really. Thanks, anyway." Sally attempted to bring a smile to her face without success, and as she continued to meet Paula's worried gaze her eyes suddenly filled. "Anthony must be under the most dreadful strain," she began unsteadily and stopped. Now the tears came, spilling out of her wide blue eyes, rolling down her ashen cheeks. Still she did not stir, nor did she utter a sound.

Paula got up and went and knelt in front of Sally, encircling her cousin with her arms. "Oh, darling, it's going to be all right," Paula murmured with the utmost gentleness, full of compassion. "Don't fight the tears. It's much better to cry, really, to get the pain out, and crying does help a bit. It's a release."

Sally clung to Paula, heaving with silent, wracking sobs, and Paula stroked her black hair, gentled her, and eventually the awful quiet heaving lessened. Soon Sally straightened up, brushing her wet face with her strong painter's hands.

"I'm sorry," she gasped, her voice strangling in her throat. She strove hard to get hold of herself, blinking the tears away. "I love him so much, Paula. I can hardly stand it, knowing what he's going through . . . He's so *alone* over there. I'm sure Aunt Edwina is no help at all. She's probably blaming all this on me." She shook her head desperately. "Oh God!" She pressed her hands to her contorted face, which expressed her anguished thoughts. "He needs me . . ."

Paula, who had returned to her chair, stiffened at these words. She held her breath, willing herself to be silent. She knew what must be said, but she was also aware that it would be wiser and kinder to wait until Sally had calmed herself further.

Emily, hovering in the doorway of the drawing room, flashed Paula a warning look and began to move her head violently from side to side. Silently Emily mouthed, *"Don't let her go over there."*

Paula nodded, motioned for Emily to come into the room. This she did at once, seating herself in a nearby chair. In a half whisper, Emily said to Paula, "No luck, I'm afraid. There's no reply from Jim's room or Winston's either. I've left messages for them to call here the minute they get back to their hotels."

Although Emily had spoken softly, Sally had heard her, and at the mention of her brother's name her hands fell away from her face. She jerked her head, looked directly at Emily. "I wish Winston were here. I feel so . . . *help-less* . . ."

"I wish he were here too," Emily replied and patted Sally's arm in her motherly way. "But you're not helpless, since you've got us. It's going to be fine, honestly it is. Paula's been super, and she's in full control, on top of everything. Try not to worry."

"I'll do my best." Sally's eyes swiveled to Paula. "I haven't thanked you—you've been wonderful. So have you, Emily, and I'm very grateful to you both."

Discerning that Sally was a little more composed, Paula said, "There is one thing I must say to you—please don't go to Ireland to be with Anthony. I know you're sick at heart, dreadfully concerned about him, but you really mustn't go over there. You can't do anything constructive, and, frankly, your presence would be highly inflammatory."

Sally was startled. "I've no intention of going to *Clonloughlin!* I know there's been a lot of nasty gossip. Anthony told me about *that* weeks ago—he tells me everything. Obviously I don't want to add fuel to the fire. But, Paula, I do think I ought to go to Ireland, either to Waterford or, better still, Dublin. I'll go tomorrow. I can leave in the morning, from Manchester Airport, and be there in several hours. At least I'll be closer to him than I am here in York-shire—"

"No!" Paula exclaimed with unusual sharpness. "You can't go. You're staying here—even if I have to put you under lock and key!"

Sally began, "But I—"

"I'm not going to let you go to Ireland." Paula threw her cousin a stern look and her mouth settled into resolute lines.

Sally stared back at Paula defiantly, and her pellucid blue eyes filled with stubbornness. Asserting herself, she said with equal firmness, "I understand your reasoning. On the other hand, what harm is there in my being in Dub-lin?" When Paula remained silent, Sally went on, "It's hundreds of miles away from Clonloughlin." She stopped again, frowned. "If I'm in Dublin, Anthony will at least know I'm within easy reach, and we can be together once the inquest is over," she finished shakily, sounding less sure of herself. The trembling started anew, and Sally clenched her hands together in her lap, striving to curb this, and then her eyes unexpectedly welled. "He needs me, Paula. Don't you understand that? Understand that I have to be with him?"

Paula commanded: "Now listen to me, and listen very, very carefully. You cannot help Anthony in any way whatsoever. In fact, you could easily do him irrevocable damage by showing up in Ireland. If Anthony were suspected of murder, you could be his motive. In Grandy's absence I am in charge of this family, and you'd better understand that I'm making *all* the rules. Therefore, Sally, I must insist that you stay here."

Sally had shrunk back in the chair, momentarily stunned by Paula's vehemence. She had not realized how formidable her cousin could be.

Paula and Emily were watching Sally and now they exchanged knowing glances. It was Emily who broke the silence. She touched Sally's arm, said, "Please take Paula's advice, Sal."

Emotionally, Sally had the desire to be with Anthony because she believed he needed her during this dreadful time. Intellectually, she was beginning to accept that going to him would be the wrong move to make. Paula *was* right in everything she had been saying. Listen to your head, not your heart, she cautioned herself.

"I'll stay here," Sally whispered finally, leaning back in the chair, passing her hands over the aching muscles in her face.

Paula let out a sigh of relief. "Thank God for that. Are you feeling up to ringing Anthony now? He's anxious to speak to you and you'll set his mind at rest, once he knows how well you're coping."

Sally jumped up. "Yes, yes, I must talk to him at once."

"Why don't you go up to my bedroom where it's quiet—private," Paula suggested kindly.

"Thanks, I will." Sally paused at the door, swung her head. She stared at Paula. "You're the most daunting person I know," she said and disappeared down the hall.

Paula gazed after her, then looked at Emily speechlessly.

Emily said, "I'd take that as a compliment, if I were you. And I think you'd better get to the phone too—don't you want to reach Henry Rossiter? It's well past eight-thirty, you know."

Together they sat on the terrace, enjoying the gentle stillness of the gardens, cloaked now by a dark-blue sky peppered with brightly twinkling stars. It was a clear night, cloudless, with a full moon, and its silvered rim was just visible above the tops of the distant trees swaying and rustling under the soft evening breeze.

"I don't know about you, but I'm wiped out," Emily said, breaking the long silence at last, peering across at Paula in the dusky, shadowy light.

Paula turned her face, and quite suddenly it was clearly illuminated in the bright glow emanating from the lamps in the drawing room immediately behind them. Emily noticed at once that the stern veil had been lifted, and a lovely softness dwelt there again and there was warmth in her cousin's expression.

Finally Paula answered. "Yes, I'm a bit done in too, I must admit. But at least all the important phone calls are out of the way." She lifted the goblet of white wine and took a long swallow. "This *was* a good idea of yours, Emily. Sitting waiting for Jim or Winston to ring us was getting awfully wearisome and frustrating."

"Yes, it was. I wonder if your father has managed to get hold of Philip yet. It must be nine-thirty by now."

Squinting at her watch, Paula nodded. "Almost. We have to give him time to get through to Australia. He'll be in touch soon." Paula cleared her throat, continued, "I do wish Sally had stayed longer. Do you think she was really all right when she left?"

"She was certainly calmer when she came downstairs, but awfully subdued."

"Well, that's understandable."

Emily made no response. Shifting her position in her chair, she picked up her drink, sipped it. "Did you notice anything different about Sally?" There was a moment's hesitation on Emily's part before she added, "I don't mean when she left, but in general."

"She's put on weight."

Emily's fingers tightened around her glass and, dropping her voice, she whispered, "I have a horrible feeling . . . well, I might as well say it . . . I think Sally's pregnant."

Paula sighed. Her worst fears had been confirmed. "That's what I was afraid you'd say, Emily. Actually, so do I."

"Oh bloody hell," Emily exploded, her voice rising, "that's all we need! I'm surprised you didn't spot her condition at the *vernissage*. Or did you?"

"No, I didn't. Mind you, she was wearing a sort of loose, tenty dress. Anyway, I was harassed, surrounded by people. But when she walked in tonight I was struck by her heaviness, especially across her bustline. Still, I was so concerned about the news I had to break I didn't dwell on her figure. I noticed her weight gain when she was standing near the fireplace, just before she left. It was most pronounced."

"That's when it occurred to me. Oh my God, Paula, the balloon's going to go up when Uncle Randolph finds out!" Emily groaned loudly. "I can't help wishing Gran were here."

"So do I, but she isn't, and I don't want her dragged back needlessly. We'll have to cope the best way we can." Paula rubbed her weary face and exhaled heavily. "Oh God, what a ghastly mess this is, and poor Sally . . ." She shook her head sadly. "I do feel sorry for her . . ." Paula left the rest of her sentence unfinished, sat staring into the shadows, filled with terrible misgivings about the situation in Ireland.

Emily said suddenly, "Well, if she is pregnant there's no problem. At least they'll be able to get married now that—"

"Emily!" Paula swung her head, glared at her cousin, horror-struck. *"Don't say it,"* she warned.

"Oh, sorry," Emily apologized swiftly, but could not resist adding with her typical unnerving bluntness, "Nevertheless, it *is* true."

Paula gave her a withering look.

Lifting the wine bottle out of the ice bucket, Emily refilled their glasses, and remarked, "I don't think I'd better mention the possibility of Sally's being pregnant to Winston."

"Don't you dare! In fact, we're not going to say anything to anyone, not even Grandy. I don't want *her* to have that kind of worry. As for the rest of the family, you know how gossipy they're inclined to be. To even hint that Sally's pregnant would be like throwing a can of petrol on a bonfire. Besides, let's face it, Emily, we don't *know* that she is expecting. She might have merely gained weight lately."

"Yes," Emily said, "there is that possibility, and we don't want to give certain people room to talk."

She fell silent, sank back into the chair, gazing out at the garden. It had acquired a magical, almost ethereal quality and the trees had turned to shimmering silver in the moonlight, which now bathed everything in its extraordinary radiance. "It's so peaceful, so beautiful," Emily murmured. "I could sit here forever. But I suppose I ought to drive over to Pennistone Royal to get my clothes for the office tomorrow if I'm going to stay here with you tonight. I told Hilda what to pack for me, and she'll have my suitcase ready, so I won't be very long."

Paula roused herself from her own reverie. "Perhaps you should pop back there, but take my car, Emily. The Jag *is* ready for the scrap heap, and I don't want you stranded in the middle of nowhere." Paula stood up. "I'll look in on the babies and then start supper. Do you really want bubble and squeak?" she asked, reaching for the ice bucket and moving into the drawing room.

"Yes, it's sort of *comforting*. It takes me back to the summers at Heron's Nest. We always had bubble and squeak on Sunday nights with Gran when we were little. Oh, for the good old days! Besides, you've a lot of leftover vegetables in your fridge. We might as well use them up. And I'm ravenous."

Paula looked over her shoulder and shook her head wonderingly. "Doesn't anything ever affect your appetite, Apple Dumpling?"

Emily, following her inside, grinned somewhat self-consciously. "I suppose not, Beanstalk," she shot back, using Paula's childhood nickname. "But listen, I'm going to scoot. I'll be back as quickly as I can, and if Winston happens to ring, give him lots of love from me."

As was usual on Sunday night, Harrogate was deserted and virtually free of traffic, and within minutes Emily was on the main Ripon road, speeding steadily along toward Pennistone Royal.

Since Paula had said she could take either of the two cars in the garage, Emily had elected to drive Jim's Aston Martin. For a while she concentrated on getting the feel of the powerful piece of machinery under her hands, enjoying its smoothness and the sense of security she felt in the well-built and beautifully designed car. It was certainly a pleasant change from her rackety Jaguar, which was so decrepit it was practically useless and probably unsafe.

Emily had clung to the old Jag for sentimental reasons, inasmuch as it had once belonged to Winston. He had sold it to her four years ago, and, until their fraternal relationship had blossomed into a love affair, driving his car had somehow seemed to bring him closer to her. It no longer held any significance because Winston himself was completely hers now that they were engaged. And the Jaguar had become a nuisance, really, always breaking down at the most inopportune times. Grandy had been after her to get rid of it for ages, and she decided she had better do so next week. She wondered what car to buy. An Aston Martin, perhaps? Why not? It was a solid car, constructed like a tank. Emily began to ponder automobiles, but after a short while her thoughts not unnaturally turned to events in Ireland.

The Land-Rover's breaking down was a rotten piece of luck for Anthony, Emily thought. If it hadn't, he would be totally in the clear. This would be an open-and-shut case. Pity he didn't go back for it before dinner, but no doubt he was trying to avoid Min. That poor woman . . . dying like that . . . drowning is the worst death . . . terrifying.

Emily shivered involuntarily as she contemplated the accident, endeavored to push away the image of cold black water eddying and swirling, dragging Min down into its murky depths. Emily swallowed, held the steering wheel more tightly. She had inherited her grandmother's fear of water, and like Emma she was a poor swimmer, assiduously avoided boats, the sea, lakes, and even the most innocuous of swimming pools. All terrified her.

In an effort to dispel the vivid mental picture of Min Standish's death, she turned on the car radio, twiddled the knob, but, unable to find the station she liked, she instantly switched it off. Through the car window she noticed the signpost which indicated she was approaching Ripley, and slowed down as she went through the small village, picking up speed as she left it behind, heading for South Stainley.

Unexpectedly, Emily felt her face tensing as a thought so distressing suddenly flashed through her mind, and she swerved, caught in the grip of apprehension. Righting the car immediately, she brought her full attention to the road, telling herself she would have an accident if she didn't concentrate.

Nonetheless, the thought would not go away. It was a question, really, and it hovered over her in the most maddening way, and she wondered why it had not reared up before now. Finally she faced it head-on: What *had* Min actually been *doing* out at the lake for some *five hours* before she drowned?

All through those summers they had spent at Heron's Nest, Emma Harte had instilled many things in her grandchildren. Chief amongst these was the importance of analyzing a problem down to the last detail, examining every single aspect of it. Now Emily's brain began to turn with rapidity in the way it had been trained by Emma.

One possible answer to the question struck her instantly—Min had not spent five hours at the lake, because she had not been there in the afternoon. It had been late at night when she had gone there for the first time yesterday. Oh my God, Emily thought, shuddering uncontrollably, that would mean Anthony is lying. That can't be so, and even if he *was* responsible for her death, why didn't he remove the Land-Rover? Why did he leave it at the lake?

Start at the beginning, Emily instructed herself. Think it through logically, and first of all work on the premise that he *could* be lying. She ran a possible sequence of events through her head.

Anthony has dinner with Edwina. He takes her home to the Dower House afterward. He returns to Clonloughlin House around ten. Min arrives unexpectedly soon after. They quarrel. He rushes out, jumps into the Land-Rover and drives off. Min follows, accosts him at the lake. They fight again, she becomes violent, following her pattern of the past few weeks. He fends her off. They struggle. He accidentally kills her. He dumps the body in the lake so that it will look like an accident. Then the Land-Rover won't start, or it conks out. He has no alternative but to walk back to the house.

It could have happened that way, Emily told herself reluctantly. But *if* it did, why didn't he return to the lake later to get the Land-Rover? The last thing he would do was leave it there.

Her mind raced as she took her original thought to its conclusion.

Anthony decides it's risky trying to tow the Land-Rover by himself late at night. He resolves to remove it early the next morning. But the estate manager is up and about at the crack of dawn and finds it first. Anthony concocts a plausible story with Edwina about Min's arriving in the afternoon, explains the Land-Rover broke down at that time. He cleverly bluffs his way through, counting on everyone to conclude, as I myself did, that only an innocent man would leave such damning evidence at the scene. On the other hand, Anthony does have an alibi for those crucial hours late at night. The housekeeper saw him. But is Bridget to be believed?

Was Anthony's story a huge pack of lies? Was this an immensely daring and brilliant bluff?

As Emily passed through Pennistone village and turned into the gates of her grandmother's estate she told herself that a man would have to be awfully cold-blooded and ruthless, would have to have nerves of steel to carry off such a scheme so successfully. Was Anthony such a man? *No.* How do you know that, Emily Barkstone? Only a few hours ago you told Paula that neither of you knew him all that *well.*

Appalled at her thoughts, Emily did her best to shake them off as she parked and climbed out of the car. She went into the house.

Hilda, her grandmother's housekeeper, was coming out of the door leading to the kitchen and the servants' quarters at the back of the house.

A broad smile flew onto Hilda's face at the sight of her. "There you are, Miss Emily," she said, and peered through her glasses worriedly. She clucked, "You're looking a bit poorly. You'd best come to the kitchen for a cup of tea."

"Thanks, Hilda, but I have to get back to Miss Paula's immediately. I'm fine, honestly, just a bit tired." Emily managed to produce a smile, then glanced around, looking for her suitcase.

"Your overnight bag's here," Hilda said, producing it from behind one of the heavy Tudor hall chairs. She carried it to her, saying, "What terrible news, just awful. It gave me a right turn, that it did. I had to sit down and have a drop of brandy after your phone call. His poor lordship . . . oh, deary me, what a tragedy for him. But then life's so unpredictable, isn't it." She nodded, her face mournful, then took hold of Emily's arm with a show of affection. Accompanying her across the hall, she said, "Does Mrs. Harte know yet? Have you spoken to her?"

"No, Hilda. Mr. David is trying to reach Mr. Philip in Australia. Don't worry, Grandma will be all right."

"Oh, I've no doubts about that, none at all, Miss Emily. But it does seem so unfair. Just when she gets a chance for a little rest, a nice holiday, a dreadful thing like this accident has to happen. Your poor grandmother's life has been full of troubles . . . I'd hoped that by now she'd be free of them."

"Yes, Hilda, I second that. But you said it yourself—unexpected things happen and we can't control life."

Emily began edging her way to the front door, looking about her as she did, savoring the beauty of the Stone Hall, but also suddenly acutely conscious of its normality. It was filled with lovely warm light, the fire in the huge hearth blazed as it always did through the autumn and winter, and pots of gold and bronze chrysanthemums were clustered in the well of the great staircase. Yes, this hall looked exactly the way it had all of her life, even to the brass urn filled with copper beech on the refectory table.

Its unchanging appearance engendered an enormous sense of security in Emily, and she felt Emma's presence so powerfully, so forcefully at this precise moment she was reassured, and her fears began to ebb away. Her grandmother was a brilliant woman with a shrewd and penetrating understanding of people. She loved and trusted Anthony . . . not because he was her grandson but because of his character and his qualities as a man.

Swinging around, Emily gave Hilda a dimpling smile. Her green eyes were serious and her voice was strong as she said, "Don't worry, Hilda, Gran will take this in her stride. And thanks for packing my bag."

"It was no trouble, Miss Emily, and you drive carefully, do you hear."

After taking her leave of Hilda, Emily ran outside to the Aston Martin, threw her bag on the back seat, and within seconds had reversed the car and was spinning down the driveway, heading back the way she had come.

On her return trip to Harrogate she kept a firm hold on the positive feelings she had experienced at Pennistone Royal, and she kept telling herself that Anthony had been truthful and that Min's death was an accident.

In fact, Emily had so brainwashed herself she was in exceptionally good spirits when she drove into the garage at Long Meadow. Although she had made the journey to Pennistone and back in record time, it had taken her a good hour, and she was beginning to feel faint with hunger. She was looking forward to a pleasant supper and her mouth watered as she thought of cold lamb, bubble and squeak, and a glass of icy white wine.

But all such thoughts were swept out of her head as she went into the kitchen. She could not fail to notice the disarray at once. Food lay abandoned on the counter top. The lamb was only half-carved, the bubble and squeak had congealed in a frying pan on top of the stove, and cupboard doors were open.

Paula sat inertly at the kitchen table and there was such a stricken look on her face Emily's worries sprang to life.

"What is it?" she cried from the doorway. "Something awful's happened at Clonloughlin. They haven't arrested—"

"No, no, nothing like that," Paula assured her, lifting her eyes. "I haven't even heard a peep out of them." Her voice was exhausted.

"Then what is it?" Emily demanded, joining her at the table, scanning her troubled face.

Paula sighed, remained mute.

Emily suspected her cousin had been crying, and leaning forward she took hold of her slender, tapering hand and patted it. "Please tell me," she said softly.

"I've had a terrible row with Jim. He phoned a little while ago and he was so snotty with me I can't get over it."

"But *why?*"

"*Sam Fellowes.* He ignored my warning and called Jim. He left three urgent messages at the hotel in Toronto. When Jim got in, he rang him back, and Fellowes told him about the accident, and my instructions not to run a story, or an obituary. Fellowes said I'd treated him in a most rude and high-handed manner, that I'd even threatened to give him the sack. Jim was obviously furious, yelled at me, *chastized* me. He thinks I handled things most undiplomatically. He said he'd had to spend twenty minutes placating Fellowes, and had finally convinced him not to resign." Paula reached for a handkerchief and blew her nose.

"I can't believe it!" Emily was aghast. "Surely Jim apologized once he understood your reasons for putting a lid on the story, when you explained about Anthony being under suspicion."

"Oh, he did ease off a bit," Paula told her morosely, "but his nose was definitely out of joint. And, no, he didn't apologize. He was more concerned about whether he could get a flight to Ireland tomorrow. He thinks he should be with Edwina and Anthony to give them moral support."

Emily made a disagreeable face. "He would." She shook her head slowly. "What's wrong with Jim? Has he forgotten Grandy's rule about the family not being mentioned in our newspapers?"

"No. At the outset of our conversation he said this was different, that since reports of Min's death would probably appear in the nationals, we'd look ridiculous if we didn't carry an obituary. Once he was fully aware of the facts, he sort of calmed down, but he still insisted I had handled Fellowes in the wrong way."

"What the hell did he expect you to do?"

Paula smiled thinly. "He said I should have told Fellowes not to run anything in the early editions, but to have the obituary prepared, and then to hold it until either Winston or he had been contacted in Canada. He told me it was their decision—his and Winston's—not *mine.*"

Emily's jaw dropped and she gave Paula a hard and baffled stare. "Doesn't he *know* that you have Grandy's power of attorney, and Winston's, to act on their behalf in an emergency?"

"I didn't see any reason to say anything before he left," Paula murmured. "I didn't want to hurt his feelings. I'd have had to break the news that I'm the trustee, with Winston and Alexander, of our children's shares in Consolidated, not him." When Emily said nothing, Paula insisted, "How could I tell him *that,* Emily?"

"Well, you should have," Emily retorted crossly.

"Perhaps," Paula admitted, ignoring her tone.

I bet she still hasn't told him, Emily thought, but said, "Is Jim *really* going to rush to Ireland?"

"I'm not certain. He was anxious to talk to Winston. Jim had been trying to reach him in Vancouver before he called here."

"You mean we were the *last* on his list, and after all the urgent messages I left?" Emily was flabbergasted.

Paula nodded. The two cousins exchanged long, very knowing looks, remembering their grandmother's strictest rule, one that had been drilled into them. Emma had told them to always check with at least one member of the family in any emergency before acting, to resist talking to strangers, to be supportive of each other, and, most importantly, to close ranks to protect the family.

Paula said hesitantly, "I suppose he thought there was something wrong at the paper—"

"He might not have been brought up by Grandy, but he sure as hell knows her rules!" Emily exploded. "He ought to have called us *first,* then he would have had the facts. It might have prevented the row you two had, if nothing else." She sat back jerkily, her annoyance with Jim apparent.

"That's true. Oh, never mind, Emily, it doesn't matter. Look, I should have told you this the moment you arrived . . . Winston rang." Paula gave her a smile, determined to forget about Jim's unreasonable behavior.

"When?" Emily asked eagerly, then added pithily, "I bet *he* didn't have long dialogues with the whole world first!"

Paula laughed for the first time in hours. "You're absolutely right, darling. And he reached me just a few minutes after I'd hung up on Jim."

"Tell me everything Winston said, and please don't leave out one single word."

Paula looked across at Emily with fond indulgence, her expression warm and caring. "Winston had been having lunch with the chairman of the board of the paper mill, at the latter's home. When he finally got back to the hotel late this afternoon, afternoon in Canada that is, he found a pile of messages. Sam Fellowes had called—*naturally*—so had Sally, Jim, and you. Since you'd left *this* number, and since Fellowes had said it was urgent they speak, Winston immediately suspected there was some sort of crisis at the paper. Naturally he wanted to talk to me or you before anyone else. Grandy's golden rule is not something any of *us* is likely to forget. Winston was really thrown off-balance when I told him Min was dead, and he was particularly concerned about Sally. 'Keep that sister of mine as far away from Clonloughlin as you can,' he repeated quite a few times. I set his mind at rest, of course, and he was awfully relieved I'd been tough with her. He asked a lot of pertinent questions, which I was able to answer, and he said I'd done the right things, and that between the two of us we'd made all the right moves, too. He was also glad you're staying here tonight."

"Does he plan to fly home?" Emily asked.

"No, not unless the situation at Clonloughlin changes—for the worst. He reminded me that we'd all been trained in the same army camp by the same general, and pointed out that he couldn't contribute anything more than you or I could, and so therefore he intended to go about his business in a normal manner."

"He's right, of course." Emily paused for a fraction of a second, before asking, "Did you say anything about the row—Jim's attitude toward you?"

"Only in passing, Emily. I didn't want to make a big thing about it, but I'm afraid Winston was fit to be tied. He was very down on Jim. He also said Fellowes was a fool, that his job had been in the balance for a long time. And then he sort of wondered aloud why Jim hadn't spoken to me before calling Fellowes back." Paula shrugged. "I told him his guess was as good as mine. In any event, he's going to talk to Jim about Fellowes, and also about going to Ireland. He thinks Jim should stay in Canada, but I got the feeling Winston wouldn't interfere if Jim insisted on leaving for Dublin tomorrow. That's about it, but he asked for you, of course, and he sends his love."

"I do wish I hadn't missed him. I was longing to talk to him," Emily said a little wistfully.

"Oh, you can do that, any time after midnight—our time," Paula immediately volunteered. "Winston's not going out this evening. He told me he would order something up to the suite, and he indicated he was going to ring Sally and Jim, and I suspect he's going to give Sam Fellowes an earful."

"I'm sure he is, and I'll give him a buzz a bit later." Emily rose, slipped out of her cardigan and hung it on the back of the chair. "What about your father? Did he reach Philip?"

"Yes, about an hour ago, only a few minutes after you'd left for Penni-stone. It was breakfast time at Dunoon and Grandy was up, having her morning tea and toast with Philip. She knows. Daddy spoke to her as well." Paula eyed Emily carefully. "What do you bet we'll hear from her before very long?"

Emily laughed. "Everything I have. It's a certainty Grandy'll ring us as soon as she's had time to think up a few penetrating questions which are bound to catch us off guard."

Paula could not help laughing too. "That's a bit naughty."

"Well, you know as well as I do that Emma Harte is always testing her grandchildren to see if they're on their toes. Why should tonight be any different?"

Throwing her a thoughtful glance, Paula said, "I don't suppose it is, and let's be thankful she brought us up the way she did. At least we're capable of handling any emergency."

"Yes," Emily agreed. "And in the meantime, I'm going to revive the bubble and squeak and make us a lovely supper."

Twenty-Five

"I'm beginning to think that Jim and I are always going to be at cross purposes, Daddy," Paula said.

David Amory, who was standing at the bar cabinet in the drawing room of his Regent's Park flat, swung around. The remark had startled him inasmuch as he had caught a most discernible hint of irritation in his daughter's voice. A dark brow lifted. "In what sense, darling?"

"He sees things quite differently than I do. Of course, that's all right, because everyone has their own vision of the world, of life, and each of us handles problems, people, and situations in our individual way, as best we can. But Jim will never admit he's wrong about anything, and he's continually accusing me of overreacting."

David made no response. A wry smile flickered and his cool, intelligent eyes held his daughter's for a split second before he turned back to the bar and refilled their glasses. Carrying them over to the seating arrangement in front of the tall windows, he handed her the vodka and tonic, seated himself opposite her.

Settling back in the chair, David took a swallow of his scotch and soda, and asked, "Does he think you've reacted too strongly to the mess in Ireland? Is that it?"

"Yes."

David nodded thoughtfully. "Do *you* think you have?"

"No, I don't."

"Good girl. I've always rather admired your decisiveness, your unwavering attitude, and you're one of the few women I know who isn't forever changing her mind. So stick to your guns, and don't let Jim upset you, especially when you're certain you've made the proper moves. We can't please everyone in life, Paula, and so the important thing is to be true to oneself. That's *your* priority.''

"I know it is." Paula leaned forward, said now with some intensity, "I have enough common sense to admit it when I'm wrong, but in this instance I'm convinced I was wise to take the precautions I did, to clap a lid on everything, to cover us for *any* eventuality. It may be a status quo in Ireland, and the national papers may have treated the story in a routine way—so far. But that doesn't mean we're out of the woods yet.''

"Naturally we're not, and we won't be until after the autopsy and the inquest." David gazed down into his drink reflectively. "I didn't particularly like the wire service story that ran today in some of the papers . . . about the police investigating the mysterious circumstances surrounding Min's death. On the other hand, there was no mention of Anthony. Thank God for the rather stringent libel laws in this country." He looked up, frowned. "I'm just praying that none of the more sensational dailies blow the investigation out of proportion. Well—" He gave her a kindly smile, finished, "We're just going to have to sit this one out, darling. And getting back to Jim, I don't wish to sound critical, but if you ask me, he's the one who has overreacted. It was quite unnecessary for him to fly to Ireland. Your mother is coping nicely.''

"Yes she is, and I'm proud of her.''

Reaching for a cigarette and lighting it, David remarked, "For what it's worth, you did exactly what Grandy would have done had she been here. Throughout the twenty-seven years I've known her, Emma has constantly told me she doesn't like unpleasant surprises, and that in her lexicon prevention is infinitely better than any kind of cure. Jim may not concur with your decisions, your actions, but Grandy, Henry, and I do, and we've all told you so in the last twenty-four hours.''

"You've been very supportive, and when Gran called me again this afternoon, just before I left Leeds, she reiterated her confidence in me, and in all of us, actually.''

"So you said. And that's the reason she's decided not to come back. Look, Paula, this may sound silly, when we're under such a great deal of tension, but please do try to relax. *I* certainly shall. And don't worry about Jim's attitude. Whilst I'm fully aware you want his approval, you'd be wise to recognize you're not going to get it, because he doesn't understand—" David stopped short, regretting this slip, not wishing to criticize his son-in-law. He had long been disappointed in Jim, but he had managed to keep his feelings to himself thus far. He had not even voiced them to Daisy.

Paula, quick as ever, said, "Were you going to say he doesn't understand my reasoning, or that he doesn't understand me?''

There was an awkward silence.

Paula stared at her father. David met her questioning gaze unblinkingly. He was convinced Jim Fairley did not have the slightest conception of his daughter's character or her business ethos, but, electing to go with the lesser of two evils, he said, "Your reasoning.''

She nodded. "I've known that for some time now. Jim can be very naïve, which is especially surprising to me, since he's a newspaperman accustomed to seeing so many of the worst aspects of people, of life. Yet his judgment is way off more often than not, and it seems to me that he looks at the world through rose-colored glasses." She let out a tiny sigh. "And, to be honest, I'm also starting to think he doesn't understand the first thing about me, or the way my mind works, or why I do the things I do."

David was conscious of the misery in her tone and he looked across at her, filling with concern at the sight of her forlorn expression and her confirmation of his own suspicions about Jim. "You can tell me to mind my own business if you want—but look here, Paula, is your marriage in trouble?"

"No, I don't think so, even though we do have our differences. I love Jim very much, Daddy."

"I'm sure you do and that he feels the same way, but love isn't always enough, Paula. You've got to be able to live with someone twenty-four hours a day, year in and year out, and comfortably so on that continuing basis. And you can only do that if there is true understanding between the two of you."

"Yes," she agreed with a faint, hesitant smile, wondering whether to pour out her troubles to her father. She decided against it. Tonight was not the right moment. Adopting a more confident tone, she assured him, "We'll work it out, I'm certain of that, because we really do care for each other. Please don't worry, and don't say anything to Mummy, will you? Promise?"

"I promise, and I'm not going to pry, but I do want you to remember that you can confide in me any time you wish, darling. I love you very much and naturally your happiness is important to me." David drained his glass, continued, "As it is to your mother too. However, you're right, she'd be disturbed if she thought your relationship with Jim was anything less than perfect."

"You've been so happy with Mummy, haven't you, Daddy?" Paula said, thinking about their long and extraordinarily tranquil marriage, which was the envy of the entire family.

"Yes. *Very*. Mind you, we've had our ups and downs." David chuckled, noticing the look of genuine astonishment registering in Paula's eyes. "It's nice to know you were never aware of our rough patches, and we *did* have a few. But then any marriage worth its salt is never all sweetness and light. There's a marvelous line in *David Copperfield* which I've always been partial to, and it's very apt when I think of my marriage to Daisy: *The strongest steel goes through the hottest fire*. Yes, my dear, we had our troubles just like most people do. Nevertheless, we overcame them."

Paula, still surprised at his revelation, said, *"Troubles*. Were they really serious?"

Shaking his head and chuckling again, David told her, "Now, when I look back, they were very piddling, but when we were suffering through them they seemed quite monumental. Which is why I'm inclined to agree with you when you say you'll work things out with Jim. I'm sure you will, and the marriage will be all that much better. But if it isn't"—he gave her a long, hard stare— "then don't be afraid to let go, to end it whilst you're still young and can find someone else. And don't fall into the trap of staying together for the children's sake if the marriage *is* seriously damaged. That kind of reasoning is cockeyed, in my opinion. In the long run, everyone's miserably unhappy, including the children. Self-sacrifice of that nature is for martyrs, and *they* usually end up being a pain in the rear end," he finished, deciding he had said enough, if not far too much, perhaps. Still, Paula was strong, sound of judgment, and determined to lead her own life. He knew she would brook no interference. And neither he nor anyone else would have much, if any, influence on her decisions. Not now or in the future.

"Thanks, Daddy, for being such a good friend," Paula said, "and for not pontificating as some fathers would. I see you've finished your drink, and I don't really want mine, so let's go to dinner, shall we?"

"Splendid idea." He glanced at the clock on the mantelpiece. "Why, yes, we ought to get a move on. I have a table for eight-thirty at Ziegi's."

They went out into the hall together and as David helped her on with her coat he bent and kissed the top of her head, making a sudden gesture of affection. She pivoted to face him, stood on tiptoe to kiss his cheek in return. "You're a truly special man, Daddy."

His eyes, usually so cool and appraising, filled with great warmth. "So are you, daughter."

Out on the street, David found a taxi at once, and after whizzing across town to Charles Street in Mayfair, they were being seated in the upstairs dining room of the famous club fifteen minutes after leaving the flat.

David brushed aside Paula's announcement that she was not very hungry, as he had so often done when she was a child. He took matters into his own hands, ordered Colchester oysters, steak Diane, and pureed vegetables for them both, perused the impressive wine list with a knowledgeable eye, finally selected a vintage Mouton Rothschild, then insisted Paula share half a bottle of champagne with him whilst they waited for the meal.

By unspoken agreement, neither mentioned the difficult situation at Clonloughlin, wanting a respite from their worry. For a while Paula did most of the talking, discussing matters pertaining to the stores, of which her father was now chairman of the board since Emma's retirement. Paula had stepped into his shoes automatically, held the title of managing director, and in consequence it was she who bore the brunt of running the chain on a day-to-day basis.

He was content to sit back and listen, enjoying her company, her wit and charm, not to mention her indisputably brilliant mind. But then his daughter had always intrigued him. When she had been growing up she had seemed, at times, more like Emma's child than Daisy's and his, in that Emma had made Paula her very own. He had vaguely resented this but had never been able to combat Emma's influence over her. Then when she was ten or thereabouts he began to understand that the child loved the three of them equally, played no one as a favorite, for with a wisdom that was remarkable, almost frightening, in one so young, she had made this perfectly clear to him, her mother, and Emma. David was amused when some members of the family implied that Emma had brainwashed Paula to such an extent she had turned her into a clone. He knew his daughter had far too strong and stubborn a mind to follow the leader blindly, to permit herself to become something she was not, to accept indoctrination without question. The truth was much simpler. Emma had indeed trained Paula in her ways, but his daughter was already so much like Emma this had hardly been necessary. The similarities of their characters aside, they had always been on the same wavelength and over the years this had become so finely tuned they appeared to read each other's thoughts, and frequently finished sentences for each other, much to everyone's amazement, including his own. But of all the qualities they shared, the one which truly impressed David was their ability to bring the most intense concentration and single-mindedness to the matter at hand. He was aware of the amount of mental and physical energy this took, and he considered it a great virtue in both women, a mark of their extraordinary genius. For genius it was.

Sometimes David had to remind himself that Paula was not yet twenty-five, as he did at this moment, struck as he was by her maturity and her keen understanding of complex business matters. As he absorbed her words, he observed her closely, noting for the second time in the last hour her elegance and refinement. He never thought of Paula as being beautiful, and she was not, at least not in the accepted sense, because of her somewhat angular features, broad forehead, and strong jawline. Rather, she was arrestingly attractive with her vividness of coloring, her translucent complexion, and her superb grooming. Yes, it's her immense elegance, he thought; that's undoubtedly what draws all eyes to her. For the half hour they had been in Ziegi's he had not failed to miss the discreet glances directed at them from time to time. He wondered, with a small flicker of amusement, if they thought she was his young mistress.

Detecting the laughter playing around his eyes, Paula abandoned the point she was making and leaned forward. "What's so funny, Daddy?"

He flashed her a wide grin. "I'm the envy of the men in this room. They most probably think you're my girlfriend."

She shrugged, smiled, eyeing him objectively. If the other diners did harbor such a thought, it was not so farfetched, really. At fifty-one her father was a good-looking man whom women found attractive and appealing. He had a strong, well-bred face, fine, clear eyes, and a head of dark wavy hair tinged at the sides with gray that did nothing to age him. He was athletically inclined, skied and played squash in winter, took to the tennis courts in summer, and in consequence was in excellent physical shape. Fastidious about his appearance, he was always beautifully dressed, a characteristic she knew she had inherited from him.

David was saying, "You do look quite lovely tonight, Paula. The dress has great style. Black has always suited you, of course. Still, few women could carry it off as well as you do. It is rather severe, and—"

"Don't you like it?"

"Very much so." He studied the Egyptian-style gold collar that encircled her long neck and partially filled out the squared neckline of the long-sleeved wool dress. Nefertiti, he said under his breath. Aloud he remarked, "I've never seen you wearing the collar before. It's beautiful. Rather striking, in fact. Is it new? A gift from Jim?"

Paula smiled mischievously, dropped her voice. "Don't tell anyone, but it's a piece of costume jewelry. From Harte's. I'm sure it's not even brass, and its color will probably turn in no time at all. But when I saw it I knew it was perfect for this dress. It gives it a bit of dash, wouldn't you say?"

"I would indeed." He made a mental note to talk to the jewelry buyer tomorrow, decided to have the collar copied for Paula for her Christmas gift. He was usually at a loss to know what to give her for anniversaries and special occasions. She was not overly fond of jewels or other baubles and because of her highly individual taste it was difficult to shop for her successfully.

As the dinner progressed, David and Paula touched on many topics of mutual interest, but eventually Paula brought the conversation back to business. Slowly, with her usual self-assurance, she began to outline an idea she had for the stores.

David sat up straighter in the chair, listening alertly, intrigued by her concept, which showed intuitive understanding of the buying public. And like so many really clever ideas it was rooted in simplicity. He wondered why no other retailer had ever thought of it.

Paula said, "You've got a peculiar look on your face. Don't you think it will work?"

"On the contrary, I think it will be a tremendous hit. Expand on it further for me, please, Paula."

She did so, finished, "But it would have to be a completely self-contained shop within the store."

"You'd need a whole floor?"

"Not necessarily. Half a floor should work very well. I thought there could be three separate salons. One selling suits, plus shirts and blouses, another for coats and dresses, and a third salon offering shoes, boots, and handbags. The key, of course, is having the individual salons adjoining each other, so that a woman can coordinate a complete outfit quickly and easily without having to trundle up and down to other floors searching for different items. It will save mistakes, not to mention time, for the shopper. And with an imaginative advertising campaign and some clever promotion I think we can do tremendous business." She sat back, watching him through keenly attentive eyes.

"It's excellent. Yes, I'm enthusiastic. Any ideas about a name for this total shop of yours?"

"There are several very obvious ones, Daddy, such as Working Woman or Career Woman. However, I've already dismissed those as being far too prosaic. We need a name that expresses exactly what we are about. We must put over the concept that we are selling clothes—good, well-designed clothes—to working women with business and professional careers, that we are offering a special service since we're making their task of putting a wardrobe together so much easier."

"What about Career Cachet?" David suggested.

"Not bad." Paula frowned. "Is it too much in the other direction? Too fancy, perhaps?" she asked, thinking aloud, and before he had a chance to reply went on, "I thought of Career Club when I was driving to London this afternoon. But I'm not sure if that says what I want to say. Well, right now the name doesn't really matter. The main thing is to get the career shop into work. So . . . do I have your blessing?"

"Naturally you do, although you don't really need it." David's eyes twinkled as he reminded her, "The Harte chain is yours, Paula, lock, stock, and barrel, and you *are* managing director."

"But you're the chairman of the board," she shot back. "And therefore you're still my boss."

"You always did have to have the last word, didn't you?" he murmured, and could not help thinking: As Emma always does.

"Sorry I'm late getting back," Paula apologized as she hurried into the executive offices at the Knightsbridge store on Wednesday afternoon at five minutes to three.

"How was your meeting with Henry Rossiter?" Gaye asked, rising, following Paula into the palatial Georgian-style office that bore Emma's inimitable stamp.

"No problems. We spent most of the time reviewing Grandy's other holdings. We hardly touched on the Irish mess, gave it only a few minutes after our business session. When we were having lunch, actually. Any further news from over there, by the way?" Paula threw her handbag on a chair, sat down behind the huge partner's desk that had once been her grandmother's.

"Yes. Your mother rang again. She wanted you to know she won't stay on after the inquest in Cork tomorrow as she had planned. She's decided to fly back to London immediately," Gaye explained, taking the chair opposite the desk.

"I'm glad she's changed her mind. Once the inquest is out of the way we'll all be able to breathe a little easier . . . I sincerely hope."

"Since the police haven't made any moves, I'm positive the hearing will be quite routine," Gaye volunteered in a quiet tone.

"Let us pray." Paula attempted a smile, then noticing Gaye's gloomy demeanor for the first time, she said, *"You're* not looking too happy. What's been happening since I walked out of here at eleven o'clock?"

Gaye cleared her throat. "Sorry to greet you with problems, Paula, but I'm afraid that's all we've got this afternoon."

"Par for the course this week, or so it seems. All right, Gaye, let's have the bad news."

"I'll start with what I think are the real priorities," Gaye said, lifting her head. "Dale Stevens rang you about twenty minutes ago. Not from Texas, though. He's in New York. At the Pierre. He sounded odd, worried, in my opinion. Certainly he wasn't his usual ebullient self."

Trouble at Sitex, Paula thought. Stifling her apprehension, she said, "Did he give you any indication why he wanted to speak to me?"

Gaye shook her head. "But he did ask me when you plan to visit Harte's in New York. I said probably not before November, and this seemed to upset him. He sort of bit back a four-letter word and asked, 'Are you sure she won't be over in the States earlier than that?' I said you wouldn't, not unless there was something urgent that needed your attention. I was fishing when I made that remark, but he didn't rise to the bait."

Paula reached for the phone. "I'd better ring him back."

Gaye said, "He's not there. He went to a meeting. The message was to call him at six our time."

"That's *all* he said?"

"Not one word more. Very cagey, our Mr. Stevens was. I can tell from your expression that you're worried, think the worst, suspect that there's something amiss at Sitex Oil. I have to agree. He did sound awfully tense, even morose."

"As you said before, that's very unusual. Dale's always so relaxed and cheerful. But there's no use speculating. Okay. Sitex at six. What's next?"

"Winston checked in from Vancouver over lunchtime. *He* was also anxiety-ridden. He has unexpected problems with the Canadian paper mill. They erupted late yesterday, after you and he had already spoken. The negotiations have stalled. He's withdrawing the offer today, as you both agreed he should if any difficulties developed. He's going to give them twenty-four hours, and if it's not back on the tracks by then he's flying to New York on Friday. He doesn't want you to bother ringing him. He said he'd be in touch—either way. But he doesn't hold out much hope of making the deal. He has a feeling it's kaput."

"Damnation, that *is* annoying! It would have been such a good acquisition for Consolidated. We'll just have to hope he can turn the situation around. Go on, Gaye."

"Sally Harte's disappeared," Gaye murmured, giving Paula a sympathetic look.

"The fool! The silly little fool!" Paula cried, sitting bolt upright. "I told her not to go rushing off to Ireland, and I bet that's exactly where she's gone. Who called? Uncle Randolph?"

"No. Emily. Your Uncle Randolph spoke to her a couple of hours ago. Emily was on her way out when she received the call. She's on her way to town right now. As you know, she has a meeting at the London office of Genret tomorrow. Anyway, apparently your Uncle Randolph is in quite a rage, although Emily says she did her best to calm him down. Emily thinks Vivienne is hiding something, knows where Sally's gone but won't talk. She suggested you tackle Vivienne when you have a moment."

Paula groaned. "I do so love Emily's advice. Why the hell didn't she speak to Vivienne when she was still in Yorkshire? This is all I need today!"

"I did ask Emily to take a minute to talk to Vivienne before setting off, but she demurred, explained that it wouldn't do any good. She said, 'Tell Paula I'm not as daunting as she is,' and she hung up before I could say another word."

"I see." The two women exchanged concerned glances. Paula looked away, focusing on the fireplace, her face reflective, and then her mouth curved down in a stern and resolute line and her eyes narrowed.

Watching her closely, Gaye could not help thinking how much Paula resembled her grandmother at this moment and she thought: I hope to God she really is as strong as Emma Harte—as we have all come to believe.

Paula brought her gaze back to her assistant. "I'll get to Vivienne later. Wherever Sally is, I can't very well remove her bodily, or force her to do as I say. Right now, business comes first. Anything else?"

"John Cross telephoned. He's in London. He asked for an appointment. Tomorrow morning, if convenient."

"Oh!" Paula exclaimed, but she was not as surprised as she appeared to be. She had been expecting to hear from the head of Aire Communications for weeks. She and her grandmother had agreed he would come crawling back eventually.

Gaye stared at her, trying to fathom her expression. It was quite unreadable. "Cross left a number, Paula," she said at last, breaking the silence. "What do you want to do? You've a fairly clear calendar tomorrow."

Pursing her lips and shaking her head, Paula admitted, "To be truthful, I'm not sure . . . There doesn't seem to be much point in seeing him. I've nothing to say to that particular gentleman. I'll let you know before the end of the day."

"Your cousin Sarah's back from Barbados, and she wants to see you. At four o'clock today. She says she has to come over to the store to see the ready-to-wear buyer and could pop up for a few minutes. She was rather insistent."

"She's back sooner than I expected. I'd better see her. It can't be anything important, so it shouldn't take very long. Sarah most likely wants to tell me about the opening of the boutique and the new hotel this past weekend. Is that all of it, Gaye?"

"It's enough, isn't it?" Gaye replied dourly.

Paula sat back, surveying her. "Do you really like being my assistant? Or would you prefer to be my secretary after all? I can demote you, Gaye, if that's what you want. I aim to please in all things," Paula teased, and laughed in spite of her many worries.

Gaye had the good grace to laugh too. "Sorry I sounded so glum. And I'm relishing the new job, honestly I am. Besides, Sheila would be hurt and affronted if she was relegated to being the junior secretary again. She's so proud she works for you personally. She's very efficient, isn't she?"

"Yes, thanks to your assiduous training over the last few years."

The telephone rang. Paula glared at it, shook her head.

Lifting the receiver, Gaye said crisply, "Mrs. Fairley's office." There was a slight pause before she added, "She's right here." Handing her the phone, Gaye mouthed, "It's okay—it's only Alexander." Gaye hurried out of the room.

"How do you like being back at the old grindstone?" Paula said into the phone.

"Bloody awful after two weeks of sunshine and indolence in the South of France. But it's a relief in one sense—I don't have to cope with my mother," Alexander answered in a sarcastic voice, rushed on, "Can you have supper with me tonight? There're a few things I'd like to discuss with you."

"Serious?"

"No. Interesting, though."

"Why don't you tell me now?" Paula pressed, her curiosity flaring.

"Too involved. Also, I'm due to start a meeting in exactly ten minutes. Since you and I are both in town and alone, I thought it was a good opportunity to get together. Fancy dining at the White Elephant?"

"That sounds like a nice change. Thanks for the invitation, and I'd love to see you, as long as we can make it around nine. I have to work late."

"Who doesn't? And nine's fine. I'll pick you up at Belgrave Square, shall I? Around eight-thirty?"

"Perfect. Oh, and Sandy, you'd better make the reservation for three. Your sister's on her way up to London, and I'm sure Emily'll insist on joining us."

"Too true. Miss Nosey Parker has to be in on everything," he responded, with a dry laugh. "See you later."

Paula rose and walked over to stand with her back to the fireplace. The weather had turned cold in the last few days and as soon as there was the slightest hint of an autumn nip in the air the fire was automatically lit every morning, as it had been for years. Paula was glad that Emma's long tradition continued unchanged. She suddenly felt chilled to the bone, and the bright blaze was warming, also brought a cheerful aspect to the handsome room.

She scowled to herself as her thoughts settled on Dale Stevens. It was not unusual for him to be in constant contact with her, since she was her grandmother's representative at Sitex. Emma, with forty-two percent of the stock, was the largest single stockholder and had always been a power in the oil company and a member of the board. Now that Paula filled this role Dale conferred with her several times a month. On the other hand, this afternoon's call had apparently not been routine. Gaye had discerned a troubled note in his voice, and she trusted Gaye's judgment. After all, it had been the redoubtable Sloane who had discovered the plot against Grandy last year. Dale is probably having trouble with the Harry Marriott faction on the board, Paula suddenly thought. He had been her grandfather's partner when Paul McGill had founded

Sydney-Texas Oil in the twenties, and he had always been difficult. Emma had managed to get him kicked upstairs as chairman of the board in January 1968, and had manipulated the board to do her will. They had voted with her, and had hired Dale Stevens, Emma's protégé, as the new president. Still, some of the board members who were Marriott's cronies resented Dale, and Paula decided that they were most likely creating an untenable situation for him.

Damn, she cursed under her breath. I wish I could reach him before six. Paula glanced at her watch. It was three-thirty. Two and a half hours to wait. Well, at least she had time to sign her letters, go over the interoffice memos piled on her desk, and speak to Vivienne Harte before Sarah Lowther appeared on the scene.

Returning to her desk, Paula flipped through the memos, saw that some of them raised questions which were too complicated to deal with quickly, and these she placed on one side. After signing the morning's correspondence, she put through a call to Allington Hall in Middleham.

"Hello, Vivienne," Paula said when her cousin answered, "how are you?"

"Oh, Paula! Hello. I'm pretty good, and you?"

"Worried, Vivienne. I just heard that—"

"If you're phoning about Sally, I won't tell you where she is! *I promised her.* Daddy can't get it out of me, and neither will you."

Paula said with firmness, "Now, Vivienne, I'm sure Sally wouldn't be upset if you told me. I'm the—"

"Oh yes she would," Vivienne interrupted heatedly. "She doesn't want anybody to know where she's gone. Not even you. Please don't badger me, put me in this terrible position."

"You *can* tell me . . . Listen, I won't say a thing to your father, or another soul, not even Winston when he calls me later. You must know I won't break my word."

"No, I don't know that . . . You're expecting *me* to break *mine,*" Vivienne retorted. "My poor sister is like a wounded bird, worn-out, too, and she needs to have a little peace and quiet. Daddy hasn't stopped ranting and raving at her since Sunday night."

"I'm sorry to hear that. Look here, you don't have to tell me where she is, but would you agree to tell me where she's *not?*"

"What do you mean?" Vivienne asked warily.

"If I name a place where Sally has *not* gone, will you tell me? All you have to say is *no.*"

Vivienne laughed hollowly. "You're trying to trap me, Paula. If I'm silent when I hear a particular name you'll know immediately that's where she's staying." Vivienne laughed again, her incredulity echoing down the wire. "Do you think I'm daft? Or green? I haven't fallen off a banana boat, you know."

"I need to know where your sister is hiding herself," Paula snapped, growing exasperated, "and for a variety of reasons which I don't propose to go into with you."

"Don't talk to me as if I'm a little kid. I'm nineteen," Vivienne cried, her own temper flaring.

Paula sighed. "Let's not argue, Viv, and I can only add this . . . If Sally's gone dashing off to Ireland, she's a bigger fool than I thought, because she will only be creating problems for herself, and for Anthony."

"Sally's hardly a *fool!* Obviously she wouldn't be stupid enough to go to Ireland—" Vivienne stopped abruptly.

Success, Paula thought with a faint smile. Her ruse had worked. She said, "If Sally happens to phone you, tell her I'm having dinner with Alexander and Emily at the White Elephant tonight. Just in case she wants to join us."

"I've got to go, Paula," Vivienne said hurriedly, after a short pause. "Daddy needs me in the stables. So I'll say good-bye now."

"Tell Sally to get in touch with me if she needs anything. Good-bye, Vivienne dear."

Paula stared at the phone for a long moment, reflecting on their conversation. Well, Sally was not in Ireland. More than likely she was not in London either, since it was not her favorite place. Could she still be in Yorkshire? If so, where? A phrase Vivienne had used echoed in her mind. She had referred to her sister as a *wounded bird.* A figure of speech to describe Sally's state? Or had it perhaps been an unconscious association in the girl's mind? Wounded birds tried to get back to their nests . . . Heron's Nest? *Of course.* Sally loved Scarborough, and many of her paintings were of the spots where they had spent so much time as children. That's where *I* would go if I wanted to hide, Paula said to herself. It's accessible, comfortable, the larder is always fully stocked, and old Mrs. Bonnyface has a set of keys.

Lifting the receiver, Paula started to dial Heron's Nest and then changed her mind. It would be infinitely kinder to leave Sally alone for the time being. Whether she was in Scarborough or not was irrelevant, really. The important thing was that she was nowhere near Clonloughlin, and this knowledge now eased Paula's anxiety about Sally Harte, of whom she was extremely fond.

"Paula?"

"Yes, Gaye?" Paula asked, leaning closer to the intercom.

"Sarah's arrived."

"Have her come in, Gaye, please."

A moment later Sarah Lowther was walking across the floor, the expression on her pale freckled face as purposeful as her step. She wore a bottle-green gabardine suit so beautifully cut it did wonders for her somewhat plumpish figure. Also, the color was a flattering contrast to her russet-red hair, which framed her face in luxuriant waves and softened her broad but not unattractive features.

"Hello, Paula," she said briskly, coming to a halt in the center of the room. "You're looking well. Thinner than ever. I don't know how you do it . . . it's a struggle for me to lose an ounce."

Paula half-smiled and, brushing aside the personal comment, said, "Welcome back, Sarah." She stepped around the desk, kissed her cousin on the cheek. "Let's sit over there by the fire," she went on. "Would you like a cup of tea?"

"No. Thanks anyway." Sarah turned smartly on her high heels and moved in the direction of the sofa. Seating herself in the corner nearest the fireplace, she leaned back, crossed her legs, and smoothed her skirt. She let her eyes rove over Paula, admiring the simplicity and elegance of the deep-purple wool dress. It was a marvel, and as head of the fashion division of Harte Enterprises Sarah knew it was by Yves Saint Laurent. Biting back the compliment which had sprung to her lips, she said, "Jonathan tells me the Irish lot are killing each other off . . . I'm surprised Grandmother hasn't hotfooted it back here."

"That's not a very nice thing to say about Anthony, Sarah," Paula gently reproved, seating herself in a chair, frowning. "Min's death was an accident, and *why* should Gran come back? The whole thing's going to be over and done with by tomorrow at this time."

Sarah gave Paula an odd look, raised an auburn brow. "Let's hope you're right."

"Tell me about the opening of the new hotel and our first boutique," Paula said, neatly changing the subject.

Sarah remained silent.

Paula insisted, "Come on, I'm longing to hear all about it."

"It went off well," Sarah said at last. "But then why wouldn't it? I've worked very hard for months to ensure that it would. To tell you the truth, the whole trip was a hard grind. I was on my feet twenty-four hours a day. Miranda was tied up with the hotel, so I had to really buckle down, supervise the unpacking and pressing of the dresses, get the windows dressed, create eye-catching interior displays," she grumbled. "But the merchandise I selected turned out to be perfect, even though I do say so myself. My Lady Hamilton dresses and resort wear appealed to everyone. They said the colors were fantastic, the fabrics superior, the designs bang on. We were jammed the day we opened, so we should do record business right through the season."

"Oh I am pleased," Paula said with enthusiasm, deciding to ignore Sarah's remarks about her contribution to the boutique, which, in all truth, had been negligible. She asked, "How's Merry?"

"All right, I suppose. I didn't see much of her. The O'Neills invited a plane load of celebrities to the hotel's gala opening weekend, so naturally she was busy rubbing noses with the famous."

Paula's back went up at this remark, which she deemed bitchy and uncalled for, but she wisely let it pass. "Did Shane fly down from New York?"

"Yes."

"And?"

"And *what?*" Sarah asked, her voice turning huffy all of a sudden. She gave Paula a challenging stare and her face settled in cold lines.

Instantly struck by the dislike in Sarah's expression, Paula recoiled in surprise. Thrown though she was, she managed to say, "Surely you saw something of Shane and Uncle Bryan? Merry may have been rushed off her feet as head of public relations, but I can't believe the O'Neills ignored you. After all, they're family, and they're not like that."

"Oh yes, I was invited to the gala evenings. But I was generally too exhausted to enjoy them. I didn't have much fun at all. That side of it was a complete bust."

Sarah glanced into the fire, remembering her mortifying weekend of embarrassment, acute disappointment. Shane had been cruel, ignoring her much of the time. And when he had deigned to notice her he had been offhand, patently disinterested in her as a woman. He wouldn't have treated Paula in such a rotten way, she thought miserably, sinking back into herself. An image of his face leapt out at her from the flames, his expression one of immense passion and love. She blinked, wanting to expunge this from her mind. That look had not been for her, but for Paula . . . that terrible day of the christening . . . She would never forget that look or that occasion. It was only then she had realized, to her horror and distress, that Shane O'Neill loved Paula

Fairley. That's the real reason he has no time for me, she said silently. Damn Paula. I detest her. Jealousy rose up in Sarah so unexpectedly and with such force she kept her face averted, willing the emotion to go away, feeling faint and sick inside.

"Well, I'm sorry you didn't have a good time," Paula murmured, attempting to be gracious, yet asking herself what she had done to engender such sudden dislike in Sarah. Paula sat back and her eyes narrowed thoughtfully. She had no reason to think that Sarah was lying about the gala weekend, but somehow she did. She considered Sarah's self-congratulatory remarks, her pleased tone when she had spoken of her hard work. How she exaggerated.

Paula could not resist adding, "So the work was grueling—that's retailing, you know, Sarah. And, let's face it, *you* were the one who insisted on going to Barbados. If I—"

"And it's a jolly good thing I did, isn't it?" Sarah interjected peremptorily, tearing her gaze from the fire, swinging her head to glare at Paula. "Somebody had to be there to organize things. We'd have been in a nice mess if we'd relied on Merry, in view of her abdication of her duties. Of if we'd left things to chance as you wanted us to do."

Paula was further astonished by this criticism and the belligerence underlying the comment. Unwilling to let Sarah get away with it, she said with some sharpness, "That's most unfair of you. I had no intention of leaving anything to chance. I had intended to fly out there myself, until you made such a song and dance about going. Anyway, you don't have to worry about the other boutiques. I've hired Melanie Redfern from Harvey Nichols. She starts next week. She will be in charge of the Harte shops in all the O'Neill hotels, and she'll be working closely with me. And Merry, of course."

"I see." Sarah shifted her position and cleared her throat. "Actually, the main reason I came to see you today is to make you an offer."

"An *offer?*" Paula stiffened, wondering what Sarah was about to spring on her.

"Yes. I'd like to buy the boutiques for my division. There won't be any problem about money. We have stacks of spare cash. You see, in view of my considerable involvement with the boutiques, I'd like to have them under my aegis, make them part of Lady Hamilton Clothes. So just name your price—I'll meet it."

Flabbergasted though she was at Sarah's ridiculous proposition, Paula retorted swiftly, "Even if I wanted to, I couldn't do that, as you well know. The boutiques belong to the Harte department store chain."

Sarah stared Paula down. Her expression hardened. "So what. I'm offering you an easy way to make a fast profit. And a big one. That should please you, since your eyes are eternally glued to the bottom of a balance sheet."

"I'd like to remind you that the Harte chain is a public company," Paula exclaimed, thinking that her cousin had taken leave of her senses. "I do have shareholders and a board of directors to answer to, in case this has escaped your notice."

Sarah smiled narrowly. "Don't talk to me about the board at Harte's. We all know about the board, my dear. It consists of Grandmother, you, your parents, Alexander, and a handful of old codgers who'll do anything you say. If you wanted to, you could easily sell me the boutiques. It's your decision. Don't expect me to believe otherwise. That board will acquiesce to your wishes no matter what, as they always did what Grandmother wanted in the past. She had them in her pocket, and so do you.''

Paula fixed a pair of immensely cold eyes on her cousin, and her voice was equally icy, as she said, ''Harte's has invested a great deal of money in the new shops, and I have personally devoted an incredible amount of time and effort to the project for many months. I therefore have no intention of selling them to you or to anyone else, even if the board sanctioned such a sale, which, believe me, they wouldn't, not at this stage. You see, Sarah, I want the boutiques for Harte's. They're part of our growth and expansion program. Also, I—''

''*Your* effort!'' Sarah cried, seizing on this particular point. ''That's a laugh. I've worked much harder than you, and I selected all of the merchandise. Under the circumstances, it's only fair that—''

''Stop right there!'' Paula warned, her face revealing her growing annoyance and impatience. ''I'm not sitting still for this nonsense, Sarah. Why, you're bloody preposterous. You walk in here, commence to criticize me, then try to take credit for the success of the Barbados shop . . . and at the moment that's a moot point. Only time will tell us how successful it really is. But getting back to *your* efforts, I think you have a real nerve. It just so happens that Emily has done a lot more for us than you. She purchased every single accessory, which was no mean feat, and I recall that *I* picked out every bit of beachwear. Furthermore, Merry and I selected all of the clothing from your company—not *you*. I'll concede that you made the best lines available at Lady Hamilton, and designed the special evening wear, and perhaps you have worked conscientiously for the past ten days. However, your contribution to the first boutique was minor, *very minor* indeed.''

Paula rose and walked over to her desk and sat down behind it. She finished quietly, ''As for trying to buy the boutiques from Harte's—'' She shook her head wonderingly. ''I can only add that that's the most foolish thing I've ever heard, especially coming from you, when you of all people know how Grandy has structured things. Look, if you want to get involved in a new project, maybe we can put our heads together—'' Paula stopped, immediately regretted her conciliatory gesture. Sarah's coldness was more pronounced than ever.

Sarah stood up without saying a thing. She made a beeline for the desk, stood facing Paula.

In a soft and uncommonly steady tone, Sarah said, ''Grandmother might have other ideas about the boutiques. She may well like the idea of selling them to me. Has that occurred to you?'' Not giving Paula a chance to reply, she continued in her oddly calm way, ''Grandy's not dead yet, and if I know her, I bet she hasn't signed over her seventy percent of the shares in Harte's to you. Oh no, she's hanging on to those, I'm *quite* certain, being as wily as she is. And so, as far as I'm concerned, she's still the boss lady around here. I want you to understand one thing . . . I'm not letting the matter rest here, with you. Oh no, not by a long shot. I fully intend to telex Grandy. *Today,* Paula. I shall apprise her of our meeting, my offer and your rejection of it. We'll see who really runs Harte stores, won't we?''

Paula gave her a regretful look through saddened eyes. ''Send a telex. Send ten if you wish. You won't accomplish anything—''

''You're not the only grandchild Emma Harte has,'' Sarah cut in, her voice biting. ''Although anyone would think it, the way you behave.''

"Sarah, don't let's quarrel like this. You're being childish, and you've always known Harte's is a public—" Paula's sentence was left dangling in mid-air. Sarah had walked out. The door closed softly behind her.

Paula stared after her, shaking her head again, not yet fully recovered from her astonishment at Sarah's preposterous proposition and irrational attitude. She sighed under her breath. Only two weeks ago she had remarked to Emily that tranquility had reigned supreme since their grandmother's departure in May.

I spoke too soon, Paula now thought, and she discovered that the most disturbing part of the meeting had been Sarah's blatant dislike of her. As Paula continued to contemplate her cousin's unexpected hostility, she asked herself if it signaled the beginning of open warfare.

Twenty-Six

Emily was awed.

"Just look at this evening gown. It's absolutely exquisite," she said in hushed tones, lifting the garment out of the large box lined with layers and layers of tissue paper.

Alexander, lolling on the bed in one of the guest rooms in Emma's Belgrave Square flat, nodded in agreement. "It also looks as if it's in perfect condition." A fond smile glanced across his serious face as Emily glided into the middle of the floor and held it against herself, carefully.

The gown was a long, slender sheath of turquoise silk, entirely encrusted with thousands of tiny bugle beads in shades of pale blue and emerald green. Emily moved slightly and the dress undulated, the beads instantly changing color as they caught and held the light. The effect was dazzling.

Cocking his head to one side, continuing to regard his sister intently, Alexander said, "You know, it contains all the colors of a summer sea in the south of France, and it certainly matches your eyes, Emily. What a pity you can't keep it, have it for yourself. It's not a bit outdated."

"Oh I know, and I'd love it, but it's far too valuable, really. Anyway, I couldn't do that to Paula. She needs the dress for her fashion exhibition next January."

"Has she found a name for that yet?"

"She's considering calling it Fashion Fantasia, with the subheading Fifty Years of Elegance and Style. I rather like it, don't you?"

"Yes." He watched Emily as she expertly folded the gown into the box and covered it with the tissue, remarking, "Imagine Gran keeping the evening dress all these years. It's easily forty-five years old, and it really pongs of mothballs." He curled his nose in distaste, then added, "But I bet our Gran looked smashing in it, with her red-gold hair and green eyes."

Emily lifted her blond head. "To say the least. And you're right about its age. Just before Gran left she said we'd find it in one of her cedar closets on the top floor, along with the other clothes. Gran told us she'd first worn it at the supper dance she gave for Uncle Frank and Aunt Natalie when they got engaged." Emily put the lid on the box, patted it down, glanced at her brother. "Do you know, there's even a pair of emerald satin slippers from Pinet to go with it, and they're in mint condition, too. They look as if they've been worn once or twice and that's all.''

"Yes, everything's been so carefully preserved,'' Alexander observed, thinking of his canny grandmother's sense of thrift which was legendary. Swinging his legs off the bed, he ambled over to the long metal clothes rack positioned near the window, ran his hand along it. Peering at the labels on the suits, dresses, and evening gowns, he read out loud, "Chanel, Vionnet, Balenciaga, Molyneux . . . these are all as good as new, Emily, and they *must* date back to the twenties and thirties.''

"They do, and that's why they're essential for the exhibition. Several other women who are noted for their elegance—Best-Dressed List ladies—are loaning similar designer clothes to Paula, and they've all accepted her invitation to come to the cocktail party at the store the night she opens the exhibition to the public.''

Emily now crossed to the dressing table, picked up a typed sheet, made a notation, slipped the sheet into its folder and said, "Thanks for keeping me company, Sandy, while I checked everything off. Well, let's go downstairs, that's all I have time to do tonight. I promised to help Paula organize the rest of the clothes this weekend, since she's snowed under at the moment.''

"Where is she, by the way?'' Alexander asked, following Emily out of the guest room onto the second-floor landing. "Don't tell me she's still at the store.''

"Oh no, she's here,'' Emily said over her shoulder, tripping down the staircase. "After we'd unpacked the clothes and hung them up to be checked for any minor repairs, she went to change her dress. She's probably popped into the old nursery.''

Alexander pushed open the drawing room door for Emily, stepped inside after her. "Are the babies here too?'' he asked, surprised.

"Yes, and Nora. Paula brought them to town with her on Monday afternoon. Oh look, Sandy, good old Parker's put out a bottle of white wine for us. Shall we have a glass now?'' She rushed over to the console.

"Why not? Thanks, Emily.'' He took a chair near the fireplace, crossed his long legs and lit a cigarette, studying his sister as she poured the wine. Although she was of average height he generally thought of her as being small, perhaps because she was so delicately made, so daintily proportioned. He nodded to himself. Emily had turned into a very pretty young woman in the last few years. How mean he and his male cousins had been to little Emily when they were children, teasing her about her enormous appetite and her totally spherical body, calling her Apple Dumpling. She was no longer anything like a dumpling. Tonight she resembled a pert china doll in the flattering pink wool dress. Some china doll, he added under his breath, ruminating on her tremendous physical and mental energy, wondering, as he so often did, where it came from. Their grandmother? Certainly it was not something she had inherited from their parents. Their mother was an indolent, bored, spoiled socialite without a serious thought in her head. Their father was a has-been who had never really made it in the first place—forever the failure. Poor Dad, he thought, he's without doubt the nicest, kindest chap I know. Alexander reminded himself to ring his father tomorrow to make a date for lunch or dinner. They didn't really see enough of each other these days.

"Gosh, Sandy, I didn't notice your lovely tan when we were upstairs,''

Emily remarked, bringing him the glass of wine, scrutinizing him closely. She flopped onto the chair opposite. "You really look super. You should sit in the sun more often."

"What? And let Harte Enterprises go to rack and ruin? Not on your life." He raised his glass. *"Santé."*

"Cheers," said Emily, and after taking a sip, she asked, "Where's old Mag?"

"She went to Scotland this morning to look at a shooting lodge that's going up for sale. The owner wants the real estate firm she works for to handle it, so Maggie's about to be given the grand tour. If she likes it, it'll go on their books. God knows who'll buy it, though. Who on earth wants a shooting lodge in this day and age, I ask you?"

"A rich American," Emily suggested. "Have you set a date for your wedding?"

"June . . . possibly."

"That's not fair!" Emily wailed, her eyes flashing. "You know Winston and I are getting married in June. You'd better make sure Maggie checks with me before you set a firm date."

"We could have a double wedding," he said, and burst out laughing at her expression. "Why are you looking at me like that?"

"If you don't know, then I'm not going to tell you," she retorted huffily. "On the other hand, perhaps I should."

"Forget that I said it. Anyway, I wasn't really serious."

"Yes, you were, and I *shall* tell you," Emily announced. "There are three good reasons. One: Every bride wants to be the center of attraction on *her* special day and she certainly can't be if there's *another bride* loitering around. Two: Gran would have a fit because she'd consider it icky . . . bad form. Three: We can't disappoint our grandmother, who's looking forward to giving *two* big super-duper extra-special weddings with all the trimmings next summer."

"You've convinced me, Emily—a double wedding is out of the question," he replied in a teasing voice. He sobered almost at once, drew on his cigarette, quickly stubbed it out, his gestures unexpectedly nervous.

Emily, forever the acute observer, exclaimed, "Is something the matter?"

"Paula might have managed to nip one scandal in the bud—over in Ireland —but I'm afraid we have another one about to explode. It's—"

"Scandal," Paula repeated quietly, entering the room. She closed the door behind her and stood staring at Alexander and Emily with a worried expression.

"Paula," Alexander said, rising and going to greet her affectionately. "Let me get you a glass of wine, and then we'll have a little powwow before we go to the White Elephant."

Paula sat down on the sofa and her gaze followed him across the room. With a scowl she asked him, "What kind of scandal, Sandy?"

He brought her the drink, returned to the chair. "It's Mother again. I'm sorry to have to tell you both." His concerned eyes swung from Paula to Emily. "She rang me this morning from Paris sounding quite hysterical. Apparently Gianni Ravioli—"

"Don't be mean," Emily remonstrated. "How many times do I have to tell you his name's de Ravello and Gianni's very sweet."

"—has started divorce proceedings," Alexander continued in a stronger tone, after throwing a chastising frown in Emily's direction, "and she's on the verge of nervous collapse, or so she says—"

"What the hell does she expect?" Emily broke in again. *"She's* the one who did a bolt with the detestable Frog."

"If you keep interrupting me, we're never going to get to dinner," Alexander pointed out, sternly wagging a finger at his sister. "In any event, our mother's distressed because of Gianni's intractability. You see, even though she's given him the evidence, he refuses to name Marc Deboyne."

"Why?" Emily asked, her curiosity piqued.

Paula said, "Who *is* he naming? Obviously that's at the root of your mother's upset."

Alexander gave her a sharp look. "Smart girl. That's it exactly." There was a slight pause before he went on, with the utmost quiet, "It seems he's going to cite a number of . . . ministers of the Crown as the corespondents. Darling Mummy must've gone through the Cabinet like a dose of salts."

"You've got to be joking," Paula cried, staring at him in astonishment and alarm.

"I wish I were," Alexander said, his gloominess mounting as he thought of the consequences of his mother's adultery, the embarrassment to the family, particularly his grandmother. *She would be mortified.*

Emily was all agog. Her eyes widened and she shrieked, "Uncle Robin's cronies, I'll wager!" Groaning theatrically, she rolled her eyes at the ceiling. "I can just see the banner headline in the *Daily Mirror:* 'Italian count cites entire British Government in society divorce.' Or what about this one in the *News of the World:* 'Socialite lays all her eggs in Government basket.' The papers are going to have a field day with this one!" She leered at them wickedly.

Paula's mouth twitched involuntarily and she could not help laughing, despite her annoyance with her aunt and the seriousness of the situation. "Stop it, Emily, you're impossible." Paula attempted to swallow her rising laughter, which she knew partially sprang from her nervousness tonight.

Alexander, who was not amused, glared at both women. "It's not funny, you know—" He broke off, shaking his head, suddenly at a loss for words. He had been seething ever since his mother had telephoned him that morning. Like Emma, he was constantly maddened by her outrageous behavior, and, being conservative, her morals were offensive to him.

In a rush, Emily said, "I'd love to know who Mummy's lovers were." A speculative gleam flashed across her face and she wrinkled her nose. "No, I can't picture the beauteous Elizabeth in bed with Fat Dabs."

"Fat Dabs?" Paula echoed in perplexity.

"Really, Emily!" Alexander exploded.

Quite undaunted by Alexander's reprimand, and adopting an exaggerated Yorkshire accent, Emily informed Paula, "Aye, Fat Dabs. That's wot t'lads at Genret call our 'Arold from 'Uddersfield." Another thought instantly occurred to Emily, and, reverting to her normal cultivated tone, she pointed out, "Robin's going to have apoplexy. Let's not forget that our charming uncle, member of Parliament for Southeast Leeds, is also one of Harold Wilson's Cabinet ministers. He's expecting to be appointed Chancellor of the Exchequer, you know, if Labor gets in again at the next election. Gosh, Sandy, you're right, there's going to be a huge scandal . . . Shades of Profumo, do you think? We'll never be able to nip this one in the bud."

"I'm not going to worry myself about Uncle Robin's precious political career," Alexander retorted with acerbity. "Oh no, not at all. Besides, he's such an opportunist he'll find a way to get mileage out of this, if I'm not mistaken. Anyway, it's probably all his fault. You put your finger on it, Emily, I'm sure Mother met the gentlemen in question through him. She was constantly dashing over to his fancy parties in Eaton Square." He shot Paula a worried glance. "Once the divorce papers are filed with the law courts the press will be onto it in no time, and Emily's not too far off the mark about those banner headlines."

Paula sat reflecting, said at last, "How much? To buy him off."

"Not sure," Alexander said.

Emily cried, "Oh, I don't think he wants anything."

Paula pinned her cousin with her cool, knowing gaze. "I'm surprised at your naïveté, Emily. We've been raised by a woman who continually told us that everyone has a price, and that it's only a question of how much. Of course he wants money. *Then* he'll do the gentlemanly thing and name Marc Deboyne."

Emily protested with fierceness, "I know him better than either of you and I don't think he's like that."

"Gran is also fond of saying that the price isn't necessarily money," Alexander was quick to remind them. "And now that I think about it, I'm inclined to agree with you, Emily. I honestly don't believe he wants lots of cash. But he does want something. *Revenge.* I'm certain he still loves our mother—although God knows why in view of her treatment of him—and he's badly hurt. So . . . he has the need to strike back, hurt her in return, and the only way he knows how is to embarrass her publicly."

"Maybe," Paula admitted, seeing the sense in Alexander's theory. "Apparently he has all the evidence he needs?" This came out as a question.

"Oh yes," Alexander told her. "Mother was quite clear that he has the goods on her. He's not making idle threats."

"Are you sure she didn't tell you who the ministers were?" Emily probed with her usual inquisitiveness.

Alexander looked at her pityingly. "Come *on,* she may be a foolish, misguided woman, but deep down she's quite crafty. Of course she didn't volunteer any names."

Paula said, "Did your mother tell you what she wanted you to do, Sandy?"

"Yes. She wants me to go and see Gianni, to persuade him to name Marc Deboyne in the suit. She seems to believe I can influence him, but she's up a bloody gum tree there. I don't know him that well, and, anyway, it's Emily he likes the most."

"Oh no," Emily shrieked, "not me!"

Alexander and Paula exchanged conspiratorial looks, and Paula said, "You might be the best person to deal with him, darling."

Emily moaned, fell back in the chair.

She found the idea of talking to Gianni about her mother's infidelity quite repugnant. On the other hand, she liked the man, and Alexander might be tactless with him. She said firmly, as she straightened up, "I simply refuse to offer Gianni money, and that's flat!"

"What will your approach be?" Alexander asked, filling with profound relief that she'd apparently agreed to take on this unpleasant task.

"I shall—" Emily thought hard and her face brightened. She said, "Why, I shall appeal to his better nature, explain that he will be hurting Amanda and Francesca more than Mummy, and he's very fond of the girls. He wouldn't want them to suffer."

Paula said with a degree of hesitation, "Very well, handle it that way . . . However, you'd better have something up your sleeve, just in case his better nature fails him."

"You do sound cynical at times," Emily declared, pursing her lips reprovingly. "I will not insult that poor, betrayed man by offering him money."

Paying no attention to Emily's irate manner, Paula shrugged, said, "You could always offer him a job—if he's adamant, if he insists on naming half the damned Government."

"A job? Where? Who with?"

"With Harte's, Emily. I've been looking for someone to run Trade Winds, the new antique accessory shop I'm planning to open in the near future. Since Gianni's an expert in that area, perhaps he'd prefer working for the family rather than that antique importing company where he's currently employed. We'd be killing several birds with one stone in a sense—ensuring he's on *our* side, if not your mother's especially, and he wouldn't really be under our feet, since he'd have to do a lot of traveling. Also, I might get myself a good man for Trade Winds. And he'll certainly earn more at Harte's."

"What a marvelous solution!" Alexander exclaimed, immediately cheering up, relaxing in his chair.

Emily bit her lip. "I shall only mention the job at Harte's if he's difficult," she warned, convinced that Gianni was not an opportunist. She added quickly, "I *know* he won't be, that he'll do the right thing. I just do."

"We'll see," Paula murmured.

Alexander stood up, strode across the room. "Now that we've dealt with Mother's love life, there's another matter I must discuss." He paused at the door. "Won't be a minute . . . I left my briefcase in the hall when I arrived."

In his absence, Emily leaned toward Paula, confided, "Gianni really is a lovely person. You just don't know him very well."

"I'm sure he is, under normal circumstances. But it's wiser to be prepared for the worst."

Emily said nothing, and a moment later Alexander returned, sat down, took a folder out of his briefcase. He handed it to Paula.

"What's this?" she asked, taking it from him.

"A report from Mr. Graves of Graves and Saunderson. But there's no need to read it now."

"Is it about Jonathan?" Paula ventured, turning the folder over, fingering it, her breath catching in her throat with apprehension.

"No. The report concerns Sebastian Cross."

"Oh." Paula put one hand to her mouth, remembering that day in the boardroom at Aire, wondering why she had a sudden sense of foreboding.

Alexander explained, "I think it'll be quicker if I give you the information in a few short sentences. The report *is* rather long, tedious in parts, which is why I suggest you peruse it at your leisure."

"Hurry up, then, tell us, Sandy," Emily ordered. "We ought to be leaving for dinner in a few minutes. I'm starved."

"Mr. Graves has been digging for months, trying to find something on Sebastian, as you're both aware," Alexander commenced. "His inquiries were business-oriented at first, since he was following Grandy's instructions. When he came up empty-handed yet again, he decided to investigate Sebastian's private life. After a number of false leads, interviews with different people in London, he went up to Yorkshire. And he stumbled on some information that's not very pleasant, I don't mind telling you. Knowing that a lot of the chaps from Aire Communications congregate at Polly's Bar in Leeds he started hanging around there. One lunchtime he struck up a conversation with a young chap who'd once worked at Aire. Graves and the fellow eventually became very chummy, got to meeting for drinks regularly over a three-week period. One night Tommy Charwood—that's the fellow's name—told Graves that Sebastian was a nasty piece of work, said he'd like to get him in a dark alley one night and give him the thrashing of his life." Alexander stopped to light a cigarette, then continued, "When Graves asked the reason, Tommy Charwood told him that he'd been courting a girl who had also worked at Aire, and that Sebastian had taken her away from him. Now, it seems that the girl, Alice Peele—"

"I've met Alice," Paula interjected quickly, her face quickening with interest. "She's in public relations, and she once came to see me about a job at Harte's."

"What's she like?" Alexander asked curiously.

"Talented in her field, rather pleasant. I remember her quite distinctly because she was well-turned-out and very striking. Tall, dark, with an unusually pretty face."

Alexander cleared his throat, pinned his grave eyes on Paula. "I'm not too sure how pretty she is these days. According to Tommy Charwood, Sebastian Cross beat her up a number of times. And so badly the last time, Alice Peele had to see a plastic surgeon. Charwood told Graves that she would have been disfigured for life without the prompt emergency treatment she received at Leeds General Infirmary. You see, Cross beat her with such a vengeance her jaw was broken, also one cheekbone, and her face was a bloody pulp."

"Oh my God!" Paula cried. "How appalling, what a horrible thing to happen!"

Emily had also blanched. Shuddering, she looked across at Paula, then whispered, "Your instincts were right about Sebastian Cross." Emily swallowed, turned to her brother. "Didn't the girl bring charges? Go to the police? Prosecute?"

"No, seemingly not. Charwood told Graves that she was terrified of Cross. Her father had wanted to go to the police, but Alice begged him not to, insisted it would only stir up more trouble. That's when Mr. Peele confided in Tommy, whom he'd remained friendly with. Tommy tried to talk Peele into going to Leeds CID—he knows a number of detectives on the force—but Peele kept wavering. In the end he decided against it. About a month after this last terrible beating, John Cross paid a visit to the Peele family, offered Mr. Peele money. Peele, who sounds like the salt of the earth, threw the money in John Cross's face. As soon as Alice was sufficiently recovered, he shipped her off to live with her married brother in Gibraltar. The brother's in the Royal Navy, helicopters I think, and is stationed permanently in Gib. Tommy Charwood believes she's still out there."

"What a ghastly story," Paula said, continuing to shiver. "I'm not surprised Alice Peele is terrified of Cross . . ." she faltered, stopped, turned away, filled with revulsion for the man.

Emily gasped, "He must be a maniac! That girl's family should have prosecuted him, regardless of what *she* said."

Alexander nodded, and his expression, reflecting Paula's, was one of immense distaste. He said with harshness, "And that's not all . . . Charwood gave Graves some additional information, after our wily private eye ingratiated himself further. Charwood swears Sebastian is into *drugs,* quite aside from being a heavy drinker, and is a congenital gambler who has suffered some big losses at the tables. At Crockford's, and God knows where else."

"And this is the man who is Jonathan Ainsley's best friend," Paula said. "This is just awful."

"Yes, it is," Alexander concurred. "And whilst the information about Cross doesn't really do *us* any good, it does reflect rather badly on Jonathan, in that he's Cross's bosom chum. Wouldn't you say?"

Paula nodded.

Emily looked from Paula to her brother. "Do you think Jonathan's also on drugs? That he gambles?"

"He'd better not be on drugs," Alexander snapped. "Not if he wants to continue running the real estate division of Harte Enterprises. Let's not forget he handles a great deal of money, and also has to make some very important decisions at times." Alexander stood up, walked over to the console, poured a glass of wine, muttered, "I'm going to have to monitor *everything* he does from now on—watch him even more closely than before. I simply can't afford to have him make any mistakes whatsoever. As for gambling"—Alexander shrugged, shook his head—"I can't hazard a guess about that. But he might be playing the tables, and that's another reason why I'm going to take a bigger interest in the real estate division. As I said, there's an awful lot of cash going through that company."

"Presumably you've instructed Mr. Graves to keep at it, Sandy. To dig deeper?" Paula said.

"Naturally."

"Oddly enough," Paula went on thoughtfully, "John Cross rang the store today. He wanted an appointment."

"Are you going to see him?" Alexander asked, returning to the chair.

"I don't know—probably not. Gaye tried to reach him at his hotel late this afternoon but he'd gone out. I expect he'll phone again in the morning."

"In one sense, I'd be curious to know what he has to say. He can't possibly imagine we'd be interested in Aire. Not now, after he's sold the building, which was the main asset of the company."

Paula shrugged, and instantly changed the subject. "Sarah came to see me this afternoon." She proceeded to recount the meeting, not missing a single detail. When she had finished, she sat back, waiting for their reactions.

Emily had been all eyes and ears throughout Paula's recital. She exclaimed, "I'd like to hear Miranda's version of the weekend, not to mention the whole ten days Sarah spent in Barbados. I have a feeling their stories will vary considerably. Sarah was always rather good at taking credit when it wasn't due her."

"Yes, I know." Paula immediately thought of their childhood days at Heron's Nest. She and Emily had been aware of Sarah's craftiness even then. Their cousin had forever tried to curry favor with their grandmother, paint herself in the best possible light, frequently at their expense.

Alexander spoke up. "Sarah's not stupid. She knows you can't sell the boutiques, not without first going to the board. She's also well aware that she can't spend the fashion division's money willy-nilly unless she has my permission. Therefore she must have convinced herself she can bypass us, succeed in her aims by going to Grandy directly. I'm certain she sent the telex, as she threatened to do."

"I am too," Emily muttered, condemning Sarah under her breath. Paula had far too many worries and problems to contend with at the moment, without Sarah creating difficulties.

Paula smiled faintly. "I won't argue with either of you. However, I can assure you that the telex ended up in the wastepaper basket. What Sarah doesn't know is that Grandy really came to believe in the boutiques before she left in May. At the last minute she suddenly saw them as a clever means to expand, and in a relatively easy way for our organization. She's convinced the boutiques will increase the value of the Harte shares—and of course they will—so she has no more intention of selling off the boutiques than I do."

"Yes, but you just said Sarah doesn't realize that," Emily pointed out quietly. "And, anyway, I've always thought she was infuriated because you got the Harte chain and not her. After all, she *is* the eldest granddaughter, and she has quite an opinion of herself as a businesswoman."

"Emily's taken the words out of my mouth," Alexander said, turning swiftly to Paula. "Sarah's visit this afternoon may have been a nasty little exercise—one specifically designed to upset you, Paula, to unnerve you, throw you off balance." As he was speaking, another thought struck him. "I say, could this be the beginning of the guerrilla war we've talked about, and have been anticipating?"

"That had crossed my mind earlier," Paula told him.

"If it is, what does Sarah hope to gain, Sandy?" Emily demanded.

"The satisfaction of knowing Paula's aggravated, under additional pressure. Also, a person who has been thrown off balance is not always thinking clearly or coolly, and frequently concentration is damaged." Alexander gave them both a very pointed look. "Sarah's been hand-in-glove with Jonathan for a long time. She bears watching as closely as he does."

Paula stood up. "Enough of *them,* for tonight at least. Let's go to dinner," she suggested, wanting to bring an end to this discussion. "It's been a difficult day, and a terrible week so far." She sighed wearily. "I'm not going to burden either of you with my problems at Sitex Oil, but I've had those to cope with today as well. I think I've just about run out of steam. I need a little light relief, such as an amusing evening at the White Elephant."

"Are they serious problems?" Alexander asked as the three of them went out into the entrance foyer to get their coats. He squeezed Paula's shoulder affectionately. "Can I be of help?"

Paula gave him a grateful smile. "Thanks, Sandy, it's sweet of you to offer. I've got things under control . . ." She hesitated before adding, "Dale Stevens was determined to resign as president this afternoon. I spent over an hour on the phone with him, convinced him to stay on. He has a number of enemies on the board, unmitigated troublemakers who try to tie his hands whenever they can." She shook her head ruefully. "What I should have said a moment ago is that he's agreed to stay on as president until the end of the year. All I've done really is buy myself a little time."

——— *Twenty-Seven* ———

"John Crawford has offered to explain the procedure in a coroner's court," Daisy said, looking from Edwina to Anthony. "He feels it will help us to be more relaxed about the inquest."

Anthony said, "It certainly would, Aunt Daisy." He stood up. "I'll go and fetch Bridget. I think she ought to hear what your family solicitor has to say. Excuse me, I won't be a moment."

As he left the library, Daisy rose and joined Edwina on the sofa. She took her half sister's hand in hers and squeezed it, looking deeply into her care-worn face. "Try not to worry, Edwina. In a few hours this tragedy will be behind us. We must go on, you know, endeavor to get on with our lives as best we can."

"Yes, Daisy, and thank you for your concern. I'll be all right," Edwina murmured in a tired voice. The last few days of anxiety and strain had taken their toll, and she looked exhausted, near total collapse. The black dress she had chosen to wear, stark and unrelieved by jewelry or any accent color, did nothing to enhance her appearance. It appeared to drain what bit of color she had from her face, emphasizing her pallor more than ever. She looked ill, and her age showed pronouncedly this morning.

Gratitude suddenly flickered in Edwina's silvery gray eyes as she added quietly, "I don't know what I would have done without you and Jim. Where is he, Daisy?"

"Right now he's on the phone to Paula, and I believe he has a few calls to make to people on the paper. But he'll join us as soon as he's finished. It's not really essential for him to be briefed. He knows the inner workings of a coroner's court since he used to cover inquests in his early days as a reporter."

"Oh yes, of course, he would understand about those things." Edwina shifted her glance to the clock on the mantelpiece at the other side of the handsome paneled room. "It's almost eight-thirty. We'll have to leave soon to drive into Cork. It'll take us well over an hour, perhaps an hour and a half, you know."

Detecting the nervousness and panic in Edwina's voice, Daisy said reassuringly, "We've plenty of time. The inquest is set for eleven, and this session with John won't take very long. He said he could cover the important points in about ten minutes. After that we can start out, drive in at a leisurely pace. Do stay calm, my dear."

"I'm fine, really. Just a little tired. I didn't sleep very well."

"I don't think any of us did," Daisy said with a slight smile. "I'm going to have another cup of coffee. Would you like one?"

"No, thank you, Daisy." Edwina sat rigidly on the sofa, twisting her hands in her lap, her chest tight with apprehension. For four days and nights she had lived with this terrible fear for her son. She could not wait to go to the county court, to get the inquest over and done with, so that the cloud surrounding him would be lifted. Only then would she be able to relax. She would willingly give her life for Anthony. He was the only person who mattered to her, and once the inquiry into the cause of Min's death was over, she would support him in anything he wished to do, even if that meant accepting Sally Harte, of whom she did not approve. Until the day she died she would regret her passive role in the trouble that had developed between Min and Anthony in the past few weeks. Anthony had asked her to intercede, to reason with her, insisting she could influence his estranged wife to proceed with the divorce as originally agreed. And perhaps she could have, but she would never know, for she had refused. Now poor Min was dead. She would still be alive if I had spoken to her, Edwina thought for the umpteenth time. The pain in her heart intensified. Her guilt soared.

Daisy brought her cup of coffee and sat down in the chair opposite. She said, "Have you decided what you want to do? Will you come to London for a few days' rest after the funeral?"

"Perhaps I should get away from here," Edwina began and stopped, looking at the door as Anthony came in with Bridget O'Donnell, the housekeeper at Clonloughlin.

"M'lady, Mrs. Amory," Bridget said, inclining her head, taking the chair Anthony indicated.

Daisy, always gracious, smiled at her. "As you know, Mr. Crawford is our solicitor and he came over from London to help in any way he can. He is going to explain a few things to us, Bridget, as I'm sure Lord Dunvale has told you. However, I just want to add that there's nothing to be alarmed about."

"Oh, I'm not worried, Mrs. Amory, not at all," Bridget answered quickly, in a clipped tone that partially obscured the lilting bur, meeting Daisy's gaze unblinkingly. "It's a very simple matter, telling the truth, and that's what I aim to do." A small smug smile flicked across her narrow pale mouth and she sat back, crossed her legs. Her red hair gleamed in the sunlight, its fiery hue contrasting markedly with her icy-cold blue eyes.

Daisy's opinion that Bridget O'Donnell was a cool customer, calculating and sure of herself, was reaffirmed. She did not particularly like this woman, whom she guessed to be about thirty-five or thereabouts, even though she did not look it.

Glancing away, Daisy turned to Anthony, but before she had a chance to say anything the door opened to admit John Crawford, the son of Emma's solicitor of many years and now a senior partner in the firm of Crawford, Creighton, Phipps and Crawford. Of medium height and build, he was nevertheless ramrod straight and had a military bearing which combined with his forceful personality to give him an aura of presence. At forty-six he had sandy hair peppered with gray, bright, informed brown eyes in a pleasant face that was oddly bland, and did nothing to reveal a razor-sharp legal brain of great brilliance.

"Good morning. Sorry to keep you waiting," he said briskly, striding forward to join them at the windowed end of the long book-filled room. Daisy offered him coffee but he declined. He remained standing behind a chair, his hands resting lightly on its back. He looked completely relaxed and untroubled, and as he always did with his clients, he endeavored to convey a feeling of supreme confidence whatever his private thoughts and opinions were.

Crawford said, "I realize this is going to be quite an ordeal for you this morning, and so I thought it might help if I gave you a rundown on the manner in which a coroner's court is conducted. Understanding something about the proceedings may lessen everyone's nervousness, I hope." His eyes swept over the four of them. "Feel free to ask any questions as I go along. Since none of you has attended an inquest before, let me first say that the coroner's court is conducted in a rather *informal* way. However—" He paused, looked at them keenly, and, speaking slowly, as if to give added emphasis to his words, went on, "I must stress that the informality in no way lessens its *importance*. It is one of the *highest* courts in the land, and it is ruled by the *law of evidence*. Any questions?" A sandy brow lifted. "All right, on to the next—"

"Excuse me, John," Daisy said, "could you please clarify what you mean by *informal*. I don't quite understand."

"Ah yes, of course. By informal I mean that the coroner is not wearing robes. He is dressed in a business suit. Also, the manner of speaking is less formal than other courts. The coroner chats informally with the interested parties before evidence is given on the witness stand under oath."

"Thank you, John. One other question. The coroner is usually a solicitor, a barrister, or a doctor with legal training, isn't he?"

"That is quite correct, Daisy. The coroner is not a judge, even though he is in fact making the ruling. He also has a very wide latitude in his conduct of an inquiry. If there are no other questions, I shall continue. I now come to a most important point, and it is this: The coroner will accept *hearsay* in this court, which is not common practice in other courts of law under British justice, where hearsay is *inadmissible* evidence."

Anthony leaned forward. "What does that mean?" He shook his head. "It can't mean what I think it does!" he went on to exclaim, his voice more high-pitched than normal.

"Yes, Lord Dunvale, it does. A coroner will listen to something a person has heard but does not know to be true . . . rumor, gossip, if you will."

"I see," Anthony said in a more composed voice, even though he was experiencing inner alarm at the thought of the gossip which had been rife in the village for months.

Edwina and Daisy exchanged worried glances. Neither said a word.

John Crawford, aware of their uneasiness, cleared his throat, continued, "Let me qualify hearsay more fully, as it applies in the coroner's court. In this instance, hearsay might be words spoken by the deceased, immediately prior to his or her death, to a member of the family, a friend, a doctor, or a solicitor. A witness might say that the deceased has threatened to commit suicide on one or numerous occasions. Or may venture the opinion that said deceased was depressed. The coroner will take note of these points. Perhaps another example would be useful. A good illustration: Based on the evidence he has gathered, a policeman could pass the opinion to the coroner that he believes the deceased has committed suicide. Or then again, a policeman might say his findings lead him to believe that death was accidental. The coroner does take such opinions into account. I would also like to stress that hearsay of this nature *does* have a bearing on the case and indeed on the rest of the questions posed by the coroner."

"Do the police question any of the witnesses?" Anthony asked.

"No, no. Never. That is not permissible in a coroner's court. Only the coroner is empowered to ask the questions." Crawford swung around as the door opened.

Michael Lamont, the estate manager at Clonloughlin, entered swiftly, closed the door behind him. Tall and heavy-set, he had a shock of dark curly hair and a merry weather-beaten face that matched a jovial manner. As he hurried across the floor he apologized profusely.

Anthony said quickly, "I'll fill you in later, Michael. John's been explaining the procedure . . . the way in which an inquest is conducted."

Nodding his understanding, Lamont sat down next to Edwina on the sofa, acknowledged the other women with a quick smile. He said, "I did attend an inquest once before, so I'm vaguely aware of the form."

"Good, good," Crawford exclaimed, with a brief nod. "I shall get on with this as quickly as possible. There may or may not be a jury of six or eight people. Either way, the coroner imposes his will, if necessary talks the jury around to his way of thinking and what he feels is right. But it *is* the coroner who decides and pronounces the verdict—of misadventure, suicide, accidental death, natural causes, or—" He paused, added quietly, "—or murder."

There was a deathly silence as this word hung in the air.

It was Anthony who broke it. "What if the coroner is uncertain? What if he can't decide whether it was suicide, an accident, or murder?"

"Ah yes, well, in that instance the coroner would have to leave an open verdict . . . He might pronounce that a person or persons unknown could be responsible for the death of the deceased and that they could be brought to justice at a later date."

Edwina, watching her son intently, gasped and turned ashen. Michael Lamont reached out and took her hand, whispered something to her.

Crawford glanced at them, then brought his attention back to Anthony. "The pathologist's report, the findings of his autopsy, usually clarify cause of death, and without any question of doubt."

"I understand," Anthony said in a low voice.

Crawford announced, "I've covered the most important points, I believe. I would like to add that I am most confident that the inquest will progress in a normal, routine manner." His eyes rested on Michael Lamont. "You will probably be the first witness, since you were the one who found Lady Dunvale's body. The Clonloughlin police sergeant will give evidence after you. Then we will hear medical testimony—from the local doctor who did the initial examination and from the pathologist who conducted the second examination and performed the autopsy. Does anyone need further clarification on any specific point?"

"Yes," Anthony said. "Just a couple. I presume I shall be questioned. But what about my mother? And Bridget?"

"I see no reason for the Dowager Countess to be called to the witness stand, since she really cannot contribute anything. You will have to give evidence, and, most probably, so will Miss O'Donnell. It's very likely that the coroner will chat to all of you in an informal way, before the main witnesses are called, as I explained earlier. Nothing to worry about." Crawford glanced at his watch. "I suggest we leave here in the next ten minutes or so." Turning to Daisy, who had risen, he asked, "Where's Jim? Perhaps you ought to let him know we're going to leave shortly to drive into Cork."

"Yes," Daisy said. "I'll tell him right away. I've got to go upstairs for my things."

Fifteen minutes later the small group left Clonloughlin House.

Edwina, Anthony, Bridget O'Donnell, and Michael Lamont traveled in the first car, with Michael at the wheel.

Jim Fairley drove the second car, and followed closely behind. He was accompanied by Daisy and John Crawford. No one spoke for the first ten minutes or so. Finally, Jim said, "Explaining the formalities was a good idea, John." He glanced out of the corner of his eye at Crawford, who sat next to him on the front seat, swung his eyes back to the road, went on to remark, "I'm sure it helped my aunt. She's a bundle of nerves. Anthony seems calm enough, though. Rather self-contained, totally in control. But he looks dreadful. This ghastly mess has aged him quite a lot."

"Yes," Crawford said laconically. He rolled down the window, peered over his shoulder at Daisy, said, "Do you mind if I smoke?"

"No, not at all." Daisy leaned forward, resting her hand on the back of the front seat, and addressed Jim: "How was Paula?"

"She's fine and sends her love." Jim's grip on the steering wheel tightened as he wondered whether to repeat Paula's final comments, which she had voiced with such anxiety he himself had become alarmed. Uncertain of what to do, he remarked, "She kept insisting we phone her immediately the inquest is over, as if we wouldn't have done that anyway."

"She'll be anxious to get in touch with Mother at once," Daisy murmured. She settled back in the corner, smoothed the skirt of her understated and restrained dark gray suit, thinking of Emma sitting in suspense at their sheep station in Australia, worrying about the outcome and about her grandson Anthony. The fact that her mother was under such strain worried Daisy. After all, she *was* eighty. Reassuring herself that Emma Harte was invincible, was really taking this in her stride, as she kept insisting when she telephoned, Daisy attempted to relax. Eventually she said, "Have you decided what you're going to do, Jim?"

"Yes. I'll stay on here for the funeral tomorrow. I think they'll appreciate the support, and it's the least I can do. I'll fly back on Saturday. I hope to persuade Anthony to come with me. He has to get away from this place for a while."

"Of course," Daisy said. "And I'm sure he'll want to see Sally." She turned to John Crawford. "I assume the inquest will be over in a couple of hours . . . David has arranged for his friend's private jet to be at Cork Airport at noon, waiting for us. You will be coming back to London with me, won't you, John?"

"Yes, thanks a lot. I appreciate the ride. And, yes, all being well, we should be through in a couple of hours. I just hope we don't have to recess for lunch. In the event that this happens, the inquest will unfortunately drag on into the afternoon."

Jim said, "You don't have any reason to believe it won't be routine, do you?"

"No, not really," Crawford replied, but there was a strange hesitancy in his voice.

Jim picked this up at once. "You don't sound as confident as you did last night, John. Is there something Daisy and I ought to know?"

"No, no, of course not," Crawford murmured.

This response did nothing to convince Jim. He decided to plunge in, confide Emily's worries, which Paula had relayed to him during their phone conversation earlier. He said, "Paula's a bit anxious. Emily's raised something . . . Apparently she woke Paula during the night and told her that ever since Sunday she has been concerned about those five or six hours Min spent at the lake, after she arrived in the afternoon and before she died late at night. Emily thinks—"

"I don't understand why those hours are important," Daisy interjected.

John Crawford pondered for a second, elected to be honest, and swung around in the front seat to face Daisy. "I must now confess that I myself have been troubled about the selfsame thing, my dear. And if *I* find that elapse of time strange—not to mention young Emily—don't you think an experienced coroner will ask himself what the deceased was doing for that extraordinary length of time?"

"Yes." Daisy frowned. "But *why* do those hours matter anyway? Look, maybe she went away and came back again."

"Or maybe she was never at Clonloughlin in the afternoon," Crawford said softly. "That possibility might easily occur to the coroner, as it has to me, and probably to young Emily too. Don't you see, Daisy, those unexplained hours raise questions . . . in regard to Lord Dunvale's story about the time his wife arrived, a story which, I might add, is only corroborated by his mother."

"You mean the coroner could think Anthony is lying—that Min came there late at night." Daisy caught her breath. "Oh good Lord, yes, I see what you mean! The coroner might jump to the conclusion that Anthony was also at the lake late at night—" She broke off and began to tremble, feeling suddenly nervous for the first time since her arrival in Ireland.

"Perhaps. But, Daisy, my dear, I do say *perhaps*. It would ease my mind considerably if we had a witness who saw the late Countess driving into the grounds of Clonloughlin in the afternoon, or leaving around that time. Unfortunately, we apparently don't have such a witness." Crawford threw Daisy a sympathetic look. He had adored her for years, wanted always to protect her. "Please don't distress yourself needlessly, my dear. I haven't mentioned my worries to you before, for the simple reason I knew I would upset you if I did." Giving her a reassuring and confident smile, he finished, "The autopsy is usually the key in this type of case. It *will* prove conclusively how she died." Crawford gave Jim a pointed look. "I'm quite certain the pathologist will pronounce it death by accidental drowning." As long as he had found water in her lungs, Crawford added to himself, praying that the pathologist had done so. If he hadn't, they were in trouble, the gravest trouble imaginable. Lack of water in the deceased's lungs would prove she had died before her body entered the water. In which case, a murder charge would be leveled at somebody . . . or persons unknown.

Jim, understanding that John wished to allay his mother-in-law's nervousness, said in a strong firm voice, "I agree with you wholeheartedly, John. I'm sure Min's death was accidental. Now, Daisy, stay calm and cool, as you have been all through this ordeal. Edwina will fall to pieces if she detects the slightest sign of distress in you."

Daisy said, "I'm all right. You've nothing to be concerned about. And I agree, I think we should all three of us be as positive as possible. Anthony and Edwina are going to find the inquest exceedingly trying, no matter what, so we must be supportive and cheerful."

Once again, Daisy McGill Amory settled back into the corner of the seat, and for the rest of the journey into Cork she remained silent, left the talking to Jim and John Crawford. She had her own troubling thoughts to preoccupy her.

Mr. Liam O'Connor, a local solicitor, was the coroner presiding at the judicial inquiry into the cause of death in the case of Minerva Gwendolyn Standish, the late Countess of Dunvale.

The inquest was being held in the small coroner's court within the county law courts in the city of Cork, county seat of Cork County.

A jury of six people sat to O'Connor's right. They were all local residents of the city who had been passing the courts that morning and had been gathered together by an official of the coroner's court. This was the custom under British law in regard to inquests. Whatever their engagements planned for that day, they had had no option but to do as bidden and enter the coroner's court to be sworn in as jurors.

The coroner said, "And now, Lord Dunvale, before I hear testimony from Police Sergeant McNamara, the pathologist, and others present, perhaps you could give the court some idea of the deceased's state of mind, prior to her tragic death. You may speak from where you are sitting. You do not have to take the stand at this moment."

Anthony said in a clear and remarkably strong voice, "My wife and I were separated and were about to divorce. In consequence of this, she had moved out of Clonloughlin House and was living in Waterford. Lately she had been in the habit of visiting Clonloughlin, and in the past month I began to realize that her disposition had changed radically. She was somewhat irrational, even quite violent both verbally and physically. I became increasingly concerned about her mental stability."

The coroner nodded. "Did the deceased ever mention suicide? Did she ever threaten to take her own life during these spells of irrationality?"

"No, she did not," Anthony replied in an even firmer tone. "Furthermore, I would like to state categorically that I do not believe my wife would kill herself, whatever her state of mind. She was not a suicidal type of person. I am convinced her death was an accident."

The coroner asked for further details about the deceased's behavior, and as Anthony answered, Daisy watched the coroner closely, listening with great attentiveness. Liam O'Connor was a small, spry man, with a deeply lined face. His expression was somewhat dour, but she noticed that he had wise and kindly eyes and a reflective manner, and these characteristics filled Daisy with a degree of relief. She was confident Liam O'Connor would brook no nonsense in his court, that he would stick to the letter of the law most scrupulously, yet she also sensed he would be eminently fair.

As the coroner continued his informal questioning of Anthony, Daisy stole a surreptitious look at Edwina. Her tension was so acute Daisy feared she would collapse any minute. She reached for Edwina's hand, held on to it tightly, wanting to give her strength and confidence.

"Thank you, Lord Dunvale," the coroner was saying. "Lady Dunvale, I wonder if you have anything you can add pertaining to your daughter-in-law's unusual behavior immediately before her death?''

Edwina was evidently surprised to hear her name mentioned. She started in her seat and gaped, speechless, at the coroner. She began to shake.

Daisy tightened her grip on her hand, whispered, "Edwina, don't be afraid. And do answer the coroner, my dear."

Clearing her throat numerous times, Edwina finally spoke in a low voice that trembled excessively. "Min . . . my daughter-in-law, that is, was . . . *was* distressed in recent weeks. Yes, that is quite true." Edwina stopped abruptly, choking on the words, and tears sprang into her eyes as she thought of the dead young woman whom she had loved like a daughter. There was a long and painful hesitation before Edwina whispered, "I'm afraid she was—was— drinking heavily lately. At least she arrived at Clonloughlin in an inebriated state numerous times over the last month. Bridget, er . . . er . . . Miss O'Donnell, my son's . . . Lord Dunvale's housekeeper—" Edwina stopped again, glanced at Bridget, then resumed: "Quite recently Miss O'Donnell had to put my daughter-in-law to bed in a guest room at Clonloughlin. I remember the occasion very clearly. Miss O'Donnell told me she was afraid Lady Dunvale would have an accident if she was allowed to drive back to Waterford in her . . . debilitated condition . . ."

Edwina swallowed. Her mouth had gone dry and she was unable to continue. Also, the effort to speak coherently and to hang on to a semblance of control had depleted her. She fell back against the seat, her face chalky and filmed with perspiration.

"Thank you, Lady Dunvale," the coroner said, sounding sympathetic. He put on his glasses, referred to the papers in front of him, looked up, removed his spectacles and surveyed those gathered before him. "Miss O'Donnell, would you give me a few more details about the particular occasion to which the Dowager Countess has just referred, please?"

"Yes, sir, indeed I will." Bridget leaned forward slightly, and in her usual clipped, precise way she confirmed Edwina's story and also the various incidents of irrationality referred to by Anthony.

Listening to her, Daisy thought that never had a better witness been heard. The woman was quite remarkable, especially in her attention to the smallest detail, and she obviously had a prodigious if not indeed a photographic memory.

"And did the deceased ever suggest to *you,* Miss O'Donnell, that she might do anything at all to harm herself?" The coroner steepled his fingers, peered out over them, fixing his keen eyes on the housekeeper.

Apparently Bridget O'Donnell did not have to think twice about this question. "Oh yes, sir, her ladyship did. Not once, but several times lately."

There were audible gasps in the courtroom.

Anthony, stiffening in his chair, exclaimed, "That can't be so—" He made to rise but was restrained by John Crawford, who hushed him into silence, aware of the stern eyes of the coroner.

The coroner motioned for silence in the court, and the hurried whisperings which had broken out ceased. "Please recount those incidents, Miss O'Donnell," he ordered.

"Yes, sir," she said without hesitation, but she did cast a swift glance at Anthony before continuing.

Daisy, whose eyes had not left Bridget's face, thought she saw an apology signaled to him silently, but she was not sure.

Bridget O'Donnell, directing herself to the coroner, said, "The late Countess was a changed woman in the last few weeks of her life, as his lordship mentioned. She was hysterical in my presence on numerous occasions, and privately she said to me that she had nothing to live for, that she wished she were dead. The last time she threatened to put an end to her life was about a week before her death. She drove to Clonloughlin one afternoon, but I was the only person who saw her. His lordship was out on the estate with Mr. Lamont, and the Dowager Countess was in Dublin. In any event, sir, her ladyship was very despondent, and she repeated over and over again that she wanted to escape the misery and unhappiness of her life by—by dying. She cried uncontrollably that afternoon, and although I tried to calm her, give her sympathy, she was beyond help, really. At one moment, when I tried to soothe her by putting my arm around her, comforting her, she struck me across the face. The minute she had done this she seemed to come to her senses, and apologized over and over again. I made a pot of tea and we sat and talked in the kitchen for a while. It was then that her ladyship confided in me about something else. She told me that the greatest tragedy of her life was that she had not had any children." Bridget, paused, took a breath, resumed: "Lady Dunvale began to weep again, but quietly, sort of desperately, and added that she was barren, that she couldn't bear children. Again I attempted to comfort her ladyship. I told her she was a young woman, had a lot to live for, and that she could make a new life for herself. This helped to calm her, and I thought she seemed more hopeful about things when she left a little later."

Bridget sat back. She glanced down at her hands. Raising her eyes she stared at the coroner, and enunciated in the clearest voice, "I think her ladyship did take her life, sir, because of the failure of her marriage and because she knew she could never have children."

The coroner inclined his head, brought his gaze back to the papers spread before him.

The court was deathly quiet. No one stirred and not one single whisper was heard.

Daisy, glancing around discreetly, saw that the jurors wore thoughtful expressions and there was no doubt in her mind that everyone had been affected by Bridget O'Donnell's story. In its full context it left little to the imagination regarding the late woman's mental state, her unhappiness and despair. Stealing a quick look at Anthony, she was struck by his extreme pallor and a pulse beating rapidly on his temple. His face was devastated.

The coroner's voice brought an end to the extraordinary stillness. Glancing at Michael Lamont, he said, "Since you are employed by Lord Dunvale to run the estate at Clonloughlin, Mr. Lamont, you obviously came into contact with the deceased in the last few weeks. Do you have anything to add to Miss O'Donnell's comments?"

Lamont cleared his throat, said in a subdued tone, "Not really, sir. I never heard her ladyship mention suicide, and I would be inclined to agree with Lord Dunvale that she was not the sort of woman to harm herself. However—" There was a moment's hesitation before he added, "I can attest to her ladyship's despondency . . . Miss O'Donnell is correct in that assertion. I spoke to Lady Dunvale about two weeks ago, and she *was* in a very depressed state." He cleared his throat nervously. "She had also been drinking. Quite heavily, I thought, that day. But what struck me the most was the deep, deep depression. She seemed burdened down by it. But that is all I can tell you. Lady Dunvale did not indicate why she was depressed, nor did I refer to it." Another pause, and then he finished softly, "I didn't think it was my place to intrude on her ladyship's privacy. As an employee of Lord Dunvale's, that would have been a presumption on my part."

"Thank you, Mr. Lamont." The coroner swiveled in his seat, focused his attention on the police sergeant. "Sergeant McNamara, can you shed any light on the disposition and mental state of Lady Dunvale?"

"Well, your honor, I'm afraid that I can't be telling you anything I've observed personally," McNamara began, rubbing his chin and shaking his head somewhat mournfully. "I haven't had the occasion to speak to her ladyship in the past few weeks. Mind you, your honor, I knew she'd been visiting Clonloughlin House. Oh yes, that she had. I'd seen her little red car going through the village. And there has been talk in the village about her very weird behavior from time to time in recent weeks, which sort of confirms the things Miss O'Donnell and Lord Dunvale have said about her stability not being what it usually was."

"Have you formed any opinion about the cause of death?" the coroner asked.

"Well now, your honor, I've had several opinions," McNamara said, straightening up a trifle importantly. "At first I believed her ladyship's death was an accident. Then later I must admit I thought of suicide. I've also wondered if foul play was involved, since her ladyship did die in mysterious circumstances." McNamara pulled out a notebook, opened it.

"You will be able to elaborate on your findings from the witness stand a little later in the proceedings, Sergeant McNamara," the coroner said.

"Yes, sir," the police sergeant replied, closing the notebook with a slap.

The coroner sat back, clasped his hands together, and directed his next words to the entire court. He said, "It is the duty and burden of this court to establish the manner, cause, and circumstance of the death of Minerva Gwendolyn Standish, the Countess of Dunvale. After hearing the evidence, the court must decide if death was of natural or unnatural causes, whether it was an accident, suicide, or a homicide committed by persons known or unknown."

Anthony was now called to the stand and was asked to recall, to the best of his ability, the events of the previous Saturday. Speaking quietly, Anthony told the court: "Late that afternoon my mother telephoned me from the Dower House. She had seen my wife's car entering the grounds and driving up to the main house. In view of the distressing scenes between my wife and myself in the preceding weeks, I decided to leave Clonloughlin House. I thought that once she realized I was not at home my wife would leave, that we would therefore avoid any further unpleasantness and disturbances. I drove out to the lake in my Land-Rover. I had not been there very long when I saw my wife's red Austin mini approaching in the distance. I was standing under a tree near the lake and I went back to the Land-Rover, intending to drive away. It would not start, the battery seemed to be dead, so I set out to walk back to Clonloughlin House, taking the long way around the estate to avoid my wife. I spoke to my mother on the telephone once I got home, and she arrived to have dinner with me a little later. Around nine-thirty I walked my mother back to the Dower House, returned home, and spent several hours working on the estate account books in the library. I then went to bed. I did not know my wife had remained on the estate at Clonloughlin until I was awakened the following morning by Mr. Lamont, who told me he had found my wife's"—Anthony's voice trembled as he finished—"my wife's body in the lake." He stopped again, took a deep breath, and his eyes were moist and despairing when he said with overwhelming sadness, "I should have waited at the lake—spoken to my wife. She might still be alive if I had."

After thanking Anthony, the coroner asked Bridget O'Donnell to be sworn in, to give her testimony. He commenced to question her about her activities on the day of the death.

"No, sir, I did not see Lady Dunvale's car that afternoon, nor did I know his lordship had left the house," Bridget said. "I was making dinner in the kitchen. Later on, I served his lordship and the Dowager Countess, and after dinner I worked between the kitchen and the dining room for half an hour, clearing up." She then spoke about her migraine, told how she had walked past the library around eleven o'clock on her way upstairs to get her pills, had noticed the Earl at his desk in the library, and had seen him again around midnight when she had retired for the night.

"I was up very early on Sunday morning, sir," Bridget O'Donnell continued. "After drinking a cup of tea in the kitchen, I drove to Waterford to attend first mass with my sister. I stayed in Waterford for lunch, and in the middle of the afternoon I returned to Clonloughlin village to see my mother. It was only then that I learned of her ladyship's death, and naturally I drove back to the estate, where I was interviewed by Sergeant McNamara."

The next person to take the witness stand was the estate manager. Michael Lamont also said that he had not seen Lady Dunvale on Saturday afternoon, and explained his movements the following morning. "I too was up and about quite early last Sunday. I was driving to my office at Clonloughlin House to retrieve some papers I had left there, which I needed to work on that day. I saw his lordship's Land-Rover parked near the lake, and I got out to investigate." Lamont swallowed. "I thought Lord Dunvale was in the vicinity. When I realized he wasn't, I turned around to go back into my jeep. It was then that I saw her ladyship's car at the far side of the lake. Before I reached the Austin mini I saw a body floating in the lake." Lamont suddenly looked discomfited, and he bit his underlip, appeared upset. Gaining control of himself almost immediately, he went on, "I jumped out of the jeep for a closer look. The body, or rather a piece of clothing, had caught on a large log near the edge of the lake. I saw at once that it was Lady Dunvale in the lake. I went immediately to Clonloughlin House to inform the Earl."

"And after you informed Lord Dunvale, you telephoned the police presumably?"

"That is correct, sir, and Sergeant McNamara arrived promptly, and we, that is Lord Dunvale and myself, accompanied the sergeant to the lake."

The coroner now called on Sergeant McNamara to report his findings. After confirming the details of Lamont's story, McNamara launched into a recital of the investigation he had conducted on the Sunday morning after the discovery of the body.

"Mr. Lamont and I retrieved the body, his lordship being too distressed by far to help. I then removed the decedent to Doctor Brennan's surgery in the village, for examination and to establish possible time of death. From there I put through a phone call to forensic in Cork, knowing there would have to be an autopsy, and to arrange for immediate transportation of the body to the forensic laboratory in Cork. I went back to Clonloughlin House, where I took a statement from his lordship, the Dowager Countess, and Mr. Lamont. I then searched the area around the lake, also Lady Dunvale's Austin. There was a silver hip flask, empty, but smelling of whiskey, in the glove compartment. Her handbag was on the seat and its contents did not look as if they had been tampered with. There was a considerable amount of money in the wallet. In the afternoon I thought I'd better return to the estate. You see, your honor, it was like this . . . I was baffled . . . and about several things. Doctor Brennan had told me he believed death had occurred around eleven-thirty at night. I couldn't help wondering what her ladyship had been doing *out at the lake alone for five hours or more*. There was something else odd. I couldn't imagine how anybody could accidentally *fall* into the lake. There is no high ground, in fact the land is rather flat, and to get into Clonloughlin Lake a person would have to *walk* or *wade* into it. It was during this second search that I found an empty whiskey bottle thrown into a clump of bushes. Now that got me to thinking, it did indeed, your honor, sir. I asked meself if death had really been accidental, as everyone was thinking. The more I pondered, the more I came around to thinking it could have been suicide, perhaps even murder." Sergeant McNamara nodded to himself. "Yes, I must admit I did wonder if her ladyship had been the victim of foul play."

"Foul play by whom, Sergeant McNamara?" The coroner stared intently at the police officer, his face more dolorous than ever.

"By persons unknown, your honor. A tramp, a stray gypsy, perhaps a stranger in the parts, up to no good, who her ladyship might have surprised out there in that lonely, deserted spot. But there were no signs of any kind of struggle, or a scuffle. No trampled bushes, no marks in the grass near the lake, marks like a body being dragged would cause, for instance. No, no, nothing like that at all, your honor. The mini was carefully parked, and, as I said, her handbag was lying there on the seat." McNamara rubbed the side of his large red nose. "Nor am I suggesting that Lord Dunvale had anything to do with his wife's death. Miss O'Donnell's statement that he was in the library at the time the decedent drowned removes any suspicion about his lordship. I had to interrogate him a second time on Sunday afternoon, mind you, your honor. That was in my line of duty." McNamara gave Anthony a careful look, as if to exonerate himself in his eyes. "Anyway, it's those five or six hours. What her ladyship was doing out there during that long period remains the greatest mystery to me, your honor."

The coroner pondered, said thoughtfully, "Of course, Sergeant McNamara, Lady Dunvale could have left the grounds of Clonloughlin House, driven back to Waterford, and returned to Clonloughlin later, on the evening in question, perhaps hoping to speak to the Earl at that time."

"Oh yes, your honor, that is true. Very true, indeed it is. *But she didn't*. I made inquiries in the village, sure and I did, and not one solitary soul saw her during those *mysterious* five hours. And she would have had to drive through the village to get to the main road leading to Waterford."

Daisy, who had been holding herself very still, hardly dared to breathe. She looked worriedly at John Crawford, who gave her a reassuring smile. But she guessed he was as concerned as she was at this moment. Drat Sergeant McNamara, she thought.

"Thank you, Sergeant McNamara." The coroner nodded his dismissal and called the village doctor, Patrick Brennan, to give evidence.

Doctor Brennan's testimony was brief: "I examined the body of the deceased late on Sunday morning, after receiving a telephone call from Sergeant McNamara and the arrival of said body at my surgery. I saw at once that rigor mortis was present throughout the entire body. I established death to be in the proximity of eleven-thirty to midnight."

"Were there any visible marks on the body of the deceased?" the coroner asked.

"Nothing other than a diagonal bruise on the decedent's left cheek, which could have been caused by the log mentioned by Mr. Lamont."

The coroner thanked the doctor and summoned the Cork pathologist, Doctor Stephen Kenmarr.

Daisy moved to the edge of her seat, scrutinizing the pathologist intently. His would be the most crucial testimony, as she and the rest of the family were aware. She felt the tension of the Dunvales and Jim enveloping her as though this were a palpable thing. The court was deathly quiet once again, so quiet, in fact, Daisy could hear her own heart thudding.

Doctor Stephen Kenmarr was as precise a witness as Bridget O'Donnell had been. He got straight to the point.

"I concur with Doctor Brennan's theory about the abrasion on the deceased's left cheek. It could have been caused by an object in the lake, which the decedent struck when entering the water, most probably the aforementioned log. On Lady Dunvale's left cheek and cheekbone was an area of ecchymosis, that is, a dark bruise, reddish blue in color. I determined that it was fresh, and not old, because of its color. For the benefit of the laymen present, a bruise changes color in stages, goes from reddish blue or dark purple to brown, then paler brown, lightens to a yellowish green and yellow in its last healing stages. Therefore, because of its dark color, I knew the abrasion was recent. I found no traumatic wounds to the skull or other injuries to the head area of the body. There were no outward, visible marks on any area of the body, no sign of a struggle, or any evidence to suggest that the deceased had been attacked physically in a violent manner or killed prior to the body entering the water. After the external examination I performed an autopsy on the decedent."

Kenmarr paused, peered at his sheaf of notes. He said, "I discovered that the deceased's bloodstream contained a large amount of alcohol and barbiturates. The lungs held a quantity of water. I therefore concluded that death was by drowning due to the excessive amount of water taken into the lungs. Death occurred at approximately eleven-forty in the evening."

"Thank you, Doctor Kenmarr," the coroner said. He slipped on his glasses and looked down at the papers before him. After a few minutes he settled back in his chair and, turning to his right, he addressed the six jurors.

"From testimony we have heard in this court today we must all be fully and most sadly cognizant of the fact that the deceased was a troubled woman who was under severe mental strain, whose normal stable disposition had been affected by acute depression, owing to the failure of her marriage and her inability to bear children." He leaned forward. "I put great store in the testimony of Miss Bridget O'Donnell, a clear, coherent, and unemotional witness, who was perhaps far more able to see the deceased in an objective light than her husband. Miss O'Donnell was most convincing, and I trust her judgment when she says that the decedent was, only days before her death, in a frame of mind that could induce her to do harm to herself. We have heard the testimony of Doctor Kenmarr, the pathologist. He has told us there were no signs of a struggle, nor any visible marks on the body, other than the abrasion, which he has explained was recent, and most probably caused by the log. We have heard his toxicology report, his findings of alcohol and barbiturates in the bloodstream. The excessive amount of water in the lungs proved conclusively to Dr. Kenmarr that death was by drowning."

The coroner's direct gaze rested for a split second on each juror. He resumed: "Sergeant McNamara has drawn our attention to the curious elapse of time between the deceased's arrival at the lake and her death some five hours later. Sergeant McNamara referred to them as *mysterious hours*—but are they, really? Let us now try to reconstruct those crucial hours when the deceased was alone at the lake—and we must presume she did remain there, since no one saw her leave the grounds of Clonloughlin House or pass through the village. Let us also consider the deceased herself—a troubled, depressed woman who was in a state of irrationality, that irrationality obviously inflamed by alcohol. She may well have been drinking before her arrival, but undoubtedly she consumed a large quantity of alcohol after she arrived. It was found in her bloodstream, and Sergeant McNamara testified that he not only discovered an empty *flask* smelling of *whiskey,* but an empty *whiskey bottle* thrown into the bushes. We have the deceased sitting at the lake, drinking, possibly hoping, indeed perhaps *expecting,* her husband to return to the lake within a short span of time. Let us not forget that his Land-Rover was parked on the other side of the water and was quite visible to her. Is it not then within the realm of possibility that she did indeed remain there? That she hoped to discuss her problems with him, to find some surcease from her pain? Let me propose the following to you: Hours pass . . . It grows dark . . . As she continues to linger, could not the alcohol have blurred her sense of time? Or even rendered her unconscious. Then again, could it not have induced in her the conviction that her husband would indeed come back to retrieve the Land-Rover? But finally, in the end, realizing her hopes were groundless, could she not have come to a most terrible and tragic decision? The decision to put an end to her life? We have been told she was unusually despondent—filled with a feeling of hopelessness about her future— and by *two* witnesses. It is quite conceivable to me that the decedent swallowed barbiturates at this most dreadful moment in time, either in a misguided attempt to ease her mental anguish, or perhaps to numb her senses before walking into that lake. Yes, I believe that the events on that evening could have progressed in exactly this way and as I have so outlined to you. There is no other feasible explanation. Medical testimony has ruled out the possibility of foul play —homicide. Sergeant McNamara has pointed out that it would be difficult for a person to accidentally fall into the lake at Clonloughlin even if a person was in a drunken stupor, befuddled and disoriented by alcohol, because of the nature of the topography of the area. There is no high ground surrounding that particular body of water." There was a split second's pause, before the coroner finished. "And so, after giving due consideration to all of the evidence presented today, I must draw the conclusion that this is a clear case of suicide." The coroner scanned the jurors for one final time. "Are there any questions?"

The jurors turned to each other, spoke together in low tones for a few seconds, and finally a clean-cut young man addressed the coroner with the apparent approval of the others. "We are all in agreement, sir. We believe as you do and that it happened the way you say."

Straightening himself up to his full height in the chair, the coroner now addressed the entire court:

"As coroner presiding in this Coroner's Court of the County of Cork I must now pronounce a verdict that Minerva Gwendolyn Standish, the Countess of Dunvale, did die by her own hand while the balance of her mind was disturbed, and while she was under the influence of alcohol and barbiturates."

There was a moment of complete silence and then a buzz began, rippling through the court. Daisy patted Edwina's hand, leaned forward and glanced at John Crawford, who smiled very faintly and nodded. Daisy's eyes rested momentarily on Anthony, who sat as unmoving as a statue on the seat. He looked stricken, disbelieving. Daisy filled with sadness and pity for him. He had so wanted Min's death to be proved an accident.

Daisy rose and helped the weeping Edwina to her feet, escorted her out into the corridor. Bridget O'Donnell caught up with them.

"I'm sorry, your ladyship," Bridget murmured.

Edwina turned, stared at her, shook her head vehemently without speaking.

Bridget went on: "I had to say what I said about Lady Dunvale because" —there was the merest fraction of a pause before she finished sullenly—"because it was the truth."

Daisy, observing her, thought: Oh no, it wasn't. Startled at herself, she wondered what had prompted her to assume such a thing, and instantly dismissed the curious idea that Bridget O'Donnell had been lying. But the thought was to recur often and the housekeeper's testimony would trouble Daisy for the longest time.

Edwina swayed against her, and Daisy turned her attention to her half sister. "Come, Edwina dear, sit down," she murmured with great gentleness and led her to a bench.

Bridget rushed to help. "I'll go and fetch you a drink of water, your ladyship."

"No!" Edwina exclaimed. "I don't want you to get me anything."

The sharpness of Edwina's tone seemed to stun Bridget, and she stepped back uncertainly. "But your ladyship—" she began and faltered.

Ignoring her, Edwina opened her handbag and took out a compact, patted her red nose and tear-stained face with the powder puff. Bridget continued to gape at Edwina, her icy blue eyes filling with perplexity, and then she edged nearer to the door leading into the coroner's court. When she saw Michael Lamont emerging she hurried to his side.

"Are you all right now, Edwina?" Daisy asked, bending over the other woman, filled with concern.

Edwina made no response. She rose and looked Daisy full in the face. To Daisy it seemed as though an immense change had been wrought in her during the passing of only a few seconds. A veil of dignity had fallen over Edwina's face and her bearing was suddenly regal, almost imperious.

Finally she spoke, and her voice was clear, unusually strong: "I have just remembered who I am. I am Emma Harte's daughter and my son is her grandson, and therefore we are made of sterner stuff than most people might think. It's about time I made them realize that, and I also think it's time that I stopped feeling sorry for myself."

A warm smile swept across Daisy's astonished face. She reached out and grasped Edwina's arm. "Welcome to the family," she said.

Twenty-Eight

Miranda O'Neill was laughing with such merriment tears sprang into her eyes.

Recovering herself after a few seconds, she flicked the tears away with her fingertips. "Honestly, Paula, I've never heard such a load of nonsense in my life."

Paula said, "You're confirming my suspicions . . . I thought Sarah was lying to me."

Searching her handbag for a tissue, Merry blew her nose, said, "Lying is rather a strong word. Let's just say that she fudged the facts. Or, to use one of Grandpop's favorite phrases, she bent the truth to suit her purpose."

"So what really happened in Barbados?" Paula probed. "She made it sound as if she worked like a galley slave."

"Oh, rubbish! She had lots of help from the two local girls I'd engaged and the young woman who's going to manage the boutique for us." Merry stood up, drifted over to the sofa positioned near the window in Paula's office at the Leeds store.

Watching her progress across the room, Paula decided she had not seen Miranda looking so well for a long time. She had caught the sun in the Caribbean and her freckled face, usually so pale, had a soft tan that was most flattering to her, gave her an extra-special glow. She wore a full-skirted wool dress of an unusual ginger shade that enhanced the color of her burnished copper hair, and her tawny eyes seemed more golden than hazel today. Paula could not help thinking of the autumn foliage in her garden at Long Meadow. Merry's natural coloring and the clothes she had chosen echoed its russet hues perfectly.

Draping herself on the sofa, Miranda explained: "The minute Sarah arrived she was obviously in that take-charge mood of hers, very superior, bossy, even demanding. I volunteered to help in any way I could, but she practically ordered me out of the shop, said she could manage, thank you very much. Frankly, I was taken aback, since she's not really involved with us in the boutiques. But I decided to let her have her way." The auburn brows met in a deep frown and her expressive face signaled her irritation. "She didn't want me around, Paula, that's the long and short of it. I *was* rather busy with other things in the hotel, but not too busy to check in several times a day by phone. And I went down every evening to see how the boutique was shaping up." Miranda's wide-set eyes rested on Paula, grew quizzical. "Surely you knew I'd be on top of things?"

"Naturally I did, silly. I'm only mentioning it because Sarah made such a fuss about the hard work she *said* she'd done. She also told me that she hadn't enjoyed herself, implied that the O'Neills ostracized her."

"Now that *is* a downright lie!" Miranda exclaimed, her annoyance more apparent than ever. "Both my father and Shane paid numerous visits to the shop, and she was invited to every single one of our special events." Miranda glanced at her hands thoughtfully, nodded to herself, and looked up at Paula. "Well, perhaps she didn't have any fun, actually. She was certainly bizarre in the way she behaved. She seemed to think it was Shane's duty to be her permanent escort, to drag her around with him wherever he went, *and* to pay constant court to her. Shane was awfully pleasant and patient under the circumstances— after all, he was preoccupied with the hotel. We were all *working,* for God's sake."

"I know you were," Paula answered. "And I didn't really pay attention to the things she said . . . but I must admit I was a bit thunderstruck at first. And why would she lie to me? Surely she knew I'd find out from you what actually transpired."

"Sarah's strange, lives in her own world." Miranda leaned forward, gave Paula a knowing stare. "Consider some of the rotten little things she did when we were children. And she's always been full of her own importance. Smug. Self-satisfied. Look, I don't think she merits this long discussion, do you? Let's—"

"There's something I haven't told you. The real reason she came to see me two weeks ago was to make me an offer . . . She wanted to buy the boutiques." Paula sat back, waiting for Merry's reaction, aware that she would be angrier than ever, but she had to be told.

"What a bloody cheek! *Our boutiques!* I've never heard of anything so outrageous in my life . . . Where was her head? I mean, you're a public company. I presume you sent *her* on her merry way and with a few choice words ringing in her ears. I hope you did!"

"Yes, of course. But she wasn't taking my *no* for an answer. She threatened to telex Grandy in Australia."

"And did she?"

"No. She telephoned her at Dunoon. Can you imagine, bothering Gran like that! Anyway, Grandy made short shrift of her." Paula's mouth worked with sudden amusement as she thought of her recent conversation with her grandmother. "When Sarah told Gran that she thought she should be allowed to buy the boutiques for her division, because of all her hard work, effort, brilliance, et cetera, Gran told me she said, 'Oh, really, Sarah, so that's what you think, is it? Well, remember what thought did—followed a muck cart and thought it was a wedding.' Then Grandy told her that her suggestion was ill-conceived, ridiculous, and out of the question. She added that it would *always* be out of the question, advised Sarah never to dare mention such a thing again."

"There's nobody quite as pithy and scathing as Aunt Emma when she wants to be," Miranda said, and leaned back. "I assume dear Sarah got the message?"

"I haven't heard a whisper from her since."

"Well, that doesn't mean anything. She's busy with the summer line right now." A look of comprehension flitted onto Miranda's face. "What you've just told me probably explains something—Sarah was awfully funny with me when I went up to Lady Hamilton Clothes the other day. I can't say she was rude, because she's always well mannered, but she was unusually standoffish, even for her. Not to digress, but it's a lovely line, by the way, and I hope you'll see it when you're in London next week. We ought to place our order soon, Paula."

"Yes, I know, and Gaye has made an appointment for me to go to the showroom. And whatever else she is, Sarah is a marvelous designer. The Lady Hamilton Collection has never been anything but stunning."

"Yes," Miranda said, thinking how generous and fair-minded Paula was, and she constantly strived to find something positive in everyone. "Incidentally, Allison Ridley was at the fashion show, and *she* was strange with me as well, treated me as if I had a social disease."

"Probably because of Winston and Emily."

"What's that got to do with *me?*"

"You're very close to Emily, and I hear that Allison's extremely cut up about Winston. Quite brokenhearted, according to Michael Kallinski, who came in to see me yesterday. He told me she and Sarah have become very thick lately, and no doubt Allison regards you as a member of the enemy camp. Anyway, Michael said Allison's thinking of moving to New York. *Permanently.*"

Miranda was surprised. "Well, well, well . . . Maybe she's contemplating going into partnership with that friend of hers—Skye Smith."

There was such a disparaging note in Merry's voice that Paula glanced at her quickly. "Don't you like Skye Smith?"

"Not particularly," Merry answered, as usual being completely open and honest with her dearest friend. "I have to admit that she has been very nice to Shane since he's been in New York. She's given a few dinner parties for him and has introduced him to some of her friends, and he seems to like her. But—" Merry's voice trailed off, and she made a face. "She's too good to be true, in my opinion, so sweet all the time, too sweet, if the truth be known. She acts as if butter wouldn't melt in her mouth, plays the innocent, but I can't help feeling she's quite experienced—where men are concerned. I said so to Shane, but he just laughed, thought it was very amusing. Winston tended to agree with me. I'm sure he's told you that Shane had a small dinner party for us both at 21 when we were in New York last week. Well, it was actually for Winston—to celebrate the deal he made with the Canadian paper mill."

"I thought he hadn't missed one detail," Paula said slowly, "but obviously he did, since he made no mention of Skye Smith."

"Oh," Merry said, thinking this omission was odd. She hurried on: "But Skye *was* there. With Shane. And I had a chance to get to know her a bit better, observe her more closely. I came away from that dinner with the most peculiar feeling. I think she has something to hide—you know, about her past."

"What a strange thing for you to think, Merry."

"Isn't it," Merry agreed. "And don't ask me *why* I think it, because I can't offer you a proper explanation. Instinct, perhaps, intuition on my part." Merry gave a tiny shrug. "Still, on the plane coming back to London with Winston, he and I had a long discussion about her, and we both decided she has a devious nature. He's not very keen on her anymore, even though he quite liked her when he and Shane first met her at Allison's in the spring."

"Is it serious? I mean between Shane and her." Paula was surprised how tight her voice sounded, and as her stomach lurched she realized that the idea of Skye and her old friend being involved troubled her. Her eyes did not leave Merry's face.

"I sincerely hope it isn't! I don't like the idea of *her* being around on a permanent basis. Winston thinks it's only platonic, and he ought to know . . . Speaking of Winston, how's Sally?"

"Oh, she's much better. Anthony came over from Ireland about ten days ago and went immediately to Heron's Nest, where Sally's been staying. I spoke to them on the phone yesterday, and they're benefiting from the peace and quiet, are glad to be alone together. Actually, Anthony's coming to see me this afternoon."

"What an awful time you must have had because of his wife's death. I would have to be out of the country, wouldn't I? I wish I'd been here to give you moral support, Paula."

"Oh, Merry, that's sweet of you. But fortunately Emily was back from Paris, and she and I managed to keep each other going. We got through it, which is the main thing."

"Yes. But you do look tired," Merry ventured, using the mildest word she could find. From the moment she had arrived at the store she had been struck by Paula's white, drained face, the dark shadows. Her friend looked quite ill to her. "Can't you take a few days off? Get away somewhere for a rest?"

"You've got to be joking! Look at this desk."

Merry made no further comment, deciding it would be wiser not to voice her worries about Paula's health. She averted her face to conceal her anxiousness. Her eyes fell on the collection of family photographs on Emma's large mahogany side table. A number of familiar faces gazed back at her—her grandparents, Blackie and Laura, on their wedding day, her father as a baby lying on a fur rug, she and Shane when they were toddlers, her parents on the day of their marriage, and Emma's children in various stages of growing up.

Reaching for the largest photograph of the handsome man in an officer's uniform, she studied it for a moment, then remarked, "Your mother looks a lot like Paul McGill. Yes, Aunt Daisy has her father's eyes. But then, so do you." Glad she had found a way to change the subject, she added, "The frame's dented, Paula. You ought to get it fixed for Aunt Emma. It's such a shame. Why this is a really lovely piece of silver. An antique." Merry held up the frame, pointed to the damage.

"Grandy doesn't want it repaired," Paula told her with a faint half smile. "When I said the same thing a couple of years ago, she laughed and told me the dent was part of her memories."

"What did she mean?" Merry asked.

"My grandfather didn't return to England after the end of the First World War. He stayed in Australia. The story is a bit involved, but one day, in a moment of rage and frustration, Gran threw his picture across the room—that particular picture in that very frame. The glass shattered, the frame was dented, but she kept it nevertheless. She told me that ever since then, whenever she looked at his photograph, she reminded herself to trust love. She thinks that if she had trusted Paul when he disappeared—*trusted his love for her*—she would have had absolute faith in him, would have waited for him to come back. She believes she would have saved herself the terrible years of heartache she suffered during her dreadfully unhappy marriage to Arthur Ainsley."

"But Paul and she did get back together in the end, had years of happiness," Merry said softly, her expression suddenly disconsolate.

"You do sound unhappy, Merry. Love problems yourself? None of your old boyfriends around, is that it?" Paula looked sympathetic.

Merry nodded. "No new ones either. I seem to have nothing but bad luck in that department these days. Most of the men I've gone out with in the last few months can't seem to see beyond the O'Neill money, my looks, and my so-called sexuality. I'm getting more leery by the minute." Merry grimaced. *"I'll* probably end up being an old maid. Emily's lucky, snagging Winston the way she did. At least she knows he's in love with *her* and not her bank balance. Especially since he's got a pretty hefty one of his own."

"Oh, Merry, not every man is after money—" Paula began and stopped, recognizing there was a grain of truth in Merry's statement. Being an heiress *did* have its manifold disadvantages, although money was only one of them.

Miranda was silent. After a moment she said, *"Perhaps.* The trouble is that the men *I* meet are simply not able to see beyond their noses, past the externals, to the person I am, to the real me. I'm not a fairy-tale princess, for heaven's sake. I work jolly hard and carry quite a load of responsibility at O'Neill Hotels International. And I have very real values, as you're aware. Shane and I were brought up to understand the value of a pound note, just as you were. And my father and grandfather aside—all they instilled—Aunt Emma certainly drilled enough sense into me during those summers at Heron's Nest."

Paula said, "Yes, I understand what you're trying to say. People do have funny ideas about us, don't they? But nothing is ever the way it seems—to outsiders, anyway."

Walking over to Paula's desk, Merry sat down in the chair opposite, her sadness mirrored in her tawny eyes. Her face became more downcast. "I'll tell you something else, Paula. I'd much prefer to marry a man I've known all my life, who loves me for *myself,* for what I am as a person, and not for what he *imagines* me to be. The other day I came to the conclusion that I don't want to get seriously involved with a fascinating stranger. To hell with fascinating strangers. They spell trouble and are frequently full of nasty surprises. If it's not the money, then it's the power they crave. Then there are the sex maniacs, the chaps who're only interested in hopping into bed." She smiled wryly. "As Shane keeps saying, sex is easy to come by but love is hard to find. That brother of mine happens to be right in this instance."

Anthony said, "It's awfully good of you to spend all this time with me this afternoon, Paula. I really appreciate it, and I'd just like to say again that you've been wonderful through this most difficult period. I can't tha—"

Paula held up her hand. "If you thank me once more I'll turf you out of my office." She lifted the teapot and poured him a second cup of tea. "I'm glad to be of help when I can, and let's not lose sight of the fact that you're a member of this family." She gave him a small, warm smile. "Besides," she added quickly, "I'm not all that busy this afternoon," resorting to a white lie in order to make him feel better. "Now, to answer your question, I think Grandy *would* be upset—very upset, actually—if you and Sally got married before she returns from Australia."

"You do, really," he murmured, his face crestfallen. He lit a cigarette, sat back in the chair and crossed his legs. He stared past her into space, focusing on the painting above the antique chest on the far wall. He seemed momentarily distracted, as if trying to work something out in his head. "And when do you think she will be getting back, in fact?" he asked eventually, bringing his attention to Paula again.

"She promised me she'd be home in time to have our traditional family Christmas at Pennistone Royal——" Paula stopped, struck by a sudden and appealing idea. Leaning over the butler's tray table between them, she exclaimed, "That's when you should marry Sally. At Christmas. Gran will love it, and you can stay with her at Pennistone Royal through the holidays."

He made no response.

Paula said in a rush, "It's a marvelous idea, Anthony. Why are you hesitating?"

Still he was mute, and as she watched him closely Paula saw a pained look cross his sensitive face, which was gray and lined with fatigue. His eyes became anxious, even alarmed. He has eyes like Jim, like Aunt Edwina. Fairley eyes, Paula thought idly. She pushed aside this inconsequential observation and, wanting to pin him down, said, "Yes, Christmas *would* be perfect, ideal. Do say yes. We can try and reach Grandy in Sydney. No, it's too late now," she muttered, thinking aloud about the time difference, glancing at her watch. It was four o'clock. Two in the morning in Australia. "Well, we can send her a telex," she announced decisively.

"I suppose Christmas will be all right," Anthony said slowly, reluctantly. "It *will* have to be a quiet wedding, Paula. Very quiet. Because by then—" His voice wavered slightly, became a low mumble as he told her, "Sally's pregnant, and her condition will be noticeable."

Aware at once of his discomfort, Paula adopted a cheerful, matter-of-fact tone. "I imagine Sally will be about six months along in December, so we'll have to make her a really lovely wedding dress that conceals her awkward figure."

Startled, Anthony said, *"You knew?"*

"No, guessed. Both Emily and I thought she had put on weight when we saw her in September, and we came to the conclusion she might be expecting. Don't worry, no one else knows, except Winston."

"Her father and Vivienne are also aware—"

"I'm talking about the rest of the family, Anthony. And as you said, it should be quiet . . . only a handful of people. The Hartes, of course, Gran, Jim and myself, your mother, and Emily. *She'd* be hurt if she didn't come."

"Yes," he said. "I'm very fond of Emily, and she was such a help . . ." He stopped, swallowed. "Under the circumstances, do you think it's indecent —my getting married again? I mean, so soon after Min's death?"

"No, of course I don't."

Anthony looked at Paula uncertainly.

She looked back, her gaze direct and penetrating.

She saw a man under great strain, and this showed in his haggard face, was echoed by his bleak manner, and the apathy she had divined in him the moment he had arrived. That he had aged in the past few weeks was transparent. He was not the same person he had been at her grandmother's birthday celebration. His fair coloring and very blond, rather English good looks had been most pronounced, and he had appeared more striking than ever in the well-tailored tuxedo, which he had worn with the same kind of panache Jim possessed. That night he had laughed a lot, been so carefree and gay, unusually outgoing, charming them all. Now he was a wreck.

Paula made a snap decision. She leaned forward, pinning him with her eyes. "Listen to me, Anthony. You were unhappily married to Min, separated from her and about to divorce. You've been devastated by her death, the circumstances of it, and understandably so. However, it was not your fault. You must put it out of your mind, otherwise it's going to come between you and your happiness with Sally, affect your future, perhaps even ruin your life." Recognizing she had spoken harshly, she softened her tone. "You must think about Sally and the baby from this moment on . . . they are your priorities."

"Oh yes, what you say is true," he acknowledged. "I'm not a hypocrite. Please don't think I'm mourning excessively for her." A quiver entered his voice when he said, "But I never wished her dead, Paula. That she had to die in such a terrible way is more than I—"

Paula stood up, joined him on the sofa. She took his hand, looked into his face, her own filled with immense compassion. "I know, I know, Anthony. And please believe me, I'm not being coldhearted, not in the least. And whatever *you* think, you *weren't* responsible. My grandmother, *our* grandmother, says we are each one of us responsible for our own lives, that we write our own scripts and then live them out to the bitter end. That *is* true, you know. Min was responsible for herself, her life, not you. Try to draw strength and courage from Grandy's philosophy."

"Yes," he said. "But it *is* hard, so very hard."

Paula was more convinced than ever that her cousin was in grave emotional trouble, and she racked her brain, wondering what to say, how to jostle him out of his present state. She was not insensitive to his feelings, but she also knew that if he allowed Min's death to dominate his life he was cutting off his chance of making that brand-new life with Sally.

Speaking so quietly, so gently that her voice was hardly audible, Paula said, "It may be difficult for you to believe me when I say that I can comprehend your feelings, but truly I can. You must put this tragedy behind you. If you don't, it will cripple you. You will also be committing a terrible sin—against your own child." Purposely she stopped with suddenness, abruptness, sat waiting, watching him.

He blinked, his eyes wide with shock. "What on earth do you mean by that?" he managed in a strangled voice. "I don't understand . . . *committing a sin against my own child.*" He was horrified.

"Yes. If you permit Min's memory, her suicide, to haunt you, to fill you with guilt, you will not be able to love that child as you should—with all your heart and soul and mind. Because Min will be there, creating a wedge between you, and, let me add, between you and Sally. Also, remember that you and Sally created this baby out of your love for each other . . . It didn't ask to be born . . . It's an innocent little thing. Don't cheat it because of *your* problems. He or she is going to need the very best of you, Anthony. To give the child anything less . . . well, yes, that would be a sin."

He stared at her for the longest moment, blinking, striving to curb his emotions so dangerously near the surface. He leapt up, strode to the window, stood peering absently into the street below. But he saw only the death mask of Min's face as it had looked when they had brought her back from the lake. He closed his eyes convulsively, needing to expunge the image. Anthony groped for his handkerchief, blew his nose, ruminated on Paula's words. And then Sally's voice echoed in his throbbing head. *Life is for the living,* she had said last night. *We can't change what has happened. We can't spend the rest of our lives flagellating ourselves. If we do, then Min will have won. And won from the grave.* The things Sally had said had been rooted in fundamental truths, he might as well admit it. Something else occurred to him, brought his head up with a swift jerk.

The woman Min had become in the last few years bore no resemblance to the girl he had fallen in love with. Min had turned sour, bitter and vindictive, and her bitterness and resentment had only served to erode his love. Sally had not broken up his marriage, as Min had so violently asserted. Only bad marriages could be shattered by another person. Those unions that were strong remained inviolate against all outside forces. Now he thought: It was Min who broke up our marriage. For a split second he believed this was a sudden revelation, but then acknowledged that he had always been aware of this in the back of his mind. He had been so busy blaming himself he had not let this fact rise to the surface. The pain in his chest began to ease, and slowly he gathered his self-possession to him. Eventually he turned and went back to the sofa and Paula.

Anthony's pellucid eyes held hers, and it was his turn to reach out, to take her hand in his. He said, "You're a very special woman, Paula. Wise, and so very compassionate, such a good and loving person. Thank you for bringing me to my senses. I shall give Sally and our child every ounce of love that I have. They will have the very best of me. I promise you that."

After Anthony had left, Paula plunged into her work with a vengeance. She was still hard at it when Agnes poked her head around the door at six-thirty.

"How late are we going to be here tonight, Mrs. Fairley?"

Paula raised her eyes, put down her pen, and sat back in the chair. "Come in, Agnes." She rubbed her aching face, picked up the cup of tea, and, realizing it had gone cold hours before, immediately put it down with a grimace. "I'll be about another half hour, that's all, but you can leave if you want."

"Oh no, I wouldn't dream," Agnes said. Conscious of Paula's drawn white face, she eyed the cup, volunteered, "Let me make you a nice cup of hot tea, Mrs. Fairley. You look dead beat."

"Yes, thanks a lot, Agnes. No, wait a minute, let's have a drink. I could use one tonight, and I'm sure you could too."

"That'll be very nice, Mrs. Fairley. But what have we got?"

Paula let out her first genuine laugh that day. "Sorry," she apologized, observing the hurt and baffled expression on her secretary's face. "You did sound droll just then. And you're right, what *do* we have . . . Very little that's palatable, I suspect. There was a bottle of sherry in the coat closet. Why don't you see if it's still there."

Agnes hurried to the walk-in closet and Paula started to shuffle her papers, slipping items into the different-colored folders spread before her, quickly bringing order to her desk.

A second later Agnes emerged from the closet, smiling triumphantly. "Bristol Cream, Mrs. Fairley." She held up the bottle with a flourish.

"Oh good, let's have a glass, and we can kill two birds with one stone, go over a few final things since it's Saturday tomorrow. I've decided not to come in, Agnes. I want to spend the day with my babies. And you don't have to be here either, you know."

"Thank you, Mrs. Fairley." Agnes beamed at her.

Ten minutes later, between sips of sherry, Paula had reduced the pile of folders on her desk. Most of them now sat on the floor at Agnes's feet.

"You can send these last three to Gaye Sloane in London. The blue folder contains all the final details for the career clothes shop. Incidentally, I've decided to use the name Emily came up with, after all. I think it's the best . . . The Total Woman says exactly what I want it to say. Do you like it?"

"I do, very much. I told Miss Emily so the other day. She was, well, sort of taking a poll around the executive offices, asking the other secretaries and typists what they thought."

"Was she now," Paula murmured, smiling to herself as she thought affectionately of Emily, her busy little bee forever trying to be of help. "The red folder has all the information for the fashion exhibition in January, and this green one has my notes for Trade Winds, plus a list of merchants we'll be buying from in Hong Kong, India, and Japan. Do you have your pad?" Paula nodded as Agnes lifted it up. "Drop a line to Gaye and ask her to make duplicates of the lists. Also, send a memo to—"

The private phone on Paula's desk began to ring and Agnes, rising and reaching over, answered it. "Yes, just a minute please," she said, depressing the hold button. She handed the receiver to Paula. "It's Mr. Stevens calling from Odessa, Texas."

"Hello, Dale," Paula said, "how are—"

He cut her off abruptly. "Paula, I'm sorry, but I have bad news."

"What's wrong, Dale?"

"The worst, I'm afraid. One of our oil tankers is in trouble. It was loading crude oil off the coast of Texas this morning at Galveston and there was an explosion in the engine room—a very bad explosion."

Gripping the phone tightly, striving to hear him through the abnormally bad static, Paula said, with rising apprehension, "No casualties, I hope, Dale?"

There was a moment of silence. "Yes, I'm afraid we've lost six of the crew . . . four other crew members badly injured—"

"Oh, Dale, this is horrendous!" Paula exclaimed. "How did it happen, for God's sake?"

"We don't know. We're investigating. Blaze ripped through the vessel. It's under control now. She's not gone down. I stress *not* gone down . . ."

There was a bad echo on the line and Paula cried, "I'm having difficulty hearing you."

"I'm here," he shouted back. "Static sure is high today. I said we don't know what caused the explosion, but there'll be an inquiry. We've lost one and a quarter million gallons of crude, and we're facing a massive cleanup job. The crude's drifting into Galveston Bay already. Seabirds and wildlife are threatened by it, also the shrimp breeding grounds. God knows how much oil spill will wash ashore."

"This is a disaster," Paula said unsteadily.

"I can't hear you, Paula!" Dale Stevens bellowed.

"I said it's a catastrophe. We're going to have everybody on our backs from the ecology people to—I dread to think who else. The families of the crew members—those poor people must be taken care of, Dale, as I'm sure you know without my telling you. Financial compensation will be small comfort. Listen, do you want me to fly over? I don't know what I could do, though, except give you moral support."

"No, no, Paula, there's hardly any point in that. I'm handling everything. I've been in touch with the insurance company. It's going to cost us millions of dollars to do a concentrated cleanup."

"How much?"

"Don't know. Depends on the spill, the damage it does. It could be anywhere between five and ten million dollars to do a proper job."

Paula caught her breath, aghast at the figure, then said, "To hell with what it costs. We have to do it. Stay in touch, Dale. I want to know how such an explosion could possibly happen. We've had such a good safety record."

"Nobody's immune. That's the oil business. I'll call you tomorrow, perhaps even later tonight if I have any further news." The line was clearer now, his voice coming over as if he was speaking from around the corner.

"I'll be home all evening," Paula said. "And, Dale, do everything you can for those bereaved families."

"It's already in the works."

"This is going to be a stain on our record."

"I know, honey. I'm going to have to hang up. Situation is pressing here."

"Dale, one more thing . . . you haven't told me which tanker it was."

"Sorry, Paula. It's the *Emeremm III*. I'm very sorry, honey."

Paula put down the phone and fell back against the chair, feeling sick inside. Her face was grim.

Agnes said worriedly, "I got the gist of your conversation, Mrs. Fairley. Something happened to one of the Sitex oil tankers." This assertion came out sounding like a question.

Paula nodded, gave her secretary the details, then explained, "The *Emeremm III* was named for my grandmother. She once owned a company called Emeremm and my grandfather loved the name—it's a contraction of emeralds and Emma. His favorite stone and his favorite lady." She unsuccessfully attempted a smile. "It was he who launched the first *Emeremm,* and then the *Emeremm II.* Ever since then it's been a tradition to have a vessel in the Sitex fleet bearing that name . . . that very special name."

"I am sorry, Mrs. Fairley," Agnes sympathized. "I know how proud you are of the company's safety record. This is just awful."

"Thank you, Agnes," Paula murmured. "It's a dreadful blow, especially since there has been a loss of lives." Pulling herself together, she exhaled, drew her pad toward her. "I'd better draft a telex to my grandmother." As she picked up her pen, Paula shivered, felt a quiver run up her spine. Although she was not superstitious by nature, she had a strange presentiment that disaster loomed. The explosion in the *Emeremm III* was a bad omen.

Twenty-Nine

"Didn't you enjoy yourself, Winston?" Emily asked, squinting at him in the muted glow emanating from the dying fire in the living room at Beck House.

Winston put down his brandy balloon and gaped at her, genuine astonishment invading his face. He shook his head in wonderment. "Paula sits there looking as if she's at death's door, hardly opening her mouth all night. Jim manages to get stewed to the gills between cocktails and the main course. My sister is so pregnant she seems about ready to drop *triplets* right there at the dinner table. Merry doesn't stop bemoaning the fact that she's on the shelf at twenty-three because all of the men she's grown up with are otherwise involved. Alexander is in a raging snit because of your mother's sexual antics with half the bloody Government. Maggie Reynolds bores me senseless, droning on about some dilapidated shooting lodge in the Outer Hebrides. And you ask a question like that. Oh yes, Emily, I enjoyed myself thoroughly. I had a wonderful time. It was one of the most exciting, entertaining evenings of my life." He began to laugh, suddenly seeing the humorous side.

Emily laughed with him. She snuggled into the corner of the sofa, tucked her feet under her, and said, "But Anthony was in good form."

"Amazingly so. Well, he seems to have *his* feet on the ground these days and is coping extremely well."

"Thanks to Paula. She told me she had a long talk with him a few weeks ago, sort of gave him a lecture, advised him to put the past behind him and get on with his life."

"She's very good at that," Winston muttered, swirling the cognac around in his glass, his face thoughtful.

"What do you mean?"

"Giving advice. Mind you, she's usually right about everything she says. If only she'd take some of her own advice."

Emily's face sobered instantly. "Yes."

Winston leaned back against the cushions, put his feet up on the coffee table, and let himself drift. The evening at Long Meadow had been a disaster, and he had been relieved to escape with Emily relatively early, to come back here to the comfort and tranquility of Beck House. But one dreary dinner party was meaningless, of no consequence. What troubled him was Paula's physical appearance and her state of mind. For some weeks now, since his return from Vancouver via New York, he had been vaguely conscious of her misery. The last few hours had confirmed his feelings. She was an unhappy woman. He was convinced her marriage to Jim was at the root of her pain.

Emily said, "You're very quiet, Winston. You're worrying about Paula, aren't you?"

"I'm afraid so, darling. Apart from the fact that she looked so dreadful tonight, she spoke in monosyllables. I know she's a bit reserved at times, not a chatterbox like you, but she's normally much more communicative, especially with the family group."

"It's not the work that's getting her down," Emily exclaimed. "She's used to pressure, long hours, carrying tremendous responsibilities. Anyway, she has the stamina of a bull—like Grandma."

"I'm aware of that, Emily. I know Paula almost as well as you do. I meant it just now when I said she looks as if she's at death's door. However, I realize she's not actually physically ill. She's emotionally disturbed . . ." He swung his feet to the floor, searched the pocket of his robe for the packet of cigarettes. "There are a lot of problems in that marriage. Want to bet?" he asked, lighting a cigarette.

"Oh, you're so right, Winston. I've tried to bring up the subject several times lately, but she just gives me funny looks and retreats into herself, or talks about something else."

"But you two have always been so close. Hasn't she said anything at all?" he asked, his voice rising an octave, registering his surprise.

"No, not really. I told you before, she was upset on that awful Sunday in September. You know, because of Jim's attitude, the way he spoke to her in regard to her problems with Sam Fellowes. And I knew she'd been crying when

I got back from Pennistone Royal. The weekend Jim returned from Ireland, when the three of us were in London, she murmured something about Jim's being irritable, even irascible with her. I started to probe a bit, and she sort of . . . shrugged it off, became as uncommunicative as she was tonight. But I've noticed that tendency a lot in the last few months, and she *is* burying herself in work. That's all she does, actually, except for spending any free time she has with the babies. She adores the twins. Actually, *I* think they've become her whole life, aside from business, of course."

"That's no good. Aunt Emma's going to be miffed—not too thrilled—when she gets back next month—seeing Paula like this." Winston shifted his position on the sofa, immediately saw the concern in Emily's face. He took her hand, "Hey, poppet, come on, don't look so miserable. It'll all work out. Life has a funny way of taking care of itself."

"I suppose so," Emily murmured, wondering if it would, deciding that it wouldn't, because of Paula's basic nature. She would cling to her marriage no matter what, because of the children and her extraordinary sense of duty to them, as well as her determination not to be defeated.

"Would you like me to talk to Paula?" Winston ventured. "I could . . ."

"God, no!" Emily cried fiercely, sitting up with a jerk. "She'd resent it, consider it an intrusion into her privacy, and, anyway, you'd only get a flea in your ear for your trouble."

Winston sighed. "I suspect that's true. Listen, if you want my opinion, I think she and Jim ought to get a divorce."

"She'd never do that! She thinks as I do about divorce."

"Oh. And how's that?" he asked, pricking up his ears. He gave her a long, hard stare.

"Well," Emily said slowly, "we sort of disapprove, really. I mean, after all, we've had a lovely example with my mother. She's had so many husbands and so many divorces I've lost count."

"Your mother's the exception to the rule, Emily."

Ignoring this comment, Emily hurried on: "Paula believes that if there are problems in a marriage they've got to be worked out. She says that people can't keep getting divorced at the drop of a hat, just because they meet a few snags along the way, that this is no solution. She thinks marriage requires a great deal of effort—"

"It takes two to tango, you know."

A reflective look washed over Emily's face as she nodded, said, "You're implying Jim might not make the effort . . . Is that actually what you mean?"

Winston hesitated. "Perhaps. But I could be wrong, and, anyway, who really knows about other people's private lives? That's why this conversation should be terminated right now. It's rather futile, Dumpling."

"Yes," she said. "Winston, don't call me Dumpling. I'm very *svelte* these days."

He laughed. "I meant it affectionately, not critically, you silly goose." He put down his drink, moved over to her side of the sofa. Putting his arm around her, he whispered against her cheek, "So I'm stuck with you for the rest of my life, it seems, in view of your opinion about divorce."

"Yes," she whispered back, "we're stuck with each other. Thank God!"

"I second that." He pulled away slightly, looked down into Emily's inno-cent young face. How pretty she was, and there *was* an innocence about her, and she was very young, and yet she had a depth of wisdom that at times took him by surprise. He said softly, "I could never be happy with anyone else, Dumpling, not now after I've had you."

"Why?" She returned his gaze through flirtatious eyes.

"Always fishing, aren't you?"

"Tell me why . . ."

"Because I know you so thoroughly and understand you, my love, and because we're so compatible sexually."

"Are you really sure we are?" she teased.

"Now that you mention it . . . well, perhaps we ought to give it another try." He smiled, loving her with his eyes. Standing up, he held out his hand. "Let's go to bed, darling, and experiment some more, just to make certain." He led her upstairs.

"It's a good thing you put central heating in this house, otherwise we'd be freezing. It's very cold tonight," Emily said half an hour later, wrapping part of the sheet around herself.

"Oh, I don't know about that. I think we're pretty hot stuff together." Winston winked, pushed a pillow behind his head, and reached for the glass of brandy he had brought upstairs with him. He offered it to Emily. "Like a sip?"

"No, thanks, I don't want any more. It gives me heart palpitations."

"Oh, damn! And I thought I was the one who caused those." He grinned, asked, "Shall I light the fire?"

"Aren't we going to sleep?"

"That wasn't part of my present plan," he said, leering at her. "Are you tired already?"

She shook her head, laughing, and her gaze followed him as he leapt out of bed, pulled on his dressing gown, and strode to the fireplace directly opposite the old-fashioned four-poster. He struck a match, ignited the paper and wood already arranged in the grate, then worked the pair of old bellows to get the blaze properly going. Emily liked watching Winston doing things. He was so clever and competent with his hands, forever repairing things in the house and on the grounds. She thought of the little bridge he had built across the pond at Heron's Nest when they were children. It had been charming, and a master-piece of intricate design and clever engineering. Yes, he had been excellent at carpentry. She still had the small jewelry box he had made for her tenth birth-day, so prettily painted and lined inside with red velvet. But he had given up his woodworking for music when he and Shane had formed the Herons.

Smiling to herself, she said suddenly, "Winston, whatever happened to your trumpet?"

He was in a crouching position in front of the fire and he swung his head, taken aback by this question which had come out of the blue. "Whatever made you think of my trumpet, for God's sake?"

"I was lying here remembering . . . you know, remembering bits of our childhood."

"Funnily enough, Sally came across it a few weeks ago, when she was poking around in one of the cupboards at Heron's Nest." He returned to the bed, threw off his robe, and climbed in next to her. "Wasn't I awful in those days? Really fancied myself on the old horn, thought I was the bee's knees."

"*I* thought you were *wonderful*. Not on the trumpet, though . . . you did stink. Gosh, I bet it was *you* who put the dead fish in my bed!" She thumped him on the arm. "You rotten thing. I'll never forget that fishy smell. Ugh!" He grabbed her, wrestled her back against the pillows, pinned her down with his hands. "You deserved it. You were a precocious little wretch." He bent into her, kissed her on the mouth, let his tongue linger on hers. As he drew away finally, he whispered, "If I'd had any sense, I should have put myself in your bed—"

"You'd never have dared, Winston Harte, so don't pretend you would! Grandma had eyes in the back of her head."

"She still does," he quipped. He moved away from her, amusement dancing in his eyes. He picked up the brandy balloon, nursed it in both hands, then savored a mouthful. He felt so good, was enjoying this friendly bit of idle banter with Emily, this relaxed break in their arduous, exciting lovemaking. He always did with her. She was so easy to be with afterward. There was never any tension between them when their passion was spent, only during their loving. Then her intensity, her endless desire for him inflamed and thrilled him. He reached for her hand lying on top of the sheet, held on to it tightly, thinking of his narrow escape. He knew now that it would never have worked with Allison Ridley. He hadn't loved her, not really, not in the way he loved Emily.

Winston closed his eyes, reliving that special Sunday night in April, when she had driven over to have the supper he was supposedly going to cook. He never did cook it. The moment Emily had arrived they had looked knowingly and longingly into each other's eyes. And they had ended up, a fast ten minutes later, in the middle of this bed, where he had proceeded to surprise himself by making love to her three times in quick succession. His cousin—third cousin, he corrected himself—had astonished him with her lack of inhibitions, her willingness to give pleasure and receive it, her unstinting generosity and joyousness in bed. At eleven-thirty, wrapped in bath towels, sitting in front of the living room fire, they had made an al fresco picnic of the odds and ends in his bachelor refrigerator, washing everything down with a bottle of Shane's vintage champagne. It had been the most wonderful evening . . .

Emily said, "Winston, please don't get cross with me, but there's something I want to tell you. It's really important."

Dragging himself away from his erotic meanderings about her, he lifted his lids, glanced out of the corner of his eye. "Why should I get angry? Go on, tell me, Dumps."

"That's even worse than Dumpling," she groused, pulling a face, pretending to be annoyed. "Why is it that the English have this ridiculous predilection for silly nicknames?"

"Because nicknames are pet names, and they express warmth, affection, familiarity, intimacy, caring. Are you going to tell me this *really important thing,* or not, Dumps?"

"Yes, I am." She pushed herself up and half-turned to face him, propping herself on her elbow, staring into his face intently. "It's about Min's death . . . the inquest."

"Oh no, Emily, not again!" he groaned and rolled his eyes in an exaggerated fashion. "You've driven Paula crazy. Now you're starting on me."

"Please listen to me, just for a minute."

"Okay, but you'd better make it quick. I think I've got myself into quite a state again."

"Winston, you're insatiable."

"Only with you, my sweet, seductive, passionate little thing."

"I'm not so little," she countered. "Listen—Sally told me Anthony is still unconvinced that Min killed herself. He thinks it was an accident, and I—"

"This is a terrible waste of time, darling," Winston interjected impatiently, wanting her desperately. "Aunt Daisy and Jim have each given us detailed accounts of the inquest. It couldn't have been an accident, from what I understand. No chance."

"I agree. I mean about its *not* being an accident. However, *I* don't believe it was suicide, either."

Winston laughed disbelievingly. "Are you trying to tell me you think it was murder? Oh, come on, Emily."

"I'm afraid I *do* think so, Winston."

"Then who did it? Certainly you can't possibly harbor the idea that it was poor old Anthony, who wouldn't say boo to a goose?"

"No. And I don't *know* who. But her death bothers me a lot . . . I can't seem to forget it. You see, Winston, it's those five hours. They've always seemed odd to me, and even that Irish policeman called them mysterious. Auntie Daisy told me so. I happen to agree with him. They are, and they're also most peculiar."

"You've missed your calling, poppet. You should have been a mystery writer," he retorted, chortling. "Maybe she just passed out from the booze."

"Laugh if you want, Winston, but I bet it'll come out one day. You wait and see," Emily shot back. Her voice was grave.

Winston sat up, paying attention. For as long as he could remember, he had always thought Emily was exceptional—bright, smart, clever, and a lot shrewder than some of the family realized. This belief had been considerably reinforced since he had become seriously involved with her. She made sense in so many ways, and he had grown accustomed to listening to her, trusting her judgment. Certainly it was she who had pushed him to go after the Canadian paper mill, insisted he persist when the talks had faltered. Lately, even some of her drive and ambition had washed off on him, and she had convinced him it was his duty to make a bigger contribution to the newspaper chain. So much so, he had actually abandoned the idea of leading the life of a country gentleman.

For all these reasons he had to take her seriously now. Slowly he said, "You say you don't know who could have killed her, and that is a tough nut, I admit. On the other hand, you've obviously thought a great deal about Min's death, so you must have some theories about what *might* have happened. Tell me. I'm all ears. Honestly, Dumps, I'm not laughing at you anymore."

Emily gave him a small gratified smile. "Nothing will ever convince *me* that Min hung around the lake for all that length of time. I think she left, *went to see someone,* where she proceeded to get horribly drunk. Whoever she was with probably helped her along, might also have given her the pills—you know, Winston, to dull her senses. Then, once she was out cold, unconscious, she was put in the lake to make it look like suicide or an accident."

"Look, I'm not ridiculing you, honestly I'm not, but this is a bit farfetched. Besides, from all the accounts we've heard, she never left the estate."

"I know, but that's a presumption. And she *might* have. She could have *walked* somewhere, left her mini at the lake."

"Oh, Emily, Emily." He shook his head, looking at her helplessly. "This doesn't make any sense. Who would want to kill Min? And why? What was the motive? I have lots of questions, and I could shoot lots of holes in your theory. I'm sure Paula did. What did she say?"

"She more or less said the same thing as you . . . then she told me to forget it, that the case was closed, that everyone had come out of it relatively unscathed. She used some terrible cliché like 'Let sleeping dogs lie,' and brushed me off. But what about Anthony and Sally having to live with the knowledge that Min killed herself because of them? And there's another thing, Winston, think of Min. If she was murdered in cold blood, which I think she was, the person who did it should be brought to justice."

Winston was silent, mulling over her words. He said quietly, "Oh, darling, don't be a crusader. There's nothing you can do, really, and Paula's right, the case *is* closed, finished with. You'd only be opening a tin of worms, putting Sally and Anthony through more unpleasantness. I could talk to you for hours about this matter, Dumps, but"—he sighed—"I just don't have the inclination or the strength at the moment."

Emily bit her lip. "I'm sorry. I shouldn't have brought it up tonight."

"Well, let's face it, darling, you did pick a most inopportune time." He touched her cheek lightly with one finger, traced a line down onto her neck, ran it diagonally across her bare chest to the edge of the sheet tucked around her. "Emily, in case you didn't realize it, I do have other things on my mind."

She smiled winningly, shoving aside her worry about the inquest. "I said I was sorry. Let's drop it."

"Your wish is my command." He turned, put the brandy glass on the side table, then swiveled his head quickly. "I'd prefer you not to mention any of this . . . your theory . . . to Sally."

"Of course I won't. I'm not a dunce."

"Far from it. Come here. I want you." He switched off the lamp.

Emily did the same, slithered across the bed, nestled into his arms opened to her, wrapped her legs around his body, fitting herself into him.

He said, "See what's happened? Your lurid murder theory has rendered me incapable of performing my duty as a devoted fiancé." He stroked her hair, which shimmered brightly gold in the light from the fire blazing up the chimney.

"Not for long, if I know you," she murmured, pulling his head down to hers, seeking his mouth, kissing him passionately.

Responding to her ardent kisses, he ran his hand over her body, touching her breasts, her stomach, her inner thighs, enjoying the feel of her silky skin. He brought his hand up swiftly, cupped one breast, lowered his mouth, let it linger around the nipple. Her hand went into his hair and he felt her strong fingers on the nape of his neck, heard the faint moan in her throat as the tip of his tongue touched the tip of her hardened nipple.

Emily held herself very still, her breathing strangled as Winston moved down and away from her breast. He began to kiss her stomach, and his hand stroked down her outer thigh, then her inner thigh, his touch sensuous, thrilling her. He knew exactly how to arouse her. But then he always had. He had acquired more expertise, more finesse, had a better understanding of a woman's body since their childhood days. His hand fluttered between her thighs, then probed, enveloped her fully. In a swift, sudden movement that momentarily startled her he pulled his hand away, dragged himself on top of her. He slipped his hands under her back, lifting her forward as he went into her and took possession of her. His mouth found hers, they locked together, her body arching to his. Emily gripped his shoulder blades, let herself be carried along by his rhythmic movements and the growing momentum of their bodies rising and falling in unison.

Sometime later, as they lay exhausted in each other's arms, Emily said, with a small smile, "I wonder who passed around that nasty and most erroneous story about Englishmen being terrible lovers?"

There was a contented sigh from Winston, followed by a deep chuckle. "Foreigners, who else," he said.

Thirty

It was a blustery day.

The leaves swirled around her feet as Paula walked down the path and across the lawn to the wheelbarrow which she had left there yesterday. The sun came out from behind the bank of leaden clouds that had piled the bitter sky with somber gray, its brilliance shafting through the autumn foliage. Suddenly the trees shimmered in the refulgence of light as they fluttered in the wind, and they looked as if they had been draped with shreds of gold and copper.

She stopped in her tracks and lifted her head, her eyes scanning the garden. How beautiful it is, even in November, she thought. Her glance traveled the length of the lawn, and this too looked as if it had been spread with a cloth of gold or perhaps an ancient tapestry woven with skeins of russet and copper, burnt ocher and chrome yellow.

Moving forward, she reached for the rake and began to scrape the leaves toward her, making a large heap, working doggedly, glad to be out of the house for a short while. Her mind was numb from worry and fatigue, and she hoped that an hour in the garden would revive her, enable her to shake off the sense of desperation which was slowly turning into a feeling of depression, an unfamiliar state of being for her. She stopped after only a few minutes, leaned the rake against the wheelbarrow, and took off her gardening gloves. She tightened her scarf, pulled her wool cap over her ears, and turned up the collar of her old tweed coat, feeling the bite of the northern wind. There was a nip of frost in the air, a hint of snow. She slipped on her gloves, started raking again, then stopped to shovel the leaves into the wheelbarrow. About half an hour had passed when she heard the crunch of footsteps behind her on the path. She went on raking, knowing it was Jim.

"Morning, darling," he called, endeavoring to sound cheerful. "You're out here bright and early."

Not wanting to look at him until she had arranged a neutral expression on her face, she continued to rake, said, "I thought I ought to clear up some of the leaves before I left for London. Anyway, the fresh air and the exercise do me good."

His footsteps finally stopped. "Yes, I suppose so, but you don't have to kill yourself. Fred can do it tomorrow. That's what he's paid for."

"It's too much for one gardener." Paula straightened up, swung around, planted the rake in the ground and leaned her weight on it, her eyes finally meeting his.

His smile was sheepish, embarrassed. "You're angry with me."

"No, I'm not, Jim."

"You should be. I got awfully drunk last night."

"It doesn't happen often," she said, then asked herself why she was making excuses for him, giving him a way out. He had been intoxicated a number of times in the last few weeks, but last night his condition and his behavior at his own dinner party had been inexcusable.

Relief flooded across his face and he stepped closer, eyeing her nervously. He placed his hands on top of hers on the rake. "Come on, let's really make up," he said shakily. "After all, what's one drink too many among friends." When she remained silent, he leaned forward and kissed her on the cheek. "I apologize. It won't happen again."

"It's all right, really it is." She pushed a smile onto her face. "It was a pretty ghastly evening anyway. Everyone was acting strangely, and I'm not a bit surprised Winston and Emily left early."

"Those two have better fish to fry." He laughed, the nervousness echoing noticeably. "I say, I hope I didn't insult Winston, or anyone else, for that matter." He seemed concerned, contrite.

"No, you didn't. You were very cordial if very drunk."

"I'm paying for my bacchanalia this morning, if that's any consolation. I feel lousy." He hunched into his overcoat, stuck his hands in his pocket, shivering. "It's bloody cold out here. I don't know how you can stand it."

She said nothing, examined his face closely. He was pale, a little drawn around the eyes. The wind whipped his hair and as it blew about in the sunshine it was shot through with silvery gold. He brushed it away from his forehead, squinting at her in the brilliant light. "Well, darling, I think I'll push off. Just came out to tell you how sorry I am about last night, give you a hug and a kiss, wish you bon voyage."

Paula frowned, asked in a surprised tone, "Where are you going?"

"Yeadon."

"Surely you're not going flying in this awful wind and with that hangover."

"The hangover will evaporate once I'm up there," he said, raising his head to the sky, "in the bright blue yonder." He dropped his eyes to hers, half-smiled. "It's nice of you to worry about me, comforting, really, but please don't, I'll be fine. I phoned the airport a little while ago and they told me the weather forecast is good. The wind is supposed to drop in an hour."

"Jim, please don't go to Yeadon, at least not yet, not until I've left for London. Let's go inside and have a cup of coffee. I'm going to be in New York for two or three weeks and I don't want to leave with things the way they are between us. I must talk to you."

"I must be a bit dense," he remarked lightly, but his eyes narrowed, turned wary. "I'm not really following you. What do you want to talk about?"

"About us, Jim. Our marriage, our problems, this awful strain between us."

"Strain?" He looked at her blankly. "There isn't any that I know of . . . we're both tired, that's all . . . and if we have problems, they're unimportant ones, very normal, actually. We both work hard and we're under a great deal of pressure, and there's been that dreadful fuss in Ireland to plague us. So . . . it's not unnatural that there are tensions at times. But they'll pass, Paula. They generally blow over. I know—"

"Why do you always do this?" she cried, her eyes blazing. "You're like an ostrich, sticking your head in the sand. We have *problems,* Jim, and I for one can't continue like this."

"Hey, steady on, don't get so excited," he said, smiling weakly. He sought a way to placate her. He was growing weary of her constant attempts to discuss and dissect their marriage, to delve into areas that were best left alone. He wondered how to forestall this impromptu chat. He wanted to flee immediately, to go flying, to lose himself up there for a while. Only then, as he soared higher and higher above the clouds, did he feel free, at peace and able to escape his mundane worries, his internal strife. Yes, those were the very best moments of his life . . . *and* being with his children . . . *and* making love to her.

Leaning forward, he took hold of Paula's arm. "Oh come on, darling, don't let's quarrel like this immediately before you go off on a trip. Everything's fine. I love you. You love me, and that's all that counts. Being away for a while will do you good. You'll come home refreshed, and we'll work out our little differences." He grinned, looking suddenly boyish. "They'll probably have worked themselves out before you even return."

"I don't think so, not unless you start talking with me, discussing our difficulties in an intelligent and mature manner. That's one of the problems— perhaps the worst—this perpetual reluctance on your part to engage in a little verbal give-and-take."

"If we have problems, Paula, as you insist, it's because of your tendency to overreact to every situation, to blow small, inconsequential incidents out of proportion. And there's another thing—you're too sensitive by far."

She gaped at him. "Oh, Jim, don't try to throw the blame on me. Why won't you admit you have trouble communicating?"

"Because I don't . . . That's something in your imagination. In any event, making love is the best way two people can communicate, and we have no problems in that area, none whatsoever."

"I think we do," she whispered so softly he barely heard her.

It was Jim's turn to look astonished. "How can you say that! We're ideally matched sexually. You know you like it as much as I do."

Paula winced, recognizing once more that he had no comprehension of what she was as a person, or any idea what she was getting at. "I have normal desires, Jim. After all, I'm a young woman, and I do love you. But sometimes you're—" She stopped, seeking the right expression, knowing she was treading on dangerous and sensitive ground.

"I'm what?" he pressed, leaning into her, fixing her with his light, transparent eyes, his interest fully engaged.

"You're a little too . . . overenthusiastic. That's the best way to put it, I think. I'm frequently exhausted when I get home from the office and not up to midnight marathons in bed." She hesitated, meeting his gaze directly, asking herself if she had been wise to embark on such a touchy subject. She now wished she had not responded initially.

He said slowly, "I've been telling you for months that you're working too hard these days. You're just going to have to slow down. It's not necessary for you to be on this foolish treadmill. My God, you're going to be one of the richest women in the world one day."

Irritated though she was by this last statement, she said as steadily as she could, "I work because I enjoy it, and because I have a great sense of responsibility, not only to Grandy because of the legacy she's leaving me, but to our employees."

"Nevertheless, if you didn't work as obsessively as you do, you wouldn't be so tired all the time." He blinked, shading his eyes against the sun with his hand. Another thought flickered in the back of his mind. He asked, and with sudden urgency, "Are you saying that I don't satisfy you in bed?"

She shook her head. "No, I'm not." There was a brief hesitation, then, against her better judgment, she added, "But my needs are a little different from yours, Jim. Women are not made exactly the same way as men. Women . . . we . . . *I* need to be led into . . . well, into the final act, and gradually. You see, it's . . ." she did not finish, noticing the change in his expression. He looked as if some basic truth had just dawned on him.

In point of fact, Jim was not certain whether he was annoyed or amused. So that's it, he thought. *Sex.* The root of all evil, or so they say. He gave her a quick glance, his eyes roving over her. "Paula . . . darling . . . I'm sorry, especially if I've been selfish, thinking only of myself. I didn't realize, really I didn't. Actually, it's your fault in one sense—because of the way you make me feel. Perhaps I'm inclined to get carried away by my own desires and drives. I'll be different in the future, I promise you." He gave a little laugh. "I must admit I've never been much of a man for the . . . er . . . er . . . the preliminaries in bed. They've always struck me as being rather unmanly. However, I will try to help you along, be less impatient, wait for you to be—" He cleared his throat. "I believe *ready for me* is the correct phrase."

Paula felt the color flooding her face. His voice had been slightly sarcastic, with a patronizing undertone, and she was mortified. *Help me along,* she thought. He makes me sound like a cripple. All I want is a little understanding in every area of our marriage. Unfortunately, he had seized on their sex life, sidetracking her, and she regretted rising to the bait. And there was another thing. Why were they standing out here having such a vital and serious talk? In the middle of the garden, for God's sake. Because he would feel pinned down indoors, she answered herself. He doesn't want to talk. If the truth be known, he wishes he could wriggle out of it yet again, slide off to go flying or occupy himself with one of his other hobbies. He's only humoring me. Paula shivered, feeling chilled now that the clouds had covered the sun and presaged rain.

"You're cold," he observed, swiftly taking her arm. "Maybe we should go indoors after all." He smiled a slow and somewhat suggestive smile. "I have a wonderful idea, darling. Why don't we hop into bed right now? I'll prove to you that I can be the most considerate lover in the world and—"

"Jim, how can you!" she exclaimed, shaking off his hand, drawing away from him, glaring. "You think sex solves all our differences!"

"You just implied we have sexual problems. I'd like to show you that that isn't true."

"I did not imply any such thing. I said I wasn't up to making love endlessly." She almost added *mindlessly,* but managed to restrain herself.

He said, "Come on," and hurried her up the garden path.

She did not protest, allowed herself to be led into the house. He turned to her in the hall, remarked quietly, "I'll get us two mugs of coffee."

"Thanks, I'm freezing." She shrugged out of her coat. "I'll be in the study." She knew her voice was clipped, but she couldn't help it. Her exasperation was running high. He said nothing, disappeared in the direction of the kitchen, and she pushed open the door to his private domain. Here a log fire blazed cheerfully in the grate, throwing off tremendous heat in the small room, one of the more cozy areas in Long Meadow.

Seating herself in a wing chair in front of the fire, she tried to relax, but when he came in a moment later carrying the mugs of coffee, she noticed at once that his face was cold and closed and her heart sank.

"All right," he said briskly, handing her one of the mugs and taking the other wing chair, "let's talk."

Although his tone did little to encourage her, she said, "Jim, I do love you, and I want our marriage to work, but very frankly, I don't think that it is—not at the moment, anyway."

"What's wrong with it?" he demanded.

She saw the bafflement on his face and wondered if he was genuinely puzzled, or faking it. "There's that lack of communication I've just mentioned," she began. "Every time I try to broach something that troubles me, you reject me out of hand, turn away from me, behave as if my thoughts and feelings don't matter." She gazed at him miserably. "Yet I know you love me. On the other hand, I feel shut out. It's as if you've built a wall around yourself. I can't seem to reach you anymore. And whenever something flares up between us, your solution is to make love. You think once we've done so all our difficulties will disappear, but they don't, they're still there afterward."

He sighed. "I'm sorry. Unfortunately, I wasn't brought up surrounded by a huge family like you were. I was a solitary little boy, with only my grandfather —an old man—for company. Perhaps I do have trouble articulating things to you, but I did think I listened to what you have to say. As far as sex is concerned, it's the only way I know *how* to patch things up between us. I thought you enjoyed it as much as I do, but if I'm forcing myself on you, then—"

"Jim, no! Stop right there!" she exclaimed. "You're misunderstanding me. Of course I want a normal sexual relationship with you—you're my husband, and I do desire you—but I can't bear it when you use sex to manipulate me. It's exploitive and unfair."

He sucked in his breath in amazement. "You see, there you go *again!* Exaggerating, imagining things. I never *manipulate* you."

Paula swallowed. She decided to take a different approach, wanting to force him into being honest with her, if she could. "I probably sound as if I'm criticizing you, and I'm not. I'm only pointing out a few things that disturb me a bit. Look—I'm sure I can be annoying at times. So . . . fair's fair. It's your turn, air your views about me. Ventilate your feelings, and let's have an intelligent exchange like two mature adults."

Jim began to laugh. "Oh, Paula, you're so intense, so irate this morning. Quite frankly, I think you're being rather silly, creating a situation where one doesn't exist. As for my views about you, why, darling, I can only say that I think you're wonderful and that I love you. If I've any complaints or criticisms . . . well . . . they're very minor ones, of no consequence."

"They are to me. Tell me what they are, Jim. *Please.*"

With obvious reluctance, he said slowly, "I do think you tend to be hard on yourself, where your work is concerned. Your hours are crippling, and they don't have to be. Just because your grandmother worked like a drudge all of her life doesn't mean that you have to do the same. Also, it seems to me that you're taking on too many unnecessary projects."

Ignoring the remark about Emma, she said, "Do you mean the new departments at Harte's, and the fashion exhibition?"

"Yes. After all, Harte's is a thriving success, and it has been for donkey's years. You don't need to—"

"Jim," she interjected impatiently, "the secret of retailing *is* constant change and growth. We need innovation and on a continuing basis, and we have to meet the public's buying needs, second-guess new trends, have the vision to know exactly when and how to expand for the future. No business can stand still, particularly a department store chain."

"If you say so, darling. You know best." Privately he believed she was absolutely wrong, killing herself with work the way she did, but he did not have the interest, energy, or desire to engage in a long discussion about her business. That would be pointless, since she always did as she wished. Instead, he felt the pressing need to curtail any further carping and probing into their relationship. He was bored to death already, growing more anxious than ever to leave. He glanced at the clock surreptitiously.

Paula noticed, said swiftly, "This is so important, Jim. We're beginning to make a good start. I think we ought to continue, thrash—"

"And *I* think you have to relax, Paula, learn to curb this compulsion of yours to turn minor problems into stupendous dramas. If you want my opinion, this discussion is really rather stupid. I can't imagine why you thought it was necessary in the first place, and especially *today,* when you're leaving for almost a month. We're very happy together, yet you insist on borrowing trouble by trying to convince me we're not."

"Oh, Jim, I only want to save—"

"Hush, darling. Hush," he said softly, smiling engagingly, taking her hand in his. "When I look around at our friends and acquaintances I know we have the most marvelous of marriages. We're very lucky, Paula, and I congratulate myself every day, knowing how compatible we are."

Dismay lodged in her stomach like a heavy stone. Observing the stubbornness settling on his face, she acknowledged there was no reason to continue. She was talking to a brick wall.

Jim said, "You *are* looking thoughtful all of a sudden. And do you know something? You think too much and far too hard." He laughed lightly, dismissively, taking the sting out of his words. "Analyzing every tiny thing the way you are prone to do isn't very smart. I discovered that years ago. Whenever one puts something under a microscope, seeking flaws, one inevitably finds them. There's nothing wrong with our relationship, Paula. Do try to take it easy, darling." He bent forward, kissed her on the cheek, then rose purposefully. "Now that we've had our chat, I'll be going, if you don't mind." He squeezed her shoulder. "Drive carefully, and phone me tonight before you go to sleep." He winked. "That's always when I miss you the most."

Paula sat staring at him, stupefied, unable to speak. Finally she managed a nod. When he turned away, her eyes followed him. There was a void in her heart as she watched him walk across the room. The study door clicked behind him. She heard the echo of his footsteps crossing the hall, the front door slamming, and a few seconds later the sound of his car as he revved the engine. She sat very still in the chair for a long time after he had left, filled with despair and an overwhelming sense of defeat.

Finally she roused herself from her troubled thoughts, pushed herself up out of the chair and left the room. Slowly, wearily, she climbed the stairs to the nursery and her children. They had always been the joy of her existence. They were her whole existence now.

Thirty-One

Paula looked from Dale Stevens to Ross Nelson. "My grandmother would never consider selling her stock in Sitex Oil. Never."

Ross Nelson smiled, his expression sanguine. "*Never* is a word I've learned to distrust. It has a way of coming back to haunt one, and that's why I hardly ever use it."

"I understand the point you're trying to make," Paula said, "but, nevertheless, I know what my grandmother's feelings are about Sitex, and she wouldn't be interested in your proposal. She promised my grandfather—" Paula cut herself short, shrugged offhandedly. "However, that's another story, and this conversation is really a waste of time—Dale's, yours, and mine."

Dale Stevens said, "Maybe you ought to broach it to Emma when she gets back from Australia next month, test the water, see what she has to say. She might like the idea. Times have changed, and let's not lose sight of the fact that she stands to make millions if she sells out."

"I don't think money comes into play here," Paula answered.

"Harry Marriott and his cronies on the board are a tough bunch, Paula," Dale remarked, giving her a pointed look, leveling his alert dark eyes at her. "They've wanted Emma out for years—resent her influence—and the situation can only worsen, get harder for you in the future. When she's no longer around, you'll find yourself—"

"My grandmother's not dead yet," Paula interjected, meeting his fixed stare with a cool glance, "and I refuse to speculate about the future and eventualities that are a long way off. I deal with business the only way I know how— on a day-to-day basis. I'm certainly not going to seek out trouble, and I'd like to remind you that Marriott is a very old man. He won't last forever, and, therefore, neither will his influence."

"There's that nephew of his," Dale pointed out quietly. "Marriott Watson's a nasty son of a bitch, a troublemaker."

"Oh, don't talk to me about nephews," Paula began and stopped, biting her inner lip. She turned to Ross, remembering that he was the nephew of Daniel P. Nelson and his heir. She laughed lightly and apologized, "Sorry, Ross, I didn't mean to sound disparaging about nephews in general. I wasn't getting at you."

He laughed with her, and there was a hint of humor surfacing in his hazel eyes. "Don't worry, I don't take offense that easily." He leaned forward, his face growing serious. "What Dale is trying to say is that those members of the board who have strained under Emma's yoke are going to be awfully rough with you, for the simple reason that you're a—"

Paula held up her hand. "You don't have to say it, Ross. I know the reason. I'm a *woman,* and a young one at that. I realize they've only listened to my grandmother all these years because they've had no option. She *is* the single largest stockholder, and my grandfather *was* the founder of the company, and obviously certain people have always hated her because of her enormous power, and, of course, because she is a woman." Paula paused. "Still, Emma Harte has managed, and managed very well indeed. She has always outsmarted that board, and so will I. I'm not without intelligence and inventiveness. I'll find a way to make them listen, take notice of me."

Ross and Dale were silent, exchanged knowing glances.

Ross spoke first: "I wouldn't want you to think I'm bigoted, a male chauvinist pig like some of those idiots on the board of Sitex, but despite the inroads women have been making in business lately, of which I totally approve, I might add, I'm afraid we have to face the facts. It's still a man's—"

Paula broke into laughter, instantly cutting him off. "I know it's still a man's world. You don't have to rub it in. And it always will be until the day women can go to the men's room."

Ross Nelson's smile was slow, amused. He appreciated her sense of humor as well as her inherent toughness and courage. She was one hell of a woman. His eyes lingered on her appraisingly. He was strongly attracted to her, fascinated by her self-control, her sharp mind, her extraordinary self-confidence. He wanted her for himself. He wondered what approach to take, the best tactics to use, how long it would take him to get her into his bed. He fully intended to do that—and the sooner the better.

He disengaged his eyes from hers, conscious of the prolonged silence. He said, with a strangled laugh, "Not all deals are made in the men's room, Paula."

"Most of them are," she shot back, throwing him that challenging look again. "Or the equivalent of the men's room," she added, making a moue with her mouth.

This further inflamed him, and he could only grin, suddenly feeling asinine, like an inexperienced schoolboy. He had the compelling urge to fasten his mouth on hers, and he would have done so if Dale had not been present.

Dale coughed behind his hand, said quickly, "Marriott Watson has been gunning for me for a long time, Paula, because I'm Emma's protégé. Don't think he won't make strong moves against me when I'm no longer under her protection. He can't wait."

"I'm well aware of that," Paula replied, her tone as sober as his. "But right now you do have her protection, and mine, for what it's worth. Also, let's not overlook those board members who are on our side. Together we wield a lot of power. In September you promised me you'd stay on as president until Christmas. Last month you agreed to continue until your contract runs out, in spite of the present harassment from certain quarters within the company. You're not changing your mind—reneging—are you?"

"No, honey, no way. I'll be right in there with you, fighting the good fight," Dale insisted with firmness. "However, I would like you to mention Ross's idea to Emma when she's back in England."

"I've every intention of doing so, and she has a right to know. Don't be concerned. She'll get a full report of this meeting." She swung her head to face

Ross. "She *will* ask me who your client is, Ross. Naturally she'll want to know who's interested in buying her stock. You haven't given me the name yet." She sat back in the chair, eyeing him speculatively.

Ross Nelson, in full control again, shook his head. "I can't tell you, Paula. At least not yet. Once you express a genuine interest in selling the Sitex stock I will, of course, do so at once. Until then, the name must remain confidential. At the specific request of our client. And I would like to repeat what I said at the outset of this meeting—that the interested party has been a client of the bank for a long time and is highly respected."

Paula was amused at his insistence on secrecy but she kept her face neutral. "It's obviously another oil company, and I doubt that it's one of the really huge ones like Getty or Standard. It must be a medium-sized company—a company such as International Petroleum, perhaps?" There was a shrewd glint in her knowing violet eyes.

Ross was impressed. His admiration for her went up another notch. She had stabbed in the dark most probably, but hit the bull's-eye nonetheless. "No, it isn't International Petroleum," he lied smoothly. "And please don't start a guessing game, because it won't do you any good." He flashed her one of his deep, warm smiles. "The name cannot be revealed until our client gives permission, and it may interest you to know that not even Dale has an inkling of who it is."

But you haven't denied it's an oil company, Paula thought. She said, "Then I suppose I may never know, since my grandmother won't be interested in selling." Paula crossed her legs, adopting a more relaxed posture, wondering if Ross had told her the truth when he had denied it was International Petroleum. She was not sure. Neither was she sure of her feelings about the man himself. Her attitude toward him had always been ambivalent. She had never been able to decide whether she liked him or not. On the surface Ross Nelson was charming, courteous, sure of himself, forever ready to oblige. A handsome man in his late thirties, he was about five feet nine, well built, fair of coloring, with an open, almost guileless face and the friendliest of smiles that flashed relentlessly to reveal his big white perfect teeth. His appearance was sleek and polished, his clothes impeccable, as were his manners.

And yet all of this was deceptive, or so it seemed to Paula. She could not help thinking that there was something concealed and predatory about him. Quietly observing Ross now, it suddenly struck her that the beautiful clothes and the insouciance he projected were mere façades to camouflage unpleasant characteristics that only came to light behind the closed doors of the bank's boardroom. As Emma had divined before her, Paula scented a cold and calculating ruthlessness in him, a grim hardness behind the charm, the smiles, and the golden boy image.

Dale and Ross had been chatting about the explosion in the engine room of the *Emeremm III,* and Paula gave the two men her entire attention.

Dale was saying, "Of course sabotage crossed my mind, Ross, but it's been ruled out. There was that recent inquiry and nothing untoward was discovered, nothing at all. Anyway, who would do such a thing?" He shook his head rapidly, frowned. "No, no, it was definitely an accident, even though we haven't been able to discover exactly what caused the explosion."

Paula thought: The disaster to the *Emeremm III* was a harbinger of bad luck, but she said, "So it remains a mystery, and a terrible stain on our safety record."

" 'Fraid so, honey." Dale's grin was rueful and his brown eyes crinkled at the corners in his leathery, weather-beaten face. "Hate to keep repeating myself, but the oil game is a high-risk business. However, the *Emeremm III* is a sturdy vessel and I just heard this morning that she's seaworthy again and back in the fleet."

"Well, that's a bit of good news!" Paula exclaimed, looking pleased, giving Dale a warm smile. The president of Sitex was a man she liked and trusted and whom she never had any qualms about. He was smart, tough, exceedingly ambitious for himself, but he was honest, and exactly what he seemed—not given to dissembling or craftiness. Studying him surreptitiously, she thought that even his clothes reflected the man himself, were good but conservative, lacked the expensive elegance of the ones that Nelson wore. She asked herself then what this wily, hard-grinding, fifty-three-year-old Texan who had risen the hard way could possibly have in common with the smooth Eastern Seaboard banker sitting next to him. The latter reeked of the old guard, pots and pots of inherited money and a privileged heritage. Yet close friends they were. Ross Nelson had introduced Dale Stevens to Emma two years ago, and it was through the investment banker that Dale was now president of the oil company.

Watching *her* watching *him,* Dale suddenly said, "I hope you don't think I lack confidence in you, because that's not true, honey."

"But I am an unknown quantity, right?" she retorted swiftly, and continued in the same mild voice, "I understand your motives, Dale, and I can't say I blame you. You're looking to the future, and you've decided that things will operate much more smoothly at Sitex if our big block of preferred stock is controlled by someone else, someone whom you believe *might* be better equipped to handle the disruptive faction on the Sitex board."

Continuing to scrutinize her closely, forever conscious of her astuteness and perception, and never one to underestimate this clever young woman, Dale decided to be truthful. "Yes," he said, giving her a direct and open look, "that's part of my reasoning, I admit that. But it's not all of it. In one sense I'm also thinking of you, your heavy burdens. It seems to me that you have your hands full with the Harte chain and your considerable business interests in England and Australia. And of course, you *are* based in England, honey."

Paula said pithily, "Telephones work, telex machines transmit, planes fly."

"But Sitex is still an additional pressure for you," he said, paying no attention to her sarcastic tone. "And do you really need it?" Dale shook his head, as if making up her mind for her. "I don't think you do, and if it were me, why, I'd persuade Emma to sell out and make a huge profit. You could reinvest the millions you make from the stock in something else—something that's less of a headache."

She said nothing.

"I concur with Dale," Ross stated, his tone flat. He cleared his throat. "Obviously I've long been aware of the difficulties at Sitex, not only through Dale, but because of Emma's confidences over the last few years. And so, when the bank's client professed an interest in buying up Sitex stock, I immediately thought of Emma's vast holdings in the company. I spoke to Dale and he agreed we should raise the matter with you immediately. The bank's client has already invested in Sitex's common stock. And with your forty-two percent—"

He stopped, offered her one of his perpetual all-embracing smiles. "Why, Paula, that would give our client real clout."

"Anybody who owns that forty-two percent has *clout,"* Paula said crisply. "Whether it's us or your client is quite beside the point. You know as well as I do that it's the actual stock, not the owner of it, that counts. And anyway, your client's common stock doesn't come into play since it's not voting stock and has no power attached to it. Obviously this client of yours—whether an individual or a company—needs my grandmother's stock to give him, or them, a voice in the running of the company. *Control* is what they're after. I understand every-thing perfectly."

Neither men responded, both acknowledging to themselves that there was no point in making denials and in so doing looking foolish.

Paula stood up and, adopting her most gracious manner, went on, "I'm afraid I have to bring our informal little get-together to a close, gentlemen. I think we've covered as much ground as we can today. I will talk to my grand-mother in December, and I'm sure you'll be hearing from her personally. And it really is up to her—her decision." Paula laughed softly, murmured, "And who knows, she might surprise even me and decide to sell after all."

Dale and Ross had risen when she had, and as Paula walked them to the door, Dale said, "I'm flying back to Odessa tonight, but just give me a holler if you need me, or need anything at all. In any event, I'll be calling you next week to touch base."

"Thanks, Dale, I appreciate that," Paula said, taking his outstretched hand.

"Are you sure you won't join us for lunch?" Ross asked.

"Thank you again, but I can't. I have a date with the fashion director of Harte's USA, and since we're going to be planning the French Designer Week promotion over lunch it's not possible for me to cancel."

"Our loss," he said, sounding disappointed, keeping his eyes focused on her, still clasping her hand tightly in his. "Unlike Dale, *I'm* not flying off anywhere, Paula. I'm staying right here in little old Manhattan. Let me know if *I* can help you with anything—anything whatsoever. And I hope I can take you to dinner one evening this week."

Extracting her hand, Paula said, "How kind of you, Ross. I'm afraid I'm rather busy this week. Every night, actually." This was untrue but she had no desire to see him socially.

"Not next week, I sincerely hope!" He leaned into her, squeezed her arm. "I'll call you on Monday and I won't take no for an answer," he warned, with a hearty laugh.

Once they had left, Paula walked slowly across the room to the desk, a great slab of glass supported by a simple base of polished steel. It was the dramatic focal point in Emma's highly dramatic office at Harte Enterprises, where Paula always based herself when she was in New York. The room was furnished with modern pieces and washed throughout with a mélange of misty grays and blues. The soft muted colors were enlivened by some of Emma's priceless French Impressionist paintings, while sculpture by Henry Moore and Brancusi, and rare temple heads from Angkor Wat, were displayed on black marble pedestals around the room. All made a strong, definitive statement, and evidenced Emma's great love of art.

Seating herself at the desk, Paula placed her elbows on it, cupped her face in her hands, thinking about the meeting she had just finished. At the back of her mind a germ of an idea flickered, began to take shape, and as it did a slow smile spread across her face. Quite unwittingly Ross Nelson and Dale Stevens had shown her a way to resolve some of her problems at Sitex, if not, in fact, all of them. But not now, she thought. Later, when I really need to make everyone keep in step to the beat of *my* drum.

As she straightened up, she laughed out loud. It was not a very nice idea, indeed, it was rather diabolical—Machiavellian—but it would be effective, and it bore Emma Harte's inimitable stamp. Still laughing quietly, she thought: I must be growing more like Grandy every day. The possibility that this was true pleased her. In a sense it helped to alleviate some of the depression and frustration she had been experiencing since her abortive attempt to talk to Jim before she had left England.

If her marriage was in a shambles, her personal life grounded in aridity, then she was going to make certain she had a fruitful career, her own successes in business to compensate for her other losses. Work had been Emma's strong citadel when *her* private life had been wrecked, and so it would become Paula's, sustaining her at all times. With her business to occupy her thoughts, and her abiding love for her children to give her emotional nourishment, she would survive, and survive well, perhaps even with style, as her grandmother had done. Her thoughts jumped to Jim, but they were neither rancorous nor condemning. She felt only a terrible sadness for him. He did not know what he had lost, and that was the pity, the tragedy of it all.

Shane O'Neill was in a quandary this afternoon.

He strode up Park Avenue at a rapid pace, dodging in and out amongst the other pedestrians, his thoughts twisting and turning at a similar accelerated rate. He was unable to make up his mind about Paula. Should he phone her or not? The knowledge that she was in New York, sitting only a few blocks away from him at this very moment, had so unnerved him he couldn't imagine what being in her presence would do to him. And if he did call her he would have no alternative but to see her, invite her out, take her to lunch or dinner, at the very least have drinks with her.

Earlier that day, when he had been talking to their London office, he had been taken aback when his father had mentioned in passing that Paula had flown to New York. "Merry and I had supper with her in London on Sunday night," his father had gone on to explain before reverting to their discussion about current business matters. And before they had hung up, his father had exclaimed, "Oh, Shane, just a minute, here comes Merry now. She wants to say hello to you."

But Merry had given him more than a greeting. She had issued instructions. "Please ring Paula," Merry had urged. "I gave her your numbers the other night, but I know she won't call you. She'd be too intimidated." When he asked her for clarification, his sister had told him that Paula had long been acutely conscious of his aloofness, as she had herself. "She'll be scared of being rebuffed," Merry had pointed out. "So it's really up to you. Be nice, Shane, she's such an old friend. And she doesn't look very well." This last statement had been announced in a grave and worried voice, and Merry had rushed on, "She seems weighted down, troubled, morose even, and that's not the Paula *we* know. Please take her out, give her a good time. Have some fun together, Shane, make her laugh again, like you used to do when we were all children."

His sister's comments had alarmed him; he had pressed for more information about Paula's state of mind and health. Merry had not really been able to enlighten him any further, and before they had said good-bye he had faithfully promised his sister he would get in touch with Paula.

But he was wavering again. Whilst he longed to see her, he knew that by succumbing to his yearning he would only be inflicting punishment on himself. She was another man's wife. Lost to him forever. To spend time with her would open up all the old wounds . . . wounds which had not exactly healed but *had* scabbed over at least, and were therefore much less painful. It will be unsettling, he thought, reflecting on the life he had built for himself in New York over the past eight months. It was not an exciting life; rather, it was dull and uneventful, with no great highs, but no debilitating lows, either. He was neither happy nor sad, in limbo in a sense, but he did have peace and quiet. There were no women around anymore. Two sorties in that direction had foundered miserably and rendered him helpless, despairing. And he had decided, yet again, that celibacy was infinitely preferable to disastrous scenes in the bedroom which ended in embarrassment, left him shaken and filled with mortification at his own inadequacies. And so he scrupulously avoided all female entanglements and spent most of his time working. More often than not, he remained at the new offices of O'Neill Hotels International until eight or nine at night, and then went home to a dreary supper in front of the television set. From time to time he made a date with Ross Nelson or with one of the other two men he had become friendly with; occasionally he took Skye Smith to a movie or the theater and then on to dinner afterward. But for the most part he led a solitary existence, with books and music as his sole companions. He was not happy, but there was no pain to deal with. He was dead inside.

As all of this ran through his head, Shane had a sudden change of heart. He really ought to see Paula, if only for appearances' sake. Should any of his other childhood friends happen to visit the city, he would wine and dine them automatically. To avoid Paula would look peculiar, pointed, actually, especially to Emma and his grandfather, who would undoubtedly ask him about her when they passed through New York next month. Besides that, Merry had said Paula was not looking well. Yes, he had better invite her to dinner, just to satisfy himself she was really all right. But she's not your responsibility, he cautioned himself, thinking of Jim Fairley. *Her husband.* Unexpectedly, a savage feeling of jealousy seized him, and he had to make a strenuous effort to fling this emotion off as he crossed Fifty-ninth Street and continued on up Park, making for the mid-sixties.

In a few minutes he would be arriving at the site of their new hotel. The construction company had almost finished rebuilding the old-fashioned interiors and momentarily he would be surrounded by the crews, the foremen, the architects, and the interior designers. All would be demanding his attention. I must make a decision about Paula. *Now.* No more procrastinating. Oh, to hell with Jim Fairley! She's my oldest and dearest friend. I grew up with her. Of course I'm going to see her. No, you can't. It will be too hurtful. Once again Shane reversed himself.

And he was paralyzed into inaction by the knowledge that he was vulnerable to her. If he so much as set eyes on the only woman he loved he would be exposing himself to pain and suffering from which he might never fully recover.

• • •

Skye Smith looked at Ross Nelson nervously, and her voice quavered slightly as she said, "But your divorce has been final for weeks now. I don't understand. I always thought we were going to get married."

"I'm afraid that has been wishful thinking on your part, Skye," Ross said, endeavoring to keep his voice level, to be courteous if nothing else.

"But what about Jennifer?"

"What about her?"

"She's your child, Ross!"

For a moment he said nothing. He had been furious when he had arrived home from Wall Street ten minutes earlier to find Skye Smith, his former mistress, sitting in his living room so coolly composed and obviously determined to fight with him yet again. He was growing exasperated with her and the constant pressuring. The moment she left he was going to fire his housekeeper for being stupid enough to allow her into the apartment.

Skye sat twisting her hands, her face white, her eyes filled with mute appeal.

Ross Nelson stared at her, his implacability increasing as he noted her agitation. Her apparent distress did nothing to engender sympathy or compassion in him. It only served to annoy him further. "You say she's my child. But is she, really?" he asked cruelly. "I've never been too sure . . . about her paternity."

Skye gasped, drew back on the sofa. "How can you say that! You know you're her father. She's the spitting image of you, Ross, and there's the blood test. And anyway, you kept me virtually under lock and key for four years. I never so much as looked at another man."

He smiled ironically. "But you're looking at one these days, and very lovingly so, aren't you, Skye? Shane O'Neill, to be precise. And since you're sleeping with him I suggest you use your considerable sexual wiles to ensnare him. You'd better lead *him* by the nose to the altar, and as quickly as possible."

"I'm not sleeping with him," she protested fiercely, her apathy dropping away, her eyes flashing angrily with sudden life.

"Do you really expect me to believe *that?*" he exclaimed, with a cynical laugh. "I know everything there is to know about you, Skye, and then some." His eyes hardened as they swept over her and his mouth lifted at the corner in a scornful smile. "You can't resist tall, husky, handsome studs, they've always been your terrible weakness, my dear. As we both know only too well. You'd be wise to marry one of them while you still have your beautiful blond looks and that extraordinarily athletic sexual ability. Shane's definitely the most likely prospect. He's getting it from you in bed, so why don't you get him to make it legal, while the romance is still in that first euphoric flush. He's your type, no two ways about it. He's also a rich man, and he's certainly available."

"Ross, I'm telling you the truth. I'm not having an affair with Shane O'Neill," she insisted.

Ross laughed in her face, reached for the silver cigarette box on the antique Chinese coffee table, slowly put a flame to the cigarette he held between his fingers.

Skye's eyes rested on him. She wondered why she had ever let herself become embroiled with him—and so foolishly—years ago; asked herself why it was her misfortune to love this man in the way in which she did. The trouble was, he knew exactly how she felt, and that was why he had lately begun to cool toward her. Ross only wanted the things in life which he could not possess, and especially women who showed no interest in him whatsoever. He's perverse, she thought, but oh God how I love him. She knew she had to make him believe her about Shane for the child's sake as well as her own. Suddenly realizing that the only way to convince him was to be open and explicit, she said quietly, "All right, I admit it. I did go to bed with Shane. *Once*. It was when I discovered you'd taken Denise Hodgson to South America with you, when I found out about your affair with her. Retaliation, I suppose. But it didn't work between us. We never made love. And we've never been near each other since, not in that way, Ross. We're friends, that's all. Chums."

"Chums," Ross spluttered, shaking his head. "Come on, Skye, it's me you're talking to, remember? I haven't known you for five years not to understand exactly how you can make a man feel, especially in the beginning, when he's not yet slept with you." He laughed derisively. "Didn't work between you, eh?" he muttered, his expression one of total disbelief.

Skye swallowed, knowing she had to continue talking, give him a full explanation if she was to make any headway, ingratiate herself with him again, somehow win him back. "Yes, that's correct, I promise you, Ross. Shane and I are simply good friends." She swallowed again. "He couldn't . . . well, the night we went to bed . . . he wasn't able to . . . you know, do anything."

Ross slapped his knee, raucous laughter rippling through him. "Do you expect me to believe Shane O'Neill couldn't get it up with you? Oh no, Skye, I'll never accept that one from you."

"But it's the truth," she whispered, remembering so clearly that miserable night, Shane's dreadful embarrassment, her own confusion. "It's the God's truth." She leaned across the coffee table, finished in a much stronger tone, "I swear it on Jennifer's head, on my child—on our child."

His laughter ceased and his eyes narrowed, observed her thoughtfully. Instantly he knew she was not lying, not when she brought the child into it. He said, "So . . . Shane's got a little problem, has he?"

She nodded. "With me at least." She hesitated. "I have a feeling he's in love with someone."

"I wonder who that could be, who the woman in question is. Do you know?"

"That's a silly thing to ask. How could I possibly know. He hasn't confided anything. Don't you see, Ross, that's why he's not available as a husband for me."

"Neither am I."

"Why?" she demanded with terseness.

"I have no desire to get married again," he said almost chattily, "not with my track record. I've had enough of grasping wives and the divorce court. Besides, I'm paying too much in alimony as it is. Hundreds of thousands of dollars a year. But if I *were* ever demented enough to take that suicidal plunge, I can assure you my bride would have to be a rich one."

"Oh come off it! Money doesn't interest you, Ross," she scoffed. "You couldn't spend your millions if you lived to be a hundred."

He said nothing.

Skye said slowly, her face growing soft, almost tender, "We've had so much together. We have a child, and I love you very much."

"You don't seem to understand—I don't love you."

She flinched but kept her hurt to herself. He had a penchant for being cruel, and his moods changed like the wind. In five minutes he might easily do a turnabout and sweep her off to bed. That had happened so many times before. A thought came to her, and she stood up, went and sat down next to him on the other sofa, laid her hand on his knee. She drew closer, whispered, "You don't really mean that, Ross darling, you know it's not true. You do love me. There's a special kind of magic between us, and there always has been." She smiled into his cold face, her eyes enticing. "Let's go to bed. I'll show you just how strong the bonds are between us."

He lifted her hand from his knee and placed it in her lap. "I didn't think you were a masochist, that you'd want a repetition of your misadventure with Shane O'Neill. It must be very humiliating for a woman like you to realize that her sexual expertise has lost its power."

She pulled away from him, gaping, and her eyes filled with tears.

Wanting to be rid of her, he went in for the kill, said in the quietest but hardest of voices, "You see, Skye, you don't turn me on anymore."

Rising, she blundered across the room to the window, flicking the tears off her cheeks, trying to stem their flow, her shoulders heaving. She knew she had lost him. Her life was in shreds.

Ross also rose and crossed to the small Regency writing table. He opened the drawer, took out his checkbook, picked up the pen and wrote. As he ripped the check out of the book she turned around, stood staring at him, puzzlement replacing the anguish on her strained face.

"What are you doing?" she asked, beginning to tremble.

"This is for you, for the child," he said, pushing himself up out of the chair, walking to her. "I will make arrangements with my accountants for you to receive the same amount every month. It should be more than enough." He stopped in front of her, held out the check.

Skye shook her head wildly. "I don't want it, Ross. *I* can support *our* child. I'm not interested in your money, and I never have been. It's only you I want. As a husband, as a father for Jennifer."

"That's too high a price for me." He tried to force the check into her hands but she refused to take it, balling her fists, backing away from him.

He shrugged, turned, walked back to the sofas in front of the fireplace. He opened her handbag, slipped the check inside, then carried her bag to her, put it in her hands. "I think it's time for you to leave, Skye. I'm expecting guests. It's over between us. There's nothing more to say."

Lifting her head, she gathered some of her shattered pride around her, and she was surprisingly cool and steady as she said, "Oh yes, there *is* something more to say, Ross, and it's this . . ." She paused, looked deeply into his face. "Things are *not* over between us and they never will be, whether we see each other again or not. And one day you're going to need me. I don't know for what reason, or why, but need me you will." She opened her bag, took out the check and tore it in half without looking at it. She let it flutter to the floor. And then she pivoted and walked away from him without a backward glance, her pace measured and controlled.

Ross picked up the torn check and pocketed it, his face expressionless. He would write another one tomorrow and mail it to her. He ambled over to the window and parted the curtain, looked down onto Park Avenue. In a few minutes she would leave the building and cross the street as she always did, heading in the direction of Lexington. He sighed. It was a pity about the child. His face softened a fraction. There was no way he could have his three-year-old daughter without the mother, and the mother he neither wanted nor needed. She was far too troublesome in far too many ways. He felt a sudden twinge about Shane and the manner in which he had maneuvered him, had tried to throw Skye into his arms. Funny coincidence, he thought, the way Skye and Shane were introduced in Yorkshire and then a week later he phoned me at the bank with an introduction from Emma Harte. The minute he had met Shane he had thought of Skye, realizing he might have found a solution to his problems with her. He had manipulated Skye, had augmented the beginning of the affair, if one could call it that. Oh well, they say all's fair in love and war. Skye's unexpected revelation about Shane's impotency *had* surprised him, though. Shocked him. Shane O'Neill, of all people. Poor son of a bitch, Ross muttered, wondering for the second time what woman had so got her hooks into O'Neill he couldn't perform with anyone else.

Ross pressed his face to the glass, saw Skye hurrying across Park, lingering on the center island, waiting for the lights to change. She was wearing the mink coat he had given her. He supposed he had loved her once. Now she bored him. He let the curtain drop, and she was instantly dismissed as he turned his mind to his present plans.

Moving toward the fireplace, Ross Nelson stood for a few minutes with his hand on the mantelshelf, staring into space, lost in his reverie, pondering Paula Fairley. He had known her for years, paid little attention to her in the past. But this morning, in her office, he had been intrigued by her. He had to have her. He was going to have her. Nobody, nothing would stop him. Now there is a powder keg of suppressed sexuality, he decided. He had spotted that at once. It was apparent in the way she held her body, from the hunger he had detected in those unusual violet-tinted eyes, so long-lashed and seductive. He would put the match to the powder keg, explode it, then lie back and let the flames of her sexuality consume them both. He began to realize that just thinking about her excited him inordinately, in a way he had not been excited for some time, jaded as he had become. He itched to get his hands on that slender body, so willowy and graceful, yet curiously boyish except for the beautiful breasts. He closed his eyes, holding his breath, recalling how taut and firm they had looked under the white silk shirt she had been wearing. He lusted for her right now, this very minute. Her image was suddenly so vividly alive in his mind he snapped his eyes open swiftly, lowered himself onto the sofa, knowing he must dispel the tantalizing picture of them in bed together. He would have a miserable evening if he did not do so immediately.

But Ross Nelson discovered she was difficult to forget, so potent was her sexual appeal to him. And then of course there was her money. He began to contemplate her great fortune, Emma's fortune, which she would inherit one day. To his astonishment the idea of matrimony was suddenly most appealing after all. There was a husband in the background somewhere, wasn't there? He would soon dispense with Fairley. Once he had bedded Paula she would be his completely. They always were, particularly those who came inexperienced and breathless with anticipation into his arms. He felt the old familiar ache in his groin. To take his mind off sex he endeavored to concentrate on Paula Fairley's huge fortune. The ache only intensified. He crossed his legs, growing uncomfortably hot. He began to laugh at himself. How fortunate it was that he had not indulged himself in his erotic imaginings about Paula earlier. Otherwise he would have been forced to take Skye to bed—for one last time.

He glanced at the phone on the writing desk, wondering why it had not yet rung. He had been expecting to hear from Paula the moment he had arrived home.

Thirty-Two

"Where on earth did those ghastly vermilion roses come from, Ann?" Paula asked, staring through the open door of the drawing room and then turning to look at her grandmother's American housekeeper.

Ann Donovan, standing next to Paula in the large entrance foyer of Emma's Fifth Avenue apartment, shook her head. "I don't know, Miss Paula. I left the card on the console, next to the vase."

She followed Paula into the room, continuing, "I wasn't sure where to put them, to be honest, the bouquet is so huge. I even wondered if I ought to leave them out here. In all the years I've worked for Mrs. Harte we've never had roses in the apartment. Don't you like them either?"

"They don't really bother me, Ann, at least not in the way they disturb my grandmother. I'm just not accustomed to seeing roses around, that's all. I never plant them, or buy them, for that matter." She wrinkled her nose, indicating her distaste, remarked offhandedly, "And that color, it's such a violent red, and the whole arrangement is overwhelming. Very pretentious."

She reached for the envelope, ripped it open, looked at the card. It had been signed by Ross Nelson. His writing was small, neat, cramped almost, and he was inviting her to his country house for the weekend. What cheek he's got, Paula thought. And what makes him think I'd want to spend the weekend with him? I hope he's not going to become a pest. She tore up the card, dropped it into a nearby ashtray, said to the housekeeper, "I really can't stand the roses, Ann, would you mind taking them out to the back, please?"

"No, of course not, Miss Paula." Ann picked up the offending vase and headed out of the drawing room, saying over her shoulder, "You received some other flowers—not very long ago. I popped them in the den."

"*Oh*. Well, I suppose I'd better go and look at them," Paula murmured, walking out after the housekeeper, who was already hurrying across the foyer in the direction of her own rooms.

Paula's face lit up the minute she saw the lovely little basket of African violets in the center of the mahogany coffee table near the fireplace. She bent over them, touched the glossy dark green leaves, then the velvet-textured petals of the deep purple flowers. How delicate, how tender they are, she thought and picked up the envelope. It was blank and she wondered who the violets were from as she opened it. She stiffened in surprise. The name *Shane* was scrawled across the front of the card in his familiar bold handwriting. There was no message, simply his first name.

Still holding the card, Paula sat down on the nearest chair, frowning to herself, not quite certain what to make of the flowers. For the first time in almost two years he had done something sweet and thoughtful, the kind of thing he used to do in the past. And she was at a loss, not sure how to deal with it. She pondered. Was the basket of violets a signal that he wanted to be friends with her again? Or merely a polite gesture, one made out of a sense of family obligation and duty? Certainly sending her flowers was a way of saying welcome to New York without his actually having to speak to her.

Paula glanced into the fire, her expression abstract. She was positive that Merry would have told him she was in the city. After all, they were brother and sister and business colleagues, and they chatted back and forth across the Atlantic on a weekly, sometimes daily, basis. Perhaps her friend had put pressure on Shane to make an effort, to be nice to her. His aloofness and remoteness still perplexed Paula. How many times had she asked herself what she had done to hurt or upset him, and how many times had the answer been a negative one. She had done nothing wrong. Yet he continued to hold himself apart, barely acknowledging her existence. And when he did do so, she knew it was because he had no alternative, considering the long and intimate involvement of their two families.

Pulling her eyes away from the fire, Paula stared at the card again and for the longest time. The simple signature without one other word was not very encouraging. In a way it was intimidating. If only he had suggested that she phone him, or hinted that they might get together before she returned to England.

Damn, she muttered under her breath, and suddenly stood up abruptly, unexpectedly filled with anger. Shane O'Neill had been her dearest friend for as long as she could remember, since she could first walk and talk. They had grown up together . . . shared so much . . . become so very close over those formative and meaningful years . . . their lives had been so deeply intertwined . . . and then he had dropped her, turned away from her, and without any kind of proper explanation. It was not logical.

I've had enough of this. I'm sick and tired of people behaving as if *my* feelings don't matter, she thought, still bridling with anger. She rushed out of the den to find her briefcase. It was on a bench in the foyer where she had left it when she had walked in from the office. Grabbing it, she sped back to the den and sat down at the desk. Snapping open the locks, she pulled out her address book, turned to Shane's New York numbers, then sat back in the chair, eyeing the phone.

I'm going to have it out with him once and for all, she decided, whether it's tonight, next week, or the very day I leave. I don't care when it is, as long as I pin him down, finally. I want to know why he ended our long friendship so cruelly. *I'm entitled to an explanation.* She reached for the receiver, then let her hand fall away, realizing it would be prudent to calm herself first. Yes, it *would* be most unwise to confront him now. She had not seen Shane since April. He had just sent her flowers. Therefore it would appear odd, even irrational, if she tackled him about their relationship out of the blue. Also, she abhorred telephone confrontations, preferred to look people right in the eye when she was thrashing out something of crucial importance, needing to observe their reactions. I ought to have insisted on a frank talk long ago, she added under her breath. I've been spineless. It suddenly occurred to her that she was not so much angry with Shane as she was with herself. She should never have permitted the breach to continue as she had. Her annoyance began to dissipate.

Sitting up straighter, she lifted the receiver, then hesitated. How would she begin the conversation? You are befuddled, really jet-lagged tonight, she told herself with a rueful smile. Obviously you'll thank him for the flowers. What else? It's the perfect opening gambit. She dialed his apartment. The phone rang and rang. There was no reply. Disappointed, she replaced the receiver. Then something his father had said to her on Sunday night flashed through her mind. Uncle Bryan had made a remark about Shane's being as addicted to work as she was these days. Paula looked at her watch. It was a few minutes before seven. Could he still be at the office? Miranda had given her two numbers for O'Neill Hotels International, and one of them was Shane's private line.

Once again she dialed.

The phone was picked up on the second ring. "Hello," a very masculine voice said.

"Shane?"

There was a pause before he answered. "Hello, Paula," he finally said.

"Why, Shane, how clever of you to recognize my voice and at once," she exclaimed with assumed flippancy. "I'm so glad I caught you. I just got back here and found your violets. They're lovely, so springlike, and it was such a dear thought. Thank you."

"I'm glad you like them," he said.

His neutral, unenthusiastic tone was so off-putting it chilled her, but nevertheless she hurried on: "It's been ages since we've seen each other, at least eight months, and now here we both are, far away from Yorkshire, a couple of tykes in New York City. The least we can do is get together—" She stopped, then taking a deep breath said, very rapidly, "—for dinner."

There was an even longer pause at his end of the phone. "I . . . er . . . well . . . I'm not sure when I could do that, actually. When were you thinking of, Paula? Which night?"

"Tonight seems as good a time as any," she said determinedly. "If you're not already busy, that is."

"I am a bit, I'm afraid. I'd planned to work late. I have an awful lot of paperwork to catch up with this week."

"You've got to eat sometime," she pointed out in her most persuasive voice. She laughed gaily. "Remember what Grandy was forever saying to Mrs. Bonnyface at Heron's Nest. All work and no play, et cetera. And you never used to argue with that sentiment."

He was silent.

Softly she said, "I'm so sorry. I shouldn't be pushing you like this. I know what it's like to be overburdened by work. Perhaps another night. I'm going to be here for about three weeks. I'll leave it up to you; call me if you have a free evening. Thanks again for the flowers, Shane. Bye." She hung up immediately, not giving him an opportunity to respond.

Pushing herself out of the chair, Paula walked over to the coffee table, picked up the card and threw it into the fire, watched it burn. He had been cold, unbending, only marginally civil.

Why? Why? Why?

Whatever had she done to Shane O'Neill to make him behave in such an unfriendly and unkind manner? She ran her hand through her hair distractedly, then shrugged as she returned to the desk. I am a stupid fool, she thought. He's probably heavily involved with Skye Smith and can't be bothered to entertain a childhood friend, especially one he no longer cares about. He might even be living with her. Merry and Winston think their relationship is platonic, but how can they really know? They're always saying he's closemouthed. Funny, though, he never was with me, nor I with him, for that matter. We never had secrets; we told each other everything.

The phone shrilled. She glanced at it, picked it up. Before she said hello he spoke.

"I couldn't make it for at least an hour, maybe a bit longer," Shane said hurriedly, sounding breathless. "I'll have to go back to my flat to change, and it's turned seven already."

"You know you don't have to bother doing that for me, of all people, for heaven's sake," she exclaimed softly, surprised but gratified that he had rung back. "After all, we're family." She laughed under her breath. He was vain about his appearance, but she didn't mind. She rather liked that trait in him. "Anyway," she went on, "you can freshen up here if you want, and, listen, we don't have to go to a fancy restaurant, a simple place will do nicely."

"All right. I'll be there around seven-thirty," he said. "See you then." He hung up as swiftly as she had done a few minutes before.

Paula sat back, staring at the phone. She felt curiously light-headed and wondered why.

Shane O'Neill sighed heavily, crushed out the cigarette he had lit before calling Paula.

Reaching for the phone again, he dialed a small French bistro he liked, made a reservation for nine o'clock, and then stood up. Hurriedly rolling down his sleeves, he fastened the buttons on the cuffs, knotted his tie which he had loosened earlier, then walked over to the closet to get his jacket and overcoat.

You're a bloody fool, he chastised himself, allowing her to get to you in the way she did. You threw your resolve not to see her out of the window, and all because she sounded so wistful when she said good-bye. And disappointed. And lonely. Desperately lonely. He had lived in that solitary and isolated state far too long not to detect it in her immediately. Besides, he knew and understood Paula much better than anyone else did, and he had always been able to accurately gauge her moods, even when she was putting up a front. Like her grandmother, she was adroit at doing that, and exceptionally deceptive. She could don that inscrutable expression at will, affect a gaiety when she spoke that did nothing to betray her real feelings. Except to him, of course. She had adopted a fraudulent lightness with him a few moments ago, he was well aware. Her laughter and flippancy had been forced. So his sister *had* been right. Paula was troubled, disturbed. But about what, exactly? Business? Her marriage? Well, he wasn't going to contemplate *that* relationship.

After slipping into his sports jacket, he pulled his overcoat off the hanger and left the offices, locking the door behind him. Several seconds later, stepping out of the building onto Park Avenue, he was relieved to see that the traffic had eased. He spotted a cab, hailed it, jumped in and gave the address on Fifth Avenue. Settling back, he fished around in his pocket for cigarettes and his lighter.

As he smoked, a sardonic smile struck his wide Celtic mouth. You're putting a noose around your neck, O'Neill, he warned himself. But then you knew that when you sent her the flowers. You expected her to call you when she received them; be honest, you did. You simply lobbed the ball over into her court. Yes, this was the truth—and yet only partially so.

That afternoon, on his way back to the office from the hotel site, he had noticed the violets as he had passed the flower shop and instantly thought of her eyes. Then, as he had hovered uncertainly outside, gazing through the window, he had been transported back in time, back to the house by the sea, and she had been there in that dreamlike villa high on the soaring cliffs . . . dreamlike child of his childhood dreams . . . the tender young girl with the garden hoe . . .

He had gone in and bought the violets, knowing how much she would love them, not giving it a second thought, swept along by the tide of his nostalgia. Only later had he questioned his motives.

Oh, what the hell, it's too late now, he thought, impatiently stubbing out his cigarette. I've invited her out. I've got to go through with it. After all, I'm a grown man, I'm well able to handle the situation. Besides, I'm simply taking her to dinner. Surely there is no harm in that.

——— *Thirty-Three* ———

Some ten minutes later Shane was alighting on Fifth Avenue at Seventy-seventh Street.

Since he had lived in Emma's apartment for the first three months he had been in New York, the doorman on duty knew him, and they exchanged greetings before the man turned to the intercom to announce him.

Riding up in the elevator to the tenth floor, Shane discovered he had a tight knot of apprehension—or was it anticipation?—in his chest. He cautioned himself to watch his step with Paula, took a firm grip on his emotions and arranged a pleasant smile on his face. When he reached the duplex, he hesitated for a split second before ringing the bell. As he lifted his hand to do so the door suddenly opened and he found himself staring into Ann Donovan's pleasant Irish face.

"Good evening, Mr. O'Neill," she said, stepping back to let him enter. "It's nice to see you."

"Hello, Ann, it's nice to see you too." He walked in, closed the door behind him, shrugged out of his overcoat. "You're looking well."

Ann took his coat. "Thank you, and so are you, Mr. O'Neill." She turned to the coat closet, and added, "Miss Paula's waiting for you in the den."

But she wasn't. She was walking across the spacious hall toward him, a bright smile of welcome on her face.

The impact of seeing her hit him in the pit of his stomach, and the shock sped down to his legs. For a moment he was rooted to the spot, unable to move or speak. He recovered himself swiftly, stepped forward, the smile on his face growing wider.

"Paula!" he exclaimed, and he was surprised that his voice was steady and perfectly normal.

"You got here in record time, Shane," Paula said. "It's just seven-thirty."

"Not much traffic tonight." His eyes were riveted on her as she drew to a standstill in front of him.

Paula looked up at him, her eyes glowing.

He bent forward to kiss her proffered cheek, took hold of her arm with one hand, drawing her closer, then he let his hand fall away quickly, afraid of even the merest close contact with her.

She began to laugh, staring at him.

"What is it?"

"You've grown a mustache!" She eyed it critically, her head on one side.

"Oh. Yes . . ." His hand went to his mouth automatically. "Of course . . . you haven't seen it."

"How could I? I haven't set eyes on you since April."

"Don't you like it?"

"Yes . . . I think so," she said haltingly, then linked her arm through his, led him into the den, continuing to talk. *"You* certainly look fit as a fiddle. My God, that tan! And all *I* hear is how hard you're working in New York. I bet if the truth were known you're really leading an idle life on the golden sandy beaches of the Caribbean."

"Fat chance of that. The old man's a slave driver."

He was glad when she let go of his arm and moved away from him, putting distance between them. She walked over to the small chest at the far side of the room. He hovered near the coffee table, watching her as she plopped ice into the glass. He noticed that she poured scotch, added soda, without asking him what he wanted. But why would she ask? She knew what he drank. He caught sight of the basket of violets and smiled and then suddenly she was beside him, offering the drink.

He took it, thanked her, asked, "Aren't you having anything?"

"Yes, a glass of white wine. It's over there. I'd just poured it when you arrived." As she spoke she sat down in the armchair near the fireplace, lifted the goblet. "Cheers, Shane."

"Cheers." He lowered himself into the chair opposite, relieved to be sitting down. He still felt shaken, unsteady, and so extremely conscious of her he was slightly alarmed. You'd better be careful, he thought, and put down his glass on the end table. He lit a cigarette to hide his nervousness, and discovered, as he puffed on it, that he was unexpectedly tongue-tied. He glanced around, admiring the room as he usually did. He felt comfortable here. Emma had used a mixture of light and dark greens, a colorful floral chintz on the sofa and chairs, and some rather handsome English Regency antiques. The ambiance gave him a sense of home, evoked nostalgic feelings in him. He said, at last, "I practically lived in this den when I was staying here."

"Funny you should say that. So do I." Paula leaned back in the chair, crossed her long legs. "It reminds me of the upstairs parlor at Pennistone Royal, although it's smaller of course, but it's cozy, warm, and lived in."

"Yes." He cleared his throat. "I've booked a table at Le Veau d'Or. Have you ever been there?"

"No, I haven't."

"I think you'll like it—like the atmosphere. It's a small French bistro, very lively and gay, and the food's excellent. I took Aunt Emma and Grandpops there one night, when they were in New York. They really enjoyed themselves."

"It sounds lovely. And talking of our grandparents, they'll be here again in a few weeks, on their way back to England, won't they? Are you coming home with them? For Christmas?"

"No, afraid not, Paula. Dad wants me to go down to Barbados for the holidays. It's a big season for the hotel."

"Everybody'll be disappointed not to see you in Yorkshire," Paula murmured, looking across at him, trying to get used to the mustache. It changed his appearance, made him seem different, a bit older than his twenty-eight years, and more dashing. If that was possible. He had always been the kind of man people looked at twice, because of his height and build, his dark good looks, the sense of presence he exuded.

"You're staring at me," he said. A black brow arched and his expression was questioning.

"I could say the same about you."

"You've lost weight," he began, stopped, reached for his drink.

Paula's brow wrinkled worriedly. "Yes, I have. And I haven't been dieting. You know I never do that. Am I too thin?"

"Yes, a little. What you need is fattening up, my girl, and since we're on the subject, you also—"

"You've been saying that to me all of your life, and *mine*," she interrupted, pursing her lips. "At least for as long as I can remember."

"True enough. I started to say you also look tired, in need of a good rest, a holiday." He brought his drink to his mouth, his gaze leveled at her over the rim of the glass, studying her. After taking a swallow, he set it on the table, leaned forward avidly. "You've done a good job with the makeup, but then you always do. However, cosmetics don't fool me. Your face is gaunt and you've got faint purple smudges under your eyes," he remarked with his usual unnerving forthrightness. "No wonder my sister and Winston are worried about you."

This comment took Paula by surprise, and she exclaimed rapidly, "I didn't know they were. Neither of them has said anything to me."

"I'm sure they haven't. In fact, I don't suppose anybody has—they're all afraid of you, afraid of upsetting you. But not me, Beanstalk. We've always been blunt with each other, and honest. That'll never change, I hope."

"So do I." She could not help thinking about his behavior lately, the break he had created in their relationship. He had been less than honest with her about that, she was quite sure. She wondered whether to take him to task about it, then decided not to do so. Another time would be more appropriate perhaps. She did not want to put him on the defensive, create trouble on their first evening. She wanted to relax with him, enjoy his company. She had truly missed Shane, now wanted him back in her life on the old footing, needed to rekindle their childhood friendship. It was vital to her. And so she said, "It's lovely to see you and I'm so glad we're having dinner together, Shane. It'll be like old times."

She gave him such a warm and loving smile and there was such eagerness in her fine, intelligent eyes, his heart missed a beat. He smiled back at her. "It already is," he said, and realized that this was the truth. His tension slipped away and he began to laugh. "I'm not very nice, or very gallant, am I? Picking on you the minute I arrive. And despite what I've just said, you do look lovely, Paula, and as elegant as always."

His eyes swept over her approvingly, took in the scarlet silk shirt and the white wool pants. A smile of amusement tugged at the corners of his mouth. "Now, if you'd only thought to add a purple kerchief, you'd look absolutely bang on, perfectly smashing."

Perplexity flashed onto her face. She glanced down at her shirt and then started to laugh with him. "The Herons! It never occurred to me when I was dressing, but of course, these were your colors."

He nodded, his black eyes merry, and then he stood up. He took his glass to the chest, added more soda water and ice to dilute the scotch. She had fixed the drink exactly right, the way he liked it, but he wanted to be especially careful tonight. Returning to the fireplace, he said in a more sober voice, "Winston told me Sally stayed at Heron's Nest during all that fuss in Ireland, and I understand everything's back to normal. But how is Sally *really?*"

"She's marvelous. Very well. Anthony is living at Allington Hall for the moment. I expect you know she's pregnant."

"Yes, Winston told me—" He broke off, looked at her alertly. "No wonder you're done in, worn out—all *you've* had to cope with." He was suddenly sympathetic, and it showed on his face.

"I managed." Wanting to keep the conversation lighthearted, and long weary of family problems, Paula changed the subject by launching into a recital about Emma, Blackie, and their travels. She regaled Shane with snippets she remembered from her grandmother's long letters, tidbits chosen at random from their weekly phone conversations. She spiced up her stories with comments of her own, peals of laughter and merriment punctuating these small asides as she warmed to her subject.

Shane's laughter echoed hers, and he nodded from time to time, listening attentively, content to sit back and let her do the talking. It gave him a chance to observe her more closely, to fully enjoy her. The familiar vivacity was there, spilling out of her, and she was humorous, pithy, and gentle by turn, displaying her love for Emma and his grandfather with every word she uttered.

If her gaiety had been forced, fraudulent—on the telephone earlier—it no longer was. He had to acknowledge that she was her natural self, open, outgoing, the girl he had grown up with and whom he knew as well as he knew himself. There was an easiness between them now, after the first few strained moments, and he felt as though he had seen her only yesterday. The rift he had created in their friendship might never have happened.

As he continued to listen to her soft musical voice, a tranquility settled over Shane. He was at peace with himself, and in a way he had not been for the longest time. But then he was generally at peace when he was with Paula. They never played silly games. There were no false barriers, no affectations, no phony attitudes. They were entirely themselves, and they were completely attuned to each other as they had been since they were children.

He studied her face quite openly, no longer bothering to hide his interest in her. Its angularity and gauntness had been softened by the warm light from the lamp behind her. It was mobile, expressive, and it articulated much about her thoughts and feelings. There were those who said Paula was not beautiful. She was to him. Her coloring was startling in its vividness, exotic, really. The shiny black hair coming to a dramatic widow's peak above her smooth wide brow, the translucent ivory complexion unstained by color, the violet eyes set wide apart, large and thickly lashed—all these features combined to create a unique kind of beauty. If he had to equate her with any of the flowers she loved to grow, he would have to liken her to an orchid or a gardenia—and yet he would never send her either—only violets. He thought of her basic nature then. She *was* retiring, reserved, and gentle. But, conversely, she was also intense, ardent, passionate about her likes and dislikes, and quick, intelligent, fair-minded, and honorable. He smiled to himself. She could be devious when it came to business, but that was a family trait, inherited from the redoubtable E.H. Now, as he pondered Paula, Shane had to admit she was the most complex of women, more complicated than any female he had ever met. Yet he loved that very complexity in her which others might easily find so baffling, even disturbing. Perhaps that was because he knew exactly where she was coming from, knew the elements and forces that had made her all the things she was.

He sat back trying to see her objectively, as another man might. His gaze lingered, then he dropped his eyes. His own emotions were intruding, blinding him, making it impossible to view her with any kind of objectivity. How could he do that? He loved her, loved her desperately. He would always love her. If he could not have her, and he knew he could not, then he would have no other woman. Second best was worse than nothing at all. Also, without another woman in his life he would not be forced into making comparisons as he yearned for Paula. And he *would* continue to yearn for her. You mustn't think of that, he told himself sharply. She is your oldest, dearest friend. You've missed her. So settle for friendship—if that's all you can have. And enjoy this evening for what it is, not what you think it could be in your imagination.

Paula was saying, "Anyway, that's all of my news about our indefatigable, globe-trotting grandparents. They're apparently having a whale of a time."

"Yes, it sounds like it," Shane agreed. "And Emma's a much more diligent correspondent than Blackie. All Grandpops does is send each one of us a weekly picture postcard with an obtuse message scribbled on the back. I have three I'll prize forever. One from Hong Kong, showing Chinese junks in an orange sunset, with a single word on the other side—*Cheers*. Another from Bora-Bora on which he'd written, *Drinking your health in coconut juice.*" Shane grinned at her. *"That's* a likely story, as we both know."

Paula giggled, asked, "And the third card?"

"One from Sydney which said, *Off to the outback today*. What a character he is, and I must say I've enjoyed hearing your news about the two of them, their activities. It brings them closer somehow."

"Yes, it does, but now it's your turn to do the talking," Paula announced. "Tell me all about your life in New York."

"There's not much to tell, Paula," he said, thinking of his lonely existence, the barrenness of his life. "I race between the office and the hotel site six, sometimes seven, days a week, fly down to Jamaica and Barbados about once a month to make sure the hotels are running smoothly. It's the usual grind, and, the truth is, I *do* work like a dog."

She nodded. "I thought you were only staying in New York for six months. It's been eight already."

"Dad and I decided it would be more practical if I remained here until the hotel is finished and open, operating properly. It's a lot more practical than flying backward and forward between New York and London. Also, the islands are closer. Now Dad has indicated he wants me to stay on in the States indefinitely."

"Well, I can understand his reasoning," she acknowledged softly. Swirling the drink around, she stared down into the glass, her face thoughtful. The idea of Shane being in New York permanently filled her with sudden and inexplicable anxiety. Then unexpectedly she thought of Skye Smith, experienced the same twinge of discomfort she had felt when Merry had mentioned her name weeks ago.

Before she could stop herself, Paula said, with a faint smile, "I suppose New York is a wonderful place to be—for a fun-loving bachelor like you, Shane. I bet the girls are falling all over you, queuing up for dates."

Astonishment crossed his face. "I'm not interested in other women," he exclaimed, and halted, recognizing his slip, instantly cursing himself. He decided to let the remark slide by, aware that the less said the better.

Not understanding that he had been referring to her, Paula nodded. "Oh yes, of course, you have a girlfriend now. Merry mentioned Skye Smith to me."

Irritated though he was with his sister and her big mouth, he nevertheless managed to grin, relieved that his gaff had gone over Paula's head. "Oh, Skye Smith's only a friend, whatever Merry has said to you. I'm not involved with her—or anyone else for that matter." He gave Paula a hard stare. "I told you, Dad's very practiced at cracking the whip these days, and I'm devoting my time to business. I don't enjoy much of a social life. I stay at the offices until all hours, stagger back to my apartment and fall into bed exhausted."

"It seems we're all on a treadmill these days," Paula said. Shane had obviously changed a great deal. He and Winston had been a couple of Don Juans, playboys, wild and reckless, according to the family gossip she had heard. But Winston had settled down. Perhaps Shane had done so as well. She was pleased he was not having an affair with Skye. Why did that woman bother her? Probably because Merry had been so scathing about her.

"Penny for your thoughts," Shane said.

She laughed. "They're not worth a farthing. Merry told me you have an apartment on Sutton Place South," she went on. "What's it like?"

"Not bad, actually. I rent it furnished, and the owner's taste is not mine exactly. But it's the penthouse, and the views are spectacular, especially at night. The whole of Manhattan is stretched out at my feet, and as far as the eye can see. I find myself sitting and enjoying those glittering vistas for hours on end. This is an exciting city, Paula, and challenging. I also happen to think it's beautiful, and the architecture never ceases to astonish me."

"I can tell from your voice that you like it here, but sometimes I wonder about the States—" She shook her head, her face growing serious, reflective.

"What do you mean?"

"I can't help thinking that it's a violent country. All those dreadful, mind-boggling assassinations—Martin Luther King, President Kennedy, and then Bobby Kennedy only last year. And this past August the ghastly Tate murders in California." She shuddered. "And the hippies and the drugs and the crime and the protests."

Shane looked across at her, said slowly, "There's a lot of truth in what you say. But it's a young country in a sense, and still going through its growing pains. Things will be all right here; they'll level off, I guarantee you that. Besides, we have hippies, drugs, crime, and protests in England . . . everywhere in the world. The sixties *have* been turbulent, but we'll soon be in a new decade. Perhaps the seventies will be more tranquil."

"I hope so. Anyway, I do hope you'll invite me over to see your apartment before I leave."

"Any time you want. And talking of leaving, I think we'd better make tracks to the restaurant. I don't want to lose the table."

"Fine, I'll just go and get my things." She was halfway across the room when she stopped, pivoted to him. "I'm not very thoughtful, am I? I said you could freshen up here on the phone and then immediately forgot all about it. Would you like to use my bathroom?"

"No, no, thanks anyway. The one down here is okay." Rising, he followed her out.

"See you in a minute then," she said, running lightly up the stairs.

Shane strode across the foyer to the guest bathroom. He washed his hands and face, combed his curly black hair, stared at himself in the mirror. He wondered whether to shave off his mustache tomorrow morning. No. He liked it. He grimaced at his reflection, wishing he had gone home to change his clothes. Oh, what the hell, I'm not trying to impress Paula, he thought, and went out.

She stood waiting for him in the foyer.

She had put on a white wool jacket that matched the pants, and had flung a white mohair cape over her shoulders. She looked impossibly beautiful to him.

He turned to get his overcoat out of the closet, gritted his teeth as the familiar longing for her surged through him. He clamped down on the feeling, knowing that the situation was useless, hopeless. She was married to Jim Fairley and very much in love with him.

All you can be is her friend, as you've always been, Shane reminded himself as they left the apartment and went down in the elevator.

Le Veau d'Or was busy, jammed with people, as Shane had known it would be.

Gérard came forward to greet them, smiling, as usual the genial host. He promised them that their table would be ready in ten minutes, suggested they have a drink at the small bar while they waited to be seated.

Shane ushered Paula forward, pulled out a stool for her and, without asking her what she wanted, ordered two *kir royales*. He lit a cigarette, watched the bartender pour the cassis into the large wine goblets, then fill both to the brim with sparkling champagne.

Once they had their drinks, Shane turned to Paula, clinked glasses with her. "To old friendships," he said, and looked down at her, his eyes warm.

"Old friendships, Shane."

"Do you know, the last time I had one of these was at La Reserve in the South of France . . . with you."

She looked at him quickly, and a smile of recollection glanced across her mouth. "I remember . . . You'd been so unkind to Emily, driving the boat at a crazy speed and with such wildness. She was terrified, poor thing. Then, to make amends, you dragged us both off, pouring *kir royales* into us with a vengeance." She shook her head, laughing. "It was about four years ago, that summer we all went down to Gran's villa at the Cap."

"But the drinks had no effect, if I remember correctly. My escapade with the speedboat cost me dearly . . . an expensive silk scarf was the price I had to pay for my lack of thought and recklessness. Still, it was worth it, just to bring the smile back to Emily's face."

"She's petrified of water—so is Gran."

"But you're not afraid of anything, are you?"

"What makes you say that?" She frowned at him.

"You were intrepid as a child, tagging along after me, doing all the things I did. You were such a tomboy, quite fearless, and you never flinched, whatever the obstacle, or its danger."

"But I trusted you. I knew you wouldn't let anything happen to me, and you never did."

And I never will, my darling, he thought, filled with love for her. A lump came into his throat, surprising him. He took a long gulp of his drink, momentarily averted his face as he placed the glass on the bar, not wishing her to see his eyes. They would reveal too much.

Paula began to chat about Emily's engagement to Winston, and once more Shane was happy to let her do the talking. It gave him a chance to marshal his feelings, get a hold on them again before they overwhelmed him. Eventually he was able to join in the conversation in a normal way, and they covered a wide range of topics. They gossiped about their mutual friends, discussed the Harte boutiques in the O'Neill hotels, wondered about Emerald Bow's chances at the Grand National. And they were still dissecting the difficulties of the Aintree course and the greatest steeplechase in the world when they were finally seated.

Settling back comfortably on the red banquette, Shane said, "All I had for lunch was a sandwich at my desk, so I'm ravenous. Knowing you, you're going to say you're not hungry, but I think we should order immediately."

"But I am hungry," she protested truthfully. For the first time in months she was looking forward to dinner. Her violet eyes, resting on him, welled with humor. "However, I'll let you order for both of us. I'll have the same as you— it's safer, don't you think?"

His mouth twitched. "I believe so. Otherwise you'll want what I have, as you always did when we were kids, and end up eating off my plate and leave me starving." He winked. "Don't think I've forgotten your bad habits . . ."

After perusing the menu, Shane motioned to their waiter, selected *saucisson chaud,* to be followed by *tripes à la mode de Caen,* and asked for a bottle of burgundy.

It was the custom at Le Veau d'Or for appetizers to be placed before the diners, to tide them over while they waited for dinner to be served. Two plates instantly materialized in front of them, and Shane exclaimed, "Oh good, mussels tonight. They're delicious. Try them, Paula." Dipping his fork into the mound of shellfish, he continued, "Will you be going to Texas while you're in the States?"

"I don't think so— Gosh, you're right, these are good." She munched on a forkful of the mussels, before adding, "I hope I don't have to go to Odessa. I met with Dale Stevens this morning, and fortunately things are relatively quiet at Sitex. Naturally, Harry Marriott is being his usual obstreperous self. That man is singularly without vision. He forever tried to block my grandfather, hated expansion and innovation, and he's constantly trying to do the same with us. He's still grousing about Sitex going into North Sea oil. But it's working extremely well, as you know. The offshore drilling paid off, and we were one of the first companies to strike oil this year. Once again, Emma Harte has proved that man totally wrong."

Shane smiled, nodded, went on eating.

Paula said, "I know Grandy gave you an introduction to Ross Nelson. What do you think of him?"

"Ross is okay. We get on quite well, actually. I suspect he's a bit of a sod when it comes to women, though. As for business"—Shane shrugged—"he's aboveboard. Very sharp, mind you, but honest. Obviously he's always looking out for the bank—that's only natural. He's been very helpful, useful to me in a variety of ways." He eyed her. "And what's your opinion of Mr. Nelson?"

"The same as yours, Shane." Paula told him about the meeting with Dale and Ross earlier in the day, confiding all of the details.

"Emma would never sell her shares in Sitex!" Shane exclaimed, when she had finished. His black brows knitted together. "I can't imagine how Ross could think that or why he is so keen for you to sell out. He can't make a profit from insider information about stock transactions, trading—it's against the law —and as a private investment banker of his standing and reputation, he would be a stickler about legalities, staying within the law, toeing the line drawn by the Securities Exchange Commission. No, financial gain has nothing to do with this, and, anyway, he's as rich as Croesus. Of course, if Ross helped to steer that kind of deal through for one of the bank's clients, he'd be a big man with that client, now, wouldn't he?" Not waiting for a response, Shane rushed on: "Yes, that's why he's interested in Sitex. From all you've just told me, his client wants control, or so it seems. Then again, if he's such a chum of Dale's, he's probably looking out for his buddy. He's trying to kill two birds with one stone."

"Yes. I reasoned things out the same way as you, after they'd left. Ross Nelson can pester me as much as he wants—I've no intention of talking Grandy into selling, which is what he hopes I'll do, in my estimation."

Shane gave her a cool and piercing look. "You'd better watch old Ross— he's bound to make a pass at you."

Paula was about to tell him about the roses, the invitation to spend the weekend at Ross's country home, and for a reason she could not immediately fathom she changed her mind. She said, with a dry laugh, "He wouldn't dare. I'm married. Also, he wouldn't want to upset Gran."

"Don't be so naïve, Paula," Shane retorted swiftly. "Your marital status and your grandmother's displeasure would not influence Ross Nelson, not one iota. He's bloody unscrupulous, if one is to believe the gossip one hears, and I'm afraid I do." Shane did not particularly like the idea of the banker hovering anywhere near Paula, and he brought the conversation around to another subject. He began to speak about their New York hotel, and continued to do so through the first course and as they waited for their main dish.

She listened with growing interest, enjoying being at the receiving end of his confidences. Earlier, before Shane had arrived at the apartment, it had crossed Paula's mind that they might feel awkward, perhaps shy with each other, discomfited and restrained even—they had not been alone or spent any time together for ages. But this had not been the case, nor was it now. It *was* like old times, as she had predicted it would be over drinks. It had not taken them long to get back on their former footing. There was warmth and affection flowing between them, and the camaraderie of their youth was much in evidence.

"So I'd like you to come over to the hotel, take a look round," Shane said, "whenever you have a spare hour this week. Some of the floors are finished and I can show you a few of the suites. I'd appreciate your opinion about the decorative schemes—I just received the renderings from the interior design firm this afternoon. You have such good taste, I'd like your opinion."

Paula's face lit up with pleasure. "Why, I'd love to see the hotel. I've heard quite a lot about it from Uncle Bryan and Merry. Actually, tomorrow's an easy day for me. I could meet you there in the late afternoon." She leaned closer, looked up into his face, hers full of eagerness. "And perhaps you'd come back with me for dinner at the apartment. Ann told me she wants to cook for you. She said something about your favorite Irish stew. And why not tomorrow evening?"

Because the more I see of you, the more I'll want you, he thought.

He said, "Thanks a lot, that'll be nice." He was startled that he had accepted her invitation so readily. Then suddenly, with a small shock, he knew that he intended to spend as much time with her as he could during her sojourn in New York.

He walked her back to the apartment.

It was a clear, bright evening, cool, but not particularly cold for November. After the warmth and noisiness of the bistro the air was refreshing, their companionable silence restful.

They were on Madison Avenue, drawing closer to Seventy-second Street, when Shane said, "Would you like to go riding on Sunday?"

"I'd love to," Paula cried, turning to glance up at him. "It's ages since I've been on a horse. I don't have my riding togs with me, obviously, but I suppose I could wear jeans."

"Yes, or you could go to Kauffman's. They're downtown and they have everything you'd need."

"Then that's what I'll do. Where do you ride?"

"In Connecticut—a town called New Milford. Actually, I own a place up there. An old barn. I've been renovating it, remodeling it for the past few months and—"

"Shane O'Neill! How secretive and mean of you! Why didn't you tell me about the barn before?"

"I haven't had a chance so far. We've had such a lot of other things to talk about over dinner—more important things, such as your business affairs, our new hotel." His laugh was deep, throaty. He went on, "Would you like to see it?"

"That's a ridiculous question. Of course I would. But I will, won't I? On Sunday, I mean."

"Yes."

"If you like I can fix a picnic lunch, and we can take it up with us. What time would we leave on Sunday?" Paula asked.

"You ought to leave fairly early. You see, I'll be there already. I've arranged for a couple of our carpenters to be there on Friday to work with me. I'm driving up on Thursday night. I plan to spend the weekend at the barn."

"*Oh.* Then how will I get there on Sunday?"

"No problem. I'll arrange for a car and driver to bring you. Unless—" He paused, exclaimed, "I have a great idea, Paula. Why don't you drive up with me on Thursday night, stay for the weekend? Surely you can take Friday off."

He gave her a quick look out of the corner of his eye, added in a jocular tone, "I'll buy you a spade. You can dig to your heart's content, make a garden for me."

She laughed. "In this weather? The ground's probably as hard as iron. But I'd love to come up for the weekend, Shane."

"Terrific." He smiled to himself.

She linked her arm through his, fell into step with him. They walked on in silence. She was thinking of their childhood days at Heron's Nest and, although she had no way of knowing it, so was he.

——— *Thirty-Four* ———

Paula woke on Friday morning to the sound of raised masculine voices and raucous laughter echoing outside.

She sat up in bed with a start and rubbed her eyes, blinking in the faint light, for a moment disoriented and wondering where she was. Then she remembered. Of course, she was at Shane's barn near New Milford. Glancing at her small traveling clock on the white wicker bedside table, she saw to her surprise that it was almost ten. She found it hard to believe she had overslept, and by four hours. Normally she was up and dressed by six o'clock every day.

Bounding out of bed, feeling rested and filled with energy, she padded over to the window, parted the red cotton twill curtains, looked down into the yard. Just below her, two men stood talking near a pile of lumber.

Shane was out of her line of vision, but she knew he was there when she heard him say, "Listen, you guys, keep the noise down, will you please? My lady friend is still asleep. And when I say lady, I do mean *lady*—so watch your language."

Half-smiling, she turned away and looked around the bedroom with interest. She had been too tired last night to pay much attention. Now she realized how charming it was, small and quaint, with white walls that stopped at a floor painted bright red, and a few pieces of white-wicker furniture. But it was the brass bed covered with a patchwork quilt that dominated the space.

Gliding into the adjoining minuscule bathroom, Paula took a quick shower, brushed her hair, put on lipstick and mascara, went back into the bedroom. She dressed in a pair of blue jeans, a pink cotton shirt, and a heavy purple sweater, then pulled a pair of knee-high red-leather boots on over the jeans. After strapping on her watch, she ran downstairs to the kitchen.

This was large, country in feeling, with rustic beams and wall-hung copper utensils, but there was every modern appliance, and it was spotless. It looked to her as if it had just been freshly cleaned. The white cabinets and countertops, along the white walls, gleamed brightly in the sunshine that filtered in through two small windows where blue-and-white checked curtains hung in crisp, starched folds. She peered out. Shane and the men were nowhere in sight.

Paula sniffed. There was a lovely aroma of coffee in the air and, spotting the bubbling percolator, she began opening cupboards, looking for a mug. She found one, filled it, then strolled through into the main living area of the barn.

She came to a halt halfway down the long expanse of space, her eyes sweeping around, trying to take in everything at once, knowing this was virtually impossible. She needed days to absorb everything Shane had accomplished here. It had looked lovely last night; this morning, filled with sunlight, it was breathtaking.

Only one room, he had said, as they were driving up from Manhattan. But what a room it was—huge, spectacular in its dimensions, with a high ceiling of exposed rafters intersected by crossbeams, a picture window on a long wall, and a gargantuan stone fireplace. A fire already blazed up the chimney, the big logs hissing and spitting.

She stepped over to the baby grand and sat down on the stool, sipping the coffee, continuing to glance up and down. He had positioned the piano in the exact center of the room, and she understood why. It created a natural demarcation between the seating arrangement next to the fireplace and the dining area near the kitchen. The color scheme was primarily white, the coolness warmed by dark wood tones. The walls had been whitewashed; two huge Chesterfield sofas and the big armchairs were upholstered in heavy white twill; the draperies matched; there were white area rugs on the polished wood floor. But pictures, prints, books, and plants added splashes of livelier color against the white background.

Shane had told her he had gone antiquing in the area, had stumbled on some genuinely good pieces. Now her eyes rested on two handsome chests she had not really noticed last night, moved on to regard a Coromandel screen that was obviously very old and rare. Its decorative panels made a striking backdrop for the mahogany dining table. I bet that screen cost a fortune, she thought.

A feeling of dismay trickled through her.

It was quite apparent that he had spent a great deal of money on the barn, not to mention time and effort. Shane had explained that most of the basic remodeling had been done by Sonny and Elaine Vickers, from whom he had bought the barn. "All I did was put in the cantilevered staircase and the plate-glass window, and add a few other finishing touches to the basic shell before I furnished," he had said.

Nevertheless, in the last few minutes something had registered, and it troubled her. The place had the look of permanence, had been made into a real home for someone who intended to live in it for a long time. Not only that, he was somewhere outside right now with the carpenters, sawing wood for shelves and cupboards. They were intended for the tiny spare room he had shown her and which he had said he was turning into a den for himself.

Did he plan to stay in America forever? Was he never coming back to England? And why did that matter to her?

Paula jumped up abruptly and hurried to the fire. She seated herself in an overstuffed armchair and placed the mug on the hearth. Her eyes fell on his cigarettes and lighter and, although she rarely smoked, she took one, lit it, sat smoking, thinking hard about the previous evening. They had arrived at nine o'clock, just as the thunderstorm had hit the area. They had been drenched after making several trips to the car to collect the bag of groceries and their suitcases, and he had insisted she change into dry clothes, immediately shooing her upstairs.

Twenty minutes later she had come back down and had stood hovering on the threshold of this room, admiring it. In her absence he had turned on all the lamps, lit the fire. The baronial expanse seemed more intimate, suffused in a warm and welcoming glow and reverberating with the strains of Bob Dylan's "Blowin' in the Wind." After wandering over to the fireplace, she had swung around to stand with her back to it, an old habit. At that very moment she had been surprised to see him emerge from the kitchen, carrying two drinks, looking spruced up and fresh in a pristine white shirt and blue jeans.

"You've been quick, doing all this and changing as well," she had exclaimed. He had given her a cheeky grin. "Training will out, as they say, and I was trained by a hard-assed general in a tough army camp, remember." She had retorted in mock reproof, "Emma Harte hard-assed! That's not a very nice thing to say about my distinguished grandmother." Handing her the vodka and tonic, Shane had clinked his glass against hers, then asserted, "Emma would appreciate my description of her, even if you don't."

They had begun to reminisce about Heron's Nest then, laughing a lot and teasing each other, and later he had brought out a huge platter of smoked salmon and a tray of cheeses. They had sat on the floor, eating off the coffee table in front of the fire, washing down their light supper with ice-cold Pouilly Fumé. And they had talked endlessly, late into the night, and about so many varied things, content to be together, at ease and comfortable in their companionship.

Toward the end of the evening Shane had noticed that she kept rubbing her neck, and in answer to his concerned glance, she had volunteered, "It's stiff —from sitting long hours at my desk, I've no doubt. It's nothing. Really." Without saying a word, he had knelt behind her, massaged her shoulders, her nape, and the base of her skull.

Recalling the scene, Paula remembered the pleasure she had felt as Shane's strong, hard fingers had kneaded her aching muscles, drawn the tension out of her. She had not wanted him to stop. And later, when he had given her a chaste good night peck on the cheek outside her bedroom door, she had felt a compulsion to put her arms around his neck. She had gone in swiftly, closed the door, her cheeks flaming.

Paula sat up in the chair with a jerk. Last night she had been baffled at herself. Now she understood. She had *wanted* Shane to touch her, to kiss her. Face it. Your so-called sisterly feelings toward him aren't very fraternal. Not anymore. *They're sexual. You're sexually attracted to him.*

This last thought so startled and shocked Paula, she leapt to her feet, threw the cigarette into the fire, and almost ran across to the picture window.

She stood staring out at the landscape, hardly aware of its beauty as she tried to calm herself. She *must* put aside these new and extraordinary feelings he had aroused in her. They shook her up, distressed her. And she had no right to be interested in Shane O'Neill—she was married. Besides, she was only his childhood friend, nothing more in his eyes.

Endeavoring to nudge thoughts of him out of her mind, she discovered that they refused to budge. They nagged at her, and then the image of Shane as he had looked last night danced before her eyes. He had seemed different, and yet his appearance and manner were exactly the same as they always were. Then it dawned on her. It was she who was different—and she had been looking at him through newly objective, newly perceptive eyes.

Why am I suddenly so aware of Shane? Because he is handsome, virile, amusing, and charming? Or because he exudes such sex appeal? But he always has, he hasn't changed. Besides, blatant sex appeal makes no impression on me. His sexuality isn't blatant, though. It simply exists as an integral part of him. My God, I must be insane, thinking in this way about Shane. Anyway, I'm not interested in sex. It turns me off. Jim has seen to that.

A little shiver ran through Paula. Jim loomed up in front of her. Merry had an expression she used to describe certain men. She called them 'the wham bam thank-you-ma'am chaps.' How apt. Paula sighed heavily, blinked in the sunshine as it pierced through the window, a blinding cataract of brilliant light. Her thoughts remained on Jim. Shane's image was demolished.

Yesterday afternoon, around two o'clock, she had telephoned Long Meadow. It had been seven in the evening in England. She had spoken to Jim, but only briefly. He had been pleasant, bland as always, but hurried, on his way out to dinner, he had informed her. He had quickly passed her over to Nora, so that she could chat to the nurse about her babies, get all the news. She missed Lorne and Tessa terribly. When she had asked Nora to put her husband back on the line, Nora had said that he had already left the house. Paula could hardly believe that he had not waited to say good-bye to her. Furious with him, she had hung up. Then the depression had set in. Seemingly Jim had forgotten their confrontation last Sunday—and what it had been about.

My God, that's less than a week ago, she thought, as the picture of them standing in the garden flashed through her head with startling clarity. Something had died in her that day. It would never be reborn. Jim had been dense, dismissive, cavalier in his attitude. And, yes, irresponsible and indifferent to her, almost callous, now that she thought about it again. He simply didn't care about her emotions, her thoughts, her needs. Once more she acknowledged that he and she were incompatible. And on every possible level, not only sexually. If sex were their only problem she would be able to cope. His attitude on the phone had only reinforced her sense of despair about him. The last vestiges of her commitment to her marriage had been swept away, and she had turned to the papers on her desk, thankful that she had so much business to occupy her.

My work and the children . . . that's where I shall direct all of my energies from now on, she reminded herself for the umpteenth time. Hurrying back to the hearth, she picked up the mug, headed for the kitchen. It was high time she went outside to find Shane, to wish him good morning and ask about their plans for the rest of the day.

But he was already in the kitchen, pouring himself a mug of coffee. "So there you are!" he exclaimed. "I bet my chaps woke you up, rowdy devils!"

Paula gaped at him, instantly conscious of his rough clothing. He was wearing shapeless, baggy corduroys, heavy work boots, a bulky fisherman's sweater, and a cloth cap set at a rakish angle on his black curls. She began to laugh, shaking her head.

"What's the matter?" he demanded, frowning, his eyes clouding.

"Your clothes!" she spluttered. "You look like an Irish navvy!"

"My dear girl, hasn't anybody told you that that's exactly what I am? Just like my grandfather."

Later in the morning they drove into New Milford.

On their way down the hill, Shane pointed out the farm where his friends Sonny and Elaine Vickers lived, told her in passing that he had invited them over for dinner that night. "He's a musician, she's a writer. They're lots of fun, you'll like them," he said, and then went on to discuss the menu with her.

By the time they were parking the car they had agreed on what she would cook—an old-fashioned North Country dinner with all the trimmings. They would start with Yorkshire pudding, have leg of lamb, roast potatoes, and Brussels sprouts for the main course, finish with an English trifle.

They went to the farm stands and various markets, bought fresh vegetables, fruit, the lamb and various other meats for the weekend, and spices, fancy candles, and armfuls of bronze and gold chrysanthemums. They staggered down Main Street, their arms laden, laughing and joking, their hilarity high.

On the return journey, Paula realized that she was being her normal self with Shane, as he was with her. But then why wouldn't he be? He couldn't read her mind, and even if he could, there was now nothing unusual to read—only friendly, affectionate thoughts, happy remembrances of their youthful past. Fortunately those strange and disturbing feelings he had evoked in her last night had entirely disappeared in the last few hours. Shane was just her old chum, her good friend, and part of the family. Everything was normal again. She felt weak with the relief.

Once they were back at the barn, Shane unpacked their purchases and put them away, while she arranged the flowers in two large stone pots. As they worked, he said, "I'm afraid it's another picnic for lunch. Is that okay with you, Beanstalk?"

"Of course. But what about your carpenters? Don't you have to feed them?"

"No. They brought their own sandwiches and they told me they were going to eat at noon, while we were out shopping. But I wonder where they are? They were supposed to start putting up some of the shelves—it's awfully silent." He began to laugh as the sound of hammering floated down from the upper floor. "I spoke too soon, it seems. They're obviously hard at it."

Lunch, eaten in front of the fire in the main room, consisted of ripe Brie cheese, thick chunks of French bread, fruit, and a bottle of red wine. At one moment Paula looked across at Shane and said, "Are you planning to live in the States for the rest of your life?"

"Why do you ask that?" He wondered why it mattered to her.

Glancing around, she said, "This place has the look of a permanent residence, and you've obviously put a lot of care and money into it."

"Yes, and it's been very therapeutic for me, coming up here whenever I could, working on the place. It's given me something to do at weekends, in my spare time. I don't have many friends, no real social life to speak of. Besides, you know I've always enjoyed rebuilding old places." He lolled back in the chair, his eyes resting on her thoughtfully. "Winston and I turned a tidy profit when we sold those old cottages we renovated in Yorkshire, and I know I'll do the same here, when the time comes for me to sell the barn." He continued to observe her. Was that relief in her eyes, or was he imagining things?

"What's going to happen to Beck House? I mean, now that Winston and Emily are getting married?" Paula asked curiously.

"When Winston was in New York he said he and Emily wanted to live there for a while, to see if Emily liked it. If she does, he'll buy me out. If she doesn't—" Shane shrugged. "There's no problem, we'll probably continue to share it as a weekend place. Or we'll put it up for sale."

"Winston told me he's asked you to be his best man."

Shane nodded.

"And I'm going to be Emily's matron of honor."

"Yes, I know."

"Won't you be in England before then, Shane?"

There it was again, that peculiar concerned expression in her eyes. He said, "I've no idea, Paula. As I explained the other day, Dad wants me to spend the Christmas season in Jamaica and Barbados, and I might just have to go to Australia next February or March."

"Australia!" She sat up straighter on the sofa, looking puzzled.

"Yes. Blackie's taken a shine to Sydney, and several times, when he's spoken to Dad lately, he has urged him to build a hotel there. I spoke to the old man yesterday morning, and he's actually received a letter from Grandpops about that very thing. So—I may have to go over there, scout the place."

"Blackie's as bad as Grandy. Don't those two ever stop thinking about business?"

"Do you? Or do I, for that matter?" He chuckled. "We're a couple of chips off a couple of old blocks, wouldn't you say?"

"I suppose so." She leaned forward, her face suddenly intent. "Do you think I work too hard?"

"Of course I don't. Anyway, it's your nature to be a worker, Paula. It's also the way you were reared—as I was reared. I don't have much time for parasites. Frankly, I'd go crazy if I had lots of free time on my hands. I love being out in the marketplace, love the rough-and-tumble, the wheeling and dealing, and so do you. There's another thing—I get a lot of gratification knowing I'm continuing the family business started by Grandpops, and you have to feel exactly the same way."

"I do."

"It's expected of us both . . . Duty has been beaten into us since our births; we wouldn't know any other way to live. Look, our respective grandparents devoted their lives to building two great business empires, strived to give us better lives than they had in the beginning, and financial security, and independence and power. How—"

"Jim says the pursuit of power leads to isolation, the death of human values and the death of the soul," Paula interjected.

This was the first time she had mentioned Jim since she had arrived in New York and Shane was momentarily thrown. He cleared his throat. He had no desire to discuss her husband but knew he had to make some sort of response. "And you? Do you agree?"

"No, actually, I don't. Wasn't it Lord Acton who said power tends to corrupt and absolute power corrupts absolutely? That's what Jim was getting at, I think. But to hell with Lord Acton, whoever *he* was. I prefer Emma Harte's philosophy. She says power only corrupts when those who have it will do anything to hang on to it. Grandy says that power can be ennobling, if one understands that power is a tremendous responsibility. And especially to others. I happen to agree with *her,* not Jim. I do feel responsible, Shane. To Gran, to our employees and shareholders. And to myself."

Shane nodded. "You're right, and so is Emma. I was going to say, a moment ago, how ungrateful and even unconscionable we would be if we were indifferent to our inheritances, turned away from them. It would be negating Blackie and Emma, and all their superhuman efforts." He stood up, glanced at the clock. "It's almost four, and since we're on the subject of responsibility, I'd better go and find my chaps, pay them, tell them to knock off."

Paula also rose, picked up the luncheon tray. "The day's disappeared! I should start preparing the food for dinner."

As they went out, Shane looked down at her, flashed his cheeky grin. "And for your information, Beanstalk, Lord Acton was an English historian, a devout Catholic, a Liberal member of Parliament and close friend of Gladstone's."

"That's nice to know," she said, laughing, and walked into the kitchen.

After stacking the dishwasher, Paula peeled the potatoes, cleaned the sprouts, prepared the lamb, smearing it with butter, adding pepper and dried rosemary leaves. Once the trifle was made and had been placed in the refrigerator, she beat flour, eggs, and milk into a batter for the Yorkshire pudding, humming happily to herself. Shane poked his head around the door several times during the hour she was working, volunteering to help, but she declined his offer, told him to scoot. She was enjoying herself in much the same way she took pleasure in gardening, using her hands instead of her brain for a change. Therapeutic, she thought, recalling his words about working on the barn.

When she eventually went back into the main room she noticed that he had laid the table for dinner, stacked piles of logs on one end of the hearth, put Beethoven's Ninth on the stereo. But he was nowhere in sight. Paula curled up on the sofa comfortably, listening to the symphony, feeling relaxed and even a little drowsy. She yawned. It's the wine. I'm not used to it at lunchtime, she thought, closing her eyes. It had been a lovely day, the nicest she had spent in a long time, and free of tension, verbal fencing. It was a relief to be herself, not to be constantly on the defensive, as she so often was with Jim.

Shane made her jump when he said, "Now, how about that walk?"

Sitting up, she covered her mouth with her hand, yawning repeatedly. "*Sorry.* I feel so sleepy. Do you mind if we scrap the walk for today?"

He stood near the sofa, hovering over her. "No. I'm wacked myself. I was up at the crack of dawn." He did not add that he'd hardly slept, knowing she was in the room opposite his, so near and yet so far removed from him. He had wanted her very much last night, had longed to hold her in his arms. He said, "Why don't you have a nap?"

"I think I will. But what are you going to do?"

"I've a few more chores, a couple of phone calls to make, and then I'll probably do the same."

She settled back against the cushions, smiling to herself as he went out, whistling under his breath. As she half-dozed she remembered she had not yet tackled him about his behavior over the last eighteen months. Oh, there's plenty of time, all weekend, she thought. I'll do it another day. Something stirred at the back of her mind. It was an incomplete thought and it slid away before she could fully grasp it. She sighed contentedly, felt herself being enveloped by the music and the warmth. Within seconds she was fast asleep.

——— *Thirty-Five* ———

It was one of those evenings which, right from the outset, was destined to be perfect.

A few minutes before seven, Paula came downstairs looking for Shane.

She was dressed in a light wool caftan which Emily had made for her. It was a deep-violet color, simply styled, loose and floating, with unusual butter-fly-wing sleeves that buttoned tightly at the wrists. With it she wore a long strand of lavender jade beads, another gift from Emily, who had bought them for her in Hong Kong.

Paula found Shane in the main room. He stood by the huge window, looking out.

She noticed that he had lit the many candles they had scattered around earlier and set up a bar on one of the small chests.

The fire blazed in the hearth like a huge bonfire, the few lamps he had turned on glowed rosily, and the voice of Ella Fitzgerald singing Cole Porter echoed softly in the background.

Walking forward, Paula said, "I can see that there's nothing for me to do but sit down and have a drink."

Shane swung around. His eyes swept over her.

As she drew closer he saw that she had stroked purple shadow on her lids, and because of this and the color of her dress, those uncanny eyes appeared to be more violet than ever. Shining black hair, brushed back and curling under in a pageboy, framed the pale face, accentuated its translucency. The widow's peak made a sharp indentation on her wide brow. It was dramatic. She was dramatic.

The strain had gone out of her face. He thought she looked more beauti-ful than she had in years. He said, "You look nice, Paula."

"Thank you—so do you."

He laughed dismissively. "You mentioned a drink. What would you like?"

"White wine, please."

Paula remained standing near the hearth, observing him as he opened the bottle.

He wore dark gray slacks, a lighter gray turtle-necked sweater and a black cashmere sports jacket. Studying him, she thought: He's the same old Shane, and yet somehow he's not. He *is* different. Maybe it's the mustache after all. Or is it me? She instantly squashed this possibility.

He brought her the drink. She caught the faint whiff of soap and cologne. He was freshly shaved, his hair well brushed, his nails newly manicured. Paula bit back a smile, remembering how his habit of looking at himself whenever he passed a mirror had driven her grandmother crazy. Emma had even threatened to have all of the mirrors removed from Heron's Nest if he did not curb his vanity. He had been eighteen that particular year and very conscious of his astonishing looks, his husky, athletic build. She suspected he was still most aware of his physical appeal, although he no longer gazed at himself in mirrors —at least not publicly. Perhaps he had learned to accept his striking appearance. She turned to the fire to hide another smile. He *was* vain, even a little conceited about some of his attributes and accomplishments, and so very sure of himself. Yet there was an inherent sweetness in him, a gentleness, and he was loving to the core with friends and family, and so very kind. How well she knew Shane Desmond Ingham O'Neill.

Shane, pouring himself a scotch and soda, called across to her, "Don't be surprised if Sonny brings his guitar. He usually does. I may accompany him on the piano—give everyone a treat. We might even have a singsong later."

"Oh God, shades of the Herons!" Paula laughed. "You really did stink, you know."

"On the contrary, I think we were rather good," he retorted, also laughing. He joined her. "You and the girls were jealous because we stole the show that summer, were the center of attraction. And you were envious of our smashing rig-outs. I'm surprised you didn't start a girls' band just to compete with us."

She laughed again. He touched his glass to hers.

Paula stared up at him towering above her, feeling dwarfed by his six feet four inches, and suddenly weak, defenseless, and decidedly female. There definitely was something irresistible about him. The weird feelings he had aroused in her last night began to stir. Her skin tingled. Her heart missed a beat.

Their eyes held.

Paula wanted to look away but his dark and piercing gaze was hypnotic.

Shane broke the contact, swiftly turning, making a show of searching for his cigarettes as he stifled the urge to kiss her. You must be careful, he told himself. He wondered if he had been wrong inviting her for the weekend. He knew he was skating on thin ice. I won't see her again while she's in the States. Inwardly he laughed. He knew he would.

A series of cheery hellos rang out. To his immense relief Sonny and Elaine walked in.

Shane hurried across the room to greet them, a huge grin surfacing. He was glad he had invited them. His tension eased.

After propping the guitar case against a chair, Sonny grasped his hand, embraced him, said, "Cognac . . . for after dinner." He handed Shane a bottle wrapped in fancy paper.

Elaine thrust a basket at him. "And here's some of my freshly baked bread for your breakfast," she exclaimed as Shane bent to kiss her cheek.

Shane thanked them, put the gifts on a chest, and brought the Vickerses over to be introduced to Paula.

The minute she met them, Paula knew she was going to like the couple. Sonny was tall, lean, and fair, with a blond beard and merry brown eyes. Elaine, softly pretty and feminine, was one of those women whose genuine sweetness is instantly recognizable. She had an open, friendly face, and her eyes were vividly blue, her short, curly hair prematurely silver.

The three of them sat down, and Shane went to make drinks for the new arrivals. Paula was glad she had chosen the caftan, even though Shane had told her to dress casually. Elaine was wearing black velvet pants with a Chinese jacket of blue brocade and looked elegant in an understated way.

Smiling at her, Elaine said, "Shane told us you're Emma Harte's granddaughter, and that you run her business now. I'm crazy about your London store. I can spend all day there—"

"She's not kidding either," Sonny interrupted, grinning at Paula. "My wife and your store are going to bankrupt me one day."

"Oh, don't pay any attention to my husband, *he's* the one who's kidding," Elaine said, and continued to rave about Harte's in Knightsbridge.

But when Shane came back with glasses of wine for Sonny and Elaine, the conversation turned to country matters and local gossip. Paula leaned back in her chair, listening quietly, sipping her drink. As the talk ebbed and flowed between Shane and his friends, she soon became aware of his liking for them, recognized how relaxed he was in their company. But then, so was she. They were easy to be with—warm, outgoing, very real and down-to-earth people. Sonny's wit was as quick as Shane's, although not quite as brilliant and astringent, and the two men were soon bouncing funny lines back and forth. There was a great deal of laughter and jollity in the air, and a festive mood prevailed.

After the first half hour, Paula felt as though she had known this engaging couple for years. Individually each of them drew her out, encouraged her to talk about her work, the stores, and both of them were particularly interested in hearing about her famous grandmother. And she, who was generally reserved with strangers, found herself chatting away. She and Sonny discussed music and his composing, and Paula discovered that he had written several Broadway musicals as well as the background music for numerous Hollywood films. Elaine, in turn, talked about her writing career and her books. And she did so in a manner that was not only informative but amusing, especially when she recounted funny incidents which had happened to her when she was on promotion tours. She told a good story, and entertainingly so, and there was a great deal of laughter and bonhomie among the four of them.

Occasionally Paula stole surreptitious glances at Shane. He was a wonderful host, constantly up and down, taking care of the drinks, changing the records on the stereo, throwing logs on the fire, and steering the conversation around to different subjects, involving them with each other. And he was obviously delighted with the way the Vickerses had warmed to her. He kept smiling across at her, nodding as if in approval, and twice when he passed her chair to do a small chore he squeezed her shoulder affectionately.

Paula had been out to check on the food once, and the second time she rose, Elaine also stood up.

"I'm letting you do all the work," Elaine said, "and that's not fair. I'm coming to help you."

"Things are under control," Paula protested.

"No, no, I insist." Elaine followed Paula out to the kitchen, and as she came through the doorway, she exclaimed, "Everything smells so delicious— my mouth's beginning to water. Now, what can *I* do?"

"Nothing, really." Paula smiled at her, bent down and took the meat out of the oven, placed it on a platter. "Well, there is one thing . . . Could you cover this with silver foil, please?"

"Consider it done," Elaine said, tearing off a large piece of the silver paper, tucking it around the leg of lamb. She stood watching Paula and, after a moment, she said, "It's a lovely evening. I'm so glad you're here. And you certainly cheer Shane up."

"Do I really?" Paula swung to face Elaine, gave her a curious puzzled look. "You make it sound as if he's been down in the dumps."

"We think he has. Sonny and I worry about him a lot. He's so nice, generous, very engaging, and pleasant and charming. Still . . ." She shrugged. "To be truthful, he's always up here alone, never brings . . . friends, and there are times when he seems despondent, melancholy." She shrugged again. "Of course, England is a long way off and—"

"Yes, I do think he gets a bit homesick," Paula volunteered, pivoting, turning her attention to the oven again.

Elaine stared at Paula's back, her brow puckering. "Oh, but I didn't mean it that way—" She stopped abruptly as Shane walked in, swinging the cork-screw in one hand.

He said, "I think I'd better open the wine, let it breathe for a while." He proceeded to do so, remarking to Paula, "I suppose the meat has to stand and bleed for fifteen minutes or so, before I carve it. Well, I might as well hang around, keep you company."

Elaine slipped out quietly, leaving them alone.

"It was a wonderful dinner," Elaine said, putting down her dessert fork and spoon, looking across the table at Paula. "And I'd love to have the recipe for this trifle. It was yummy."

"And the recipe for the Yorkshire pudding," Sonny suggested. He flashed his wife a sly but loving grin, added, "And I know Elaine won't take offense when I tell you that her puddings come out like great lumps of soggy dough."

Everyone laughed.

Paula said, "I'll write them out for you tomorrow." A smile of pleasure tugged at her mouth. "You're both very good for my ego. I've never had so many compliments about my cooking."

"That's not true," Shane exclaimed. "I've been giving you praise for years. You never pay attention to anything I say, that's your trouble," he groused, but there was laughter on his face.

"Oh yes I do," Paula shot back. "And I always have."

Chuckling, Shane pushed back his chair. "I'd better retreat to the kitchen, make the coffee."

"I'll assist you," Sonny said, springing up, walking out after him.

Elaine sat back in the chair, studying Paula. How arresting and unusual her looks were. She wondered how old she was. Earlier, Elaine had decided she must be in her late twenties, perhaps even thirty. But now, in the soft candle-light, Paula looked much younger than that; her face held the vulnerability of a little girl's, and she was most appealing. Conscious she was staring rudely, Elaine said, "You're a beautiful woman, Paula, and so very accomplished. No wonder he's miserable most of the time."

Paula instantly stiffened, put down her glass unsteadily. "I'm afraid I'm not following you."

Elaine blurted out, "Shane . . . he's crazy about you! It's written all over his face, and reflected in everything he says. What a pity you're so far away in England. That's what I was getting at earlier—when we were in the kitchen."

Paula was stunned. She managed, "Oh but, Elaine, we're just old friends, childhood friends."

For a split second Elaine thought Paula was joking, continuing the banter which had punctuated the good talk during dinner. Then she saw the horrified expression on Paula's face. "Oh my God, I've said the wrong thing obviously.

I'm so sorry. I just assumed you and Shane were having . . ." Her voice trailed off miserably.

Paula pushed back her sense of dismay. "Please don't look so stricken, Elaine. It's all right, really it is. I understand. You've simply mistaken Shane's brotherly affection for me, read it to mean something else, something entirely different. Anybody could make that error."

There was an awkward silence as the two women regarded each other. Both were at a loss for words.

Elaine cleared her throat. "Now I've gone and spoiled a lovely evening . . . me and my big mouth." Her expression was chagrined, apologetic. "Sonny says my mouth's always open and my foot's always in it. He's right."

Wanting to make her feel comfortable, Paula murmured softly, "Oh please, Elaine, don't be embarrassed. I'm not. I like you, and I do want us to be friends. And look here, why wouldn't you jump to conclusions. After all, I am staying here with him, living under the same roof, and we are rather free and easy with each other. But then we grew up together, and we've been around each other all of our lives. There's a certain kind of naturalness between us, and it could easily be misinterpreted. But our relationship is not what you think." Paula attempted a laugh, glanced down at her hands. "I've just realized I'm not wearing my rings tonight, and we haven't discussed my personal life, so you couldn't possibly know that I'm married."

"Oh well, then that explains everything!" Elaine cried, immediately flushing. She shook her head. "There I go again . . . Forgive me, Paula. My apologies. I'm saying all the wrong things tonight. I've probably had far too much to drink."

Paula summoned another light, dismissive laugh. "I think we ought to talk about something else, don't you? Shane and Sonny will be back at any moment."

"Agreed. And please don't say anything to Shane . . . about what I assumed. He'll think I'm a real busybody."

"Of course I won't say anything," Paula reassured her. She rose. "Let's go and sit by the fire."

As the two of them walked across the floor, Paula slipped her arm through Elaine's companionably, said in a low voice, "Try not to look so upset, so worried. Shane'll spot that straightaway. He's very intuitive. It's the Celt in him, I suppose. When I was little I actually believed he could read my mind . . . he was always second-guessing me in the most maddening way."

Elaine merely smiled at this remark as she lowered herself into a chair. Although she had recovered some of her composure, she was cursing herself under her breath. How stupid she had been to presume they were having an affair. But who wouldn't think that . . . there *was* an intimacy between them, a kind of bonding, and Shane devoured Paula with his eyes, hung on to her every word. It was transparent that he was in love with her, no matter what Paula believed. And who's *she* kidding? Only herself. Well, self-delusion is a very human trait, Elaine thought, and stole a look at Paula, who sat in the chair opposite. Whether she knows it or not, she adores him. And not just as an old friend would . . . it's much more than that, more complex, and it runs deeper. Still, perhaps she hasn't realized the extent of her feelings for him. And *I* ought not to have said anything. Elaine chastised herself again.

But a few seconds later, when Shane brought the tray of coffee to the fireplace, Elaine saw Paula's eyes instantly fly to his face, detected curiosity and a new and avid interest glittering in them. Elaine thought: Who knows, maybe I wasn't so foolish—maybe I've done them both a big favor by speaking out of turn.

Shane served the coffee. Sonny poured cognac, and ten minutes later he fetched his guitar and began to play. He was a classical guitarist and immensely talented, and the others sat back, captivated by his playing and his music, entranced by the magic he created for them.

Paula was only half-listening. She was thankful not to have to make conversation. Her mind was in a turmoil. Elaine had stunned her, and much more than she had permitted the other woman to see. But the shock was receding and she tried to sort out her troubled thoughts.

She was positive that Elaine had simply misunderstood Shane's attitude, his behavior toward her. On the other hand, what if Elaine was correct? Elaine had asserted that her marriage explained everything—meaning, of course, that it explained Shane's unhappiness, which they had apparently detected. Paula suddenly remembered the incomplete thought she had had that afternoon when she had been dozing on the sofa. She had been dwelling on the past few days, thinking that Shane was his old self, the way he was before her marriage. Something had clicked in her head, but then she had fallen asleep. Now that thought became whole, fully formed. *Shane had changed, had dropped her, the moment her engagement to Jim had been announced.* Why? Because he was jealous. That was the obvious explanation. How stupid she had been not to recognize this before tonight. But why hadn't Shane made it clear to her that he cared for her, when she was still free? Perhaps he had not understood that, until it was too late. It all made sense suddenly.

Paula leaned back in the chair, shattered by her conclusions. She closed her eyes, letting the music lap over her. She thought of Shane. He sat only a few feet away from her. What were his thoughts and emotions at this moment? Was he really in love with her? Crazy about her, so Elaine had said. Paula's heart clenched. And what about me? How do I feel about Shane? Am I unconsciously responding to vibrations emanating from him? Or am *I* in love with *him?* . . . Have I always been in love with him without knowing it? She tried to examine her innermost emotions, take stock of her feelings. She floundered.

They left at eleven forty-five.

Shane saw them out.

She knew what she was going to do.

Rising, she walked over to the chest, retrieved the bottle of cognac, carried it back to the fireside. She refilled their brandy balloons, placed the bottle in the center of the coffee table, threw a couple of logs onto the fire.

Then she sat down on the sofa to wait for him.

A few minutes later she heard his step, glanced around as he came in. She smiled across the room at him.

Shane faltered, surprised to see her sitting there, holding another drink. He frowned. "Are you planning to stay up all night? I would've thought you'd be half dead by now. It's been a long day, you worked so hard in the kitchen, shouldn't we go—"

"I just got a second wind!" she cried, cutting him off before he suggested they go to sleep. "I'm having a nightcap. I've poured one for you. Aren't you going to join me?" When he did not reply, she laughed gaily. "Oh, don't be such an old spoilsport, Shane."

He hesitated fractionally. He was afraid of being alone with her. He had been much too aware of her this evening. His desire for her had flared time and time again. His emotions were near the surface. He had sunk a lot of booze. He suddenly wasn't sure whether he could trust himself with her. This thought instantly annoyed him. He wasn't a callow youth, out on his first date, itching to make a conquest. He was a grown man. And he was with the girl he had known all his life. Yes, he loved her. But she trusted him. He was a gentleman. And he could handle himself. Still, I ought to put an end to the evening now, he thought. He said, "Well, just one for the road. I'd planned for us to go riding tomorrow morning—bright and early."

He strolled over to the fireplace, striving to appear offhand. He reached for the drink she had poured, stepped away from the coffee table, planning to sit in the chair next to the hearth.

Paula patted the sofa. "No, sit here, Shane, next to me. I want to talk to you."

He tensed, looked at her alertly, searching her face. Her expression was neutral, placid even. It baffled him. She was usually much more animated. "Okay." He sat as far away from her as possible, squashed himself into the opposite corner of the sofa.

"Cheers," Paula said, leaning closer, knocking her glass against his.

"Cheers." Their hands accidentally touched as they lifted their glasses. He felt a spark of electricity shoot up his arm. He pushed himself even farther into the corner, crossed his legs. "What do you want to talk to me about?"

"I'd like to ask you a question."

"Go on, then . . ."

"Will you tell me the truth?"

He eyed her, suddenly wary. "It depends on the question. If I don't like it, I might be evasive in my answer."

She gave him an odd look. "You and I always told each other the truth when we were children. We never dealt in lies then . . . I'd like it to be like that between us again."

"But it is!"

"Not really, Shane." She saw the surprise registering in his eyes. "Oh yes," she said, "it's been like old times this week, I admit, but there has been an estrangement between us for almost two years. Please don't even try to deny that." There, it was out at last. "In fact," she went on quickly, "you've been cold and distant with me for the longest time. When I asked you about your remoteness, your absence from my life, oh, ages ago now, you brushed me off with silly excuses. Pressure of work, travel, you said." Paula placed her drink on the coffee table and stared hard at him. "I never really believed you in my heart of hearts. And that brings me to my question"—she paused, her eyes stayed on his face—"and it's this: What awful thing did I do to you, to drive you out of my life? *You*—my oldest and dearest friend."

He stared back at her, unable to make any kind of response. If he told her the truth he would reveal himself, his real feelings. If he lied, he would hate himself for doing so. Anyway, she was clever. She would spot the lie immediately. He swallowed, put his drink down, looked ahead at the fire, his face reflective. Better to be silent.

Neither of them spoke for a while.

Paula, her eyes fixed on him, knew suddenly what his terrible dilemma was. Oh my darling, she thought, open your heart to me, tell me everything. Her love for Shane flowed through her, sweeping all else aside. She caught her breath in astonishment as she finally acknowledged her feelings. She longed to put her arms around him, to expunge the sadness on his face with her kisses.

The silence lengthened.

Paula said softly, "I realize how difficult it is for you to answer my question." There was only the merest hesitation before she finished, "And so I will do it for you. You dropped me because I became engaged to Jim and then married him shortly afterward."

Still he did not dare open his mouth, afraid of giving himself away. So she had guessed. But exactly how *much* had she guessed. He blinked, continuing to focus on the dancing flames. He knew he could not let her see his face until he had wiped it clean of all emotion.

Eventually he half-turned to her, said slowly, in a voice that was strangely hoarse, "Yes, that's the reason I put distance between us, Paula. Perhaps I was wrong to do that. But . . . you see . . . I thought . . . that Jim would resent me, yes, and that you would too. After all, why would either of you want an old chum like me loitering on your doorstep . . ." He left the sentence unfinished.

"Shane . . . you're not telling me the truth . . . you know you're not, and so do I."

It was the inflection of her voice that caught his attention, prompted him to swing his head. In the bright glow of the firelight the pallor of her face had acquired a curious luminosity, a pearly sheen. The violet eyes had darkened, burned with an unfamiliar look he could not fathom. He noticed a vein pulsing rapidly in her neck. She parted her lips as if to say something, but remained silent. *That expression in her eyes.* Again it struck him with unusual force. His desire for her raged through him. His heart thudded, an internal shaking gripped him. It took all of his self-control to remain seated, to stay away from her. Then he knew what he must do—he must get up, walk out, leave her. But he found he could not move.

They gazed at each other.

Paula saw his love, no longer concealed, leaping out from his brilliantly black eyes. Instantaneously Shane saw her love fully revealed, saw the yearning on her face, the longing and desire that hitherto had been only his to disguise, to withhold.

The shock of recognition transfixed him.

And then with sureness, absolute certainty, they moved at precisely the same moment.

They were in each other's arms. Their mouths met. Her lips were warm and soft and they parted slightly, welcomed him. Their tongues grazed, caressed, lay still. He pushed her down onto the mound of pillows, his left hand holding the nape of her neck, his right smoothing her hair away from her face, stroking her cheek, her long neck. Her hands pressed into his shoulder blades, then moved up into his hair, strong and firm on his scalp. He began to kiss her as he had wanted to kiss her for so long, with passion and force, his mouth hard and demanding on hers, his tongue thrusting, their breath, their saliva, mingling. But unexpectedly his kisses became gentle, tender, as he moved his hand onto her breast. He held it firmly, then slowly stroked it until the nipple sprang up hard under his fingers. His heart was slamming against hers.

They pulled apart at last, their breathing labored. He looked down into her face. His eyes impaled hers. She reached up, touched his face, traced one finger across the line of his long upper lip under the mustache.

Shane stood up, undressed rapidly, flung his clothes onto the chair. Paula did the same, and they came together on the sofa with extreme urgency, their hands clutching at each other. He took her in his arms and held her tightly against his chest, kissing her face, her hair, her shoulders. Then he pushed himself up on one elbow, bent over her. How well he knew this body. He had watched it grow from infant to child to young woman. But he had never seen it like this—entirely naked, every inch of it exposed to him, waiting for him. He let his hand slide down over her high, firm breasts, onto her flat stomach, along the edge of her outer thigh, then her inner thigh, smoothing, caressing, touching every part of her until they came to rest on that soft black vee of hair that concealed the core of her womanhood. He covered it with his entire hand, moved his body so that he could rest his face against her thigh. His fingers seemed to move of their own accord, gently seeking, probing, learning her. And finally he brought his mouth down to join with his fingers in their tender exploration.

Shane felt her immediately stiffen. He stopped, lifted his head, stared up along the slender stretch of her body, met her widening eyes. She was watching him intently, her expression baffled, alarmed. He smiled. So much for her marriage. His way of loving her, giving her pleasure, was seemingly new, and most transparently so. This sudden insight, the thought of her inexperience, delighted and thrilled him. At least no other man had touched her thus.

Her tenseness increased. She tried to raise herself on her elbows, opened her mouth to speak.

He murmured, "Be still, let me love you."

"But you, what about you?" she whispered.

"What's a few more minutes after all the years I've waited for you."

Paula fell back against the cushions, sighing lightly. She closed her eyes, let her body go limp, allowed him to do as he wished with her. Her senses were beginning to reel, not only from the suddenness with which they had come together, but from his passion and sensuality. The way Shane was kissing and touching every part of her was unfamiliar, erotic. With his knowledge, expertise, and sensitivity he knew exactly how to arouse her fully. He excited her as she had never been excited before, and she opened up to him uninhibitedly. Quiver upon quiver ran through her as his mouth and fingers loved her with delicacy, then fervency, and always with consummate skill. They seemed to transmit a scorching heat, struck the core of her being with an exquisite sensation that she had never known had existed until this moment. The heat was spreading, searing her body. "Oh, Shane, Shane, please don't stop," she gasped, unaware that she had spoken.

He could not answer unless he stopped, and he could not stop now. He was being carried along by her mounting excitement. It matched his own. He was aroused as he had never been before, and her desire for him was thrilling, a powerful aphrodisiac. He intensified his concentration on her, savoring the warmth of her, bringing her to the pinnacle of ecstasy. He knew that any moment she would spasm. She did, and he lifted himself on top of her, joined himself to her with a power and force that made them both cry out. She clung to him, screamed his name. He brought his mouth down hard on hers. She cleaved to him, her body arching. They began to move in unison, their mutual passion rising.

Shane opened his eyes. The room was brilliant with light. And he who had so recently craved darkness now wanted that light . . . blinding, glittering light. He wanted to see her face, catch every flicker of emotion that crossed it, needed to know that it truly was she whom he was loving. He pushed himself up, his hands braced on each side of her, and she lifted her lids, staring into his face. He stared back. He began to move again and with rapidity and she followed his lead and not once did his searching eyes leave hers. Suddenly he slowed the rhythm, wanting to prolong their joining.

He suddenly understood that this went far, far beyond mere sexual possession. He was possessing her soul, her heart, her mind, as she was possessing his. She was his dreamlike child of his childhood dreams . . . in his arms at last . . . truly his at last. She belonged to him now. He held the world in his arms. The pain he had lived with ceased abruptly. His old life fell away . . . down . . . down . . . into a dark void . . . A new life was beginning . . . he was someone entirely new. He was a complete man . . . made whole as he came up . . . up into the blinding, blinding light where she waited in the center of the radiance.

They were mesmerized by each other. Their eyes locked, became wider as their scrutiny intensified. They looked deeper, deeper still, endeavoring to convey the extent and strength of their emotions, and they saw into infinity, saw their own souls and each other's. And everything was made clear.

She is my life, he thought. *And oh the blessed peace of it.*

She thought: *There is only Shane. There only ever has been Shane.*

He started to move against her, slowly at first and then more urgently and without restraint. She matched him, was as unrestrained as he. Their bodies entwined. Their mouths joined. They became one.

As he felt his life's essence flowing through him into her, he cried out, "I love you, I have always loved you, I will love you until the day I die."

Shane's bedroom was much larger and more spacious than the one he had given her, but it was warm because the entire barn was centrally heated.

As in her room, a huge brass bed dominated the space. Paula now lay propped up against the mound of snowy pillows, a down comforter tucked around her chest, only her bare shoulders revealed. She sighed, filled with contentment and an extraordinary feeling of inner peace, and of completeness. The physical release she had experienced with Shane was wholly new to her. She had never achieved satisfaction before, and she marveled at him, at herself, and at their lovemaking. How unselfish and tender he was, and oh how she had responded to his emotion, to his yearning desire for her. And because of his genuine understanding of her, his caring, their loving had been natural, uninhibited, full of exultation and joyousness, a true bonding in every way.

When they finally doused the lights in the main room and crept upstairs carrying their clothes, she had believed their mutual passion was entirely spent. Exhausted, they had lain here in this great bed, their bodies touching, holding hands under the sheet, and they had not stopped talking. And then quite suddenly their desire for each other had flared unexpectedly, and they had made love for the second time with the same urgent need and breathlessness.

Shane had turned on the lamp, thrown back the bedclothes, telling her he must look at her, know that it was really she, must witness the emotions he was evoking in her. The kissing, the touching had been unhurried and voluptuous, and again he had brought her to that blissful state of fulfillment before taking her to him, and had led her into new regions, murmuring what he wanted, showing her how to further excite him, love him as he had loved her. And she had done so willingly, lovingly, taking pleasure from his pleasure. But he had stopped her when he was on the brink, had pulled her on top of him, his body thrusting upward to join with hers. And together they had reached greater heights of rapture than the first time.

Shane had finally switched off the lamp and, wrapped in each other's arms, they had tried to sleep, but it had eluded them. They were too keyed up and conscious of each other, needed to prolong their newfound intimacy. And so they had begun to talk in the dark, and then a few minutes ago Shane had gone downstairs to make tea for them.

Paula leaned forward and glanced at the clock on the small campaign chest at his side of the bed. It was nearly four. We made love endlessly, she thought, but not mindlessly. Oh no, not mindlessly at all. She had not realized until tonight how beautiful the sexual union between a man and a woman could be. In fact, she had always thought that sex was not what it was cracked up to be. How wrong she had been. But it has to be the right man with the right woman, she said under her breath. She sank into the pillows, another sigh escaping as she waited for Shane to come back.

He did so a moment or two later, carrying a laden tray and singing at the top of his voice.

"Who do you think you are? A pop star?" she cried, sitting up in bed, grinning at him.

His answer was to gyrate his body at her several times and leer in an exaggerated fashion.

He brought her the mug of tea and the plate of ginger biscuits she had requested, put his own tea and chocolate biscuits on his bedside chest. Continuing to hum the melody, he slipped off his robe, threw it across a nearby chair.

She looked at his broad back, massive shoulders, and strong arms, and admiringly so. He was a big, well-built man, and she had seen him in swimming trunks for years. So why did his powerful physique seem so startling to her tonight? Because now she really *knew* him? Because she had learned about his body as he had hers, and in the most intimate way?

As he swung around he noticed that she was staring at him.

"What's wrong?" he asked.

"Nothing. I was just thinking I've never seen you so brown." She giggled. "But you've got a white bottom."

"And you too, madame, will have a brown back and a white bottom by this time next week." He strode over to the bed, unself-conscious in his nakedness, and got in next to her, kissed her cheek. "If I've got anything to do with it, that is."

"Oh," was all she said, gazing at him.

"Yes. I have to go to Barbados on Tuesday. Come with me, Paula." His eyes appealed.

"Oh, Shane, what a lovely idea. Of course, I'll come with you." Her face instantly dropped. "But I couldn't get away until Wednesday."

"That's all right." He turned to get his mug of tea, took a sip. "It'll give me a chance to do some of my work. Actually, I will have to spend some time every morning in the administrative offices. But we'll have the afternoons . . . and all those beautiful nights." His smile was suggestive, his dancing black eyes wickedly teasing.

She said, with a small smile, "I've been dying to go to Barbados—to see the Harte boutique."

He lifted his brows. "Aha, so that's why you agreed, and so readily. And I thought you were after my body again."

Paula gave him a light, playful punch on his arm. "Oh, you!" She drank her tea. It tasted good, hot and refreshing. And she felt good. No, wonderful. And filled with wonderment. She reached out, took a chocolate biscuit from the plate on his lap, munched it, then took another.

"I wonder what a psychiatrist would make of that?" Shane said.

"Make of what?"

"This constant desire of yours to eat off my plate. You've been doing it all of your life, and perhaps it has some hidden sexual meaning. Do you think it's a form of oral gratification, linked in some way to me and your feelings for me?"

She threw back her head and laughed, enjoying him, being with him. "I don't know. And I'll try to stop doing it, but childhood habits are hard to break. As a matter of fact, very seriously, I've really got to curb my appetite. I haven't stopped eating since I've been with you. Anyone would think I've been on a starvation diet."

Shane merely smiled, thought: You have, my darling, in more ways than you know.

They finished their tea and biscuits, continuing to chat about the trip to Barbados, and Shane was delighted she was so obviously thrilled and excited about the prospect of spending five days with him in the sun. At one moment Shane got out of bed, found his cigarettes, and opened the window. "You don't mind if I smoke, do you?" he asked, climbing back into bed.

"Not at all." Paula edged closer to him, so that their legs touched and their shoulders grazed, wanting the closeness of him.

"Happy, darling?" he asked, glancing at her through the corner of his eye.

"Very happy. Are you?"

"As never before."

There was a short silence, then Paula confessed, "I've never made love like that before."

"I know you haven't."

"Was it that obvious . . . my inexperience?"

He chuckled, squeezed her hand, said nothing.

She said, "But you're *very* experienced, Shane." She stole a look at his face. Jealousy, an unfamiliar feeling, trickled through her. "You've had a lot of women."

He was not certain if this last remark was a question or a statement. "You've heard all the gossip about me and my romantic escapades over the years."

"The stories were all true, then?"

"Yes."

"Why not me, Shane?"

"That's fairly obvious, easy to answer. Because of Emma and Blackie, their relationship, the closeness and involvement of our two families. But even if I'd understood my true feelings for you, Paula, I wouldn't have dared come near you, tried to make love to you. I'd have been skinned alive, and you know I would." He thought of Dorothea Mallet's words, added, "Before your marriage, you were sort of—well, the crown princess of the three clans. And, therefore, inviolate. A man doesn't sleep with a woman like you, have an affair with her. He proposes marriage. Sadly, regrettably, I didn't know that I wanted you desperately, or how I felt about you when you were available, unattached. I was too close to you, I suppose."

"I understand." She looked at his face. A feeling of possessiveness came over her, and the jealousy intensified. She asked softly, "Those other women . . . did you make love with them the same way you made love with me tonight?"

He was momentarily startled by the question. He was on the verge of lying, not wishing to hurt or upset her, and then he knew he should be honest. Opting for the cold truth, he said, "Yes, sometimes, but not always, not with all of them. You and I made love in the most personal and intimate way there is, Paula. Most of my former girlfriends didn't arouse that kind of desire, that need in me—as you do. Oral sex is . . . well, *extremely* intimate, as I just said. I've got to be very emotionally committed to want that." He half-smiled. "It's not something I have ever been able to do indiscriminately, Paula."

She nodded. "I think that it probably springs from the urge and the desire and the compulsion to totally possess the other person."

"Oh yes, yes, it does." He gave her a penetrating glance.

"Since you've been in New York—" She paused, hating herself for prying, but she could not help it. She cleared her throat. "Have you had a lot of affairs?"

"No."

"Why not?"

"Because of you." Shane drew on his cigarette, exhaled, said, "My bedroom liaisons have been pretty disastrous ever since the day I understood that I loved you." He turned his head, looked deeply into her eyes. "Actually, I've had a lot of trouble in that direction . . . I've been impotent."

He saw the surprise and dismay cross her face. She stiffened against him slightly, but she said not one word.

Shane went on, "I managed to make it occasionally, if the room was dark and my partner did not shatter my fragile fantasy . . . my fantasy that it was you whom I was with. If I could hold the image of you in my mind, then it was all right. But for the most part it's been bloody difficult."

Without mentioning names, he told her then about his experience in Harrogate the afternoon of the christening, and recounted other devastating incidents. He felt neither shame nor embarrassment talking to Paula in this most self-revealing manner. He was glad to unburden himself, and as he continued to speak he acknowledged that he was only following his old pattern of confiding in her, sharing his secrets with her as he had when they were children.

Once he had finished, Paula reached up, put her arms around his neck, held him close. "Oh, Shane, Shane darling, I'm so sorry I caused you such pain and heartache."

He stroked her head, pressed it closer to his shoulder with one hand. "It was hardly your fault." He then asked softly, "When did you discover how you felt about me?"

"I've been very conscious of you since I came to New York. Last night, then again this evening, the strangest feelings began to stir in me. I realized I desired you sexually, wanted you to make love to me, and I to you. Suddenly— when we were talking after Elaine and Sonny left—it dawned on me that I was in love with you."

He did not speak for a few seconds, then he said, "I didn't bring you up here to seduce you, Pau—"

"I know that!"

"I just wanted to be with you, spend time with you. I've missed you very much." There was a short pause. "I've had a golden rule for years—no married women. I never wanted to take something that belonged to another man."

"I believe I belong to myself," she said.

Shane was silent. He was eaten up with curiosity about her marriage, and his jealousy of Jim was rife, but he was reluctant to embark on this subject, afraid of spoiling the mood that presently existed between them.

Paula remarked evenly, "Surely you know I wouldn't be here with you like this, Shane, if I were happy in my marriage."

"Jesus, Paula, of course I do! You're not promiscuous. I know you'd never play around just for the sake of it." He scowled, eyed her closely through his narrowed gaze. "It's not working, then?"

"No. I've tried, Shane, God knows I've tried. I'm not blaming Jim. I think it takes two to create a disaster. I don't hate him, he's not a bad person. We're not right together, that's all there is to it. We're incompatible in every way." She bit her inner lip. "I'd like to leave it at that . . . for tonight, anyway. All of a sudden I don't want to talk about my marriage."

"I know, darling, I know."

For a short while they were silent, lost in their own reflections. But eventually Paula murmured, "Oh, Shane, what a mess I've made. If only we could turn the clock back."

"Ah, but that's not possible . . . and time is not so important, you know. And you mustn't think about yesterday or tomorrow, only today. Anyway, time isn't portioned out and then encased in little capsules. Time is like a river. The past, the present, the future all flow together to become one long continuing and never-ending stream. We get echoes of the past every day of our lives, and we see images of the future as we live in the present. Time gone and time yet to come is all around us, Paula, and time is a dimension unto itself."

She looked up into his familiar and well-loved face, and in her mind's eye she saw the man as he had been as a boy, recalled his preoccupation with the Celt in himself and his Celtic forebears and Celtic legend. That old dreamy look born of his mysticism filled his eyes, and his deep introspection was evi- dent in his expression and she knew that he was lost somewhere in the far, far distant past. And then he blinked, gave her a funny little lopsided smile—one she remembered so well. The man instantly became that small boy at Heron's Nest, and their childhood was all around them, encompassing them, filling this room. And she knew that Shane was correct in the things he had said about time being like a flowing river, and she reached out and touched his arm and told him this.

He said slowly, thoughtfully, "And there's another thing, Paula. Life has its own intricate pattern . . . There is a grand design, really. What has already happened in our lives was meant to happen, perhaps to show us the way, lead us to each other. And the future is already here with us, *now,* at this very moment, whether we're aware of it or not." He put his hand under her chin, lifted her face to his, looked deeply into her eyes. "And we're not going to think about anything except this weekend. We'll take each day after that as it comes." He leaned into her, kissed her lightly, drew back. "Don't look so serious. Life has a way of taking care of itself, and I have a feeling that we are going to do just fine together."

Her throat tightened with a rush of emotion. She clung to him, whispered, "I love you so much, Shane. How could I have ever not known that!"

"You do now, and that's all that matters, isn't it?"

Thirty-Six

She arrived in Barbados on Wednesday afternoon.

As she walked out of customs, carrying her suit jacket over her arm and clutching her traveling bag, she thought that he had not come to meet her after all. Disappointment replaced anticipation. She looked around, seeking a chauffeur or someone wearing the uniform of the Coral Cove Hotel whom he may have sent in his place.

The porter trailing behind her, carrying her large case, asked if she wanted a taxi. She explained she was expecting to be met, then peered again at the blur of people crowding the busy airport entrance.

Paula saw Shane before he saw her.

He came barreling through the main glass doors, looking anxious. She stood stock still, taut with excitement. Her heart began to clatter unreasonably. She had been with him on Monday night. Two days ago. But seeing him now was a shock. Every detail of his appearance leapt out at her, as though she was observing a total stranger, someone she did not know. His wavy hair, longish and curling down onto his neck, the well-defined brows and the distinctive mustache all appeared much blacker, and his brilliant eyes were like pieces of onyx in his tan face. Even the cleft in his chin seemed more pronounced. She saw that he wore a beautifully cut cream silk suit, a cream shirt with fine burgundy stripes and a burgundy tie. A silk handkerchief of the same wine color flared in his breast pocket. His brown loafers gleamed. He was immaculate from head to toe. But he was the same old Shane. It was she who was new. The new Paula who was in love with him. He was the only man she wanted.

Finally he spotted her and pushed through the crowd, purposeful, confident. He was there, towering above her, grinning, his eyes filled with laughter.

She felt weak at the knees.

"Darling," he said, "I'm sorry. I cut it fine, as usual."

She could not speak, just stood there, smiling up at him inanely.

He bent to kiss her cheek, and then took her arm, motioned for the porter to follow them, bustled her outside.

A chauffeur leaning against the hood of a silver-gray Cadillac sprang forward, opened the passenger door, stowed the suitcase in the trunk. Shane tipped the porter, helped her into the car, climbed in after her. He pressed a button. The glass partition behind the driver's seat closed. As the car slid noiselessly away from the curb he put his arm around her, tilted her face to his. He stared at her, as if he had not seen her for years. She stared back, saw her own reflection mirrored in his glistening black eyes. Her mouth went dry as he bent toward her. And as his tongue slid past her parched lips to touch hers, blood rushed through her. She felt dizzy. His grip on her tightened. Her arms went around his neck. Her hands slipped up into his thick hair. She knew he was terribly excited. But then, so was she.

Shane held her away from him, shaking his head, half-laughing. "I think I'd better exercise a bit of restraint here, otherwise I'll end up making love to you on the back seat and that would cause a scandal." He held her eyes. He seemed unexpectedly amused at them both. "You do get me hot and bothered, lady."

"It works both ways, you know."

Smiling, he lit a cigarette, asked her if she had had a good flight, and then began to talk effortlessly about the island, pointing out interesting landmarks, giving her a brief history of Barbados. For the next half hour or so he talked incessantly, reached out to squeeze her hand from time to time.

"Coral Cove is on the west side of the island," Shane was saying. "It's not far from the Sandy Lane Hotel, which we'll be passing in a few seconds. I'll take you there to lunch one day—it's a lovely spot. Anyway, our place is located in the area known as the Platinum Coast, so called because of its sandy white beaches. I hope you're going to like it."

"Oh, Shane, I know I will, but I'd be happy anywhere with you, darling."

His eyes instantly swiveled to hers. "Would you really, Paula?"

"Yes, Shane."

"Love me?"

"Madly."

"You'd better."

"And you?"

"I'm crazy about you, darling. So crazily, overwhelmingly in love with you I'll never let you go," he replied, his voice light. And then he took hold of her hand tightly and his expression and his voice changed. "I mean that, Paula. I won't let you go. *Never.*"

Startled, she swallowed, not knowing what to say. England and her life there, momentarily forgotten in her euphoria at being with him, loomed hideously. She met his piercing gaze, said haltingly, "There're a lot of prob—"

He covered her mouth with his large, sunburned hand, shook his head. "Sorry, darling, I shouldn't have said that. At least, not now." He gave her his cheeky, boyish grin. "We're not going to even think about problems, never mind talk about them, for the next few days. There'll be plenty of time for that when we're back in New York."

And before she could reply, the car was slowing down. The chauffeur turned in through iron gates and as the Cadillac swept on she caught a glimpse of the name Coral Cove. A moment later, at the end of the short driveway, they came to a standstill in front of the hotel.

The intense heat hit her as Shane helped her out of the air-conditioned car. She looked around. Coral Cove was larger than she had expected, painted white and pale pink on the outside. She could see it was set in the middle of lush, exotic gardens. Just beyond the edge of the green lawns lay a stretch of silver sand and the turquoise ocean glittering in the sunshine.

"Oh, Shane, it's beautiful," she exclaimed as he looked at her expectantly, his eyes eager.

He nodded, took her elbow. "I think so—and thanks. But come on, it's bloody hot outside at this time of day."

He led her through the spacious, airy lobby, washed in white and furnished with rattan pieces and immense tropical plants in ceramic tubs. Ceiling fans whirred pleasantly, creating a gentle breeze, and the ambiance was cool, shady, welcoming.

Even though she wanted to stop and look around, Shane would not permit her to linger.

He whisked her smartly up to the suite, and once they were inside he pulled her into his arms roughly, began to kiss her, his hands hard on her body. Paula clung to him, returned his kisses. A loud rapping on the door interrupted this moment of intimacy, forced them apart.

Shane called, "Come in, Albert," and hurried forward to take her suitcase from the bellboy.

When they were alone, Shane said, "All this kissing's going to lead to something else any minute. And since I don't want you to think I'm a sex maniac, I'm going to show you around." He drew her into the center of the room. "Listen, I've got a whole program mapped out for you. Sun and sleep" —the impudent grin flashed, as he went on—"and Shane. Lots and lots of Shane. Day and night, nonstop. How does that sound to you?"

"Scrumptious," she said, laughing. "And so is this suite."

"I knew you'd like this particular one, Paula."

She glanced about with pleasure, noting the coral and lime accents highlighting the cool whiteness of the room, the handsome wicker furniture, the comfortable sofas covered in a pretty floral fabric.

He had filled the room with masses of flowers. Bowls and bud vases held all manner of exotic blooms that were a blaze of stunning color. "Shane . . . the flowers . . . they're beautiful." She smiled at him, reached out to touch a delicate purple spray. "Just exquisite. Thank you."

"Those are miniature orchids . . . wild orchids. But most likely you know that. They grow all over the island. Come on, let me show you the bedroom."

He propelled her through the open door and she found herself standing in another large white room, this one accented with yellow and pale blue. The furniture was of white-lacquered wood; there was a big bed, curtained in white muslin, which faced out toward the terrace that ran the length of the suite. More flowers abounded here, but something was missing, and as her glance swept from wall to wall she realized that the bedroom, like the living room, looked curiously unoccupied. It had an unlived-in air.

She turned to him. "Do you have another suite for yourself, Shane?"

"Yes, the adjoining one. I thought it was more discreet." He smiled wryly.

"Not that anyone will be deceived—hotel staffs are notorious for knowing everything that's going on." He took a key out of his pocket, opened a door, motioned her to follow him.

His suite was similar to her own, but here his possessions were strewn all over; his briefcase was on a table, a yellow sweater was thrown across the back of a chair; papers and his work littered the small desk; a bottle of scotch, an ice bucket, and glasses were arranged on a tray on a white wicker console.

"Then why bother to have another suite, if that's the case?" she asked. "I mean, our families would never be suspicious of us—we're supposed to be like brother and sister."

"Then if this is incest, give me incest anytime."

She laughed.

He sobered, added, "But you never know . . . I think it's wiser . . . just for appearances' sake, the switchboard, and the hotel register. Let's not borrow trouble unnecessarily. I've instructed the switchboard to monitor all calls for both of us. That way we won't be taken off guard." He put his arm around her, walked her through to her suite. "Don't fret, I've every intention of staying in here with you. All the time. Now, do you want to freshen up, have a drink or a cup of tea? Or would you like to pop down to see the boutique?"

"Oh, Shane, let's do that." She gave him a studiously prim look. "After all, that's the real reason I came to Barbados."

"*Rat.*"

The Harte boutique was situated on the far side of the main garden nearest to the hotel. It was the central building in a semicircle of five shops which looked out onto a grassy lawn. Here a fountain played in the center. Flower beds added bright splashes of color around the edge of the smooth clipped lawn.

A feeling of excitement trickled through Paula. There it was, the familiar and distinctive lettering that read *E. Harte,* staring out at her above the bright pink door. The large windows on either side were well dressed, eye-catching, most professionally done.

She grabbed Shane's arm. "I know it's only a boutique, and nothing like our large department stores, but I feel so proud, Shane. Here we are—in the Caribbean! Harte's has another branch. I do wish Grandy could see it. She'd be as thrilled as I am."

"Yes, she would, and I know what you mean. It's a combination of things —pride of ownership, gratification, a sense of tremendous satisfaction. And don't forget, this is *yours,* Paula, as the other boutiques in our hotel chain will be."

"Merry thought of the idea, Shane, not I."

"You did all the work."

"Not according to Sarah."

"I told you last week to forget Sarah Lowther. She's jealous of you."

"Because I'm running the stores?"

"Yes. She's a nitwit. She could never handle Emma's business, and Aunt Emma has always known that. She picked the best man she had . . . you."

"If anybody else but you had said that, I'd accuse him of being a male chauvinist."

"Sorry, you know I didn't mean it the way it came out. Just a figure of speech." He gave her a pointed look. "There's nothing masculine about you, my darling, let me assure you of that. Come on, let's go inside."

He pushed open the door to the sound of tinkling bells.

Together they stepped inside and Paula caught her breath. The central area of the boutique was white with lots of chrome fixtures and the floor was made of white ceramic tiles. There was a paucity of clutter, but this starkness made an ideal background for showing off the colorful clothes and accessories. A small cantilevered staircase led to an upper floor. It was cooled by the many ceiling fans.

"Oh, Shane, you've outdone yourself," Paula exclaimed.

He gave her a delighted grin, turned to introduce her to Marianna, the manager, and the three assistants who worked for Harte's. Paula chatted to them enthusiastically as she was given a tour. The young women were all pleasant, outgoing, well informed about fashion, and Paula found herself warming to them as they showed her the various displays, gave her a rundown on current sales, showed her the latest sales figures.

At the end of an hour, she said to Shane, "I have to buy a few things. I simply didn't get a chance to pick up everything I needed at the New York store. But, look, you don't have to wait. I can meet you back at the hotel."

"Oh, I'm in no hurry," he said with a nonchalant smile. "I haven't seen you since Monday night. You're not getting rid of me that easily. Besides, I may have something to say about the things you're going to buy."

After trying on swimsuits and other beachwear, and having received a nod of approval from Shane, Paula began to look at cocktail dresses. She threw a number of casual summer evening outfits over one arm, and then Shane joined her, picked out several items he liked. Handing them to her, he gave her a conspiratorial wink. "What about these?"

Paula made a face. "I'm not sure they're really *me*."

"Yes they are. Trust my judgment."

Not wishing to cause a fuss in the shop, she took them from him. As a child and a young girl, Paula had always striven to please Shane, to cater to his wishes, and she found this desire surfacing. It overcame her objections to the outfits he had chosen. All of the dresses and evening wear bore the Lady Hamilton label, and as Paula went back into the dressing room she could not help thinking of Sarah. Shane was correct about her cousin. Instantly she dismissed Sarah from her mind, not wanting to spoil her lighthearted mood by dwelling on unpleasant memories of their last encounter. She tried on one of the outfits and returned to the main area of the boutique.

As she swung around, she suddenly liked her reflection in the long mirrored wall. He obviously did. He was nodding emphatically. He told her she looked sensational.

Paula stood in front of the glass, studying the dress. It was short, made of the deepest blue chiffon, and was simply styled, with only one shoulder and a ruched effect over the bodice. Though it lacked the hard-edged chic she usually favored, it was flattering, feminine, and curiously sexy in the way in which it clung to her body. It was a wholly new look for her, but the color was glorious.

Shane enthused over a white silk pant suit he had selected but told her to forget the short red dress he had pulled off a rack. In the end, she bought two of his choices, the blue and the white, and a long yellow shift made of silk jersey trimmed with violet ribbons. He waited patiently as she tried on sandals, settled on several pairs, and then picked up a couple of straw hats and added these to her purchases. After complimenting Marianna on the way she was running the boutique, Paula promised to visit them the following day.

They meandered around the semicircle of boutiques, window-shopping. Paula said, "Our layout is stunning, Shane. Merry showed me the renderings, but one can never really tell from drawings. Thank you for making our boutique so special."

"I'm notorious for pleasing those I love and adore," he said.

Slowly they strolled back to the hotel. Shane could not help smiling as he noticed the way Paula's eyes swung from side to side, scrutinizing the many and varied tropical plants, flowering shrubs, and unusual blooms indigenous to the island.

"Well," he said, "I'll know where to find you—if you're missing in the next few days. Did you pack a trowel?"

"No, and it's odd, Shane, I have no desire to do any gardening." This was true, and she was surprised at herself. She glanced up at him. "All I want is to be with you."

He put his arm around her shoulder, kissed the top of her head. "Let's go up to the suite, shall we?"

She lay within the circle of his arms.

The bedroom was dusky, shadow-filled. The filmy muslin curtains around the bed stirred gently in the soft breeze, and beyond the open louvered doors leading out to the terrace the sky had turned to a deep pavonian blue. The only sounds were the rustling of the palm trees and the faint distant roar of the ocean.

The bosky stillness was soothing after their frantic and impassioned love-making, and she luxuriated in it, and in her own sense of fulfillment. How surprising she was with him. Whenever they made love she felt completely satiated as they drew apart, exhausted, staring in astonishment. But the minute Shane was aroused again, so was she, and her feverishness echoed his. And each time he took her they reached a greater pitch of excitement and the ultimate in gratification.

A tiny sigh of contentment trickled through Paula. She could no longer recognize herself. Only a few days of loving Shane . . . being loved by him . . . and she would never be the same woman again. Shane had somehow helped her to shed her old self. He had re-created her. And in so doing he had made her his.

On Tuesday she had worked frantically to be able to leave for Barbados today. She had raced between the apartment, the store, and Harte Enterprises, and had worked until three in the morning. He had rarely been out of her mind, and whatever she was doing he insinuated himself into her thoughts. Their relationship had reverted to what it had been when they were growing up. With added dimensions—sexual adoration and a deep, abiding love, that of a man for a woman, a woman for a man.

There were no jarring notes or irritating habits to contend with. Shane was a communicator. He venerated the language, verbalized everything that came into his fertile, agile, searching mind. And he never shut her out. He shared, confided, never ever withheld. She did the same. His secrets were her secrets now. Hers had been conveyed to him and in explicit detail. His responses, his thoughts, and his understanding were her great consolation. He made her feel whole, and completely female. A total woman.

She stole a look at his face. It was in repose. He drowsed. Her heart filled. What a mixture he was: impetuous, extravagant, and vain in some ways, yet intelligent, tender, loving, thoughtful, and passionate in everything he did. There was that strangely fey, mystical side to his nature which she knew sprang from the Celt in him, and he could be melancholy and brooding at times. And, yes, he had a terrible temper. In the past they had had their violent quarrels. As a child she had often been the victim of his whims and moods and temperamental outbursts. But Shane was flexible, and he could disarm and enchant her with his self-deprecating humor, his dry wit, and his sweeping, natural charm. As a man he was as complex as she was as a woman.

Suddenly she endeavored to evaluate their relationship as it stood at this moment. It was so unusual she could think of no way to describe it to herself. And then she thought: Shane and I have an intimacy of the heart and mind as well as the body. Together we are complete. I feel more married to Shane than I do to Jim.

She held herself very still, appalled at this thought. Gradually she eased herself back into it and acknowledged that it was the truth. Her mind swung to Jim.

Why did you marry him? Shane had asked her the other night in New York. *Because I was in love with him,* she had responded. Shane had admitted that she probably had been, but he had also suggested that Jim's fatal attraction might have been his name. *A Fairley was forbidden to you because of Emma's past,* Shane had ventured, and possibly he was right. She *had* believed herself to be in love with Jim, and yet now she understood that her feelings for him had never equaled her tremendous emotional bonding to Shane. She and Jim were totally different; she and Shane were incredibly alike. And she had never known what sex was all about, had never really enjoyed participating until Shane had made love to her. She had told him this. He had said nothing, had simply sighed and held her more tightly in his strong and loving arms.

Her life, her responsibilities, the complications of her business and family intruded. Suddenly the future glared her in the face like a terrible specter. She was frightened. What was going to happen to them? What would she and Shane do? Release the fear, fling aside these distressing thoughts, she told herself. For God's sake, don't dwell on your problems now. You'll spoil the next few days if you do. Enjoy this time with Shane, enjoy being free, unfettered.

She nestled closer to him, slipped her arm across his stomach, let her fingers curl against his side, bent herself into the shape of his body.

Shane stirred, opened his eyes, looked down at her. He smiled to himself, his heart full of love and tenderness for her. His dreamlike child of his childhood dreams had become his dreamlike woman. Except that she was no dream. Paula was reality. His reality. His life. She had extinguished all pain, all hurt, all of the anguish in his heart and mind. And with her he could truly be himself, expose himself, warts and all, and in a way he had never been able to do with any other woman. There had been legions of women until two years ago. Too many, really, and of too little quality. Now he belonged to Paula—as he always had in his soul and heart and his imagination. He would belong to her for the rest of his life. She owned him.

She opened her eyes, looked up at him, smiled. He smiled back, bent to kiss her, stroked her rounded breast, moved his hand down to nestle between her thighs. She reached out to touch him, knowing how much he took pleasure from the feel of her hand on him. Within the space of a few minutes they were both aroused, craving each other. Shane rolled on top of her, slipped his arms under her back, took her to him. He began to move against her slowly, looked down into her unnaturally blue eyes, marveled at the joy that lit her face. He whispered her name, spoke his love for her, his heart leaping at her swift and ardent responses. He closed his eyes, as did she, and they lost themselves in each other and their love.

The jangling telephone bell pierced the silence.

They stopped, startled, snapped open their eyes, gaped at each other. "Oh Christ!" Shane groaned. He disentangled himself, switched on the light, shot another look at her as she clutched his arm fiercely.

Sitting up, Paula exclaimed, "Maybe I'd better answer it, since we're in my suite."

"It's all right, don't look so alarmed. I told you the switchboard's monitoring all of our calls." He lifted the receiver on the fourth ring. "Shane O'Neill." He paused. "Thanks, Louanne. Put him through." He covered the mouthpiece with one hand. "It's my father," he said.

"Oh." Paula tugged at the sheet, covered herself.

Shane began to chuckle. "He can't see you lying here naked, you know."

She had the good grace to laugh. "But I feel funny. Exposed."

"You'd better be—to me." Shane said, then shouted into the phone, "Dad! Hello! How are you? What's up?" As he began to listen, he cradled the phone between his ear and his shoulder, lit a cigarette, shuffled himself up against the pillows.

"Well, I have to admit I've been expecting it, Dad, and, let's be honest, the idea does have a lot of merit. But look here, I can't go over there right now. Certainly not until January or February. I've got my hands full in New York. You know the hotel's at the most crucial stage. It would be disaster if I left. And I thought you wanted me down here in the islands over the holidays. Jesus, Dad, I can't be in two or three places at once."

Shane flicked his cigarette ash, relaxed against the pillows, listening once more. "Oh good," he interrupted. "Yes, yes, I agree. And you'll enjoy the trip. Why don't you take Mother with you?"

Paula slipped out of bed, found her dressing gown in the bathroom, slipped it on, returned to the bedroom. She began to pick up their clothes, which were scattered all over the floor. We were in a terrible hurry when we first went to bed, she thought, then sat down on a chair, watching him.

Shane, silent again, winked at her, blew her a kiss, then again he interrupted his father. He exclaimed, "I say, Dad, Paula's just this minute walked in and she wants to say hello."

Paula shook her head. She felt ridiculously—and irrationally—self-conscious.

Shane put down the phone and his cigarette, leapt out of bed, grabbed her and dragged her to the phone, whispering, "He doesn't know we've been making passionate love for the last two hours, you silly thing. It's only seven-thirty here. I'm sure he thinks we're having drinks before dinner."

Paula had no option but to take the phone. "Hello, Uncle Bryan," she said in the most normal voice she could summon. Then she fell quiet, listening to Shane's father. "Oh yes," she said after a moment, "I got in this afternoon. The hotel's simply beautiful, so is the boutique, Uncle Bryan. Shane's done a marvelous job. He's very talented. I'm most impressed." She sat down on the bed, as Bryan commenced to relay his news from London.

Eventually Paula had a chance to reply: "Then you'll be seeing Grandy before me. And Uncle Blackie. Do give them both my love. And lots of love to Auntie Geraldine and Merry. See you soon, Uncle Bryan, and have a safe trip. Here's Shane again."

He took the phone from her and she lolled across the end of the bed. Shane resumed his business conversation with his father, but after only a few minutes, he said, "All right, Dad, that's it, then. I'll be here until Monday morning. After that you can get me in New York. Love to Mother and Merry, kiss little Laura for me, and take care of yourself. And, listen, don't forget to give my love to Grandpops and Aunt Emma. Bye, Dad."

Shane hung up, looked at Paula, rolled his eyes. They burst out laughing. "Come here, you witch, you," he exclaimed, dragging her up from the end of the bed, wrapping his arms around her.

She struggled with him, still laughing and rumpling his hair. They rolled over and over on the bed, their merriment accelerating. He gasped, "My father certainly picks the wrong time to call, doesn't he? Just as we were about to have another few minutes of lovely passion."

"Few minutes!" she shrieked. "More like an hour, you mean."

"Are you complaining, or is that a testimonial?" He kissed her ear, chuckled again, mimicked her, saying, "Shane's done a marvelous job, Uncle Bryan. He's very talented. I'm most impressed." Reverting to his own voice, he murmured against her neck, "I sincerely hope Shane's done a marvelous job, that he's talented, and that you're truly impressed, sugar."

"Oh, you!" She beat her fists lightly against his chest. "You vain conceited impossible gorgeous man!"

He caught her wrists, held them tightly in his hands, peered down into her face. "But oh how that man loves you, darling." He released her suddenly, sat up.

Paula did the same. She said, "Imagine Blackie deciding to buy a hotel in Sydney. I'll bet you anything that that grandmother of mine was goading him on." She gave him a long look. "Uncle Bryan wanted you to go to Sydney, didn't he?"

"Yep. Grandfather hasn't actually bought the hotel yet. That's why he wants either Dad or me to fly there immediately, give it the once over. What I said's true, Paula, I can't get away. I'm jammed. And you don't think I'm going anywhere while you're still in New York, do you? It'll do Dad good to get away for a week or two. He said he might fly back to New York with Blackie and Emma early in December. But we'll see. I hope he takes my mother along, they'll have a good time."

Shane kissed the tip of her nose. "I'd better go and shower, get dressed, wander downstairs, check up on a few things."

He sprang off the bed, pulled her to her feet. "Would you mind meeting me downstairs when you're ready?"

"No, of course not. Where will I find you?"

"How long will it take you to dress?"

"About three quarters of an hour."

"By then I'll be waiting for you in the bar off the main lobby. You can't miss it—it's called the Aviary." He chucked her lightly under the chin. "I would've called it the Bird Cage, but I didn't want to be accused of stealing someone else's idea."

At Shane's twenty-fourth birthday party, early in June of 1965, Emma had made a comment to Paula. She had said that he had an intense glamour. Paula had not understood exactly what her grandmother had meant four years ago. She did now.

Paula was poised at the entrance to the Aviary, viewing him with unprecedented objectivity. He was at the far end, stood leaning with one elbow on the bar, one foot resting on the brass rail that encircled the base of the bar.

He was wearing black linen trousers, a black voile shirt, and a jacket of silver-gray silk. Although he was tieless, he nevertheless looked extremely well dressed, as impeccably groomed as usual. But the aura of glamour her grandmother had spoken about had little to do with his clothes, as Paula was realizing as she continued to study him unobserved. It emanated from his height and build, his natural good looks, and the force of his personality. He was in command of himself—and this room. And he has abundant charisma, Paula thought, that's what it is, and it's the kind that every politician in the world would give his eyeteeth to possess.

Shane was talking animatedly to a couple, obviously guests of the hotel, his face alive, expressive. The woman was entranced, hanging on his every word. But then, seemingly so was the man who accompanied her.

Shane happened to swing his head. He saw Paula, straightened up, excused himself graciously.

The bar was fairly busy and as they walked toward each other Paula was aware that more than one pair of female eyes followed his progress.

"I'm glad you wore the blue dress," he said, catching hold of her hand when he reached her side. He led her swiftly to a reserved table in the corner. "It looks wonderful on you. You look wonderful."

Her radiant smile, her shining eyes conveyed her pleasure and her thanks.

He said, "I thought we'd have champagne, since it's a celebration."

"What are we celebrating?"

"Finding each other again."

"Oh, Shane, that's a lovely sentiment."

A waiter appeared, opened the bottle which already stood on the table in an ice bucket, poured a little into Shane's glass. He tasted it, nodded, "It's perfect, Danny. Thank you."

"You're welcome, Mr. Shane." The smiling waiter filled their glasses, quietly moved away.

"To us," Shane said, raising his glass.

"To us, Shane." After a few seconds Paula's eyes roamed around the bar discreetly, taking in the decor. "I can see how this spot acquired its name . . . it looks exactly like the cafe in the Leeds store." Her expression was teasing.

"Our birdcages aren't half as nice as yours, though." He grinned at her. "Mind you, the artist did a good job with the murals. I must admit I do love exotic birds." His eyes swept over her suggestively.

Paula laughed at the innuendo.

Shane moved in his chair, reached into his pocket for his cigarettes. His shirt was partially open down the front and she suddenly caught the gleam of gold against his suntanned chest. She peered at him. "Goodness, is that the St. Christopher medal I gave you?"

He looked down, fingered it. "The very same."

"You haven't been wearing it, though—before tonight."

"I haven't worn it for a couple of years. I found it in the flat on Monday night when I was packing. The catch was broken. I brought it with me, had it repaired in Holetown. They just delivered it back to me half an hour ago."

"I'm glad you're wearing it again."

"Do you remember when you gave it to me?"

"When you were twenty. For your birthday eight years ago."

"And what did I give you when you were twenty?"

"A pair of antique amethyst earrings." She frowned, then laughed lightly. "Did you think I'd forgotten, Shane O'Neill?"

"I was sure you hadn't forgotten. However, I bet you don't remember what I gave you when you reached the ripe old age of five."

"Oh yes I do. A bag of blue marbles."

He sat back, looking pleased. "Correct. Which you promptly began to lose, one by one. You cried so much I had to promise to buy you another bag. But I never did, and so"—he put his hand in his jacket pocket—"here's the replacement. Sorry it's taken me so long to fulfill a boyhood promise." He dropped a small opaque plastic bag in front of her.

Laughing, enjoying his mood and flirting with him, Paula picked it up, opened the bag, dipped into it. "You are a fool, but a most adorable one—" She stopped. A pair of sapphire-and-diamond earrings, beautifully cut and of superb quality, lay glittering in her hands. "Oh, Shane, they're absolutely exquisite. Thank you, thank you so much." She kissed his cheek, added, "But you're awfully extravagant."

"So I've been told. Like them?"

"Like them! I love them. And most especially because they're from you." She pulled off the gold studs she was wearing, slipped them into her silk evening purse, took out a small mirror and put on the sapphires. She glanced at herself, admiring the earrings. "Oh, Shane, they *do* look lovely on me, don't they?"

"Almost as lovely as those uncanny eyes of yours."

She squeezed his hand. She was touched by the unexpected present, overwhelmed, really. Her throat tightened. She recalled the gifts he had given her when she had been a child. He had always been uncommonly generous, saving his pocket money for months to be able to buy something special. And he had had a knack for giving her exactly the right thing—like the earrings tonight. For a reason she could not comprehend, her eyes filled with tears.

"What's the matter, darling?" he asked gently, leaning across the table.

She shook her head, blinking. "I don't know, aren't I silly." She groped in her bag, found a handkerchief, blew her nose, gave him a watery smile.

He watched her silently, waiting for her to compose herself.

"I was thinking of our childhood," she commenced after a few seconds. "At the time, it seemed as if it would never end—all those lovely summers at Heron's Nest. But it did come to an end, just as those summers did." Before she could stop herself, she added, "As this will come to an end too."

He put his hand over hers. "Oh, darling, don't be sad."

"Our days here in the sun, this magic time . . . it's just a brief sojourn, really, Shane."

Squeezing her hand, entwining his fingers with hers, he said slowly, *"You* talk of endings . . . *I* think of beginnings. That's what this is, Paula, a beginning. Remember what I said about time? Well, this *is* the future. It's here, now. All around us. Part of the flowing river of time."

She was silent, her eyes resting on him, searching his face.

"I hadn't wanted to get into a discussion about the mess we've found ourselves in, Paula, at least, not down here. But perhaps we'd better have a talk. Would you like to do that?"

Paula nodded.

The smile settling on his face was confident, very sure. "You know how much I love you. I said in the car, earlier today, that I'd never let you go, and I won't, Paula. Our feelings for each other are too strong to be ignored. We're meant to be together for the rest of our lives. Do you agree?"

"Yes," she whispered.

"Then it's obvious what you're going to have to do. You'll have to get a divorce so that you can marry me. You do want to marry me, don't you?"

"Oh yes, Shane, very much."

He saw that her face had paled, and that her very bright supernaturally blue eyes had darkened with apprehension. "Tell me what's troubling you, Paula."

"You said I was intrepid when I was a child—but as a grown woman I'm not. I'm frightened, Shane."

"What about?" he asked, his gentleness increasing. "Come on, let's have it. If anyone can chase your fears away, surely it's me."

"I'm afraid of losing my children and of losing you."

"You know that will never happen. The three of us will be with you always."

Paula took a deep breath, plunged in. She said, "I don't think Jim will agree to a divorce."

Shane pulled back slightly, eyeing her askance. "I can't imagine his taking that attitude. Not once he knows you want to end a bad marriage."

"You don't know Jim," she interjected, her voice tense. "He's stubborn, and he can be difficult. I have a horrible feeling he's going to adopt an inflexible stance. I told you, he doesn't think there's anything wrong with our marriage. He'll use the children as a wedge, and especially if he thinks there's another man."

"He's *not* going to think there's another man in your life," Shane said quietly. "I'll be the only man you're seeing, and nobody is going to be suspicious of *me.*" He attempted a laugh. "Me, your childhood playmate!" His brows shot up. "Come on, darling, don't be so gloomy."

Paula sighed heavily. "Yes, perhaps I shouldn't anticipate." She shook her head. "Poor Jim. I feel sorry for him, actually."

"I know. But you can't build a relationship on pity, Paula. There's no reward in that for either party. You'll start regarding yourself as a martyr and he'll sink under his humiliation. You'll end up genuinely hating each other."

"I suppose you're right," she admitted, seeing the truth in his words.

"I *know* I'm right. And look here, don't start feeling guilty, either. That's another wasted emotion." He tightened his grip on her fingers. "And, anyway, you don't have one single reason to feel guilty, Paula. You've given your marriage your best efforts, done your damndest to hold it together, from what you've told me. It simply hasn't worked. And so you must end it—for Jim's sake as well as your own."

Paula bit her inner lip. Her worry flared. Then she murmured, "It may take me a while to work everything out, to get things settled properly."

"I'm aware of that, these emotional situations are never easy, but I'll wait, I'll be a model of patience. I'll be there to give you moral support. And there's another thing, we're both young. We have all the time in the world."

"Don't tempt providence, Shane!"

Shane shook his head, scoffed lightly, in amusement, "I'm not, I'm merely stating facts." Whilst he trusted her judgment, privately concurred with her assessment of Jim, he did not want to burden her further by acknowledging this. Not tonight. Instead, he wanted to dispel her gloominess by making light of her worries. And so he produced his most assured smile, adopted his most engaging manner. He exclaimed, "Let's make a pact—like we used to when we were kids."

"All right. What kind of pact?"

"Let's agree not to discuss our problems, and they *are* mine as well as yours, for the next few weeks. Two days before you return to England we'll have a long session, thrash things out. Together, we'll decide how you're going to proceed. What do you say?"

"Yes, it's a good idea. We mustn't let things get to us, must we? Otherwise we won't enjoy this precious time we have together."

"That's my girl. Shall we drink to our pact? We've hardly touched this champagne."

She nodded. He poured. They clinked glasses. Their hands automatically entwined.

His eyes were tender and warm as they rested on her. He said, after a while, "You must trust me. Trust my love, Paula."

She looked at him in surprise, remembering how her grandmother had once said that it was important to trust love. As she met Shane O'Neill's dark and steadfast gaze, saw the depth and strength of his feelings for her, Paula's fears slowly began to evaporate. Her depression lifted.

"I do trust your love, and you must trust mine." A small smile played around her mouth. "Everything *is* going to be all right. It really is, Shane, because we have each other."

But Paula was wrong. Her troubles were about to begin.

Thirty-Seven

Emma Harte stared hard at Paula, a frown knitting her brow. "I'm not sure I'm following you," she said. "What exactly do you mean when you say Christmas is going to be difficult?"

Paula said quickly, "Before I explain, I just want you to understand that he's all right, actually—"

"Who's all right?"

"Jim, Grandy. I'm afraid he's had an accident. A rather bad accident, and he's—"

"Not in that plane of his?" Emma cried, and straightened up in the chair jerkily, her frown intensifying.

"Yes. He crashed. Two weeks ago. It happened a couple of days after I got back from New York, at the beginning of December," Paula said in a rush. Wanting to allay her grandmother's worry, she hurried on, "But he was lucky, in one sense at least, since the plane came down at Yeadon Airport. They were able to pull him out of the plane before it exploded in flames."

"Oh my God!" Emma's hackles rose as she thought of Jim's narrow escape. He could so easily have been killed, and Paula might have been in the plane with him, might not have survived. Leaning forward, she asked in an urgent voice, "How badly is he injured?"

"He's broken his right leg and his left shoulder, and his ribs are cracked. He's also badly bruised. But there are no injuries that are permanently disabling or life-threatening. Obviously, though, those he has sustained are serious enough."

"No internal damage?"

"None, thank heavens, Grandy. Jim was rushed to Leeds Infirmary immediately, and he stayed there for five days, having all kinds of tests—neurological, what have you. Fortunately, the doctors didn't find a thing. Every injury is external." Paula paused, looked across at her grandmother. Worry ringed her face. She said, "He's in two casts and his ribs are taped. I've had to hire a male nurse to look after him. You see, Jim can't dress himself and he finds it awkward, almost impossible, to do the most normal things."

Emma exhaled, still reeling from the news. She exclaimed, "Why on earth didn't you tell me about this when I was in New York? Or yesterday, when I arrived in London?"

"I didn't want to worry you when you were still on your holiday, and so far away. And last night you were so excited about being back I didn't want to spoil your homecoming and the little supper my mother had planned for you here. I'd intended to mention it on our way in from the airport but—" Paula shrugged, gave her a small apologetic smile. "I decided it could easily wait until today."

"I see." Emma sat back, shaking her head. "I am sorry, Paula, this is just dreadful, simply dreadful. But we must be thankful it's not any worse, more serious than it is. He's going to be out of action for months, of course."

"Yes," Paula murmured. "The casts have to be on at least six weeks. Then he'll have to have intensive physical therapy. The muscles will atrophy from lack of use. The doctor has explained that Jim won't be able to lift his arm or put weight on his leg until those dead muscles have been built up again. It seems it'll be a good six months before he's back to normal."

"Broken bones are a lot more serious than people realize," Emma said quietly. She fixed Paula with a steely glance. "And how did it happen?"

"The engine stalled. Jim tried to land as best he could, and thankfully he was on the approach to Yeadon airstrip. But—well, he couldn't control the plane. It plunged down, virtually broke in two when it hit the ground. He's been awfully lucky."

"He has indeed." Emma's mouth tightened. "I always knew he'd have an accident in that damned plane one day, Paula. It's worried me to death." She shook her head again, her dismay apparent. "Whilst I'm upset and sorry that Jim's been hurt, I can't help feeling he's been somewhat irresponsible." She gave Paula a long and careful look. Her eyes narrowed. "He's a married man with two children, and he should not have been taking that kind of risk. Utter foolishness on his part. If only he'd given up that pile of junk when I asked him, this wouldn't have happened."

"Well, Jim is inclined to be a bit stubborn."

"That's the understatement of the year," Emma snapped. "I don't mean to sound callous or unsympathetic, but it strikes me he was putting himself in unnecessary physical danger. And why *I'll* never know. Perhaps that husband of yours will listen to me *now*. And I insist that we buy a corporate jet if we must have a plane in the family. I will not permit Jim to waltz around the skies in a flimsy light aircraft ever again. Oh no, not under any circumstances." Emma leaned back in the chair, her face grimly set in its rigid determination.

"Yes, Grandy." Paula glanced down at her hands, recognizing the implacability in that dear and familiar voice. Her grandmother was furious, and she could not blame her. Jim did lack a sense of responsibility and he had most willfully ignored everyone's pleas to get a more stable, up-to-date plane.

Suddenly realizing she had sounded harsh, Emma said rapidly, in a softer tone, "I expect poor Jim is in a lot of pain, isn't he, lovey?"

"Excruciating. The shoulder's driving him crazy. He says he's not sure which is the worst, the persistent nagging ache in the shoulder itself, or the cramp and stiffness from having his arm permanently bent in the cast. It's constricting, you know." Paula winced, recalling the past ten days, knowing how much he was genuinely suffering. Once her initial shock and fright had subsided, exasperation with him had surfaced, only to be replaced by compassion. Being inherently kind, she was doing her utmost to make him as comfortable as possible. And she had shelved the discussion about a divorce. She would have to wait until he was in better physical condition to talk about her freedom.

Emma said, "Surely the doctor has given him painkillers."

"Yes, and they help. But he says they make him feel doped up, woozy, a little out of it."

"I hate pills myself. Still, if they ease the pain, he ought to stay on them. I see what you mean about Christmas being difficult, Paula. Oh dear, this is such an added burden for you—on top of all of your work during one of our busiest seasons at the stores. Not only that, we have so many family things planned at Pennistone Royal . . . our traditional Christmas Eve with the O'Neills and the Kallinskis, lunch on Christmas Day, and Sally's wedding to Anthony—" Emma cut herself short.

Her green eyes became thoughtful. An idea came to her, and she made a snap decision. Taking command in her usual way, she exclaimed, "Running back and forth between your house and mine is going to become the bane of your life, and transporting Jim hither and yon will prove tiring. I think you'd better move everyone in with me . . . Jim, the babies, Nora, and the male nurse. I've plenty of room and, in fact, I'd rather enjoy having you all with me after my eight-month absence."

"Oh, Gran, what a wonderful idea!" Paula cried, swamped with relief. "And it's a marvelous solution." A smile broke through as she confided, "I've been panicky, wondering how I would ever cope."

Emma laughed quietly, amusement flickering on her mouth. "You'll always cope, my girl, that's your basic nature. But I don't see why your life shouldn't be made as easy as possible, since you carry enough responsibility to bury three people. Now that I'm back home, I aim to see to it that things run smoothly for you. You've had a rough few months, between business problems and all the family upsets."

"Thank you, Gran. What a lovely thought, moving into Pennistone Royal, being with *you*. Why ever didn't I think of it?"

"I suspect you've had enough on your plate these past few weeks. I'm sure Jim is not a good patient . . . too active a man to be confined in this way. Is he getting around at all?"

"No. Ever since he came home from Leeds Infirmary he's been sleeping in his den, virtually living in it—he can't navigate the stairs, for one thing. He's awfully frustrated being disabled. Even more frustrated because he can't go to the paper. He misses it."

"I'm sure he does. But he won't be able to go to work for a long time. No use fussing over that. Well, he certainly won't be able to manage the staircase at Pennistone Royal. It's too long and steep. But never mind. Hilda can turn the small parlor next to the dining room into a bedroom for him. Now, Paula, please try not to worry anymore. What's done is done. We'll have to make the best of it."

"You're right, Grandma, and moving in with you is going to make my life so much easier," Paula said, thinking that being surrounded by people was going to be a real blessing. Jim was becoming fractious because of the pain, his helplessness. He had started to complain about her work more vociferously than ever, forever grumbled about the hours she kept. And he was drinking more than he should.

Rising, Emma now walked across to the fireplace, stood with her back to it, warming herself. She and Paula were having coffee in the charming study of her Belgrave Square flat where they were both staying until they journeyed to Yorkshire the following day.

Paula glanced up at her grandmother, thinking how rested and well she looked this morning after yesterday's transatlantic flight. Emma wore a coral wool dress and pearls. Her silver hair was beautifully styled and immaculate and her makeup perfectly applied. There was a freshness and vitality about her. Paula thought: It doesn't seem possible that she is eighty years old. She looks ten years younger at least.

"You're scrutinizing me very intently," Emma said. "What's wrong with my appearance?"

"Nothing, Gran, and I was admiring you, really. You're positively blooming this morning."

"Thank you. I must admit to feeling marvelous. I'm not a bit jet-lagged." She glanced at her watch. "It's only ten o'clock. I'd better not ring Blackie just yet. He may still be sleeping. Bryan's driving him back to Harrogate later in the day, you know."

"So Merry said last night at the airport."

"It was nice having Bryan and Geraldine in Sydney for a couple of weeks," Emma now volunteered with a smile of fond recollection. "And they really enjoyed themselves. However, I was a bit disappointed that it wasn't Shane who came to negotiate the deal on the hotel they've bought."

"From what Shane said to me, November was a difficult time for him."

"Yes, Bryan mentioned it." Flashing Paula a warm and loving glance, Emma continued, "I'm glad you were able to find time to pop down to Barbados to see our boutique when Shane was there. It did you good, seemingly. You're positively blooming yourself, Paula. You look better than I've seen you for years."

"I enjoyed the trip, the little rest," Paula said, keeping her voice very steady. "I still have traces of my tan, so perhaps that's it."

Emma nodded. She studied her favorite granddaughter. Paula has become as inscrutable as I am, she thought. I'm actually having difficulty reading her at this moment. Clearing her throat, Emma said, "So . . . you and Shane are good friends again. I *am* happy about that."

Paula made no comment.

Emma, riddled with curiosity, probed, "And did he explain what it was all about, finally?"

"Pressure of work, his schedule, his traveling, as he's always said, Gran. However, I do think he was afraid of intruding—" Paula met her grandmother's quizzical gaze with a cool, direct look of complete innocence. She added in a calm voice, "You know what I mean—intruding on a couple of newlyweds. I think he was simply being diplomatic and considerate."

"Really," Emma said. A snowy brow arched. She did not believe his reasons, but she said nothing else, moved in the direction of the desk. Seating herself, she gave her attention to the three different folders Paula had arranged there earlier. Emma opened one, stared at the memorandum on top, but she was not actually reading it. Instead, she was contemplating Paula and Shane. Ever since she had heard about their rapprochement, which was no great secret, she had wondered if Shane had finally made an overt move. She had never forgotten that look on his face at the christening. A man who loved a woman the way Shane O'Neill loved her granddaughter would be unable to repress his feelings indefinitely. He would have to come out in the open. One day. He would not be able to help himself. Had he already done so? And if so, what had his reception been? She could not hazard a guess. Shane had been unreadable in New York, as Paula was now. She concentrated on Shane, whom she knew like one of her own, and thought of his nature. He was impetuous, impulsive, passionate. And what of Paula? Of course Paula would have spurned him. Would she? Yes, Emma answered herself. She is happily married. But is she?

Partially raising her eyes, Emma stole a look at Paula, surreptitiously, over the top of her glasses. There was something different about her granddaughter —she had noticed it last night. She seemed more womanly, more feminine than usual. Had there been a radical internal change? Or was it merely her outward appearance? The longer hair, the extra weight, the general air of softness she had acquired? Had a man's influence been at work? Shane's? Or was her current look simply a new style she had formulated for herself. I'm damned if I know, Emma thought. And I refuse to pry. Her life is her own. I will never interfere. I dare not. If she has anything to tell me she will do so . . . eventually.

Paula said, "I asked Alexander and Emily to prepare those reports for you, Grandy, and I've written one myself. Each folder—"

"So I see," Emma interrupted, glancing up. "Are they simply summations of business matters over the past eight months? Or have you included anything I don't already know about?"

"Oh no, Grandy, we've simply recapped everything for you, the matters we telexed you about, or discussed on the phone. There's nothing new at the moment, but I thought you ought to have the reports just to refresh your memory. Later, at your leisure."

"I don't have to refresh my memory," Emma exclaimed dryly. "I forget nothing. Thank you for going to all this trouble, though. I'm sure it goes without saying that I trust the three of you, and I'm very proud of you and your cousins. You've handled yourselves in the most exemplary manner, been extremely diligent, and, I might add, very smart in a number of instances." Emma's eyes gleamed shrewdly under the hooded lids. "And how's Gianni what's-his-name working out at Trade Winds?"

Paula could not help grinning at her grandmother's knowing expression. "He's the best antique expert Harte's has ever had," she said. "And he's done a terrific job on his trips to the Orient recently. He's worth every penny we're paying him."

"I sincerely hope so . . . Presumably he's now giving Elizabeth the divorce without causing a scandal?"

"Yes, he is, Gran."

"Alexander never did explain fully about that fuss and bother with his mother, when he rang me in Australia." Emma's eyes sharpened. "Who was Gianni going to cite instead of Marc Deboyne?"

"Oh, some Cabinet minister, I believe," Paula said, striving to sound offhand, not wanting to go into the outrageous details. "Alexander was worried that a well-known politician being involved in the divorce would simply draw additional press attention to the case, to the family."

"Good thinking." Leaning over her desk, Emma now remarked, "Talking of politicians, or rather a politician's son, have you anything to tell me about Jonathan?"

"Not one thing, Gran." Paula hesitated. "But Mr. Graves of Graves and Saunderson dug up some unpleasant personal information about Sebastian Cross." Paula grimaced. "Alexander has the report. I'm sure you don't want to read it—it's rather disgusting. Alexander will explain it to you better than I."

"I've lived with unpleasantness all of my life, Paula. However, obviously *you* prefer not to discuss it, so we'll let it go for now. I'll take it up with Alexander when he gets here later. And what about your cousin Sarah? Is she behaving herself?"

"I haven't seen her, but Emily tells me she's very snotty with her, and holding herself aloof. Apparently Sarah's become rather chummy with Allison Ridley, Winston's old girlfriend. Emily thinks that's the reason for Sarah's coldness toward her."

"I'm rather surprised," Emma muttered. "Why would Sarah take umbrage at Emily?" She looked across at Paula, and began to laugh at herself. "That's a pretty stupid comment on my part, when I think of the terrible things members of this family have done to each other." She sat back in the chair, went on, "Would you mind giving me another cup of coffee, please?"

"Of course not. Coming right up, Gran." After filling the cup, adding milk and sugar, Paula brought the coffee to the desk, hovered. She said slowly, "Look, this isn't a criticism of Emily, you know how much I love her, but she's got a ridiculous bee in her bonnet about the mess in Ireland. I'd like you to talk to her—"

"Oh, she's already mentioned it to me, Paula," Emma interrupted. "Last night, when you were on the phone to Long Meadow." Emma swallowed a smile as she observed Paula's serious expression. "Murder most foul and all that nonsense, right?"

Paula nodded.

Emma said, "I gave her a little lecture. I don't believe she'll ever bring it up again. However"—Emma eyed her granddaughter closely—"you know, your mother mentioned something about Ireland too last night. When you were out of the room. She doesn't believe the housekeeper was telling the truth . . . I mean about Min's craziness and drinking."

Paula exclaimed fiercely, in irritation, "Good God, the two of them are incorrigible! Honestly, Grandma, I hope you've nipped their imaginative chatter in the bud. It's a load of tripe and can only lead to further trouble. Loose tongues are dangerous."

"Agreed. But whether it's tripe or not is beside the point, Paula. What matters, in reality, is that the case is closed. *Firmly closed.* Min's death was a suicide. That was the coroner's ruling and it's good enough for me. And for John Crawford. Don't worry, neither your mother nor Emily will mention anything about murder in the future. I've seen to that."

"Thank heavens you have." Paula came around the desk and hugged Emma tightly, kissed her cheek. "Oh, Gran darling, I'm so glad you're back. I've missed you so much. It's positively awful when you're not here."

Emma smiled up at her, patted her hand. "If you've said that once since I stepped off the plane, you've said it a hundred times, darling. But thank you, it's nice to hear. And I've missed you too—all of you. I've enjoyed myself, traveling the world with Blackie, seeing so many, many wonderful things. I've had a little fun for once. He was sweet. And he pampered me in a way I've not been pampered for years. Not since your grandfather died. But no more gallivanting off to foreign parts."

"I didn't begrudge you the wonderful trip around the world, Gran, please don't think that . . . but you seemed to be so far away most of the time."

"I was always here in spirit, Paula."

"Yes, I know, but it's not quite the same as having you here in the flesh!"

"Alexander should be arriving in a few minutes." Emma glanced at the carriage clock on the mantelpiece. "Then Emily at noon. I thought we would lunch at one." Her mouth twitched. "I suggested to Parker that we have fish-and-chips—and from the local fish shop. That's the one thing I missed when I was away."

Paula chortled. "Oh, Gran, you are lovely, and you haven't changed."

"And it's hardly likely that I will, not at my age."

"I'll just have time to dash across to Harte's, deal with a few things, and get back for lunch."

"Yes, do run along, dear. I know what it's like . . . I used to feel exactly the same way when I was your age. I couldn't wait to get to the store."

"See you later, then." Paula bent to kiss Emma's cheek.

"Yes. Oh, and by the way, Paula, I had lunch with Ross Nelson the day before I left New York. I haven't had a chance to tell you—but I scotched that idea about selling my Sitex stock."

"Good for you. He was getting to be a pest—in more ways than one, if you want the truth."

Emma pursed her lips, staring at Paula with sudden alertness. "Was he now," she said. "Well, yes, I must admit I did get the feeling he was rather keen on you. Tiresome man. Full of himself, and his so-called fatal charms, wouldn't you say?"

"He's the worst kind of bore. The deadliest, really. And so transparent. I'm afraid I can't stand him."

Paula walked to Harte's in Knightsbridge.

It was a frosty day. The etiolated sky was bloated with snow, but its bleached-out quality made the light seem curiously luminous despite the fugitive sun.

She was hardly conscious of the weather as she hurried along. She was thinking of Shane. She always thought of him. He was rarely out of her mind for very long. Today was the twentieth of December. When she had spoken to him yesterday he had said he would ring her at seven New York time. Noon in London. Immediately afterward he was taking a plane to Barbados, since it was the height of the season at the Coral Cove Hotel.

Paula sighed under her breath as she cut down a side street, heading for the main thoroughfare. Jim's accident had thrown all of their plans askew.

But this aside, he had nearly been killed and all because of his ingrained pigheadedness. Her mind leapt back to the dreadful weekend two weeks ago. She had arrived in London on Saturday, having taken an overnight flight from the States, and had been driven straight to Yorkshire by her grandmother's chauffeur.

When she got to Long Meadow in the early afternoon her first stop had been the nursery. To her distress the twins and Nora were suffering from streaming colds. At four o'clock, when Jim had walked in from the newspaper, he had muttered he was coming down with it himself, and had retired to bed immediately. She seized the opportunity to vacate their bedroom. That night she had slept in one of the guest rooms, explaining she could not afford to get sick, not with the whole household under siege and a business to run. He had not complained.

On Sunday, Jim had been much better, certainly well enough to get up for lunch, eat a hearty meal, and drink half a bottle of red wine. She had been aghast when he had insisted on going off to fly that dangerous little plane, had begged him to stay at home. Jim had laughed, told her she was being ridiculous, protested he was neither drunk nor sick. When the phone call had come through from the airport later that afternoon her heart had stopped beating for several seconds, and then she had leapt in the car and rushed to Leeds Infirmary to be with him. At odds with him though she was, and in love with Shane O'Neill, Paula still harbored affectionate feelings for her husband. She had once cared deeply for him, he was the father of her children, and she wished him no harm.

But later, when she could think clearly, she had realized there was no excuse for his behavior. The crash need not have happened. He had been reckless. At heart Paula doubted his story about the engine stalling. He had been taking pills for his cold; he had demolished half a bottle of wine. If he had not been drugged or drunk exactly, he had hardly been in a fit condition to take up the plane.

When she had telephoned Shane in New Milford, later on that fated

Sunday, he had been distressed for her. But he had been understanding of her dilemma, had agreed they could not make their moves until Jim was well enough to cope with her news. She was going to tell him she wanted a divorce.

As she swung into Knightsbridge, she prayed that Jim would agree. The worry that he might fight her nagged at the back of her head constantly.

Don't think about it, don't be so negative, she told herself firmly. All you have to do is get yourself through the next few months. She and Shane had made new plans this past week, changing their business commitments to accommodate each other. They needed to be together as often as they could. In January she would go to New York to be with him. During February and March he would visit Australia to start work on the rebuilding of the hotel the O'Neill chain had just purchased. He would stay with her brother Philip. Shane would come to England in April to see Emerald Bow run in the Grand National, but she would be with him in London before and after the race. At the end of April he would return to New York. They had decided that Jim ought to be on his feet again by then, and once Shane had left for the States she would tackle her husband. In May she would finally tell her grandmother everything, move herself and the twins into Pennistone Royal.

May, Paula repeated under her breath. Such a long way off. No, not really. And, anyway, Shane and I have the rest of our lives ahead of us.

Her pace automatically quickened. She ached for the sound of his voice. Thank God for the telephone, she thought, as she went into the staff entrance at Harte's. At least we can talk every day.

Thirty-Eight

It snowed heavily for the next four days.

Yorkshire was quickly covered with a mantle of white. The countryside around Pennistone Royal looked particularly picturesque. Drystone walls disappeared under monstrous drifts, trees were weighted down by their laden branches, rivers and streams were glazed over with blue-tinted ice.

But the snowstorm ceased with abruptness on the afternoon of Christmas Eve. Suddenly the blindingly white landscape had a crystalline beauty as the sun broke through. There was a diamond-bright dazzle to the sky, a sparkling crispness in the air.

By nightfall the fields and the fells and the rolling moors were ethereal under a clear winter moon that coated them with a silvery sheen.

Emma, standing at the window of her bedroom, was momentarily transfixed as she gazed down at her gardens. The snow and the ice had created the most magical effect, enveloping the land in a strange white silence, an overwhelming stillness that seemed like a palpable thing to her. But despite the breathtaking beauty spread before her, Emma knew that beyond the great iron gates of her house, the roads and country lanes were dangerous, very treacherous in this kind of weather.

As she turned away and walked through into the upstairs parlor, she could not help but worry, thinking of her family and friends who were currently driving on those roads. All were courageously braving the icy conditions in order to spend this special evening with her. It had been a tradition for many years, and none of them wanted to miss it. She hoped each of them would arrive safely and without any mishaps.

Emma already had a full house.

Once they were back in Yorkshire, Paula had lost no time in moving her family into Pennistone Royal. Jim, the babies, the nanny, and the male nurse were already ensconced. Emily had brought Amanda and Francesca home from Harrogate College earlier in the week. David and Daisy had taken the train from London yesterday, accompanied by Alexander and his fiancée, Maggie Reynolds. Edwina and Anthony had flown into Manchester Airport from Dublin that morning, had reached the ancient house in time for a late lunch.

Pausing at her desk, Emma picked up the guest list, scanned it quickly. Her sons and their wives had been invited, but she was quite certain they would not come. Well, it did not matter anymore. She was adjusted to their absence from her life. Kit and Robin would avoid her again. She knew why. They were as guilty as hell about their treachery toward her. Elizabeth was not coming either, was remaining in Paris with Marc Deboyne, but at least her daughter had been gracious when she had phoned to decline and to wish her a happy Christmas. I hope this is the last husband *she's* going to have, Emma thought, her glance traveling on down the list.

Her eyes rested briefly on Jonathan's name. He had accepted. So had Sarah. They were driving over from Bramhope together. She could not help wondering about their current chumminess. Were they up to something? Now, Emma Harte, no bad thoughts tonight, she cautioned herself. It instantly struck her that she was unutterably weary of intrigue. It had dogged her all of her life. She was getting too old to pick up the sword again.

A thoughtful look settled on her face as she remained standing at the desk, clutching the guest list. *She was eighty.* She had paid her dues long ago. Her time was now far too precious to indulge in battles. Let them get on with it, she muttered. As I shall get on with my life—what's left of it. All I want is to have peace and quiet and to be with my dear old friend. We'll march on together into the future. Blackie and I . . . a couple of old war-horses. She felt as if a great burden had been lifted as she suddenly acknowledged that she *had* abdicated eight months ago. She *was* out of the fray. She was determined to stay out.

Emma finished perusing the list. Blackie, who was spending Christmas with Bryan and Geraldine in Wetherby, was due to arrive with them and Miranda shortly. The entire Kallinski clan had also promised to come early. The Hartes would be out in full force tonight. Randolph, too, had a house full, since his mother, Charlotte, and his Aunt Natalie, were staying at Allington Hall with Sally, Vivienne, and himself. Winston was a self-invited guest at Pennistone Royal, had walked in at four o'clock with his suitcase and three large shopping bags top-heavy with gifts. Only Philip and Shane are missing, Emma murmured to herself, putting down the list. But perhaps next year they will be here. We'll all be together. Then the three clans will really be complete.

The clock struck six.

The chimes roused her from her meandering thoughts. She gazed down at the one remaining present that lay on the desk. Earlier all of the others had been taken downstairs to the Stone Hall to be placed under the tree. Sitting down, Emma thought for a moment, then inscribed the card carefully.

There was a knock on the door. "Cooee, Gran, it's me," Emily called, floating in on a cloud of perfume.

Emma lifted her head, smiled at her granddaughter. "And don't you look lovely!" she exclaimed, scrutinizing her intently. "That's the dress tartan of the Seaforth Highlanders," Emma remarked, referring to the long taffeta skirt Emily wore, immediately recognizing the plaid. "My father's old regiment, and Joe's and Blackie's when they were in the First World War. It certainly looks smart with your white silk shirt."

"Yes, I thought so too." Emily planted a kiss on Emma's cheek, said quickly, "You seemed a bit surprised when Winston arrived this afternoon. I could have sworn I'd told you he was coming to stay."

"No, you didn't. But that's all right." Sitting back, Emma pursed her lips, gave Emily a pointed look. "I expect it's too much to ask you to behave yourselves, but *please,* do be discreet if you're bedroom-hopping."

Emily's face flushed. "How can you think a thing like that, Grandma?"

"Because I was young once, believe it or not, and I know what it's like to be in love. But be careful, dear. After all, we do have a lot of house guests. I wouldn't want your reputation besmirched."

"In this family! Good God, nobody can afford to throw any stones—" Emily stopped. "Sorry, I didn't mean to be rude, Grandma."

"Don't apologize for speaking the truth, Emily. But remember what I've just said."

Nodding and looking relieved, Emily drifted over to the fireplace, stood observing her grandmother. "You should always wear dark green velvet. It's very becoming on you, especially with all your emeralds."

"Goodness me, Emily, you make it sound as if they're dripping from every pore. I'm only wearing Paul's ring and earrings and Blackie's little bow. But thank you for the compliment, and, tell me, what's happening downstairs?"

"Amanda and Francesca are finishing trimming the tree, at least the top half which I started earlier. Little monkeys, they haven't helped me one bit today. All they've done is loll around in their room, listening to the Beatles and shrieking their heads off, or alternatively swooning and being silly. I routed them out an hour ago and set them to work."

"Good for you. I'm going to have to take those two in hand during the holidays, put my foot down. There has to be a limit on the time they spend listening to those records. Apart from anything else, the racket was deafening this afternoon. Anyone else down yet?"

"Auntie Daisy, looking gorgeous in a red silk pant suit and masses of rubies and diamonds—"

"Why do you always exaggerate?" Emma shook her head, faintly reprimanding, but her eyes were fond. "She doesn't have masses of rubies and diamonds, to my knowledge."

"Well, a pair of beautiful earrings," Emily admitted, wrinkling her nose. "She was helping to set up the bar. Jim's there, in the new wheelchair you got for him, having a drink and—"

"He's started a bit early, hasn't he?" Emma exclaimed, a silver brow lifting in surprise.

"What do you mean, started early? He hasn't stopped since lunch."

Emma was dismayed. "Ought he to be drinking?" she asked. "He's on painkillers—so Paula told me. That combination can be awfully dangerous." Her eyes grew flinty with a mixture of concern and annoyance.

Emily nodded. "I mentioned that to him a few minutes ago, so don't *you* say anything. He told me to mind my own business. He's awfully grouchy. I don't envy Paula one bit."

"I've noticed his moodiness. Still, we have to make allowances, I suppose. Has Paula come home from the store yet?"

"No, but she should be here any minute."

"Oh dear, the roads are so bad tonight . . ." Emma's voice faltered.

"Don't fret, Gran, she's a careful driver. Besides, she went over to the Harrogate store this afternoon. However, knowing Paula, she'll probably stay until closing time. But at least her driving time has been cut in half."

"I'll rest easier once she gets here. Well, continue, who else has made an appearance?"

"Maggie. She's sorting the Christmas tree decorations, helping the girls. Alexander and Uncle David are hanging mistletoe. Hilda and Joe are preparing the refectory table for the buffet, and Winston's stacking gifts under the tree." Emily grinned. "Oh yes, and Aunt Edwina is making herself useful for once. She's instructing Winston exactly *how* to arrange the packages for the best effect, as if it mattered."

"At least she's talking to a Harte for a change. That's certainly a step in the right direction." Emma motioned to Emily. "Come here, dear, I want to show you something."

As Emily joined her, Emma lifted the lid of an old leather jewelry case and then handed it to her granddaughter.

Emily gasped, staring down at the beautiful diamond necklace lying on the dark red velvet. It was a glittering lacy web of brilliant, perfectly cut and mounted stones. The diamonds had such fire, such life, such matchless beauty, Emily gasped again. "This is extraordinary, Grandma, and obviously very old. Where did it come from? I don't think I've ever seen you wear it."

"No, you haven't, because I never have. I haven't even tried it on since I've owned it."

"I don't understand," Emily said, her eyes perplexed.

"I've never wanted to wear it, and I only bought it when it was auctioned because—well, it was a sort of symbol to me. It represented everything I never had when I was a young girl—when I was a maid at Fairley Hall." Emma took the case back from Emily, lifted out the necklace, held it up to the light. "Yes, it's superb. Superb. It belonged to Adele Fairley, Jim's great-grandmother. I can still recall the night of a big dinner when I helped Adele to dress, fastened this around her throat. I was very bitter that night. The necklace, you see, represented the grinding toil and drudgery of the villagers, and of my father, my brother Frank, and me." Emma shook her head. "When the Fairleys went down the drain, after Adam died, Gerald put this up for sale." Her shoulders lifted in a shrug. "I outbid everyone," she explained and placed the necklace in its case.

Emily said, "But why have you never worn it, Grandy?"

"Because it was suddenly meaningless to me once I owned it . . . I preferred the things which had been given to me with love, by those who loved me."

"What are you going to do with it?" Emily eyed the fancy wrapping paper and silver ribbon on the desk. "Oh, I know! You're going to give it to Paula because she's married to Jim."

"No, not Paula."

"Then who?"

"Edwina."

"Edwina. Why her? She's always so awful to you!"

"So what. And just because she behaves badly doesn't mean I have to do the same. Anyway, throughout my life I've tried to rise above that sort of thing. Always remember that it is far better to be gracious in difficult situations, Emily, than to sink to the level of others. Anyway, Paula wouldn't want this. She might bear the name of Fairley, but I don't believe she considers herself to be one, no, not at all. On the other hand, Edwina *does.* The Fairley name is important to her, and I think she, above everyone in the family, would appreciate owning this and—"

"But Gran," Emily began.

Emma held up her hand. "Edwina was denied her birthright because she was illegitimate, and I know how much the circumstances of her birth troubled her, perhaps still do. I feel it is only proper that she has something that belonged to them—this kind of family heirloom. *I* don't want it, since it has no meaning for me. Neither am I trying to ingratiate myself with her, or redeem myself in her eyes. I simply want to give it to her, and that's all there is to it. She will enjoy wearing it, of that I feel sure. Now, perhaps you would be kind enough to wrap it for me, Emily."

"Of course I will. May I sit at the desk? It's easier to work there."

"Yes." Emma rose, walked across to the fireplace, stood with her back to it.

Emily glanced at the necklace again, closed the case, began to wrap it, thinking what an extraordinary woman her grandmother was. There was no one like her in the whole world. She was so generous and so very forgiving. Damn Edwina, she thought. I wish *she* would make just one gesture of love toward Gran. That would make *me* feel better.

There was a tap on the door. It opened and Paula looked in, exclaimed, "Hello, you two! I'm frightfully late, I'm afraid. The Harrogate store was mobbed all day, like bedlam when we closed. Then the roads were ghastly. See you both in a while. I must pop in on the babies and Nora before I change."

"Thank heaven you got here safely." Emma was filled with relief at the sight of Paula's smiling face. "And take your time, dear. Nobody's going anywhere."

"I will." Paula closed the door softly.

Emma said to Emily, "Once you finish wrapping the necklace I think we'd better go downstairs. The O'Neills and the Kallinskis will be arriving momentarily."

"It's finished." Emily clipped off the end of the silver ribbon, sat back to admire her handiwork. She lifted her dancing green eyes, focused them on her grandmother. "I bet old Edwina has a heart attack when she opens this later, Gran!" she said, grinning mischievously.

"Really, Emily, sometimes . . ." Emma shook her head, tried to look disapproving, without much success.

• • •

The Stone Hall at Pennistone Royal derived its name from the local gray stone which had been used throughout—on the ceiling, the walls, the floor, and the fireplace façade. But it was more than an entrance hall, had the over-tones of a huge sitting room with its handsome Jacobean and Tudor furniture which partially underscored the architecture of the house.

Dark wood beams crisscrossed the stone ceiling, introduced a touch of warmth, as did the faded Aubusson carpets on the floor, the antique tapestries and oil paintings on the walls. The baronial overtones were further diminished by the blaze of rosy light from the chandelier and wall sconces, and the huge fire crackling up the chimney back. Pots of yellow, pink, and purple chrysan-themums and deep-orange amaryllis sparked some of the wood surfaces, and tall brass urns filled with dark green holly, bright red berries, graced several cor-ners.

But taking pride of place and dominating the hall tonight was a giant Christmas tree. This was nine feet tall, with wide spreading branches, and it towered up to touch the edge of the minstrel gallery at the far end of the hall.

Emma, descending the staircase with Emily, paused halfway, stood for a moment admiring the scene. "Oh, doesn't it look festive!" she cried. Not waiting for a response, she hurried down, glided across the floor to join the throng of family members, her eyes sparkling, her face wreathed in smiles.

"Hello, everyone," she said. "And well done. You've obviously worked hard to make the hall look beautiful tonight. Thank you."

They came to greet her in turn, kissed her, told her she looked wonderful. Winston took the gift she handed him and put it under the tree. Jim, who had trouble maneuvering the wheelchair, could only wave.

Emma hurried over to him, rested her hand on his good shoulder, squeezed it, bent to kiss him. "How are you feeling?" she asked, her concern for his well-being apparent in her expression.

"Bloody awful, but I'll survive." He gazed up at her through his light silvery eyes, then grimaced. "What a rotten way to spend Christmas."

"Yes, I know, dear, and you must be terribly uncomfortable. Can I get you anything?"

"No, thanks. Where's Paula? She should be home by now. It's almost six-thirty." His voice was unexpectedly querulous, and he scowled at Emma, his mouth twisting into an angry line which he could not manage to conceal. Before she had a chance to answer, he exclaimed, "I don't know why she had to go to the store today. It's ridiculous the way she works, and it is Christmas Eve. She ought to be here with her family. The babies need her, and, further-more, so do I—crippled as I am in this way. I think she's inconsiderate."

Emma drew back, amazed at his words, his nasty tone, his sudden burst of petulance. She knew he was not feeling well, but she could not help thinking that he was overdoing it a bit. She said softly, "It's because it *is* Christmas that she had to be at the stores today, Jim. You know this is her busiest period."

"She should have left at noon," he groused, "come home to me. After all, the circumstances are a little exceptional, wouldn't you say?"

Emma bit back a sharp retort, knowing she must excuse him, blame his irascibility and immaturity on his condition. She said, more quietly than before, "I was never an absentee landlord and I doubt that Paula will ever be one either. And, as a matter of fact, she just got back. She'll be down in a few minutes. She's changing into a cocktail dress. I see you have a drink and your cigarettes, Jim, so if you'll excuse me I'll go and deal with those two rowdy teenagers."

Hurrying over to the tree, where Amanda and Francesca stood on two stepladders quarreling furiously, Emma exclaimed, "Now, girls, stop that and come down. At once, do you hear!"

"Yes, Grandma," Amanda said dutifully, quickly doing as she was bidden.

Francesca lingered. She placed a silver bell on the tip of a branch, craning her neck to study it.

Amanda, having reached the bottom of the ladder, took a step back, watching her sister. She shrieked, "Not there, you clot! It's right next to a silver icicle. You need more color on that branch. Put the red star you're holding in that spot instead of the bell."

"Go to hell!" Francesca retorted. "I'm sick of you tonight. You're a dimwit. And far too *bossy.*"

"That's enough!" Emma snapped. "Get down, Francesca, and immediately. Otherwise you'll spend this evening in your room."

"Yes, Grandy," Francesca mumbled, clattering down the stepladder to join her sister, who was standing next to Emma.

"Now, upstairs, both of you." Emma gave them a disapproving glance. "You look like a couple of street urchins. I want you out of those disgusting jeans and grimy shirts and into more suitable clothes. *Instantly.* And wash your faces and brush your hair. I've never seen you both in such an appalling state. And please don't dress alike. I'm getting sick and tired of this twin-sister act of yours. You're like a music hall turn."

"Yes, Grandmother," Amanda murmured meekly.

"What do you want us to wear?" Francesca asked, eyeing Emma boldly, giving her a cheeky grin.

Quite unexpectedly, Emma wanted to laugh, but she controlled herself, said sternly, "You can put on your red velvet frock, Francesca. And *you,* Amanda, had better wear your blue silk. That should do it. If nothing else, at least I'll be able to distinguish you from each other. Now run along."

Emily, who had witnessed this little scene, laughed when her half sisters were out of earshot. "Thanks, Gran. They've been extremely bolshie these last few days. I almost threatened to send them to Paris to join our mother, but it would've been an idle threat. I wouldn't have the heart to do that to them—as tiresome as they are."

"They're just trying the two of us on for size, you know, seeing how much they can get away with." Emma chuckled.

"I know. Would you like a drink?"

"Why not, Emily. Perhaps you can ask Winston or your brother to open a bottle of champagne. I think I'd like a glass. And let's have some music." Emma swung around as Emily hurried off to fetch the wine, and called across to David Amory, "Please pop a record on, David dear, one of those selections of Christmas carols. No, not the carols just yet. I rather like that Bing Crosby record . . . *White Christmas,* I believe it's called."

"Right away, Emma. And it's certainly appropriate this year."

Emma turned to the box of tree decorations, started to dress the lower branches, which were relatively bare and unfinished. She had been working only a few seconds when she felt a hand touch her arm tentatively. She swiveled, found herself face-to-face with Edwina.

"May I help, Mother?"

"Yes, I'd like that," Emma said, camouflaging her surprise. "Root around in the other box. Perhaps you'll find something sparkling and pretty for these low branches. It seems to me that the most beautiful ornaments generally end up on the top of the tree." Emma's eyes roved over her eldest daughter. She nodded. "Blue has always suited you, Edwina. You look lovely tonight, and that's a beautiful frock."

"Thank you . . . Daisy talked me into buying it." Edwina hesitated. "You look very elegant, but then you always do, Mother." Edwina offered her a smile that was as tentative as her touch had been.

Emma smiled in return, wondering what to make of the unprecedented compliment, then reached for a gold *papier-mâché* pear, hooked it onto a branch, frowning to herself. Edwina was certainly most cordial, all of a sudden. Still, she had to admit she was pleased at this show of friendliness.

After a moment, Edwina tapped Emma's arm, held out a blue glass star. "Here you are, Mother, would you like to hang this one? Maybe over there, next to the angel. Or wherever you think it would look right."

Taking it from her, Emma searched her daughter's face.

For a split second she was transported back in time . . . to a Christmas long, long ago. *December of 1915.* Joe Lowther had still been alive. It was the year before he had been killed in the Battle of the Somme. They had lived in the avenue called the Towers in Armley. In her mind's eye the memory flashed so vividly Emma caught her breath. Edwina had been nine years old and exceptionally pretty with her long blond hair, her silvery eyes so like Adele's, her delicate features inherited from Edwin Fairley, her father. But the little girl had believed Joe to be her father and she had adored him. Worshiped him, really.

The three of them had stood in front of a giant fir, very similar to this one, and on a snowy Christmas Eve such as this. Dim echoes of their joyous laughter reverberated in Emma's head. But it had been the child and the man who had laughed, shared the delight and fun of dressing the splendid tree. She had been the interloper, unwanted by her daughter. Edwina had spurned her, slighted her every time she had offered that beautiful but disdainful child a pretty bauble to hang on the tree. And she had left the room, her heart almost breaking. She had put on her coat and run down the short avenue to Blackie and Laura's house, and her dearest Laura had comforted her, helped to take the sting out of the child's spitefulness.

Edwina said, "Are you feeling all right, Mother?"

Emma blinked. The memory dissolved. "Yes," she said, "oh yes. I'm fine. I was just remembering something."

"What were you remembering?"

"Oh, a Christmas . . . so long ago now you've surely forgotten it." Emma smiled faintly. "But I've never forgotten it—not really."

"You were thinking about the Christmas of 1915, weren't you?" Edwina moved closer to Emma.

"Yes."

"Mother . . ." Edwina looked deeply into Emma's old wise eyes. "I've not forgotten that Christmas either." She paused, seemed to consider, and then reached out and took hold of Emma's hand impulsively. "Forgive me, Mother, please, please forgive me for that terrible Christmas," she whispered.

Emma stared back at her daughter in stupefaction. And then she instantly knew what Edwina was trying to say. She wanted to be forgiven for all of her transgressions over the years, and not just that particular Christmas. Emma said slowly, "You were such a little girl, so young. You didn't understand . . . understand how things were in an adult world. You had no conception of pain or heartbreak."

"Please say you forgive me, Mother," Edwina begged, her sincerity evident. "It's become so very important to me."

"Why, of course I forgive you, Edwina. You are my daughter, my first-born child. And I told you months ago that I've always loved you. My love has never wavered or changed, though you have doubted me."

"I don't anymore." Tears swam in Edwina's pale eyes. "Can we be friends at last—so late in our lives—do you think?"

"I know we can." Emma smiled her incomparable smile that always filled her face with radiance. "Why, we already are, my dear," she said, clasping Edwina's hand tightly.

Jonathan Ainsley was beginning to realize how dangerous the conditions were after he left the main Ripon road and maneuvered his Aston Martin down a narrow side lane, taking a shortcut to the village of Pennistone Royal.

"You shouldn't have come this way," Sarah complained. "The lane twists and turns too much. We'll have an accident, if you're not careful."

"This is the fastest route," Jonathan replied. A cold smile touched his mouth. "I don't want to miss anything tonight. I think it's going to be—" He broke off as he felt the wheels sliding on the ice. The car was going into a skid. He gripped the steering wheel tighter, turning the car into the skid in an effort to avert it, gently pressing his foot on the brake as he did.

Sarah, stiffening with fright, grabbed his arm.

Angrily Jonathan shook off her hand, managed to right the Aston in the nick of time, shouted, "You'll have us in a bloody ditch!" He slowed his pace to a slow crawl. "For God's sake, don't ever do a thing like that again, Sarah. It's very dangerous."

"I'm sorry. It *was* a silly reaction. Don't be angry with me. You know I can't bear it when you lose your temper."

"Okay, okay, let's forget it," he muttered, pushing his annoyance to one side. The last thing he wanted was to upset Sarah. He needed her too much to incur her disfavor. He peered ahead, watching for new ice patches in the glare of the headlights.

Neither of the cousins spoke for a while.

Sarah shrank into the corner of the seat, pulling her silver fox coat around her, hoping his good humor would soon be restored.

Jonathan concentrated on the road, driving now with the utmost care. The Aston Martin was new, not even paid for yet. A bashed-up hood or a damaged fender would be costly. He relaxed a fraction as he hit a clear stretch, but still he did not increase his pace, determined to be cautious. His mind swung to his cousin sitting next to him. He wondered how to persuade Sarah to put up more money, invest another few hundred thousand pounds in the company he secretly owned with Sebastian Cross. Sarah was their partner now. Her money was vital to them. Urgently needed. They had had a lot of bad luck lately. And Sebastian had made some disastrous deals, which negated the good ones he had closed. But they would pull out of it. One good deal would do the trick.

A grimness settled on his face as his duplicitous brain continued to turn at a rapid rate. Maybe he would have to steer one of the deals he was handling for Harte Enterprises into Stonewall Properties, his own company. *Why not?* The thought tickled him. Jonathan Ainsley was aware that he had larceny in his heart, accepted that he was avaricious, greedy for the good things in life, hungry for power. He also knew he was not a good sport, despite his grandmother's efforts to instill in him the importance of playing the game. Who wants to play the game? he now asked himself. He was a bad loser. He didn't care. But he would be damned if he would ever be the loser again. He was going to be the winner . . .

Sarah said, "We're almost at the end of the lane, Jonny."

"Yes, I know." Jonathan began to ponder her. He had been manipulating Sarah for months, playing on her hatred for Paula, feeding her jealousy, envy, and bitterness. But she had every reason to be bitter. Just as he did. Paula was the favorite, the Crown Princess. She was getting everything, damn her. And so was Alexander. A small tremor of fury shot through Jonathan. He instantly curbed it, warning himself to stay cool tonight. He had schooled himself not to show his hand to the family, and least of all to his grandmother. Bloody old witch, he thought. My father's right, she's never going to kick the bucket. We *will* have to shoot her in the end. Poor Dad—he was cheated out of his inheritance. But he's a great politician and one of the greatest men in England. He might even be Prime Minister one day. He's so smart. He thought my idea of starting my own business was brilliant. He gave me his blessing. Jonathan wondered if his grandmother suspected him. Never. She was too old, getting senile. Once Emma Harte was dead he would inherit the New York apartment. The bequest to him was in her will. It had to be worth five million dollars at least. And Sarah was to get the Belgrave Square house. I'll make her sell it, invest the cash with me. The mere thought of this enormous amount of money cheered him. He tingled with excitement. His mood became sanguine. He felt much better all of a sudden, and quite up to facing his boring family. He wished he could park and smoke a joint before they reached the house. He did not dare. Sarah would disapprove. She was such a bore. A pain, really. Better cater to her. He needed her support, her continuing friendship. Sebastian had recently had the idea of marrying Sarah. Jonathan was not sure that he should encourage this. He despised Sarah, but Sebastian was a strange bird, and the gambling had grown worse and he was growing ever more reckless. Besides, Jonathan did not want to lose control of Sarah, or, more precisely, her money.

At the end of the lane Jonathan drew to a standstill, flicked his lights, then pulled out onto the main road. He said, "That was a bumpy ride, but like all bumpy rides it was worth it. At least we won't be all that late."

"Why are you so anxious to get to Grandy's early? What are you afraid of missing?" Sarah asked, filled with curiosity.

"*Family dramas.*" Jonathan chortled. "And there are bound to be some, with that motley crew in attendance. There'll be our peer of the realm hovering over his pregnant mistress. Christ, Sarah, Anthony's been lucky. He's just missed standing trial for murder, and by the skin of his teeth. I hear Sally Harte's blown up like a helium balloon, got his bun in her oven all right, and for all the world to see."

"Do you always have to be so crude?" Sarah said with her usual primness.

He glanced at her quickly out of the corner of his eye and, undeterred, said, "And there'll be our two lovebirds, billing and cooing inanely. I always knew Emily was itching to get into Winston's trousers when we were kids. She's a bloody little sexpot if you ask me, just like her randy mum."

"Allison Ridley's devastated about Winston," Sarah remarked as evenly as she could, brushing aside his vulgarity. "She's moving to New York in a few weeks. I can't say I blame her. Our crowd is too close-knit . . . she'd always be running into Winston."

"He's certainly riding high at the moment, got *his* hands on the newspaper company because of Jim's accident." Instantly Jonathan saw a way to inflame Sarah, added swiftly, "That plane crash was a bit odd, don't you think?"

"In what way?"

"It struck me at the time that Jim might have been trying to do himself in —you know, end it all in one dramatic moment."

Sarah was shocked. "Jonathan! That's a terrible thing to say! Why would Jim want to kill himself, for heaven's sake?"

"Who wouldn't—being married to the Ice Queen?"

"Yes," Sarah muttered, "she is a cold bitch. Probably frigid."

"Oh, I wouldn't say *that*—" Jonathan stopped, waiting for Sarah to take the bait.

"I thought you hated Paula as much as I do."

"I haven't changed," he reassured her.

"But you just implied that she's not cold, Jonny."

"I heard something about her that leads me to think otherwise—" Again he broke off, wanting to further intrigue Sarah.

"Oh! Tell me the gossip."

Jonathan sighed. "I shouldn't have started this conversation with you, Sarah dear. The last thing I want to do is upset you on Christmas Eve."

Sarah said, "I won't be upset . . . Come on, don't be mean, give me all the dirt on Paula. I'm certainly all ears."

"No, I'm positive I oughtn't to continue." He smothered a gleeful laugh, enjoying this cat-and-mouse game. He always did. It gave him a sense of power.

There was a small silence.

"On the other hand, you're a big girl—" He patted her hand. "And of course it might *not* be true at all."

"For God's sake, tell me . . . this is driving me crazy," Sarah cried.

"Paula was in Barbados in November, as you know. But were you aware that Shane O'Neill was there at the same time?"

Sarah tensed. She sucked in her breath, obviously taken aback. "So what?" she managed after a moment. "He was down there when *I* went out to supervise the opening of the boutique. His presence on the island doesn't mean a thing."

"Perhaps not—on the surface. But you were the one who told me you'd seen him ogling her, looking all hot-eyed and turned-on at the christening."

"He was!"

"Well, Rodney Robinson, my old school chum from Eton, was in Barbados at the same time as Paula. He was staying at the Sandy Lane Hotel, and he told me he saw her having lunch at the hotel. She was with a man—"

"It may not have been Shane," Sarah said swiftly. She could hardly bear to think of Shane with her cousin. It made her physically ill.

"It *was* Shane," Jonathan said steadily. "Rodney thought he looked familiar. After they'd left, old Rod spoke to the head waiter, asked him if he knew the name of the man with the tall, dark, striking young woman. The head waiter told him it was a Mr. O'Neill who owned the Coral Cove Hotel."

"Having lunch together isn't anything unusual. They've always been close friends," Sarah protested, willing the pain in her chest to go away.

"Oh, I agree, love. Except for one thing. Rodney told me they were looking extremely cozy. Intimate, was his word. In fact, he said Shane was practically getting it off with her at the table."

"P-p-please," Sarah stammered, "y-y-you know I loathe it when you're vulgar."

"Oh, sorry, love." He patted her hand again. His glee spiraled. "They were drooling all over each other and in the most disgusting way. So Rodney said. Obviously our Ice Queen isn't so icy after all, nor is she the little Miss Goody Two-shoes she pretends to be. Poor Jim. I'm not surprised he almost plunged to his death."

Sarah swallowed. She was overwhelmed by jealousy, hardly able to breathe.

Jonathan, aware of her feelings for Shane O'Neill, continued relentlessly, "Yes, methinks there's something rotten in the state of Denmark, to quote old Will Shakespeare. *Adultery,* perhaps? Rocking the House of Fairley." He chuckled sarcastically.

"They can't be having an affair," Sarah moaned. "Paula wouldn't dare. She'd be too scared that Grandy would find out. Anyway, she's in love with Jim."

"A hundred to one that you're entirely wrong, Sarah, my poppet."

"I don't think we should talk about this anymore. I *am* getting upset after all. Actually, I feel rather queasy."

"I do hope you're going to be all right," Jonathan murmured softly, pretending to be concerned. "I knew I shouldn't have told you. But you've always been able to twist me around your little finger. Thank God, we have each other, Sarah. We'll fight those cousins of ours and to the bitter end. We'll come out on top, you'll see. Sebastian and I have the company really rolling now. You're going to make millions with us, and be as rich and powerful as Paula bloody Fairley."

There was no response from Sarah, who sat hugging herself, fighting back the tears. She loved Shane so much it was painful hearing these things about him and Paula. She did not doubt Jonathan.

Jonathan said, "Cheer up, love. And remember one thing—Shane is a Roman Catholic. He'd never marry a divorced woman. And *if* he is involved with the lady, he's bound to tire of her soon. He's a real stu—" Jonathan cleared his throat, quickly corrected himself by substituting, "Ladies' man." He continued, "And he's still sowing his wild oats. That's what this affair with Paula is. Shane's bound to calm down soon, and, *voila!* you'll be there waiting for him. Rich, too, as you walk to the altar with him. By the way, I've been meaning to tell you, you're looking very beautiful these days, Sarah, since you lost so much weight. Shane won't be able to resist you. I'm going to help you, don't worry. I'm going to make certain you get the man you love."

"Oh, Jonny, you're always so nice to me," Sarah said, instantly cheering. "Everything you say is true, I just know it is. I will end up with Shane. And I am glad about our real estate company." She peered at him in the dim light of the car. "Am I really going to be as wealthy as Paula?"

"Absolutely. I guarantee it. Incidentally, after Christmas, Sebastian and I want you to come to our first real board meeting. We'll show you the books, go over our various deals, explain the new ones that are pending. You may have to invest a little more money, but it'll be worth it. Think of the dowry you'll take to Shane. I realize that sounds old-fashioned, but don't let's be foolish enough to dismiss money in this instance. Shane O'Neill is bloody ambitious, and he'd never look twice at a poor woman. So . . . I'm going to make sure you are loaded, Sarah."

"What would I do without you?" Sarah sighed, blissful at the prospect of her rosy future. "I'm feeling tons better now." She giggled. "It must be the thought of lauding it over Paula in the not too distant future, and snatching Shane out from under her nose."

"That's the spirit, Sarah! When should I arrange for us to get together with Sebastian Cross?"

"Any time you like. And of course I'll put up some more money. I trust you, Jonny. You've always been on my side, been my best friend."

"And as you have been mine, my pet."

Within minutes Jonathan was turning into the gates of Pennistone Royal. As he parked he noticed the long lineup of cars, and realized that they were probably the last to arrive. Secretly laughing up his sleeve at Sarah's gullibility, he nevertheless managed to keep his face straight as he helped her out of the car, ran around to the trunk to collect their gifts for their grandmother.

Puffed up with self-congratulation at his adroit handling of his cousin, he put his hand under her elbow, arranged a suitably insouciant smile, and escorted her inside.

Joe, the houseman, was on duty, and he wished them a happy Christmas as he took their coats. They returned his greeting. Jonathan's sharp, ever-quick eyes darted around as he and Sarah went down the short flight of steps leading into the Stone Hall. The party was in full swing. Everyone was present. The air was filled with the sound of Christmas music playing on the stereo, and the high-pitched buzz of chatter intermingled with bursts of jolly laughter. The fire roared, the giant tree blazed with lights, and the familiar faces which turned to greet them were ringed with happy smiles.

Jonathan smiled back, nodded, but did not stop. He propelled Sarah on a steady course down the hall. He saw Paula sitting on the arm of Blackie's chair, talking to the old man very earnestly, her face tender. If I exaggerated Rodney's story to goad Sarah, I know I wasn't far off the mark, Jonathan commented silently. I bet Shane O'Neill has got her where he wants her. In his bed. Good old Rodney. I owe him one.

Now Jonathan noticed Jim, trapped in the wheelchair, talking to Anthony. They had a strong look of each other. Fairley blood, he thought. He felt the sardonic laughter rising in his throat, almost choking him. He swallowed, made sure his charming smile was intact. As soon as Jim's alone, I'll go over and talk to him, sow a few seeds of doubt in his mind about that holier-than-thou wife of his. In the meantime, I'd better find the old dragon, go over and genuflect.

• • •

Jonathan's predictions to Sarah to the contrary, there were no dramas at Pennistone Royal that evening.

Emma's traditional Christmas Eve party progressed without a hitch. However, Emily's comment about Edwina's being shocked to death when she saw the diamond necklace proved to be no exaggeration.

After the buffet supper had been served and eaten, and before the carol singing began, Emma distributed her generous tokens of her affection to her family and friends. They were thrilled and touched by their presents, recognizing the amount of time she had spent in selecting something extra-special for each of them. Even the malcontents were pleased—Jonathan with his gold-and-jade cuff links, Sarah with the pearl-and-jade necklace she had received.

But it was Edwina who was genuinely stunned, momentarily rendered speechless as she gaped in amazement at the Fairley necklace. Observing her closely, Emma thought her daughter was indeed going to keel over from a heart attack. Instead, Edwina collapsed in floods of tears.

After she had composed herself, Edwina began to realize that the Fairley heirloom she had been given was a gesture of unselfish love, that of a mother for a daughter, and she was more than thankful she had made the initial move to end her estrangement from her mother earlier. She remained at Emma's side for the rest of the evening.

The happy mood prevailed until midnight. Only Paula felt out of it at times, when her thoughts turned to Shane. She was attentive to Jim and his needs, and chatted with everyone, but she constantly found herself gravitating to the O'Neills, needing to be in the midst of Shane's family. Somehow it seemed to bring him closer.

Next year, she kept thinking. Next year. We'll be together next year.

———— *Thirty-Nine* ————

It was a rainy night in the middle of January.

Jim Fairley sat in the Peach Drawing Room, sipping a straight vodka, gazing at his favorite painting, the Sisley he loved so much and longed to possess for himself. So rapt was he in his contemplation of it, he did not realize that Emma had appeared in the doorway of her drawing room.

She stood observing him closely.

Her worry about Jim was increasing daily, and she could not help thinking now that she was watching the slow but steady disintegration of a man. He had changed so radically during her absence abroad and over the last six weeks, he was hardly recognizable as the personable young editor she had first employed. She had tried to talk to him, but her words seemed to flow over him, leaving him untouched. He continued on his downward slide.

He was drinking steadily. Ever since she had chastised him about this a few days after Christmas he had endeavored to conceal his tippling. Still, she was aware he was consuming great quantities of liquor—day and night.

She thought of his family. Every single one of the Fairleys had been drinkers. His great-grandmother Adele had fallen down the staircase at Fairley Hall in a drunken stupor, breaking her neck. The shattered wineglass had been scattered around her body, on that dreadful morning when Annie, the maid, had found her.

Emma frowned to herself. She wondered if alcoholism was congenital. Jim was not yet an alcoholic, but she was convinced he was well on the way to becoming one. And then there were the painkillers. He had not really persuaded her he had stopped taking pills. And yet she could not for the life of her imagine where he was getting them from. Continuing to study his face in profile, thinking how good-looking he was despite the ravages of drink, medication, and his physical pain, a phrase Blackie had used recently leapt into her mind. They had been at Allington Hall stables, looking over his string of racehorses. "The breeding's there, but no stamina," Blackie had said, referring to one of his thoroughbreds. An appropriate analogy, Emma mused. Loath though she was to condemn Jim, it was apparent to her that he was weak, lacked strength of character. But had she not always suspected this?

Emma cleared her throat, said in a cheerful voice, "Good evening, Jim." She walked into the room purposefully.

She had startled him. He swung his head quickly. He gave her a half smile. "I wondered where you were," he exclaimed, forcing a conviviality he did not feel. "I didn't wait for you but I hope you don't mind." He glanced at the drink. "This is my first today, Grandy."

That's a downright lie, she thought. She said, "I was delayed on the telephone, but now I'll join you in a cocktail before dinner."

Pouring herself a glass of white wine, Emma continued, "I was just speaking to Daisy. She rang from Chamonix. They're so sorry you're not with them. David misses you on the slopes." She brought her drink and sat down near the fire. "Daisy's not much of a skier, as you know, and David is feeling lonely without you, his boon companion. Well, never mind, you'll be able to go with them next year, Jim."

"I sincerely hope so." He moved his broken shoulder slightly, gave her a quirky little smile. "It's a relief to have this in a sling, I can tell you that, and Doctor Hedley's going to take the cast off my leg tomorrow."

She knew all about this but faked surprise, not wanting him to know she was constantly consulting with the family doctor about him. "That's *wonderful* news. You must start therapy immediately, get those muscles in shape again."

"Try and stop me." He gave her a long, careful look. "Did Paula call you from New York today?"

Emma's eyes flickered. "No, she didn't, but I wasn't expecting to hear from her. Surely she told you last night, when she called, that she was flying to Texas today. Sitex business, you know."

"Oh, that's right. I'd forgotten."

Emma wondered if he really had, but let the comment pass. "Emily just told me that Winston's coming to dinner after all. That'll be nice for you, Jim —a little male company should cheer you up. It must be very boring for you— surrounded by women."

He laughed. "You're all very attentive, but it'll be nice to see Winston, hear what's happening in the outside world. I feel so cut off, and weary of this inactivity. I hope I can get back to the paper in a couple of weeks. What do you think?"

It struck Emma that this would be a wise move, and she said swiftly, "I'm all for it. I've always found that work is a wonderful cure for what ails *me.*"

Jim cleared his throat. "Talking of the newspapers, Emma, there's something I've been meaning to ask you for the longest time."

"Oh, and what's that, Jim?"

He hesitated briefly, then said in a low voice, "When I came back from Canada in September, Paula and I had a bit of a quarrel about Sam Fellowes, and the instructions she had given him in my absence, you know, about suppressing the stories dealing with Min's death."

"Yes, she mentioned something about it—her decision, not your quarrel." Emma gave him a questioning look.

"Paula told me that she has your power of attorney, and Winston's, to act on your behalf or his, if the need comes up."

"That's quite true."

"I couldn't help wondering why you didn't give those power of attorneys to me?"

Emma sat very still, was silent for a second, and said gently, "Jim, when you resigned as managing director of the Yorkshire Consolidated Newspaper Company you forfeited your right to any power in that company, other than the editorial power you have as managing editor, of course. Since you said you were not interested in the administrative side of the newspapers, it seemed patently obvious to me that those power of attorneys had to rest in the hands of someone who was ready, willing, and able to act, to take charge, if the situation arose—*administratively* take control, I mean."

"I see."

Watching him closely, she saw his face stiffen in annoyance, his eyes cloud over with resentment. "You did resign of your own accord, Jim," she remarked evenly, in that same gentle voice.

"I know." He took a long swallow of the vodka, placed the drink on the end table, stared into the fire. Finally he swung his eyes to hers. "Paula is also the trustee of my children's shares in the newspaper company, isn't she?"

"She is."

"Why, Grandy? Why didn't you make me the trustee for them? I am their father, after all."

"It's not as simple as it seems, Jim. The shares which I am leaving to Lorne and Tessa are not in a separate trust but in their overall trust fund, into which I have placed many other shares from my different holdings. It seems clear to me that such a giant trust must be managed by one person. It would be ridiculous to have a number of different trusts, have each one handled by a different individual. Far too confusing."

He nodded, made no comment.

Emma gave him a discerning look, recognizing that he was not only put out, but furious, even though he was doing his best to conceal this emotion from her. Whilst she knew she had no obligation to explain her actions to anyone, she nevertheless wanted to make him feel better about himself.

She said, "My decision to appoint Paula is no reflection on you, or your ability. She—and she alone—would be the trustee of her children's trust fund whomever she was married to, Jim."

"I understand," he murmured, although deep down he did not. He felt he had been passed over. But then he had no one to blame but himself. He suddenly realized he should never have resigned as managing director of the newspaper company.

Ignoring his moody expression, his angry silence, Emma remarked, "If Emily and Winston have children before I die, and if I created a trust fund for their offsprings, which of course I *would*, Winston will be in the same position as you are. So would Sarah's husband, should she marry whilst I'm still alive. I'm not singling you out."

"I said I understand, and I do, Emma. Thanks for explaining things to me. I appreciate—"

There was a tap on the door, and Hilda came in, said, "Excuse me, Mrs. Harte, but Mr. O'Neill is on the phone. He said that if you're busy you can ring him back. He's at Mr. Bryan's, in Wetherby."

"Thank you, Hilda, I'll take it." She rose, smiled at Jim. "Excuse me, dear, I won't be a moment."

He nodded, and the minute he was alone he trundled himself over to the Regency sideboard and filled his glass with vodka, plopped in ice. He put the drink in his left hand, which peeped out from the sling, then pushed his chair back to the fireplace with his right.

He drank half of the vodka quickly, so that Emma would not know he had refilled his glass, then sat pondering her words. Suddenly everything was clear to him. Emma was placing all of her power in the hands of her grandchildren. She was ensuring it stayed within the family. And absolutely so. He had thought he was family. He was an outsider, after all.

Sighing, he lifted his eyes to the Sisley. The painting had always had a hypnotic effect on him. Again, he wished it was his, as he always did when he gazed on it. He wondered what exactly it was about this particular landscape that so enthralled him. There were other Sisleys in the room, and Monets. All were worth millions.

Suddenly, and with a small stab of acute horror, Jim understood. This painting represented wealth and power to him. That was the reason he coveted it—the *real* reason. That the Sisley was heart-stopping, lyrical, a great piece of art which appealed to his sensibilities more than the others, was beside the point. His hand trembled and he put the drink on the table, closed his eyes, blocking out the painting.

I want the money. I want the power. I want it all back . . . all that my great-grandfather and my great-uncle so foolishly squandered or lost, and which Emma Harte took from the Fairleys. Instantly Jim was appalled at these thoughts and at himself. I've had too much to drink. I'm getting maudlin. No, I'm not. I've not had that much vodka today. I've been very careful about my intake.

The trembling seemed to seize his whole body, and he opened his eyes, gripped the sides of his wheelchair to steady himself. The image of Paula flashed through his mind. He had married her because he was madly in love with her. He had. He knew he had. *No.* There was another reason. He had wanted her because she was Emma Harte's granddaughter. Wrong again. Because she was Emma Harte's principal heir to her vast fortune.

For a split second James Arthur Fairley saw himself as he truly was. It was his epiphany. And he did not like what he saw in that intense flash of clarity. *It was the truth.* He did love his wife, but he craved her money and her power. He groaned aloud and his eyes filled. This sudden self-revelation was insupportable. He was not the man he had believed himself to be all of his life. His grandfather had brought him up to be a gentleman, to look to the higher things in life, to be unconcerned about material wealth and position. Edwin Fairley had brain-washed him. Yet secretly he had always longed for the power, the glory, and the riches. There was a dichotomy in his nature. That was the true cause of his internal strife. I've deluded myself for years, he thought. I've lived a lie.

He groaned again and ran his hand through his hair. I love Paula for herself, I really do.

The nagging pain in his shoulder intruded, and so insistently he winced in agony. It was the rainy weather. His shoulder was like a barometer. He groped around in his pocket for a pill, washed it down with vodka.

"Blackie's so excited," Emma said from the doorway, hurrying in, laughing gaily. "He's making such elaborate plans for the Grand National. He's taking *all* of us to Aintree for the steeplechase. It's the first Saturday in April." Emma sat down, took a sip of her wine. "And so you'll be able to come with us, Jim. You'll be as fit as a fiddle by then."

Forty

"What are we going to do, Shane?" Paula stared at him, her expression troubled.

"We're going to take this one step at a time, get through each day as best we can," he said confidently. He gave her one of his reassuring smiles. "And we're going to make it."

They sat in her office in the Leeds store. It was an afternoon in the middle of April of 1970. Shane had just returned from a quick trip to Spain, where he had been to supervise the remodeling currently in progress at their Marbella hotel.

Now he edged closer to her on the sofa, put his arm around her, held her tightly in his arms. "Try not to worry so much, darling."

"I can't help it. The situation hasn't improved—it's just worsened. And everything's dragging on interminably. I'm beginning to think I'll never be free of my problems."

"Yes, you will." Moving away, he lifted her face, looked deeply into her eyes. "We've both got innumerable business pressures right now, a load of responsibilities, and we're just going to have to concentrate on those, keep ourselves busy, knowing that ultimately we'll be together. And when we are, it will be for always. Think of the future, Paula, keep your eyes trained on that."

"I try, I do try, Shane, but . . ." Her voice wavered and stopped. Her eyes filled up.

"Hey, come on, love," he said, "no tears. We've got to keep moving ahead, and purposefully so. I keep telling you, time is on our side. We're both young, and we are going to win in the end."

"Yes." She brushed her eyes with her fingertips, forced a more cheerful expression onto her face. "It's just that—oh, Shane, I miss you so much."

"I know, I know, and I miss you too. It's sheer hell being apart. But look here, I *would* have to go to New York next week, and then on to Sydney for two months, even if your situation was straightened out. There's no way I can change those circumstances. And it's not been so bad, has it? We were together in New York for part of January and we've managed to grab some time together these past few weeks. So . . ."

"I can't help feeling that it's not fair to you. I'm keeping you dangling and . . ."

His laughter obliterated her words. "I love you, and only you. I'll wait for you, Paula." He hugged her fiercely. "What kind of a man do you think I am, you silly, silly girl. None of this is your fault. It's beyond your control. Life intrudes, that can't be helped. We're just going to have to battle it through."

"I'm sorry, Shane. I *am* being mournful today, aren't I? Perhaps that's because you'll be leaving in a few days. I feel so desperately alone when you're not in England."

"But you're *not* alone, Paula. You have me, my love and my support—*always*. I carry you in my heart wherever I go, and you're never out of my thoughts, not for a single moment. We talk on the telephone practically every day, and if you need me urgently I'll come to you as fast as I can. You know I'd be on the first plane out, whether I'm in Australia or the States." He gazed at her, his black eyes quizzical all of a sudden. "You *do* know that, don't you?"

"Yes, yes, of course I do."

"Remember what I said to you in Barbados?"

"That I must trust your love for me."

"That's right. *As I trust yours for me.* Now, are you going to change your mind and come to dinner at Beck House tonight? It'll do you good, and Emily was so disappointed when you declined her invitation."

"Perhaps I will, after all." Paula frowned. "Do you think she and Winston suspect anything about us?"

"No way. They believe we've become good friends again, and that's all."

Paula was not entirely convinced he was correct. However, she had no wish to implant troublesome ideas in his mind, and she said, "I couldn't get there until eight. I want to go home to see Tessa and Lorne, and then I have to go to the nursing home to see Jim."

"I understand."

"You really *do,* don't you, Shane?"

"Of course, and I wouldn't expect anything less of you, Paula. You're far too good and too compassionate a woman to turn your back on Jim at a time like this. You said over lunch that he was a bit better. What's the general prognosis?"

"The doctor told me yesterday that he could be out of the nursing home in a few weeks, *if* he continues to improve the way he has. He's not as depressed as he was and he's responding well to treatment, to the psychiatric help." She shook her head and her worry flared up in her. "But you never know with a nervous breakdown. I mean, some people recover quickly, others take months, and it's not unusual for a person to have relapses." She hesitated, murmured in a low, almost inaudible tone, "I can't bring myself to say anything to him just yet —about my freedom."

"I'm aware of that, you don't have to keep repeating yourself," Shane said rapidly, but with gentleness. "We agreed that we must wait until Jim's back to normal, truly capable of handling things, before you tell him you want a divorce. I'm not reneging on our agreement. What else *can* we do? I'd like to be able to live with myself in the future, and I know you would too."

"Yes. Oh, Shane, thank you, thank you so much for your understanding, and most of all for your love. I don't know what I'd do without you."

He took her in his arms and kissed her, and they sat holding each other for a few minutes. Finally he released her. "I've got to get back to the office. I've a couple of meetings scheduled, and with Dad in London at the international hotel conference I've got my hands full. Then I want to stop off and see Grandpops on my way home to Beck House."

They rose and she walked him to the door. "Give my love to Uncle Blackie," Paula said, looking up at him. She offered him a brighter smile. "I feel much better—now that I've seen you."

Shane touched her face lightly. "You'll be all right, darling, *we'll* be all right. Just so long as we stay cool and keep a positive attitude. We musn't let anything rattle us or throw us off our course."

Several hours later, when Shane pushed open the door of the library in his grandfather's house, he found Blackie standing in front of an antique chest. He had a soft yellow duster in his hand and was carefully rubbing away at the silver trophy which was now his pride and joy.

Shane smiled. If his grandfather polished it once a day, he did so at least half a dozen times. Of all the things Blackie owned, it had become his proudest and most treasured possession. At the beginning of April, Blackie's eight-year-old mare, Emerald Bow, had run at Aintree and had won the Grand National. Winning the greatest steeplechase in the world had been the fulfillment of Blackie's lifelong dream. Curious, though, Shane now thought, that of all the horses he owns it had to be the one Emma gave him which finally won the most coveted prize for him. There has to be something prophetic in that.

Moving forward, Shane said, "Hello, Grandpops, sorry I'm late."

Blackie turned around, his face lighting up. The sight of his handsome, strapping grandson warmed his heart. "Shane, me boy!" he cried and ambled across the floor.

The two men embraced. But as his arms went around his grandfather in a bear hug, Shane realized, with a small shock, that Blackie had lost weight since he had last seen him. My God, I can feel his bones through his suit. He's suddenly become so frail, Shane thought with a spurt of worry mingled with sadness. They drew apart and Shane looked into Blackie's face, his eyes scanning it swiftly. The weight loss was evident in the sunken cheeks, the scrawny neck. His shirt collar looked too big for him, and Blackie was unnaturally pale tonight. His ebony black eyes were cloudy, seemed to have a milky film.

"Are you feeling all right, Grandfather?" Shane asked, his scrutiny fixed on the old man.

"Never felt better."

"That's good to hear," Shane answered, but he reminded himself that his grandfather usually said this. Not wishing to press him further about his health, Shane eyed the cloth in Blackie's hand. "If you're not careful, you're going to rub a hole in that thing with your constant polishing, and then where will you be?"

Blackie snorted in amusement, followed Shane's glance, which was directed at the trophy. He lumbered over to the chest where it reposed, his pace as slow as before. Putting the cloth down, he rested his hand on top of the symbol of Emerald Bow's great triumph.

"I won't go so far as to say that winning this was the crowning moment of my life, but it was certainly the most thrilling." Blackie nodded to himself. "It truly was."

Shane smiled across the room at his grandfather. "And mine too," he asserted.

"Aay, lad, but you're going to have greater triumphs in your life than I've ever had. That's in the cards, sure and it is." Stepping up to the small console, Blackie picked up a crystal decanter and poured whiskey in two glasses. "Let's drink to that foregone conclusion with a drop of me good Irish."

Shane joined him, took the tumbler, clinked it against Blackie's and said, "To future triumphs—for us both, Grandpops."

"Yes, indeed. And to Emerald Bow and next year's Grand National. You never know, she could win again." Blackie shot Shane a knowing look, went over to the fireplace and sat down in his favorite wing chair.

Shane followed him, struck once more by his grandfather's slow gait, which was almost a shuffle, and his fragility. Concern mounted in Shane, but he pressed down on it. Perhaps his grandfather was merely tired this evening. Also, the excitement of the Grand National, winning, and all the partying that had ensued might easily have taken its toll. And, after all, he was an old man, very old now. He was eighty-four years old.

Blackie sat musing to himself for a second or two, gazing into the flames, an abstracted look in his eyes, then he said to his grandson, "I don't think I'll ever forget the finish." Swinging his head, he leaned forward with a burst of energy and eagerness, his glass clasped tightly between his hands, his eyes shining brightly as he relived the race in his mind's eye.

He exclaimed excitedly: "There they were, Shane, coming to the last fence! Emerald Bow with two other big horses alongside her! *Almost neck and neck.* Steve Larner, tough little sod that he is, going hell-for-leather. High in the stirrups, pushing her forward, a grim look on his face. Me heart was in me mouth, aye, it was that, Shane. I thought she wasn't going to make it. Sure and I believed one of the other two would beat her to it, if only by a hairsbreadth. When Highland Boy went first, sailed up but hit the top of the fence, rolled over and was out of the race, just like that, well, I couldn't believe me eyes. And then King's Gold went the same way, catapulting over and landing on his back. I knew he'd taken it too close to the roots of the fence. Me old eyes were glued on Emerald Bow. And only a fraction of a second after the others had fallen, there she was, me valiant little mare, jumping the fence like a gazelle and finishing two hundred yards in front of the field. Aye, Shane, it was the most spectacular finish I've ever seen, and I've been to a hell of a lot of horse races during my long life." Blackie's face was flushed, and he fell back against the chair. He was breathless, but recovered himself in a matter of moments.

"I was there, Grandpops. I saw it all, remember."

Blackie winked at him. "Sure you saw it, but I can't help reliving it with you, lad. It gets the blood flowing through me veins again, and you know your father doesn't understand how I feel—not really. It's you, Shane, who has inherited my love of horses, and you've got as good an eye as me when it comes to spotting a thoroughbred."

Blackie paused, and his eyes danced merrily as another thought struck him. "Poor Emma, how she suffered that day, in one way and another. Worrying because I was getting overly excited, concerning herself with thoughts of my disappointment if Emerald Bow lost, and she even got hurt in the process. I grabbed hold of her so hard at the finish she was bruised for days, at least so she tells me. Said I'd almost crushed some of her fragile old bones. Still, she did enjoy it, no two ways about that. And she was as excited as I was. As I still am, if the truth be known."

"And why not, Grandpops, it was a wonderful victory for you, and so well deserved."

Blackie sat back, took a sip of his whiskey. His face sobered and he became reflective. After a moment he said, "Randolph was always right about Emerald Bow, you know, from the day Emma gave her to me. He never stopped telling me she had the stamina required for the National. It's a hard race, bloody carnage, too, when you consider that out of the forty horses that start, only about eight finish. If that. Thirty fences to jump, and twice over Becher's Brook. So many horses are injured, and it's exhausting for those that last. The stuffing's knocked out of them by the time they're coming into the final stretch."

"The National's also a hell of a *fast* race," Shane volunteered. "It's over in about ten minutes."

"Aye, it is, it is." Blackie peered at Shane. His expression was one of self-congratulation and gratification. "The party I threw at the Adelphi Hotel after the race was one of the best ever given, so I've been told. It *was* a grand bash, wasn't it?"

"Smashing! And so was the welcome we received when we got back to Middleham on Sunday lunchtime. The huge banner congratulating Emerald Bow stretched across the main street, the boys coming out of the pubs when you and Randolph paraded her around the town, and then the luncheon at Allington Hall—memorable, all of it, Grandfather. I was so pleased and proud for you, I wouldn't have missed it for anything."

"I know you wouldn't, but still, I admit I was a bit worried when you got bogged down with work in Sydney, early in March. I held my breath, I did indeed. I thought you mightn't make it, and that would have been a severe blow to me, my boy." Blackie sighed and a look of true contentment crossed his face. "It's been a wonderful twelve months when I look back now. The trip around the world with me darlin' Emma, and now this—" He broke off, glanced at the trophy, the smile lingering on his face. "Imagine *me* winning the greatest race in existence."

"You're not still talking about the Grand National are you?" Emma exclaimed sharply, walking into the library in her usual brisk way. "We're never going to hear the end of it, I can see."

Laughing, Blackie pushed himself up, went to greet her, kissed her cheek. "Now, mavourneen, don't spoil me bit of fun." He held her away from him and studied her closely. "Bonny as always, and I see you're wearing my emerald bow." His face filled with genuine pleasure as he gestured to the brooch pinned onto the white-silk shawl collar of her gray wool dress. "I notice you haven't had this off since we won. Now if that's not an emblem of the National, I don't know what is, mavourneen."

Emma laughed, squeezed his arm, turned to Shane as he walked across the floor to join them.

Shane said, "Hello, Aunt Emma, and Grandfather's right, you do look lovely tonight." He bent forward, kissed her cheek.

"Thank you, Shane. How was the trip to Spain? I see you're keeping that tan of yours going strong."

"I try," he said, grinning. "And the trip was very successful."

Returning to the chair by the fire and drawing Emma along with him, Blackie said, "Shane will get you a drink. What would you like to have, Emma?"

"Sherry, thank you."

"And where's Emily?" Blackie asked. "I thought she was coming in for a drink. Is she parking the car?"

"No. She dropped me off and went on her way. She had to get over to Beck House early. She sends you her love, and her apologies. Apparently she's cooking dinner for Shane and Winston tonight."

"Oh, I am disappointed not to see her. I was looking forward to her visit —I've got a soft spot for young Emily. She always gives me a good chuckle, no one quite as pithy and blunt as Emily—except for you, of course." Blackie reached for a cigar, clipped off the end.

Frowning at him, Emma exclaimed fiercely, "Should you be smoking that thing? You promised me you were going to cut them out." He gave a throaty chuckle, grinned at her. "At my age!" Shrugging, he went on, "I keep telling you, I'm living on borrowed time. I don't aim to deprive myself of me last few pleasures. *This*"—he waved the cigar under her nose—"and me drop of whiskey."

Emma let out a long-suffering sigh, knowing there was no use arguing with him.

Shane carried the glass of sherry over to Emma, sat down on the sofa. His grandfather and she had begun to talk about Emily's wedding, which was to take place in two months. He sat back, lit a cigarette, listened, his mind straying to Paula. He worried about her constantly, and even though he presented a patient and understanding demeanor to her, he was extremely anxious for Jim to make a quick recovery from whatever ailed him. And what did ail Fairley? Booze and pills, Shane thought. He was convinced that this lethal combination had contributed to, if not caused, Jim's recent collapse. Emma, Winston, and Emily tended to agree with him, and Paula had confided in January that she thought Jim was an alcoholic.

"Winston tells me you won't be able to be his best man after all," Emma said, drawing Shane into the conversation. "We're so disappointed."

"No more than I am, Aunt Emma. But Dad wants me to go to Sydney again, after I've spent a couple of weeks in New York, and I'll have to remain there through the end of May into June. Nothing much I can do about it— somebody has to supervise the building of the new hotel."

"Yes, so Winston explained."

Shane said, "Michael Kallinski's standing in for me, and I can't think of a better man for the job."

"I hear his father's not been too well," Blackie interjected worriedly. "Have you spoken to Ronnie in the last few days, Emma?"

"Yes, and he's up and about. He's had a bout of pneumonia, but he's feeling much better. This April weather has been most treacherous. So sunny, but the wind has been awfully cold, hasn't it? I've felt nithered to death these last few days."

"That's nothing new," Blackie announced, sitting back, contemplating her fondly. "You suffered from the cold even when you were a slip of a girl. I remember how you used to shiver and complain about being frozen stiff at Fairley Hall."

The two of them were soon engaged in a discussion about the past, which Shane had noticed they were prone to do quite frequently these days. He listened for a while, but when the clock on the mantelpiece struck he glanced at it, saw that it was six-thirty. After stubbing out his cigarette and downing the last drops of his drink, he stood up. "I'm going to push off, leave you two lovebirds to your own devices. Don't do anything I wouldn't do, Grandpops."

"That gives me a lot of rope then," Blackie retorted, winking broadly.

"Several hundred yards at least," Shane answered, his tone jocular. He bent over the chair and kissed his grandfather in the tenderest way, touched his shoulder. "Take it easy, and I'll come and see you tomorrow."

"Yes, please do, my boy. I'll be looking forward to it, and have a nice evening."

"Thanks, I will, Grandpops." Shane stepped over to Emma. He thought how pretty she was despite her grand age. After kissing her, he said, "Keep an eye on this old warrior for me, Aunt Emma. I know he's a handful—but, then, you've had his number for years."

The look Emma gave Shane was full of love. "I will."

"Humph!" Blackie's eyes traveled from Emma to Shane. "And don't think I haven't got *her* number. I've always had it!"

Their laughter followed Shane as he walked to the door. He looked back over his shoulder as he went out, saw that they were already contentedly chatting away, retreating into their own private world, sharing their memories. He closed the door softly behind him.

Blackie glanced at the door, leaned forward, and said in a conspiratorial whisper, "Do you think Shane's still leading a wild life and chasing fast women, like he used to do, Emma?"

"No, I don't," Emma reassured. "I'm perfectly sure he doesn't have time for that, Blackie dear, not the way he works."

"Everyone's getting married and he's still single. And at twenty-eight," Blackie complained, sounding unusually fretful. "I'd hoped to see him settled down before I died, but it doesn't look as if I will. No chance of bouncing *his* babies on my knee."

Emma threw him a chastising look, clucked softly, said, "Of course there is, you silly old thing. What's got into you tonight? You're the one who's forever telling me you're going to live to be ninety."

"Ah, I've grave doubts about that, mavourneen."

Ignoring this comment, Emma hurried on, "Shane *will* settle down, but only when *he's* good and ready."

"Aye, I suppose so." Blackie moved his great white leonine head from side to side. A look of helplessness spread across his face. "This generation—I don't know, Emma, they baffle me at times. They make such messes of their lives, or so it seems to me."

Emma froze in her chair, watching him closely, her eyes growing sharper. Was he generalizing or was he referring to anyone in particular? Surely he had not guessed about Shane's feelings for Paula. She said: "Were we any different? Our generation was just as bad, Blackie dear."

He was silent.

"Think about it—you'll have to agree that I'm correct, you know that." She smiled and her shrewd green eyes danced. "Now who made a bigger mess than me at different times in her life?"

He had to laugh. "That's true. And here I am, going on about Shane, and I haven't even asked you how Paula is faring. Is she all right?"

"Coping, poor girl. She does seem to have her hands full at the moment. However, Jim is on the mend, I think. I sincerely hope he is, for their sakes. She's been worried to death about him, and so have I."

"I was about to ask you about Jim." Blackie gave her an odd look and there was a small pause before he asked, "How long is he going to have to stay in the mental asylum?"

"Psychiatric clinic," Emma corrected. "About another month, maybe six weeks."

"That long! Oh dear, Emma, that is a terrible burden for Paula." He rubbed his chin, gave her a piercing stare. "He will get better, won't he?"

"Of course!" Emma said in her most positive voice, but she couldn't help asking herself if he would. Her mind strayed to his family's troubled history.

As if he had read her thoughts, Blackie reflected out loud, "A funny family, the Fairleys." He looked at her again and for the longest moment. "Adele Fairley used to seem a shade demented to me . . . the way she wandered around Fairley Hall like an apparition. And then there was the dreadful way she died. Tragic. I can't help thinking that this illness of Jim's might be—"

"I'd prefer not to contemplate something like that, if you don't mind, dear," Emma said firmly. "It's all too depressing and worrying for everyone concerned."

Leaning forward, Emma now smiled her most winning smile and changed the subject. "You and I agreed that we wouldn't go gallivanting off again, but I was wondering if you'd like to come and stay with me at my house in the South of France? This summer, Blackie, perhaps in the middle of June, after Emily's wedding, and before Alexander's in July. What do you think?"

"That is a tempting idea. These old bones of mine could use a bit of warming sunshine. Like you, I've been feeling the bite of the northern wind this past week or so. To tell you the truth, I thought I was coming down with the flu."

"Aren't you feeling well?" Emma's quick darting glance betrayed her concern for him.

"Oh, sure and I am, me darlin'. Don't be fussing over me, Emma, you know I've never been able to stand that." His wide Celtic mouth curved up in a smile of tenderness. "Let's face it, we're not spring chickens anymore. We're both very old now." He chuckled, eyeing her in amusement, his eyes suddenly teasing. "Two bags of ancient bones, that's what we are, Emma."

"Speak for yourself," she retorted, but her expression was as loving as his.

They were interrupted by Mrs. Padgett, Blackie's housekeeper, who came in to tell them that dinner was served.

As they walked across the library and out into the lovely circular entrance hall, Emma noticed, as Shane had done earlier, that Blackie's steps were belabored this evening. She had to slow her own pace so that he could keep up with her, and this troubled her deeply.

During dinner she realized that he was picking at his food, not really eating. He seemed to have no appetite, and he hardly touched his glass of red wine, which was most unusual. But she made no comment, deciding instead that she would take matters into her own hands. Tomorrow she would telephone Doctor Hedley, ask him to drive over to give Blackie a thorough examination.

For a short while Blackie talked about the Grand National, and Emma let him ramble on, knowing how important winning had been to him. But at one moment he unexpectedly dropped this subject when he said, "It's always seemed strange to me that Shane was never interested in one of your girls, Emma. There was a time, when they were growing up, that I thought he and Paula might end up marrying each other . . . one day."

Emma held her breath. For a split second she was on the verge of confiding in him, and then instantly changed her mind. It would only distress him if he knew about Shane's love for her granddaughter. Particularly since she had now come to the conclusion that Paula did not reciprocate Shane's feelings. Blackie would not be able to bear the thought of Shane's heartache.

Emma leaned over and patted his hand lying on the table. "I suppose being together all of their lives makes them feel like brother and sister."

"Aye, most probably, but it would've been lovely if they'd married, wouldn't it, me darlin'?"

"Oh yes, Blackie, it would have been wonderful."

As they left the dining room, Mrs. Padgett reminded Blackie she was taking the rest of the evening off, and bid them good night. Slowly he and Emma walked back through the hall and went into the library. Emma poured a cognac for him, a liqueur glass of Bonnie Prince Charlie for herself.

They sat in silence for a while, sipping their drinks, lost in their own contemplations, as companionable tonight as they had been all of their lives. But eventually Blackie roused himself. "Don't you think it would be nice to play some records, Emma? Listen to a few old tunes, the ones we used to love."

"What a good idea." Emma rose and went over to the small cabinet that housed the stereo, looked through the stack of records. "My goodness, I didn't know you still had this . . . that John McCormack selection of old Irish ballads I gave you years ago. Shall I put it on?"

"Aye, why not." Blackie gave her a small grin as she returned to her chair, boasted, "I still have a good voice you know. I'll sing along with the music, if you like."

"I always did love that rich baritone of yours."

They listened to the selection and, true to his word, Blackie did sing a few snatches of the old songs now and then, but his voice was feeble and quavering, and so he mostly hummed the melodies.

When the record came to an end, Emma remarked, "Those songs bring back a lot of memories . . . especially 'Danny Boy.' I'll never forget that night I came looking for you, after I'd run away from Fairley Hall. I found you at the Mucky Duck, singing that ballad as if your life depended on it. Oh, Blackie, you looked so marvelous, standing there next to the piano, and, goodness me, you were *so* theatrical. A real ham."

He smiled.

Emma's eyes rested on him affectionately, took in the wavy hair, still thick but white as driven snow, the craggy features, the broad face marked by the signs of age, and suddenly, in her imagination, she saw him as he had been in his youth, as he had looked that night in the pub. Vibrant black curls rippling back from a tanned face, black eyes dancing, white teeth flashing between rosy lips, his superb looks prominently highlighted in the glare from the burning gas lamps.

Leaning forward, Emma asked, "Do you remember that particular night, Blackie?"

"How could I ever forget it, Emma? We went and sat together in the Saloon Bar and you drank a lemonade. I had a pint of bitter. Ah, such a little snippet of a lass you were . . . and you told me you were pregnant . . . and I asked you to marry me. Perhaps you should have."

"Yes, perhaps. But I didn't want to burden you . . ." Emma did not finish, and she picked up her liqueur, took a sip.

Blackie settled back in his chair, a faint smile playing around his mouth, and then he nodded to himself, said, "You do look bonny tonight, Emma. You're the most fetching colleen in the whole county."

"You're prejudiced," she murmured, returning his unwavering gaze, his gentle smile.

Blackie sat up a little straighter, peering across at her in the soft dim glow of the muted light in the room. "I'll never be able to tell you what our holiday has meant to me, Emma. Those eight months with you have made up for all the bad things that ever happened to me in my entire life—the pain, the heartache, the sorrow. And I do thank you, me darlin'."

"What a lovely thing to say, Blackie. But it is I who should thank you for making your Plan with a capital P."

"It was a good plan—" Blackie stopped short and grimaced.

Instantly Emma was on her feet, leaning over him. "What's the matter? Are you ill?"

He shook his head. "It's nothing . . . just a twinge of indigestion."

"I'm going to ring the doctor, and then I'm going to get you upstairs to bed." She turned away from him, made a movement toward the desk near the window.

"No, no." He tried to restrain her but his hand fell away weakly. "I won't make it, Emma."

"Yes, you will," she insisted. "I'll help you."

Blackie shook his head very slowly.

"I *am* going to telephone Doctor Hedley," Emma announced with a show of her old firmness.

"Sit down here with me, Emma. *Please,*" he begged. "Just for a minute or two."

Emma pulled up a hassock, seated herself, took his hand in hers, searched his face. "What is it, Blackie?"

He squeezed her fingers, then smiled at her. Suddenly his eyes opened very wide. "All my life," he whispered hoarsely, "I've known you all my life. We've been through so much together, Emma."

"Yes," she said, "we have and I don't know what I'd have done without you, Blackie."

He sighed a very long, slow sigh. "I'm sorry to have to leave you alone. So very sorry, mavourneen."

Emma could not speak. Tears rushed into her eyes, fell down her wrinkled cheeks, splashed over the white silk collar and the emerald bow, and onto their entwined hands.

Blackie's eyes widened again, and he stared at her more acutely, as if memorizing her face. And then he said in a surprisingly clear voice, "I've always loved you, me darlin'."

"And I have always loved you, Blackie."

A fleeting smile struck his pale mouth. His eyelids fluttered, closed, lay still. His head fell to one side. His hand went slack in her tenacious grip.

"Blackie," she said. *"Blackie!"*

The silence overwhelmed her.

She held onto his hand tightly, closing her eyes. The tears seeped out from under her old lids, ran down her face in streaming rivulets. She lowered her head and rested it on their clasped hands, drenching them with her tears.

"Good-bye, my dearest friend, good-bye," she said at last. She continued to weep quietly, unable to stem the tears, and she sat there for a long time, her aching heart full of love for him.

But eventually she lifted her head, let go of his hand, and pushed herself up onto her feet. She bent over him, gently smoothed his snow-white hair back from his forehead, and kissed his icy lips. How cold he is, she thought.

Emma's pace was slow and her step faltering as she moved blindly toward his chair near the window, where he had so often sat lately looking out at his garden. She took the small wool blanket patterned with the tartan of the Seaforth Highlanders and brought it to him and covered his legs and tucked it around him.

And then at the same snail's crawl she went to his desk. She lifted the phone and with trembling hands dialed Beck House.

It was Shane who answered. "Hello?" he said.

On hearing his strong and vibrant tone her tears began to flow once more. "It's Blackie," Emma said through her tears, in a voice that shook. "He's gone . . . Please come, Shane."

Shane arrived within the hour, bringing Paula, Emily, and Winston with him.

They found her sitting on the hassock next to Blackie, her hand resting on his knee, her silver head bowed. She did not turn nor did she move at all, merely went on sitting there, staring into the fire.

Shane hurried to her, put his hand on her shoulder lightly, brought his face to hers. "I'm here, Aunt Emma," he said in the kindest of voices.

She made no response.

Shane took her hands in his and brought her to her feet slowly, gentleness flowing out of him.

Emma finally lifted her face to look up into his, and she began to weep and Shane took her in his arms and held her close, soothing her.

"I miss him already and he's only just died," Emma said with a small heartbreaking sob. "Whatever am I going to do without Blackie?"

"Hush, Aunt Emma, hush," Shane murmured and then he led her over to the sofa, motioning with his eyes to Paula, who stood in the doorway white-faced and trembling. She came and sat with her grandmother, began to comfort her, and Emily joined them.

Shane stepped over to Blackie. His throat was thick with emotion and the sorrow rose in him and tears ran down his cheeks. He gazed at Blackie's face and saw how peaceful it was in death, and then he leaned forward and kissed his withered cheek.

"Godspeed, Grandfather," he said in a low and saddened voice. "God-speed."

Forty-One

Paula began cautiously, "It's your birthday in two days, Grandy, and I thought we might have a—"

"Oh dear," Emma interrupted softly, with a small frown, "Don't bring that up. Blackie's only been dead a couple of weeks and I'm not in the mood for a celebration."

"I know, and I wasn't talking about a big party. Just a small dinner here at Pennistone Royal. There would only be me, Emily, Winston, and my parents. We thought it would cheer you up."

"Cheer me up," Emma repeated hollowly, and then reached out and patted Paula's hand. "I don't think anything would cheer me right now. But I suppose I have to keep plodding on. All right then . . . just the five of you, though. Please don't invite anyone else. I'm not in much of a mood for people right now. They tire me."

"I promise I won't invite another solitary single soul," Paula assured her, pleased that the suggestion had met with success.

"And no presents, Paula. I don't want any presents. As far as I'm concerned, reaching eighty-one is cause for lament not receiving gifts and whooping it up."

"Don't worry, Grandma, we'll keep it very simple and casual. And it'll be nice for you to have Mummy and Daddy here for a few days."

"Yes," Emma murmured. She glanced down at the album on her lap. She had been looking at it when Paula had arrived a short while ago. She stared at the old photographs absently, her thoughts drifting into the past for a few seconds. Then she lifted her head, pushed the album toward Paula, remarked, "Look at us here—Blackie, Laura, and me. We're standing outside my first shop in Armley. That's me—in the tam-o'-shanter."

"Yes, I recognize you." Paula had seen this picture many times, knew the pages of the album by heart, but wanting to humor her grandmother, she said, "Let's look at some of the others, and you can tell me a few of your lovely stories about your early days in business. You know how I like hearing them."

Emma nodded and at once began to talk with sudden animation as they leafed through the book, and for the next twenty minutes the two of them sat side by side in the upstairs parlor, reliving parts of Emma Harte's life.

At one point Emma broke off, peered at Paula, and said, "How long do you think I'm going to live?"

Taken aback at this question, Paula stared at her grandmother askance, filling with sudden alarm. She cleared her throat, said firmly, "A long time, darling."

"You're very optimistic," Emma said, and turned away, looked out into space, a faraway expression settling on her face.

Paula exclaimed, "You're extremely fit for your age, remarkable, really, and not a bit forgetful. You have years ahead of you, Grandy, as long as you take care of yourself."

Emma brought her ancient and wise green gaze to meet Paula's troubled face, and she smiled slowly. "Yes, yes, you're quite right. I don't know what's got into me today—I'm being morbid, aren't I? Blackie's death has been such a terrible blow to me, but I suppose I must be positive." She let out a chuckle. "Anyway, I might be old and a trifle weary these days, but I don't want to leave this world yet."

"That's the spirit, Grandy."

Emma did not reply. She rose and walked over to the oriel window, stood looking down at her gardens and the daffodils blowing in the breeze. It's such a beautiful afternoon, she thought. Another perfect spring day . . . just like the day of Blackie's funeral. How eternal the land is, constantly renewing itself. Yes, in death there is always life. Sighing again, Emma returned to the fireplace and sat down in the chair next to it. She said, "It was lovely of you to come over to see me, Paula dear. But I think I'd like to be by myself for a while, to have a little rest before dinner."

Paula came to her, kissed her cheek, her heart full of love for Emma. "All right, Gran, and I'll pop in tomorrow with the babies."

"That'll be very nice," Emma answered, and settled back in the chair as her granddaughter left the room. Her mind turned inward. The young don't really understand, she thought. Paula tries, and tries very hard, but she doesn't know what it's like to be the sole survivor, the only one left of one's contemporaries. They've all gone now. They're all dead and buried. My dearest friends, my loved ones. Even my enemies are no longer around to get my goat and spark the will in me to fight. I'm so alone without Blackie. We kept each other going all these years—he and I. Rambling on together into our twilight years. We had so many memories to share, a lifetime of experiences, and so much love and friendship to give each other. Why, my whole life has been lived out with my sweet Irishman. I didn't expect him to go like that. Such a shock. I knew he was old, as I am old, but he seemed so strong, and indomitable, like me. Funny, I always thought I would die first. Whatever will I do? However will I manage without him?

Emma's grief and enormous sense of loss overcame her again, as it had done so frequently in the last two weeks since Blackie's sudden death. Tears came into her eyes and she choked back a sob, brought her hand to her trembling lips. I miss Blackie so much. Such a void without him. There are so many things I didn't tell him and now it's too late. I ought to have told him about Shane and his love for Paula. I didn't want to upset Blackie. He would have worried. But I do wish I had told him after all.

Emma wiped her damp cheeks with her hand and rested her head against the chair. She was filled with an aching loneliness she could not endure. She closed her eyes and, after a few minutes, began to drowse, drifting off into a gentle sleep.

After leaving her grandmother, Paula had gone downstairs in search of Emily. She had found her in the library, and now they sat together discussing Emma.

"She's putting up a good front, of course," Paula said, "but she's really suffering inside."

Emily frowned worriedly. "I agree with you. She's absolutely lost without Blackie. I think all the fight's gone out of her. To tell you the truth, the other day I even wished we *had* found something on Jonathan. At least that might have captured her interest, made her angry enough to lift her out of this resigned mood."

Paula said, "She was very busy with the plans for your wedding before Blackie died. Can't you get her involved again?"

"Don't think I haven't tried. But she seems so distracted, almost absent-minded, which is not like her."

"You know something, Emily, there's only one thing for it!" Paula leaned forward eagerly. "Emma Harte has been a workhorse all of her life, and her business was her strong citadel in times of grief and sorrow and trouble in the past. We've got to persuade her to come out of retirement . . . get her back in the harness again."

Emily sat up with a jerk, her face brightening. "That's the best idea I've heard in weeks. And Grandma used to say she intended to die with her boots on. Oh, let's do it, Paula." Instantly Emily's face fell, and she bit her inner lip, shaking her blond head. "I'm not sure she'll agree. She might not want to intrude on us . . . she can be very funny, you know."

"We have to make a stab at it. Personally, I think that it's her only salvation. She'll just fade away and die if we don't encourage her to be active, come back to work."

"Agreed, and you can count on me. There's another thing—" Emily hesitated, gave Paula a careful look, then rushed on, "Why don't you move back in here with Nora and the babies? At least until Jim comes out of the nursing home."

"Oddly enough, I thought of that when I was with Gran a little while ago. There's nothing like a couple of babies to liven things up, and perhaps having her great-grandchildren with her will give Grandy a new lease on life."

"Absolutely. And together you and I can jolly Gran out of her despondency, don't you think?"

"Oh God, I hope so, Emily."

"When do you think you could move in to Pennistone Royal?"

Paula laughed. "How does tomorrow sound?"

"Terrific. I'll come over and help you, if you like."

"I'd love it. And then on Monday morning I'm going to vacate Grandy's office at the Leeds store, move back into my old one. That evening, when we have the dinner for her birthday, you and I can make our proposal to her. I'll alert my parents, and they might be able to add a few words of persuasion." Paula stood. "I'd better go, Emily. I want to stop off at the nursing home. I promised Jim I'd come by later today."

The two cousins left the library and walked across the Stone Hall to the front door.

Emily caught hold of Paula's arm just before they reached the short flight of steps. She said in a low tone, "Jim's been in there for ten weeks now. How much longer, Paula?"

"Another month to six weeks. If he continues to improve. Otherwise—" She shrugged wearily, added, "Then it could be longer, of course."

Emily stared at Paula, said swiftly, "Look, I hope you don't mind my saying this, but I hope that Jim knows what drink does to him now. I mean, he won't be able to touch a drop ever again and—"

"He knows," Paula interjected. "And you can be damned sure *I* know. Thanks for being concerned, Emily. One step at a time right now—that's the only way I can live my life, get through each day without losing my sanity. And, very frankly, our grandmother is my priority at the moment."

"Yes," Emily said. "I understand, and she's mine too. You can rely on me to help you any way I can."

They cajoled, pleaded, challenged, and attempted to bully her, using every ruse they knew to get Emma Harte to return to work.

But consistently, and quite categorically, she refused to be budged. Her stance was inflexible. She would shake her head emphatically, repeat over and over again that she had retired and that was that.

Eventually Paula and Emily gave up, at least on the surface. But they were forever dropping pointed remarks and making asides at mealtimes. They continued to seek her advice, even when they did not really need it, using every opportunity to gain her interest and induce in her the desire to take an active role in her business once more.

Emma was fully aware of their ploys, and she would smile to herself, touched by their love and concern for her, but she remained resolute in her determination to lead a quiet life at Pennistone Royal.

And then one morning in the middle of May, Emma awakened early. She discovered that she was filled with her old energy and restlessness and drive. This surprised her, and she lay in bed for a while pondering to herself.

"I'm bored silly," she said to Hilda, when her housekeeper brought up her breakfast tray at eight o'clock.

Placing the tray on Emma's lap, Hilda clucked sympathetically. "Of course you are, Mrs. Harte. You've been such an active woman your entire life, this drifting along, doing nothing, doesn't sit well on you. Perhaps you ought to let Tilson drive you into Leeds today. You could have lunch with Miss Paula or Miss Emily. Getting out of this house would do you the world of good, I just know it."

"I've got a better idea, Hilda," Emma said thoughtfully. "I think I'll start going to the office for a short while every day. I know I don't want to get involved with my business on a day-to-day basis. On the other hand, I would like to keep busy." Emma shook her head, looking regretful. "I ought to be helping Emily plan that wedding of hers. I've been awfully neglectful, a selfish old woman, now that I think about it . . . feeling sorry for myself because my old friends are dead." A look of comprehension flitted across the wrinkled face. "Why, Hilda, my grandchildren are my friends, aren't they?"

"You can be sure they are, Mrs. Harte," Hilda replied. "And Miss Emily will be delighted to have your help with her wedding, what with her mother living in Paris and seemingly not all that interested. She's such a lot to do, and time is running out on her. June fifteenth is not so far off, you know, madam." Hilda beamed. "I shall go downstairs right now and ask Tilson to bring the car around at ten-thirty. How does that sound?"

"It sounds wonderful, Hilda. Thank you very much."

It was ten minutes to twelve when Emma Harte walked into her large department store in Leeds. She looked smart in a tailored navy-blue dress and matching coat. Milky pearls encircled her throat. Diamonds glittered in her ears. Her silver hair was perfectly dressed and her makeup artfully applied.

Emma hurried through the cosmetics department on the street level, her step purposeful and brisk, a wide smile ringing her mouth. And as she stopped to greet the various sales assistants she discovered she was almost moved to tears at the genuine welcome she received from them all.

She took the lift to the executive offices, and then hesitated for a moment outside the door leading into her own private suite. She could not help asking herself what Paula and Agnes would say. She turned the knob and stepped inside.

Paula and Agnes were standing next to the latter's desk deep in conversation. Both women automatically glanced at the door as it swung open. They were speechless at the sight of Emma, obviously completely taken by surprise.

"Well," Emma said, "I'm back. And I'm here to stay." She began to laugh at their stunned expressions, and reverting to the vernacular of the North, she added, "Don't stand there gaping at me like a couple of sucking ducks. Say something."

Paula grinned with pleasure. "Welcome, Grandy," she said, moving forward, catching hold of Emma's arm. "Come on, your office is waiting for you —it's been ready for weeks."

It seemed to Emma that the next few months sped by before she hardly had a chance to catch her breath. Every day she arrived at the Leeds store at eleven and stayed until four o'clock. She was soon in the swing of things, and taking a renewed interest in her colossal business empire, although she left the daily running of it to her grandchildren. She strenuously refused to take back the reins, pointing out, yet again, that she had retired the previous year and had no intentions of resuming her role as head of her various enterprises. She did agree to be a sounding board whenever they needed one, and she was always available to them, offering astute advice. And she was as smart and alert and agile as she had ever been.

And so, whilst she kept a canny eye on the business, she devoted most of her time to planning the two weddings due to take place in June and July. Emily was vastly relieved to have her grandmother's help, as was Maggie Reynolds, Alexander's fiancée. Maggie's mother had been dead for a number of years, and her father, a retired army colonel, had not been in the best of health lately. Nor was he the type of man to embroil himself in such a feminine matter as his daughter's wedding, being gruff and taciturn by nature.

With her inimitable brand of efficiency, and her extraordinary ability to concentrate totally on the matter at hand, Emma plowed ahead, making elaborate arrangements. She dealt with the invitations, the guest lists, the caterers, the florists, the dress designers, and the musicians who were to play at the two receptions. Several times she visited the Dean of Ripon, the Very Reverend Edwin LeGrice, to discuss each marriage ceremony, which he was personally to perform in Ripon Cathedral. Emma spoke to the organist and to the choirmaster at great length, and she helped the two future brides and their grooms select the appropriate music for their nuptials.

Not even the slightest detail was left to chance. Emma Harte wanted perfection and she aimed to have it, whatever it cost in time, energy, and money. Winston said to her one evening, "Well, Aunt Emma, it's good to have you back in command, playing the general again, *and* cracking your whip like you used to at Heron's Nest. Whatever would we do without you?"

"Manage, I'm sure," Emma said in her pithy way, but she laughed, pleased by Winston's remark. She wanted to be wanted, enjoyed feeling useful. And *they help to keep me young and alive and cheerful,* she thought later that same evening, as she was getting ready for bed. She also acknowledged that planning the weddings had helped to take her mind off Blackie's death, had eased her sorrow and her sense of loneliness. *Positive action,* she muttered under her breath as she slipped on her nightdress. *And happy occasions. That's what every old person needs to give them a reason to go on living.*

It was with a heart bursting with love and pride and joyousness that Emma watched Emily walk down the great aisle of Ripon Cathedral on the arm of her father, Tony Barkstone, at noon on June fifteenth.

To Emma, her young granddaughter looked her most beautiful that day. She resembled a delicate Dresden figurine in her wedding gown made of white taffeta. It was styled like an old-fashioned crinoline, the overskirt lifted at the hem, draped and caught with tiny sprigs of forget-me-nots and lilies of the valley. A mixture of these same flowers, also made of silk, had been woven into a small coronet which held her flowing veil in place. Her only pieces of jewelry, other than her engagement ring, were the teardrop diamond earrings Emma had given her in 1968, and Great-Aunt Charlotte's string of pearls which had been *her* engagement present from Emma's brother, Winston, immediately after the First World War. Emily's half sisters, Amanda and Francesca, were her bridesmaids and were charming in blue taffeta gowns, wearing wreaths of honeysuckle in their hair.

The reception was held in the gardens of Pennistone Royal, and as Emma moved amongst her family, friends, and the many guests she kept telling herself how fortunate she was to be here on this most special day in Emily's life and her own. The weather was glorious. The sky was a bright China blue, and the sun brilliant. Emma decided, as she glanced about, that her gardens had never been so stunning in their beauty, the many flowers a vivid blaze of riotous color against the fresh greenness of the lawns and the trees. That afternoon she had an acute awareness of everything, and she saw nature's loveliness and the people present through eyes that were more penetrating than ever in their perception. The smallest things suddenly took on a new importance and significance, and at one moment Emma knew that she was filled with a contentment she had not hitherto felt.

As she sat drinking her tea, watching the young people dancing, she thought of her hard life, her struggles, the sorrow and pain she had endured, the defeats and losses she had suffered. Quite suddenly they were all quite meaningless. *I've been so lucky,* she commented to herself. *Luckier than most, in fact. I've experienced a great love, had dear and loving friends, achieved enormous success, amassed colossal wealth, and enjoyed good health all of my life. And, most important of all, I have grandchildren who love me, care about me now in my old age. Oh yes, I've been lucky to have all that I've had.*

Five weeks later, at the end of July, Emma experienced similar emotions when her grandson was married to Marguerite Reynolds. Maggie made another lovely bride, was elegant and svelte in a simply styled gown of heavy cream satin. It had a high neck, long tight sleeves, and a slender skirt that extended out into a long train. With it Maggie wore a satin pillbox hat encrusted with seed pearls and a veil of Brussels lace. The glorious weather of June held for the July ceremony at Ripon Cathedral and for the reception, which was again held on the grounds of Emma's great old house.

One Sunday, about a week after the second wedding, Emma and Paula went for a walk through the gardens of Pennistone Royal. Emma said suddenly, "Thank you for chivying me out of my despondency after Blackie died. If you hadn't, I might not have been around to witness those two wonderful occasions, to see Emily settled with Winston and Sandy with Maggie." She winked mischievously at Paula, and added, "Now, with a little bit of luck, I might still be here to welcome a couple of new great-grandchildren into my family in the not too distant future.

"You'll be here, Grandma!" Paula exlaimed, returning Emma's smile. "I'm going to make damned sure of that."

Emma linked her arm through Paula's as they continued to meander up the Rhododendron Walk. After a short while, Emma said quietly, "I'm pleased Jim came out of the nursing home in time to attend Alexander's wedding, at least."

"So am I, Grandy." Paula turned to Emma, remarked evenly, "And he's much better. Poor Jim—he's been down at the bottom of the pit. He can only go up from now on."

"Yes, darling, let's hope so." There was a slight hesitation on Emma's part before she murmured, "I've tried to speak to him about the nervous breakdown because I wanted to understand what brought it on. But I'm afraid he's not very forthcoming, is he?"

"No. He doesn't seem able to talk about it, not even with me. I decided it was better not to press him. I'm sure he'll open up later." Paula sighed. "In some ways Jim's very introverted, Gran. Doctor Hedley told me that the psychiatrist at the nursing home has been somewhat baffled too. Apparently he hasn't really been able to get to the root of Jim's despondency."

Emma made no comment and the two of them walked on in silence and finally sat down on the bench at the top of the hill. Emma stared ahead, still thinking of Jim. Her expression changed, became sad as she wondered why he was so bottled up inside and seemingly incapable of unburdening himself to the psychiatrist, a doctor who might well be able to help him.

Paula, watching her grandmother, said, "What are you thinking about, darling? You look so pensive all of a sudden."

"Nothing of any great importance," Emma murmured. "I'm glad Jim went to my house in the South of France with Daisy and David. I think the holiday will do him a lot of good. The sun, the fresh air, outdoor activities, plenty of good food and rest always seem to work wonders. When he comes back at the end of August he'll be able to go back to the newspaper." When Paula was silent, Emma glanced at her curiously. "He will, won't he? You're not hiding something from me, are you, dear?"

"No, no, of course I'm not," Paula exclaimed, dragging herself out of her own worrying thoughts. "And like you I'm happy he agreed to take the holiday with my parents."

"I'm surprised he didn't insist you went with them," Emma ventured, eyeing her with greater interest.

"I promised Jim I'd join them for a week in the middle of August, if that's all right with you. In fact, I was hoping you'd come too."

"Oh no, I don't want to start gadding off again. I shall stay here, and keep my eye on those great-grandchildren of mine." Emma paused, reflected, then remarked as casually as she could manage, "It'll be nice for me if you'd stay on at Pennistone Royal, Paula. If Jim's agreeable and would like to live here, of course. The house is so big, and it's going to seem rather desolate without little Emily." Emma burst out laughing. "I'd better not call her that anymore, had I? After all, she's a married woman now."

"And very much aware of it," Paula said, also laughing. "I'd like us to live here with you, Grandy. I'll talk to Jim when I'm at the Cap." Paula was on the verge of telling Emma that she also fully intended to talk to Jim about a divorce. She stole a look at her grandmother, and changed her mind. Why worry her. Far better to get everything settled with Jim first.

Forty-Two

It was a hot afternoon at the end of August.

Emma sat at her desk in her office at the Leeds store, checking a list of sales figures for Paula. Quite suddenly she had the feeling she was not alone. She looked up quickly and glanced at the open door leading into Paula's office, expecting to see her granddaughter standing there.

There was no sign of Paula.

"I'm beginning to imagine things," Emma said out loud, and then laughed under her breath. I'm also talking to myself, she thought. I hope I'm not getting senile. That state of affairs I couldn't bear.

She put down her pen and stared at the sheet of figures on her desk. She was filled with distaste, found she no longer had any interest in them whatsoever. She peered at her watch. It was almost five. Paula usually slipped out onto one of the floors around this time, and perhaps she had gone to meet Emily in the Rayne-Delman shoe salon. Emily had said something about buying shoes when she had phoned from her office at Genret earlier in the day.

A smile of intense pleasure touched the corners of Emma's implacable mouth, softening its resoluteness. They were having a girls' evening at Pennistone Royal tonight, as they often did on Fridays. Just the three of them and Merry O'Neill.

Emma leaned back in her chair, ruminating on the evening ahead, looking forward to it, and then she blinked in the brilliant light which was streaming in through the windows. How bright the sun is all of a sudden, blinding, really, she muttered to herself. Rising, Emma walked over to the sofa and sat down.

She closed her eyes, wanting to shut out that harsh light which was flooding the room. But it seemed to penetrate through the thin skin of her old lids and she lifted them, stared out into that most extraordinary and unnatural radiance. Emma's eyes narrowed as she shaded them with her hand. How very dazzling it is, she thought again. I must tell Paula to get blinds for this office. It's quite unbearable in here on such a sunny day.

To avoid the intense glare Emma turned her head. Her gaze rested on the photograph frames on the table next to the sofa. The silver and the brass and the glass glittered sharply in the luminescence that now washed over her office, and there was a curious luster to those well-loved faces that stared back at her and so hauntingly. Yes, they *had* been haunting her lately . . . Laura and Blackie, her brothers Winston and Frank, and Paul. Oh yes, always her dearest Paul. In the last few days their faces had been so vividly clear in her imagination, their voices so strong and vibrant in her mind. They were as real to her as when they had been alive.

It seemed to Emma that the past had started to acquire a greater and more pronounced reality than the present. She was constantly invaded by memories, memories of years gone by, and they rushed at her with a force and clarity that stunned. They engulfed her, led her into other regions of time, and frequently she felt that time itself had been suspended at some juncture long ago when she had been a young woman. Yes, her dear, dead loved ones had begun to completely tenant her waking moments, encroach on her restless nights. For the past week she had dreamed so many strange dreams and *they* were there with her in those dreams.

Emma reached for Paul's picture, smiling to herself. She held it tightly between her hands, looking down into his face. How often she had picked up this particular photograph in the last forty-eight hours, irresistibly drawn to it, continually magnetized by his smile, his laughing eyes.

The intensity of the coruscating light sharpened so markedly Emma blinked again. Her whole office was glowing with a shimmering iridescence. It was as if thousands of lights had been turned on and were focused on the very center of the room. She hugged Paul's picture close to her body and gazed wide-eyed into that supernatural light, no longer disturbed by its refulgence. It was glorious and it had an aura of splendor.

But after a few moments of gazing into it she leaned her head against the cushions and closed her eyes. Emma let out a tiny sigh of pleasure. She was filled with happiness, the kind of happiness she had never known before or believed existed. A feeling of warmth began to spread through her body. How lovely it is, she thought. And she, who had suffered from the cold all of her life, was suffused with that warmth and with a peacefulness that was perfection itself. She felt drowsy, enervated, without strength. And yet somehow Emma recognized she was stronger than she had ever been in her whole life. And gradually she became aware of something else. He was here. In this room with her. That was the presence she had felt a few minutes ago.

He walked through the light, coming toward her, growing closer and closer. But he was so young . . . he looked exactly the way he had that night when she had first set eyes on him at the Ritz Hotel during the First World War. He was wearing his army uniform. Major Paul McGill of the Australian Corps. He was standing over her, smiling that engaging smile of his, the blue eyes so wide and clear and spilling his love for her. "I knew I'd find you here in the office, Emma," Paul said, "but it's time for you to stop. Your work on this earth is finished. You have accomplished all you had to accomplish, done everything you had to do. And now you must come with me. I've waited for you for over thirty years. Come, my Emma." He smiled at her and held out his hand. Emma sighed through her smiles. "Not yet, Paul," she said. "Don't take me yet. Let me see them again . . . Paula and Emily. They'll be here any minute. Let me say good-bye to my girls. Then I'll come with you and willingly so. I want to be with you now. I too know it is time for me to leave." Paul smiled and moved away from the sofa, stepped into the core of the glorious shining light. "Paul, wait for me, my darling," Emma cried. He

answered, "Yes, I'm here. I'll never leave you again. You're safe now, Emma." She
reached out her arms to him, straining toward him.

The photograph fell out of her arms, crashed to the floor, the glass shattering. Emma felt so weak she did not have the strength to pick it up. She did not
even have the strength to open her eyes.

Paula and Emily, entering the adjoining office, heard the sudden noise.
They looked at each other in panic and ran into their grandmother's office.

Emma lay quite motionless against the cushions. In repose her face was so
still, so quiet, they were both unnerved. Paula put a calming hand on Emily's
arm and together they approached the sofa. They stood looking down at their
grandmother in apprehension.

"She's just having one of her little snoozes," Emily whispered, instantly
filling with relief. She noticed the photograph on the floor, picked it up,
returned it to its given place.

But Paula was regarding the still and gentle face more closely. She saw the
pinched nose, so white around the nostrils, the pale lips, the chalky pallor of the
cheeks. "No, she's not dozing." Paula's mouth began to tremble uncontrollably. "She's dying, Grandy's dying."

Emily's face paled and she went rigid with fear. Her green eyes, so like
Emma's, welled. "No, no, it can't be so. We must call Doctor Hedley immediately."

Paula's throat tightened and tears sprang into her eyes. She flicked them
away with a trembling hand. "It's too late, Emily. I think she only has a few
minutes." Paula repressed a sob and knelt at Emma's feet, took one of her frail
old hands in hers. "Gran," she said softly. "It's me, Paula."

Emma's lids lifted. Instantly her face lit up. "I waited for you, darling, and
for Emily. Where is she? I can't see her." Emma's voice was feeble, fading.

"I'm here, Grandma," Emily gasped, choking on her words. She too knelt
down and took Emma's other hand in hers.

Emma saw her, half-inclined her head. She closed her eyes but opened
them at once. She straightened up with a small burst of energy and stared
directly into Paula's tear-stained face. Her voice was very weak yet clear, almost
youthful, as she said, "I asked you to hold my dream . . . but you must also
have your own dream, Paula, as well as mine. And you too, Emily. And you
must both hold on to your dreams . . . always." She lay back against the sofa
as if exhausted and her eyelids drooped.

Her two granddaughters gazed at her speechlessly, clinging to her hands,
seared by their grief, their strangled sobbing the only sound in the room.

All of a sudden Emma opened her eyes for a second time. She smiled at
Paula and then at Emily before looking away. She directed her gaze into the far,
far distance, as if she saw a place they could not see and someone who was
visible only to her.

"Yes," Emma said, "I know it is time now."

Her green eyes stretched, became very bright and shining, and they
glowed with the purest of inner light. And she smiled her incomparable smile
which illuminated her face with radiance, and then her expression became one
of rapture and perfect joy as she looked for the last time on her granddaughters.
Her eyes closed.

"Gran, Gran we love you so much." Emily began to weep as if her heart
would break.

"She's at peace," Paula whispered, her mouth twisting in pain and sorrow. Tears were trickling down her face. After a moment she stood up. Leaning over her grandmother, she kissed her on the lips, her tears dripping onto Emma's cheeks. "You'll always be in my heart, Gran. All the days of my life. And you are the very best part of me."

Emily had been kissing Emma's small hand over and over and over again, and now she too rose. Paula moved to one side so that her cousin could also bid Emma farewell.

Reaching out, Emily stroked her grandmother's cheek, then she kissed her on the lips. "As long as I'm alive you'll be alive, Gran. I'll love you always. And I'll never forget you."

Paula and Emily automatically drew together, put their arms around each other. The two young women clung together for a few minutes, weeping, sharing their grief, endeavoring to comfort each other. Gradually they became a little calmer.

Emily stared at Paula. Tremulously she said, "I've always been afraid of death. But I'll never be afraid of it again. I'll never forget Grandy's face, the way it looked as she was dying. It was filled with such radiance, such luminosity, and her eyes were brimming with happiness. Whatever it was our grandmother saw, it was something beautiful, Paula."

Paula's throat constricted. "Yes," she said shakily. "She did see something beautiful, Emily. She saw Paul . . . and Winston and Frank . . . and Laura and Blackie. And she *was* happy because she was going to join them at last."

Forty-Three

In death, as in life, Emma Harte was in full command.

After summoning Doctor Hedley to the store, telephoning members of the family, and then accompanying Emma's body to the undertakers, Paula and Emily finally drove out to Pennistone Royal.

A tearful Hilda greeted them in the Stone Hall.

The housekeeper handed Paula a letter she was clutching. "Mrs. Harte gave this to me a few weeks ago. She asked me to hold it for you, Miss Paula, until her death." Hilda, who had worked for Emma for over thirty years, burst into tears again. "It doesn't seem possible that she's gone," Hilda said, wiping her eyes. "She looked so well this morning when she left for the store."

"Yes, she did," Paula murmured quietly. "And let's be glad she had her faculties until the end, and that her death was so peaceful, quite beautiful, really, Hilda." Paula and Emily spent the next few minutes comforting the sorrowful housekeeper, and gave her the full details of Emma's passing, which seemed to soothe her.

Finally pulling herself together, Hilda said, "I know you both must have a lot to do. I'll be in the kitchen if you need anything."

"Thanks, Hilda," Paula said. Slowly she walked across the Stone Hall and mounted the great staircase, clasping the letter to her chest. Emily trailed in her wake.

They went into Emma's upstairs parlor where a fire blazed and the lamps glowed. They sat down on the sofa together and it was with shaking hands that

Paula opened the sealed envelope and read the four pages covered with Emma's neat yet elegant handwriting. The letter was neither maudlin nor sad, but brisk and matter-of-fact, and it contained Emma's instructions for her funeral. She wanted a short and simple service, only one prayer and two hymns, one of them to be sung by Shane O'Neill. She forbade a eulogy, but suggested that if Paula so wished there could be one. It had to be spoken by Randolph, her nephew, and no one else.

It was the very cheerfulness that brought the tears to Paula's eyes. Swallowing, she passed the letter to Emily. "These are Grandy's last wishes. She doesn't want the funeral service to be long or drawn out, and it mustn't be overly religious. We must do as she asks, Emily."

Emily also wept as she read the letter. After mopping her streaming eyes and blowing her nose, she asked in a quavering tone, "Whatever are we going to do without Grandy, Paula?"

Paula put her arm around Emily and comforted her. After a while she said firmly, but with gentleness, "We are going to do what she wants us to do, take charge, and bury her the way she requested. And from now on we are going to be strong, and very brave. She wouldn't expect less of us. After all, that's the way she raised us. She taught us to stand tall, as she did throughout her life, and so we *must*. We can't let her down. Not now. *Not ever.*"

"Yes, you're right." Emily took a deep breath. "Sorry, I don't mean to be a burden to you. I know it's just as hard for you as it is for me." Emily frowned and then added, "Did you notice the date on the letter?"

"Yes. She wrote it a few days after Alexander's wedding—only a month ago."

"Do you think Grandy knew she was going to die soon?"

"Perhaps, but I can't be sure. Still, they say old people do see death approaching. Blackie going so suddenly shook her up, as you know, and it made her feel vulnerable, even more conscious of her own mortality." Paula forced a watery smile. "On the other hand, I'd like to believe that *our* Gran was just being her usual efficient self, thinking of every contingency when she wrote the letter. You know as well as I do that Emma Harte never left one single thing to chance."

These comments seemed to cheer Emily. "That's true. And at least Gran died the way she wanted to die—at the office, with her boots on."

Both young women glanced around as the door opened suddenly.

Winston hurried into the parlor, his face grave, his eyes red-rimmed. "Sorry I'm late. I've been on the phone for ages," he said. He kissed his wife, squeezed her shoulder comfortingly, and then bent down and kissed Paula on the cheek. "You both look as done in as I feel. How about a drink?"

"Thanks, Winston. I'll have a vodka and tonic," Paula said.

"The same for me, darling," Emily said.

He brought them their drinks, took a chair next to the fire and lit a cigarette.

Paula passed Emma's letter to him, explaining, "These are Emma's last instructions, her final wishes."

After reading it, he said, "Emma's been very explicit and precise. Thank God. It'll save a lot of family discussions and arguments about her funeral, especially with Robin. You know what he's like, so vociferous about everything, too bloody opinionated."

Paula looked across at him curiously. "I hardly think he would volunteer an opinion about his mother's funeral—not under the circumstances. Surely he wouldn't dare."

Winston grimaced. "He might, knowing him. But her letter spells it out and that's that."

"And you can be sure Grandy's funeral is going to be exactly the way she herself planned it," Paula exclaimed.

Winston nodded, asked, "What did Doctor Hedley say after he examined Aunt Emma?"

"Heart failure," Emily volunteered. She gulped. "Gran's poor old heart just gave out, stopped beating."

Winston drew on his cigarette and looked away, his eyes suddenly swimming. There was a tremor in his voice as he remarked, "Grandfather Winston always used to tell me that his sister had a heart as big as a paving stone, and Emma did, she surely did." He sighed softly. "At least she went peacefully, and for that we must all be grateful." He brought his eyes back to Paula. "When is the funeral? Have you decided yet?"

"I'm afraid we can't have it until Tuesday at the earliest. Mainly because of Philip's getting here from Australia," Paula told him. "Fortunately Pip was in Sydney, not out at the sheep station in Coonamble, when I rang him tonight. He said he'd leave first thing in the morning. Very early. He's chartering a private jet. He thinks it'll be quicker than taking a commercial flight. I also spoke to my mother. Naturally she was as devastated as we are, and she wants to get home as quickly as possible. So she, my father, and Jim are flying from Nice directly to Manchester tomorrow morning. Alexander and Maggie will be arriving then, too."

Emily said, "I spoke to Mummy in Paris. I told her she didn't have to come until Sunday or Monday. I also talked to Robin and Kit. They're here in Yorkshire, so there's no problem. We managed to contact everyone on our list, including Sarah and Jonathan. What about you, Winston?"

"I got hold of Dad at the hotel in London. He'll be on a train in the morning. Vivienne's at Middleham, of course. Sally and Anthony were both at Clonloughlin. But Aunt Edwina is in Dublin. Anthony told me he'll reach her later this evening. They'll fly over on Sunday. You're going to have a house full, Paula."

"Yes, I know."

Winston said reflectively, "I think Emily and I ought to move in here with you for the next few days. What do—"

Paula interjected. "Oh yes, please do. I'd appreciate it."

Clearing his throat, Winston now asked in a muffled tone, "When are they bringing her body—I mean, bringing Aunt Emma back to Pennistone Royal?"

Paula blinked rapidly as her eyes moistened. "Tomorrow afternoon. I'm going to take the dress she wanted to wear to the undertaker in Leeds first thing in the morning." Paula turned her head, pressing back her tears with her fingertips. After a second, she went on, "Emily and I didn't want to leave her there all alone for the next few days. It may sound silly, but we didn't want— her to be lonely without us. And so her coffin will be brought here, to this house, her home, the one place she truly loved on this earth. We've decided to let the coffin stand in the Stone Hall. She liked the hall so much . . ." Her voice trailed off.

Emily said, with a little burst of anger, "You wouldn't believe how stupid the undertaker was, Winston! So bureaucratic. He actually tried to argue with us earlier this evening, when we insisted on accompanying Gran to—his place."

"Oh, I know, darling," Winston murmured sympathetically. "There's always a lot of stupid red tape. But you got your way, which is the main thing."

"You can bet your last shilling we did," Paula asserted. "By the way, Emily reached Merry just as she was leaving the office, to come to dinner here, and she went to tell Uncle Bryan about Emma. Apparently he was so heartbroken she had to drive him home to Wetherby."

"I'm sure he was, and is," Winston replied. "Aunt Emma was like a mother to Bryan when he was a child growing up."

"Merry rang us back at the office," Emily said. "The O'Neills are popping over at about nine o'clock to be with us."

"Incidentally, I tried to get hold of Shane. He was due back from Spain this afternoon." Winston fixed his eyes on Paula. "But when I rang the London office at six forty-five there was no reply. I guess I missed him—"

"I caught him there," Paula interrupted. "At six. He'd just walked in from the airport. He's on his way to Yorkshire right now—driving. He'll come straight here, and he should arrive about eleven."

There was a knock on the door and Hilda walked into the parlor. "Excuse me, Miss Paula," she said, "but I'd already prepared the usual cold buffet for tonight, as I always do on Friday. You know, before you rang me about—" The housekeeper stopped, covered her mouth with her hand. She took a breath, and her voice wobbled as she finished, "About Mrs. Harte passing away." She stared at Paula helplessly, unable to utter another word.

"I'm sorry, Hilda, but I don't feel like eating." Paula glanced at Emily and Winston. "Do either of you?" They both shook their heads, and Paula added, "I think we'd better skip dinner tonight. Thanks anyway, Hilda."

"Oh, I understand, Miss Paula." Hilda made a face. "I can't eat either. To tell you the truth, I'd choke on the food," she muttered and disappeared.

"Blunt as ever, Hilda is," Winston said. "But I know what she means. I feel the same way." He rose and went to the console, where he poured himself another scotch and soda. He turned suddenly, looked first at his wife and then at Paula. He said thoughtfully, "This may seem like a peculiar thing to say, rather farfetched even, but now that Aunt Emma's dead I feel her presence more acutely than ever. I don't mean because I'm here in this room, which was her favorite, but in general. She's—well, she's just *with* me. I've felt her closeness ever since you called me at our Harrogate office to tell me that she'd died."

Emily nodded and emphatically so. "It's not farfetched, Winston. Paula and I discussed that very thing when we were driving back here tonight."

For a moment Paula sat silently reflecting, and then she said in a quiet voice, "We all feel her presence because she *is* here with us, Winston. She's all around us. And inside us. She made us what we are, gave us so much of herself that we're full of her." A sudden and lovely warm smile spread across Paula's tired face. "Grandy will be with each one of us for all of our days. And so, in a sense, she'll never really be dead. Emma Harte will live on forever through us."

• • •

Emma Harte's funeral was held in Ripon Cathedral, as she had requested. It took place at one o'clock on the Tuesday following her death.

Her entire family was present, along with friends, colleagues, employees, and most of the inhabitants of the village of Pennistone Royal, where she had lived for well over thirty years. The cathedral was packed to overflowing and if there were some present who were dry-eyed, they were far outnumbered by those who were tearful and sorrowing.

Her coffin was borne down the nave and through the great chancel to the altar by the six pallbearers she herself had chosen. Three of them were her grandsons, Philip McGill Amory, Alexander Barkstone, and Anthony Standish, the Earl of Dunvale. The other three were her great-nephew Winston Harte and Shane O'Neill and Michael Kallinski, the grandsons of her two dear friends from her youth.

Although her coffin was not heavy, the six young men walked at a slow, measured pace, their steps keeping time with the organ music that swelled to the rafters of the ancient cathedral. Finally the pallbearers came to a stop in front of the magnificent altar and it was here that they rested Emma's coffin amidst a profusion of exquisite floral bouquets and wreaths. The central area where the coffin stood was bathed in light from the many flickering candles and the sunlight pouring in through the jewel-colored stained-glass windows.

The family occupied all of the front pews. Paula sat between Jim and her mother. Her father was on Daisy's other side. He, in turn, had Emily on his right side. She was mothering Amanda and Francesca, who cried continuously into their damp handkerchiefs. Although Emily was as distressed as her sisters, she somehow managed to keep a firm grip on herself, endeavoring to comfort the heartbroken teenagers.

Once the pallbearers had been seated with the rest of the mourners, the Dean of Ripon, the Very Reverend Edwin LeGrice, began the short service. He spoke beautifully about Emma, his words eloquent and moving, and when he stepped down from the pulpit ten minutes later, his place was taken by Emma's nephew Randolph Harte.

Randolph gave the sole eulogy. He had difficulty at times, his strong voice cracking with emotion, and he choked on some of his sentences, his sorrow and sense of loss rising to the surface. Randolph's words about his aunt were very simple and loving, spoken from the heart and with genuine feeling. His eulogizing of Emma was limited to a recital of her attributes as a human being. He made no mention of her business career as one of the world's greatest merchant princes. Instead, he touched on her generosity of spirit, her kind nature, her understanding heart, her great acts of charity, her loyalty as a friend and relative, her extraordinary qualities as a woman of remarkable character and strength and indomitable will.

After the eulogy, which had caused many to weep, the Ripon Cathedral choir rose and gave their beautiful harmonized rendition of "Onward, Christian Soldiers," one of the two hymns Emma had learned as a child, and which she had wanted sung today.

As the choir sat down, the Dean of Ripon returned to the pulpit. He led the mourners in a single prayer, before offering up his own brief prayer for Emma Harte's soul and for her eternal life. When he brought this to a close he asked all of those present to say their own personal and private prayers for Emma during the next few minutes of absolute silence.

Paula, her head bowed, squeezed her eyes tightly shut, but the tears seeped out anyway and dripped onto her clasped hands. The cathedral was perfectly still now, its peacefulness enveloping them all. But occasionally the silent hallowed space echoed with a muffled sob, a small gasp of grief, or a strangled cough.

And then suddenly his voice rang out, so true and clear and pure Paula thought her heart was going to burst. She had known Shane was going to sing "Jerusalem," since this was one of Emma's last wishes, but nevertheless she was startled. She brought her handkerchief up to her face, wondering how she could ever bear this part of the service.

Shane O'Neill stood alone in a far corner of the cathedral and he sang William Blake's old hymn without accompaniment, his rich full baritone echoing to every corner of the church.

As he came to the end of the first verse and commenced the second, Paula experienced a sudden and extraordinary feeling of peace and release as the words washed over her. He held her enthralled.

Shane's lilting voice reached out to touch everyone present as he now sang:

> "Bring me my Bow of burning gold:
> Bring me my Arrows of desire:
> Bring me my Spear: O clouds unfold!
> Bring me my Chariot of fire!
>
> I will not cease from Mental Fight,
> Nor shall my Sword sleep in my hand:
> Till we have built Jerusalem,
> In England's green and pleasant Land."

As Shane's voice faded away, Paula unexpectedly understood the need, the significance, and the importance of the ritual and ceremony of death. Somehow they were helping her to endure her sorrow. The prayers, brief though they had been, the choirboys and then Shane singing so melodiously, the masses of flowers, and the extraordinary beauty of this ancient cathedral had given her a degree of ease from her overwhelming pain. The presence of the Dean, whom she had known for years, was calming, comforting to her. It suddenly struck her that when grief could be shared in this way the burden of the heartbreak became slightly lighter to bear. She knew the service had been a shade more elaborate than her grandmother had intended, but somehow she felt it has been extremely consoling to those who genuinely cared about Emma and mourned her truly. We did her honor, we gave her a wonderful tribute as she leaves this earthly life, Paula thought. It has been our way of saying our loving good-byes. Paula felt a new strength flowing through her as she lifted her head.

Instantly she became conscious of her mother's terrible anguish. Daisy was sobbing unrestrainedly against David's shoulder. Paula put her hand on her mother's arm, whispered, "It's all right, Mummy. Draw comfort from knowing that she's safe at last. She's gone to your father, to Paul, and now they're together for all time, for eternity."

"Yes," Daisy gasped. "I know, darling, I know. But I shall miss her so much. She was the best. The very, very best there is in this world."

The organ music began again and rose to a crescendo as her coffin was lifted by the pallbearers. They brought it back through the chancel and down the nave and out of Ripon Cathedral. Emma's immediate family walked behind her coffin and then they stood outside, watching as it was placed in the hearse and covered with a blanket of flowers for her last journey.

Paula noticed that Edwina was as stricken and tearful as her mother and impulsively she went over, placed her hand on her aunt's arm. "I'm glad you made your peace with Grandy," Paula said in a shaky voice. "Really glad, Aunt Edwina."

Edwina turned to Paula, her light gray eyes brimming. "It was too late. I should have done it years ago. I was wrong. So very wrong, Paula dear."

Paula said, "She understood. She always understood everything, that was the beauty of Emma Harte. And she was so pleased you and she became friends —overjoyed, if you want to know the truth."

"That helps a little," Edwina said softly. "And you and I, Paula, we must be friends too. Can you forgive me?"

"Yes," Paula said very simply, and bent forward and kissed Edwina's wet cheek.

A long line of cars followed the cortege out of Ripon and on to Harrogate. They soon left the bucolic Dales behind, passed through the city of Leeds, the seat of Emma's power, and traveled through the grimy industrial valleys of the West Riding. But eventually the procession came up onto the high moorland road that cut through the great Pennine Chain of hills.

On this sunlit afternoon in early September, those grim and savage Yorkshire moors had lost their blackened and daunting aspects that could so appall the eye. Dark and implacable for most of the year, they now blazed with sudden and glorious splendor. As it always did at the end of the summer, wave upon wave of purple and magenta heather undulated across the great sweep of wild, untenanted moors. It was as if a cloth of royal purple had been rolled out, and it rippled gently under the light breeze. High above floated a resplendent sky that was as blue as speedwells and brilliant with that incredible clarity of light so peculiar to the North of England. The air was pure and bracing. Larks and linnets wheeled and turned with a rush and fluttering of wings and their sweet trillings pierced the silence, and there was the fragrant scent of harebells and wildflowers and heather on the lucent air.

Finally the cortege began its descent, leaving the moorland behind, and several hours after its departure from Ripon it progressed slowly into the village of Fairley. The hearse came to a standstill outside the quaint Norman church where, eighty-one years ago, Emma had been christened.

Her six young pallbearers, representing the three clans, shouldered her coffin for the last time. Moving at a slow pace and with great care, they carried her through the lych-gate into the cemetery, where the vicar, the Reverend Huntley, was waiting at the graveside.

Against the dry-stone walls and under the blowing trees and along the winding paths stood the villagers of Fairley. They were silent and grieving, the men with their caps in their hands, the women and children holding sprays of wildflowers, and heather, for remembrance, and all had their heads bowed and most of them were weeping quietly. They had come out of love to pay their last respects, to say farewell to this woman who was one of their own, she who had risen so high in the world but had never once forgotten them.

After a brief ceremony under that wide and shimmering sky which she had believed to be unique, Emma Harte was buried in the benign earth which had for so long sheltered her loved ones. Her grave was between those of her mother and Winston, her final resting place overshadowed by the moors she had so loved and wandered over as a child, and where she had never felt lonely or alone in her solitude.

BOOK THREE

Tycoon

*Cease to ask what the morrow will bring forth, and
set down as gain each day that Fortune grants.*

Horace

Forty-Four

"I still think there's something fishy going on," Alexander muttered, pacing the floor of Paula's office at the London store.

"So do I," she agreed, her eyes following him as he progressed up and down between the fireplace and her desk. "But having suspicions is simply not good enough. We need concrete evidence of some kind before we can make a move against Jonathan. And Sarah, perhaps. I'm still not certain whether she is being treacherous or not."

"Neither am I. But we do need to get the goods on him, you're quite right. Until then our hands are tied." Alexander rubbed his chin, his expression thoughtful. He came to a stop in front of Paula's desk and leveled his gaze at her. "My gut instinct tells me that Jonathan's double-dealing is staring me in the face, and you can bet it's going to *hit* me in the face one day very soon." He shook his head. "And to borrow a phrase of Grandy's, I don't like unpleasant surprises."

"Who does?" Paula sighed, her worry growing more acute. She knew Alexander was the most conservative of men and not prone to exaggeration or flights of fancy. Besides, their grandmother had been convinced of Jonathan Ainsley's duplicity until the day of her death five weeks ago. But like them, Emma had not had the proof. Settling back in her chair, Paula said, "Whatever it *is* that he's doing, he's obviously been very clever about it, since the accountants haven't found anything wrong after checking the books."

"Naturally he is, and you know he's always been bloody devious. He doesn't let his right hand know what his left is doing, for God's sake. He hasn't changed much over the years." Alexander gave her a pained look. "Don Littleton thinks I'm stark raving mad. If I've had him go over the books once, I've had him do it a dozen times." Alexander lifted his shoulder in a helpless shrug. "Don and two of the other accountants with his firm put the real estate division under a microscope. There's nothing untoward—not one single thing that seems suspicious. At least, not as far as money matters are concerned."

Paula leaned forward, rested her elbows on her desk, propped her chin in her hands. "He wouldn't be stupid enough to *steal,* Sandy, and he's smart. He'd cover his tracks wherever they led. I wish we could think of some way to lure him out into the open, get him to show his hand . . ." Her sentence remained unfinished as she considered this idea, racked her brains for likely possibilities.

Her brother Philip, who sat on the sofa at the other side of the room, had been listening intently for the last fifteen minutes. Finally breaking his silence, he said, "The only way you'll ever trap our dear cousin is to set him up as a target."

Alexander pivoted on his heels. "How?" he asked.

Philip rose and strolled over to join them. Of all of Emma's grandsons,

Philip McGill Amory was the most handsome. He was the spitting image of his grandfather and had the McGill coloring that his mother and his sister had inherited. His hair was the same glossy black, his eyes that uncanny blue which bordered on deep violet, and he was as tall, virile, and dashing as Paul McGill had been. Although only twenty-four, Philip also happened to be the shrewdest of Emma's grandsons, since he had been blessed with Paul's extraordinary business acumen and financial genius, as well as a great deal of his grandmother's not inconsiderable brilliance. He had been diligently trained by Emma since the age of seventeen and, after taking over the vast McGill empire in Australia, he had proved himself to be worthy of her trust many times over. He was known as a man to be reckoned with, and one who had a wisdom beyond his years.

Drawing to a stop next to Alexander, he put his hand on his cousin's shoulder and said, "I'll tell you *how* in a minute, Sandy." Lowering himself into one of the chairs facing his sister, he remarked, "That detective Gran hired—Graves—hasn't been able to dig up a thing on Jonathan. However, *I* still believe that it's very probable he has his own company—one that is being run by straw men, and—"

"Don't think I've dismissed that possibility," Alexander fiercely interrupted, "because I haven't."

Philip nodded. "Okay, so let's start with the assumption that he *does* indeed have a real estate company, and that he's been funneling deals into it—big deals that by rights should be going to Harte Enterprises. That in itself is enough to hang him." Philip sat forward urgently, looked first at his sister and then at Alexander. "I propose that *we* put the noose around his neck. And I'll tell you how. It's very simple, really. We have to get someone to present a deal to Jonathan as head of the real estate division of Harte Enterprises. Now, here's the twist . . . we have to make the deal so attractive, so juicy, he won't be able to resist putting it through his own company. Naturally it must be extremely appealing, and so very big, so tempting, his greed will far outweigh his judgment. If the stakes for himself are high enough he'll act rashly, believe me, he will."

Sitting back, Philip crossed his long legs, glanced from Alexander to Paula and back to Alexander. "Well, what do you say?"

Alexander now sat down heavily in the other chair, nodded slowly. "I must admit, it's a smart ploy, and I'll go along with it, providing you can answer a couple of questions."

"*Shoot.*"

"Philip, let's be practical, where the hell are *we* going to find this tempting deal to dangle like a carrot in front of Jonathan? That's for openers, and, second, who are *we* going to get to offer it to him?" Alexander smiled narrowly. "Let's not underestimate our wily cousin . . . he'll spot the holes immediately."

"Ah, but there won't be any," Philip replied evenly. "I have someone who can offer the deal to Jonathan, a close friend who has his own real estate company here in London. So that answers your first question. As far as the deal itself is concerned, I believe my friend may have something up his sleeve that would be most appropriate, and tempting. All I need is your approval, and then I'll talk to him."

"I suppose it's worth having a go," Alexander said, fully aware of Philip's inbred shrewdness and discretion. He turned to Paula. "What do you think?"

Paula said, "I'm all for it, if you are, Sandy." She eyed her brother. "What's the name of your friend?"

"Malcolm Perring. Surely you remember old Malcolm—we were at Wellington together."

"Vaguely. I think you introduced us once, when I came down to visit you at half term."

"I did. Anyway, he and I remained relatively close friends after we left school, and he was out in Australia for a year and—"

"Jonathan's bound to smell a rat," Paula said sharply. "You and Malcolm were at the same public school, then he was in Australia. Jonathan'll put two and two together."

"I doubt it," Philip said, sounding assured and confident. "Malcolm's been back here for a couple of years. He inherited his brother's real estate company after that poor chap dropped dead of a heart attack at thirty-nine. Besides, Jonathan's not going to ask a lot of personal questions, and Malcolm can be adroit and evasive, believe me, he can."

"I trust you. I know you wouldn't embroil somebody in our affairs whom you couldn't rely on to be absolutely discreet. And you *will* have to take him into your confidence," Paula remarked.

"Obviously. But Malcolm *is* reliable . . . true blue, Paula." Philip chuckled. "I'm sure he has a deal that is ready to go—Perring and Perring is a huge company—and wouldn't it be ironic if we were able to kill two birds with one stone? Catch Jonathan red-handed and do a bit of smart business for Harte Enterprises at the same time."

Alexander began to laugh dryly, tickled at the idea. "Oh, how Grandy would love this!"

Paula half-smiled. "Perhaps we should go ahead, then, Philip, since Alexander is all for it. And actually it must be his decision—as managing director of Harte Enterprises."

Alexander exclaimed, "We don't have anything to lose, and, very frankly, I'm relieved we're taking aggressive action. This sitting around waiting for Jonathan Ainsley to tip his hand is most frustrating. I feel we must force him out in the open, if we can."

"I shall talk to Malcolm first thing tomorrow morning." Philip glanced at his watch. "If we're going to grab a bite of lunch before we go to John Crawford's office, I think we ought to leave. It's eleven-thirty. We have to be at John's at two-thirty, don't we, Paula?"

"Yes." She stood up, brushed a piece of lint off her black dress. "I'm not looking forward to this afternoon," she began and stopped. Her upper lip quivered and her eyes filled with tears. She glanced away quickly. After a moment she managed to compose herself, and she smiled weakly at the two men.

"I'm so sorry," she said. "That happens when I least expect it. I think of Gran and just choke up. I can't get used to her not being here. It's just awful, such a gap in my life . . . all of our lives, I suppose."

"Yes," Philip agreed. "Alexander and I feel the same way as you do. In fact, we were discussing it last night at dinner. It's hard to realize that she's not going to suddenly swoop down on us with a bit of unorthodox but frighteningly clever advice, or make one of those blunt or pithy comments of hers."

Philip walked around the desk and took hold of Paula's shoulders gently, looked down into her white face. "The reading of the will *is* going to be dreadfully upsetting, Paula, because it emphasizes the reality of her death. But you must be there . . . we all must." He attempted a bit of levity as he finished, "Grandy will be mad at us if we're not."

Paula nodded, smiling faintly at his remark, knowing he wanted to cheer her up. Her sadness did ease slightly. "I'll tell you one thing—it gets my goat when I think of the leeches who are going to be present later." She sighed. "Ah well, there we are, nothing we can do about it, and my apologies to the two of you again. I think the less said about this afternoon the better. Now, come on, let's go to lunch. Emily's joining us—I've booked a table at the Ritz."

"The Ritz!" Philip exclaimed in surprise. "A bit fancy, isn't it, for a quick snack?"

She tucked her arm through her brother's, glanced up at him and then across at Alexander, a hint of genuine gaiety surfacing. "Not really. It *was* one of Grandy's favorite places. And I chose it because it has such happy associations for the four of us . . . all those lovely treats she used to give us there when we were children." Paula laughed, now addressed her brother. "Besides, you and I might not be here if Emma and Paul hadn't indulged in a bit of romantic dallying at the Ritz over sixty years ago!"

"Correct," Philip answered with a laugh. "And in that case I think lunch had better be on Paul McGill! Consider this my treat."

"Jolly decent of you," Alexander said as they left Paula's office and went out to the staff elevator. Alexander engaged Philip in a few seconds of conversation about his friend Malcolm Perring as they rode down. Satisfied with Philip's answers, confident that his cousin had selected the right man to help them corner Jonathan, he asked, "By the way, how long are we going to have the pleasure of your company?"

"I'll be here until the end of October, when I'm apparently going to Texas with Paula. So she told me before you arrived. Sitex business. From there, it's back to Sydney for a few weeks, and then I'm coming home again—for Christmas."

"Oh!" Paula exclaimed. "You didn't tell me."

"I only just decided at breakfast this morning. I haven't had a chance to mention it. Mum's so done in at the moment, I think I ought to be here. It'll cheer her up. I've also agreed to go to Chamonix with them in January, and of course they're both delighted about that."

"And so am I—this is great news." Alexander beamed. "Maggie and I have been invited to join Auntie Daisy and Uncle David." He shot Paula a quick glance. "Are you going to change your mind, now that Philip's coming along?"

"*No.* When *I* take a vacation I want to lie in the hot sun and bake myself to a crisp dark brown. The ski slopes have never appealed to me, as you both well know. Also, I have to be in New York in January. We're doing a big promotion of French and Italian couture fashions at the store, and I'm opening the Total Woman Shop at our Fifth Avenue branch then." She gave them a wicked grin as they stepped out of the elevator. "Somebody has to work in this family."

Laughing, they bustled her outside into Knightsbridge and into a taxicab and headed for the Ritz Hotel.

Emily was already waiting for them at a table in the restaurant. Elegant in a black suit, which was most flattering and showed off her blond beauty to perfection, she nevertheless wore a mournful expression. Her green eyes were wistful as her cousins and brother sat down with her. "I'll be glad when today's over," she muttered to Alexander. "The thought of hearing the will is so depressing."

Alexander said, "Come on, Emily lovey, cheer up. Philip and I have just been through the same recital with Paula." He squeezed her arm. "Grandy wouldn't approve. In fact, she'd be bloody furious if she could see us sitting around moping. Remember what she used to say?"

"Which particular thing?" Emily asked pensively.

"The remark she often made when we'd had some sort of failure or disappointment. She usually told us to forget yesterday, think of tomorrow, and keep forging ahead without looking back. Don't you think that's what we should do, especially today?"

"Yes," Emily admitted, giving her brother a more cheerful smile.

"Good girl," Alexander said.

Philip said, "I'm going to order a bottle of champagne and we're going to drink to the memory of that remarkable woman who gave us life, taught us everything we know, and made us what we are."

He motioned to the wine waiter.

After Philip had ordered a bottle of Dom Pérignon, and whilst they waited for it to be brought to the table, Paula leaned closer to Emily. She whispered, "Philip has had a clever idea, thought of a way to possibly flush Jonathan out into the open. Once we've toasted Grandy, he'll tell you about it."

"I can't wait," Emily exclaimed. Her glistening green eyes narrowed with sudden shrewdness as she contemplated Jonathan's downfall. "Now that would be a fitting tribute to Gran—if we can uncover his treachery to her and deal with him as she would have done."

───── *Forty-Five* ─────

John Crawford, Emma's solicitor, and a senior partner in the firm of Crawford, Creighton, Phipps and Crawford, hurried into the large conference room.

He glanced about and nodded with satisfaction. The twenty-four chairs which were permanent fixtures around the long mahogany table had been rounded out to twenty-nine with the addition of five more. His secretary had rustled these up from other offices within the law firm, and the room could now accommodate himself and the twenty-eight people who were due to arrive momentarily.

John strode down the floor, placed the last will and testament of Emma Harte on the table in front of his chair at its head. His eyes rested on it briefly but thoughtfully. It was a bulky document and he was facing a long session. No matter, he thought and, half-shrugging, stepped over to the window, parted the curtains, and looked down into Upper Grosvenor Street.

A few seconds later he saw a taxi pulling up outside the front door. David Amory alighted, followed by Daisy and Edwina. Even from this distance he could see that Daisy looked drawn, very sad, but she was still as beautiful as ever. He sighed under his breath. No wonder his marriage had failed. It was impossible to be married to one woman whilst worshiping another. He had been in love with Daisy for as long as he could remember. Most of his adult life, really. No hope there. She had married young, and she had only ever had eyes for David. How special she was, so sweet and unaffected, and not a bit spoiled by that extraordinary wealth. They were good friends, and spent two days a month working together, since it was Daisy who ran the Emma Harte Foundation, a rich organization devoted to charity. Daisy frequently needed his legal advice on other matters, and sometimes he was lucky, was able to spend a few extra hours with her. He was grateful for these small crumbs of her time, and looked forward with eagerness to their business luncheons.

He swung away from the window at the sound of his secretary's voice as she showed the Amorys and Edwina into the conference room. Smiling, he went to greet them, struck by Edwina's ghastly appearance. Like Daisy, she wore black and in consequence her face looked utterly colorless and drained of life. But this aside, she had become an old woman in the last few weeks. Emma's death had apparently affected her deeply.

He stood chatting to the three of them for a few minutes, and then they took their seats as the others began to arrive in rapid succession. By two-twenty everyone was present except Jim and Winston. They came hurrying in five minutes later, apologizing, and explaining they had been held up in the traffic on the way from Fleet Street.

At precisely two-thirty John brought the room to order. He said: "It is a very sad occasion that brings us all together today, but as Emma said to me the last time I saw her at the beginning of August, 'No long faces after I'm dead. I've had an extraordinary life, known the best and the worst, and so there hasn't been one dull moment. Sing no sad songs for me.' However, before I proceed with the business at hand, I would like to say that I personally mourn a very good and dear friend, who was the most remarkable woman—no, correction, person—I've ever been privileged to know. She will be sorely missed."

There were a few scattered mutterings of approval at the expression of these sentiments before John said in a more solemn voice: "This is the Last Will and Testament of Emma Harte Lowther Ainsley, who shall, hereafter, be known simply as Emma Harte throughout the reading of the will." He cleared his throat, and his tone became more conversational as he said, "Before her death Mrs. Harte told me that members of her immediate family were aware of certain of the contents, since these were revealed to them by her in April of 1968. However, since the will covers the disposal of her entire estate, and because there are other beneficiaries, I must read the will in its entirety. Also, that is the law. I must therefore ask you all to bear with me. It is a long document, I'm afraid, and one of some complexity."

Paula, who sat between Jim and Philip, leaned back in her chair, folded her hands in her lap and directed her attention on the family solicitor. Her face was expressionless.

The first five or six pages dealt with Emma's bequests to the staff employed in her various homes, and all were generous, showed Emma's special consideration for each individual and their needs. Paula was genuinely gratified when she heard that Hilda was to receive a substantial pension when she retired, as well as the deed to one of the cottages Emma owned in the village of Pennistone Royal.

Hilda was not present, but Gaye Sloane was, and Emma's former secretary looked across at Paula and gave her a surprised smile of delight, after John had read out the details of Emma's gift to her. Gaye was to receive two hundred thousand pounds and a pair of diamond-and-gold earrings with a matching brooch.

The second portion of the will was concerned with Emma's considerable art collection. John explained, "In the will drawn in 1968, Emma Harte left all of the art works to her grandson, Philip McGill Amory, with the exception of the paintings hanging at Pennistone Royal. This bequest has been modified." He swung his eyes to Philip. "Mrs. Harte told me that she discussed this change with you and gave you her reasons for making it, and that you were fully understanding of her motives."

"Yes," Philip said. "Grandmother was seeking my approval and I told her this was not necessary, that she must dispose of her art as she so wished, since it was hers and hers alone. I am totally in accord with her."

John nodded, glanced down at the document and read out Emma's words: " 'In recognition of their many years of devotion, loyalty, and friendship, I do give and bequeath to Henry Rossiter the Van Gogh landscape; to Ronald Kallinski the Picasso from the Blue Period; to Bryan O'Neill the Degas ballet dancer, each of which currently hangs in my Belgrave Square residence. To my beloved nephew Randolph Harte, in appreciation of his love and friendship, I bequeath the four horse paintings by Stubbs and the two Barbara Hepworth sculptures, which are at present housed at Pennistone Royal. All of my other art works, *excluding* those hanging at Pennistone Royal, I give to my grandson Philip. Also *excluded* from this bequest to Philip is the painting entitled "The Top of the World" by Sally Harte.' "

Philip leaned into Paula and whispered, "Uncle Randolph and the others are very touched. I'm glad she made those gifts to them, aren't you?"

Paula nodded, gave him a small smile.

John Crawford said, "Regarding the matter of the Fabergé Imperial Easter Egg—" The solicitor paused to take a sip of water, and went on to explain that Emma wished the Fabergé object of art to be auctioned, the money returned to her grandchildren who had purchased it for her as a gift for her eightieth birthday. Any balance of money left over, should the Imperial Easter Egg bring more than they had paid for it, was to be donated to charity in accordance with Emma's wishes.

Paula's eyes were surreptitiously wandering around the conference room. She had been aware of the mounting tension for the last fifteen minutes, had noticed the anxiety written on the faces of Robin, Kit, and Elizabeth. Edwina, on the other hand, seemed oblivious to the proceedings, sat twisting her hands in her lap. She appeared more dolorous than ever.

As John began, "I now come to the trust funds Emma Harte created for her children," Paula could almost feel the anxiousness and nervousness emanating from her two uncles and her aunt. She quickly averted her eyes, trained them on John once again.

Leaning back in his chair, the solicitor said, "The trusts, which became effective some years ago, have not been rescinded or changed in any way, shape, or form by Mrs. Harte. They remain intact, and the beneficiaries, Edwina, Kit, Robin, and Elizabeth, will continue to receive the income from their trusts."

John's voice droned on as he elucidated further details of the trusts, and just as she had sensed the apprehension in three of those four earlier, Paula was conscious of their profound relief. Robin and his twin, Elizabeth, were unable to conceal their jubilance. Kit's face was sober, but his eyes betrayed him as they flickered with triumph. Only Edwina was unaccountably distressed, weeping copiously into her handkerchief. Paula realized that her aunt was undoubtedly thinking of Emma, understanding yet again how eminently fair her mother had been.

"I will move on to the trusts which Emma Harte created for her grandchildren," John announced, and Paula's grave face became very alert. She could not help wondering if Grandy had changed these. It soon became clear that Emma had not. Emily, Sarah, Alexander, Jonathan, Anthony, Francesca, and Amanda would continue to benefit from the trust funds which Emma had provided for them in April of 1968. After spelling out the terms of the trust, the solicitor paused, shifted his position in his chair.

His glance rested on Paula, then moved on to regard Anthony. He remarked, "At this point in the proceedings I must tell you that Emma Harte created three additional trust funds. These are for her great-grandchildren, Lorne and Tessa Fairley, son and daughter of Jim and Paula Fairley, and Jeremy, the Viscount Standish, son of Anthony and Sally Standish, the Earl and Countess of Dunvale. Each trust for these three great-grandchildren is in the amount of one million pounds."

Picking up the will, John once more launched into a relatively long recitation of Emma's wishes, which were couched in her own language. When this section was dispensed with, he moved on briskly, introduced the portion of the will that dealt with the dispersal of Emma's vast business enterprises and the enormous McGill fortune. She had again left the 1968 bequests intact. Alexander received fifty-two percent of Harte Enterprises and was formally appointed head of this company for life. His sister, Emily, as well as Sarah and Jonathan, each received sixteen percent of the shares. In the event of Alexander's death or disability, Emily would automatically assume control of the company, holding this position for her lifetime.

Paula eyed Jonathan and Sarah, and asked herself if they knew how lucky they had been. Jonathan could hardly conceal his glee, Sarah was smiling smugly, Paula noticed, and her face became closed and cold.

At the mention of her own name Paula gave John her full attention, even though she expected no surprises. She listened as he repeated Emma's words, written by her in 1968. Paula received all of Emma's shares in the Harte Stores, which gave her total control of the company.

The entire McGill fortune went to Daisy McGill Amory, with the stipulation that her son, Philip, was to continue as Chief Executive Officer of the McGill Corporation of Australia, a conglomerate that owned the diverse McGill companies. Paula was to remain as her mother's representative in all matters pertaining to Sitex Oil. Upon Daisy's death, the McGill holdings were to be equally divided between Paula and Philip. Daisy inherited Pennistone Royal, all land and property attached to the house, all of its furniture, furnishings, and works of art, as well as the McGill emeralds. The house, its contents, the land, and the jewels were to pass to Paula on her mother's death. Paula received the remainder of her grandmother's considerable emerald collection.

"Mrs. Harte's other jewelry is, for the most part, to be divided among her granddaughters. However, there are other bequests—to Marguerite Barkstone, Alexander's wife, Sally Harte Standish and Vivienne Harte, her great-nieces, and Rosamund Harte Ellsworthy, her niece," John told them. "Emma made the selections for each individual, and these are as follows: 'To my dearest granddaughter, Emily Barkstone Harte, I do give and bequeath my sapphire collection, comprising of . . .'" John intoned as he commenced to read from the long list.

It took the solicitor almost an hour to complete the reading of this part of the will, since Emma had owned a huge collection of jewelry, and those who were not beneficiaries became restless. There were rustlings and small muffled sounds as people moved around in their chairs. Cigarettes were lit. Someone poured a glass of water. Edwina blew her nose several times. Robin coughed behind his hand.

John Crawford was perfectly calm, as he always was, and oblivious to the scattered shufflings and odd noises. He read slowly, precisely, and it was obvious to everyone that he had no intention of being hurried. At last he finished: "That completes the details of the disposal of Mrs. Harte's collection of jewelry. I shall now proceed with the portion of the will that covers some of her real estate, mainly the house in Jamaica, British West Indies; the Avenue Foch apartment in Paris; the villa at Cap Martin in the South of France."

The solicitor explained that the bequests Emma Harte had made in April of 1968 were unchanged. Emily Barkstone Harte was to inherit the Paris apartment, her brother Alexander Barkstone the villa on the Riviera, and Anthony was to get the house in the Caribbean.

At this juncture, John suddenly put down the will. His eyes roved from face to face and then his own face changed perceptibly as he brought himself up in his chair.

He enunciated in a most careful tone, "It is now my duty to inform you that Emma Harte changed the remainder of her will."

There were several audible gasps and the majority of those present stiffened in their seats. A number of worried glances were exchanged. Paula felt Philip's hand on her knee and she looked at him swiftly, her dark brows lifting before she brought her eyes back to Crawford. He was turning the page he had just read and perusing the one following.

Paula felt the tension flowing around her as it had earlier, and there was a sense of great anticipation mingled with apprehension in the air. Her chest tightened as she clasped her hands together, wondering what bombshells were about to burst. I always knew it deep down, Paula thought. Unconsciously I knew that Gran would have a few surprises up her sleeve. She could hardly wait for John to continue.

The silence in the room was deathly.

Twenty-eight pairs of eyes were fixed unwaveringly on the solicitor.

Finally John looked up. He scanned their faces a second time, noting the expressions on each. Some were fearful or anxious, others avidly curious, a few merely interested. He smiled and read out in a strong voice:

" 'I, Emma Harte Lowther Ainsley, hereafter known as Emma Harte, do hereby declare that the codicils attached to my Last Will and Testament on this Twenty-fifth Day of April in the Year of Our Lord Nineteen Hundred and Sixty-nine are made whilst I am sound of body and mind. I do further hereby declare and attest that no undue pressure or influence was brought to bear on me by any person or individual to make said changes in my Last Will and Testament and are solely of my own volition and doing.' "

There was a brief pause on John's part as he turned the page, then gave his entire attention to the legal document in his hands.

" 'Codicil One. I do give and bequeath to Shane Desmond Ingham O'Neill, grandson of my dearest lifelong friend, Blackie O'Neill, the diamond ring given to me by his late and aforementioned grandfather. I also bequeath to Shane O'Neill the painting known as "The Top of the World," which I also received from his grandfather. Further, I do give to Shane O'Neill the sum of one million pounds in the form of a trust which I have had created for him. I make these gifts to Shane out of love for him, and in appreciation of his constant love and devotion to me.

" 'Codicil Two. I give to Miranda O'Neill, granddaughter of my friend, Blackie O'Neill, the emerald bow brooch, presented to me by her grandfather. I do also make a gift to Miranda O'Neill of all other pieces of jewelry which were given to me by her grandfather during his lifetime. List of said pieces is attached to the end of these codicils. Further, I do give and bequeath to Miranda the sum of five hundred thousand pounds in the form of a trust. I do so in recognition of her affection and love for me and in memory of my dearest friend, Laura Spencer O'Neill, her grandmother.

" 'Codicil Three. I do bequeath to my great-nephew, Winston John Harte, grandson of my beloved brother Winston, the property known as Heron's Nest in Scarborough, Yorkshire, and the sum of one million pounds, held in a trust similar to the aforementioned trusts. Also, I bequeath to Winston Harte fifteen percent of my shares in my new company, Consolidated Newspapers International, which he and I formed in March of 1969. I make these bequests to Winston Harte as a gesture of my love, and because of his love, devotion, and uncommon loyalty to me over the years and because of his marriage to my granddaughter Emily, for the benefit of them both and any offsprings of their marriage.' "

At this point John stopped, took a quick sip of water, and, aware of the taut atmosphere which now prevailed, hurried on:

" 'Codicil Four. I give to James Arthur Fairley, husband of my grand-daughter Paula Fairley, ten percent of my shares in Consolidated Newspapers International. This is a personal bequest to Jim Fairley and is in no way related to the trusts established for my great-grandchildren, Lorne and Tessa. This bequest is to show my appreciation of his dedication to me and my interests at the Yorkshire Consolidated Newspaper Company, and is also given as an expression of my affection for him.

" 'Codicil Five. To my great-niece Vivienne Harte, granddaughter of my dear brother Winston, and to my niece Rosamund Harte Ellsworthy, daughter of my dear brother Frank, I do give and bequeath five hundred thousand pounds each in the form of trust funds which I have had drawn up for them. I do this out of my considerable affection for them both and in memory of my brothers.

" 'Codicil Six. I do give and bequeath to my granddaughter Paula McGill Amory Fairley, and my grandson, Philip McGill Amory, my Fifth Avenue apartment in New York and my Belgrave Square house, both properties to be owned jointly by them. I make these gifts to Paula and Philip because the aforementioned residences were bought for me by their grandfather, Paul Mc-Gill. After long and careful consideration, I have decided that Paul McGill's grandchildren should rightfully inherit these homes. For this reason I have rescinded the original bequest made in my will drawn in April of 1968.

" 'Codicil Seven. I give to my granddaughter Paula McGill Amory Fairley the remainder of my estate, including all motorcars, clothing, furs, and cash in my current checking accounts. Further, I do give and bequeath to Paula Fairley all assets held in my private company, E.H. Incorporated. Said assets include my personally owned real estate, my personal stocks and shares, and cash balances. Total value of these assets is estimated at six million, eight hundred and ninety-five thousand pounds, six shillings and sixpence.' "

The solicitor lifted his head, said to the gathering, "That concludes the reading of the Last Will and Testament of Emma Harte Lowther Ainsley, except for—"

"Just a minute!" Jonathan exploded. Seething, he jumped up. His eyes were wild, his face as white as bleached bone. "I'm going to contest this will! I was left the Fifth Avenue apartment in her original will and it's mine by rights. I'm going to—"

"Please be so kind as to sit down, Jonathan," the solicitor exclaimed coldly, glaring at him. "I have not finished."

Bristling, his rage apparent, Jonathan did as he was asked but not without crying, *"Dad!* Don't you have anything to say about this?"

Robin, also infuriated, nevertheless shook his head, motioned for his son to be silent.

Crawford continued: "I was about to read the final statement made by Mrs. Harte at the end of her will. I will now proceed to do so, and I must ask that there be no further unruly outbursts of this nature. This is Mrs. Harte's last statement: " 'I truly believe that I have been right, proper, and fair in the disposal of all my worldly goods and possessions. I sincerely hope that my heirs understand why some of them are receiving greater inheritances than others.

" 'However, should any of my heirs feel that they have been cheated or passed over for other members of my family, I must state again that this is not the case. Furthermore, should any member of my family contemplate contesting this will, I must caution them most strongly not to do so. Once again I attest that no undue influence, or influence of any kind, was brought to bear on me at any time. No one, other than my solicitor, John Crawford, knew of these changes and codicils, which are entirely of my own creation. I must also state that I am not senile, nor is the balance of my mind disturbed. Attached to this document, which is my Last Will and Testament, are four affidavits signed by four doctors. These doctors were hitherto unknown to me before the date of this will, and are therefore uninterested parties. Two general practitioners and two psychiatrists examined me on the morning and afternoon of April Twenty-fifth of Nineteen Sixty-nine, prior to this will being drawn on the evening of that same date. The results of their examinations are contained in the affidavits and confirm that I am in excellent physical condition and perfect health, that I am mentally stable, and that none of my faculties are impaired.

" 'Therefore, I must now point out that this will is irreversible, irrevocable, and absolutely watertight. It cannot be contested in a court of law. I appoint my beloved and devoted daughter, Daisy McGill Amory, as executrix of my estate, and Henry Rossiter of the Rossiter Merchant Bank and John Crawford, of Crawford, Creighton, Phipps and Crawford as the co-executors of my estate.' "

John sat back, waiting for the storm to erupt.

It did so instantly.

Everyone began to talk at once. Jonathan was on his feet and almost running down the long stretch of the conference room, looking as if he was about to physically accost John Crawford. Robin had also risen, and so had Kit Lowther and Sarah. These three also bore down on John, their expressions furious, their rage unconcealed as they began to rail at him shrilly.

Jonathan was apoplectic, shouted that the O'Neills had been favored in his place and that Paula and Philip had stolen his inheritance. Sarah began to weep. Her mother, June, hurried to her, endeavoring to console her, and trying to hide her own considerable embarrassment without success.

Bryan O'Neill leapt to his feet. He went over to Daisy and, as the sole member of his family present, protested that the O'Neills did not wish to accept Emma's legacies to them, in view of Jonathan's comments.

The brouhaha swirled around Paula. Jim, who had the seat in front of her, turned his head and said, "Wasn't that lovely of Grandy to leave me the shares in the new newspaper company?"

"Yes, it was," Paula said, noting his shining eyes, his gratified smile.

Philip, who sat on her left, tapped her on the shoulder and leaned closer. Paula swung her eyes and stared at her brother. They gazed at each other knowingly for a protracted moment. Paula tried to keep her face straight but had difficulty doing so. She compressed her lips to prevent herself from laughing out loud. She murmured, "Good old Grandy, as usual she thought of everything. What a brilliant stroke of genius that was, attaching those medical affidavits. The malcontents can do nothing—their hands have been firmly tied by Emma Harte."

Philip nodded. "Yes, but there will be trouble with them, you mark my words. On the other hand, knowing Jonathan's temperament, this sudden turn of events could easily make him behave in the most irrational way. He might even act rashly. And we will probably uncover his treachery to Gran sooner than we think."

"Let's hope so. Perhaps Grandy realized that too, Philip. I don't doubt her sincerity about leaving the McGill residence to us because we're McGills, but let's not forget how shrewd and wily she was." Paula could not help smirking. "You have to agree that Emma Harte has had the last laugh."

"I would call it a loud guffaw," Philip replied, chuckling.

Daisy pushed back her chair and came around the table rapidly. She bent over Paula and said, "Poor John . . . he's being verbally castigated and most unfairly. Mummy's will was her own doing, not his. He's only the family solicitor. Can't you put a stop to their disgusting behavior? The Lowthers and the Ainsleys are getting out of hand."

"Perhaps Daddy can say something," Paula muttered.

"No," Daisy answered firmly. "Emma Harte made you the head of this family. It's your responsibility, darling. I'm sorry, but that's the way it is."

Paula nodded and stood up. "Please, everybody, do be quiet for a moment."

Her natural reserve made it difficult for Paula to assert herself in a large group such as this, but when none of the rowdy troublemakers paid any attention to her, she leaned forward and banged her clenched fist on the table. She exclaimed fiercely, "Shut up! All of you! And sit down!"

The Ainsleys and the Lowthers looked at her with antipathy and, although they did not budge from their positions around John Crawford's chair, they did stop quarreling amongst themselves.

"Thank you," Paula said more evenly, but her voice reflected her icy eyes. She drew herself up to her full height and her inbred hauteur and imperiousness reached out to momentarily stun them all.

"How dare you behave in this unconscionable manner!" she reprimanded sternly. "You're perfectly reprehensible, the lot of you. I think you might show a little respect for Emma Harte. My God, she's only been dead a few weeks and here you are, behaving like vultures, picking over her bones." Paula's eyes were now riveted on Jonathan and Sarah, who stood together. "My grandmother knew what she was doing, and I think she has been overly generous to certain members of this family."

Paula gripped the back of the chair tightly and continued in a tone that was almost threatening: "Don't any one of you dare to even *think* about contesting Emma Harte's will. Because if you do, I shall fight you to the bitter end —if it takes every hour of my time and every penny I have."

The entire gathering stared at her. Most of those present were admiring of her, a few were condemning, but all were mesmerized by the aura of power she conveyed.

Winston edged closer to Emily and touched her arm. He whispered to his wife, "Just look at her . . . she's Emma Harte personified. I think the legend lives."

———— *Forty-Six* ————

Shane and Paula walked across the British Airways terminal at Kennedy Airport, took the escalator to the second level, and went into the First Class lounge.

They found a quiet corner.

After helping her off with her wild mink cape, Shane shrugged out of his trench coat and threw it on a chair nearby.

"Let's have a drink," he suggested. "We have time before your flight."

"That'll be nice. Thank you, darling."

Shane smiled down at her, and ambled over to the bar at the other side of the lounge.

Paula watched him. How marvelous he looked. So darkly handsome and commanding, in absolute control. Her expression became soft; her eyes filled with love for him. In the year they had been having their love affair her feelings for him had only grown deeper. He was so much a part of her now she felt lost when they were separated and only half-alive without him. He never ceased to surprise her. Although she had known him all of her life, she had never fully realized how truly dependable he was in every circumstance or emergency. He had a tremendous sense of commitment to her, and to every single thing that was important in his life. His strength of character was almost awesome. He has iron in his soul, she thought.

She gazed at him lovingly as he returned with their drinks. Shane smiled back, handed her the vodka and tonic, and took the seat next to her.

He touched his glass to hers, said, "Here's to next month, Paula, to the beginning of the new year."

"To 1971," Paula said.

"It *is* going to be our year, darling. Everything will be worked out with Jim. You'll be free, and, just think, you'll be back here in January, not too long, really. We can start making our plans for the future. *Finally*."

"Won't that be wonderful," she said, but her luminous eyes darkened with incipient worry.

Shane noticed. He frowned. "I don't like that look on your face, Paula. What's wrong?"

She shook her head, laughed gaily. "Nothing. I'll just be glad when I've talked to Jim, settled matters with him. He's so frustrating, refusing to admit anything's wrong, burying his head in the sand. I know you probably think I've been ineffectual in dealing with the situation. However, it's hard to talk to someone who simply will not listen." She reached out, squeezed his arm. "Sorry. I'm going over old ground, repeating myself."

"That's all right. I understand. But you'll tackle him when you get back." A grin surfaced as Shane added, "You should get him in a room, lock the door and pocket the key. That way he'll have to hear you out."

"If necessary that's what I *will* do. I promise. I'm very determined to thrash this out once and for all. Of course, it's not a good time, with Christmas only two weeks away. On the other hand, I suppose there is never a *right* time for discussing divorce . . . emotional situations are always difficult."

"Yes." He leaned forward urgently. "I know it won't be easy, Paula. I wish I could be in England with you, there in the background if you need me, but I have to go to the islands. I've no option. However"—he stopped, stared at her intently—"I'll fly to London immediately, if you can't cope alone."

"I know you will, but I'll manage. Really, I will, Shane." There was a small silence and then she said, "Thank you for this past month. It's been wonderful. And having an uninterrupted period of time with you has worked miracles for me. I feel so much better than I did when I arrived in November . . . in every way."

"So do I. And look here, Paula, it's been a triumphant month for you, if you think about it. Getting Dale Stevens's contract renewed and defeating Marriott Watson on so many of the issues at Sitex ought to make you feel good. And perhaps your success augers well for the future. You've had a lot of sadness to deal with."

"*You* pulled me through, Shane, you truly did. You've been so supportive and consoling. I'm stronger than I ever was because of you, your love and your understanding. And talking of Sitex . . ." Her voice trailed off lamely. She eyed him carefully and wrinkled her nose. "I know that *you* won't laugh when I tell you this, since you're such a superstitious Celt at heart . . ." Again she stopped. Her eyes did not leave his face.

"I never laugh at you. So go on, tell me."

Her fine mouth curved up into a light smile and she shook her head, suddenly laughing at herself. "Well, when I first heard about the explosion in the *Emeremm III* I couldn't help thinking it was a bad omen, a sign of more hideous disasters looming ahead. And in a way I was right. Looking back, these past fourteen months have been fraught with problems . . . Min's death, the trouble in Ireland around the time of the explosion. Grandy's growing suspicions about Jonathan; Sarah's nastiness to me personally, her scheming to get her hands on the Harte boutiques. My marriage falling apart. Aunt Elizabeth's awful behavior; the fear of scandal because of her divorce and Gianni's attitude. The continuing difficulties with Sitex, the internal fighting in that company, not to mention Jim's plane crash, then his nervous breakdown. The suddenness of Blackie's death, and Grandy going so soon after him, and all that horrendous quarreling in the family about her will." She pursed her lips. "I feel as if someone put a curse on me, or, rather, on Emma's family."

Shane took her hand in his. "In a sense, you *have* had more than your fair share. But let's be objective. First of all, Blackie was eighty-four and Emma was eighty-one, so it was to be expected that they would die soon. And they did have peaceful deaths, Paula, after long and productive lives. Second, you've put an end to the screaming and shouting about her will in certain quarters. You've settled many of the problems at Sitex, and Sarah's scheming against you was nipped in the bud by Emma. Jim has apparently recovered. Anthony and Sally are happily married and have a lovely son. Even your Aunt Elizabeth got off scot free and is seemingly happy with Marc Deboyne. As for your marriage, it was doomed long before the *Emeremm III* exploded."

He put his arm around her, kissed her cheek, then drew away, looking into her face so close to his. "What about adding up the positives? Blackie and Emma were able to celebrate her eightieth birthday together, and they did have a wonderful eight months traveling the world. Emerald Bow won the Grand National, which was a triumph for Grandpops. Edwina was reconciled with Emma, who lived long enough to see Emily married to Winston, Alexander to Maggie. There have been many happy occasions, and a lot of good things have happened along with the bad."

"Oh, Shane, you're so right. How silly I must sound."

"Not at all, and, as you said, there's nobody more superstitious than I. Still, I do try to look for the rainbow. There usually is one, you know." His face changed slightly and he peered at her through dark eyes grown quizzical. "When you phoned me that night in October, after the reading of Aunt Emma's will, you said she'd made me one of her heirs because she loved me like one of her own, and because of her lifelong friendship with my grandfather. And I know you keep repeating that, but—" He sat back, groped in his pocket for his cigarettes, took one, lit it. He smoked for a second or two, staring into the distance.

Observing him closely, her interest piqued, Paula probed, "What are you getting at, leading up to, Shane?"

"I can't help wondering if Emma had other reasons, or, more precisely, *one* other reason."

"Such as what?"

"Maybe Emma knew about us, Paula."

"Oh, Shane, I don't think so!" Paula exclaimed, giving him a curious stare. "I'm sure she would have mentioned something to me. You know how close I was to Grandy. Anyway, she would have told Blackie, I know she would, and *he* would have certainly brought it up with you. He wouldn't have been able to resist doing so."

Shane flicked ash into the ashtray. "I'm not quite as positive as you are. Emma was the smartest person I've ever known. I doubt that she *would* have said anything, under the circumstances. For one thing, she wouldn't have wanted to intrude on my privacy, or yours, and she wouldn't have told Grandpops because she would have been afraid he'd worry. Let's face it, she did leave me the engagement ring. Hoping that *I* might end up giving it to *you* one day?"

Paula said, "Perhaps she simply thought you were entitled to own the ring, that it was rightfully yours, considering from whom it came. It is very valuable. Besides, she left you the painting, which was another gift from your grandfather."

"True. But, Paula, a million pounds in trust for me . . . that's one hell of a hefty present by anybody's standards."

"Agreed." Paula smiled at him and her bright blue eyes, flickering with violet lights, filled with tenderness and warmth. "My grandmother cared for you very much, Shane. She thought of you as another grandson. And, look here, what about Merry? Grandy was awfully generous to her, too."

"Yes." Shane let out a small sigh. "I'd love to know the real truth. But I don't suppose I ever shall." Sudden laughter bubbled in his throat and his eyes danced mischievously. "I must confess *I* like to think that Emma *did* know about us, and that she approved."

"Well, that's one thing I can be sure of, Shane. I know she would have given us her blessing. Also—" Paula stopped abruptly when an announcement was made over the loudspeaker. She glanced at him and pulled a face. "That's it, darling, they're announcing the departure of my flight." She made a motion to stand up.

Shane restrained her. He took her in his arms and whispered against her hair, "I love you so much, Paula. Remember that in the next couple of weeks."

"How could I ever forget? It's part of my great strength. And I love you, too, Shane, and I will for *all* of my life."

Emily said, "No, Jim, she hasn't arrived yet. I'm expecting her shortly, though." Balancing the receiver between her ear and her raised shoulder, Emily zipped up her skirt as she continued to listen to Jim. He was phoning from Yorkshire and had caught her just as she was dressing.

After a few seconds, Emily exclaimed with impatience, "I *know* the plane has landed. I checked with Heathrow and it *was* on time. It touched down at seven-thirty *exactly*. Paula has to clear customs and then get into town, you know." Emily glanced at the clock on the bedside table. "It's only *nine,* for heaven's sake, Jim. Look, I have to go. I'll tell her to ring you back the minute she walks in."

"I'm about to leave the office, Emily," Jim said. "I'm driving up to London. Tell Paula not to bother coming to Yorkshire as she planned. I'll see her at Belgrave Square tonight. And you and Winston as well. Let's have dinner together, make it a *bon voyage* party."

"Oh yes," Emily muttered, "I see what you mean. Because Winston's going to Canada tomorrow."

"Yes . . . and I'm going with him, Emily. I just finished talking with him at our London office, and he's delighted that I've decided to tag along."

"Oh," Emily said, taken aback. "Well, yes, it will be company for him, I suppose. I'll see you tonight, Jim. Bye."

"Good-bye, Emily."

She dropped the receiver in the cradle and stared at it for a moment. She grimaced, wondering if Winston was really as pleased as Jim thought. She doubted it. Neither of them had much time for Jim Fairley these days.

The phone rang again. Emily picked it up quickly, feeling quite certain it was her husband. "Yes, Winston?" she said.

Winston laughed. "How did you know it was me?"

"Because I was speaking to Jim a moment ago. He was looking for Paula. He told me he's going to Toronto with you. Aren't you thrilled to bits?" she asked sarcastically.

"Like hell I am," Winston said. "There's really no reason for him to come with me, but I couldn't very well tell him to get lost. He does own ten percent of the new company, and he's curious about the latest acquisition, wants to look the new newspaper over. You know how odd he is these days, a real fusspot, and, frankly, he's getting to be a pain in the arse."

"What a bore for you, Winston." Emily sighed. "Look, I hope he doesn't start messing around with the Toronto *Sentinel.* Editorially, I mean. That could delay you. You'd better be back here for Christmas, Winston."

"I will, don't worry, lovey. As for Jim, well, I shall make short shrift of him if he starts interfering."

"He suggested we all have dinner tonight. A *bon voyage* party, he called it. I'd prefer to be alone with you, but I suppose we'll have to join them," Emily said, her tone grudging.

"We've no choice. Anyway, I only rang to tell you about Jim coming to Canada with me. Must dash. I'm about to start a meeting."

After saying good-bye, Emily took her suit jacket out of the armoire and slipped it on. She hurried down the stairs in the Belgrave Square maisonette, where she and Winston had been staying for the weekend, heading in the direction of the study.

The lime-and-white room with its bright yellow and peach accents was filled with cold December light on this dreary Monday morning. Yet it had a cheerful feeling because of the bowls of fresh flowers, the blazing fire, the many lamps that glowed warmly. Emily noticed that Parker had brought in a tray of coffee and three cups and saucers. Her brother was due to arrive at ten o'clock, soon after Paula was expected.

Seating herself at the desk, Emily telephoned her secretary at Genret's London office and explained she would not be coming in that day. As she hung up she heard Parker greeting Paula in the foyer. She leapt to her feet and ran out to welcome her cousin.

"What a lovely surprise to see your smiling face," Paula said warmly, rushing to embrace Emily. "I didn't expect you to be in London, Dumpling. What are you doing here?"

"I'll fill you in shortly."

Paula turned to the butler. "Tilson's keeping the luggage in the car, Parker, since he's driving me to Yorkshire later today."

Emily said, "Oh, er, Paula, Jim rang a bit ago. He's on his way to London. He wanted you to know that, and suggested you stay here tonight."

Paula bit back an exclamation of annoyance and murmured, "I see." She smiled weakly at the butler. "Would you please ask Tilson to bring my luggage in after all, Parker."

"Yes, madame." Parker went to the front door.

Paula threw her mink cape on a hall chair and stepped after Emily, following her into the study. She closed the door, leaned against it and said heatedly, "Damn it! Jim knew I was anxious to go *straight* to Yorkshire to see Lorne and Tessa! Did he say why he's suddenly coming up to town?"

"Yes. Winston's going to Toronto tomorrow, to review the situation at the new newspaper. Jim has decided to tag along."

"Oh no!" Paula cried, her face tightening. She walked over to the fire and sat down heavily on the sofa. Her anger flared inside her. Jim was doing a disappearing act again, as he had in October when he had gone to Ireland to stay with Edwina. Did he have a sixth sense? Did he somehow *know* when she was about to broach the subject of divorce?

Emily stood near the fireplace, scrutinizing her cousin closely. Finally she said, "You look awfully upset, Paula. Is something wrong?"

Paula hesitated, then confided, "I don't suppose you'll be surprised, Emily, if I tell you that Jim and I have a lot of personal problems to discuss. And resolve. I'd hoped to get down to brass tacks in the next few days. Now he's leaving. *Again.* Unless I can persuade him to cancel the trip with Winston, I'm going to have to wait until he gets back from Canada to talk to him."

Emily lowered herself onto the sofa and patted her hand. "I've known for a long time that things were difficult between the two of you, Paula. And you *should* talk to Jim—about a divorce, if you want my opinion. Winston happens to agree."

Paula searched Emily's face and with alertness. "So it's that apparent, is it?"

"Oh no, not to everyone, but certainly to those closest to you."

"My parents?" Paula asked swiftly, sitting up straighter.

"Your father is aware there is great strain and he's concerned about the situation, but I'm not sure about Aunt Daisy. I mean, I don't think she realizes how bad it is, Paula. She's so nice, always making allowances for everyone."

Paula sighed wearily. "Do you think I can persuade him not to go to Canada?"

"No, I definitely don't. Because of those shares Grandy left him, Jim feels very much a part of the new company, and he wants to get his fingers into the pie. He's a bit of a meddler, these days."

"I know." Paula rubbed her face, feeling suddenly fatigued. She blinked. "I hate these overnight transatlantic flights."

Emily nodded. She took a deep breath, then said, "You wouldn't be able to go to Yorkshire today anyway, Paula. Alexander needs you here in London. As a matter of fact, he'll be arriving in a few minutes to have a meeting with us."

"What's happened?" Instantly, a look of comprehension flashed. "Not Jonathan?"

"Yes, I'm afraid so."

"Tell me all about it." Paula stared at Emily anxiously, thoughts of Jim and the divorce momentarily swept to one side.

"Alexander prefers to fill you in, Paula. He asked me to ask you to wait until he gets here. It's rather involved. And that's why I'm in London—because of Jonathan. Alexander wanted me to be here for the meeting with you. Actually, Alexander and I have thrashed the situation to bits for the past two weeks—"

"You mean you've known all this time and you didn't let me know?"

"We wanted to be sure, and get a plan together. Also, we had to talk to Henry Rossiter and John Crawford. We needed their advice. We're going to have to take drastic steps, Paula."

"Is it that bad?"

"Pretty serious. However, Sandy and I have it well under control. Sarah is involved to a certain extent."

"As we thought." Paula sighed. Her dismay increased.

The door opened quietly and Alexander walked into the study. "Morning, Emily. Welcome back, Paula." He came over to the sofa, kissed them both and took a chair facing them. "I wouldn't mind a cup of coffee, Emily," he said to his sister. "I walked over from Eton Square and the weather's beastly this morning. I'm frozen."

"Yes, of course." Emily lifted the silver pot, poured. "What about you, Paula?"

"Yes, thanks, I might as well." Her eyes were penetrating as they rested on Alexander. "You ought to have let me know."

"To be honest, I thought about doing so, Paula. Emily and I discussed it at great length, and we finally decided there wasn't much point. You would have worried and you couldn't have contributed very much from New York. Besides, you had your hands full with Sitex. I didn't want to drag you back to London. Furthermore, I only just got to the root of it all at the end of last week. Well, more or less."

Paula nodded. "Tell me everything, Sandy."

"Well, here goes. Philip's plan worked. Malcolm Perring helped me to flush Jonathan out, but I had another source of information. It was this source that enabled me to really nail him. But I'm jumping ahead of myself. I'd better begin at the beginning."

"Please," Paula said.

"Malcolm Perring *did* eventually come up with the perfect property deal for Harte Enterprises. He took it to Jonathan, who expressed considerable interest. Then nothing happened. Malcolm kept ringing him over a two-week period, and Jonathan stalled. However, in the middle of November, Jonathan invited Malcolm to come over to the office for a meeting. Apparently Jonathan waffled on for a while about its being an excellent deal, but finally he turned it down. He said Harte Enterprises could not handle it at that particular time. He suggested Malcolm take the deal to a man called Stanley Jervis at a new company, Stonewall Properties. He explained that Jervis was an old friend, very reliable, and in the market for big real estate deals."

"Don't tell me," Paula muttered, "that Stonewall Properties belongs to Jonathan Ainsley."

"Correct. And get this—Sebastian Cross is his partner."

"That odious man. Ugh!" Paula shuddered.

"Sarah also has money in the company," Alexander told her. He shook his head. "Foolish girl."

"She's been duped by Jonathan again, just as she was when she was a child," Paula remarked softly.

"Precisely," Emily interjected. "Only this time there are far-reaching consequences for her."

"Yes." Paula scowled in perplexity, now demanded, "But how did Malcolm Perring manage to find all this out?"

Alexander answered, "He didn't. I did. Malcolm Perring went along with Jonathan's idea, since that was the whole purpose of our plan—catching him with his hand in the till, so to speak. Malcolm had two meetings with this Jervis chap, and then suddenly Sebastian Cross was on the scene. He's pretty much up-front in the company now, even though Jonathan is obviously hiding behind straw men, his men, since his name doesn't appear anywhere."

Alexander lit a cigarette, continued: "Malcolm started negotiations with Cross and Jervis, playing them along, inducing them to believe he was prepared to close the deal with Stonewall. He didn't take to either of them, and suspected that the company was shaky financially. He did a bit of investigating, talked to people around town, and his suspicions were soon confirmed. As planned, Malcolm began to back off, much to the astonishment of Jervis and Cross. They were scared of losing the deal, and started to boast about the big business transactions they had recently handled. Malcolm brought this information to me. I went through the files in our real estate division late one night and discovered that we could have made all of those deals. Jonathan had passed them over to Stonewall. That cinched it for me, Paula. I knew positively that he was as guilty as hell. Malcolm finally cut off negotiations with Stonewall, explaining that another real estate company had come in with an enormous offer, one which his partners were insisting the firm accept."

"And they bought it?" Paula asked.

"They had no choice. I was ready to swoop down on Jonathan, and then quite unexpectedly some other information fell into my lap, and within forty-eight hours I had enough on Jonathan to hang him."

"Where did the new information come from?" Paula leaned forward eagerly, riddled with curiosity.

"John Cross."

"Alexander, you can't be serious!" Paula's astonishment was evident. "John Cross," she repeated, and her eyes widened as she drew back, looked at Alexander askance. "I don't believe it."

"It's the truth."

"But why would he confide in you?"

"Actually, Paula, John Cross was looking to confide in you. He only got in touch with me because you weren't around. He asked me to come to Leeds to see him . . . he was in St. James's Hospital."

"Oh," Paula said. "What was wrong with him? Was he very sick?"

"Poor old man," he murmured. "He died, Paula. John Cross died just a few days after I saw him. It was cancer, I'm afraid. He was riddled with it, and obviously in great pain."

"Oh, Sandy, how awful." Paula pursed her lips. "Poor man. I wouldn't wish that on anyone. And he wasn't so bad. Weak, a little misguided maybe, and under the thumb of that rotten son of his."

Alexander cleared his throat. "I immediately drove to Leeds and went to see John Cross at the hospital. I was with him for almost four hours. The doctor allowed me to stay that length of time, because—well, he was dying. John Cross talked about you for a while. He said he had a great deal of respect for you, Paula, admired your honesty and fairness. He then explained that you'd been very courteous to him in the autumn of 1969 when you saw him in London. I told him I knew about your meeting. He commented about your patience and your kindness to him that day, and said he understood why you hadn't been interested in reopening negotiations for the acquisition of Aire Communications . . . because his company no longer had any real assets since the building had been sold. That's when he started to open up. To be honest, I was flabbergasted when he confided that Stonewall Properties had bought the Aire building for five hundred thousand pounds. Apparently his son persuaded him to sell. He insisted that he'd been cheated by them, because the building was worth a million at least. I had to agree with him. John Cross became very upset, and he said this to me, Paula: 'Imagine my shock when I discovered six months ago that it was my son who robbed me, who ruined me, ruined any chance for Aire Communications to make a recovery. I was heartbroken that Sebastian could do such a terrible thing to me. My son . . . my only child.' He began to weep, and I can't say I blamed him."

"What a ghastly thing to happen to him . . . So Grandy was always right about Jonathan . . . She was very suspicious of him at the time of the Aire Communications negotiations," Paula said.

"And with good reason." Alexander crossed his legs, sat back. "Mr. Cross wanted *you* to know, *us* to know, that Jonathan was Sebastian's partner and that he had been working against Emma Harte for years. He mumbled something about despising family treachery, said that he wanted to die with an easy conscience."

Paula sighed, rubbed her weary face. "What else did he reveal about Stonewall Properties?"

"Not a lot, at least nothing I didn't already know through Malcolm. Mr. Cross confirmed that Jonathan had been moving deals away from Harte Enterprises and into Stonewall, and he confessed that his son had bled him dry, taken every penny he had. The old man was very bitter when he explained that it was only because of his sister's generosity that he was able to have a private room at St. James's, and private doctors. You see, Paula, old Mr. Cross was destitute."

Paula sank back against the cushions and, for a reason she would never fully understand, her eyes filled with tears. She coughed behind her hand and reached for one of Alexander's cigarettes. "How sad that he had to end his days in such a frightful way . . . betrayed by his own son."

Emily announced, "Sebastian Cross is a bastard. And Jonathan Ainsley is no better, is he, Sandy?"

"No." Alexander gave Paula a long look. "John Cross told me something else, and this is the worst part of all. However, because of it, I *am* going to get Jonathan, really *get* him, Paula. In an effort to bail out Stonewall Properties, which is in grave financial difficulties, Jonathan borrowed a lot of money—against his shares in Harte Enterprises."

Paula was momentarily dumbfounded and thrown off balance. She gaped at her cousins, then gasped, "But he's not allowed to do that!"

"Exactly!" Emily cried. "Don't you see, because he did that we can nail him . . . Actually, he's nailed himself to the cross, hasn't he?"

Paula nodded, asked sharply, "Are you sure there's no mistake?"

"None," Alexander replied. "John Cross knew about the loan, don't ask me how, but he did. He wouldn't reveal his source, nor did he realize the true importance of his information to us. He merely wanted to alert us to our cousin's activities. In a funny way, I think he blamed Jonathan for his son's transgressions, although I'm not so sure he's correct there. However, he *was* able to give me the name of the finance company that made the loan to

Jonathan. Obviously Jonathan couldn't borrow from a bank—they'd want to know too much."

"I can't believe he would be so foolhardy," Paula said. "He's fully aware he's not permitted to use his shares in Harte Enterprises as collateral, nor can he sell those shares unless it's to another shareholder—"

"That's right," Alexander interrupted. "He can only sell them to me, Emily, or Sarah. Those are the company laws, which are very precisely spelled out in the articles of incorporation by Grandy. She wanted to ensure that Harte Enterprises remained a private company, a family concern, with no strangers or outsiders involved, and she made damned certain that that was the way it would be."

"Which finance company did he get involved with?"

"Financial Investment and Loan."

"Good God, Sandy, they're crooks," Paula exclaimed, horrified. "Everyone knows that they're a shady outfit. How could he be so stupid?"

"I told you, he couldn't go to a bank. A bank would want to know everything, as far as those shares are concerned, as would a reputable finance company."

"How much did he borrow and against how many shares?" Paula demanded.

"He put up seven percent of his shares, just under half of his sixteen percent, and he raised four million pounds against them. However, the loan company gave him a poor deal. Those shares are worth twice that much, except, of course, that they cannot be sold to anyone—except to one of us. Still, the finance company wasn't aware of that at the time they made the loan. They are now."

Paula experienced a sudden sense of relief and her troubled expression lifted. "You paid off his note and retrieved the shares, didn't you, Sandy?"

"I did. Last Thursday Emily and I met with the managing director of that dubious little company, along with Henry Rossiter and John Crawford. It was all very troublesome, and there were a lot of strong words, heated arguments, and general unpleasantness. We returned again on Friday, all four of us, and I paid them back their four million pounds and they returned the shares. There was some interest due, but Henry and John were adamant, refused to let me pay that. They told the managing director to go after Jonathan. And there you have all the gory details."

"Where did you and Emily get the four million from? Did you use your own money?"

"No. John Crawford figured out a way for Harte Enterprises to buy the shares back, rather than an individual. As you know, Paula, Grandy drew up a number of legal papers in regard to Harte Enterprises just before she died. I have extraordinary powers, a free hand in many instances, especially if the overall good of the company is involved. John and Henry agreed that this situation with Jonathan was such an instance. However, I told them that Emily and I are perfectly willing to purchase those shares if they decide, at a future date, that this is the proper thing to do."

"I see." Paula stood up and walked to the fireplace. A thought struck her. "Are Sarah's shares involved?"

"No. Stupid she might be, but she would never risk her shares," Alexander replied.

"What are you going to do about Jonathan and Sarah?" Paula asked, her eyes sharpening.

"I intend to fire them both. At noon today. I've called a meeting. I'd like you to be present, Paula."

Forty-Seven

There was a sanguine air about Jonathan Ainsley as he walked into Alexander's office at Harte Enterprises.

Being an egotist who was convinced he was smarter and shrewder than everyone else, it never occurred to him that his double-dealing might have been uncovered.

"Hello, Alexander," he said, strolling nonchalantly across the room, shaking his cousin's hand. "Sarah told me she's been asked to come to this meeting too. What's it all about, then?"

Alexander sat down in the chair behind his desk and said, "There are some important matters I have to discuss. It won't take long." Alexander's clear blue eyes, so intelligent and honest, rested on Jonathan, but only briefly. He shuffled the papers on his desk, filled with contempt and loathing for the other man.

Walking over to the sofa, Jonathan sat down, lit a cigarette, and lolled back against the leather cushions. He glanced at the door as Emily came in, and gave her a warm smile. This was entirely fraudulent, since he disliked Emily. But the feeling in no way matched his virulent hatred for Paula, and that hatred flared when she hove into view, stood in the doorway a split second later.

Rising, he greeted Emily with a degree of cordiality, but his voice turned a shade colder as he said to Paula, "You're not involved in the day-to-day running of Harte Enterprises, so what are you doing here?"

"Alexander invited me, since I have a family matter to talk about."

"Ah yes, family matters do seem to preoccupy you these days, don't they, Paula?" he said, his sardonicism echoing. He lowered himself into a chair, muttering, "Not the will again, I hope."

"No, not that," Paula replied, her voice calm, betraying nothing. She followed Emily over to the sofa and sat down. Ever since his bitter outburst at the reading of the will, Jonathan had dropped all pretense with her. He did not bother to conceal his animosity and a minute ago she had seen the antipathy flickering. She had also noted that his anxiety had slipped through the bland façade he was trying so hard to hold in place. Paula looked down at her hands, half-smiling to herself. Her presence had unnerved him, try though he had not to show it. After a second or two she lifted her head, studied him surreptitiously, her eyes objective. How attractive his appearance was. So fair of coloring and fine of feature. Yes, he *was* very clean-cut, and there were times, such as now, that he had the look of an innocent choirboy. Yet she knew he was a schemer who would stop at nothing to gain his own ends.

Sarah swept in grandly, scanned the room. "Hello, everyone," she murmured coolly, and then spoke to Alexander directly: "I'm in rather a hurry. I have a luncheon date at one o'clock with a very important buyer. I hope this isn't going to take long."

"No, it won't," Alexander said. "I intend to make our meeting as short as possible."

"Oh, good." Sarah swung away from the desk, looked at Emily and Paula on the sofa, and purposely chose a chair near Jonathan. Sitting back, she offered Alexander a sweet smile.

He stared at her for the longest moment. Not an eyelash flickered and his face was suddenly cold and implacable. Sarah's smile slipped and she frowned at him, obviously puzzled by his manner.

"It seems odd to me," Alexander began, "that Stonewall Properties has such severe, such grave, financial problems." He focused on Jonathan. "Bad management, do you suppose?"

Jonathan felt a tightening of his stomach muscles and all of his senses were alerted for trouble. Secure in the knowledge that he could not be linked to Stonewall, he managed to keep a composed demeanor. He shrugged. "How would I know? And don't tell me you've dragged us here to discuss another company?"

"Why yes, that is one of the reasons." Alexander leaned forward, peering at Sarah. "Were you aware that Stonewall Properties is likely to go belly-up in the near future?"

Sarah opened her mouth and closed it swiftly. The disturbing information about the secret company, which she had invested so much money in, had stunned her. She did not doubt its truth, since it came from the reliable Alexander. She was anxious to speak to Jonathan alone, but she dreaded tackling him. He could be so difficult, and now it was fear of his wrath that made her hold her tongue.

Alexander continued to regard her unwaveringly. She had paled under this fixed observation and her eyes were suddenly alarmed. He knew Sarah would crack if he increased the pressure.

But he addressed the room at large. "What really baffles me, though, is how they managed to get into this state. Stonewall have closed an amazing number of genuinely good deals. I can't imagine why they are foundering so badly. Unless, of course, somebody has had a hand in the till."

Rattled by this remark, Sarah cried, "Do you think that's possible, and if—"

Jonathan interjected peremptorily, "Now look here, Alexander, let's forget about the problems at Stonewall and get on with our own business."

"Oh, but Stonewall *is* our business," Alexander said in a murderously quiet voice. "And you know it, since Stonewall Properties is your company, Jonathan."

There was an involuntary gasp from Sarah, and then she shrank back in the chair.

Jonathan laughed dismissively and threw Alexander a look that was both challenging and threatening. "What bloody nonsense you do talk. I've never heard anything so preposterous."

"Jonathan, I know everything there is to know about Stonewall. The company is jointly owned by you and Sebastian Cross, and Sarah has invested a great deal of money in it. It's run by Cross and Stanley Jervis, along with a number of straw men put in there by you. Cross and you formed the company in 1968. You've been channeling real estate deals intended for Harte Enterprises into your own company. You've lost us an enormous amount of business, important and highly profitable business, Jonathan, and you queered Grandy's pitch when she was in negotiations with Aire Communications. I'm appalled. You have been disloyal and a traitor to this company. You have betrayed Grandy's trust in you, and therefore I have no alternative but to—"

"Just try to prove it!" Jonathan shouted angrily, leaping to his feet. He slapped both his hands on the edge of Alexander's desk and bent over it, glaring into his cousin's face. "You'll have the greatest difficulty doing so. There is not one shred of evidence to support or substantiate these ridiculous accusations."

"You're absolutely wrong. I have all the evidence I need," Alexander shot back evenly, but his tone was glacial, his look condemning. He patted the file of folders on his desk, which in fact had nothing to do with Stonewall, and said, with a thin smile, "It's *all* here, Jonathan. Then, of course, there is your partner in"—Alexander lifted his hands and shrugged—"shall we *say,* crime, for want of a better word. Yes, there she sits in stunned silence . . . Sarah Lowther."

"Now you're trying to bring poor Sarah into this plot of yours," Jonathan shouted. "Yes, that's what it is—a plot to discredit us both. You've always been out to get me, Alexander Barkstone, ever since we were kids. And Sarah as well. But you're not going to get away with it. I'll see you in hell first. I shall fight for my rights, and for Sarah's. So just beware," he threatened.

Alexander leaned back in the chair, and his blue eyes, so cold and hard a second before, instantly changed when he gave Sarah a look of pity. "Yes, *poor* Sarah indeed," he remarked softly. "You've been duped, I'm afraid. Your money has gone down the drain, Sarah. Sad for you, really, but there's nothing you can do about it now."

"A-A-Alexander," Sarah stammered, "I-I-I don't—"

"Be quiet, and let *me* do all the talking, Sarah dear. He's a crafty devil. He'll trap you into saying the wrong thing." Jonathan brought his blazing eyes back to the other man. His lip curled. "You're the biggest bastard alive!"

"All right, that's enough!" Alexander was on his feet behind the desk. "Don't you dare call *me* a bastard."

"Cut you to the quick, have I?" Jonathan laughed nastily. "But that's what you undoubtedly are, and so is that sister of yours. You would do well to remember that it is *your* mother who sleeps around, not mine."

"You're fired!" Alexander exclaimed, his anger spiraling into pure rage.

"You can't fire me." Jonathan threw back his head and guffawed. "I'm a shareholder in this company and—"

"Your holdings in this company have been considerably reduced," Alexander interrupted in a steadier tone, taking full control of himself. "By exactly seven percent." He lifted the top folder and took out the share certificates, waved them under Jonathan's nose. "I just retrieved these . . . last Friday. It cost Harte Enterprises exactly four million pounds to pay off your loan to the finance company you borrowed from, but I was happy to do it in order to get these shares back."

Jonathan had blanched. He stood gaping at Alexander in stupefaction. For once in his life he could think of nothing to say. For a moment he thought he was finished, and then he exclaimed, with a scornful smirk, "I still own nine percent of this company. Furthermore, there's no way you can fire me. Under the company laws, a shareholder cannot be fired."

"Grandy made that ruling in 1968, when she drew her will and divided her one hundred percent between the four of us. However, *she* still owned her one hundred percent until the day she died, and, therefore, she owned the company outright. And as the sole owner of Harte Enterprises, Emma Harte could do anything she wanted, as you well know. And so, just before she went to Australia, Grandy changed all of the company laws. Actually, what she did was to reconstruct the company and cause new articles of incorporation to be drawn. Under the new company laws, I, as managing director, chairman of the board, and majority shareholder, can do practically anything I wish. I have extraordinary powers. I can buy out a shareholder, if that shareholder is agreeable. I can hire. I can fire." Alexander leaned over his desk and impaled Jonathan with his eyes. "And so I am firing *you.*" He looked past Jonathan, fixed his gaze on Sarah. "You're also fired, Sarah. Your behavior has been as shoddy as Jonathan's."

Sarah could not speak. She seemed to have turned to stone in the chair.

"We'll see about all this bloody nonsense," Jonathan railed. "I'm going to pay a visit to John Crawford the minute I leave here, and I'm taking Sarah with me. There's—"

"Do go and see him by all means," Alexander cut in, dropping the share certificates on the desk. He slipped his hands into his trouser pockets and rocked back and forth on his heels. "He'll be perfectly happy to confirm what I've just told you. As a matter of fact, he does want a word with you anyway. He was with me at the two meetings I had with Financial Investment and Loan, and John was a little bit disturbed about the interest you owe to them. They're a shady bunch, Jonathan. You'd better pay up, and smartly."

Jonathan opened his mouth, and then snapped it shut, glaring at his cousin.

Sarah, having partially recovered, hurried to the desk. She appealed to Alexander tearfully, "I haven't done anything with my shares . . . I haven't done *anything* wrong. Why are you firing me?"

"Because you *have* done something wrong, Sarah. You invested in a company which was in direct competition with the real estate division of Harte Enterprises. You've been disloyal, a traitor like Jonathan. I'm sorry, but as I just told you, I cannot condone your behavior."

"But I love Lady Hamilton Clothes," she gasped, and began to sob.

"You should have thought of that when you threw your lot in with your reckless cousin here," Alexander answered steadily, quite unmoved by her tears. "And God in heaven only knows why you ever did."

Jonathan cried irately: "I intend to take this matter to another solicitor. I'm not convinced those papers Grandmother drew are quite as legal as you seem to believe."

"I can assure you that they are . . . *very, very legal.* John Crawford and Henry Rossiter, as directors of Harte Enterprises, approved them, as did I. Don't try to challenge anything Emma Harte did, because, believe me, you won't get anywhere. She outsmarted you."

Suddenly Jonathan went berserk. He yelled, "I'll get you for this, you bloody sod!" He swiveled on his heels and shook his fist at Paula, "And you too, you bitch!"

"Get out." Alexander made a move toward Jonathan. "Before I personally take you by the scruff of your neck and throw you out."

Paula jumped to her feet and ran to Alexander, put a restraining hand on his arm.

She stared at Jonathan and Sarah, pressing back her disgust and disdain. She said, very quietly, "How *could* you? How could you do it to *her?* She who gave you so much, who was so fair and generous. She suspected you, Jonathan, for a long time before she died, and you, Sarah, latterly. And yet she gave you both the benefit of the doubt because she had no real proof. She did not rescind your trust funds, nor did she take back the shares in Harte Enterprises she so generously gave you." Paula shook her head sorrowfully. "You are both everything Grandy loathed and despised . . . treacherous, devious, and dishonest, and liars and cheats besides."

Neither of them spoke. Jonathan's face was ringed with bitter hatred, and Sarah looked as if she was going to pass out from shock.

Paula's voice took on a new note, one of calm resoluteness as she said, "I'm afraid I'm not as forgiving as Emma Harte was. She tolerated your fathers long after their treacherous treatment of her. But I will not tolerate either of you. I only have this to add . . . neither of you are welcome at family gatherings in the future. Please remember that."

Sarah, still white and trembling, became hysterical at Paula's words of banishment. She turned on Jonathan and cried accusingly, "This is all your fault. I should never have listened to you. I've not only lost my money, but Lady Hamilton Clothes and the family as well." She started to sob anew.

Jonathan ignored her. He leaned closer to Paula, his eyes baleful, his face contorted in a mask of hatred. "I'll get you for this, Paula Fairley. Sebastian and I will bloody well get you!"

Alexander finally lost his temper completely. He sprang past Paula, grabbed Jonathan's arm roughly, and dragged him to the door. "I think you'd better leave before I give you the thrashing of your life."

Struggling out of his cousin's tenacious grip, Jonathan yelled, "Keep your filthy hands off me, you sneaky sod. And don't think you're immune. Don't forget what I said. We'll get you too, Barkstone. If it takes all my life I'm going to make certain you get yours." Jonathan flung open the door and stormed out.

Sarah ran to Alexander, who still stood near the doorway. "What am I going to do?" she wailed, brushing her hands over her wet face.

"I really don't know, Sarah," Alexander answered in a cold and quiet voice. "I really don't know."

She looked at him helplessly, then brought her gaze to Paula and finally to Emily. She knew from their closed faces that her plight was hopeless. Cursing Jonathan under her breath, she found her handbag and left the office as quickly as she could, striving to quell her tears.

Alexander walked across the room, seated himself behind his desk and took a cigarette. He saw that his hands shook as he struck a match and lit it, and he was not surprised. "That was all rather unpleasant," he said, "but no worse than I expected. I have to admit, I couldn't help feeling Sarah was in over her head, and without knowing it."

"Yes," Paula agreed, and took the chair opposite his desk. She turned and glanced at Emily. "There was a moment when I actually felt sorry for her, but it passed when I thought of Gran, and the wonderful things she did for them all their lives."

"I didn't have one ounce of sympathy for Sarah!" Emily cried indignantly. "She deserved everything she got. As for Jonathan—he's despicable."

"He'll try and make trouble, but he won't succeed," Alexander announced. "He'll huff and he'll puff, but he'll never blow our house down. All he did was make idle threats." Alexander grinned. "I couldn't believe it when he shook his fist at you, just like the villain in a Victorian drama."

Paula laughed nervously. "I know what you mean. On the other hand, Sandy, I don't think we should dismiss Jonathan quite so lightly. Not with Sebastian Cross—my enemy—in the background, egging him on to do heaven knows what. I've told you before, I have a very low opinion of Cross."

Alexander sat back, observing her quietly, musing on her words.

Emily hurried over and stood next to Paula. She said, "Honestly, Alexander, Paula's right. We've not heard the last of Jonathan Ainsley, Sarah Lowther, and Sebastian Cross—not by a long shot."

Leaning over his desk, Alexander smiled warmly and confidently. "Forget the three of them, please. There's nothing they can do to us . . . not now or in the future. They're quite powerless."

Paula was not so sure about this, but she said, "Spoken like a true grandson of Emma Harte's." Pushing aside her worry, adopting a positive attitude, she exclaimed, "And as she would have said, let's get on with it. We've got a lot more to accomplish today. Now, Sandy, who do you have in mind to run Lady Hamilton Clothes?"

"As a matter of fact, I was thinking of putting Maggie in there. She has a good business head, and with a bit of help from the two of you . . ." He stopped, looked at his sister and his cousin. "Well?"

"It's a terrific idea!" Emily cried.

"I second that," said Paula.

Forty-Eight

The old nursery at Pennistone Royal, slightly shabby though it was, glowed with comfort and warmth. A huge fire crackled in the grate, lamps shone brightly, and there was a feeling of gaiety and lightheartedness in the air.

It was early evening on a cold Saturday in January of 1971. Emily, sitting on the window seat observing Paula and her children, was filled with delight as she witnessed the happy scene being enacted in front of her. Paula was so very carefree tonight, and her eyes, which had been unusually troubled of late, sparkled with laughter. There was a new tranquility in her face and, as always when she was with the children, her demeanor was gentle and loving.

The twins, who would be two years old next month, had already been bathed and were dressed in their nightclothes. Paula was holding their hands, and the three of them formed a circle in the center of the floor.

"All right, ready, set, go!" Paula cried and slowly began to move, taking small steps, leading the children around and around. Their freshly scrubbed faces shone with joy and their smiles were vividly bright, their eyes glowing.

Paula now began to sing: "Half a pound of tuppenny rice, half a pound of treacle, mix it up and make it nice—*Pop* goes the weasel!"

As they came to a standstill, Lorne broke free and flopped down onto the floor, giggling and laughing and rolling about. "Pop!" he shouted loudly. "Pop! Pop!" He continued to chortle and kick his legs in the air with the abandonment of a frisky puppy.

Tessa, clinging to Paula's hand, stared down at him and then up at her mother. "Silly," Tessa said. "Rorn . . . silly."

Paula crouched on her haunches and smiled into the solemn little face regarding her so intently. "Not silly, darling. Lorne is happy. We're all happy after such a lovely day. Try and say Lorne, sweetheart."

Tessa nodded. "Rorn," she repeated, unable as yet to properly pronounce her brother's name.

Paula's heart was bursting with love. She reached out and stroked the child's porcelain cheek with one finger. The green eyes surveying her reminded her of Chartreuse liqueur that had been only slightly diluted, so startling was their depth of color. She took Tessa in her arms and hugged her close, rumpling her burnished red-gold curls. "Oh, you're such a darling, Tess."

Tessa clung to Paula for a moment longer and then wriggled free. She pushed her face at her mother, craning her neck, and pursing her lips. "Mama . . . Mama," she said, and made small smacking sounds with her mouth. Paula smiled, leaned into her daughter and kissed her, ruffled her hair again. "Run and give Auntie Emily a kiss, sweetheart. It's well past your bedtime."

Paula watched Tessa march purposefully across the floor. In her white flannel nightdress and blue robe she looked adorable, resembled a cherub. Turning to Lorne, Paula knelt on the floor and began to tickle him. He squirmed and kicked, enjoying every minute of the game, his peals of laughter slicing through the gentle silence. Finally Paula stopped and lifted him to her. She stroked his flushed cheek and swept back his hair, which was a slightly darker red than his sister's, and endeavored to calm him. "Mummy's the silly one, Lorne, getting you so excited, and just when it's time for bed."

He cocked his head to one side and looked at her with great interest. "Me," he said. "Mam . . . Mam." Lorne now held up his face to be kissed, pursing his lips in the way his sister had done. This was a nightly ritual with both children, and Paula took his head between her hands and kissed his cheek, the tip of his nose, and his damp rosy lips. She drew back. "You're such a good boy, Lorne," she murmured, straightening the collar of his pajama jacket, overwhelmed by tenderness for her little boy.

Lorne reached up, touched her face, and then flopped against her, grabbing her arms tightly with his small hands, rocking to and fro. Paula held him close, also rocking, and smoothing her hand over his copper head, shining so brightly in the firelight. But after a few seconds she gently disentangled herself, rose, and pulled him up off the floor with her. Taking his hand, she walked him over to Emily and Tessa, who were cuddling on the window seat.

"The Sandman's about to arrive, Auntie Emily," Paula announced, making this sound most important. "Shall we go into the bedroom to welcome him?"

"What a lovely idea," Emily said, taking Tessa's hand, helping her down off the seat. "I haven't seen the Sandman for years."

Together the four of them went into the adjoining bedroom, where a small night-light glowed on the table between the two beds.

"Off with your dressing gowns," Paula instructed, "and into bed with you both. Quick! We don't want the Sandman to go away because two little poppets dawdle."

Tessa and Lorne struggled with their belts, and Paula and Emily went to their assistance. The twins scrambled into their beds and Paula pulled up the bedclothes, tucked them in, and gave them a kiss in turn.

"Take a seat, Auntie Emily, and be very, very quiet or you'll frighten the Sandman away," Paula cautioned as she pulled up a stool and sat down between the two beds.

"I'll be as quiet as a mouse," Emily whispered, going along with the game, seating herself on the bottom of Lorne's bed.

Paula gazed at her children. "Sssh!" she said softly, bringing a finger to her lips.

"Pom," Tessa said, "pom . . . Mam."

"All right, I'll say the Sandman's poem for you, but snuggle down and close your eyes, both of you."

Each child did as she said. Lorne put his thumb in his mouth and Tessa clutched at the white lamb lying next to her in the bed, and began to suck on its ear.

Paula began to recite in the softest of voices:

> "The Sandman has the swiftest wings
> And shoes that are made of gold,
> He calls on you when the first star sings
> When the night is not very old.
> He carries a tiny silver spoon
> And a bucket made of night,
> He fills your eyes with bits of moon
> And stardust that's shiny and bright.
> He takes you on a ship that sails
> Through the land of dreams and joys,
> And tells you many wondrous tales
> Of dragons and magical toys.
> So come now and rest your sleepy head
> And close your eyes very tight,
> For should you stay awake instead
> The Sandman won't pass by tonight."

Paula stopped, stood up, and went to peer at the twins. Both were already fast asleep. A tender smile flickered on her mouth. They had had an unusually hectic day and were worn out. Gently she kissed each of them and moved the stool out of the way. Emily went to Lorne and Tessa, also bent and kissed them, and the two young women crept out of the bedroom on their tiptoes.

By seven o'clock Paula was beginning to wonder what had happened to Jim. Emily had left over half an hour ago, after having a quick drink with her in the library. She had seated herself at the desk, intending to do some paperwork, but her worries had intruded.

It was the fifth of January—the day she had set aside to have a serious talk with Jim. Her parents and Philip had returned to London three days ago, after spending Christmas at Pennistone Royal. They had already departed for their skiing holiday in Chamonix.

Christmas had been exceptionally quiet. Randolph and Vivienne had accepted an invitation to visit Anthony and Sally at Clonloughlin, and the

O'Neills had made a last-minute decision to join Shane in Barbados. Emily and Winston, along with Alexander and Maggie, had come to stay for a few days, and the entire Kallinski clan had driven over on Christmas Eve. But the whole holiday period had been sad and depressing for everyone without Emma. She had always been the catalyst, the mover and the doer, and without her things were not the same.

Paula had somehow struggled through, making a supreme effort for the children and her parents, whilst counting the hours until today. And then Jim had suddenly rushed off to the newspaper this morning before she had had a chance to open her mouth.

Suddenly Paula swung around in the chair and jumped up as she heard the sound of a car on the gravel driveway outside. She stepped up to the window behind her chair, cupped her hands against the glass and peered out. The light over the back door shone brightly, clearly illuminating Jim's Aston Martin.

With a small intake of breath she held herself rigid as her eyes fell on the pair of skis sticking out of one of the back windows. So that was why he was so late. He had gone to Long Meadow first—to collect his skiing gear. He was going to Chamonix after all.

It's now or never, Paula muttered under her breath and flew across the library. Wrenching open the door, she stepped out into the Stone Hall, waiting for him, suppressing her exasperation.

Jim came in a moment later and headed in the direction of the main staircase at the other end of the hall.

"I'm in here, Jim," she exclaimed.

Startled, he pivoted swiftly, stood regarding her with uncertainty.

"Can you spare me a few minutes?" she asked, striving to bring her voice down to a lower pitch, not wanting to alert him or scare him off.

"Why not? I was just going up to change. Had a rather hectic day," he announced, walking toward her. "Surprisingly busy for Saturday."

Not so surprising, she thought, stepping back, opening the door wider. You've been clearing your desk in readiness for your imminent departure. But she said none of this.

Jim strolled past her into the library, without kissing her or making any gesture of affection. There was a great deal of strain between them, and this had lately turned into real coldness.

Paula closed the door firmly, thought of locking it, but changed her mind. She followed him over to the fireplace.

Sitting down in a wing chair, Paula glanced up at him, hovering near the fire. "Dinner's not until eight. You've plenty of time to freshen up. Make yourself comfortable, Jim. Let's chat for a while."

Throwing her an odd look, he nevertheless took the other chair, pulled out his cigarettes and put one in his mouth. After lighting it he smoked in silence for a second, staring ahead at the fire. Then he said, "How was your day?"

"Fine. I spent it with the children. Emily came over for lunch and stayed all afternoon. Winston had gone to a football match."

Jim said nothing.

Paula kept her voice very low as she said, "So you *are* going to Chamonix."

"Yes." He did not look at her.

"When are you leaving?"

He cleared his throat. "I thought I'd drive up to London late tonight, around ten or eleven. The roads will be virtually empty. I can make it in record time. That way I can catch the first flight to Geneva tomorrow."

Anger rushed through her, but she clamped down on it, knowing that she had to keep a cool head and must not inflame him if she was to accomplish anything. She said, "Please don't go, Jim. At least not for a few days."

"Why?" Now he swung his head, leveled his silvery gray eyes on her, and a blond brow lifted in surprise. He said, "You're going to New York."

"Yes, but not until the eighth or ninth. I told you, when you came back from Canada, that I wanted to discuss our problems. You put me off because it was Christmas and we were expecting guests. You promised you wouldn't go to Chamonix until we had settled things, thrashed out our problems."

"Your problems, not mine, Paula."

"Our problems."

"I beg to disagree. If there are any problems in our marriage, you have created them. For over a year now you've been looking for trouble, insisting we had difficulties when we didn't have any. Also, you are the one who has . . . left the marital bed, not I. You, and you alone, Paula, are the one who has brought about the present untenable situation." He smiled faintly, eyeing her more closely. "Because of *you* we have only half a marriage, but I'm prepared to live with it."

"We have no marriage at all."

He laughed hollowly. "We do have two children, though, and I'm prepared to share the same house with you for their sakes. They need us both. And talking of houses, when I come back from Chamonix we are *all* going to move back to Long Meadow. That is *my* house, *my* home, and *my* children are going to be brought up there."

Paula stared at him aghast. "You know very well Grandy wanted—"

"This is not your house," he cut in rapidly. "It belongs to your mother."

"You know very well Mummy and Daddy have to live in London so he can go to Harte's every day."

"That's their problem, not ours."

"Grandy didn't want Pennistone Royal to be left unoccupied half of the year. It was always a foregone conclusion that I would live here most of the time, that my parents would come for weekends when they could, spend the summer months and special holidays at the house."

"I have every intention of moving back into Long Meadow. With the children," he said in a rush. "You are very welcome. Of course, I can't force you to move in with us—" He broke off, shrugged. "It's your decision."

Paula looked at him, biting her inner lip. She said, "Jim, I want a divorce."

He said coldly, "I don't. I will never agree to one. *Never.* Furthermore, I think you should know that if you decide to take such a step I will fight you for custody of Lorne and Tessa. *My* children are going to be with me."

"Children need their mother," she began, and shook her head. "Surely you of all people know that. Naturally, you would have full visitation rights. I would never keep the children away from you, Jim. You would see them whenever you wanted, and they would come and stay with you."

He smiled narrowly as he snapped, "You're priceless, do you know that? Quite extraordinary, and the most selfish woman I've ever known. You want it *all,* don't you. Your freedom to do what you want, to live where you want, and the children as well." His eyes became icy. "Do you also want to take my job away from me?"

Paula sucked in her breath. "How can you think a thing like that! Of course I don't. Grandy renewed your contract before she died, and your job is safe for the rest of your life. And you also have the shares in the new company."

"Ah yes," he mused softly. "The new company. I rather like Toronto . . . lovely city. I might move there for a few years. That idea had crossed my mind in December. I'd enjoy running the Toronto *Sentinel.* Naturally the children would go with me."

"No!" she cried, her face paling.

"Oh yes," he countered. "But it *is* up to you, Paula. If you persist in this ridiculous idea of getting a divorce, if you break up *my* family, I will settle in Toronto, and I have every intention of taking *my* children with me."

"They're also mine."

"Yes," he said, "they are. And you are *my* wife." He softened his tone, gave her a warmer look. "We're a family, Paula. The children need you, I need you." He reached out, took her hand in his. "Why can't you stop all this nonsense, put aside your silly and *unfounded* grudges against me, make an effort to patch up our marriage. I'm willing to try." He flashed her his bland smile. "Why not start right now—*tonight."* He tightened his grip on her fingers and leaned closer to her, added in a suggestive tone, "There's no time like the present, darling. Come on, let's go upstairs and make love. I'll prove to you that all of these differences you're forever talking about are imaginary, exist only in *your head.* Come back to my bed, come back into my arms, Paula."

She did not dare say a word.

There was a long and painful silence.

Finally Jim murmured, "All right, not tonight then. Pity. Listen, since I'm going off to Chamonix and you're about to head for New York, let us both take the rest of this month to come to terms with ourselves during our separation. And then, when we're both back home in a few weeks, we'll start afresh. We'll move into Long Meadow and begin again, build a better relationship than we ever had before."

"There's nothing left between us, Jim, and therefore there is nothing to build on," she whispered miserably.

He let go of her hand and gaped into the fire. After a short while he said, "Psychologists call it compulsive repetition."

Not understanding what he was suddenly talking about, Paula frowned and said, "I'm not following you."

Jim turned to face her, and repeated, "Psychologists call it *compulsive repetition."*

"What's that supposed to mean?" she asked sharply, wondering if he was attempting to sidetrack her, as he so often did.

"It refers to the pattern of behavior some people adopt—an offspring actually *reliving* the life of a parent or grandparent, repeating that life, mistakes and all, as if he or she is guided by some terrible inner compulsion."

Paula gaped at him speechlessly. But she quickly found her voice. "Are you trying to say that I am reliving my grandmother's life?"

"Exactly."

"You're absolutely wrong!" Paula cried. "I am my *own* person. I am living my *own* life."

"Think that if you wish, but it's not true. You are compulsively doing everything Emma Harte ever did, and with great precision. You work your fingers to the bone, devote every moment of your time to that wretched business, selfishly flitting around the world, wheeling and dealing and neglecting your duties as a wife and mother. You make everybody toe the line, *your line,* and you lack emotional stability just as she did."

Paula was furious. "How dare you! How dare you criticize Grandy! You're making her out to be something she was not, she who was so good to you! You've really got a bloody nerve. Furthermore, I don't neglect my children, and I never neglected you. Our estrangement came about because of the things which are lacking in you, Jim. I'm not emotionally unstable, but it strikes me that you are. I wasn't the one in a—" Paula stopped herself, clenched her hands together in her lap.

"I knew you'd never let me live that down," he said, his face darkening. "Has it ever occurred to you that you might be responsible for my nervous breakdown?" he challenged.

Paula gasped, "If anybody's compulsive, you are. You continually want to blame *me* for everything that you yourself do."

Jim sighed. He glanced away, ruminating for a few seconds, and then he brought his eyes to Paula. He gave her a penetrating stare. "Why are you so keen to get a divorce?"

"Because our marriage is over. It's ridiculous to continue," she murmured, adopting a calmer, more reasonable tone. "It's not fair to the children, to you, or to me, Jim."

"We were in love," he mused almost to himself then asked, "Weren't we?"

"Yes, we were." She took a deep breath. "But being in love doesn't guarantee happiness, Jim. Two people have to be compatible and able to live with each other on a day-to-day basis. Being in love is never enough, I'm afraid. A marriage needs a solid foundation based on genuine friendship."

"Is there another man?" he demanded. His eyes remained fixed on hers.

Unexpected though the question was, Paula managed to keep her neutral expression in place. Although her heart missed a beat, she said in her most convincing voice, "No, there isn't, Jim."

He did not say anything for a few seconds. And then he got up, went and stood over her chair. He gripped her shoulder. "There had better not be, Paula. Because if there is, I will destroy you. I'll countersue you for divorce, and I'll have you declared an unfit mother. I'll get custody of my children, never you fear. No judge in England is going to give the children of a broken marriage to a woman who willfully broke up that marriage and who is neglectful of those children, who travels the world in pursuit of her business interests to the detriment of those children." He brought his face closer to hers and, tightening his hand on her shoulder, added, "Or one who is screwing around with another man."

Paula managed to throw off his vise-like grip. She leapt to her feet, her face blazing. "Try it," she said in a cold voice. "Just try it. We'll see who wins."

He stepped away from her and laughed in her face. "And you don't think you're reliving Emma Harte's life. That's the joke of the century. Just look at you—why you sound exactly like her. And you think the way she did. You too believe that money and power make you invulnerable. Sadly, my dear, they don't." He swung around and walked toward the door.

"Where are you going?" Paula called after him.

Jim stopped in his tracks and turned to face her. "To London. There's not much point in my staying here for dinner—we'll only continue to fight. Frankly, I'm weary of it all."

Paula ran after him, took his arm, gave him a pleading look, "But there is no real reason for us to quarrel in this way, Jim," she said in a shaken voice. "We can work this out like civilized people, like adults who are mature and intelligent. I know we can."

"It's really up to you, Paula," Jim said, also speaking in a more reasonable voice. "Think about everything I've said, and perhaps when I get back from Chamonix you'll have come to your senses."

Forty-Nine

John Crawford, the family solicitor, had been listening to Paula for over an hour.

He had not interrupted her once, deeming it wiser to let her unburden herself before asking any relevant questions. Also he had discerned, in his astute and insightful way, that she had not discussed her disastrous marriage with anyone else before tonight. Certainly not at great length, and he decided that in a sense talking to him was a catharsis for her. He believed that by talking, opening up, she would feel better.

Paula finally paused for breath. He instantly detected a relaxation in the way she held her body, a sudden slackening of her rigid facial muscles, and relief was mirrored in her startling blue eyes. "That's about it," she said, smiling a bit uncertainly. "I don't think I've missed anything."

John nodded, continuing to observe her. He recognized she was in total control, calm enough to accept what he was about to say. He cleared his throat. "I don't want to alarm you, and this is only a suggestion, but perhaps we ought to make the children wards of court."

Although she was startled, Paula said steadily enough, "Oh, John, surely that's far too drastic a step. It might even be begging for trouble. It's so inflammatory."

John, who had long harbored a visceral dislike of Jim Fairley, clasped his hands together and brought them up to his face. He looked at her over them, his eyes reflective. "It seems to me, from the things you've told me, that Jim virtually threatened to take those children out of the country, to Canada to be precise, if you don't do as he wants. Isn't that so, Paula?"

"Yes," she admitted.

"By making children wards of court one prevents their physical removal from their country of domicile by a disgruntled and angry parent involved in this kind of distressing emotional situation."

"Yes, John, I know what it means. But Jim believes I will change my mind about getting a divorce. He's not going to suddenly swoop down, grab the children, and fly off to Toronto. He would certainly try to ascertain what I'm going to do first. Besides, he's in Chamonix."

"And you, Paula, are going to the States in a couple of days. He knows that. He could easily try to pull something whilst you're absent. After all, Geneva is only a few hours away."

"I'm sure he wouldn't—" She stopped abruptly, alertly searching the solicitor's face. "From your expression you obviously think he might."

"There is that possibility." John stood up and walked across the drawing room, poured himself another dry martini from the jug on the bar cart, swung around and apologized: "I'm sorry, I didn't ask you if you wanted another drink. Do you?"

"No, thanks anyway."

Returning to his seat, John sat down, continued: "I'm going to ask you a very blunt question, Paula, a crucial question, and I would like you to think most carefully before you answer."

She nodded.

He said: "Do you believe that Jim is mentally stable?"

Without hesitation, Paula replied. "Oh yes, John, I do. I realize he was in a nursing home an awfully long time after his nervous breakdown, but he's fully recovered now. He's behaving quite normally." She smiled ruefully. "If you can call his attitude to me normal, that is. He's stubborn, pigheaded, really, but then he always has been. He blinds himself to the truth, to reality. He's convinced our problems are figments of my imagination, as I just told you. However, I'll say it again, I do not believe he is unstable. Upset at the moment, yes, but that's all."

"Very well, I trust your judgment, and I also understand your reluctance to take steps that would inflame him. However, I think it would be advisable for you to talk to Daisy, alert her to the situation. If Jim should leave Chamonix unexpectedly, she must contact me at once."

"No, not Mummy," Paula exclaimed. "I'd prefer not to worry her. Anyway, I've never confided in her, or anyone, to be truthful. Well, actually, I have spoken to Emily and my father a few times lately, and they know how bad the marriage is, and, in fact, Emily and Winston have urged me to get a divorce. The point is this . . . Emily and Winston are going off to Chamonix the day after tomorrow. They'll be there for the next two weeks. I'll speak to her before she leaves, explain everything, and ask her to ring you if anything untoward happens."

John's face brightened. "Good, good. Emily is levelheaded and smart. I feel more confident knowing she's going to be staying at the chalet. As your grandmother always said, there're no flies on Emily. So in view of that, and because you're against it, I'll drop the idea of having you make the twins wards of court." He gave her a funny little smile. "It's crossed my mind that you may think I'm paranoid, but I'm not. Still, I am prudent and fully aware that it's often wiser to take precautions to avert trouble." He leaned forward intently. "That's why I suggested the idea in the first place. Also, it struck me that you were worried about the children yourself, otherwise you wouldn't have brought them to London with you yesterday."

"Yes, I was a bit concerned," Paula agreed. "I was badly shaken up on Saturday night after Jim left. On Sunday morning I decided I ought to have Lorne and Tessa with me. They looked so small and defenseless, so vulnerable, John. They're only babies, and I do love them so much. I even thought of taking them to New York with me, but that would be uprooting them unnecessarily. Nora is quite happy to spend a few weeks in London, and at least the weather's better here than it is in Yorkshire. They'll be fine, and Nora has Parker and Mrs. Ramsey as backup at the London flat."

"Yes, they're both very reliable. Try not to worry, my dear. I'll keep an eye on things at Belgrave Square. Make sure Nora has my telephone numbers, though, and explain that she must ring me if Jim arrives on the scene."

"I'll do that tonight." Paula gazed past John, staring at the dark green damask draperies, her face suddenly thoughtful. She said a little haltingly, "Jim can't take them away from me, can he, John?"

"Of course not. Don't even contemplate such a thing!" John patted her hand and, wishing to reassure her, said, "Jim can threaten all kinds of things, in an effort to make *you* do as *he* wishes, but threats are meaningless in the long run. Thankfully, we do have courts of law in this land and they are eminently fair, which is more than I can say about the judicial systems in a lot of other countries."

"Yes," she murmured, then let out a tiny sigh of weariness. "He says I want it all, want everything my way."

John laughed. "That's like the kettle calling the pot black, Paula. Hasn't it occurred to you that Jim wants it *his* way?" Not waiting for an answer, the solicitor hurried on, "He's being selfish, expecting you to toe *his* line, regardless of your own feelings, and despite the fact that you have a disastrous marriage. It's already playing havoc with you emotionally, and it will inevitably start affecting the children. The only thing to do with a marriage that has failed so miserably is to end it immediately, for everyone's sake. Stop the flow of blood, in a manner of speaking. I ought to know."

Paula looked across at him. "Poor John, you went through hell too, didn't you?"

"To put it mildly, my dear," he replied. "However, those troubles are behind me, and Millicent and I are good friends these days, most amicable, really."

"I do hope Jim and I can be friends eventually," Paula said, as if musing aloud. "I don't hate him, far from it. To be honest, John, I feel rather sad for him . . . because he just cannot face reality." She lifted her shoulders in a light shrug. "But, look, I came here to talk to you about a plan of action, and I want to say now that I wish to be scrupulously fair with him in every way. I want him to have total access to the twins, and of course there's no question about his staying on at the newspapers." She scowled at the solicitor. "I was stunned when he suggested I would take his job away."

John stared into his glass for a moment, slowly lifted his eyes, which were grave and intent. "I don't want to delude you into thinking we're going to have an easy time with Jim, because we are not. I *know* we're going to have a fight on our hands. It's patently obvious, from what you've said, that he doesn't want to let you go, that he is prepared to put up with the worst kind of marital situation to remain your husband. Understandable, perhaps. You are the mother of his children, you are a desirable and accomplished young woman, with immense wealth and power. What man wouldn't want to hang on to you? Also—"

"But Jim isn't interested in my money or my power," Paula cut in rapidly. "Why, John, he resents my business, does nothing but complain about my career."

"Don't be naïve!"

Paula stared at him, her brows drawing together as she sat back, her expression changing to one of total disbelief. She opened her mouth, and then quickly closed it, wanting to hear what else John had to say.

"Of course he cares about your money and your power, Paula," the solicitor remarked quietly. "And he always has, in my opinion. Jim is not quite as altruistic as you seem to believe. As your solicitor I feel it is my duty to point this out to you, however unpalatable that might be to you. Jim has apparently been complaining very vociferously about your work, but he knew long before he married you that you were Emma's chief heir. He was also aware that you would not only inherit most of her wealth, but *all* of her tremendous responsibilities as well. He's merely using your career as an excuse to get at you, to hurt you, to punish you. At the same time, it enables him to paint a picture of himself as the long-suffering, neglected, and injured husband. In other words, he strikes a pose that will gain him sympathy. Please, my dear, do be aware of that for your own sake, and for your own peace of mind."

"Perhaps you're right," she conceded, knowing that John Crawford was a shrewd and brilliant lawyer and a man with great psychological insight into people. She leaned forward. "If Jim *is* interested in money, as you imply"—she shook her head and laughed—"no, *insist,* then let us give him money. I'm prepared to make a large financial settlement on him. Suggest an amount, John, and let's set a date when we can have a meeting with Jim. He'll be back at the end of the month, as will I, and I would like to put things in motion."

"I can't come up with an amount tonight, off the top of my head," John explained. "That wouldn't be fair to anyone. It requires careful thought." He took a sip of his martini, put the glass down, and stood up. He walked over to the humidor on a side table, and took a cigar, not wanting her to see the cynical smile that had touched his mouth involuntarily. If my assessment of Jim is correct, and I'm sure it is, money will do the trick, John decided. Clipping off the end of the cigar, he strolled back to his chair, contemplating the settlement. It was a good card to have up his sleeve and would be a powerful negotiating weapon if Jim did prove to be intransigent.

Striking a match, John puffed hard on the cigar until it ignited, then told her: "As far as a meeting is concerned, we can get together any time you wish—" He did not complete his sentence, but began to shake his head in a negative fashion.

"What's wrong?" Paula asked, clasping her hands together, experiencing a stab of apprehension.

"Nothing for you to look so concerned about, my dear. I think, however, that you're going to have your job cut out for you—getting Jim to meet with me, I mean. He's so dead set against the divorce, and obstinate by nature. Maybe it would be better if I simply dropped by for a drink one night when he's in town. On his way back to Yorkshire after the Chamonix trip, perhaps?"

"Yes, that is a good idea," Paula agreed. "He did mutter something about seeing me in London in two weeks, before he left Pennistone Royal on Saturday." Paula pushed herself to the edge of her chair and her face filled with sincerity as she reminded him, "Don't forget that I want to be fair with Jim about the children, and I am willing to be very generous when it comes to money. It's important to me that Jim is financially secure for the rest of his life."

"I'll remember everything," John assured her. "And whilst you're in New

York I'll work on the terms of the divorce and make them most acceptable to Jim, I promise." He gave her a fond smile. "Not many women would be as kind as you. He's very lucky."

"I'm sure *he* doesn't think that right now," she ventured, rising to her feet. "Thank you for being so understanding. I feel better after talking to you and much more positive about the future. And now I'm going to leave you in peace to have your dinner. I've taken up far too much of your evening as it is."

He squeezed her arm affectionately as he escorted her across the drawing room and out into the small foyer. Loving her mother as he did, he considered Paula to be the daughter he had never had. He felt inordinately protective of her sometimes. Shrewd and clever in business though she was, she had had little or no experience with men, had been protected all of her life by Emma Harte and her parents. In many ways, the harsher aspects of everyday living were unknown to her, and she might well be an easy target for an unscrupulous man.

As they reached the door, John turned her to face him. He bent forward, kissed her cheek and, with a chuckle, said, *"You* can take up my time whenever you wish, my dear. It does a crusty old bachelor like me a lot of good to see your beautiful face. I'm only sorry we were meeting to discuss such a sad matter."

Paula hugged him affectionately. "You're not a crusty old bachelor," she declared, smiling at him. "You're the most wonderful friend—to all of us. Thank you for being that, and for everything, John. I'll speak to you before I leave for New York."

"Please do, my dear." He opened the door, then caught her arm as she went outside. "It's going to be all right, Paula, really it is. Do try not to worry."

"I will." She ran down the short flight of steps in front of his house in Chester Street, turned and waved. John lifted his hand in response, went inside and closed the door, pressing back his concern for her.

Paula hurried down the street, making for Belgrave Square, which was only a few minutes away. She had meant it when she had told John Crawford she felt relieved after talking to him. But this was not the only reason why her depression of the last forty-eight hours had lifted so unexpectedly. Making a decision, taking positive and constructive action, had worked wonders for her. Paula never vacillated. Like Emma before her, she was expedient by nature, always preferring action and commitment to waiting. In consequence, marking time for the past year—because of Jim's plane crash and subsequent sojourn in the mental home—had been unendurable. But she was nothing if not prudent, and she had schooled herself to be patient, had acknowledged months ago that if waiting was debilitating, it was infinitely preferable to making rash moves she might live to regret.

But now, as she walked at a brisk pace, she experienced a great sense of release. The act of talking to John, of putting matters in his hands, was liberating. She was confident he would work out an equable divorce agreement, and surely Jim would be convinced she was serious, in deadly earnest, when he knew she had taken this final step.

Paula glowed with a new optimism as she crossed Belgrave Square and went into the great mansion purchased so many years before by her grandfather, Paul McGill. She slammed the heavy exterior glass-and-wrought-iron door behind her, climbed the short circular staircase that led up to the front entrance of the maisonette, and let herself in with her key.

Slipping off her tweed coat, she hung it in the hall closet and turned as Parker came hurrying out of the back quarters and into the large entrance foyer.

"Oh, Mrs. Fairley, I was just wondering whether I ought to telephone you at Mr. Crawford's house. Mr. O'Neill is in the drawing room. He's been waiting for you for quite a while. I gave him a drink. Would you like anything, madam?"

"No, thank you, Parker."

Wondering what Uncle Bryan wanted, why he had arrived so unexpectedly and without ringing first, she pushed open the drawing room door and stood stock-still on the threshold. Fully expecting to see Bryan, she was thrown at the sight of Shane. He stood up, grinning like a Cheshire cat from ear to ear.

"My God!" she cried. "What are you doing here?" She pushed the door closed with her foot and ran into his arms, her face wreathed in delighted smiles.

Shane kissed her, took her by the shoulders and held her away from him. "I was so worried about you after those awful phone conversations on Saturday and Sunday that I decided to come home. I arrived at Heathrow about two hours ago."

"Oh, Shane, I'm sorry I worried you . . . but it is a wonderful surprise to see you, and several days sooner than I expected." She drew him over to the sofa and they sat down, continuing to hold hands. Paula said, with a bright little laugh, "But I'm leaving for New York the day after tomorrow, and you know that—"

"I thought we'd fly back together," he interjected, his dark eyes roving over her lovingly. "As a matter of fact, I concocted a rather good plan in the last half hour. I thought I'd sidetrack for a few days, whisk you off to Barbados for the weekend on our way to the States. What do you think?"

"Oh, Shane," Paula began and hesitated, her face sobering. She said gravely, "I told you Jim asked me if there is another man. And even though I denied it, I don't know that he's entirely convinced. What if someone should see us in Barbados? Or even traveling together? I don't want to do anything that would jeopardize my position and my custody of the children. He would be vindictive, I just know he would."

Shane said, "I understand your worry, darling, and I'd taken those points into consideration earlier. Now look, Paula, he's never going to be suspicious of me. It would be like his suspecting your brother Philip, for God's sake. Also, you do own a boutique in Barbados. You've every reason to go there, to check on it. And, finally, no one will see us on the plane, and we can lay low once we get to Coral Cove."

"Nobody will see us?" she repeated. "What do you mean?"

"I have another surprise for you, Beanstalk. I finally took delivery of the private jet Dad and I decided to buy for the company. I just whizzed across the Atlantic in it, but let's forget that, and pretend our trip to the Caribbean is really its inaugural flight. Come on, say yes, sweetheart."

"All right, then," Paula agreed, making a snap decision. Surely it was safe to travel with Shane. He was her childhood friend, after all. The grave expression fled and her violet eyes lit up. "It's just what I need to give me a lift after the upsetting weekend."

"Yes, it is." He beamed at her. "We have to think of an appropriate name for the jet, you know. Any ideas?"

"No, but I *will* bring a bottle of champagne and break it on the side, wet its bottom so to speak, even if we don't have a name," she announced, enjoying the sudden and unexpected fun, the joyousness of being with him. Her heart soared with love for him, and she felt the old dizziness, the lightheadedness she experienced when she was with him again after a separation. Shane made all the difference in the world to her. And he made everything seem possible. The residue of her depression fell away so completely it might never have existed.

Shane now pulled her to her feet. "I told Parker you were going out to dinner. I hope you don't mind my taking you over." He gave her his boyish grin and kissed her forehead. His face immediately turned serious. "I want to know about your meeting with John. We can talk about it over a bottle of good wine and a pleasant meal at the White Elephant."

Fifty

The chalet was deserted.

Emily realized this as she ran lightly down the stairs and stood poised in the circular entrance hall, her head cocked on one side as she listened for the usual morning sounds. Generally voices and laughter reverberated and the radio was always playing in the background. But all were absent on this Saturday morning late in January.

Swinging to her left, Emily went into the dining room. Her mother was standing near the window, holding a small hand mirror and peering at her face in great concentration.

"Good morning, Mummy," Emily called in a cheery tone from the doorway and meandered across the floor.

Elizabeth turned with swiftness, smiled, and said, "Oh, Emily, there you are. Good morning, darling."

After planting a kiss on her mother's cheek, Emily sat down at the long rustic table and lifted the coffeepot. She asked, "Where is everybody?"

For a moment Elizabeth did not answer, continuing to examine her face in the bright sunlight pouring in through the window, and then, sighing under her breath, she joined her daughter at the table. "The devoted skiers left ages ago, as they always do. You've just missed Winston. He decided to go skiing at the last minute, and hurried off, hoping to catch up with the others. Apparently you were sleeping so soundly he didn't have the heart to wake you. He asked me to tell you he'll see you at lunch."

"I just couldn't get up early this morning," Emily murmured, stirring her coffee, eyeing the croissants longingly. They smelled delicious. Her mouth watered.

"I'm not surprised. It was awfully late when everyone left last night. I'm paying for it myself this morning—" Elizabeth cut herself short, glanced at Emily quickly. "Do you think I need to have my eyes done?"

Laughing, Emily put down the coffee cup and leaned across the table, staring at her mother's eyes. She was accustomed to such questions and aware that she had to pay the strictest attention when they were asked. She shook her head several times. "No, of course you don't. Your eyes are marvelous."

"Do you really think so, dear?" Elizabeth lifted the mirror and gazed at herself again.

"For heaven's sake, Mummy, you're a young woman, only fifty—"

"Not so *loud,* darling," Elizabeth muttered. She placed the mirror on the table and went on: "I must admit I have been toying with the idea lately. I think my lids look a bit wrinkled. Marc is so conscious of a woman's looks, and being older than he is—"

"I didn't know he was younger than you, Mummy! He certainly doesn't look it."

This seemed to cheer Elizabeth and her face brightened. "I'm glad to hear that, Emily, but he *is* younger, I'm afraid."

"By how many years?" Emily reached for a croissant, no longer able to resist temptation, and broke it in half.

"Five."

"Good heavens, that's nothing. And forget about having facial surgery, Mum, you're a beautiful woman and don't look a day older than forty." Emily plunged her knife into the mound of creamy butter, lavishly spread it on a portion of the breakfast roll and added peach jam.

Elizabeth, distracted from her constant preoccupation with herself for a moment, stared at her in disapproval. "You're not really going to eat that, are you, dear? It's loaded with calories."

Emily grinned. "Of course I am. I'm ravenous."

"You know, you must watch your weight, Emily. You've always had a tendency to get plump very quickly, ever since you were a child."

"I'll starve myself when we get home."

Elizabeth shook her head in exasperation, but knowing it was useless to argue, she remarked, "Did you notice Marc flirting with that French countess at the party last night?"

"No, I can't say I did. But he flirts with everyone, Mother. He can't help it, and it doesn't mean anything, I'm sure. I wish you'd relax about that man. He's lucky to have you."

"And I'm most fortunate to have him. He's very good to me, the best husband I've had, if you want to know the truth."

Emily doubted this, and before she could stop herself, she exclaimed, "What about *Daddy?* He was wonderful to you. It's a pity you ever left *him.*"

"Naturally you're prejudiced about Tony. He *is* your father. But you have no conception of how it was between us, dear. Latterly, I mean. You were only a small child. Anyway, I don't propose to start regurgitating all the details of my first marriage with you, Emily, picking it over and examining it under a microscope."

"That's very *wise* of you," Emily said with acerbity and munched on the roll, conscious they were touching on an explosive subject.

Elizabeth gave her daughter a sharp look, but she, too, sagely held her tongue. She poured herself another cup of coffee and lit a cigarette, sat observing Emily, thinking how pretty she looked this morning in her emerald green sweater and pants. They intensified the color of her eyes. After almost two weeks in the French Alps, her hair was a lighter, brighter blond and her delicate face had the hint of a suntan. Elizabeth was suddenly glad that she and Marc had accepted Daisy's invitation to join them at the chalet they had rented. She had enjoyed being with her children and she had derived a great deal of satisfaction from Marc's attentiveness to them, especially to Amanda and Francesca.

Between bites, Emily said, "I think I'll go into the town later. I need to buy a few things."

"That's a good idea," Elizabeth remarked. "And perhaps you'll drop me off at the hairdresser's, darling."

Emily burst out laughing. "You don't need your hair done, Mummy. You were there yesterday."

"Now, Emily, let's not get into a long discussion about my hair. *You* paddle your canoe and *I'll* paddle mine."

"Okay." Leaning forward, Emily propped her elbows on the table and continued: "I have a vague remembrance of Amanda and Francesca's barging into our room at some ungodly hour this morning and smothering Winston and me with kisses. I assume Alexander dragged them off to Geneva—screaming at the top of their lungs, no doubt."

Elizabeth nodded. "They *were* rather obstreperous. Neither of them seems to like the finishing school on Lake Geneva, and I can't imagine why. But they settled down when they knew Daisy was going to Geneva with them. She wanted to do some shopping and decided to go along with Alexander. They're planning to take the girls to lunch at the Hotel Richemond before returning them to the school. I do love that hotel, Emily, and in fact I promised the twins I'd fly up to Geneva from Paris at Easter to spend a few days with them." Elizabeth had a sudden thought, and it brought a warm smile to her face. "Why don't you and Winston join Marc and me, as my guests at the Richemond? It would be fun, Emily."

Pleasantly surprised at this unprecedented gesture, Emily said, "That's a lovely thought, Mother, and very kind of you to invite us. I'll ask Winston and let you know later." Emily reached out, her hand hovering over another croissant.

"Please don't eat that, darling!"

Looking slightly shamefaced, Emily pulled back. "Yes, you're right. They are awfully fattening." Emily rose. "I think I'd better go upstairs and get ready to go into the town. I know if I sit here chatting with you I'll demolish that entire plate."

"I'll come up too," Elizabeth said. "I want to change."

Emily groaned. "You look perfectly gorgeous, Mummy. You don't have to bother . . . you're only going to the hairdresser's."

"One never knows whom one might meet," Elizabeth countered. Glancing at her watch, she added, "It's not quite eleven. I'll only be half an hour. I promise."

To Emily's relief, her mother was true to her word for once, and a few minutes after eleven-thirty she was turning the key in the ignition and pulling away from the chalet. This was located in a small hamlet on the outskirts of Chamonix, the lovely ancient town that nestled at the foot of Mont Blanc. As Emily swung out onto the main road and cruised along at a steady speed, she could not help admiring the extraordinary scenery which never failed to make her catch her breath.

The Valley of Chamonix, bounded on one side by the Mont Blanc range and on the other by the Aiguilles Rouges chain, was like a natural platform from which to view the highest peak of Europe. And now, as Emily peered ahead at Mont Blanc and the surrounding mountains, she could not help feeling overawed by their grandeur and majesty. Their glittering snow-covered pinnacles thrust up into a high-flung sky that was a clear cerulean blue, filled with white puffball clouds and brilliant sunshine.

As though reading her daughter's thoughts, Elizabeth exclaimed, "Impressive, isn't it, Emily! And it's such a glorious day."

"Yes," Emily agreed. "I bet our skiing enthusiasts are happy as larks, enjoying themselves on the slopes." She glanced at her mother through the corner of her eye. "By the way, did Marc go with Uncle David and the others?"

"Yes, and Maggie."

"Oh," Emily said, surprised. "I thought she was driving to Geneva with Alexander."

"She wanted to go skiing instead, make the most of it, I suppose, since they're leaving tomorrow for London."

"Jan and Peter are traveling back with them, so Jan told me last night," Emily remarked, referring to the only nonfamily members who were houseguests of her aunt and uncle.

"I tried to persuade them to stay on for a few days longer," Elizabeth explained. "I rather like them, and *he's* such a charmer."

"Peter Coles! Honestly, Mummy, you do have funny tastes. I think he's a crashing bore. So pompous." Emily giggled. "But he is especially attentive to you, and I've seen Marc give him more than one filthy look during the ten days they've been here. I do believe the old Frog is as jealous as hell."

"Please don't refer to Marc as an *old Frog,* darling, it's a very unkind description and most inappropriate," Elizabeth chastised. Then she laughed with sudden gaiety. "So you think Peter makes Marc jealous. That's nice to know. *Mmmm.*"

"Very." Emily smiled to herself, realizing how happy this bit of irrelevant information made her mother feel. But maybe it wasn't so irrelevant to her. The poor woman was dotty about Marc Deboyne. That snake in the grass, Emily thought. She detested him and wouldn't trust him as far as she could throw him.

Elizabeth now launched into a glowing recital about her new husband's manifold qualities, and Emily nodded and made small agreeable sounds, as if concurring. But she was only half-listening. Her mother was quite irritating when she went on and on about him in this ridiculous way, and Emily was pleased when she saw the town of Chamonix looming immediately ahead.

After leaving the Citroën in the parking lot, Emily and her mother walked briskly down one of the main boulevards, heading in the direction of the small square where the hairdressing salon was situated. When they arrived at its door, Emily said, "How long will you be?"

"Oh, just about an hour, dear. I'm only having a comb-out. Why don't you meet me at that little bistro over there at the other side of the square. We'll have an aperitif before going back to the chalet for lunch."

"All right. Bye, Mummy."

Emily sauntered leisurely around the square, glancing in the shop windows. She only had a few things to buy and an hour to waste, so she took her time. After traversing the entire square, she continued down the boulevard, making for a boutique that sold highly original *après ski* clothes, and went inside. The sales assistants knew her and she wasted twenty minutes chatting to them and trying on evening tops, none of which she liked enough to buy.

Back on the street, Emily wandered down to the pharmacy, purchased the small items she needed, tucked them in her shoulder bag, and left the shop. Slowly she retraced her steps, remembering she wanted to pick up some picture postcards to send to friends in England.

To her astonishment Emily saw Marc Deboyne coming toward her. He was hurrying, looked deeply preoccupied, and he had obviously not seen her.

As they drew level with each other, Emily said archly, "Fancy meeting you, Marc. Mummy thinks you've gone skiing."

Marc Deboyne, caught off guard, was both startled and embarrassed. Quickly recovering his equilibrium, he exclaimed, "Ah, Emilee, Emilee, my dear," and caught hold of her arm, squeezed it affectionately. He added, in his Gallic-accented but perfect English, "I changed my mind. I decided to go for a walk. I have a headache."

Leaning into him, Emily said pointedly, "It's not the only thing you have, Marc. You've also got lipstick on the neck of your sweater."

His smile was indulgent but his eyes reproved, and then he chuckled. "Emilee, what *are* you implying? It's undoubtedly your mother's lipstick."

Ignoring this remark, she said, "Mummy's having her hair done. I'm meeting her at the bistro opposite for a drink. At one o'clock. She'll be disappointed if you don't join us." Emily's tone was all sweetness. Her eyes were chips of green ice.

"I would not disappoint Elizabeth. I shall meet you there. *Ciao,* Emilee." He gave an odd little salute and moved on, walking at the same rapid pace.

Emily stared after him, watched him as he crossed the road and cut down a side street. She wondered where he was going. Bastard, she thought. I bet he was having a quickie with that ghastly countess from the party last night, who is no more of a Frenchwoman than I am. Filled with dislike for him, Emily grimaced in distaste and turned on her heels, marching up the street in search of a newspaper shop. She found one within minutes and browsed for a while, flipping through the latest magazines, still endeavoring to pass the time. Finally peeking at her watch she saw that it was almost one o'clock, almost time to meet her mother. Stepping up to the metal rack holding cards of Chamonix, she selected four and went to pay for them.

Putting the cards and the change in her shoulder bag, Emily smiled at the woman behind the counter. *"Merci, madame."*

The woman started to respond and then stopped abruptly, cocking her head. At that precise moment there was a sudden, extraordinary rumbling sound that rent the air around them and increased to thunderous and deafening proportions within the space of a split second.

Emily shouted, "That sounds like a terrible explosion."

The woman gaped at her through terrified eyes, screamed back, "No! Avalanche!" She swung her plump body, grabbed the telephone.

Clutching her bag, Emily ran out into the street.

Shop doors were opening and people were emerging, all of them wearing the same frightened expressions, as were the passersby.

"Avalanche!" a man cried to Emily and pointed in the direction of Mont Blanc as he sped on down the street.

Emily stood transfixed, mesmerized by the sight. Even from this distance she could see that great fractures boomed across the slopes of Mont Blanc and half the mountainside was rumbling down in a tremendous swath that looked to be hundreds and hundreds of feet across. Gargantuan slabs of snow were hurtling forward, gaining momentum as they tumbled on their precipitous downward journey, sweeping aside all that lay in their path. And rising up into the brilliant blue air were enormous billowing clouds of powdered snow that had been pulverized by the turbulence of the slide into millions of tiny snowsmithereens.

Two police cars, their sirens screaming, raced along the street at breakneck speed. Their high-pitched wails broke the hypnotic spell that had momentarily held Emily in its grip. She blinked several times and then the blood seemed to drain out of her. *Winston was up there. Everyone was up there. David. Philip. Jim. Maggie. Jan and Peter Coles.*

She began to shake like a leaf and she could not move. Her legs turned to jelly as the fear rushed through her, swamped her, overwhelmed her. *"Oh my God! Winston!"* Emily cried out loud. *"Winston. Oh God! No!"*

It was as if the sound of her own voice galvanized her. She began to run, racing along the pavement, her head thrust forward, her feet flying over the stones as she ran faster and faster, making for the large cable-car terminal she knew was only a short distance away.

Her heart pounded in her chest, her breathing was labored as she hurled herself on, blinking again, squeezing back the tears that stung her eyes. *Oh God, let Winston be safe. Please let Winston be safe. And the others. Make them all safe. Oh God, don't let any of them be dead.*

Emily became aware of other running feet, other people pressing around her. Some were outstripping her as they pounded past. They were also making for the terminal, which was now in her line of vision. A man jostled her as he leapt ahead, and she almost tripped and fell. But she recovered her balance and went on running, her fear propelling her.

She thought her heart was bursting when she finally reached the terminal. Only then did Emily slow down and come to a standstill, gasping for breath. She pressed her hand against her heaving chest. Rasping noises emanated from her throat. She leaned against one of the police cars parked near the cable-car depot and fumbled in her shoulder bag. She found her handkerchief, wiped her sweating face and neck, endeavored to marshal her swimming senses, willed herself to stay calm.

After a few seconds, her breathing was more normal and she straightened up, looked around. Her eyes were frantic as they swept over the crowd that had already gathered in the space of fifteen minutes.

Emily hoped against hope that Winston had finished skiing before the avalanche had struck, prayed that he was somewhere among the tourists and townspeople milling around. She threw herself into their midst, her eyes darting from side to side, seeking him, her anxiety paramount. Instant dismay lodged in the pit of her stomach. He was nowhere in sight.

Turning away, Emily pressed her hands to her mouth, choking. Terror seized her, held her in a vise. She stumbled back to the police car, leaned against its hood, her heart clenching. *How could anyone have survived that avalanche? It hurtled down at such speed and force it would have crushed anything that stood in its way.* Emily closed her eyes. She ought to go and speak to someone, ask about rescue teams, but she had no strength. She closed her eyes. She felt her legs slipping and sliding under her as if she had lost all control of her body.

Suddenly two strong arms gripped her, pulled her upright.

"Emily! Emily! It's me."

Her eyes flew open as she was spun around rapidly. It was Winston. She grabbed at his ski jacket, weak with relief, and then her face crumpled as she burst into tears.

Winston held her close, supporting her limp body and soothing her at the same time. "It's all right, it's all right," he kept repeating over and over again.

"Thank God! Thank God!" Emily gasped. "I thought you were dead. Oh, Winston, thank God you're alive." She searched his worried face. "The others?" she began and stopped when she saw his grim expression, the clenched jaw.

"I don't know whether they're safe or not. I hope to God they are. I pray they are," Winston said, putting his arm around her.

"But you—"

Winston interrupted fiercely, "I didn't go skiing this morning. When I got here I'd just missed a cable car. I waited around for a while, planning to take the next one, but I got fed up. I had a bit of a hangover and I was beginning to feel queasy. So I left, went in to the town. I bought the English papers, stopped at a cafe and had a Fernet Branca. By the time I felt better it was too late to go skiing, so I did a bit of shopping. I was actually in the parking lot, stowing the stuff in the car, when I heard a *whoomp* that sounded like a blast of dynamite. There was an American parked next to me, and he shouted something about an avalanche, that his daughter was on the slopes, and then he ran like hell. I followed him, knowing"—Winston swallowed—"knowing that everybody from the chalet, well, practically everybody, was up there too."

An unexpected feeling of hope soared in Emily. She exclaimed, "Perhaps they decided to ski on that other range."

Winston shook his head. His face was bleak.

Emily grabbed hold of him. "Oh, Winston!"

He calmed her. "Come on, Emily, you must be strong, very brave—" He broke off and swung his head as he heard his name being called. He spotted Marc Deboyne and Elizabeth running in their direction and lifted his hand in a wave, looked down at his wife and said, "Your mother and Marc are coming."

Elizabeth almost flung herself at Winston and embraced him, crying. "You're safe, you're safe. I was petrified for you, Winston." She looked at him through anxious eyes. Her white face was stark, but she was exercising immense control. She hugged Emily, then said, "What about the others, Winston? Have you seen any of the family, or Jan and Peter?"

"No. You see, I didn't go skiing this morning. I changed my mind."

There was a sudden flurry of activity in the area. They all turned around. The rescue teams had arrived, professional skiers wearing backpacks and controlling a number of German shepherds. With them were additional police, a group of French soldiers and town officials.

"I will go and ask a few questions," Marc muttered and strode off purposefully.

Winston exclaimed, "It's stopped! Do you realize the avalanche has stopped."

Elizabeth stared at him. "It stopped when Marc and I were running down here. After that deafening noise the silence was awful, deathly."

Before Winston could reply, Marc was back with them, explaining: "The teams are going up now. They've got the best equipment in those backpacks. Listening devices, probing rods, and the dogs, of course. Let us be hopeful."

"Is there any hope?" Winston asked in a low, intense tone.

Marc hesitated, tempted to lie. But he elected to speak the truth. "It's doubtful," he murmured quietly. "The avalanche must have been traveling at enormous speed, anywhere between one hundred and twenty to two hundred miles per hour . . . and then there is the force, the weight of the snow. And yet"—he attempted an encouraging smile—"people have been known to live through avalanches and snowslides as bad as this one. It depends where they are on the slopes when it strikes. Those near the bottom would have the best chance, providing they knew to throw away their skis and poles, make swimming motions with their arms. That creates air pockets in front of the face. Even if a person is felled by the snow, it is vital to keep the arms moving in that manner to provide air around the body. People have lived for days under the snow—because they had those air pockets."

Emily said worriedly, "David, Jim, and Philip are experienced skiers, but *Maggie*—"

Elizabeth suppressed a cry of fear. She gasped. "We must have courage and keep our hopes high. Please don't let's talk so mournfully—it makes me nervous. I must continue to believe that they are *all* alive."

Marc put his arm around her protectively. "You are right, *chérie*. We must be positive."

Winston said to Emily, "I think you ought to take your mother over to one of the nearby cafes. Wait there. There's nothing you can do here."

"No!" Emily cried heatedly, glaring at him. "I want to be here with you. Please, Winston."

"Yes, we must stay here," Elizabeth insisted. She blew her nose and got a grip on her diminishing composure. Silently she began to pray.

Exactly one hour after the avalanche had struck, the rescue teams and the dogs went up in the cable cars.

In just under an hour they returned with the first eight people they had found. Five of them were dead. Three were miraculously alive. Two were young girls. One was a man.

"It's Philip!" Emily screamed and, breaking away from Winston and her mother, began to run toward her cousin.

Philip was being supported by a member of the rescue team. As he limped across to her, Emily saw that one side of his face was scraped and covered with congealed blood, and his bright blue eyes were dazed. But otherwise he looked as if he had escaped with no really serious injuries.

"Philip!" Emily exclaimed, drawing up beside him. "Thank God, you're safe. Are you hurt at all, do you think?"

He shook his head. Despite the odd glazed look in his eyes, he recognized her, reached out to her.

A second later, Winston, Elizabeth, and Marc were also by his side, asking questions. Philip simply went on shaking his head helplessly, remained mute.

The skier who had found him said in halting English, "This man, your friend, has been lucky . . . he knew what to do. He did not panic. He discarded his poles . . . the skis . . . did the swimming. Yes, he was most fortunate . . . this man was at the bottom of the slope . . . had completed his run. He was covered with only ten feet of snow . . . the dogs . . . they found him. Now . . . if you please. We go. To the first aid station over there."

Philip finally spoke. He asked, in a hoarse voice, "Dad? Maggie? The others?"

Winston said, "No news yet."

Philip closed his eyes, then opened them quickly, allowed himself to be helped away.

Turning to Emily, Winston said, "You and your mother had better go along with Philip, lovey. Marc and I will wait here. Once you've ascertained that he has no internal injuries, I want the three of you to go back to the chalet."

Emily started to protest. Winston cut her off sharply. "Please, Emily, don't argue. Look after Philip. And somebody *should* be at the chalet . . . when Daisy and Alexander get back from Geneva."

"Yes," Emily acquiesced, realizing the sense he made. She kissed him and ran after her mother, who had walked ahead with Philip and the skier.

Winston and Marc stood around for another hour, smoking incessantly, occasionally talking to each other, and striking up conversations with other people who were keeping the same distressing vigil at the terminal.

The rescue teams continued to go up and down in the cable cars. Four more survivors were brought to safety, to be followed by nine who were dead.

At four o'clock one of the rescue teams which had been long and endlessly searching the higher part of the mountain returned. They brought with them five more vacationing skiers who had been trapped by the avalanche. The bad news spread quickly. All were dead.

"We must go over and check," Winston said, throwing his cigarette on the ground, grinding his toe on the butt. Bracing himself, he swung to Marc. "Will you come with me?"

"Yes, Winston. No use putting it off."

The bodies were being laid on stretchers. When he was a few feet away from them, Winston came to a sudden halt. His strength ebbed out of him, but somehow he managed to take several more steps forward after this brief pause.

He felt Marc's strong hand under his armpit, heard the Frenchman say sorrowingly, "I am so sorry, so very sorry. This is a tragedy for the family."

Winston found he could not speak.

He gazed down at the five people who lay on the stretchers. Two of them he did not know, but the other three . . . For a moment his mind floundered. It did not seem possible that they were dead. Only a few hours ago they had all been laughing together at breakfast.

Sucking in his breath, and brushing his hand across his brimming eyes, Winston went to identify the bodies of David Amory, Jim Fairley, and Maggie

Barkstone, fatal victims of the avalanche. And he thought of Daisy and Alexander, driving back from Geneva, and of Paula, who was in New York, and he wondered how he was ever going to break the devastating news to them.

———————— *Fifty-One* ————————

Shane O'Neill stood in the kitchen of the barn in New Milford, waiting for the second pot of coffee to brew.

After lighting a cigarette, he reached for the wall phone and dialed the farm. When Elaine Vickers answered, he said cheerily, "Top of the morning to you."

"Hi, Shane," Elaine replied. "We thought you weren't coming up this weekend when we didn't hear from you last night. But Sonny saw your car earlier this morning, so we knew you'd made it."

"It was late when we arrived," Shane explained. "The farm was in darkness and I thought twice about waking you. Paula didn't get back from Texas until early evening, and it was after nine when we left the city. Sorry I didn't ring you before now, but we got off to a slow start this morning."

Elaine laughed. "I'll say you did. It's almost noon. But the way you two work you deserve to take it easy occasionally. I hope we're going to see you for dinner tonight," she went on. "We've been looking forward to it all week."

"We'll be over around seven-thirty as planned," Shane assured her.

Elaine exclaimed, "Oh, Shane, you'll have to excuse me. That was the oven bell. My bread's going to spoil if I don't take it out immediately. See you tonight."

"Bye, Elaine." Shane dropped the phone in its cradle, stubbed out his cigarette and went to the sink. He rinsed the two mugs and dried them. He was just about to pour the coffee when the telephone began to ring. Putting down the pot, he picked up the receiver. "Hello?"

There was no response at the other end of the phone, only the sound of static and a hollow echo. "Hello? Hello?" Shane said again in a stronger tone.

Finally a muffled voice came down the wire. "It's me. Winston. I'm phoning from Chamonix. Can you hear me, Shane?"

"I can now. Winston! How—"

Winston cut him off. "Something terrible has happened here, Shane, and I don't know where Paula is, where to reach her, and I thought I'd better speak to you first anyway."

Shane gripped the receiver tighter, frowned to himself. "Actually, she's staying here with me for the weekend. What's wrong, Winston?"

"There has been a disastrous avalanche on Mont Blanc, at about one o'clock today, the worst in years," Winston began, his voice sounding more muffled and gruff than ever. "Some of the family have been killed." Winston's voice cracked and he was unable to continue.

"Oh, Jesus!" Shane steadied himself against the counter, waiting to hear the worst. His heart had begun to thud in his chest and intuitively he knew that Winston was about to impart news that would devastate Paula. He knew it in his Celtic bones.

Thousands of miles away, in the dining room of the chalet on the outskirts of Chamonix, Winston Harte stood at the window gazing into the distance. Mont Blanc loomed up into the darkening sky, looked so peaceful now in the twilight after the havoc it had wrought only five hours ago. He got a grip on himself, said in a controlled voice, "Sorry for breaking down. It's been the worst day of my life. Look, Shane, I'm going to give it to you straight because it's the only way I know how." Winston took a deep breath and began to speak, relaying the tragic news to his friend.

As he listened, Shane felt the shock strike him like a body blow, and ten minutes later, when Winston finally hung up, he was still reeling. He stood with his hand on the phone, staring blankly into the middle of the room. He began to blink as bright sunlight streamed in through the windows. How normal everything seemed here in this kitchen. It was so tranquil, peaceful. And it was such a pretty day outside. The sky was a bright blue, clear and without a single cloud, and the sun was radiant. But over in France the family he had been so close to for his entire life were living with unexpected death and sorrow. How abruptly, how suddenly lives had been changed, almost in the flicker of an eyelash. Oh dear God, Shane thought, how am I going to tell Paula? Where will I find the words?

He heard her step in the hall outside and swung around to face the door, then held himself very still, waiting.

She was laughing as she came in and said in a teasing voice, "That's the last time I'll ever ask you to make the coffee. You've been on the phone for ages. Who were you talking to, darling?"

Shane took a step toward her. He tried to speak but nothing came out. There was a parched, gravelly feeling in his throat and his mouth went dry.

"You've got the oddest look on your face, Shane. What's wrong?" Paula demanded, instantly tensing.

He put his arm around her shoulder and propelled her out of the kitchen and into the big living room, leading her to the fire. She demanded again, and with fierceness, "Shane, what's happened? Please tell me."

"I will, I will," he said hoarsely, pressing her down on the sofa, seating himself next to her. He took her hands in his, held onto them tightly, and looked into that face he had loved all of his life. He saw the worry, the sudden apprehension invading it.

Shane's heart clenched as he said in the softest of voices, "I just got some very bad news, some dreadful news, Paula darling. From Winston. There was the most hideous accident in Chamonix around one o'clock today. An avalanche on Mont Blanc. Some of the family have been killed."

Paula gaped at him. Her eyes, opening wide, were pinned on his. He saw the horror mirrored in them and the draining away of all color from her face. It turned chalky white. *"Who?"* she asked in a strangled whisper.

Shane's grip increased, his fingers biting into her flesh. "You must be brave, my darling," he said. "Very brave. I'm here, I'll help you through this." He paused, swallowed hard, sought the right phrases, the right words. But there were no such things, he knew that.

Paula, her mind racing, thought of the most dedicated skiers in the group. She cried harshly, "Not Daddy? *Not my father?*"

Shane's throat constricted. He nodded. "I'm so sorry. So very sorry, my darling," he murmured in a dim and shaken voice.

For a moment Paula could not say a word. She continued to stare at

Shane, stunned and stupefied, almost uncomprehending, unable to conceive what he was saying—or accept it.

Aware that it would be kinder to tell her everything at once, quickly, and without further delay, he said in the same saddened tone, "Paula, I don't know how to tell you this, and I'm so sorry, but Jim was also killed. And Maggie. They were on top of the mountain with your father when it happened."

"No!" she said. "No!" She wrenched her hands out of his and clapped them over her mouth, looking around the room frenziedly, as if seeking escape, as if trying to run from this new and dreadful knowledge. Her eyes stretched and stretched in her ashen face. She jumped up jerkily and shouted in a frantic voice, "It can't be so! *No!* It just can't be so! Oh my God! *Philip. My brother.* Was he—"

"He's all right," Shane exclaimed, also leaping to his feet, wrapping his arms around her. "Everyone else is safe, except for Jan and Peter Coles. They haven't been found yet."

Paula pulled away from him roughly, staring up into his face. Her violet eyes were black with the pain and horror of it all, and her face twisted in a grimace of grief and anguish and heartbreak. She began to tremble violently, but as Shane reached for her once more, wanting to help her, to comfort her, Paula ran into the middle of the room, moving her head from side to side, denying, denying. Suddenly she wrapped her arms around her body and doubled over in agony.

She began to make small but high-pitched mewling noises like a terrified animal in immense pain. It was a keening, really, and it did not cease. Grief and shock continued to assault her, swept over her like giant tidal waves and engulfed her finally. She slipped to the floor unconscious.

The private jet owned by O'Neill Hotels International sliced through the dark night sky high above the English Channel. It was set on a steady course for London airport where it would soon be landing after a seven-hour flight across the Atlantic.

Shane sat opposite Paula, who was stretched out on one of the banquettes and wrapped in several light wool traveling rugs. He watched her closely, hardly daring to take his eyes off her. Occasionally he leaned over her, soothed her gently, as he had throughout the long and difficult trip. She tossed about restlessly despite the sedatives she had been given at intervals since he had told her about the tragedy in Chamonix.

The local doctor in New Milford, instantly summoned by Shane after she had collapsed, had treated her for shock. He had injected her and given Shane a small box of additional sedatives in tablet form. Before leaving the barn, he had instructed Shane to administer them during the flight whenever he considered it necessary, but to use his discretion.

Shane had rapidly come to realize that Paula was fighting the tranquilizing drugs, just as she had fought him at times during the night. Twice over the Atlantic she had tried to struggle up off the banquette, her eyes filled with panic and fear. She had vomited once, retching until there was nothing left inside. He had tended to her every need with infinite patience, tenderness, and love, helping her in every way he could, murmuring consoling words to her, trying to ease her mental turmoil, ensure her physical comfort.

Now, as he sat observing her, Shane's worry accelerated. She had not broken down or cried once, and this was abnormal for her, she who was such an emotional woman by nature. Nor had she spoken to him, and it was this extraordinary and protracted silence, plus the wild and febrile look in her eyes, that frightened him so much.

He glanced at his watch. They would be on the ground in no time at all. His father and Miranda would be there to meet them with a private ambulance and Paula's London doctor, Harvey Langen. Thank God for Harvey, Shane thought. He'll know what to do, the best way to treat her condition. And then he asked himself how a doctor could treat the overwhelming grief and anguish she was experiencing, and he acknowledged miserably that he had no ready answers.

Shane sat in the small study of the Belgrave Square flat with his sister Merry. His expression was morose, his black eyes abstracted as he sipped his third cup of coffee, then drew on his cigarette.

Parker, the butler, had prepared breakfast a short while ago, but none of them had been able to eat a thing, and Shane had been chain-smoking since he had entered the room.

Bryan O'Neill, who had been showing the doctor out, came back in and hurried over to Shane. His hand rested on his son's shoulder, and he said in an optimistic tone, "You were mistaken, Shane. Harvey says Paula's definitely not in catatonic shock. I tackled him about that, as you asked me to. She is in shock, of course, we're all aware of that, but Harvey believes she'll be pulling out of it later today, or tomorrow at the very latest."

Shane looked at his father and nodded. "Oh God, I hope so, Dad. I can't bear to see her like this, suffering so much. If only she would speak to me, say something."

"She will, Shane, very soon," Bryan said, squeezing Shane's shoulder affectionately. Sighing, he lowered himself into a chair, and continued: "This kind of catastrophe is devastating, and sudden death, sudden loss, is always the hardest to bear because of its very unexpectedness, apart from anything else."

"If only I knew how to help her," Shane exclaimed. "But I'm floundering right now. I haven't been able to get through to her, get a reaction from her, and yet I know she is in the most dreadful agony. I must find a way to ease the burden of her sorrow and pain."

Miranda said, "If anyone can help her it's you, Shane. You're the closest to her, and perhaps when you come back tonight she'll be out of the shock, as Harvey said she would. She'll talk to you then, I just know it. You will be able to console her, let her know that she's not alone, that she has you."

Shane stared at his sister. "What do you mean *come back tonight?* I'm not leaving her. I'm going to be right here until she sleeps off the drugs . . . I wouldn't let her wake up alone."

"I'll stay with you," Merry announced. *"I* won't permit *you* to be alone."

Bryan, who had been listening to this exchange between his children, instantly understood so many things that had baffled him in the last year. He said slowly, "Shane, I didn't know—I didn't realize you were in love with Paula, that you loved her so profoundly."

"Love her," Shane repeated almost wonderingly, glancing across at his father in astonishment. "Why, Dad, she's my whole life."

"Yes," Bryan said. "Yes, Shane, I realize that now, seeing you like this.

She'll recover, please believe me, she will. People have enormous inner strength in times of trouble, and Paula is no exception. In fact, she's stronger than most —one of the strongest women I know. There's a lot of Emma in her. Oh yes, she'll pull out of this eventually. In time everything will be all right."

Shane threw him a dismal look and his eyes reflected his own pain. "No, it won't," he said in the bleakest of voices. "You're wrong, Dad. Quite wrong."

Fifty-Two

The harsh winter had passed.

The spring came, bringing a new and wondrous greenness to her gardens at Pennistone Royal. And then, before she knew it, the summer was filling the air with its sweet fragrance as the flowers burst into bloom under warming sunlight and skies that were as blue as speedwells and filled with that glorious northern light.

She was alone now. Entirely alone except for her children. Lorne and Tessa filled every waking moment of her time, and she drew consolation and joy from their laughter, their carefree spirits, and their childlike pleasures.

The grief that had shattered her at the end of January had been brought under control.

Paula had reached deep inside herself, had drawn on her inner resources for sustenance and strength in her time of loss and pain and trouble. She had had no option really. Too many people were dependent on her.

Her mother and Alexander had returned from Chamonix grief-stricken and crushed by sorrow. They had automatically turned to her, had needed her comfort and her support, her immense fortitude, to help them through the difficult period of the funerals and the distressing weeks that followed. They were plunged deeper into mourning as their shock receded and reality took over. Her children had also needed the security of her love and devotion, every bit of attention she could give them, now that they were without a father.

And finally her enormous empire required her to be at the helm, guiding its course at all times, and she devoted herself to the great legacy she had inherited from her grandmother, working around the clock to ensure that it remained safe and only increased in importance and wealth. And work had become her strong citadel in the way it had been Emma's in the past.

But as the grief lessened, grew a little easier to bear, her guilt only increased and intensified. And it was the guilt that continued to cripple her now, so many months after the tragedy that had decimated the family.

It was a many-faceted guilt . . . survivor guilt that she was alive when her father, Jim, and Maggie were dead . . . guilt that she and Jim had parted with such animosity the day before he had left for Chamonix . . . and, worst of all, guilt that she had been with Shane when those three people she cared about had met their untimely and hideous deaths.

As they had been suffocating under thousands of tons of snow, she had been in Shane's arms, transported by passion and the ecstacy of fulfillment. Illogical as it was, she nevertheless felt responsible, blamed herself for their deaths. Intellectually she knew that she was not to blame, that it was wrong to feel this way, but emotionally she could not come to grips with true reality.

And she never wanted to make love again because in her mind the act of love was now associated with death and dying. In consequence, the mere thought of sex appalled her. She was desensitized, without feeling, and emotionally and physically frigid, incapable of giving of herself as a woman.

Slowly Paula had come to realize that she had nothing to offer Shane O'Neill. He was too virile, too passionate a man to settle for only a small part of her, and since she could not participate in lovemaking, she believed the relationship to be doomed.

And so she sent him away. She knew his heart was broken, and she loathed herself for inflicting pain and heartache on him, but she had convinced herself that she was doing the best thing for him, for them both ultimately.

Shane had remained by her side through February, always there when she needed him, giving her his continuing love and friendship. Sensitive by nature and knowing her as well as he did, he never made demands on her whatsoever. He shared her grief, her pain and her anguish, was consoling, became kindness itself. But after a month's sojourn in London and Yorkshire, he had had to resume his business activities. He had flown off to Australia to supervise the building of the new O'Neill hotel which Blackie had purchased on his trip with Emma.

Around this period, Paula had conceived the idea of sending her mother to Sydney with Philip, who was returning on the O'Neill private jet with Shane. At first Daisy had demurred, had protested that she must remain in England to be with Paula and the twins, but Paula had persuaded her to go. At the last minute Daisy had hurriedly packed and traveled across the world with the two men. Her mother was still in Australia, trying to pick up the threads of her life without David, acting as Philip's hostess and taking an interest in the McGill holdings. And Paula was aware that her mother was starting to throw off her own pain and function again.

But Shane had returned to England in April and had come again to Yorkshire to see her. Once more, as was his way, he had been understanding of her dilemma. He had explained that he recognized that she needed time to adjust herself to the loss of her father, to whom she had been so close, to the loss of her husband, who though estranged from her, was still the father of her children.

"I only wanted my freedom, a divorce from Jim. I never wished him harm or wanted him to die. He was so young," she had whispered on the day Shane was setting off for New York with Miranda.

"I know, I know, darling," Shane had said with gentleness. "I'm there whenever you need me. I'll wait for you, Paula."

But she had not wanted him to wait, for she knew deep within herself that she would never be ready. She could never be Shane's wife. In a sense that part of her life was over, and she had adjusted herself to the knowledge that she would live alone with her children, would never share herself or her life with a man. It was not possible anymore.

She had not told Shane about the dreadful nights when she awakened from the same terrifying nightmare, the nightmare that she was suffocating, one which constantly haunted her. It was so real she would sit up in bed with a start, her trembling body bathed in sweat as she cried out in terror and fear. And always in the center of her mind there wobbled the horrifying image of her father and Jim and Maggie being swept away by the avalanche, being buried under that icy snow that had smothered them, snuffed out their lives with such suddenness and so pointlessly.

But Shane O'Neill was no fool, and it soon became apparent to him that Paula had changed toward him, and she *knew* that he knew. How could he not. She could not help her attitude or her demeanor, nor could she alter the circumstances that had wrought the shift in her emotional balance. Her remoteness, her detachment, her preoccupation with her children and her work combined to stun him initially, and then they eventually told him everything he needed to know.

Sometimes she was lonely, frequently she was sad and sorrowing, and occasionally she was afraid.

She stood alone. Her grandmother and her father, the two people from whom she had received so much support and love, were dead. She was the head of the Harte clan. Everyone looked to her, deferred to her, came to her with their problems, both personal and business. There were times when her responsibilities and burdens were crushing, overwhelming, too much for one woman to bear. But then she would think of Emma and draw strength from the memories of that beloved woman who was so much a part of her and whose blood ran in her veins. And every single day she thanked God for Winston, who was her rock, and for Emily, who was her greatest consolation, her dearest friend and her most loving, loyal, and devoted cousin. Without them her life would be very bleak indeed.

The old familiar sadness enveloped Paula on this Saturday morning in August as she strolled slowly up the Rhododendron Walk which she herself had created. It seemed so long ago now—that spring when she had planted these bushes. So much had happened to her in the last few years . . . . so many losses, so many defeats . . . and yet so many triumphs and gains as well. She smiled to herself as she suddenly thought of the children and the happiness and love they gave her. Her sadness lifted slightly and her smile widened. An hour ago Emily had arrived to take them and Nora off to Heron's Nest for the next three weeks. They would spend the remainder of August and the first two weeks of September in the old villa by the sea, whilst she herself was in Texas and New York on business. They loved their Auntie Emily and their older counterparts, Amanda and Francesca, who would be joining them for the holiday in Scarborough. They had been so excited as they had toddled down the steps to the car, clutching their buckets and spades. And they had looked so adorable in their cotton sunsuits and matching sun hats. Little monkeys, she muttered affectionately, recalling the scene which had been enacted in the driveway a short while before. For once they had not been a bit concerned that they would be apart from her. After kissing her hastily, they had clambered into the car and had been driven off without so much as giving her a backward glance.

No matter, she thought, as she turned and retraced her steps down the steep walk. They will enjoy the sun and the sea air and have a rare old time with Emily. And I know they are truly in safe hands in my absence.

Paula paused when she came to the lily pond at the bottom of the long sloping lawn. She stood reflecting as Shane edged into her mind.

The last time she had seen him, the two of them had sat here on the stone bench near the pond. It had been a very hot sunny day toward the end of June.

Almost two months ago. She had been exhausted, careworn on that Saturday, after a debilitating week rushing between the Harte stores in Leeds, Harrogate, and Sheffield. He had arrived after lunch, unexpected and unannounced, and they had ended up having a violent quarrel. No, that was not actually true. They had not quarreled. But he had lost his temper with her, and she had simply sat there, letting his anger roll over her, aware that there was nothing else she could do. She had often been subjected to his outbursts as a child, and she had never won with him. It was always better to remain silent, let him rant and rave and get everything off his chest. That Saturday he had been justified. It would be wrong of her not to admit this.

Lowering herself onto the stone bench, Paula stared ahead, and it was as if she was watching a piece of film as she sat back and saw herself and Shane as they had been on that stifling June Saturday only a few weeks ago.

"I can't go on like this, Paula," Shane had exclaimed suddenly in the middle of their conversation. His voice had risen to an unnatural level for him these days as he had burst out, "I know it's only been five months, and I understand your pain, understand what you're going through. But you don't give me any hope for the future. If you did that, perhaps I *could* go on coping. But without hope a man has nothing. You turned away from me on that ghastly day at the barn, and you're drawing further away as you retreat deeper into yourself."

"I can't help it," she had murmured. "I'm sorry, Shane."

"But why? For God's sake, tell me *why.*"

She had taken a while to reply. Then she had murmured in her quietest voice, "If only I hadn't been with you . . . and I mean *with* you in the most intimate way, then perhaps things would be different now. But Shane, we were making love at seven o'clock on that Saturday morning. It was one o'clock in France, the moment the avalanche struck. Don't you see, I can't face making love ever again. I just can't. When I envision doing so, I fall apart emotionally. I link it to the tragedy, to the awful way Daddy and Jim and Maggie died."

He had stared at her helplessly, his face tensing. "I knew it. I knew that was it," he had finally remarked in a curiously hoarse, choked voice.

There had been a short silence, and then she had told him, had spelled out in actual words what she had long believed he knew within himself, understood in his heart of hearts. "Shane, it's better that we don't see each other again," she had whispered. "Not even as friends. I have nothing to offer you, not even friendship right now. Look, it wouldn't be fair to you if we continued in this way. Perhaps one day I will be able to resume our friendship, be your friend, but . . ." Her voice had trailed off.

He had stared at her hard, his eyes piercing into hers, and she had seen the shock and hurt, the disbelief, and then the sudden anger reflected on his handsome face.

"I can't believe you're saying this to me!" he had cried heatedly, his face blazing. "I love you, Paula, and even though you want to deny it at this moment, *you love me.* I know you do. We've had so much and have so much together. That deep closeness that has grown from childhood affection to the mature abiding love of two adults, and compatibility in every way, and passion. Yes, I understand how you feel about sex because of the last time we made love, but that awful memory of the catastrophe will eventually fade. It has to. It would be abnormal if it didn't go away."

She had shaken her head, remained mute, her hands clasped in her lap.

"You blame yourself!" he shouted, losing patience with her. "Now I understand your attitude even more. You actually *blame* yourself and you're punishing yourself! Punishing me! You're so wrong, Paula. So wrong. It wasn't your fault. The avalanche was an act of God. You didn't cause it to happen. And now you think that by flagellating yourself, leading a chaste life, you'll redeem yourself! *Is that it?*" Not waiting for her response, he had rushed on, "Whatever you do, Paula, you can't bring them back. Accept that. Accept that life is for the living. You have every *right* to be happy. And so do I. So do *we*— together. You need a husband, you need *me,* and Lorne and Tessa need a father. I love the twins. I want to be a loving father to them, an adoring husband to you. You cannot be alone for the rest of your life. It would be a waste, the most terrible and wanton waste."

He had paused for breath at this point, and she had reached out, touched his arm gently. "Please, Shane, don't upset yourself like this."

"Upset myself! That's a joke, Paula! Here you are, telling me we must part . . . forever, seemingly, and you use a word like *upset.* Jesus Christ, I'm *shattered,* don't you realize that? You are my whole life. I have nothing if I don't have you."

"Shane," she had begun, reaching out again.

He had shaken her hand off his arm and leaped to his feet. "I cannot continue this ridiculous discussion. I have to go, get away from here. God knows how I'll ever find peace of mind again, but I don't suppose that's your problem, is it, Paula? It's mine." He had stepped away from her, gazed down at her, his expression one she could not quite read. "Goodbye, Paula," he had said in a shaking voice, and as he had turned away, she had seen the tears glittering in his black eyes.

She had wanted to run after him as he had bounded up the steps to the terrace. But she had restrained herself, knowing that there was no point. She had been cruel to Shane, but at least she had told him the truth, and perhaps one day he would understand her motives. She hoped he would come to realize that she had given him his freedom because she could no longer continue to hurt him by dangling the future in front of his nose. It was a future that did not exist.

Now, as she rose and went up the stone steps to the terrace in front of Pennistone Royal, Paula remembered how oddly detached she had felt that day. It had troubled her then, and it troubled her now. Was she always going to be like this?

Sighing under her breath, she went in through the open French doors, crossed the Peach Drawing Room, and hurried down the length of the Stone Hall. As she ran lightly up the grand staircase, heading for the upstairs parlor, she put all private and personal thoughts to one side. She was driving to London later in the day, taking a plane to Texas on Monday. She was about to do battle at Sitex, and her plan of action needed every ounce of her attention, her total concentration.

Fifty-Three

"Anyway, Shane, when John Crawford told me he was going to Australia to spend a month with Daisy and Philip, I was delighted," Winston said across the luncheon table to his closest friend.

"So am I." Shane lifted his glass, took a sip of red wine, and continued, "Daisy was looking much better, and she was certainly in brighter spirits when I saw her in Sydney in August. I think she's adjusting to life without David."

"Daisy's a sensible woman." Winston eyed Shane, and then he laughed quietly. "I must admit, I've always had a sneaking suspicion that John had a crush on Daisy." Shrugging lightly, he added, "Who knows, maybe he can give her a bit of love and companionship. After all, she's still a young woman."

"Yes." Shane's face changed. His expression turned morose and brooding as he gazed across the restaurant absently. He was lost in his thoughts, pondering his future, as he so often did of late.

Winston leaned forward and said slowly, carefully, "Despite Paula's attitude at this moment, she could easily reverse herself, you know. Women are unpredictable creatures at the best of times."

"Not Paula," Shane said after a few seconds of consideration. "She's very strong, and once her mind is made up, it's made up." He shook his head sadly. "I'm going to have to do my damnedest to forget her, Winston, and make a fresh start. It won't be easy, but I'm certainly going to give it a try. I can't go around carrying a torch for her the rest of my life. There's not much to be gained from that."

"No, there isn't."

Shane brought out his cigarettes, offered one to Winston. They sat smoking for a few minutes, and then Shane said, "I'm glad you stopped off in New York for a couple of days on your way back to London. It's been a—"

"So am I," Winston interjected and chuckled. "I rather like the idea of flying home in style on that private jet of yours. Not to mention having you for company. And thanks again for delaying your plans, waiting for me. I appreciate it."

"Yes, and what I started to tell you is that I've appreciated having your company." Shane pursed his lips, gave Winston a pointed stare. "As you're aware, I've never talked about women or my love affairs to you, but I needed to confide my feelings for Paula, to unburden myself to someone I trust and respect. You've been very patient and helpful. Thanks, Winston."

Winston sat back, finished his wine, and then puffed on his cigarette, looking thoughtful. Finally he murmured, "I should have told you this the other night, but you seemed done in after your marathon session on the subject of Paula. Anyway, you weren't really telling me anything I didn't know. I mean about you being in love with Paula. I've known that for the longest time now. So has Emily."

Shane said, very startled, "And I thought no one knew. Just goes to show you, doesn't it."

Winston said softly, "Emma knew too, Shane."

"She did!" Shane's astonishment was more pronounced, and for a split second he was speechless; then he smiled faintly. "Funnily enough, I've had the strangest feeling since she died that she was aware of our relationship. But Paula pooh-poohed the idea, dismissed it out of hand."

"Aunt Emma didn't know you were involved, that's true," Winston exclaimed rapidly. "And to tell you the honest truth, neither Emily nor I were too sure about that either. Aunt Emma spotted a look in your eyes when you were observing Paula at the christening two and a half years ago. That's when Emily and I also realized how deeply you felt about Paula."

"I see." Leaning across the table, Shane gave Winston a hard and questioning stare, then asked, "Obviously Aunt Emma discussed it with you. What did she say?"

"She was worried about you, Shane. She loved you a lot, you know, like one of us, one of her own. I think it was a disappointment to her that you hadn't spoken up earlier, before Paula married Jim. But she was philosophical about it really and knew she couldn't interfere. However, if she were alive, she wouldn't be a bit surprised to know that Paula reciprocates your love for her— that I can guarantee you."

"*Reciprocated* in the past tense, mate," Shane muttered and made a sour face. "The lady has chosen to walk a solitary path."

"She might change her mind," Winston shot back, wanting to cheer him up. "I keep telling you, women do that half a dozen times a day. Besides, it's only been nine months. Give her a chance, a bit longer to pull herself together. Look, Shane, I have an idea. Don't fly back to London with me this afternoon. Stay here in New York. Paula's been in Texas for a week, and I know she's due back in the city in a couple of days, either tomorrow or Wednesday. See her again, take her out, wine and dine her, talk to her. You can be very persuasive and—"

Shane held up his hand and shook his head with firmness. "No, Winston, it won't do any good. She made it very clear to me in June that it was over. *Finished*. Besides, I can't delay my return any longer. Dad's due to go out to Sydney later this week. His turn, you know, and with Merry running this hotel, I have to be on the scene at home for a few months. I'll be racing between Leeds and London but spending more time in Yorkshire, I hope."

"Emily's looking forward to having you at Beck House on weekends, Shane, as soon as she's back from Scarborough. I hope you're not going to disappoint her, or me for that matter."

"No. I'll be staying with you at weekends when I can, and thanks a lot. I want to spend some time at your father's stables, talk to him about Emerald Bow and our racing program for next year. Grandpops left me the racehorses to race, not to put out to pasture. And I haven't been on a horse for months. I'm itching to get into the saddle, give War Lord and Celtic Maiden a few good workouts."

"That's great, Shane, it'll be—" Winston stopped, grinned from ear to ear and waved. To Shane he said, "Here's that gorgeous sister of yours."

Shane swung around, and his face lit up when he saw Miranda, who was hurrying across the restaurant looking as if she had something of vital importance to tell him. He smiled at her extraordinary costume, for that was all he could call it. She resembled a redheaded gypsy in her colorful patchwork cotton dress and masses of gold chains. Taking over as head of their New York operation had not induced her to change her spectacular style of dressing. Good for you Merry, Shane thought. Stick to your guns. Be your highly original self, one of the genuine free spirits of this world.

"Hello, you two gorgeous men, and don't get up," Merry exclaimed as they both made to rise. She flopped down into the empty chair and said, "Come closer. I've something interesting to tell you." Giving them both a conspiratorial look, she went on, "You'll *never* guess who I've just seen. Not in a million years!"

Winston looked amused. "Then tell us, Merry darling. It'll save a lot of time."

"Yes, do," Shane remarked. "Would you like a glass of this?" He lifted the bottle of wine, showed it to her.

"Thanks, that'll be lovely." Merry settled back in her chair, waited until her brother had poured the last of the wine into their three glasses, then said, "I was in the Terrace Café, talking to the *maître d'* when I spotted them . . . talk about the Terrible Trio!"

Both men looked at her blankly.

Grinning, Miranda wrinkled her freckled nose and hissed, "Allison Ridley, Skye Smith, and—*Sarah Lowther.* All lunching together and looking very, very chummy, to say the least. Can you believe it!"

"Sarah!" Winston chuckled sardonically. "Well, well, well, that's very interesting. I wonder what she's doing in New York. Paula and Emily haven't heard anything about her for months, or Jonathan either, for that matter, since he went to the Far East."

"Don't mention that bastard," Shane said, scowling. "He's always been a troublemaker and as devious as the devil."

Winston nodded in agreement.

Merry said, "I suppose I ought to have gone over and spoken to them, but quite frankly I beat a hasty retreat. I wanted to warn you both that a couple of your old girlfriends were floating around our hotel. Thank God they didn't decide to lunch in here—then where would you have been?"

Winston said jokingly, "Allison would have probably slipped a Mickey Finn in my drink."

"Skye Smith was *never* a girlfriend of *mine,*" Shane announced and winked at Merry. "Not my type."

"We all know *you* don't like blondes, that you prefer dark exotic beauties like my darling Pau—" Miranda bit off the name and gave her brother an apologetic and concerned look. "Sorry, Shane, I didn't mean to rub salt in the wound."

"That's all right, Merry, and I'm a big boy. I might be still licking my wounds, but at least I've managed to stem the flow of blood finally."

"Yes, I know." Merry took a small swallow of her wine and began to talk about their impending flight to London, making an effort to change the subject. Despite Shane's flippancy, the front he put up, she was aware that he was deeply hurt and still suffering inside. He yearned for Paula. He would all of his life—that was the depressing part. If only Jim had not been so tragically killed, Merry thought. Paula would have eventually been divorced, and Shane and she would have married. Now Paula had put herself on a rack. And Shane too. Why is she doing this? Miranda asked herself. I don't understand her anymore.

Shane said, "Daydreaming suddenly, Merry? You started to say something about the car."

"Oh yes, sorry," Merry said, smiling at him. "I arranged for the limousine to be outside at three o'clock. That gives you plenty of time to get to Kennedy before the rush hour."

Skye Smith was the first to excuse herself after lunch. She could not wait to escape, and it was with a sigh of relief that she crossed the elegant lobby of the Plaza Towers Hotel, property of the O'Neills, and hurried out into the street.

She peered at her watch. It was just turning off two-thirty, and she had plenty of time to get back to the antique shop for her next appointment at three.

As she strolled toward Park Avenue, she thought about Sarah Lowther. She did not particularly like Sarah and could not help wondering what Allison saw in her. Sarah was the bitchiest woman she had ever met and not very bright in some ways.

On the other hand, Sarah had inadvertently dropped a gold mine of information onto the table over lunch, and had opened up in such a personal way about her private affairs that Skye was still slightly taken aback.

She smiled cynically as she waited on the corner for the traffic lights to change before crossing Park. *So Paula Fairley was the mystery woman, the love of Shane's life, the lady who had got her clutches into him. And so much so he was incapable of making it with any other woman.*

This news had staggered Skye. When Sarah had discovered that Skye had occasionally dated Shane, the Englishwoman had turned to stone at the luncheon table. Skye had thought for a minute that Sarah was going to scratch her eyes out, so venomous was the look on the redhead's face. It had become patently obvious to Skye that Sarah was madly in love with Shane, and she had quickly assured Allison's friend that they had only ever had a platonic relationship. This had seemed to appease Sarah, and she had relaxed again, confided more dirt about the family, and in particular about Paula. The hatred Sarah harbored for her cousin was frightening. Hell hath no fury like a woman scorned, Skye thought, hurrying along. I ought to know.

She hardly ever saw Shane O'Neill these days. He had become a world traveler as their holdings had increased, and apparently he spent a great deal of time in Australia. He was only in New York on rare fleeting visits since his sister had been made the president of their American hotel corporation. He had called her once, almost a year ago now, and they had had a drink together, but he had seemed preoccupied and restless, and she had decided against pressing him to take her to dinner.

Ross, on the other hand, was always taking Paula Fairley to lunch, especially in the last six months or so. He had let that slip accidentally. When she had teased him about Paula, Ross had said that it was strictly business. And at heart she knew there was a great deal of truth in this. Ross had been close to Paula's grandmother, as had his uncle, Daniel P. Nelson. Still, Skye knew Ross as well as she knew herself. Business it might indeed be, but he no doubt hankered after the woman. Paula Fairley was everything Ross craved. Good-looking. Young. Rich. Powerful. And available—now that she was a widow. Ross probably had some scheme up his sleeve, a plan to propel Paula Fairley into his bed and possibly into matrimony. He had once told her that if he ever married again, he would make sure his intended bride was wealthy. Yes, Ross would always continue to repeat his old patterns. He desired what he could not have. And after the things Sarah had told her, there was no question in her mind that Paula Fairley had held herself apart, had not succumbed to Ross's charms. And why would she with Shane O'Neill in the background—her lover of long standing?

Skye now thought about her dinner date with Ross on Wednesday night and laughed under her breath. They dined once a week since they had become friends again. It had taken her a long time to forgive his shoddy treatment of her, but in the end she had forgiven him. She had done so because of their daughter Jennifer. When Ross had come begging to see their child, she had consistently and categorically refused to permit this. The longer she had remained cold and unbending, refused to reverse her decision, the more his need to see his little girl had increased. How typical of him. What he could not have he did persist in chasing and forever tried to attain. She had taken great pleasure in making Ross implore and crawl on his hands and knees to her. And that he had eventually done—well, almost.

With reluctance she had finally given in but only because she had come to understand how much Jennifer loved her father, longed to see him on a continuing basis and to spend time with him. She could not deprive the child because of the man and his character.

The laughter bubbled up in Skye again as she continued walking at a steady pace, heading for her shop on Seventy-third and Lexington. What fun she would have with Ross at dinner later in the week. She would adroitly drop a few spicy tidbits about Paula Fairley and Shane O'Neill at the right moment, and then sit back and watch Ross choke on his food. It would drive him crazy when he knew that the sorrowing *widder* was in reality the Merry Widow, waltzing to Shane's tune and bestowing her very special favors on him. Although Ross and Shane had done business together in the past, Ross had always been disparaging about Shane behind his back, constantly referring to him as the stud.

Although she was not an unkind woman, Skye Smith was bitter about Ross Nelson. A cold gleam entered her eyes as she contemplated making her former lover squirm. I knew if I waited long enough I'd be able to twist the knife in Ross's back one day, she thought. And he deserves it after all the pain and humiliation he's inflicted on me. I forgave him for our daughter's sake. But I've never forgotten and I never will.

She did not understand that she wanted Ross for herself.

Ross Nelson's sanguine expression vanished. His light hazel eyes clouded and narrowed slightly as he leaned back in his leather chair and stared harder at Dale Stevens.

Finally Ross cleared his throat and asked, "Exactly what do you mean when you say Paula changed her mind?"

"She's decided not to sell her Sitex stock," Dale told him and shrugged. "We both misread her, I guess. And badly."

"She reneged? Reneged on our deal?" Ross exclaimed in a cold, tight voice. "And where the hell were you, Dale, when all this was happening?" When Dale did not reply, he continued in a sharper accusatory tone, "This is one hell of a disaster! I'm going to look like the biggest fool in the world. Milt Jackson is going to have apoplexy when he finds out."

Dale sighed and crossed his legs, waiting for the banker to cool down.

The two men sat in Ross Nelson's private office in his bank on Wall Street. It was early on Thursday afternoon in the first week of September, the day after Dale had flown up from Texas with Paula.

"What am I going to say to him?" Ross pressed, leaning forward urgently across his huge partner's desk, endeavoring to control his considerable annoyance.

"Tell him the truth. That's all you can do."

"Why didn't you call me after the board meeting yesterday, give me a chance to collect my thoughts, come up with a reasonable story?" Ross demanded tersely.

"I felt it was better to tell you in person."

"I just can't believe this," Ross muttered angrily, shifting his weight in the chair. "I was certain she was going to sell, was convinced of it. I could wring her neck after the merry dance she's led us."

Dale sighed wearily. "Nobody was more surprised than I was when she pulled her stunt at the board meeting. But last night, when I could think dispassionately, I began to realize that she simply blinded us—with words, sweet talk, charm, and a lot of dissembling. And you know something, Ross, she *didn't* renege. I had time to analyze the situation last night, and as I ran everything through my head, replayed every meeting we've ever had with her, and particularly in the last six months, I suddenly saw things very clearly. Yes, she talked incessantly about her problems, her worries, the burdens of running the Harte chain, and she did keep intimating she wanted to sell her mother's stock. But she never actually came out and said she would do so. In my anxiousness to render Marriott Watson helpless, have International Petroleum take over the company, and in your *own* anxiousness to please Milt Jackson, your valued client, we *assumed* she would unload. If anything, we're at fault, believing we could push her around, get her to do our bidding."

"She listened to us both so attentively," Ross exploded. "She asked for our advice, seemed to be taking it. Not only that, she insisted on knowing who the prospective buyer was, and against my better judgment I told her!" Ross groaned. "Oh Jesus, what a fool I've been! I should never have arranged those meetings between her, Milt Jackson, and us." The banker reached for a cigarette and lit it nervously. "Milt thinks Sitex is in the bag. Jesus Christ, he's going to be convinced I misled him or that I've suddenly developed flawed judgment in the prime of my life. We've got to come up with a plausible story to tell him."

"I repeat what I just said, we have to tell him the truth, explain that *she* misled *us*. He'll have to accept it. There's nothing else he *can* do," Dale insisted.

Ross drew on his cigarette and then stubbed it out. He rose, walked around his desk, and began to pace up and down, his hands behind his back as he contemplated the meeting with Milton Jackson, chairman of the board of International Petroleum and an important client of the bank. Suddenly he stopped in his tracks and fixed his eyes on Dale. "If this gets out, we're going to look like the biggest idiots in Wall Street. Two grown men, seasoned businessmen, shrewd, tough, and hard-assed, taken by a slip of a girl." He ran his hand through his blondish hair and grimaced with disgust at himself and Dale. "Talk about Emma Harte. Paula Fairley puts her to shame. The double-dealing little wretch. I would never have believed it of her. I really thought she was taking our guidance."

"I had my doubts about that on several occasions," Dale remarked dryly. "And then I admit I began to readjust my thinking about her, particularly in view of the events over the past year. There was Emma's death—that knocked her for a loop—and then she lost her daddy and her husband. She was in shock. You witnessed her state with your own eyes. So there she was, all alone, and suddenly I believed it would be a cinch. I genuinely thought she would unload the stock. She indicated she'd be happy to do that, would be relieved to get out of the oil rat race. What a foul-up."

Ross said in a rush, "I'm going to tell Milt that she *did* in fact renege. To hell with it. Guys renege on deals every day in the street and in the oil business. Why should a woman be any different? More likely to change her mind, in my opinion. I can't afford to lose Milt Jackson as a client of this bank or International Petroleum as a corporate account."

"Okay," Dale concurred. "Basically he's your baby anyway. I don't owe him an explanation." The oil man brought out a cigar, fiddled with the end, finally struck a match, and brought the flame to the cigar. He said, "You do realize my hands were tied at the board meeting, don't you, Ross? There was nothing I could do."

"Sure, sure," Ross mumbled and returned to his chair. "Tell me exactly what happened on Tuesday."

"Be happy to, Ross. Paula arrived looking like a demure little nun, wearing a black dress with a white collar and cuffs. She was unusually pale, even for her, and it gave her a waiflike look. She had a sort of innocence about her."

"Save me the description, God damn it! I'm interested in what she said, not how she looked."

"Her appearance is important," Dale replied. Paula had played her role very well. He had realized as he had sat in the Sitex boardroom in Odessa that there was something of the actress in her. "Don't you understand, Ross, she looked like a little girl, easy to handle; and some of those old buzzards on the board, who don't know her very well—why, they were rubbing their hands with glee. Metaphorically speaking, that is. Yes, Marriott Watson's cronies thought they were going to eat her alive."

"As we did," Ross muttered softly.

Dale smiled faintly. "We weren't the only guys who were fooled, Ross. Take comfort in that, cold as it is. Before we got down to general business—the North Sea oil situation and the renewal of my contract—Paula asked to make a statement to the board. Naturally Marriott Watson had no choice but to agree. She said that it was her duty to inform her fellow board members that she was about to sell her mother's stock. The entire block—the entire forty percent of it. Everyone was taken aback, and that was when Jason Emerson piped up."

Ross nodded. "He's still sharp, smart as hell, despite his great age."

Dale agreed. "Tough old wildcatters like Jason don't change, not in my experience. I sat back, enjoying every minute, thinking it was going our way. It was only later that I began to realize Paula had made good use of the week she had spent in Texas, prior to the board meeting. She had done a lot of lobbying, entertained a number of the directors socially. Especially Jason. He was primed by her, no doubt in my mind about that. Still he was close to Paul McGill in the thirties and had remained loyal to Emma for forty years."

"I know about that," Ross snapped.

"Jason Emerson asked Paula who she was selling the stock to and when she intended to sell. She told him very sweetly that she was selling all forty percent to International Petroleum. *Immediately*. I thought that some of the board members were going to have a collective coronary. Holy hell broke loose. I said nothing, pleased at the way she had handled herself. There was a lot of heated talk about International Petroleum and Milt. It's no secret in the oil business that he has that company on a growth-and-expansion program and that once he gets a foothold in a company, he does his damnedest to swoop down and take it over. Also, certain board members seemed to be aware that Milt has been buying up Sitex's common stock and that he now holds an enormous amount of it. Only a dunce could fail to miss the implications."

"If I'm following the script correctly, as I think I am, presumably Jason spoke up again and asked her not to sell to International Petroleum."

"You've got it, old buddy." Dale shook his head regretfully. "Sure as God made little green apples, once the shouting had died down, old Jason started to persuade her to reconsider her decision. It was a bit of real craftiness, I can tell you, Ross. Before I had a chance to jump in with a few comments of my own, the majority of the board was singing his tune. Except Marriott Watson. He looked as if he was about to spit blood. I'm not certain, but he may have deduced that the tough negotiating between Paula and Jason had been set up in advance."

"And she capitulated of course."

"Not at first. She said she would reconsider not selling her block of stock, providing she was guaranteed a stronger voice on the board and if certain conditions were met. *Her conditions*. To be precise, the continuation of the North Sea drilling and the renewal of my contract."

"She blackmailed the board!" Ross shouted.

Dale shook his head very slowly, and a gleam of admiration now entered his brown eyes. "No, Ross, I wouldn't call it blackmail. It was the most brilliant bit of manipulation I've seen in a long time. In one way I've got to take my hat off to her because that's what business is all about—manipulation."

"That's true," Ross acknowledged. "At least you got what *you* wanted despite everything. Your contract has been renewed again and is secure for two years, Marriott Watson is temporarily muzzled, and you have a free hand. But what's your position with Paula now, Dale?"

Dale grinned. "My position remains the same. I'm president of Sitex Oil, she controls the stock of her mother and is the largest single stockholder. Paula has more power on the board than she ever had. Naturally I'll continue confiding in her as I always have. I intend to remain friendly. You never know, she still might decide to sell her stock one day. International Petroleum isn't going anywhere."

"Points well taken." Ross laughed unexpectedly. "Business is business. Not every deal works out the way one would wish. There's no point in my being immature about this. The bank still handles some of her business in the States. Anyway, if I can't succeed with her in the boardroom, maybe I'll get lucky—in the bedroom."

Fifty-Four

Paula Fairley was late.

Ross Nelson glanced at the carriage clock on the mantelshelf of his living room for the umpteenth time. He was growing impatient. When she had telephoned at six-thirty to say she was delayed, he had told her to take her time. But he had expected her to arrive before now.

He strolled across the antique Chinese carpet and hovered in front of the bar contained in the ebony and gilt Chinese chest. He poured himself another dry martini, dropped in an olive, and walked to the window, looking down onto Park Avenue. His thoughts continued to dwell on Paula.

She was one of the few women he had not been able to fathom. Or coax into his bed. He had desired her for the longest time now. Since the fall of 1969, when he had first become aware of her potent sexuality. She had always managed to keep their relationship on a cool businesslike basis. At first he had believed he would win her over. Women generally fell for him. Later he had become annoyed as she continued to be uninterested. But he had kept up his battery on the telephone, constantly invited her out to dinner, and bombarded her with flowers. Since he was conceited and had enjoyed much success with women from all walks of life, Ross convinced himself that Paula would one day be his alone.

After Jim Fairley had been killed in the avalanche, Ross had played the role of a concerned good friend whenever she had been in New York. In the past nine months, he had seen more of her than usual, since she had wanted to divest herself of some of Emma Harte's holdings which she had inherited. He had been on hand to help the sorrowing widow handle her business. He had hoped to persuade her to sell the Sitex stock—and seduce her as well. Her grief and curiously distant manner had induced him to hold himself in check. He had bided his time. But he had no intention of doing so any longer. Not now, not after Skye Smith's revelations last night.

He focused on the gossip Skye had relayed about Paula and Shane O'Neill. He had been stunned and disbelieving, had demanded to know the source. Skye had been only too ready to confide further. At the end of the evening he had walked home, bridling with anger and riddled with frustration. All these months, as he had held her hand and comforted her, Paula had been sleeping with Shane O'Neill. He knew Skye had not lied. After all, Sarah Lowther, Paula's cousin, had been the one who had spilled the beans.

He was delighted that Dale and his wife had been called back to Texas so unexpectedly. They had planned a foursome for dinner. He relished the idea of being alone with Paula tonight. His way was clear with her. *Finally.* At long last he was going to possess this most elusive of women.

Ross sat down on the sofa, put his martini on the Chinese coffee table, and took a cigarette, suppressing the sudden grin that had begun to spread across his face. He had not told Paula that Dale and Jessica had returned to the ranch. Why alert her, give her the opportunity to cancel? But he had given his housekeeper the evening off and telephoned the restaurant to change the reservation to ten o'clock. That would give him ample time to make his moves.

Thoughts of her slender boyish body, the voluptuous breasts intruded, brought a sudden flush to his neck. He lifted the glass, downed the rest of the drink, and went to the bar to pour another one. It was his third. He hesitated. Oh what the hell, he muttered. I can handle my liquor. Ross prided himself on his ability to drink gallons and remain a potent lover. His glance fell on the bottle of champagne in the ice bucket, and he smiled confidently. After a few glasses of that and a little of his sweet talking, Paula Fairley would be much more susceptible to his masculine appeal.

Ross Nelson had almost demolished that third martini when the intercom rang. Leaping to his feet, he rushed out into the foyer to answer it, hardly able to contain himself. He told the doorman to send Mrs. Fairley up and stood waiting for her.

A few minutes later he was kissing Paula's cool cheek, ushering her across the hall and into the living room.

She paused in the entrance and swung her head, looked up at him, her violet eyes quizzical. "Haven't Jessica and Dale arrived yet?" she asked before she moved forward.

He gazed after her, watching the fluid movement of her body, the shapely outline of her long legs through the thin silk of the pale gray cocktail dress. He almost salivated with longing. He could hardly wait to remove the dress, to strip her naked and revel in her beauty.

Paula turned to face him, catching him off guard. He blinked rapidly, hurried into the room, explained, with a nervous laugh, "They had to fly back at the last minute. An illness in the family." He stepped up to the bar, began to open the bottle of champagne. "Dale sends his apologies, and he told me to tell you he'll phone you tomorrow."

"I see," Paula said, seating herself on the sofa. "I'm disappointed they're not having dinner with us. I did have a few more things to discuss with Dale." She gave him a small smile. "Never mind."

"Yes," Ross murmured and carried the drink over to her. Seating himself in the chair opposite, he lifted his own glass and grinned at her. "Well, Paula, congratulations! You've certainly pulled off a coup at Sitex!"

"Cheers, Ross," Paula said, took a sip of the champagne, and then eyed him speculatively. "You're probably annoyed with me, angry that I finally decided to hold on to the Sitex stock. But—"

"Of course not," he lied blandly, wanting to keep the atmosphere cozy and totally free of conflict. "It was your choice. Dale and I could only advise you. We only wanted to help you, Paula. As Dale said to me at the bank this afternoon, International Petroleum is not going anywhere. I think Milton Jackson would always be interested in buying you out."

"I'm sure they would," Paula responded quietly. "And I do want to thank you for your concern, all of your help with the Sitex matter, and with my other American business. I'm most appreciative."

"My pleasure."

Paula leaned back on the sofa and crossed her legs, trying to hide her surprise at his attitude. She had expected Ross to be furious, knowing how much he valued Milton Jackson as a client of the bank. Dale, she knew, would always give her his support. But Ross Nelson was another kettle of fish. She was relieved that he was being so agreeable. He was always agreeable though, wasn't he? She sighed, realizing she would have to spend the next few hours alone with him. There was no way she could get out of dining with him. She decided to be gracious and get through the evening as best as she could.

Ross began to talk about her brother Philip, whom he had met the previous autumn when they had both been in New York. And for the next half hour the banker kept up a steady stream of conversation about the family in general, her grandmother, and Harte Enterprises. In between he kept refilling her glass, downed another martini, and lit endless cigarettes.

At ten to nine Paula cut him short suddenly and asked, "Shouldn't we be leaving, Ross? For the restaurant, I mean?"

"No, not just yet. I'm afraid I had problems with the reservation at Twenty-One. They couldn't give me a table before nine-thirty, ten o'clock. We might as well relax here."

"Oh all right," Paula said, but she was irritated. She disliked eating when the evening was almost over.

As he talked, believing he was being entertaining, Ross continued to drink. He also scrutinized Paula intently, admiring her elegance and beauty. The dress she wore was simple, with a draped cowl collar and short sleeves. She wore emerald earrings and, apart from a watch, these were her only pieces of jewelry. She looked stunning, and the gray silk molded her figure in all the right places. Suddenly he was unable to keep his distance.

He rose, strolled to the bar cabinet, topped his glass, and joined her on the sofa. He rested his arm on the back and sipped his drink. His eyes held hers, and he smiled a slow warm smile. "You're looking exceptionally lovely tonight, Paula."

"Thank you, Ross." She returned his gaze, and her brow puckered. There was something in those hazel eyes of his that instantly alerted her, and she drew back slightly, pressed herself closer to the arm of the small sofa. She felt a sense of panic.

Ross placed his glass on the coffee table, and in one swift move he pulled her into his arms, brought his mouth down hard on hers. She struggled with him, tried to push him away, but his grip was firm as he held her tightly. He forced his tongue against her mouth, forced her mouth open, and began to suck on her tongue and her lips. Heat ran through him, and he moved slightly so that he could grasp her left breast with his right hand. He squeezed it, pinched the nipple, increased the pressure of his fingers.

Paula continued to struggle, tried to disentangle herself from his arms, but he was a big man and strong, and she had no chance against him. He somehow managed to pull her forward, sliding her body down the sofa into a supine position, and then he fell on top of her, working his tongue on her mouth again. She clamped her teeth shut and moved her head to one side rapidly. He ran his hand over her thigh, lifted her skirt, slid his hand underneath, stroked her upper leg, and then worked his fingers against her crotch.

Paula, lying under the weight of Ross Nelson, was in a state of shock. She struggled hard to break free from his tenacious hold on her. He had leaped on her so unexpectedly, taken her totally by surprise, and only a split second after she had noticed the lust burning in his eyes. She was horrified and revolted by him, and also terribly frightened. She knew she had to escape from him, from his apartment. Quickly. If only she could get her hands up to his face to scratch him. They were trapped under his bulk. She moved her head from side to side again, frantically avoiding his mouth without success. His hands were now ripping at her panty hose, and dimly through the roaring in her head she heard the nylon tear as he tugged at the crotch of the hose. Oh my God! His fingers were against her skin, pushing into her as he slobbered against her face, his mouth slack and wet. Shudders rippled through her. She thought she was going to vomit. He was hurting her, trying to penetrate her with his fingers.

Tears sprang into her eyes, induced by the fear, the shock, the revulsion, and the pain as he pushed his hand harder between her legs. He stopped kissing her at last, drew back for breath.

Paula opened her mouth and began to scream.

Ross was jarred from his exploration of her body, and he sat up swiftly, looked down into her tear-stained face, and clamped one hand over her mouth.

"Shut up," he hissed. "You know you like this, you bitch. Don't play the innocent with me. You've been getting it from Shane O'Neill for months. Now it's old Ross's turn."

He laughed loudly, and Paula realized that he was very drunk. She struggled, moving under him violently, easing herself to the edge of the sofa.

To pull her back, he had to remove his hand from her mouth. The minute he did she began to scream again. Once more he covered her face with his large hand, wrapped one of his heavy legs around her body, and pinioned her under him. "You've been playing the grieving widow with me far too long, Paula," he gasped, his glazed eyes roving over her lasciviously. His lust was mounting by the minute, inflamed by the fight she was putting up. It brought a flushed and congested look to his face. "Come on, let's go to the bedroom," he mumbled, his words slurred. "You know you want to screw me."

Paula had been waiting for the right moment, and now she endeavored to nod her head, as if acquiescing to this suggestion. She acknowledged him with her eyes, softening her gaze.

"No more screaming," he muttered. "Okay?"

She nodded again.

He took his hand away from her mouth and leaned into her as if to kiss her.

Paula whispered, "I thought you wanted to go into the bedroom?"

He grinned at her drunkenly. "That's the idea, baby."

"What are we waiting for?"

Still grinning he got up off the sofa. Before Paula had a chance to do the same, he bent down, took hold of her arms, and pulled her to her feet.

She did not dare struggle, knowing his great strength. She would have to pick the right moment to flee. She swallowed as he dragged her to him and nestled his face against her hair. "You're going to have to tell me everything liddle old Shane did to excite you, baby. Whatever old Shane can do, Ross can do better. And then some, baby."

Swallowing her disgust and fear, summoning all of her strength, Paula pushed him away from her. Drunk, believing she was playing along with him, Ross was taken by surprise. He lost his balance, staggered back, and flopped down on the sofa.

Paula reached for her solid gold evening bag on the coffee table and swung around.

He was far too fast for her and grabbed her again. They struggled in the middle of the room. She kicked his shin, and he yelled in pain, instantly loosened his grip on her. Finally she was able to pull away from him.

Ross snatched at her dress. The cowl collar ripped under his hand.

Paula kicked him again as he took a step toward her, his expression threatening, and then in a swift movement she raised her hand and smashed the heavy gold bag into his face with all her might.

He cried out in pain as the precious metal struck his cheek and backed off, stumbling against the Chinese coffee table immediately behind him. He went sprawling on the floor. "You bitch!" he screamed, bringing his hands to his bleeding face.

Gasping for breath, shaking and terrified, Paula dashed into the foyer. The Chinese area rug skidded under her, but she recovered her balance, hitting her face against the edge of the tall cabinet as she did. But ignoring the stab of pain, she flew to the door, jerked it open, and banged it after her as she ran out. She pressed the button for the elevator, cowering against the wall, praying he would not follow her.

Tears rushed to her eyes as she fiddled with the collar of her torn dress. She pushed them back, attempted to compose herself. When the elevator doors rolled open, she almost fell into the car, avoided the curious glance of the uniformed operator. She moved further back, retreated into the shadow, opened her bag, and took out her compact. She ran the powder puff over her face and then smoothed her hand over her hair, aware of her disheveled appearance.

Within seconds she was stepping out into the marble lobby of the building, hurrying across it at her fastest pace, and then hailing a cab on Park Avenue.

—————— *Fifty-Five* ——————

Paula somehow managed to keep a grip on herself until she reached the Fifth Avenue apartment.

After letting herself in quietly, she tiptoed upstairs, not wishing Ann, the housekeeper, to see her in this terrible condition and nervous state.

She slipped into her bedroom, locked the heavy carved-wood door, and leaned against it, finally beginning to breathe a little easier. Her body was taut, rigid still with the fear that had swamped her when Ross Nelson had so unexpectedly launched his physical attack on her.

Eventually she found the strength to move forward on her trembling legs, and her hands shook as she unzipped her ruined dress and pulled it up over her head and discarded it. Once she had removed her underwear and her ripped stockings, she stumbled blindly into the bathroom.

Paula stood in the shower stall for ten minutes, soaping herself over and over again, letting the hot steaming water sluice down over her body. She felt battered and unclean, had the urgent need to erase the smell of him, the touch of him.

When at last she stepped out and looked at herself in the mirrored side wall, she saw that her body was bright pink, red in parts as if she had scalded herself or damaged the skin. But at least she felt cleansed of Ross Nelson. Pulling on a toweling robe without bothering to dry herself, she went over to the washbasin and peered at her face in the mirror. Her cheekbone was bruised where she had struck it against the cabinet. It would be black and blue tomorrow.

She continued to stare at herself.

Her blue eyes were dark, almost black, and they held the look of a wild hunted deer, were wide with fright and shock. She squeezed them tightly shut, wanting to forget what had happened to her only a short while ago. But she could not, and she lifted her lids. His lustful face danced before her eyes, was reflected in the mirror as if he was standing behind her in the bathroom. Paula shuddered and gripped the edge of the sink as she remembered how his hands had wandered so roughly over her body, how his horrible wet mouth had slobbered against hers, how his weight had trapped her under him. She had felt as though she was being suffocated.

Anger blazed through her. Ross Nelson had virtually tried to rape her. That he had been dreadfully drunk was no excuse. There was no excuse for that unconscionable behavior. He was a disgusting specimen of a man. The worst. He was not a man. He was an animal. The shuddering intensified. How violated, how damaged she felt.

Nausea rose up in Paula. She began to vomit in the washbasin, retching until she had nothing left inside. The dry heaving continued for a while and then eventually subsided. Lifting her head, she wiped her streaming eyes and her sweating face with the damp washcloth, then leaned her head against the cool tiles of the wall. Her head throbbed, her eyes ached, and her muscles were sore from struggling with him, fighting him off.

Blocking out the image of him, she closed her eyes, gulping air, calming herself as best she could, and when she was steadier on her legs, she moved away from the washbasin and blundered back into the bedroom. She lay down on the bed.

It was only then that Paula Fairley fell apart.

Quite suddenly she was gripped by an internal shaking, and then her whole body began to shake as if she had palsy. She pulled the eiderdown up over her. Her teeth began to chatter and she shivered as icy chills swept through her. Clutching at the pillow, she buried her face in it, and she began to sob as if her heart was breaking.

Paula cried without restraint for the next hour.

And all of the pain and sorrow she had suppressed since the tragic deaths of her father, Jim, and Maggie broke free at last.

Her terrible grief overwhelmed her, but she let it wash over her, envelope her completely, gave herself up to it, recognizing finally that it had been wrong and foolish of her to bottle it up inside. But she had not known what else to do. She had had to be strong, so very strong for her mother and Alexander and her children. And so she had deliberately buried the grief. It had lain there dormant, yet it had gradually gnawed away at her, eating her alive, rendering her helpless in so many aspects of her life.

As Paula Fairley wept the bitter tears she should have wept nine months ago but had not, she began to experience a measure of ease, a genuine relief from the searing heartache and anguish that had engulfed her since the avalanche.

When she had no more tears left inside her, she lay quietly on the bed, her body limp and exhausted, her eyes red and swollen, wide open, staring up at the ceiling.

Slowly, but with her usual intelligence and analytical powers, she began to sort out her muddled thoughts, sift through the painful memories, examine her emotional and physical frigidity with a new and stunning objectivity.

It was as if the shock of Ross Nelson's violent assault on her had cleared her brain, startled her out of her state of frozen containment. She started to see herself with new objectivity, and she knew with sudden sureness that the burdensome weight of her enormous guilt had crushed all feeling in her, all emotional response to others except her children. *She had no reason to be guilty. She was not to blame for anything. Not one single thing.*

Shane was correct in everything he had said.

How cruel she had been to him, inflicting pain on him because her own pain had blinded her to the truth, to reality. *Shane.* She saw his face in her imagination, transferred it in her imagination to the ceiling. If only he were really here now. She longed to have the comfort and security of his strong arms around her, keeping her safe.

Tears rushed into Paula's eyes. She had sent him away, had been so willful in her determination to tread her solitary lonely road, believing it to be the only road for her. She wondered if he would ever be able to forgive her.

Ross Nelson's hideous, grinning, drunken face nudged Shane's to one side, obliterated him. Paula shuddered violently and sat up in bed. Fury ripped through her, momentarily stunning her. *He had tried to rape her.* Never in her entire life had anything quite so disgusting happened to her. But then she had never been exposed to the harsher side of life. She had always been so protected. By Grandy. By her parents. By her large family. And by all that power and wealth. She did not know the streets, the hard world where other women had to live and fight and hold on to their sanity somehow, despite the burdens they had to carry, the punishment certain kinds of men made them endure.

Certainly she had never been exposed to men—not men like Ross Nelson, who were exploitive, pursued their own ends relentlessly. There had only ever been Jim. He had been her first lover, and then she had married him. If he had been selfish and self-involved, and he undoubtedly had, if he had been swept along by his own needs, most certainly he had never been violent with her. He had never really forced himself on her, not once in all the time they had been married.

And then there had been Shane . . . theirs had been the grandest of passions, but physical desire had blended in with their deep abiding love, that love which he had said had grown out of their childhood affection and friendship. With Shane there had been a true bonding and on every level.

The brutalizing experience she had suffered at the hands of Ross Nelson had been terrifying. It was the worst kind of violation a man could inflict on a woman—an invasion not only of the body but of the mind and the heart and the soul as well. It had been cruel, painful, and humiliating. She realized how lucky she had been to escape before he had committed that final act, and a small series of shivers rippled over her, and her anger surfaced yet again.

And yet his violence with her *had* shocked her into reality, brought her back to life, released the dam of her grief, destroyed the shell she had so carefully and deliberately built around her. But the carapace had cracked open, and she was permitting herself to crawl out of it, to come back into the real world, to live again. Yes, she wanted to start afresh, to move forward, to put the past behind her, to look ahead to the future. Don't look back, forge ahead, Emma had always said to her. And that was what she must now do.

It was dawn when Paula finally fell asleep.

She slept deeply, as if she had been drugged. Not once during the night did she awaken and sit up in sudden fear, crying out in terror as she felt herself being buried alive under tons of cold snow that brought with it icy death.

The nightmare that had haunted her nights for so long had been exorcised, along with so many ghosts, so many troubled memories.

When she arose the following morning, after only a few hours of rest, she discovered she felt lighter, freer. It seemed as if a great weight had been lifted, and she recognized then that the guilt she had carried had started to dissolve. That too would disappear entirely . . . one day in the future.

A new strength came into Paula as she dressed to go to the store on Fifth Avenue. And with that strength came a steadiness, a calmness, and a sure and thrusting knowledge that reached deep into her heart. She knew where she must go, what she must do, and as she stood in front of the mirror she nodded to herself. Her way *was* clear. She was about to set out on a new road.

——— *Fifty-Six* ———

He sat on one of the ancient ruined walls of Middleham Castle, daydreaming on this warm Sunday afternoon in September.

The high-flung canopy of the sky was a pewter color, overcast and presaging rain, despite the sun which was valiantly trying to push through. It finally emerged from behind the bank of cumulus, and great rafts of brilliant silver light streamed across the heavens.

Shane lifted his head, looked up, was struck at once by the supernatural quality of that blinding light. It seemed to emanate from some hidden source behind those wild implacable hills, and it held a shimmering clarity, a pure radiance that was unearthly, made him catch his breath.

His dark brooding eyes swept across the sky, and then he glanced away, focused his attention on the ruined arch of Warwick's once great stronghold, his mind turning inward. He was lonely and alone, and yet he knew within his heart that he would find a measure of peace here in Yorkshire. He had made a decision when he had flown home from New York with Winston, at the beginning of this past week.

Shane O'Neill was going to end his long, self-imposed exile at last. There was too much pain in his life now to bring additional pain on himself, and that he would surely continue to do if he persisted in exiling himself. When he was not traveling the world, he would live here, surrounded by the beauty he had grown up with and which he so dearly loved. It was the one spot on this earth where he felt truly happy.

It would be hard for him at first, but he would manage somehow. He was a man, mature, intelligent, and he had always been strong. Somewhere he would find the courage to create a new life for himself without her. And he fully intended to live out that life here.

War Lord was tethered nearby, and he whinnied. Shane swung his head, looked about, expecting to see hikers or tourists. But he was still entirely alone. The ruined castle was deserted today, and there was little sign of life except for the occasional call of a kingfisher or a curlew, the *gawk-gawk* cry of a seagull which had flown in from the North Sea. His eyes lifted to the rolling moors, ranged up against the skyline, glorious today as the heather bloomed and rippling below were the lush green slopes of the Dales.

Shane sat there for a long time, feasting his eyes on the landscape, enjoying its stunning beauty. The grandeur and majesty of this place never failed to touch his Celtic soul, which was so atuned to nature.

Suddenly he blinked, lifted his hand to shade his eyes. He saw a speck moving across the line of the hills, coming steadily down the bridlepath, heading in the direction of the castle.

When the lone horse and rider drew close, he stiffened on the wall and stared ahead, focusing his vision.

The rider was a young woman. She trotted at a brisk pace, handled the horse beautifully, showing great equestrian skill. Her long dark hair was blowing in the light breeze, streaming out behind a pale intense face.

In the passing of a moment, he felt his heart leap and begin to clatter abnormally against his rib cage. The rider was spurring the horse forward. He recognized his own mare, Celtic Maiden, and he knew that girl, so clearly visible in that shimmering northern light that washed the sky and the hills and the castle walls with its penetrating radiance.

It was his dreamlike child of his childhood dreams . . . riding through the dreamlike landscape of his childhood dreams . . . riding through the sunlight and the shadow . . . drawing nearer . . . nearer . . . nearer . . . raising her hand in greeting. His dreamlike child of his childhood dreams was coming to him . . . at last. But she had grown to womanhood now . . . as he was a man now . . . she was the dreamlike woman he loved, had always loved, would always love until the day he died.

The thud of the hooves on the rich dark earth drowned out the clattering of his heart. Slowly, disbelievingly, he rose from the wall, his eyes full of questions. But his face was still and without expression.

She swung down out of the saddle lightly, threw the reins over the tree stump where War Lord was tethered, took a step toward him, and stopped.

"I thought you were in New York," Shane heard his voice say. He was surprised that he sounded so controlled, so normal.

"I took the overnight flight from Kennedy to Manchester on Friday. Tilson picked me up yesterday and drove me back home . . . to Pennistone Royal."

"I see." Shane stepped back involuntarily, sat down on the wall, feeling weak.

She joined him on the old graystone wall and studied him for a long moment.

Neither of them spoke.

Finally Shane said, "What's happened to your face?"

"I fell. It's nothing."

"What are you doing here?"

"I came looking for you. Randolph told me where you were. I came to ask you something, Shane."

"Yes?"

"Would you please give me the ring . . . the ring Blackie gave to Emma?"

"You can have it if you want, Paula. She should have left it to you in the first place."

"No. She meant you to have it. *She* never made mistakes like that. And I wasn't asking you to give me the ring as . . . you know, as a gift." She hesitated only for the briefest second. "I want you to give it to me as your future wife."

He gaped at her.

She smiled at him.

Paula's uncanny violet eyes grew enormous in her pale face. "I want to spend the rest of my life with you, Shane. If you still want me."

He was incapable of answering. He put his arm around her and held her close to his shaking heart. And then he began to kiss her hair, her eyes, and finally her soft and tender lips. The kiss was deep and passionate, yet there was tenderness in it and a depth of feeling that sprang from the recent pain they had both endured.

They sat for a long time on the ruined wall of Middleham Castle, their arms around each other. They did not speak, lost for a while in their own thoughts.

Paula felt safe at last now that she was with him. She would never leave him again. They would be together always until the end of their days. They belonged together, were part of each other.

Shane, his eyes scanning the gaunt bleak silhouette of the castle, was filled with a sense of timelessness that he always experienced here. And then slowly he was enveloped in a new and wondrous peacefulness, and he knew it would never leave him now that she was to live with him for the rest of his life.

Paula murmured, "If only Blackie and Emma knew . . . if only they could see us together."

He looked into her face and smiled, and then he lifted his eyes to the dark hills, resplendent in that extraordinary supernatural light, his glance sweeping across the sky.

Then the Celt in him rose up, and he reached out and touched her face with gentleness. "Perhaps they can, Paula," Shane said, "perhaps they can."

To Be the Best

For Bob
who is.
With my love.

CONTENTS

———✦———

Prologue 479

Lovers and Strangers 485

Saints and Sinners 627

Winners and Losers 691

Epilogue 759

PROLOGUE

To be on my team, you've got to be the best.
And to be the best, you've got to have character.
Emma Harte in *A Woman of Substance*

Paula left Pennistone Royal just before dawn.

It was still dark as she eased the car out of the tall iron gates and turned left, heading for the moors. But as she came up onto the road which cut through the Pennine Chain of hills, the sky was already beginning to change. Its blurred mass of anthracite grays was giving way to amethyst and pink and a cold and fading green, and on the far horizon the first rays of the sun shimmered like shards of silver against the dark rim of the moors. It was an eerie hour, neither day nor night, and the silent spacious moors seemed emptier and more remote than ever. And then unexpectedly there was a sudden burst of radiance and that crystalline light so peculiar to the north of England filled the entire sky and day finally broke.

Paula rolled down the window and took a deep breath, then leaned back in the seat, relaxing as she pushed the car forward at a steady speed. The breeze that blew in was cool, but then it was always cool up here on the "tops" whatever the time of year and hardly the right place to gauge the weather. She knew it would be a scorching day again, and she was glad she had set out for Fairley early.

It was the end of August when the heather always blooms in Yorkshire and the wild, untenanted moors were glorious. Grim and daunting for most of the year, they were breathtaking in their beauty this morning, a sea of violet and magenta rippling under the wind, rolling ahead as far as the eye could see. On an impulse Paula stopped the car and got out, glancing around, filling her eyes. The landscape was awesome . . . stunning. She felt her throat tighten with emotion. Grandy's moors, she murmured, thinking of Emma Harte. I love them just as much as she did . . . as my own daughters, Tessa and Linnet, have grown to love them too.

Paula stood for a moment by the car, savoring her surroundings, looking and listening. She could hear the sharp trilling of the larks as they soared and wheeled high on the clouds and in the distance was the tinkling of water as a little beck rushed down over rocky crags, and on the cool and lucent air were the mingled scents of heather and bilberry, wildflowers and bracken. She closed her eyes briefly, remembering so many things, and then she lifted her head and looked up. The inverted bowl of a sky was China blue and filled with white puffball clouds and brilliant sunshine. The beginning of a pretty day, she thought, smiling inwardly. There is nowhere like the moors when the weather is beautiful, nowhere in the whole world. It was a long time since she had been up here. Too long really. My roots are here, just as Grandy's were, she thought, lingering a moment longer, the memories flooding her fully, carrying her back . . .

Abruptly, Paula turned away, got into her Aston Martin DB 2-4, and drove on, following the winding moorland road for another hour until it finally started its descent into the valley below, and Fairley. Because it was so early, the village still slumbered. The streets were entirely deserted. Paula parked in front of the ancient gray stone church with its square Norman tower and stained-glass windows, then she alighted, went round to the passenger door, and opened it. She had wedged the cardboard box on the floor near the seat, and now she lifted the vase of summer flowers out of the box and closed the door with her knee.

Carrying the vase with both hands, she pushed through the lych-gate that led into the cemetery adjoining the church.

Her steps carried her down the flagged path until she came to the far corner, secluded, bosky, infinitely still. Here, near the ancient moss-covered stone wall and shaded by a gnarled old elm tree, were a cluster of graves. For a while she stood staring at one headstone.

Emma Harte was the name engraved upon the dark green marble, and below were the dates *1889–1970*.

Eleven years ago, Paula thought. She died eleven years ago today. Whatever has happened to the time? It has spun away from me so fast . . . it seems like only yesterday she was alive and vigorous and running her business and ordering us all around in her inimitable way.

Moving closer to her grandmother's grave, Paula bent down, placed the flowers on it, then straightened and stood motionless with one hand resting on the headstone, staring out toward the distant hills. There was a reflective look in her eyes, and she was lost for a moment in the sweep of her thoughts.

I've got to do something, Grandy, something drastic you wouldn't like. But I'm certain you'd understand my reason . . . that I want to create something of my own. If you were in my position you'd do exactly the same thing. I know you would. And it'll come out right. It must. There is no room for doubt.

The striking of the church clock split the silence like thunder, made Paula start, and brought her out of her reverie with a jolt.

After another moment or two she turned away from Emma's grave and let her eyes roam over the other headstones. They came to rest on David Armory's, then moved on to regard Jim Fairley's . . . her father . . . her husband . . . who had lain here for ten years. They had both been far too young to die. Sadness struck at her with such sharpness she caught her breath in surprise and her heart filled with an old familiar ache. She steadied herself, spun around, and continued along the path, clamping down on the pain and sadness the memories engendered in her. She reminded herself that life was for the living.

Paula broke her rapid pace only once, when she passed the private plot which stood close to the church. Encircled by iron railings, it was filled with the graves of Jim's forebears . . . Adam and Adele . . . Olivia . . . Gerald. So many Fairleys . . . just as there were so many Hartes buried here. Two families whose lives had been entwined for three generations . . . bound together in a bitter feud . . . and in love and hate and revenge and marriage . . . and finally in death. Here they lay, together in their eternal resting place under the shadow of the windswept moors, at peace at last in this benign earth . . .

As the lych-gate clicked behind her, Paula straightened up, threw back her shoulders, and hurried to the car, a new determination in her step, a new resoluteness in her expression. There was so much ahead of her, so many challenges, so much she had to accomplish.

She got into the car and settled herself comfortably for the long drive ahead of her.

The tape was on the passenger seat where she had placed it earlier that morning in readiness for the journey. After slipping it into the player in the dashboard, she turned up the volume. The strains of Mozart's *Jupiter* Symphony filled the car . . . rich, melodious, so full of spirit and vivacity and, for her at least, a soaring hope. It was one of her favorites. Tessa had bought the tape for her a few weeks ago. It was the latest recording. Herbert von Karajan conducting the Berliner Philharmoniker. Paula shut her eyes, letting the music wash over her, thrilling to the first movement . . . *allegro vivace* . . . it made her feel . . . uplifted.

A moment passed, and then another, and she opened her eyes finally, turned on the ignition, and coasted down the hill, making for the Leeds-Bradford Road, which would lead her onto the M1, the motorway going south to London. She swung onto it thirty minutes later and saw at once that the traffic was light. There were only a few stray cars on the road and no trucks at all. If she was lucky and continued to have a clear run, she would be sitting behind her desk at Harte's in Knightsbridge within four hours.

Picking up speed, Paula roared ahead, her foot hard down on the accelerator, her eyes fixed on the road.

The symphony swelled to a crescendo, fell away, rose again, enveloping her in its beauty, transporting her with its magic. She experienced a surge of real happiness. Her mind was vividly alive. She could see the months ahead very clearly, knew with a sureness that thrust deep into her soul that she was right in everything she intended to do.

She increased her speed. The Aston Martin flew forward along the motorway as if it had wings and were airborne. She was enjoying the feel of this superb piece of machinery under her hands, enjoying the sense of control she felt . . . control of the car, of herself, of the future. She had made her plan. *Her master plan.* She intended to execute it as soon as possible. It was watertight. Nothing could possibly go wrong . . .

Lovers and Strangers

Call no man foe, but never love a stranger.
                                    Stella Benson

Be not forgetful to entertain strangers:
for thereby some have entertained angels unawares.
                                    The Bible: Hebrews

My true-love hath my heart, and I have his,
By just exchange one for the other given:
I hold his dear, and mine he cannot miss,
There never was a better bargain driven.
                                    Sir Philip Sidney

One

Paula walked into her private office at the London store with her usual briskness, and after removing several folders from her briefcase, she sat down at the
antique partners' desk in the corner. It was precisely at this moment that she
noticed the buff-colored envelope propped against the antique porcelain lamp.

Marked PERSONAL, it had apparently been hand-delivered, and she
recognized the writing at once. She felt a small shiver of pleasure. Eagerly, she
reached for the envelope, slit it open with the gold-and-jade paper knife, and
took out the folded piece of paper.

The note was boldly penned.

Meet me in Paris. Tonight, it said. *You're booked on Flight 902. British Airways.
6 p.m. I'll be waiting impatiently. Usual place. Don't disappoint me.*

Paula frowned. The tone was peremptory, commanding, and implicit in
his words was the assumption she would go. Mild irritation at his high-handed-
ness flared and diluted the flush of pleasure she had experienced a second
before. Of course she wouldn't go. She couldn't. She must spend the weekend
with her children as planned, *wanted* to spend it with them, in fact.

Still clutching the note, she leaned back in the chair and gazed into space,
thinking about him. Bossy . . . conceited . . . those were the adjectives
which sprang into her head. They were certainly appropriate. A trace of a smile
surfaced, flickered on her mouth. She was suddenly amused by the invitation
and sorely tempted to accept. Admit it, you'd love to spend the weekend in
Paris with *him.* But then you'd love to do a lot of things you constantly pass up,
a small voice at the back of her head reminded her. And she smiled again,
though this time with wryness, a hint of regret even, knowing that she could
never be indulgent with herself. Perish the thought! Duty had to come first.
That little rule of Emma Harte's had been inculcated in her since childhood,
although sometimes she wished her grandmother had not been so thorough.
But Grandy had schooled her well, had taught her that wealth and privilege also
meant responsibilities, and that they had to be shouldered without flinching, no
matter what the cost to oneself. And since she was now thirty-six, almost
thirty-seven, her character was hardly likely to change at this stage in her life.

Paula sat up, slipped the note back into its envelope, sighing under her
breath as she did. A romantic interlude in her favorite city with that very special
and exceptional man was infinitely appealing but decidedly not possible. No,
she would not go to Paris for a weekend of love and intimacy and pleasure.
Instead, she would go to her children and be a good mother. Her children
needed her. After all, she had not seen them for two weeks. On the other hand,
she had not seen him either . . .

"Damn and blast," she muttered out loud, wishing he had not sent the
note. It had thrown her off balance, made her feel unexpectedly restless, and at

a moment in time when she could not afford to have distractions of any kind. The months ahead were going to be extremely complicated, and they would be crucial months.

And so she would phone him later, tell him she was not coming; she must also cancel the airline reservation he had made for her. On second thought, perhaps she ought to call British Airways immediately.

As she reached for the telephone it began to ring.

She picked up swiftly, said, "Hello?" and glanced at the door as her assistant, Jill, hurried in with a cup of coffee.

"Hello, Paula, it's me," her cousin Alexander was saying at the other end of the phone. "I came into the Leeds store looking for you, only to find that on the *one* day I'm up here, *you're* in London."

"Oh Sandy darling, I *am* sorry to have missed you," she exclaimed, then covered the mouthpiece, murmured her thanks to Jill, who placed the coffee in front of her, smiled, and disappeared.

Paula went on, "Were you in Yorkshire last night?"

"Yes. I got in around six-thirty."

"I was still at the store, Sandy. You should've called me. We could've had dinner."

"No, we couldn't. You see, I had to get out to Nutton Priory as early as possible. My estate manager's going off on holiday today and we had a lot to go over." Alexander paused, cleared his throat. "You were at Grandy's grave this morning . . . those *are* your flowers, aren't they, Paula?"

"Yes," she said, her voice growing softer. "I went there very early, before driving to London."

"I was close on your heels." He laughed faintly. "I suppose we just weren't meant to meet up today. Well . . . my loss."

Paula loved her cousin dearly and thus was sensitive to his moods. She had caught something odd in his voice, a nuance that disturbed her. "Sandy, do you have some sort of problem?" she asked quickly. "Do you want to talk to me about anything?"

There was only the slightest hesitation before he exclaimed with a certain firmness, "No, no, not at all! I merely thought it would be nice for us to lunch together, I haven't seen you for weeks. I realize you've been busy . . . however, I do miss our tête-à-têtes, old thing."

Paula had been listening attentively, straining to catch that peculiar inflection she had noticed a moment ago, but now it was absent. His voice sounded perfectly normal—well-modulated and controlled, as it always was.

She said, "Yes, I miss them too, Sandy, and it has been a bit hectic for me this summer, what with all the flying to the south of France and back, and staying ahead of the game with the business. And look here, whilst I have you on the phone there's something I've been meaning to say to you for ages." She took a quick breath, and her voice was a trifle sterner when she continued, "I'm terribly cross with you, Alexander. You've hardly spent any time with us at Cap Martin this year, and it is *your* house for God's sake. Besides, I do think you—"

"You're not the only person who works for a living!" he shot back curtly, then added, in a rush of words, "I've had a lot on my plate, too, you know, so please, Paula darling, don't nag. Emily's become quite the expert at that technique. *She's* beginning to get on my nerves."

"Your sister thinks you don't get enough relaxation. She wants you to take it easy, enjoy life a bit more. And I happen to agree with Emily. Wholeheartedly, I might add."

Ignoring these comments and her reproachful tone, Alexander said, "I expect you're going down to the villa this weekend, aren't you?"

"Yes. I'm catching the nine o'clock plane to Nice tomorrow morning, returning early on Monday. Sandy! I've just had a wonderful idea! Why don't you come with me? You'll enjoy it, you know you will, and the children will be so thrilled to see you. So will Emily."

"I really do have to be at Nutton Priory for the next few days. Honestly I do, Paula. I'd love to join you, but there's far too much that needs my attention on the estate. Look, let's have lunch on Tuesday." His voice was suddenly eager.

"Oh God, I *can't*," she groaned. "I'm taking the Concorde to New York first thing on Tuesday morning, and at the end of the week I'm flying from New York to Sydney. I'll be gone for the whole of September."

"Oh. I see."

His disappointment communicated itself to her so acutely, she exclaimed, "Why don't we make a date now? For October." As she spoke she opened her engagement book, flipped the pages. "How about the first Wednesday in the month?"

"I'm sure it's fine, but let me look at my pocket diary. Hold on, Paula."

There was a clatter as he put down the phone.

Paula lifted her cup, took a sip of the hot coffee.

A moment later, Sandy was back on the line, his voice bright and chipper. "All free and clear, darling. I'll see you in October then. And I'll be looking forward to it."

"Oh so will I! And Sandy . . ."

"Yes?"

"Take care of yourself."

"I will, and you do the same, Paula. My love to everyone at the villa."

After they had hung up, Paula sat drinking her coffee, frowning, and staring at the telephone, her mind on her cousin.

She felt a pang of genuine regret for having let the summer slide by without putting more pressure on him to come to the Riviera with them. On the other hand, would her insistence have done any real good? Most likely not. After all, Emily had been relentless with him since Easter, using all of her not inconsiderable wiles and doing everything in her power to persuade him to join them at the Villa Faviola. He had flown down twice, but only for brief stays and then only to please his sister. This had been quite evident to both her and Emily.

Still, she could not help feeling guilty now, recognizing that she had neglected Alexander of late. There had been so much to cope with this past year; so many things had encroached on her free time, interfered with her various friendships. Sandy had been a casualty of the merciless work ethic she had adopted for herself. Poor Sandy, she hadn't had time for him, that was the sad truth, and she admitted it freely.

Perhaps that was why he had sounded strange. No, that was not the reason at all. The peculiar inflection in his voice, which she knew she had not imagined, had been tension pure and simple. No, it had been strain. Or anxiety? Yes, that was it. *Anxiety*. And it had alerted her to something . . . to trouble.

As she came to this realization, Paula thought, with a sinking feeling: *Everything's not right with Sandy*.

A curious unease took hold of her. It was an odd sensation, one that made her sit up in her chair, and she held herself tensely, worriedly asking herself what could possibly be wrong. Frowning again, she ran things through her mind at the speed of light. There could be nothing amiss at Harte Enterprises. Emily would have known and would have told her. Sandy's health was good. He certainly had no financial problems. And even though he was not wooing anyone special—according to Emily, who knew everything about everyone in the family—he did not appear to lack for female companionship whenever he felt the need of it. His social life was not spectacular. But then again, this seemed to be his preference, the manner in which he chose to live his life these days.

He must often be lonely though, she mused, wishing for the hundredth-or-so time that Sandy had remarried.

After Maggie's death in the avalanche at Chamonix he had been grief-stricken and inconsolable for so long. Then slowly he had pulled out of it, had regained his self-possession, and painstakingly, he had put himself back together. But it was as if he had assembled all of the pieces of himself in a new and wholly different pattern. He had not seemed quite the same ever again.

The avalanche affected us all, Paula reminded herself, thinking in particular of her brother, Philip. He had also been skiing on the mountain that day. But he had been the one family member who had lived . . . the sole survivor. And then there was her mother, who had lost a husband. And *I* lost a father; and my children lost a father. Yes, the avalanche wreaked havoc on the entire family. It damaged us, changed us, and irrevocably so. Each one of us has been decidedly odd ever since . . .

She began to laugh under her breath. And *me* most of all, she thought, as she endeavored to shake off that sense of unease she had felt about her cousin a moment ago. Wasn't she being overly imaginative, perhaps? After all, she and Sandy had been close as children, had remained close over the years. If there truly *was* something troubling him, he would have confided it to her on the telephone. I'm being irrational about this, and unaccountably so, she decided, and made a resolute effort to dismiss her worries about Alexander.

Her gaze came back to the papers on her desk.

The quickest of glances told her there was nothing particularly urgent to be dealt with, and she was relieved. Problems that arose on Fridays usually had a way of impinging on her weekends—and ruining them. This did not matter so much in the winter, but in the summer, when the children were home from their respective schools for a long period, it was distressing for them. They treasured their weekends with her, guarded them jealously, and resented any intrusions on their time, just as she did.

Once she had read the morning's mail and a memorandum from Jill, which detailed suggested structural changes in the Designer Salon, she checked the pile of purchase orders, then reached for the telexes. All had emanated from the New York store and were signed by her American assistant, Madelana O'Shea. They had come in late last night and only one required an answer.

Pulling a yellow pad toward her, Paula began to draft a reply. When this was done, she opened the thickest of the folders she had brought with her from Yorkshire and took out the top sheet of paper. It was the only thing which interested her at this moment. On it were the salient points of her master plan. A single sheet of paper . . . but it was the key to so much . . . the key to the future.

Within seconds she was so immersed in her work, so busy making additional notes on the pad, that all thoughts of her cousin Sandy fled. But months later Paula was to recall this day only too well. She would remember her uneasiness about him with great clarity and vividness, and she would fervently wish she had paid more attention to her intuition. Most of all, she would bitterly regret that she had not pressed him to confide in her. Knowing about his problems would not have enabled her to change the inevitable outcome, but at least she could have revised her travel plans. In so doing she would have been able to help him, simply by being there for him whenever he needed her.

But on this scorching morning in August of 1981, Paula had no way of knowing any of this, and that sense of impending trouble—a foreboding almost —which she had experienced earlier had already been squashed by the force of her will. Also, like her grandmother she had the enviable knack of pushing everything to one side in order to concentrate on her business priorities, and this she now did. Head bent, eyes riveted on the page, she fell deeper and deeper into her concentration, as always so totally absorbed in her work she was oblivious to everything else.

Twenty minutes later, Paula finally lifted her head, stapled her notes together, and put them in the folder along with the single sheet of paper; she then locked the folder in the center drawer of her desk for safekeeping over the weekend. Half smiling to herself, satisfied that she had thought of everything and was prepared for any contingency, she sat holding the key for a split second longer before placing it carefully in her briefcase.

Pushing the chair back, she rose, stretched, walked across the floor, feeling the need to move around. Her body was cramped, her bones stiff from sitting— first in the Aston Martin and then here at her desk. She found herself at the window and parted the curtains, looked down into Knightsbridge below, noticed that the traffic appeared to be more congested than ever this morning, but then Fridays were usually wicked in the summer months.

Turning, Paula stood facing the room, a look of approval washing over her face. From her earliest childhood days she had loved this office, had felt comfortable within its confines. She had seen no reason to change it when she had inherited it from her grandmother, and so she had left everything virtually intact. She had added a few mementos of her own and photographs of her children, but that was the extent of it.

The office was more like a drawing room in an English country house than a place of business, and this was the real secret of its great charm. The ambiance was intentional. It had been created by Emma Harte some sixty-odd years earlier when she had used valuable Georgian antiques and English oil paintings of great worth instead of more prosaic furnishings. Classic chintz fabrics on the sofas and chairs and at the windows introduced glorious color against the pine-paneled walls, while antique porcelain lamps and other fine accessories lent their own touches of elegance and distinction. The decorative look aside, the room was spacious and graceful, and it had a beautiful old Adam fireplace which was always in use on cold days. The office never palled on Paula, and she was delighted when people entering it for the first time exclaimed about its beauty and uniqueness.

Like everything else she did, Grandy got this room exactly right, Paula thought, walking across the threadbare but priceless Savonnerie carpet, drawing to a standstill in front of the carved pine fireplace. She gazed up at the portrait of her grandmother which hung above it, painted when Emma had been a young woman. She still missed her, quite intensely at times, but she had long drawn comfort from the feeling that Emma lived on in her . . . in her heart and in her memories.

As she continued to stare at that lovely yet determined face in the portrait, she experienced a feeling of immense pride in Emma's extraordinary and most singular achievements. Grandy started out with nothing and created one of the greatest business empires in the world . . . what incredible courage she must have had at my age. *I* must have her kind of courage and strength and determination. *I* must not falter in what *I* have to do . . . my master plan must succeed just as her plan did. Paula's mind raced, leaped forward to the future, and she was filled with excitement at the thought of what lay ahead.

She returned to her desk, realizing she must get on with the day's business. She flipped on the intercom. "Jill . . ."

"Yes, Paula?"

"My things *were* brought up from the car, weren't they?"

"Some time ago, actually, but I didn't want to disturb you. Do you want me to bring everything in now?"

"Please."

Within seconds Jill's bright auburn head appeared around the door and she hurried through into Paula's office, holding aloft Paula's garment bag in one hand, a suitcase in the other. Jill was tall, well built, an athletic type of young woman, and she appeared to manage these items with the greatest of ease.

"I'll put these in your dressing room," she said, disappearing through the door leading to this adjoining area as she spoke.

"Thanks," Paula murmured, and when her assistant returned to her office, she went on, "Sit down for a minute, would you, please, Jill? I'd like to go over a couple of things with you."

Jill Marton nodded, took the chair on the other side of the desk, sat watching Paula through warm and intelligent brown eyes. Jill had worked for her for over five years and she never ceased to admire her, forever marveling at her extraordinary energy and stamina and drive. The woman opposite her was a powerhouse, not to mention astute and inspired and frequently daring in business. Jill had never worked for anyone like her. Those at the store who had known the legendary Emma said that Paula was a chip off the old block. Jill suspected this was the truth, that the traits she so admired in her boss were inherited from the famous founder of the Harte chain. Yes, it's all in the genes, Jill thought, continuing to observe Paula surreptitiously.

"Ah, here it is . . . your memo about the Designer Salon," Paula said, picking up the piece of paper she had been searching for on the desk.

Jill sat up straighter in her chair, looked at Paula with alertness. "I hope it makes sense to you," she said.

"It does indeed. Your recommendations are excellent. I've nothing to add.

You can put the structural alterations into work immediately and make the other changes as well. They'll do wonders for the salon, Jill."

On hearing this compliment Jill felt vivid color staining her neck and cheeks, and with a flush of pleasure she took the memo which Paula had slid across the highly polished surface between them. She said, "I'm so glad you approve," and beamed.

Paula returned her smile. "Send this telex to Madelana later, and here's the morning mail . . . nothing important, as you already know. You can deal with it easily. I've initialed these purchase orders." She tapped them with a bright red fingernail, then asked, "Now, did any of last week's advertisements come up from the art department yet?"

Jill shook her head. "But they'll be on your desk immediately after lunch. I spoke to Alison Warren earlier, and they're almost ready."

"Good. And speaking of lunch, did Michael Kallinski confirm? Or let you know where I'm supposed to meet him?"

"He called a bit earlier. He didn't want me to bother you, since you'd just arrived when he rang. That's why I didn't put him through. He's picking you up at twelve-fifteen."

"Oh." Paula looked at her watch, rose and walked over to the dressing room, paused at the door, glanced down at her wrinkled cotton pants. "In that case, I'd better change. I want to go out onto the floor, check a few things before Michael arrives, and I don't have too much time. Excuse me, Jill."

"Of course." Jill scooped up the papers on the desk and headed to her own office. "Let me know if you need anything."

"I will," Paula said, closing the door behind her.

The dressing area had been the filing room in Emma's day, but Paula had revamped it, adding floor-to-ceiling closets with mirrored doors, excellent lighting, and a dressing table. She sat down at this, freshened her makeup and brushed her hair, then she slipped out of the shirt, pants, and sandals she had worn for driving from Yorkshire.

Within seconds she was dressed in the clothes she had brought with her in the garment bag: a black silk shantung suit, designed especially for her by Christina Crowther, classically simple, tailored, and smart, worn with a white silk camisole, dark, sheer stockings, and high-heeled black patent pumps. The jewelry she added was equally simple but effective: A three-strand pearl choker with a diamond clasp at the front encircled her neck, and large *mabé* pearl studs ringed with diamonds glittered on her ears.

Staring at herself in the mirror, eyeing her reflection critically, Paula decided she liked the way she looked. The suit was crisp and businesslike without being overly severe and was therefore perfect for the store; it was also chic enough to go to lunch at an elegant restaurant. And no doubt they would be going somewhere smart. Michael always took her to the best places.

The staff elevator whizzed her down to the main floor.

Paula crossed the jewelry department and headed in the direction of cosmetics and perfumery, looking about as she did.

The store was crowded this morning.

But then it was generally thronged with shoppers from the moment it opened its doors at ten until it closed them at six. Over the decades it had become a famous landmark in London, and people from all over the world flocked through its great portals, to walk around its renowned halls and simply *look* as well as to buy the merchandise.

Paula loved the bustle, the activity, the crowds, the high-pitched buzz of the voices, so many of them foreign, the excitement that seemed to hang in the very air. She usually experienced a small thrill when she returned after an absence, however short it had been, and this morning was no exception. The Yorkshire shops were important entities in the chain, just as those in Paris and New York were, but this was the flagship store, and the one she loved the most.

Emma Harte had opened it in 1921.

In three months they would be celebrating its sixtieth anniversary. And what a celebration she had planned. It would be a tribute to her grandmother, one of the greatest merchant princes who had ever lived, as well as a salute to sixty years of superlative retailing and a record unchallenged by any department store, in any city, in any country in the world. Harte's of Knightsbridge was the best. The only one of its kind. A legend.

A sense of exhilaration at being back on this very special territory, her favorite bit of turf, brought an extra spring to her step as she walked into Perfumery and drew to a stop.

Eagle-eyed as always, she stood seeking out imperfections but found none. This pleased her. The area had recently been redesigned under her close supervision, and even though she said so herself, the results were smashing.

Glass panels etched in the manner of Lalique, many mirrors, masses of chrome and silver accents, crystal chandeliers and wall sconces . . . all these elements combined to create a shimmering effect that was stunning. The scheme made the perfect backdrop for the eyecatching displays of cosmetics, perfumes, and beauty products. Opulent, glamorous, inviting, the department was designed to lure women into spending tons of money, and it had succeeded brilliantly, just as she had known it would when it was still on the drawing boards.

Good merchandising and marketing, that's what it's all about, Paula commented to herself, moving on briskly, making a detour through lingerie on the way to the Rayne-Delman shoe salon. She was reveling in her morning walk through her store . . . the finest department store in the world. It was the seat of her power, her strong citadel, her pride and joy. In fact, it was everything to her.

─────────── *Two* ───────────

For the second time that morning the portrait of Emma hanging in Paula's office was undergoing a close and fixed scrutiny.

The man who had just drawn to a standstill in front of it was in his late thirties, fair-haired with light blue eyes and a summer tan. He stood about five feet eight, but appeared taller because of his lean, trim build. Also, his clothes added to the illusion of height. He wore a white shirt and a burgundy silk tie, and his dark blue suit, made of the finest imported raw silk, was so flawlessly cut, so unerringly tailored, it hung on him perfectly, obviously a work of art from Savile Row.

His name was Michael Kallinski and he stood examining the alluring face captured in oils on the life-sized canvas, his eyes narrowed in concentration as he ruminated on the formidable Emma Harte.

It suddenly struck him as quite curious that a woman who had been dead for over a decade—eleven years to this very day to be exact—was always spoken about as if she were still alive, and by most people at that, not merely her immediate family. He supposed that someone of Emma's charisma and brilliance, who had made such a vivid and powerful impact in her lifetime, *would* be on the short list for immortality. After all, the dent she had made on the world—in her personal relationships, in international business, and through her many philanthropies—was enormous.

Michael stepped back, tilted his head to one side, trying to ascertain how old Emma had been when she had sat for this portrait. Most probably in her late thirties, he decided. With her chiseled features, flawless complexion, reddish-gold hair, and those extraordinary green eyes, she had been a great beauty as a young woman, there was no doubt about that whatsoever.

Little wonder his own grandfather had been madly in love with her those many years ago, and ready and willing to leave his wife and children for her— according to Kallinski family gossip, at any rate. And from what he understood from his father, David Kallinski had not been the only man to fall under her mesmeric spell. Blackie O'Neill had apparently been bewitched by her, too, in their youth.

The Three Musketeers. That's what Emma had called them—his grandfather, Blackie, and herself. In their early days together, at the turn of the century, they had been considered an unlikely trio . . . a Jew, an Irish Catholic, and a Protestant. Seemingly they had not paid much attention to what people thought of them or their friendship, and they had remained close, almost inseparable, throughout their long lives. And what an unbeatable trio they had proven to be. They had founded three impressive financial empires which straddled half the world and three powerful family dynasties which only went from strength to strength with the passing of time.

But it had been Emma who had been the real mover, the doer and the shaker, always pushing ahead with vision and enterprise, the two men following her lead. Anyway, that was the way his father told it, and Michael had no reason to disbelieve him. And he knew from his own experience of her that Emma had been absolutely unique. As far as the younger members of the three clans were concerned, she had certainly left her imprint on each one of them, himself included. Her indelible stamp, his father called it.

Michael smiled to himself, remembering exactly how Emma had been thirty-odd years ago . . . rounding them up as children and carting them off to Heron's Nest for the spring and summer holidays. They had called her "The General" behind her back, and the house in Scarborough had been affectionately referred to as "the army camp." She had put them through their paces and instilled in them her own philosophy of life, had taught them the meaning of honor and integrity, the importance of the team spirit and playing the game. And all through the years of their growing up she had given unstintingly of her love and understanding and friendship, and they were better people now for having known her then.

A look of love washed over his face, and he touched his hand to his forehead, giving the portrait a small salute. She had been the very best

. . . just as her granddaughters were the best. A rare breed, the Harte women, all of them, and most especially Paula.

The sound of the door opening prompted him to swing around quickly. His face lit up at the sight of Paula.

"I'm sorry to have kept you waiting!" she exclaimed, looking apologetic, hurrying forward to greet him.

"You didn't, I was early," he replied, going to meet her in the center of the floor. He gave her a huge bear hug, then held her away, stared down into her face. "You're looking wonderful." He glanced over his shoulder at the portrait, then brought his gaze back to hers. "And you're beginning to resemble *that* legendary lady more than ever."

Paula groaned, gave him a look of mock horror as they drew apart.

"Oh God, Michael, not you too! *Please.* There are enough people who call me the Clone behind my back without *you* giving voice to the idea." She shook her head. "That's all I need from a dear friend . . ."

He burst out laughing. "I sometimes think you're all clones, actually. The lot of you . . . Emily and Amanda, as well as you." He swiveled to face the portrait. "And when was that painted, by the way?"

"In 1929. Why?"

"I'd been trying to figure out how old Emma was when she sat for it."

"Thirty-nine. It was started and finished just before her fortieth birthday."

"Mmmm. I guessed as much. And she *was* beautiful then, wasn't she?" Not giving Paula a chance to reply, he went on, with a small grin, "Do you realize that you and I would have been related if David *had* left my grandmother Rebecca and run off with Emma?"

"Let's not get into all that history today," she said with a light laugh, moved rapidly toward the desk, sat down, and added, "Anyway, I feel as if we are, don't you? Related, I mean."

"Yes."

He followed her across the room, seated himself in the chair facing her.

There was a brief silence, then he remarked quietly, "Blood might *not* be thicker than water as far as some families are concerned, but it is when it comes to the three clans. Our grandparents would've killed for each other, and I think their kind of loyalty has been passed down to our generation, hasn't it?"

"I should say so—" She cut herself short when the phone rang, and she reached to answer it. After saying hello and listening for a second she put her slim, tapering hand over the receiver, explained, "It's the manager of the Harrogate store, I'll only be a minute."

He nodded, sat back in the chair, waiting for her to finish her call, quietly studying her as he had studied the painting only a few minutes before.

Michael Kallinski had not seen Paula for over two months, and because he had been away, her uncanny resemblance to Emma had struck him more forcibly than ever when she had walked in. Her coloring was different from Emma's, of course. Paula had hair as black as pitch and eyes of the deepest darkest blue. She had inherited Emma's clear, finely wrought features, though, and the famous widow's peak, which was extremely dramatic above those large eyes set wide apart. With the passing of time the two women seemed to merge more and more, to become identical, to him at least. Perhaps it had something to do with the expression in Paula's eyes these days, her mannerisms, her pithiness, the way she moved—swiftly, always in a hurry—and the habit she had of laughing at her misfortunes. These characteristics reminded him of Emma Harte, just as her attitude in business did.

He had known Paula his entire life and yet, oddly enough, he had not really known her until they were both in their thirties.

When they had been children he had not liked her one little bit, had considered her to be cold, standoffish, and indifferent to them all, except for her cousin Emily, that roly-poly pudding of a child whom she had forever mothered, and Shane O'Neill, of course, whom she had always striven to please.

Privately, Michael had called her Miss Goody Two Shoes, because she had been just that, a child who appeared to have no faults whatsoever, one who was always being clucked over, praised, and held up as an example to them by their respective parents. His brother Mark had had his own name for her . . . Paragon of Virtue. He and Mark had secretly laughed at her, made fun of her behind her back, but then again, they had scoffed at *all* the girls from the clans, had never wanted to spend time with them, had preferred to be roistering around with the other boys. They had banded together with Philip, Winston, Alexander, Shane, and Jonathan, who had been their boon companions in those days.

It was only in the last six years that he had come to know Paula and he had discovered that this shrewd, hardworking, and brilliant woman hid a deep emotional side behind her cool air and her inbred refinement. The aloof manner was merely an outward manifestation of her shyness and natural reserve, those traits he had so misunderstood in childhood.

Discovering that Paula was quite different than he had believed her to be had come as something of a shock to him. To his astonishment, he found she was so very, very human. She was vulnerable, loving, fiercely loyal, and devoted to her family and friends. Terrible things had happened to her over the past ten years, devastating things which would have felled most other people, perhaps even destroyed them. But not Paula. She had suffered deeply, yet had found strength from adversity, had become a most compassionate woman.

Since they had been working together they had drawn closer, and she was his staunch supporter in business and an ally in every way, whenever he needed one. It occurred to Michael now that he would not have been able to cope with his messy divorce and his dreadful personal problems without Paula's friendship. She was always willing to listen to his woes at the end of the phone, or make herself available for a drink or a meal when the going really got tough. She had cornered a special place in his life, and he would be forever grateful that she had.

For all her success and sophistication and self-confidence, there was something about Paula—an endearing little-girl quality—which tugged at his heart, made him want to do things for her, want to please her. Frequently he went out of his way to accomplish this, as he had in New York recently. He wished the interminable phone call from the Harrogate store would come to an end so that he could impart his news.

Suddenly it did.

Paula put down the receiver, made a little moue.

"Sorry about that," she apologized. Leaning back in the chair, she went on, in an affectionate tone, "It's lovely to see you Michael . . . and how was New York?"

"*Terrific. Hectic.* I was up to my neck with work, since our business is going well over there right now. Still, I also managed to enjoy myself, even had a few weekends out in the Hamptons." He leaned closer to the desk. "Paula—"

"Yes, Michael?" she cut in, eyeing him astutely, alerted by the urgency in his voice.

"I think I may have found it . . . what you've been looking for in the States."

Excitement flew onto her face. She sat forward slightly, her eagerness only too apparent. "Private or public?"

"Private."

"Is it for sale?"

"Isn't everything—if the price is right." There was a hint of mischief on his face as he held her eyes.

"Come on, don't tease me!" she exclaimed. "Is it actually *on* the market?"

"No, it isn't. But what does that mean in this day and age of the takeover? The owners can be approached . . . it doesn't cost anything to do that."

"What's the name of the company? Where is it? How big is it?"

Michael chuckled. "Hey, steady on, I can only answer one question at a time. The company is called Peale and Doone and it's in the Midwest. It's not big, only seven stores . . . suburban stores. In Illinois and Ohio. But it's an old company, Paula, founded in the 1920s by a couple of Scotsmen who settled in the States and at first dealt only in Scottish imports. You know, woolen goods, tartans and plaids, cashmeres and the like. They extended their inventory during the forties and fifties. But the merchandise is supposedly stodgy and the company's in the doldrums, management-wise that is. Quite solid financially, or so I've been led to understand."

"How did you hear about Peale and Doone?"

"Through a lawyer friend who's with a Wall Street law firm. I'd asked him to be on the lookout for a chain and he heard about this company through a colleague in Chicago. My chap thinks they're ripe for a takeover."

Paula nodded. "Who holds the stock?"

"The heirs to Mr. Peale and Mr. Doone."

"There's no guarantee they'd sell, Michael."

"Correct. On the other hand, often stockholders don't *know* they want to sell until they're actually approached to do so."

"That's true, and it's worth investigating further."

"You bet it is, and although this chain is small, it might well be perfect for you, Paula."

"It's just a pity the stores are in the boondocks," she murmured, and with a grimace, thinking out loud. "Big cities like Chicago and Cleveland would be more my speed."

Michael gave her a sharp stare. "Look here, with your flair and expertise you can easily put your own special cachet on any store *anywhere,* and you *know* that. Besides, what's wrong with the boondocks? There's plenty of money to be made out there."

"Yes, you're quite right," she answered quickly, suddenly realizing she may have sounded ungrateful after the effort he had made on her behalf. "Can you get some more information, please, Michael?"

"I'll ring my friend in New York later in the day and ask him to pursue this further."

"Does he know you were inquiring about retail chains for *me?*"

"No, but I can tell him if you like."

Paula said very briskly and firmly, "No. I think not. At least not for the moment, if you don't mind. It's better no one knows. The mention of my name could send the price skyrocketing. *If* there's going to be a price, that is."

"Point well taken. I'll keep Harvey in the dark for the time being."

"Please . . . and thank you, Michael, for going to all this trouble for me." Her smile was warm, sincere, as she added, "I really do appreciate it."

"I'll do anything for you Paula, anything at all," he replied, his eyes filling with affection for her. Then he glanced down at his watch. "Oh, it's getting late! We'd better be going," he announced and promptly stood up. "I hope you don't mind, but the old man's invited himself to lunch."

"Of course I don't mind," she said, her voice rising slightly. "You know I adore Uncle Ronnie."

"And the feeling is mutual, I can assure you." He threw her an amused look. "The old man dotes on you . . . he thinks the sun shines out of you."

She picked up her black patent bag and moved across the room. "Come on then, let's go. We don't want to keep him waiting, do we?"

Michael took her arm, escorted her out of the office.

As they went down in the elevator he could not help thinking about his father and Paula, and their special relationship which had developed over the past few years. The old man treated her like a beloved daughter, whilst she seemed to revere him. Certainly she behaved as if he were the shrewdest man alive, which, of course, he was. Dad's become her rabbi, Michael thought suddenly with an inner smile, and also a substitute for her grandmother. Not surprising that some people considered their friendship peculiar and were jealous. Personally, he applauded it. Paula filled a void in his father's life as he did in hers.

Three

Sir Ronald Kallinski, chairman of the board of Kallinski Industries, walked across the impressive marble lobby of Kallinski House at a leisurely pace.

Tall, slender, and a man of dominating presence, he had black wavy hair, heavily frosted with white, and a saturnine face. He had inherited the eyes of his father David and his grandmother Janessa Kallinski; they were of the brightest cornflower blue and seemed all the more startling because of his weather-beaten complexion.

Renowned for never appearing ruffled or disheveled, no matter what the circumstance, he was always perfectly groomed and elegantly attired. This morning he was wearing a charcoal gray three-piece suit with an impeccable white shirt and a pearl-gray silk tie. Although he was almost seventy, he was in such robust health and was so vigorous for his age he looked like a much younger man.

As he strolled through the vast entrance foyer, he nodded graciously to several people who recognized him, and paused to admire the Henry Moore reclining figure in the center, which he had commissioned from the great English sculptor who also happened to be a Yorkshireman born and bred. Sir

Ronald was as proud of his north country origins as he was of his Jewish heritage.

After a brief moment of contemplation in front of the imposing piece of bronze, he continued on his way, pushed through the swing doors, and stepped out into the street. He drew to an abrupt halt after taking only two steps, recoiling as the intense heat hit him. He had not realized how hot the day had become.

Sir Ronald could not abide heat of any kind. Upstairs in his executive suite, a series of handsomely furnished rooms spanning the entire top floor of the giant office complex bearing his name, the atmosphere was icy cold, thanks to the air conditioning that was permanently turned up high and the well-shaded windows. This area of Kallinski House was generally referred to as "Antarctica" by those who occupied it with him. Doris, his secretary of twelve years, had grown used to the freezing temperature by now, as had other executives who had been with him for more than a year or two, and none of them bothered to complain anymore. They counteracted the chill simply by wearing warm sweaters in their offices. Even in winter, Sir Ronald kept the executive suite and his various homes as cold as he possibly dared without eliciting violent protests from staff, family, and friends.

Earlier that morning he had contemplated walking to the Connaught Hotel; now he was relieved he had changed his mind and had ordered his car up from the garage. It was sizzling out here, and oppressive, hardly the kind of weather for sauntering through the busy streets of Mayfair.

His chauffeur had spotted him the instant he had emerged from the building and was already standing stiffly to attention next to the back passenger door.

"Sir Ronald," he said, inclining his head respectfully, and opened the door wider.

"Thank you, Pearson," Sir Ronald responded with a half smile, stepping into the burgundy-colored Rolls Royce. "The Connaught, please."

The car pulled away from the curb and he settled back against the seat and stared absently ahead. He was looking forward to lunching with Paula and Michael. He had not seen her for several weeks and his son had been in New York for over two months and he had missed them both . . . in different ways.

His son was his good right hand, his alter ego, and his favorite. He loved his younger son, Mark, very much; but Michael had a special hold on his heart. He was never quite sure why this was so. How could one explain these things? Sometimes he thought it was because his son was very much like his own father. Not that Michael *looked* anything at all like David Kallinski, being so much more Anglo-Saxon in appearance with his fair complexion and blondish hair. It had to do with a similarity of character and personality, and just as Sir Ronald had enjoyed a marvelous camaraderie with his father until the day of David's death, so did he now with his son. It had been thus ever since the boy's childhood, in fact, and he noticed Michael's absences most acutely these days, was frequently lonely when his firstborn was traveling.

As for Paula, she was the daughter he had never had, or rather, the surrogate for the daughter who had not lived through her childhood. Miriam, their second child, born after Michael and before Mark, would have been thirty-four this year, if she had not died of encephalitis at the age of five. How they had grieved, he and Helen; they had not understood why she had been taken from them at such a tender age. "God works in mysterious ways, His wonders to perform," his mother had said to them at the time, and only in old age had he come to terms with *that* extraordinary belief.

Paula was the smartest woman he had ever known, except for Emma, and he appreciated her sharp and clever mind, her quickness, her business acumen. But she could also be very female at times and he missed her femininity as much as he relished his role as her sounding board and, on occasion, her advisor. He had a lot of admiration for Paula. She was a good mother as well as a successful executive. Hers was a hard road and she trod it most adroitly, rarely ever stumbled.

He wished his daughter-in-law were half as practical and down to earth as she was. The trouble with Valentine was that she lived in another world. She was a bit flighty, and forever discontented. Nothing was ever *enough* for her, or ever *right,* and he understood only too well Michael's feelings. His son's frustration had grown to monumental proportions over the years and the inevitable explosion, when it had come, had been violent. He had not been surprised. He had never approved of Valentine as a wife for Michael, not because she was a *shiksa*—differences in religion scarcely mattered to him—but because she was so shallow, unworthy really. He had always known this, but how did one tell such a thing to a young man in love? In any event, the divorce agreement had been concluded finally, after much bitter wrangling and the exchange of vast amounts of money. Michael, most fortunately, had succeeded in getting what he wanted—a decree *nisi* and joint custody of his three children, the boy, Julian, and the two younger girls, Arielle and Jessica.

A smile softened Sir Ronald's stern face as he thought of his little grand-daughters. If only Helen had lived to see them, it would have made her so happy. But his wife had died eight years ago. He had never stopped missing her, and when he had been given his knighthood by Harold Wilson in 1976, his joy had been tempered by sadness because Helen was no longer with him.

This singular honor had come as a genuine surprise to him. He had never asked for nor sought a title, nor had he tried to buy one by making heavy donations to charity. He *was* philanthropic, and he had his favorite causes, had contributed generously to medical research and the arts, but this had been done discreetly and without fanfare.

To be on the Prime Minister's honors list was flattering, and especially since everyone knew the title had been earned and was therefore deserved. Kallinski Industries was one of the largest and most successful conglomerates in Great Britain, and as such it not only provided much-needed jobs for thousands but was a major exporter of British goods abroad. Ronald Kallinski had devoted his life to bringing the company to its present dominant position, and he was proud of his accomplishments. So was his country apparently, since this was the reason the knighthood had been bestowed upon him.

Sir Ronald was enormously proud of his title. He was not the first York-shire Jew to be knighted; others had been singled out by grateful prime ministers over the years . . . men like Montague Burton and Rudolph Lyons. But nevertheless he prized the honor, as if he *had* been the first, and most especially when he contemplated the Kallinski family's early history, thought of his grandfather Abraham fleeing Russia and the pogroms in the last century, set-tling in the ghetto in Leeds, and eventually opening his tailoring shop in North Street. That little factory turning out piece work for the John Barran Company

—the first ready-made clothiers to start in Leeds after Singer invented the sewing machine—had been the beginning, the nucleus of the billion-pound empire that Kallinski Industries was today.

On the morning of his investiture his one regret had been that Helen, Abraham, his father David, Emma, and Blackie had not been present to share his pride and happiness. The four old-timers in particular would have appreciated the significance of the ceremony at Buckingham Palace, truly understanding how far the Kallinskis had risen since Abraham, the young refugee from Kiev, had first set foot on English soil at Hull in 1880.

The Rolls Royce came to a sudden stop in Carlos Place.

Sir Ronald shook off his thoughts, leaned forward, addressed his chauffeur: "Please pick me up around two-thirty, Pearson," he said as the uniformed doorman outside the Connaught Hotel stepped up to the car, opened the door for him, helped him alight.

They "Sir Ronalded" him to death as he went from the front steps to the dining room, and a faint smile touched his eyes as he was shown to the table his son had reserved. Five years ago he had wondered how he would ever get used to being addressed by his title. But he had—and in no time at all.

After he had ordered a dry sherry, he took a sip of the iced water a waiter had placed before him, then sat back to wait for Paula and Michael.

Sir Ronald did a double take.

Paula and his son were heading across the restaurant in his direction, and she looked so much like Emma at a comparable age it was quite amazing.

He realized, as she drew closer, that she was sporting a new hairdo, and that it was this which underscored her already-pronounced similarity to her grandmother. Her dark glossy hair had been cut short in a sort of sleek bob. It was chic and obviously of the moment, and yet to him it had the look of the 1930s. It brought to mind the film stars of his youth . . . and the elegant Emma he had known and admired as a boy.

He rose, took Paula's outstretched hand in both of his, shared her broad and loving smile, kissed her cheek. They exchanged affectionate greetings, seated themselves next to each other, and at once started chatting animatedly.

Michael went to the other side of the table, took a chair, motioned to the waiter. After Paula and he had ordered aperitifs, he asked for the menus.

Turning to Paula, he said, "You're always in such a hurry, so let's order . . . then we can relax."

"Why not?" she laughed and took the menu from the captain.

The latter hovered next to the table, explaining the specialties of the day, and making his own recommendations. After a cursory glance at their menus, Paula and the Kallinskis followed the captain's advice. All three asked for the cold poached salmon and cucumber salad, and Michael ordered a bottle of Sancerre.

The aperitifs had materialized in front of Paula and Michael whilst they had been ordering lunch, and once the captain had disappeared, Sir Ronald raised his glass. He looked directly at Paula. "To the memory of your grandmother."

"To Emma," Michael toasted.

Paula smiled at them both. "Yes, to Grandy."

They clinked glasses, sipped their drinks.

After a moment, Paula said, "I thought you'd remember what day it is today, Uncle Ronnie."

"We both remembered!" Michael exclaimed.

Sir Ronald remarked, "How could anyone forget the passing of such a great woman. And she'd be so proud of you, my dear. You've never let her down, and you've held her dream wonderfully well."

"I hope so, Uncle Ronnie . . . I've certainly endeavored to guard everything she built . . . and make it stronger."

"And you have," Sir Ronald said, regarding her warmly. "You're as much of a genius at retailing as Emma ever was. You've displayed a great deal of vision over the years, and I can only commend you on everything you've done with the stores."

"Thanks, Uncle Ronnie," Paula said, smiling, enjoying his approval.

"And I second everything Dad says," Michael declared emphatically. He took a sip of his Cinzano Bianco, then winked at her over the rim of his glass.

Paula's violet-blue eyes filled with laughter. "You're prejudiced, Michael. Actually, you both are."

Sir Ronald settled back in his chair, said in a more confidential tone, "One of the reasons I invited myself to lunch is to seek your advice, my dear."

Paula's curiosity was instantly piqued, and she quickly asked, "But how can I possibly advise *you?* Why, you're the wisest person I know, Uncle Ronnie."

He made no response to this remark. It was almost as if he had not heard it. A preoccupied expression invaded his face; he took a sip of his sherry, then gave her a long and careful look. "Ah, but you can advise me, Paula. About Alexander. Or to be more precise, you can give me an opinion." Sir Ronald briefly paused, before asking, "Do you think Sandy would sell Lady Hamilton Clothes to Kallinski Industries?"

This was the last thing Paula had expected to hear, and she was taken aback. She stared at Sir Ronald without speaking for a moment. "I'm quite sure he wouldn't," she said at last in a surprised voice. "That division is far too important to Harte Enterprises. And to Harte stores, for that matter."

"Yes, it had great value to Sandy, and to you too, of course, since the Lady Hamilton line is made exclusively for Harte's," Sir Ronald said.

Michael interjected, "He may want to unload it, Paula—for the right price, and to the right people. Let's face it, Sandy has been terribly overburdened ever since that family debacle, when he fired Jonathan and Sarah. He and Emily really have their hands full, and they have to work awfully hard running Harte Enterprises—"

"Oh, I don't know," she cut in swiftly, "they seem to manage quite well, Michael."

"In any case, we'd be prepared to pay top money for that division," Michael added, determined to get his point across.

"I'm sure you would," Paula replied evenly, "and I'm just as sure Sandy wouldn't even consider it, no matter what you offered." She looked from the younger Kallinski to the older, rapidly and with quickening interest. *"Why* do you want to buy Lady Hamilton Clothes, Uncle Ronnie?"

"We'd like to have our own women's fashion division," Sir Ronald explained. "And to supply your stores with women's ready to wear in much the same way we supply your men's clothing, and to sell to your boutiques in the hotels. Just as importantly, we wish to start to build up a strong export line."

Paula nodded slowly. "I see."

"Obviously, we wouldn't sell the women's fashions in countries where you own retail stores," Michael pointed out. "We're thinking of trading only in Common Market countries—"

"Excluding France," Sir Ronald interrupted, "since you have a store in Paris."

"Oh I know you'd never do anything to damage my business, that goes without saying," Paula murmured. "And I can see why you'd like the acquisition, Uncle Ronnie, it makes a lot of sense."

She glanced at Michael. "But *you* know how conservative Sandy is, and bound by tradition. Those are just two of the reasons Grandy gave him control of Harte Enterprises. She knew it would be safe in his hands because he would never do anything to *weaken* its basic structure. Such as selling off a very, *very* profitable division," she finished dryly, but her mouth twitched with sudden amusement.

Both men laughed.

"Touché," Sir Ronald said.

"Yes, I do know *exactly* what kind of person Sandy is," Michael acknowledged, shifting in his chair. "And that's why I suggested to Dad that we got your reading on the matter first."

At this moment the waiter arrived with the food, and Michael changed the subject. The three of them chatted about inconsequential things for the next few minutes, and once they had been served, the *sommelier* poured the chilled white wine for Michael. After tasting it, he nodded approvingly. "It's excellent," he said to the wine waiter, who immediately proceeded to fill the other glasses.

Sir Ronald and Paula sipped their wine and both of them commented on its fresh dry taste and lightness, and then Sir Ronald put his goblet down. *"Bon appetit,"* he said, and picked up his fork and cut into the poached salmon.

"Bon appetit," Paula and Michael responded almost in unison.

They ate in silence for a while, but at one moment Paula swung her gaze between the two Kallinski men, and asked curiously, "Uncle Ronnie, Michael, why don't you simply start your own women's clothing division? Certainly you've got all the necessary resources."

"We thought of that, my dear," Sir Ronald admitted. "But quite frankly we'd prefer to buy a well-established brand. So much easier, you know. And it would save us an enormous amount of time—and money, of course, in advertising and promoting a new product."

"And surely there must be lots of manufacturers who would jump at the chance to sell to Kallinski Industries!" she exclaimed.

"I'm perfectly certain there are." Sir Ronald gave her a pointed look. "But I'm interested in Lady Hamilton Clothes because it was founded by Emma and my father all those years ago. He had a soft spot for the company long after he sold his shares to your grandmother, and so do I." Sir Ronald smiled wryly, and finished, "I must admit, I do feel rather sentimental about it."

Paula placed an elegant, beautifully manicured hand on Sir Ronald's arm,

squeezed it affectionately. "But Alexander has no reason to sell that division
. . . at least, not one *I* can think of, Uncle Ronnie. His sister's been running it
successfully for a number of years now." Her arched black brows drew together
in a small frown. "Besides, what would she *do* if he sold Lady Hamilton?
Amanda would be out of a job, and Sandy would always take that into consideration. You know how he fusses about her."

"She need not necessarily be out of a job," Michael was quick to announce. "Amanda's terrific at what she does. She'd remain with the company
and run it for us."

Paula made no comment. She toyed with the cucumber salad on her plate,
suddenly acknowledging to herself that if Lady Hamilton were ever up for grabs
Sandy ought to sell it to the Kallinskis. In a way they were entitled to it.

Sir Ronald dabbed his mouth with his napkin and ventured, "I'd like to
pose a hypothetical question, Paula."

"Of course." She looked at him alertly, wondering what was on his mind
now.

He said, "Let us just suppose that Alexander did want to sell Lady Hamilton, was anxious to do so, in fact. *Could he?* Or would he have to go to the
other shareholders, get their agreement?"

"Oh no. There's only Emily, and she would go along with anything her
brother wanted to do. She always has, you know."

Puzzlement flickered in Sir Ronald's eyes and he leaned back in his chair,
regarding Paula thoughtfully. After a second, he said slowly, *"Only Emily . . .*
But surely you told me several years ago that Sarah and Jonathan still owned
their shares in Harte Enterprises, even though they were thrown out of the
company because of their shoddy behavior."

"That's perfectly true, they do. They draw their dividends, receive the
company reports and balance sheets, but they have no power whatsoever. But
then, neither does Emily, now that I think about it."

Sir Ronald appeared to be more baffled than ever.

Recognizing this, Paula said, "Let me clarify things for you, Uncle Ronnie, and for you too, Michael."

Father and son nodded and Sir Ronald said, "Please do, my dear."

"My grandmother left fifty-two percent of Harte Enterprises to Sandy.
The remaining forty-eight percent was split three ways among Emily, Jonathan,
and Sarah, who each received sixteen percent. As chairman of the board and
majority stockholder, Sandy can do virtually anything he wishes in the company, or with it, for that matter. This is the way Grandy set it up. Whilst she
wanted all four of them to draw income from the company, she knew Sandy
must have absolute power to prevent any bickering among the four cousins. She
felt Sandy had earned, and also deserved, the bulk of the shares in her privately
owned company. She gave total control to him because she knew that he would
always abide by her wishes."

"Ah, yes, I can see the sense in everything your grandmother did." Sir
Ronald never failed to be impressed by the late Emma Harte's clever strategy.
He went on, "As usual, Emma was shrewd—and most prudent, I might add.
Certainly Sandy has guided Harte Enterprises through some rough periods and
done admirably well in the past few years."

Quickly Michael said, "Look, Paula, I know you're adamant about Sandy
not being interested in selling, and perhaps you're right. At least about his

attitude at present. But he may well change his mind and decide to pare down Harte Enterprises . . . one day in the future . . .'' Michael paused. There was a speculative expression on his face as he added, *''No?''*

Paula could not help smiling at his dogged persistence. "So you'd like to talk to him anyway, explain that Kallinski Industries are standing in the wings, if ever he decides to get rid of Lady Hamilton Clothes. Is that what you're trying to say?'' she asked with a laugh.

Michael nodded. "That's exactly it. You wouldn't object if Dad did have a word with him, would you, Paula?''

"No, of course not. There's no harm in letting Alexander know about your interest in the division." She swung to the older man. "Are you going to Yorkshire this weekend, Uncle Ronnie?''

"Yes, I am, my dear.''

"Then why don't you drive over to Nutton Priory, and have a chat with him. He's always much more relaxed when he's in the country.''

"I think I shall do that,'' Sir Ronald said. "And my thanks to you, Paula, you've been most helpful.''

Michael flashed her one of his engaging smiles. "Yes, thanks, we really do appreciate your input." He sipped his wine and his light blue eyes grew thoughtful and after a moment he asked, "By the way, just out of curiosity, is Sarah Lowther still married to that French painter? Or don't you hear anything about her anymore?''

"Obviously not directly, since I kicked her out of the family along with Jonathan,'' Paula murmured, the gaiety on her face instantly fading. "But there was a piece on Yves Pascal in a French magazine about six months ago . . . *Paris Match,* I believe. Anyway, amongst the many photographs was one of Sarah and Yves and their five-year-old daughter, Chloe. Seemingly they live in Mougins in the Alpes Maritime. They own an old farmhouse; that's where he has his studio. He's known as the *enfant terrible* of French art, and he's become very big, immensely successful.''

Michael said, "He's a damned good painter actually, although his work's not my cup of tea. Having been raised on the school of French Impressionist painting, all this ultra-modern stuff leaves me utterly unmoved. Give me Monet, Manet, Sisley, and van Gogh any day of the week.''

"Absolutely,'' Paula agreed.

"And talking of Sarah, whatever happened to her partner in crime, Jonathan Ainsley?'' Michael stared at Paula, frowning. "Is he still lurking in the Far East?''

"I believe so, but not even Sandy knows for sure,'' Paula said, her voice low and unemotional. "Friends of Emily's reported seeing him in Hong Kong, and then Singapore on another occasion. Jonathan's dividends and the balance sheets of Harte Enterprises go to a firm of accountants here in London who handle his business seemingly." She made a sour face. "Just so long as he doesn't show up in England, that's all that matters to me. As Emma would have said, *good riddance to bad rubbish.''*

"Christ, yes!'' Michael began to shake his head wonderingly. "I've never been able to understand why he did what he did. He was such a fool—bloody stupid if you ask me. He had everything going for himself and he threw it all away.''

"Perhaps he believed he would never get caught,'' Sir Ronald ventured to

Michael. "But then I'm sure he hadn't bargained for this one here." He glanced at Paula through the corner of his eye, patted her arm, and finished with a chuckle, "He met his match in you, my dear, no doubt about that whatsoever."

Paula attempted to laugh with him but it came out sounding forced and artificial, and for a moment she did not trust herself to speak. She was hating this discussion about Jonathan Ainsley, her cousin, her deadly enemy of long ago.

Michael pressed, "And so nobody in the family knows what he's doing for a living?"

Paula stared at Michael through eyes grown bleak and flat. She gave him a long and careful look, and pursed her lips, a habit she had picked up from her grandmother years before. After a split second, she said with a certain pithiness, "Jonathan Ainsley doesn't have to *earn* a living, since he receives a very sizable income from Harte Enterprises." There was a small pause before she thought to add, "And nobody's ever bothered to find out about his personal or business life . . . because none of us *care* what's happened to him." Now frowning in perplexity, and pinning Michael with her vivid blue gaze, Paula asked testily, "Why the sudden preoccupation with Jonathan anyway?"

"I don't know, I haven't thought about him in years, and now, unexpectedly, I'm riddled with curiosity," Michael admitted with a rueful grin.

"I'm not." Despite the warmth of the Connaught dining room, Paula shivered. She had never forgotten the last words Jonathan had spoken to her . . . *I'll get you for this, Paula Fairley. Sebastian and I will bloody well get you,* he had screamed, shaking his fist at her in the most ridiculous way, like the villain in a Victorian novel. Well, Sebastian Cross could not "get her" since *he* was dead. But Jonathan would if he could. Sometimes she had nightmares about her cousin, nightmares in which he did her terrible harm. He was certainly capable of it. Capable of almost anything. She knew that from their childhood. Once, a few years ago, she had confided her fears in Sandy, who had laughed and had told her to dismiss Jonathan from her mind. Sandy had reminded her that Jonathan was a bully and, like all bullies, a coward. This was true; nevertheless, she had never been able to expunge the memory of the day Sandy had fired him. It was only too easy to recall the baleful look in Jonathan's eyes, the mask of hatred contorting his face, and instinctively, ever since then, she had known he would always remain her unremitting enemy until the day they buried him. Ten years had passed and she had not set eyes on him again, none of them had, in fact, and yet deep down inside her was this small kernel of fear.

Suddenly becoming aware that Michael and Sir Ronald were watching her, were waiting for her to say something, she turned toward Michael. Adopting the lightest of tones, she said, "Master Ainsley turned out to be a bad penny, and the least said about *him* the better."

"Quite so, my dear, quite so!" Sir Ronald muttered. He had grown conscious of the change in her demeanor whilst they had been discussing Ainsley and he decided it would be wise to change the subject. And so he said with a rush of genuine enthusiasm, "I received your invitation to the dinner dance you're giving for the sixtieth anniversary of the store, Paula, and I'm looking forward to it immensely. Now, tell me more about the other celebrations you've planned."

"Oh I'd love to, Uncle Ronnie, I have some really special things coming up—" She cut herself off as the waiter drew to a standstill at the table. "But perhaps we should order dessert first," she went on, accepting one of the menus being thrust at her.

"Splendid idea, and I do recommend the sorbets," Sir Ronald said. "It's really far too hot for anything else, isn't it?"

Paula nodded. "I think that's what I'll have. Michael will you join us?"

"Only coffee for me."

As the waiter went off with their order, Michael's eyes swept over Paula appreciatively. He grinned as he remarked, "It seems to me *you* can eat anything and never put on an ounce . . . I'm afraid I have to watch myself these days."

Paula shook her head and laughed with him. "Oh I don't know, you're trim enough, Michael."

Swiveling to face his father, she now picked up the conversation where they had left off a moment ago, and launched into a recital about the forthcoming events to be held at the Knightsbridge store later that year.

Michael had settled back in his chair, toying with his wineglass. He was only vaguely listening to Paula.

His mind remained focused on Lady Hamilton Clothes and the endless possibilities the company held for them, *if* they were lucky enough to buy it back from Harte Enterprises. Amanda Linde, Sandy's half sister, had been creating the line for a number of years now, and in his opinion she was a far better designer than Sarah Lowther had ever been. Her clothes were easy and comfortable to wear, and yet they had a special kind of elegance because she always managed to give them a touch of the Harte class. Her designs would sell as well in other Continental countries as they did in France, of that he was quite certain.

Sir Ronald and Paula continued to chat about her celebratory plans for the store's anniversary. Their voices were a faint murmur, barely audible against the buzz of the lunchtime crowd in the busy restaurant.

The waiter came back and served the dessert, poured the coffee.

Michael picked up his cup, further ruminating on the talented Amanda. If they bought Lady Hamilton, whether now or in the future, she would have to remain as head fashion designer and managing director. That was an imperative. If she was in any way reluctant to stay on, to work for them, he would have to come up with some special inducements—

Paula's sudden laughter reverberated on the warm air, cut into his myriad thoughts. It was a full, throaty, curiously sexual laugh and it caused Michael to lift his head swiftly.

He glanced across the table at her. She was spooning sorbet into her mouth. A small glob of it clung to her upper lip and she licked it off with the tip of her tongue and went on eating. He watched her, fascinated, and as he did he experienced the most extraordinary physical attraction to her. His reaction unnerved him. Michael held himself perfectly still in the chair, dropped his eyes, and stared into his coffee cup.

When he eventually looked up she had finished the sorbet and her face was averted as she responded to something his father had just said. He blinked, not understanding himself at all. He must be mad to think of Paula in this way.

Brilliant sunshine was pouring in through the window immediately behind her and it encircled her with shimmering light, brought her into focus as if she were under a pinspot on a stage. Her coloring appeared to be more vivid than ever . . . the black hair, the violet eyes, the incomparable skin touched with a faint tan like the golden bloom on a summer peach. How vibrantly alive she was at this moment . . . and how very sexual.

Michael, who had never felt anything but fraternal affection for Paula, was filled with a fierce desire to make love to her. He took a steely hold of his feelings, which had flared so suddenly, and lowered his head, fearful that something would show in his face, that his eyes would betray his lust for her. *Why?* he asked himself. Why do I want to take her to bed *now* after knowing her for so many years? He gazed intently at the small vase of flowers in the center of the table, his face unreadable as he endeavored to quell his emotions.

Sir Ronald was saying, "And I shall be in Paris next weekend, Paula, en route to Biarritz, and if you're going to be over there, visiting the Paris store, perhaps we could dine together."

"No, I won't be in Paris next weekend—" Paula began, and came to an abrupt halt. "Oh damn!" she exclaimed, sitting up jerkily in her seat, frowning, remembering the note on her desk. She had forgotten to cancel the Paris airline reservation which had been made for her for later in the day.

"Is something wrong?" Sir Ronald asked in concern.

"No, no, it's nothing," Paula assured him, making a mental note to telephone British Airways the minute she returned to her office. "I forgot to do something before lunch, but there's no problem, really there isn't, Uncle Ronnie."

Michael, who had managed to extinguish his erotic thoughts about Paula, gave his father a puzzled look. "Why are you going to Biarritz at this time of year, Dad? The season's over."

"Yes, I know it is . . . but I'm going to look at an Imperial Russian Easter Egg by Fabergé," Sir Ronald announced with obvious pleasure.

He beamed at them both. "My art dealer in Paris has a client in Biarritz. A very old lady. A White Russian. She is apparently ready to sell her jeweled egg at long last. And quite naturally, I want to get there first, before the American publisher Malcolm Forbes or any other serious collector hears about it and snaps it up before I do. You know how extremely rare the Fabergé eggs have become." Sir Ronald peered at his watch, clucked to himself, and before Michael had a chance to comment, he rapidly went on, "And that reminds me, I have an appointment at Wartski's in fifteen minutes. Kenneth Snowman recently acquired a cigarette box which belonged to Czar Nicholas the Second. It's by Perchin, one of the greatest of the Fabergé designers, and I promised I would pop in to see it this afternoon."

"I'm delighted for you, Dad, and I hope that you manage to get both items," Michael said with real sincerity, knowing how important collecting these beautiful objects had become to his father. What had begun as a vague hobby had turned into a grand passion. The Kallinski Fabergé Collection was renowned, and was frequently on exhibition with the Sandringham Collection, which had been started by King Edward VII and Queen Alexandra, sister of the Czarina Marie Feodorovna, later added to by Queen Mary and now owned by Queen Elizabeth II.

Michael smiled at his father. "Since you're in a hurry, I'd better get the bill, Dad," he said, and motioned to their waiter.

Sir Ronald glanced at Paula. "If you wouldn't mind dropping me off at Wartski's first, my car can then take you back to the store, my dear."

"Thanks, Uncle Ronnie, that'll be lovely."

"Michael, can I give you a lift too?"

"Oh no," Michael said, suddenly having no wish to be around Paula any longer than was necessary today. "Thanks anyway, Dad, but I prefer to walk."

Four

She went to Paris after all.

It was a sudden decision, made when she returned to the store at three o'clock. She had picked up the phone and begun to dial British Airways, ready to cancel her reservation, when she had changed her mind and had let the receiver drop back into its cradle.

It had been a scramble then to finish her work and stuff several silk dresses into the garment bag and get out to Heathrow to catch the six o'clock plane. She had made it with ten minutes to spare and the flight had been smooth and fast with the wind behind them and exactly one hour and five minutes after takeoff they had landed serenely at Charles de Gaulle Airport.

Her luggage had come through without much delay and she had passed customs quickly and with no fuss, and now she sat comfortably in the back of the chauffeur-driven car he had sent to meet her, being whizzed toward Paris and their rendezvous.

For the first time since lunch at the Connaught with the Kallinskis earlier in the day, Paula began to unwind. And as she did she realized that it had not been such a sudden decision to come here . . . she had known from the first moment she had read his note that she would go to him, hadn't she? Hadn't it been a *fait accompli* even then? Of course it had. But, very simply, she had not wanted to admit this to herself and so she had clouded the issue with thoughts of duty and responsibility.

Paula leaned into the corner of the seat and crossed her long and shapely legs, and a smile flitted across her face as she recalled something her grandmother had said to her many, many years before. "When the right man beckons, a woman will always go running to him, no matter who she is, no matter what her responsibilities are. And no doubt you'll fall into that same trap one day, just as I did when I met your grandfather. You mark my words, Paula," Grandy had remarked in her knowing way. As usual, Emma had been correct.

The smile lingered on Paula's face as she turned her head to glance out of the window. With the hour's difference in time between London and Paris it was now nearly nine and already growing dark.

The car was leaving the Boulevard de Courcelles at a good clip, following the other traffic through the Etoile without slowing, and as it whirled at a dizzying speed around the Arc de Triomphe, that giant monument to a nation's valor, Paula cringed. She wondered how all these fast-moving automobiles, being driven as if they were in a miniature Grand Prix, would make it safely without crashing into each other and creating a major disaster. That seemed to be almost an impossibility.

But suddenly their car was free of the traffic jam, jostling bumpers, screeching tires, and madly hooting horns, and was pulling onto the Champs Elysées, and she caught her breath in delight as she usually did upon seeing this glittering avenue.

Whenever she returned to Paris she remembered the very first time she had come here and all the other times after that, and there was always something of those times caught up in her feeling for it. Memory and nostalgia were woven into her love for the City of Light, her favorite city, the most beautiful city in the world. It was full of evocations of the past and of all those who had been with her and who had made those occasions so very special: Grandy, her mother and father, her brother Philip, Tessa, and her cousin Emily, who had been her dearest companion on so many trips when they had been girls.

He was very much bound up with her remembrances of Paris, too, and in a short while she would be seeing him and she made up her mind not to spoil the weekend by worrying about the children or having regrets that she had changed her plans to be with him instead of them. That would not be fair, and anyway, she had always considered regrets to be pointless and a waste of valuable time.

They were on the Rond-Point now and ahead she could see the Egyptian obelisk built in the reign of Ramses II and transported from Luxor to rest in the immense rectangle of floodlit stone that was the Place de la Concorde. How spectacular the sight was . . . a breathtaking scene that was forever etched in her mind. She felt a sudden thrill of pleasure at being back here, was glad she had told the chauffeur to take the longer route to the hotel.

But within a matter of minutes they were entering the Place Vendôme, that quiet gracious square of perfectly proportioned buildings designed in the reign of Louis XIV, and coming to a standstill in front of the Ritz, and Paula was alighting and thanking the chauffeur and asking him to deal with the luggage.

She moved swiftly through the grand and elegant lobby, down the seemingly endless gallery filled with display cases from Paris shops, making for the Rue Cambon section of the hotel—known as *côté Cambon,* just as the other side where she had entered was called *côté Vendôme.* When she reached the smaller lobby she took the lift to the seventh floor and ran the length of the corridor to his suite. She found she was taut with excitement when she reached the door. It was slightly ajar, in anticipation of her arrival, and she pushed it open, went in, closed it softly, leaned back against it, catching her breath.

He was standing behind the desk, his jacket off, the sleeves of his white shirt rolled up, his dark tie dangling loose around his neck. He was talking on the telephone and he lifted a sunburned hand in greeting, his face lighting up at the sight of her. He paused in what he was saying into the receiver, listened carefully to his caller, and finally said in a low rapid tone, *"Merci, Jean-Claude, à demain,"* then hung up.

They moved toward each other at precisely the same moment.

As she passed the small Louis XV table holding a bucket of champagne and two crystal glasses she gaily twirled the bottle resting in the ice and said in a light voice, *"You* were sure of yourself, sure I'd come, weren't you?"

"Of course," he said, laughing, "I'm irresistible."

"And so terribly modest."

They met in the middle of the room, stood facing each other for a split second.

Quickly she said, "I almost didn't . . . I was worried . . . worried about the children . . . they need me—"

"Madam," he said, "your husband needs you too," and reaching out he pulled her into his arms. He bent down and kissed her deeply on the mouth and she returned his kiss, clung to him, and he held her hard and very tightly for the longest moment after they stopped kissing.

"Oh Shane," she said at last against his chest, "you have me."

"Yes, I know I do," he answered. And then with a deep chuckle he drew away from her, held her by the shoulders, and looked down into her face upturned to his. He shook his head slowly.

"But you're always surrounded," he continued, the residue of laughter clinging to his mellifluous voice. "By children and relatives and secretaries and staff, and I can never seem to get you alone for very long, or have you entirely to myself for a while these days. And that's why I decided early this morning, when I was flying up to Paris for a meeting with Jean-Claude, that we were going to have this weekend together. *Without* our usual encumbrances. A bit of private time for us, before you leave for New York. We're entitled to that, aren't we?"

"Yes, we most certainly are." Paula gave him a small, rueful smile. "Coming in from the airport I vowed I wouldn't say anything about the children, and I've only been here a few minutes and already I've—"

Shane gently placed his hand over her mouth. *"Sssh!* I know how much you wanted to see the kids before going away, and you shall."

"What do you mean?" she asked, giving him a puzzled look.

"Tonight and Saturday belong to us, and then on Sunday morning Kevin will fly us down to the Riviera to spend Sunday and Monday at the villa with the brood. You'll have to go to New York one day later, that's all. On Wednesday instead of Tuesday. Okay?"

"Oh darling, yes, of course! What a marvelous idea and how lovely of you to think of it, to think of pleasing them as well as us," she exclaimed.

He grinned at her. "They're my kids, too, you know."

"But you've been coping alone with them for the last two weeks and you must have had your fill of them by now."

"Only too true . . . in some ways. On the other hand, they've really been looking forward to seeing you, and I don't want them to be disappointed, or you to think I'm an *entirely* selfish sod. So, I'm prepared to share you with our offspring . . . After all, you are going to be gone from us for five or six weeks."

Paula gazed up at him, loving him. "Yes, I am . . ." She paused, hesitated, then asked softly, almost tentatively, "How's Patrick? Is he all right, Shane?" A worried frown knotted her dark brows together and her clear blue eyes turned cloudy and apprehensive.

"He's wonderful, Paula, and as happy as a sandboy enjoying every minute of the day and having lots of fun," Shane reassured her, his tone very positive. "Please, darling, don't *worry* so much." He put his hand under her chin, tilted her face to his, and added, "Patrick manages very well, really he does."

"I'm sorry, Shane, I know I fuss about him, but he's such a little boy and so diffident . . . and different. And the others can be so boisterous at times, and I'm always afraid he'll get hurt when he's out of his usual environment . . ."

She let her sentence trail off, not wanting to express the thought that anything might ever happen to their firstborn child. Patrick, who was seven, was slow, retarded actually, and she could not help being concerned about him when he was not under her sharp and watchful eyes.

Although Shane was equally protective of their son, he was constantly—if gently—chastising her for being overly anxious. Deep down, she knew Shane was right and so she tried very hard to control her anxiety, to treat Patrick as if he were perfectly normal, like his five-year-old sister, Linnet, and his half-brother and half-sister, Lorne and Tessa, the twelve-year-old twins fathered by Jim Fairley.

Shane, observing her carefully, understanding her complex feelings about Patrick, said with a confiding smile, "I haven't mentioned this to you before, but Linnet's become a real little mother while we've all been down at the villa. She's taken Patrick under her very small but very loving wing and, actually, without you around, she's even turned a bit bossy. And you know how Lorne is with Patrick . . . he adores him. So all is well, my darling, and—" Shane broke off at the sound of knocking, exclaimed *"Entrez,"* and moving away from Paula, he went hurrying to the door as it was being pushed open in response to his command.

A genial-looking porter came in carrying her garment bag and small suitcase, and Shane dealt with him briskly, showed him through into the bedroom, told him where to put the luggage and tipped him.

Once they were alone again, Shane strode over to the table, began to peel the metal paper off the champagne cork.

"Listen," he said, "enough of the kids. They're absolutely fine with Emily and Winston."

"Yes, of course they are, darling."

A moment before, Paula's thoughts had swung to their youngest child, and now she started to chuckle and her eyes crinkled up at the corners in amusement. "So Linnet's *true* character has finally emerged, has it? I always suspected that that daughter of ours had inherited a bit of Emma's imperiousness, that she also had the makings of a general."

Shane glanced up, pulled a face, rolled his eyes heavenward. "Another general in the family! Oh my God, I don't think I can stand it! Oh well, I suppose *all* of my women compensate for their bossiness by being so easy on the eye." Winking at her, he said, "And by the way, Emily sends her love. When I rang her earlier this evening, to tell her I'd sidetracked you to Paris, that we wouldn't be at the villa until Sunday, she was tickled to death about our weekend alone together. She thought it was a smashing idea, and she says you're not to be concerned about a thing. Now, how about a glass of this marvelous stuff, before we get ready for dinner?"

"That'd be lovely, darling."

Paula had seated herself on the sofa whilst he had been dealing with the porter, and she kicked off her shoes, curled her legs under her, and sat back, watching him.

It did not matter whether they had been apart for four days or a fortnight, she was always a little startled when she saw Shane after an absence and overwhelmed by the sheer physical presence of him. It had much to do with the force of his personality—that extraordinary charisma he possessed—as well as his height and build and natural dark good looks. Sixteen years ago, at his twenty-fourth birthday party, Emma Harte had said that Shane O'Neill had an intense glamour, and this had never been truer than it was today. He was the most dazzling of men.

Shane had celebrated his fortieth birthday this past June and he was in his prime and looked it. He had a powerful physique with a broad back and massive shoulders, he had stayed lithe and trim, and his sojourn in the sun with the children had given him a deep tan. There was a touch of gray at his temples now, but curiously, this did not age him. Rather, in combination with his bronzed complexion, the gray seemed to underscore the youthfulness of his strong and virile face. And in contrast to his hair, there was not a strand of gray in his mustache, which was as coal black as it had always been.

I've known him all of my life and it's never changed, this extraordinary feeling I have for him, Paula thought, continuing to quietly observe him. He's the only man I've ever loved. The only man I will ever want . . . for the rest of my life . . . my husband, my lover, my closest friend.

"Hey, Beanstalk," he said, using his childhood nickname for her as he walked across the room. "You're a million miles away." He handed her the glass of champagne, sat down next to her on the sofa, and gave her a quick quizzical glance.

"Just daydreaming," she replied, clinking her glass to his when he held it out.

He leaned into her and fastened his eyes on her face. "Emma would've approved of this weekend of ours . . . she was a thorough-going romantic, just as I am."

"Yes, that's very true."

"She was on my mind earlier today and for the obvious reasons," Shane went on, "and it suddenly struck me how quickly the time has passed since her death. It's frightening, really, the way the years have sped by. It seems like only yesterday that she was ordering all of us around—"

"I was thinking *exactly* the same thing when I was at the cemetery this morning!"

Their eyes met. They exchanged slightly startled glances and then smiled knowingly at each other. This frequently happened, the shared thought when they were apart, or when they were together, the sudden voicing by one of them of a sentiment that the other had been about to express.

As a small child, Paula had believed Shane had the ability to read her mind and that he knew her every thought, and she still believed this. But it no longer surprised her; they were too much a part of each other now and she took their closeness for granted and considered it perfectly natural that they were on the same wave length.

Looking across at him, she said in a voice that rose slightly, as if she were suddenly surprised, "It doesn't seem possible that we'll have been married for ten years in November, does it?"

"No . . ." He lifted his hand and touched her cheek lightly. "But we have, and every single day I've been your husband has been meaningful to me, and I wouldn't have missed one of them, not even the really bad days. Better to be with you, no matter what the circumstances, than without you."

"Yes, I feel the same way," she said and her eyes signaled her deep and abiding love to him.

Shane returned Paula's unwavering gaze and the expression in his brilliant black eyes echoed the one in hers.

A silence fell between them.

It was a compatible and harmonious silence, one of those quiet interludes they often shared when they discovered words were not necessary to communicate their feelings.

Paula sat back and sipped her drink and unexpectedly thought of what it would be like to be without him, and she felt herself shriveling inside, appalled at the idea. It was Shane who gave true meaning to her existence. He was the substance of her life, her rock, and he was always there for her, just as she was for him. She was glad he had devised this weekend, that they had this bit of special time together before she went off on her business trip to the States and Australia. She smiled inwardly, thinking of the clever and masterful way he had planned the interlude for them, adoring him for it.

Shane, studying her, became aware that the tensions of the day were slowly ebbing out of her face, and this gladdened his heart. He frequently worried about her, knowing how hard she worked, but he never interfered. She was like Emma. Protesting about her unremitting schedule would only be a waste of *his* breath and an irritant to *her*.

He eased his large frame into the corner of the blue velvet Louis XVI sofa, settled back to enjoy his drink; he, too, was finally able to relax, to let go for the first time since leaving the villa that morning. From the moment he had stepped off the O'Neill corporate jet, until Paula's arrival in the suite, he had been busy with Jean-Claude Soissons, the head of O'Neill Hotels International in France. But he had no intention of letting business intrude any further, either tonight or tomorrow, which was why they were not staying at the hotel he owned in Paris. Whenever he wanted Paula to himself, to spend some quiet private time with her, he always took a deluxe suite at the Ritz where he knew no one would disturb him.

Now, as Paula had done a moment before, he turned his gaze inward, contemplating the next thirty-six hours and the joy they would derive from being together—and completely alone.

There was something very special between these two.

It had always been there, even as children, this spiritual oneness, this closeness, this bonding together, and what had begun in infancy had come to full flower with their sexual union as adults.

For a period of time, during Paula's disastrous marriage to Jim Fairley, Shane had been at odds with her, but the bond between them had never *really* been broken. When they had patched up their friendship and had subsequently become lovers at long last, they had been profoundly shaken by the strength and force of their physical passion for each other. But they had recognized how right it was, knew they had always been meant to be together in this way, and they felt whole and complete for the first time in their lives.

Shane realized how utterly worthless his liaisons with countless other women had been, and at once understood that without Paula his life would be meaningless; Paula finally knew that Shane was the only man she had ever loved, saw how empty and loveless her marriage to Jim was, and acknowledged that to continue to live this lie would be like killing herself. And she accepted that she must end the marriage if she was to save her life—and keep her self-respect and sanity.

Expecting to meet opposition from Jim, Paula had, nevertheless, been staggered by his vituperativeness and the spiteful way he had behaved once he knew she wanted a divorce. They had battled, locked horns, reached an impasse.

In the middle of one of their worst crises, Jim had done a bolt to Chamonix for a winter holiday with her parents at their rented chalet. Paula had been furious with him for going skiing at such a crucial time in their lives. And then he had been fatally struck down on Mont Blanc by the avalanche that had decimated the family, and she did not have to worry about getting a divorce anymore because she was suddenly a widow at the age of twenty-six.

Jim's death had come between Paula and Shane, and she had sent him away out of her great and terrible guilt. But eventually she had come to her senses and had found her true self again. She had gone to him, had told him she wanted to spend the rest of her life with him, and they had been reconciled immediately, for Shane O'Neill had never stopped loving her.

Two months later, with Emily and Winston Harte as their witnesses, they had been married at Caxton Hall registry office in London.

And they both knew deep in the innermost recesses of their hearts that they had finally fulfilled their destiny.

The antique ormolu clock on the white marble mantelpiece began to chime loudly.

Paula and Shane both started in surprise and glanced across at it, and Shane exclaimed, "Good Lord, it's nine-thirty already, and I booked a table at the Espadon for quarter to ten. Can you get ready in fifteen minutes, darling?"

"Yes, of course," Paula said, putting down her glass, stretching, then smothering a yawn behind her hand.

Shane stared hard at her and scowled. "You're terribly tired," he said in concern. "How thoughtless of me to expect you to go downstairs to the restaurant. It's a hot bath for you, my girl, and immediately. We'll have a snack from room service tonight."

"Don't be silly, I'm fine," Paula began and paused, yawning again. "Well, to tell you the truth, it has been a long day," she admitted. "Perhaps you're right about eating in the suite."

"I know I am."

As he spoke, Shane stood up, reached down, took her hands in his, and pulled her to her feet. He laid his arm around her shoulders and propelled her toward the bedroom door. "I wish I'd canceled Kevin's weekend off and sent him with the plane to collect you this evening—"

"I'm jolly glad you didn't cancel it!" Paula cried, giving him a sharp, almost reproving look. She was fond of Kevin Reardon and was aware that the pilot's devotion to them frequently caused him to neglect his personal life. "Kevin's been looking forward to his girlfriend's birthday party tomorrow night for weeks now. Anyway, he made a good messenger, didn't he? It *was* Kevin who delivered your note to the store this morning, wasn't it?"

"Yes, it was." Shane grinned as he proceeded to bundle her into the bedroom. "Come on, get undressed and take a hot bath, and whilst you're relaxing I shall order supper. What do you fancy?"

"Oh anything you like . . . I'll leave it to you, darling."

"How about a picnic . . . with some of your favorite things? And another bottle of bubbly."

Paula laughed gaily. She said, "If I drink any more champagne I might *just* pass out."

"That's permissible," Shane shot back. "You have your husband here to look after you."

"True. And a very special husband at that." She stood on tiptoe, kissed his cheek.

Shane's arms went around her and he caught her to him for a moment, tightening his grip, kissing the top of her dark head, and then he let go of her abruptly, stepped away from her.

"I'd better be a good boy and go and order supper, otherwise you never know *what* might happen. After all, I have been deprived of you for two whole weeks, and I don't mind telling you, I've missed you like bloody hell, my love . . ."

"Oh Shane darling," she said slowly, very softly. "Yes . . . I know what you mean . . ."

It was the inflection in her voice, the sudden longing flaring on her face that made him instantly take a step forward.

She reached out her hand to him.

He took it.

Their clasped hands tightened and they moved into each other's arms swiftly. He bent his face to hers, seeking her mouth, and felt the sudden hotness of her cheeks, and the knowledge that she always wanted him as much as he always wanted her aroused him, made his heart begin to clatter erratically. They kissed, a long deep tantalizing kiss, and he let his tongue explore her mouth, and she did the same; then their tongues lay still, and they shared a feeling of the most profound intimacy.

Paula was suddenly trembling in his arms and together they swayed on their feet as if they were intoxicated, and of course they were—with each other —and then they half stumbled, half walked in the direction of the bed, their arms still wrapped around one another.

Shane stripped her of her clothes.

She went and lay down on the bed, waiting for him, and her eyes never once left his face as he flung off his shirt and trousers. As she watched him intently she was hardly able to contain herself, wanting him so much, and when she saw how excited he was she felt a shiver trickle down her spine.

And as Shane stared back into those violet eyes turning inky black with longing for him, he was possessed by such a violent desire for her it sent the blood rushing to his head and made his heart begin to pound against his rib cage. He felt dizzy and light-headed as he walked across to the bed and stretched out beside her.

Pushing himself up on one elbow, he bent over her, looked down into her face.

She gazed up at him.

Their eyes locked and held for the longest moment of the most intense and adoring communion, and then he touched her cheek with two fingers, moving their tips across her brows, her eyelids, her nose, and onto her mouth; slowly he traced the outline of her lips and parted them and rested his fingertips against her tongue. She sucked on them and the sensuality of this little act inflamed him, made the fire leap through him. Immediately, he crushed his mouth to hers. It was hard and insistent and their teeth grazed and he kissed her with mounting passion, and as he did he moved his fingers away from her lips, slid them along the elongated line of her lovely throat. They did not linger there, but moved on to fondle her voluptuous breasts, then slipped farther down to flutter lightly across her flat concave stomach until they were finally resting between her thighs.

Shane began to stroke her lovingly, languorously, in slow motion, and with such tenderness he seemed hardly to be touching her at all. But he could feel the velvet softness of her increasing and he continued to stroke, to explore, until his fingertips came to nestle against that precious part of her that was the fountainhead of her womanhood.

Instantly, Paula twisted herself into him, bringing her body closer to his, her slender hand reaching out for him, and she began to caress him as delicately as he was her. Shane felt his hardness growing as she unexpectedly moved her hand with greater rapidity and he had to bite back a cry as he began to throb under her touch. He grasped her wrist, stilled her hand, and then he intensified the pressure of his fingertips and she tensed, and held her body rigid. He explored further, slipped deeper into the velvet folds of her, and as he did he heard a strangled cry in her throat.

He leaned over her satin-smooth breasts, very taut and upright, and savored the hard, erect nipples with his mouth, first one and then the other. She started to gently undulate under his expert fingers, his loving mouth, and she sighed and murmured his name softly, over and over. Now her hands went out to him again, were strong and hard on the nape of his neck and in his thick hair, and they suddenly moved on to grasp his wide shoulders as her excitement accelerated.

Paula stiffened and gasped. She was filling with an exquisite warmth. His touch quickened, became ever more nimble and deft, and she cried out in her excitement, "Shane, oh Shane, my darling husband, I love you so much!" And he said against her throat, in a voice thickened by desire, "You're my true love, Paula, my own true love. Come to me, my darling, so that I can take you to me." And she gasped again and said, "Yes, oh yes," and gripped his shoulders more tenaciously than ever.

Shane thought he was going to explode as she opened up to him like an exotic flower unfolding soft lush petals, moaning his name and shuddering. He was unable to contain himself, and he moved onto her, took possession of her swiftly, raging with the same kind of molten heat that was suffusing her.

He lost all reserve and she was as unrestrained as he. Her arms went around him and were full of strength as she held him to her. And he pushed his hands under her body and lifted her to him and they cleaved together, were joined, became one.

As Shane thrust deeper, lost himself completely in her and in the joy of her, he suddenly thought, *I want to make her pregnant tonight. I want another child.*

This idea, unexpected as it was, sent such thrills surging through him he moved against her violently and she responded with unbridled ardor, matching his passion equally, and they quickly found their own rhythm as they had all through the years of their marriage. But for Shane, tonight was suddenly like the first time they had ever made love and in an instant the years fell away. He was back in Connecticut, in the barn he had once owned, taking her to him as he had yearned to take her during the years of her marriage to another man, loving her as he had never loved any other woman, as only he and she were meant to love.

And then he was reaching up . . . reaching into the light . . . the light was surrounding him . . . she was at the center of the light . . . waiting for him . . . his dreamlike child of his childhood dreams. And she was his now. Nothing, no one, could ever separate them again. They belonged together for all time, into eternity. He felt weightless . . . he was soaring higher and higher . . . rising up into that timeless light . . . floating into infinity. And he was carrying her with him, holding the world in his arms, calling her name, just as she called his.

And together they crested on waves of ecstasy in the golden shimmering light . . . were blinded by it and then could see . . . and oh the blessed peace of it . . .

Shane woke up abruptly.

He moved his head to the right and looked at the bedside clock. In the dim light he could see that it was almost five.

Paula slept soundlessly by his side.

He braced himself on one elbow, bent over her, touched her face lovingly, but very lightly, so as not to awaken her from her exhausted sleep, and lifted a strand of hair away from her eyes. Then he settled down again, stretched out on his back, and closed his eyes, but before many minutes had passed he decided he was not going to fall off again quite so easily, or as quickly as he had just imagined he would. He was suddenly wide awake. Still, he had slept very deeply for the past few hours, as he always did when he was with Paula, as if he were more content and at peace when she was in his bed. Well, of course he was.

He turned over onto his side, made an arc of his body around hers. She was his whole life, and now, lying next to her in the darkness, adoring her in the silence of his heart, he wondered if he had made her pregnant. Weeks ago they had agreed she should stop taking the pill.

Tonight he had planted his seed in her and he prayed that the seed had taken hold and would come to flower as a child . . . a true love child conceived at the height of passion and spiritual joining. He stifled a sigh, thinking of Patrick. He loved his little boy with a deeply tender and protective love, but he could not help being sad that their firstborn was not normal. He dare not let Paula perceive his feelings, for fear of underscoring her own pain. They were never far from the surface and yet, somehow, he always managed to conceal his sorrow from her.

Instinctively, Shane lifted his right arm, put it around her, drew closer, burrowed his face in her fragrant hair, overflowing with his love for her. He closed his eyes again, let himself drift into sleep. Yes, he thought, now is the time for our next child. And he wondered, as he finally dozed off, if that was the real reason he had sidetracked her to Paris.

Five

The Villa Faviola was situated in the town of Roquebrune-Cap-Martin, approximately halfway between Monte Carlo and Menton.

It stood in its own small park at the end of the little peninsula of Cap-Martin, sheltered by pines at its back, with its many tall windows facing out toward the sea.

Built in the 1920s, it was a lovely old house, sprawling, airy, and gracious, with a curving driveway bordered by pines, spacious green lawns that swept down from the terrace past the swimming pool, up to the edge of the rocky promontory and the glittering Mediterranean Sea beyond.

Its exterior walls were painted a soft melon, but in a tone so pale it was almost sand, and the canvas awnings shading the windows were of a deeper melon, partnered with shutters of pristine white.

A wide terrace stretched along the side of the house facing the sea. Made of white stone and marble, it appeared to float gracefully above the verdant gardens where flowers grew in riotous color and fountains sparkled in the shimmering sunlight. Scattered along the terrace were several round white-metal tables topped by melon-colored parasols; matching white chairs, swing-sofas with sun-awnings, and chaises all had cushions of cream. Because only these soft integrated tones had been used, nothing jarred the harmonious flow of pale color across the lovely facade.

The Villa Faviola had been purchased by Emma Harte in the late 1940s, just after the end of the Second World War, and it was she who had originally created the gardens surrounding the house and intersecting the lawns. But in recent years, Paula had enlarged the flower beds and borders. She had planted a wide variety of small flowering trees, shrubs, and exotic plants, cultivating the entire park to its present beauty—and a magnificence that was renowned along the Côte d'Azur.

Inside Faviola its cool, lofty rooms were filled with lovely filtered sunlight and furnished with a simple yet distinctive elegance. Charming old French Provincial pieces made of dark woods or bleached oak were mingled with vast sofas, comfortable chairs, chaises, and ottomans. Occasional tables held small pots of African violets, pink and white cyclamen, and the latest magazines and books.

Floors of highly polished parquet and rose-veined cream marble were either bare or were covered here and there by old Aubussons and plain rugs of cream wool. Throughout the house, colors were pale and cool. Cream, vanilla, and white predominated, flowed over the walls, were repeated in the fabrics that fell at the windows, covered sofas, and chairs; accent colors were variations of melon and peach and sand. And there were touches of *café au lait,* that lovely milky brown that was so typically French.

Spilling vivid color into these monochromatic-toned rooms were romantic, lyrical paintings by such noted contemporary French artists as Epko, Taurelle, and Bouyssou and huge Baccarat crystal urns overflowing with a great abundance of flowers and foliage from the gardens.

But none of the rooms were so imposing or so grand that guests and children were intimidated and felt they were in a museum. On the contrary, Emma had designed the house as a vacation home, one to be lived in and enjoyed, and it had an easy grace that was all its own. It also happened to be one of those houses that had always had a warm, welcoming atmosphere, and there was a lovely serenity about its sun-drenched rooms and the inviting pine-shaded park with its glorious gardens.

Alexander Barkstone owned Faviola, having inherited it from Emma along with its contents—with the exception of the Impressionist art, which his grandmother had bequeathed to Philip in Australia. But Sandy rarely came to the villa, preferring his country estate in Yorkshire. It was mostly used by his sister Emily and her family, his cousins Paula O'Neill and Anthony Dunvale, and their respective spouses and children. Occasionally his mother, Elizabeth, and her French husband, Marc Deboyne, came down from Paris for long weekends, usually when the season was over.

But of all of them, it was Emily who loved Faviola the most—and with an enduring passion.

As a little girl some of the happiest times of her childhood had been spent at the villa with her beloved Gran, and she had always believed it to be an enchanted and magical place. She knew every cranny, every corner, of every room on every floor; every inch of the park and the garden and the beach below the rocky promontory. After she had married her cousin, Winston Harte, in June of 1970, they had flown down to the Riviera for their honeymoon and the first two weeks of their life as man and wife had been spent at the villa. The lovely carefree days and romantic evenings were so blissful, Emily's deep feelings for Faviola were only intensified, and ever since then the villa had been her haven which she could escape to at odd times during the spring and winter, either alone or with Winston, and always in the summer months with their children, Toby, Gideon, and Natalie. She had never grown tired of it and she knew she never would; she thought of the villa as the most perfect place in the world to be.

But in contrast, Sandy's visits to the house had grown fewer and fewer after his wife's death; in 1973, recognizing how much Emily loved the place, he had asked her to take over from him, to supervise its general management. He had been relieved and happy when she had promptly and enthusiastically agreed.

Inevitably, Emily had put her individual stamp on Faviola over the years, but she had not tried to turn it into a replica of an English country house. Instead she had retained its Gallic flavor in every possible way, and if anything she had even enhanced the predominantly Provençal feeling with her inimitable touches. But as involved with it as she had become in the last eight years, Emily never considered the villa to be her own, never once forgot that it was the property of her brother. And yet it *was* hers in a certain sense, because of the time and the care and the great love she constantly lavished on it, and certainly everyone thought of Emily as *la grande châtelaine* of the Villa Faviola.

When Emma Harte was living, the day-to-day running of the villa had been in the capable hands of a local woman from Roquebrune, one Madame Paulette Renard. Engaged by Emma in 1950, she had moved into the pleasant and roomy caretaker's house in the private park—known as *la petite maison*—and had looked after the Harte family with unfailing care for the next twenty years.

But with Emma's death in 1970, Madame Paulette had decided the time had come for her to retire and she had handed over her responsibilities and her keys to her daughter, Solange Brivet, who wished to leave her job as the housekeeper at a hotel in Beaulieu. Madame Paulette was a widow, and the Brivets and their children had been living with her in *la petite maison* for a number of years, and so there had been no great upheavals or sad good-byes. And since it was only a short walk across the vegetable garden to the villa, Madame Paulette was always on hand to give her expert advice or air her considerable knowledge.

Over the past eleven years, the management and running of Faviola had become something of a Brivet family affair. Solange's husband, Marcel, was the chef, two of their three daughters, Sylvie and Marie, were the maids, and their son, Henri, was the butler and, as Emily put it, "our general factotum *par excellence,*" while Marcel's nephews, Pierre and Maurice, were the gardeners. These two drove over from Roquebrune in their little Renault every morning, bringing with them another Brivet, Cousin Odile, who worked in the kitchen as assistant to Marcel, and it was Odile who carried with her the huge basket of breads from her mother's *boulangerie* . . . fresh *croissants* and *brioche,* which Marcel served warm for the family's breakfast, and *baguettes,* those long French loaves with a hard crust which the children especially loved.

Madame Solange, as she was called by everyone, had been trained at the Hotel de Paris in nearby Monte Carlo, and she ran the villa in the grand Riviera style, rather in the manner of a great hotel, with efficiency, meticulous attention to detail, and with the same kind of loving devotion her mother had expended before her. And in all the years she had been employed, she and Emily had worked together in harmony, with rarely, if ever, a cross word.

The phrase, "Thank God for Solange," was forever on Emily's lips, and she was muttering it under her breath on this Monday morning in August as she hurried into the kitchen, stood in the center of the floor, glanced around, and nodded to herself, looking pleased.

They had had their annual, end-of-the-summer dinner party last night, but no one would have known it from the look of the large, old-fashioned kitchen. As usual, the hanging pots and pans sparkled, the wood countertops were scrubbed to gleaming white, the terra-cotta tile floor shone, and every-thing else was spotless and back in its given place.

Solange must have really cracked the whip to get everything so ship-shape for this morning, Emily thought, recalling the mess in the kitchen the night before, after the last of their guests had finally departed. Smiling to herself, she took a glass from the cupboard, went to the refrigerator, poured herself some Vichy water, and carrying the glass she walked back through the pantry, across the dining room, and out of the French doors onto the terrace, the clicking of her sandals the only sound on the warm, still air.

Emily was always the first one to be up and about every morning, some-times as early as dawn.

She treasured this private time before the family awakened and the staff started to arrive. She liked being entirely alone to enjoy the gentle quiessence of the silent slumbering house, to savor the early morning smells and colors of the Mediterranean landscape.

It was also her hour for reviewing the paperwork she invariably brought with her, making notes for her secretary in London, whom she phoned several times a week, working out the day's menus, and planning activities for the children. But frequently she just sat quietly on the terrace, glad to have a few moments of solitude and introspection before the excitement of the day began and a horde of children descended on her, dragging a kind of chaos in their wake.

It was not so bad when she had only her own three to cope with, but when Paula's four and Anthony's three children were at Faviola, often bringing with them a number of young guests, it was rather like having an unruly juvenile football team underfoot. But Emily had her own system and she managed to control them far better than anyone else. It was not for nothing the children called her "The Sergeant Major" behind her back.

Now, taking sips of Vichy as she walked, Emily went up to the edge of the terrace and leaned against the balustrade, looked out across the gardens to the sea. It was a dark metallic blue and choppy, and the sky that surged above it was a curdled cloudy gray that seemed ominous.

She hoped the weather was not going to change again, as it had last week when the mistral, that dry north wind that blew down out of the Rhône Valley, had brought several days of mean weather with it. Without exception, all of the children had been restive, moody and difficult. Solange had immediately blamed the mistral, reminding Emily that this wind usually disturbed everyone's equilibrium. Emily had agreed, and they had both been relieved when it had finally blown out to sea. The weather had changed for the better—and so had the children. They were much calmer, almost their normal selves again. Even Emily felt more at ease. She had been edgy and irritable during those dull, incredibly windy days; she now had to admit there was probably a lot of truth in what Solange—and the locals—said about the mistral and its peculiar effect on people. She glanced at her watch. It was only twenty minutes past six. By nine o'clock the sky would be a perfect cerulean blue, the sun would be out, and the sea would be as still as a pond, she decided, as always the eternal optimist, as her grandmother had been before her.

Turning away from the balustrade, she stepped up to the table where she had laid out her papers earlier, and sat down. As far as work was concerned, her immediate priority was her impending trip to Hong Kong to buy merchandise for Genret, the import-export trading company she ran for Harte Enterprises. She opened her diary, glanced at the dates in September she had tentatively selected some weeks ago. She flipped the pages backward and forward several times, carefully studied her schedule, penciled in the changes she now wished to make; then she began to scribble a note for Janice, her secretary in London, outlining her new itinerary.

A few minutes later, Emily almost jumped out of her skin as a strong cool hand came to rest firmly on her shoulders. She started up in her chair and swung her head swiftly, her eyes wide with astonishment. "My God, Winston! You mustn't creep up on me like that! *So silently.* You scared me!" she cried.

"Oh, sorry, darling," he apologized, then bent over and kissed her cheek. "Good morning," he added as he walked across the terrace and leaned against the balustrade, where he stood regarding her lovingly for a moment before proffering her a warm smile.

Emily smiled back. "And tell me, what are *you* doing up so early? You're usually dead to the world until ten o'clock at the earliest."

Winston shrugged his bare shoulders, put the towel he was holding on the balustrade. "I couldn't sleep this morning. But it's always the same with me, isn't it, Em? I mean, on our last few days here I seem to want to cram every-thing in, enjoy every single second, just like the kids."

"And as I do, too."

"Yes, that's true . . . you do love this place so. But then it loves *you*, Emily . . . why, you're positively blooming."

"Thank you, kind sir," she said.

He eyed the glass in front of her. "I suppose that's water you're drinking . . . aren't you going to make coffee?"

Emily shook her head. "No, Winston, I'm not," she said very adamantly. "Because if I do, I'll also make some toast and I'll butter the toast and put jam on it and then I'll eat it, and when Odile arrives at seven, with all that scrump-tious stuff from the bakery, I'll have another breakfast, a *second* breakfast, and you know perfectly well that I've got to watch my weight."

"You look pretty terrific to me, Mrs. Harte," he said with a chuckle and leered at her. "I don't half fancy you."

"Honestly, Winston, at this hour!"

"What's wrong with this hour? It's still very early . . . come on darling, let's go back to bed."

"Oh don't be so silly, I've a thousand things to do this morning."

"So do I," he remarked lightly, giving her a pointed look, leering again. Then his face changed suddenly, and he leveled a swift appraising glance at her, liking what he saw. Emily was now thirty-four and, in his opinion, one of the prettiest women alive. She was blonder than ever and brown from the sun and her brilliant green eyes, so identical in color to his own, sparkled with a vivid intelligence and a *joie de vivre* that were uniquely hers. She was wearing a lime-green-and-pink cotton shift over her bikini, looked impossibly young and fresh and delectable this morning.

"Winston, you're staring. And very *rudely*. What's wrong?"

"Nothing. Just admiring you, that's all. And thinking that you look like a delicious ice cream . . . and good enough to eat."

"Oh pooh!" Emily laughed, but her neck turned bright pink and she dropped her head, stared at her engagement book intently.

There was a tiny silence.

Winston swallowed a smile, both amused and pleased that he could still make her blush after eleven years of marriage, but then that was his Emily and he adored her for her girlishness, her femininity, and her softness. Odd, he thought, that she can be so tough in business and yet she has such a soft edge to her in her personal life. Like Paula, of course, and Aunt Emma, when she was alive. It was just this dichotomy in their natures that made the Harte women so original. He had known that for a long time.

Emily raised her head. At once, she saw the contemplative expression on her husband's face and asked, "And what are you thinking about *now*?"

"I was just wondering what all this is in aid of this morning?" Winston murmured, strolling over to join her at the table. He flopped down in the chair opposite and held her eyes as she looked across at him.

"What do you mean?" she asked, puzzled.

"Why are you going at the work hammer and tongs today, when you'll be back in London at the end of the week? It hardly seems worth it, love."

"I'm not working, actually, I'm trying to figure out the dates for my buying trip to Hong Kong and Mainland China," Emily explained. "If I leave on the tenth of September, instead of the sixth as I'd planned, I'd still be there when Paula breaks her return journey back to the States from Sydney. We were talking about it yesterday afternoon, and decided it would be nice to have a couple of days in Hong Kong. Relaxing . . . doing our Christmas shopping . . . and then we could fly on to New York together, spend a day or two there before taking the Concorde home to England. What do you think?"

"It sounds good to me, if that's what you feel like doing. I've certainly no objections, I don't have to be in Canada until the first week of October. Presumably you'd be back in England before I left?"

"Yes, of course I would. I've taken your Canadian trip into consideration and planned around it."

"Then it's fine, darling," Winston answered with a smile and stood up, went to get his towel. "Well, if you're not going to take pity on your poor husband and make him a cup of coffee, I think I'll go for a swim before that tribe of fiendish little monsters invades the area and ploughs down everything in sight."

Emily couldn't help laughing at the expression on his face. "Oh I don't know, darling, they're not *so* bad," she protested, feeling the sudden need to defend the younger generation.

"Oh yes they are!" he retorted. "They're bloody awful most of the time!" A wide grin glanced across his face. "But I must admit, I do love 'em . . . especially the three that are mine." He kissed her quickly, loped off in the direction of the swimming pool without another word, nonchalantly swinging the towel and whistling merrily.

Emily watched him go, thinking how fit and healthy he looked with his tanned body and face, his reddish hair turned to gold by the Riviera sun. The summer here had done him good. He worked extremely hard running the Yorkshire Consolidated Newspaper Company and its Canadian subsidiaries, and she was always after him to slow down a bit. But he paid not the slightest attention to her, merely commented that they *all* worked like demons, which was true, of course. It was the way her Gran had brought them up. Emma had only disdained slackers; naturally they had all become overachievers.

How lucky I am to have Winston, Emily mused, settling back in the chair, idly drifting with her thoughts, putting off preparing the menus for that day's meals for a few moments longer.

Sometimes, when she turned her gaze back into the past, she realized she had managed to catch him by the skin of her teeth, understood how easily she might have lost him to another woman.

Emily had been in love with Winston since she was sixteen. They were third cousins. His grandfather and namesake, Winston Harte, had been her grandmother's brother. Although Winston was five years older than she they had been bosom pals as children. But once he had grown up he had hardly noticed her again, at least not as an attractive young woman with whom he might become romantically involved.

He had gone off to Oxford with his best friend, Shane, and the two of them had rapidly acquired reputations as terrible womanizers. Almost everyone had been scandalized by their disreputable antics. *She* had ached with a mixture of jealousy and longing, wishing *she* were one of the girls Winston chased and bedded. Only her Gran had been sanguine. Emma had simply laughed, had said they were merely young bucks sowing their wild oats. But then neither Winston nor Shane could do much wrong in Emma Harte's eyes. She had had a special fondness for them both.

And so Emily had worshipped Winston from afar, hoping that one day his glance would fall on her again. But it hadn't, and much to her profound dismay he suddenly became seriously involved with a local girl, Alison Ridley. At the beginning of 1969 the gossip going around the three clans was that he was about to get engaged to Alison. Emily had thought her heart was going to break.

Then everything had changed. Quite miraculously, Winston had noticed her at the christening of Paula and Jim Fairley's twins in March of that same year. And all because of an incident with Shane which had upset her grandmother. She and Winston had been called into the library at Pennistone Royal and had been grilled by Emma about Shane's feelings for Paula. When they had finally escaped, they had gone for a walk in the gardens to recover from their ordeal, and for some reason Winston had been prompted to kiss her. This action on his part had been as sudden as it was unexpected. Even Emily, loving him though she did, had been as stunned as he by their intense physical reaction to each other as they had sat on the bench by the lily pond, entwined in each other's arms. The world had turned dizzingly and wonderfully upside down for them both.

Winston, in typical Harte fashion, had wasted little time. The moment their affair had begun he had broken off with Alison; shortly thereafter he had asked her grandmother if they could become engaged. Emma had given her consent, thoroughly approving of the match between her granddaughter and her great nephew. One year later, when her Gran had returned from Australia, they had been married in the quaint old church in Pennistone village. Gran had given the most beautiful wedding reception for them in the gardens of Pennistone Royal and her life as Winston's wife had begun. . . . It was the best life any woman could ever want.

Emily sighed with contentment, brought her thoughts back to the present, picked up her pen, and began to write out the menu for lunch. When she finished, she started on the one for dinner, but stopped abruptly as an idea occurred to her. Tonight, she and Winston, Paula and Shane, would drive over to Beaulieu and have dinner at La Reserve. Just the four of them. Without the tribe. That would be much more peaceful. Not to mention romantic. Winston will approve, she thought, and smiled a small secret smile.

Six

"You clot! You unbelievably stupid clot! Look what you've *done!* You've splashed my beautiful painting and ruined it!" Tessa Fairley yelled at the top of her lungs, glaring at Lorne, adopting an angry stance, waving the paintbrush in the air.

"The side of the swimming pool is hardly the proper place to set up an easel and start painting," Lorne rejoined loftily, returning her glare. "Especially when everyone's leaping in and out. It's your own fault the watercolor's been splashed. And one more thing—I'm *not* a stupid clot."

"No, you're a stupid *cretin,*" his twelve-year-old twin shot back, then sucked in her breath with a horrified gasp. "Don't do that, Lorne Fairley! Don't shake yourself like that! Oh! Oh! you *rotten* thing. You've spoiled my other pictures. Oh, God, you've made them all *trickly.* Mummy . . . *Mummy* . . . tell Lorne to stay away from my paintings," she wailed.

"I want this," Linnet announced matter-of-factly and snatched Tessa's large yellow sun hat from the chaise near the easel, placed it on top of her bright red curls, and happily marched off, dragging a rubber duck on a string behind her and pushing the hat up as it kept sliding down over her eyes.

"Bring that back at once, you naughty girl!"

When her five-year-old sister paid not a blind bit of notice, Tessa exclaimed to no one in particular, "Did you see that? She took my hat without my permission. Mummy . . . *Mummy* . . . that child's spoiled rotten. You and Daddy have ruined her. There's no hope—"

"Pompous, pompous, Tessa's being pompous, just like Lornie, she's parroting Forlornie," Gideon Harte taunted in a sing-song tone from the relative safety of the pool.

"I won't dignify *that* ridiculous remark," Lorne sniffed, lowered himself onto a mattress, picked up his copy of Homer's *Iliad* and buried his face in the book.

"Bring my hat back!" Tessa screamed, stamping her foot.

"Oh for God's sake, leave her alone," a faintly disembodied voice admonished from the pool, and Toby Harte's reddish-gold head bobbed up over the side. The ten-year-old grinned at Tessa, who was his favorite girl cousin, and then hauled himself out of the water, being careful not to splash her or her paintings, having no wish to incur her wrath. "After all, she's only a little itty bitty *baby.*"

"*Not* a baby," a muffled voice informed them from underneath the large sun hat.

"And why do you care so much, Tess? It's only a cheap bit of rag you bought in Nice market," Toby said.

"It's not! It's *beautiful!* And it cost me a whole week's pocket money, Toby Harte!"

"More fool you," called out eight-year-old Gideon.

"What do you know about anything, Gideon Harte! You're a *cretin* like my brother."

"Is that the only *stupid* word you know, *Stupid?*" Gideon shouted back and stuck his tongue out at her.

"Brat! Brat!" Tessa yelled at him. "You're a spoiled brat, too!"

"Oh shut up, both of you," Toby admonished in a bored voice. "Listen, Tess, can I borrow one of your old Beatles' albums?"

"Which one?" Tessa asked, suddenly wary, squinting up at him in the bright sunlight.

"*Sgt. Pepper's Lonely Hearts Club Band.*"

"Oh no, I can't possibly lend you that one! It's become a . . . *classic.* When Auntie Amanda gave it to me, she told me it'd be very, *very* valuable one day. She'd had it since before *we* were even born. But . . . well . . . because it's *you* I'll make an exception, so—"

"Gosh, thanks, Tess," Toby cut in, his freckled face lighting up.

"—you can rent it if you want, it's ten pence an hour," Tessa finished, sounding as magnanimous as she now looked.

"*Ten pence an hour!* That's highway robbery!" Toby spluttered. "No thanks, Tessa, I'm not going to help you become a capitalist."

"In this family, everybody's a capitalist," Tessa declared smugly.

"Forget it, I'll play my new Bee Gees."

"Suit yourself."

"Aunt Paula. *Aunt Paula* . . . your daughter's turned into a really nasty little sharpie this summer," Toby exclaimed and threw a disgusted look in Tessa's direction.

"Mummy . . . I'm taking my knickers off, they're all wet," Linnet cried from the depths of the sun hat.

"You see what I mean, Mummy," Tessa sniggered. "She's the only five-year-old *I* know who still wee-wees in her pants."

"I don't! I didn't, Mummy!" a clear voice shrilled as the hat was pushed back and Linnet's round flushed face appeared.

"Auntie Paula, may I have one of these ginger snaps, please?" three-year-old Natalie Harte asked and took one and crunched on it before she was forbidden to do so.

"Mummy! Look at her now! She's *dragging* my gorgeous sun hat in the puddles. Stop it, you little monster. *Stop it!* Mummy, make her stop. *Mother* . . . you're not listening. If you throw that hat into the pool, I'll kill you, Linnet O'Neill! Gideon! Get my hat! Quick, before it sinks!"

"Okay, I will, but it'll cost you plenty."

Tessa ignored this threat. "Wait until I catch you, Linnet," she screamed after the small, plump figure retreating swiftly in the direction of the pool house.

"Mother . . . *Mother* . . . will you *please* tell Tessa to stop screeching like a banshee? I'm getting a frightful headache," Lorne murmured languidly from the mattress where he lay reading.

"Auntie Paula, Natalie's eaten *all* of the ginger snaps," India Standish gasped, and turning to her cousin, she added in the most dire tone a seven-year-old could summon, *"You're* going to be *sick*. Horribly, horribly sick, and it serves you right, you greedy little girl."

"Have this, India," Natalie said with a winning smile, pulling a half-eaten chocolate out of the pocket of her sundress, dusting it off, and offering it to the older girl, whom she adored.

"Ugh! *No thanks*. It looks icky!"

"Auntie Paula, there's a dead *something* at the bottom of the pool," Gideon shouted, coming up for air with a splash, triumphantly holding the sodden sun hat aloft.

"Oh my God! Mummy, she's ruined my *expensive* hat. *Mummy*, did you hear what I just said?"

"Where's the dead *something?*" Patrick asked, throwing himself flat on the ground, dangling his dark head over the pool, so that he could peer down into the depths. "Can't see it, Gid."

"I've got to dive for it," Gideon explained, plunging under water again like an agile little dolphin.

"Will you take five pence an hour for *Sgt. Pepper's Lonely Hearts Club Band?*" Toby negotiated hopefully.

"Eight pence . . . *perhaps.*"

"No thanks, Miss Sharpie. You can go and shove it up your . . . jumper."

"Oh Mummy, Mummy, look! A Bird. *Dead,*" Patrick cried. "Oh poor birdie. Funeral. Can we have a funeral?"

"Auntie Paula, please make Gideon get rid of that disgusting, revolting object," eleven-year-old Jeremy Standish exclaimed. "It pongs to high heaven and it's contaminating the air."

"No, it *isn't!*" Gideon glared at his cousin. "We're going to bury it, like Patrick wants, aren't we, Auntie Paula? Auntie Paula, cooee! *Auntie Paula,* we *can* bury it, can't we?"

"*Mummy,* can birdie have a funeral?"

"*Mummy,* I want some dry knickers."

"*Mother,* look at Linnet now. She's waving her knickers in the air. Mummy. Mummy! *Mother!*"

"For Christ's sake, Tessa, stop screaming," Lorne shouted. "How can I concentrate on my Homer with you bellowing in my ears. I'll be jolly glad to get back to school next week and away from you. You're a bloody little pest."

"If Daddy hears you swearing, you'll catch it."

"And who's going to tell him, Miss Tattletale?"

"I've never split on you yet, you *moron.*"

"If I'm a moron, then so are you, *twin!*"

"Don't bring that smelly disgusting *thing* anywhere near me, Gideon, or I'll punch you on the nose," Jeremy threatened.

"Auntie Paula! Auntie Paula! Natalie's being sick! I *knew* she would be," India cried.

"Gideon Harte, I'm *warning* you. Keep your distance or I'll thump you!"

"*Auntie Paula,* tell Toby to let go of me!" Gideon screamed. "He's *hurting* me."

"And it's *my* turn next," Jeremy threatened with sudden manic glee.

"Mummy, *Mummy,* make the boys stop fighting," Linnet shrieked.

Paula threw down her book and angrily leaped to her feet.

She began to chastise them vociferously, but her voice was drowned out by a series of strange booms that reverberated on the warm air, and as the echoes died away, Paula was able to ask, "What on earth was *that?*"

"The gong," Linnet said.

"*Gong,*" Paula repeated in perplexity, and it instantly struck her how chastened the children seemed.

"What gong? Whose gong?"

Lorne explained, "Auntie Emily's gong . . . she bought it—"

"From the house up the mountain," Tessa quickly interjected, then volunteered to her still-baffled mother, "The old lady who owned the house died, and there was a sale two weeks ago. We all went with Aunt Emily, she thought we might find some bargains."

"But all we found was the gong," Jeremy muttered.

"Mummy uses it to signal us," Toby said. "One strike means that breakfast's ready, two is for lunch, three is to summon us inside, to get ready for dinner, and—"

"When she bangs and bangs and *bangs,* like just now, it means we're going to *catch* it," Linnet confided and grimaced. "For being *bad*. For something *terrible* we've done."

"I see," Paula said and her shrewd eyes swept over the group of youngsters yet again. It was more apparent to her than ever that each child was suitably intimidated—even the most recalcitrant of them. She turned away to hide a smile, thinking how terribly clever Emily was.

"We're definitely in for it," Lorne muttered, jumping up, edging away.

"You're right," Toby agreed. "Come on, Troops, let's skedaddle before my mother starts giving us stupid chores to do, or worse still, thinks up idiotic activities to keep us properly occupied."

Within the space of seconds, the older children had raced after Lorne and Toby, as always the ringleaders, who were heading at breakneck speed for the steps that led down to the beach below the promontory. Only Patrick, Linnet, and Natalie remained with Paula in the pool area.

Silence finally reigned.

Paula sank gratefully into her chair, delighted to have peace and quiet for the first time that morning. She had done her utmost to ignore them, had remained aloof from their endless bickering—as she had learned to do over the years—at least until Toby and Gideon had started fighting and Jeremy had seemed about to join in the *mêlée*. She couldn't permit that to happen. Anthony and Sally Dunvale's eldest son had not been well, and the last thing his father had said, before leaving for Ireland earlier that morning, was for them to make sure the boy did not overtax himself for the rest of his stay at the villa. Paula knew that if Jeremy went home to Clonloughlin looking as if he had been scrapping with the boys, she and Emily would never hear the end of it from his mother. Their cousin Sally fussed a great deal about her firstborn, the heir to the Dunvale title, lands, and fortune.

Paula took a deep breath, and was about to give her small daughter a lecture about removing her underclothing in public, when she saw Emily hurrying down the path between the lawns.

"Cooee! Cooee!" Emily called, waving.

Paula waved back.

A moment later, Emily drew to a stop and she and Paula exchanged knowing looks. They began to laugh hilariously.

Emily said, "I know it's noisy, but it's *very* effective."

"And *how*," Paula agreed. "I've never seen them silenced quite so quickly. *Never*. It was an inspired buy on your part."

"Yes," Emily chuckled, "so it's proved. My God, they were kicking up such a racket, I'm surprised you don't have a splitting headache by now. I know I could hardly hear myself think when I was in the kitchen, talking to Marcel about the meals for today."

"Mummy, I've been sick," Natalie announced, going over to Emily, tugging at her shift. "I frowed up."

"Don't talk like a baby, you're a big girl. And it's *threw* up," Emily corrected. She looked down at her youngest child, frowning, and put a hand on her forehead in concern. "Are you feeling all right? Are you better now, angel?"

"I don't know, Mummy."

"It's because she ate *all* the ginger snaps," Linnet said.

"Now, now, Linnet, you know it's wrong to tell tales out of school!" Paula reprimanded sharply, scowling at her daughter. "And let's not forget that you've been very naughty this morning. First, flinging Tessa's sun hat in the pool, and then taking your knickers off in public. I'm terribly cross with you, and ashamed of you, Linnet." Paula shook her head, trying hard to look appropriately angry without much success, but nevertheless, she added, "You've disgraced yourself, and the only reason you haven't been punished *yet* is because I'm still trying to think of a *suitable* punishment."

Linnet bit her lip, adopted a sorrowful expression, and wisely said nothing.

Emily looked from her daughter to her niece and then glanced at Paula. She exclaimed, "Why do I do such stupid things? Such as letting both nannies have the same day off, so they can go up to Grasse to buy perfume. And today of all days—the last chance you have to get a bit of rest before you go to New York on Wednesday. I'm sorry, Paula."

"It's all right, really it is, lovey."

Sighing under her breath, Emily now took hold of Natalie's hand. "Come along, let's go inside and get something to settle your tummy. And you'd better come along, too, Linnet, for a pair of clean underpants."

"Oh thanks, Emily," Paula murmured, settling back in her chair.

"Lunch is at one," Emily said, "and I've booked a table at La Reserve for dinner tonight. Just the four of us."

"I should jolly well hope so." Paula laughed. "And it sounds absolutely lovely. It's ages since we've been over there . . . it's one of my favorite places."

"Yes, I know," Emily replied, looking pleased as she turned away. She took a couple of steps, stopped, and said over her shoulder to Paula, "Oh by the way, I've got to go into Monte Carlo this afternoon, to pick up a repair from my antique porcelain man. Do you want to drive in with me? I'll only be a few minutes with Jules, and then we could take a stroll around the town and have tea at the Hôtel de Paris . . . watch the world go by for a while, like we used to do with Gran."

"What a nice idea, Emily, yes, I'd like that."

Emily gave her a sunny smile, then bustled her charges forward, half bending down, talking to them as they made for the villa.

Paula watched the three of them go up the path together, the two little girls walking on either side of Emily, clinging to her hands. Linnet and Natalie bore a strong resemblance to each other, could easily be mistaken for sisters since they had both inherited the famous Harte coloring—Emma's red hair and vivid green eyes and English rose complexion. They were dazzling children, really. A couple of Botticellis.

Patrick now came to Paula, stood by her chair, touched her arm, stared deeply into her face. "Mummy . . ."

"What is it, darling?"

"Mummy . . . poor birdie. Gid took it. No funeral now." The child shook his head and looked sad.

"Of course we'll have a funeral," Paula said gently, taking his small, rather grubby hand in hers and looking into his angelic face. His black O'Neill eyes were bright and lively for once, not devoid of expression and vacant as they so frequently were. Her heart lifted with joy to see such life in them today.

She gave her son a reassuring smile, and went on, "I know Gideon will bring the little bird back, and we'll ask Madame Solange for one of her old tin biscuit boxes to put the birdie in, and then after lunch we'll have the funeral. I promise, darling."

Patrick put his head on one side and studied her carefully. "Bury it in the garden?" he asked, and gave her a slow, tentative smile.

"Yes, that's *exactly* what we'll do. Oh darling, *look* who's coming!"

Patrick swung his head, and when he saw Shane approaching, his face lit up and he extracted his hand from his mother's and ran to meet his father.

Paula called out worriedly, "Patrick, do be careful. Don't fall."

Patrick did not answer. He sped ahead as fast as his little legs would carry him, shouting, "Daddy! Daddy! Daddy!"

Shane caught his son in his arms and swung him up high in the air, then placed him on his shoulders, and the two of them laughed merrily as Patrick rode Shane back to the pool area, crying, "Gee-up, gee-up. Nice horsey. Gee-up, gee-up."

"I'm going to take him for a swim. Is that okay, darling?" Shane called. He knelt down and carefully lowered Patrick to the ground.

"Yes, of course," Paula called back.

She sat up straighter, so that she could see the two of them better, shading her eyes with her hand.

Shane jumped into the shallow end of the pool, holding Patrick tightly in his arms, and immediately they began to frolic in the water, still laughing, and shouting with glee, and Patrick's face was bright with excitement and happiness and so was Shane's.

From this distance, her son seemed like any normal seven-year-old; the problem was that he would always have the mind of a seven-year-old. His body would grow and age, but his mental capacities would remain as they were now for the rest of his life. He would never be any different; they had given up hope of that. When they had first discovered Patrick was retarded, Paula had blamed herself, believing she carried some flaw in her genes which had been inherited from her grandfather. Paul McGill had had a legitimate son, Howard, by his legal wife, Constance, in Australia, and the boy, dead now for a number of years, had been retarded. She had so convinced herself that this was the case, she had told Shane she dare not risk having any more children. But Shane had immediately pooh-poohed her theory, and he had insisted they see Professor Charles Hallingby, a leading geneticist.

They had both been tested and the results had proved conclusively that neither she nor Shane had passed on any kind of deficiency to their son. Patrick's condition was inexplicable, simply a terrible fluke of nature. Professor Hallingby, having studied their family histories, had pointed out to Paula that her grandfather's son may well have suffered prenatal damage because of Constance McGill's heavy drinking during her pregnancy, a possibility her mother, Daisy, had mentioned innumerable times. She had finally conceded that the professor and her mother could be right. Not unnaturally, the knowledge that Professor Hallingby had imparted had helped to ease her mind. Shortly after, she had conceived again, and when Linnet was born she was a perfectly normal baby.

Paula loved her children equally, and tried not to have a favorite, but deep in the innermost regions of her heart she was aware that Patrick was special to her, that he had a unique place in her affections. There was a terrible fierceness about her love for her afflicted child, perhaps, in part, *because* of his affliction, which made him so vulnerable and dependent.

His siblings also loved him dearly, and took great care with him, and for this she was thankful. Often she thought how heartbreaking it would have been if they had despised him or shunned him, as sometimes happened in families where there was a retarded child. But Lorne, Tessa, and even little Linnet were as protective of Patrick as she and Shane were and, in fact, so were his many cousins. Not one single child in the family had ever made Patrick feel that he was in any way different to them. It was a tragedy that her little Patrick had not been born a perfect child, that he was damaged in the way he was. But Paula recognized that his inherent sweetness and his loving disposition compensated for so many things and endeared him to the family, and certainly he brought out the best in all of them.

An afflicted child is like a bruise on the heart—one never quite gets rid of the aching pain, Paula suddenly thought, and she sighed under her breath and held herself very still, pressing down on her sadness, continuing to watch the two dark heads bobbing around in the water. Her husband, her son. Oh how she loved them both, and with a love that was heart-stopping at times.

It did her good to see how much they were enjoying their nautical games. Shane could be very gentle and tender with Patrick, or roughhouse with him, as he was doing now, and from the joyous shrieks and the whoops of delight filling the air, she knew the little boy was having the best time with the father whom he worshipped. A great rush of happiness filled her to the brim, displaced the sorrow she had felt a moment ago.

Paula lay back and closed her eyes, feeling a measure of contentment, but she lifted her lids almost immediately and sat up at the sound of Winston's voice.

He walked into the pool area carrying a large tray of plastic tumblers, and trotting dutifully behind him was his nephew, Giles Standish, second son of his sister Sally, the Countess of Dunvale. Giles was carefully holding a large jug of lemonade with both hands.

"Bon jour, Tante Paula. Voilà! Ici citron presse pour toi," the nine-year-old Giles said, showing off his little bit of French, as he had been doing all through the summer. He was having special tutoring in the language and made a point of speaking it whenever he could, much to the irritation of the other children, who were not as fluent as he was becoming. But their constant ribbing rolled off his back; he was independent by nature, so he paid no attention and went on speaking French whenever he felt like it.

Giles put the jug down on one of the tables in the shade, and politely stood aside to make way for his uncle.

"How delicious it looks, Giles dear," Paula said. "Just what I need, I'm getting quite parched from this heat. Did your parents get off all right?"

"Yes, but Nice Airport was jammed, wasn't it, Uncle Winston?" Giles said, reverting to English.

"It was bloody awful, Paula," Winston asserted, pouring lemonade into a tumbler and bringing it to her. "Chaotic. I've never seen so many people. Sally and Anthony were thankful they were returning on Shane's private jet, and I must say, that plane's turned out to be a real godsend. I'm certainly glad Emily and I will be able to use it to get the mob back home at the end of the week. Now, Giles, do you want a glass of this?"

"No, thank you very much." Giles glanced around. "Where are Jeremy and India, Auntie Paula?"

"I believe your brother and sister decamped to the beach. With the rest of the troops."

"Oh goody! I bet they're all fishing or looking for *oursins*. I'm going down there too!" Giles squealed excitedly. "Please excuse me, Auntie Paula, Uncle Winston," and so saying he took off, leaping across the grass in great bounds, making for the long flight of steps.

Winston stared after him, and said to Paula, "That kid's got the best manners of the whole bunch of them. If only some of the others—mine in particular—would borrow even *half* a page from his book, I'd be happy." He lowered himself onto a nearby chair, took a long swallow of lemonade, and continued, "Emily told me every single one of them was raising hell earlier."

"It did start to get a bit out of hand, actually, Winston. But Emily finally put a stop to their bickering with that wonderfully effective gong." She glanced at her cousin through the corner of her eye, and chuckled. "Trust Emily to come up with something ridiculous like that. Still, it really works, and I must admit, I wish I had a handle on them the way she does."

Winston grinned. "Don't we all."

Seven

"I adore old-fashioned hotels, especially when they're in the *belle époque* style and have a grandiose splendor," Emily said to Paula as they turned into the Place Casino in Monte Carlo later that afternoon. "You know, like the Hôtel de Paris here, the Negresco in Nice, the Ritz in Paris, and the Imperial in Vienna."

"Not to mention the Grand in Scarborough," Paula said, laughing, tucking her arm through Emily's companionably. "I can well recall how attached you were to that place when we were little. You never stopped pestering me to take you there for afternoon tea, and you couldn't wait to stuff your fat little face with cucumber sandwiches and cream puffs and scones with strawberry jam and clotted cream," she teased, her violet eyes dancing merrily.

Emily shuddered at the remembrance and made a gruesome face. "My God, all those fattening things! No wonder I've had to work so hard to keep my weight down ever since. Too much ballast as a child, methinks!" She grinned at Paula. "You shouldn't have permitted me to eat like that."

"How could I stop you! I tried very hard to keep you out of the Grand Hotel, using every kind of ruse, even pretending I didn't have any money on me. But you always had an answer for everything, even for that . . . 'Scribble on the bill like Grandma does,' you used to tell me. You were a very enterprising child, you know."

"And so were you."

They both stopped at precisely the same moment and automatically swung to face each other and they shared a smile, thinking of those lighthearted happy days when they were growing up together in Yorkshire and London. There was a brief and loving silence before Emily said, "We *were* lucky, weren't we, Paula?

We had such a wonderful childhood, and especially when we were with our Gran."

"Yes, it was the *best,*" Paula agreed. "And she was the *best.*"

They started walking again, lost in their own thoughts as they crossed the pleasant square, heading in the direction of the Hôtel de Paris, which was situated in the far corner, opposite the renowned Casino de Monte Carlo.

It was a lovely afternoon, filled with dappled sunlight and soft white clouds scudding across the azure-blue sky, and there was a refreshing breeze blowing up from the sea. It ruffled the skirts of their summer dresses, puffed them out like tulip bells, and made the white sails on the boats in the harbor billow about, and the brightly colored flags on the masts ripple and dance gaily.

Emily had driven them down to Monte Carlo in her powder blue Jaguar, after a family luncheon on the terrace at the villa, and then the burial of the dead bird in the garden, which everyone had attended, much to Patrick's satisfaction.

Once they had arrived in the Principality of Monaco they had parked the car and gone to Jules et Cie, the antique shop where Emily frequently bought old porcelain, to pick up a Limoges plate Jules had repaired for her. The charming old man had chatted to them at length about antique china and glass, and had shown them his private collection of rare items, and they had browsed for a while before leaving the *antiquaire's* to stroll around the main streets and window-shop on their way to the famous hotel for afternoon tea.

"It's impossibly grand, even a bit gingerbready, but it's irresistible, at least to me," Emily said, pausing on the pavement outside the Hôtel de Paris, looking up at it, beginning to laugh at herself as they climbed the front steps. Almost instantly the laughter died in her throat, and she grabbed Paula's arm so tightly her cousin winced and followed her gaze.

Heading toward them down the steps was a tall woman with an abundance of flaming red hair and the kind of elegance that was indisputably French. She wore a white silk dress, very chic and severely tailored, with a black-silk rose pinned to one shoulder, black-and-white high-heeled shoes, a matching bag, and white gloves. She carried a black straw picture hat, and she was holding the hand of a little girl of about three years, also dressed entirely in white, who had the same natural, bright red hair. The woman was bending over the child, saying something to her as they moved forward, and she had not seen them.

"Christ Almighty! It's Sarah!" Emily gasped and squeezed Paula's arm again.

Paula sucked in her breath, but she had no chance to make any response, nor could she and Emily turn around and hurry away.

A split second later their cousin had drawn level with them. The three women were standing on the same step, gaping at each other, and they were so stunned they were utterly speechless, rooted to the spot.

It was Paula who finally broke the uncomfortable silence.

"Hello, Sarah," she said, very quietly, in a soft voice. "You're looking well." She stopped, took a deep breath. "And this must be your daughter . . . Chloe, isn't it?" she added, forcing a smile, looking down at the child, whose upturned face was solemn and filled with curiosity. And Paula saw, on closer inspection, that this was a true offspring of Emma Harte.

Sarah had regained her self-possession, and she gave Paula a look that was deadly. "How dare you speak to me!" she cried, not bothering to sheathe her hostility and loathing. "How dare *you* attempt to make a friendly gesture toward *me*." Leaning closer, she hissed in Paula's face, "You have a bloody nerve, behaving as if nothing happened between us, Paula O'Neill, and after what you did to me, you rotten bitch!"

The undisguised hatred on Sarah's face, and her threatening manner, made Paula recoil in shock and dismay.

"You'd better stay away from me and mine!" Sarah exclaimed, her face turning brilliant red. She looked almost choleric, and her voice was unnecessarily loud and shrill. "And you too, Emily Harte, you're no better than she is," she scoffed, her scarlet lips curling in scorn. "You two turned Grandmother against me, and then you cheated me of what was rightfully mine! You're both *thieves*. Now, get out of my way! Both of you!"

Tightening her grip on the child's hand, Sarah pushed between Paula and Emily, almost knocking Paula over. And she swept on grandly down the remainder of the steps without a backward glance, the child hurrying and stumbling to keep up with her mother, exclaiming, *"Maman, Maman, attendez!"*

Paula had gone cold all over, despite the heat of the day, and there was a queasy feeling in the pit of her stomach. She was momentarily paralyzed, powerless to move. Then suddenly she grew conscious of Emily taking hold of her arm.

Emily said, *"Phew!* That was awful. She's not changed, has she?"

"No, she hasn't," Paula agreed, rousing herself. "Let's go in, Emily, people are staring at us." Paula extracted herself, flew up the steps and through the doors of the hotel, wanting to put distance between herself and those passersby who had witnessed the scene. She was mortified and still shaking inside.

Emily ran after her and found her cousin waiting inside the door, striving to calm herself. She slipped her arm through Paula's and drew her forward into the hotel, saying, "At least we didn't *know* any of those people who were listening and gawking at us, darling, so forget it. Come on, let's go and have a nice cup of tea. It'll do us both good."

Once they had been shown to a secluded table in the lounge area of the vast lobby, and had settled down and ordered a pot of tea, Emily sat back and expelled a great sigh. "What a nasty performance that was," she said.

"Yes. Ugly. And embarrassing. I could hardly believe my ears when she started to shout at us like a fishwife, not to mention the ghastly things she was saying."

Emily nodded and gave Paula a careful look. "Why on earth did you speak to her in the first place?"

"I didn't know what else to do. We were eyeball to eyeball. It was terribly awkward, you know that, Emily," Paula replied, and paused. A contemplative expression settled on her face and she shook her head slowly. "I suppose I've always felt a bit sorry for Sarah. She *was* Jonathan's pawn, and his victim, in a certain sense. He duped her, used her and her money. I've never really considered her to be wicked like Jonathan. Just rather stupid."

"I agree with you—about her stupidity—but I don't feel sorry for her, and neither should you," Emily exclaimed. She drew closer, continued, "Look here, Paula, you're far too nice, always trying to be fair-minded and compassionate, and seeing everyone else's point of view. That's all very well when you're dealing with people who deserve your concern, but I don't think Sarah does. Stupid or not, she knew it was wrong to back Jonathan, to put up money for his private company. That truly was going against Harte Enterprises—and the family."

"Yes, it was," Paula admitted. "But I still think that in some ways she's more dense than anything else, and I'm sure Jonathan pulled the wool over her eyes."

Emily said, "Maybe he did." She sat back, crossed her legs, and went on, "Don't you think it's odd that we haven't run across Sarah before now. I mean after all, she's been living up the coast near Cannes for about five years, according to that story we saw in *Paris Match,* and Mougins isn't that far away."

Paula was silent.

After a moment she leveled her steady gaze at Emily, and murmured, "What's also kind of odd is that for the first time in years Michael Kallinski was talking about Sarah and Jonathan on Friday and—"

"Why?" Emily cut in peremptorily.

"No special reason, other than his own curiosity. We'd been talking about Lady Hamilton Clothes, as I told you yesterday, so I suppose it was natural for him to inquire about Sarah's whereabouts. Still . . ." Paula broke off, shook her head.

"Still *what?*" Emily pressed.

"I was just thinking that his talking about them was almost prophetic." Paula gave a curious, rather nervous little laugh as she stared pointedly at Emily.

"Gosh, it was! And I hope to God we don't run into Jonathan next. I'm not sure I could survive an encounter with *him* quite as coolly as the one with Sarah."

"I know I couldn't." As she spoke, Paula shivered involuntarily, and she felt the hackles rise on the back of her neck and goose flesh speckle her arms. She sat back in the chair, biting her inner lip, wishing the mention of Jonathan's name would not upset her the way it did.

Fortunately, the waiter arrived with the laden tea tray, and Paula was glad for the distraction as he commenced to place the cups and saucers on the table in front of them and speak in rapid French to Emily, whom he apparently knew by sight. Paula declined the many delicious pastries being offered, and stole a surreptitious glance at Emily, wondering if her cousin would succumb to temptation.

Emily looked longingly at the cakes, but she also shook her head, and as Paula poured the tea, she said, "Don't think I didn't want one of *everything,* because I did. I could have cheerfully made a meal out of the chocolate eclairs and the vanilla slices, but you saw how I resisted. All for the benefit of my figure. And Winston. He likes me to be svelte, so I've developed a will of iron when it comes to nasty fattening things like cream buns. You should be very proud of me," she finished, irrepressible laughter bubbling up in her.

"And so should Winston," Paula said, also laughing. Their sudden gaiety helped to dissipate the unpleasantness of the scene with Sarah, which still lingered in their thoughts, and it changed their mood, brought them back to normal. Almost at once they began to talk about spending a few days in Hong Kong together next month, and made their plans.

At one moment, between sips of tea, Paula said, "You and Shane are right, Emily, I think I will take Madelana to Australia with me."

"Oh I am glad you agree with us, darling. If the boutiques really are in a mess, she'll be of tremendous help."

"Yes, that's true, and I think she'll be thrilled to come with me, don't you?"

"Who wouldn't be—it's a marvelous trip, and anyway she's devoted to you."

"She is. It was a smart move on my part, promoting her to be my assistant a year ago. She's proved herself to be invaluable." Paula glanced at her watch. "It's five o'clock . . . eleven in the morning in New York. I'll give her a ring later, explain that I want her to come with me. She'll have her hands full this week, clearing the decks in order to leave with me on Saturday, so the sooner she knows, the better."

"You could call her from here, if you wanted to, Paula," Emily suggested, never the one to waste any time if she could help it.

"No, no, that's all right. I can do it when we get home to Faviola. The six-hour time difference gives me plenty of leeway."

Emily nodded, and then right out of the blue, she said, "I bet you anything that dress she was wearing was a Givenchy."

"I've no doubt it was. Sarah always did have a flair for clothes."

"Mmmm." Emily turned thoughtful, sat looking into the distance for a few moments. Finally, she asked Paula, "Do you think she ever hears from Jonathan?"

"I can't even hazard a guess."

"I wonder what did happen to him, Paula? Where he's living?" Emily said softly, thinking out loud.

"I'd prefer not to know. Or to talk about him, if you don't mind, Emily. You know very well that Jonathan Ainsley's not my favorite subject," Paula answered sharply.

"Oh gosh, sorry, darling," Emily said, suddenly regretful that she had started talking about their cousins again. Changing the subject, she said quickly, "Well, I'd better pay and we'll get off home, so you can call Madelana at Harte's in New York."

"Yes, let's go," Paula agreed.

Eight

She was the kind of woman that men looked at twice. And women, too, for that matter.

It was not that Madelana O'Shea was very beautiful. She was not. But she had what the French call *je ne sais quois,* that indefinable something that made her special and caused heads to turn wherever she went.

Tonight was no exception.

She stood outside Harte's department store on Fifth Avenue, patiently waiting for the radio cab she had ordered from her office a short while before. It was eight o'clock on a Thursday and the store was still open. Everyone who hurried in and out stole a glance at her, obviously wondering who she was, for she had style and there was a touch of regality in her bearing.

A tall young woman of about five feet eight, and slender, she had a willowy figure and legs that were long and shapely. Her thick, chestnut-brown hair was shoulder length, worn full and loose around her heart-shaped face. She was a little too bony to be called pretty, but the smooth forehead and high, slanting cheekbones, sharp as blades, gave her the look of a thoroughbred, as did the finely drawn aristocratic nose sprinkled faintly with freckles. She had a wide Irish mouth, with a full, somewhat voluptuous bottom lip, and a lovely smile that filled her face with radiance, but it was her eyes that fascinated and compelled. They were large, widely set, and of an unusual pale gray the color of chalcedony, their marvelous transparency emphasized by the dark brows arched above them. They were highly intelligent eyes, and filled with a determination that could turn steely at times, but there was also laughter in them and sometimes a hidden recklessness.

Madelana had a flair for clothes and wore them well. She looked smart in anything she put on, gave it her own cachet; it might be the way she knotted a scarf, snapped down the brim of a hat, wrapped a length of oriental silk into a unique cummerbund or twisted antique beads around her long and slender neck. And it was this great personal chic in combination with her svelte good looks that made her appearance so arresting.

The evening was stifling, humid as only New York in the middle of summer can be, and everyone seemed worn down and wilted in the oppressive weather as they toiled up Fifth, or stood at the edge of the sidewalk, looking for a yellow cab or waiting to cross to the other side.

But not Madelana O'Shea. Her tailored cream silk tunic, with its simple round neckline and three-quarter-length sleeves, worn over a straight black silk skirt, was as crisp as it had been when she had set out for work that morning, and she looked cool, untouched by the heat, and as elegant as usual.

The burgundy radio cab pulled up in front of the store, and she hurried forward with an ease and lightness of movement that bespoke her childhood ballet and tap lessons. She was limber, and had the agile grace of a dancer, and this, too, was part of her immense appeal.

After opening the taxi door, she put the large Harte's shopping bag on the seat and slid in next to it.

"West Twenty-fourth Street, right, miss?" the driver said, moving off down Fifth.

"Yes, between Seventh and Eighth, in the middle of the block, please."

"Okay, miss."

Madelana sat back, rested her hands on the black patent bag in her lap, her mind racing as it almost always did, no matter where she was or what she was doing.

Ever since Monday afternoon, when Paula had called from the south of France to tell her she was going to Australia, she had felt as if she had been running in a marathon. She had had to complete her current work, cancel her business appointments for the next few weeks, along with the few personal dates she had made, plan ahead for a possibly protracted absence from the store, and select appropriate clothes and accessories for the trip.

And then Paula had arrived in New York on the Concorde, early on Wednesday morning, and had come directly to the store. The two of them had worked like demons for two solid days, but they *had* accomplished miracles, and they would have a relatively normal business day tomorrow, before leaving on Saturday on the first leg of their journey. Tonight she would go over the files of papers she had stacked in the shopping bag and finish working on them, and tomorrow night she would pack.

I'm ahead of the game, Madelana thought with sudden relief, and nodded to herself, feeling gratified. She glanced out the window, hardly noticing the tawdry glitter and squalor of Times Square with its hustlers and peddlers and drug addicts and pushers and undercover cops and hookers on the make. As the cab slid swiftly through this clamoring rinky-tink wedge of real estate and headed on downtown toward Chelsea, her mind focused on the trip to the other side of the world.

They were going first to Sydney, then on to Melbourne and perhaps even to Adelaide after that, before returning to Sydney, where they would spend most of their time. From what Paula had told her, they had a lot of work to do, and it would be a grueling two or three weeks. But the prospect did not faze her. She and Paula O'Neill worked well together, had always seemed to understand each other right from the beginning, and they were compatible.

It struck her, and not for the first time, how strange it was that she, a poor Irish-American Catholic girl from the South, and an aristocratic Englishwoman, heiress to one of the world's great fortunes and a noted international business tycoon, could be so similar, and in so many ways. They were both workaholics and had boundless energy, were sticklers for detail, disciplined, dedicated, driven, and extremely well organized. In consequence, they did not grate on each other's nerves, or create problems for each other, and they seemed always to be in step. It's like dancing with Fred Astaire or Gene Kelly, she thought and smiled inwardly, liking her analogy.

In the year she had been Paula's personal assistant, she had not put a foot wrong and she did not intend to, not ever, and especially not on their forthcoming trip to Australia. Paula was the key to her future. Her goal was to become president of Harte's store in New York one day, and with Paula's help she would achieve it.

Ambition. She was loaded with it. She knew this only too well, and she was pleased that she was. She considered it to be a plus not a minus. It had goaded her on, helped her to arrive where she was today. Her father had occasionally complained that she was too ambitious. But her mother had merely smiled her lovely Irish smile at him, and behind his back had winked at her and nodded maternal approval and encouraged her at every opportunity.

She wished her parents were still alive. And her little sister, Kerry Anne, who had died at the age of four. And Joe and Lonnie. Her two brothers had been killed in Vietnam. She missed them so very much, just as she missed her baby sister and her parents, and at times she felt as though she had no roots, no center to her life, with all of them gone from her. They had been close knit as a family, and very loving of each other. She considered her losses over the past few years, thought of her sorrow, and her heart clenched. Resolutely, she pushed the pain away.

Madelana took several deep breaths, keeping absolute control of herself and her emotions, as she had taught herself to do after her father had been buried four years ago. Only when he was lying in the ground did her sense of aloneness truly overwhelm her, and only then did she fully comprehend that she no longer had any family left, except for Aunt Agnes, her father's sister, who lived in California and whom she hardly knew.

The cab drew up outside the Residence Jeanne D'Arc. She took the receipt from the driver, said goodnight, grabbed her shopping bag, and alighted. She ran swiftly up the steps and into the building.

The minute she walked inside, Madelana felt herself relaxing.

This place was so familiar and welcoming . . . she had lived here in one of the rooms when she had first come to New York, had stayed for three years. She still thought of it as home, even though she now had her own apartment uptown in the East Eighties.

She crossed the small entrance foyer and turned right, heading for the office.

"Hello, Sister Mairéad," Madelana said to the nun behind the counter, who was in charge of the office this evening. "How are you?"

"Why, Madelana, it's nice to see you, and I'm just fine, very fine indeed," the sister replied, the faint Irish lilt echoing softly in her voice, her rose-apple cheeks dimpling with pleasure. The sister had had a soft spot for Madelana when she had lived here, and she was always delighted to see this lovely young woman who was such a credit to her parents, God rest their souls, and who in every way exemplified her good Catholic upbringing.

"Sister Bronagh's expecting me," Madelana said with a smile, and put the large Harte's bag on the counter, took out a gift-wrapped package, and looked at the sister. "Can I leave my shopping bag with you, please?"

"Of course you can, Madelana. Sister Bronagh said for you to go to the garden. She'll be up to join you in a few minutes. I'll let her know you've arrived." Sister Mairéad beamed and picked up the phone, began to dial.

"Thank you, Sister," Madelana murmured, heading for the small, boxlike elevator that would take her up to the fifth floor and the stairs that led to the roof of the building.

Surprisingly, the roof garden was empty.

Usually in the summer, on pleasant evenings, some of the girls who lived at the residency came up here to chat and socialize with each other, and with the sisters, to share a drink of wine or juice, or read a book or simply be alone.

It was a charming spot, planted with rambling ivy, and there were vines growing on trellis panels, and window boxes of bright red and pink geraniums, and pots of yellow and peach begonias, and the sisters grew vegetables up here. Scattered about were chairs and several small tables, and the atmosphere was inviting and suggested conviviality.

She paused to look at the statue of the Blessed Virgin, surrounded by masses of flowers as it generally was in the summer, recalling how often she had tended the flowers when she had been living here. She had always thought of this spot as an oasis, a lovely patch of green-growing things in the middle of the concrete canyons of Manhattan, and it had given her a feeling of well-being, had nourished her soul.

Gliding forward, she went to one of the tables, put down the gift and her handbag, and seated herself in one of the chairs facing uptown. Straight ahead of her, in her direct angle of vision, were the Empire State and the Chrysler Buildings thrusting up above the higgledy-piggledy roofs and chimney pots of Chelsea and the less-distinguished skyscrapers of the city.

Dusk was already falling, and the lavender-and-gray tinted sky was changing as a deep cobalt blue seeped in like ink and slowly extinguished these paler hues. The lights that washed over the towers of the two dominating buildings had been turned on, but the grandeur of the architecture would not be properly visible until the sky was pitch black. Then these towers would be thrown into relief, would shimmer magnificently against the dark velvet backdrop of the sky, and it was a sight that never failed to make her catch her breath in delight.

Even in winter, Madelana had enjoyed coming up here when she had lived at the residency. Wrapped in warm clothes, she had huddled in a sheltered corner, admiring these two extraordinary edifices and a skyline that stunned with its unique beauty.

The Chrysler, with its Art Deco sunburst motif on its elegant tapering tower, was only ever flooded with clear white light that gave it a pristine beauty and underscored the purity of its design, whereas the Empire State changed its colors to suit the season and the holidays. At Thanksgiving, the two tiers and the slender tower above were flooded with amber, gold, and orange; at Christmas with red and green. The lights changed to blue and white for Chanukah and other Jewish holidays, became yellow at Easter, green on St. Patrick's Day, and red, white, and blue for the Fourth of July. And if the Chrysler Building really was the more beautiful of the two, then certainly the Empire State was the most eye-catching when it blazed with a celebratory selection of its rainbow colors.

"Good evening, Madelana," Sister Bronagh called as she walked across to the table, carrying two glasses of white wine.

Madelana sprang up at the sound of her voice.

"Hello, Sister." She hurried forward, smiling, and took the glass being offered to her, and the two women clasped hands affectionately, before sitting down together at the table.

"You're looking extremely well," Sister Bronagh said, peering at her in the gathering dusk.

"Thank you, I feel good."

They touched glasses and sipped their drinks.

"This is for you, Sister," Madelana said, after a moment, and slid the gift across the table.

"For me?" Sister Bronagh's eyes suddenly twinkled merrily behind her spectacles, her face wreathed in smiles.

"That's why I came tonight . . . to bring you the present and to say good-bye. I won't be able to come to your farewell party next week. I'll be in Australia by then."

"Australia! My goodness, so far away, Madelana. But exciting, I think, for you. I'm so sorry you won't be at the party . . . your absence will be noticed. It always has been, when you haven't been able to make one of our little get-togethers. And thank you for the gift, it was thoughtful of you. May I open it now?"

"Of course," Madelana said, laughing, enjoying the sister's obvious delight in the small token she had brought.

Sister Bronagh untied the yellow ribbon, dispensed with the wrapping paper, and lifted the lid of the Harte's silver cardboard box. Underneath the layers of tissue paper were three different-sized toilet bags made of deep blue silk and trimmed with a lighter blue welting.

"Oh, how lovely they are!" Sister Bronagh exclaimed, taking one out, turning it over in her hands, opening the zip, and looking inside. Her small, birdlike face was bright with sudden happiness and she took Madelana's hand resting on the table and squeezed it. "Thank you so much, my dear, they're just what I need."

"I'm glad you like them. I wanted to get you something that was pretty but also useful." Madelana grinned at her. "I *know* you . . . how practical you are. Anyway, I thought these would be perfect for traveling." She rested her elbows on the table. Her fingers toyed with the glass of wine. "When *do* you leave for Rome?"

"On the tenth of September, and I'm becoming excited about going. It'll be a challenge, helping to run the residency over there. It's situated not very far away from the Vatican, and that's an added joy for me, being so close to the Holy See." There was a lovely glow about her as she continued, "I must confess to you, Madelana, I was thrilled when Sister Marie-Theresa picked me to be the one to go."

Madelana nodded. "Everyone here at the residency is going to miss you, though, me included."

"Oh and I shall miss you, too, Madelana, and the other old girls who still come to see me, and the ones living here now, and the sisters." There was a brief pause. A fleeting sadness touched Sister Bronagh's eyes, and they grew moist, and then she cleared her throat quickly, sat up, straightened the collar of her white blouse. She gave Madelana a warm smile. "Tell me about your trip to Australia. It's rather sudden, isn't it?"

"Yes. I'm going on business with my boss, Paula O'Neill. We're leaving for Los Angeles on Saturday morning, and we'll spend the night there, since she thinks we'll both be in better shape if we break the trip instead of flying direct. We take the Quantas flight to Sydney at ten o'clock on Sunday night."

"And how long will you be gone?"

"Two or three weeks, perhaps even four. Paula may have to leave me behind to follow through for her. We're going out there because of the boutiques in the hotels. She's concerned they're not being run properly. The manager has been sick, and her assistant seems to either panic or flounder on alternate days."

"You've done well at Harte's, Madelana, I'm proud of you."

"Thank you. Anyway, my career's very important to me, as you know . . ." Madelana stopped, and there was a hesitation in her manner, and she looked down at her hands resting on the table. Shortly, she went on in a more muted, thoughtful tone, "But working so hard these past few years has also helped me to keep grief at bay, to come to grips with my losses . . ." Her voice suddenly trailed off.

The sister reached out, took Madelana's hand in hers, and there was a sense of comfort in this gesture. "Yes, I know it has. But then so has your great faith, Madelana. Always remember that God has His reasons, and that He never gives us a burden that is too heavy to carry."

"Yes, you've told me that many times before." Madelana tightened her grip on Sister Bronagh's hand. There was a short silence between them. She lifted her head then, and smiled faintly at this devout and gentle middle-aged woman who had been so warm and loving to her when she had lived here, who had singled her out for special attention.

"I couldn't let you leave for Rome without coming to see you, Sister Bronagh, to thank you from the bottom of my heart for helping me to get through so much pain and sorrow, for making me feel so welcome when I first arrived. You gave me courage."

"No, no, I didn't, Madelana," the sister said swiftly. "The courage was within you, already part of you then. As it is now. And as it will always be. If I did anything at all, it was simply to show you that it *was* there, to make you understand that all you needed to do was to reach inside of yourself, and to draw on it."

"Yes . . . But I'll never be able to thank you enough for all you've done for me. And for all you've taught me—especially about myself."

"You were always very special to me, my child," Sister Bronagh replied in a soft voice. "If I had not chosen this way of life, had not chosen to be in service to God, to do His work, and if I had married and had a daughter, I would have wanted her to be exactly like you."

"Oh Sister Bronagh, what a beautiful thing to say, thank you, thank you so much!" Madelana experienced a sudden rush of emotion and there was the unexpected sting of tears behind her eyes and she blinked them away, not wanting to break down. She realized how much she would miss Sister Bronagh after the nun had departed for her new job in Rome.

Now Madelana said, "Your belief in me has been so important, Sister, it's mirrored the faith my mother had in me. She encouraged me the way you have. I'll try never to let you down."

The sweetest of smiles brushed across Sister Bronagh's pale mouth and she said slowly, to give greater emphasis to her words, "The important thing is never to let yourself down, Madelana."

———— *Nine* ————

It was a long, hot ride uptown from the residence Jeanne D'Arc to East Eighty-fourth Street, and for the first time that day Madelana felt uncomfortably warm and damp when she finally alighted in front of the small apartment building where she lived.

"Hi, Alex," she said, greeting the doorman breezily as he helped her out of the cab.

The doorman responded in kind, and there was an admiring look in his eyes as he watched her walk rapidly across the sidewalk with her usual ease of movement. She swung into the building before he could rush to open the door for her, and appeared to float across the lobby, her feet hardly seeming to touch the marble as she sped ahead.

She stopped to collect her mail and then took the elevator to the seventeenth floor. The phone was ringing inside her apartment when she put the key in the lock. She hurried in as the phone continued its strident shrilling in the cool silence of the empty apartment.

Snapping on the light in the minuscule entrance hall, she dumped her things unceremoniously on the floor and ran to pick up the nearest extension.

This was on the desk in the yellow-and-white living room, which opened directly off the tiny foyer, and snatching the receiver, she exclaimed, "Hello," only to discover that there was no one at the other end. All she could hear was the faint burring of the dial tone; the caller had obviously disconnected a split second before she had reached the phone.

Oh well, she thought, whoever it is will call back, if it's important, and she dropped the receiver into the cradle with a shrug of her elegant shoulders, then hesitated, pivoted to look at the phone. She was on the verge of picking it up again, wondering if it had been Paula calling her, concerned with some last-minute bit of business. Or about something they had forgotten. It was hardly likely, since it was almost ten o'clock. She immediately dismissed the idea of calling her boss at her Fifth Avenue apartment. That would be an unwarranted intrusion, and anyway, Paula always went to bed early when she first arrived in New York, in an effort to counteract jet lag.

Madelana shivered, becoming aware of the chilly temperature. The air-conditioning had been running at its highest all day, and the apartment was like a freezer. But her body would soon adjust, and she welcomed the coolness after the humidity of the stuffy, airless streets of Manhattan.

She went to retrieve her things, and carried them back to the living room, sat down on the yellow velvet sofa, and glanced at her mail. There was nothing of any importance and she put it on the glass-and-brass coffee table, rose, and went into the adjoining bedroom to change her clothes.

A minute or two later she emerged, barefooted and wearing a long pink cotton caftan, and hurried into the kitchen to prepare a light supper for herself, before digging into the work she had brought home from the store.

The kitchen in her small apartment was long and narrow, and it had reminded Madelana of a ship's galley the first time she had seen it, just a year ago this month. And for this reason she had decorated it in various shades of blue with lots of white and dashes of brilliant red. She had covered the walls with nautical prints, ranging from Boston whalers, nineteenth-century sailing ships, and Mississippi riverboats to ocean-going liners and modern yachts. All were framed in brass, and there were other touches of brass in small accessories; copper molds hung above the stove and the sink, and these added their own sparkle.

At one end, near the window, she had placed a small, drop-leaf table and two bentwood chairs, an ideal spot for a snack. A small window box on the sill was filled with feathery spider ferns, and the kitchen had a gaiety and a charm which owed more to her ingenuity and flair than to the amount of money she had spent.

One of the colorful yachting prints caught Madelana's eye, and she smiled to herself, thinking of her friend Patsy Smith. Patsy was a Boston girl who had lived at the residency at the same time that she had, and two years ago Patsy had invited her to the Smith's summer home in Nantucket for the long Fourth of July weekend. They had done a lot of sailing over those four glorious days, and Madelana had loved every moment she had been on the water. It had been a new and exhilarating experience for her, and much to her amazement she had discovered she had a great affinity for boats and the sea.

Perhaps one day I'll do it again, she thought, turning to the refrigerator, taking out the ingredients for a salad.

The telephone on the wall behind her rang. She reached for it. "Hello?"

"So, you're finally home."

"Oh Jack, hi. Yes, I was—"

"You canceled our date in order to work, or so you said," he interrupted rudely, sourness curling around the edge of his beautiful, resonant voice. "But you ain't been home, kiddo, I've been calling you all night."

Madelana felt herself stiffening at his accusatory tone, and she resented the fact that he had obviously been checking up on her. But she took a deep breath, managed to muster a reasonable tone, to say evenly, "I had to go down to the residency. To see Sister Bronagh."

"I suppose that's as good an excuse as any."

"But it's *true,* and please don't take this attitude with me. I don't like it, Jack."

"You don't expect me to believe that's where you *really* were, do you? Visiting a nun?" He laughed hollowly. "Come on, babe——"

"I'm not a liar," she cut in, bristling with anger. Her voice rose, and she added coldly, "Nor do I appreciate being called one."

He ignored this remark. "Why won't you tell me *who* you were with tonight?"

"I was with Sister Bronagh." She tightened her grip on the phone to steady herself. Her exasperation was running high, her patience growing thin.

He laughed again, this time more sardonically. "Sister Bronagh indeed! Come on, babe, don't start getting holier than thou with me. It's Jack you're talking to. *Me. Jack.* Jack your lover, Jack the big man in your life. But is he the *only* man in your life? That's the question."

She realized then that not only had he been drinking again, but that he was, in fact, quite drunk. Although there was no slurring of his speech, she could recognize the signs these days. He became sarcastic, argumentative, and suspicious of her, and all of his insecurities started to show. And of course he enjoyed baiting her, which only infuriated her further. Jack was a bad drunk. In the last few months she had learned that firmness was the only way in which to deal with him, and that if she adopted the stern posture of a school teacher she could somehow get the upper hand. But she didn't want the upper hand with Jack. She wanted an equal partnership, a balanced relationship in which neither one of them was manipulating or controlling the other.

Sounding crisp and cool, she said, "Good night, Jack. Go to bed. I'll call you in the morning."

There was a sudden silence at the other end of the phone.

She heard him suck in his breath, as if he were taken aback that she was about to hang up on him.

She said again, her voice very firm and colder than ever, *"Good night."*

"Hey, wait a minute, Madelana, how about dinner tomorrow night? A quick, quiet little dinner. At my place. Or yours. Or somewhere in your neighborhood. Come on, say yes, honey," he cajoled, unexpectedly much less hostile, almost contrite.

"You know I can't, Jack. I explained earlier in the week that I have to pack on Friday night. In case it's slipped your mind, I'm going to Australia on Saturday morning."

"That's *right! Of course!* I keep forgetting that you're the little career girl dedicated heart and soul to work. Or should I say *big* career girl. Much more appropriate, no? Ah yes, indeedy, *big* career. *Big* job. *Big* ambitions. But tell me one more thing, babe, is work going to keep you warm in bed on cold nights?" He laughed thinly. "I doubt it. You don't need a *big* career, babe. You need a *big* man. Like me. Listen, I've got a great idea. Why don't I come over right now and——"

"Y'all've had too much to drink, Jack Miller! Why you're drunker than a skunk that's been suckling at the moonshine barrel!" she cried, inadvertently slipping into the idiom of her Southern childhood, as she sometimes did when she was angry or overly excited. "Go to bed," she instructed fiercely, "I'll call y'all in the morning." She replaced the receiver quietly, even though she felt like slamming it down hard. She was humiliated by his attitude toward her, and resentful and angry.

I hate the way he makes me feel these days, she said under her breath, opening the cupboard, taking out a small metal strainer. Furiously, she tore the lettuce apart, dropped it in the strainer standing in the sink, let the tap water run on the broken leaves.

She stared morosely at the wall, her mind intently fixed on Jack Miller.

He's a jerk, she thought, and I'm a bigger jerk for continuing to see him. I've known for weeks that the two of us are not making it together. We're going no place fast. I can't tolerate his possessiveness and his accusations, and the drunken scenes he's been creating lately are insupportable.

She ran her hand through her hair distractedly. And he makes me madder than a wet hen in a thunderstorm. Damn it, why do I take this from him?

Opening a drawer, she took out a sharp chopping knife, but her hands were shaking so much she put it down, for fear of cutting herself.

Leaning against the sink for the longest moment, she endeavored to still her fulminating anger.

It's all over between us.

As this unexpected thought penetrated her brain like an arrow hitting its given mark, she felt her tension lessen. And very slowly the shaking began to subside.

It was true. There was nothing left. At least, not for her. Even her sexual desire for him had diminished. His bad behavior was turning her off ever more frequently. I'll break up with him when I get back from Australia, she decided. There's no point in wasting my time with him. I must get on with my own life. I can't baby-sit Jack Miller, which is what I've been doing for several months now. No, I'd better tell him tomorrow. That'll be much kinder than waiting until I come back. Now, why am I trying to be kind to *him?* That dude's led me a real merry dance of late.

Madelana expelled a wearisome sigh. Jack seemed to want to punish her these days. Or was it someone else he was punishing? Himself, perhaps? He had been out of work for several months, and that was proving extremely hard on him. When he worked he was a different man. A whole man. He stopped carousing in bars with his friends and never touched a drop of liquor.

Poor Jack, she thought, the anger unexpectedly falling away. He has so much. Good looks and charm, talent and even brilliance. But he's wasting it all, letting it drain away down the neck of a bottle. It was the boozing that troubled her; and it was the boozing that had come between them. Invariably, he was full of chagrin afterward, and apologetic, but this did not take the sting out of the way he had behaved, the hurt he had inflicted.

It struck her then that he needed her pity more than anything else. Broadway actor, almost but not quite Star, he was a virtuoso performer who could have made it very, very big if he had wanted, gone to Hollywood, conquered the silver screen as he had the legitimate theater, which was his forte. His clean-cut handsomeness and silver-gilt hair and those marvelous baby blues were arresting and made him exceptionally photogenic. And he even had movie star charisma—when he wished to exercise it. He could have been another Paul Newman, or so his peers constantly informed her. It was always on the tip of her tongue to ask "Then why isn't he?" but she never did. Yes, his friends were most admiring of Jack Miller . . . he was an actor's actor, they said. The best. In the same class as Al Pacino and Jack Nicholson. But to her way of thinking, there was something missing in him, something gone askew in his character. If only he were different of temperament.

It seemed to her that Jack wasn't driven, and certainly he wasn't ambitious enough. Maybe that was the reason he was always jabbing at her, why he resented her career . . . because she had an overabundance of ambition, while he had none. Maybe he had had it once, but he didn't anymore.

Madelana let out a knowing laugh. Jack resented her career because at heart he was a male chauvinist. In his oblique way, he had told her that more than once, hadn't he?

She picked up the knife and began to slice a tomato, and she was gratified to see that her hands no longer shook.

Later, after Madelana had eaten her chicken salad, she sat drinking a glass of iced lemon tea in the living room, aimlessly staring at the television set, not really seeing the mindless movie that was playing, and certainly not listening to it.

Lolling back against the cushions, she realized that she was brighter of disposition, and much lighter in spirit. The constricted feeling in her chest had dissipated, and she had to admit that she was full of relief and felt better because she had finally resolved to terminate her relationship with Jack Miller.

Also in the last half hour, she had come to understand that this decision had not been quite so quick or so sudden as she had previously imagined. She had wanted to cut the cord between them for some time, but she had simply not had the guts to do so before.

She wondered why, wondered if she had stayed with Jack these last months out of the fear of being absolutely alone once more?

Patsy Smith had gone back to Boston to live, and Madelana didn't have too many other close friends in New York. Then again, because she worked so hard and kept such long hours, she had hardly any time for socializing with the few women she knew and liked.

But Jack was a different matter.

Since he was in the theater, his leisure hours started after the ten o'clock curtain had dropped. Their odd time schedules had somehow dovetailed neatly.

Several times a week she had stayed late at the store, or taken papers home with her and worked there, until she had met him at Joe Allen's or Sardi's for supper at eleven. And on other nights he had often come up to her apartment after the show, and she had cooked for him, and he had stayed over; and they usually spent Sundays together at his place on East Seventy-ninth Street.

But when he was not in a play, like now, he wanted to see her every night, regardless of her work. That wasn't possible, and she religiously stuck to her own schedule, refusing to be budged by him, and that was when the trouble started. He loved acting with a passion; in a way, it was the center of his life. Yet he couldn't seem to grasp that her work was just as important to her as his was to him. And thus there was conflict between them.

Patsy had introduced them. She had known him for two years now, and she *had* loved him, and he *was* the one person she had grown truly close to in the time she had lived in Manhattan. In a way, he was almost like family, and perhaps that was why she had continued to cling to him when her deepest instincts had told her to run for her life.

Family, she thought again, turning the word over in her mind, then she swung her head and looked at the framed color photograph on the end table. They were all in it . . . her brothers, Young Joe and Lonnie, herself with baby Kerry Anne sitting on her knee, and her mommy and her daddy. How young they looked, even her parents, and there was such joy and love on their sweet and shining faces. Her family would have been charmed by Jack Miller, would have found him entertaining and likable, because he *was* those things, but they wouldn't have approved of him. Not as a boyfriend for her, at any rate.

Her parents and her siblings had considered her to be unique and great things had been expected of her, especially by her mother, and for as far back as she could remember. "You're the one who's going to go out and do it, ma-vourneen," her mommy would tell her in that lovely lilting voice that had never lost its beguiling Irish brogue. "You're the clever one, Maddy, the one who's been blessed . . . kissed by the gods, to be sure, me darlin'. Why, you're one of the golden girls, Maddy."

Madelana became motionless, as if turned to stone on the sofa, suddenly hearing their voices echoing in her inner ear, every voice so clear and distinct and individualistic . . . Joe . . . Lonnie . . . Kerry Anne . . . her mommy . . . and her daddy . . .

They were dead, yet she still felt very close to them.

Each one of them had left little pieces of themselves behind in her. They were deeply embedded in her heart, and they were with her all the time. And she had such good memories to cherish and they sustained her and gave her enormous strength.

For a time she drifted off, as if in a trance, traveling back into the past in her mind, but after a short while she roused herself and stood up. She turned off the television, went and got her guitar, and brought it back to the sofa.

Tucking her bare feet under her, she played a few chords, adjusted the strings, then began to strum lightly, thinking of her family, reliving those happy times they had spent together. Each of the O'Sheas had been musically gifted, and they had enjoyed many lovely evenings over the years, playing their various instruments, harmonizing together, or singing solo.

And now, quietly, almost to herself, Madelana started to hum one of the old folk ballads which she and her brothers had sung, and when she finally got the feel of it, found the exact beat she wanted, her voice rang out true and pure in the quiet apartment.

"On top of old Smoky, all cover'd with snow, I lost my true lover, for courtin' too slow. Now courtin's a pleasure, but partin' is grief, a false-hearted lover, is worse than a thief. A thief will just rob you, and take what you have, but a false-hearted lover will send you to your grave. On top of old Smoky, all cover'd with snow, I lost my true lover, for courtin' too slow."

Ten

She had arrived in New York shaking the dust of Kentucky off the heels of her silver kid boots.

That was in the autumn of 1977, when she was twenty-three years old. It was probably her wry sense of humor that made her characterize herself as "just a poor country girl, a hillbilly who knows nothing much about anything," since, in point of fact, she was neither.

Her full name was Madelana Mary Elizabeth O'Shea, and she had been born just outside Lexington, in the very heart of bluegrass country, in July of 1954.

She was the first daughter of Fiona and Joe O'Shea and she had been adored from the moment she had opened her eyes to the world. She had two older brothers, Joseph Francis Xavier Jr., so named after his father, who was eleven at the time of her birth, and Lonnie Michael Paul, who was then seven. Both boys fell passionately in love with their beautiful baby sister, and it was a love that never dimmed during the boys' tragically short lives.

Everyone petted and indulged her throughout her childhood, and it was a miracle that Madelana grew up to be so unaffected and unspoiled, and this was due in no small measure to her own strength of character and sweetness of nature.

Her father was third-generation Irish-American, and a Kentuckian through and through, but her mother had been born in Ireland, and had come to America in 1940, at the age of seventeen. Fiona Quinn had been dispatched by her older sister and brother to stay with cousins in Lexington, in order to escape the war in Europe. "I'm an evacuee from the old sod," she would say with a bright smile, her green eyes sparkling, enjoying being something of a novelty amongst her cousins and their friends.

Joe O'Shea was twenty-three in 1940, and an engineer who worked for his father in their small family construction business, and he was the best friend of Liam Quinn, Fiona's cousin. It was at Liam's house that Joe first met Fiona, and he had immediately fallen in love with the tall, lissome girl from County Cork. He thought she had the prettiest of faces and the most dazzling of smiles it had ever been his great good fortune to see. They had started courting, and to Joe's delight, Fiona soon confessed that she reciprocated his feelings and they were married in 1941.

After their honeymoon in Louisville, they set up house in Lexington, and in 1943 their first son was born, just a few weeks after his father had embarked for England to fight the war in Europe.

Joe, who was in the U.S. 1st Infantry Division, was initially stationed in England, and later his unit was part of the Omaha Beach Assault Force that landed in Normandy on D-Day, the sixth of June, 1944. He was lucky and survived this and other Allied offensives in the European theater of war, and came home safely at the end of 1945, proudly wearing a Purple Heart pinned to his battle dress.

Once he had settled down to civilian life in Kentucky, Joe had again gone to work in his father's small business, and slowly life for the O'Sheas had returned to normal. In 1947, Lonnie was born, and with the addition of Maddy seven years later, Fiona and Joe decided it might be wisest not to have any more children, wanting to give as much as they could to the three they already had. Most especially, they were thinking of the cost of college educations for the two boys and Maddy. Joe's father had retired, and Joe had taken over the little family business and was making a decent living. Whilst they were not poor, they were not rich either. "Middlin' comfortable," was the way Joe would put it, and he would always add, "But that's no cause for celebratin', or for bein' extravagant."

Joe O'Shea was a good husband and father, Fiona a tender, loving wife, and the proudest of mothers, and they were a happy family, unusually devoted to each other.

Young Joe, Lonnie, and Maddy were inseparable—"the terrible trio," Fiona called them.

Madelana was something of a tomboy when she was growing up and wanted to do everything her brothers did; she swam and fished in the creeks with them, went hunting and trekking in the hills, always tagging along on any expedition, but invariably holding her own.

Riding was her favorite sport and at this she excelled. She became an accomplished equestrian at an early age, being fortunate enough to work out at various horse farms in and around Lexington where thoroughbreds were trained, and where her father did jobs from time to time.

She loved horses, had an understanding of them. Like her father and her brothers, she was keen on racing, and her greatest thrill was to accompany them to Churchill Downs in Louisville when the Kentucky Derby ran. And it was she who cheered loudest of all when a horse they favored won.

From a young age, Maddy was determined never to be outstripped by her brothers, and they, so adoring of her and immensely proud of her good looks, intelligence, independence, and daring do, forever encouraged her. But their mother, constantly shaking her head at the blue jeans and plaid work shirts, and the boyish, boisterous antics, tried to instill in her more ladylike ways.

"Whatever's going to become of you, Maddy O'Shea?" Fiona would demand, clucking with exasperation under her breath. "Just look at you . . . why, to be sure, anybody could be mistakin' you for a stable lad in that getup, and your friends so bonny and feminine in their pretty dresses. You won't be finding a nice young man to go a-courtin' with, no, not looking like that, you will not, me girl. I aim to enroll you in Miss Sue Ellen's dancing class if it's the last thing I do, so you can be learnin' a bit about deportment and gracefulness and femininity. I swear I will, Maddy O'Shea. Be warned, me girl."

Maddy would respond with a vibrant laugh and a jaunty toss of her chestnut head, for this was an old threat. And she would hug her mother tightly then, and promise to mend her ways, and they would sit down at the kitchen table for a cup of hot, steaming chocolate, and talk and talk their hearts away, and they were never anything but the best of friends.

And eventually, just to please her mother, Madelana did attend Miss Sue Ellen's School for Dancing and Deportment in Lexington, taking ballet and tap. As it happened, she had a natural aptitude for dance, and enjoyed her lessons, and it was here that she quickly learned to move with lightness and elegance, where she acquired the dancer's agile grace that she would never lose.

In later years, when she looked back, Madelana took comfort from the fact that she and her brothers had had such a marvelous childhood. There had been large doses of the Catholic religion rammed down them by their mother, and a good deal of discipline from their father, and they had had to work hard at school and to do chores in the house and yard, but it had been one of the happiest times of her life, and it had made her all the things she was.

Nobody was more surprised than Fiona when, toward the end of 1964, she learned that she was pregnant again, and the following year, at the age of forty-one, she gave birth to Kerry Anne.

Although the child had been unexpected, she was loved, and her christening was a happy affair. The only thing that slightly marred their joy that day was Young Joe's imminent departure for his tour of duty in Vietnam. He was a private in the U.S. Army and just twenty-two years old.

Sometimes tragedy strikes a family many times in quick succession, and it is so incomprehensible, so inexplicable, it defies belief. So it was with the O'Sheas.

Young Joe was killed at Da Nang in 1966, one year after he had shipped out to Indochina. Lonnie, who had joined the Marines and was also serving in Vietnam, lost his life during the Tet offensive in 1968. He was twenty-one.

And then to their further horror and heartbreak, little Kerry Anne died of complications following a tonsillectomy, shortly before her fifth birthday in 1970.

Reeling from shock and stunned by their enormous grief, Fiona, Joe, and Maddy cleaved to each other, were barely able to handle their anguish and the pain of their sudden and terrible losses over five short and fatal years. It seemed to them that each new blow was more ferocious than the one before, and it was a suffering they found unendurable.

Fiona was never really to recover, remaining forever after bereft and grieving, but despite this, and even though she needed her only living child by her side, she insisted Madelana continue her higher education at Loyola University in New Orleans, when she became eighteen.

Madelana had set her heart on going there some years before, and her parents had approved of this small college run by the Jesuits. Even so, she was reluctant to leave her parents, in particular her mother, who was so dependent on her, and she was more than willing to change her plans.

But Fiona would have none of it, since it had been a long-cherished dream of hers that Madelana attend college. She knew by this time that she was suffering from cancer, but she and Joe scrupulously kept this devastating news from their daughter.

However, four years later, toward the end, Fiona became so debilitated it was no longer possible to hide the medical facts from Maddy, who struggled through her last few months at Loyola fighting despair and endeavoring to hold sorrow at arm's length. The only thing that kept her going during this excruciatingly painful time was the determination not to let her mother down.

Fiona lived long enough to see Maddy graduate with a bachelor's degree in business administration in the summer of 1976. She died two months later.

"Kerry Anne's going was the last nail in your mommy's coffin," Joe kept saying all through the winter of that year, until the words began to sound like a dreadful litany to her.

Or he would sit and stare at Maddy, then ask, with tears welling in his eyes, "Wasn't one son enough to give to my country? Why did Lonnie have to get massacred too? For what?" And before she could say anything in response, he would add with anger and bitterness, "For *nothing,* that's what, Maddy. Young Joe and Lonnie both died for *nothing.*"

Madelana would take his hand and try to comfort him whenever he talked like this, but she never had any answers for her father, and certainly she had none for herself either. Like the majority of Americans, she had scant understanding of the war they were fighting in Vietnam.

After graduating from Loyola, Madelana had found herself a job in the offices of Shilito's Department Store in Lexington.

Despite her hoydenish ways and lack of interest in feminine things as a child, she had fallen in love with clothes in her late teens, and had recognized that she had a great deal of flair when it came to fashion. Retailing attracted her, and when she had been attending college, she had decided she wanted to carve out a career for herself in this field.

Madelana's job in the marketing department at Shilito's had proved to be challenging, and she had found it stimulating and absorbing as well. She had thrown herself into the work, and divided her time between the store and the family home, where she had continued to live with her father.

Joe had begun to worry her considerably in the early part of 1977, for he had grown more morose than ever, and apathetic, since her mother's death, and unlike her mother, he seemed unable to draw solace from religion. He still continued to mutter to Maddy that his sons had died in vain, and she would frequently find him staring at their photographs on the mantelpiece in the living room, his eyes filled with hurt and bafflement, his face grown painfully thin.

Maddy's heart ached for him, and she did everything possible to take him out of himself, to give him a reason to go on living, but it was to no avail.

By the spring of that year, Joe O'Shea had become a shadow of the handsome, jocular man he had once been, and when he died suddenly of a heart attack in May, Maddy realized, in the midst of her searing grief, that she was not really surprised. It was as if he had willed himself to die, as if he had desperately wanted to join Fiona in the grave.

Once she had buried her father, Madelana began to sort out and settle his business affairs. He had left everything in order and so this task was relatively easy for her to do.

His small construction company had been in the black for a number of years, and she was able to sell the equipment, the materials, and the "goodwill" to Pete Andrews, who had been her father's right-hand man and wanted to keep the business going for himself and the handful of old employees. And though it was wrenching for her, she had also sold the house where she had grown up, along with most of her mother's furniture, and moved into an apartment in Lexington.

It was not very long after this that she had started to understand just how difficult living in Lexington was going to be for her from now on. As much as her beloved bluegrass country was part of her, in her blood, each day grew increasingly painful. Wherever she went, wherever she looked, she saw their

faces . . . her parents, Kerry Anne, Young Joe, and Lonnie. She yearned for
them and for the past, and for the way things once were.

Her father's passing had opened up her old grief for the others who had
died before him.

She knew she had to get away. Perhaps she could come back one day and
rejoice in the past. But now she had to put distance between herself and this
place. The heartbreak was too fresh, too potent, and her emotions were far too
near the surface for her to draw any kind of solace from the memories of her
family.

Only through the passing of time would her pain lessen, and only then
would she be able to draw a measure of comfort from her remembrances, and
find peace in them.

And so Madelana made the decision to move to the North, to go to New
York City, to start a whole new life.

She was very brave.

She had no job, knew no one, had no contacts, but at least she had a roof
over her head when she arrived in Manhattan. This had already been arranged
for her before she had left Lexington.

The Sisters of Divine Providence, a teaching order of nuns from Kentucky, and one of the first such orders to be founded in America, maintained a
residency in New York. Rooms could be rented at a nominal charge, and were
available to Catholic girls and young women from all over the world.

And it was to this residency, the Jeanne D'Arc, that Maddy went in October of 1977.

Within a week of her arrival at West Twenty-fourth Street, she had settled
in and was beginning to get her bearings.

The sisters were warm and helpful, the girls friendly, and the residency
itself was pleasant, convenient, and well run. It had five floors of rooms, with
showers and bathrooms on each floor. There was a small but rather beautiful
chapel, where the young residents and the sisters could pray or meditate, and
close by were the common rooms—a library and a television parlor. Other
facilities included a kitchen and a canteen in the basement, for the cooking and
serving of meals, plus a laundry room, and lockers for the storage of personal
belongings.

One of the first things Maddy had done was to put her nest egg of forty-
thousand dollars in the bank, opening both checking and saving accounts. After
this she had had her own phone installed in her room on the fourth floor. Patsy
Smith, who lived across the corridor from her, had recommended that she do
so, explaining that it would simplify her life.

She had then gone looking for a job.

Ever since she had decided to make a career for herself in retailing,
Maddy's role model had been the late Emma Harte, one of the greatest merchant princes of all time. In the past few years she had read everything about
the renowned Emma that she could lay her hands on, and Harte's in New York
was the only store where she wanted to work. But she quickly discovered there
were no vacancies when she went for an interview. The personnel manager had
been impressed with her, however, and had promised to be in touch if something suitable came up. Her résumé and application had been duly filed for
future reference.

By the end of her third week in the city, Maddy had managed to find employment in the business offices of Saks Fifth Avenue.

Exactly one year later there was finally an opening at Harte's and she had grabbed it immediately, filled with enthusiasm at the opportunity to work there, and within six months she had made her mark.

And she had come to the attention of Paula O'Neill.

Paula had spotted her in the marketing department, had been struck by her personal style, pleasant demeanor, efficiency, and vivid intelligence. Thereafter, Paula had constantly singled her out, given her a variety of special assignments, and had ultimately moved her to work in the executive offices. A year after this, in July of 1980, Paula had promoted Maddy to be her personal assistant, actually creating this job for her.

With this big promotion and a sizable increase in salary, Madelana had at last felt secure enough to look for her own apartment. She had found one she liked in the East Eighties, and had had her possessions shipped up from the storage warehouse in Kentucky. And she had finally left the residency, feeling a little pang as she had said good-bye to Sister Bronagh and Sister Mairéad.

The first meal she had cooked at the new apartment had been for Jack and Patsy one Sunday night, just before Patsy had gone back to Boston to live.

It had been a lovely evening, very celebratory, and Jack had kept them amused and laughing. But she and Patsy had grown a bit sad toward the end, knowing they would be living in different cities soon. They had promised faithfully not to grow apart, and they had corresponded on a fairly regular basis ever since.

With her new promotion, Madelana's life had changed in other ways, and a whole new world had been opened up to her. Paula had brought her over to London so that she would understand the inner workings of the famed Knightsbridge store, and she had visited the Harte stores in Yorkshire and Paris. And twice Paula had taken her to Texas, although this had been on Sitex business rather than Harte's. She had discovered how much she enjoyed traveling, going to new places, and meeting new people.

Her first year as Paula's assistant had fled by, filled with excitement, challenges, and continuing successes, and very quickly Maddy had begun to recognize that she had found her niche in life. It was at Harte's of New York, where she was a star.

Eleven

Playing some of her favorite old folk songs had soothed Madelana. She was feeling at ease with herself at last.

Earlier in the evening, she had half expected Jack Miller to call her back, had been dreading that he would. But he had not. Now, at last, she was filled with a peacefulness, and she was completely calm. She got up, put the guitar to one side, and went over to the desk near the window.

The files she had brought home with her from the store were stacked and waiting for her attention. She sat down, glanced at the clock, saw that it was almost midnight. But that did not matter to her. She was wide awake and full of energy. Stamina had always been one of her strong suits, and she knew she could complete the work quite easily within two or three hours.

Picking up her pen, she sat back in the chair, staring at the wall, thinking for a moment.

The needlepoint sampler which hung there, and which her mother had made for her when she had been a little girl, suddenly held her attention. It had hung above her bed in her room in Lexington, and it was one of the things she had brought with her when she had first moved to New York.

If your day is hemmed with prayer it is less likely to unravel, her mother had stitched in royal blue wool against the beige background, and she had bordered the sampler with tiny flowers in brilliant primary colors.

Madelana smiled inwardly, seeing Fiona's lovely image in her mind's eye. I think she'd be proud of me, proud of what I've made of my life, and of where I am today. I know she wouldn't approve of Jack, of course. I don't believe I do, either. Not for me. Not anymore. I'll call him in the morning, ask him to have lunch, and I'll end it face to face, she added to herself, reiterating her earlier decision in her mind. That's the only decent thing to do. I can't tell him over the phone.

She put down the pen and began to shuffle through her files, looking for the one which held her notes and the material for the fashion exhibit.

Each of these folders pertained to the forthcoming celebrations for Harte's sixtieth anniversary. Paula's theme was simple, but clever in its simplicity: sixty years of stylish retailing from the jazz age to the space age.

Paula had put her in charge of the anniversary program at the New York store, and she was responsible for the overall planning of different events and shows, and telexes had been flying back and forth across the Atlantic for many, many months. Ideas had been approved, or knocked down, by Paula, and merchandise ordered, campaigns put in work, advertising art completed, brochures and invitations printed. The files represented endless hours of work and thought and dedication, and she must complete the last few memorandums about each event and campaign tonight.

Maddy's own special projects included Fragrance Month; a stylish art show in the gallery of the store, highlighting decorative objects from the Art Deco period; an exhibit of real and costume jewelry from the Art Deco period to the present, featuring some of the world's greatest jewelry designers. These included Verdura, Jeanne Toussaint of Cartier, and Renée Puissant of Van Cleef and Arpels, and their work from decades past; Alain Boucheron and David Webb were two of the designers of the present who would be showcased. At the other end of the price scale, she had decided to highlight the unique costume jewelry and fabulous fakes designed by Kenneth Jay Lane, along with a collection of paste pieces from the nineteen thirties.

Her hands came to rest on the fashion folder at last. This held information and details of the fashion exhibition which Paula planned to hold at the London store next spring. Maddy had convinced her to bring it over to New York in the late summer of 1982. Having agreed, Paula had then suggested she try to expand the exhibit, by adding clothes borrowed from American women who had either been on the best dressed list at some time or other, or who owned a garment by a top couturier, whether living or dead. And this she had done— with great success.

The nucleus of the couture exhibition were clothes which had once belonged to Emma Harte, and which Emma had kept in good condition for years before her death. Paula had also preserved these clothes after they had been in the Fashion Fantasia exhibit at the London store some ten or eleven years ago.

Emma's clothing in the show dated as far back as the early twenties, and included a Paquin evening coat of brown velvet trimmed with a huge fox collar, a short evening dress with a big bow on the back, designed in 1926 by Poiret, and a blue-and-green beaded evening gown by Vionnet. This was apparently in extraordinary condition, and looked stunning in the photograph the London marketing department had sent over. It seemed hardly dated at all to Madelana.

Sifting through the other drawings and photographs, she poured over Emma's Chanel suits from the twenties, a huge collection of her hats by French and English couturiers, outfits by Lanvin, Balmain, and Balenciaga, two Fortuny pleated silk evening gowns, evening pajamas by Molyneux, and an exquisitely cut coat by Pauline Trigère, designed in the fifties but as chic now as it had been then. There were other modern outfits by Dior, Givenchy, Yves Saint Laurent, Bill Blass, and Hardy Amies.

Maddy began to make her notes, creating the exact order in which she wanted the drawings and photographs to appear in the catalog. She had already put this into work with the art department, and they were pressuring her for these illustrations.

One of Maddy's favorites was a charmeuse evening dress by Mainbocher, which according to Paula, her grandfather Paul McGill had bought for Emma in New York in 1935. It was trimmed with clustered silk flowers stitched as epaulets on the shoulders, and worn with a matching muff made of the same clustered silk flowers.

Picking up a photograph of Emma wearing the dress, Madelana studied it for a moment. God, what a beautiful woman she was, she murmured to herself, and decided to lead off with this particular picture.

After she had finished with the fashion exhibit file, she dealt with the information required for the Fragrance Month, and then tackled the Art Deco show, leaving the final details of the jewelry exhibit until last. She worked relentlessly for another hour and a half, making sure there could be no mistakes whatsoever while she was in Australia.

At two in the morning she stood in her little kitchen waiting for the kettle to boil for a cup of instant coffee. And as she carried this back into the living room a moment later, she braced herself for at least another hour of work.

Well, Maddy thought, seating herself at the desk, if Emma Harte could work around the clock, then so can I. After all, she has been my inspiration and my idol for years, and I want to emulate her in every way I possibly can.

Twelve

"How did you manage to complete everything?" Paula asked, eyeing the files she had just read, then glancing across at Madelana.

"I stayed up until three-thirty this morning."

"Oh Maddy, you didn't have to do that. We could have finished the files together on the plane, and telexed our final instructions from Australia.'' As Paula spoke, she could not help feeling slightly relieved that they would not have to do this.

"But it's better this way, isn't it, Paula?" Madelana asked. "We'll have free minds, and we'll be able to concentrate that much more keenly on the boutiques with this stuff out of the way."

"That's perfectly true," Paula agreed. "And I must say, your hard work, what you've accomplished, is very commendable." Paula's violet eyes narrowed and she studied the other woman closely, then began to laugh. "And what's even more remarkable is that burning the midnight oil doesn't show on your face."

"Doesn't it?" Madelana laughed with her boss, whom she not only admired and respected, but genuinely cared for. "Thank you, it's nice of you to say so."

Paula tapped the folders. "I like the way you've managed to tie in so many different products and merchandise. By pulling everything together in the way you have, you've also strengthened my theme considerably. To be truthful, when I came up with the idea of calling our sixtieth celebration *From the Jazz Age to the Space Age,* I wondered if I was making it far too broad to be effective. But you've helped to prove yet again that I wasn't, and frankly, you've even gone a step further than Marketing has in London. That's what has been so exciting for me this last hour as I've read your memos."

Paula was a firm believer in giving credit where it was due, and now she added, "Congratulations. Some of the things you've thought of are brilliant, and I'm delighted with your efforts."

Madelana filled with satisfaction and her face was wreathed in smiles. "Thanks, Paula, but don't let's forget that your theme *was* clever, and very challenging. And everything was already there really, just waiting to be pulled out of the reference books and the research files."

"Not to mention your clever little head!" Paula exclaimed. She picked up the folder marked FRAGRANCE PROMOTION and opened it, took out the top sheet.

After glancing at the paper again, she said, "Some of this stuff's really fascinating. For instance, *I* never knew that Chanel actually considered the number five to be her lucky number, and that that was the reason she called her first perfume *Chanel No. 5.* Nor was I aware that Jean Patou created *Joy* in 1931, and that Jeanne Lanvin brought out *Arpège* in 1927. Here we have three of the world's greatest perfumes, which are still enormously popular today, and they are actually fifty years old."

"Quality always lasts, doesn't it," Madelana said. "And I thought some of those odd little items were kind of interesting, too. Perhaps we can use them somewhere in our promotional material, or in our advertisements."

"Absolutely. That's a terrific idea. And you might tell the art department to make up display cards featuring a few of the items, for the counters in Perfumery."

"Okay. Talking about displays, could you spare me a minute, please? I'd like you to see a piece of artwork I had created, I hope for use here in the store. If you approve."

"Let's go and look at it then." Paula jumped up, followed Madelana into the adjoining office.

An easel had been placed in one corner, near the window which looked out onto Fifth Avenue. Madelana picked up a large display card and put it on the easel. She said, "I'd like to use this on silk banners throughout the store, and if I could get a yea or a nay from you now, I'd appreciate it. The banners have to be ordered today, at the *latest* on Monday, if they're going to be ready for the commencement of the celebrations in December."

"I understand. So come on, let's see it."

Madelana flipped the tracing paper that protected the hardboard card, and then stepped aside.

Paula stood staring at the bold lettering, which read: FROM THE JAZZ AGE TO THE SPACE AGE: 1921 TO 1981.

Underneath the giant-sized slogan was a smaller subheading: *Sixty years of style and elegance at Harte's.*

Paula continued to study it.

This was her slogan, the words she had written down over a year ago, when she had first started to plan the anniversary celebrations and special events. The only thing which made this suggested banner different to the ones created by the marketing department in London was a portrait of Emma Harte etched in shadowy form behind the lettering.

Paula said nothing. Her eyes grew thoughtful.

Watching her intently, and anxiously, waiting for her reaction, Madelana held her breath. When Paula remained silent, she said worriedly, "You don't like it, do you?"

"I'm not sure, to be honest," Paula murmured, then hesitated. She moved around the office, looking at the board from different angles. "Yes . . . yes . . . I think I do," she finally said, her voice more positive. "But I wouldn't want to use my grandmother's image on *every* banner in the store. I think that would be in poor taste, and overkill, really. And I certainly don't want to go over the top. But the more I look at this, I think we *could* use it, in a *limited* way . . . in some of the big halls in the London and Paris stores, and on the first floor here. Oh, and in the Leeds store, too! That's a *must,* I suppose, since that's where it all began."

"Are you really sure? You still sound a bit uncertain."

"No, I'm positive. You can order the banners, and why don't you get enough for the other stores. We might as well have them made in New York. They can be shipped out air express to London and Paris when they're ready."

"Good idea. And I'm glad you approve of the things we've done. Everyone's going to be thrilled that you're so pleased, and that we can now go forward with these plans."

Paula half smiled. "Well, I suppose that's about it, as far as the special events are concerned. Come back to my office for a moment, though, would you, Madelana, there's something I wish to discuss with you."

"Yes," Maddy said, hurrying after her, wondering what this was all about. All of a sudden there had been an anxious note in Paula's voice, which was unusual for her, and therefore disconcerting.

Paula walked around her desk and sat down.

Madelana took the chair facing her, perched on the edge, and looked across at her boss, asking herself if trouble was brewing.

Paula sat back, steepled her fingers, and contemplated the tips of them for a moment. Then she said, "I want to take you into my confidence about something, Madelana, but I must stress that it *is* confidential. I haven't mentioned it to Shane or Emily yet, although actually that's really because I haven't had the right opportunity. However, since you work so closely with me, I thought you should know immediately."

"You have my confidentiality, Paula. I'd never discuss your business with anyone. That's not my way."

"I'm aware of that, Madelana."

Paula sat back, her eyes serious. She said carefully, "I've had several phone calls from a Harvey Rawson during the past few days, which I'm sure you know, since you put a couple of those calls through to me."

Madelana nodded.

"He's a lawyer with a Wall Street firm, and a friend of Michael Kallinski's. He's been doing some work for me. Private work."

"You don't have a legal problem, do you?"

"No, no, Maddy. For a long time I've wanted to go into an expansion program in the United States . . . I've wanted to take Harte stores right across the country, and I've been looking for an existing chain to buy, with that purpose in mind. Michael's known about this, and he put the word out some time ago, without mentioning my name, of course. Last week he heard about a small suburban chain through Harvey Rawson. Before I left for New York, I spoke to Michael, and told him he could tell Harvey I was the one interested in the chain and to get in touch with me directly."

"So Harvey Rawson's actually representing you in the buy out," Madelana asserted, sitting up straighter in the chair, pinning her eyes on her boss.

"It's not a buy out yet. But yes, he is representing me, inasmuch as he's approaching the chain, but without saying I'm the interested party."

"Yes, I understand. That would jack up the price, and then some, if they knew it was you. But I think this is a wonderful move you're making, Paula, and very visionary." Madelana's excitement was reflected on her face and she leaned forward with eagerness. "What's the name of the chain? Where are the stores located?"

"The chain is called Peale and Doone, and there are seven stores altogether, in Illinois and Ohio," Paula explained. "This is not the type of chain I was originally looking for—I'd prefer my stores to be in big cities. Still, Peale and Doone would be a beginning."

"Are they a public company?"

"No, private. And next week Harvey will ascertain whether or not the stockholders are interested in selling, and then we'll take it from there. He'll be in touch with me, and with Michael, and they both have the Australian itinerary, at least the part of it that's planned," she finished, sitting back in her chair.

Standing up, recognizing that Paula had just brought this conversation to a close, Madelana said, "Thanks for telling me about your plans, Paula, for sharing with me. I'm flattered, and I'm looking forward to working with you on the expansion program."

"Good. I hoped you would be. I want you to be very involved with me in this, Maddy." Paula also stood. Lifting the stack of files off her desk, she brought them to Madelana.

Together the two women walked across the room, paused at the door to Madelana's office, turned to face each other.

Paula remarked, "You seem to be finished, so there's no reason for you to come back after lunch, if you don't want to. I don't need you for the rest of the day, and I'm sure you've plenty to do between now and tomorrow morning."

"Oh thank you, that's nice of you, Paula, but I'm sure I'll be back, and anyway, I want to pick up a couple of track suits in Active Sportswear. Didn't you say that was the only way to fly? To Australia, I mean."

Paula laughed. "It is, and I'm afraid the suit is not very elegant, but it *is* very practical. And don't forget your Reeboks or a pair of tennis shoes. Los Angeles to Sydney is around thirteen to fourteen hours flying time, depending on the winds, and every part of the body seems to swell up. Not only that, I find that I sleep much more comfortably when I'm dressed in a track suit."

"Then I'll be sure to get myself properly outfitted after I've had lunch with Jack—" Madelana broke off, and her face instantly changed, grew taut with anxiety.

Paula did not miss this. She frowned, asked softly, in concern. "Is something wrong?"

Maddy shook her head. "Not really," she began and again stopped abruptly. There was a closeness between Paula and herself, and they had always been open and forthright with each other. "I shouldn't say that, Paula, because it's not true. Things are pretty lousy between Jack and me, and I'm going to break off with him. I want to get it out of the way before I leave. That's why I'm having lunch with him."

"I am sorry," Paula murmured, giving her a small, sympathetic smile, touching her arm lightly. "I thought everything was working well between the two of you. At least that's the impression you gave the last time we spoke about him when you were in London."

"It was then, and he's a nice guy in many ways. But there's such a lot of conflict between us. I think he resents me these days, and resents my career." Madelana shook her head. "There's no future in it as far as I can see."

Paula was silent, remembering words of Emma's, words uttered at a time when she had been where Madelana was today. She said quietly, "Many years ago, when I was having great difficulties in my first marriage, my grandmother gave me a bit of advice that I've never forgotten. She said, 'If something's not working, then don't be afraid to end it whilst you're still young enough to start again, to find happiness with someone else.' Grandy was a very wise woman. And I can only reiterate those words of hers to you, Maddy, and add that you must trust your own instincts. From what I know of you, they've never let you down yet."

Paula paused, gave her a quick, penetrating look, and went on, "Personally, I think you're about to do the right thing. The best thing for you."

"I know I am. And thanks for caring, Paula. I'll break up with Jack today, make it clean and swift. And then I want to concentrate on my career."

Thirteen

It rose up against the azure sky like some great monolith, an immense, unyielding structure of black glass and steel. It was a statement of wealth and privilege, prestige and power, and a glittering monument to the founding fathers of a gargantuan business empire.

The McGill Tower was its name, and it dominated the skyline of Sydney.

The man who had conceived this extraordinary and beautiful edifice, and caused it to be built, occupied the tower in the manner of a magnate from a time long past, completely in control, overseeing and operating all that he owned from this stylish, modern command post, and doing so with a shrewdness, wisdom, and fairness that went far beyond his years.

The black glass tower was his true domain.

He worked there from early morning until late at night, and during the business week he frequently lived there. His executive offices and his penthouse flat were situated one above the other, and occupied the entire two top floors of the building.

Late on this Monday afternoon, the man stood with his back to the immense sweep of plate glass which formed the window-wall at one end of his private office, and which offered a panoramic view of Sydney Harbour and the city. With his head tilted to one side, his eyes narrowed in concentration, he was listening attentively to his visitor, a young American businessman.

Always the most handsome of Emma Harte's grandsons, at thirty-five Philip McGill Amory was in his prime and at his full power. He had magnetism, and a mystique in international business circles and with the press, and to many people he was an enigma. Like his mother and his sister, he had inherited Paul McGill's coloring. His hair was the same glossy black and his eyes were that uncanny blue which was almost violet, and he possessed the vitality and virile looks and height which had made his grandfather such an arresting man.

Today he was wearing a stone-colored light gabardine suit that was fashionably cut, and he was perfectly groomed from the collar of his deep-blue shirt to the tip of his dark brown loafers that gleamed like highly polished glass.

"And so," his visitor was saying, "that's the story. And before I put up a couple of million dollars—U.S. dollars that is—I thought I'd better high-tail it over here and get your advice. Shane told me, before I left London, that if I felt the need, I *should* come and talk things over with you, because you know more about opal mining than anybody else."

Philip let out a deep chuckle.

"Not quite, Mr. Carlson. I'm afraid my brother-in-law tends to exaggerate, but I'm fairly knowledgeable, yes. We've been mining opals for years—among other things. One of our subsidiaries, McGill Mining, was founded by my great-grandfather in 1906, a few years after the famous black opal field at Lightning Ridge was discovered around 1903. But to get back to your situation, from what you've told me so far, I don't believe you've been getting the best guidance. If I were you, I'd move with some caution, think twice before putting your money into this syndicate you've been telling me about."

Steve Carlson sat up straighter, gave Philip a questioning look. "You don't think it's some sort of scam, do you?" he asked, his voice rising nervously, sudden anxiety filling his eyes.

Philip shook his head. "No, no, not at all," he answered swiftly and emphatically. "But we've heard of Jarvis Lanner, and whilst he's honest enough, as far as we've been able to ascertain, he's hardly the right man to be advising you about opal mining in the outback."

"That's not the way he presents himself."

"Maybe not. But he's a pommy jackeroo, for God's sake!"

Carlson looked baffled. *"Pommy jackeroo.* What's that?"

Philip tried, unsuccessfully, to smother a laugh. "Sorry, I shouldn't be confusing you by using Australian slang. It means an English immigrant who's a greenhorn."

"Oh, I see." Carlson nodded, then continued, "It did strike me, a few days ago, that Jarvis Lanner didn't know as much as he professed, that's why I came running to you, I guess."

Philip made no comment. He strolled over to his desk, stood behind it, regarding the young man for a moment, feeling sorry for him. Now here was a jackeroo, if ever he'd seen one. Wanting to help him, and also to bring the meeting to a close, Philip now said, "I think the best thing I can do for you, Mr. Carlson, is to put you in touch with a couple of reputable mining experts and some leading geologists. They'll be able to steer you in the right direction. Would you like me to do that?"

"Well, gee, yes, I guess so, and I really appreciate that you've taken the time and trouble to see me. But just as a matter of interest, what's *your* opinion of Queensland, as far as opals are concerned? Don't you think it offers as much as I've been led to believe?"

"I wouldn't say that, no."

Philip sat down, pulled a pad toward him, reached for his gold pen. "A lot of prospectors and miners will tell you that the Queensland fields still have a lot to offer, and I suppose that's true, in certain ways. But I doubt you'll find much precious opal there. That's very rare. Plenty of common opal, of course, in the Queensland fields. Jarvis Lanner was not lying to you when he told you that. But I do stress *common* opal. You indicated to me that you want to mine *quality* stones."

"Yes." Carlson got up off the sofa, meandered over to the desk, took the chair facing it. "Where do *you* think I should do my mining, Mr. Amory?"

"There are any number of places," Philip responded with a light shrug of his shoulders, not wanting to be drawn on this one, or held responsible for making a recommendation that might turn out to be the wrong one for young Carlson. But he had no wish to appear discourteous either, and so he said, "Our company's still mining at Lightning Ridge in New South Wales, and also at Coober Pedy. That's actually Australia's largest opal center where we get our exquisite light opal from. Then there's Mintabie, in South Australia. Prospectors have been mining there very successfully since about 1976."

"So it's a new field."

"No, it was discovered in 1931, but lack of water, very harsh conditions, and bloody awful equipment made it hard to coax the opal out of the ground, prevented proper mining for many, many years. Today's modern machinery has opened it up pretty good. In any case, let me give you the names and phone numbers of the experts I mentioned. Go and talk to them. I'm confident they'll put you on the right track. They'll also be able to tell you whether or not you should invest in the syndicate Lanner recommended to you."

"Do you think that group might be A-okay then?"

"I never said there was anything wrong with the syndicate, merely that you should think twice about investing your money with it," Philip was swift to remind the other man. "And I pointed out that you'd not received the best advice from Lanner." Philip smiled faintly, and not giving Carlson a chance to say anything, he murmured, "Excuse me," picked up the gold pen for the second time, and began to write in his neat, rapid hand.

"Sure, go ahead," Steve Carlson said, somewhat after the fact, and sat back in the chair, his scrutiny keen. He was impressed with this man who had agreed to see him so quickly and without fuss. Admittedly, he'd had the best introduction. On the other hand, tycoons of Amory's caliber and power were hard to get to personally, even when members of the family opened the door. They were usually too busy, up to their eyeballs in high finance and balance sheets, to be bothered with strangers wanting advice. Invariably they had assistants stand in for them. But not this cowboy, who seemed like a decent enough guy, unaffected, with no bullshit about him. He'd been struck dumb when he'd first met him an hour ago. Philip McGill Amory was so goddamned good looking he ought to be in front of a movie camera in Hollywood, for God's sake, not behind a desk. That handsome face, those mesmerizing blue eyes, the gleaming teeth, and the very deep tan had to be seen to be believed. And what about the fabulous suit he was wearing and the custom-made voile shirt, not to mention the sapphire cuff links? Why, this guy was larger than life, more like a superstar than a businessman. He hadn't expected Amory to have a mustache though. He decided it was dashing, gave the tycoon the look of a riverboat gambler . . . no, a buccaneer.

Steve Carlson suppressed the laughter rising in his throat, thinking that there were surely plenty of pirates around these days—all plowing the waters of Big Business. But Amory didn't have the reputation for being a predator, one of those modern-day corporate raiders who swooped down on other companies and commandeered them for their own ends. Amory didn't need to raid anybody, did he? Not with a conglomerate the size of the McGill Corporation to play with, and keep him busy. It was worth millions, no, billions.

Carlson shifted in his chair, gave Philip a glance that was full of speculation. *I bet this cowboy has one helluva private life, a real ball,* the young American thought with a stab of envy tinged with admiration. *With his physique and looks, all that power, all that dough, women probably drool all over him. Boy, oh boy, what I wouldn't give to be in that pair of handmade Italian loafers just for one night.*

Philip flipped the intercom. "Maggie?"

"Yes?"

"Mr. Carlson is about to leave. I'm giving him a list of names. Please affix the appropriate telephone numbers, will you?"

"Certainly."

Philip strode around the desk.

Carlson jumped up, took the sheet of paper being offered, walked with him to the door.

Philip shook the young man's hand firmly. "Lots of luck, Mr. Carlson. I'm certain it'll all pan out."

"Gee, thanks, Mr. Amory. I sure am grateful for your time, and the advice you've given me."

"My pleasure," Philip answered, and motioned to his secretary, who was standing waiting near her desk. "Look after Mr. Carlson, would you please, Maggie?" he added before stepping back into his inner sanctum and closing the door firmly behind him.

Alone at last, and glad to be, Philip ambled over to the plate glass window-wall and looked out toward the harbor. It was the beginning of spring and the weather had been glorious all day. Any number of sailboats were out there on the bright water, racing in front of the wind, their multicolored spinnakers billowing straight out, the mainsails set out wide over the sides, catching every bit of the wind following behind them.

What a beautiful sight it was . . . Sydney Harbour Bridge so majestic in the distance, the white racing yachts and their colorful spinnakers, the glittering, sunlit sea, and off to the side, the Opera House with its unique roof of curved white demidomes that from this angle looked like the giant sails of a galleon set against the edge of the sea and the powder-blue sky.

A smile touched Philip's eyes. He had loved this city since he was a boy, and to him there was no sight in the world quite like the Sydney harbor. It never failed to give him pleasure, especially when he surveyed it from this vantage point.

As he turned away from the window, he made a mental note to have the spinnaker on his own racing yacht checked. The big parachute was made of gossamer-thin nylon and attention had to be paid to it and to the other sails. He smiled wryly to himself. Yacht racing was an expensive hobby these days. A full suit of sails, ranging from the light-weather spinnaker to heavyweight Kevlar for a storm mainsail, cost just under a million Australian dollars.

There was a knock on the door. It opened, and Barry Graves, his personal assistant, poked his head around it, grinning. "Can I come in?"

"Sure," Philip said, walking over to his desk.

"Got kangeroos in his top paddock then, has he?" Barry asked, a brow lifting eloquently.

The two men exchanged knowing looks and then they both started to laugh.

"No," Philip said, "he's not crazy. Carlson's just young and inexperienced. He's been bitten by the adventure bug, I guess. Apparently he heard somewhere that Australia supplies ninety-five percent of the world's opals, and he decided to come over here, try his luck, and invest his inheritance in opal mining."

"Another jackeroo." Barry sighed. "Poor sod. Oh, well, I guess there's one born every minute. What's he to Shane?"

"Nothing really. Carlson's brother-in-law is one of Shane's top executives at O'Neill International in New York, and Shane was just trying to do the guy a favor. The kid went to see him in London and Shane told him to check with me before he did anything wild."

"Good thing he did, too." Barry hovered at the side of the desk, went on rapidly. "I just came in to say goodnight, Philip. If you don't need me for anything else, I'd like to push off. Committee meeting at the tennis club tonight."

"Go ahead, Barry."

"Thanks. Oh, there's just one thing—do you want me to send a car to pick Paula up at the airport tomorrow morning?"

"No, thanks anyway, but it's not necessary. My mother's taking care of that."

"Good-o." Barry headed for the door. He paused as he went out, swung to face Philip. "Don't stay too late tonight."

"I won't. I'm driving out to Rose Bay in a little while, to have dinner with my mother."

"Give Daisy my best."

"I will."

"See you tomorrow, Philip."

Philip nodded, turned to the papers on his desk, and began to work. Just before six o'clock he buzzed Maggie on the intercom and told her to go home.

"Thanks, Philip."

"Oh and Maggie, please call down to the garage and tell Ken to have the car outside at seven."

"I will. Good night."

"Good night, Maggie." He flipped off the intercom, and went on working on his papers with the diligence and dedication that had been instilled in him by his grandmother years before.

From the moment he had taken his first breath, in June of 1946, it had been understood by his mother and father, and everyone else in the family, that Philip McGill Amory would be raised and groomed to run the McGill Corporation in Australia.

Before he had shot himself to death in 1939, after being partially paralysed in a near-fatal car crash, Paul McGill had drawn a new will. In it he had bequeathed everything he owned to Emma Harte, his common-law wife of sixteen years.

His immense personal fortune, personal real estate, and other personal possessions in Australia, England, and America he left directly to Emma, to do with as she wished. But the business empire in Australia and his big block of shares in Sitex Oil of America, the company he had founded in Texas, were to be held in trust by Emma for Daisy, the only child they had had together, and any offspring Daisy herself might one day have.

From 1939 until 1969, Emma herself had run the McGill Corporation, both at close range in Sydney, and long distance from London. She had managed to do this successfully with the help of trusted appointees, some of whom had worked for Paul McGill until his death. These men, the managing directors of the various companies within the conglomerate, carried out her instructions and were responsible for the day-to-day running of their divisions. These were diverse, ranged from the mining of opals and minerals to coal fields, land development, and commercial real estate, and included the family sheep station at Coonamble.

The McGill family's vast business enterprises, which were now the responsibility of Philip, had begun with that sheep station, one of the largest in New South Wales. Called Dunoon, it had been founded in 1852 by Philip's great-great-grandfather, Andrew McGill, a Scottish sea captain, who was a free settler in the Antipodes. The McGill Corporation, as such, had been created by his great-grandfather, Bruce McGill, and later expanded to become one of the most important companies in the world by his grandfather, Paul.

When he was still only a very little boy, Emma had begun to talk to Philip about Australia, telling him of the wonders and beauty and riches of that extraordinary land. And she had filled his head with adventurous yarns about his grandfather, speaking to him about Paul so beautifully, so vividly, and with such an enduring love she had brought the man to life for the small child. Certainly Philip sometimes felt as though he had actually known his grandfather.

As he grew older, Emma had explained that one day Paul's mighty empire, which took *her* so frequently to Australia, would belong to him and Paula, but that he would run it, as she herself was doing on behalf of their mother and them.

Philip had been six years old when Emma had first taken him out to Sydney with his parents, Daisy and David Amory, and his sister, and he had fallen in love with it from the first moment he had set foot on Australian ground. That love had never waned.

Philip had been educated in England, attending Wellington, his grandfather's old school, but at seventeen he had rebelled, had told Emma and his parents that he wanted to leave school, that he had no intention of going to a university. He had explained, and in no uncertain terms, that the time had come for him to start learning about the business he was supposed to run when he was old enough.

Eventually his father had given in, had shrugged philosophically, knowing he was not going to win the day.

Emma's attitude had been somewhat similar. She had brought Philip to work with her, hiding a smile on that first day, knowing that her grandson had not the slightest idea of what was in store for him. And so it had begun— Emma's relentless training program which demanded complete dedication. She was stern, exacting, and the hardest taskmaster he had ever met. She insisted on excellence in all things, and diligence and concentration, and his life was hers until the time came when he had absorbed the precepts of her business ethos.

But Emma was eminently fair, and Philip had eventually come to understand that his grandmother's unremitting pounding on himself, his sister, and his cousins was merely her way of ensuring they would be able to hold their own when they were out on their own, and when she was no longer there to guide or protect them.

During the years of his training, Philip traveled constantly to Australia with Emma, and whenever possible he spent his holidays there, invariably going up to Dunoon at Coonamble, wanting to learn as much as he could about their sheep station. Sometimes Emma went with him, and he enjoyed it even more when she did, because she would reminisce about the old days, the times she had spent there with Paul, and he was always captivated by her stories.

In 1966, when he was twenty, Emma sent Philip to live permanently in Australia.

She wanted him to learn firsthand about the business empire he would operate and control as chief executive officer and chairman of the board.

At the end of three years, Philip had proved himself to be worthy of Emma's belief in him.

She had not been unduly surprised, since she knew that he had inherited her astuteness, her canny Yorkshire ways, and her instinct for making money, and that he had the ability to turn situations to his own advantage, as she had done all her life. Also, Emma was aware that quite aside from being the spitting image of his grandfather, Philip was blessed with Paul's acumen and financial genius.

Philip was soon entrenched professionally and socially in Sydney, and he made a good life for himself in Australia. The country of his McGill forefathers, which had so fascinated and intrigued him since those childhood visits, became his true home. He had not the slightest desire to live anywhere else in the world.

Two of Emma's appointees, Neal Clarke and Tom Patterson, had been instrumental in Philip's training in Australia, and they had earned his genuine respect and affection. However, it was usually Emma to whom Philip turned for guidance and counsel when he was uncertain, or when he faced a crisis. After his grandmother's death in 1970, his father took her place, inasmuch as he became his confidante and sounding board whenever Philip deemed it necessary to seek advice outside his own organization. David Amory's untimely death in the avalanche at Chamonix in January of 1971 had robbed Philip not only of his beloved father, but of a wise counselor and guiding hand.

When Philip had returned to Sydney in March of that year, fully recovered from the minor injuries he had suffered on the mountain that fateful day, he had been an extremely troubled young man of twenty-five. He was not only grieving for his father, but filled with anxiety and concern about the future. He had a mighty business to run, enormous responsibilities to shoulder, and he was entirely alone with Emma and his father now dead.

Paula, never anything but devoted and loyal, had her own problems to contend with, and he could not inflict his terrible worries on her.

His mother, Daisy, who had returned to Australia with him at Paula's urging, was crushed by sorrow at the loss of her husband. And although the McGill Corporation was hers, technically speaking, she had never been involved in business, and he knew she could be no help whatsoever. In fact, he was aware that she was looking to him for strength and support.

But quite apart from these problems, Philip was grappling with another emotion at this particular point in his life: *survivor guilt.*

Few people would be left unaffected after surviving an avalanche in which other members of the family had been killed, and Philip was no exception. He had floundered, been unable to come to grips with himself. Why had *he* been singled out to live when the others had died? This question had dominated his thoughts, jostled for prominence in his mind.

He had no ready answer.

However, gradually, he had recognized that he must get over the traumatic experience, put it behind him, and if at all possible, somehow turn it positive. His mother and sister needed him, and he had the conglomerate to run, he repeatedly reminded himself in the ensuing months. And so he focused on the future, and hoped that perhaps the reason for his survival, the purpose of it, would one day be revealed to him.

With the blood of Emma Harte and Paul McGill coursing through his veins, Philip was nothing if not a hard and dedicated worker, and as he began to marshall his turbulent emotions, he directed his full energies into the McGill Corporation. Work blocked out problems and worries, and as far as he was concerned, it was also the most satisfying way to lead his life, to fill his days and nights.

And so by 1981 Philip McGill Amory had become one of Australia's leading industrialists, an important man in his own right, and one to be reckoned with.

The conglomerate had had its ups and downs in the eleven years since Emma's death. But he had held the helm firmly, kept it steady, and steered the company ahead. He had divested himself of losing divisions, diversified his holdings, purchased other companies which mined iron ore and harnessed natural resources, and he had branched out into communications with the acquisition of newspapers and magazines, radio and television stations.

Under Philip's aegis, the company founded and brought to prominence by his forefathers, and immeasurably strengthened by Emma during the years of her trusteeship, had moved forward into the 1980s with greater power and financial growth than it had ever known in the past.

The phone on Philip's desk buzzed several times. He picked it up.
"Yes?" he asked, glancing at his watch.
"It's Ken, Mr. Amory, I have the car waiting."
"Thanks, Ken, I'll be right down." Philip replaced the receiver, put a pile of financial statements, other documents, and *The Asian Wall Street Journal* in his briefcase, snapped it shut, and left his private office.

His wine-colored Rolls Royce stood outside the McGill Tower on Bridge Street, and Ken, his driver of the last five years, leaned against the hood.
"Evening, Mr. Amory," Ken said, straightening up, opening the back door for him.
"Hello, Ken," Philip replied and stepped into the car. A second later they were pulling away from the curb, and he instructed, "Rose Bay, please, Ken. Mrs. Rickards' house."
"Right you are, sir."

Philip settled back into the soft, beige-leather upholstery, endeavoring to shed the general preoccupations of the business day.

He closed his eyes, relaxing, letting the tension ease out of him. He thought of Paula and experienced a small rush of happiness, knowing she would be arriving in Sydney in the morning. He missed her. So did their mother. Philip's mind swung instantly to Daisy. He had not seen her for the past week, since she had been in Perth with her husband, Jason Rickards, and had only returned to the city late last night. But he had no doubt she was hardly able to contain herself, impatiently waiting for Paula's arrival.

He was aware that the only thing casting a faint shadow across their mother's happiness these days was being so far away from her daughter and grandchildren. But she did have Jason, and for that he was extremely thankful.

What a vital role timing plays in life, Philip suddenly reflected. He had introduced his mother to the Perth industrialist in 1975, when Jason had finally recovered from his messy divorce of three years earlier, and when his mother was at last ready to enter into a relationship with another man. Despite their busy lives and their many commitments, both Daisy and Jason had been lonely, and they had welcomed the introduction. And then, lo and behold, much to everyone's surprise but his, these two had fallen in love and had married a year later.

Seemingly it was a good marriage. Jason had a permanent smile on his rugged face and his mother never looked anything less than radiant these days, and she had put her sorrow truly behind her. But then his mother was a wise woman.

In the years immediately following his father's death, she had done her best to make the most of her new life in Australia. She had acted as Philip's hostess, had then gone on to create her own social circle, and she had eventually thrown herself into charity work with a great deal of zeal and dedication to her chosen causes, mostly to do with the welfare of children. This had given her tremendous satisfaction, added purpose to her existence.

As the only child of Paul McGill, who had been one of the richest men in Australia, heiress to his great fortune, and half Australian herself, Daisy believed that doing good works was her duty, the responsibility of wealth and privilege such as hers. She had created the McGill Foundation, had endowed millions to medical research, children's hospitals, and education. Yes, living in Sydney had been good for his mother, just as she, in her way, had been good for Sydney.

Jason Rickards was an added bonus in her life, in all of their lives, really. He was well liked by everyone, was very much a part of the family. Childless, Jason had thrown himself heart and soul into being an adopted grandfather, and Paula's children adored him.

Yes, timing *was* on their side, Philip thought. *And luck . . . lots of it.*

He opened his eyes, pulled himself upright on the seat, smiled ruefully. *His* timing was invariably wrong and *he* never had any luck when it came to women. Just the opposite. But he didn't really care. He had no desire to get married, much preferred the life of a bachelor. There were, after all, worse fates.

Fourteen

The balmy night air drifting in through the open French doors was fragrant with a variety of mingled scents . . . honeysuckle, wisteria, rambling roses, and eucalyptus, and inside the room there was a faint hint of *Joy,* Daisy's favorite perfume, the one she invariably wore.

A Chopin *étude* played softly on the stereo in the background, and silk-shaded lamps added their mellow glow to the gracious drawing room, where peach, white, and pale green predominated, and where a certain gentle calm prevailed.

Philip sat facing his mother across the antique Chinese coffee table made of hand-carved ebony, enjoying a snifter of cognac after the delicious dinner they had just shared. Fernando, the Filipino chef, had prepared Barramundi, his favorite fish, and Daisy had made an English trifle, which had always been a special treat when he was a child. Now he was feeling well satisfied, replete with good food and vintage wine, and completely spoiled as he relaxed on the comfortable sofa.

He brought the brandy balloon up to his nose and sniffed, appreciating the strong, almost harsh bouquet of the alcohol. He took a mouthful, savored it, then sat back, nursed the balloon in his hands, nodding from time to time as he listened to her softly modulated voice, giving her his entire attention.

"And since Jason will be back from Perth on Thursday, I thought it would be nice to take Paula up to Dunoon for the weekend. Don't you, darling? And you will come with us, won't you?"

Philip put the balloon down on the end table and frowned.

"Do you honestly think she'll want to start traveling the minute she gets here, after she's flown halfway across the world?" He shook his head. "I doubt it, Mother." Instantly a grin surfaced, replaced his frown. "Besides, if I know *my* sister, *your* daughter, she'll have her nose to the grindstone on Saturday, trying to bring order to the boutique at the Sydney-O'Neill. That's why she's flying out here, remember."

"Oh but she's coming to see us as well!" Daisy asserted, giving him a sharp look. She wondered if either of her children ever thought about anything else except business. She doubted it. They took after her mother.

Daisy's face changed, became reflective, and after a moment, she said, "But perhaps you're right, Philip. It is *rushing* her a bit, I suppose. Maybe we can go up to the sheep station the following weekend."

"Yes, why not, Mother," he agreed, humoring her.

The smile flicked into Daisy's vivid blue eyes again, and she leaned forward, her face full of enthusiasm and eagerness. "Jason and I have decided to spend an extra month in England, Philip. We're leaving at the beginning of November instead of December, and we won't be back until January. Three months . . . and I'm *so* looking forward to them, to being in London and at Pennistone Royal. Christmas in Yorkshire with Paula, Shane, and the grand-children, and the rest of the family as well, is my idea of sheer bliss. It's going to be like old times . . . when Mummy was alive."

"Yes," Philip said. A brow lifted as he next asked, "Can Jason afford to be away so long though?"

"Of course. And it's one of the reasons he's been spending so much time in Perth these last few weeks, making sure everything will run smoothly during his absence. And in any case, he has every confidence in his staff, just as you do." She smiled at him. "You're coming too, aren't you? To England for Christmas, I mean."

"Well, I'm not sure," he began, and stopped abruptly when he saw his mother's expression. Her face had dropped.

"I hope I can get away, darling," he said noncommittally, having no desire to make a decision about Christmas so far in advance, or to promise her anything. She would hold him to it.

"Oh Philip, you must! You *promised* Paula! Have you forgotten about the sixtieth anniversary of Harte's? You *have* to be at the dinner dance she's giving on New Year's Eve. Everyone's going to be there, and it will look simply awful if you're not."

"I'll do my damnedest, Mother, okay?"

"Yes, all right," she responded quietly, leaning back against the big pillows on the sofa, smoothing the skirt of her silk dress, sighing under her breath. After a moment, Daisy raised her eyes, studied Philip, trying to gauge his mood, wondering if she dare mention his current girlfriend. He could be touchy at times, especially when it came to his private life.

Deciding to take a chance, she said in her low, even tone, "If you do come to England, I think it might be rather nice if you bring Veronica with you. She's such a lovely young woman."

Philip started to laugh, gave his mother an odd look.

Daisy stared back at him in surprise, perplexity flitting across his face. "What is it?"

Still chuckling and catching his breath, Philip finally managed to say, "Honestly, Mother, you *are* behind the times. I broke up with Veronica Marsden weeks and weeks ago. It's over . . . finished . . . caput."

"You didn't tell me," Daisy replied, sounding reproachful. She filled with dismay. "Oh darling, I *am* sorry. As I said, she is a lovely person, and frankly, I thought the two of you were quite serious about each other. But never mind, I expect you know best, Pip," she murmured, using the diminutive of his childhood.

Her look became quizzical when she ventured, "Perhaps you'd like to bring the current favorite?"

"There isn't a current favorite, Mother. And please stop trying to get me married off!" he exclaimed crossly. At once conscious of the hurt invading her eyes, he softened his harsh tone, added, with a light laugh, "You just want to get me hitched so that you can have lots of grandchildren to fuss over here in Australia."

"Yes, there's some truth in that," Daisy admitted.

She lifted her cup, took a sip of the lemon tea, and fell silent, slipping down into her thoughts. And she asked herself why her son continually broke off with suitable young women at the most crucial time in his relationship with them. She remembered Selena, his girlfriend before Veronica, who had come to see her after she and Philip had parted company last year. Selena had confided that Philip had the need to end a relationship the moment it became serious, or rather, became *threatening* was the way Selena had put it. Daisy wondered if the girl had been correct. She stifled another sigh. Her son was as baffling to *her* as he was to many other people. There were those who said he was an enigma, and wasn't that the absolute truth?

Philip, watching her closely, said, "Hey, Ma, what are you cooking up in that head of yours? I can almost see your mind working."

"Nothing, nothing at all, darling." Then Daisy gave a little laugh, and went on confidingly, "Actually, I was asking myself if you would ever marry."

"I have the reputation of being the biggest playboy in the Western world. I aim to keep the title." Lifting the brandy balloon to his mouth, he winked at her over its rim, his expression mischievous.

"Hardly a playboy, not the way you work, Philip. That's an exaggeration, and merely the press pinning a label on you, because you're so eligible."

Now Daisy shifted on the sofa, crossed her long legs, and a new seriousness entered her voice as she continued, "But I can't bear to think of you being alone later in your life, Philip. That's a terrible prospect for you, and not a very comforting one for me to envisage either. And I certainly don't want you to become a crusty old bachelor."

Daisy paused, gave him a penetrating stare, hoping her words would sink in. "Not like poor John Crawford," she finished, thinking of her solicitor in London. He had once had a crush on her, had wanted to marry her after David's death. But she had harbored only friendship for John, nothing deeper than that.

"Yes, poor John indeed," Philip agreed. "He is a bit of a sorry case these days. Yearning after you, Ma, I do suspect. But me *crusty*? Never. The ladies will keep *me* young and merry into my old age." He gave her a cheeky grin. "You know what they say . . . variety's the spice of life, and so I shall always make sure I have a pretty girl on my arm, even in my dotage."

"I don't doubt it," Daisy conceded, laughing with him. But privately she wondered if these fleeting liaisons with countless women were ever going to be enough for her son in the final analysis. If that was what he wanted, then she supposed they would be. On the other hand, he was missing so much, not being married. She longed to continue the conversation in this vein, to speak to him seriously about his personal life, his future, and the future of the McGill Corporation if he did not produce heirs. But instinct, and her better judgment, told her to keep quiet. After all, Philip was thirty-five and answerable to no one but himself, and he might easily resent her probing.

The phone trilled in the adjoining library, and a second later Daisy's Filipino houseman, Rao, appeared in the arched doorway to the living room. "Excuse me, madam, it's Mr. Rickards."

"Thank you, Rao," Daisy said, and glanced across at her son. "I won't be a moment, darling."

There was a faint swish of silk, a whiff of *Joy,* as Daisy rose and hurried out.

Philip's eyes followed her.

He could not help thinking how young his mother looked tonight. She had celebrated her fifty-sixth birthday in May, but she appeared to be years younger. She had a slim, almost girlish figure, and her lovely face was quite unlined, and because she had stayed out of the sun most of her life, she had preserved her flawless English complexion. There was a freshness, a youthfulness about her still, and even the few strands of gray streaking her black hair did nothing to age her. She was remarkable, but then Emma had been well preserved too.

Philip was finishing the last of his cognac when Daisy returned to the living room.

She said, "Jason sends his love, Pip. I told him what you said about dragging Paula to Coonamble, and he tends to agree with you that it wouldn't be fair. Perhaps we'll have a little dinner party for her on Saturday. Is that all right with you? You will come, won't you?"

"Of course! I wouldn't miss being with old Beanstalk for anything. Listen, Mother, I'd really like you to take a look at the financial statements and balance sheets I brought with me. I want to go over them—"

"You know very well that's not necessary, Philip," Daisy interrupted. "I don't know a blessed thing about business, yet you constantly force these papers on me."

"But the McGill Corporation is *your* company, Mother."

"Oh fiddlesticks, Philip, it's yours and Paula's, except in name, and you know that. And obviously I trust you implicitly. Good Lord, darling, my mother trained you all those years ago to do the job properly. *She* had immense faith in your judgment and business acumen, and so do I."

"Thanks for that lovely vote of confidence, Ma, but I insist you look at the papers. Let me go and get them." As he was speaking he hurried out to the foyer and returned at once with his briefcase.

Reluctantly, Daisy took the papers he offered, and settling back on the sofa, she began to read them slowly, although she did so only to please her son.

For his part, Philip sat observing her quietly, thinking that she looked stunning in the silk dress she was wearing. It was a peculiar bluish-purple, like the wisteria growing in her garden, and it underscored the blueness of her eyes. So did the sapphires on her ears and at her throat, a recent gift from Jason, she had told him over dinner. Jason Rickards is a lucky man, Philip thought, and then as his mother lifted her dark head, looked across at him, he smiled and handed her a second sheaf of papers.

"Oh God, not more of them," Daisy groaned, making a face. "This is a pointless exercise, you know, they're double Dutch to me."

Philip merely grinned. This was now an old story between them.

"Here, let me explain," he said, and went to join her on the sofa. For the next half hour he patiently walked her through the balance sheets, striving hard to explain everything in the simplest of terms, as he had been doing for years.

He did not return to the city that night.

He went instead to his house at Point Piper. Earlier, he had phoned, and had told his housekeeper he would be arriving later, but not to wait up for him. She and the rest of the staff were in their own quarters when the car dropped him off at eleven.

He went straight to his den, laid his briefcase on the sofa, and strode over to the bar, where he poured himself a brandy. Carrying it out to the terrace, he stood leaning against the balustrade, sipping the drink and staring out at the ocean, dark as pitch now under a moonless sky.

His mother's words reverberated in his head.

She wanted him to get married because she did not want him to end up a lonely man. That was a belly laugh. Being married didn't necessarily prevent loneliness. Sometimes it even underscored one's very aloneness. He'd never been married, but he had lived with a woman at one point in his life, and he was well aware that the company of another person did not change a damn thing. Certainly it did not chase the devils away.

He had had an unconventional private life for years now. It worried Daisy, and he understood why. But there was nothing he could do about changing it. He sighed. Too many women over too short a period lately, and too damn many even for me, he thought, filling with sudden distaste.

As he examined his life with a new objectivity, he saw that it was as arid as the Great Sandy Desert. A meaningful relationship with a woman *had* eluded him. It would *always* elude him. But did that really matter? Long ago he had decided it was simpler to settle for sex. A physical relationship was reasonably uncomplicated. Anyway, he was a loner by nature. At least he could live comfortably with himself.

As he swallowed the last drop of brandy, swung around, and walked back into the house, Philip McGill Amory had no way of knowing that his life was about to change, for better and for worse. And forever.

Fifteen

"I want to sell the Sitex stock."

Paula's words fell like an exploding bomb into the quiescence of her mother's beautiful peach drawing room, and she realized she had startled herself as much as she had her mother and her brother.

Daisy and Philip were obviously flabbergasted, and neither of them spoke; they simply stared at her for the longest moment.

Paula glanced from one to the other. She had not meant to tell them tonight, nor had she meant to be so blunt about it, but since she could not take the words back, she might as well finish what she had started.

She took a deep breath, but before she could continue, her mother broke the short, uncomfortable silence.

Daisy said, "I don't understand, Paula. Why do you want to sell the stock all of a sudden?"

"Any number of reasons, Mummy, but mainly because oil prices have dropped considerably, and since there's currently a glut of oil on the world market, I feel they're going to drop even lower. And anyway, you know that Sitex has been a pain in the neck to me for years now, so I think we ought to get out, once and for all. Sell our entire forty percent and be done with it."

"I see," Daisy murmured, puckering her eyebrows. She swung her head, stared at Philip.

Philip returned his mother's questioning glance, but remained silent.

He rose, walked over to the French doors, stood gazing out across Rose Bay to the lights of Sydney glittering in the distance. The McGill Tower, soaring up into the starlit sky, dominated the cityscape even at night.

Paula's unexpected announcement puzzled him, and he wondered what was *really* behind it. He turned slowly, his eyes sweeping over her as he returned to his chair. Despite her tan, she looked drawn and tired, and he thought she ought to be in bed, not discussing business at this hour. However, her eyes told him she was waiting for some sort of comment from him.

"The situation's bound to change, Paula, it usually does," Philip said at last. "Oil prices have always fluctuated, sometimes even wildly, and in my opinion, if we're going to sell, it should be at a more auspicious time than now, when we can get the most for the stock, don't you think? When oil is at a premium and prices are high, for instance."

"And when will that be, Philip? I just told you, there's an overabundance of oil in the world today, but you know that as well as I do." Paula sighed, shook her head wearily. "Hundreds of thousands of barrels are being stored up, yet the world demand for oil has dropped by fifteen percent—ever since those artificially high prices were imposed by the cartels in 1979. I honestly believe the demand for oil will continue to fall. It'll go down, down, *down*. You'll see, this current trend will go on for several years . . . in my estimation until 1985."

Philip laughed. "Come on, darling, your outlook is awfully bleak."

Paula said nothing. She sat back on the sofa, rubbed her neck, feeling very tired, once more wishing she had not begun this.

Daisy, whose blue eyes were still troubled, turned to her daughter and said, "But I promised my mother I'd never sell our Sitex stock, Paula, just as she promised the same thing to Paul all those years ago. My father told her to hang on to it, insisted that she never let it go, no matter what, and—"

Cutting in, Paula muttered, "Times have changed, Mummy."

"Yes, they have, and I'm the first to acknowledge that. On the other hand, I would feel very funny about selling our interest in Sitex. Uncomfortable really."

Paula gave Daisy a pointed look. "I bet if Grandy were alive today, she'd agree with *me,*" she asserted, and stifled a yawn. She felt dizzy, woozy actually, and the room seemed suddenly to swim before her eyes, and she thought that if she didn't lie down soon she would collapse right there on the peach sofa. But Philip had started to say something else, so she endeavored to focus on him, to listen to his words.

He was saying, "What does it matter if the shares bring in lower dividends for a year or two, or even three or four. Mother doesn't need the additional income."

"That's absolutely true, I don't," Daisy concurred. "In any case, Paula darling, I really don't think we should be discussing this matter right now. You look exhausted and seem about ready to keel over. I'm not a bit surprised either —as usual, you've done far too much since you arrived yesterday," she chastised gently.

Paula blinked again. "Too true, Mother, and the jet lag generally hits me hard on the second night, doesn't it?" She was struggling to keep her eyes open as waves of exhaustion almost engulfed her. "I think I do have to go to bed. Right now. I'm so sorry, I shouldn't have brought this up . . . we'll have to finish our chat about Sitex another day."

Pushing herself to her feet, Paula went and kissed her mother goodnight.

Philip, who had risen at the same time, put his arm around her and walked her across the drawing room and out into the entrance foyer.

They stood together at the bottom of the staircase.

"Shall I help you upstairs, Beanstalk?" he asked, his eyes kind, full of brotherly affection.

Paula shook her head. "Don't be daft, Pip, I'm not *so* decrepit that I can't make it to my bedroom." She covered her mouth with her hand and yawned several times, then grasped the bannister, put a foot on the first step. "Oh dear, I *think* I can make it . . . I shouldn't have had the wine with dinner."

"It'll make you sleep like a top."

"Gosh, I don't need anything to do that," she murmured, then leaned forward and kissed his cheek. "Good night, love."

"Night, Paula darling, and let's have lunch tomorrow. I'll meet you in the Orchid Room at twelve-thirty. Okay?"

"You're on, brother o' mine."

When she got to her room, Paula was so bone tired she hardly had the strength to undress and take off her makeup. But she managed somehow, and within minutes she was pulling a silk nightgown over her head and gratefully sliding into bed.

As her head touched the pillow, she admitted to herself that she had made a tactical error, *had* picked the wrong time to discuss Sitex. With a sudden flash of insight, she knew her mother would never agree to sell the stock, no matter what *she* said, and that this would drastically interfere with her plans.

Or would it? Her last thought, before she fell asleep, was of her grandmother. "There's more than one way to skin a cat," Emma had been fond of saying. Remembering this, Paula smiled to herself in the dark before her eyelids fluttered and closed.

Silence reigned in the back office of the Harte Boutique in the Sydney-O'Neill Hotel the following morning.

Paula and Madelana sat facing each other across the large desk, their heads bent and close together as they poured over two ledgers.

It was Madelana who looked up first.

"I can't imagine how Callie Rivers managed to make such a mess," she said to Paula, shaking her head, her face a picture of disbelief. "It took some sort of perverse genius to create a muddle of these proportions."

Paula raised her eyes, looked at Madelana, and grimaced. "Either she's totally dense and my judgment was haywire when I hired her, or her illness debilitated her to such an extent, she just hasn't known what she was doing these past few months."

"It had to be her illness, not you, Paula. You're far too smart not to spot a dud the minute you see one," Madelana said confidently, and closed the ledger in front of her with a degree of finality. "I've checked these figures three times now . . . twice with the calculator and once by hand. You're right, I'm afraid. We are in the red here . . . and the red is *very* red."

Paula took a deep breath, expelled it, stood up, and began to pace for a few seconds, her face reflective. Returning to the desk, she took the ledgers, put them in the filing cabinet and locked it, then dropped the key in the pocket of her gray linen jacket.

"Come on, Maddy, let's go back to the stock room and try to make some sense there."

"Good idea," Madelana answered, rising immediately, following Paula out of the office and into the main area of the three-level boutique.

"We'll be downstairs, Mavis," Paula informed the assistant manager, and swept on across the floor without pausing, making for the heavy glass doors which opened into the hotel lobby.

"Yes, Mrs. O'Neill," Mavis answered quietly, staring after Paula, her gloomy face reflecting her worry.

Madelana merely nodded to the young woman.

But once she and Paula were crossing the dark-green marble lobby, she confided, "I think Mavis is all right basically, Paula. Just out of her depth. Callie Rivers should never have made her the assistant manager. She doesn't have what it takes to run a boutique of this size, and she's not very imaginative either. Still, she *is* honest, and that counts for a lot, I guess."

"Everything you say is quite true," Paula agreed, walking briskly into the empty elevator as the door opened, pushing the button for the floor below. "Callie left her a mess to cope with, and she didn't know what to do to correct it, I realize that now." Paula glanced at Madelana through the corner of her eye. "I don't hold Mavis responsible, you know. I just wish she'd had the sense to tell me everything. She knew she could phone me, or telex me, any time she wished."

The two women stepped out of the elevator, and Paula went on, "Let's face it, if the hotel manager hadn't mentioned it to Shane on the phone a few weeks ago, I still wouldn't be any the wiser."

"Yes, it was a good thing he found out there were problems, and that Mavis was in a panic and floundering. I think we just got here in time to avert a real disaster."

"You can say that again," Paula muttered.

The stock room which belonged to the Harte Boutique was located on the mezzanine floor of the hotel, and was actually a series of rooms. These included an office with filing cabinets, a desk, chairs, and telephones in the entrance, and several large storage rooms behind this. Racks of clothes were kept there, along with chests of accessories ranging from costume jewelry, scarves, hats, and belts to handbags and shoes.

Madelana grimaced as she and Paula paced along the lines of bulging racks, looking at the stock for the second time since their arrival, but only now doing their first proper assessment. Groaning, she eyed her boss. "We're going to have one hell of a job making inroads into this lot. It's worse than I realized yesterday."

"Don't I know it," Paula responded grimly. "And I dread to think what awful secrets those chests over there hold." She shook her head, and her annoyance and dismay rose to the surface yet again. "This is partially my fault. I shouldn't have let Callie persuade me to carry several less expensive lines, as well as the Lady Hamilton Clothes. But she convinced me she knew this market better than I did, and fool that I was I gave her a good deal of leeway. And so here we are today, looking at clothes she bought from other manufacturers and which haven't moved."

"I think we do have to have a sale, like you suggested yesterday," Madelana volunteered.

"Yes. We must get rid of the old merchandise, including the remainder of the Lady Hamilton line from last season. A clean sweep, that's the only thing to do—and then we can start again from scratch. I'll telex Amanda this afternoon, instructing her to send as much Lady Hamilton stock as she has available. She can air freight it out to us. We need spring and summer merchandise, of course, since Australia's heading into those seasons now." She broke off, staring at the clothes hanging there, a look of anxiety settling on her face.

"What's wrong?" Madelana asked, as always quick to sense any change in Paula's demeanor.

"I hope we *can* move these clothes in a sale, and make *something* on them, however little that is."

Madelana exclaimed, "Oh I'm sure we will, Paula, and I've got an idea . . . why not make it a Grand Sale. Capital *G*, capital *S*, and advertise it as being comparable only to the one at Harte's of Knightsbridge. That's the world's most famous sale—so let's cash in on it. Surely the agency here in Sydney can come up with some clever copy for the newspaper advertisements." Maddy thought for a moment, and when she continued, it was with a rush of enthusiasm. "I think the message we want to convey to the public goes something like this . . . *You don't have to fly to London to go to the Harte's sale of the year. It's right here on your own doorstep.* Well, what do you think?"

For the first time that morning, a genuine smile flickered on Paula's mouth. "Brilliant, Maddy, I'll put a call into Janet Shiff at the ad agency this afternoon, and have her start working up some of her snappy copy. Now come on, let's sort through these clothes, and pick out as much as we can for the sale."

Madelana needed no further encouragement. She dashed over to one of the other racks, and began her own ruthless process of selection and elimination.

The Orchid Room of the Sydney-O'Neill Hotel was considered to be one of the most beautiful places to lunch or dine in the city. It was also a very *in* spot where people went to be seen and to see, and so it had acquired a certain cachet in local society.

Situated on the top floor of the hotel, two of its walls were made entirely of plate glass running floor to ceiling, and thus it appeared to float, as though suspended between the blue sky and the sea far below, and offered a sweeping view for miles around.

Breathtaking giant-sized murals of handpainted white, yellow, pink, and cerise orchids covered the other two walls, and there were real orchids everywhere . . . arranged in tall cylindrical glass vases, planted in Chinese porcelain pots, and clustered in bowls on every table.

Paula was particularly proud of the room, since Shane had conceived it and had taken an active part in its planning with the architects, at the time the hotel was being designed and constructed. He liked to use animals, birds, or flowers endemic to a country as the motif for a lobby, a dining room, or a bar in his foreign hotels, and since orchids grew in such profusion in the forests, heaths, and woodlands of Australia, this species had seemed appropriate to him. Also, because of the orchid's various shapes and sizes, and lovely, vibrant colors, the flower lent itself to any number of artistic effects and decorative themes.

Paula sat in the elegant, sun-filled restaurant, sipping a mineral water before lunch, and she glanced around admiringly, realizing she had forgotten how truly magnificent the real orchids were, and how brilliantly the hotel florist arranged them in the room, so that they were shown off to their best advantage. Talented gardener that she was, she could not help wishing she could grow these exotic blooms in England.

"Penny for your thoughts," Philip said, peering at her across the table.

"Oh sorry, I didn't mean to drift off like that . . . I was just thinking about the possibility of growing orchids at Pennistone Royal, but I don't think it's feasible."

"Of course it is. You could have a greenhouse built in which to cultivate them . . . you know, like growing tomatoes." He chuckled and there was mischief in his bright blue eyes, and he went on teasingly, "After all, *you* have so much free time on your hands these days."

Paula smiled at him. "If only I did . . . Gardening is very relaxing for me though. And why not a greenhouse? That's a very good thought of yours."

"Oh Lord, what have I done now?" her brother groaned in mock horror at himself. "Shane'll kill me."

"No, he won't, he loves me to garden, to grow things, and he's always giving me new seed catalogs, and packets of seeds and bulbs, and similar stuff. I shall tell him I want an orchid greenhouse for Christmas. How about that?" she finished, laughing, her eyes as merry as her brother's.

"If *he* doesn't give it to you, *I* will." Philip sat back in his chair and went on, "By the way, Mother phoned me just before I left the office. She's thrilled you're spending the weekend at Dunoon. But you proved *me* wrong, you know."

"What do you mean?"

"When Ma told me she wanted you to go up there, I said you wouldn't be interested, not after stepping off a fourteen-hour flight from L.A." He studied Paula for a moment. "And I must admit, I was a bit surprised that you agreed to go. And so readily, she said. I thought you'd be hard at it in the boutique on Saturday. Don't tell me that you've already sorted out the mess there?" This came out sounding like a question and he raised his brows.

"Not completely, Philip, but I'm on my way to doing so."

"Good for you! So come on, tell me the real story, Beanstalk."

Paula quickly filled him in, then explained, "And after I've had the sale next week, I'll do new window displays with the Lady Hamilton stock I'm bringing in from London in a hurry, and I'll back the merchandise with a fresh advertising campaign. With the spring-summer season ahead of me here, I think I can turn the boutique around again in a relatively short period of time."

Philip nodded. "You're one terrific retailer. If you can't do it, no one can, darling. And what about your manager? You're not having her back, are you?"

"I can't, Pip, even though I do believe that some of the mistakes she made were because she wasn't in good health. Obviously I've lost my faith in her, and I know I'd be worried to death if I put her in charge again."

"I can't say I blame you. What's happening at the boutiques in the hotels in Melbourne and Adelaide? They're not affected, are they?"

"Fortunately not. They seem to be all right, from what the managers told me yesterday. Callie was no longer involved with them, thank God. If you remember, I set up a new system some time ago, made each manager autonomous, answerable only to me. However, since I am here in Australia, I'm going to fly down there later next week, just to make sure all is well."

"Good idea. And you shouldn't have too many problems finding a new manager for the Sydney boutique. There are plenty of excellent people around."

"Yes, so I understand. I hope to start interviewing on Monday, and if I haven't found anybody suitable before I leave in a couple of weeks, Madelana O'Shea will follow through for me. In any case, she's staying on for a while, to work with the advertising agency, and get the Sydney boutique organized and running properly. I trust her judgment, and I've every confidence in her."

"So you've said before. I'm looking forward to meeting her sometime."

"It'll be this weekend, Pip. I've invited her to Coonamble. Are you flying up with us tomorrow night?"

"No, I can't. You'll be going with Mother in Jason's plane, and I'll come in on Saturday morning. I'm glad we're going to have the weekend together, and it'll do you good. You can have two days complete rest, and lots of fresh air."

Paula smiled faintly, and leaned across the table, pinning her gaze on her brother. There was a slightly different nuance in her voice when she asked, "Do you think Mummy will change her mind about the Sitex stock?"

"No, I don't," Philip was swift to reply. "Ma's attitude about the stock is all tied up with her emotions about her father. You know as well as I do that she worshipped him, and she just can't bring herself to go against his wishes. And she believes that is what she *would* be doing if she sold the stock. It may sound farfetched, but it happens to be the truth."

"But those were Paul's wishes over forty years ago, for God's sake!" Paula cried vehemently. "His view of the situation would be quite different today, just as Grandy's would be."

"Maybe so, but I know Mother won't budge." Philip gave Paula a searching look. "Anyway, why *do* you want her to sell the stock? *Why* are you so anxious about it?"

Paula hesitated fractionally, wondering whether to tell her brother the truth, but decided against it. "I gave you the reasons last night," she said, keeping her voice neutral. "Although I do have to admit I'm also rather fed up with Marriott Watson and his cronies on the board. They do everything they can to obstruct me, to make my life as difficult as possible."

Philip gave her a curious look. "But Paula, they always have—that's nothing new, is it? Furthermore, they were always at loggerheads with Grandy." He paused, scowling, and rubbed his hand over his chin, reflecting for a moment. "Still, if their behavior is beginning to get to you, perhaps I should explain this to Ma, and—"

"No, no, don't do that," Paula cut in rapidly. "Look, let's forget about selling the Sitex stock. I'll cope with Marriott Watson and the board."

"Yes, I know you will," Philip said. "You always have. You're very much like me. It's impossible for you not to do your duty—it goes against the grain." He flashed her a loving smile. "Now come on, let's order lunch."

Sixteen

Sunlight filtering through the shaded windows awakened Madelana.

Blinking, she sat up abruptly in the antique four-poster bed, feeling at once both startled and disoriented, wondering where she was. And then she adjusted her eyes to the gentle, hazy light and looked around, took in the details of the lovely room, and remembered that she was at Dunoon, the McGill sheep station near Coonamble.

She turned her head, glanced at the little carriage clock on the taffeta-skirted bedside table, saw that it was early, only six o'clock. But that did not matter; she was accustomed to rising at the crack of dawn. Anyway, last night Daisy had told her she could get up whenever she wished, that she should make herself at home, explaining that she would find the housekeeper in the kitchen after six-fifteen. From that time on, such things as freshly squeezed juices, coffee, tea, toast, and fruit were always set out in the breakfast room; after seven, when one of the two cooks arrived, she could order a hot breakfast if she wanted, Daisy had added.

Throwing back the sheets, Madelana leapt out of bed, and hurried into the adjoining bathroom to shower.

Ten minutes later she emerged, wrapped in her white toweling bathrobe, and went over to the windows. She pushed up the shades on both of them, stood for a moment looking down into the gardens below. They were brilliantly green, filled with an abundance of vivid flowers planted in spectacular herbaceous borders, and in huge central flower beds cut into the rolling lawns. It was a radiant day, very sunny, with a bright blue sky scattered with billowing white clouds that looked like handfuls of cotton candy.

The excitement and anticipation she had experienced on arriving the night before flowed through her again, and she could hardly wait to go outside and investigate her immediate surroundings. Most especially she wanted to walk through those inviting gardens, which she knew Paula had had a hand in creating some years earlier.

Seating herself at the kidney-shaped dressing table positioned between the two soaring windows, Madelana began to brush her thick chestnut hair before applying her makeup, and as she wielded her brush, her thoughts centered on this unique place where she had come with Paula, and Daisy and Jason Rickards, to spend the weekend.

Dunoon was unlike anything Madelana had expected, or had imagined it to be.

It was approximately five hundred and seventy kilometers from Sydney, situated in the North West plains region of New South Wales, and the flight in Jason Rickards' corporate jet had been short and fast. They had left Sydney at five yesterday afternoon and had landed on the private airfield at Dunoon just after six o'clock.

Tim Willen, the station manager, had met them, greeting them jovially, and laughing and joking with them as he had helped the pilot and the steward load their luggage into the vintage station wagon.

Ten minutes later, when they were driving off the airfield, Madelana had been startled to see several different types of planes resting in the huge hangars they passed, as well as two helicopters parked on the nearby helipad.

She had voiced her surprise to Daisy, who had explained that it was easier to use air power to get around Dunoon, especially if there was some kind of sudden emergency. On the flight up, Daisy had told her that their fully operating sheep station covered thousands upon thousands of acres, and from the air it had looked like a small kingdom. Seeing the planes and the helicopters had only confirmed this sense of vastness to Madelana.

The main house was five miles away from the airfield, and on the way there Madelana had sat with her nose pressed to the window, frequently feeling awestruck by the things she was seeing. Daisy had been her guide last evening, had pointed out a variety of interesting sights as the station wagon rolled along the wide tarmac road, which cut through the huge property and also encircled it.

At one point they had passed a cluster of buildings which resembled a small village, and Madelana had learned from her hostess that these included sheep-shearing sheds, barns for storing the raw wool shorn from the Merino sheep bred and raised on Dunoon, sheep pens, a smithy, a small abattoir for slaughtering the livestock used for consumption on the station, a small freezer plant for preserving the sides of lamb, mutton, and beef, and a series of other large barns where feed, hay, and grain were stored. There was also a water tower off to one side, and a generator which provided the sheep station with its own electrical power.

A short distance beyond these buildings were several fenced-in paddocks shaded in parts by beautiful golden elm trees and willows. Here cattle and horses grazed contentedly in the luxuriant grass, and overlooking the bucolic paddocks was a compound of attractive houses built on a slight rise against a backdrop of golden elms and thick old oaks.

Tim had slowed down so that she could see everything better, and he had told her that he and his wife lived there, as did the station hands and some of the indoor staff from the main house; adjoining the compound were tennis courts and a swimming pool for the sole use of the staff and their families.

A quarter of a mile farther along the main road, they drove past indoor and outdoor riding rings, where the horses were trained, and close by were large stables.

These buildings had captivated Madelana. Low, rambling and very rustic in appearance, they were made of dark gray and black stone, and were partially covered in creeper. They seemed very old to her, and she had mentioned this to Daisy, who had explained that the stables dated back to the 1920s and had been built by her father, Paul McGill.

The landscape had made a deep impression on Madelana during the drive from the airfield to the house. Somehow, she had not expected the countryside to be so beautiful, had not anticipated such green lushness in Australia. Until she had arrived here, she had always pictured the continent as being arid and dry, and composed almost entirely of scrub-laden outback once the great coastal cities had been left behind.

But Dunoon was glorious, set amidst lovely, undulating hill country, where gentle slopes fell down into verdant valleys, wide paddocks, and wooded areas. It was truly a pastoral landscape, with the Castlereagh River running through its dark rich earth, and where everything seemed to flourish.

The driveway leading up to the main residence, known simply as the manor, was half a mile long, and the minute they had pulled into it, Daisy had rolled down one of the windows. Instantly the station wagon had filled with the all-pervasive scent of lemon. "It's the *Eucalyptus citriodora,"* Daisy had explained, gesturing to the trees towering up above them and bordering the drive on both sides. "They stretch all the way to the house, and they're very aromatic." And Paula had added, "When I smell lemons, no matter where I am in the world, I immediately think of Dunoon." Madelana had nodded. "I can understand why," she had murmured, breathing in the lovely sharp fragrance of citrus.

The manor had blazed with lights to welcome them in the dimming light of gloaming, and when Madelana had alighted from the station wagon and had looked up at the house, she had been momentarily dazzled, and transported back to her beloved bluegrass country. Instantaneously filling with nostalgia and a flock of memories, she had choked up, had had to blink back incipient tears. The manor at Dunoon was built in a classical style reminiscent of the great plantation houses of the American South, somewhat antebellum in feeling, and it was magnificent.

Its front facade was mainly of white-painted wood, with sections of very dark red brick. Wide verandas swept around its four sides, shading the walls in summer but allowing the sun to reach them during the winter months. Standing at the edge of the front veranda were eight elegant white columns, four on each side of the front door made of polished mahogany. These columns were tall, stately, and soared up past the first two stories to support a terrace that encircled the entire third floor.

The green foliage of wisteria growing against the manor's white paintwork contributed greatly to the feeling of cool serenity, as did the many leafy trees shading the graceful house in the back. Lawns bordered with huge pink and white azalea bushes sloped away from the gravel driveway, and the flower gardens were situated beyond these smooth and spacious greens.

Once inside the manor, Madelana had discovered that the interiors did justice to the exterior architecture. The rooms were furnished with choice antiques, crystal chandeliers, fine old carpets, and marvelous paintings, many of them French Impressionists. Later she learned that the collection had been Emma Harte's and included works by Monet, van Gogh, Gauguin, Cézanne, and Degas.

Paula had brought her upstairs to this charming bedroom located next door to hers. Decorated in delicate shades of apricot, lime, and pale blue, it was large and airy, with a high ceiling, a white marble fireplace, and watercolors of Dunoon hanging on the walls. The antique four-poster took pride of place, and there was a loveseat and two chairs arranged in a grouping in front of the fireplace.

Fresh flowers in vases had been placed everywhere and they permeated the room with the mingled scents of the gardens outside. The flowers were potent this morning, but Madelana did not mind.

She peered at herself in the dressing-table mirror, smoothed the brush over her hair again, and then went over to the armoire, took out tailored, gray flannel slacks, a white silk shirt, and a hand-knit jacket of a bluish-gray mohair.

After she had dressed in these clothes, she slipped her feet into a pair of brown leather moccasins, put on her gold watch and a pair of gold Tiffany shrimp earrings, and left the bedroom.

It was just after six-thirty when she pushed open the door of the breakfast room and looked inside.

The housekeeper, Mrs. Carr, whom she had met last night, was nowhere in sight, but Madelana's nose twitched from the tantalizing aromas of coffee and warm bread and ripe fruit. She noticed that these were set out on the table placed against the far wall underneath a painting of a circus clown. The round table in the middle of the octagonal-shaped room was covered with a fresh white organdy cloth and had been set with pretty floral china for four people.

Madelana went over and poured herself a cup of black coffee. She stared at the painting of the clown. Oh, it's a Picasso, she thought, as she turned away, not at all surprised. Nothing about Dunoon could surprise her anymore. It was a magical place.

She carried her cup of coffee outside, sat down on the steps of the back veranda, and drank it slowly, enjoying the smell of the grass and green-growing things, the lemony tang of the eucalyptus trees pervading the air, listening to the stillness of nature. The silence was broken only by the twittering of the small birds and the faint rustling of the leaves under the soft breeze.

How peaceful it was here. It was the kind of peace which was only ever found in the country, and she had forgotten it existed. It's such a luxury, she thought, and closed her eyes, allowing the peace to penetrate her bones, to settle deep inside her. And she realized, quite suddenly, that she had not known a peace like this since her childhood.

A little later, Madelana went back into the house, deposited the cup and saucer in the breakfast room, and then wandered out to the main entrance hall. Earlier, when she had been doing her makeup, she had intended to take a stroll through the gardens in front of the house, but now she hesitated.

Opening off the other end of the foyer was the gallery. Paula had pointed it out last night on their way upstairs; they had not had time to go in then, since they were in a hurry to change for dinner. As they had mounted the grand, curving staircase together, Paula had said, "The gallery is hung with portraits of our McGill ancestors, but there's also an extraordinary painting of Emma in there. You must see it, Maddy, before you leave Dunoon."

Her curiosity of last night was aroused again, and Madelana decided to take a peak at Emma's portrait. She would go for her walk afterward.

The gallery was much longer than she had envisioned, with a high ceiling and a huge window at one end. The polished wood floor was bare, the walls were painted white, and a dark oak refectory table stood in the middle. A Chinese porcelain horse, quite large in size, had been placed on the table, and this appeared to be yet another priceless antique to Madelana.

She hurried down the length of the gallery, barely glancing at the portraits of the McGills, mainly interested in finding the one of Emma Harte.

When finally she stood in front of it, she caught her breath. It was extraordinary, just as Paula had said, so very lifelike, and so much better than any of those she had seen in the Harte stores, and even superior to the one at Pennistone Royal in Yorkshire.

She gazed at it for the longest time, marveling at the vividness of the painting, and the exceptional brushwork. It had obviously been painted in the 1930s, and the evening gown Emma wore was of the period and made of white satin, and Madelana felt that if she reached out, touched the painting, her fingers would rest against the real fabric. Emeralds blazed around Emma's throat, at her ears and wrists, and there was a square-cut emerald on her left hand, and the stones echoed the color of her radiant eyes.

What small hands she had, Madelana thought, stepping closer, peering at the picture. Why, they're so tiny, they're almost a child's hands.

The portrait which hung next to Emma's was of a darkly handsome man, elegant in a white tie and tails. He had the most piercing blue eyes she had ever seen, a strong, arresting face, a black mustache, and a deep cleft in his chin. Clark Gable, Maddy thought, and then smiled to herself, knowing it could not possibly be the late movie star. It was undoubtedly Paul McGill.

Tilting her head to one side, she studied the painting carefully, thoughtfully, wondering what kind of man he had been. A match for Emma Harte, she had no doubt.

Philip came running downstairs as the grandfather clock in the entrance foyer was striking seven.

He crossed the vast hall, heading in the direction of the breakfast room, when he noticed that the double mahogany doors leading into the gallery were slightly ajar. He walked over, intending to close them, and immediately saw the young woman inside. She stood at the far end, and she was leaning toward the painting of his grandfather, studying it, and he realized she must be Paula's American assistant.

As if she sensed his presence, she swung around swiftly. When she saw him in the doorway, her eyes opened very wide and a look of astonishment crossed her face. She stared at him intently. He found himself staring back.

And in that instant his life changed.

It seemed to Philip that all about her was the light. Not simply the bright sunlight pouring in through the big window, but the light which emanated from within her. She was an incandescent being.

He knew at once that he wanted her, and that he would have her. Philip could not comprehend how he knew this, but it flashed through his brain like a bolt of lightning, and he accepted it as the undeniable truth.

Slowly he began to walk forward, his riding boots clattering loudly against the wood, and the noise was overwhelming to him, a dreadful intrusion on the perfect stillness enveloping her. She stood there waiting for him, not moving, appearing hardly to breath, still watching him intently. And his eyes did not leave her face.

She was a stranger, yet entirely familiar to him, and he experienced a deep sense of predestination—of fate—as he finally drew to a standstill in front of her.

Looking up into his face, she smiled a slow, tentative smile, and he was aware that something stupendous was happening to him, and what startled him the most was that it was happening here, in his own home, in the one place he truly loved on this planet. She continued to smile up at him, and he felt as though a burden was lifting from his shoulders, and there was the total cessation of pain, and a sense of peace flowed through him.

Dimly, as though from far away, he heard his own voice. "I'm Philip, Paula's brother," he was saying, and he was surprised he sounded so normal.

"I'm Madelana O'Shea."

"So I'd guessed."

She put her hand in his, and he clasped it firmly, knowing he had been waiting for her all his life.

——— *Seventeen* ———

It was a great effort for Philip to let go of Madelana's hand, but finally he did so.

Immediately, Madelana slipped it into her pocket quickly. The feel of his strong fingers lingered, as though their imprint had been permanently burned onto hers. She shifted on her feet, and glanced away. Philip McGill Amory unnerved her.

Philip, watching her closely, said, "You looked surprised when I appeared in the doorway. I'm sorry, I didn't mean to startle you."

"I thought for a minute that Paul McGill had suddenly sprung to life—"

His vibrant laughter cut into her sentence, echoed around the quiet gallery, and he glanced at the painting through the corner of his eye, but made no comment.

"Also," she went on, "Paula said you wouldn't be arriving from Sydney until around noon today."

"I changed my mind, decided to fly up last night. I got in at eleven-thirty, but everyone was already in bed."

She nodded, said nothing, stared up at him.

"You were studying my grandfather's portrait very closely." He gave her a lopsided grin and his bright blue eyes were full of laughter, danced teasingly. "Did it reveal anything to you? Secrets of his character, perhaps?"

"I was thinking that he must have been very special, a true man, to have won Emma Harte and to have married her."

"From what my grandmother told me about him, Paul McGill was everything you or I could ever imagine him to have been. And *more,* I suspect," Philip said. There was a slight pause, before he went on in a softer tone, "But they were never married, actually . . . his wife wouldn't divorce him. So they took matters into their own hands, flouted convention, and lived together for about sixteen or seventeen years. Until his death in 1939, in fact. I suppose what they did was considered quite scandalous in those days, but they didn't care." Philip shrugged. "They were madly in love, wildly happy, and apparently they never regretted a thing. And naturally they adored their only child, my mother." There was another pause, then Philip said, "She's illegitimate, of course."

Madelana was taken aback. "I didn't know that, or any of the things you've just told me. Paula has never said anything about your grandmother's personal life. And what I've heard or read has been to do with her business achievements."

"Yes, she had quite a success story, didn't she? She was so far ahead of her time. A brilliant and truly emancipated woman who showed a lot of other women the way . . . into big business and the corporate world. And I'm glad she did. I for one don't know what I'd do without the women executives in our company."

Philip chuckled, suddenly looked amused again. "But I'm sure everybody's forgotten about Emma's private life by now. After all, it happened so long ago. Anyway, she has become something of a mythical figure. A legend. And there are any number of keepers of the flame around, both in the family and out . . . who don't want her image tarnished in any way." He pursed his lips, shook his head. "Of course, as far as I'm concerned, nothing could tarnish Emma's image, least of all living out of wedlock with a man she truly loved— and with all her heart."

"I agree with you. But *why* wouldn't she divorce him? His wife, I mean."

"Her religion got in the way, and rather conveniently, *I* think. Constance McGill was a Roman Catholic, and *I* feel she simply hid behind the church and its teachings in order to frustrate Paul. She didn't want him, but she didn't want anyone else to have him. And she didn't want him to be happy, that's an *absolute* certainty. So, she put a bunch of priests and a lot of ridiculous religious mumbo-jumbo in the middle of their marital affairs, merely to confuse the issue, in my opinion."

"Oh—"

Philip was acutely aware of Madelana, and he immediately saw the oddest look entering her eyes. Sensitive, possessing real insight, he knew instinctively that he had blundered. "I've offended you . . . you're a Roman Catholic, aren't you?"

"Yes, I am, but you haven't offended me. Honestly."

"I'm so sorry."

"It's all right, really, Philip . . ." Her voice trailed off. She glanced up at him.

Their eyes met and held. Neither of them could look away. The silence between them deepened.

As he stared into her luminous eyes, silvery, curiously transparent, Philip understood that it *was* all right. She meant exactly what she said, and would always mean it. For there was no guile in her. She was open and honest, and this pleased him. Once more, he had that peculiar feeling of familiarity. It was as if he had known her long ago, had been separated from her, and had found her again. He felt natural with her, comfortable as he had never been with any other woman, and completely at ease. *I want her,* he thought for the second time that morning. *And I aim to have her.* But go slowly, go very slowly, a voice inside him cautioned.

Madelana, held by his mesmeric blue gaze, was also filled with strange feelings, ones she had hitherto never experienced. Her throat was constricted and dry, she had a tight pain in her chest, and she was shaking inside. She was reacting strongly to Philip, physically and emotionally, and in a way she never had in her entire life, not even with Jack Miller. But then she had never met anyone like Philip McGill Amory before. He was so masculine, so potent, and there was all that charm. Fatal charm. He threw her off balance. And worse still, he frightened her.

Inexplicably, Madelana thought she was about to burst into tears. She averted her head swiftly, broke the eye contact between them. She had begun to tremble, and afraid that he would notice, she walked to the other side of the gallery.

Clearing her throat, she said, without looking back at him, "And which ancestor is this?"

Philip followed her across the room.

He stood directly behind her, breathing in the fragrance of her hair, her perfume. It was something spicy, musky almost, and he found it provocative. He had the sudden urge to put his arms around her, and he had to exercise enormous constraint not to do so.

In a tightly controlled voice, he said, "Oh, that's Andrew, the Scottish sea captain, who came to Australia as a free settler in 1852, and that's his wife, Tessa, in the portrait next to his. Andrew was the founding father, settling here on this land, starting the sheep station, and putting down the original foundations of this house, which he called Dunoon, after the place he came from in Scotland."

"It's a very beautiful house," Madelana murmured in a husky voice, so conscious of Philip's proximity she could barely speak.

"Thank you . . . I think so, too. But actually, it was Andrew's son, Bruce, my great-grandfather, who gave the manor its feeling of the American Old South in the early 1900s, after a trip to America. He built the new facade, added the pillars, and superimposed the look of the plantations of Georgia and Virginia."

"And Kentucky . . . it reminds me of home."

Philip walked around her so that he was able to see her face, and his dark brows lifted in surprise. "You come from bluegrass country?"

Madelana nodded.

"But you don't sound at all Southern."

"And you don't sound particularly Australian," she said, and then she laughed for the first time since meeting him, and this eased the tension which had been building inside her. "I was born and raised in Lexington."

"Then you must have grown up around horses. You *did*, didn't you? And you *do* ride, don't you?"

"Yes."

His eyes lit up, and his voice was buoyant as he exclaimed spontaneously, "Come riding with me! *Now.* I want to show you the land, take you over the station . . . you can't have seen very much last night, especially in the dusk." He glanced at her clothes. "I'm sure we have breeches and boots to fit you."

"I brought my own riding things," Madelana said, then explained, "Before we left New York, Paula told me we'd probably be coming here for a weekend, and to be prepared. In fact, she told me exactly which clothes to bring."

"Smart girl, my sister," he said, the lopsided grin sliding onto his mouth again. "Come on then, what are we waiting for!"

Philip grabbed hold of her hand, hurried her out of the gallery and into the hall, adding, "I'll have a quick cup of coffee in the breakfast room while you're changing. I'll be waiting for you in there."

"I'll only be a few minutes," she said quietly, swept up by the power and magnetism of this man.

True to her word, she arrived in the breakfast room within the space of ten minutes.

When she appeared in the doorway so quickly, he was surprised, but pleasantly so. Women who fussed about their hair and their makeup, and dawdled and kept him waiting, had always been an irritant to him. He was accustomed to the Harte women, who rarely primped but always looked smart, and he was glad Madelana fit into this mold.

As he rose and went over to her, admiration flickered in his eyes. He liked the way she was dressed. She was obviously a genuine horsewoman, not an amateur who merely fancied herself in the getup and did not take riding seriously. Her clothes announced this to him. Her man-tailored, red-and-purple-plaid wool shirt and cream breeches were in good condition, but by no means new, and her black boots, as highly polished as his own, were well worn and obviously a few years old.

Smiling broadly, taking her elbow, he led her out of the house and across the back courtyard to the garage.

As they walked past the collection of vintage automobiles lined up against the wall of the roofed-in walkway, he asked, "Which way did you drive to the manor from the airfield last night?"

"Tim Willen brought us on the main road," Madelana answered. "I saw quite a lot of the station—the sheep pens, the shearing sheds, and that whole area of work buildings, as well as the compound."

"Good-o . . . then we can get out to the countryside immediately, go for a *real* ride, instead of just puttering around," he announced, helping her into his dark blue Maserati.

Philip had phoned through to the stables while she had been changing, and when they arrived at the old buildings which she had so admired the night before, their horses were already saddled.

The head groom was waiting for them, and after Philip had introduced her to Matt, he took her over to the stalls. "This is Gilda," he said, opening the stall gate, leading out the roan mare. Handing Madelana the reins, he went on, "She's all yours. You'll find she's gentle, but with enough spirit not to be too boring for you."

Philip stepped away from the horse, and resisted the temptation to help Madelana mount.

"Thanks, and she's beautiful," Madelana said, looking at the roan appreciatively. She began to stroke and fondle the young mare's nose and head, and nuzzle her, then she whispered in her ear, endeavoring to make friends, as the grooms in Kentucky years before had taught her always to do with a strange horse. After a couple of minutes of this play, Madelana felt that they knew each other well enough, and she put her left foot in the stirrup, swung herself up into the saddle.

Philip had watched her performance with Gilda, nodding to himself at her expertise, and smiling inwardly. Now he mounted Black Opal, his glossy ebony-colored stallion, and led the way out of the cobbled stable yard, across the main road, and down a dirt track that sloped toward a small copse.

They trotted single file along the narrow track overhung with golden elms and willows, and soon came out into a wide meadow where the green grass rippled under the light breeze. For a while they cantered side by side, and then unexpectedly Philip broke into a gallop, spurring Black Opal forward, leaving Madelana behind.

"Come on, Gilda girl, come on, mah honey," Madelana cooed, leaning forward on the mare's neck, rising slightly out of the saddle, standing as she broke into a gallop and streaked after Philip.

She caught up with him, and they galloped together through several adjoining meadows, jumping fences, racing neck and neck, until Philip finally slowed and reined in Black Opal.

Madelana instantly followed suit, knowing that she must take his lead, since she was on strange ground and in unfamiliar surroundings.

As they caught their breath, they looked at each other.

"That was great. You're terrific," Philip said. "But we've got to cool it now, we're coming to the sheep and cattle grazing fields."

"Yes, I understand," she said.

They wandered at a gentle pace through the beautiful pastoral countryside, passing herds of cattle and flocks of sheep roaming the meadows and the lower slopes. They skirted copses filled with the ever-present golden elms and eucalyptus, and traveled along a deep and lovely valley, following the winding, silver thread of the river Castlereagh for a short way, and finally they went slowly up into the green hills of Dunoon.

They spoke intermittently.

Madelana asked the odd question now and again, and occasionally Philip volunteered bits of information, but for the most part they were quiet.

This pleased Philip. He did not always wish to talk, was frequently introspective and preoccupied, and women who chattered nonstop got on his nerves. Her silence was like a balm. He was conscious of her in every respect, yet she was not an intrusion on him or his inbred sense of privacy, and there was no awkwardness between them, at least as far as he was concerned. In fact, just simply riding along with her like this made him feel lighter, happier than he had been in years.

Madelana was having similar feelings.

The anxiety and tension she had experienced in the portrait gallery had lessened when she was in her room changing her clothes, had dissipated almost entirely during the time she had been out here in the open air with him.

Although New South Wales was as far away from Kentucky as anyone could get, she felt closer to home than she had since leaving her beloved bluegrass country four years ago. The stillness of the gardens, which had struck her so forcibly earlier that morning, was even more pronounced in this vast landscape, and the overwhelming peacefulness was filling her with a sense of tranquility. And because she was relaxed, she was unexpectedly at ease with herself and with Philip.

They rode together across his land for almost two hours.

At last they came to the place he had been heading for since they had left the stables. It was the highest point on Dunoon, and Philip led the way up the steep incline. When he reached the top of the hill, he jumped down off Black Opal, stood waiting by the side of the horse for Madelana, who was only a short distance behind him.

She came up onto the crest, handling the roan beautifully and with the skill of a seasoned equestrian. Nevertheless, he wanted to help her dismount, but once again he refrained. He was afraid to touch her.

As she swung out of the saddle, dropped lightly to the grass, he strolled over to the huge oak that spread its ancient branches across the hilltop like a giant parasol of lacy green.

Madelana joined him, and he told her, "My great-great-grandfather planted this oak over a hundred years ago, and this is my favorite spot. It was Emma who first brought me up here when I was a little boy—she loved it, too. You can see for miles around. Just look!" he exclaimed, flinging his arm out in a sudden sweeping gesture. Then he shaded his eyes with his hand, gazed out across the undulating terrain, and there was pride and love in his voice when he said, "There's nowhere in the world like it, at least not for me."

"It is staggeringly beautiful," Madelana replied, meaning her words. Everything seemed more vivid to her at Dunoon . . . the sky looked infinitely bluer, the clouds whiter, the grass and trees greener, the flowers more colorful. It was a paradise, as he had said earlier when they were riding through the valley. She took several deep breaths. The air was crystal clear up here, and so pure and bracing.

Philip took off his wide-brimmed hat, threw it down, ran his hand through his thick black hair. "Let's take a rest before heading back," he suggested, then motioned to the ground and sat down.

Madelana nodded and also seated herself, enjoying the dark green coolness under the shady tree after their long ride in the sun.

They were both silent for a short while, and then Philip said, "It must have been wonderful to feel the way they did, don't you think?"

"Yes," Madelana said, understanding immediately that he was referring to Paul and Emma.

"Have you ever been in love like that?" Philip asked.

"No, have you?"

"No." He immediately fell silent, slipped down into his thoughts, and Madelana was quiet.

"Are you married?" he asked suddenly.

"No, I'm not . . . nor have I ever been."

Philip gave her a sidelong glance. He wanted to ask her if she was involved with anyone special, but he did not dare. Already the conversation had been more breathtakingly personal than he had intended.

As if aware that he was studying her surreptitiously, she turned her head, gave him a long look through those quiet, unwavering gray eyes.

He smiled at her.

She smiled back. Then she pulled her knees up to her chest, rested her chin on them, sat staring out into the blue-and-white haze of sky and cumulus clouds, drifting.

Philip leaned back, rested his head against the gnarled tree trunk. Intuitively, he knew that she knew about his reputation as a playboy. He stifled a sigh. It had never bothered him in the past. Now it did.

Eighteen

The evening had turned suddenly cool, and a strong wind was blowing down from the hills above Dunoon, ruffling the curtains, making them billow about wildly, and chilling the air in her bedroom.

Paula shivered, rose from the dressing table, and went to close the window.

Once seated again, she picked up her pearl choker, fastened it around her neck, put on the *mabé* pearl-and-diamond earrings, and then sat back, staring at her reflection in the mirror. Not bad, she thought, for an overworked executive and harassed wife and mother of four who's knocking thirty-seven.

She turned her head, glanced at the color photograph on the dressing table. It was of Shane and herself with Lorne, Tessa, Patrick, and Linnet, taken by Emily on the terrace of Pennistone Royal in the spring. Her heart tightened imperceptibly when she thought of her two youngest children; in their different ways they were both so vulnerable, and they needed her.

They had been in bed and fast asleep when she had phoned Shane earlier that morning. With the difference in time between Australia and England she was actually one day ahead, and it had been almost midnight on Friday when she had reached him at Pennistone Royal. He had just returned from dinner with Winston at Beck House; Emily had already left for Hong Kong, on her buying trip for Genret, and apparently the two best friends had enjoyed a rare bachelor evening together.

It had been wonderful to hear his loving and reassuring voice, to know that all was well at home. Lorne and Tessa were now properly settled in at their respective boarding schools, and Nanny Pat, back from her week's holiday in the Lake District, was once again in command of the nursery and her young charges.

"No problems, darling," Shane had said, sounding so close he might have been in the next room. "I'll spend the weekend here with the kids, then push off to London on Sunday night. And listen, angel, I heard from Dad today. He phoned to tell me he and Mother are definitely coming for Christmas, and so young Laura will be with us too, and Merry and Elliot have also accepted. It looks as if we're going to have quite a mob with us up here in Yorkshire . . . It'll be like the old days when Blackie and Emma were alive. And we'll have a wonderful time."

His news had delighted her, and they had chatted for another half hour about the Christmas plans, the children, and other family matters, and Shane had promised to ring her in a couple of days. She had felt much better when she had hung up. She missed him and the children enormously when she was traveling, was never completely at ease when she was separated from her family. She tried not to worry, but invariably she did, and she suspected she would never change. Her nature, after all, was her nature.

Paula glanced at her watch, saw that she had ten minutes to spare before going downstairs for drinks. Rising, smoothing down the skirt of her silk cocktail dress, she walked across to the writing desk where she began to sort through the papers strewn there. Among them were the Christmas lists she had started in Sydney earlier in the week. Shane's family were marked down for major gifts, but not for stocking stuffers and tree presents. She must add their names, now that they were coming to Yorkshire, along with ideas for suitable little tokens, since she planned to do all of her Christmas shopping in Hong Kong when she met Emily there in ten days.

Paula's thoughts focused on Shane's parents as she leaned over the desk, rapidly making notes for herself. She was truly thrilled that Bryan and Geraldine were coming to England in December; they had been ambivalent about it for a number of weeks. Ever since Bryan's heart attack five years ago they had been living in Barbados. Bryan kept an eye on the other O'Neill hotels in the Caribbean, but for the most part he took it easy these days, and was semiretired at Shane's insistence.

She missed them, and there had been a void in all their lives since the O'Neills had lived abroad. She missed Miranda, too. She and Shane's sister had been close friends from childhood, and although they managed to see each other in New York, they were forever grumbling that they never had enough time together these days. As head of O'Neill Hotels International in the United States, Merry was a busy executive, and now that she was married to the noted American architect, Elliot James, she wanted to spend any free time she had with him at their homes in Manhattan and Connecticut. In consequence, Merry had not been to England much lately, and even her business trips were brief. "Hit and runs," Merry laughingly called them.

For once all the O'Neills would be under one roof at the same time, along with the Hartes. Sir Ronald and Michael Kallinski had already accepted to come for Christmas dinner, so the three clans would be represented, and for the first time in years. This thought made Paula smile with pleasure.

Clipping the sheaf of papers together, she slipped them into her briefcase for safekeeping. When she had another free moment, either later tonight or tomorrow morning, she would make a few more notes, allocate bedrooms at Pennistone Royal, do the menus for the holiday period, and start the guest lists for the parties she wanted to give. Christmas was three months away, but that was not really very long, not with the schedule she had, and all she had to accomplish. Planning ahead, being well organized, was the only way she knew how to cope with everything. That was how she had been brought up by her grandmother, and sometimes she wondered if this was indeed the secret of her success.

Paula believed herself to be the first one downstairs when she stood in the doorway of the living room a few minutes later. It was so hushed, so still.

But then Jason Rickards stepped into the room from the veranda, closed the French windows, locked them firmly, and swung around. His tanned, craggy face lit up when he saw her.

"Hi there, sweet'art," he said, striding across the floor toward her.

Lean and rangy, Jason had the gait of a man who had spent years on a horse, a weatherbeaten complexion from being constantly outdoors, and dark hair silvered at the sides. He was in his early sixties, but looked younger. Tonight he wore a navy blue cashmere jacket and dark gray pants, with a white shirt and a navy tie, and was as impeccable as he generally was, but to Paula he seemed to be uncomfortable when he was dressed up for the evening. It was as if more formal clothes constrained him, and she couldn't help thinking that

Jason would much prefer to be in blue jeans, riding boots, and an open-necked shirt.

Coming to a standstill, he caught one of her hands in his, twirled her around. "My, you look pretty, Paula. And red suits you as much as it does your mother."

"Thank you, Jason." Paula smiled up into his face, tucked her arm through his, and walked with him to the fireplace. "Where is Mummy, anyway?"

"Upstairs, finishing dressing. She'll be down in a minute. Now, me darlin', let's have a drink together. What would you like?"

"If that's a bottle of champagne I spy over there in the silver bucket, then that's what I'll have, please."

"Good-o." He loped over to the console, where a tray of liquor, glasses, a bucket of ice, and the champagne stood, and proceeded to open the bottle of Louis Roederer Crystal.

Paula watched him, her eyes full of warmth. She thoroughly approved of Jason, had grown very fond of him, admired his down-to-earth attitude toward life. Her respect for him was immense, not only because of his brilliance as a businessman, but for his personal qualities as well. He was kind and thoughtful. Like Philip, she was overjoyed that her mother had become his wife. Despite the disparities in their backgrounds, they got along beautifully and he was a devoted husband. A self-made man, Jason had married late for the first time, and had lost his wife from cancer after only seven years; he had then had a brief, disastrous second marriage. "Third time lucky," was his favorite expression these days, and he was most adoring of Daisy, as she was of him. Sometimes they reminded Paula of a couple of young lovers, and this pleased her.

Pouring champagne into a Baccarat crystal flute, then mixing a scotch and soda for himself, Jason remarked, "It's damn windy out there tonight, Paula. I bet you there's one helluva damn storm down in Sydney."

"I hope it doesn't hit here," she said, accepting the glass from him when he brought it to her.

"I doubt it will, and if it does, it'll soon blow over. We always get a drop of rain in the spring, you know. And we'll have a nice sunny day tomorrow, never fear." He clinked his glass to hers. "Cheers, darlin'."

"Cheers, Jason."

They stood together in front of the fire, perfectly at ease, and full of affection for each other.

Suddenly Jason eyed her speculatively. "There you go again, Paula, smilin' quietly, and looking mighty damn pleased with yourself." He chuckled. "As your mother would say, you look like the cat that's swallowed the canary."

Paula could not help laughing. Jason had adopted many of her mother's expressions, almost all of which Daisy had learned from *her* mother, but they did not sound quite the same without Emma's pithy delivery.

She said, "I'm thrilled about the way Christmas is shaping up, Jason, that's all. It's going to be the biggest get-together we've had in years, now that Shane's parents and sisters are coming."

"Your mother's worried that—"

"What am I worried about?" Daisy asked from the doorway, and floated into the living room on a cloud of *Joy* perfume and a swirl of purple silk.

"Sweet'art, you look gorgeous!" Jason exclaimed, his dark brown eyes glowing with love and admiration. He hurried to Daisy, took her arm, ushered her over to the fireplace. "What can I get for you, sweet'art? Champagne, or a vodka tonic?"

"Champagne, please, Jason darling."

"Jason's right, you *do* look fabulous tonight, Mummy," Paula said. "I've not seen you in purple for years. It's a great color for you, and simply marvelous with those exquisite opals. Are they new?"

"Thank you, dear, and yes, they are. Jason gave them to me on Thursday night. They're from his mine in Coober Pedy."

"Lightning Ridge," Jason corrected, grinning, bringing her the drink. "They're very rare black opals, Paula."

"Thanks," Daisy said, taking the glass. She repeated, "And what am I worried about, Jason?"

"Philip."

Daisy frowned, sat down on the sofa, raised her flute. "Cheers."

"Cheers," Paula and Jason said in unison.

Daisy took a sip of the champagne, peered quizzically at her husband over the rim. "And *why* am I worried about him?"

"Because he's so reluctant to commit himself . . . about coming to England with us for Christmas," Jason explained. "Paula was just remarking how thrilled she is about the big family reunion and I was on the verge of telling her that her brother was undecided about his plans."

"Oh I think he'll come now," Daisy murmured with a small, but knowing smile.

"You *do?*" Jason sounded surprised and he stared hard at Daisy. "What's happened to make you change your mind, sweet'art? You were pretty damn adamant about it when I got back from Perth on Thursday night, and that's only two days ago."

"At lunch today Paula invited Madelana to go to London for Harte's sixtieth anniversary dinner and dance at the Ritz, and she also invited her to spend Christmas with us in Yorkshire. And Madelana accepted, didn't she, Paula?"

"Well, yes, she did, Mummy." Paula seemed slightly baffled, and she frowned. "But what's that got to do with anything?"

Daisy sat back, beamed first at her daughter, and then at her husband, and said, "It has everything to do with Philip coming to England in December."

Both Jason and Paula gaped at her, but neither of them said a word.

"Haven't you noticed how Philip looks at Madelana?" Daisy asked softly. "When he thinks no one else is watching, of course. And haven't you also noticed how he was behaving around her today . . . at the pool, during lunch, and at teatime? *So very solicitous.* And they were out riding *all* morning, you know, Paula. For about four hours or so."

"Oh Mummy, honestly, you're such a romantic!" Paula exclaimed. "He was merely being a good host. After all, you brought him up to be well mannered. He's a gentleman." Paula laughed dismissively. "He's only known her for *one* day! Not even that, for heaven's sake!"

"So what?" Daisy said, and took another sip of champagne.

Paula frowned at her mother, then looked at Jason, raising a brow.

Jason let out an amused chortle. "I'd only known your mother for one hour when I realized I wanted to marry her, and I was hell-bent on getting her,

I don't mind telling you, Paula. I think a man and a woman *know* immediately if they've clicked in a special way, *know* how they truly feel about each other. It's kind of . . . well, it's kind of an instinctive thing. And *time,* as such, doesn't make a helluva lot of difference. You can know a person for years, yet never really know them, feel nothing for them. Or you can suddenly meet someone, and *bang!* That's it!" He glanced across at Daisy. "What's that French expression, sweet'art?"

"Coup de foudre . . . a clap of thunder, an unexpected blow . . . meaning love at first sight," Daisy replied. "And you're absolutely right, Jason, I agree with everything you say." She smiled at him lovingly.

"Madelana and Philip," Paula muttered. "Oh no!" Her heart sank. She adored her brother, but the last thing she wanted was for him to become involved with Madelana. For Madelana's sake. She did not want her to get hurt. Also, she had her own important plans for her assistant in the future.

Paula said slowly, "He might be interested in her, Mother, but you know what he's like with women. He thinks they're a dime a dozen. Why, he's told me that so many times, and *you* also know better than *anyone* that he breaks off with them the minute the relationship starts developing into something more meaningful than a romp in the hay." She shook her head. "I hate to say this about him, but Philip is actually only interested in one-night stands."

"Really, Paula, how can you make a statement like that! He went out with Veronica Marsden for almost three months," Daisy exclaimed vehemently, although she kept her voice muted.

Paula groaned wearily. "Yes, that *is* about the duration of his affairs, isn't it? *Three months.* I sincerely hope he *doesn't* get involved with Maddy, because he'll only cause her heartache, and that I couldn't bear. She's had too much pain in her life already. Please don't encourage him, Ma. Promise me."

Daisy's face dropped. "Yes, I suppose you're right, as usual, Paula." She let out a heavy sigh. "Oh, dear, and I do like her so much. I was so happy today when I saw how keen he seemed to be . . ." Her voice tapered off lamely.

Paula insisted, "Mummy, please promise me you won't encourage Philip. I'm very *serious* about this."

Daisy nodded swiftly. "Oh, I do, dear, I do." She instantly noticed Paula's stern, almost forbidding expression, and added, *"I promise."* Daisy recognized that her daughter was only reiterating what she herself had been thinking earlier in the week, and dismay lodged in the pit of her stomach. She could not bear to think that her son was destined to be a playboy for the rest of his life. What an empty and shallow existence that would be for him.

Jason said, "I think we'd better get off this subject mighty damn sharpish, I'm sure they'll both be down any minute."

"Of course, Jason," Daisy was quick to agree. "And it really isn't very nice, talking about them in this way, is it?"

"No," Paula muttered, still feeling disturbed, and wondering why *she* hadn't noticed Philip's behavior around Madelana, the attention he had supposedly paid to her. Renowned in the family for being eagle-eyed, for never missing a trick, she suddenly asked herself if she was slipping.

Jason strolled over to the console, refilled his glass, and remarked, "By the way, Paula, when are you planning to go to Hong Kong?"

"Not for about ten days or so. It really depends on what I find in Melbourne and Adelaide. Madelana and I are flying down there on Wednesday, once we've got the Sydney boutique organized for the sale. But why do you ask, Jason?"

"One of my executives, Don Metcalfe, has to go over to the crown colony around that time. It occurred to me that you might like a lift on the corporate jet."

"Gosh, Jason, that would be wonderful," Paula exclaimed, smiling at him. "If our dates coincide, of course."

"Don can leave any time around the twenty-first, the twenty-second, or even the twenty-third of September, whichever suits you, darlin'."

"Thanks so much, I'll let you know."

"You never did say why you're going to Hong Kong, dear," Daisy murmured, giving Paula a questioning look.

"To meet Emily, Mummy. She's there now, on one of her buying trips for General Retail Trading, and we thought it would be fun to have a few days together, relaxing, doing our Christmas shopping. Then we'll continue on to New York, spend a day or two there, return to London on the Concorde."

Daisy smiled somewhat ruefully. "I don't know, Paula, here you are, the head of one of the greatest department stores in the world, and you have to do your shopping in Hong Kong." She shook her head, looking a trifle perplexed. "It doesn't make sense to me."

Paula grinned at her mother. "It's much more fun shopping in foreign places—" She cut her sentence off when Madelana appeared in the doorway. "There you are, Maddy! I was just beginning to wonder what happened to you. I was thinking of sending out a search party," Paula teased, her expression affectionate.

In view of the previous discussion, three pairs of alert and curious eyes automatically fastened on Madelana as she glided across the floor with her usual gracefulness, her elegant and beautifully cut dress moving with fluidity around her long legs.

"Forgive me for being so late," Madelana apologized. "I decided to have a rest earlier, and promptly fell asleep. It must be all the fresh air I've had today . . . and the riding. I haven't been on a horse in a coon's age."

"Then you'll feel it tomorrow," Jason warned. "You'll have damn sore muscles. Take a very hot bath filled with Epsom salts tonight, that'll help a bit. I know Mrs. Carr has plenty of salts in the kitchen. We'll get a box or two for you before you go to bed. Now, what can I get you to drink? A glass of champagne?"

"Thanks, Jason, but I'd prefer a mineral water for the moment," Madelana murmured, and joined Paula in front of the fireplace.

Paula eyed Madelana's cocktail dress. It was a superb piece of clothing, made of cut velvet on silk chiffon, and was a light gray color that emphasized the silvery lights in her eyes. Paula said, "That dress is perfection on you, Maddy. It's a Trigère, isn't it?"

"Yes, it is, and thank you very much." Madelana smiled at her boss. "You're pretty elegant yourself . . . that's a Christina Crowther."

"Yes, but an old one which I left here a couple of years ago. Still, it's not a bit dated is it? Like Pauline Trigère's clothes, Christina's have a wonderful timelessness."

Daisy was smiling approvingly at Madelana. "Paula just took the words right out of my mouth, Maddy, you *do* look particularly lovely tonight." Patting the sofa, she added, "Come, sit next to me, dear."

Madelana did so, and the two of them immediately fell into a conversation about clothes, and the merits of various fashion designers in New York, Paris, and London.

Paula continued to hover in front of the fire, only half listening to Daisy and Maddy. She had the distinct feeling that her mother *would* encourage Philip in his pursuit of Madelana, if indeed he was interested, despite Daisy's promise to her to the contrary. Her mother was desperate for him to get married, and it was patently obvious she thought Madelana was the perfect candidate for daughter-in-law.

Jason brought Madelana a Perrier water, carrying the champagne bottle in his other hand. He topped up Paula's glass, then Daisy's, and as he walked back to the console, he said over his shoulder, "Philip's late coming down, Paula. I hope everything's all right on the station. That wind is damn strong, more like a gale, if you ask me."

Paula said, "I'm sure there's nothing wrong, Jason. Oh, here he comes now."

Philip sauntered into the living room a split second later, looking nonchalant, without a care. He apologized for being late, adding, "Tim Willen kept me on the phone longer than I expected."

"Any problems with the weather?" Jason asked.

"None at all," Philip assured him. "How about fixing your old cobber a scotch on the rocks, since you're standing right next to the bottle, Jason?"

——— *Nineteen* ———

The cautionary voice inside his head had warned Philip to go slow with Madelana. But on this Wednesday night, ten days after meeting her at Dunoon, he was asking himself if he had perhaps gone *too* slowly.

He walked across the living room of his penthouse atop the McGill Tower and stood looking out the window absently, for once not seeing the magnificent view of the harbor which he so loved. He was thoroughly preoccupied with his interior meanderings.

Instinctively, he had known not to rush Madelana, had recognized that he had his reputation as a womanizer to overcome with her. If she had thought she was merely going to be another notch on his belt, she would have undoubtedly fled from him. But she was rarely if ever out of his thoughts. He was obsessed with her, and his longing to know her more intimately had created the most enormous tension within him, and there had been times lately when he had felt as though he was about to explode.

I *should* have made my moves before, he thought dismally, regretting the way he had delayed, acknowledging that time was running out on him. She would be leaving soon for the States. On the other hand, even if he had decided to go more quickly with her, it would have been difficult to do so with Paula around.

His sister had become Madelana's self-appointed chaperone during the weekend at Dunoon. She had not left them alone for one minute on Sunday.

Wherever they went, she went too, and then she had spirited Madelana off to Melbourne and Adelaide for most of the following week, and the two of them had not returned to Sydney until Friday evening.

In their absence, he had hit on the idea of showing Madelana the sights of Sydney, thinking that at least he would get to know her *better,* if not more intimately. But Paula had accompanied them on their jaunts around the city, and whilst it had been fun, it had not been what he had originally planned. Although seduction had not been his intent, he had thought a bit of mild flirting would enable him to test the waters. But once they were a threesome this was impossible.

A wry smile touched Philip's mouth as he reflected on the past few days. Just as Paula had striven hard never to leave them alone together, so his mother had done everything in her power to push him toward Madelana. Without appearing to do so, of course. But he had seen through Daisy's discreet little ploys. Sadly, none of them had worked, because of Paula's vigilance.

Finally, his sister had left this morning for Hong Kong.

He had driven her to the airport himself, and on the way there he had told her that he intended to invite Madelana out for dinner that evening.

"Yes, I suspected you would," Paula had said. There had been a small silence between them, before he had exclaimed, "She's twenty-seven, Paula, and a grown woman. Not to mention extremely intelligent, and quite capable of making her own decisions. You shouldn't have done her thinking for her . . . you haven't been fair to me, or to her. And that's so unlike you, darling."

At once, his sister had apologized, had admitted that he was absolutely right, and she had endeavored to explain her protectiveness. "I care about Madelana," Paula had said. "She's one of the most special women I've ever met, and I couldn't bear it if you, of all people, did anything to cause her grief." She had then gone on to tell him something about Madelana's past, the tragedies that had befallen her family, her dreadful losses, and he had been profoundly touched. He had promised Paula he would do nothing to hurt her assistant, and he intended to keep his promise.

Philip glanced down at his watch. It was seven-forty and time to go. Turning away from the floor-to-ceiling window, he hurried across the huge, modern living room decorated entirely in shades of white and cream, and went on through the marble foyer at the same rapid pace. He was going to be alone with Madelana at last and he could not wait to get to her.

As he rode down in his private elevator, it suddenly struck him that he had no idea whether Madelana was interested in him or not. Her behavior had not revealed her thoughts or her feelings; her calm gray eyes had told him nothing. In fact, the only certain thing was the way he felt about her. And it was quite possible that she would consider his overtures repugnant and so reject him.

The same wry smile flickered in the cool blue eyes. He would soon find out exactly where he stood with her . . . if anywhere at all.

Madelana's suite at the Sydney-O'Neill was on the thirtieth floor of the hotel. It covered a corner of the building, and the L-shaped expanse of windows in the sitting room offered panoramic vistas.

She stood at one of the windows, looking out toward the Opera House on Bennelong Point and the Sydney Harbour Bridge beyond. It was almost eight o'clock, and the night sky was aglow with stars and the myriad lights of the city.

The spectacular view was familiar to her by now, and she was beginning to feel at home here, had become enamored of Sydney and its people. She had quickly discovered she liked the Australians, who were down to earth, open, and friendly, and she had come to understand, through Philip, that their sardonic humor was simply an insurance against pomposity and pretentiousness. "It goes way back, to the early settlers, the Cockneys in particular," he had explained.

Walking over to the sofa, Madelana sat down. Spread out on the coffee table were the photographs which had been taken last weekend on their sightseeing tour of the city. She began to sort through them, selecting the best for the album she had bought that afternoon.

Memories of the weekend brought a smile to her face. Here was one of Paula and herself at Taronga Park Zoo. They were standing next to a kangaroo with a joey in its pouch, and again it struck her how much the roo reminded her of a deer with its narrow, sensitive face and soulful eyes. She had not realized they were such gentle animals until her visit to the zoo on Saturday morning. The photo was good and she put it on one side to include in the album later.

Picking up a shot of Philip and Paula, which she had taken in the rain forest aviary at Taronga, she marveled again at the jewel-colored parrots and other brilliant, exotic birds shown in the background. This was another must for the album. Next she reached for the small stack of pictures taken on Philip's boat, the *Saraband.* He owned two yachts. The one called *Dunoon,* after the sheep station, was used solely for racing; the *Saraband* was for cruising and entertaining. Magnificently decorated and appointed, it slept six and had a permanent crew.

To Madelana, Sunday had been the best day of the weekend. Certainly she had reveled in their jaunt up the coastline, past Philip's house at Point Piper, and Daisy's and Jason's at Rose Bay. Loving the sea as much as she did, the excursion on the water had been wonderful for her. Deciding that the yachting trip should take pride of place in the album, she selected a handful of snaps of the three of them on board the *Saraband,* and fanned them out in front of her.

A shot of Philip caught her eye, and she picked it up, studied it for a moment.

Paula had not told her very much about him before they had left New York, and what little she did know had been gleaned from various magazines, where she had also seen pictures of him from time to time. Now, staring at the snap in her hand, she realized that nothing could have prepared her for Philip McGill Amory. His presence overwhelmed her. There was something about him, something within him, that reached out to her, moved her in a way she had never been moved before by any other human being. Her reaction to him had been intense from the first moment she had set eyes on him at Dunoon. She felt unsteady when she was with him, and breathless, almost as if she had been punched in the stomach.

Peering closer at the picture, she could not help thinking how debonair and dashing he looked, standing there on the deck of the beautiful *Saraband.* His sailing whites emphasized his tan, his vivid coloring. It had been windy on

Sunday, and his black hair was ruffled, his laughing blue eyes screwed up against the glare of brilliant sunlight and glittering sea. How irresistible he seemed.

She was most powerfully drawn to him, and this disturbed and worried her for a number of reasons. He was her boss's brother, but quite aside from this, he was hardly likely to be interested in her. He was immensely powerful, immensely rich, and devastatingly attractive, and therefore he could have any woman in the world he wanted. His reputation as a playboy only verified this as a fact. A career girl like herself, who was not a member of the international social circles he moved in, was hardly a candidate for one of his romantic interludes. Nor did she care to be. The last thing she wanted was a quick fling. She was not cut out for brief encounters. No, Philip McGill Amory was not the kind of man a woman like her should *ever* become involved with. He was too dangerous, guaranteed to wreak havoc and heartbreak.

I don't need any more problems with beautiful, difficult men, she thought, remembering her recent experiences with Jack Miller. Her career was her priority now. And in any case, she would be leaving Sydney in ten days, and that would be that. She and Paula had fortunately found a manager for the boutique yesterday. The young woman met all of Paula's requirements, and had already started working on a week's trial. Providing all went well, she would soon be winging her way back to New York . . . far, far away from Mr. Amory.

The telephone on the writing desk shrilled and she went to answer it. "Hello?"

"It's Philip," he said, "I'm in the lobby."

"I'll be right down," she said, and replaced the receiver. Picking up her bag, her silk shawl, and the doorkey, she left the suite.

Going down in the elevator, she wondered what the evening would be like. She had accepted his invitation against her better judgment, and only because he had been so gracious, and just a little bit insistent on the phone that morning. Also, being who he was, she had not wanted to offend him. But this was the first time she was going to be alone with him, since they had gone riding at the sheep station, and sudden nervousness invaded her.

She saw him the moment she stepped out of the elevator.

He wore a dark blue blazer, a pale blue shirt and tie, and gray slacks. He dominated the lobby with his height and his arresting looks, his inbred confidence, and his commanding air of authority.

When he saw her he raised a hand in greeting, and strode toward her.

She instantly tensed up in the way she had when she had met him in the portrait gallery, and she almost missed a step as she walked across the marble floor. Then she took hold of herself, and pushed a bright smile onto her face, and as they came together in the middle of the lobby, she extended her hand, still smiling.

Philip took it, gave it a small squeeze, instantly released it. Looking down at her, he returned her smile, and said, "It's nice to see you, Madelana, you look lovely, as usual." He glanced approvingly at her full, black wool skirt and the tailored, white silk shirt.

"Thank you. You did say to dress simply."

"Yes," he murmured, escorting her across the lobby, then explained "I've booked a table at Doyle's . . . it's a fish restaurant on the beach. Very casual, lots of fun, and they have the best fish and chips in Sydney, not to mention the most wonderful view of the city skyline from there."

"It sounds terrific."

They went out into the street. His wine colored Rolls-Royce was parked immediately in front of the hotel, and after helping her inside, Philip strode around to the driver's side, got in, turned on the ignition, and pulled away from the curb.

"Doyle's is out at Watson's Bay," he informed her. "It'll take us about half an hour. So sit back, relax, and enjoy the music." As he spoke he turned on the tape in the dashboard and the voice of Mel Torme singing "Moonlight in Vermont" filled the interior of the car.

Madelana tried to do as he suggested, not even attempting to make conversation. She could think of nothing to say to him. Unexpected panic choked her, made her throat dry. She did not know how she would manage to get through the evening. Sitting here next to him, in such close proximity, she was filled with some awful kind of terror, and she fervently wished she had not accepted his invitation.

"Relax," he said, as if reading her mind.

She looked at him through the corner of her eye, and laughed nervously.

"I am relaxed."

"No, I don't think so."

She was silent. She bit her inner lip.

Now it was his turn to laugh, and he sounded as nervous as she had.

Eventually, he murmured in a low voice, "We both work too hard, I suspect, and I suppose you've had as rough a day as I have. It takes a while to unwind . . . and I haven't been very thoughtful. I should have taken you for a drink at the bar in the hotel first."

"No, I'm fine," she told him, and realized that this was partially true. The feeling of panic was easing somewhat. Anyway, she was being silly, wasn't she? He had no way of knowing how attracted she was to him. Thank God. She had cultivated a bland face for the past few days, worn an inscrutable expression especially for him. Anyway, he was obviously only being polite, taking care of her for Paula. Undoubtedly, it was her boss who had asked him to take her out. Paula was always so thoughtful, so solicitous of her welfare.

The exterior architecture of Doyle's had lovely Victorian mannerisms. Made of red brick and beige stone, the building was two stories high, and its upstairs balconies were decorated with fancy, pierced-wood valances painted white, and these were repeated around the edge of the front portico. The rooms inside were bright and cheerful, simply furnished, and there was a pub-like atmosphere.

It was busy when they arrived, but Philip was quickly shown to a table in a quiet, windowed corner overlooking the beach and the dark sea curling away to the edge of a dim horizon. He insisted Madelana take the chair facing toward the city, and just as he had said earlier, the view of Sydney from Watson's Bay was breathtaking, with the McGill Tower dominating the skyline.

He ordered a bottle of Pouilly Fuisse, dry and cold and refreshing, and as they sipped it he asked her about the new manager, and how the Grand Sale was going at the boutique. She felt on safe ground, talking about business, and as they chatted she began to relax further, and so did he. He answered her questions about their opal mines at Coober Pedy and Lightning Ridge, told her about opal mining in general, and he talked at length about the various divisions of the giant conglomerate he ran. The McGill Corporation fascinated her, and she gave him her entire attention, as always intrigued by big business. Before either of them realized it almost an hour had passed.

"I think we'd better order," Philip said, when the waitress appeared at their table for the third time.

"I'll have the same as you, please," Madelana murmured, after a quick glance at the menu.

He grinned. "Fried fish and chips . . . how does that sound?"

"Just great. Thanks."

Once he had ordered dinner, he asked her exactly what she did for Paula at Harte's in New York, and she told him a little about her work, how she had been planning and organizing the special events for the sixtieth anniversary of the stores.

When she finished, he laughed, shook his head. "And I thought Paula was a workaholic! My God, you're as bad as she is!"

"I guess I am," Madelana agreed, also laughing, enjoying being alone with him; her earlier apprehension had entirely dissipated.

"And tell me, how do you manage to have a private life, working the way you do? Doesn't your boyfriend object?"

"I don't have one."

"Oh." A black brow lifted. "A girl like you . . . so beautiful . . . so bright . . ." He did not finish, merely stared at her intently.

Ignoring his compliments, she said softly, "I just broke up with someone."

"I'm sorry."

"You don't have to be. It was for the best . . . I'd made an error in judgment."

Now the black brows drew together in a frown. "What do you mean?"

"I mistook personality for character."

"Ah, I *see,*" he said, liking the shrewdness of this observation. He was suddenly eaten up with curiosity about the man she had so recently been involved with, and he couldn't help probing. "What does he do? You know, for a living?"

"He's an actor. A rather brilliant one, too. On the Broadway stage."

"Famous? Would I know him?"

"Possibly . . . probably. Jack Miller."

"Oh sure, I saw him in something a couple of years ago when I was in New York. A Eugene O'Neill play, I think."

Madelana nodded.

"What went wrong between the two of you?"

Madelana bit her inner lip, glanced away.

But after a brief moment, she brought her eyes back to his, smiled faintly. "Mah daddy used to say there's nothing worse than the ole moonshine for killin' a romance and curin' a woman of fanciful ideas she might be havin' about a dude. Ah doan know that a truer word has ever been spoken."

Philip smiled, loving the sudden, Southern intonation in her voice. It was soft, beguiling, very feminine. "Now you really sound as though you come from Kentucky," he said. "And I must admit, I agree with your daddy . . . about a drinking man."

"It wasn't just the booze," she now said in her New York voice. "Jack was always a bit odd with me . . . about my work, I mean. He is a male chauvinist, by his own admission, and he resented my career. Anyway—"

At this moment the waitress arrived with their food, and Madelana changed the subject by asking him about yacht racing. Since this was Philip's favorite sport and his only genuine hobby, he was happy to discuss it with her. And when he finally paused, she told him how much she loved the sea, and how she had first gone sailing with the Smiths at Nantucket.

"I met Patsy Smith the first day I arrived at the residence, and we became friends instantly. And we're still close, even though she's gone back to Boston."

"What's the residence?" Philip asked, between mouthfuls of fish.

She proceeded to tell him about Sister Bronagh, the other nuns, what life had been like at the residence, and her early days in New York.

Philip listened carefully, nodding from time to time, occasionally laughing at her anecdotes. But he did not interrupt her once. She was truly opening up to him tonight, revealing a great deal about herself for the first time, and he wanted to encourage this. He needed to know everything there was to know about this woman. She was under his skin.

It was later, over coffee, that Philip suddenly said, "I thought you might like to come up to Dunoon this weekend, Madelana. It'll do you good after all your running around with Paula, all your hard work. And it *is* your last chance, since you're leaving at the end of next week. Aren't you?"

"Yes, I am." She lifted her cup, took a sip of the coffee.

He waited a moment, then pressed her. "Say you'll come, Madelana. I want you to . . . so very much."

An odd nuance in his voice made her glance at him more closely, and she saw there was a curious expression in his eyes, one she could not quite fathom. And then intuitively she knew he was interested in her, and she felt a sudden tightening in her chest. She found it impossible to speak. Her throat went tight and dry again. She instantly understood that to go to Dunoon with him would be playing with fire. Therefore she must refuse his invitation. To protect herself. That was the only wise thing to do.

She said, "Yes, I'd love to come. Thank you very much, Philip." As these words left her mouth, she sat back in the chair, surprised at herself, and at her perversity. You fool, she thought. You're just asking for trouble.

Philip was beaming at her and saying, "We can fly up tomorrow afternoon."

"No, no, I can't go then," she exclaimed quickly. "I've got to be at the boutique. I couldn't possibly come until Saturday."

"Friday," he insisted, holding her with his eyes. "You can come up Friday morning. Everything will be all right at the boutique. Don't worry so much."

She swallowed hard, wondering why she had ever accepted. "I must go into the boutique for a couple of hours at least," she compromised.

"Okay, if you say so," Philip agreed. "But Ken will collect you there at eleven, drive you out to the airport. My plane will be waiting, and if you leave Sydney at noon, you'll get to the station in time for lunch." Philip smiled deeply into her eyes, reached out, took her hand, held it in both of his.

Madelana nodded, not trusting herself to speak.

Twenty

Philip took off his soaking wet sweater and shirt, and threw them to one side. Hooking his right foot into the boot jack, he pushed off one riding boot, and then the other, stripped down to his underpants, and hurried through into the bathroom, feeling chilled to the bone.

He took a very hot shower, letting the steaming water sluice down over his body for a few minutes, until his blood was tingling and he felt warmer. Stepping out of the shower stall, he dried himself, pulled on his toweling robe, and walked over to the sink. He stood in front of the mirror, combing his wet hair, slapping on cologne, and thinking of Madelana.

What a pity the thunderstorm had blown up when it had, so suddenly, about an hour ago. It had curtailed their ride. They had been up in the hills above Dunoon, and he had begun to sense a lessening of the tension in her out there in the peaceful countryside. Certainly she appeared to be more at ease with him today. When she had arrived yesterday at lunchtime, she had been very quiet, and so taut he thought at one moment that she might snap in half, and she had remained tense for the rest of the day. She had seemed a bit better in the evening though, had evidently enjoyed their dinner with Tim and Anne Willen.

By the time they had gone riding this afternoon she had been light-hearted, almost gay, and she was opening up to him once more, and he knew he was gaining her confidence. So much so, he had been on the verge of telling her how strongly he felt about her when the weather had changed abruptly. The sky had grown overcast and dark. Heavy torrential rain had started to fall, and they had mounted their horses and galloped back to the stables at top speed. Even so, it had taken them a good twenty minutes to get there. Matt had been waiting for them with one of the other grooms, and they had led Gilda and Black Opal off to the tack room; he had driven Madelana up to the manor in the Maserati, the two of them drenched to the skin and shivering. She had become very white, her teeth chattering uncontrollably as they had dashed into the house, and now, as he went through into his bedroom, Philip hoped that she had not caught a cold.

He stood warming himself in front of the fire for a few minutes before crossing to the black lacquer Chinese cabinet, which contained a small, fully stocked bar. He poured two cognacs into small brandy balloons, gulped one down, then went to dress, pulling on a thick Fair Isle sweater and socks, and heavy gray flannels. He slipped his feet into a pair of brown loafers, collected the other brandy balloon, and left the room with it.

A second later he stood in front of Madelana's door. He was about to knock, but hesitated fractionally, wondering if he had given her enough time to shed her wet riding clothes, shower, and change. Deciding that he had, he rapped softly.

"Come in," she called.

He did so, stood hovering on the threshold.

She was huddled in front of the fire, seated on the floor with her back to the sofa, dressed in a track suit and thick socks, sipping the tea he had asked Mrs. Carr to have sent up to her a short while before.

"I thought you might want to drink this," he said, holding out the brandy balloon. "It'll warm you through."

"Thank you." She put the cup she was holding back in its saucer on the end table. "Yes, I'd like it, Philip." There was a pause. "Thank you," she said again.

He pushed the door closed with his foot, walked over to her, handed her the glass. She took it from him, and as she did, their fingers grazed. She jumped slightly, as if surprised, drew back, pushed herself harder against the sofa. Then she lifted her eyes to his.

It was still raining outside, and somber, and she had not turned on the lamps, and in the shadows of the dim room she looked ethereal, illuminated as she was by the blazing fire. Her face shimmered with an incandescent, fragile beauty, and her eyes were huge, transparent, and shining.

He found it impossible to look away.

They continued to gaze at each other. For a split second Philip thought he was looking deep into her soul. Finally he dropped his eyes. He did not trust himself with her, and he swung around without a word, walked back to the door, intending to leave her alone until dinner. But he could not help turning to glance at her before he went out, his eyes irresistibly drawn to hers once more.

She returned his long, penetrating stare steadily, solemnly. Her face was infinitely quiet. She did not move, nor did she speak. The air was hushed, very still between them.

He took a step forward, then another. "I want to be with you," he said in a voice that was unexpectedly hoarse. "Please don't send me away."

"I'm not going to."

At first he thought he had not heard her correctly, and he looked at her swiftly, through narrowed eyes.

She put down the brandy glass, lifted her arm, held out her hand to him.

He hurried back to her, took the slender hand in his, brought it to his mouth, brushed his lips over her long fingers. Then he knelt down on the floor by her side.

"Oh Maddy," he said, using the diminutive of her name for the first time. "Oh Maddy."

"Philip," she whispered in a voice so low it was hardly audible.

He pulled her forward. She was in his arms, clinging to him, saying his name over and over, and he held her close to his body, tightening his grip. With one hand he stroked her hair. His mouth found hers, and he kissed her as he had wanted to kiss her from the very first day, deeply, fiercely, passionately, his tongue thrusting as if he was taking possession of her with his mouth. She returned his kisses, and her tongue grazed his, and he realized that her ardor for him matched his own for her. This knowledge sent a thrill searing through him.

There was no going back, he knew that. They must make love at once, now, here, on the rug in front of the fire. There was no time to waste . . . too much time had been wasted already. He pulled her down under him, slid his hand under her loose top. When his fingers closed around one of her breasts she let out a long sigh; he stroked her gently, smoothed the tips of his fingers across her nipple, caressed it lovingly. Almost instantly, he felt it harden under his fondling, and this inflamed him even more. He tugged at her top, wanting to lift it over her head.

She sat up, pulled it off. He tore at his own clothes, flung them to one side. Suddenly they were stretched out next to each other on the rug, completely naked. They began to kiss again, frantically, more urgently than ever, and they could not keep their hands off each other. They reached out hungrily, longingly, to touch, to explore, to caress, to excite. The urgency between them grew and intensified as they became more and more aroused.

There was a violence in his desire for her, and he sensed the same turbulent emotion in her. She wanted him as desperately as he wanted her, and she was making that quite clear. And so he fell across her, slid into her. As he did he felt her tense, gasp, and then relax.

He braced his hands on either side of her, rose up above her, looked down into her face. It was full of yearning and desire, and the wild expression that blazed in her eyes mirrored exactly what he was feeling, and his breath caught in his throat in surprise and pleasure.

Philip began to move against her, very slowly, expertly, and she thrust her body forward to meet his, cleaving to him.

Their rhythm grew faster and the urgency of their passion spiraled up into total abandonment, and they were on a dizzying climb, rising higher and higher together, out of control. He had fantasized about her for days. Now his fantasy had become his reality, and he was unable to hold back. He flowed into her, gave himself to her, and then his mouth was on hers, devouring hers. And she was flying with him on that dizzying flight, and she cried his name suddenly and stiffened, and they began a slow slide down over the edge, down into scorching white heat.

Her arms and legs were woven around him, binding him in their silken vise. He was welded to her, part of her, and she was part of him, and the miracle was that they had become one single being . . .

Entirely spent, they lay still, locked in each other's arms. There was no sound except for their labored breathing, the crackling of the logs on the fire, the faint ticking of a clock somewhere in the background.

Philip stirred first. He buried his face in the mass of her chestnut hair, murmured against her neck, "I've wanted you since I first saw you downstairs in the portrait gallery, Maddy."

When she made no comment, he asked, "Didn't you know that?"

"No, I didn't," she whispered. With a small smile, she confessed, "I wanted you too."

"You certainly hid it very well," he exclaimed quietly.

She said, "And so did you."

They both laughed, but fell silent immediately, caught in the webs of their own thoughts. After a short while, Philip released his hold on her, got up, took her hands in his, pulled her to her feet. He slipped an arm around her, and they stood together in front of the fire, gazing at each other as though mesmerized. He tilted her chin, bent down, kissed her on the mouth, lightly, gently, and then reached for the brandy balloon. He offered it to her. She shook her head. He took several swallows, placed the glass on the table, and as he led her over to the large four-poster bed, he said, "I do hope you don't think that I'm a drinking man, too . . ."

Madelana laughed, said nothing, slid under the bedclothes. Philip joined her, wrapped his arms around her. She curved her body into his, relaxing her shoulders against his broad chest, filled with a rare joy. It had as much to do with the pleasure she had given Philip as the fulfillment and release he had brought to her. The tension which had been building in her for days had disappeared. She felt as though she were wrapped in a cocoon of peace and contentment and happiness. And she knew it was because of him, all the things he was.

Philip continued to hold her close to him, nuzzling his face into the nape of her neck, her hair, the space between her shoulder blades. To his surprise he was suddenly at full arousal again. He threw the bedclothes to one side, pushed himself up on one elbow, looked down at her.

Madelana smiled up at him. Her face was radiant.

He smiled back, lifted one hand, began to stroke her cheek, his eyes spilling with emotion. The truth was, he loved her. He had fallen in love with her that very first day. He was glad it had happened at Dunoon, and that they had first made love here. It seemed very right to him that something as important as this had taken place in his home. He knew that he would always love her. This was not a passing thing. There could be no other women in his life now. Never, ever again.

"You look thoughtful," she said, her eyes quizzical.

He leaned over her, answered in a low voice, "It was too quick, Maddy. I'm sorry . . . anxiety on my part, I'm afraid." He laughed lightly, ruefully. "But I'd ached for you for days . . . fantasized about you."

"You were wonderful."

"Perhaps you're prejudiced, darling."

He brought his mouth down to her breasts, began to kiss them, whilst stroking her body, running his hands all over her. Her skin felt like satin to him, and in the firelight it had a lovely roseate cast to it. He marveled at the beauty of her lithe body, so slender, so delicately formed, her long legs, the heavy, voluptuous breasts, taut now under his touch.

Lifting his head, he brought his mouth to her mouth, kissed her deeply, traced a line down her stomach with one finger, until his hand came to rest between her thighs. He caressed her lightly, adeptly, and she reached out for him, began to stroke him. As he felt her tense and spasm, he pushed her hand away from him, entered her, and again they were instantly swept away by the intensity and urgency of their passion for each other.

They were together for a long time, and then he got up and left the bed. He strode over to the fireplace where he had discarded his clothes earlier, began to dress.

She watched him as he moved around in front of the fire, thinking what a beautiful man he was. He had a wonderful body. He was over six feet and broad shouldered with a barrel chest, and there was not an ounce of extra flesh on him, and he was tanned from being constantly in the sun.

Madelana had the sudden curious feeling that she had known him before . . . long ago. There was something so very familiar about him to her that it was startling. And yet they *were* strangers . . . albeit *intimate* strangers now.

He came back to her, sat down on the edge of the bed, moved a strand of hair away from her eyes. Bending over her, he kissed her lightly, said, "This is just the beginning, Maddy darling."

"It's the beginning of the end—" She stopped abruptly, stared up at him, her eyes wide with surprise at her words.

He scowled. "What an odd thing to say. What do you mean?"

"I don't know," she exclaimed. "It was a thought that flashed through my head, and I said it without thinking."

"I'm not going to talk about the *end* of anything." He laughed dismissively, and pulled her into his arms, hugged her tightly. Then he let her go, stood up. "I'll see you downstairs shortly. Dress casually, darling, it's just the two of us."

"Yes," she said.

She lay there for a while after he had gone. There was an indentation on the pillow next to her, where his head had been, and she reached out to touch the spot, slithered to his side of the bed, buried her face in the pillow. It smelled of him . . . of his hair and his cologne. She began to weep.

An enormous sense of loss overwhelmed her and she was afraid.

——— *Twenty-One* ———

Hong Kong glittered. It was all color and light and movement and noise.

From the moment Jason Rickards' private jet had thundered down the runway at Kai Tak Airport five days ago, and Paula had alighted, she had been caught in the spell of the British Crown Colony.

She had not been there for fourteen years, and she had forgotten what it was really like. It overpowered in every sense.

Visually it reminded her of Manhattan, with its towering skyscrapers, air-conditioned shopping emporiums, boutiques, banks and businesses, stylish restaurants, and elegant hotels. Yet withal, Hong Kong had a rhythm that was uniquely its own, a tempo that was rapid, pulsating, full of excitement and tumult.

Paula felt movement all around her. Wherever she looked she saw perpetual motion. Great jets soared up into the misty blue skies above Victoria Peak; sailing boats and sampans, yachts and junks, hydrofoils and ferries plowed the busy harbor waters around Central and Kowloon; automobiles, trams, buses, and rickshaws surged through the streets; and people jostled each other in swarming crowds as they rushed about their business. It was overpopulated. Space was at a premium, on land and sea, and there was so much teeming life and deafening noise that Paula had begun to feel slightly battered by it.

Yet in contrast, there were lovely little pockets of calm and tranquility that caught her by surprise . . . the quiet hills of the New Territories, that rural area between Kowloon and mainland China . . . the temples and shrines . . . and even a spot down near the Star Ferry Pier, where every morning a group of Chinese men performed the slow, meditative movement of t'ai chi.

To Paula, it was the many contrasts which so startled, and which made the deepest impression on her.

Nowhere on earth was there such limitless wealth and grinding poverty within the same few miles, such breathtaking beauty rubbing shoulders with sickening squalor. Ritzy high life was perilously juxtaposed against dangerous low life. Grand and ancient families lived in close proximity to desperate refugees. Hong Kong was a place of old money and taipans, over one hundred and forty years of British rule and colonial traditions, newly made fortunes, stunning success stories, and mind-boggling business bonanzas. It also had one of the highest suicide rates in the world.

It had captivated Paula, and she fully understood its extraordinary allure for residents and visitors alike.

Until Paula's arrival, Emily had been ensconced in the Peninsula in Tsimshatsui on Kowloon side. This was the hotel where she invariably stayed on her buying trips. It was convenient for her business dealings with mainland China, since she had ready access to the factories which manufactured the varied products she purchased for Genret.

The night before Paula had flown in with Don Metcalfe of Rickards International on the company plane, Emily had "moved Hong Kong side." She had checked into the vast and beautiful suite she had booked in the famous Mandarin Hotel in the heart of the Central District.

"I've finished all my business, and Central's much more convenient for us, and what we want to do," Emily had explained to Paula when she was settling in after her arrival. "It's the shopping mecca of Asia, and anyway, I think it's much more interesting for you to be on Hong Kong Island itself." Paula had nodded and agreed. "Whatever you say, Emily. You're in charge."

Emily had planned a program which hardly left them a moment to breathe. Nevertheless, Paula had been enthusiastic about doing everything, and tremendously energized by the sight-seeing, the shopping, the visits to various restaurants and several of the other smart hotels, not to mention their tour of night clubs in Wanchai.

The first evening she was there, Emily had taken her to Gaddi's for dinner. It was considered to be the finest European restaurant in Hong Kong, and Rolf Heiniger, the renowned maître d'hôtel had lived up to his reputation for knowledge and attentiveness, had suggested the most delicious dishes and the finest wines.

The following morning they had gone browsing and shopping in Emily's favorite boutiques, shops, markets, and galleries. "Don't forget, I'm an old China hand," she had confided to Paula with a grin. "Trust me and you'll get the best bargains. Quality merchandise at the right prices."

Paula had laughed, had exclaimed, "Oh I trust you all right, Emily. You had a sharp eye even as a child. I think that's one of the reasons Grandy gave you Genret to run."

In the course of several hectic days they did all of their Christmas shopping, buying important gifts as well as stocking stuffers and tree presents. They purchased pearls, jade jewelry, cuff links for the men in the family, embroidered silks and brocades, Chinese evening jackets and cheongsams, beaded evening bags, unusual wooden toys, cloisonné, hand-embroidered linens, trinkets, and knickknacks.

Emily had suggested they pay a visit to Hollywood Road, just above Central, explaining that this was an imperative, and Paula quickly discovered that she was right. Many of the more important antique shops and art galleries were located here, and as they had gone on the rounds, Paula had been enchanted by the artifacts on display. She had bagged an ancient nefrite vase for

Jason, who collected oriental art, and a beautiful antique jade necklace for her mother.

And in between the shopping expeditions and all manner of exotic meals in unique restaurants, Emily had arranged a few other fascinating excursions. She had taken Paula to Aberdeen Harbour, where thousands of Boat People lived and worked on junks and sampans; they had made a trip to the New Territories on Kowloon side; had driven up to the top of misty Victoria Peak to see the spectacular view; and visited various temples and shrines.

On the flight from Sydney, Paula's traveling companion, Don Metcalfe, had said he would like to take her and Emily out to dinner before they left for New York. And this he had done the previous night. They had gone with him on the hydrofoil to Macau, the Portugese enclave at the entrance to the Pearl River, just fifty minutes away, where they had dined in an elaborate restaurant before visiting some of the famous gambling casinos. It had been a memorable evening. They had enjoyed themselves tremendously with Don, who had kept them laughing and entertained; Emily, in particular, had been excited by the trip to Macau, where she had never been and had always wanted to go.

In the early hours of the morning, when Paula had finally fallen into bed exhausted, it struck her that they had packed in more in a few days than she had imagined possible. Every minute of her stay in Hong Kong had been enjoyable, and being alone with Emily had been an added bonus. It reminded her of the trips they had taken together as girls, and she felt young again, lighthearted, almost carefree.

Today was their last day in Hong Kong; they were taking the night flight to New York. Emily had been determined that she see the beautiful Regent Hotel in Kowloon, and the unparalleled view of Hong Kong Island from this vantage point. And so they had gone there for lunch. She had had to get up very early to do her packing first, but it had been worth making the effort. The lunch and the view would linger in her mind and memory for a long time.

Immediately after lunch, they had caught the Star Ferry back to Central. Emily had made for the hotel to finish her suitcases; Paula had returned to the jewelry shop where she had seen a pair of exquisite earrings, which she wanted to buy as a Christmas gift for Emily.

Once inside the shop, Paula had bargained in the way she had seen Emily doing it for the last few days. Much to her surprise, and enormous delight, she had won the earrings at a far better price than she had expected. And now, as she walked the short distance to the hotel, she was filled with a great sense of satisfaction at this small success.

Hurrying across the lobby of the Mandarin, Paula realized she was twenty minutes late to meet her cousin for tea. And so she headed straight for their point of rendezvous, the Clipper Lounge, which floated like a gallery above the lobby on the mezzanine floor, and ran lightly up the steps.

Emily saw her, raised her hand in greeting.

Paula waved back.

A moment later she was sitting down in one of the comfortable chairs facing Emily.

"Sorry I'm late. The last hour just flew by," Paula said with an apologetic smile.

"It's all right. I've not been here long, and you know I love this place. I feel as if I'm on a boat, what with the brass portholes and all this mahogany. Oh, and before I forget—'' Emily opened her handbag, fished around, handed Paula two small envelopes, and finished, "These were in the suite waiting for you when I got back after lunch.''

"Oh, telexes! Thanks, darling." Paula took them, opened the first, scanned it quickly, then read the second. She pursed her lips, filling with disappointment. One was from Michael Kallinski in London, the other from Harvey Rawson in New York, and both effectively said the same thing: Peale and Doone, the small chain of stores in the Midwest, had been sold right under their noses to another buyer. *Too bad*, she thought, *the chain would have been a good beginning for my expansion program. On the other hand, she had never been quite as enthused as Michael about the locations of the shops.* This thought consoled her a little.

Emily was watching Paula closely. She said, "Is something wrong at home?"

"No, no, nothing like that," Paula responded quickly, reassuringly. "These are business telexes."

"Oh. Who from?" Emily probed, as usual inquisitive.

"One's from Michael, the other from a Wall Street lawyer who was doing some work for me." Paula smiled faintly. "A deal we wanted didn't come off. Now, let's order. I think I'm going to have the mulberry tea again. I've grown rather partial to it."

"Yes, I'll have the same." Emily swung her blond head, caught the attention of the waiter, motioned to him.

Once she had given the order, she leaned across the table, leveled her shrewd green eyes at her cousin. "What kind of deal didn't come off?" When Paula did not immediately answer, Emily remarked, "It must have been something important to you. I noticed how put out you looked."

Paula nodded. "Actually, I *was* disappointed, Emily. I was hoping to buy a small chain of stores in the States. Unfortunately, we missed getting them by a hair's breadth."

"Why do you want to buy more stores?" Emily was perplexed, and she frowned.

"I've been wanting to expand Harte's in America. Buying an existing chain seems to be the best way to go about it to me, Emily."

"One store in America was enough for Gran. Why would *you* want more?"

"Times have changed radically. You know that as well as I do. I must expand, darling, it's the only way to survive as a retailer today."

Emily said, in her blunt way, "I think you're biting off more than you can chew, if you ask me."

Paula laughed. "Now how many times did our grandmother tell us that everyone said *that* to her, and throughout her life, too, and *she* never paid a blind bit of notice."

Ignoring this comment, Emily said strongly, "I bet Shane agrees with me. What does *he* think about this expansion idea of yours?"

"Well, very frankly, Emily, I haven't had a chance to tell him yet. This summer, the south of France was so hectic, and there seemed no point in bringing it up until there was a chain available. And the week we were together, before I left for Australia, was so rushed, you know."

"I don't think he'll like it, Paula. You've enough to keep you pretty busy, what with Harte's in London, Paris and Yorkshire, Sitex Oil, and the boutiques in the hotels."

"Grandy used to tell us that organization was the key to everything, and that an organized woman had the world by the balls."

"That's true, she did say that. Nevertheless, Shane *won't* be happy. And there's something else, Paula. I don't think Gran would approve of this idea of yours if she were alive."

"Nonsense! Of course she would! She'd see the wisdom behind everything I plan to do," Paula cried spiritedly, sounding confident. She drew closer to Emily, and began to outline her plans for the future of the Harte stores in the United States.

Emily listened attentively, nodding from time to time.

They were so absorbed in their conversation that neither of them saw the man who was regarding them intently from the stairs leading up to the Clipper Lounge.

He was stunned at the sight of the two women, and was momentarily rooted to the spot. Recovering himself rapidly, he pivoted, ran down the steps, sped across the lobby, and went out through the front door.

The blood rushed to the man's head, and he filled with a fulminating rage as he raced back to Pedder Street, dodging in and out, pushing past people almost violently in his haste and anxiousness to put distance between himself and the Mandarin.

Exactly two minutes after leaving the hotel, he was standing in an elevator, riding up to the top floor of the skyscraper where his company, Janus and Janus Holdings Ltd., was housed. Avoiding the front entrance, and in so doing bypassing the large outer offices where his staff worked, he hurried down the long corridor, let himself in through the private door.

This opened into a foyer, handsomely furnished with Chinese antiques, which in turn led through double mahogany doors to his inner sanctum, luxuriously appointed, with a stunning view of Victoria Harbour visible through a wall of plate glass.

Going straight to the small mirrored bar, he poured himself a straight vodka. To his annoyance his hand shook as he lifted the glass to his mouth. He downed the drink, strode over to his desk, flipped on the intercom.

"Yes, sir?" his English secretary said.

"Please have Lin Wu bring the Daimler around to the front, Peggy. I'm leaving early today. And I'll sign my letters now."

"Yes, sir, I'll be right in with them."

He arranged a suitably inscrutable expression on his face, and sat down, willing his anger to subside.

Twenty-Two

His rage lingered.

He carried it with him in the Daimler on the drive up the Peak to his home. It was still with him now as he sat in the library of his elegant duplex apartment, going through his personal mail. The rage was of a kind he had not experienced for the longest time, and the fact that he had reacted so strongly when he had seen the two women had unnerved him. He seethed inside, and with good reason. However, he knew he must bring the anger under control. He dare not allow emotion to cloud his vision or flaw his judgment.

Exhaling, he put the half-dozen or so social invitations, various thank-you notes, and personal letters to one side, pushed the carved rosewood chair away from the antique rosewood desk, went out into the gallery.

It was from this long and spacious hallway that the other rooms in the apartment flowed; a staircase at one end led up to the second floor. He crossed the flowing space, walking in the direction of the drawing room, thinking how restful the gallery was after the busy activity of his offices. It never failed to give him pleasure. The floor was stained ebony and highly polished, the walls white and hung with his collection of very fine Chinese paintings by past masters, dating from the fifteenth century to the present.

Drawing to a standstill in front of an ink-on-paper painting by Sun Kehong, dated 1582, he straightened it, then stood back, regarded it for a prolonged moment, smiling, nodding to himself in appreciation of its refinement, elegance, and simple beauty.

Moving slowly, he continued along the gallery, admiring the art he had so lovingly assembled. The gallery was sparse, the only piece of furniture a console table made of ebony upon which rested a carved celadon vase with a cover from the Qianlong period, balanced by two white nefrite rams carved in the Song spirit. At the far end, against a short wall, glass shelves suspended on brass chains from the ceiling appeared to float, held his prized collection of rare Ming bronzes.

Recessed ceiling spots, discreet, strategically placed, illuminated the art; these were the only lights, and this area of the apartment was dim, shadowy, tranquil. He lingered, allowed the peacefulness to penetrate his bones, calm his turbulent spirit, in the way he had learned to do over these many years.

After a short while, he entered the drawing room, and his face changed, lit up, and so lost some of its tightness. He hovered in the doorway.

It was early evening, and the mist was rolling down the Peak. Outside the long wall of window, the sweeping view of Hong Kong, Victoria Harbour, and Kowloon across the water was slightly obscured. Familiar images were smudged, indistinct, wrapped in a haze of grayed blues and whites, the color combination reminding him of the faded glaze on a piece of ancient Chinese porcelain. Ah Qom, the Chinese amah who had looked after him and his home since the beginning, had turned on the silk-shaded carved jade lamps and lighted the fire, and this airy graceful room of perfect proportions was bathed in warm and mellow light. It welcomed him.

Huge overstuffed sofas and chairs, covered in pale blue and lavender and gray Thai silks by Jim Thompson, were balanced by Chinese cabinets, chests, and tables of varying sizes and shapes made of black or dark red lacquered wood. Wherever he looked, his eyes rested on an object of rare beauty. His possessions were meaningful to him. They nourished him, helped to restore his mood when he was feeling out of sorts.

He felt this lightening now, and a return to normal, and he moved forward across the antique Chinese silk carpet, sat down on the sofa. He knew that in a moment, Ah Qom's niece, Mee-Seen, would bring his jasmine tea, as she usually did half an hour after he had been home, no matter what time he returned from the office. It was a ritual, as so many things were a ritual here.

This thought had no sooner passed through his head than the pretty, delicately formed Chinese girl in her black silk cheongsam came hurrying in with the tray.

Smiling and bowing, she placed it on the low table in front of him.

He thanked her graciously, inclining his head.

Smiling and bowing, she departed.

He poured the fragrant tea into the small, paper-thin porcelain bowl, drank it quickly, poured another, sipped this more slowly, let his mind relax and empty itself of all thoughts. After savoring a third bowl, he placed it on the dark red lacquer tray, leaned his head against the sofa, and closed his eyes.

Gradually the last shreds of his anger drifted away.

He had been half dozing, and awakened with a start when the antique chiming clock on the mantelpiece struck the hour of six.

Sitting up, stretching his long frame, he realized he must go upstairs to shower and change for Lady Susan Sorrell's dinner party at her house in Recluse Bay.

Immediately pushing himself to his feet, he walked swiftly across the drawing room, but stopped suddenly in front of the long console next to the coromandel screen. The silver-framed photographs arranged there glittered brilliantly in the light from the adjacent lamp. He stared at the photograph of his father, then let his glance wander to the smaller picture of the woman.

His hatred for her had never dimmed. It rose up in him again. Impatiently, he shoved it away. Nothing must impinge on his newfound calmness, or ruin the evening ahead, which he had been anticipating for several days.

He had never intended to keep a photograph of *her* in his home, where every single object was perfect, chosen by him, the perfectionist, for its very perfection. But his better judgment had triumphed over emotion when he had unexpectedly found the picture amongst a trunk full of old possessions years ago. He had been on the verge of throwing it away when he had recognized its great usefulness.

Hong Kong was a place of status, of keeping face. Both were of paramount importance. And so it did him no harm whatsoever to be known as the grandson of that late great international tycoon, Emma Harte. However, tonight he could not bear to see that diabolical old woman's face, and he pushed her picture behind the larger one of his father standing outside the Commons. Being the son of Robin Ainsley, respected Labour politician, Member of Parliament, and former Cabinet Minister, had done him no harm either. His family ties had made him eminently acceptable, had propelled him into the highest echelons of local society.

Returning to the library, Jonathan Ainsley seated himself at the desk, took a ring of keys from his jacket pocket, opened the bottom drawer. He lifted out the folder marked HARTE'S and opened it, let his eyes scan the top sheet covered with several columns of meticulous figures in his own neat handwriting.

A smile of triumph brought a lift to his mouth, and he chuckled quietly. He generally laughed when he reviewed this list, reminded himself exactly how much stock in the stores he now owned. Harte's shares were traded on the London Stock Exchange, and for years he had been buying shares through nominees: his Swiss bank and other financial institutions. Today he was a major shareholder in the Harte department store chain, although only he knew this.

Closing the folder, he set it down on the desk, leaned back in the chair, and steepled his fingers, gloating to himself. Paula O'Neill would make a mistake one day. No one was infallible. Not even she. And then he would strike.

Jonathan reached down into the drawer for another folder, this one unidentified, and slipped out a sheaf of papers. They were detailed reports from the London detective agency he had been employing for a number of years.

Since 1971, Jonathan had had his cousin Paula O'Neill watched on a regular basis. Nothing scurrilous about her had ever been turned up, and he had not expected it to be. On the other hand, it suited his purpose to know as much as possible about her and her life, her family, her friends, and any business moves she made.

From time to time, he had had Alexander Barkstone and Emily Harte watched and reported on as well. Like Paula, they were pristine. In any case, he was not particularly interested in them. As long as his cousins continued to run Harte Enterprises on a profitable basis, and he continued to get his large dividend check every quarter, that was all that mattered to him. After all, it was Paula O'Neill who was his target.

He glanced at the last report which had come in from the agency in London. It placed her at the Villa Faviola in late August. He supposed that was why he had been so startled to see her in the Clipper Lounge of the Mandarin Hotel earlier. Obviously she was either on her way to Australia, or going back to England from there.

Damn her, he thought. He returned the folders to the drawer, locked it, and hurried out, climbed the stairs to his bedroom, having no wish to become enraged again. Thinking about that bitch made his blood boil.

He paused on the landing, breathing deeply, exhaling, cleansing his mind of her infuriating image.

As he went into his room, Jonathan expected to see his valet, and was surprised to find the room empty. Tai Ling was nowhere in sight, although his pleated dress shirt, black tie, and black silk socks had been laid out on the bed. Undoubtedly Tai Ling was downstairs in the laundry, steaming his dinner jacket, and would reappear at any moment. Humming to himself, he strolled over to a Ming chest, emptied his pockets of keys, credit card wallet, and money, and began to undress.

Like the other rooms in his home, the bedroom was furnished in excellent taste, with the emphasis on all things Chinese and unique oriental objects of art. It was understated, masculine in feeling, a trifle cold and austere, and the women who were brought by him to his bed soon discovered that the ambience reflected something in Jonathan's nature.

Taking a dark blue Chinese silk robe from the armoire and slipping it on, he went into the adjoining bathroom, wondering who it was that Susan had invited to the dinner party especially to meet him. She had sounded mysterious on the phone the other day, but it was bound to be an interesting woman. Susan knew his taste very well.

He sighed, thinking yet again how much he missed the arrangement they had had for almost a year. It had been purely sexual, a relationship convenient for them both. Although they had also enjoyed each other on an intellectual level, there had been no emotional involvement to spoil things. Just sex and intelligent talk. Perfect, to his way of thinking.

Three months ago, when she had told him her husband was suspicious of her, that they must end their affair, he had believed her, had immediately agreed to do as she wished. He had not realized at the time that there would be such a void in his life when she was no longer available to him. It was not particularly the sex he missed, even though she was very good in bed, since sex was an easy commodity to find anywhere in the world these days. Rather, he missed their conversations, their repartee, their shared English upbringings and backgrounds.

But he had not tried to pursue Susan, or reinstitute the affair. The last thing he wanted was to be cited as co-respondent in a messy divorce, or spotlighted as one of the chief players in a nasty little scandal in the crown colony. After all, he was a man of great standing here, and it was his home.

He stared at himself in the mirror over the washbasin, ran his hand over his chin. He had risen very early to play squash before a business breakfast at seven, and there was a hint of blond stubble on his chin. The electric razor was handy, and he plugged it in, ran it over his jawline. As he did, he thought of his cousins Paula O'Neill and Emily Harte, but ever so fleetingly. And with a sudden rush of pride he congratulated himself on all that he had accomplished in eleven years. He had come a long way.

When Jonathan Ainsley had alighted in Hong Kong in 1970, he knew at once that he had found his natural habitat and his spiritual home.

The air was full of excitement, mystery, adventure, and intrigue. Anything —and everything—seemed possible. Furthermore, he smelled money. Vast amounts of it.

He had come to the Far East licking his wounds, after being ignominiously kicked out of Harte Enterprises, where he had been head of the real estate division. Alexander had fired him; Paula had banished him from the family. And forever after he had blamed her for everything, believing that Alexander did not have the guts to stand up to him without her encouragement and support.

Before he had left England, Jonathan had done three things. He had dissolved his partnership with Sebastian Cross; sold his interest in Stonewall Properties to Sebastian for an excellent price; put his real estate holdings in London and Yorkshire on the block, and had made a tidy profit in the process.

When he had set out on his travels he had had two overriding goals—to amass a great fortune and to wreak revenge on his cousin Paula, whom he loathed.

Jonathan had been attracted to the Eastern world ever since his youth. Its religions, philosophies, and customs fascinated him; he drew aesthetic pleasure from its art, decorative objects, and furniture. And so he decided to do a tour of this part of the world before settling in Hong Kong, which he had concluded was the most logical place to set up in business. For the first six weeks of his self-imposed exile he had wandered around, sight-seeing and enjoying being a tourist. He had stopped off in Nepal and Kashmir, gone hunting in Afghanistan, made a leisurely trip through Thailand, before proceeding to the crown colony.

Prior to leaving London, he had taken the precaution of collecting letters of introduction from friends in the city and in real estate. Within a few days of arriving at the Mandarin Hotel, he had begun to call on those to whom the letters were addressed. At the end of his second week he had met a dozen or more bankers, businessmen, owners of land and construction companies, as well as a number of wheeler-dealers whom he considered to be dubious and not worth pursuing.

Two of the men he was particularly drawn to were a fellow Englishman and a Chinese. Separately, they had decided to help Jonathan get started, for their own reasons and to suit their own ends, and they were to prove invaluable to him. The Englishman, Martin Easton, was a real estate developer; the Chinese was a highly respected banker by the name of Wan Chin Chiu. Both were highly influential in their own circles, professionally and socially, but it was Jonathan who brought them together.

Exactly four weeks after he had landed at Kai Tak Airport, he had set himself up in business. With the help of his new associates he had found small but attractive offices in Central, had hired a small staff consisting of an English secretary, a Chinese expert in land and construction, and a Chinese book-keeper, and had formed his own company, Janus and Janus Holdings Ltd. In Greek mythology Janus was the god of portals and the patron of beginnings and endings, and Jonathan had selected the name with relish—tongue in cheek— deeming it highly appropriate under the circumstances.

Luck was on his side when he started out in Hong Kong. It was to hold for over a decade.

This extraordinary luck, and the guidance and patronage of his two very powerful friends and backers, were the keys to his immense success. And timing played an important role.

It just so happened that when Jonathan arrived in the crown colony in 1970, land and construction were on the upswing. Since his expertise was in real estate, he knew he had accidentally landed on his feet. Shrewd enough to recognize a grand opportunity when he saw it, he plunged into local business with a gambler's instinct for the main chance, and a certain amount of courage, in that he was risking almost everything he had, plus the money invested in Janus and Janus by Martin Easton and Wan Chin Chiu.

Afterward he was to realize that he had been unable to throw the dice wrong once, figuratively speaking. His number always came up.

He made a considerable profit in the first six months, and in 1971, when the really big boom in property and land hit Hong Kong, he was well positioned. Suddenly there was a great deal of activity on the Hang Seng Index, the major index for the Hong Kong Stock Market. Like many others, Jonathan took advantage of the market activity. He cashed in quickly by taking his company public.

His two advisors, who had been guiding him all along, but independently of each other, warned him to start easing off a few months later. He continued to do a considerable amount of wheeling and dealing through the end of 1971 and 1972, but he had reduced his investments in the Hong Kong Stock Market by the beginning of 1973. Wan Chin Chiu, who had his ear to the ground and seemed to know everything, had been more cautionary than Easton, and wisely Jonathan had followed his advice scrupulously.

In any case, he had already made a killing, and was on his way to parlaying those profits into a huge personal fortune. He never looked back from that moment on.

By 1981 he had become a force to be reckoned with in Hong Kong and the world of Far East Asian business. He was a millionaire many times over, owned the skyscraper where his offices were located, the duplex on the Peak, several expensive cars, and a string of Thoroughbreds which he raced at the Happy Valley racetrack in Hong Kong.

Some years earlier, he had bought out Martin Easton, who had decided to retire to Switzerland, but he had remained closely associated with Wan Chin Chiu until his death two months ago. Tony Chiu, the American-educated son of the banker, had taken his father's place, and Jonathan's association with the bank continued to flourish. His personal outside investments were secure, and Janus and Janus Holdings was rock solid.

Business aside, he was socially prominent, one of the most eligible European bachelors in the community, and considered to be something of a catch. Except that no woman had managed to get anywhere near catching him.

Jonathan sometimes wondered about his own elusiveness, asked himself if he was far too fastidious, too much of a perfectionist when it came to the kind of woman he wanted to marry. Maybe no such woman existed. Yet he had discovered he was unable to alter his disposition.

Perfect, Jonathan suddenly thought, remembering the word Susan Sorrell had used to describe the young woman who was to be his dinner partner tonight.

"She's just the girl for you, Jonny darling," Susan had said, sounding sincere. "She's divine. Simply *perfect.*" He had laughed, had pressed for more information, but Susan had merely murmured, "No, no, I won't tell you anything at all. Not even her name. You must wait and see for yourself." Well, he *would* see very shortly.

Now he stepped back from the full-length mirror on the door of the armoire, took a last look at himself. He adjusted his bow tie, straightened the black silk handkerchief in the breast pocket of his white dinner jacket, and shot down his cuffs.

At thirty-five, Jonathan bore a strong resemblance to his grandfather, Arthur Ainsley, who had been Emma's second husband. He had inherited Arthur's blond hair and coloring, his light eyes, his polished, rather refined good looks, and like Arthur, he was tall, slender, and extremely English in his appearance. If anything, he looked better than he ever had. He had aged well and knew it.

But fair and handsome though he was, Jonathan's character had changed little in the decade that had passed. He was as devious and as manipulative as ever, and despite his unquestioned success, he was profoundly bitter about his ousting from Harte Enterprises. Nevertheless, he was able to camouflage his innermost feelings behind a facade that was a combination of his own natural blandness, an inscrutability learned from his Chinese friends, and a manner that was insouciant and charming.

He glanced at the paper-thin Patek Philippe watch on his wrist. It was not quite seven. He had to leave in a few minutes. But within half an hour he would be arriving at Susan's house in Recluse Bay. And finally, meeting the mysterious lady she had found for him.

As he hurried out of the bedroom and ran down the stairs, he grinned. He hoped she lived up to Susan's description, hoped she was indeed perfect. But if she was not, no matter. He would date her a couple of times anyway, and see what happened. Besides, she was obviously a newcomer to Hong Kong. *A stranger.* And strangers were always fascinating, weren't they?

Twenty-Three

He spotted her at once.

She stood at the far end of the living room, just near the French doors leading out to the terrace, talking to Elwin Sorrell, Susan's American banker husband.

He hesitated on the threshold for a moment, before going in, scrutinizing her intently. Her face was in profile and in the shadows, and it was difficult to ascertain whether she was beautiful or not.

And then suddenly Susan spotted him and glided over to greet him, and he thought again, as he had so often in the past, how beautiful *she* was. Her red hair was like an aureole of bright amber light around her lovely tranquil face, and her eyes were vividly blue tonight and full of her irrepressible laughter.

"Jonny darling," she exclaimed as she closed in on him, "I was just beginning to wonder where you were."

She lifted her face to be kissed. He pecked her cheek quickly, perfunctorily, but squeezed her arm in a more intimate fashion. "I'm only a few minutes late," he said. Dropping his voice, he whispered, "Can't you find a way to meet me one afternoon at the flat? Or at my office? We can be just as private there. I've missed you."

She shook her head rapidly, looked around the room, smiling brightly. "I daren't," she muttered as she brought her gaze back to him. Tucking her arm through his, she laughed gaily, said in her normal voice, "By the way, Jonathan, I forgot to mention that Elwin and I are going to San Francisco the day after tomorrow. For a couple of months. That's the real reason for tonight's dinner party. A sort of farewell get-together with a few of our favorite people."

"We'll all miss you," Jonathan said, following her cue, aware that several of the other guests were looking across at them.

One of the Chinese houseboys came up to him with a tray of champagne, and he took a glass, murmured his thanks, turned to Susan. "Cheers," he said as he took a sip. "Now, tell me about the mystery lady. That's her, isn't it, talking to Elwin in the doorway?"

"Yes, but I can't tell you much, because I don't know her well. I've only met her once, at Betsy Androtti's house last week. I was instantly struck by her. She's extremely attractive, charming, well turned out, and intelligent. Naturally I thought of you immediately."

"You used the word 'perfect' on the phone."

"I think she *is* perfect. For you at any rate. There's something about her that will appeal to you tremendously." Susan paused, gave him an appraising stare. "I *do* know you very well, you know, Jonny."

His mouth twitched with sudden hidden laughter, and he asked, "Didn't Betsy give you *any* information about her?"

"Betsy doesn't know her either. She came to the dinner with some visiting banker. German, I think. And seemingly *he* met her last summer in the South of France. Or was it Sardinia? Oh dear, I'm not sure."

"So she's truly the mystery lady, eh?"

Susan laughed. "I suppose she is. On the other hand, that makes it more fun, doesn't it? And anyway, a stranger in our tight little group always elicits a great deal of curiosity, wouldn't you say?" She eyed him knowingly and, not giving him a chance to respond, rushed on, "Some of the single men are bound to be interested in her. That's why I wanted to nab her at once for this dinner. And for my darling Jonny."

"How very thoughtful of you." He stared at her speculatively for a split second, then murmured *sotto voce,* "I'd much rather have you though."

"But I'm married, Jonny," she shot back softly, her tone as low as his had been. "To Elwin. And I always shall be married to him."

"I wasn't proposing to you. Merely propositioning you, my love."

Looking highly amused at his retort, she made a moue, but did not comment.

Jonathan went on, "Anyway, what's the mystery lady doing in Hong Kong? Seeing the sights?"

"She's living here now. She told me she's opened a small antique shop and gallery on Hollywood Road."

"Oh really!" he exclaimed, pricking up his ears, looking at Susan alertly. "What kind of antiques?"

"Jade, I think. I got the impression she's an expert. That's another reason I thought the two of you would hit it off. So come along, my darling, don't let's loiter here in the doorway. Let me take you over to meet her. After all, that's why I invited her to this dinner in the first place. For you. Before any of the other young blades could scoop her up and carry her off."

"Lead the way," he said, following his hostess—and former lover—across the room.

Elwin Sorrell's face lit up at the sight of Jonathan. They were good friends and Jonathan was convinced that the American had never once suspected him of a dalliance with his wife.

The two men greeted each other warmly, and then Susan said, "Arabella, I'd like to introduce Jonathan Ainsley. Jonathan, this is Arabella Sutton."

"Hello," she said, stretching out her hand. "I'm so pleased to meet you."

He took her hand, shook it, half smiled. "I'm delighted to meet you, too, Arabella." He paused, then added, "You're English."

"Yes."

They stared at each other, sizing each other up.

She had silver-gilt hair, parted in the center, that was absolutely straight and fell in smooth fluid folds around her face and down her back to the top of her shoulder blades. Her face was extremely pale, without a spot of color in the cheeks. It looked carved from alabaster, the features cleanly defined. She had a narrow nose, high cheekbones, a rounded chin with a cleft, and her mouth, wide, sensual, was painted brilliant red. At first glance this was startling in the very white face, yet somehow it was right on her. A young woman of medium height, and slender, she was dressed in an elegant white silk dress that shouted Paris and *haute couture* to his discerning eye.

Thirty, thirty-two, or thereabouts, Jonathan thought, and decided that her looks were more interesting than beautiful. It was her eyes that held him. They were large, curiously elongated, almost but not quite almond-shaped. Dark as pitch, they seemed bottomless.

Arabella was studying Jonathan as intently as he was her.

She had heard a lot about him, knew he was from a famous family, and the grandson of the legendary Emma Harte. She had not expected him to be so prepossessing, though. His blond good looks were arresting. He was well groomed, expensively dressed, and he had an air about him—something indefinable. And then she realized that it *was* definable. He had the air of a man who was accustomed to authority and power and money, and the things money bought.

She liked what she saw.

So did Jonathan.

Susan said, "Why don't you two get better acquainted? Come along, Elwin, let's mingle with our other guests."

Suddenly Arabella and Jonathan found themselves standing alone. He put one hand under her elbow and guided her out to the empty terrace. He said, "That's the most extraordinary piece you're wearing, Arabella."

She looked down at the large carved jade pendant hanging on a string of carved jade beads. "It's of the Daoguang period," she told him. "Very, very old."

"I realize that. Susan told me you have an antique shop, that you're a dealer in jade."

"Yes, jadite jewelry and nefrite carved pieces."

He smiled inwardly, immediately noting the way she had made the distinction between the two types of jade, something only a real expert would do. He said, "Where do you find your jade? Do you buy it here in Hong Kong from other dealers? Or on the mainland?"

"Both. I've been finding some wonderful things in Shanghai, especially jade jewelry like this piece"—she paused briefly, fingered the pendant—"and snuff bottles and vases. I came across some old nefrite belt buckles from the Qing period last week, and I've started to collect the multicolored Beijing glass. Mostly the deep yellow."

"Very clever of you, buying the glass, I mean. It's become highly prized because it's so difficult to craft. I'm interested in those nefrite belt buckles, by the way. I'd like to come over to your shop to look at them. Tomorrow perhaps?"

"Oh, but I haven't actually opened yet! I've been busy buying, collecting stock. My official opening is a week from this coming Monday." Noticing the disappointment registering on his face, she added, "Do come tomorrow. It's still a bit of a mess, but I'd love to show you some of the truly rare objects of art I've managed to find in the last couple of months."

"I'd enjoy that, Arabella. Would you care to dine with me afterwards?"

There was only the merest hesitation on her part before she said, "Why yes, Jonathan. Thank you very much."

He nodded. "Give me the address later, and I'll be there about six." He shifted his weight slightly, looked down at her. "I understand from Susan that you're an expert in Chinese jades and antiques. Where did you actually study?"

"Oh, I didn't—I mean everything I know I sort of taught myself, and I've read a great deal. I also took several courses at Sotheby's in London, at different times during the past three years." She shook her head, laughing. "But I'm hardly an expert. Just knowledgeable. And I hope I learn more here in Hong Kong."

"Oh, you will. Indeed you will," he murmured and averted his face, not wanting her to see the predatory gleam entering his eyes.

"Susan told me you have quite a collection of Chinese antiques yourself, Jonathan, including some marvelous bronzes."

"Yes, I do. Would you like to see them? We could go to my flat for drinks before dinner tomorrow. Would you enjoy that?"

"It would be nice. Thanks."

"Where do you come from, Arabella?" he asked suddenly, changing the subject.

"Hampshire. My father's a doctor. And you're from Yorkshire, aren't you?"

"Among other places." Jonathan smiled thinly, put his hand under her elbow, and ushered her into the living room. "I think we'd better join the others now, don't you? I've not said hello to any of my friends yet. Besides, I mustn't monopolize you."

Arabella smiled up at him, thinking how easy this had been, much easier than she had anticipated. She felt a rush of success, allowed her eyes to linger on him for a brief moment. And then she drifted off to talk to Vance and Marion Campbell, whom she vaguely knew and who had given her a lift to the dinner party. She was determined to leave with them at the end of the evening.

Susan had placed Arabella opposite Jonathan at the table, and he was able to study her surreptitiously throughout the dinner.

He was seated between Susan, who was at the head of the table to his left, and Marion Campbell, on his right. He paid enough attention to them both so as not to appear rude.

Mostly though, he watched Arabella Sutton and listened to her, and he was impressed in a variety of ways. He was captivated by her voice. It was husky, very beguiling. And her presence was hypnotic. Elwin seemed entranced, and so did Andy Jones, seated on her other side.

Jonathan noted how poised she was, and she was articulate, well informed on many subjects, not just Chinese art. He liked her intelligence, her sophistication. She had obviously traveled extensively, had done a good bit of living, and this pleased him. He did not care for women who were gauche or inexperienced, whether in bed or out of it. He preferred women to be his equals. To match him.

The more Jonathan studied her, the more he realized that she *was* beautiful. It was an unusual kind of beauty, different, intriguing. In the candlelight her face had become oddly mysterious and highly sexual.

It was the perfect curve of the rounded cheek, the depth of the sloe eyes, the lusciousness of the full mouth, the silken sheen of the silver-gold hair that made her such a sensual-looking woman. To him there was something exceedingly erotic about her, and the sexuality was not only visible in her face and in the seemingly perfect body under the white gown, but was even apparent in her hands.

Jonathan had never seen hands like hers before. They were extraordinary.

Slender, very white, with tapering fingers, and the long, perfect nails were painted brilliant red to match her inviting mouth.

He wanted those hands on him, wanted her. But thinking about seducing her was too tantalizing, anticipation too dangerous a game at this particular moment. And then, before he could switch gears in his head, he was aroused and fully so, much to his amazement. Getting an erection at a dinner table had not happened to him since he had been a schoolboy. How remarkable, he thought, feeling hot under the collar.

Shifting his gaze from the fascinating—and potent—Arabella, he brought his attention to Andy Jones and began to talk to him about sports.

"Why do you do it?" Jonathan whispered in Susan's ear as they strolled across the living room after dinner. They came to a stop near the fireplace, stood waiting for the Filipino butler to serve the coffee.

"Do what?" she asked, swiveling her eyes around the room, making sure Elwin was fully occupied elsewhere.

"Procure for me," Jonathan replied and surreptitiously ran his hand down her back, let it rest in the hollow above her buttocks.

"Don't do that, Jonny, someone might see you," she whispered.

"Come on, confess. It turns you on, doesn't it?"

"Of course not!" she hissed. Sudden anger made her swing to face him. Then, catching herself swiftly, she adopted a bland expression, took a deep breath, said in a steady voice, "Perhaps it's because I still feel guilty about ending our affair the way I did. I want to make it up to you, Jonny. You've always been very special to me, and you were such a wonderful lover. The best I've ever had. Besides, this is the first time I've procured for you, as you so crudely put it. *I* prefer the word 'introduce.'"

He grinned, said nothing, wondering what it would be like to take the two of them to bed together. Arabella and Susan would be quite an interesting and exciting combination. But he knew neither of them would go for it. English women were not a bit adventurous when it came to sex. And especially these two—the daughters of an earl and a doctor. No way.

Susan was saying, "I was right though, wasn't I, Jonny? Arabella is perfect, isn't she?"

"Outwardly, on the surface, yes." He waited for a second, eyed her carefully, and continued softly, suggestively, "However, I can't really give you an assessment, a truthful answer until I've stripped off those elegant clothes and bedded her."

His gaze had not left Susan's face and he saw the sudden flicker, the expression at the back of her eyes. Jealousy? Anger? Or a mixture of both perhaps? The idea that he might have hurt her, if only ever so slightly, pleased him. He had not wished to become involved in a marital scandal, but deep down it rankled that she had dumped him the way she had.

There was a painful silence.

Eventually she said in an amused voice, "What a pity I won't be in Hong Kong to hear your report."

"You probably will be."

"Oh." Now her eyes were surprised.

"I'm going to see Arabella's antique shop tomorrow. In the late afternoon. And then I'm taking her to my flat for drinks. Before dinner, an intimate little dinner at home. And perhaps we'll get down to something even *more* intimate later in the evening. I have high hopes. I really do."

"Bastard," she muttered under her breath, but loud enough for him to hear.

"But my love, you started all this," he retorted, grinning, now understanding that he was glad she had. Arabella Sutton was a challenge. He had not had a challenge in the longest time.

Much later that evening, Jonathan sat near the window in his bedroom, brooding and still, his eyes focused on the cloudless night sky sprinkled with countless stars. The room was in total darkness, the only illumination coming from the very bright full moon that cast a silvery sheen over everything.

He held a pebble of mutton-fat jade in his hands, turning it over and over, rubbing it between his fingers occasionally. It was his talisman, his lucky piece, and he had owned it since he had first come to the British Crown Colony.

He was contemplative for a long while, considering the two women he had encountered today.

His cousin, Paula O'Neill.

The stranger, Arabella Sutton.

In their different ways they haunted him now. He separated the images in his head, and as he did he made two promises to himself.

The first woman he would destroy.

The second he would conquer and own.

The vows made, he sighed deeply, filled with a curious sense of satisfaction. Rising, he slipped off his blue silk Chinese robe and walked slowly over to the bed. He could not resist smiling smugly to himself. There was not the slightest doubt in his mind that he would succeed.

It was only a question of time.

Saints and Sinners

A lure more strong, a wish more faint,
Makes one a monster, one a saint.
                                 Walter Learned

'Tis the eye of childhood that fears a painted devil.
                                 William Shakespeare

Riches and power are but gifts of blind fate,
whereas goodness is the result of one's own merits.
                                 Héloise

Twenty-Four

Success was in the air.

From the moment the dance had begun, Paula had known the evening was going to be magical.

Everything was exactly right.

The grand ballroom at Claridge's had been decorated by the design staff of Harte's to her specific instructions, and it was stunning. Extraordinary, really. Forsaking the staid, the traditional, she had had them create a color scheme of silver and white and crystal, developed with silver lamé tablecloths, white candles in silver sticks, crystal bowls filled with mixed white flowers. More white flowers—lilies, orchids, chrysanthemums, and carnations—were banked around the room in great masses and spilled out of huge urns standing in various corners.

To Paula the ballroom looked like a winter ice palace, all silvery and glittering, yet it had a neutrality that made a splendid backdrop for the guests in their finery—the women in their colorful, stylish evening gowns and fabulous jewels, the men in their impeccable, well-cut black dinner jackets.

She was delighted that everyone she had invited had come to this very special party. In attendance was a mixture of family and close friends, executives from the Harte stores and Harte Enterprises, honored guests, and celebrities.

Glancing about yet again, she could not help thinking that in particular the women in the family looked especially beautiful tonight.

Her cousin Sally, the Countess of Dunvale, lovely in delphinium-blue taffeta and the famous Dunvale sapphires that exactly matched her eyes . . . Emily, a vision in dark ruby silk and a superb ruby-and-diamond necklace and earrings Winston had given her for Christmas . . . Emily's half sisters, the twins Amanda and Francesca, pert and pretty in magenta chiffon and scarlet brocade respectively . . . her vivacious red-haired sister-in-law, Miranda, a law unto herself when it came to fashion, striking in a russet-satin column, stark, simple, strapless, worn with a long matching stole and an antique topaz-and-diamond necklace that fell down from her neck in a lacy cobweb of a bib.

Paula's gaze shifted over to the three sisters.

They were sitting at a nearby table, talking amongst themselves. Her mother, Daisy, dramatic in dark green chiffon and the magnificent McGill emeralds that Paul had bought for Emma almost half a century ago . . . Aunt Edwina, the Dowager Countess of Dunvale, in her seventies, white-haired, frail, yet regally elegant in black lace and the Fairley diamond necklace, presented to her by Emma the last Christmas she had been alive.

These two were the youngest and the eldest daughters of Emma Harte, both born on the wrong side of the blanket, bonded together, more than likely, by similar circumstances of birth and by her mother's deep compassion for the older woman. And seated between them was the legitimate daughter, the middle one . . . Aunt Elizabeth. Still a raven-haired beauty and looking half her age, she was positively stunning in silver lamé and a king's ransom of rubies, diamonds, and emeralds.

The three sisters were the only children of Emma Harte who were present tonight. Paula had not invited Emma's two sons, Kit Lowther and Robin Ainsley, and their wives. They had been *persona non grata* for years because of their treachery to Emma and the treachery of their children, Sarah and Jonathan.

A nest of vipers, she thought, remembering something her grandmother had said to her once. How horribly true that statement had turned out to be. Paula pulled her thoughts away from those despicable family members, whom she had no time for, and lifted her glass, took a sip of champagne.

The evening was drawing to a close, and it suddenly struck her that this dinner dance, the first of the celebrations she had planned to mark the sixtieth anniversary of the opening of the Knightsbridge store, was going to be the talk of the town tomorrow. The newspapers would be full of it. The stunning backdrop, the delicious food, the fine wines, the designer clothes and fabulous jewels, the celebrity guests, Lester Lannin and his orchestra . . . all added up to glamour with a capital G, something the press and the public could not resist.

Paula was pleased. Good publicity was a tremendous boost for the store. She smiled inwardly. It was New Year's Eve. The end of 1981. The beginning of a New Year. And she hoped the beginning of a new and brilliant era of retailing for the chain stores founded by her grandmother.

Leaning back in the chair, she silently made a New Year's resolution: *The stores were going to be greater than ever in the coming decade*. She owed that to her grandmother, who had had such faith in her, and to her own daughters, who would one day inherit the chain from her.

Shane, who had been chatting to Jason Rickards and Sir Ronald Kallinski, cut into her thoughts when he suddenly turned to her, murmured, "You look as though you're miles away, darling." He took hold of her hand, leaned closer. "You can relax. The evening's an assured success, and everyone's having a wonderful time. It's a smashing party, Paula."

She gave her husband a radiant smile. "Yes, it is, isn't it! And I'm so glad I decided on the ballroom at Claridge's, rather than a series of private rooms at the Ritz. This has worked so much better."

Shane nodded. Then he half groaned, half laughed, and exclaimed, "Oho! Here comes Michael! Obviously I'm about to lose you again, and you only just sat down a few minutes ago."

"They are keeping me busy tonight, aren't they? Actually, it's a bit exhausting, but I *am* the hostess, Shane, and I have my duty to do." Her mouth curved up with laughter. "I'm doing enough dancing to last me for the whole of 1982. I hope this is it, that we won't be going to any more dances for a long time. Remind *me* not to plan any, darling." Despite these words, her face was still covered with smiles and her eyes were sparkling.

Shane gazed at her, loving her. Admiration flooded his face. He thought she had never looked more ravishing than she did tonight in all the years he had known her. She wore an elegant evening gown of midnight blue velvet, beautifully cut, but understated with long sleeves, a round neckline, and a straight skirt. It had been designed by Christina Crowther especially for her, and it emphasized her height and her slenderness. Pinned to one shoulder was the large pansy brooch he had commissioned Alain Boucheron, the Paris jeweler, to make for her. Composed entirely of sapphires, it echoed the bright blue of her eyes, as did the matching sapphire earrings. He had given the set to her on Christmas Eve, had known from the look on her face how much she liked them, how thrilled she was, even though she protested he had been overly extravagant. "After all, you had the orchid greenhouse built for me. That is enough," she had said. He had grinned, had told her the greenhouse was a present from the kids as well. "They all chipped in, darling," he had explained.

Michael drew to a standstill next to Paula's chair. "Come on, shake a leg, Paula . . . you promised me the first slow number, and I have a feeling this one's it. Possibly for the rest of the evening." He grabbed Shane's shoulder. "You don't mind, do you?"

"Not half I don't," Shane shot back swiftly, but in a jocular tone. "However, since it's you, okay."

"Philip's wife is a beautiful woman," Michael said as he steered Paula around the ballroom floor. "He's a lucky chap."

"Yes, he is," Paula agreed.

"But his gain is your loss."

Paula laughed. "Too true, Michael, in some ways." She looked over his shoulder, focusing on Philip and his new bride gliding ahead of them to the strains of "Strangers in the Night." "But I've never seen him so happy. He adores her. As she does him. And I may have lost the best personal assistant I've ever had, but I've gained a lovely, and very loving, sister-in-law."

"Mmmm," Michael murmured, moving nearer to Paula. Instantly he checked himself, pulled back, realizing that he was taking chances, holding her in such an intimate way. Her presence continued to inflame him, and being entwined on the dance floor was dangerous. Physically dangerous, for him at least. Their proximity was far too close. Also, it might cause tongues to wag. And besides, joke though Shane might, his eyes seemed to have been on *him* all evening. If Shane suspected him of being enamored of Paula, *she* certainly did not. She was blithely unaware of his romantic interest in her, continued to treat him like an old shoe, the childhood friend, familiar, dependable, trustworthy. And that was the way he wanted it.

Paula was saying, "Anyway, Maddy's going to continue working when they return to Sydney. I've made her the managing director of the Australian division of Harte's. She'll be supervising the running of the boutiques in Shane's hotels out there. But I *will* miss her in New York, no two ways about that, Michael. On the other hand, their happiness is so important to me . . . it must come first." Leaning away from him, she smiled into his face, finished, "Those two are madly in love, you know."

"That's patently obvious."

They danced in silence for a few minutes.

Michael grimaced to himself. He wished he had the same kind of private life and personal happiness as Philip Amory. But he had not been so fortunate. Valentine had been a strikeout as a wife, and he had never found anyone else who had the necessary attributes. He wondered then if he was in love with Paula or merely turned on by her. There was no doubt in his mind that he was sexually attracted to her and would like to take her to bed. But love? He wasn't sure.

Immediately squashing this thought, he said, "Daisy seems to be over the moon about Philip and Madelana."

"She is. Of course, she was disappointed they got married in New York at the beginning of December and only told the family after the fact. We all were, actually. But Mummy's relief at knowing her wayward, playboy son is finally hitched has canceled out the disappointment, I'm absolutely sure of that."

"I wanted to give a dinner party for them, but Philip was telling me earlier that they're leaving in a couple of days. Off on their honeymoon."

"Yes. To Vienna, West Berlin, and then down to the South of France and the Villa Faviola."

"Pretty coolish in those places right now. I would have thought they'd have chosen somewhere warm. Like Shane's hotel in Barbados, for instance."

"Philip's always loved the Imperial in Vienna, ever since Grandy took us there when we were children. He and Emily think it's one of the greatest hotels in the world, in fact, and he wanted Madelana to see it. They're going to be staying in the Royal Suite, which is quite magnificent. It was Maddy who suggested that they then go on to Berlin, ending up at Faviola. She's heard a lot about it from me and Emily. Anyway, Maddy seems to have an obsession about Grandy, is wildly curious about every blessed home she owned. So naturally Faviola is a *must*."

Michael laughed, fully understanding why Madelana was obsessed with Emma Harte. So many people had been, throughout her life and after her death, which was why she was a legendary lady. Unexpectedly, he felt an easing of the tension within himself. "I haven't had a chance to tell you, Paula, but I think you've done Aunt Emma proud tonight," he said. "This is a fabulous party, one of the best I've been to in the longest time, and—"

"Mind if I take over, old chap?" Anthony said with a huge grin.

"Every time I dance with you, one of your male relatives cuts in," Michael grumbled, relinquishing her to the Earl of Dunvale. "No doubt about it, Paula, you're the belle of the ball tonight."

Paula laughed, winked at him mischievously.

Michael stepped to one side, ambled off, went in search of young Amanda.

Anthony took Paula in his arms and whirled her into the middle of the floor. After a couple of seconds, he said against her hair, "Any chance of talking you and Shane into coming over to Ireland for a long weekend soon? It's been ages since you've visited Clonloughlin, and Sally and I would love to have you. You could bring Patrick and Linnet with you."

"What a lovely idea, Anthony, and thanks for asking us. Perhaps we *can* make it . . . at the end of January. I'll talk to Shane. As far as I know, neither one of us is planning any foreign trips."

"What a change that is!" Anthony answered in an amused voice. "You two are worse than a couple of gypsies these days, forever trotting off around the world, wheeling and dealing. I can hardly keep track of you both."

Before she had an opportunity to answer, Alexander was tapping Anthony on the shoulder, exclaiming, "You're monopolizing the lady. It's my turn, Cousin."

So saying, Sandy maneuvered her into his arms and they swept away from Anthony. The latter stood gaping at them, a surprised look settling on his face.

They danced without speaking at first, enjoying being together on the floor. As children they had favored each other as dancing partners. They had been in step then, as they were now.

Eventually, Alexander murmured quietly, "Thanks so much, Paula."

She looked up at him in puzzlement. "What for, Sandy?"

"Christmas at Pennistone Royal, and this evening. For a short while you've turned the clock back for me, brought back so many lovely memories . . . of the past . . . of people whom I truly loved. Gran . . . my darling Maggie . . . your father . . ."

"Oh Sandy, you sound so sad!" Paula exclaimed. "And I wanted the Christmas holidays and tonight to be happy occasions for each one of us. I didn't—"

"And you succeeded admirably, Paula! They have been wonderful. And I'm not a bit sad. Quite the contrary, in fact."

"Are you sure?" she asked in concern.

"Positive," he lied smoothly, smiling at her.

Paula offered him a warm and loving smile in return, moved closer into his arms, gave his shoulder a squeeze. Her cousin Sandy had always been very special to her, and she was determined not to neglect him in the future. He needed her as much as he needed his sister, Emily. He was quite lonely, really. She realized that more than ever.

Sandy stared ahead, glad that they were on the floor, which was dim and crowded, since he was no longer able to keep the bleak look out of his eyes, the grim expression from his mouth. But Paula could not see his face, and everyone else was too preoccupied to notice, and for these small mercies he was thankful. They finished the dance to the end, and, to his relief, not once did his step falter.

Sandy was a devastated man, and it was only a matter of weeks before the others knew this. They would have to know. He had no alternative but to tell them. He dreaded the day.

"Well, Paula, what do *you* think? Can the modern woman have it all?" Sir Ronald asked, looking at her quizzically, his eyes twinkling. "You know— career, marriage, and children."

"Only if she's one of Emma Harte's granddaughters," Paula quipped with a wicked grin.

Sir Ronald and the others seated at the table chuckled, and then Paula went on, "But seriously, Grandy did teach us to be well organized, and that's my secret and Emily's too. So my answer is *yes,* the modern woman can have it all, provided she plans her life properly and is a past master of organization."

"There are many who would differ with you, Paula," Sir Ronald countered, "who would say you can have *two* of those things, but not all three. However, don't get me wrong, my dear, I applaud the way you and Emily run your lives. You're both quite remarkable, quite remarkable indeed."

Paula said, "Let's ask Maddy what she thinks . . . here she comes now . . . and if anyone personifies the modern woman of the eighties, then she certainly does."

Several pairs of eyes focused on Madelana and Philip, who were approaching the table. She was glowing and radiant in a Pauline Trigère evening gown of deep purple chiffon overpatterned with swirls of purple cut velvet. With it she wore a magnificent diamond-and-pearl choker and matching chandelier ear-rings, which had been wedding presents from Philip. Her hair was upswept, and, if anything, she was more striking than ever. Added to her natural grace-fulness and poise was a new and lovely serenity.

She clung to her husband's arm as if never to let him go, and Philip looked equally possessive and proud of her as they drew to a standstill at the table.

"Join us," Paula said, beaming at them.

They did so, and Philip said, "Congratulations, darling. This has been a smashing evening, truly remarkable, and it was an inspiration on your part to fly Lester Lannin in from the States."

"Thanks, Pip." Turning to Madelana, Paula went on, "Listen, Maddy dear, Uncle Ronnie just asked me if the modern woman can have it all . . . marriage, career, babies. And I said who better to answer that than you . . . the career girl newly married."

"I *hope* I can have it *all*," Madelana laughed, glancing at Philip out of the corner of her eye. "Philip wants me to continue working, to have a career, and I think I'd like to do so even after I have a child."

"Anything that makes my wife happy is perfectly all right by me," Philip announced, endorsing her words. He reached for her left hand, on which she wore a platinum wedding band and a flawless thirty-carat diamond that blazed in the candlelight.

Madelana returned Philip's squeeze, looked from Paula to Sir Ronald, said quietly, "I think it's a terrible waste for an educated woman with a career to stop working when she has a baby. I believe one can do both . . . it's all a question of juggling. And of course it depends on the woman, to a certain extent."

Shane exclaimed, "This is it! The last waltz!"

He sprang up, walked around the table, took hold of Paula's arm. Leading her off, he said, "I wasn't going to let anyone else grab you for this one, my love."

"I would have refused anyone who asked."

They moved into each other's arms, and Shane held her tightly as they waltzed. Paula relaxed against his body, feeling safe and content with him, as she had since childhood. They were lucky, she and Shane. They had so much together. Their deep and abiding love. Their children. Shared interests. A com-mon background. And he understood her so well, understood her immense need to fulfill her destiny as Emma Harte's heir. She wished she had pointed out to Sir Ronald a few seconds ago that a woman could only *really* have it all if she were married to the right man. She was.

She thought of Jim then, but in the most fleeting way. He had become a dim figure in her mind, and her memories of him were fragmented, blurred by events that had taken place since his death, by those whom she loved, those who now peopled her life, by time passing. It seemed to her that she could not remember when she had not been Shane's wife. But the years *had* flown by since their marriage. This sudden thought made her draw away, look up at him.

He stared down at her, his black brows knitting together.

"What's the matter?"

"Nothing, darling. I was just thinking that very soon a new year will begin, and I expect that it, too, will disappear in a flash, as all the others have."

"Too true, my love. On the other hand, look at it this way—1982 is only the *first* of the next fifty years we're going to spend together."

"Oh, Shane, what a lovely thing to say, and it's a beautiful thought with which to start the new year."

He brushed her cheek with his mouth, tightened his arm around her, swirled her around several times, and moved her out into the middle of the ballroom. Paula smiled inside, loving him so very much. Then she peered around the ballroom, seeking members of the family, her closest friends. It truly was a gathering of the clans . . . the Hartes, the O'Neills, and the Kallinskis were all represented tonight.

She spotted her mother dancing with Jason, looking as much in love as Madelana, who dreamily floated by in Philip's arms. Her father-in-law, Bryan, was leading Shane's mother in a sweeping, old-fashioned waltz, and Geraldine winked at her as they went sailing grandly past. Emily and Winston were coming onto the floor, followed closely by Michael and Amanda. She saw her Aunt Elizabeth gazing into the face of her French husband, Marc Deboyne, who was obviously enjoying himself tremendously tonight; even her old Aunt Edwina was on her feet making an effort, being solicitously shepherded around by a gallant Sir Ronald.

The music stopped abruptly, and Lester Lannin was saying into the microphone, "Ladies and gentlemen . . . it's almost midnight. We have BBC radio on the hotel's relay system. Here it comes . . . here's Big Ben . . . the countdown to midnight commences."

Everyone had stopped dancing to listen to the orchestra leader, and the ballroom was quiet, perfectly still. The chimes of the great clock in Westminster boomed out again and again. When the last stroke finally reverberated, there was a resounding drumroll, and Shane was hugging Paula, kissing her, wishing her a happy new year, to be followed by Philip, then Madelana, doing the same thing.

Paula returned Madelana's affectionate embrace.

"Let me say it again, Maddy . . . welcome to the family. And may this be the first of many happy years for you and Philip."

Maddy was touched by Paula's lovely words, but before she had a chance to respond the orchestra struck up "Auld Lang Syne."

Paula and Philip grabbed hold of her hands, pulled her forward as they began to sing.

Encircled by her new family, Maddy felt their love flowing out to her, and she wondered how *she* had ever been so lucky to become one of *them*. But she had, and she would be forever grateful. For years she had had nothing but sadness and loss. Now at last everything had changed.

Twenty-Five

Madelana lay with her head resting on Philip's shoulder.

The bedroom was shadow-filled, quiet except for the sound of his even breathing as he dozed, the faint rustling of the silk curtains, the ticking of the ormolu clock on the antique French Provincial chest.

The weather was somewhat mild for January, springlike almost, and earlier

Philip had opened the tall window. Now the night air blowing in was fresh and cool, laden with the tangy salt smell of the Mediterranean, the freshness of green-growing things in the sprawling gardens of Faviola.

She slipped out of bed, glided over to the window, leaned against the sill, looked out at the grounds, enjoying the gentle silence that pervaded the landscape at this late hour. She lifted her eyes. The sky was a deep pavonian blue that was nearly black and resembled a canopy of velvet, high flung like a great arc above the earth, and it was filled with brilliant stars. Earlier, clouds had obscured the moon, but they had drifted away, and she saw that it was full tonight, a perfect sphere, and clear.

A long sigh of contentment trickled through her. They had been at the villa for ten days, relaxing, taking it easy after their trips to Vienna and Berlin. They had done very little since they had been here except love each other, sleep late, go for walks in the gardens and on the beach, and take leisurely drives along the coast. They had spent most of their time at the villa, where Solange fussed over them like a mother hen, and Marcel cooked imaginative and delicious meals, and was forever thinking up some new dish with which to tempt them.

And they read and listened to music. Sometimes she played her guitar for Philip and sang her favorite Southern folk songs. He listened as if enraptured, and Madelana was pleased and flattered that he found her music entertaining. "It's been ten days of absolute bliss, doing nothing in particular, having you all to myself," Philip had said to her that morning, and she had told him she felt exactly the same way as he did.

A special tranquility abounded here at Faviola, just as it did at Dunoon, and she drew enormous strength, as well as pleasure, from the quietness and the natural beauty of both places. *Dunoon*. It was her home now, just as the penthouse atop the McGill Tower in Sydney was her home. But it was the house on the sheep station at Coonamble that she loved the most. She had fallen in love with it at first sight. As she had with Philip. And he with her.

Madelana shivered and goose bumps spreckled her arms, as she remembered the first time they had made love. She had lain in bed, weeping into his pillow after he had left the room, because when she had tried to envision the future with him she had seen no future. How foolish she had been that day . . . and how wrong. She *did* have a future with Philip McGill Amory. She was his wife. And, as Paula had said, 1982 was only the first of many happy years to come. They had a lifetime together stretching out before them.

She loved him . . . loved him so much it seemed almost unbearable at times. When he was absent from her, she felt an enormous sense of loss and experienced genuine physical pain, a tightness across her chest that only went away when he returned. Fortunately they had not been apart much since he had followed her to New York last October. He had suddenly arrived without warning, two weeks after she had left Sydney, had breezily walked into her office at Harte's on Fifth Avenue, unannounced, grinning from ear to ear. But his eyes had been anxious—she had noticed that immediately.

He had swept her off to lunch at "21," then taken her to dinner at Le Cirque, and it had been wonderful to be with him again. The minute she had left him at the airport in Sydney, she had suddenly known how much she cared. And on the long flight home there was a yearning for him in her heart that she knew would never go away. Never, not as long as she lived. The love she felt for Philip superceded everything in her life, even her career, if she had been asked to choose.

Later that same night, as they lay enfolded in each other's arms, after making love in the privacy of her apartment, he had asked her to marry him. She had not hesitated, had accepted his proposal at once.

They had talked well into the night, making their plans for the future. He had insisted they keep their engagement a secret. "But only because I don't want a big fuss," he had carefully explained. Equally as strong-willed as he in certain ways, she had endeavored to persuade him to tell Paula. "Because she will have to find a replacement for me. I can't—I won't—leave her in the lurch, Philip. She's been far too good to me. Besides, that's not my way of doing things. I have a responsibility to her, and to myself."

Philip had understood her sentiments. Nevertheless he had pointed out that she could find a replacement without informing Paula, and he had been so tough with her about it she had had no option but to agree. And, oddly enough, she had not had to look far in the end. Cynthia Adamson, who worked in Marketing, had been a protégé of hers and a favorite of Paula's for some time. The young woman showed extraordinary promise, was quick, intelligent, diligent, and devoted to Paula and Harte's.

Maddy had realized that Cynthia could handle most of her work when she left, had the necessary potential to become Paula's personal assistant eventually. This had put her mind at ease to some extent, and she had made a point of bringing Cynthia into her orbit for the remainder of her time at the store.

Philip had stayed on until the end of the month, had then gone back to Australia for two weeks to attend to certain business matters, and had finally returned to New York at the end of November.

The minute he had arrived, he had announced that they were going to get married immediately. To have a big wedding, with his family in attendance, would have meant too much of a delay for him, he had explained. And far too much excitement. "But we ought to give them a chance to come over. And we ought at least to inform your mother. And Paula," Maddy had pointed out, filled with discomfort about excluding them.

He had been adamant. "No, I won't wait for them to make their endless plans, to take over. It's got to be now." He had laughed then, had said lightly, "I'm afraid of losing you, don't you see? I must marry you at once." Despite that laughing face, the carefree tone of voice, she had noticed the anxiety dwelling there once more, clouding his clear blue eyes. She had agreed to do anything he wished . . . just to make that panic-stricken look go away. She could not bear to see him troubled or upset.

And so they were married quietly at the beginning of December, in a Roman Catholic ceremony at St. Patrick's Cathedral on Fifth Avenue, with only her Boston friend, Patsy Smith, and Miranda O'Neill and her husband Elliot James present. She had worn an elegant winter-white wool dress with a matching coat by Trigère, and had carried a trailing spray of pink and yellow orchids; afterward Philip had taken them all to lunch at Le Grenouille.

"I think we'd better consummate this marriage at once," he had said teasingly later in the day, when they had returned to their vast suite at the Pierre Hotel. And only after they had made love did he finally agree that they could telephone his family in England.

They had spoken first to Daisy, who was staying at Pennistone Royal in

Yorkshire, and then to Paula, who was at the house in Belgrave Square. His mother and his sister had not sounded particularly surprised, and they had been overjoyed at the news, if somewhat disappointed to have missed the actual wedding. And both of them had welcomed her warmly into the family. She had felt their sincerity and love coming across the transatlantic wire as they had reached out to her.

And then it had begun . . . a whole new life for her.

Philip loved her as deeply, as desperately, as she loved him. This not only manifested itself in his physical passion for her, his tenderness and kindness, but in the manner in which he showered gifts on her, spoiled her outrageously, and in countless ways. The flawless diamond engagement ring, the pearl-and-diamond choker and chandelier earrings had been only the first of many valuable jewels he presented to her. There had been other gifts as well . . . furs, Hermès bags, and couture clothes. But he was just as likely to show up with a pair of gloves, a silk scarf, a favorite book or tape he wished to share with her, a bottle of perfume, a bunch of violets, or some other such small yet meaningful token.

But the most important aspect of her new life was her husband. Philip filled the empty spaces of her heart, and he gave her such a sense of security and of belonging that she no longer felt so alone.

There were times when she had to pinch herself to make sure this was not all a dream. That it was real, that he was real . . .

She did not hear Philip get out of bed, and she started in surprise when he wrapped his arms around her. She swiveled her eyes to look up at him.

He kissed the top of her head. "What are you doing, standing here at the window? You'll catch cold, darling."

Madelana turned around within the circle of his arms so that she was facing him. She reached up to touch his cheek. "I couldn't sleep, so I got up to look at the gardens. They're so beautiful in the moonlight. And then I started thinking—"

"What about?" he interrupted, gazing down at her.

"Everything that's happened in the last few months. It's like a dream, Philip. And sometimes I have the awful feeling I'm going to wake up and discover none of it is true, and that you're not real."

"Oh but I am very real, my darling, and this is not a dream. It's reality. *Our reality.*" He drew her closer to him, held her tightly against his bare chest, stroked her hair. There was a long moment of silence between them, before he said, "I've never known peace like this. Or such love. I cherish you, my lovely Maddy. And I want you to know I will always be constant. There will never be another woman in my life, not ever again."

"I know that, Philip. Oh darling . . . I do love you so . . ."

"Thank God for that! And I love you, too."

He bent down, kissed her gently on the lips.

She clung to him.

He found himself involuntarily sliding his hands down her back, over her lovely, small, rounded buttocks. The satin of her nightdress was smooth and cool and curiously erotic to him. He pressed his body closer to his wife's, and in an instant he was aroused.

Madelana began to tremble, wanting him again, as she knew he suddenly wanted her, even though they had made love only a short while before. They were always like this, reaching out to each other, unable to keep their hands off each other. She had never known this kind of aching, all-consuming physical desire, this overwhelming passion, this constant need to possess and be possessed. The depth and strength of her feelings for him were unlike anything she had ever experienced in her life.

The heat was flowing through her, rising from her thighs, from the very core of her, spreading through her body up into her neck and face. Her cheeks were flaming. She kissed his chest, then put her arms around him tightly. Her fingers pressed against his shoulder blades, smoothed down over his broad back.

Philip was conscious of the heat from her body, and it seemed to scorch him. He reached for one of her breasts, began to caress it, and as he did he kissed her neck, then brought his mouth to hers once more. Their kisses were deep, sensual, and they stood in front of the window, locked in a fierce embrace, welded together as if never to be separated. And then finally, unable to contain himself any longer, he lifted her in his arms and carried her over to the bed.

They slipped out of their nightclothes, and he ran his strong but gentle hands over her slender body, marveling at its beauty. Moonlight was flooding the room, and in its soft and muted light her skin was taking on a silvery sheen and she looked ethereal, of another world.

He bent over her, kissed the cleft between her breasts, trailed his mouth down her stomach, and she shivered and reached for him. And quickly, with little preamble, he took her to him, joined himself to her, and they loved each other for a long time.

She told him two days later.

It was a radiant day, bright and hard as a diamond. The sky was a sharp azure blue and cloudless, the glittering Mediterranean Sea the color of lapis, the sun a golden orb, but without any warmth. And despite the beauty of the day there was a nip in the air, a hint of snow coming down from the Alps.

They were sitting on the terrace overlooking the vast sun-filled gardens of Faviola, bundled up in thick sweaters and warm coats. Earlier they had gone for a walk, and now they were sipping an aperitif before lunch. Philip had been talking about their travel plans for the next few weeks. Maddy had listened, said little, even though he had given her the opening she'd been looking for, and a small silence had fallen between them.

She broke it when she said, "I don't think we should go on to Rome, Philip. I think it would be better if we returned to London."

He looked at her swiftly, struck by the odd note of tension in her voice, a nuance that had been absent for weeks. A black brow arched. "Why, darling?"

Madelana cleared her throat, said softly, "There's something I've been wanting to say for a few days . . . I have a strange feeling . . ." She stopped, cleared her throat, and after a slight hesitation, finished quietly, "I think I'm pregnant."

He looked startled for a moment, taken aback, and then a smile broke through and his vivid blue eyes sparkled with joy. His excited voice echoed the expression on his face, when he exclaimed, "Maddy, this is the most wonderful news! The best I've had since you said you'd marry me."

Reaching for her, he brought her into his arms, kissed her tenderly, then pressed her head close to his chest, stroked her hair.

After a moment, he murmured, "But you said *think*. Aren't you sure, darling?"

Drawing away from him, she looked up into his face and nodded. "Pretty sure. All the signs are there, and when I see a doctor I know he'll confirm it. That's the reason I'd like to go back to London instead of continuing on to Italy."

"Absolutely, darling. You're right. That's what we must do. Oh Maddy, this is just marvelous."

"Then you're happy about it?" Her voice was low.

"Thrilled." He gave her a puzzled glance, frowned. "Aren't you?"

"Of course . . . I just thought you might think it's a bit too soon."

"To have a son and heir! You must be kidding. I'm elated, angel."

"It might be a girl . . ."

"Then she'll be a daughter and heir. Let's not forget, I'm the grandson of Emma Harte, and she never drew distinctions between men and women when it came to heirs. And neither did my grandfather Paul. He made my mother his heir, you know."

Madelana nodded, half smiled.

But there was a quietness about her that gave Philip reason to pause for a moment. He studied her, then asked, "What's wrong, darling?"

"Nothing. Truly, Philip."

He was not so sure about this. He said, "Are you worried about your career? About running Harte's in Australia?"

"No, I'm not."

Still unconvinced, he went on quickly, "Because if you are, you mustn't be. You'll have no problems with me about working. My grandmother went to business when she was pregnant. So did Paula and Emily, and neither Shane nor Winston objected. That's the way the men are in this family, since we were raised and trained by the famous matriarch."

"I know all that, darling."

"So what's wrong? You seem so quiet, almost deflated."

Reaching out, she took hold of his hand, held it very tightly. "I've been worrying about telling you for days, worrying that you would think the timing was wrong, that it was too soon in our marriage, that we needed more time alone together, to get to know each other better before a child came along. I suppose I thought you might be annoyed, think I'd been careless."

"It takes two to tango," he murmured.

"Yes." She paused, smiled at him tremulously. "I love you so much, Philip . . . you're everything in the world to me. And I want you to be happy with me . . . I want to please you . . . always."

He saw the sudden glitter of tears in her lovely gray eyes, and his heart twisted inside. He brought his hand to her cheek, stroked it lovingly. "You *do* please me. In every way. And you make me very happy. You're my life, Maddy. And the baby will be my life."

Unexpectedly, he threw back his head and began to laugh, entirely changing the mood between them.

Baffled, she looked at him curiously. "What is it?"

"To think that the dyed-in-the-wool international playboy is now very much a married man and an expectant father! Who would have believed it?" he asked, eyeing her merrily, chuckling again.

Maddy laughed with him. He always managed to assuage her worries, to lift her spirits.

He jumped up, took her hand in his, pulled her to her feet. "Come on, love. Let's go inside. I want to make some phone calls."

"To whom, darling?"

"The family, of course."

"All right."

They walked along the terrace toward the French doors, their arms wrapped around each other.

Abruptly, Madelana stopped, turned to Philip.

"Once I've seen the gynecologist in London, and we've spent a few days in Yorkshire with your mother, as we promised, I'd like to go home, Philip . . . home to Australia. Home to Dunoon."

He hugged her to him, loving her more than ever for saying this. "Yes, my darling, we'll go home," he said, "and make ready for our first child . . ."

Half an hour later he was still on the phone in the library.

He had spoken first to Daisy and Jason in Yorkshire, then to Paula at the store in London, passing along the news about her pregnancy. And each time he had brought her to the phone to have a word.

There had been many congratulations and lots of love sent, and Daisy, in particular, had been ecstatic, knowing she was to become a grandmother again.

Now Philip was talking to his cousin Anthony at Clonloughlin in Ireland.

She had not anticipated this, had not expected him to shout their news to the world in this way. Philip was such a private man when it came to his personal life, and, after all, he had insisted on a secret engagement and marriage. Maddy knew then, with a sudden flash of insight, why he had excluded his family from their wedding. It had been for her to save her from undue heartache, to balance the situation. He had a vast family; every member of hers was dead.

How painful her wedding day might have been . . . Philip would have been surrounded by his loved ones; she would have been alone, with no one from her side to witness that very special and important day in her life. And she would have longed for her parents and little Kerry Anne, for Young Joe and Lonnie.

Philip had understood all this. Of course he had. Everything was suddenly clear to her.

Madelana curled up on the big, comfortable sofa, listening to him speaking, watching him, thinking what an extraordinary man he was. Shrewd, brilliant, tough in business, yet so sensitive and loving when it came to his feelings for her.

She blinked, sat back, held her head to one side, trying to visualize him objectively for a split second. What a handsome man he was. It was his vivid coloring that so startled her at times—the dark glossy hair, the black mustache, the tanned face, the eyes so supernaturally blue. He seemed larger than life. And he was so wonderfully alive and vital, and he positively glowed with well-being at this moment.

He must always be like this, the way he is today, she thought. Full of laughter and life and joyousness. And I must never be the one to cause him pain.

——— *Twenty-Six* ———

There was no question in Arabella's mind that Sarah considered her to be a usurper of sorts.

No, that's too strong a word, she thought, impatiently throwing down the magazine she had been reading, unable to concentrate. I'm the . . . *interloper.* Yes, that's the right word. Until I strolled into his life, Sarah had him all to herself whenever he came to Europe. The woman enjoys being the center of attraction. That was only too apparent at lunch today.

Arabella rose, glided across the sitting room of the guest suite of the farmhouse in Mougins, stood looking out of the window for a moment.

It had been a glorious day, but now dusk was falling, and the gardens below were bosky, mysterious, almost eerie in the dimming light. A faint, vaporous mist shrouded everything in a mantle of gray and opal tints, and the trees in the apple orchard beyond the white fence were inchoate, illusory.

She shivered, filling with melancholy, feeling unexpectedly sad. She shrugged these feelings away before they took hold. She had no reasons to be sad. She had everything. Arabella smiled a small, secret smile. Well, not *every-thing*. But she was getting there.

Swinging around, she returned to the fireside, settled herself on the sofa once more, enjoying the warmth and cheerfulness of the blazing logs. She liked a fire. There was something comforting about it . . . perhaps because it re-minded her of her childhood in Hampshire, the big old house where she had grown up.

After a few moments reflection and several adjustments to her plans for the next few weeks, she glanced around for the umpteenth time since they had arrived that morning, admiring the room again.

Here and in the adjoining bedroom, ancient, dark wood ceiling beams, white, half-timbered walls, and old brick fireplaces had been left intact. In combination with the slightly slanting ceiling, they gave this top floor under the eaves a coziness and character. Thick wool carpet stretched wall to wall, and its *café-au-lait* beige was the perfect backdrop for the lovely English chintzes on the huge sofa and the chairs, the French Provençal country furniture made of ripe woods polished to a mellow gleam. The same coffee-colored carpet flowed through into the bedroom, where Porthault linens dressed the bed, upholstered the antique headboard, and hung as curtains at the mullioned windows.

The suite was as fresh as a flower garden, overflowing with diverse floral patterns that somehow blended well together, and it was infinitely comfortable. A fortune had been spent on the entire farmhouse, and all of the rooms had been put together with taste, discernment, and an eye to color and design.

Whatever else Sarah Lowther Pascal might be, she is certainly a clever homemaker, Arabella decided. She had done wonders with the sprawling old farm perched on a hillside high above Cannes, had decorated it with flair, given it undeniable cachet and charm. And in the grounds outside she had turned a series of decrepit barns into one huge, superb studio for Yves, had covered the central section with a roof of glass to let in the maximum amount of light.

Yves Pascal's paintings hung everywhere in the farmhouse. They were bold, modern, not to Arabella's taste, which ran to Old Masters and the traditional. But the artist was a powerhouse in the international art world, and his paintings were in great demand; apparently others liked his works, even if she did not. These days they were commanding huge prices.

On the other hand, she had really taken to the small, wiry Frenchman from the moment she had met him. He was a bit of a peacock, a strutter, and obviously rather hyper. But nonetheless, he was the possessor of an inordinate amount of Gallic charm. She did not quite understand his relationship with Sarah. They seemed to be poles apart. Yet he adored his wife and their child, Chloe—she had noticed that immediately.

Jonathan had told her that the little girl had his grandmother's looks and coloring. He had not volunteered much about the legendary Emma Harte in the four months she had known him, but from a remark Sarah had made at lunch, she had gathered that the two of them were at loggerheads with their cousin, Paula O'Neill. After lunch, later that afternoon, she had asked Jonathan why there was a feud in the family, and he had muttered something about Paula turning their grandmother against them, persuading her to make certain changes in her will. He had seemed suddenly upset, even angry, and after murmuring a few sympathetic words, she had wisely let the matter drop. She had not wanted to underscore his unprecedented agitation. She had never seen him like that before.

Her thoughts centered on Jonathan.

She had been led to believe he would be difficult to ensnare. But this had not proved to be the case. He had immediately and heavily fallen for her, had courted her assiduously in Hong Kong. She had withheld herself in every way in the beginning. Then slowly she had opened up, both mentally and physically. She had let him see her intelligence, her knowledge about art and antiques, her sophistication; and she had tempted him with her body. Their fraternal good night kisses had led to deeper kissing, then petting and increasingly intimate touching, until she had finally succumbed to his potent sexuality, had allowed him to take her to bed.

All along she had never pretended to be a virgin, had let him know there had been other men before him. But she had carefully pointed out that she was discriminating, not promiscuous, and wanted to be certain of her feelings, his feelings, before they embarked on an affair. He had applauded her candor and had confided he was only interested in women who were as experienced and worldly-wise as he. And he had shown patience with her.

A knowing look slid into Arabella's pitch-black eyes. She had expertise. She knew how to give him pleasure in countless ways . . . ways he had no comprehension of as yet. She did not want him to know just how experienced she was in the art of sex. She wanted him to become totally besotted with her, to fall truly in love with her first. Only then would she take him to heights he had never dreamed of, as only she knew how.

And so she continued to lead him along gently, and little by little it was all happening . . . every day he became more committed to her. There was a new warmth in him, and he could not get enough of her. In bed and out of it. He wanted her with him all the time.

Arabella looked down at the plain gold wedding band on the third finger of her left hand. It was gleaming brightly in the firelight. Jonathan had wanted to give her a circle of diamonds. She had asked for this plain, old-fashioned gold ring, telling him that it was more symbolic. He had been surprised, yet obviously touched, by her sentiments.

How thunderstruck Tony had been when Jonathan had married her so quickly in Hong Kong just before Christmas, then swept her off to Europe on their honeymoon. He had been startled to discover she was suddenly going to be out of reach for several months. Very put out, in actuality. And she had taken great satisfaction in being able to ruffle Tony's infuriating equanimity for once.

Her new husband had wanted to take her to Paris. But there was so much of her past in that city, so much sadness to be recalled, she was not excited about honeymooning there. Nor did she particularly want to take the chance of running into someone who had known her in the old days. She did not need to deal with friends long since departed from her life, nor confront memories gone stale and cold. And so she convinced Jonathan they would enjoy Rome more, had suggested that they then go on to Mougins in the South of France, to visit his cousin Sarah, whom he had spoken about so warmly. This had delighted him, and he had readily agreed to her travel plans.

Rome had been fun. Since she knew the city like a native, she had been able to take him sightseeing, and to the chicest restaurants and clubs, which were well off the usual tourist track, patronized by local society and the international jet set.

And she had been very loving, sexually pliable, catering to his desires, more than ready to please him, and this had made him extremely happy.

It was in Rome that he had bought her yet another wedding gift, an extraordinary necklace he had presented to her as a surprise on their last night in the Eternal City, before they had left for France. Composed of a single strand of large black pearls, it had a cream-colored, teardrop pearl hanging from a ten-carat diamond in the center of the strand.

Although she had some good jewelry of her own, the black pearl necklace was not only rare but surpassed everything in her possession. Except, of course, for the huge Burmese ruby-and-diamond ring Jonathan had given her when they had become engaged.

The chimes of the little carriage clock brought Arabella out of her reverie. She glanced at it, surprised to see it was seven. Jonathan, who had gone to Cannes with Yves, had said he would be back by seven-thirty. She must be ready for him.

Rising, she hurried into the bedroom, took a sheer, black-chiffon nightgown trimmed with coffee-colored lace out of the armoire, then went into the bathroom to undress and freshen up.

A few minutes later, wearing the glamorous nightgown and a matching black chiffon peignoir that floated around her in a cloud, Arabella seated herself at the dressing table. She had worn her silver-gilt hair in a severe chignon all day; now she pulled out the pins and let it fall around her face and down her back. She brushed it until it gleamed.

Leaning forward, she peered at herself in the glass. Sometimes she was startled by her own beauty, by the lack of lines around her eyes and other telltale signs of aging, by the suppleness of her skin, the flawlessness of her complexion. Life had left hardly any marks on her face, and nothing seemed to mar its youth and beauty. Even when she was ill with a cold, or some other minor complaint, she appeared to be in blooming health. How lucky she was. She looked much younger than her thirty-four years.

After scrubbing off her bright red lipstick with a tissue, she toned down her flushed face with creamy foundation and transparent powder until she was very pale, almost wan-looking. She added extra eyeliner to her lids, emphasizing their natural, almond shape. Smoothing on black shadow, she then highlighted the bones under the brows with touches of purple and silver, and instantly her eyes stood out like huge, dark coals in her face. Once she had blotted her lips, she smeared on colorless salve, and sprayed herself generously with the musky perfume Jonathan preferred. She then lifted the black pearl necklace out of its leather case and clasped it around her neck. Jonathan liked her to wear jewelry in bed. It was a fetish of his.

Hurrying now, she stepped over to the armoire, opened it, stared at herself in the full-length mirror, approving of her reflection. She looked so young, like a girl of sixteen, her face full of innocence—and promise. Yet in contrast her body was the body of an alluring woman, shapely, sensual, and provocative in the revealing nightgown.

The black chiffon was taut across her breasts. Her nipples and their dark aureoles were faintly visible through the filmy chiffon and lace. She had had the nightgown made in Hong Kong, and the seamstress had cut it to fit her body perfectly, and so it clung to her in all the right places. And in the most tantalizing way.

Stepping into a pair of high-heeled, black-satin mules, she went through into the sitting room where she stood for a moment warming herself in front of the fire. And then she stretched out on the Chesterfield sofa to wait for her husband.

As the minutes ticked by, Arabella began to realize she was anxious for Jonathan to return, looked forward to seeing him, even though he had only been gone for a couple of hours. She hoped he would want to make love before they went down to dinner.

Startled by these thoughts, she sat upon the sofa with a jolt, frowned, reached for a cigarette, lighted it.

As she smoked, her mind turned over at a rapid pace, and it dawned on her how much she liked Jonathan's blond good looks, his lovely manners, the finesse with which he did things, his very Englishness. It was such a change, such a relief, to be with an Englishman after the foreigners she had known. She also enjoyed the avid attention he paid to her, his passion for her, his sexual prowess. Jonathan Ainsley, her husband, was as good a lover as she had ever had, if not, indeed, the very best.

She suddenly suspected she was falling in love with him, and she was further surprised at herself.

Fifteen minutes later Jonathan hurried into the sitting room. It was dimly lit, but the logs blazing in the hearth cast a roseate glow throughout.

Arabella was standing in front of the fireplace, and he thought she looked quite extraordinary tonight. This brought him to a standstill.

He paused in the center of the floor, staring at her, appreciating her beauty, her sensuality. How inviting she was in the black-chiffon negligée. He could faintly make out parts of her body through the delicate fabric . . . the high, full breasts, the slender waist, the blond mound of Venus below. Black was a color that suited her well. It brought out the creaminess of her incomparable skin, the silver lights in the cascade of glorious, shimmering blond hair.

She held out her arms to him, half smiling.

Her black eyes seemed to burn right through him, and they held an expression he had never seen reflected there before. But curiously enough, whatever the expression meant, it excited him. As he moved forward he felt his desire for her stirring.

"I've missed you, darling," she murmured in her low, husky voice as he came to a stop next to her.

"I've not been all *that* long," he replied. Nevertheless he was pleased. He reached for her, took her in his arms, kissed her on the mouth. When they finally drew apart, he held her away from him, gripping her shoulders firmly with both hands, gazing deeply into her face.

"What is it?" She asked at last.

"You are so very, *very* beautiful tonight, Arabella. More beautiful than I have ever seen you, I do believe."

"Oh Jonathan . . ."

He leaned into her, kissed the hollow in her throat, and as he did he slipped the peignoir off her shoulders. It slid to the floor. Next he pulled at the narrow nightgown straps tied in bows, and as they came undone this garment, too, fell in a swirl of chiffon at her feet.

She stood before him naked except for the black pearls encircling her slender throat.

Jonathan stepped back. Of all the women he had ever had, she was the most experienced sexually, and therefore the most exciting, the most desirable . . . Of all the objects of art in his collection, she was the most beautiful thing, the biggest prize of all . . . his greatest possession. She was perfection itself. And he owned her. Owned every part of her. No, that was not quite true. She was still withholding. This continued to surprise him. But soon she would give herself up to him completely, abandon herself fully. He was confident of his powers . . . and his power over her.

Arabella said slowly, "Jonathan, is something wrong? You're looking at me oddly."

"No, of course there's nothing wrong," he replied. "I'm just admiring you, thinking how lovely you look . . . wearing only my black pearls. How white your body is in contrast." As he spoke, he reached out, ran a finger down one of her breasts.

Suddenly he thought he would explode. He was terribly excited. The blood rushed to his face, and he trembled as he moved closer to her, put his hands around her neck, unclasped the necklace.

"There, that's much better," he said, slipping it into his pocket. "You need no adornment, Arabella. You are perfect as you are . . . like a Grecian statue exquisitely chiseled out of the finest alabaster."

He removed his sports jacket, threw it on a chair. Then, taking hold of her hand, he led her toward the sofa. "Come, let us lie here together for a while. Let us love each other, enjoy each other," he said. "I want to know you more intimately than I already do, possess even more of you. And then more . . . and more. Will you let me, Arabella?"

"Yes," she whispered huskily. "If you will do the same."

"Ah, Arabella, we are so alike, you and I, and in every conceivable way." He chuckled softly. "A couple of sinners, I do believe."

Jonathan held her with his eyes. A knowing look crossed his face. He pressed her down onto the cushions with one hand. With the other he began to unbutton his shirt.

——— *Twenty-Seven* ———

"I'm not quite sure how to tell you this," Alexander began, looking from his sister, Emily, to his cousins, Paula O'Neill and Anthony Standish, the Earl of Dunvale.

The three of them were seated on the two sofas in front of the fire, sipping the drinks he had poured for them a short while before.

"In fact," Alexander went on, "I've wracked my brains for weeks now, seeking the right words, the best way of explaining—"

Breaking off, he rose from his chair, walked across the drawing room, stood at the huge, bow-shaped window that soared to the ceiling, overlooked the small garden behind his Mayfair house.

He suddenly wished that he hadn't asked them to come over, that he didn't have to tell them . . . *fervently* wished that he could simply . . . let it happen. But that would be unthinkable. Unfair of him. And besides, there were too many things to be decided, too many legalities involved.

Alexander was tense, held himself stiffly, his shoulders hunched underneath his jacket. He took a deep breath, summoning his courage. This was perhaps the most difficult thing he had ever had to do in his entire life.

Emily, watching him intently, had detected the strained note in his voice when she had first arrived at the house. And now she noticed how taut he was. They had been unusually close throughout their lives, and she knew him as well as she knew herself. Intuitively she felt that something was radically wrong.

Pressing back her alarm, she said, "You sound awfully serious, Sandy."

"Yes," he responded, continuing to stare out of the window, wondering how to begin. In the gathering dusk of this January evening, the patch of garden looked sad and bereft with its blackened skeletal trees, empty flower beds frosted with old snow turned gray by London soot. It seemed to him that this bit of earth echoed his bleak mood.

The three cousins were waiting for Alexander to continue, to explain why he had invited them here, had actually *insisted* they come tonight. And they exchanged concerned glances behind his back.

Paula swung her head, focused on Anthony, lifted a brow questioningly.

The Earl shrugged, half raised his hands in a helpless gesture, indicating his own considerable bafflement.

Next Paula peered at Emily on the sofa opposite. Emily tightened her lips, shook her head rapidly, expressing her own puzzlement. "I don't know what this is all about either," Emily mouthed silently to Paula. After a moment, she cleared her throat, ventured aloud, "Sandy dear . . . Gran always said that if a person had something difficult to explain, or unpleasant to say, the best thing to do was simply to blurt it out. Why don't you do that?"

"That's not as easy as it sounds," her brother answered quietly.

"Whatever problems you have, you know you have our full support," Anthony volunteered in his most reassuring voice.

Alexander pivoted on his heels, stood with his back to the great window, regarding the three of them thoughtfully, "Yes, I do know that, Anthony, and thanks," he said at last. A faint wavering smile touched his mouth, then faded instantly.

Paula, studying him alertly, saw something strange in the back of his light blue eyes, the emptiest of expressions, and it made her heart tighten. "There's something awfully wrong . . . it's . . . it's bad, isn't it, Sandy?"

He nodded. "I've always prided myself on being able to handle anything, Paula. But this . . ." He discovered he was unable to finish his sentence.

Paula remembered then, remembered the telephone conversation she had had with him at the end of August last year. She had sensed he had a problem that particular morning, had then dismissed it as being merely her vivid imagination at work. But she had been right after all, she was sure of that. She clasped her hands together tightly, feeling unaccountably nervous and filling, unexpectedly, with apprehension.

Alexander said slowly, "I asked the three of you to come round this evening . . . because of our closeness over the years, the special relationship I have with each one of you." He waited, took a breath. "I do have certain problems. I thought we could discuss them rationally and that perhaps you would help me to come to a few decisions."

"Of course we will," Anthony said. His cousin was behaving out of character and he was desperately worried. He fixed his clear, steady gaze on the other man, wanting to convey his affection and devotion. They had helped each other over some rough terrain in the past and would no doubt do so again.

Leaning forward with a degree of urgency, Anthony asked, "Is it to do with business? Or is it a family matter?"

"Personal really," Alexander answered.

He moved away from the window, walked slowly across the elegant, period drawing room, lowered himself into the chair he had vacated a short while before. He knew there was no point in putting it off any longer. They simply had to be told.

Alexander let out a deeply weary sigh. He said, in a controlled voice, "I'm very ill . . . I'm dying, actually."

Emily, Paula, and Anthony gaped at him. None of them had expected to hear anything as devastating as this. They were stunned.

Alexander went on hurriedly, "I'm sorry to have told you in such a blunt manner, but I took Emily's advice. And Gran *was* right, you know. It *is* the only way . . . best to blurt it out, get it said without too much preamble."

Paula was so shaken she was unable to respond. Blindly, she groped for Anthony's hand.

He took it, enfolded it in his comfortingly. He was as stupefied as she, at a complete loss. There were no words. A great sadness flowed through him. What an appalling thing to happen to poor Sandy, who was in his prime. He would notice it most acutely when his cousin was gone. Sandy had been such a source of strength during his own travails over the years. And most especially at the time Min had been found drowned in the lake at Clonloughlin. Anthony reached for his glass of scotch-and-soda on the end table. He suddenly needed a drink.

Emily was ashen with shock.

She sat perfectly still, staring at her brother in disbelief, her eyes dark with sudden pain. She felt as though all blood had drained out of her. Then taking hold of herself, she got to her feet a bit shakily, and went to him. Kneeling down next to his chair, she took his hand in hers, clung to it.

"Sandy, it's not true! It can't be!" she cried in a low but vehement tone. "Oh please say it isn't . . ." Emily's voice quavered, came to a stop, and her green eyes brimmed. "Not you, Sandy, oh please, not *you.*"

"I'm afraid so," he said in the steadiest voice imaginable, "and there's not much I can do to change this one, Dumpling. It's out of my hands."

His use of her old nickname made her choke up, and long-forgotten memories came rushing back unbidden, evoking their childhood years together, and she remembered how he had protected her, looked after her, and her throat suddenly ached and her heart felt as if it was being squeezed in a vise. She closed her eyes for a split second, striving to come to grips with her brother's tragic and frightening news.

"You say you're d-d-dying." She stumbled on this last word, had to take several deep breaths before continuing, "But of what? What's wrong with you, Sandy? You seem perfectly well to me. What are you suffering from?"

"I have acute myelogenous leukemia . . . it's also known as acute granulocytic leukemia."

"Surely that can be treated!" Anthony exclaimed, sudden hope leaping onto his worried face. "Tremendous strides have been made in medicine today, especially in the treatment of cancer, and perhaps—"

"There is no cure," Alexander interrupted.

"But what actually is it?" Emily demanded, anxiety making her voice rise, giving it a shrillness abnormal for her. "What on earth *causes* it?"

"A malignant change in cells that produce granulocytes, one of the types of white blood cells made in the bone marrow," he explained, so well educated about his disease that the details were now readily on the tip of his tongue. "They multiply and survive longer than normal cells. Very simply put, they destroy. As their numbers increase, they invade the bone marrow, enter the bloodstream, and eventually attack the organs and tissue."

"Oh God, Sandy—" Paula began and came to a halt. Her feelings got the better of her. The words she had been about to say strangled in her throat. She steadied herself; somehow she managed to hang onto her self-possession. After a few moments, she went on, "I'm so sorry, so very sorry, darling. I'm here for you, we're all here for you, whenever you need us, day or night."

"Yes," he said, "I know you are. I'm counting on it, actually, Paula."

"Isn't there any chance of at least *arresting* the leukemia?" Paula probed, her manner gentle, her sympathy and compassion reflected in her eyes.

"There really isn't," Alexander replied.

With sudden fierceness, Emily said, "I realize you must have been to the best doctors in London, but we must go farther afield. We really must. What about the States? Sloan-Kettering in New York, for instance? We can't just stand by and *allow* this to happen, Sandy. We must do *something.*"

"I agree with you, Emily," Anthony said. "There has to be some sort of advanced treatment in this day and age. *Somewhere.* I can't accept this either, Sandy. I won't." He averted his face, struggling with his feelings.

Alexander shook his head, and it was with a finality that was unmistakable.

"I understand how the three of you feel. I was exactly the same as you in the beginning. Looking for a cure, full of hope, but the hope rapidly changed to frustration, then anger, and finally to *acceptance*. You see . . ." He stopped, took several deep breaths, continued slowly, "There is absolutely nothing that can be done for me. And believe me, I *have* been to the very best specialists in London, New York, and Zurich. What I'm suffering from *is* fatal. I'm having treatment, of course, but there has been hardly any remission."

A grim silence settled in the drawing room.

Alexander sat back in his chair, relieved at last to have finally told them. He had resigned himself to his fate some time ago, but he had worried greatly about the family and how they would take it, most especially Emily.

For their parts, his sister and his cousins were trying to come to grips with the heartbreaking news he had just imparted, striving to absorb it and to get a hold of their emotions as well. They each, in their different ways, loved Alexander, and although they did not know it, they were sharing the same thought at this precise moment. All were asking themselves why it had to be Alexander who had been stricken in this manner. He was the finest, the kindest, the most loving of men. The very best. He had always been there for them, whenever they had needed him, no matter what the problem, and that was how he had been since childhood. The three cousins believed him to be the one truly *good* man they knew. If anyone was a saint, it was Alexander.

Paula eventually spoke. "You've known for some months, haven't you?"

Alexander nodded, then picked up his glass of white wine, took a sip.

"Was it the end of August last year when you found out you were ill?" she asked.

"No, it was October. But you're close enough, Paula." He gave her an odd look. "How did you know?"

Paula's grave face was infinitely still. "I didn't. Not really. But I did have a queer feeling things were not right with you, when you phoned me from Leeds —the day we missed each other at Fairley. There was such a peculiar nuance in your voice, it prompted me to ask you if there was a problem, and, if you recall, you said no. So I dismissed it. I thought it was my imagination getting the better of me."

"You were very perceptive that morning," Alexander murmured. "I felt uneasy, wanted to talk to you. I was already starting to have symptoms. I was becoming fatigued quickly, and it worried me, and I discovered I bruised and bled very easily . . . if I merely knocked myself against something."

Alexander got up, went to fetch the bottle of wine, refilled Paula's and Emily's glasses and his own, took the bottle back to the silver ice bucket on the console.

The others waited in silence, dreading what else he had to say to them.

He went on as he sat down, "I was doing a lot of work on the estate at Nutton Priory in late September, and I was baffled. I wondered if I'd become a hemophiliac overnight—if that was possible. Then early in October I developed the most frightful ulcers in my mouth. I was growing more alarmed than ever, and that's why I canceled our lunch date, Paula. I finally went to see my doctor. He immediately sent me to a specialist in Harley Street. The tests and the bone marrow biopsy were quite conclusive."

"You say you're having treatment," Anthony said. "It must be doing you some good, Sandy, having some effect. You don't look as though you're dreadfully ill. You're a trifle pale perhaps, thinner, but—"

"All it's doing is keeping me going for the moment," Alexander interjected.

Emily looked at her brother closely. "What sort of treatment is it?"

"Transfusions of red blood cells, and platelets when I need them. I also take antibiotics from time to time, to help reduce the chances of my getting infections."

"I see." Emily bit her inner lip nervously. "You just said the treatment is keeping you going . . . for . . . for . . . how long?" she asked in a voice that shook. She was filled with fear for her brother.

"Four to five months at the outside, I think. Not many people last much longer than a year after this type of leukemia has been diagnosed."

Emily's mouth trembled. "I can't bear it. Not *you*. It's just not fair. Oh Sandy, you can't be dying!" She endeavored to push back the tears, knowing he wanted her to be strong, to face this with the same kind of courage he was displaying. She was unable to do so.

She jumped up, hurried out of the drawing room, suddenly aware that she was about to break down completely.

Twenty-Eight

Emily stood at the bottom of the staircase in the entrance hall, holding the bannister, filled with an internal shaking. And slowly the tears slid down her cheeks unchecked as she quietly wept for her brother. He was only thirty-seven. Her mind balked at the thought of his imminent death. It was unacceptable to her.

After only a matter of seconds, the drawing room door opened and closed softly. Emily felt Alexander's arms encircling her. He turned her around to face him, took a handkerchief out of his pocket, wiped the tears from her face.

"Come on, Dumpling, try to hang in there. For me," he said. "I can't stand to see you so upset. It doesn't help me. I realize this has been a ghastly shock for you; on the other hand, there is no *easy* way to break this kind of news. How *do* you tell those you love that you're dying?"

Emily was incapable of responding. Her eyes welled again, and she buried her face against his chest, held on to him tightly.

He said, very softly, "I'm glad you reminded me of Gran's attitude . . . you know, about just blurting it out. It *did* help me to screw up my courage and get it said. I'd been putting it off for weeks."

Alexander smoothed his hand over her hair, and there was a pause before he remarked, "I've hidden my illness from you for a very long time, old thing. However, it is going to start showing very soon. So you *had* to be told. And there are a lot of things which must be properly dealt with. *Now*. They can't be put off any longer . . . time does go so *quickly,* especially when one is trying to hold on to it."

Emily swallowed hard, wanting to be strong, but finding it difficult. She stood very still, snapping her eyes shut.

After a moment, when she had regained a little of her self-possession, she said, "Nothing will ever be the same again, Sandy, not when you're . . . gone. Whatever will we all do? Whatever will *I* do?" As the words left her mouth, she realized how selfish she was being, but she could not take them back. They had been said, and to apologize to him would only make matters worse.

He said softly, in a confident tone, "You'll be all right, Emily. You'll keep going, and with the strength and courage you've always had . . . Gran's kind of fortitude. She taught you how to soldier on when you were a little girl. And you have Winston and your family." A long sigh trickled through Alexander, and as if thinking aloud, he murmured against her hair, "Francesca's all right, too, now that she's married to Oliver, but I do worry about Amanda. She's such a vulnerable young woman, so impressionable, really. You will keep an eye on her, won't you?" For the first time Alexander's voice held a slight tremor. He glanced away, hid his face from her, then coughed behind his hand.

Emily said, "You know I will, darling."

They stood together for a few minutes longer.

Alexander held her closer, gathering as much of his diminished strength as possible, aware that he had a great deal to say in the next half hour. He was not looking forward to it. But it had to be done, and the best way, he had decided earlier, was to be very businesslike about everything.

Emily could feel Sandy's bones through his clothes, and she realized how thin he had grown. She drew away, stole a quick glance at him, took note of his pallor, the faint purplish smudges under his eyes, and her heart sank. She could not understand why she had not noticed signs that he was ill before now, and she cursed herself angrily for not having paid more attention in the last few months.

Alexander finally released her, and taking out his handkerchief once more, he blotted her damp cheeks. A fleeting smile touched his eyes. How blond and small and dainty she was. She had always reminded him of a fragile piece of Dresden china. Yet she had a backbone of steel, and there was an indomitability about her that reminded him of their grandmother. And he knew that as distressed as she was now, in the long run she would be strong for everyone. He could count on his sister. Like Emma Harte before her, she had grit.

Emily was acutely aware of Alexander's intense scrutiny. She returned it, said, "I'll be fine, Sandy," as though she had read his mind.

Alexander smiled at her, nodded.

There was a brief silence before Emily went on slowly, in a low voice, "You've not only been a wonderful brother to me, but mother, father, best friend as well. You've been . . . everything to me, Sandy. I've never *really* told you before how I feel, but I do want you to know that I—"

"I'm very aware of how you feel," he interrupted swiftly, unable to deal with any more emotion at this time. "And I love you too, Emily. Now we'd better go back to the drawing room, join the others, don't you think? There are arrangements to be made. For the future."

"I'd like to talk about business first. About Harte Enterprises to be specific," Alexander said once they were all gathered around the fire again.

"Yes, of course, anything you wish," Paula answered. Her eyes were red and watery, and betrayed her, despite her air of calmness. It was obvious that she had wept whilst her cousins had been out of the room, but she now appeared to be in total control of herself.

"I've had time to think things out," Alexander began, "and I'd like to share some of my thoughts with you before I come to my final decisions. I suppose I'm looking for your input before I put my plans into motion."

"But I'm not involved in any of the family businesses," Anthony immediately reminded him. "Are you sure I'm not in the way?" His expression turned quizzical.

"No, you're not. And anyway, you're the eldest of Emma Harte's grandchildren, and you ought to—"

"Paula's the head of the family, though," Anthony countered. "And thank God she is, too. It's not a job I'd relish, I don't mind telling you."

Alexander smiled with a certain wryness. "I know what you mean. But to continue, you're my closest male friend, and very simply put I want you here. Let's just say for moral support, shall we, old chap?"

The Earl nodded, got up, strode over to the console where he refreshed his scotch-and-soda. He glanced across at Paula and Emily. "Do either of you want another drink?"

Both women shook their heads.

"How about you, Sandy?"

"I'm fine right now, thanks."

Alexander waited until Anthony had returned to the sofa before he turned to Emily, and went on, "I'm sorry I called this meeting when Winston is in Canada, but I had to have it this week because I'm going into the hospital tomorrow for treatment. He ought to have been here, of course, as head of the Yorkshire Consolidated Newspaper Company and our Canadian papers. On the other hand, the divisions he runs are not actually relevant to this discussion."

"He'll understand, Sandy." Emily leaned forward, pinned her brother with her green eyes. "How long are you going to be in the hospital?" she asked, her worry instantly showing.

"Only a few days, and don't be concerned about it. The treatment does help me. Now, I would like to move along. Look, I know what I'm going to talk about is somewhat unsettling. But please, *don't be upset*. It must all be said, and I want my affairs to be in order . . . a Harte family trait, I believe."

Alexander's gaze swept over the three of them, and he went on to explain in a thoughtful tone, "I've analyzed Harte Enterprises in every conceivable way over the past couple of weeks, trying to decide what to do with the company. I considered selling it, knowing it would fetch hundreds of millions of pounds, which we could reinvest in the market. Then I thought of selling off only certain divisions, keeping others. And then it struck me how unfair I was being to you, Emily."

Before she had a chance to say anything, he rushed on, "After all, you run Genret, which is one of our biggest money-making divisions, and you're the only other shareholder—"

"Except for Jonathan and Sarah," Emily cut in. "And I don't suppose they're of any consequence."

"No, they're not," Alexander agreed. "In any event, Emily, I realized it was rather imperious of me to make decisions without consulting you. And it was certainly wrong of me to assume, as I did initially, that you might not want to run Harte Enterprises yourself. A few days ago, yet another thought occurred to me . . . what would Grandy have wanted us to do with Harte Enterprises in view of my illness? I instantly concluded that she would not want us to sell it. The company is too solid, too rich, too important to the family as a whole for us to relinquish it. Don't you agree?"

"Yes," Emily managed, more aware than ever of what the future without her brother would actually mean.

"Paula, what is your opinion?" Alexander asked.

"You're absolutely right about everything," Paula said, striving to sound normal. "Grandy did have very strong feelings about Harte Enterprises. She would want Emily to continue in your stead. That *is* what you have in mind, isn't it?"

"Yes, I think Emily should become chairman of the board and chief executive officer within the next few weeks. That way we can make a smooth transfer of power in the company and I can step down. Fairly soon, too, I hope."

"I suppose you'll want Amanda to run Genret," Emily ventured.

"With your agreement. And the one division I think we should sell is Lady Hamilton Clothes."

"To the Kallinskis presumably," Paula interjected.

"Yes." Alexander cleared his throat, reached for his glass, took a sip of wine. "If anyone is entitled to buy Lady Hamilton Clothes, it's Uncle Ronnie. For sentimental reasons, and because of our long involvement with the family for over seventy years. I say let's keep everything in the three clans. As you both know—" He looked from Emily to Paula, continued, "Uncle Ronnie is prepared to meet our price. I'm not worried about that aspect. My only real concern is that you're comfortable with the deal, Paula. Whilst you're not involved with the running of Harte Enterprises, Lady Hamilton does supply the Harte stores and the boutiques."

"Uncle Ronnie assured me they would continue to do so, and on an exclusive basis, when we discussed the idea of Kallinski Industries buying the fashion division last August," Paula told him.

"Well, Emily?" Alexander peered across at her, lifted a brow.

"Yes, it's all right with me. But what about Amanda? She loves her division, Sandy."

"I know she does. But under these unexpected circumstances I'm sure she'll understand the necessity for making certain changes, for streamlining the company to an extent. Grandy's philosophy was that we must be loyal to the company as a whole, not just to our own divisions. I believe that, too, as you and Amanda are aware. Anyway, Genret will be a challenge to Amanda, just as it was to you when you took over from Len Harvey twelve years ago."

"That's true . . . yes . . ."

"What's the matter, Emily?" Alexander asked, frowning at her. "You look and sound rather hesitant."

"I'm not really. It's just that I'm not terribly well informed about the real estate division of Harte Enterprises. And that worries me."

"There's not *really* a problem, darling. Thomas Lorring is my right hand in that division, and he's been virtually running it for several years. And you *know* that he has, Emily." He leveled a long, very direct look at her. "He'll do the same for you, when you take over from me . . . and you *will*, won't you?"

"Of course I will." Emily sat back on the sofa jerkily, wishing she did not have to step into her brother's shoes. If only things could suddenly be the way they were yesterday. She longed suddenly for Winston, regretted her husband was not here, that he would not be returning to England for another week. The thought plunged her into deeper dismay.

Paula said, "You've made some very sound judgments, Sandy."

He rose, paced to the window, glanced out at the garden almost absently. He said, without turning around, "I think they're the most logical moves, given the situation." He remained motionless in front of the flaring bay for a few seconds longer.

No one said a word.

Finally Alexander returned to the fireplace, where he stood with his back to the blazing logs, warming himself.

And then without any preamble, he announced in a brisk and businesslike voice, "About my will. I intend to leave this house to Francesca and Nutton Priory to Amanda. Naturally, the Villa Faviola is yours, Emily."

"Oh Sandy—" She stopped abruptly. She could not speak. Her throat closed on her. She blinked back sudden tears.

He hurried on relentlessly, "Fifty percent of my personal wealth will be divided by the three of you, Emily, and the other fifty percent will go to the children in the family. And not just my nephews and nieces, but to your children, Paula, and yours, Anthony."

They both nodded their understanding.

Anthony looked away, not wanting Alexander to see the anguish suffusing his face. He stared fiercely at the painting on the opposite wall.

Paula twisted her wedding ring nervously, gazed down at her hands, thinking how uncertain life was. Only that afternoon she had been congratulating herself on so many things accomplished lately, and she had been happy. Now, without warning, she was miserable, filled with worry and concern, and facing the untimely death of a beloved cousin, who was also a dear friend and important business associate. The implications of Sandy's fatal illness were manifold and on a variety of levels.

"Now, Emily," Alexander proceeded, determined to be done with everything tonight, so that there would be no need for this kind of discussion again. "Next we come to my holdings in Harte Enterprises. To be precise, the fifty-two percent of the shares Grandy left me. I am going to give thirty-two percent to you and twenty percent to Amanda. I am not leaving any of my shares to Francesca since she does not work for the company."

"Yes, I see . . . thank you," Emily said in the steadiest voice she could muster. "But I'm just wondering . . . is that quite fair to Amanda, darling?" She asked this softly, not wishing to argue with him, but at the same time wanting her half-sister to be fully involved and totally committed to Harte Enterprises. After all, it would be just the two of them running it eventually.

"I believe it is *eminently* fair," Alexander was quick to respond. "Grandmother insisted that one person had control of this particular company, to prevent any dissension among us, and that is how I want it, why I have divided my shares in the way I have. You will be the majority shareholder and head of Harte Enterprises, as I am now." His tone was unusually firm and uncompromising and it left no room for doubt about his feelings or for further conversation on the matter.

Emily made no comment, directed her gaze to the fire, grappling with her overwhelming sadness, still finding it difficult to comprehend that her brother would not be with them for much longer, that next year at this time he would be dead. Her heart was heavy, and once more she longed for her husband and his comforting presence, the emotional security Winston gave her.

Anthony now spoke up at last. He said, "When you've finished your treatment, I want you to come and stay with us at Clonloughlin, Sandy. And for as long as you can."

"Yes, I *would* like that. It'll do me good to be with you all. And then afterward, Emily, I'll work with you for a few weeks, take you through every aspect of the job. Mind you, I do believe you'll be capable of doing it blindfolded."

Emily bit her lip, nodded rapidly, glanced at Paula, her eyes full of mute appeal.

Paula quickly bridged this tense moment, when she said in a warm and cheerful voice, "Is there anything I can do, Sandy? Anything that will make things easier for you?"

"Not really, Paula, thanks anyway. Oh wait! Yes, there is one thing you can *all* do for me!" His intelligent, light blue eyes roamed over them, and he shifted on his feet, slightly changed his stance in front of the fire. "I'd like you to keep the news of my illness quiet, if you don't mind. I really don't wish it to become a topic for discussion in the family. And I certainly don't want to have to cope with sadness and sympathy, or be surrounded by a lot of long, gloomy faces."

A stricken expression settled in Emily's eyes. "I appreciate your feelings," she said and paused. Her voice wavered as she went on, "I'll try not to tell Winston, but I think it'll be ever so hard for me . . ."

"Oh, but of course, you must tell him!" her brother exclaimed. He looked at Paula and Anthony. "And naturally you must tell Shane and Sally. I didn't mean you to exclude them, only your children. And yours, Emily, and our half-sisters, I don't want Amanda and Francesca to know—at least not just yet."

"What about Mummy?" Emily asked, worry flaring. "Has she got to be kept in the dark, too?"

Alexander inclined his head. "Oh yes, very much so. It's better Mother doesn't know anything at all. She has a tendency to become hysterical about the slightest thing. She would only upset me."

Striding over to the Georgian console table, Alexander picked up the bottle of white wine, brought it to Paula and Emily. "Well, that's about it," he said as he refilled their crystal goblets. "I've covered everything I think. Incidentally, Emily, John Crawford knows about the situation. Obviously, as my solicitor, he had to be told, and he'll help you with any and all legalities after I'm . . . er . . . when I'm no longer around."

"Yes," she said in the smallest of voices, and she clenched her hands together in her lap, wishing he would not keep alluding to his impending death.

"This has been a terrible burden for you to carry alone, Sandy," Anthony said a short while later.

Emily and Paula had left together, and the two men were finishing their drinks in the drawing room before going out to dinner.

Looking across at his cousin intently, the Earl added, "You ought to have told me before, you know."

"Perhaps I should have," Alexander admitted. "But to be honest, *I* had to come to grips with my illness first. As I explained earlier, I went through any number of different emotions—disbelief, anger, frustration, and acceptance. Then the fury came back, and the frustration, and the sense of total *helplessness.* I was on an emotional seesaw for the longest time, and naturally it was impossible for me to confide in anyone until I could handle myself properly. And, of course, I did want to pursue every avenue, look for a cure, if there was one to be found. I soon discovered there was absolutely nothing I could do except take the treatment and seize a bit of borrowed time."

Alexander smiled faintly, shrugged. "I am resigned to it now, Anthony, and completely in control. That is why I was finally able to tell you tonight. And now that that ordeal is over, I can relax, get on with my life for the next few months. I aim to make the most of it . . ."

"Yes," Anthony said, then discovered he could not go on. He took a quick sip of his scotch. What a bloody waste, he thought, and asked himself if he would have been able to handle himself with the same kind of courage and grace his cousin was displaying if he had been in similar circumstances. He was not sure. It took an awful lot of character to cope with one's own imminent death with such extraordinary stoicism.

Alexander said, "Come on, Anthony, don't look so morose. And please don't start getting maudlin on me. I couldn't cope . . . I had a difficult time dealing with Emily's emotion this evening. I realize how rough it is on all of you . . . but it's not quite as rough as it is on me."

"So sorry. Do forgive me, old chap."

"Nothing to forgive . . . I want everything to be as normal as possible. That makes it so much easier for me. I must now endeavor to ignore my illness, go about my business as best I can, and in the most controlled manner. Otherwise it'll be pure hell."

"You will come to Clonloughlin, won't you?"

"Yes, in about two weeks' time."

"Marvelous. Sally and I will enjoy having you. How long do you think you can stay?"

"Ten days, two weeks perhaps." Alexander swallowed the last of his wine, put the glass down on the end table near the fireplace. "I've booked a table at Mark's Club for nine o'clock. Perhaps we should stroll down there shortly, have a drink in the bar—"

Alexander rose at the sound of the phone ringing in the library which adjoined the drawing room. "Excuse me," he said as he hurried to answer it. He returned a second later. "It's for you, Anthony . . . Sally calling from Ireland."

"Oh yes, I expected to hear from her. Thanks."

"Don't tell her anything now. Not over the phone," Sandy instructed.

"I wouldn't dream of it," Anthony reassured him as he strode across the floor, went through the double mahogany doors and into the library.

Left alone, Alexander sat down on one of the sofas and closed his eyes. The last couple of hours had been trying, had vitiated his energy. Even though the others had striven hard not to display their feelings, to be brave, they *had* been terribly upset. As he had known they would be. That was why he had so dreaded telling them. He had only managed to get through the ordeal of breaking his bad news by being utterly detached and matter of fact.

He accepted his death with equanimity now, had come to terms with his fate. And in so doing he had been able to confide in those closest to him, because he could help *them* to do exactly the same thing. It was going to be hardest on Emily, of course. They had been as close as two peas in a pod when they were growing up. They had relied on each other in a certain sense. Their mother had been so flighty in those days, running from man to man and marrying all sorts of disreputable characters. And their sweet but weak-willed father, crushed by the burden of his broken heart, had scarcely seemed aware of their existence. Alexander sighed under his breath. What a catastrophe his father's life had been. And his mother's, too. But wasn't life itself a catastrophe?

Alexander instantly let go of this thought, not wanting to sink into deep philosophical ruminations this evening, as he had been so wont to do of late. Grandy wouldn't approve, he said to himself and smiled, remembering Emma Harte. How invincible *she* had been, and right up to the end. Life for her had been a triumph. So much for *his* theories . . . but then perhaps life *was* rooted in doom and tragedy for some.

Opening his eyes, Alexander glanced around the room, blinking. It looked beautiful tonight in the glow of the lamps and the warming firelight. Maggie had decorated this room just after their marriage, and he always thought of it as a bit of English spring, whatever the time of year, with its primrose and daffodil yellows, pale blues and greens. Whenever it needed redoing, he simply had the scheme repeated. He had been doing so since her death . . .

His cousin interrupted his musings when he said, "I say, Sandy, are you all right?" Anthony hovered over him, looking concerned.

Alexander pushed himself upright on the sofa. "Yes, I'm fine. I was re-couping . . . the last few hours have been a little wearing."

"Of course they have. Come on, let's go to Mark's."

Within the space of ten minutes the two cousins were leaving Alexander's house in Chesterfield Hill and heading for Charles Street where the club was located.

It was a chilly night and windy, and Alexander hunched further into his overcoat, shoved his hands in his pockets, shivering slightly. "Anyway, how was Sally?" he asked, falling into step with Anthony.

"Wonderful, as usual. She sends her love. I told her you were coming to stay . . . but that's all I said."

"Quite."

They walked on in silence. Suddenly Anthony remarked, as if to himself, "There was something odd though . . ."

"Oh, in what sense?" Alexander asked, looking at him curiously.

"Sally told me that Bridget has been pestering her . . . wanting to know when I'm returning to Clonloughlin. According to Sally she seems rather anxious to talk to me. In fact, Sally said she seemed a trifle agitated today."

"That *is* odd. On the other hand, I have always found your housekeeper to be somewhat eccentric, if you don't mind me saying so."

"Have you really? Mmmm. Perhaps she is . . . and a bit fey too, like most of the Irish. Well, it can't be anything important," Anthony finished as they crossed Charles Street in the direction of the club.

But he was wrong. Events that had happened a decade ago were about to come back to haunt him.

——— *Twenty-Nine* ———

It was raining at Clonloughlin the first morning Anthony was back, and there was a faint mist that softened the dark skeletal trees and the tall chimneys of the house etched so starkly against the leaden sky.

As he walked up the central path carved out between wide lawns he thought how lovely it looked even on this bleak winter's day, with its symmetrical, harmonic proportions, soaring windows, and the four white Palladian pillars supporting the front portico. Georgian in origin, it was a stately looking mansion situated on a small rise in the middle of a splendid park, with excellent views from its many windows. There were three hundred and sixty-five of them altogether, one for each day of the year, a fine madness on the part of his ancestor, who had built the house in the eighteenth century. But it was a madness that Anthony had always secretly applauded. The many windows were unique, gave the exteriors a certain gracefulness, opened up the interiors to the pastoral landscape, filled those beautiful rooms with light and air the whole year round and hazy sunshine in the summer months.

Anthony loved Clonloughlin with a fierce and abiding passion. It was his ancestral home and the only place he had ever wanted to live. He had been born here forty-five years ago and he would die here when his time came. And his son Jeremy would continue in his place, the Standish line unbroken as it had been for centuries.

His mind swung to Alexander and a rush of sadness engulfed him as it had last night when he had been talking to Sally. Although she had met him at Cork Airport, he had resisted giving her the grave news about Sandy on their drive home. He had not even told her when they finally reached Clonloughlin, had waited instead until they were in the privacy of their bedroom suite.

Sally had been dreadfully upset once she had heard the stark facts about Sandy's illness. She had wept and he had comforted her. And then, to cheer themselves up and trying to be as positive as possible, they had made extensive plans for Sandy's stay with them after he left the hospital. But later, when Sally had fallen asleep in his arms, her cheeks had been tear-stained once again. She and her brother Winston had grown up in Yorkshire with Sandy and Emily. They had been unusually close, and Sandy was one of the godfathers to Giles, their nine-year-old son.

Anthony now veered to the left as he drew nearer to the house, and went around to the other side, entered through the back door. Inside the small indoor porch he shed his barbour and tweed cap, which were both drenched with rain, hanging the oilskin and the hat on the coat stand to drip. Seating himself on the wooden chair, he pulled off his green Wellington boots, slipped into a pair of brown loafers, then hurried down the back passageway to the library.

The house was very quiet.

It was early, only seven, and Sally was still asleep, as were the younger children on the nursery floor. Settling himself at the desk near the window, he pulled a pile of correspondence toward him, began to sort through the mail that had accumulated in the week he had been in London on business.

He did not hear the housekeeper come into the room until she spoke.

"Good morning, your lordship," said Bridget O'Donnell. "I didn't expect you to be up so early after your late arrival last night. Excuse me for not having the fire going in here."

"Ah, good morning, Bridget," Anthony said with a quick smile as he looked up. "It's not a problem. I'm not cold."

"The kettle's boiling. I'll just be putting a match to the fire, and then I'll be back with your pot of tea and toast."

"Thank you," he murmured, glanced down at the papers, wondering whether to ask her what it was she wished to discuss with him, then decided against it. Far better to wait until he had been fortified by his light breakfast. Bridget had a tendency to be garrulous at times, which required an enormous amount of patience on his part. He was not in the mood for her this morning.

He heard matches being struck, a faint *whoosh* as the paper and wood chips ignited and flames flew up the wide chimney back. Then there was the sound of bellows being pumped, the scraping of metal against stone as she placed the guard around the fire and finally departed to the kitchen.

Anthony reached for the letter addressed to him in his son's handwriting. Jeremy had only just returned to boarding school after the Christmas holidays, and as he slit open the envelope he wondered what his eldest son and heir had to say to him. There would be a request for cash, no doubt. Eleven-year-old schoolboys were forever hard up. He smiled. Jeremy was exactly as he had been at the same age. But the boy worried him at times. Jem was not strong physically, did not have the robust health of his brother, Giles, and his sister, India, and Anthony had to constantly resist the temptation to mollycoddle him, as did Sally.

Anthony scanned the letter quickly. It was, as usual, a sketchy, imprecise report of Jeremy's activities over the last few days since he had been back at school, with a postscript, underscored, to *please send money urgently, please, Daddy, please.*

Bridget came sailing in with the breakfast tray sooner than he had expected, and Anthony put the letter down as she approached.

"Where would you like this, your lordship?"

"You can put it here on the desk," he answered her, pushing aside the papers he had been perusing a moment before.

She did so, then went around to the other side of the large partners' desk, stood looking at him.

Lifting the teapot, he poured tea into the oversized breakfast cup, added milk, then glanced at her. "Yes, what is it, Bridget?"

"I've got to talk to you, Lord Dunvale. About something important."

"Now?"

"Yes, sir, I think so . . . I'd like to get it out of the way . . . this morning."

Anthony smothered a sigh. "All right." He spread his favorite thick-cut Frank Cooper marmalade onto the buttered toast, crunched on it, took a sip of tea. When the housekeeper was silent, he said, "Go on, Bridget, get it off your chest. And don't hover there, you know I detest people who do that. Please, do sit down."

She lowered herself into the chair, sat facing him, twisted her hands together nervously in her lap, focused her dark blue eyes on him.

The Earl finished his slice of toast as he waited for her to begin. Finally he raised a brow.

Bridget said slowly, "I'm not quite sure how to tell you this," and stopped abruptly midsentence.

Anthony, who had his cup halfway to his mouth, put it down with a clatter, stared at her in alarm. This was the second time in the space of several days that someone had begun a sentence with those words. First Sandy, and now Bridget, and it seemed like a bad omen. "You really ought to be able to tell me anything, Bridget. After all, we've known each other since we were children."

The housekeeper nodded. "Well, your lordship . . . what I have to say . . . Well, it is about Lady Dunvale."

"Oh." He sounded surprised and his eyes narrowed.

"Not this Lady Dunvale. The first one."

"My mother?"

"No, no, not the Dowager Countess. Your first wife . . . that's who I mean . . . the Lady Minerva, sir."

Startled, Anthony sat back in his chair and gave Bridget a long, probing look. "What *about* the late Lady Dunvale?" he asked at last.

"It's . . . er . . . er . . . about her death."

For a moment he could not speak or move. Instinctively, he knew that something awful was about to be said, and he braced himself before muttering, "Is it important to discuss her death now . . . so long after the event?"

"Yes," Bridget said tersely.

"Why?" he probed, unable to resist the question, yet conversely not wanting to hear a word she had to say.

"Because I don't want it on my conscience anymore," Bridget replied. "I have to tell you what really happened . . . it's been a burden for me to carry, a nightmare still, even after all these years."

His mouth had gone very dry.

"It wasn't suicide like they said it was at the inquest."

He frowned, at first uncomprehending, not fully understanding her meaning. "Are you trying to tell me that Lady Dunvale fell into the lake, that she had an *accident,* as I've always maintained? That she didn't take her own life?"

"No, she didn't, she—" Bridget cut herself off, pursed her lips, then muttered, "She was *put there.*"

"By whom?" His voice was barely audible.

"Michael Lamont. They had a quarrel that fateful Saturday night, those two did, and he struck her. She fell, hit her face on the brass fender in his living room. If you remember, she did have a bruise on her face. The pathologist and Doctor Brennan mentioned it at the inquest. Well anyway, Lamont couldn't revive her. She appeared to be unconscious. Within seconds he realized she was actually dead. He said she'd had a heart attack or something. All that liquor she had drunk continually through the afternoon and evening, the tranquilizers she was forever swallowing . . . the combination killed her, he said. So Lamont took her and put her in the lake to cover everything up, and the next morning he drove past, pretended to have found her body . . . then he came up to the mansion to tell you there had been an accident, and he sent for the police and no one ever suspected *him* of being involved in any way. But they did suspect you, though. At least, Sergeant McNamara did."

Events that had happened over a decade ago came rushing back to hit Anthony between the eyes, and he remembered every tiny detail with great vividness and clarity. He felt as if he had been kicked several times in the stomach, and he began to tremble all over, clasped his hands together to stop them from shaking, took several deep steadying breaths. He said at last, "And how do you know all this, Bridget?"

"I had seen her ladyship that afternoon, when she had driven over to Clonloughlin from Waterford. You know she came to the estate quite a lot, even though you had forbidden her to do so and were in the middle of the divorce. But Lady Min couldn't stay away, she loved Clonloughlin so much. She often came to see me. And *him*. We had tea together that afternoon, and she drove off around five, told me she was going down to the lake . . . she'd always been drawn to the lough, even when she was a small girl. Don't you remember the picnics the three of us used to have there when we were children? In any case, sir, you saw her little red car at the edge of the lake, after your Land-Rover had stalled, and you'd decided to walk home, taking the long way round in order to avoid her. And her ladyship also took a walk . . . over to Michael Lamont's house. She'd told me she was going to have dinner with him, but explained that she wouldn't be staying the night. You see, your lordship, they were—"

Bridget took a gulp of air, rushed on in breathless haste, the words pouring out of her, "They were having an affair. Lady Min had told me she would come by the kitchen at ten-thirty to say goodnight to me. She never *ever* left Clonloughlin without doing that. When she hadn't arrived by eleven-thirty, I got worried, so I went down to Lamont's house looking for her."

Bridget paused and her face crumpled and she almost broke down. She was suddenly thinking of their childhood, remembering how close they had been . . . she and Lady Minerva Glendenning, daughter of the Earl of Rothmerrion and the young Lord Anthony Standish, now the Earl of Dunvale. So long ago. And yet those days were as clear to her as yesterday, and they had been the best part of her life.

Watching her, Anthony saw the distress on Bridget's face, the anguish in her eyes, and he was about to make a sympathetic gesture toward her, but inexplicably changed his mind. He said, a trifle harshly, "Continue, Bridget, tell me everything. *I must know.*"

She nodded, swallowed. "When I got to Lamont's door, it was locked and the curtains were drawn, but I could hear them. Screaming at each other like banshees they were, saying horrible things, vile they were, and her ladyship . . . well, she sounded very drunk. Out of control. And then suddenly everything was quiet. There was absolute silence. I was frightened. I banged hard on the door, called out that it was me, and Michael let me in. He had no option, did he. Besides, he knew how close I was to Lady Min. When I saw her lying on the floor, my heart stopped. I ran to her, tried to revive her. But she was gone. It was then that Lamont dreamed up the idea of putting her in the lake, so as to make it look as if she had drowned herself. You see, he didn't want you to know that he'd been sleeping with Lady Min for all those years. He was afraid you'd sack him if you found out. He couldn't afford to lose his job. And even though he hadn't had a hand in Lady Min's death, it might have *looked* as if he had. That's what he said to me, your lordship. And he kept repeating it, over and over again, and he told me that circumstantial evidence can be very damning."

Anthony was appalled and outraged. "Why in God's name didn't you come up to the mansion to get me?" he demanded furiously, his voice rising in anger and disgust. "Why did you go along with Lamont?"

Bridget compressed her lips, said nothing.

He saw the stubborn set of her jaw, the defiance in the ice-blue eyes and he knew he was wasting his breath. She had been independent and difficult as a child; she had changed little over the years. If she did not want to confide her reasons for her silence at the time of Min's death, and for so many years after, then nothing could drag it out of her.

Sitting back in the chair, he studied her thoughtfully, trying to still his rage, the urge to shake her violently. And then suddenly a terrible thought occurred to him, one so unacceptable he tried to squash it, was barely able to face it. But he found himself saying carefully and with great deliberation, "Why were you so sure Lady Min was actually dead?" He leaned forward, fixed his probing, steely eyes on her. "Lady Min may only have been *unconscious,* Bridget. In which case, Michael Lamont did murder her if he put her in the lough whilst she was still alive."

"No, no, she was dead, I know she was dead!" Bridget cried excitedly, her eyes wide and flaring. "I know she was dead!" she insisted, verging on hysteria.

"Do you not recall the pathologist's report? Doctor Stephen Kenmarr said that when he did the autopsy he discovered an excessive amount of alcohol and barbiturates in her bloodstream and a quantity of water in her lungs. This led him to conclude that her death had been by drowning. And since her lungs were full of water, she could not have been dead when she was placed in the lake. I don't believe a dead body can take in water."

As the implications of his words sank in, Bridget paled. She had loved Minerva like a sister, had mothered her from the first moment she had set eyes on her as a child.

"No!" Bridget shouted. "She wasn't alive. She was dead. I would never have harmed *her.* I loved her. I loved her. You know I did. The water must have somehow seeped into her lungs afterward."

Anthony wondered if this was actually possible. He decided it might be, depending on the length of time Min had been dead before she had been submerged in the lake. He rubbed his forehead wearily, looked across at the housekeeper, asked in a quiet, very controlled voice, "Was her body still warm when Lamont took her out to the lake?"

Bridget nodded, not able to speak, shaken by the Earl's horrifying suggestion.

"Rigor mortis doesn't set in for about two to four hours after death. I suppose she might have been able to take water into her lungs for a short time after she died. Maybe for half an hour. But no longer, I'm absolutely sure of that. Still, only a pathologist could give me a truly accurate answer," Anthony said softly, almost to himself, as if thinking aloud.

Bridget stared at him, twisted her hands in her lap.

There was a long and deadly silence. The strain between them was a most palpable thing; it hung heavy in the air.

Eventually the Earl spoke. Pinning his eyes on the housekeeper, he said, "Why did you suddenly decide to speak up, to confide in me now, after so many years? Tell me that, Bridget O'Donnell?"

Bridget cried, "But I already told you . . . I couldn't have it on my conscience any longer . . . I mean about you not knowing the truth, not knowing the real circumstances of Lady Min's death. I realized how much it troubled you . . . the idea that she had committed suicide while the balance of her mind was disturbed. You'd blamed yourself for years, blamed her death on your decision to leave her and get a divorce. And I was sure you believed your relationship with your cousin Miss Sally Harte had been a contributing factor in your wife's death."

Anthony flinched. There was a certain truth in all this.

Bridget gave Anthony a hard stare. "I wanted to put your mind at rest, your lordship," she finished.

Like hell you did, Anthony thought, not for one moment believing her. And then, in a flash of sudden insight, he understood. There was no question in his mind that Bridget had been having an affair with Michael Lamont. But Lamont was leaving Clonloughlin in a few days and he was never coming back. He was going to America to work for Mrs. Alma Berringer, the young American widow who had recently returned to her horse farm in Virginia after renting Rothermerrion Lodge for the past year. Lamont and Mrs. Berringer had been friendly, but Anthony had not realized just how intimate they had become until Lamont had given his notice a month ago, announcing that he was moving to the States.

Anthony rose, walked over to the huge stone fireplace, picked up the poker, and stirred the logs. His expression was ruminative. He was convinced he was right. Slowly he spun around, stood facing Bridget, studying her with infinite care. Never really pretty, she had, however, been arresting when she was younger, with her blazing red hair and milk white skin and cornflower blue eyes. Her striking coloring and long legs and lissome figure had always caught men's attention. But sadly she had not aged well. The red hair was a faded salt-and-pepper auburn rapidly turning gray, her figure had lost its willowy appeal. Only those bright blue eyes remained unchanged, vivid, and youthful. And very calculating, he decided. Yes, Bridget O'Donnell was always manipulative and devious even when she was a child. And oh, how she had dominated poor Min. Odd that he had never realized this until now.

"There's an old saying, Bridget," Anthony remarked in an icy, contained voice. "Hell hath no fury like a woman scorned."

"I'm sorry, sir, but I'm not following you."

"You're in love with him. You've always loved him since the first day he came to run the estate for me. That's why you helped him, protected him since my wife's death. And after she was dead, *you* became involved with him. And now, because he's leaving you, going off, chasing after another woman, you want your revenge. You're sticking the knife between Michael Lamont's shoulder blades with a real vengeance, aren't you? That's what all this is about, isn't it?"

She stared him down. "No," she said flatly. "It isn't. I simply wanted to put your mind at rest. I didn't want you to blame yourself for Lady Min's death."

"But I don't," Anthony said coldly, in all truthfulness, "and I haven't for years. You're pointing a finger at Lamont because he's found somebody younger and prettier than you. Let's face it, Bridget, your lover has passed you over."

At these words she flushed deeply, looked down at her hands.

Anthony knew his words had struck home.

After a moment, she asked in a low, subdued voice, "What are you going to do about Michael Lamont? Are you going to have it out with him?"

Anthony looked at her with steadiness for several seconds, then slowly walked across the floor, resumed his position behind his desk. He leaned over it, looked deeply into those blue eyes so warily returning his penetrating gaze.

"Obviously I shall confront Lamont. The facts you have given me cannot be ignored. As you know they cannot. That's why you told me in the first place." There was a small pause before he said, "However, I may also go to the police and open up the investigation into my wife's death again. And I wonder, Bridget, if it's ever occurred to you that you helped to tamper with evidence in a sudden and questionable death. And that you perjured yourself under oath. Also, if my first wife *was* alive when Michael Lamont put her in the lake, then you are also an accessory after the fact. *An accessory to murder.*"

Once Bridget had returned to the kitchen, Anthony made a telephone call to Cork. It lasted for ten minutes and mostly he listened. When he quietly put the receiver back in the cradle, his face was white and his expression was grim.

Glancing at the clock on the mantle, he rose to his feet, left the library, and went down the passageway to the indoor porch. After putting on his Wellingtons and his barbour, he took his tweed cap off the coat stand and went outside.

He looked up. It had stopped raining, but the sky was still overcast and a light mist persisted. Walking at a brisk pace, he took the path which led to Michael Lamont's house. It was just a few yards away from the lake, set back against a copse of trees next to a field. When he reached the front door, he barged inside without knocking, strode through the hall, across the living room, and into the adjoining office.

Lamont, a dark-haired, heavy-set, but good-looking man, was seated behind the desk, entering figures in a large estate ledger. He looked up in surprise as the door was flung open unceremoniously and a gust of air caused the papers on his desk to flutter and lift.

"Good morning, Lord Dunvale," he said pleasantly, his weatherbeaten face breaking into a smile. And then the smile vanished as he became aware of Anthony's dire expression, his angry stance.

"Is something wrong?" Lamont asked, rising.

Anthony did not at first reply. He stepped into the room, closed the heavy oak door behind him firmly, leaned against it. He studied the estate manager through icy eyes. Lamont had worked for him for almost twenty years, and he suddenly wondered what in God's name made him tick. Anthony had always believed he knew Lamont inside out; apparently he had not known him at all. He had considered him to be a trustworthy and devoted employee and a good friend. Now he was filled with loathing for him.

At last Anthony said, "Bridget had rather a strange tale to tell earlier this morning. About the late Lady Dunvale's death."

Taken by surprise and off guard, Lamont gaped at him, opened his mouth to speak, then closed it. He walked away from the desk swiftly, moved to the far end of the room, hovered near the fireplace, wanting to put distance between himself and Anthony. Reaching for a cigarette, he lit it, then pivoted to look at the Earl.

Lamont's expression was one of uncertainty and his dark brown eyes flickered with apprehension. "What exactly are you getting at?" he asked finally.

"Bridget told me everything, confided every little detail about what happened here in this house that tragic evening." Anthony stepped forward, drew closer to the estate manager, let his eyes rest on him for the longest moment.

Lamont flinched under this intense and unwavering scrutiny. Blinking, he eventually glanced away, took a long drag on his cigarette, inhaling deeply.

"How could you be so certain Min was dead after she collapsed?" Anthony demanded in a hard voice. "You're not a doctor, Lamont."

Lamont's face turned brilliant red, and he cried out angrily, "She *was* dead! I'm telling you, she was dead!" Unexpectedly he began to cough, excessively so, and it took him a few minutes to recover. When he finally caught his breath, he added, "I might not be a doctor, but I do know when somebody has stopped breathing." He puffed on the cigarette again and then, with nervous intensity, exclaimed in a shaky voice, "I tried to revive her, to breathe life into her with mouth-to-mouth resuscitation, but she was gone. I loved Min. Which is more than you ever did."

Anthony took another step forward. His hands were clenched tightly at his sides, his knuckles shining white in the pale morning light. He wanted to ram his fist into Lamont's red, boozy face, smash it to a pulp until it was unrecognizable. But he resisted the impulse, hung on to his self-possession with a masterful control.

"You don't know the meaning of the word 'love,' Lamont. You're a philandering, double-dealing bastard and a menace to any decent woman."

"*You* talk to *me* about philandering. What about you!" Lamont snorted. "Certainly you drove Minerva into my arms with your constant womanizing and years of neglect."

Anthony held himself taut. He was once more afraid that he might do Lamont bodily harm. He said slowly, "Why didn't you come for me when my wife collapsed? Or at least call a doctor? Why did you take matters into your own hands? Your behavior was unconscionable and nothing short of reckless."

Michael Lamont was not the most brilliant of men, but he had sufficient native shrewdness to recognize that Bridget O'Donnell had done her work well. He decided there was no point in lying, and so he spoke the absolute truth when he mumbled, "I was afraid. Afraid that once you knew what had been going on between us you'd get rid of me. I couldn't lose my job. It also occurred to me that you might blame me for her death. Circumstantial evidence has condemned more than one innocent man. Don't you see," he finished in a whining tone, "I had no choice, I *had* to cover everything up."

Disgust and revulsion swamped Anthony as he continued to observe the estate manager with a steely gaze. "I wonder how you've been able to look me in the eye all these years, knowing the terrible things you did, knowing how you lied to everyone to protect your own skin. You're despicable, Lamont. Monstrous.''

Lamont did not respond. How stupid he had been not to leave Clonloughlin years ago. He had stayed because of Bridget O'Donnell, the terrible hold she had over him. He had never really trusted her. Apparently he had been right not to do so. When their long relationship had ended by mutual consent, he had believed himself to be finally free of her. There had been no rancorous feelings on her part, or so he had thought. He had been wrong. The minute he had taken up with another woman, she had struck out at him like a viper, wanting to destroy him. She had succeeded.

"I ache to give you the biggest thrashing of your life,'' Anthony was saying. "But I'm not going to lay a finger on you. I shall let the law do my work for me.''

Lamont started, drawn out of his thoughts. He peered at Anthony. *"What? What are you saying?''*

"I fully intend to reopen the investigation into my wife's death. I believe you killed Lady Dunvale. And I aim to see that you pay for it,'' Anthony said with cold deliberation.

"You're mad, stark raving mad!'' Lamont shouted, his dark eyes popping out of his face, his expression one of sudden fear. "You don't know what you're talking about, Dunvale. Min poisoned her system with all that muck she was forever swallowing. She died within a few minutes of collapsing.''

"That's where you're quite wrong,'' Anthony said in a voice that was murderously soft. "She was in a deeply unconscious state, which was indeed induced by excessive amounts of alcohol and barbiturates. But when you placed her in the lake, she was very much alive, and—''

"I don't believe you! You're lying! Inventing all this!''

"I am not!'' Anthony shot back with ferocity. "When Bridget confided in me this morning, I was not absolutely sure about certain medical facts! So I telephoned Forensic at the hospital in Cork, where I located Doctor Stephen Kenmarr. The pathologist who did the autopsy on Min's body, who discovered her lungs were full of water and testified at the inquest that she had died of drowning.''

Anthony paused, finished emphatically and very slowly, as if to give added weight to his words, "Doctor Kenmarr confirmed to me what I already suspected . . . *that water cannot be inhaled by a person who is dead.* Therefore, Min was alive when you placed her in the lake. You drowned her.''

Michael Lamont felt his hackles rising, and he was so shocked, so stunned by Anthony's dreadful accusation he could barely stand. He swayed slightly on his feet, reached out, supported himself against the mantelpiece. The idea that he might have actually caused Min's death struck horror in him, and he was reeling. Over the years he had suffered greatly, had been haunted by his deceit, the lies he had told, the cover-up he had wrought, and he had never stopped wrestling with his guilt and his conscience.

Now he cried out in protest, "No, Dunvale, no! She had no pulse, no heartbeat!'' He choked on his words and tears came into his eyes and he broke down completely. "I could not have done anything to hurt her,'' he sobbed. "I loved her. Talk to Bridget again. *Please. Please.* She'll verify that I'm telling the truth. Min was dead . . . and Bridget O'Donnell knows that she was.''

"She was alive, Lamont!''

"No! No!" Demented, Lamont rushed at Anthony, his arms flailing in the air, his face apoplectic. He felt a sudden and excruciating pain shoot across his temple and along the side of his face, but he did not let it slow him down. He lunged at Anthony. As he did, another searing pain blinded him. The blood rushed to his head and everything went black. He fell sprawling to the floor and then was still.

Startled, Anthony stood looking down at him, momentarily rooted to the spot, unable to move. He had noticed the sudden and dreadful change when Lamont had rushed toward him, had instantly realized that the other man was having some sort of seizure.

Pulling himself together, Anthony bent down, felt Lamont's pulse. It was erratic, faint, but it *was* there.

Hurrying to the telephone, Anthony dialed the cottage hospital in the village of Clonloughlin.

"Dunvale here," he said to the duty nurse when she answered. "Could you please send an ambulance immediately. To the estate manager's house. Michael Lamont has just had a stroke, I think. But he's still alive. If you hurry, we can probably save him."

To see justice done, Anthony thought as he hung up.

Thirty

"I've really got to take it over!" Paula exclaimed, tightening her grip on Michael Kallinski's arm. "It would be nothing short of criminal if I let it slip through my fingers."

"Yes, I know it would." Michael looked at her through the corner of his eye. "Six hundred and fifty million dollars is a hell of a lot of money, though."

"That's true, it is. On the other hand, it isn't *really*, not if you consider what I'm actually buying. A chain of department stores that has a fine reputation, great prestige, with invaluable real estate assets and a balance sheet that's in the black. And it's a perfect chain for me, Michael. Thanks so much for bringing it to my attention." She leaned closer, added in an emphatic tone tinged with excitement, "Larson's locations couldn't be better for me if I'd hand-picked them myself. Westchester, Philadelphia, and Boston cover the Eastern Seaboard. Chicago and Detroit the Midwest. Los Angeles and San Francisco the West Coast. It's a deal made in heaven, as far as I'm concerned."

"If you make a deal."

Paula gave him a hard stare. "Is there a chance I might not?" she asked, her voice instantly changing, rising slightly in sudden concern.

"I suppose there's always that chance, Paula.

"But I don't think you have too much to worry about in this particular situation. As far as I know, there's no one else after the company, and I understand from Harvey in New York that the chairman of the board is willing to start talking, to open negotiations whenever you're ready. And what Millard Larson says goes, since he's the majority stockholder as well as C.E.O. If I were you, I'd make plans to fly to New York as soon as possible."

"I agree with you, and I want to go. But I can't . . . at least not for two weeks. Lorne and Tessa are both coming home from their schools tomorrow. It's the Easter break. I just can't be away right now."

"Oh God, I had forgotten about Easter! I have the same problem as you, I'm afraid, so I'll have to stay put, too."

"Oh." Puzzled, she frowned, asked, "Are you planning a trip to the States, Michael?"

"I thought I should be there in case you need me," he explained, his voice vibrant with enthusiasm, his face lighting up. "After all, I'm the one who introduced you to Harvey Rawson, found the Larson chain for you, set everything in motion." He gave her a small, confiding smile. "Besides, I have to be in New York on business sometime this month, and if I go when you're going I can kill two birds with one stone, so to speak." When she did not initially respond, he asked, "What do you think?"

"Well . . . yes . . . I suppose so." She realized how hesitant she sounded and rapidly nodded her head. "Yes, yes, why not," she added in a more positive tone.

"Good, it's settled then," he exclaimed, looking delighted, congratulating himself on his adroit little maneuver. The thought of being alone with her in New York excited him. But he said in the most neutral voice, "Now we'd better concentrate on Dad's exhibition. He's been giving us peculiar looks for the last ten minutes. I have a feeling he's a bit miffed."

Paula laughed. "I'm sure he is. We have been rather rude, standing here in the middle of the floor deep in conversation. Not only ignoring him and everyone else, but all these priceless art treasures as well. Come on, we must go and join him at once. He wants to show me around the exhibition himself, tell me about each piece of Fabergé he owns. And I must admit, I am rather staggered by all this. His collection is much larger than I ever imagined it to be."

"Not every piece on display belongs to him," Michael was quick to point out. "The Queen and the Queen Mum have loaned some of their Fabergé objects, as have Kenneth Snowman, the great British expert on Peter Carl Fabergé, and Malcolm Forbes, who's another avid collector like Dad."

"I know. Your father explained. Still, he does have a superb collection."

"I'll say. And it's given him a truly consuming interest other than business these last few years."

They moved together down the long salon, one of two in the Royal Academy of Art at Burlington House where the reception for the opening of the Fabergé exhibition was in full swing on this April evening. The event had been organized by Sir Ronald Kallinski to benefit one of his favorite charities, and the gallery was packed.

A waiter drew to a standstill in front of them.

Michael took two glasses of champagne from the silver tray being proffered, murmured his thanks, and handed a flute of Dom Pérignon to Paula.

When Sir Ronald spotted them coming toward him, he extracted himself from a small group of people and hurried to meet them.

"I know you two are committed to business and rarely think of anything else, but do you really have to have a confab during my reception?" he asked, obviously quite put out. But then his eyes became warm with affection and twinkled brightly as he took Paula's arm and led her along the gallery, his irritation instantly forgotten.

"Now, my dear," he said, "let me take you around. I have many new acquisitions, none of which you have seen. Neither have you, Michael," he added, glancing over his shoulder at his son.

"I've been looking forward to this for weeks," Michael replied in all sincerity. "And I'm sorry we got caught up with our business discussion the way we did. My apologies, Dad."

"Accepted, accepted, my boy," Sir Ronald answered briskly, striding down the salon with Paula, Michael dutifully in tow. Suddenly he came to a stop in front of a display case.

Turning to Paula, he said, "This is not one of my pieces. Sadly, I might add. It was graciously lent for the exhibition by Her Majesty the Queen. And it happens to be a particular favorite of mine. It's called the Mosaic Egg, and I think it's perhaps the most poignant of all the Imperial Easter Eggs. It was presented to Czarina Alexandra Feodorovna by Nicholas II on Easter morning of 1914. As you can see, it's a gossamer platinum shell which has been 'embroidered' with flowers made of precious stones . . . rubies, sapphires, diamonds, and emeralds, the whole encircled with bands of pearls. And look, there on the little gold stand are the miniature sepia profiles of the Imperial children."

"It's exquisite," Paula said admiringly, leaning forward, peering at the egg. "And the stand is concealed inside the egg, isn't it, when not on display?"

"Correct." Sir Ronald took her arm, and the three of them progressed down the gallery slowly, pausing to admire other treasures in the show. "That's the beauty and genius of the Fabergé objects of art," he went on, "those extraordinary and very often magical surprises contained within the egg itself. Like that dazzling little golden chanticleer which emerges from the translucent blue-enameled Imperial Easter Egg your grandmother once owned," Sir Ronald reminded her, smiling.

Paula smiled back at him. "Oh yes, that egg is the most beautiful—at least that's what I think, Uncle Ronnie. And I'm glad it's in your collection, that you won it at the auction. At least it's still in the clans."

He chuckled. "I don't think I'll ever forget that day at Sotheby's. There was such competitive bidding for the egg. But it was exciting. And gratifying when I suddenly realized *I* owned it. Naturally it's on display tonight. Let's go and have a look at it, and then we can go through into the other salon. There are more breathtaking examples of Fabergé masterpieces, which were made for the Imperial family before the Romanov dynasty came to its tragic end."

"I didn't know Amanda was coming to the exhibition!" Michael exclaimed in surprise a short while later, when he spotted her standing in the doorway, glancing around, obviously looking for them.

"Oh, I forgot to tell you," Paula murmured. "I sent her a ticket and she said she would do her best to make it."

"I'll go and get her, bring her over to join us," Michael said, hurrying across the room.

Paula's eyes followed him and she smiled to herself, then looked at his father and winked.

Sir Ronald regarded her closely for a moment, then said slowly, "I'm not wrong in thinking you're playing *shadchan,* am I, Paula? *Matchmaking?*"

"And why not?" she answered, laughing. "Anyway, she has such a crush on him . . . wouldn't it be lovely if Michael reciprocated her feelings, Uncle Ronnie?"

Sir Ronald seemed initially startled, then suddenly pleased, and he nodded. "It would indeed. Amanda's a lovely young woman. Clever, too. Emily and Alexander have trained her well. She's certainly made our takeover of Lady Hamilton Clothes very smooth. But of course you know that, my dear. As I was telling Emily the other day, my people are terribly impressed with her. We're all sorry she won't be staying on to run the company for us. Emily explained she's needed at Harte Enterprises and I do understand that. Still—" He cut himself short, and a look of infinite sadness crossed his face fleetingly.

Paula was aware that he was thinking of Alexander, who had taken Uncle Ronnie into his confidence. She experienced a rush of sadness herself. Sandy had retired at the beginning of March, and now Emily was chairman of the board and chief executive officer. Amanda had moved over to become head of Genret, whilst Winston continued to run his own division, the Yorkshire Consolidated Newspaper Company and its subsidiaries, of which he was a part owner. They had become a close-knit triumvirate, and Harte Enterprises was running as efficiently as it always had, but Paula knew that they missed Alexander terribly. She missed him herself now that he was living quietly at Nutton Priory, although they did speak quite a lot on the telephone.

"Hello, darling," Paula said, greeting Amanda warmly as she and Michael joined them. "You look stunning."

"Thank you, Paula," Amanda said, smiling at her cousin, pecking her on the cheek. "Hello, Uncle Ronnie. Sorry I'm late, but the traffic was ghastly tonight."

"That's all right, my dear," Sir Ronald said, taking her hand in his, giving her a quick kiss. "Now, Michael, do the honors, my boy, and get a glass of champagne for Amanda, would you please?"

"I certainly will. Be back in a jiffy."

Amanda turned to Paula, and it gave Sir Ronald a chance to study her surreptitiously, appraisingly, for a brief moment. Tall, slender, and blond, Amanda was a lovely looking young woman who bore a strong resemblance to her half-sister, Emily. Tonight she was wearing a smartly tailored red silk suit with a diamond Victorian bow broach pinned onto one lapel and antique diamond earrings. Chic but discreet, Sir Ronald thought, and very well bred. Suddenly he saw her through new eyes. As a potential daughter-in-law. The idea strongly appealed to him. Amanda was ideal for Michael, an intelligent, charming, and outgoing girl with perfect manners, like all of Emma's granddaughters. Just the sort of wife his son needed. The possibility that the Kallinski and Harte clans might finally be united in marriage thrilled him. He would encourage this friendship, as apparently Paula was intending to do. Yes, Amanda and Michael must become husband and wife. He would have a long chat with Paula later; together they would map out a plan of action. Michael needed to be gently guided into this relationship. His son tended to vacillate when it came to women. And he had been single far too long since his divorce.

——— *Thirty-One* ———

The garden was still her most magical place.

Ever since childhood Paula had found satisfaction and reward in planting and weeding, pruning and hoeing. Working outdoors was soothing to her—it never failed to put her in the best of moods.

Also, she had discovered long ago that she often did her best thinking in her gardens at Pennistone Royal, and today was no exception. It was a bright April afternoon, just after Easter, sunny and brisk with a light breeze and a powder-blue sky that was cool and cloudless.

As she worked on the new rockery she was creating, she focused her thoughts on business, in particular the Larson chain in the United States. The deal was already in the first stage of negotiation, and Millard Larson was expecting her in New York next week, when they would sit down at the conference table and hammer out the terms and conditions of the sale.

When she had first had the idea of expanding her operations in the States, long before the possibility of Larson's had come up, she had made the decision to purchase any new retailing company that caught her eye with her own money.

Six hundred and fifty million dollars, she thought now, mulling the figure over in her mind whilst concentrating on the alpine plants she was sorting through. It *was* a lot of money, no doubt about that, and she had been wondering for several days which financial combination would work best for her.

Paula sighed under her breath. If her mother had agreed to sell the Sitex stock last year, her problem would have been solved. Under the terms and conditions of her grandfather's will, she and her brother Philip would automatically have received one third of the proceeds of that sale—hundreds of millions of dollars each. But her mother had refused to sell the oil stock and continued to be adamant about not doing so. Paula had acknowledged months ago that she would have to raise the necessary cash another way, once she found the right department store chain to buy.

She ran several possibilities through her mind, then dismissed each one as convoluted and complex, went back to her original idea. To her way of thinking, the best solution was to sell ten percent of her Harte shares which Emma had left her. They would realize between two hundred and three hundred million dollars on the market, but without making much of a dent in her holdings. She would still be the majority stockholder with forty-one percent, as well as chairman and chief executive officer of the Harte chain. The remainder of the money she could easily raise from the banks, by borrowing against the retail chain she was acquiring, pledging its assets, in particular its real estate holdings which were valuable.

Suddenly, after days of indecision, she made up her mind. She *would* do that. And she would put everything in motion at once. First thing on Monday morning when she got to her office in the Leeds store, she would speak to her stockbroker.

A bright smile broke through, expunging the worried and preoccupied expression she had worn all day, and she continued to smile to herself as she finished planting the small alpine species in the narrow crevices of the rocks.

"Mummy! Mummy!"

Paula lifted her head alertly at the sound of Patrick's voice. He and his sister, Linnet, were running as fast as their legs would carry them along the gravel path that sloped down from the long terrace at the back of Pennistone Royal.

They both wore sweaters and jeans under their duffel coats and mufflers, and she could not help thinking how healthy and fit they both looked today. Especially Patrick. That vacant expression which so often dulled his eyes was absent, as it had been for some weeks. This pleased her, raised her hopes that he was improving mentally, if only ever so slightly. She loved her sensitive, damaged, and beautiful child so very much.

"Patrick! Do be careful! You're going to fall!" she called out. "And you too, Linnet! Do slow down, both of you! I'm not going anywhere, you know." She rose as she spoke, picked up the basket full of her gardening tools, and carefully climbed down from the top of the clustered rocks.

Patrick hurled himself against her body, clinging to her, panting hard and trying to catch his breath.

She pushed his dark hair away from his temple and clucked quietly. "Dear, dear, you are a one, aren't you? Running so hard, I—"

"Puffed, Mummy," he interrupted her, raising his solemn little face to hers. "Linnet puffed too."

"I'm *not!*" Linnet protested fiercely, glaring.

Ignoring her, Patrick went on, "Horsey, Mummy. Patrick wants horsey."

Puzzled, Paula swung her eyes to her six-year-old daughter, as she so often did when Patrick spoke in riddles and she wanted edification. She gave Linnet a questioning stare.

Linnet explained, "The horse in the attic, Mummy. That's what Patrick wants. I said he couldn't take it, not without asking Daddy. And Daddy said to ask you."

"Horse in the attic. What on earth are you talking about, darling?"

"The cresel horse . . . the one that goes round and round and around and round. To the music, Mummy."

"The carousel, the horse on the carousel. Now I understand." Paula smiled at them both. "But I don't remember there being a carousel in the attic. I suppose it must be, since you've apparently seen it."

"It's in a trunk," Linnet rushed on excitedly. "We saw it just now. Daddy let us play in the attic after our walk this afternoon."

"Did he now." Paula pulled off her gardening gloves, threw them on top of the basket, and, taking a small hand in each of hers, she led her children back to the house.

A short while later the three of them were rummaging in the old trunks which had been stored in the attics of Pennistone Royal for many years. Patrick had already taken possession of the carousel, which Paula had immediately given to him, and he was turning the small key, making it work in the way she had shown him.

The horses on the merry-go-round were moving up and down to the strains of the "Carousel Waltz," and the little boy was fascinated, his happy, eager face a pleasure for Paula to witness.

Linnet and Paula left him to play with the carousel on his own, and they soon had their heads and their hands in another trunk which Paula had pulled out and opened.

Busily they sorted through the toys that brimmed to the top, taking out a large, painted wooden soldier, a box of bricks, a scruffy teddy bear with one arm and no eyes, several stuffed animals, various jigsaw puzzles, a box of tin soldiers, and various rag toys.

Paula's hands finally came to rest on a beautiful china baby doll at the bottom of the trunk, and lifting it out she caught her breath in surprise and pleasure. She remembered it very well. Her grandmother had given it to her, and she had taken great care of it, had loved this doll more than any of her other possessions. Years ago she had packed it carefully away when she had moved from Long Meadow to Pennistone Royal after Jim's death. She had meant to give the doll to Tessa but had somehow forgotten all about it during the troubled year after the avalanche.

Sitting back on her haunches, she held the doll up, smoothed its golden curls, straightened its dainty ecru-colored lace dress. She was amazed that the doll was in such good condition and looked almost new.

Linnet was watching her closely, her eyes lingering with longing on the doll. "Was it yours, Mummy?" she asked at last.

"Yes, darling, it was. My grandmother gave it to me when I was your age."

"You mean Grandy Emma?"

Paula nodded.

"So you wouldn't want to give that doll to anybody then, would you? Not if *Grandy Emma* gave it to you," Linnet said gravely, her eyes still fastened on the doll.

Paula laughed. "Well, perhaps I would give it to a girl whom I knew would look after it, would take good care of it as I did."

"Tessa," Linnet said a trifle sadly in a small and quiet voice.

"No. I think her name's Linnet."

"Oh, Mummy! Mummy!"

"Here you are, my darling, it's for you." Paula held out the doll. "I used to call her Florabelle."

"Then I shall, too." Linnet struggled to her feet, took the doll, her eyes shining, her smile brilliant.

"Thank you, Mummy, oh thank you." Hugging the doll tightly in her arms, she leaned into Paula, nuzzled her nose against her cheek. "I love you, Mummy," she whispered. "Oh you do smell nice. Like a bunch of flowers." Linnet put her head on one side and observed Paula thoughtfully. Then she reached out, touched Paula's cheek gently with her small hand. "You won't get lost, will you, Mummy?" she asked, her voice unexpectedly wistful, almost fretful.

Paula's brows puckered together into a jagged line. "What do you mean, lovey?"

"Sometimes when we're waiting for you to come home, Daddy says, 'I think your mother must have got lost. I don't know *where* she can be.' And then he goes to the window and looks out. And I worry till you get home and so does Patrick. Well, I think he does."

"Oh darling, it's merely a *saying*. It doesn't mean that I'm really lost," Paula said and smiled at her daughter reassuringly.

"Are you sure, Mummy?"

"Of course I am."

"Oh. That's all right then."

Paula smoothed a hand over her daughter's red-gold hair and sat back on the floor, watching her as she played with the doll. How easy it is to please children, she thought at one moment. As long as they receive love and care and kindness and discipline, that's all that really counts. Their needs are really very simple. If only adults could be the same . . .

"So this is where you're all hiding!" Shane exclaimed from the doorway, making the three of them start in surprise.

Paula pushed herself to her feet. "We've been finding all sorts of lovely treasures in the trunks," she explained, hurrying over to him. "A carousel for Patrick, and my old doll Florabelle for Linnet."

Shane nodded, put his arm around his wife. "But now I think you have to come downstairs . . . Nanny has tea waiting in the nursery . . . for all of us."

"That was such fun, and the kids enjoyed it too," Shane said to Paula that evening as they were dressing for dinner. "It's ages since we've had a nursery tea with them. We must do it more often."

"You're absolutely right, darling," Paula agreed, leaning forward, looking into the mirror of her dressing table, smoothing the silver brush over her sleek black hair. Putting the brush down, she outlined her mouth with bright red lipstick, then sprayed on Christina Crowther's *Blue Gardenia* perfume, one of her favorites. "And I'm really thrilled with Patrick, the progress he's making, aren't you?" She half-turned to look at Shane.

"I am indeed. He's so much better in every way, and there's been a vast improvement in his understanding of things. It's the new tutor. Mark is doing wonders for the boy."

"Yes, he is," Paula said.

Shane slipped into a dark blue blazer, adjusted his tie, walked across the floor. He stood behind Paula with his hands resting lightly on her shoulders, smiling at her in the mirror.

"You look beautiful, Beanstalk," he said, his lopsided grin surfacing briefly. "So stop titivating yourself. Come on, let's go into the upstairs parlor. I put a couple of bottles of champagne on ice earlier, and we can have a quiet drink together before Emily and Winston arrive for dinner."

"That's a lovely idea," Paula exclaimed, pushing back the dressing table stool, rising to her feet, reaching up, kissing him on the cheek. "But then *you* usually *do* have the best ideas."

She tucked her arm through his, and together they walked across the floor into the adjoining room.

The upstairs parlor at Pennistone Royal had been Emma Harte's favorite room in the great old house in Yorkshire, and Paula loved it as much as her grandmother had. Its impressive architectural details and splendid furnishings belied the name 'parlor,' but for some reason it had never been called anything else. The soaring dimensions gave it a singular grandeur, and its high ceiling was Jacobean in style, decorated with elaborate plasterwork. Tall, leaded windows flanked an unusual oriel window, and there was a carved fireplace of bleached oak and the floor was of parquet. Emma had years ago balanced its imposing detail and size with a mellow charm, intimacy, and comfort, as well as her own brand of understated elegance.

Paula had never felt the need to change the room, even though it would be sacrilege to do so, and the decor was the same as it had been for nigh on fifty years. Since the day Emma had bought it in the 1930s, in fact. The primrose colored walls were repainted every year to the same shade, and new slipcovers and draperies were made when they were required; otherwise it was exactly the way it had been throughout Emma's lifetime.

The priceless Turner landscape filled with misty blues and greens hung above the mantelpiece, and the only other paintings in the parlor were excellent portraits of a young nobleman and his wife by Sir Joshua Reynolds. The three oils were in perfect harmony with the Georgian antiques, the Savonnerie carpet, and the rare Rose Medallion china in the Chippendale cabinet. Brightly patterned yellow chintz fabric covered the two huge sofas in the center of the room, which faced each other across a mahogany butler's tray table, and the antique porcelain lamps were shaded in cream silk, and everywhere there was the gleam of silver and crystal.

The lamps had been turned on and a huge fire blazed in the hearth. The warmth had opened up the narcissi, daffodils, and hyacinths planted in bowls, and the air was fragrant with their mingled scents.

As she moved toward one of the sofas and sat down, Paula thought the parlor had never looked more beautiful than it did this evening. It was dusk and the light was changing. Outside the great soaring windows, the sky was turning to navy blue tinged with lilac bleeding into amethyst and deeper purple. A strong wind had blown up, was rustling the trees, and distant thunder heralded a storm.

But here in the gracious room there was a sense of peacefulness and tranquility. To Paula, the parlor had a timeless quality, never changing. It was full of her past, her entire life really, and so many cherished memories . . . memories of her childhood, her youth, the days of her growing into womanhood. And there were memories of the most special people in her life . . . those dead and living . . . her father and Grandy . . . her mother . . . Philip . . . the special friends of her youth . . . and her cousins Emily, Winston, and Alexander. And Shane, too, was caught up in the memories which were held captive in this room. *Home,* she thought. *The parlor represents home to me, and my roots, just as it did to my grandmother. And that's why I could never be happy living anywhere else . . .*

"Penny for your thoughts," Shane said, looming over her, making her jump. He handed her the crystal glass brimming with icy, sparkling champagne.

"Oh darling, thank you," she said, taking the glass from him. "I was just thinking how lovely this room is, and it's truly filled with the past, isn't it?"

"All the days of our lives actually," he said, touching his champagne flute to hers. "Since we were very little."

They smiled into each other's eyes, loving each other, and then Shane moved across to the other sofa, where he sat down, settled into the plump chintz cushions, relaxing.

Paula leaned forward, focused her violet eyes on him. "Talking of the past

—I've been thinking of the *future* in the last few days, Shane, and I'm definitely going to go ahead and buy the Larson chain in the States."

Shane looked at her sharply. The expression in his black Irish eyes changed slightly, became anxious, but he said in the same even, well-controlled voice, "If that's what you want, then I'm glad you've made the decision to go ahead, darling." Privately he believed she might well be taking on too much responsibility, but he never interfered in her business, remained neutral and uninvolved. It was one of the reasons their marriage was so solid.

She said slowly, "Six hundred and fifty million dollars is a fair price for the chain, I think." She raised a shapely brow. "No?"

He nodded. "Yes, I agree with you. It is."

"Well, anyway . . . I've decided to buy it myself, with my own money," she added, giving him a direct look.

For the fraction of a second he was quite floored and gaped at her in astonishment, but once again his tone was even, steady, as he said, "Have you now. And what are you going to sell to raise the necessary cash to pay for it?"

"I'll borrow from the banks, take out a mortgage on the Larson real estate, pledge some of the chain's other assets. I'll probably be able to borrow about three hundred million dollars or so. And to raise the other half of the money I need, I intend to sell ten percent of my Harte shares."

"Paula!" he cried, askance. "Do you really think you should?" Holding her with his eyes, he asked swiftly, "Isn't that rather *risky?* Far be it from me to interfere in your business, darling, but those Harte shares are a great weapon—and your security—in as much as they give you absolute power in the company. If you sell ten percent of your fifty-one percent, you're reducing your holdings in the company. You're leaving yourself wide open to challenge."

"Gosh, don't be silly, Shane. Whoever's going to challenge me!" she laughed. "I have the full support of my board and my shareholders. They're behind me. Good Lord, the store is *mine.* Nobody would ever dream of going against me, neither the board members nor stockholders. I *am* Harte's, just as Emma was."

"Well . . . I don't know . . ." Shane began and stopped. He had finally broken the rule he had made the day he had married her. He had promised himself he would never give her any business advice, and he never had. She was far too much like Emma Harte to take it anyway. Paula was stubborn and independent. And usually infallible in her judgments, as her grandmother had been before her. He took a deep breath, resisted arguing against this planned move on her part.

"I can see from your face that you've made up your mind to do things your way," he said carefully. "You're confident, determined, and your attitude is admirable, the only one you *should* have when you embark on a venture like this." Shane smiled at her, and he meant every word when he added, "I'm behind you all the way, Paula."

"Oh Shane, darling, thank you . . . thank you for believing in me. That means such a lot. I was only saying so to Michael the other day."

"Were you?"

She nodded. "I told him I hoped you'd approve of what I'm doing. By the way, he'll be in New York next week when I'm there."

"That's a coincidence . . . or is it?" He gazed at her intently, his dark eyes narrowing.

"No, darling, it's not. Michael does have to be in New York some time this month, but he has made his plans to dovetail with mine. He thinks he should be there to give me any help I might need with the Larson takeover."

Stiffening, Shane held himself rigid on the sofa, and for a moment he did not respond. Then he cleared his throat. "You've never needed help with deals in the past. Not from anyone. Why *now* all of a sudden?"

She shrugged, laughed. "I don't need any help, but Michael introduced me to Harvey Rawson, found me the Larson chain, as you know. *He* thinks he ought to be there, and I don't want to hurt his feelings by telling him not to come over specially for me."

"I see."

Shane sprang to his feet, strode over to the console, not wanting her to see his sudden anger. He poured himself another glass of Dom Pérignon, pushed back the jealousy he was feeling, endeavored to arrange a suitably unconcerned expression on his face. Michael was irritating him of late. He had an instinctive, gut feeling that the other man was interested in his wife in a more personal way than she realized. He trusted Paula implicitly, knew that she loved him with all her heart. But he was no longer certain that he trusted Michael Kallinski. Certainly he did not want Paula to be placed in an awkward or embarrassing situation when she was in New York, and that might possibly happen. Or was he being unfair to Michael? After all, his old friend was a gentleman, wasn't he?

Shane made a snap decision and pivoted to face his wife, flashed her a brilliant smile. "I was keeping this as a little surprise, but I might as well tell you: I'm going to be in New York too next week, Paula darling," he improvised. "Miranda needs me to go over there. I know we try not to be away at the same time, for the sake of the children, but this trip is unavoidable. I do have some pressing problems to deal with."

"But how marvelous!" Paula cried, her face filling with happiness. "And Patrick and Linnet will be perfectly all right with Nanny and Mark . . ." Paula stopped, chuckled quietly. "It just so happens that Amanda is going to be in the States as well, on a buying trip for Genret. I plan to give a few dinner parties for her . . . and Michael. You see, Shane, Amanda's quite potty about him, and Uncle Ronnie and I think they would make a perfect couple."

"I'm not so sure that Michael is interested in matrimony at the moment," Shane remarked as he strolled back to the sofa and sat down. "Not after that debacle with Valentine. Still, I'm rather inclined to agree with you and Uncle Ronnie about Amanda being ideal for him." Shane leaned back on the sofa, feeling a curious sense of relief. He added, as an afterthought, "I think we'd better fly separately though, as we usually do."

"Yes, of course, that is wisest. Anyway, Shane—" Paula stopped mid-sentence as the door opened and her daughter, Tessa, came into the room.

"Goodnight, Mummy, Daddy." She hovered in the doorway, blew them kisses. "I'm off to Melanie's party now. Her brother's just arrived to drive me over there."

"You're not going looking like that!" Paula exclaimed and stood up.

Tessa frowned. "What do you mean, Mummy?"

"You know very well what I mean." Paula beckoned with one finger. "Come over here, Tessa, I want to look at you."

"It's only a bit of blush-on," Tessa muttered, throwing her mother a hostile look, not budging from the door. "Everybody wears it these days."

"I'd hardly say that. Please come over to the fire, Tessa."

Reluctantly the girl did as her mother asked. Paula took hold of her shoulders and gently turned her into the light emanating from the lamps on the tables on either side of the fireplace. She shook her head, grimaced. "Just a little blush-on, you said. But you're wearing mascara and lipstick as well."

"It's a very *pale* pink lipstick," Tessa protested.

"You're only *thirteen!*" Paula shook her head in dismay. "I can't allow you to wear cosmetics. Now run up to your room and wash your face, please."

"No! I won't! I'm not going to take it off! You're just old-fashioned! That's what's wrong with you!" Tessa cried angrily, and she glared at Paula, then tossed her head.

"Steady on, Tessa!" Shane warned, sitting up straighter on the sofa, throwing the girl a cautionary glance. "Don't speak to your mother in that way. You're being extremely rude. I will not have it."

"She *is* old-fashioned, Daddy. Out of date. All the girls in my class wear makeup after school."

"I sincerely doubt that." Paula took a step backward, regarded her daughter through freshly objective eyes. My God, she thought, Tessa could easily pass for seventeen. She's grown up all of a sudden. Whatever's happened to the years? It seems like only yesterday that she was a baby in her pram.

Adopting a conciliatory manner, softening her voice, Paula now murmured, "Please do as I say, darling."

Tessa compressed her lips in a stubborn line and her silver-gray eyes became defiant. "I won't go to the party if you make me take my makeup off. I'll look childish, ridiculous. The other girls will be made up, and they'll laugh at me."

Mother and daughter stared at each other.

Paula shook her head slowly. "No, they won't."

"Mother, please . . . you're being stupid!" Tessa wailed.

"No, I'm not. And as long as you live in this house and are supported by us, you will live by our rules," Paula said quietly, but with great firmness.

Tessa looked down at her feet, thinking hard. She admitted to herself that her mother had the upper hand; nevertheless, she was quite determined to get her own way. She took another approach when she said, "I'll make a deal with you. I'll—"

"No negotiating," Paula shot back.

"But the ability to negotiate is often the secret of business success," Tessa pointed out, quoting Paula to Paula.

Her mother swallowed a smile and glanced away to hide the merriment unexpectedly brimming in her eyes. Shane was less successful at concealing his amusement, and he burst out laughing.

Paula looked over at him and shook her head; then she turned to Tessa. "All right, you can wear the blush-on. But that's all. And for this concession on my part you must promise to spend an extra hour practicing the piano. You've been neglecting it lately."

"Okay, I promise. But please let me keep the mascara on. My eyelashes are so pale. I look awful. Bleached out. I'll double my piano practice, and . . . and . . . I'll take Linnet off your hands on Nanny's day off."

"That's tomorrow, you know," Paula pointed out, and relenting, she added, "All right, it's a deal. But no lipstick. *Understood?"*

"Yes. Thanks, Mums." Laughter touched Tessa's face and she danced lightly across the room, pirouetting until she reached the door.

"And don't be late," Paula instructed.

"I won't. Bye."

The door slammed behind her with such a crash that Paula grimaced, then winced as the Rose Medallion china trembled in the Chippendale cabinet. She murmured, "Tess looks older than thirteen, doesn't she, Shane?"

"Yes, she's suddenly becoming quite the young lady, and she's growing up a little too fast for my liking. I think it's time we considered taking her out of Harrogate College, Paula, sending her to Heathfield, as we've always intended."

"I'll get in touch with the headmistress next week. I agree that the sooner Tess goes there the better."

"I told you years ago that she was a maverick, Paula. She and Lorne are very different, even though they're twins. She's going to need a strong hand in the next few years."

Paula nodded, recognizing the truth in everything Shane said. She fell into her thoughts. Her daughter was headstrong, willful, reckless, and even defiant at times. She was a loving girl, warm, outgoing, and she was clever at school. And yet she could be temperamental, and to Paula this was a negative. Her daughter was very much a Fairley, had inherited many of their characteristics, not the least of which were the personal vanity, preoccupation with self that had always been Fairley flaws. There's not a great deal of Harte in her, Paula thought with a little stab of dismay. She even looks like her great-great-grandmother Adele Fairley, with her pale blond hair and those silvery, enigmatic eyes. Paula shivered unexpectedly and gazed into the fire.

"You've got the oddest look on your face, Paula," Shane said. "Is something wrong, darling?"

"No, no, of course not," she exclaimed, rousing herself from her ruminations. "Can I have another glass of champagne, please?"

"I *was* right, wasn't I?" Emily said, glancing from Paula to Winston. "Now come on, the two of you, have the good grace to admit it."

"You were right about *everything*," Paula acknowledged. "And I'm sorry I pooh-poohed your theories all those years ago." She lifted her wine glass, took a swallow of the claret. "Is that good enough for you, Dumpling?"

Emily grinned.

Winston said, "I apologize for ever thinking you were slightly bonkers when you kept on insisting that Min had not committed suicide."

"Apologies accepted." Emily smiled at her husband and then at her cousin, picked up her knife and fork, cut into the slice of spring lamb on her dinner plate, and ate a mouthful.

Shane, sipping his wine thoughtfully, said, "You always suspected it was murder, didn't you, Emily?"

"Yes."

"Why?" Shane probed curiously.

"It was the missing five hours that troubled me, Shane." Emily put down her cutlery, sat back in the chair. "I simply couldn't understand where Min had been from about six o'clock, when Anthony first saw her at the lake, until the time she died around eleven. Her car had remained at the lake, so I was sure she had been visiting someone . . . either in the village of Clonloughlin or on the estate. I even thought of a lover . . . but I was unable to figure it all out . . . it was a great mystery to me."

"One that has been solved at long last," Winston added. "And my sister, for one, is vastly relieved. For years poor Sally has believed that she and Anthony somehow drove Min to her death. Thank God that's finally been cleared up. A cloud has been lifted from the Dunvale family."

"Did Anthony explain why Michael Lamont suddenly confessed to accidentally killing Min?" Shane asked, leveling his eyes at Winston.

"Anthony told us that Lamont couldn't go on, that his conscience was troubling him so much it was making him ill," Winston said. "Apparently he went to Anthony, told him the truth about that night. When Anthony pointed out that a dead person couldn't take water into the lungs, and therefore Min had to have been alive when he put her in the lake, Lamont went berserk, was so shocked, so devastated, he had the stroke."

"At least Lamont's subsequent death enabled Anthony to bury the whole matter with him," Paula murmured. "It would have been ghastly for the family if Anthony had been obliged to reopen the case. Not to mention for Lamont, who would have been standing trial for murder, I've no doubt."

"I always felt that Bridget O'Donnell knew more than she was admitting," Emily remarked. "But when Anthony was here last week, I asked him about her, and he looked at me in the most peculiar way. He told me Bridget had known nothing about Min's death, that she had been suffering from a migraine in her room that night, just as she had said at the inquest, when she also gave Anthony his alibi. Still—"

"Excuse me, Mrs. O'Neill," the housekeeper said, coming into the dining room, "I'm sorry to interrupt you during dinner, but there's an important telephone call for you."

"Thank you, Mary," Paula said, pushing back her chair, rising. "Excuse me, chaps, I won't be a moment."

Paula hurried out to the Stone Hall and the nearest telephone, wondering who could be calling her at this hour on a Saturday night. Lifting the receiver, she said, "Hello?"

"Mrs. O'Neill, it's Ursula Hood here."

Paula tightened her grip on the receiver at the sound of Mrs. Hood's voice. She was Alexander's housekeeper at Nutton Priory, and all of Paula's senses were instantly alerted to trouble. Her throat was slightly dry when she said, "Good evening, Mrs. Hood. How can I help you?"

"Mrs. O'Neill . . . I'm calling because . . . well, something dreadful has happened." The woman's voice cracked. She was unable to go on, and there was a small silence before she continued quietly, "Mr. Barkstone went out hunting in the woods early this evening. He . . . he . . . accidentally shot himself."

The short hairs rose on the back of Paula's neck and she began to tremble. She asked shakily, "Is he badly injured, Mrs. Hood?"

Mrs. Hood cleared her throat. "Oh, Mrs. O'Neill . . . he's . . . he's . . . Mr. Barkstone's dead. I'm so sorry. So very sorry."

"Oh God, no!" Paula cried and steadied herself against the oak table, trying to absorb the shock, blinking back the tears that had sprung into her eyes.

Mrs. Hood said softly, "I can't believe he's gone . . . Such a lovely man." The housekeeper broke down again, but managed to get a grip on herself, to explain: "I'm ringing *you* because I don't have the heart to get in touch with his sisters . . . I just wouldn't know how to tell Mrs. Harte or Miss Amanda and Miss Francesca . . . I wouldn't . . ."

Paula said slowly, "It's all right, Mrs. Hood, I understand. And Mrs. Harte is here for dinner this evening. I'll break the news to her and to her sisters. But please . . . can you tell me . . . a little more about . . . what happened?"

"Not really I can't, Mrs. O'Neill. When Mr. Barkstone didn't come down for dinner this evening, I sent the butler up to his bedroom. Mr. Barkstone wasn't there. It seemed that no one in the house had seen him return from the woods. The butler, the houseman, and the chauffeur then went out to look for him . . ." Mrs. Hood blew her nose, finished, "They found him lying under one of the big oaks, the gun by his side. He was already dead."

"Thank you, Mrs. Hood," Paula managed to say, striving hard to control her feelings, to contain them as best she could. "I'll handle things here, and my husband and I will drive up to Nutton Priory within the hour. I'm sure Mr. and Mrs. Harte will come with us."

"I'll be waiting for you, Mrs. O'Neill, and thank you."

Paula put the receiver back in the cradle and stood for a moment longer in the Stone Hall thinking of her cousin. Oh Sandy, Sandy, why did you have to die like that? All alone in the woods. Her heart clenched. And then a most terrible and unacceptable thought flashed through her mind, stunning her. *Had he taken his own life?* No. Never. He wouldn't do that, she told herself. Sandy wanted so much to live. He fought so hard to keep going. Every minute was precious to him. He told me that so many times lately. She dismissed the idea of suicide, blocked it out of her mind.

Taking several deep breaths, Paula walked slowly back to the dining room, bracing herself to break the shocking news to Emily.

——— *Thirty-Two* ———

It was a bleak day for April.

Great clouds, curdled and gray, rolled with gathering speed across the lowering sky which merged into the grim and blackened Yorkshire moors. Lonely and implacable, their daunting aspects appalled the eye, cast dark shadows over Fairley this morning. There was not a drop of sunlight to soften those savage windswept reaches, the cold bracing air held a strong hint of rain and a thunderstorm seemed imminent.

Along the moorland road that cut through this great Pennine Chain of hills, a line of cars moved slowly, following the funeral cortege. Soon the cortege left the moors, began its slow descent into the village, and within fifteen minutes it was coming to a stop in front of the lovely little Norman church. Here the new vicar, the Reverend Eric Clarke, was waiting to greet the family and friends of the deceased on the ancient porch.

There were six pallbearers to carry Alexander's coffin. Anthony Standish, the Earl of Dunvale, and Winston Harte, his cousins; Shane O'Neill and Michael Kallinski, and two of his friends from school. They had known him most of their lives, and so it was fitting that they were with him at the end, had brought him to his last resting place in this old churchyard.

The six men lifted Alexander's coffin, shouldered it lightly, carried it through the lych-gate into the cemetery, moving at a slow and dignified pace down the flagged path. Their hearts were heavy and their sorrow was etched on their grieving faces. In their different ways, they had cared deeply about this man they had come to bury.

The pallbearers brought the coffin to the graveside where the vicar was now standing with Alexander's sorrowing sisters, Emily, Amanda, and Francesca, and his distraught and weeping mother, Elizabeth, who was being physically supported by her French husband, Marc Deboyne. At the other side of the grave stood the rest of the family and many friends, all of them dressed in mourning.

Anthony looked burdened down, his face morose and stark, as he walked over to join his wife, Sally, and Paula, who was next to her. He hunched further into his black overcoat, shivering in the gusting wind blowing down from the moors. It was making the new leaves on the trees rustle and ruffling the flowers in the wreaths. Anthony stared at them. They were a reminder that it *was* spring . . . tender blossoms, so colorful against the dark earth . . . the vivid yellow and purple of jonquil and crocuses, the transparent white of pale narcissi . . . the dark blood red of tulips. He was barely listening as the vicar began the burial ceremony, his mind awash with troubling thoughts.

Sandy's funeral was evoking memories of the one he had attended only a few weeks ago in Ireland. He was still disturbed about the way Michael Lamont had keeled over on that dreadful morning in Clonloughlin, when he had confronted him about Min's death. Lamont had died in the cottage hospital several days later, the victim of a massive stroke. He would have been a vegetable if he had lived. In a curious way, Anthony felt somehow responsible for the death of the estate manager. On the other hand, as Sally kept pointing out, Lamont had been saved the agony and disgrace of a trial, which, she insisted, he would never have survived anyway. Perhaps she was right. He tried to erase Lamont from his mind, partially succeeded.

A long sigh trickled through Anthony, and he turned his head, looked at Sally, gave her a faint smile as she slipped her arm through his, drew nearer to him. It was as if she understood everything. She did, of course. They were very close, as close as two people could ever be.

He stole a glance at his mother, Edwina, the Dowager Countess, wishing she had not insisted on coming over from Ireland with them for Sandy's funeral. She had not been well lately, and how frail she *did* look, a white-haired old lady in her seventies. She was the first-born child of Emma Harte, the daughter of Edwin Fairley.

There is so much history in this graveyard, it's awesome, Anthony thought all of a sudden, his eyes roaming over the gravestones. The ground was full of Hartes and Fairleys. Generations of them. He was both Harte and Fairley, as well as part Standish. It struck him then that it had all begun here in the quaint little church looming up behind him . . . begun with Emma Harte when she had been christened here in April of 1889. Almost a hundred years ago. Good Lord, his grandmother would have been ninety-three at the end of this month, if she had lived. He continued to miss her even after all these years.

An image of Emma slipped into his mind. What a unique and brilliant woman she had been. She had loved each one of her grandchildren, but he was aware she had had a special sort of relationship with Alexander. But then they all had, hadn't they? And Sandy had managed to bring out the best in them. Yes, they *were* better people for having known him.

Now his thoughts swung back to his cousin. The letter was in the inside breast pocket of his jacket. He had kept it on him ever since he had received it the day after Sandy's death. He already knew that Sandy was dead before the letter came in the morning post, because Paula had telephoned him from Nutton Priory the night before to tell him and Sally. Nonetheless, the letter had been a shock at first. Until he had understood and had accepted the words.

He had reread it so many times by now, much of it was committed to memory. He felt as if it were engraved on his mind. It was not a long letter, and it was level-headed, matter-of-fact, really, so like Sandy, and Sandy had meant it only for his eyes. That was why he had not shared it with his wife, close as they were, or with Paula, who, after all, was head of the family. But there was no need for them to see it.

Closing his eyes, he saw Sandy's handwriting in his mind's eye . . . and that particular fragment of the letter which had so moved him.

"I wanted you to understand why I am doing this, Anthony," Sandy had written in his careful script. *"Mostly it is for myself, of course. A chance to go at last. But it will save everyone the agony of my protracted dying. I know none of you could bear to see me suffer. And so before I take my life, I say goodbye, dear cousin, and friend. Know that I am happy to shed my mortal coil . . . I escape . . . I am free . . ."*

And Sandy had scribbled a postscript: *"You have been such a good friend to me, Anthony. You have helped me through my private hells more than once, perhaps without even knowing it. I thank you. God bless you and yours."*

Anthony realized it would be unwise to keep the letter, yet he had been incapable of destroying it. But he *must* do so. Today. After the funeral, in fact, when he returned to Pennistone Royal. He would go to the bathroom in their suite of rooms and burn it, then flush the charred pieces down the toilet. Only he knew that Sandy had carefully planned his death, had gone out into the woods hunting, and after bagging several rabbits and hares, had shot himself but rigged it to look like an accident. He would never reveal Sandy's secret to anyone. There had been an inquest, of course, and the coroner had returned a verdict of accidental death, exactly as Alexander had intended. No one suspected the truth.

So be it, Anthony said under his breath, looking out toward the distant moors, continuing to dwell on Sandy, so many memories seizing him . . . carrying him backward in time for a few more moments longer.

Unexpectedly, brilliant sunshine burst through the dark clouds and the leaden, somber sky was filled with a most marvelous radiance that seemed to emanate from below the smudged horizon. Anthony caught his breath at the sudden beauty and raised his eyes to the heavens, and he smiled. And in the quietness of his gentle, loving heart he said farewell to Sandy. *His pain is over,* Anthony thought. *He's at peace at last. Gone to his beloved Maggie.*

The brief ceremony was coming to an end.

The coffin was being lowered into the rich Yorkshire earth where Sandy's ancestors lay, and Anthony turned away from the grave as the vicar closed his prayer book.

He took Sally's arm. "Let's go back to Pennistone Royal for a drink and lunch," he said.

Sally nodded. "Yes, we do need something to warm us up. It's freezing this morning."

Paula, walking with them, shivered, looked from Shane to Anthony, and muttered. "I detest these hearty meals after funerals. They're barbaric."

"No," Anthony said in a muted voice, "they're not." He linked arms with her as they fell in step, went down the flagged path to the lych-gate and the waiting cars. "The lunch today gives us a chance to be together for a while, to console each other . . . and to remember Sandy as he was. To take comfort from having known him and known his love. And to celebrate his life."

Paula was to remember those words.

They were still echoing in her ears a week later, on the morning she was being driven out to Heathrow to take the Concorde to New York.

Amanda sat next to her on the back seat of the Rolls Royce, sad and withdrawn, hardly speaking. A few minutes before they arrived at the airport, Paula reached out, took her cousin's hand in hers, squeezed it.

Swinging her head, Amanda frowned slightly, and then she returned the pressure of Paula's hand.

Paula said, "You're thinking of Sandy, aren't you?"

"Yes," Amanda whispered.

Patting her hand lovingly, Paula murmured, "Grieve for him, by all means, and get the grief out. That's so very necessary . . . part of the healing process. But also take comfort from your lovely memories of Sandy, the years you had with him when you were growing up. Be glad he was your brother, that he gave you so much love, so much of himself."

"You're very wise, Paula. I will try . . ." Amanda's lips trembled. "But I miss him so much."

"Of course you do, it's only natural. And you will—for the longest time. But I also think you should take solace from the fact that Sandy is out of his suffering now." Paula paused, then added softly, "Let him go, darling, let him rest."

It was difficult for Amanda to speak, and she simply nodded several times, swung her head, stared out of the car window. She felt too emotional to respond coherently, and she knew that Paula would understand and would respect her silence.

But a short while later, when they were sitting in the Concorde lounge, sipping coffee before the flight, Amanda suddenly leaned closer to Paula, said in a low voice, "Thanks for being such a good friend. I do appreciate it." She looked off into the distance, before murmuring softly, "How uncertain life is, isn't it, Paula? None of us know what might happen to us next . . . people's lives can change in the flicker of an eyelash . . ."

"Yes . . . life *is* tenuous. But it's also quite marvelous, you know. And life is for the living. We must get on with it."

"Grandy always said that!" Amanda brought her gaze to Paula's and a smile broke through. "I had the most amazing phone call from Francesca last night . . . she's pregnant."

"That *is* lovely news! We'll have to do some shopping for baby clothes in New York." Paula picked up her cup, took a swallow of coffee, and eyed

Amanda thoughtfully over the rim. Placing the cup in its saucer, she said carefully, "Forgive me for prying, but you're rather keen on Michael Kallinski, aren't you?"

Amanda looked at her, surprise flashing in her light green eyes. A faint blush tinged her neck, swept up into her pale cheeks. "Is it *so* apparent?"

"Only to me. I'm very observant and intuitive, and don't forget, I've known you since the day you were born."

"He's not interested in *me,* though," Amanda asserted.

"We'll see about that."

"What do you mean?"

"Michael's spent a great deal of time with you lately, but always on business, dealing with their takeover of Lady Hamilton Clothes. Now he ought to see you in a different light, in social situations, with other men flocking around you . . . which they generally *do,* so don't shake your head in that way. Whilst you're both in New York, Shane and I are going to be giving a few dinners and cocktail parties . . . I want to make certain Michael gets to know you even better. And in a more personal way."

"Oh" was the only thing Amanda could think of to say.

"Trust me. Your future looks very bright you know, from my vantage point."

"And so does yours," Amanda was swift to say. "I feel certain you're going to get the Larson chain."

"I sincerely hope you're right," Paula said and crossed her fingers.

As the British Airways Concorde flight took off for New York, a Quantas flight from Hong Kong was simultaneously landing at Heathrow.

Within an hour the passengers had disembarked, the luggage had come down on the carousel, and Jonathan Ainsley, looking like the prosperous business tycoon he was, walked through customs and out into the arrival hall.

His eyes scanned those people waiting near the barrier, and he raised his hand in greeting when he saw the flaming red hair and beaming face of his smartly dressed cousin, Sarah Lowther Pascal.

Sarah waved back, and a moment later they were embracing affectionately.

"Welcome home, Jonny," Sarah said as they drew apart, looked each other over appraisingly and with mutual approval.

"It's nice to be back. It's been ages." He grinned at her, motioned to the porter to follow with his luggage, and grabbing Sarah's arm, led her out to the car park.

"I *am* glad your trip to London coincided with mine," Jonathan was saying some ten minutes later as they rolled comfortably toward London in the large chauffeur-driven limousine Sarah had hired to meet him.

"So am I," she said. "Yves wanted me to come to see the gallery that represents him here, and I had some business of my own to attend to this week. So it was perfect timing, Jonny."

"And how is Yves?" Jonathan asked.

"Extremely well," Sarah answered, her voice full of enthusiasm. "Painting with great brilliance at the moment."

"And selling very well too," Jonathan murmured and glanced across at her. "And not stinting you, I see, if the jewelry is anything to go by . . . and that *is* a Givenchy suit, isn't it?"

Sarah nodded, smiled with pleasure at his compliments. "He's very generous, but my own investments have been paying good dividends . . ." She gave Jonathan a sidelong glance. "And how is Arabella?"

"Wonderful!" Jonathan's face instantly lit up, and he began to talk about Arabella and their life in Hong Kong in great detail, hardly drawing breath.

Sarah wished she had never brought up the woman's name. She hated her cousin's wife.

Settling back against the butter-soft, wine-colored leather of the car, she appeared to give her attention to Jonathan, nodding from time to time, looking as if she was absorbing every word he uttered, but, in point of fact, she was not listening to one single thing he was saying.

She's innocence, all innocence, Sarah thought, her mind focused on Arabella. But I spotted her type the minute I met her. She's clever and crafty and out for the main chance. And she's got a past, that one. I'm sure of it. I just wish I could warn him about her, but I daren't. She found it hard to believe that Jonathan had been taken in by Arabella Sutton. Even Yves, usually uninterested in other women, had appeared to be bewitched by her when Jonathan had brought her to stay at Mougins earlier in the year. Of course, she *was* charming. And beautiful. All that silver hair, the sloe eyes, the sensational figure. A sex pot, I bet, Sarah thought disparagingly, loathing her irrationally. What did it matter to her whom her cousin married. Except that she cared about Jonny, cared about his well-being.

She had her own family now, an adoring husband, an angelic and gifted child. But Jonathan represented her past, her ties in England. Her parents were alive and so were Jonny's, her Aunt Valerie, and Uncle Robin. But somehow Jonathan was the one she loved the most, even though he was mostly responsible for her estrangement from their other cousins and aunts and uncles. The rift in the Harte family had so distressed her. Although she harbored dislike for some of them, she nonetheless felt the sting of banishment, minded that she was no longer a member of that distinguished clan.

Arabella fascinated Jonny—that was quite obvious. Sarah hated competing for his attention. She had had to do that when Sebastian Cross was alive. Bosom chums they had been, from their days at Eton. And they had stayed close. She used to wonder why. Sebastian had not been very nice. Sleazy, in her opinion. And he had had such a strange fixation about Jonny. If she had not known otherwise, she would have sworn Sebastian was gay. But his reputation as a womanizer had preceded him. Now she wondered if that had actually meant anything. Sebastian had been such an odd bird. He had died of an accidental overdose of cocaine. He had had nothing but bad luck after Jonathan left England, had made nothing but disastrous business deals. She had heard that he died flat broke.

Jonathan touched her arm, exclaimed crossly, "You seem far away, Sarah. Haven't you been listening to me?" He peered into her face, his pale eyes narrowing shrewdly.

"Yes, yes, of course I have," she protested, now truly giving him her fullest attention, not wishing to displease him. Jonny had quite a temper, was easily provoked.

"Is something bothering you?" Jonathan pressed, as usual attuned to her as if he could read her mind. He had always managed to unnerve Sarah because of this ability.

"Actually, I was just thinking about Sebastian Cross," Sarah admitted. "It was odd the way he died, wasn't it?"

Jonathan was quiet for a fraction of a second.

"Yes," he said at last. "Very odd indeed." There was another pause, before he volunteered quietly, "He was bisexual. I didn't know, of course." He looked Sarah fully in the face, confided, "He only admitted that to me when he flew out to Hong Kong to see me, the first year I was there . . . he confessed that I was . . . well, the object of his passion, shall we say?"

"Oh dear," Sarah said, not particularly surprised by this sudden revelation. "How frightful for you."

Jonathan smiled narrowly. "In all truth, it was, Sarah. But he took my rejection of him very well indeed. Or so I believed at the time."

Sarah said not a word, watched him acutely.

He asked, "Do you think that's why he died, Sarah? Do you think that the overdose was intentional . . . you know, an *accident on purpose?*"

"It has occurred to me from time to time."

"Sad really."

"Yes."

"How rude of me, darling, I forgot to ask after that adorable child of yours. How is little Chloe?" Jonathan abruptly changed the subject, not wishing to dwell on Sebastian Cross, to rake over the past. He was only interested in the future, which he had been looking at very closely of late.

"Chloe is simply wonderful," Sarah said, glowing as she launched into a recital about her daughter, one of her two favorite subjects, the other being her husband. "She fell in love with her Uncle Jonny . . . and before I left France earlier this week she made me promise I'd bring you back to Mougins for the weekend. You will come, won't you?"

"I'll certainly try."

"Good," Sarah half turned in her seat, gave him a long and searching look. "What did you mean when you phoned me from Hong Kong and said our day would come, that we'd soon get our own back on Paula?"

Jonathan leaned closer. A wicked and knowing smirk spread across his bland face. "I believe that no one is infallible, that even the smartest tycoons can make flawed judgment calls at times. And I have always known that Paula O'Neill would make a mistake one day. I've been waiting . . . and watching . . . and my gut instinct tells me she's about to do something foolish. The odds are there, you see. She's had too good and too long a run for her money. And when she makes her fatal error, I shall be there. Ready to pounce."

Sarah gave him a penetrating stare, her green eyes quickening. "What do you mean? How do you know? Tell me, Jonny, tell me more!"

"Later," he said, squeezing her arm in the very intimate way he had with her. "Let's wait until we're in the privacy of my suite at Claridge's . . . and then I shall explain how I aim to destroy Paula O'Neill."

Sarah shivered with pleasure and anticipation at the thought of Paula's downfall. "I can't wait to hear your plan. I'm sure it's brilliant . . . and how I've longed to get *my* revenge on that cold, frigid, thieving bitch. She stole Shane from me, quite aside from everything else."

"Of course she did," Jonathan concurred, fanning Sarah's festering hatred of Paula, as he had for years, needing an ally in his scheming, if only for moral support.

He put his hand in his jacket pocket, and his fingers curled around the pebble of mutton-fat jade. His talisman. It had brought him great good luck in the past. He had no reason to doubt that it would do so again.

Winners and Losers

Unnatural deeds do breed unnatural troubles.
           William Shakespeare, *Macbeth*

One must therefore be a fox to recognize traps,
and a lion to frighten wolves.
                   Machiavelli, *The Prince*

All or nothing.
                       Henrik Ibsen, *Brand*

Thirty-Three

"You really are the best thing that ever happened to Philip," Daisy said, filled with love and respect for the young American woman who was her daughter-in-law.

Madelana's face lit up, and she laughed lightly and with gaiety, and settled herself more comfortably on the sofa. "Thank you. That's a lovely thing to know."

They were sitting in the drawing room of the house at Point Piper in Sydney, which Philip had owned for a number of years, and where he and Maddy now lived for most of the week when they were not at Dunoon. It was August and a lovely afternoon, even though it was still the winter season in Australia, and earlier Madelana had opened the French doors leading out to the terrace and the garden beyond. A soft breeze drifted in, made the silk draperies flutter and whisper, carried with it the mixed scents of honeysuckle and euca-lyptus and the salt tang of the sea.

After a moment, Madelana smiled at her mother-in-law and added, "Any-way, I have to say the same thing about your son, Daisy. He's made me a whole person again, chased all my sorrow and gloom away, and given me so much love there are times when I think I might just burst with happiness."

Daisy nodded, understanding exactly what she meant. It had always pleased her that Maddy was so open, without guile, and so readily able to articulate her feelings, with considerable eloquence at times. Also, it was grati-fying to know that her son was such a good husband, had adjusted to being a married man after years of playing around, and that he and Maddy were so blissfully happy.

"When a marriage truly works there's nothing else like it in the world, nothing that can take its place," Daisy said with great feeling. "And it's pure joy to have a relationship with a man who gives so much of himself . . . as both Philip and Jason do."

Daisy paused, glanced to her left, stared at the various photographs of her late husband taken with Philip, Paula, and her twins, Lorne and Tessa, and with herself. Happy, loving family pictures which Philip kept grouped on a small side table near the fireplace. She was thoughtful for a moment, remembering her life with David, and when she swung her head and smiled across at Maddy it was with a certain ruefulness.

"When David was killed in the avalanche, I thought the world had come to an end for me. And of course it had in so many ways," Daisy confided, speaking to Maddy about her first husband in a more intimate way than she ever had before.

"You see, Maddy, I'd shared a perfect marriage with my darling David . . . ever since I'd married him at eighteen. I believed it could never be repeated or recaptured with another man, and it couldn't. For the simple reason that no two men are the same, no two women are either, for that matter, and every relationship is different, has its own strengths and weaknesses. Leaving England, coming out here, helped me to start over again, and my charity work for sick and needy children especially helped to give me a purpose. But it was Jason who made me come alive again as a woman. *He* made *me* whole, Maddy."

"He's a wonderful person," Maddy acknowledged in all sincerity, thinking of the gruff Australian's many kindnesses and loving gestures to her over the past few months. "We both lucked out, finding ourselves a couple of genuine forty-carat dudes."

"I'll say we did!" Daisy exclaimed, laughing, as usual amused by Madelana's quaint expressions. She couldn't wait to tell Jason of Maddy's assessment of him, which, she decided, was absolutely spot on. Continuing to smile, Daisy leaned forward, picked up her cup of tea, took a sip of it.

A compatible silence fell between these two women, who sprang from such different echelons of society, from such different worlds, yet who had grown to care deeply for each other in the year they had known each other. Their great common bond was the love they both felt for Philip and Paula, and Maddy's obsessional admiration of Emma Harte. Daisy was devoted to the memory of her mother, and she enjoyed answering Maddy's never-ending questions, speaking about Emma, recounting anecdotes about the legendary tycoon, and she had a rapt and enthralled listener in her daughter-in-law. And finally there was the bond created by the child Madelana was carrying. Philip's child . . . and the heir to the McGill empire Daisy had longed for.

Daisy thought of the baby now as she sipped her tea and quietly studied Madelana. She wished the baby would arrive. It was nearly two weeks late, and everyone was growing more impatient by the day. Except for Maddy, who was tranquil and healthy . . . and somewhat amused by their constant fussing.

"I'm glad you didn't have the amniocentesis test after all," Daisy said, breaking the silence, "even though I can't wait to know whether I have a grandson or a granddaughter inside that tummy of yours."

Madelana grinned. "I don't think I've ever wanted to know . . . I prefer to be surprised." She placed her hands over her stomach, feeling the baby, the gesture protective, and then she started to laugh. "However, I have a peculiar feeling that she's a girl, Daisy."

"Do you really?"

Maddy nodded, leaned forward, announced, "And if it's a girl we're going to call her Fiona Daisy Harte McGill. Rather a long name, isn't it? But we did want to name her after my mother and you, and to include the surnames of her great-grandparents."

"I'm touched and honored—and terribly flattered," Daisy responded, pleasure lighting up her vividly blue McGill eyes, which were so like her father's had been.

Madelana shifted her weight on the sofa, pushed herself into the pile of cushions, seeking a more comfortable position. She felt awkward and ungainly, slightly cramped all of a sudden.

"Are you all right?" Daisy asked, noticing Maddy's grimacing, her pained expression.

"I'm fine, just a bit stiff today. But to tell you the truth, I, too, wish the baby would come now. I feel like a giant-sized, overripe watermelon that's about to go plop! And I'm lumbering around after Philip as if I'm a fish out of water . . . a huge beached whale, or something of the sort!''

Daisy burst out laughing. "And what if you have a boy? Have you chosen a name yet?"

"Paul McGill. After your father."

"Oh, Maddy, how lovely of you and Philip. I'm delighted, thrilled actually."

Daisy got to her feet, walked across to the console where she had left her handbag when she had arrived earlier in the afternoon. She opened it, took out a small leather box, brought it over to Madelana. Handing it to her, she said, "This is for you."

Madelana looked up at her mother-in-law in surprise, then brought her eyes down to the jewel box in her hands. The leather was worn and scratched, the gilt-embossed edge faded by time. She lifted the lid and caught her breath when she saw the emerald bow lying on the black velvet.

"Why, Daisy, it's simply beautiful. *Gorgeous.* Thank you, thank you so much. It's old, isn't it?"

Daisy, who had seated herself next to Madelana on the sofa, nodded. "It dates back to the 1920s. I've wanted to give you something very special for the longest time, and I finally—"

"But you have!" Madelana interrupted. "I've had so many extraordinary gifts from you and Jason, as well as from Philip. You all spoil me."

"We love you, Maddy. But as I was saying, I wanted to give you something that would be truly meaningful to you at this particular time . . . and so I picked the emerald bow from my collection. Not only because it's exquisite and will suit you admirably, but also because it belonged to my mother. I felt you'd appreciate that, that you'd appreciate the sentimental value attached to the brooch more than anything else."

"I do. But I can't take it after all, Daisy . . . why it's a family heirloom."

"And what are *you,* if not family? Darling, you're Philip's *wife,*" Daisy said softly but emphatically. She took the brooch out of the box, and together they looked at it, admiring the exquisite workmanship, the beauty of the design, the luster and depth of color of the emeralds.

Presently, Daisy said, "There's a lovely story about this piece of jewelry . . . would you like to hear it?"

"Oh yes, I would."

Daisy smiled to herself as she laid the brooch in the velvet-padded box and settled back on the sofa. She was thinking of her mother, envisioning her as a little girl at the turn of the century, as she had so frequently done in the past, forever marveling at her extraordinary character.

"The story actually began in 1904," Daisy explained. "As you know, Emma was a servant girl in service at Fairley Hall in Yorkshire, where she had worked since she was twelve. One Sunday afternoon in March of that year, her best friend Blackie O'Neill arrived to see her. He had bought her a green glass brooch shaped like a bow for her fifteenth birthday at the end of April. He was going away, you see, and he wanted her to have something from him before he left. Anyway, Blackie explained to Emma that when he had noticed the bow in the window of a shop in Leeds the stones had reminded him of her emerald eyes. Naturally, young Emma was enchanted with the brooch, cheap as it was, because she had never had anything like it. She thought it was the most beautiful thing in the world. And that afternoon, Blackie made a promise to her . . . he told her that one day, when he was rich, he would buy her a replica of the brooch, and that it would be made of emeralds. He was true to his word. Many years later he gave her this . . . *this* is Blackie's emerald bow," Daisy finished. She thought to add, "When my mother died, she left the brooch to me, along with her collection of emeralds which my father had given her over the years."

"What a lovely story, and the bow *is* beautiful, but I'm still not sure I should accept it, Daisy. Ought it not to go to Paula in view of its history?"

"No, no, she and I want you to have it!" Daisy insisted, reaching out, squeezing Madelana's hand affectionately. "I've spoken to Paula, and she thinks it's a most fitting gift for you. As I do. And I know that if my mother were alive she would want you to have it, too."

Madelana realized there was no point in protesting further, that it would even be ungracious to do so, and she murmured her thanks again, permitted her mother-in-law to pin the emerald bow to her maternity smock. Then pushing herself up, she went to the mirror over the fireplace, looked at herself. The bow was an extraordinary piece, and she was greatly moved because Daisy had given her something which had once belonged to Emma Harte.

Madelana went back to the sofa, and after a moment Daisy leaned back against the cushions. "Speaking of my daughter, do you think she's made a mistake buying the Larson chain in the States?"

"Of course not!" Madelana cried, sitting up straighter on the sofa, returning Daisy's penetrating gaze. "She's a brilliant businesswoman and I've never known her to make a wrong move yet."

"I just wish she'd told me *why* she wanted me to sell the Sitex stock when she suggested I do so last year. Or at least given me the chance to let her have the additional money she needed for the takeover of Larson's." Daisy sighed heavily. "Paula can be awfully stubborn and she's determined to do everything her own way. She's so like my mother. Oh dear, I don't know . . . business does baffle me most of the time."

Daisy rose, moved to the fireplace, stood with one hand resting on the mantel. "And I don't understand Shane, if the truth be known. I can't imagine why he didn't tell me or Philip about her plans long ago. And why on earth didn't he advise her? After what he said last night, I think he should have, don't you?"

"I'm not sure anyone can advise Paula. She's so confident and self-assured and so truly brilliant in business that she doesn't need advice from anyone. Besides, Shane would never interfere. He would remain aloof . . . that would be the wisest course for anyone to take, as I'm sure he realizes by now."

Daisy frowned. "I was surprised by some of the things I heard over dinner last night, weren't you?"

"Not really," Madelana answered truthfully. "Don't forget, I was Paula's assistant at the New York store, and she has been after an American chain for a long time. In any event, as I said before, I trust her judgment implicitly. And so should you. I know Philip does, and from what Shane said at dinner, he does too." Madelana gave Daisy a look she hoped was reassuring. "There's one more thing I'd like to add. Hasn't it ever occurred to you that Paula might want to own something of her own?"

"But she does, Maddy dear," Daisy exclaimed in a startled tone. "The Harte chain, not to mention—"

"But that was founded by Emma," Madelana was quick to point out. "In fact, everything Paula runs she inherited from her grandmother. Perhaps emotionally she has the need to . . . to . . . well, to *create* and *build* something of her very own and with her own money.

"Is that what she indicated to you when you worked together in New York?"

"No, it's just a feeling I have, knowing her as well as I do."

Daisy looked further surprised and fell silent, ruminating on her daughter-in-law's words. Eventually, she said, "Perhaps you're right, Maddy dear. I hadn't looked at it quite like that. Nevertheless, apart from anything else, I do think she has taken on an enormous amount of responsibility in addition to everything else she has to do."

Maddy said in a loving voice, "Try not to worry about Paula and her expansion program in the States. She'll be fine; it'll be fine. Philip believes she's a chip off the old block, and you said only a few minutes ago that she's like your mother. Being another Emma Harte can't be all that bad, can it?" Maddy finished on a teasing note, raising a brow.

Daisy had the good grace to laugh. "No, it can't," she said.

Thirty-Four

Later, after her mother-in-law had left to return to her house in Rose Bay, Madelana put on a thick, white wool cape and went outside. She walked slowly through the gardens as she did twice a day, enjoying the exercise and the air.

Although the wind had dropped, it had turned cold and dusk was falling, and in that lovely half light, neither day nor night but hovering somewhere in between, everything appeared to be softer, gentler.

The pristine sky of earlier had lost its sharp, icy blue-and-white tints, was slowly darkening, and its rim at the edge of the horizon was streaked with flaring ribbons of amber and rose as the sun sank into the sea. And in those hushed and silent gardens, where not a single thing stirred, the only sound was the lapping of the waves against the rocks of the jutting headland on which the mansion was built.

When she reached the end of the wide path, Madelana stood for a moment gazing out across the endless stretch of inky water. It looked cold, forbidding, bottomless, and she shivered despite the warmth of her cape. Turning swiftly on her heels, she hurried back up to the house. She could see that lamps were being turned on in some of the rooms, and narrow corridors of light were streaming out from the windows, illuminating her way.

How warm and welcome her home looked in contrast to the daunting sea behind her. She increased her pace, wanting suddenly to be inside. Within minutes she was closing the French doors of the library, walking through the room and out into the foyer, still shivering slightly.

As she hung her cape in the hall cupboard, she heard the chatter of voices coming from the kitchen area of the house. It was the two maids, Alice and Peggy, and Mrs. Ordens, the housekeeper, twittering away together like a flock of chirpy sparrows. The three women took care of them exceptionally well, eased the burden of running two homes in Sydney—the house out here at Point Piper and the penthouse atop the McGill Tower. She took a step toward the door, then decided to change her clothes in readiness for the evening before going in to speak to them.

A little sigh of happiness trickled through Madelana as she climbed the staircase leading to the upper floors. She had been experiencing a lovely sense of contentment in the last few days. It was Philip's love and the baby she was carrying that filled her with such abundant joyousness. Soon they would be three instead of two. She could hardly wait . . . she longed to hold her child in her arms.

The rosy glow of the fire greeted her when she pushed open the door of their bedroom and went in. This was one of the two rooms in the house she had redecorated after her marriage, and she had used a mixture of soft greens and a striking white chintz splashed with pink peonies, scarlet roses, yellow lilies, and dark green leaves. The play of greens in the overall scheme and the airy chintz, lavishly used, served to endorse the spaciousness of the bedroom. There was a sweeping bay window overlooking the gardens and the sea, a curving, cushioned window seat underneath, and a huge four-poster bed.

A small antique writing desk was positioned in a corner near the fireplace, and Maddy went and sat down, picked up the letter she had been writing to Sister Bronagh in Rome when Daisy had arrived for tea earlier than expected.

She read it quickly, added a last sentence and her love, then signed it. After sealing it in an envelope and addressing it, she propped it up with the others going to Sister Mairéad in New York, Patsy Smith in Boston, and Paula in London. Maddy was a diligent correspondent, regularly penned entertaining epistles with her latest news to her four favorites. After lunch today she had decided to get the letters written before she went into the hospital to have the baby; she was positive their child would be born this week.

Leaning back in the chair, Maddy began to ruminate on the past year. How extraordinary it had been. *Wondrous.* That truly was the only word to describe it. But it's not even a year, she suddenly thought. I didn't meet Philip until September, and it's only August. What a lot has happened in that short span of time. She rested her hands on her lap, linked her fingers under her large tummy, thinking again of the baby, making endless plans for the future.

Eventually she lifted her eyes, let them rest on the little sampler she had owned since childhood. It had been shipped out to Australia with her other possessions and it hung on the wall above her desk.

"If your day is hemmed with prayer it is less likely to unravel," her mother had stitched so meticulously in bright blue wool all those years ago.

Oh Mom, she thought, everything did turn out beautifully for me, just as you said it would when I was little. I *am* your Golden Girl after all. I *have* been blessed.

Maddy swiveled her eyes to the photographs framed in silver standing on her desk . . . her parents, Kerry Anne, Young Joe, and Lonnie. You've been gone from me for a long time now, but I carry each one of you in my heart and I always will, she whispered to herself.

As she continued to gaze at her family, she realized her memories were much sweeter, far less painful than they had ever been. This was surely because she was a fulfilled and happy woman who no longer felt lonely or alone. At last her keen sense of loss was muted if not totally eradicated.

Maddy left the bedroom half an hour later, freshly made up and immaculately groomed, dressed in a well-cut navy blue silk tunic over loose, pajama-style pants of the same dark silk. Emma's emerald bow was pinned to one shoulder. With it she wore a strand of perfectly matched pearls, large pearl earrings, and her wedding and engagement rings. On her arm was a navy blue shawl of heavy jacquard silk, thickly fringed, and she carried a navy silk evening purse into which she had just popped her letters. She would mail them later at the Sydney-O'Neill Hotel.

Before going downstairs, she paused at a door a little farther along the corridor, turned the handle, and went inside. Switching on the nearest lamp, she beamed with pleasure as she looked around the former guest room, now transformed into the nursery. Philip and she had decorated it together. It was done in a cheerful combination of yellow and white, with shocking pink as a lively accent color. They had decided on this particular scheme since it was neither feminine nor masculine, and therefore suitable for a girl or a boy.

Lovingly she smoothed one hand along the edge of the crib, went over to the window wall to straighten a slightly crooked nursery rhyme print, moving around the large and pleasant room slowly, checking everything for the umpteenth time. Then she turned off the lamp, closed the door behind her as she went out, smiling beatifically, satisfied that everything was perfect and in total readiness for their child.

Maddy ran into Mrs. Ordens in the entrance hall.

"Oh there you are, Mrs. Amory," the housekeeper said, giving her a warm smile. "I was just coming up to tell you Ken has arrived with the car to take you into Sydney."

"Thanks, Mrs. Ordens," Maddy said, smiling back, "but there's plenty of time. Let's go into the kitchen for a minute. I'd like to go over a few things with you before I leave."

Shane decided that he had never seen Madelana looking more beautiful than she did tonight. She was obviously more head over heels in love with Philip than ever, and he with her, and their happiness was reflected in everything they did and said.

The first thing he had noticed when he had arrived in Sydney several days ago was the way her face had filled out since he had last seen her in Yorkshire in January. It was no longer quite so bony, and the extra bit of weight suited her. Her cheeks were slightly flushed, her large gray eyes filled with sparkling lights, and there was a special radiance about her which he found utterly breathtaking. She seemed lit from within. No wonder some of the other people in the restaurant kept glancing in their direction. But then Philip was a handsome son of a gun, very distinguished-looking, and his face was well known in Australia. That might also explain the numerous surreptitious looks. These two made a striking couple; they had an aura of glamor about them.

It had been a merry evening from the outset.

The three of them had laughed a lot over dinner in the Orchid Room of the hotel. In fact, from the moment she had arrived at Shane's suite, where Philip was having an aperitif with him, hilarity had been in the air. Philip had fussed over Madelana, pressed her into a comfortable chair, poured cool Evian water for her, and generally behaved like the besotted man he was. And she had been warm and loving and somewhat placid in her general demeanor, the beatific smile intact. Shane was happy for them, knowing full well what a good marriage meant. They were as lucky as he and Paula.

Philip was saying, "Anyway, Shane, we're not going to Dunoon this weekend. The baby is *so* overdue now, Doctor Hardcastle wants us to stay in Sydney. He's positive the birth is imminent, and so is Maddy, for that matter, and he thinks it's best we stay put."

"He's absolutely right, too," Shane said. "And from a strictly selfish point of view, I'm glad you'll be in the city. Perhaps I'll come out to Point Piper on Sunday, spend the day with you both, if you'll have me, and if the little scalawag still hasn't budged, of course."

Philip grinned. "That's what we had in mind, although we hoped you'd come for the whole weekend. You could drive out with me on Friday evening; it'll give you a chance to relax, get away from the hotel and its problems."

"That's a splendid idea—I'll do that. It'll be nice being with you, taking it easy, doing nothing much except read and listen to music. I don't seem to have had a minute's peace since I arrived."

Maddy exclaimed, "Oh, I am glad you're going to stay with us, Shane! And Mrs. Ordens is a wonderful cook. She'll make all your favorite dishes if you tell her what you'd like."

Shane laughed, shook his head. "No fancy meals, darling girl. Paula's put me on a strict diet. She seems to think I gained weight in the South of France this summer. Mind you, Beanstalk's always been so bone-thin I suppose anyone looks fat next to her." He eyed Madelana, his expression merry and teasing. "You're pretty skinny yourself—when you're not pregnant."

"Yes," she agreed, "I think Paula and I both burn off pounds when we're working. It's all that nervous energy being expended, I guess."

"Talking of work, are you still planning to run Harte's-Australia after the baby's born?" Shane asked curiously.

"Oh yes, I think so," Maddy told him. "I plan to have a month or two off with the baby, since I can do paperwork and phoning from the house or the penthouse until I start keeping regular business hours again . . . nine to five and all that."

"Actually, I'm having a suite decorated for Maddy, next to my office in the McGill Tower," Philip said. "That way, she's only one flight down from the nursery we've designed in the flat upstairs."

"Paula has often hauled one of ours into the office with her . . . and so has Emily," Shane laughed. "It's a trait of the Harte women, I do believe. You might as well join the club, Maddy!"

She gave him a huge smile, which turned into a languorous yawn. She endeavored to stifle it without much success, brought her hand to her mouth, yawned again several times.

Philip did not fail to miss this. "I'd better get my lady home to bed," he announced, instantly rising, helping Maddy to her feet. "I hope you don't mind having an early evening, Shane, but I do think we should be making tracks."

"Of course I don't mind." Shane also pushed back his chair, stood. "I'll come down with you, and anyway it won't do me any harm to get to bed at a reasonable hour for once."

Shane escorted them through the Orchid Room, down in the elevator, across the dark green marble lobby to the front doors. "There's Ken with the car," he said as they stepped out into the street. He kissed Maddy goodnight, embraced his brother-in-law, and slammed the back door firmly shut when they were inside, waved them off.

As the Rolls-Royce pulled away from the curb, Philip put his arm around Madelana, drew her close to him on the back seat. "Are you feeling all right, sweetheart?"

"Yes, I'm fine, Philip. Very tired, that's all." She rested her head against his body. "It just suddenly hit me . . . the feeling of total and absolute exhaustion, I mean."

"Do you think the baby's coming? Do you have any labor pains?"

"Not a one." She smiled against his chest, slipped her arm inside his jacket and around his back, wanting to be even closer to him. "I'll let you know, and in no uncertain terms, the minute I get the slightest twinge," she promised.

He stroked her chestnut hair, brought his face down, kissed the top of her head. "Oh God, I love you so much, Maddy. I don't believe I can ever convey to you exactly how much you mean to me."

"Mmmmm, that's lovely," she said, smiling again, then stifling another series of long yawns. "I love you, too . . . I'll be glad when we get home . . . I can't wait to put my head on the pillow." Her eyelids felt so heavy she could hardly keep them open. They drooped and finally closed, and she dozed intermittently all the way to the Point Piper house.

After breakfast the following morning, Philip went back upstairs to say good-bye to Maddy.

But she was still fast asleep in the great four-poster bed, her chestnut hair tumbled across the pillow. In repose her face was tranquil, relaxed, devoid of the quickness and mobility that gave it such vivacity when she was awake.

How beautiful my wife is, he thought, bending over her, kissing her lightly on the cheek. He did not have the heart to awaken her. She had been almost speechless with fatigue the night before, and she needed her rest this morning. He moved a strand of hair away from her face, kissed her again, quietly crept out of the bedroom.

Ken was waiting in the driveway with the Rolls when Philip walked out of the house just before seven o'clock, and within seconds they were en route for Sydney. Philip opened his briefcase, went over the most urgent documents he had collected from his desk last night, preparing himself for the day's business as he usually did during the half-hour drive into the city. He made a number of quick notations on his pad; studied a detailed memorandum from Tom Patterson, head of their mining division and one of the world's great opal experts; perused other communications from various executives who worked for the McGill Corporation, eventually returned all the documents to his case. He sat back, mulling over everything he had read for the remainder of the drive.

When he strode into the executive offices of the McGill Corporation atop the McGill Tower, it was exactly seven-thirty. His personal assistant, Barry Graves, and his secretary, Maggie Bolton, were both waiting for him. After greeting each other affably, the three of them went into Philip's inner sanctum for their usual early morning confab.

Lowering himself into the chair behind his desk, Philip said, "The most important meeting on our agenda today is going to be the one with Tom Patterson. Presumably he got in all right from Lightning Ridge last night?"

"He did," Barry said. "He phoned about ten minutes ago, and I confirmed that we were expecting him around eleven-thirty this morning, and that lunch would be with you in your private dining room here."

"Good-o!" Philip said. "I'm looking forward to seeing my old cobber, talking to him. It's been months since Tom's been to Sydney. He had a lot of pertinent things to say in his memo. I went over it again in the car on the way in, and I want him to elaborate on a number of points he's raised. But better not go into that right now." Philip glanced over at Maggie, sitting at the other side of the desk, her pad in her hand, her pencil poised.

"Anything special in the post today?" he asked, dropping his eyes to the pile of papers in front of him, then looking at her again.

"Nothing of any great consequence—mostly personal letters, a few invitations, charity requests, the usual daily stuff. Oh, and a cheery note from Steve Carlson. He's still in Coober Pedy. And doing quite well," Maggie finished with a small grin.

Philip couldn't help grinning with her. "So much for *my* assessment of him! The jackeroo seems to have turned out to be quite smart."

The three of them exchanged knowing glances, chuckling, remembering the young American they had characterized as a greenhorn when he had come seeking Philip's advice about opal mining a year ago.

Barry said, with a touch of acerbity, "Beginner's luck, that's all it is. You mark my words, he'll come a cropper yet." He opened one of the folders he was holding, went on briskly, "I now have all the information you require on the newspaper chain in Queensland. The boss man over there seems to be interested in selling. I've prepared a fact sheet, Philip, with all the salient details. Also, Gregory Cordovian phoned just a few minutes after you left the office last night. He wants to set up a meeting with you."

"Does he now!" Philip exclaimed, surprise echoing in his voice. He eyed Barry quizzically. "Could it be that he finally wants to call a truce?"

"Hard to say. He's a cagey sod, that one is. But I kinda got the feeling he was receptive to having a friendly little natter with you. More so than he's ever been in the past. Could be that he even wants to sell the television stations in Victoria. And listen, Philip, *he* called *us,* didn't he? I take that as a good sign."

"It is. And you may well be right—about the television stations."

Barry nodded, tapped the other folder he was holding. "Reports here about our natural energy companies, our Sydney real estate, and our other mining interests. You'll have to go over most of them before next Thursday week, when we have that series of meetings with the executives of these companies."

"I will. Leave the folders with me, Barry. Anything else from you, Maggie."

His secretary flipped back to a previous page on her pad. "Ian MacDonald called late yesterday afternoon. He has a full suit of sails for you, including the spinnaker and the Kevlar for the storm mainsail. He wants to know when you can get out to see him? Wonders if you'd like to lunch with him at the yard?"

"Tomorrow or Friday . . . I am free, aren't I?"

"Tomorrow you are, yes. But not on Friday. You have a meeting with your mother and the board of trustees of the Daisy McGill Amory Foundation. A working lunch here at the Tower in the private dining room."

"Oh that's right, I'd totally forgotten." Philip pondered a moment. "Perhaps you'd better make a date with Ian for next week sometime. That'll be more convenient."

"All right." Maggie stood up. "That's it for me, I'll leave you two alone. Buzz me if you want a cup of coffee, Philip."

"Thanks, I will."

Barry strode over to the desk. "I don't have anything else either at the moment. I want to get back to my office, dig into the report I'm preparing for you on your mother's foreign holdings. I'm still behind on it."

"Okay, go ahead, Barry, do what you have to do. In any case, I have enough to keep me busy with that lot," he said, gesturing to the folders Barry had just placed on his desk. "I'll see you at the meeting with Tom. Let me know the minute he arrives."

"Sure thing, Philip."

Left alone, Philip turned his attention to the two reports on their iron-ore mining interests. Settling back in his chair, he began to read the first one, which consisted of fifteen typed pages. He was still reading the second and making copious notes an hour later when Maggie brought him a cup of coffee, and he did not start on the report about their Sydney real estate until ten o'clock. He was halfway through this when Maggie's voice came over the intercom.

"Philip . . ."

"Yes, Maggie?"

"Sorry to disturb you, but I have your housekeeper on the phone. She says it's urgent."

"Oh . . . okay, put her through." The phone on his left immediately began to ring. He picked it up. "Yes, Mrs. Ordens?"

"Something's the matter with Mrs. Amory," the housekeeper said, getting straight to the point, her anxiety and concern echoing down the wire.

"What do you mean?" Philip demanded sharply, instantly alarmed. He sat up straighter, gripped the phone hard.

"I can't wake her. I looked in on her at nine-thirty, as you told me to, but she was sleeping so soundly I decided to leave her be for a while. I just brought her breakfast tray up, and I've tried for the past ten minutes to rouse her, but it's no good, Mr. Amory. I think she must be unconscious."

"Oh my God!" Philip sprang to his feet, alarm signals going off in his head. "I'll be right there!" he exclaimed. "No, no, that won't help. We must get her into the hospital. The emergency room at St. Vincent's. I'll send an ambulance. You must go with her. I'll meet you there with Doctor Hardcastle, but I'll call you back in a few minutes. Are you in the bedroom now?"

"Yes."

"Then stay there until the ambulance comes. And don't leave my wife alone for one moment."

"No, I won't. But please hurry, Mr. Amory. I know there's something terribly wrong."

—— *Thirty-Five* ——

A private ambulance transported Madelana to St. Vincent's Hospital in Darlinghurst, about fifteen minutes away from the Point Piper house. It was the hospital closest to the eastern suburbs of Sydney, and the only one in the city with emergency facilities.

Mrs. Ordens rode with her in the ambulance, holding onto her limp hand, watching over her as she had promised Philip she would. Not an eyelash flickered against that wan face, but Madelana's breathing was even, and for this at least Mrs. Ordens was thankful.

The moment the ambulance arrived at the hospital, Madelana was rushed straight into Emergency, and Mrs. Ordens was shown into a private office which had been made available at the request of the patient's doctor.

Rosita Ordens sat down to wait for Philip Amory. He was on his way from the McGill Tower with Malcolm Hardcastle, the noted Sydney gynecologist who had been a close friend of Philip's for several years.

Clasping her hands together, Rosita Ordens focused her eyes on the door expectantly. She wished her boss would arrive. He would soon get to the bottom of this situation, find out exactly what was wrong with his wife. One thing was certain—she had not liked the peculiar looks exchanged by the two ambulance men when they had first seen Madelana Amory.

Rosita bowed her head. She focused her thoughts on the lovely young American woman whom she had grown so fond of in the last eight months, *willing* her to be all right, to open her eyes, to speak to the doctors now examining her.

A Catholic like Maddy, Rosita began to pray under her breath. "Hail Mary, full of grace, the Lord is with thee, blessed art thou amongst women, and blessed is the fruit of thy womb, Jesus . . . Hail Mary, full of grace, the Lord is with thee, blessed art thou . . . Hail Mary, full of grace . . . Hail Mary . . ." She went on repeating these words over and over again. Praying helped Rosita, gave her solace in times of trouble. Moreover, she was devout, believed her prayers would be answered by her merciful God.

Suddenly she lifted her head with a start as the door was flung open. "Oh Mr. Amory, thank goodness you're here!" she cried at the sight of Philip, jumping up, going over to him.

Philip took hold of her hand. "Thanks for phoning me when you did, Mrs. Ordens, and for acting so promptly. I'm grateful."

"Have you seen Mrs. Amory yet?"

"Very briefly, with Doctor Hardcastle. He's examining her himself. Naturally, he's concerned about the baby. And after he's conferred with the doctors in Emergency, I'm sure he'll be able to tell me what has caused her condition."

"She is unconscious then?"

"I'm afraid so."

Rosita Ordens sucked in her breath quickly. "I do wish I'd tried to waken her earlier, that I—"

"Don't blame yourself, Mrs. Ordens," Philip interrupted swiftly. "That serves no purpose, and you did what you believed was right. After all, she did appear to be merely in a deep sleep. I also thought that myself."

Rosita Ordens nodded glumly. Her worry knew no bounds.

Philip went on, "Ken's outside with the car. He'll drive you back to the house. I'll phone you the minute I have more news."

"Please do, Mr. Amory. I'll be anxious until I hear from you. So will Alice and Peggy."

"I know." He escorted the housekeeper over to the door. "Ken's parked in front of the main entrance . . . he's waiting for you."

"Thanks, Mr. Amory." Rosita slipped out of the office, knowing her employer wished to be alone.

Philip sat down, sank at once into his troubled thoughts. His mind raced, seeking answers. It was not natural for anyone to fall into unconsciousness in the way Maddy had. Something serious had induced this state in her—he was convinced of that. Radical action was needed. He would bring in a team of specialists, send his private jet to get them if necessary, wherever they were. Yes, he would do it immediately. *Now.* Suddenly he stood up, then sat down again, his nerves on edge. He pushed back the awful panic swarming over him once more. He must stay calm, handle things with cool intelligence. Yet he could hardly contain himself. He wanted to rush back to Emergency to be with Maddy, to look after her, to stay with her until she was her normal self. But there was no point, not at this moment. He was helpless, could do nothing. And she was in the best hands for now. Philip believed in allowing the experts to do their jobs. He was not going to play doctor.

After what seemed like an eternity to Philip, but was in reality only twenty minutes, Malcolm Hardcastle entered the office.

Philip was on his feet immediately, striding across the floor. He stared sharply at the gynecologist, searching his face, his own anxious and full of questions. Urgently he asked, "What caused Maddy's condition, Malcolm?"

Taking hold of Philip's arm, the doctor led him back to the group of chairs. "Let's sit down for a minute."

Philip was astute, and when Malcolm did not give him a direct reply he was instantly alert for trouble. Fear for Maddy gripped him. "What do you think happened to my wife between last night and this morning?" he asked fiercely, his blue eyes flaring.

Malcolm did not know how to break the news. After a split second of hesitation, he said, very quietly, "We're fairly certain that Maddy's had a brain hemorrhage."

"Oh my God, no!" Philip gaped at the doctor. He was stunned, shocked. "It can't be so . . . it just can't be!"

"I'm so sorry, Philip, but I'm afraid all the signs are there. Two very respected brain surgeons have now seen Maddy since she was admitted. I've just consulted with them, and—"

"I want a second opinion! Specialists brought in!" Philip interjected, his voice rising harshly.

"I guessed you would. I asked Doctor Litman to try and contact Alan Stimpson. As I'm sure you know, he's Australia's most renowned brain surgeon and considered to be one of the best in the world. Thankfully he lives in Sydney." Malcolm put his hand on Philip's arm, added in a most reassuring tone, "And even more fortunately for us, he happened to be at St. Margaret's

Hospital out here in Darlinghurst this morning. Doctor Litman managed to catch him just as he was leaving to go back to the city. He should be joining us in a matter of seconds."

"Thanks, Malcolm," Philip said, calming down somewhat. "And excuse me for being snappish. I'm fraught with worry."

"That's understandable, and you don't have to apologize to me, Philip. I know the strain you're under."

There was a knock, and the door opened to admit a tall, slender, sandy-haired man with a freckled face and sympathetic gray eyes.

Malcolm Hardcastle leaped to his feet. "That was fast, Alan. Thanks for coming. I'd like to introduce Philip McGill Amory. Philip, this is Doctor Alan Stimpson, whom I was just speaking to you about."

Philip, who had also risen, greeted the renowned surgeon. They shook hands, and then the three of them sat down together.

Alan Stimpson was a direct man who believed in getting to the crux of the matter at once. "I've just spoken to Doctor Litman, Mr. Amory, and I will examine your wife in a moment." His gaze was steady, level, as he went on, "However, I hadn't realized the baby's birth was so imminent, that the child is actually now two weeks overdue." He glanced at Malcolm. "Have you explained to Mr. Amory how dangerous a brain scan would be to the unborn child?"

Malcolm shook his head. "No, I haven't. I was waiting for you."

"Could you elucidate further, please?" Philip said to Alan Stimpson, his alarm increasing. He clasped his hands together to stop them trembling.

"There would be danger of radiation from a brain scan, Mr. Amory. It would most probably injure the unborn child."

Philip was silent briefly. Then he asked, "Do you have to do a brain scan on my wife?"

"It would enable us to ascertain the true extent of the cerebral damage."

"I see."

Doctor Stimpson continued in the same gentle tone, "However, before we make a decision about that, I must give Mrs. Amory a very thorough physical examination. I will then consult with my colleagues, and we'll decide on the best course of medical action to take."

"I understand," Philip said. "But I hope some fairly fast decisions are going to be made. Surely time is of the essence?"

"It is," Alan Stimpson replied. He stood. "Please excuse me." When the brain surgeon reached the door, he glanced back at the gynecologist. "I'd like you to be at this examination, Malcolm, and consult with us, in view of your patient's pregnancy."

Malcolm jumped up. "Of course, Alan." He turned to Philip. "Hang in there . . . and try to stay calm . . . take it easy."

"I will," Philip muttered, but he knew that this was the last thing he would be able to do. His gaze turned inward as he dropped his head into his hands, worrying about Maddy, becoming more anxious than ever for her. He was reeling from the shock. He could not believe this horrendous thing had happened. She had been so well last night. He felt as if he was living in some horrifying nightmare to which there was no end.

• • •

Ten minutes later Philip jerked his head up, found himself looking at the worried face of his brother-in-law, Shane O'Neill, who stood framed in the doorway.

Shane exclaimed, "I came as soon as I heard! I was out of the hotel. Barry tracked me down. He said to tell you he hasn't been able to contact Daisy yet."

"Thanks for coming," Philip murmured, relieved to see him.

"Barry told me the housekeeper found Maddy unconscious this morning. What happened, Philip? What's wrong with her?"

"The doctors think she's had a brain hemorrhage."

"Oh Jesus!" Shane was aghast. He stood staring at Philip, disbelief washing over his face.

"It occurred during the night most probably," Philip thought to add. His voice was hardly audible.

Shane took the next chair. "But she seemed perfectly normal last evening at dinner! Do they *know* what caused the hemorrhage?"

Philip shook his head. "Not yet. But Doctor Stimpson is examining her right now. He's one of the world's foremost brain surgeons. We're damned lucky he wasn't abroad, that he was actually out here at a nearby hospital in Darlinghurst this morning."

"I've heard of Alan Stimpson," Shane said. "He has an extraordinary record, has performed some miraculous brain operations. From what I've read about him, there's nobody better."

"Yes, he *is* brilliant." Philip turned to Shane. "I don't know what I'll do if anything happens to Maddy," he blurted out shakily. "She's the most important thing in my life . . ." He bit off the end of the sentence, unable to continue, averted his head so that Shane would not see the sudden tears glittering in his eyes.

"Maddy's going to be all right," Shane asserted, his voice confident, strong. "Let's not dwell on the worst, but think of the best instead. We've got to take a positive attitude, Philip. And you're not going to lose her. We must hold that thought."

"Yes . . . I'm glad you're here, Shane. It does help."

Shane nodded.

A silence developed between the two men.

All of Philip's thoughts and his mind and his heart were with his wife in Emergency. He kept envisioning her face. It had been pale, still, devoid of expression when he had seen her a short while before. He could not forget the limpness of her hand when he had held it in his. There had been something so lifeless about Maddy. His mind balked at the idea that she might slip away from him. He refused to contemplate this.

From time to time, Shane looked at Philip. His heart went out to his brother-in-law. But he did not say a word, not wishing to intrude on Philip's privacy. It was obvious that he wanted to be quiet, to be left alone. He was faraway, his handsome face ringed with worry, and his bright blue eyes, so like Paula's, were filled with growing anxiety.

Shane sat back. Silently he offered up a prayer for Maddy.

When Daisy came into the office a little later, Shane was on his feet and across the room to her immediately. She was white, and there was a stricken expression on her face. Shane put his arm around her protectively.

She looked up at him questioningly. "What has happened to Maddy?" she asked tremulously, clutching at him.

Shane explained in a muted voice, "It looks as if she may have had a brain hemorrhage."

"Oh no! Not Maddy! Philip—" She flew across the room to her son, sat down in the chair Shane had just vacated, reached out her hand to him, wanting to give him comfort.

"I'm all right, Ma," Philip said, taking her hand in his, squeezing it. "The doctors are with Maddy now . . . Malcolm Hardcastle, two doctors from the hospital, and Alan Stimpson, the famous brain surgeon."

"He's wonderful," Daisy said, relieved to hear that this man was in charge medically. Her hopes for Maddy soared. "I've met him several times through the Foundation . . . he's the very best. You could not ask for a finer doctor to take care of Maddy."

"I know, Ma."

Daisy swung her eyes to Shane, hovering nearby. "Barry is very anxious . . . he hasn't heard from either of you. You must call him, Shane, let him know what's going on. He can then get in touch with Jason, who went to Perth last night."

"Oh God, yes, I did forget to phone him," Philip muttered. "I'll do so now, and I'll call Mrs. Ordens at the house. She and the maids are as concerned as we are."

"I'm sorry, Mr. Amory, but there is little question that your wife has suffered a cerebral hemorrhage," Doctor Stimpson told Philip forty minutes later. "Her condition is very grave."

Philip, who was standing near the window, thought his legs were going to give way under him. He sat down heavily in the nearest chair. He was unable to speak.

Shane had been introduced to the two doctors by Daisy a moment before, and he took charge, addressed the brain surgeon. "What's your recommendation, Doctor Stimpson?"

"I would like to do the brain scan as soon as possible, and then trepan her skull. That operation would at least relieve the pressure of the blood clot on her brain. Also, I should point out that without the trepanning of her skull she might never regain consciousness. She could be in a coma for the rest of her life."

Philip stifled an anguished cry. He clenched his hands, digging his nails into his palms. *Maddy never to be conscious again.* The thought of this was so appalling, so terrifying he could not—would not—countenance it, let alone accept it.

Alan Stimpson, compassionate, saw the agony on Philip's face, the mixture of pain and apprehension now flickering in those startlingly blue eyes. He was silent, waiting for the other man to marshal his swimming senses.

At last Philip whispered, "Please go on, Doctor Stimpson."

"There is the complication for the baby, Mr. Amory. If your wife were only a few weeks or even a few months pregnant, I would recommend aborting the child. Obviously that is not possible at this late stage of the pregnancy. And . . . well, she could go into labor at any moment. Therefore, the child must be delivered by caesarean section. I recommend that this be done without further delay."

"I can perform the caesarean immediately," Malcolm said.

"Will that endanger my wife's life?" Philip asked quickly.

It was Alan Stimpson who answered him. "Quite the contrary . . . I'd say she could be in more danger if Malcolm doesn't perform the caesarean. Also, in another sense it would be very helpful, in that I could perform the scan and the operation without fear of doing injury to the unborn baby."

"Then go ahead with the caesarean. Now," Philip answered rapidly, wanting no further procrastination. "But I would like Maddy sent to a private hospital . . . if she can be moved, of course."

"We can arrange to transfer Mrs. Amory to St. Vincent's private wing next door," the surgeon said.

"Then let's do that." Philip rose to his feet. "I want to go to my wife now, to be with her. And I'll accompany her next door."

Thirty-Six

At a few minutes past two o'clock that afternoon, Malcolm Hardcastle performed a caesarean section on Madelana Amory.

The child he delivered was perfect. But the mother did not know this. She remained in a coma.

Malcolm brought the news to Philip.

He was waiting impatiently with Shane and Daisy in a private room adjacent to the one he had taken for Maddy at St. Vincent's Hospital.

"You have a baby girl. A daughter, Philip," Malcolm announced.

Philip was pacing the floor.

He stopped, pivoted to face the gynecologist. "Is Maddy all right? Did she come through it all right?" he demanded, his wife his first priority.

"Yes, she did. And her condition is the same as it was when she was taken to St. Vincent's this morning. I'm afraid she still hasn't regained consciousness. On the other hand, she has not taken a turn for the worse."

"Is that a good sign? Hopeful?" Shane probed.

"Yes . . . she seems . . . quite stable."

"Can I see her?" Philip asked.

"Not just yet . . . she's in Recovery."

"But when?" he asked again in the same soft yet demanding tone.

"In an hour. Now, about your daughter . . . she's perfect, just beautiful, and she weighs seven pounds ten ounces."

Philip remembered his manners. He grasped Malcolm's hand tightly. "Thanks for everything you've done, Malcolm. I'm grateful to you, relieved that the baby's all right."

"Can we at least see the child?" Daisy looked at Malcolm, then shifted her gaze to her son standing next to him. "I'd like to welcome my granddaughter into the world."

"Of course you can see her, Mrs. Rickards."

The four of them left the room together, walked down the corridor to the glass-windowed hygienically controlled nursery where new babies were taken immediately following their births.

"There she is!" Malcolm was exclaiming a few seconds later. A duty nurse, catching sight of the noted gynecologist, had already lifted a baby from a crib and was bringing her over to the window for them to see her.

"Oh Philip, she is beautiful," Daisy murmured, her eyes lighting up. "And look, she's got a little tuft of reddish blond fluff on top of her head. I think we're going to have another redhead in the family."

"Yes," her son responded laconically, staring at the baby through the glass. He wished he could be more enthusiastic about the child. But he was so sick at heart about his wife nothing else seemed to matter to him.

Eventually, he brought his gaze away from the nursery window, drew Malcolm to one side. "What happens next? When is Stimpson going to do the brain scan?"

"Shortly. Now, why don't you go outside and get some air? Or take your mother and brother-in-law for a cup of tea or coffee."

"I won't leave the hospital! I won't leave Maddy!" Philip exclaimed. "Perhaps I can persuade them to go. But not I, oh no. Again, thanks for everything you've done for my wife and my child, Malcolm," he said as he turned away.

Later, when they had returned to the room in the private wing of the hospital, Philip suggested to Shane that he accompany Daisy to the Point Piper house, to relax and take some sort of refreshment. "You don't have to keep vigil with me," he muttered, throwing himself into a chair.

"We do," Shane shot back quickly. "We're not going to let you go through this alone."

"We're staying, Philip, and that's flat!" Daisy said in a voice that was as resolute as her mother's had ever been. "My God, Shane and I couldn't stand it, being away from you and from Maddy. We're worried enough as it is without being isolated at the Point Piper house, not knowing what's going on."

Philip did not have the energy to respond, never mind argue with Daisy or Shane.

For a time he nervously paced the floor, then the corridor outside, his agitation increasing. In an effort to stem his spiraling anxiety, he returned to the room, phoned his offices in the McGill Tower, spoke to his secretary, Maggie, and to Barry, his assistant. He made the occasional comment to his mother and Shane, but for the most part he was silent, stood staring morosely out of the window.

He was accustomed to being in control and master of his own fate. All his adult life he had been a man of action, a decision maker, a mover, a doer. He was not used to standing idly by in an emergency, no matter what the emergency was. But at this moment, perhaps the most crucial in his life, he had no alternative. He was not a doctor, and therefore he could do nothing to help the woman he loved beyond all reason. His frustration mounted, drew level with his fear.

Just before three o'clock he was permitted to see Maddy in Recovery. She was unresponsive, unaware of his presence, still in a coma. He returned to the private room filled with fresh anguish and distress and a burgeoning despair.

Daisy and Shane endeavored to comfort him, to reassure him, but they were not very successful.

"I know there is no wisdom at a time like this," Daisy said, going to

Philip, taking hold of his arm, filled with compassion for her son and concern for her daughter-in-law's well-being. "But we must try to be brave and have hope, darling. Maddy is strong. If anyone can pull through this, why she can."

He looked down at Daisy and nodded, then turned away from her so that she would not see the pain and heartache flooding his face.

Alan Stimpson arrived at four and quietly told them he had performed the brain scan on Madelana.

"Your wife did have a massive brain hemorrhage, as I originally thought when I first examined her, but I wanted to be absolutely positive," he reported.

Philip swallowed. His worst fears had been confirmed. His voice shook slightly when he asked, "Have you any idea what might have caused the hemorrhage?"

Alan Stimpson was silent for a split second. "It may very well have developed because of her pregnancy. There have been similar cases."

Appalled, Philip had no words.

"I want to operate, to trepan her skull now, Mr. Amory. I thought you would wish to see her before she is prepared for surgery."

"Yes, I do." Philip glanced at his mother. "We ought to have sent for Father Ryan. Maddy would have wanted her priest here, no matter what the outcome of the operation. Could you call him for me, Mother?"

Unnerved though she was by this sudden request, which underscored her own considerable fears for Maddy, Daisy nodded. "Yes," she said as steadily as possible, "I'll do it now, darling."

"There is every chance the operation will be successful," Alan Stimpson said confidently, looking with swiftness from Daisy to Philip. "And I will do everything in my power to save her life."

"I know you will," Philip said.

The two men were silent as they walked down the corridor together. The brain surgeon showed Philip into the anteroom, which was a few steps away from the operating theater, and closed the door softly behind him.

Philip walked over to Maddy.

He stood gazing down at her, loving her with all his heart. How small and defenseless she looked, lying there on the narrow hospital bed. Her face was chalk white, the color of the sheets. Earlier, Alan Stimpson had told him they would have to shave off her hair. That beautiful chestnut hair. He did not care as long as they saved her life. It was fanned out on the pillow around her face. He touched it, feeling its silkiness, and then he bent, kissed a strand.

Seating himself on the chair, he took her hand in his. It was listless. He brought his face close to hers, kissed her cheek. Against her hair, he whispered, "Don't leave me, Maddy. Please don't leave me. Fight. Fight for your life, my darling."

Finally lifting his head, he stared at her for the longest moment, hoping and praying for a flicker of understanding, a sign that she had heard him.

He knew she had not. She was so very still.

He kissed her again and left. He felt as if his heart was cracking in half.

"My watch has stopped," Daisy said to Shane. "What time is it?"

Shane glanced at his wrist. "Almost six. Shall I go and rustle up a pot of tea?"

"Yes, I think I could use a cup. What about you, Father Ryan?"

Maddy's priest, who had arrived a little while ago, lifted his eyes from the prayer book in his hand. "Thank you, Mrs. Rickards, that's very kind. I'll join you."

"Philip?"

"I'd prefer a cup of coffee, Ma, if—" he began and stopped short when Alan Stimpson entered the room.

The surgeon closed the door behind him, leaned against it. He was dressed in his green cotton surgical gown and pants, had obviously come straight from the operating theater. He remained standing by the door, not speaking, his eyes riveted on Philip.

Philip stared back at him. There was such an odd expression on the surgeon's face, one he could not quite fathom . . .

Alan Stimpson said, "I'm sorry, so very, very sorry, Mr. Amory. I did everything within my skill to save your wife . . . but I'm afraid she just died on the operating table. I'm so sorry."

"No," Philip said. "No."

He reached for the chair he was standing behind, gripped it to steady himself. The knuckles of his tanned hands turned white. He swayed slightly.

"No," he repeated.

Father Ryan rose, helped Daisy to her feet. Tears had sprung into her eyes, and she clamped a hand over her mouth to hold back the sob rising in her throat. She moved rapidly toward Philip, followed by Shane and Father Ryan.

Daisy's heart was breaking for her son. She dared not contemplate the effect Maddy's death would have on him. He had worshiped his wife. Life is not fair, Daisy thought, her eyes brimming. Maddy was too young to leave us.

Philip sidestepped his mother, Shane, and the concerned priest, shaking his head violently from side to side as though denying the surgeon's words. His blue eyes were stunned, uncomprehending. He got hold of Alan Stimpson's arm. "Take me to my wife," he rasped.

Stimpson led him back to the small anteroom near the operating theater where he left him alone with Maddy.

Once more Philip stood gazing down at her. How peaceful she looked in death. There was not a trace of pain or suffering on her face. He knelt beside the bed, took hold of her hand. It was icy. Irrationally, he tried to warm it.

"Maddy! Maddy!" he suddenly cried in a low voice raw with agony. "Why did you have to die? I have nothing without you. Nothing at all . . . Oh Maddy, Maddy . . ."

He bent his head and his scalding tears fell on his fingers, which were tightly holding hers, and he stayed there with her for a long time until Shane came and led him away.

Thirty-Seven

He took her back to Dunoon.

After a short private service at St. Mary's Roman Catholic Cathedral in Sydney, he flew her body to the sheep station at Coonamble. He sat next to her coffin the entire way. Shane accompanied him.

His mother and Jason followed in Jason's corporate jet, bringing with them Father Ryan and Barry Graves.

Once Philip's plane had landed, he had her coffin driven up to the manor where it was placed in the long gallery amidst the portraits of his ancestors. It rested there overnight.

The following morning dawned bright and clear with a sky vividly blue and spotless, and in the brilliant, shimmering sunlight the gardens and grounds of Dunoon looked magnificent. But Philip saw nothing. He was numb with shock, doing the things he had to do automatically, by rote, and for the most part he was oblivious to those around him.

To carry her coffin on the last stage of its journey he chose as the pallbearers Shane, Jason, Barry, Tim, the station manager, and Matt and Joe, the grooms, who had become devoted to her in the brief time she had lived there.

At exactly ten o'clock on Saturday morning, the six men shouldered her coffin and carried it out of the manor. They followed Father Ryan down the winding path that cut through the spacious lawns and flower gardens and led to the little private cemetery beyond. It was in a sheltered glade surrounded by trees and enclosed by an old stone wall. Here Andrew McGill, the founding father, was buried along with his wife, Tessa, and all of the other Australian McGills who were descended from them, their graves marked by simple marble headstones.

Philip had chosen the plot next to Paul for his wife.

The first day he had ever set eyes on Madelana O'Shea, she had been gazing at Paul's portrait, had later said that she thought it was the great man himself suddenly sprung to life when she had seen *him* hovering in the doorway of the gallery. Maddy had often teasingly remarked that he looked like a riverboat gambler, just as his grandfather had, and she had been as fascinated by Paul McGill as she had been by Emma Harte.

And so he thought it appropriate, very fitting, that her final resting place was with his grandfather. In the most curious way, it was oddly comforting to him to know that they lay close together in this patch of earth.

The priest and Philip and the pallbearers finally came to a standstill by the open grave. It was in a corner of the cemetery, shaded by the lovely golden elms and lemon-scented eucalyptus trees she had come to love, just as she had come to love Dunoon and the glorious land upon which it stood, and which had so reminded her of her native Kentucky.

Daisy was waiting with Mrs. Carr, the housekeeper, the household staff, and the other men and women who worked on the sheep station, their spouses and their children. Everyone was dressed in black, or wore black arm bands on their most somber clothes, and the women and children carried sprays of flowers or held single blooms in their hands. And as they stood with their heads bowed, listening to Father Ryan conduct the Roman Catholic burial service, they openly wept for Madelana, whom they had held in great affection, and who had lived with them at Dunoon for far too short a time.

Philip's grief had turned inward.

It was frozen inside him, and he was dry-eyed throughout the ceremony. He stood stiffly, his body rigid, his hands clenched at his sides. There was a grim moroseness about him, and his vivid, cornflower eyes were hollow, empty, his handsome face thinner, wiped clean of all expression. He was a forbidding figure, and there was an aloofness about him that held everyone at bay.

When the final prayer for Maddy's soul had been offered up by Father Ryan, and her coffin had been lowered into the earth, he accepted the whispered, heartfelt condolences of his employees, then strode swiftly back to the manor.

Shane and Daisy hurried after him. He spoke not at all until they were inside the house. Turning to them in the great hall, he muttered, "I can't stay here. I'm going, Ma. I have to be by myself."

Daisy looked up at her son. Her face was drawn, white, her eyes red from crying. She touched his arm gently. "Please don't let it be like it was when your father was killed in the avalanche, Philip. You must get the pain out, you must grieve for your Maddy. Only then will you be able to function properly again, go on living."

He looked at Daisy as if not seeing her. His eyes pierced right through her, focused on some distant image that was visible only to him. "I don't want to live. Not without Maddy."

"Don't say such a thing! You're a young man!" Daisy cried.

"You don't understand, Mother. I've lost everything."

"But there's the baby, your daughter, Maddy's daughter," Daisy said swiftly. She was wretched, heartsick, and her feelings were only too transparent on her troubled face.

Once more Philip stared right through his mother. He made no comment, swung around, crossed the entrance hall, and left the manor without a backward glance.

Daisy watched him go, filled with the most enormous pain for her son. She began to weep quietly, turned to Shane. There was a dreadful helplessness about her. She did not know what to do.

Shane put his arm around her, led her into the drawing room. "Philip will be all right," he assured her. "He's in shock right now, not thinking straight."

"Yes, I know that, Shane, but I'm so afraid for him. So is Paula," Daisy said tearfully. "She told me so yesterday when she phoned from London. She said, 'He mustn't let his grief fester inside him like he did when Daddy died. If he does, he'll never recover from Maddy's death.' I know exactly what she means. And she's right of course."

Daisy sat down on the sofa, fished around in her bag for her handkerchief, wiped her eyes, blew her nose. She glanced at Shane standing by the fireplace, added pointedly, "Perhaps we made a terrible mistake, stopping Paula from flying out here."

"No, Daisy, we *didn't*! It's much too long a trip for her to make for only three or four days! Philip was the first one to say so. He was quite adamant that she stayed in England."

"She might have been able to help him. They've always been close, Shane, you *know* that."

"True, she might," Shane agreed, softening his tone. "On the other hand, I don't think that even *her* presence would have diminished the shock, eased his suffering. It's the terrible suddenness, the unexpectedness that has so thrown him, quite aside from his awful pain. And that's perfectly understandable, when you consider that less than a week ago Maddy was in blooming health, awaiting the birth of their child. Everything was wonderful for them, and they were so much in love. And then *wham!* Overnight she's dead. He's been hit between the eyes, he's literally staggering from this tragedy, Daisy. But he *will* recoup. He has to . . . he's no alternative. We just have to give him time."

"I don't know," Daisy said doubtfully, "he worshiped Maddy."

"That he did," Jason said, striding into the drawing room, hurrying to be at Daisy's side. "And he'll suffer for a very long period. But Shane *is* correct, darlin', Philip will recover. *Eventually.* Somehow we all do, don't we?"

"Yes," Daisy whispered, remembering David.

Jason seated himself next to her, placed an arm around her comfortingly. "Now, sweet'art," he went on, "try not to worry about him."

"I can't help it." She looked at Shane. "Where do you think he's gone?"

"Most likely to Sydney . . . to be by himself. Like an animal in pain, he wants to lick his wounds in private."

Jason volunteered, "Philip has a huge conglomerate to run and he's very conscientious, Daisy. You'll see, he'll be at the helm on Monday, as usual, and if I know him as well as I think I do, he'll throw himself into business with a vengeance."

"And the work will be his salvation," Shane interjected quietly. "He'll use it as an antidote to grief yet again, as he did when David was killed, and it'll help him to keep going until the healing process starts."

"I hope he *will* come to grips with his sorrow, and that he'll make some sort of life for himself in the future," Daisy said.

She looked from her husband to her son-in-law with a worried frown. "Philip can be so odd. He's been an enigma to many people for years, including me at times." She sighed, and then unexpectedly her eyes filled again. "Poor Maddy, I loved that girl so very much. But then we all did, didn't we? And she was like a second daughter to me. Why did *she* have to die?" Daisy shook her head, and before either man could comment, she continued softly, "But it's always the good ones who go, isn't it? It's all so unfair . . . *so unfair.*" Tears spilled from Daisy's eyes, trickled down her cheeks.

Jason drew her into his arms. "Ah, me darlin', me darlin'," he murmured, wanting to soothe her, to calm her. He was at a loss, had no words. He knew only too well that words were cold comfort at a time like this.

After a moment or two, Daisy took hold of herself, sat up straighter, blew her nose, patted her eyes. Her expression was one of sudden resolve, and she said in her bravest voice, "We must be as strong as we possibly can to help Philip pull through this tragedy."

"He knows we're here for him," Shane said, giving Daisy his most cheerful smile, trying to be as reassuring as he could. "Take heart."

"Yes, yes, I will." She swiveled to face Jason. "Where is Father Ryan?"

"He's in the library with Tim and his wife, and some of the others. Mrs. Carr is serving coffee and cake and drinks for those who prefer something stronger."

"How rude of us! We should be there!" Daisy announced, immediately rising. "We must stand in for Philip." She hurried out.

Jason followed on her heels with Shane in his wake.

Privately, Shane was desperately worried about Philip, despite his encouraging words to Daisy. He could not wait to leave Dunoon on Monday morning. He was impatient to get back to Sydney, wanted to be close to Philip, to keep a watchful eye on him.

● ● ●

No one ever knew where Philip had gone that weekend after he had left Dunoon with such abruptness on the day of Maddy's funeral.

When Shane had tried to reach him later that night at the Point Piper house, Mrs. Ordens had said he was not there. Nor was he at the penthouse in the McGill Tower, according to José, the Filipino houseman.

Whether or not these two were lying on behalf of their employer, Shane could not quite determine; he did not even try very hard, knowing that if Philip wanted to hide behind the domestic help he would do so. He could be as stubborn as Paula. It was a family trait inherited from Emma Harte.

And then on Monday morning, Philip had walked into his suite of offices in the McGill Tower as he always did at seven-thirty precisely, and called Maggie and Barry into his inner sanctum for their usual early morning confab.

There was an air of such cold containment about him, and he appeared to be so formidable in his iron-clad grief, both Maggie and Barry dare not make a consoling gesture toward him, or venture any kind of personal comment whatsoever.

As Jason had predicted, Philip threw himself into work, and with a fury that defied description. As the days passed, his hours grew longer and longer. He rarely went upstairs to the penthouse before nine or nine-thirty in the evening, where he ate a light supper prepared by the Filipino houseman. He then retired to his bedroom, rose the following morning at six, was back in his office at seven-thirty, never once deviating from this relentless schedule. He had no social life, no contact with any persons other than his employees. In fact, he shunned everyone who was not directly involved with him in business, including his mother and Shane, to whom he was the closest. They became increasingly troubled by his behavior, but were helpless to do anything.

Barry Graves, who was with Philip most of the time during business hours, kept expecting him to make some sort of reference to Maddy, or to her death, or to the child, but he never did. And, to Barry, he appeared to become colder and more introverted as time passed. There was a sheathed anger in him that Barry knew would have to erupt in some form or another before very long.

Finally, in desperation, Barry called Daisy at her Rose Bay house one afternoon, and spoke to her confidentially, and at length, about her son and his concern for him.

The minute she hung up on Barry, Daisy telephoned Shane, who had just returned from a two-day trip to Melbourne and Adelaide, where he had been visiting the O'Neill hotels.

"I have to come into Sydney today . . . in a short while, in fact. May I pop in to see you, Shane?" Daisy asked.

"Of course," he said. "That'll be fine." He glanced at the clock on his desk. It was exactly five minutes past three. "Come by in about an hour. We'll have tea together and a nice chat, Daisy dear."

"Thanks, Shane, I appreciate it."

Promptly at four, his secretary showed his mother-in-law into his private office in the Sydney-O'Neill Hotel. Shane rose, went around the desk to greet her.

After kissing her on the cheek, he held her away, eyed her closely. "You look lovely, as usual, Daisy. But troubled," he said soberly. "About Philip," he added, leading her over to the sofa in front of the wall of plate glass overlooking Sydney Harbour.

Daisy made no comment.

They sat down together. She reached out, took hold of his hand, stared into his face. She had known him all his life, since the day he was born, and she loved him like a child of her own.

She said, after a moment, "You've always been such a good friend to me, Shane, not to mention a wonderful son-in-law. You were a great comfort to me when Mother died, and I don't think I'll ever forget how supportive you were at that most awful time in my life—when David was killed. You've been a rock for me, and for Paula, too. Now, yet again, I must ask you to help me, to do something else for me."

"You know I'll do anything I can, Daisy."

"Go to Philip," she said, leaning closer to Shane with some urgency. "Talk to him. Try to get through to him. Make him see that he'll become ill if he goes on like this."

"But he won't see me!" Shane exclaimed. "It takes me all my time to get through to him on the phone! You know I ring him every day. Maggie literally has to force him to take my calls. It's one hell of a tussle, I don't mind telling you. And when I ask to see him, beg almost, he hides behind pressure of work, business meetings, and the like."

"Oh yes, I know, I'm having the same problems with him myself. And encountering the same type of resistance. But I believe you're one of the two people who *can* get through to Philip. The other is Paula, but she's not here. So it has to be you. Please, please do this for me, and for Philip. Help him to help himself," she pleaded, her desperation surfacing.

Shane was silent, ruminative.

Daisy said swiftly, "Go over to the penthouse tonight! Force your way in! Actually, that won't be necessary. I'll phone José, alert him that you're coming. He'll let you in, and once you're inside the penthouse, Philip will see you, I'm sure of that."

"All right," he agreed. "I'll go. I'll do my best."

"Thank you, Shane." She tried to smile without success. "Barry's been helpful," Daisy now explained. "But there's only so far he can go with Philip. He's awfully worried about him. He says Philip's full of anger. Rage, really. Rage that Maddy died. He doesn't seem able to accept it, or place her death in any kind of perspective."

"It's been the worst shock to him . . . a very severe shock."

Daisy opened her mouth, closed it, bit her inner lip. Then she said softly, "Oh Shane, he hasn't even been to see the baby since Jason and I brought her to our house from the hospital, or asked me about her either."

Shane was not altogether surprised to hear this. "Give him time on that one," he said and paused thoughtfully. He chose his words with care when he added, "He may well blame the baby for Maddy's death, and therefore himself, since he is the father of the child. Remember what Alan Stimpson said—that Maddy's pregnancy might have caused her to have the brain hemorrhage. I haven't forgotten how appalled Philip looked on hearing those words."

Daisy nodded. "Neither have I, and I'd thought of that, too. Blaming himself, I mean." She sighed heavily. "Barry says Philip sinks into the most awful depressions. Maddy's death is a terrible scar on his heart, one that will take months to heal."

If it ever does, Shane thought gloomily, although he did not voice this opinion to his mother-in-law, seeing no reason to worry her unduly. Instead, he said, "Now, tell me about the baby, Daisy."

Instantly her face changed, lit up. "Oh Shane, she's the most adorable little thing. Actually she reminds me of your Linnet and Emily's Natalie. She's definitely going to be another Botticelli redhead . . . she's a real little Harte through and through."

Shane smiled and nodded and listened, giving Daisy every ounce of his attention. He knew how important it was for her to speak about her new granddaughter, the long-awaited heiress to the great McGill empire. Poor kid, he thought suddenly at one moment, she's come into this world under a cloud and carrying a rotten burden . . . her mother's death. Shane knew then that he had to do everything within his power to make Philip accept and love the baby. For both of their sakes. The father needed the daughter just as much as the daughter needed him.

After Daisy finally left, Shane waded through an enormous amount of paperwork that had been accumulating over the past week. He then penned a quick but loving note to Paula, and wrote postcards to Lorne, Tessa, Patrick, and Linnet. He finished just before six o'clock, when he went into a meeting with Graham Johnson, managing director of the O'Neill hotel chain in Australia, and three of the other top executives in the company. The main subject on the agenda was the new O'Neill hotel currently under construction in Perth.

At seven-thirty Shane brought the meeting to a close, and he and Graham walked over to the Wentworth for dinner. When Shane was in Sydney, he always made it a point to visit other hotels in the city. He liked to take stock of the decor, food, drink, service, and conditions in general, in order to make comparisons between the competition and his own hotel. He had always liked the Wentworth, and he and Graham spent a pleasant couple of hours together over a delicious meal of roast baby lamb with the most succulent vegetables, and an excellent bottle of local red wine. For the most part they spoke about business, covering various aspects of the new hotel in Perth. Shane agreed to fly out to Western Australia with Graham the following week, before returning to London.

It was ten o'clock when the two men exited the hotel. Graham took a taxi home, and Shane strode off in the direction of Bridge Street where the McGill Tower was located. He needed the walk and the fresh air, after being cooped up in the executive offices of the hotel all day; also, he wanted to be certain Philip had finished dinner and was relaxing when he arrived at the penthouse. Daisy had suggested that he get there around ten-thirty and he had taken her advice.

A little while later, as he approached the black-glass skyscraper, Shane steeled himself for the impending encounter with his brother-in-law. He knew it was going to be difficult—painful, emotional, and upsetting. Riding up in the elevator, he asked himself what kind of wisdom he could offer Philip in his pain and sorrow, and he realized that he had none. All he could do was talk to the other man with compassion, give him his understanding, his support, and his love.

• • •

As prearranged by Daisy, the houseman, José, let Shane into the apartment as soon as he rang the doorbell.

The Filipino showed him into the beautiful cream-and-white living room that floated high over the city. It was dimly lit tonight, permitting the spectacular view to dominate. Bowing politely, the houseman said, "I tell Mr. Amory you here, sir."

"Thank you, José." Shane strolled over to a chair and sat down.

A split second later José was back, bowing again. "Mr. Amory says please wait."

"Yes, all right. Thanks again."

The Filipino smiled and bowed and hurried out on silent feet.

After fifteen minutes had elapsed, Shane grew restless, wondering what was keeping Philip. He got to his feet, walked over to the bar set against the far wall, poured himself a small cognac. He carried this back to the chair, where once more he sat down to wait. Sipping the drink, he mentally prepared himself for Philip, seeking the right words to use, the proper approach to take with him. One thing was vital. No matter what else he accomplished tonight, he must persuade Philip to go to Daisy's house with him tomorrow. To see the baby. He had made that promise to Daisy, and he himself knew how important it was that Philip put aside any feeling of blame, all guilt. Shane was convinced the baby was the key to Philip's well-being. Once he accepted her, he would love her, and only then would he begin to recover from his grief for Maddy, the loss of her.

It was another fifteen minutes before Philip finally emerged from his study. He stood hovering in the entrance to the living room, silently staring at Shane, his demeanor morose.

Shane rose at once, took a step forward, then stopped abruptly with a quick intake of breath. It took all of his self-control not to exclaim in concern when he saw his brother-in-law's appearance. Philip had lost weight, and there was an air of exhaustion about him, but it was his face that so appalled. It was ravaged. The cheeks were hollow, gaunt, the bright blue eyes dulled and red-rimmed, the purplish shadows beneath resembling dark bruises. The most startling thing of all, perhaps, was his black hair. It had turned pure white on either side of his temples.

There had never been any question in Shane's mind that Philip had taken Maddy's death badly; he had merely miscalculated the extent of his agony. The man was lacerated inside, suffering more horribly than even Shane had imagined. He understood then that whatever exterior equanimity Philip may display to the world it was utterly fraudulent. His cold containment and aloofness, so described by Barry, were his only defenses against total collapse. All this instantly became clear to Shane as he regarded Philip, and his heart went out to him.

Shane moved forward, and the two men clasped hands with their usual familial warmth.

Philip said, "I almost sent you away." He let go of Shane's hand, shrugged wearily, walked to the bar where he poured himself a large vodka, added ice cubes from the silver bucket.

"But there was no point—I suddenly realized that," he went on without turning around. "I knew you'd be back tomorrow or the day after and that my mother would come. And Jason. And then it occurred to me that one of you might have the insane idea of dragging Paula out here, so I decided I'd better see you . . ." Philip did not bother to finish his sentence. His voice was drained. He was worn out from lack of sleep, and his tiredness became apparent as he lethargically ambled over to the sofa and sat down. His usual vitality and vigor had fled.

Shane observed him quietly for a moment, then murmured, "It's been three weeks since Maddy was buried, and in that time you've seen me only once, Daisy only once. Your mother is worried about you, Philip, and so am I, for that matter."

"Don't be! I'm okay!" Philip said snappishly, with more spirit than he had displayed thus far.

"That's not true! You're not okay!" Shane shot back.

"Oh for God's sake, I'm fine."

"*I* don't think you are. And, very frankly, you need your family around you at a time like this. You need me and Daisy and Jason. Don't shun us, please. We want to help you, Philip, to comfort you as best we can."

"There is no comfort for me. I'll survive—everyone survives, I suspect. But the sorrow will stay with me forever . . . she was so young, don't you see? One expects old people to die . . . that's the life cycle. When we bury the old, time heals the pain eventually. But when we bury the young, the pain never, ever goes away."

"It will, please believe me, it will," Shane answered in his most compassionate voice. "And Maddy wouldn't want you to be like this. She would want you to take strength from—"

"I don't want you to make one religious statement to me, Shane!" Philip exclaimed with a flash of irritation.

"I wasn't going to," Shane replied gently.

Philip let out a long wearisome sigh, leaned back against the sofa, closed his eyes.

A silence drifted between the two men for a short while.

Suddenly, Philip got to his feet, went over to the bar, plopped more ice into his glass. He gave Shane a most penetrating stare, said in the bleakest of voices, "I can't remember anything about the past year, Shane. That's the most horrendous thing. It's . . . it's . . . *blank*. She's gone as if she never existed in my life." His voice broke, and he said hoarsely, "I can't remember *her* . . . I can't remember Maddy."

"That's the shock," Shane was quick to say, speaking with assurance, knowing this was the truth. "Really, it's only the shock, Philip. She'll come back to you."

Philip shook his head with vehemence. "No, she won't. I know she won't."

"The body is dead, but you have the spirit," Shane told him. "She's alive in you. Her spirit is in you, and in the child. Only her body's gone. Please believe that. Maddy is in your heart and in your memories, and she will be with you always. And there is the child."

Philip made no response.

He moved away from the bar, slowly crossed the room to the window, moving like an old man. He stood looking out. He had listened carefully to Shane, had absorbed his words. Now he was trying to come to terms with them, to accept them. Were they true? Was Maddy's spirit in him? Would she be with him always?

He sighed. He found no solace in anything Shane had just said to him. He had acknowledged the finality of death days ago, had acknowledged that his Maddy was gone from him forever. She had meant everything to him. She had been his life. Maddy had made the pain inside him stop, and just thinking about her had given him the happiest feeling, had warmed his heart. Now he could not even recall her face in his mind's eye. He had to look at a photograph to remember her. He did not understand why this was so. He had loved her so very much.

He snapped his eyes tightly shut, rested his aching head against the glass. He had killed her. He had killed the woman he loved more than life itself through the very act of love . . .

Shane said something, and Philip opened his eyes, but he did not answer. He had not been listening to his brother-in-law.

He stared at the night sky. How magnificent it was tonight, a deep midnight blue, velvet smooth, cloudless, filled with diamond stars and the bright, winking lights of the city's many skyscrapers. And off toward the eastern suburbs the sky was a curious amethyst spreading into the most vibrant of golds and a warm, glowing red.

It will be a beautiful day tomorrow, Philip thought absently. *Red sky at night, shepherd's delight, red sky at morning, shepherd's warning.* How many times had his grandmother said that to him when he was a little boy growing up. Emma had always been fascinated by skies and the light in them. Unexpectedly, the beauty of this evening's sky brought a lump to his throat and he did not comprehend exactly why. And then he remembered. Maddy, too, had forever commented about the clarity of light, cloud formations, the changing colors of the day as it moved into night.

Suddenly Philip stiffened, stepped closer to the window, frowning, his eyes focused on a dark cloud mass moving up above the skyscrapers several blocks away. How odd it looked. He couldn't quite make out what it was. "Oh my God!" he exclaimed a split second later. "Oh my God!"

Shane was on his feet, hurrying over to him. "What's wrong? Don't you feel well?"

Philip swung around, grabbed Shane's arm, pulled him over to the window. "Look! Over there! The black smoke, the red glow. Oh Christ, Shane, you've got a fire! The Sydney-O'Neill is on fire!"

Shane tensed. The breath caught in his throat as he followed Philip's gaze. He did not know the Sydney skyline as well as his brother-in-law, and it took him a moment to distinguish the smoke, find its source. He knew at once that it *was* his hotel going up in flames. He had just located the huge expanse of glass window wall that fronted his famous Orchid Room.

Without a word he pivoted, shot across the floor.

Philip followed, fast on his heels.

Together they took the elevator down, staring at each other speechlessly and in horror. As the elevator doors slid open, both men hit the lobby simultaneously, raced out into Bridge Street.

They began to run in the direction of the Sydney-O'Neill, the sound of their pounding feet drowned out by the screaming sirens of the three fire engines hurtling past them at breakneck speed.

——— *Thirty-Eight* ———

As Shane ran on, heading for the hotel, he was not sure what to expect when he got there. Disaster, obviously, but to what extent and degree he was uncertain.

Only a hotelier understood the true horror of a hotel fire and its nightmarish consequences. So all of Shane's senses were alert to the greatest possible danger, endless problems of the most appalling kind. There would be panic, fear, chaos, and every type of injury. Smoke inhalation, burns, broken bones, trauma, shock. And death.

Rounding the corner of the street, he came into full view of the Sydney-O'Neill, his favorite hotel in the international chain. What he saw brought him to a complete standstill. "Oh God! No! No!" he gasped out loud. He was momentarily stunned, rooted to the spot.

His hotel was an inferno.

Flames, black smoke, heat confronted him. Helicopters circled and hovered over the top of the burning building, lifting people off the roof. Fire engines were in full operation with swarms of fire fighters manning hoses from the ground and from ladders; others were using ropes and ladders to rescue those trapped on some of the high floors.

There were ambulances and police cars parked at various strategic points. Doctors, paramedics, and the police were doing everything in their power to help those in need. Three ambulances carrying the injured sped past him, their sirens wailing as they headed to the nearest hospital.

Shane pulled his handkerchief out of his pocket, wiped his damp face. He was sweating profusely from running, the sudden intense heat, and fear for those who might still be trapped in the hotel. The scene before him was appalling, just as he had anticipated. Everywhere there was broken glass, debris on the ground, blinding smoke that was lethal in itself, the raised voices of police and hotel staff shouting orders, the sounds of crying and moaning from those in distress. A group of hotel guests, many of them in their night clothes, looked unnerved and frightened as they huddled together near a police car. Shane was about to go over to them when he saw two of the hotel's porters assisting them. They were taken over to the ambulance set up as a first-aid unit; here they would be treated for minor injuries, shock, and trauma.

Covering his mouth with his handkerchief, Shane pushed his way through the people milling around—hotel staff and security guards, police officers, paramedics, and ambulance drivers. He had to get closer to the hotel, knew he must take command of the situation immediately.

A policeman stopped him. "You can't go any nearer than this, sir. It could be dangerous."

"Thanks, officer, for your warning. But I'm Shane O'Neill, the owner of the hotel. I must get through, do what I can to help."

"Go right ahead, Mr. O'Neill," the officer said, suddenly recognizing him. He gave Shane a sympathetic look as he let him pass through the wooden barricade that had been erected.

Almost at once Shane spotted Peter Wood, the night duty manager. He grabbed his arm.

Wood swung around almost violently. A look of relief spread across his grimy face when he saw it was Shane. "Mr. O'Neill! Thank God you're okay! We tried to ring you when the first alarm went off around eleven o'clock. We realized you weren't in your suite. But we didn't know whether you were somewhere else in the hotel. We've been as worried as hell, keeping our eyes peeled for you."

"I was out of the hotel," Shane said. He gave the night manager a hard stare. "Do you know how many casualties there have been?"

Peter Wood shook his head. "Not exactly. But I'd say about fifteen people injured." He paused, dropped his voice. "And four dead, I think."

"Oh Jesus!" Shane drew Wood to one side as several guests were being shepherded to safety by a hotel security guard. When they were out of earshot, he asked, "Do we know what started this?"

"No. But I have my own ideas."

Shane peered at him swiftly, frowning. "You're not suggesting arson?"

"No, no. Why would anyone want to set the hotel on fire?"

"A disgruntled employee, perhaps? One who'd been sacked recently?"

Wood said very firmly, "No, Mr. O'Neill, I'm sure it's nothing like that. If you want my opinion, I believe it was an accident."

"I see. Where did it start, Peter?"

"On the thirty-fourth floor." Wood gave Shane a pointed look. "You were lucky, Mr. O'Neill. You had a narrow escape."

Shane stared at Wood, the full impact of the manager's words suddenly hitting him. His own suite was on that floor, along with a number of other private apartments leased out on a permanent basis. There were rooms and suites for hotel guests on the thirty-fifth floor, and situated on the thirty-sixth floor, at the very top of the building, was the famous Orchid Room.

Shane exclaimed, "I can only thank God that I closed the entire thirty-fifth floor and the Orchid Room for redecoration last week. Otherwise this disaster would have been ten times worse if we'd had guests on the thirty-fifth floor, not to mention two hundred people dining and dancing in the restaurant tonight."

"Yes, we've all been saying the same thing."

"I presume most of the guests have been evacuated to emergency facilities in other hotels?"

Wood nodded. "To the Hilton and the Wentworth. We're lucky in another sense, sir. The O'Neill was not filled to capacity this week."

Philip ran up to them at this moment. He was out of breath, perspiring. "I've been looking for you," he said to Shane, then turned, nodded to Peter Wood. "What can I do to help?"

"Not very much," Shane replied. "From what I can see, the actions of my staff and the various agencies called to the scene have been tremendous. It *looked* like chaos when I arrived a few minutes ago, but it's not. They seem to have things under control." He glanced toward the hotel, his expression pained. Two of the middle floors were still burning, but reinforcements had been brought in; additional fire fighters were tackling the blaze with renewed energy, would soon have it put out.

Philip said, "Perhaps I can—"

Neither Shane nor Peter Wood heard what he said next. His voice was drowned out by a thunderous explosion that sounded like several huge kegs of dynamite going off. It rent the air, made all of them jump. They swung to stare at the hotel. Shock and apprehension flooded their faces.

"What the bloody hell was that?" Philip cried.

"Windows blowing out from the intense heat within the shell of the hotel," Shane said, shuddering. He dreaded to think that there might be more casualties.

"But I don't see any broken glass falling," Philip muttered, looking baffled.

"Neither do I," Shane said. "But I'm sure that's what it was."

Peter Wood volunteered, "It's probably the windows on the other side of the building, Mr. Amory, the rooms facing Sydney Harbour."

A young woman wearing a dressing gown, her face streaked with dirt, hurried up to them. She appeared distracted, afraid. "Please help me," she said, tugging at Philip's arm. "Please, please help me. I can't find my little girl. She's lost. I can't find her. I know we got her out. I know we did." The woman's face crumpled. She began to weep hysterically.

Philip put his arm around her. "I'm sure she's in a safe spot. Come along, I'll help you to find your child."

"She's only four," the woman sobbed. "A baby, just a baby."

Philip attempted to comfort her as he led her off. His own agony, his all-consuming grief were forgotten in the horrendous tragedy of the fire.

By four o'clock in the morning the fire was out.

All of the injured, numbering some twenty-five, had been taken to the emergency room at St. Vincent's Hospital and to other hospitals in the city. The dead, totaling nine men and women, were in the morgue.

Fire fighters, police, and hotel staff were bringing complete order to the area. Shane had been in command for several hours, handling everything with cool authority and decisiveness.

The Sydney-O'Neill was a smouldering ruin, blackened by smoke, a burnt-out hulk against the skyline. Shane and Philip stood together in the rubble as dawn broke, looking up at it, both of their faces grim.

"What a horrible tragedy this has been," Shane murmured, turning to his brother-in-law. "So many injured and dead. It should never have happened. All I can think about are the families of those who died." He sighed heavily. "Well, I'm glad you were able to help that young woman. She was quite demented. Where *did* you find her little girl?"

"In one of the ambulances, being looked after by a paramedic. She wasn't injured, thankfully. Just scared after becoming separated from her mother." Philip took hold of Shane's arm, wanting to console him. "I'm sorry this disaster had to happen to you, Shane. You're suffering terribly because of the loss of lives, and for those who have been injured. But quite aside from that, I know how much you prided yourself on your safety systems."

When Shane was silent, Philip added, "I understand what this particular hotel meant to you. I'm so very sorry. I'll do anything I can to help you."

"Thanks, Philip." Shane rubbed his tired face, shook his head with weariness. So much for Blackie's dream, he thought, remembering how excited his grandfather had been about building the Sydney-O'Neill. It was he who had found and bought the land on a visit to Sydney with Emma years before, he who had decided it would be the flagship hotel in the Antipodes. Blackie had not lived to see it constructed, but he had approved of the first architectural blueprints before he died. Now his dream had gone up in smoke in the space of a few hours.

"I'll build it again," Shane said, as if making a promise to his grandfather.

"I know you will," Philip answered. "Now, come on back with me to the penthouse to clean up. You're going to need clothes and the like. It's a good thing we're about the same size."

Later that morning, showered, shaved, and wearing his brother-in-law's clothes, an exhausted Shane set up headquarters in the boardroom of the Mc-Gill Corporation.

It was here that he held his first meeting, began the investigation into the cause of the fire at his hotel. Present with him were Peter Wood, the night manager who had been on duty when the fire broke out; Lewis Bingley, the general manager; Graham Johnson, managing director of the O'Neill hotel chain in Australia, various executives from the Sydney-O'Neill, and Fire Chief Don Arnold, who had been in charge of the fire fighters the night before.

Once introductions had been made, greetings exchanged, Shane went straight to the heart of the matter. "We're looking to you for information at this moment, I'm afraid, Chief Arnold," he said. "I understand that you and your men have talked at length to many members of the hotel staff. Have you any idea how the fire started?"

"Through carelessness on the part of someone staying in the hotel," the chief said. "From what we found on the thirty-fourth floor, where it began, and from what we've since discovered, we're certain it was started by a cigarette. One that most probably fell into a sofa in a suite on that floor. One of the private jobs you lease out. In this instance, the suite leased to the Jaty Corporation."

"Could you go into a few more details, please, Chief Arnold?" Shane asked.

"Sure thing. One of the room service waiters came forward in the early hours of this morning. He told me that he remembered noticing an ashtray perched on the arm on a sofa in that particular suite. That was when he went to remove the dinner trolley around eight o'clock. I believe that the ashtray remained on the arm of the settee, that it was used several times before the couple occupying the suite went to bed. The ashtray later fell into the sofa, and a cigarette, which was not quite out, set light to the sofa. More than likely, it smouldered for a couple of hours until it actually burst into flames. Only seconds after waking, the two people in that private suite were dead."

"How do you know that?" Shane asked quietly.

"Two of my firemen found them huddled in the bedroom. They were not burnt. They were poisoned by the fumes from the foam stuffing in the sofa. It's so highly flammable that within seconds it creates the kind of inferno you had in your hotel last night. And those flames are so hot, so very intense, they can punch a hole in a wall or a ceiling, and shatter windows. The foam also gives off the most fatal fumes, chiefly cyanide and carbon monoxide."

Shane was horrified. He looked at Lewis Bingley, and exclaimed sharply, "Regulations against the use of foam in furniture were passed by the British

Government in 1981. I've had foam banned in all my hotels for the past year. How come it was used here?"

Lewis Bingley shook his head. "We followed your instructions, Mr. O'Neill, we really did. There is no foam in any of the furniture used in the hotel. You know we replaced all the furniture."

"But you just heard what Chief Arnold said! That sofa in the Jaty Corporation suite was upholstered with foam!"

The general manager pursed his lips nervously. "I can only think that it crept past us. *Somehow.* You see, Mr. O'Neill, the president of the Jaty Corporation used his own interior decorators, and they furnished the suite for him."

"Were they told of our new regulations?" Shane demanded.

"Oh yes. But they apparently ignored them," Bingley muttered.

"That is outrageous!" Shane exploded. "And in any case, we were remiss for not going back, checking that the decorators had heeded our warning about the foam." He tried to quiet his boiling anger, turned to the fire chief. "Who were the couple who died in the suite? Have they been identified yet?"

"The son and daughter-in-law of the president of the Jaty Corporation."

Shane shook his head sadly. His face was grave, troubled. "That's your analysis of how the fire began. But what happened next, Chief Arnold?"

"I think the sequence of events went like this." Don Arnold then explained, "To quickly recap, the cigarette set the sofa alight. The foam smouldered, eventually burst into flames. That would have been around ten forty-five, ten-fifty, in my estimation. The flames had such intensity they blew out the windows within seconds. The sudden, new supply of oxygen created a wall of fire that burned right through the doors of the suite. Fuelled by the oxygen, the fire gained murderous force as it roared along the corridor of the thirty-fourth floor. It all happened in the space of minutes. Ten or fifteen, I'd say. Fire travels with the speed of light."

Shane nodded his understanding. He was unable to speak for a moment. He was shocked by what he had just heard. Negligence, he thought. First on the part of the decorators and then on the part of my management. They should have had that private suite checked once it was furnished. This tragedy might well have been avoided if they had. He sighed under his breath again. He had to hold Lewis Bingley accountable.

"One thing's for sure, Mr. O'Neill," Chief Arnold was saying, "your safety systems are the very best. The smoke detectors, the fire doors, and the sprinklers all worked like clockwork. If the hotel hadn't been as perfectly maintained for safety as it was, you would have had an even worse disaster on your hands."

Jason said, "This place gives me the joes."

Shane stared at him. "What do you mean?"

"It makes me depressed. It's so damn gloomy, the shades drawn, the lamps turned low." Jason eyed the half empty bottle of scotch on the coffee table. "And drinking in the middle of the afternoon, that's not you, Shane. Come on, mate, the booze ain't going to get you anywhere."

"I'm stone cold sober. But frankly, I feel like getting drunk. Bloody pissed to the gills, if you want to know the truth."

Jason shook his head. "You've had kronk mozzle, Shane, real bad luck. But you ain't no jackeroo. You know things like this can happen."

"I can't believe the hotel burned to the ground," Shane began and stopped. He sprang up, began pacing the floor as he had been doing off and on for days. *"Negligence! Sheer bloody negligence!"* he fumed. "If I'm not breathing down their necks every minute of the day, things start to go wrong—"

"You shouldn't be in business if you don't want the agro. And aggravation *is* the key word these days, mate. Still, I know what you mean. The fire's been a bleedin' horrible tragedy. I can well understand why you're angry."

Shane exclaimed, "I pay the best wages, big bonuses, they get all kinds of benefits and God knows what else, and they can't check out the furniture in a bloody private suite. It's criminal, Jason. Criminal. You know as well as I do that the fire would never have happened if they'd been on top of the situation. Those poor people would not have died or been injured, if my managers had done their jobs properly. That's what makes my blood boil. So much pain and suffering for all those concerned. And I'm going to be up to my eyeballs in lawsuits and lawyers, not to mention insurance company investigators. Now *they're* about to start their own investigation into the fire."

"Well, that's to be expected, Shane," Jason was quick to point out. "And you *know* that. Anyway, they're going to come to the same conclusions as the fire chief, I'm sure. And look, there's no reason why you can't start making plans for the rebuilding of the Sydney-O'Neill, get the architects working on the blueprints already."

"I don't think I'm going to rebuild."

Jason was shocked. "You have to build a new hotel, Shane! You owe it to your grandfather. More importantly, you owe it to yourself."

Shane made no response. He sat down heavily on the sofa, dropped his head in his hands, this gesture full of weariness and despair.

Jason looked down at him, suddenly worried. He had never seen Shane like this, disheveled and unshaven, still wearing his pajamas and dressing gown in the middle of the afternoon. What was wrong with these young guys? Didn't they have any balls? First Philip had fallen apart after Maddy's death, and now Shane looked as if he was about to go to pieces, too.

Jason cleared his throat. "You were so abrupt with Daisy on the phone earlier, she asked me to come over to see what was going on here. She wants you to come out to Rose Bay for dinner tonight."

Shane lifted his head, shook it. "I have to work." He shoved the pile of folders on the coffee table in front of him. "I have all this paperwork about the fire to deal with."

"It's Saturday. You've got to take a break sometime. And by the way, where's Philip?"

"I honestly don't know, Jason. And if you'll forgive me, I really can't worry about him right now. Frankly, I've got enough problems of my own to contend with."

"Yes, I know. That's why Daisy and I want you to come over for dinner. It'll do you good to get out, to be with people."

"No, I want to be alone. And really, it's best that I am. I've a lot to do. And a lot of thinking to do."

"You know you can come over any time, if you change your mind."

"Yes. Thanks, Jason."

Shane picked up the bottle of scotch and poured himself another drink.

Jason shook his head sadly as he left the study, crossed the foyer, and quietly let himself out of the penthouse.

——— *Thirty-Nine* ———

Alone, he rode across his land.

He was mounted on Black Opal, his ebony-colored stallion. Keeping pace at his side was a riderless horse. It was Gilda, the roan he had given Maddy after their marriage. Before leaving the stables he had strapped on Maddy's favorite silver-chased saddle, and turned the stirrups backward to symbolize that her owner would never ride her again.

It was the first time he had been back to Dunoon since he had buried Maddy here four weeks ago.

When he had arrived on Friday night, Tim and everyone else on the sheep station had welcomed him warmly, and it was apparent they were glad that he had at last returned. So was he.

Maddy's death had torn him apart, and he was filled with an unendurable sorrow. He had been afraid that it would be too painful to come here. They had been so happy together at Dunoon. But now, as he rode through the lovely, pastoral countryside on this Sunday afternoon, he felt a certain kind of peace settling over him. He knew that in part it was due to the tranquility, the gentleness, the stillness that abounded here.

He followed the Castlereagh River for a long time, then branched off, crossed several meadows, and took the winding track that led through the green hills of Dunoon. When he reached the crest of the steep incline, he dismounted, walked over to the great oak, stood gazing out across the extraordinary landscape.

How beautiful it looked after two days of rain. Everything was green and shimmering. It was the end of August, almost the end of winter. In a few weeks it would be spring; already the weather was superb, mild for this time of year. Philip lifted his eyes. The sky was a bright, polished blue, radiant with sunlight. The very perfection of the day seemed to underscore his sadness. It was a day to share . . . with someone . . .

Philip turned away, went and sat down under the oak, propped himself against its ancient trunk. Taking off his flat-brimmed hat, he threw it to one side, endeavoring to relax. His thoughts were scattered, chaotic still, his mind fogged by pain. But perhaps here he would be able to find a little ease.

This was his special place; it always had been since his childhood. Maddy, too, had grown to love it up here on this high land. She had said it was like being part of the sky. He smiled to himself at the remembrance, then recalled the morning he had met her in the portrait gallery, not quite a year ago.

They had ridden out here, had sat for a while under this leafy old tree. He had said some extremely personal things to her, which had even startled him at the time. But she had not seemed to mind. She had looked at him for the longest moment, her lovely, intelligent gray eyes so quiet and unwavering, but she had made no comment. And at that precise moment he had known he would marry her.

Madelana had been unique among the women he had ever met. From the outset of their relationship there had been a strange familiarity about her. It was as if he had known her, been separated from her, then reunited with her again. He realized now that he had felt this way because he had been looking for someone like her all his life, that she was the woman he had idealized in his mind. He had found her finally, only to lose her . . . so quickly.

Maddy had had such inner grace. That, perhaps, had been the source of her radiance . . . she had been an incandescent being. A fragment of a poem by Rupert Brooke flashed through his mind . . . *All about you was the light that dims the greying end of night, . . . and, in the flowing of your dress, undiscerning tenderness.*

Philip sighed and closed his eyes, allowed himself to drift with his myriad thoughts, and slowly the memories came flooding back. He began to remember every little thing about their relationship . . . every single moment he had ever spent with her was suddenly crystal clear. He recalled the hours, the days, the weeks, the months. Each and every detail was precise and exactly in place, as if a reel of film was being projected before his eyes. And on that hillside, where he had been taken by Emma Harte as a boy, he found his Maddy again. He saw her as she had been the instant he had first set eyes on her in the gallery, her image intact. He smelled the fragrance of her hair, heard the laughter and joyousness in her voice, felt the gentle touch of her hand on his. And the tears came then, and he wept for her, and he remained on the hillside until the light began to fade.

And as he rode back to the manor, down through the green hills of Dunoon, the riderless horse at his side, he felt her presence everywhere, and he knew he would never lose his Maddy ever again. She was in his heart, and she would be a part of him for as long as he lived. Shane *had* been right. Her spirit *was* in him.

He flew back to Sydney late that night. Early on Monday morning he went out to Rose Bay.

His mother was startled to see him standing in the middle of her living room, and her surprise showed as she hurried to greet him.

Cool sunlight was pouring in through the windows, illuminating Philip's face most painfully. Daisy felt herself flinching inside and her heart shriveled. He looked as if he hadn't slept for weeks. His face was a study in desolation. There was a haggardness about him that startled her, as did the streaks of white in his black hair. It seemed to Daisy that he was a shadow of the man he had once been, his looks gone, his vigor and energy vitiated completely.

She wanted to take her son in her arms and comfort him, but she did not dare. He had pushed her away, held her at arm's length since Maddy's death, and she had respected his wishes, had had no alternative but to leave him alone in his sorrow.

And so she was further surprised when he took a step forward, wrapped his arms around her. He held on to her tightly, as he had done when he was a small boy needing consolation, and she clung to him, loving him with all her heart. Neither spoke. This long embrace was enough; words were not needed. And Daisy understood deep within herself that the healing process had started for him. And she thanked God.

Eventually he released her and said, "Well, Mother, I thought I'd better come out to see you . . ."

"I'm so glad you did, Philip."

"I'm sorry for the way I've behaved, Ma. I realize I've been impossible, difficult with you, and with everyone else for that matter. But very simply, I couldn't help myself."

"Oh darling . . . I understand, truly I do. You've been suffering so very much."

"Yes." He hesitated a moment, then continued slowly, "Seeing Maddy's young life cut tragically short has been heartbreaking for me, and I honestly thought I would never be able to sustain the loss of her. It's been pure hell, Ma. But then last night, flying back from Dunoon, I began to realize there was also a degree of self-pity in my grief. I was not only mourning for Maddy, but mourning for myself as well . . . and mourning for the life we'll never have together now."

"That's only natural," Daisy murmured softly, her vivid blue eyes filling with sympathy and understanding.

"Yes, I suppose it is." He moved away from her, edged toward the door, then swung to face her suddenly. There was a little pause before he blurted out, "I've come to get the baby."

Daisy looked at him swiftly. Her heart lifted. "Fiona's with the nanny. The young Englishwoman Maddy engaged before she—" Daisy cut herself off, looked at Philip uneasily.

"Don't be afraid to mention Maddy's death, Ma. I've accepted it."

Daisy could only nod. She was reluctant to speak in case her voice trembled.

She led the way upstairs. "This is Mr. Amory. My son," Daisy said to the nanny as they entered the room.

"Yes, I know, Mrs. Rickards. We met when I went for the interview with Mrs. Amory."

Philip shook the nanny's hand, murmured a greeting, then strode over to the crib in the corner of the bedroom which was serving as a nursery.

He stood staring down at the baby.

He had not seen her since the day she was born. She was already a month old. After a few seconds, he bent down, reached into the crib, picked her up somewhat tentatively, looking trepidatious, as though he thought she might break in half.

Holding her away from him, he gazed into her small face. A pair of solemn gray eyes stared back at him unwaveringly. Maddy's eyes, he thought, and choked up. Bringing the baby to his chest, he held her tightly in his arms, close to his heart, one hand on her head protectively. This was Maddy's child. His child. A wave of love for the baby swept through him.

Slowly, Philip walked across the floor, still holding Fiona in his arms. He paused at the door, swung around.

"I'm taking my daughter home," he said. He glanced at Daisy. "Don't look so worried, Ma. It's all right. I'm all right." A small smile glanced across his mouth. "And *we're* going to be all right. We have each other."

Forty

"I tried to stop you coming over, Emily," Paula said as her cousin hurried into the study of the house in Belgrave Square. "But I was too late. Your house-keeper told me you'd just left."

Emily paused in the middle of the antique Aubusson carpet. She squinted across at Paula, who was sitting on the sofa in a pool of September sunlight. "Don't you want me to go with you to Heathrow after all?"

Paula shook her head, looking regretful. "I just hung up on Shane a short while ago. He doesn't want me to fly out to Sydney. So I've canceled my trip."

Emily was amazed. "But why doesn't he want you to join him? You said he was all for it the other day, when you suggested it, urging you to come, in fact."

"He was, and *I* believe I *should* be with him at a time like this, but he now says he can handle things by himself, insists he's over the shock of the fire. Anyway, he thinks I ought to be here with the children. You know he's always had a bee in his bonnet about one of us being at home for their sakes."

"Winston feels the same way. But then so do we," Emily reminded her. She eyed Paula carefully. "Let's not forget that Grandy taught us to be responsible parents. She said that when we had children we should put them first, consider their needs above all else. In fact, she was adamant about it, most probably because she so frequently neglected her own."

"Emily! That's not a nice thing to say!"

"But it's true. And Grandy said so herself. She was so busy empire build-ing, her kids took second place. Except for your mother. Aunt Daisy was the lucky one. Probably because Gran had made it by the time she was born."

Paula had the good grace to laugh. "Yes, you're right as usual, Emily." She let out a long sigh. "As much as I really want to be with Shane, I'm afraid it has to be his decision." A wry little smile touched her mouth. "Still, I can't help wishing I'd missed his phone call this morning. You see, I do think he needs me, despite what he says, if only for moral support."

"Then why not just *go,*" Emily suggested.

"Come on, Dumpling, you ought to know better than that!" Paula laughed hollowly. "Shane would be furious with me—you know how bossy and dictatorial he is—and the trip would then serve no purpose whatsoever."

"I suppose you'd better do what he says," Emily agreed, knowing how difficult Shane could be at times. She sat down in the chair opposite Paula, glanced at the breakfast tray on the antique Georgian coffee table positioned between them, saw that it was set for two. "It was jolly nice of you to include a cup for me," she said, smiling at her cousin. As she lifted the teapot and poured, she contemplated the basket of fancy French breakfast rolls. "You don't want that brioche, do you?"

"No, I seem to have put on weight in the past week. But you shouldn't eat it either," Paula warned.

"I know I shouldn't," Emily said and promptly reached for it. She looked thoughtful as she munched on the brioche. After a sip of tea, she sat back, said slowly, "Look here, Paula, perhaps Winston ought to go to Sydney. At least he would be able to keep Shane company, and I'm certain he could be very helpful in innumerable ways. He's leaving Toronto this afternoon and he'll be in New York tonight. Instead of going to Rochester to look at that printing plant, he could fly to L.A. From there he could continue on to Sydney, take that night flight you always rave about. I'll phone him right now."

"It's four o'clock in the morning in Canada!"

"So what. This is an emergency."

"No, it isn't, Emily, not anymore. Besides, I don't think Winston should go. Shane will be fine, he's a very strong person. He was just badly shaken up by the fire. And frankly, who wouldn't be? He was devastated that so many people were killed and injured. He kept repeating that every time he called, and you know he's hardly been off the phone to me since it happened. I think he went into a depression for several days—at least, that's the impression Mummy gave me. But he's pulled out of it now; I can tell by the tone of his voice. As I said, I'd prefer to go, to be with him, but I must do what *he* thinks is best."

"Yes," Emily said slowly; then she added, "And of course he does have a lot of strength—you're correct there. If anyone can cope, it's Shane."

"I *know* he can, Dumps. And remember, it's not as if he's alone. There's my mother and Jason, and Philip, of course."

"Is Philip better then?" Emily asked.

"Yes, I'm glad to report. Shane told me Philip went over to my mother's the other day and took the baby home with him at long last."

"Thank goodness for that! I was getting a bit worried, I must admit. I had visions of Aunt Daisy and Jason having to raise Fiona. Imagine, at their ages!"

Paula smiled faintly at this remark. "Shane believes the disastrous fire and all it entailed shocked Philip out of his frozen state, brought him back to reality."

"I'm sure he's right. Shane's got a lot of insight into people, knows what makes them tick." She shook her head sadly. "Poor Maddy . . . dying in that way, so suddenly. It's been hard for me to accept."

"I know what you mean." Paula fell silent, thinking of Maddy. There was a dull ache in her heart for her sister-in-law. She missed her terribly, and her own grief had still not entirely abated. There were times when her eyes would fill up, even at work, and she had to excuse herself if she was with people, hurry away to be alone, to regain her composure. Maddy had been a most unusual woman and she had affected all of their lives.

Paula settled herself against the cushions, gazed off into the distance. Her eyes held a faraway look.

Emily watched her, but said nothing, not wishing to intrude on her at this moment. She knew Paula was thinking of Madelana, whose death had so shocked her, upset her so badly.

Out of the blue, Paula murmured in a voice suddenly turned gloomy, "I'm beginning to think there's a curse on this family."

Struck by the seriousness of her tone, Emily sat up in the chair and gaped at her. "Paula! How superstitious of you! You sound positively Celtic . . . some of Shane's Irishness must be rubbing off on you!"

"Well, just consider the past year, Emily. There's been the regurgitation of that old deception in Ireland, which ultimately led to the death of the estate manager. It was all very upsetting for Anthony and Sally, having to relive Min's death. And Anthony's felt responsible for Michael Lamont's stroke ever since it happened."

"It's better Michael Lamont keeled over from a stroke and died, rather than face a trial for murder."

"Good God, Emily! You fair take my breath away at times, some of the things you say!"

"But it's true, and I'm not a hypocrite."

"I know that, but you're so *blunt.*"

"Like Gran."

"Yes, like Gran," Paula agreed. There was a short pause before she continued softly, "Then there was Sandy's fatal illness, his shooting accident, followed by Maddy's brain hemorrhage and subsequent death, and last week the Sydney-O'Neill went up in smoke. Surely that's enough to make anybody think there's some sort of curse on them. Anyway, look at the terrible things that happened to Grandy throughout her lifetime. And what about the avalanche that killed Daddy, Jim, and Maggie? And there's my little Patrick, who was born retarded." Paula gave Emily a pointed stare. "It's as if we're being punished for something."

Not wishing to encourage Paula in these sudden, dire thoughts, Emily exclaimed dismissively. "Oh pooh! I don't believe that! We're a big, sprawling family—like the Kennedys. All sorts of awful things happen to people during their lives, but when there are a lot of you, as in our case, disasters only appear to be so much more numerous than in a small family. And despite everything, *I* happen to think we've been lucky . . . and in so many countless ways."

"Granted we're all fabulously successful and rich, but we've had more than our fair share of tragedies."

"And I suppose we'll have many more."

"My God, Emily, you sound like Job's comforter."

"Oh sorry, darling, I don't mean to; nor do I mean to make light of the dreadful things that have recently happened in Australia. But I won't subscribe to superstition, and I'm surprised at you. Cursed indeed." Emily grinned, shook her head as if highly amused. "I can tell you this—if our Gran were alive, she'd have a real belly laugh."

"What do you mean?"

"She'd pooh-pooh you, too. She often said that we write our own scripts, live in what we ourselves create, and that we're ultimately responsible for everything that happens to us."

"*I* don't ever remember hearing her say that." Paula stared at Emily, frowning. Her eyes were puzzled. "Are you sure it was Grandy who said it?"

"Oh yes."

Paula nodded, and then she changed the subject.

But later that night she was to recall those words, and as she acknowledged their basic truth she did so with growing apprehension.

Paula spent the rest of the morning and most of the afternoon out on the floor of the store in Knightsbridge.

As she walked back into her private office, just after three-thirty, her private line began to shrill. Hurrying to the desk, she leaned across it, snatched up the phone, half expecting it to be Shane. Sydney was ten hours ahead of London, and he frequently rang her before going to sleep.

Her voice was therefore light, cheerful, as she said, "Paula O'Neill here," and clutching the phone to her ear, she walked briskly around the desk.

"It's Charles Rossiter, Paula."

"Hello, Charles! How are you?" She was disappointed, but she kept her voice gay.

"Er . . . I'm fine, thank you."

"You got my message then?"

"Message?" he sounded vague, slightly impatient.

"I telephoned you this morning, to let you know I'm not going to Sydney after all. So we can still have lunch on Friday, as we'd originally planned."

"Oh yes, of course I received it—"

There was a sudden pause, a hesitation on the part of her banker, and Paula said, "That *is* why you're calling, isn't it? To confirm our lunch?"

"No, actually, it's not."

She caught an odd note in his voice. "Is there some kind of problem, Charles?"

"I'm afraid so."

"But I thought those new documents were in order, and that—"

"It's nothing to do with your usual banking business with us, Paula," Charles interrupted. "Something very urgent has come up. I think you must come down to the bank for a meeting this afternoon. Say at five o'clock."

"Why, Charles? What's going on? You sound very mysterious."

"I received a telephone call a bit earlier this afternoon from Sir Logan Curtis. I'm sure you've heard of him, and of Blair, Curtis, Somerset, and Lomax."

"Of course. They're a very prestigious firm of solicitors, and Sir Logan is distinguished as one of the foremost legal brains in the country."

"Quite. Sir Logan requested a meeting today. Here at the bank with me. He wishes you to be present."

"Why?" she asked, surprised.

"Seemingly he represents your cousin, Jonathan Ainsley. The latter is visiting London from Hong Kong, where he has apparently lived for the past ten or twelve years. According to Sir Logan, it is actually Ainsley who wants the meeting with us. To discuss a matter of business he has with you."

Paula was so startled she almost dropped the receiver. She was speechless for a moment, before exclaiming, "I have no business dealings with Jonathan Ainsley! As you are well aware, Charles. You've been my banker for years. My cousin draws dividends from Harte Enterprises, of course, but that is his sole involvement with the family. And with any of our businesses."

"Not according to Sir Logan."

"But you know otherwise!" she cried, her voice rising shrilly. "Sir Logan has been misinformed."

"I don't believe so."

"Charles, what on earth do you mean?" Aghast, she sat down in the chair.

"Look here, Paula, I'd really prefer not to go into it any further over the telephone. Quite aside from the confidentiality of the matter, I just stepped out of our annual board meeting to phone you, after I'd made the decision to accede to Sir Logan's request for a meeting. I'm very pressed. I must go back to the boardroom at once. However, I will say this, it is *imperative* that you are present."

"I don't understand."

"Whatever Jonathan Ainsley's business is with you, seemingly it could affect this bank, the other banks you deal with in the city, and the Harte stores."

"I'm more puzzled than ever! You must explain in greater detail!"

"I'm afraid I can't, Paula," Charles exclaimed, trying to keep his voice down. "I'm not being evasive. Please believe me, I'm not. Sir Logan gave me only the broadest outlines. He, too, did not wish to have a protracted conversation about confidential business over the phone. However, he did stress the importance of the matter to all of us. That's why I'm agreeing to the meeting. It sounds critical. Furthermore, I deem your presence to be crucial."

"I'll be there, Charles. At five sharp."

"Good. One more thing . . . I must forewarn you, Paula, Jonathan Ainsley will be in attendance this afternoon."

"I see," she answered grimly.

After she had said good-bye and hung up, Paula leaned back in the chair, pressed her fingers to her eyes. She was so stunned it took her a few minutes to gather her scattered thoughts, to get her mind working properly again.

She focused her concentration on her cousin. *Jonathan Ainsley,* she thought. *Why has he come back? What does he want?* She had no answers for herself. But she did remember the threat he had made against her years before, and her blood ran cold.

Forty-One

It was exactly five minutes to five when Paula walked into the Rossiter Merchant Bank in the City.

Charles Rossiter's private secretary was waiting for her in the reception area and took her into Charles's office at once.

The chairman of the bank, who was an old family friend, hurried to greet her, kissed her on the cheek.

"Have they arrived?" Paula asked as they drew apart, stood regarding each other worriedly in the middle of the room.

"Yes, about fifteen minutes ago. They're waiting for us in the boardroom."

"Do you know more about all this now, Charles?"

"A little. Sir Logan discussed it with me briefly."

"Jonathan Ainsley owns shares in Harte's, doesn't he?"

Charles nodded.

"He bought some or all of my ten percent which I put on the market recently, didn't he?"

"Yes. *All of it.*"

"I thought so. I figured that much out on the way here," Paula murmured, giving the banker a bleak little smile.

"He wants a seat on Harte's board of directors."

"He can't ask that! Owning ten percent of the shares doesn't give him the right to ask that! He can go to hell!"

"He's demanding it, Paula. And in my estimation he's out to make trouble for you."

"Obviously, Charles. Otherwise he wouldn't have bothered to come all the way from Hong Kong. Now, shall we go in? Get it over with?"

"Yes, let's do that," Charles agreed, escorting her across the room. He opened the side door which led directly into the oak-paneled boardroom of the bank.

Sir Logan Curtis, small, gray-haired, younger-looking than she had expected, came forward as they walked in.

"Mrs. O'Neill, I'm Logan Curtis," he announced before Charles had a chance to make the introduction. He smiled as he offered her his hand.

Paula took it. "How do you do," she said in a businesslike tone. Out of the corner of her eye she could see Jonathan seated at the conference table. He did not rise, neither did he greet her, and she did not acknowledge him.

Sir Logan said, "Your cousin wishes to speak with you privately, Mrs. O'Neill. We will withdraw, leave you alone together." He glanced pointedly at Charles Rossiter as he walked over to the door.

The banker, who did not appreciate being pushed around in his own boardroom, was suddenly seething inside. He turned to Paula, "Is that all right with you?" he asked, his expression one of concern for her.

"Yes, of course, Charles," she responded evenly.

Charles Rossiter could not help admiring her coolness, her extraordinary poise under the circumstances. Nevertheless, he felt bound to add reassuringly, "I'll be next door in my office if you should need me, Paula."

"Thanks, Charles, you're most considerate." She smiled at him as he slipped out and closed the door quietly behind him.

Alone in the room with her cousin, she turned slowly, walked toward the conference table.

Jonathan's eyes did not leave her face. He was elated, knowing he had the upper hand, enjoyed playing cat-and-mouse with her. He had waited a long time to get his revenge on Paula O'Neill, and now at last it was within his grasp. Earlier, he had resolved not to get up or ask her to sit down. He was not going to pay tribute to this cold, calculating bitch, who was the reincarnation of his diabolical grandmother, Emma Harte.

Paula came to a stop a few feet away from the table. She returned his stare unflinchingly. Her blue eyes were cold, steely.

Jonathan spoke first. He said in his smoothest voice, "It's been a long time since we faced each other across a conference table. I do believe the last time was twelve years ago, when the saintly Alexander gave me the sack, and you kicked me out of the family."

"I'm perfectly certain this meeting wasn't arranged in order that you and I could reminisce about old times," Paula snapped. "So let's get to the point, shall we?"

"The point is that I have—"

"I know you hold shares in Harte stores," she said sharply, cutting him off. "Ten percent. I also know that you think you're entitled to a seat on the board. The answer is *no,* you're not. And now that you have my answer, I will leave."

Paula pivoted, walked back to the door. Her superior intelligence and shrewdness told her that he had more up his sleeve, so she was not surprised or perturbed when he said, "I haven't finished with you, Paula. I have something else to say to you."

She paused, turned to look at him. "What is it?"

"Over these many years I've been purchasing Harte shares through various nominees. Altogether, I now hold twenty-six percent."

Although this startled her, she managed not to show it. She kept her face still, her eyes steady, decided to make no comment. She watched him alertly. Instinctively, her guard went up.

Jonathan went on, "Furthermore, I also have the voting power over another twenty percent—" He paused for dramatic effect, and a smug smile slowly spread itself across his face. "Just think, Paula, forty-six percent in my hands! And you only have forty-one percent now." He laughed triumphantly. "I actually control more shares in the Harte stores than you do!" A gloating expression slid into his crafty eyes. "How unwise of you to put yourself in such a vulnerable position . . . just to buy the Larson chain in the States."

The shock Paula felt was so enormous she thought her legs were going to give way under her. But she managed to keep herself upright and steady, despite the tremors running through her whole body. She dare not allow any reaction to show.

Keeping her voice low, composed, she remarked, "And whose twenty percent do you control?"

"The shares left to James and Cynthia Weston, by their grandfather, the late Samuel Weston."

"They are minors. Those shares are in the control of their solicitors, executors of their grandfather's estate. And traditionally Jackson, Coombe, and Barbour have always voted those shares with me, as Sam Weston did when Emma Harte was alive."

"Allegiances can change, Paula."

"I find it hard to believe that Jackson, Coombe, and Barbour would involve themselves with you."

"Believe it . . . it's true."

"You're bluffing."

"Not at all." He rose, strolled down the other side of the room. Halfway to the door he stopped, swung around. "It's only going to take me a week or two to buy the five percent I need to get control of Harte's. You'd better start packing your things, lady, and clear out of your office. I'm moving in." He gave her a cold, penetrating stare, his bitter loathing for her surfacing. "I'm putting you on notice. I am going to make a takeover bid for Harte's. And I promise you, I will succeed. I will be the winner this time! And *you* are going to be the loser, Paula O'Neill!"

She did not deign to answer him.

He slammed the door behind him as he left the boardroom.

Paula sank into the nearest chair.

She was filled with an internal shaking, and she clutched her bag in her lap to keep her hands from trembling. It seemed to her that all her strength had drained away.

Charles Rossiter appeared in the doorway. He rushed across the room to her, his face as white as hers, his expression grave, his eyes reflecting his apprehension.

"I knew we had trouble brewing this afternoon when I received that phone call. But I didn't anticipate that it was going to be this bad," he cried. "Sir Logan Curtis just briefed me fully on Ainsley's intentions. I'm flabbergasted."

Paula nodded, unable to speak for a moment. Her composure was shattered.

Charles peered at her. "Let me get you a brandy. You look awful."

"Thanks, but not brandy, Charles. I don't like it. Do you have vodka?"

"Yes, I'll go and get it. I need a drink myself."

He returned in a moment with a bottle and two glasses from the bar in his private office. He poured, handed her a glass. "Just knock it back. It'll do the trick."

She did as he said, felt the sting of the alcohol in her throat, then a warm sensation. After a moment, she said slowly, wonderingly, "I find it difficult to believe that a staid, old-fashioned firm of solicitors like Jackson, Coombe, and Barbour have done this. Thrown their lot in with Jonathan. *Could* he be bluffing, Charles?"

"I doubt it. Anyway, why *would* he? Besides, having Sir Logan Curtis at his side was a maneuver on his part to show you—*to show me*—that he is absolutely above board, very legitimate, and that everything he is trying to do is perfectly legal. Sir Logan told me he is rich, a tycoon in his own right, head of a big company, Janus and Janus Holdings, in Hong Kong. He and his wife have been staying at Claridge's for some weeks. No, Paula, I am afraid this is no bluff."

She exclaimed irately, "But why would Arthur Jackson go against me? Agree to vote those shares he controls with Jonathan's?"

"There is no question in my mind that Ainsley has offered Jackson a fabulous inducement to vote with him, something very beneficial to those children. Ainsley must have some sort of agreement with the law firm, Paula. He wouldn't have come here today if he hadn't been holding all the cards."

She nodded miserably, knowing he was correct.

Charles continued, "He wanted to undermine your reputation as C.E.O. of Harte's with our bank, of course, shake our confidence in you. That's why he asked for the meeting to be held here. Clever devil, isn't he? However, I just want to say this . . . *I* am behind you, Paula. This *bank* is behind you. As we were always behind your grandmother."

"Thank you, Charles." She stared at him morosely. "I'm in a mess."

"Yes, you are." He paused thoughtfully, added, "The mere *rumor* of a takeover bid for Harte's could be disastrous for you."

"I know." Abruptly, she jumped up.

Charles was taken aback. "Where are you going?"

"I have to get some air. I'm going back to the store."

"But surely you want to talk with me further, work out some sort of strategy, Paula."

"I'd prefer to do that tomorrow, Charles, if you don't mind. I feel the need to be alone right now, if you'll excuse me."

She sat at her desk in her office at Harte's in Knightsbridge, the world's most famous department store, her special territory, her citadel.

She was unable to move or think or focus on anything except the terrible problems facing her. She felt as if she had been bludgeoned about her head and her body. Her brain was still reeling, and from time to time waves of panic swept through her, blocking all rational thought.

For the first time in her life, Paula O'Neill was afraid.

She was frightened of Jonathan Ainsley, of the power he had over her, so suddenly, so unexpectedly. His specter loomed like a black cloud. And she detested the feelings of helplessness, of powerlessness, but she was fully aware they would not readily disappear.

He has me cornered, she thought, endeavoring to quell the nausea rising in her again, as it had been doing off and on for the past hour. *He's going to ruin me, as he threatened he would all those years ago. And I've no one to blame but myself.*

The queasy feeling intensified and she ran into the bathroom in the adjoining dressing area. Leaning over the washbasin, she retched and retched until she thought there was nothing left inside her. When she finally straightened, looked at herself in the mirror, she saw that her face was the color of putty; her eyes were red, watery, her cheeks streaked with mascara. After cleaning them with a damp tissue, she filled a glass with cold water, drank it gratefully. The vodka made me sick, she told herself, all the while knowing this was not so. It was nerves and fear and panic that were having such a dire effect on her system.

Returning to her office, she moved quickly toward the desk, then came to a halt in the center of the room. The portrait of her grandmother hanging over the fireplace caught her attention, brought into focus as it was by the picture light on top of the frame. Aside from the lamp on her desk, this was the only illumination in the shadow-filled room. Consequently, the portrait stood out in bold relief. Walking over to it, she stood staring up at the beloved face of Emma Harte, captured with such lifelike precision in oils.

Oh Grandy, what have I done? How could I have been so stupid? I've jeopardized all that you built, put myself in jeopardy. You asked me once to hold your dream, and I've done just the opposite. I've let you down. Oh Gran, whatever am I going to do? How can I regain the advantage to prevent the stores from falling into the wrong hands?

The beautiful face in the portrait gazed back. The smile was benign, but the green eyes were watchful and shrewd.

If only she were alive, Paula thought, suddenly choking up. Tears came into her eyes. She felt so alone.

Patting her eyes with her handkerchief, she sat down on the sofa, continuing to study her grandmother's face. She began to twist the hankie in her hands fretfully, asking herself how the brilliant Emma Harte would have extricated herself from an appalling situation such as this.

But no sudden insights or clever solutions came to Paula, and in her anxiety she began to shred the lace hankie into tiny pieces. She was strung out, paralyzed by apprehension. She leaned back against the sofa, closed her eyes, trying to compose herself, hoping to bring some order to her turbulent and disturbing thoughts.

The chiming of the hour made Paula sit up swiftly. She glanced at the clock on the chimney piece. To her astonishment it was nine o'clock. Where had the time gone? Had she dozed? She realized she had been sitting on the sofa for over an hour.

Rising, she went to the desk, picked up the phone, instantly dropped the receiver back into the cradle. There was no point in calling Shane. He had enough to cope with right now. Her news would only distress him. Far better to wait until tomorrow or the day after to tell him, when she had worked out some sort of strategy. And she would most certainly have to do that: find a way to block Jonathan Ainsley's takeover bid for Harte's. *She could not let it happen.*

Unexpectedly, the feeling of claustrophobia she had experienced in the boardroom of the Rossiter Merchant Bank gripped her again. She felt as if she was suffocating, had the sudden pressing need to escape this room, to be outside, to breathe in fresh air.

Snatching up her bag, she flew out of the office, took the staff elevator down to the ground floor. And with a brisk goodnight to the security guard on duty, she left the store.

The air was crisp on this Wednesday evening, rather chilly for September. But Paula welcomed the coolness, found it refreshing. Certainly it seemed to revive her as she hurried away from the main thoroughfare of Knightsbridge, headed in the direction of her house in Belgrave Square.

Ever since she had left the bank in the city, she had felt dazed, unnerved, and panicked. But slowly, as she walked, these negative feelings were starting to lift. She had no idea what she would do, how she would proceed with Jonathan Ainsley, but she did know it was going to be an all-out war between them. And she was determined now to fight him with everything she had, do everything in her power to win. She could not afford to lose. Her cousin would be a calculating, cool, and devious adversary—she had no doubt about that. His threat had not been an idle one. He was in deadly earnest, would stop at nothing. He wanted the Harte stores. Equally as important, he wanted—no, *needed*—to ruin her. Manifold emotions were tangled up in his drives. And not the least of them was his overwhelming jealousy of her, which he had harbored since their childhood.

Unexpectedly, it occurred to her that there were several possible ways to outmaneuver Jonathan. But would they work? She wondered if one of them was even legal. She was not sure. She would have to check Harte's papers of incorporation tomorrow. She made a mental note to call John Crawford, her solicitor, when she got home. She was obviously going to need legal counsel.

Her brain was functioning again. This realization gave her a great sense of relief. Her mind began to race, and so intent was she on her mental machinations, she was unaware that she had bypassed her house until she found herself crossing Eaton Square.

She knew at once exactly where she was going: to see Sir Ronald Kallinski. Her Uncle Ronnie, her wise rabbi. He was the only one who could help her, guide her as Emma Harte would have guided her had she been alive.

——— *Forty-Two* ———

Wilberson, Sir Ronald Kallinski's butler, opened the door of the Eaton Square house a few seconds after Paula rang the bell.

A look of surprise crossed his face when he saw her standing on the front steps. "Why, Mrs. O'Neill, good evening," he said, inclining his head politely.

"Is Sir Ronald at home, Wilberson? I must see him urgently."

"But he's entertaining guests this evening, Mrs. O'Neill. A dinner party is in progress."

"This is an emergency, Wilberson. Please tell Sir Ronald I'm here." Before the butler could stop her, she had walked right past him into the marble entrance hall hung with antique French tapestries. "I'll wait in here," she said firmly, pushing open the door of the library.

"Yes, Mrs. O'Neill," Wilberson said, sheathing his annoyance but looking pained as he hurried across the vast foyer and knocked on the dining room door.

It was only a matter of seconds before Sir Ronald hurried into the library to join her. Paula's unannounced arrival at nine-thirty in the evening had startled him. But his surprised expression changed to one of concern when he saw her face.

"You look frightful, Paula! What on earth is wrong? Are you ill?"

"No, I'm not, Uncle Ronnie. And I do apologize for bursting in on you like this. But something awful has happened. I'm in serious trouble and I need your help. There could be a takeover bid for Harte's. I could lose the stores."

Sir Ronald was thunderstruck. He understood at once that she was not exaggerating. It was not in her character to do so. "Excuse me for a moment, Paula. Let me explain to my dinner guests that I have an emergency, and ask Michael to hold the fort for a while. I'll be right back."

"Thank you, Uncle Ronnie," she said, and sat down on the leather Chesterfield sofa.

When he returned, almost immediately he took a seat opposite her. "Begin at the beginning, Paula, and don't leave anything out," he instructed.

Slowly, precisely, with her usual attention to detail, she told him everything that had happened that day. She had a prodigious memory, was able to repeat every conversation verbatim. She started with Charles Rossiter's phone call to her and finished with her confrontation with Jonathan Ainsley at the bank.

Sir Ronald had been listening to her attentively, his chin resting on his hand, nodding from time to time. When she had finally given him all the facts, he exclaimed angrily, "My father had a name for a man like Jonathan Ainsley!" He paused, leveled his gaze at her, pronounced with contempt, "A *gonif.*"

"Yes, he *is* the biggest thief alive." Paula cleared her throat. "But actually, I've only got myself to blame. I set myself up for the likes of him." She sighed, shook her head. "I forgot that Harte's is a public company, forgot that I had stockholders. I believed it was mine, believed that no one would ever challenge me. I was over confident. Relaxed in too many ways. And that's always when the sharp knives come out, isn't it?"

He gave a slight nod, sat scrutinizing her closely. He loved her like a daughter, admired and respected her more than anyone he knew. She was daring, brilliant, and intuitive in business. It had taken a lot of guts to say what she had just said, to admit her mistakes. Nevertheless, he had been stunned at the outset of their conversation, when she had told him she had liquidated some of her Harte stock. It had been an error of the worst magnitude.

"I'll never understand why you sold that ten percent, Paula," he found himself saying with sharpness. "Never, as long as I live. Very flawed judgment on your part."

She looked down at her hands, fiddled with her wedding ring. When she finally looked up at him, she gave him a faint smile of chagrin. "I know. But I wanted to buy a chain of stores with my own money . . . So that it would really be mine."

"Your ego got in the way."

"That's true."

Sir Ronald exhaled heavily, adopted a softer tone. "But then nobody's infallible, Paula, least of all business executives like us. People seem to think that we're cut from a different cloth, that we're a special breed, with immunity from human frailties. They think we must be hard-headed, passionless, without any weaknesses to be able to wheel and deal, make fortunes the way we do. But none of it's true." He shook his head, finished, "In your case, some sort of genuine emotional need got in your way. And it distracted you."

"I think I had to prove something to myself."

A costly way of doing it, he thought, but said, "Recriminations and regrets are a waste of valuable time. We must turn disadvantage to advantage, make certain you come out the winner. Let's examine your options."

She nodded. His words reinforced her own attitude, which had grown more positive since she had been with him. "I could go and see Arthur Jackson, at Jackson, Coombe, and Barbour, appeal to his better instincts, get him to reverse his decision to vote the shares he controls with Jonathan's," she said. "I might even be able to find out what inducement Jonathan used, come up with a—"

"Telephone Jackson, by all means," Sir Ronald interrupted. "But don't be surprised if he turns a deaf ear. He's not beholden to you, and he doesn't have to tell you anything."

"Uncle Ronnie, he's behaved unethically!"

"It may seem that way, but it's not necessarily so. Arthur Jackson is the executor of Sam Weston's estate. He has only one obligation. To those children whose interests he protects. If he can strike a lucrative deal, or make additional income for them, he will."

"I think that's what he's done with Jonathan, don't you?"

"Most likely. Ainsley's always been a crafty operator. He's probably offered to pay a big cash dividend out of his own pocket to the Weston estate, as long as the law firm votes the stock they control with his." Sir Ronald rubbed his chin, pursed his lips, ruminated. Then he added, "I'll do a little fishing tomorrow. I have ways and means of finding things out. There are no secrets in our world, you know. Hold off on your phone call to Arthur Jackson for the moment."

"Yes, I will. Thanks, Uncle Ronnie." She leaned forward eagerly. "Is there any reason why I can't launch a bid to take Harte's private? Buy out my stockholders?"

"Yes, one very good reason. I won't let you."

"But it *would* be legal?"

"It would. But to take your company private, you would have to offer money publicly, in the open market, to your stockholders. And you would immediately expose yourself to every predator and corporate raider in the City and in Wall Street." He shook his head with great vehemence. "No, no, I won't permit you to do that, Paula. There would be other takeover bids, possibly hostile ones. And anyway why should your stockholders take your money? They may prefer to take Sir Jimmy Goldsmith's money or Sir James Hanson's or Carl Icahn's or Tiny Rowland's . . . or *Jonathan Ainsley*'s. You'd all be bidding against each other, accomplishing nothing except pushing up the price of the shares."

Her face changed ever so slightly and she glanced away, biting her lip. After a moment she looked at him and asked in a tired voice, "Then what *can* I do, Uncle Ronnie?"

"You can start looking for a few small stockholders who among them hold ten percent of the Harte shares. Perhaps four or five, maybe even as many as twelve. Track them down, buy them out—at a premium, if necessary. You've already got forty-one percent. You only need fifty-one to have control."

"God, I'm so stupid, Uncle Ronnie! What's wrong with me tonight? I keep losing sight of things. Obviously I'm not thinking straight."

"That's understandable, you've had a nasty shock. Also—" He paused thoughtfully before continuing, "I think there's one other thing you *must* do, my dear."

"What's that?"

"You must dispose of Jonathan Ainsley."

"How?"

"I don't know at this moment." Sir Ronald pushed himself to his feet, walked over to the window, stood staring out into Eaton Square, his analytical mind examining various possibilities. Eventually he swung around. "What do we know about this *gonif?*"

"Not much, I'm afraid, since he left England and went to live in Hong Kong."

"Hong Kong! So that's where he ended up after Alexander turfed him out. A very *interesting* place, Hong Kong. Now, tell me what little you do know."

Paula did as he asked, repeating the information Charles Rossiter had given her, which he, in turn, had learned from Sir Logan Curtis.

"Start digging, Paula," Sir Ronald told her, "and dig deep. Do you have a particular private investigating firm you use for business matters? If you don't, I can recommend one."

"No, that's all right, thanks. I use Figg International and have for years. They handle all of my security at the stores, provide guards—you know, the usual thing. They happen to have a private investigating division with offices and agents all over the world."

"Good. Hire them immediately. A *momzer* like Jonathan Ainsley must have more than one skeleton in his closet—" Sir Ronald bit off the end of his sentence when the library door flew open.

Michael walked in, and when he saw Paula he exclaimed, with a laugh, "Oho, so you're the emergency!" Instantly, he realized how serious Paula and his father were and continued in a more sober tone, "From the way you both look, it *must* be an emergency." His eyes rested on Paula. He took in her extreme pallor, her tired eyes. "What's wrong? It's not something to do with the fire in Sydney, Paula, is it?"

"No, Michael, it's not," Paula said quietly, then glanced across at his father.

Sir Ronald said, "Jonathan Ainsley has returned, and he's in London. To make trouble for Paula."

"How can he do that?" Michael demanded.

"Uncle Ronnie will explain."

Once his father had acquainted him with the facts, Michael went to sit next to Paula on the sofa. He took hold of her hand affectionately. "Dad's made some excellent suggestions, but what can *I* do to help you?" he asked.

"I honestly don't know, Michael, but thanks for offering. Right now I'm going back to the store. I must start checking the records, go over the computer printouts. I must find those crucial stockholders. And as fast as possible."

"I'm coming with you to help you," Michael announced.

"Oh, you don't have to, honestly. Uncle Ronnie has guests. I've interrupted your dinner party."

"You can't do a job like that alone," Michael protested fiercely. "You'll be at it all night."

"I was going to phone Emily."

"Good idea. Let's call her from here. We'll meet her at Harte's. The three of us can handle it together."

"But—"

"Do let Michael go with you, my dear," Sir Ronald interjected. "*I* will feel better, knowing he's at the store with you."

"All right." Paula rose, kissed him on the cheek. He hugged her to him, and she murmured, "I can't thank you enough, Uncle Ronnie."

He smiled down at her. "We're *mishpocheh,*" he said.

Forty-Three

"*Know thine enemy,*" Paula said. "That's what this is all about, Jack, why I asked you here."

Jack Figg, managing director of Figg International, nodded quickly. "I get the picture."

"The situation is critical. I wouldn't have dragged you to the store at eleven-thirty at night otherwise."

"That's no problem. I'd come out at any time for you, Paula."

Jack Figg, who ran the biggest and most successful security and private investigating company in Britain, sat back in the chair facing her. He pulled an Asprey leather jotting pad out of his sports jacket and said, "All right, Paula, *shoot.* Give me as many facts as you can."

"That's just it, I don't have very many. However, it's my understanding that Jonathan Ainsley has lived in Hong Kong for about twelve years. That's when he left England. He owns a company called Janus and Janus Holdings. More than likely it's to do with real estate; that's always been his area of expertise. He's married, but I don't know to whom. Charles Rossiter told me that they're presently staying at Claridge's. Oh, and he mentioned that the wife is pregnant." Paula lifted her shoulders in a shrug. "I can't tell you more than that."

"Hong Kong is obviously our jumping-off point. But I'll also have him watched here, so we know what he's up to."

"That's a good idea, and, as I just said, the situation is *critical.*"

"I understand. And no doubt you needed the information yesterday."

"No, five years ago, if the truth be known," Paula answered quietly.

Jack Figg gave her a knowing look. "But actually, how long *do* I have?"

"Five days—at the most. I'd like your report on my desk by Monday."

"Good God, Paula! You're asking for miracles! I can't deliver in that short a time!"

"Jack, you have to—otherwise the information will be worthless to me. It'll be too late." She leaned across the desk, her face tense, her blue eyes focused intently on him. "I don't care how many agents you put on. It can be a hundred, if necessary—"

"If I do that, it's going to cost you a lot of money," Jack interjected.

"Have I ever haggled with you, Jack?"

"No, of course you haven't—it's not your style. But digging deep, doing a complete profile of this nature can become very expensive. Very quickly. Especially when there's a time element involved. To gather the kind of information you want, I have to turn Ainsley inside out. I *will* have to put a lot of operatives on. It'll also be necessary to move a number of my agents from other Far East countries into Hong Kong. That in itself will send the costs skyrocketing. Then there'll be all kinds of payoffs, bribes—"

Paula cut in, "I don't need to know the details, Jack. Just do it. *Please*. Get me as much information on Jonathan Ainsley as you can. I need ammunition against him in order to defend myself. There's got to be some skeletons in his closet."

"Maybe not, Paula. He might be as clean as a whistle."

She was silent, knowing this was true.

"But I hope he's not," Jack added swiftly, "for your sake. And look, I'll try to get back to you on Monday. However, it could be Tuesday."

"Do your very best, Jack."

"I'll get to it tonight," he promised, impatient to start working the telephones and the telex machine. He stood up. "The Far East is already open for business."

After Paula had walked Jack Figg to the staff lift and thanked him once again, she hurried into the office where Emily and Michael were working on the records of Harte's shareholders.

"Any luck yet?" she asked from the doorway.

"Not yet," Emily answered. "But never fear, we're bound to come up with some names before too long. How did it go with Jack Figg? Is he on the job?"

"He is. And I have a lot of confidence in him. If there's anything to find, Jack will find it."

"Oh, I'm sure there's *sleaze* in Jonathan Ainsley's life!" Emily exclaimed. "He always was weird and mixed with a strange bunch when he lived here. Like that awful Sebastian Cross."

Paula felt a cold little shiver run through her. "I'd rather not think about *him,* if you don't mind."

"Why should *he* bother you! He's dead. Anyway, don't stand there looking like a sucking duck. Come and help us."

"Of course." Paula joined them.

Emily gave her a batch of computer printouts. "Start on these, but before you really dig in, let me get you a cup of coffee and one of the sandwiches I brought with me. You haven't eaten all night, Paula."

"I'm not hungry, darling. But I will have a cup of coffee. Thanks, Dumps."

Paula concentrated on the top sheet, running her eyes quickly down the page of names. Harte's had hundreds of small stockholders who held nominal amounts of shares, as well as those others who had acquired larger blocks over the years. Suddenly, her heart sank. This *was* an endless task, as Michael had said earlier. It might even take longer than one night—several days perhaps—to find the people they needed. Jonathan had boasted that he was quickly going to buy up the five percent he needed. But it was not a boast. She knew he fully intended to do exactly that.

"I bet Jonathan has his stockbrokers and all kinds of flunkies skittering around, trying to buy Harte shares!" she exclaimed, voicing her thoughts, looking at Michael.

He returned her glance. "I'm sure he is. But you have the advantage, Paula. You have the inside information—these records."

"Yes," she said dully, starting to read again.

Emily brought coffee for the three of them, sat down next to Paula. "Cheer up, lovey. We'll get the results soon. As Gran used to say, many hands make light work. But oh boy, do I wish Winston and Shane were here to help us."

"Oh, so do I, Emily. I miss Shane so much and in so many different ways. I can't wait for him to get back from Australia. I feel as if half of me is missing when he's not here."

"Are you going to phone him tomorrow, tell him about this?" Emily inquired.

"I think I have to—he'd be hurt if I didn't. I only hope it doesn't upset him too much. I couldn't bear that. Poor darling, he's had too much to contend with lately."

It was the gentle tone, the loving nuances, the look of longing in her eyes that stabbed at Michael. *She worships Shane,* he thought with a flash of insight. *He is her life.* At that precise moment Michael knew what a fool he had been to think she would ever entertain any advances from him. The mere thought of what he might have done in a foolish moment caused him acute internal embarrassment.

He dropped his head, pretended to concentrate on the sheet of names to hide his sudden discomfiture. His sexual desire for her had not waned in the past year. He had constantly fantasized about her, but how ridiculous he had been—he saw that now. She was happily married to his friend. How could he have ever thought that she would be interested in him, or any other man for that matter. It had always been Shane since their childhood.

Michael felt as if a veil had been lifted. He saw everything with sudden clarity. He understood then what she had been doing earlier in the year . . . she had been persistently pushing Amanda at him. He ought to have recognized that months ago in New York, known that Paula was out of his range. But he had been so caught up in the fantasy in his own head, he had been blind to many things, most especially reality.

"Here it is!" Emily shrieked. "I've found a shareholder with quite a substantial number of shares."

"How many?" Paula asked, hardly daring to breathe.

"Four percent. Gosh, she must be a fairly wealthy woman."

"Who is she?" Paula asked excitedly, her voice echoing Emily's enthusiasm.

"A Mrs. Iris Rumford of"—Emily traced her finger across the printout—"Bowden Ghyll House, Ilkley!"

"A Yorkshire woman," Michael said quietly. "Perhaps this is a good omen, Paula."

On Saturday morning at ten o'clock, Paula sat opposite Mrs. Iris Rumford in the handsome drawing room of her lovely old manor house in Ilkley.

It was obvious to Paula that Mrs. Rumford was a woman of considerable means, and she had been graciously received and offered coffee on her arrival minutes before.

Paula had accepted a cup, and the two women had exchanged pleasantries, discussed the weather. Now, as she finished her coffee, Paula said, "It was very kind of you to see me, Mrs. Rumford. As my assistant told you, I wanted to talk to you about your shares in Harte's stores."

"Yes. And it's my pleasure, Mrs. O'Neill. Anyway, it was the least I could do, in that I had tea with your cousin, Jonathan Ainsley, on Thursday."

Paula almost dropped the coffee cup. She put it down carefully on the end table. This was the last thing she had expected to hear, and she gave Iris Rumford a sharp look. "He also came to see you about your shares in Harte's presumably?"

"Yes, Mrs. O'Neill. He did. He offered me an excellent price for them, went very high actually."

Paula felt her throat tighten, and she swallowed several times before saying, "And did you accept his offer, Mrs. Rumford?"

"No, as a matter of fact, I didn't."

Paula relaxed. She smiled at the older woman. "Then I can make you an offer for them, can't I?"

"You could, yes."

"Name your price, Mrs. Rumford."

"I don't have a price."

"But you must know how much you want for your shares."

"No, I don't. You see, I'm not all that keen to sell them. My late husband bought them for me in 1959." She gave a funny little laugh. "I'm sort of sentimentally attached to them. Harte's is my favorite shop in Leeds. I've always patronized it."

Paula held herself still, pressing back her annoyance. She had obviously come here on a wild goose chase. But she could not afford to antagonize this woman; she needed her too badly. Paula said, "Well, of course I'm glad you like the store, that you're a satisfied customer. But look here, I do wish you would consider my offer. I will purchase your shares at the same price Mr. Ainsley quoted to you."

Iris Rumford studied her for a moment, frowning slightly, as if she were trying to make up her mind about something. Then she said, "Is there going to be one of those big battles? The kind I read about in the financial pages of the Sunday *Times?*"

"I sincerely hope not," Paula exclaimed quietly.

Unexpectedly, Iris Rumford pushed herself to her feet.

Paula also rose, realizing the conversation was suddenly at an end.

"I'm sorry, Mrs. O'Neill," Mrs. Rumford murmured. "Perhaps I should not have let you come to see me. I've wasted your time, I'm afraid. You see, I thought that I might sell my shares, but now I've changed my mind."

"I'm truly sorry to hear that." Paula stretched out her hand, trying to be cordial.

Iris Rumford shook it. "I can see you're angry. And I can't say I blame you. Forgive my vacillation. And please excuse the indecisiveness of an old lady."

Paula said, "It's all right, really it is. But if you should change your mind again, please ring me."

All the way back to Leeds, Paula fumed.

She was baffled and irritated by the woman's odd behavior, as well as being disappointed. Had Iris Rumford just wanted to be important for a brief moment in her life? Or was it a case of simple curiosity on the part of a lonely old woman? Had she merely wanted to meet Jonathan and herself? Paula wondered how Jonathan Ainsley had found Iris Rumford, how *he* knew that *she* owned a block of Harte shares.

She sighed with some exasperation as she pressed her foot hard on the accelerator, and headed the Aston Martin in the direction of Leeds. Going to see Iris Rumford *had* been a waste of time.

Paula spent most of the day working in her office at the Leeds store.

Several times she went out onto the floor, but mostly she kept herself busy with paperwork. And she strove not to think about Jonathan Ainsley, the possible takeover bid, or dwell on the frightening prospect of losing the stores to him.

When she did become tense, she reminded herself that in the last forty-eight hours her stockbrokers and Charles Rossiter had between them managed to acquire another seven percent of Harte shares on her behalf. They had bought them from nine small stockholders Emily and Michael had pinpointed on the computer printouts.

Only three percent, that's all I need now, she kept saying under her breath whenever she needed to lift her sagging spirits. The words consoled her.

At four o'clock she placed a pile of papers in her briefcase, locked her office, and left the store. She usually stayed until six, even on Saturdays. But Emily was coming over to Pennistone Royal for dinner that evening, and Paula wanted to spend an hour with Patrick and Linnet before she arrived.

It was a lovely September afternoon, very sunny, and Leeds had been busy all day. The traffic was heavy on Chapeltown Road as shoppers returned to the outskirts after a day in town. But Paula was an excellent driver; she dodged in and out between the other cars, was soon on the open road going to Harrogate.

She was approaching the roundabout in Alwoodley when the Cellnet phone in her car rang. Reaching for it, she said, "Hello?" half expecting it to be Emily.

"Mrs. O'Neill, it's Doris at the store."

"Yes, Doris?"

"I have a Mrs. Rumford of Ilkley on another line," the switchboard operator said. "She insists it's very urgent. Apparently you have her phone number."

"I do, Doris. But it's in my briefcase. Please give her the car number, ask her to phone me at once. And thank you."

Only a few minutes after Paula had hung up, the car phone rang again. It was Iris Rumford, and she got straight to the point. "I wonder if you could come and see me tomorrow? To discuss those shares again."

"I really can't, Mrs. Rumford. I have to drive to London tomorrow. In any case, since you don't want to sell, there doesn't really seem to be much point, does there?"

"I might reconsider your offer, Mrs. O'Neill."

"Then why don't I drive over now?"

"All right," Iris Rumford agreed.

"You don't know who I am, do you?" Iris Rumford was saying to Paula an hour later.

Paula shook her head. "Should I? Do I know you?" Her brows knitted together in perplexity. She fixed her gaze intently on the other woman. Iris Rumford was thin but sprightly, with silver hair and a ruddy complexion, and she looked to be in her seventies. Paula was certain she did not know her. "Have we met?" she asked with another frown.

Iris Rumford sat back and returned Paula's penetrating stare. At last, she said slowly, "No, we haven't met. But you knew my brother. Or at least, you were acquainted with him."

"Oh," Paula said, lifting a black brow. "What was his name?"

"John Cross."

This name so startled Paula that she almost exclaimed out loud. She managed to say in a normal tone, "We met when he owned Cross Communications." As she spoke, Paula thought of his late son, Sebastian, once her deadly enemy and Jonathan's best friend. She realized immediately how Jonathan knew about Iris Rumford and the stock she owned in Harte's.

"You were very kind and courteous to my brother at the end of his life," Iris Rumford continued. "He told me about you when he was dying. He respected you, thought you were very fair. It was your other cousin, Mr. Alexander Barkstone, that I met briefly, when my brother was in St. James's Hospital in Leeds." Iris Rumford looked into the fire. There was a short pause. "You and Mr. Barkstone . . . well, you're different from Jonathan Ainsley . . ." She brought her eyes to Paula, half smiled.

Paula waited, wondering what was coming next. When Mrs. Rumford made no further comment, she said, "Yes, I do believe we are. I hope so. But sadly, Mr. Barkstone is now dead."

"I'm sorry to hear that." The old lady gazed into the flames again. She muttered, "It's funny, isn't it, how people in families can differ so very much. He was wicked, evil, my nephew, Sebastian. I never had much time for him. John, of course, idolized him, the only son, the only child. But he killed my brother, drove him into his grave with all that wickedness. And Jonathan Ainsley was just as wicked. *He* hammered quite a few nails into my poor brother's coffin. Bad lot, Sebastian and your cousin."

Suddenly, Iris swung her silver head, focused her eyes on Paula once more. "I wanted to meet you, Mrs. O'Neill, to judge for myself what kind of person you are. That's why I asked you to come this morning. You're a sincere woman—I can tell that from your eyes. Anyway, I've never heard anything bad about you hereabouts. Mostly they say you're like Emma Harte. She was a good woman. I'm glad you take after her."

Paula had no words. She held her breath.

"And so, if it will help you personally, I *will* sell you my Harte shares."

For a moment Paula thought she might burst into tears. "Thank you, Mrs. Rumford. It would help me, very much so. I would be most grateful if you sold them to me and not to my cousin."

"Oh, I never intended to sell them to him. I just wanted . . . well, wanted to look him over again, satisfy myself that I'd always been right in my judgment. Also, I got a bit of satisfaction from dangling the carrot in front of him and then snatching it away." She shook her head. There was a shrewd glint in her wise old eyes. "When you both phoned me about selling the shares, I got a feeling he was out to make trouble for you. Well, never mind, he'll get his comeuppance one day."

"Yes." Paula leaned forward, said, "I told you this morning I would purchase the shares at the price Jonathan Ainsley had offered. That still stands, of course."

"Good Lord, that doesn't matter! I wouldn't dream of holding you up, Mrs. O'Neill. You can have them at market value."

Forty-Four

Paula stood in front of the fireplace in her office at Harte's in Knightsbridge, below the portrait of Emma. It was three-fifteen on Tuesday afternoon, and she was waiting for Jonathan Ainsley.

Generally she wore black to work. Today she had chosen a bright red wool dress, simply tailored with long sleeves. She thought the color was appropriate. It was strong, defiant, bold, and it echoed the way she felt.

She had turned disadvantage to advantage. She was about to demolish her enemy.

But when Jonathan appeared a few minutes later, she realized that he misguidedly believed *she* was going to capitulate to *him.* Everything about him indicated this. He sauntered in, looking sanguine, his demeanor arrogant, his smile superior.

He halted in the middle of the floor.

Adversaries, they did not greet each other.

He said, "You sent a message. I'm here. You have something to say to me?"

"You've lost!"

He laughed in her face. "I never lose!"

"Then this is a first for you." She lifted her head slightly, the gesture one of confidence and pride. "I've acquired additional Harte stock . . ." She paused for effect. "I now hold fifty-two percent."

This information threw him. He recovered himself. Displaying no emotion whatsoever, he sneered, "So what. I have forty-six percent. I'm the *second* largest stockholder and entirely within my rights in demanding a seat on the board. I shall do so formally today. Through my solicitors. I also intend to proceed with my takeover bid." His eyes swept over her coldly. "This will be my office in the not too distant future."

"I doubt it!" she shot back. "Furthermore, you don't have forty-six percent. Only twenty-six."

"Have you forgotten that I control the shares held in trust by Arthur Jackson for the Weston children?"

"I forget nothing. And I am absolutely certain Arthur Jackson will not be doing business with you after today."

"Don't be so ridiculous!" His expression turned smug. "I have an agreement with him, with the law firm. A written agreement."

Paula took a step forward, reached for a manila envelope on the coffee table, stood holding it in her hands. She tapped it with a bright red fingernail. "When Arthur Jackson finishes reading this report, which was delivered to him an hour ago, I feel quite confident he will be shredding the agreement."

"What report is that?" he asked, his expression now one of disdain.

"An investigation into your life in Hong Kong."

He threw her a look of contempt, said with scorn, "You have nothing on me. I'm clean."

Paula studied him thoughtfully. "Funnily enough," she said after a short pause, "I'm inclined to believe you. But nobody else will."

"What are you implying?"

Ignoring this question, she continued, "You have a partner in Hong Kong, a silent partner, one Tony Chiu, son of Wan Chin Chiu, who died last year. The older man was your mentor, your advisor, and also your silent partner from the moment you arrived in the crown colony. Pity the son's not as honorable and reliable as the father."

"My life and my business in Hong Kong have nothing to do with you!" he spluttered. He was irate, trying to hold himself in check.

"Oh yes it does. It has a great deal to do with me when you are trying to take over Harte's."

"And I will take it over!"

"No you won't!" Her eyes narrowed, and she proceeded in a soft but deadly voice, "It was very interesting to discover that Tony Chiu has a sideline. A very profitable sideline. He's alleged to be the biggest dealer of opium in the Golden Triangle, with a huge network spreading through Laos and Thailand. Convenient, isn't it, that he can apparently launder the drug money through Janus and Janus Holdings without anyone being the wiser about what he's up to. What a wonderful front for him. But I wonder how the Hong Kong Government and the Hong Kong police would react, what they would do about it —if they knew the real facts."

He gaped at her. "You're lying!" he screamed. "That report you're clinging onto for dear life is a pack of lies! Tony Chiu is not a drug dealer, he's a respectable and *respected* banker. And he certainly has not been using my company to launder drug money. I would know about it. He could not do a thing like that and hide it from me."

She smiled sardonically. "Don't be naive. You have Chinese employees who are his men, placed there by him even when his father was alive. He handpicked them in readiness for the future, for the time he would take over his father's banking concerns. And those men are his spies in your organization."

"Bullshit!"

"Your wife, Arabella, knows all about it. She is his business partner, has been for years. And he's financed many of her businesses at various times, including the antique shop she now owns in Hong Kong. She, too, is his spy. That's why she married you. To spy on you."

Jonathan was livid with rage, unable to speak coherently. He wanted to hit Paula O'Neill in the face for saying such unspeakable things about Arabella. He took several deep breaths, gasped angrily, "Someone with a vivid imagination has written a piece of fiction for you. *It's all lies, lies, lies!*" His breathing was ragged as he finished, "He is my silent partner. We are never seen together. My wife does not even know Tony Chiu."

"Why don't you ask her?"

His lip curled and his pale eyes filled with hatred for her. He shifted his gaze to the portrait of Emma Harte above her head, and his loathing for the two of them intensified. "You bloody bitch!" he hissed. "You're just like that old cow used to be! I piss on her grave! I piss on yours!" he cursed.

His words denigrating her grandmother incensed Paula. She went in for the kill. With meticulous care, she said, "The beautiful Arabella Sutton, doctor's daughter from Hampshire, is not quite what she seems to be. No doubt you are aware she lived in Paris for years. But did you know she was a 'Claude girl'?" Paula laughed coldly, taunted, "Don't tell me a sophisticated man like you doesn't know all about Madame Claude. She ran the most successful, indeed the finest, sex operation ever known in Paris. And until 1977 . . ."

Jonathan gaped at her. He was dumbfounded.

". . . Arabella Sutton, *your wife,* was one of Madame Claude's call girls. She went by the name Francine."

"I do not believe you," he shouted. "Arabella is—"

"Believe it!" she shouted back. She flung the envelope at him. It landed at his feet. "The report and copies of certain official documents attached to it will make interesting reading for you."

Jonathan saw it out of the corner of his eye, but he made no move to pick it up.

Paula said in an icy voice, "Instead of trying to knock my house down, go and put your own in order."

He opened his mouth to say something, then closed it. He glanced at the envelope at his feet. He longed to show her what he thought about her report by walking away from it. But he could not. His overriding desire, his consuming need to see the official documents she had just alluded to got the better of him. He bent down, picked it up, swung around, and strode to the door.

"I've won!" Paula called after him. "And don't you ever forget it!"

He halted, looked back at her. "We'll see about that," he said.

Paula walked back to her desk, sat down, reached for the phone, changed her mind. She sat thinking for a while. There was one more thing she had to do to ensure complete success, but it required her to be utterly ruthless, more ruthless than Emma Harte had ever been. She was still balking at the idea. She glanced over at the portrait of her grandmother, then brought her eyes back to the photograph in the silver frame on her desk. It was of Shane and the children. They, too, were Emma's heirs. She had to protect Harte's for them, no matter what it took.

Without any further hesitation, she reached for her private phone, dialed Sir Ronald on his direct line.

He picked up the phone after two rings. "Kallinski here."

"Uncle Ronnie, it's me again. Sorry to keep bothering you today."

"You're not, my dear." There was a slight pause. "Has he left?"

"Yes. Shaken, but not conceding anything. In fact, he was obviously determined to keep on fighting me. And so I will dispose of him in the way we discussed. A copy of the report will go to the authorities in Hong Kong. But honestly, Uncle Ronnie, I—"

"No regrets I hope, Paula."

"It makes me far more ruthless than Grandy ever was."

"That's not true, my dear. Emma could be *extremely* ruthless, too, when there was something for her to be ruthless about . . . such as Harte's, the business empire she built from nothing, and those she loved."

"Perhaps you're right."

"I know I am," Sir Ronald murmured, speaking in a softer voice. "I told you last night that Jonathan Ainsley will never be off your back. He'll always keep trying to get the stores. That's the nature of the man."

When she remained silent at the other end of the phone, Sir Ronald added, "You have no option but to stop him now. To protect yourself."

"Yes, I realize that, Uncle Ronnie."

He sat in the corner of Claridge's foyer, where afternoon tea was being served. But he scarcely heard the rattle of tea cups, the violins, or the varied background noises. He was reading far too intently to notice anything.

Jonathan had read the report twice.

At first he had wanted to dismiss it as pure invention, a vindictive interpretation of the facts on someone else's part, and especially the sections about Tony Chiu. But now he was finding this difficult to do. There was too much genuine information included to dismiss the entire thing as bogus. He had been amazed to read a whole page about his affair with Lady Susan Sorrell. That had been such a clandestine relationship he could hardly believe his eyes when he had come across her name. He was convinced Susan would not have talked about their sexual relationship when it was in progress. Or after it finished. She was terrified of gossip and of invoking her husband's wrath. Divorce from her rich banker was the last thing she wanted.

He came out as clean as he had insisted he was to Paula O'Neill, despite the information about Tony, which disturbed and alarmed him. If it *was* actually true, then he could be implicated in something he knew nothing about. Janus and Janus could be in jeopardy, as he might be himself. It could turn out to be serious. He would have to fly back to Hong Kong as soon as possible, start his own investigation there.

The thing which truly distressed him, however, was the detailed account of Arabella's past. This was backed up with photostats of documents relating to her years in Paris. Her whole life in France had been tracked and meticulously recorded in these pages of typescript. There was no longer any question in his mind that she had used the name Francine and that she had been one of Madame Claude's girls. Quite aside from the documentation, there were so many other things which made him give credence to the report. There was her sexual expertise and knowledge, her overall attitude toward a man, which smacked of the courtesan's trade, her sophistication, her worldliness, her elegance . . . Madame Claude's girls had all been like her.

Carefully sliding the papers back into the envelope, he got to his feet, hurried out to the lift. There was nothing productive he could do about Hong

Kong at this moment, but he could go upstairs and confront the woman he was married to.

As he rode up in the lift to the tenth floor, his suppressed anger bubbled up in him, spiraled into a terrible fury. He was ashen-faced and shaking inside when he entered the suite. He went in quietly, but she heard him and came out into the foyer, smiling.

"Jonathan darling, how did it go?" she asked, coming over to him, kissing him on the cheek.

Jonathan was devastated by what he had just read about his wife, and he could hardly bear for her to touch him. He had to hold himself rigid in order not to react to her kiss or to strike her.

He had loved her, had considered her to be his most perfect possession. She was soiled now, damaged, worthless.

Again she said, "How did the meeting go at Harte's?"

"So-so," he said noncommittally, controlling himself even though the rage boiled inside him.

Arabella looked at him oddly, detecting a sudden coldness in him; then she immediately dismissed this as irritation with Paula O'Neill, his *bête noir*.

Turning, she walked back into the sitting room where she had been reading, settled herself on the sofa. Her knitting bag was next to her, and she opened it, took out the baby's jacket she was making, began to ply the needles.

Jonathan walked in after her, put the envelope down on an end table, went over to the bar, where he poured himself a neat vodka.

He stood sipping it, regarding her, thinking how heavy with child she looked this afternoon. The baby was due any moment, and as much as he wanted to confront Arabella head on, he knew he must restrain himself. He did not want her anymore, and he would divorce her as quickly as possible, but he certainly wanted his child . . . his son and heir.

He said conversationally, "Did you ever know a man in Hong Kong called Tony Chiu?"

If Arabella was startled by this question, she did not show it. "No, why do you ask?" she murmured, all calm contentment.

"No special reason. His name happened to come up at lunch with my solicitors today. I thought you might have run across him in your travels, know something about him."

"I'm afraid I don't, darling."

He finished the vodka, reached for the envelope, and crossed the room. Taking the chair facing her, he said, "You lived in Paris for years . . . but you never want to go there. Why is that?"

"It's never been my favorite place," she said, lifting her eyes from the knitting, smiling at him lovingly.

"Then why did you live there for almost eight years?"

"My work was there. You know I was a model. And why all these questions about Paris, Jonny darling?"

He said slowly, "Are you afraid to go to Paris?"

"Of course not. And why are *you* being so strange? I don't understand you."

"Are you afraid you'll run into some of your old . . . paramours, is that what it's all about, *Francine?*"

Arabella gazed at him. Her pitch-black eyes were full of innocence. "I don't know what you're getting at, or why you're calling me Francine." She laughed lightly, shook her head.

"Because that's the name you used when you were a call girl."

"What on earth are you saying?" she cried, looking at him askance.

"Don't deny it! The documentation is all here, courtesy of Paula O'Neill. You can read it for yourself," he said, pinning her with his eyes. "It's an investigation into my life, and they've done quite a number on yours, too."

Arabella had no alternative but to take the documents he was thrusting at her.

"Read them."

She was suddenly terrified. She saw the dark gleam in his eyes, the cold implacability on his face. He could be cruel, dangerous when crossed; she knew that, knew all about his temper. She did as he said, scanning the pages swiftly, not wanting to read them, knowing the papers were damning. But words jumped out at her; she took in the general contents, and her heart tightened in her chest.

She handed them back to him. Her face was the color of chalk. Tears glittered in her eyes. "Darling, please, you don't understand. Let me explain. Please. My past has nothing to do with today, with now, with you, with us. It happened so long ago. I was very young. Only nineteen. I left that life behind me long ago, Jonny darling."

"I'm going to ask you one more time," he said. "Do you know Tony Chiu?"

"Yes," she whispered.

"Did he back your antique jade business in Hong Kong?"

"Yes."

"Why?"

"We've been in business before at different times. He's a bit of an entrepreneur."

"And he put you on to me, didn't he? Set me up as a target for you. He wanted you to ensnare me, to marry me so you could keep an eye on me. For him."

"No, no, that's not true. Oh Jonny, I fell in love with you! I did! You know I did."

"Admit you set me up. I know everything," he railed at her.

She began to shake. Floundering, she cried, "Yes, I did try to ensnare you that night at Susan Sorrell's, when we first met. But very soon after that, I became involved with you. I didn't want to do anything but love you. *Truly.* You must know that from our time at Mougins, from our extraordinary intimacy there, the way we became almost one person."

"I can't believe anything you say," he exclaimed, going to pour another drink.

She watched him go, return to the chair. Once he was seated again, she said, "I told Tony I couldn't give him any information about you. *That I wouldn't.* And that decision was reinforced more strongly than ever when I became pregnant with our child . . . I love you," she repeated, meaning this, her eyes riveted to his face.

"And are you involved in the drugs with him?"

"I don't know what you mean," she cried, truly baffled.

"For God's sake, don't keep denying things!" he shouted. Something in him snapped. He jumped up, took hold of her shoulders, shook her violently. "Whore," he shouted at her, "tart, *putain*. I loved you—no, adored you. I thought you were the most perfect thing, the most beautiful woman in the world, without blemish. But you're nothing . . . dirt."

Arabella began to weep uncontrollably. "You've got to believe me, Jonny. I love you with all my heart, and I've told him nothing—"

"Liar!" he screamed at her.

She reached out to him, grabbed his coat sleeve.

He shook her hands off him, his face filling with contempt and hatred. "Don't touch me."

Suddenly Arabella's face twisted and she brought her hands to her stomach. "The baby! I think the baby's coming. I'm having a contraction. Oh please help me . . . help me, Jonny. Get me to the hospital. *Please,*" she begged.

Arabella was in labor by the time he got her to the London Clinic. She was taken to the delivery room immediately.

Jonathan went to wait in the lounge reserved for expectant fathers in the famous private clinic. An hour and a half later his son was born. A nurse came to inform him of this, explaining that he could see his wife and child shortly.

He did not care about Arabella. His only interest was in his son. The heir he had always wanted. He would take the child away from her as soon as he could. Women like Arabella—whores—were not interested in children. The boy would be brought up as an English gentleman. Suddenly his mind turned to schools. He would send the boy to Eton, where he had gone, and then to Cambridge University.

Settling into his thoughts, he sat quietly, waiting patiently to see his child. He realized he was excited, that he looked forward to holding the baby in his arms. His father and mother would be happy. This was their first grandchild. Perhaps he would call the boy Robin. After the christening, the reception would be held at the House of Commons. As a leading politician and member of Parliament, his father could easily arrange that.

He switched gears, contemplated Paula O'Neill, considered the problem of the Harte stores. More than ever he was determined to go through with his plans to wrest control of the chain from her. He must. There was his son and heir to consider now.

A nurse came to fetch him sooner than he expected. He followed her down the corridor to the private suite he had booked for Arabella a month ago. The nurse showed him in, disappeared, murmuring she was going to get the baby.

Arabella was in bed, propped up against the pillows. She looked pale, exhausted.

"Jonny," she began, reaching out her hand to him. Her eyes were imploring. "Please don't be like this with me. Give me another chance, for the sake of our child. I've never done anything to hurt you. Never. I love you, darling."

"I don't want to talk to you," he snapped.

"But Jonny—" She broke off as the door opened. The same nurse walked in, this time carrying the baby wrapped in blankets and a lacy cashmere shawl.

He hurried over to the bed as the nurse placed the baby in Arabella's outstretched arms. They looked down at their child together.

Jonathan stiffened. The first thing he saw was the epicanthic fold of the eye, the little bit of skin covering the inner corner that was unmistakably oriental.

The shock on his face mirrored the stunned expression on hers. Arabella looked up at him speechlessly.

"This is not my child!" Jonathan shouted, his rage exploding. "It's Tony Chiu's! Or some other Chinaman's, you bloody whore!"

He pushed past the incredulous nurse, half stumbled, half ran out of the suite, wanting to put as much distance between himself and Arabella as he could.

The uniformed chauffeur turned on the ignition and the stately, silver-gray Rolls Royce pulled noiselessly away from the Claridge Hotel, rolled off on its way to the London airport.

Jonathan leaned back, sank into the glove-soft leather of the seat. His rage was monumental, would not abate. He could not get over the shock of Arabella's past, her duplicity, her treachery, and the knowledge that she had been sleeping with another man whilst married to him. An oriental man. There was no way she could ever deny that. The baby was living proof. *Tony Chiu,* Jonathan thought for the umpteenth time. Her old friend and benefactor was the most likely candidate.

He glanced at his briefcase next to him on the back seat, and his mind zeroed in yet again on the report. He was not sure how much truth there was in the information it contained about Tony Chiu's activities. But if the man was laundering money through Janus and Janus, he was going to put a stop to it. Immediately. And somehow he would find a way to even the score with his Chinese partner.

Jonathan could not wait to get back to Hong Kong. He glanced at his watch, saw that it was only nine-thirty. He had plenty of time to catch the midnight flight that would take him to the British Crown Colony.

Slipping his hand into his pocket, he automatically curled his fingers around the pebble of mutton-fat jade. He brought it out, stared at it in the dim light of the car. His eyes narrowed thoughtfully. It no longer looked the same. Somehow it had lost its luster. But it *was* his talisman. He laughed hollowly to himself. Some talisman. It had brought him no luck recently. Only bad joss. Very bad joss.

Rolling down the window, Jonathan flung the pebble out into the street, watched it roll away into the gutter.

The car sped on. He sat back, smiled to himself. He was glad to be rid of the jade piece. Now, perhaps, his luck would change.

EPILOGUE

We are each the authors of our own lives . . .
there is no way to shift the blame
and no one else to accept the accolades.
Paul McGill in *A Woman of Substance*

They sat together on the rocks at the Top of the World.

It was a glorious Saturday afternoon in late September. The sky was the color of speedwells and glittering with sunlight, and below them the implacable moors were softened by wave upon wave of purple heather. Somewhere in the distance there was the sound of rushing water as a stream tumbled down over rocky crags, and on the lucent air there was the smell of heather and bracken and bilberry.

They had been silent for a while, lost in their own thoughts, enjoying being together again, being up here where it was so peaceful.

All of a sudden Shane put his arms around Paula, held her close to him. "It's wonderful to be home, to be with you," he said. "I'm lost when we're apart."

She turned her head, smiled at him. "I feel the same."

"I'm glad we came up to the moors today," Shane went on. "There's nowhere like them in the whole world."

"Grandy's moors," Paula said. "She loved them, too."

"Especially up here, at the Top of the World."

"Grandy once said that the secret of life is to endure," Paula murmured and looked at him quizzically. "I hope *I* will."

"Of course, you will, my darling. *You have.* In fact, you've not only endured, you've prevailed. She'd be very proud of you. Emma always wanted you to be the best. And you are."

"You're prejudiced."

"I am indeed. But that doesn't make my statement any less true."

"I almost lost Harte's, Shane," she whispered.

"But you didn't. And that's what counts, Paula."

He jumped off the rocks, took hold of her hands, helped her down. "Come on, we'd better get back. I promised Patrick and Linnet we'd share their nursery tea."

They walked through the heather, holding hands, buffeted forward by the wind as they headed for the car parked on the dirt road. Paula stole a look at him, loving him, relieved and happy that he had returned from Australia. He had arrived in Yorkshire last night, and he had not stopped talking since, full of his plans for rebuilding the Sydney-O'Neill Hotel.

Paula came to a sudden halt.

Shane also stopped, turned to look at her. "What is it?" he asked. "Is there something wrong?"

"I hope not," she replied, starting to laugh. Her eyes were bright with happiness. "I've wanted to tell you since last night, but you haven't given me the chance—"

"Tell me what?" he probed.

She leaned into him, looked up into his face, that face she had known and loved all her life. "We're going to have another baby. I'm almost three months pregnant."

He pulled her into his arms and hugged her, then held her away. "That's the best welcome-home present I've ever had," Shane said, smiling at her.

And he continued to smile all the way back to Pennistone Royal.

Act
of
Will

Dedicated with love to the memory of my parents,
Freda and Winston Taylor. She gave me the greatest
gift a mother can give a child, the desire to excel.
He taught me to be strong of heart and to stand tall.

It is also for my husband Bob, whose love and support
has equalled theirs, with all of my love.

PROLOGUE

Audra, Christina and Kyle
1978

Prologue

Audra Crowther sat on the sofa in the living room of her daughter's Manhattan penthouse. She held herself tense and clenched her hands together so hard that the knuckles shone white as she looked from her daughter Christina to her granddaughter Kyle.

The two younger women stood in the middle of the room, their faces pale, their eyes blazing as they glared at each other. Their angry words of a few minutes ago still reverberated on the warm afternoon air.

Audra felt increasingly helpless. She knew that to remonstrate with them, to attempt to make them see reason, was a waste of time, at least at this moment. Each was convinced she was right, and no amount of persuasion would make them reverse their positions or endeavor to understand the other's point of view.

Even their clothes were like distinguishing uniforms, underscoring their intrinsic differences, further separating them: Blue jeans and sneakers for Kyle, the white Swiss voile shirt her only concession to style, the combination giving her an oddly vulnerable, childlike look, with her scrubbed face and long hair hanging loose. And for Christina, an expensive, beautifully cut dress and tailored jacket of matching raw silk, without doubt bearing her own couture label; the silver-gray of the silk the perfect foil for her chestnut hair shot through with reddish-gold lights, the gray also emphasizing her lovely smokey eyes which had always been her best feature. She was slender and impeccably groomed, not showing her forty-seven years in the least.

Tycoon versus student . . . role model versus rebel . . . mother versus daughter, Audry thought, smothering a sigh. Well, it wasn't the first time a mother and daughter were at odds with each other; that was an age-old conflict.

Suddenly Kyle broke the protracted silence when she snapped, "And there's another thing, Mother, you had no right to drag poor Grandma into this debacle, drag her all the way from England, especially since—"

"I didn't!" Christina shot back. "It was your father who telephoned my—"

"Oh yes, go on, blame Dad," Kyle cut in, her voice scathing.

"But it *was* your father who phoned my mother," Christina protested. She appealed to Audra. "Isn't that so, Mummy?"

Audra focused her attention on her granddaughter. "That's quite true, Kyle."

Kyle tossed back her mane of black hair, then thrust her hands in the pockets of her jeans, her movements brusque, defiant. Her huge brown eyes, usually doelike and soft, continued to flash rebelliously. "I suppose he thought we needed a mediator. Well, we don't . . . there's nothing to mediate—" She brought herself up short, swung her long-limbed body toward Audra and gave her a half smile. "Sorry, Grandma, I don't mean to be rude, but you shouldn't have been forced to travel halfway around the world just because my parents have discovered they can't *influence* me, or *handle* me anymore." Kyle let out a laugh that was abnormally harsh. "You see, the trouble is my parents treat me like a child, Grandma. Anyone would think I'm nine years old, not *nineteen,* for God's sake, the ridiculous way they're carrying on."

Before Audra had a chance to comment on these strident assertions, Kyle pivoted to face Christina. Her voice rose shrilly as she rushed on, "Nothing will induce me to change my mind, Mother. *Nothing.* And *nobody.* Not even Grandma. I'm going to live my life the way I want. It's my life and no one else's. You and Dad can cut me off without a nickel. I don't give a damn. I'll get a job to support myself while I'm studying. I don't need any help from you!"

"Neither your father nor I has ever said anything about cutting you off," Christina exclaimed, furious that Kyle was even suggesting such a thing. *"Your* problem is your inability to discuss this matter intelligently. And *calmly*. You fly off the handle every time we attempt to have a reasonable conversation with you."

"Listen who's talking! You're not calm either!"

Christina's mouth tightened in aggravation, but she tried to curb her increasing exasperation with her daughter. "That's not so surprising, is it?" she countered in her coldest tone. "I have built an enormous empire, an international fashion business worth millions and millions of dollars, and you're my only child, my *heir*. It's always been understood that you'd succeed me one day. Understood by *all* of us. Why, you're being trained with that in mind . . . and now, out of the blue, you announce that you don't want the company. I'm flabber—"

"No, I don't!" Kyle shouted. "Can't you get that through your head *yet,* Mother? I've been saying it for days! I'm not in the least bit interested in your stupid business empire! It can go to hell, *collapse,* for all I care! It's your problem, not mine!"

Recoiling, Christina drew in her breath sharply. She was as much stunned by Kyle's vehemence and manner as by her words.

Audra, registering shock, admonished swiftly, "Steady on there, Kyle."

Immediately, Kyle knew she had gone too far, and she bit her lip in embarrassment. Bright hot color blotched her neck, sped up into her smooth young cheeks. She glanced at her grandmother, so pale and still on the sofa. She saw the sadness and disappointment reflected in Audra's candid blue eyes, saw the gentle reproach on her sweet face. Discomfort tinged with shame swept over her. She recognized that she had discredited herself with her grandmother, whom she adored, and this she could not bear. She burst into tears and fled before she disgraced herself further, slamming the door behind her.

Christina stared at the door speechlessly.

She was mortified, enraged, and so taut her shoulder blades protruded through her thin silk jacket. "Can you believe this!" she exploded and took a step forward, obviously intent on following Kyle.

"No, no, let her go," Audra said firmly, pushing herself up, hurrying across the room. She took hold of Christina's arm and led her back to the sofa.

Gently forcing her daughter down next to her, she went on, "There's no point in continuing this. You're only inflaming each other, and you know very well that the things we say when we're angry are difficult to retract later, and you must admit you're both overwrought at the moment."

"Yes, I suppose we are." Distractedly, Christina ran a hand through her hair, then slumped against the cushions, feeling miserable and frustrated. But after only a moment she jumped up, restlessly began to pace back and forth in front of the fireplace.

As she watched her, Audra's worry intensified. She had never seen Christina quite like this before—so agitated, with her temper so close to the surface and her patience so tightly stretched. Normally she was in control, no matter what the circumstance. But then her world had never been rocked as it was rocked now; and Audra knew, too, that Kyle's words, thoughtlessly uttered in the heat of the moment and without any real malice, had nevertheless been hurtful to Christina.

Wishing to assuage that hurt as best she could, Audra said in her most reassuring voice, "Kyle didn't mean it, Christie. You know, about not caring if the business collapsed. Of course she cares, and she does love you, dear."

"She has a fine way of showing it," Christina grumbled without looking at her mother, continuing to pace, her mind still fogged by the pain her daughter had inflicted.

Audra sighed and, understanding everything, remained silent. She settled back in the corner of the sofa, waiting for Christina to calm herself, relieved that the shouting had stopped. There was hardly any sound in the room now, only the faint murmur of silk against silk, as Christina's legs moved, the ticking of the brass carriage clock on a chest between the French windows, the muffled rumble of the traffic on Sutton Place spiraling up through those windows, standing wide open on this balmy day in the middle of May. She glanced toward the terrace, mottled with sunlight, blooming with greenery and flowering plants, absently wondering how well the pink azaleas would do out there.

Then she brought her eyes back to the interior, let them roam around. For a split second her anxiousness was diluted as she absorbed the loveliness of the setting awash with tones of peach and apricot and cream, the beauty surrounding her, enveloping her . . . the priceless art on the walls: two Cézannes, a Gauguin . . . the fine English antiques with their dark glossy woods . . . bronze sculpture by Arp . . . the profusion of flowers in tall crystal vases . . . all illuminated by silk-shaded lamps of rare and ancient Chinese porcelains.

What marvelous taste Christina and Alex have, Audra thought and experienced a burst of motherly pride in her daughter and son-in-law. This was not induced merely by the graciousness they had recently created in this room but was a genuine pride in what they were as people, for all that they had achieved in their life together. They had a harmonious relationship, and their marriage had only gone from strength to strength over the years, and for that Audra was thankful.

Her thoughts settled on Alex Newman. He was a gentle man, one of the most thoughtful people she had ever met. He had been like a loving son to her. How she wished he were here at this moment. He might not have succeeded in quelling the trouble which had erupted between his wife and daughter, but with his tact and good humor, and worshipping Christina the way he did, he always had a tranquilizing effect on her.

Audra turned her head, looked over at the carriage clock. To her disappointment, it was only ten minutes to five and Alex never got home from work before seven. On the other hand, perhaps he would arrive earlier today, since they were going out to dinner at eight. As she contemplated the evening stretching ahead, her heart sank. Unless there was a radical change in Kyle's disposition in the next few hours, it was going to be an awkward evening.

Now, as though she had zeroed in on Audra's thoughts, Christina said, "I don't much relish the idea of going to dinner at Jack and Betsy Morgan's, nice though they are, and so fond of you, Mummy. No, not with Kyle in this bolshy frame of mind."

Drawing to a standstill at last, Christina looked directly at her mother and smiled ruefully, her gray eyes filled with concern. For the first time she noticed the weariness etched on Audra's face and she bit her lip, frowning.

"You must be bone-tired and terribly jet-lagged, darling," she exclaimed. "How selfish we've been since you arrived yesterday! We haven't given you a chance to catch your breath. I'd better pack you off for a rest before we go out to dinner."

"No, not just yet, Christie. I'm all right, really I am," Audra said.

Christina crossed to the sofa, sat down next to Audra and took her hand. She held it tightly, looked into her mother's lined face, swamped by the deep and abiding love she felt for her. She shook her head and her smokey gaze was tender as she said, "Kyle's judgment might be cockeyed about some things, but she could easily be right about dragging you all this way, *needlessly*—" Abruptly she stopped. Guilt flooded through her. Her mother was seventy years old, almost seventy-one, and should not be exposed to their problems at this time in her life. She and Alex ought to be capable of dealing with their recalcitrant daughter themselves. Irritated at the thought of their ineptitude, Christina cried, "We haven't been fair to you, expecting you to cope with us and our mess when you could be at home pottering around in your garden, or going off on your little day trips to the seaside—certainly leading a tranquil life. You must think Alex and I are a couple of imbeciles!"

"Don't be so silly." Audra squeezed Christina's slender tapering hand, so different from hers, gnarled as it was by arthritis. "I'd come to you no matter what it entailed if you needed me, and even if I had to walk the three thousand miles to get here. I love you, Christie, and I love that granddaughter of mine, and Alex. I can't bear to see you all so unhappy."

Christina confided in a tense voice, "It's so wrong of Kyle to abandon her courses at the Fashion Institute and to spurn my business the way she is doing. Having her take over from me one day has always been a cherished dream of mine." These last few words caught in her throat, and she had to steady herself before she could continue, "Oh Mum, what's it all been *about*? What's all my hard work been *for,* if Kyle walks away?" Christina's eyes welled with tears and she averted her head, blinking.

Audra felt a pang of sympathy, and her heart went out to her daughter. In an effort to comfort her, she murmured, "But Christie darling, you've derived a great deal of pleasure and satisfaction from your designing, and making a name for yourself in the fashion world has always been important to you, as well as a challenge. What you've accomplished, your staggering achievements and success—why surely these things must be gratifying to you . . ." Audra let her sentence trail off. She was incapable of finishing it. How hollow the words are, she thought.

I, and I alone, know what Christina sacrificed, what it cost her to create the business. She paid a high price, a terrible price, really. That's why she's so emotional about it, why she can't stand Kyle's rejection of it now.

Having regained her composure, Christina was remarking in a more level voice, "The last two weeks have been sheer purgatory with Kyle, Mother. She's downright stubborn; her implacability astounds me. Unnerves me, actually. I've never met anyone like her."

Oh, Audra thought, *haven't you?* She threw her daughter a startled glance, but she wisely said nothing. This was not the time to start delving into ancient events; there was already far too much emotional turbulence in this family. And so adopting a positive manner, Audra said, "Kyle and I have always been such good friends since she was a child, and that's one of the reasons we decided I should come to New York, isn't it? Anyway, I promised to spend the day with her tomorrow. I'm sure she wants to unburden herself to me, and I am more than ready to listen."

"But you will *talk* to her, won't you? I mean as well as listen." Without waiting for a reply, Christina plunged on, "She pays attention to you, wants to please you. So you will make her see reason, won't you, Mummy?"

Audra nodded, although she had her misgivings, and managed to say encouragingly, "Yes, I will, and somehow we'll sort this out, Christie."

For the first time in days Christina felt a little of the heaviness lifting from her and her tired eyes brightened. She leaned into Audra, kissed her wrinkled cheek, then rested her head on her mother's shoulder. "I'm so glad you're here, Mam. You're such a comfort, and I know you'll make everything come out right, as you always have."

Mam, Audra repeated silently. For years it had been Mummy or Mum or Mother. *Mam* was the childhood name. Hearing it now, suddenly, after all these years made Audra flinch. It evoked so many memories, not all of them happy ones. Then a rush of warmth and love filled her throat and for a moment she could not speak. Automatically she lifted her hand and stroked Christina's glossy hair. It's true, old habits die hard, Audra thought, bending down, kissing the top of her daughter's head. All that money, all that power, all that fame, but she's still my little girl. I can't stand to see her distressed in this way. But then there is also Kyle, my only grandchild, and *her* unhappiness is insupportable. What a dilemma. Skating on thin ice between the two of them. Oh dear God, wherever will I find the wisdom and strength to help each one without somehow inflicting hurt on the other?

Growing conscious that her daughter was waiting for a response, Audra clamped down on her worries. "I can only *try* to make things come out right for you, Christie," she said softly. "I told you, when I arrived, that I'm not going to take sides. Anyway, Kyle is correct about it being *her* life. And she does have the right to live it the way she sees fit."

Straightening up, Christina nodded slowly. "Yes," she replied evenly, "I know what you mean. But she's very young and inexperienced, and she can't possibly know her own mind. Not yet, at any rate." Rising, Christina walked over to one of the French windows, stood gazing out at the terrace. Then she swung around and gave Audra a penetrating look. "Rejecting my business out of hand is not only foolish but irresponsible of her, wouldn't you say?"

"Well, yes," Audra felt bound to agree, yet she had the need to defend her granddaughter, and could not help adding, "Still, Kyle is intelligent, as well as being a spirited and independent girl. And, you know, I also find her wise for someone her age." Audra paused, thinking: Well, in for a penny, in for a pound, and I might as well say it all. Taking a deep breath, she finished in her firmest manner, "I just want you to give some consideration to *her* needs, *her* desires, as well as your own. Promise me that you will."

Christina was startled, and there was a brief silence before she muttered, "All right . . . yes . . . I promise."

It struck Audra that there was a lingering reluctance in this promise. Slowly and very carefully, she said, "Once a long time ago, I told you that a child is only lent to you, Christina. Don't ever forget that."

Christina stared at Audra and the strangest expression crossed her face. She opened her mouth to speak and then closed it. She swung away, focusing her eyes on the terrace once more as she reflected on her mother's words.

Absently, Audra pushed a strand of silver hair away from her face and sat back, watching, waiting. She saw her daughter's shoulders droop in dejection, saw at once the pensive expression settling on her pretty mouth. Yes, she's remembering, Audra thought. And I've said enough for today. It would be wiser to let things rest where they are for the present.

Gripping the arm of the sofa, Audra pulled herself to her feet a bit unsteadily, exhaustion finally getting the better of her. "I think I will have a rest before dinner, perhaps try to get a little sleep," she said.

"Yes, yes, you should," Christina responded. She went quickly to Audra's side, put her arm around her shoulders lovingly, and escorted her out of the room.

Half an hour later Audra was still wide awake, much to her irritation. Try though she had to sleep, she was unable to do so. Christina had accompanied her to the guest suite at the far end of the penthouse, had closed the curtains, plumped up the bed pillows, and generally fussed until Audra had impatiently waved her out. Glad to be alone at last, Audra had undressed, slipped on a robe and stretched out on the bed. She had done so gratefully. Every bone in her body ached, she was debilitated by jet lag and her hands and knees throbbed painfully as her arthritis flared. But the moment her head touched the pillow, her mind had started to race.

Mostly Audra was worried that she had made a mistake in coming to New York. Might it not have been more prudent to refuse Alex's request and leave them alone to battle it out among themselves? And it *was* going to be a battle, Audra was quite positive of that. It would be a trial of strength. Christie would worry it through, refusing to let go, tenacious to the end; Kyle would dig her heels in, equally as stubborn and determined to win no matter what the cost to everyone involved. The stakes were so high neither of them could possibly act in any other way. Where was it all going to end? In disaster, she suspected. They couldn't both win. And the loser would be bitter and resentful.

I have to find a way to help them settle this, Audra now told herself; then with a stab of dismay she wondered how. If Alex, who was diplomatic and persuasive, had been unable to arbitrate their differences, then surely she would not be able to influence them either. I *must* find a way, she muttered.

With a sigh of weariness, Audra opened her eyes, acknowledging that sleep was going to evade her. The spacious bedroom looked as tranquil as it always did in the gentle light seeping in through the curtains. Usually the blue-and-white color scheme, elegant furnishings and opulent comfort engendered a sense of well-being in her. But these feelings were sadly absent tonight.

Audra shivered. The early evening breeze blowing in through the window came up off the East River. It was cool now and there was a sharp tinge of dampness in the air that seemed to penetrate her joints. Shivering again she drew the quilt up over her body and reached for her pills. Putting one in her mouth, she washed it down with a sip of water, reminding herself that this was her third; the doctor had warned her not to take more than four in one day.

Sometimes she wondered about her arthritis, wondered if her hard life had not contributed to her present condition. Doctor Findlay said it hadn't, but when she thought of the endless scrubbing and cleaning and washing and ironing, the drudgery that had been her lot for so many years, she could not help pondering. Well, those days had long since gone. In her old age she had a life of ease.

As she put the tumbler back on the bedside table her glance fell on the photograph standing near the cobalt-blue glass lamp. Audra turned on her side, rested herself on one elbow and gazed at it thoughtfully.

Three faces stared back at her. Christina's, Kyle's and her own.

The picture had been taken last summer, in her rose garden in Yorkshire. What a wonderfully happy day that had been . . . her seventieth birthday. The weather had been glorious, as the color photograph attested.

After a little tea party on the terrace, Alex had insisted on taking this picture. In honor of the occasion and for posterity, he had laughingly said as he had lined them up near the old stone sundial, a few steps to the right of her best hybrid tea roses.

Three generations, she murmured under her breath. But we don't look as if we're related. We might easily be strangers, as disparate in appearance as any three women could be. And yet we are very much alike deep down within ourselves.

Almost half a century ago I was told that I had an implacable will, that I was relentless and propelled by a terrible driving force within myself. I had been angry and hurt. But it was the truth. And they have inherited those characteristics from me . . . my daughter, my granddaughter. When Christina was a child, I committed an act of will that changed all of our lives irrevocably. And then, when she was a young woman, Christina repeated the pattern, performed an act of will of her own that was as powerful as mine. Now it is Kyle's turn . . . she is on the verge of doing the same. And, as before, our lives won't ever be the same again.

Audra sat up with a jolt, sudden comprehension flickering on her face. "I am to blame," she said aloud to the silent room, and then she thought: If I had done things differently, things would be different now. Everything that is happening *now* harks back to when I was a young woman. *Cause and effect.* Every act we commit, trivial or important, has its inevitable consequences. It's like throwing a pebble into a pool and watching the ripples spread out . . . farther and farther, ever far-reaching.

Audra sank back onto the pillows and lay there, allowing herself to drift with her thoughts. They were centered entirely on Kyle.

Slowly the pain in her hands and knees began to ease, and her body grew warmer under the quilt. Audra closed her eyes at last.

Nineteen twenty-six, she mused drowsily . . . such a long time ago . . . but not so long that I can't remember what *I* was like then . . . when *I* was Kyle's age.

Audra
1926 to 1951

One

Today it was her birthday.

It was the third of June in the year 1926 and she was nineteen years old.

Audra Kenton stood at the window of her room in the Fever Hospital in Ripon, in Yorkshire, where she worked as a nurse, gazing out at the back garden. Absently she watched the play of light and shadow on the lawn, as the sunlight filtered through the leafy domes of the two great oaks that grew near the old stone wall. There was a gentle breeze, and the leaves rustled and trembled under it, and shimmered with green brilliance as they caught the sun. It was radiant and balmy, a day that invited and beckoned.

Matron had given Audra the afternoon off for her birthday. The problem was that she had nowhere to go and no one to spend it with. *She was entirely alone in this world.*

Audra only had one friend, Gwen Thornton, another nurse at the hospital, but Gwen had been summoned home to Horsforth yesterday. Her mother had been taken ill and she was needed. Weeks ago, Gwen had arranged to exchange her day off with one of the other nurses, so that she could be with Audra, celebrate this important occasion with her, and the two of them had planned a very special day. Now their elaborate plans were laid to waste.

Leaning her head against the window frame, Audra sighed, thinking of the empty hours looming ahead. Unexpectedly her throat tightened and she felt the tears gathering behind her eyes as sadness mingled with bitter disappointment trickled through her. But after only a few seconds she blinked and cleared her throat, managed to take hold of herself. Resolutely she pushed aside the negative emotions momentarily invading her, refusing to feel sorry for herself. Audra despised self-pity in others, considered it to be a sign of weakness. *She was strong.* Her mother had always told her that she was, and her mother had rarely been wrong about anything.

Turning away from the window, she walked over to the chair and sat down heavily, wondering what to do with herself.

She could read, of course, or do a little embroidery, or even finish the sketch of the blouse she was designing, and which she intended to make—when she could afford to buy the fabric. On the other hand, none of these occupations had any real appeal for her. Not today. Not on her birthday.

She had been so looking forward to the outing with her friend, to enjoying a few carefree hours of pleasure for once in her life. Audra had little to celebrate these days, and festive occasions were a thing of the past, a rarity indeed. In fact, her life had changed so radically, so harshly, in the last few years, she hardly recognized it as her own.

It suddenly struck her that resorting to one of those mundane hobbies, normally used to pass the time when she was off duty, would be infinitely worse than just sitting in this chair, doing nothing. They're poor substitutes, all of them, for the plans Gwen and I made.

Audra had long since trained herself not to notice the room where she lived in the hospital. But now, seeing it so clearly illuminated in the bright sunshine, she became painfully aware of its ugliness and lack of comfort. Having been born into gentility, albeit somewhat impoverished, Audra was a young woman of breeding and refinement. She possessed taste in abundance, had strong artistic leanings, and the austerity of the spartan furnishings and institutional color scheme suddenly stabbed at her discerning eyes. They offended her sensibilities.

Confronting her were walls painted a dismal porridge-beige which ran down to a floor covered with dreary gray linoleum. The iron bedstead, rickety night stand and chest of drawers were notable only for their shabbiness and utilitarian design. The room was chillingly bleak, intolerable at any time, but especially on this sunny afternoon. She knew she had to escape its oppressive boundaries for a short while, no matter where she went.

Her gaze fell on the dress lying on the bed, where she had placed it a short time before. It was new. She had saved up for a whole year, putting away a shilling every week, in order to buy herself a present for her birthday.

She and Gwen had gone to Harrogate two Saturdays ago with this in mind. They had wandered around for several hours, mostly window shopping and admiring the beautiful things they saw and which they knew they would never be able to afford. Audra filled with warm and affectionate feelings for Gwen as she thought of that day now.

Gwen was especially attracted to jeweler's shops, and Audra had found herself constantly cupping her hands and dutifully peering through glass at some bauble that had caught Gwen's attention. *"Oh Audra!* Just look at *that!"* Gwen kept crying, pointing to a brooch or a ring or a pendant. At one moment she had clutched Audra's arm fiercely and whispered in awed tones, "Have you ever seen anything like that gorgeous bangle, Audra! Why the stones could be *real* the way they sparkle like diamonds. It *would* suit you, Audra. Let's go in . . . it doesn't cost anything just to *look."*

Audra had half smiled and shaken her head, not saying a word, and she had thought of her mother's jewelry, which had been much more beautiful than any of these tawdry imitations of the real thing.

Gwen's excited exclamations and urgent proddings continued a bit too long for Audra that afternoon, and she had eventually grown exasperated, had silenced her friend with a stern look and a sharp admonition to be quiet. Immediately regretting her shortness, she had quickly apologized to Gwen. And she had gone on to explain to her, for the umpteenth time, that *she* had no money to spare for frivolous items like brooches and bracelets and nonsensical hats and bottles of Devon Violets scent, which were just a few of the things Gwen constantly craved.

"You *know* I only ever buy clothes for myself," Audra had said, and had added, with a tiny rueful laugh, "and usually the most *practical* clothes I can find, at that, Gwen. Things I know will last me for a very long time."

And then, not ten minutes after she had uttered these words, Audra had seen the dress in the window of Madame Stella's gown shop. She had fallen in love with it instantly. It was a frock destined only to go to parties, a bit of airy, gossamer muslin. Effectively draped on a stand in the center of the window, it was the one piece of clothing displayed. Next to it, accessories were scattered on the floor: a picture hat of cream leghorn, a parasol of ruffled cream silk and three long strands of pearls. All had epitomized true elegance to Audra, but most particularly the dress. It was highly impractical, obviously costly and very, very beautiful. She had gazed at it for ages, not knowing when or where she would ever wear it and yet aching to own it just the same.

Even so, she had hung back, would not budge when Gwen, shrewdly observing the expression of longing on her face, had pushed open the door and insisted they go in and ask the price. Despite Audra's reluctance and her adamant refusal to enter the shop, Gwen had obviously had no intention of being thwarted. She had taken Audra's arm in a viselike grip and frog-marched her into Madame Stella's.

Although both girls had expected the dress to be expensive, the two of them had been stunned, nevertheless, when they had learned that it cost three guineas. Audra had made to leave at once. But the redoubtable Gwen had restrained her, had somehow managed to maneuver her into the fitting room before she could make a graceful escape. Not wanting to create an embarrassing scene in front of the saleslady, Audra had had no option but to try on the dress.

It was the color that captivated her—a clear bright blue that had reminded her of the delphiniums at High Cleugh. She had not needed Gwen to tell her that it suited her to perfection; she had seen herself in the cheval mirror.

Indeed, Audra had been momentarily taken aback by her own reflection that afternoon. For the first time in some years she had acknowledged to herself that for once she looked quite pretty. Mostly she referred to herself as a Plain Jane, which she genuinely believed to be the truth. But in this she did herself an injustice.

Audra Kenton was not beautiful in the strictest sense, but then neither was she plain. She was in a category somewhere in between. There was a certain stubbornness in her well-defined face. This was reflected in the determined set of her chin and in her firm and resolute mouth, which was quite beautiful, however, when she smiled. Her best features were a faultless, creamy complexion, glossy light brown hair glazed with a golden sheen in the summer, and lovely eyes. In actuality, these were the most spectacular things about her. They were large, set wide apart, thickly fringed with golden-brown lashes and accentuated by finely arched brows. But it was their color that was so memorable and caused people to look at her twice. They were of a blue so deep and so vivid it was startling.

As Audra had stared back at herself in the mirror of the fitting room, she had not failed to notice how the blue of the muslin intensified their depth of color. She also saw that the "flapper" style of the dress was flattering and did wonders for her. Audra was small, only five feet two inches, and her lack of height was a constant source of irritation to her. Yet despite her diminutive size she was nicely proportioned, and the simple cut of the frock emphasized her pretty figure, whilst its short skirt, cut on the cross so that it flared out, drew attention to her shapely legs and slender ankles.

And so in the end, after some indecision on her part because of its price, and worried whisperings with Gwen, she had finally bought the dress. To make up the three pounds, three shillings needed, Audra had used her entire savings of two pounds twelve shillings, every other penny in her purse—which was all she had in the world—plus one and six borrowed from Gwen.

"Don't look so glum," Gwen had whispered whilst they had been waiting for the saleslady to wrap the dress. "It's worth every penny. Besides, it's about time you treated yourself to something nice."

There was no question in Audra's mind that the dress was the most beautiful thing she had owned since she was a child. And a memory had stirred, a memory of another time when she had come to Harrogate shopping—with her mother and Uncle Peter. It had been 1919, just after he had returned from the Great War. She had been twelve and he had bought her a pink party frock which had entranced her just as much as the blue muslin.

As they had left Madame Stella's, Audra had told Gwen of that particular trip and the pretty pink frock, had confided more about her past life, and Gwen had been agog and full of questions. Audra, who was reserved by nature, had nonetheless answered some of them, not wanting to offend Gwen by appearing secretive. Later, arms linked, they had taken a leisurely stroll along The Stray, the stretch of green common carpeted with lovely flowers which made a natural tapestry of brilliant color underneath the shady trees. Then Gwen had taken them to Betty's Cafe, the posh tearoom on The Parade overlooking The Stray, and had generously paid for them both, since Audra had spent all of her cash. She had also loaned her the money for her ticket back to Ripon, just as she had promised she would when Audra had been wavering in Madame Stella's. And Audra had reminded herself yet again how lucky she was to have Gwen for her friend.

At the end of their day's excursion, on the way to the bus stop, they had passed the Arcadian Rooms, where tea dances were held every afternoon in the Palm Court. Everyone knew that this was *the* place to go, the smart spot in town where the local swells foxtrotted and tangoed to the strains of Stan Stanton and His Syncopated Strollers.

Both young women had been itching to visit the Palm Court for weeks, and Gwen, who had learned the Charleston from her brother, had been teaching it to Audra in their off-duty hours. Audra had been astonished and thrilled when Gwen had announced she was taking them to a tea dance at the Palm Court on her birthday. "It'll be my treat, my birthday present," Gwen had said, beaming at her. "And you'll wear your new dress and everyone will admire you in it." The two of them had been bursting with excitement and anticipation as they had ridden on the bus back to Ripon, and they had been counting the days ever since.

But there would be no trip to Harrogate after all. No tea dance at the Palm Court of the Arcadian Rooms. No one to admire her or the new dress. Audra sighed. Earlier she had planned to wear it just for her own pleasure, although she had not been quite sure where she would *go* in it all by herself. But now she changed her mind.

Audra was nothing if not practical, and it struck her that it would be foolish to risk ruining it or getting it crumpled and soiled. Far wiser to save the frock for another special occasion, she reasoned. And there's bound to be one in the future, now that I have a friend like Gwen. Perhaps we'll go to the church Garden Fete in August, and then there's Gwen's birthday in September. We must celebrate that. Yes, something's bound to come up, she reassured herself, her natural optimism surfacing as it invariably did.

Audra was blessed with a sunny disposition and a cheerful personality, and it was these traits, coupled with her strong will and intelligence, which had saved her in the past. They helped her to cope with her problems in the most positive way. She never let her troubles burden her for very long, sought always to solve them with expediency. And if this was not feasible, she tried not to dwell on them unnecessarily.

Now she roused herself, took the blue frock off the bed and returned it to the clothes closet in the corner of the room.

After she had slipped out of her blue-and-white-striped nurse's uniform and put it away, she peered at the other garments hanging there, wondering what to wear for her walk in the country.

Although she did not have an extensive wardrobe, the clothes she did own were of good quality, and because she was fastidious, they were never anything but immaculate. For economic reasons, Audra made all of her summer clothes herself, and these were mostly lightweight dresses in the darker spectrum of colors; to her practical turn of mind these were guaranteed to wear better than the paler shades. Finally her hand came to rest on a navy cotton dress with a dropped waistline and a sailor collar trimmed with white. She pulled it out, found her black leather walking shoes with flat heels and began to dress.

Suddenly Audra thought of Gwen. How self-centered I'm being, she chastised herself. Here I am, concerned about my birthday, when Gwen has a sick mother to nurse. Audra wished she could go to Horsforth today, to help Gwen, but it was much too far to travel with only an afternoon free. Poor Gwen must be run off her feet, not to mention dreadfully worried, she thought. Then her face brightened as she adjusted the collar of her dress and pivoted to look at herself in the small mirror standing on the chest of drawers. Gwen's father was a doctor, and her brother Charlie was a medical student at Leeds University. Mrs. Thornton was in good hands. She would soon be well again, and Gwen would be returning to the hospital in no time at all.

As she left her room and hurried down the corridor, it struck Audra how truly attached she had become to her friend. Ever since Gwen had come to work at the hospital a year ago, her life had changed for the better, and it was much more bearable now. Until then none of the other nurses had ever attempted to be friends with her. Audra knew that this was mainly because of her background, her manners and her cultured way of speaking.

The other nurses thought she was stuck-up and unapproachable. But this was not true at all. It was her shyness that held her somewhat apart, prevented her from making the first gesture.

As if she had instinctively understood this, happy, laughing, gregarious Gwen had paid not the slightest attention to her reserve. Having singled Audra out as the one girl she wanted as her friend, she had persisted and had broken down the protective walls Audra had built around herself. Within the first week of knowing each other they had become inseparable.

I don't know what I'd do without Gwen, Audra thought, banging the front door of the hospital behind her. She's the only person I have in the world.

———— *Two* ————

She had not intended to go to High Cleugh.

But before she realized it she was almost there.

When she had set out from the hospital, Audra had had no particular destination in mind. She had taken the road that led to Sharow and Copt Hewick, both small villages on the outskirts of Ripon.

There was no special reason for her to go there, other than that they were pleasant little spots; also, the route was picturesque, the surrounding landscape pastoral and unusually pretty at this time of year.

Arriving at Copt Hewick, Audra wandered slowly up the cobbled main street, thinking how well-kept everything looked on this hot June afternoon. The dainty gardens in front of the neat cottages were bright with nasturtiums and marigolds and dahlias; white lace curtains glowed behind sparkling windows; every doorstep was newly scrubbed, each step outlined with yellow scouring stone.

Glancing up ahead at the Blackamoor Inn, Audra noticed that it, too, was spruced up. Its white walls and black shutters had been treated to fresh coats of paint, and even the sign swinging over the front door appeared to have been artistically embellished with a few colorful daubs from somebody's paintbox.

Audra hesitated at the Blackamoor pub, which was the juncture of several roads, wondering whether to take the main thoroughfare to Boroughbridge or the secondary side road that led to Newby Hall and Skelton. She chose the latter, although she did not follow the road to its end. Instead she veered off to her right when she was halfway down, favoring a narrow lane flanked on either side by drystone walls.

After only a few steps along the lane, she stopped dead in her tracks, immediately understanding exactly where her feet were leading her. She half turned, wanting to go back the way she had come. She discovered she could not.

High Cleugh drew her toward it like a powerful magnet.

With every step she took, Audra Kenton told herself she was making a mistake, exposing herself to heartache, especially today of all days, yet still she continued to walk, almost against her own volition.

By the time she came to the bottom of the long, twisting lane, she no longer cared whether she was being foolish or not. She was conscious only of her yearning to see the one place she loved above all others on this earth. She had stayed away far too long.

She climbed over the stile set in the wall, jumped down into the long pasture and ran through the tall grass. It rippled and swayed like an undulating sea of green under the light breeze which had blown up. Unexpectedly, a couple of cows lazily lumbered across her path, and she dodged around them, plunging ahead, her young face taut with anticipation, her long hair flying out behind her as she ran.

Audra did not break her pace until she came to the huge sycamore tree at the end of the pasture. Upon reaching it, she stooped down and stepped under its spreading branches which formed a canopy of green, shutting out the sky.

She leaned her body against the tree, pressed her face to its trunk and closed her eyes. She was out of breath and panting with exertion.

After only a few moments, she began to breathe more evenly. Slowly, she smoothed her hand over the tree, felt the rough texture of the bark under her fingertips, and she smiled to herself. This was her tree. Her place.

She had named it the Memory Place in her mind. For that was exactly what it was—the place to remember *them,* to relive the past, to recall the happiness and joy that had once been hers and was no more.

Frequently they had come here together. Her mother. Her brothers, Frederick and William. And Uncle Peter. And when she was here at the tree they were with her again, and her misery was vanquished for a brief while.

Audra opened her eyes, blinking in the cool green darkness of the sycamore's shade, and then she moved out from underneath its branches. Circling the tree, she came to a standstill at the edge of the little slope that fell away to the banks of the River Ure just a few feet below her. Finally she lifted her head and gazed out across that narrow band of swift-running water to the wooded valley on the opposite side of the river. There it was, nestled in the palm of a natural dell set amidst the trees.

High Cleugh.

The small but lovely old manor where she had been born nineteen years ago today. The house where she had grown up, had lived for the best part of her life. Her beloved home until five years ago.

She feasted her eyes on it, struck as always by its simplicity and gentleness, which, to her, were the things that made it compellingly beautiful.

High Cleugh was an eighteenth-century house, long and low, with a fine symmetry that gave it an incomparable gracefulness. It was built of local gray stone and had many leaded windows that winked and glinted now in the bright sunlight. These faced out onto a terrace made of the same ancient stone; running the length of the house, the terrace was broken in the center by a very long flight of steps that sliced its way through lawns tilting to the river. Herbaceous borders, wide, rambling, grew beneath the terrace walls, splashed vivid hues against the dark stone and verdant grass.

But it was the massed delphiniums which caught the eye, entranced. These flourished in great abundance at the bottom of the lawns near the river's edge, their blossoms blanketing the ground with a breathtaking mixture of blues. Cobalt bled into a powder blue so delicate it was almost white, this tint giving way to cornflower, then a luscious violet-blue that in turn brushed up against lavender and the purple tones of belladonna.

Her mother's delphiniums . . . planted with such care and nurtured so lovingly over the years. Audra's heart clenched with a bittersweet mixture of pleasure and pain. Oh how she longed to be in those gardens once again! It would be so easy for her to slip over to the other side of the river. All she had to do was follow the path along the bank until she came to the stepping stones. These giant flat slabs, worn smooth by running water and time, stretched across the shallowest part, led directly to the copse adjoining the manor.

But she could not go to High Cleugh. If she did, she would be trespassing. Another family lived there now.

She sat down on the springy grass, pulled her knees up to her chest, rested her chin on them and clasped her arms around her legs.

For the longest time Audra stared at High Cleugh.

There was no sign of life. It appeared to slumber in the brilliant sunshine as if it were not inhabited at all. A peacefulness lay over the motionless gardens. Not a blade of grass, not a single leaf stirred. The wind had dropped and the air was warm and languid. There was no sound except for the faint buzzing of a bee somewhere nearby and the gurgle and splash of water rushing over dappled stones as the Ure wended its way below her.

Audra's gaze became more intense than ever. She saw beyond the exterior walls to the inner core of the house. She closed her eyes, let herself sink down into her imagination, remembering, remembering . . .

She was inside the house.

She stood in the hall with its apricot-colored walls and worn green-velvet bench and the palm in the pitted brass pot. All was shadowy, quiescent. She listened for a while to the stillness. Then she stepped forward, her footsteps echoing with a metallic ring against the marble. Slowly she climbed the staircase. It twisted upward in a graceful curve. She paused on the first landing. Her room was here. She went inside, closed the door, sighed with pleasure.

Familiar walls of the palest green surrounded her, reminded her as always of a summer sea on a misty Yorkshire morning. The polished wood floor gleamed like glass under her feet as she stepped up to her four-poster bed. She reached out, touched the tulips printed on the worn coverlet, traced a finger around their once-red petals long since washed out to the color of old rust. Burnt sienna it was called in her paintbox. She glided to the window, looked out across the Dales, heard the rustle of the curtains as they flapped about in the breeze. The scent of carnations filled the summer air. She turned her head, saw a cloud of pink petals in the blue willow-patterned bowl that stood on the oak chest. Their perfume drifted away, was replaced by a sweeter, headier fragrance. October roses lifted full-blown heads from the bowl, shining yellows against the blue. It was autumn now. The time of the harvest.

How well she knew the changing seasons of this house.

The air had grown chillier. The fire crackled in the grate. She felt the warmth of the flames on her face. Snowflakes fluttered against the window pane. The gardens were made of white-icing sugar.

She was no longer alone in the house.

She caught the sound of her mother's laughter, the swish of her silk gown as she joined her by the fire. The Beautiful Edith Kenton. That was how they always spoke of her hereabouts.

Sapphires blazed at her throat, on her cool white arms. Blue fire against that translucent skin. Hair the color of new pennies, an aureole of burnished copper light around the pale heart-shaped face. Warm and loving lips were pressed down to her young cheek. The smell of gardenias and Coty powder enveloped her. A slender, elegant hand took hold of hers, guided her out of the room.

Frederick and William waited in the hall, sang carols as they descended the stairs. Rowdy, loving brothers and devoted sons. Uncle Peter stood behind them in the entrance to the drawing room. He embraced her with his smile and ushered them all into the room.

She stood transfixed.

The room had acquired a magical quality this Christmas night. Its faded elegance had taken on a curious new beauty in the muted, golden light. Candles glowed on a sturdy little fir. Logs hissed and spurted up the chimney. Sprigs of holly decorated the paintings, draped the mantel, hung in great beribboned swags in front of the windows. Mistletoe fell from the cut-glass chandelier. Paper chains were inverted rainbows looped across the ceiling. The air was redolent with new aromas that assailed her senses. She smelled pine cones and wood smoke and eggnog, and succulent goose cooking and chestnuts roasting on the fire.

They crowded around the fireplace.

They sang carols and drank the eggnog from little crystal cups and lifted the steaming chestnuts from their bursting shells. And their laughter reverberated through the house.

Three red-felt stockings hung from the mantelpiece. They opened them . . . she and Frederick and William. In hers there was a treasure trove. An orange, an apple, a bag of nuts and a new penny tied in a scrap of silk; a sachet of potpourri, Pears soap and yards of silk ribbons for her hair plus a box of Egyptian dates, lavender water and a book of verse with the name "Edith Kenton" written on the flyleaf in her mother's flowing script. Little things which had cost nothing but whose value was priceless to her.

Snowdrifts were banked outside the house.

Sleet and bitter winds rattled against the window panes and heralded the new year. The Christmas decorations had disappeared. The house was hushed and desolate without her mother's laughter. It was the time for Uncle Peter to go away again. She saw the sadness on his face, and her mother's eyes, blue like the sapphires she wore, were filled with tears . . .

Audra's face was wet with tears . . . she had not realized that she had begun to cry. She straightened up and brushed her eyes with her fingertips, tearing her gaze away from High Cleugh.

She lay down and buried her face in the cool, sweet-smelling grass, then squeezed her eyes tightly shut as she felt the sharp prick of tears once more. But now she did not bother to suppress them; instead, she allowed herself the luxury of weeping.

And she wept for those she had lost and for the past and for the way things had once been.

Eventually her tears ceased. She lay there quietly, staring up at the China-blue sky, absently watching the drift of the scudding clouds, ruminating on her beloved family and all of the things which had happened in the last few years.

Three

Audra's father was a shadowy figure in her mind.

He had died in 1909, when she was only two years old, and her memories of him were indistinct.

But the images of her mother, and of Frederick and William, were potent and so very vivid to her the three of them might have been standing there, looking down at her lying on the grass. And Uncle Peter was as indelibly imprinted on her heart as the other three were.

How inexorably their lives and their destinies had been bound up with his.

Peter Lacey had died in 1920 whilst still a young man. He had been an officer in the British Army during the Great War, and had fought in the trenches of France, where he had been badly gassed in the Battle of the Somme. His lungs had been so seriously damaged that his health had never been the same, and that was why he had died. Or so they said at the time.

Audra's mother, the Beautiful Edith Kenton, had been inconsolable. She had followed him to the grave less than a year later, in July of 1921. She had been thirty-seven.

Frederick, Audra's elder brother, had told her that their mother's death was due to heart failure, but she had recently substituted *heartbreak* for the latter. Audra had come to believe that their mother really *had* died of a broken heart as she had pined away for Peter Lacey; since Audra had grown to young womanhood, she had come to understand their relationship so much better. They had been lovers, of course. There was no longer any doubt in her mind about that.

As a child Audra had never questioned his presence. He was their Uncle Peter, a distant relative of their father's—a third cousin, she had been led to believe—and he had been there for as long as she could remember.

After their father Adrian Kenton had died of consumption, Uncle Peter had become an even more frequent visitor, staying with them at High Cleugh for a week or two at a time. Because of his business interests and financial affairs, he had returned to London at regular intervals, but he was never absent for very long. And whether he came for an extended visit or a brief few days, he never came empty-handed. There were usually presents for them all.

"Isn't it wonderful the way Uncle Peter looks after us," her mother had said once to Audra. "I am a great burden to him, I fear. He is such a busy man . . . but very kind and generous, and most uncommonly thoughtful. He *wishes* to take care of me, and of you and your brothers. He insists, and will not have it any other way." Edith had sighed, then smiled her shimmering smile. "He was devoted to your father, of course. That is the reason why he has made *us* his responsibility, Audra."

But it was not devotion to their father at all, Audra had come to realize. It had been adoration of their mother that had caused Peter Lacey to become their benefactor and protector.

Once she had come to understand the reality of their life together, Audra had accepted the truth about them, and she had never blamed or censored her mother and her uncle in her heart. They had been very much in love. He had also loved Edith's fatherless children and behaved as a father would toward them; he had taken care of the Kenton family to the best of his ability and his financial means. There had been a wife somewhere in the background, and two children, a boy and a girl; otherwise Edith Kenton and Peter Lacey would have married.

Audra and William had not comprehended the situation when Edith and Peter were alive, but Audra had lately come to wonder if Frederick had ever had his suspicions. After all, he *was* the eldest. He had been seventeen when Edith had died, and William fifteen, and Audra had just celebrated her fourteenth birthday the month before.

The Kenton children had been stunned and heartbroken at the unexpected death of their mother, and disbelieving. It had been sudden. And then, only a short hour after her coffin had been lowered into the ground, they had suffered another terrible blow.

They were so shocked they were unable to speak, when they learned that Edith had died penniless, and that they were not only destitute but without a roof over their heads. High Cleugh was not their property as they had always believed. It had never belonged to their father, in fact. He had merely rented it from the owner—Peter Lacey. Peter had permitted Edith to live on at High Cleugh, and without paying rent, since 1909.

Apparently a codicil in his will had protected Edith after his death—but not them. High Cleugh was to remain her home for as long as she lived; after her death it must revert to his estate. The annuity he had left her also ceased when she died.

There was no separate provision for them, most probably because Peter Lacey had not anticipated that their mother would die at such an early age. Obviously neither had she, despite her great sorrow at his passing, since she had not left a will.

The three orphans were told all this by their mother's cousin, Alicia Drummond. She had taken them back to her house, The Grange, after the funeral service at St. Nicholas's Church and the burial in the adjoining cemetery in the village of West Tanfield. She had hurried them into the library, a cheerless room filled with gloomy shadows, dolorous paintings and ponderous Victorian furniture, where tea was to be served later. Aunt Alicia's husband, Uncle Percival, her daughter, Cousin Winifred, and her mother, Great-Aunt Frances Reynolds, had attended the funeral and had joined them for tea afterward.

Although the Kenton children disliked the Drummonds intensely, they held a certain affection for their great-aunt, who had always shown a particular fondness for Edith, her only niece, and the Kentons. And so they automatically gravitated to the Chesterfield sofa next to her chair. Here they aligned themselves in a row. They were a staunch little trio, wearing their best Sunday clothes and black arm-bands of mourning, sitting stiff-backed and controlled. Somehow they managed to hide their sorrow behind expressionless faces.

Aunt Alicia had poured tea from a Georgian silver pot, and the maid had passed around the delicate china cups, then offered them plates of watercress sandwiches and carraway-seed cake. They were not able to eat a thing.

Audra was the first one to speak up, after Aunt Alicia had delivered her devastating news about their impecunious state. "What's going to happen to us? Are we to be sent to the workhouse?" she asked in a small but curiously steady voice, fixing Alicia Drummond with a penetrating stare.

Great-Aunt Frances, shocked, exclaimed, "Of course not, dear child!" and then she reached out and patted Audra's hand. She was a much nicer person than her daughter, and she continued in a kindly tone, "I'm too old to take you in, I'm afraid. However, you will all come and live here at The Grange. Your Aunt Alicia and Uncle Percival have very generously offered to provide a good home for the three of you."

The Kenton children, with no other living relatives, had been obliged to accept this offer, dubious though they were about moving in with the Drummonds. After only a few days at The Grange, they realized just how much they were going to detest living there. The large Victorian mansion was as cold and as forbidding as Alicia Drummond herself, who was also a snobbish, bigoted, avaricious and crafty woman. The house was run on ludicrous timetables; the rules were rigid; the atmosphere was depressing and unpleasant; the food, mediocre at best. The Kenton children had been brought up with a great deal of love and freedom by a woman who was also an excellent cook, and they were shocked by life at The Grange.

A week after Edith Kenton's funeral, some of her furniture and other possessions from High Cleugh were sold at the auction rooms in Ripon, to pay for her funeral expenses and settle her debts. At least, this is what her children were told by their aunt. The best pieces of furniture, a number of good paintings, and choice items of silver were removed to The Grange by Alicia Drummond. "I shall be happy to store these things for you until you are old enough to have them," she had explained to the three young Kentons.

Despite the fact that this sounded reasonable enough to Frederick and William, Audra, who was far smarter than her brothers, did not trust the woman. And her distrust only increased when, several days later, she noticed her mother's things appearing in various rooms of her aunt's house. And so that night, when everyone was asleep, she had crept down the corridor to the room which Frederick and William shared. She had awakened her brothers, and, curling up at the bottom of Frederick's bed, she expressed her concern to them both, whispered that they must make an inventory of all of their mother's possessions which were now in this house.

William, who knew Audra was much cleverer than he or his brother, nodded in agreement. But Frederick blanched in alarm, afraid that they would be thrown out if they so much as put one foot wrong. "She'll take offense," he whispered back, frowning. "We can't do it, Audra. It would be throwing aspersions on her character—as if we think she's dishonest."

Sweeping aside his protestations, Audra hissed, "I'm sure she is, so we *must* do it. To protect ourselves. And what about Mother's jewelry? The sapphires in particular? Does *she* have those too, Frederick?"

Frederick shook his head vehemently. "No, she doesn't, and that I know for an absolute fact. But they *have* disappeared. I looked everywhere for them the day after Mother died, and to no avail. When I was searching her drawers, I suddenly remembered that I hadn't seen her wear them since Uncle Peter's death. She must have sold them, Audra, and used the money to help support us over the past year. It's the only possible solution."

"Why didn't you tell me about the sapphires before now?" Audra demanded in a low but fierce voice, throwing him a reproachful look.

"Because I didn't want to worry you," Frederick whispered back, and then his voice sank as he added, "But Aunt Alicia does have Mother's other jewelry. She took the box away from me . . . for safekeeping, she said."

Although she had faithfully promised Frederick she would not do anything rash, and so risk incurring their aunt's disfavor, Audra was determined, nevertheless, to have her own way about the inventory. Alicia Drummond did not intimidate her, but after thinking it through, she wisely decided to wait for the right moment to introduce the subject to her aunt. This presented itself much sooner than Audra had anticipated.

On Sunday of that week, Great-Aunt Frances returned with them for lunch after church services. And it was the old lady herself who inadvertently gave Audra the perfect opportunity. They were all seated in the dark and depressing library, where Uncle Percival proceeded to pour careful glasses of sherry for the adults, when unexpectedly their great-aunt brought up the matter of Edith Kenton's jewelry.

Out of the blue, she said, "I think Audra is old enough to have something of dear Edith's, a memento of her mother. Perhaps the cameo brooch. Please be kind enough to fetch me Edith's jewelry box, Alicia." Aunt Alicia, tight-lipped and sheathing her annoyance, did so.

Smiling at Audra warmly, the old lady took out the cameo and pinned it on the front of her summer frock. "Take care of it, child—it was a favorite of your mother's," she said.

Audra promised that she would and thanked her great-aunt for allowing her to have it now. Then she shrewdly seized the moment. "Frederick, William, come and look at Mother's jewelry. You must have your share of it when we grow up."

As her two brothers joined her at their great-aunt's side, Audra exclaimed to Frederick, "Perhaps I ought to make a list of these things, so that we can talk about them later and decide what we'd each like to have. That's only fair, isn't it, Frederick?"

There was a startled silence.

Frederick gaped at her, aghast, and bit his lip, knowing what she next had in mind. William tried to hide his delight in her audacity without succeeding; his eyes danced mischievously.

And then, before anyone could make a comment, Audra ran to the desk, found a pencil and scrap paper, and returned to her great-aunt's chair, where she pored over the box. At one moment, as she scribbled away, Audra looked up at the silver-haired old lady, and remarked in an off-hand manner, "Great-Aunt Frances, do *you* think I should also list Mother's furniture and her possessions which Aunt Alicia is storing for us here? You know, so that my brothers and I can divide everything else properly."

Great-Aunt Frances gave her a surprised look, and then she smiled slightly. "Well, Audra, you are a practical child, it seems. I think that's an excellent idea, especially since poor dear Edith did not think to make a will. This way the three of you can discuss the division of your mother's property at leisure, and make your decisions. Why don't you take an inventory next week, my dear?"

Audra nodded solemnly, camouflaging her triumph behind a bland expression. "Yes, I think I will, Great-Aunt."

In the days which followed this conversation, Frederick, quaking in his boots, had warned Audra that there were bound to be repercussions. *He* had noticed the calculating look in Aunt Alicia Drummond's mean little black eyes when they had all been in the library, even if his brother and sister had not.

But nothing untoward had happened in the end, and the long, hot summer had slithered into a cool autumn; then winter had come finally, and life at The Grange had continued uneventfully. And as miserable as the Kentons were in the unloving environment of their aunt's home, even Audra felt bound to agree with William, her favorite, that they were fortunate in one respect: The three of them were together. They had each other to love, and for companionship and consolation.

It was the week before Christmas that Audra chanced to hear a strange remark, one that worried her briefly; its true meaning was to baffle her for some time thereafter.

Late one afternoon, knowing that Great-Aunt Frances had come to visit, Audra went looking for her.

She was about to push open the drawing room door, which was already ajar, when she heard Aunt Alicia mention her mother's name in the most scathing manner. She did not catch what her aunt said next because Alicia lowered her voice. But Audra stiffened as Great-Aunt Frances suddenly exclaimed in a horrified tone, "You cannot punish the children for the sins of the mother, Alicia!"

Instantly, Audra's hand dropped from the knob and she quickly backed away, not wishing to hear any more, and knowing that it was wrong to eavesdrop anyway.

She crept down the dark passage to the back parlor, where she sat for a while, pondering her great-aunt's odd remark. Audra knew that it had to do with them—that much was patently obvious. But she could not fathom its meaning. *How* had her mother sinned? At once she told herself that her mother had not committed a single sin in her entire life. As young as she was, Audra was perceptive and she had long known that Alicia Drummond had always been jealous of her mother's classical beauty, her charm and her refinement. So much so, she had never lost a chance to demean Edith Kenton during her lifetime. Seemingly she could not resist doing the same thing after her death.

For the next few days Audra continued to wonder why Alicia wanted to punish them, but eventually she managed to curb her worry. She consoled herself with the knowledge that whatever punishment *she* had had in mind for them, their great-aunt had obviously found a way to put a stop to it.

But as it turned out, Frances Reynolds' words had apparently meant little or nothing. Certainly they had not been a deterrent to her daughter.

For in the end they had been punished.

Two months later, in February of 1922, Frederick and William were dispatched to Australia as emigrants, and Audra was sent to work at the Fever Hospital for Children in Ripon.

Their fierce protestations and anguished pleadings to stay together had made no impression. They were helpless in the face of their aunt's determination. And so, against their wishes and those of their Great-Aunt Frances, they had been forced to do as Alicia Drummond said.

It was a wrenching moment for the three young Kentons when Frederick and William took leave of their sister on that bitter winter morning. Before setting out for London and the boat to Sydney, they had huddled together in the front hall, saying their goodbyes, fighting back their tears.

Audra clung to William, whom she secretly loved the most. Emotion welled up in her, and her throat was so tight she could barely speak. Finally she managed, "You won't forget about me, will you, William?" And then she started to sob brokenly and her eyes streamed.

Swallowing his own tears, endeavoring to be brave, William tightened his arms around his adored little sister. She looked so young and vulnerable at this moment. "No, I won't. *We* won't," he said reassuringly. "And we'll send for you as soon as we can. *I promise,* Audra."

Frederick, equally emotional, stroked the top of Audra's head lovingly, and repeated this promise. Then her brothers stepped away from her, picked up their suitcases and left the house without uttering another word.

Audra snatched her coat from the hall cupboard and ran out. She flew down the drive, calling their names, needing to prolong these last few minutes with them. They stopped, turned, waited for her, and the three of them linked arms and walked on in silence, too heartbroken to speak. When they arrived at the gates, the two boys silently kissed Audra for the last time and tore themselves from her clinging arms.

Holding one hand to her trembling mouth, stifling her sobs, Audra watched them stride courageously along the main road to Ripon until they were just small specks in the distance. She wanted to run after them, to shout *"Wait for me! Don't leave me behind! Take me with you!"* But Audra knew this would be useless. They could not take her with them. It was not her brothers' fault they were being separated from each other. Alicia Drummond was to blame. She wanted to rid herself of Edith Kenton's children, and she did not care how she did it.

Only when her brothers had finally disappeared from sight did Audra drag her gaze away from the empty road at last. She turned back into the driveway and wondered, with a sinking heart and a sickening feeling of despair, if she would ever see her brothers again. Australia was at the other end of the world, as far away as any place could possibly be. They had promised faithfully to send for her, but how long would it take them to save up the money for her passage? A whole year, perhaps.

As this dismaying thought wedged itself into Audra's mind, she looked up at that bleak, grim house and shivered involuntarily. And at that precise moment her dislike for her mother's cousin hardened into a terrible and bitter hatred that would remain with her for the rest of her life. Audra Kenton would not ever find it in her heart to forgive Alicia Drummond for her cold and deliberate cruelty to them. And the memory of the day her brothers had been sent away would stay with Audra always.

The following afternoon, white-faced and trembling, and fretting for her brothers, Audra had gone to live and work at the Fever Hospital. Since there were no vacancies that year for student nurses, she had been taken on as a ward maid.

Audra Kenton's life of drudgery had begun. She was still only fourteen years old.

She had been awakened at dawn the next morning. After a breakfast of porridge, drippings and bread, and tea, eaten with the other little ward maids, the daily routine had commenced. Audra was appalled at the hardship of it, and she, who had never done a domestic chore in her entire life, had found that first day unspeakable. Balking at the tasks assigned to her, she had asked herself despairingly how she would manage. Yet she had not dared complain to her superiors. Being intelligent and alert, she had understood within the space of a few hours that they were not interested in the likes of her. She was inconsequential in the hierarchy of the hospital, where everyone—doctors and nurses alike—worked extremely hard and with conscientiousness.

On her second morning she had gritted her teeth and attacked her chores with renewed vigor, and she had learned the best way she could, mainly by observing the other maids at work. At the end of the first month, she was as efficient as any of them, and had become expert at scrubbing floors, scouring bathtubs, washing and ironing sheets, making beds, emptying bed pans, cleaning lavatories, disinfecting the surgical ward and sterilizing instruments.

Every night she had fallen into her hard little cot in the maids' dormitory, so bone-tired she had not noticed her surroundings or the uncomfortable bed. She was usually so exhausted in these first weeks she did not even have the strength to weep. And when she did cry into her pillow, it was not for her state of being or for her mean and cheerless life. Audra wept out of longing for her brothers, who were as lost to her now as her mother and Uncle Peter lying in their graves.

There were times, as she scrubbed and polished and toiled in the wards, that Audra worriedly asked herself if *she* had brought this disastrous state upon her brothers and herself. Guilt trickled through her when she remembered how insistent she had been about taking those inventories of her mother's possessions. But generally her common sense quickly surfaced, and Audra recognized that they would have been punished no matter what. In fact, she had come to believe that Alicia Drummond had callously determined their fate on the very day their mother had died.

When Audra had been pushed out of The Grange and sent to the hospital, Aunt Alicia had told her that she could visit them every month, on one of her two weekends off, and spend special holidays with them. But Audra had only ventured there twice, and then merely to collect the remainder of her clothes and a few other belongings. For as far back as she could remember, she had felt uncomfortable in that appalling house; furthermore, she understood she was not welcome. Also, Audra's hatred for her aunt was another powerful reason for her to stay away.

The second time she went to fetch the last of her things, she had had to steel herself to enter The Grange, and she had made a solemn vow to herself. She had sworn she would never set foot in that mausoleum of a place again, not until the day she went back to claim her mother's property. And so, over those early months of 1922, as she had learned to stand on her own two feet, she had kept herself to herself. She had continued to do her work diligently, and she had stayed out of trouble at the hospital.

If her daily life was dreary and lacked the normal small pleasures enjoyed by most girls of her age, she nevertheless managed to buoy herself up with dreams of a pleasanter future. Hope was her constant companion. No one could take *that* away from her. Nor could anyone diminish her faith in her brothers. She was absolutely convinced that they would send for her, that she would be with them in Australia soon. Three months after Frederick and William had left England, their letters had started to arrive, and these had continued to come fairly regularly. They were always full of news, good cheer and promises—and the pages had soon grown tattered from her constant reading of them. Audra treasured her letters; they were her only joy in those days.

The hospital routine had scarcely varied during Audra's first year. The work was hard, even for the strongest of the girls. Some of them had left because their daily chores had worn them down and inevitably demolished their interest in nursing. Only the truly dedicated remained. Audra, with nowhere else to go, stayed out of sheer necessity.

However, there was also something very special in Audra Kenton, call it grit, that made her stick it out until she could graduate to nurse's training. Small though she was, she had unusual physical stamina, as well as a mental energy and toughness of mind that were remarkable in one so young. Despite her youth, she possessed inner resources which she was able to draw on for courage and strength. And so she had continued to scrub and clean and polish endlessly . . . run up and down endless stairs and along endless wards . . . forever on her feet or on her knees.

The toil and monotonous grind of her days quite apart, Audra could not complain that she was ill treated in any way, for she was not. Everyone at the hospital was kind to her and the other little ward maids, and if the food was plain, at least there was plenty of it. No one ever went hungry. Audra, plodding along and braced by her stoicism, would tell herself that hard work and stodgy food never killed anybody.

But by the end of the year she was looking to better herself. Her thoughts were focused on the day she would take a step forward and start climbing the ladder. She had been sent to work at the hospital against her will, but slowly, as she had mastered her chores, she had had a chance to look up, to observe and absorb. Gradually she had begun to realize that nursing appealed to her.

Audra knew she would have to earn a living, even if she went out to join her brothers in Sydney; she wanted to do so as a nurse. According to William, she would have no trouble finding a position in a hospital. He had written to tell her that there was a shortage of nurses Down Under, and this knowledge had fired her ambition even more.

It was in the spring of 1923, not long after Audra had commenced her second year at the hospital, that her chance came. Matron retired and a successor was appointed. Her name was Margaret Lennox, and she was of a new breed of woman, very modern in her way of thinking, some said even radical. She was well known in the North of England for her passionate espousal of reforms in woman and child welfare, and for her dedication to the advancement of women's rights in general.

With the announcement of her appointment there was a flurry of excitement, and everyone wondered if the daily routine would be affected. It was, for, as was usually the way, a new broom swept clean and a new regime, in this instance the Lennox Regime, was swiftly instituted.

Audra, observing everything with her usual perspicacity, decided that she must waste no time in applying for nurse's training at once. From what she had heard, Margaret Lennox favored young and ambitious girls who wanted to get on; apparently she went out of her way to give them her unstinting support and encouragement.

Two weeks after Matron Lennox had taken up her duties, Audra sat down and wrote a letter to her. She thought this was the wisest tactic to use, rather than to approach her personally. Matron Lennox had been in a whirlwind of activity and surrounded by a phalanx of hospital staff since her arrival.

Less than a week after Audra had left the letter in Matron's office, she was summoned for an interview. This was brisk, brief and very much to the point. Ten minutes after she had walked in, Audra Kenton walked out, smiling broadly, her application approved.

With her superior intelligence, her ability to learn quickly, Audra swiftly became one of the best student nurses on the hospital staff, and earned a reputation for being dedicated. She found the new work and her studies challenging; also, she discovered she had a desire to heal and, therefore, a real aptitude for nursing. And the young patients, with whom she had a genuine affinity, became the focus of the love she had bottled up inside her since her brothers had gone away . . .

Now, remembering all of this, as she lay in the grass on the crest of the slope above the River Ure, Audra thought not of her diplomas and nursing achievements over the past four years, but of Frederick and William.

Her brothers had not sent for her in the end.

They had not been able to save up the money for her passage to Australia. Things had not gone well for the Kenton boys. Frederick had had two serious bouts with pneumonia and seemed to be in a state of physical debilitation a great deal of the time. Apart from the problems with his health, he and William were unskilled and untrained. They had had a hard time scraping a living together.

She sighed and bestirred herself, then sat up, blinking as she opened her eyes and adjusted them to the brightness. Poor Frederick and William had had nothing but bad luck really. Their letters, which arrived less frequently these days, were permeated with defeat. Audra had all but given up hope of going out to join them in Sydney. She continued to fret and to miss them, and she supposed she always would. They were her only family, after all, and she loved them very much.

Her work at the hospital gave her satisfaction, and for this she was grateful, but it was not enough. Her sense of isolation, of not belonging to anyone, or more precisely, of not being part of a family contributed to the aridness of her life. Sometimes she found it unbearable, despite her treasured friendship with the devoted Gwen.

Audra stood up, then cast her gaze to the other side of the river.

The light had changed in the last few hours, and High Cleugh now looked as if it had been built from polished bronze stones. It was bathed in a sort of golden glow, appeared to shimmer like a mirage in the distance, and even the gardens had a burnished sheen in the rosy sunset. All of her life thus far—at least the best, the happiest parts of it—and her dearest memories were bound up with that old house. A rush of feeling swept over Audra, and she suddenly knew that she would never cease to yearn for High Cleugh and all the things it represented.

Four

Here they were, sitting in the Copper Kettle in Harrogate. She and Gwen.

Audra could hardly believe they were finally meeting after all these weeks. The two girls had not seen each other since the beginning of June. On this hot and muggy Saturday it was already the end of August, the end of the summer, and the first time Gwen had been able to travel from Horsforth for a visit with her best friend.

Even so, Gwen had not been able to make it as far as Ripon, and in her letter she had asked Audra to meet her halfway. Audra had agreed to this request immediately and had sent off a note by return post.

Now, flushed with happiness, Audra looked across the table and broke into a smile. "It's lovely to see you, Gwen. I've really missed you."

"So have I—missed you, I mean." Gwen's cherubic face, covered with freckles and vividly alive, was filled with laughter; it signaled her own pleasure at their reunion. "I still feel ever so *awful* about not being able to spend your birthday with you—" Gwen broke off, reached down for the fabric shopping bag at her feet and proceeded to rummage around in it. She pulled out a package wrapped in royal blue paper and tied with scarlet ribbon.

With a gay flourish, Gwen handed it across the table to Audra. "Anyway, this is your birthday present, lovey. I never did get to take you to one of the fancy tea dances at the Palm Court of the Arcadian Rooms, so here, I bought you something instead."

"You didn't have to, you shouldn't have!" Audra protested, but it was easy to see she was thrilled to receive the gift. It had been a long time since she had been given a present, and there had been nothing on her birthday. Her face lit up, and her bright blue eyes danced as she tore off the ribbon and paper with the excitement of a small child.

"Oh Gwen! *A paintbox!*" Audra looked up and beamed at the other girl. "How lovely. And how clever of you. I really needed a new one. Thank you so much." She reached out and took hold of Gwen's hand lying on the table, and squeezed it affectionately.

It was Gwen's turn to look pleased. "I wracked my brains, trying to think of something . . . something . . . well, *just right.* You being ever so particular as you are. As it happened, I was looking at that watercolor you painted for my mother last Christmas . . . the tree reflected in the pond at Fountains Hall, and it suddenly occurred to me. The paintbox, I mean. I thought to myself, that's exactly the thing for Audra. It'll appeal to her practical side, but it'll give her pleasure as well."

Gwen sat back and wrinkled her pert, very freckled nose. Her gaze did not leave Audra's face as she asked, "It will, won't it?"

"Oh yes, Gwen, lots and lots of pleasure." Her eyes widened and she nodded several times, as if to give added weight. She lifted the shiny black lid and looked inside at the small blocks of bright color. She repeated some of the familiar names under her breath: *Chrome yellow . . . rose madder . . . cobalt blue . . . jade green . . . burnt sienna . . . crimson lake . . . Saxe blue . . . royal purple . . . burnt umber . . . Malaga red.* Audra loved the sound of the names almost as much as she loved to paint.

It had been her favorite hobby since her childhood. Her father had been a gifted artist, and his paintings had sold fairly well, but then he had fallen gravely ill just as he was becoming known. Adrian Kenton had not really had a chance to make a name for himself before he had died. She had inherited his talent—or so her mother had always told her.

Audra closed the lid of the paintbox and raised her eyes to meet Gwen's soft hazel-amber gaze. How pretty she looks, Audra thought, so blond and golden from the sun. Gwen's fairness and her flaxen hair, cut short in a halo of curls around her head, added to the angelic impression she gave; so did the pale blue frock with its big white Quaker collar, which she had chosen to wear today. She reminds me of a choirboy, Audra thought, and smiled at this analogy. With her beautiful bosom and lovely figure, there was nothing very boyish about Gwen Thornton.

Audra noticed that for once Gwen looked restrained in her mode of dress. Usually she glowed and glittered with all kinds of jewelry; necklaces and beads, earrings and bangles and rings. Obviously she had made a big effort to be both understated and dignified for this trip to Harrogate. She wants to please me, Audra decided, and her warm and loving feelings for Gwen soared.

Leaning forward, Audra said, "I'm going to paint a very special picture for you, Gwenny. For your room at home. Would you like a scene—the kind I did for your mother? Or a still life, such as a bowl of flowers? Oh, I *know* what I'll paint for you. The Valley Gardens here in Harrogate. You've always said that's your favorite spot when all the flowers are in bloom. Would you like that?"

"Yes, that'd be ever so nice. Thanks very much, Audra. I'd treasure one of your paintings—Mum says they're masterpieces. The Valley Gardens would look lovely on my wall. So I'd—"

"Can I take your order, miss?" the waitress interrupted rather peremptorily. She looked first at Gwen, then at Audra, her pencil poised impatiently above her pad.

"We'd like to have tea," Audra said pleasantly, ignoring her huffy manner and angry stance. "For two, please."

"A pot? Or the set tea?" the waitress asked in the same snippy tone and licked the end of her pencil.

Gwen said, "You oughtn't do that. I hope that pencil's not indelible. You'll get a purple tongue, and probably lead poisoning."

"Get on with you, I won't get no such thing!" the waitress scoffed disbelievingly, then gave the two of them a worried glance. "Will I?" she muttered and carefully examined the tip of her pencil. "Oooh bloomin' heck! It *is* indelible."

Gwen nodded solemnly. "I thought it would be. You'd better go and see a doctor immediately if you develop peculiar symptoms tonight, especially if they're at all like convulsions."

"Convulsions!" the waitress repeated in a shrill voice and turned as white as her apron.

Audra, taking pity on the young woman, said, "We're nurses and we know about these things. But I'm sure you won't get lead poisoning from licking that pencil a few times."

The waitress, appearing slightly relieved, nodded her head.

"You'll be perfectly all right," Audra reassured, and went on briskly, "Now about our order, I think we'd better have the *set* tea. I suppose that means it includes everything . . . sandwiches, scones, jam, clotted cream, cakes—all of the usual things?"

"Yes," the waitress said laconically. She brought the pencil up to her mouth, then dropped her hand quickly and edged away from their table.

When she was out of earshot, Audra stared at the merry-faced Gwen and shook her head a bit reprovingly. However, she could not help grinning at Gwen's gleeful expression. "You're incorrigible, Miss Thornton. And that really *was* a little mean of you. Why, you've gone and ruined that poor young woman's day."

"I jolly well hope I have!" Gwen cried with a show of indignation. "She's a right Tartar, that one, Audra."

"Perhaps she has bad feet—or a bad love life."

"I don't know what she's got. Yes, I do—a nasty manner, that's a certainty."

There was a small silence, and then Audra reached for her handbag, took out some coins and placed them on the table in front of Gwen. "Before I forget, this is what I owe you. The one and six I borrowed when I bought the blue dress."

Gwen was about to say it didn't matter, to refuse the coins; then she thought better of it. Audra was very proud and might even be insulted; and that Gwen could not bear. And so she picked up the money and said, "Thanks very much, lovey."

"I am glad your mother has recovered her health at long last," Audra said with genuine feeling. "I know these last few months have been very worrying for you, and such hard work as well."

Gwen let out a tiny sigh. "Yes, Mum's out of the woods, thank goodness. But I don't mind telling you, she's been a trying patient, Audra. Hard to keep in bed. The minute she felt stronger she wanted to be up and about." Gwen pursed her lips and sighed again. "Well, you know what Mum's like, a typical Yorkshire woman, very tough, who believes it's a crime to be ill. My father has finally convinced her she must take it easy, so that's all right then. But listen, Audra, enough of this . . . tell me *your* news. You didn't say much in your letters, except for boring bits and pieces about the *boring* hospital."

"There wasn't anything special to tell," Audra replied, amused at the eager and expectant expression which had suddenly appeared on Gwen's dimpled face. "Certainly nothing startling. It hasn't taken *you* very long to forget that Ripon's a sleepy old backwater, not a great big metropolis like Leeds."

Gwen giggled. "Course I haven't forgotten, silly. But what I meant was how're your brothers? What've you heard recently?"

"Frederick's health has seemingly improved. At least, so William wrote and told me. I was very upset with them both in June, though." Audra's face changed slightly and the light in her eyes dulled. "I thought they had forgotten all about me . . . and my birthday, but then their card finally did arrive . . . two weeks late."

"That's brothers for you, Audra, they're a bit daft at times," Gwen said swiftly, wanting to make her friend feel better. And it struck Gwen once more how sad Audra's nineteenth birthday had been. She vowed to make it up to her on her birthday next year.

Audra said, "Anyway, how are your brothers?"

"In top form. Jem's got himself a job as a copy boy on the Leeds Mercury, Harry's going to be apprenticed to one of the leading architects in Leeds, and our Charlie's flying high, feeling very chuffed with himself." A huge grin spread across Gwen's face.

Audra looked at her curiously. "Why is Charlie so pleased?"

"Because he got *very* high marks in his exams, Audra. Dad's really proud of him, and so am I. Anyway, old Charlie can't wait to get back to medical school now that the summer hols are just about over. Oh, and that reminds me, he asked to be remembered to you." Gwen's eyes took on a wicked twinkle and she brought her fair head closer to Audra's, whispered in a conspiratorial manner, "As I keep telling you, I think our Charlie really fancies you, Audra. And quite a bit, at that."

Audra blushed furiously. "Don't be so silly, Gwen, of course he doesn't."

"He does too! He's always asking questions about you!" Gwen shot back with unprecedented fierceness, giving her friend a stern glare. "He's *definitely* interested in you, I just know he is."

"Oh" was the only thing Audra could think of to say, feeling flustered all of a sudden.

"Well, you could do worse, you know."

"Yes," Audra murmured, and then clamped her mouth shut as the waitress hove in view.

Much to Audra's relief the young woman headed straight for their table, carrying a laden tray. She began to unload the tea things with a great deal of fuss and clattering, and this naturally curtailed their conversation for a few moments.

Once the waitress had departed, she picked up the large brown pot and began to pour tea into Gwen's cup, remarking, "I suppose I could say *she's* just had the last word."

"Oh no she hasn't, not by a long shot," Gwen said with a sly little smile. "Wait until it's time for her tip."

Five

Gwen Thornton was an affectionate girl, open-hearted and generous of nature, and she genuinely cared for Audra Kenton.

From the first moment she had met her, Gwen had been drawn to Audra. She had recognized there was something very special about the delicate-looking girl with the extraordinary blue eyes and the shy smile that could dazzle at times.

Gwen had quickly come to understand what it actually was that made Audra stand out in a crowd. It was her background and upbringing. Coming from an ordinary, though solid, middle-class family as she did, Gwen knew that Audra's air of breeding was downright impossible to imitate. You either had it or you didn't. It simply could not be acquired. And it not only gave Audra distinction, but it explained her aristocratic aloofness, her manners and her self-assurance, which were bred in the bone.

However, Gwen admired and loved Audra for a variety of other reasons, all of which added to her uniqueness. She was a superior young woman in every way, one who was inordinately loyal and loving; she was also the most indomitable person Gwen had ever met.

Yet despite these commendable traits, Gwen could not help worrying about Audra sometimes. She chiefly worried because Audra was without a family. Gwen knew more than anyone how much this bothered Audra. She sorely missed her brothers, yearned to *belong* in the way she had when her mother had been alive. This was why Gwen went out of her way to make her best friend feel like a real member of the Thornton clan, to make her truly understand she was as much loved as her baby sister Jenny-Rosalie, and her brothers, Charles, Jeremy and Harry.

Ever since Charlie, the eldest, had shown an interest in Audra, Gwen had been encouraging him, endeavoring to foster a relationship between them. But from time to time, Gwen had had to admit to herself that the interest was a trifle one-sided thus far; and she sometimes wondered if her sweet but rather dull brother was the right match for Audra. But inevitably, Gwen managed to convince herself that he really was ideal. Certainly there was no question in her mind that Charlie was a good catch, since he was such an admirable young man, and one with an assured future. He would not stay a bachelor for very long, once he had qualified as a doctor, and he would make a wonderful husband and father. Gwen had always known in her bones that Charlie was cut out to be a family man.

And in Gwen's mind, the crucial word was indeed *family*. This was what

Audra longed for the most, and so she was going to help her dearest friend acquire a family of her very own. And, of course, Charlie was the key.

All of these thoughts, which had frequently preoccupied Gwen during the past few weeks, had started to swirl around in her head again this afternoon.

She and Audra were now strolling through the beautiful Valley Gardens. Both girls were glad to be out in the open air, after being cooped up inside the noisy cafe.

Gwen cast a glance at Audra as they headed down the sloping path. She decided she would be very hard-pressed indeed to find a sweeter or prettier candidate for a sister-in-law. Audra looked particularly attractive today, wearing a primrose-yellow print dress patterned with primroses, and a straw boater with a yellow silk band and matching ribbons fluttering down at the back. The boater gave her a jaunty air, whilst the simple cut of the frock and its sunny color were flattering to her.

She might be small, Gwen thought, but she's quality through and through. And then, before she could stop herself, she said out loud, "Yes, good stuff in a little room." Gwen could have bitten her tongue off, instantly regretted repeating this comment Charlie had made about Audra, who hated any reference to her height or lack of it. She cleared her throat nervously.

Audra said, with a puzzled look, "Excuse me, I don't quite understand what you're referring to, Gwen."

Deciding it would be smarter not to mention Charlie, Gwen explained, "Oh it was just something my mother said about you—good stuff in a little room means that a small person often has a lot of wonderful qualities. Haven't you heard the expression before? It's very Yorkshire."

Audra shook her head. "No, I haven't, but it's a nice compliment."

"Yes," Gwen said, delighted that she had taken it so well, and tucked her arm through Audra's companionably. "And talking of Mum, she says I can have a party for my birthday, so I hope you'll come and stay with us at The Meadow, the third weekend in September. There'll be Charlie, Jem and Harry, of course, and I can invite a *few* friends. But only a few. 'Cause Mum couldn't cope with a big crowd after her illness. You *will* come, Audra, won't you? It wouldn't be the same without you."

"Of course I'll come. It'll be a lovely treat for me, and I always enjoy staying at your house. Thank you for inviting me."

Gwen laughed gaily. "You'll get to wear your gorgeous blue dress. *Finally.* Why, Audra, you'll be the belle of the ball. All the boys will be after you." Especially our Charlie, Gwen added to herself, and hoped he wouldn't be rejected.

Audra glanced up at Gwen, who was a few inches taller, and joined in her laughter. *"You'll* be the belle; after all it's your birthday party. But I must admit, I am dying to wear my new dress. And what frock are you going to wear, Gwenny?"

"Oh, I don't know. I'll find something suitable, I expect. Now, who else do you think I should invite?" Not giving Audra a chance to reply, Gwen hurried on, "I'll tell you what, let's go and sit over there on that form and talk about the party. You're so clever, Audra, I'd like your advice about a few things. You know . . . such as what kind of food and drinks to serve, and your suggestions in general. Come on, lovey."

Gwen steered Audra in the direction of a park seat positioned under one of the lovely weeping willows which were planted throughout the Valley Gardens. Here the two girls sat themselves down and brought their heads together. They chatted animatedly about Gwen's twentieth birthday party for the next half hour, covering all the different aspects of it, planning the menu and the guest list.

Finally Gwen said, "Thanks Audra, you've been a great help. It'll be a nice party . . ."

Audra turned her attention to the passersby, thinking how smart some of the women looked, dressed in their finery and out for a stroll before dinner at one of the swanky hotels. They were obviously from London, judging by their clothes, and were visiting Harrogate to "take the cure." It had been a renowned Spa since Victorian times, and people came from all over the world to drink from the variety of the forty waters available in the Pump Room and visit the hydros at the Royal Baths. Her mother had always loved Harrogate for its elegance, and the Beautiful Edith Kenton had called it a throwback to Victorian times and a more civilized age.

Their mother had often brought them here for the day. Audra recalled a memorable afternoon in 1911 when they had come to get a glimpse of the queens of England, Russia and Poland, who had all been visiting Harrogate on the same day. Their Uncle Peter had been with them, and he had lifted her up on his shoulders so that she could see above the crowds. There had been lots of excitement and flags waving and a band playing . . . Audra drifted along with her remembrances of things past.

Gwen, however, was thinking of the future and wondering how to break her awful news to Audra. Earlier, she had toyed with the idea of not saying anything, of writing a letter at a later date. But Gwen knew that Audra, who had so much integrity and was such a fair person, deserved better from her than that. She decided there really was only one way to do it, and that was to jump right in, both feet first.

Reaching out, she touched Audra's arm tentatively, and said in an unusually subdued voice, "There's something I want to tell you before we go to the bus station for our buses . . ."

Audra looked at her, instantly coming back to the present. "You sound very serious all of a sudden, Gwenny. Is there something wrong?"

Gwen swallowed and cleared her throat. "I've wanted to tell you this all afternoon, but I haven't known how to begin. Well . . . look, it's like this, Audra . . . I won't be coming back to work at the Fever Hospital. I'm ever so sorry."

Audra gaped at her friend, flabbergasted at this announcement. It was a bombshell, the last thing she had expected to hear. "Oh Gwen," she murmured, so softly it was a whisper.

Observing her closely, detecting the misery now flooding her bright blue eyes, Gwen cried anxiously, "Please, oh *please* don't be upset, Audra. *I'm* not going to *Australia.* I'll only be a couple of hours away, either in Leeds or Horsforth. We can see each other all the time, and listen, Mum wants you to come and stay for Christmas, like you did last year. And we'll be together on my birthday next month."

Audra, considerably shaken by Gwen's news, was only able to nod.

"You see, it's like this, Audra. Dad wants me to be nearer home, because of Mum's weak heart. He says I have to apply for a position at the Infirmary or

St. James's Hospital, and until I get something at either place, I've got to stay at home with Mum. Dad's ever so set on it, Audra, I can't make him change his mind."

Audra, always sensitive to the feelings of others, heard the distress in Gwen's voice, and she smiled faintly and nodded. "I understand, Gwenny," she said. But her heart sank at the prospect of being all alone in Ripon. She felt as though she was being abandoned once more.

Gwen had a sudden idea. She exclaimed, "Look, Audra, why don't you apply too? For a hospital job in Leeds, I mean." She drew closer, took hold of Audra's small hand and was surprised how cold it was on this muggy day. She clutched it tightly, begged, "Say you will. Please, lovey."

"I'm not sure whether I should—"

"Why not?" Gwen demanded, her voice rising. "There's not one good reason for you to stay in Ripon."

Audra blinked and returned Gwen's hard stare, realizing immediately that her friend was absolutely right. She began to nod her head emphatically. "Yes, I'll do it, Gwenny!" And a smile broke through at last, expunged the sadness which had darkened her lovely eyes.

Gwen threw her arms around Audra. She hugged her tightly, bursting with happiness and filled with relief. The thought of leaving her beloved friend behind at the Fever Hospital had been more than the girl could bear.

Six

"Matron wants to see you, Kenton," Sister Rogers said, drawing to a standstill, fixing a stern eye on Audra. "She did say *immediately,* so you'd better look sharp."

Audra, who had just finished taking a child's temperature, nodded. "Thanks. I'll go up at once."

Moving away from the bed, Audra glanced around at her young patients with her usual concern. The small isolation ward was occupied by children suffering from whooping cough, and she was worried about each of them on this icy December morning.

As she and the head nurse walked down the ward toward the door, Audra dropped her voice and said, "They're all a bit restless, especially the little one over there by the window. He's exhausted from the whoop, and he's not been able to keep his breakfast down because of his excessive coughing, and Doctor Parkinson is a bit concerned about him. Can you send a junior nurse in to keep an eye on him? And on the others, of course?"

"Don't worry about it, I'll stay here myself until you get back. I'm sure you won't be very long with Matron." A slight smile touched the head nurse's mouth and there was an unprecedented softening in her attitude toward Audra, and she remarked in a quiet tone, "Your diligence really is commendable, Kenton. You've turned out to be a good nurse."

These were words of praise indeed, coming from this most senior member of the nursing staff, who had worked herself up from ward maid and who was renowned as a disciplinarian. Audra, surprised, returned her smile and with a little burst of pride, she drew herself up to her full height. "Thank you, Sister," she said. "I do try."

Sister Rogers inclined her head and turned away.

It was a dismissal of sorts, and Audra crossed the front hall and ran up the wide main staircase, hoping that Matron had good news for her at last. After making the decision to leave Ripon and find a nursing job in Leeds, Audra had confided her intentions in the head of the hospital and had asked for her advice. Matron had given it and had generously offered to do everything she could to help Audra. Unfortunately, they had not been successful so far. It seemed there were no vacancies in any of the hospitals in Leeds or the surrounding districts.

Audra, however, was not overly dismayed about this situation, since Gwen herself had only just managed to find a place at Leeds General Infirmary. Lonely though she was at the hospital without her dearest friend for companionship in her off-duty hours, Audra remained cheerful and optimistic as she went about her duties.

For the past three months, Audra had held the firm conviction that something would turn up eventually, and now, as she came to a stop outside Matron's office, she wondered if it finally had materialized. She tugged at her cuffs to straighten them, smoothed her hands over her starched white apron, then knocked on the frosted-glass panel of the door. At Matron's bidding she went in.

Margaret Lennox sat behind her large, paper-strewn desk.

She was wearing the navy-blue tailored dress and small white muslin cap that signified the highest nursing rank in the hierarchy of every hospital, and she seemed more formidable than ever. But Audra knew from experience that this stern-looking woman had the kindest of hearts.

Matron raised her eyes. She smiled at the sight of Audra, who was a particular favorite of hers, and for whom she had a great deal of respect and not a little admiration. She was aware of Audra's history from the hospital files, and she never ceased to marvel at this girl's strength of character and inner fiber.

"Ah, Audra," she began pleasantly, "do come in and sit down. I have a matter to discuss with you."

"Yes, Matron." Audra stepped up to the desk briskly and lowered herself onto the wooden chair where she sat straight-backed as always, her hands clasped in her lap. Her wide blue eyes were riveted to the matron's face.

Margaret Lennox glanced at the letter in her hand, then put it down on the desk. "Well, Audra, I think I might have a position for you in Leeds."

A look of delight flew onto Audra's face and she opened her mouth to speak.

But before she could say anything, Matron lifted her hand and exclaimed, "Just a moment! Don't get too excited . . . at least not yet. I must explain that this is not the type of nursing job you've been looking for, Audra. It's not in a hospital, I'm afraid."

"Oh," Audra said. "I see," and her face fell.

"I know you're disappointed that I have not been able to get you situated somewhere appropriate," Matron went on in a sympathetic way. "However, I do think you should consider this private position, especially since you are so very anxious to move to Leeds."

"Of course I will, Matron."

"Good girl. Now, Audra, I have had a letter from a Mrs. Irène Bell, who is the wife of a well-known Leeds solicitor. She's looking for a nanny and has been in touch with me about finding a suitable candidate here at the hospital. Naturally, Audra, I thought of you at once."

Matron Lennox then went on to explain that she had originally met Mrs. Bell through her work with the suffragette movement before the Great War, and that they had remained friendly over the years. Then she continued, "I cannot speak highly enough of Mrs. Bell. She has many wonderful achievements to her credit, and I have a strong feeling you and she would be compatible. In any event, from what she says in her letter, it's not a difficult job. There is only one child to look after, a little boy of five years. The other three children are grown up, away at school I believe." Matron's brow lifted questioningly. "What do you think, Audra? Are you interested?"

Audra had been listening avidly, and she knew she would be foolish if she turned down this opportunity without investigating it further. So she immediately said, "Yes, I am, Matron."

Matron nodded, as though confirming something to herself, and said, "I am confident you can handle a job such as this with the greatest of ease." She sat back, brought her hands together and steepled her fingers, contemplated Audra over them for a few moments, before remarking: "You have such a wonderful way with children, I know you will do well as a nanny. But you are an *extraordinary* nurse, Audra, a true healer, and that's rare. Don't ever forget that you have this remarkable ability . . . one might even call it a gift."

"No, I won't," Audra said, flushing with pleasure. She murmured her thanks to Matron for her kind words and the confidence she expressed in her.

Margaret Lennox went on, "I did have special plans for you here at the hospital, Audra, and I had envisaged promotions coming your way quickly." She smiled at the young woman with obvious fondness, then lifted her shoulders in a small resigned shrug. "Well, there we are . . . I for one shall be *most* sorry to see you go, if you *do* decide to leave, Audra. But, as I've told you all along, I would never presume to stand in your way."

"Yes, I know that, Matron, and I do appreciate everything you've done for me."

Matron half smiled, then finished in a more businesslike tone, "I will give Mrs. Bell a ring today and arrange for you to go over to Leeds for an interview. I'll let you know the details as soon as I have them. In the meantime, you had better return to your duties on the ward, Audra."

"Yes, Matron," Audra said, standing up. "Thank you again."

She was on her way to Leeds.

To meet Mrs. Irène Bell of Calpher House, Upper Armley.

Audra had the feeling that this was going to be an auspicious occasion. She laughed at herself under her breath. It was only an interview for a job after all. On the other hand, if everything went well there would be big changes in her life at long last. It might even be the beginning of a brand-new life.

This thought brought an extra spring to her step as she crossed the Market Place in Ripon, making her way toward the small country railway station on North Road. Audra's eyes sparkled with such radiant light, and there was such a glow on her fresh young face this morning, several people turned to look at her as she passed them by. But she did not notice this. Nor was she conscious of the weather. It was a harsh day, exceptionally cold, and the sky was sullen, laden with snow. But it might have been the middle of spring, for all she knew or cared, so intent was she in her purpose. She was also filled with anticipation and excitement. A week ago she had never heard of the Bell family, and now, here she was, journeying halfway across Yorkshire to seek a post with them.

What if she did not like the Bells?

At this thought her step faltered, but only for a split second. Stepping out as briskly as before, she told herself she would make a polite excuse and leave at once if the people at Calpher House did not appear to be suitable employers.

The ticket collector at the station gave Audra a cheerful greeting as he punched her ticket and handed her the return stub. He touched his cap politely, and she nodded in acknowledgment, then hurried down the platform where the Leeds-bound train was already standing, puffing out steam and whistling. She boarded it swiftly and went into the first empty First Class carriage she saw. She took a corner seat near the window with only a few minutes to spare before the guard blew his whistle and the train shunted out.

Audra soon began to realize that it was warmer in the carriage than she had anticipated. She pulled off her gray woolen gloves and unbuttoned her coat, then settled back, making herself comfortable for the journey.

Audra knew she looked smart today.

For her trip to Leeds she had chosen to wear her best gray Melton topcoat. Although it had been purchased in a sale and was already two years old, it was still fashionable, a wrap-around style with long, rolled lapels fastening at the hip with a huge button. Underneath the coat she had on a straight skirt made of gray wool and a matching gray jumper that came down over her hips. Together they created a slender tubelike effect, and she believed that this long line and her black court shoes with Cuban heels made her look taller. This pleased Audra, who was always trying to gain a few inches. Her only jewelry was her mother's cameo brooch, which she had pinned onto the front of her jumper, and her second-hand but treasured watch.

When Audra had been visting Gwen in September, her friend had given her a cloche made of plum-colored brushed felt. "My worst buy ever!" Gwen had said when she had shown the hat to Audra. "It's like a pea on a drum. I look awful in it, but I bet it suits you to a T, lovey." Gwen had been correct. The cloche *was* perfect on Audra, and she had treasured the hat for a special occasion. In fact, she had not worn it until today.

But now she wondered if the hat was too frivolous for the interview with Mrs. Bell, and she opened her bag, took out her mirror. Her reflection reassured her at once. The cloche, which was very much the rage, gave her a stylish up-to-date look, and the rich plum tone of the felt added just the right touch of necessary color to her all-gray ensemble. Her clothes were definitely sober and dignified, and she felt sure she would make a good impression on Mrs. Irène Bell.

Audra repeated the first name under her breath. It was spelled in the French way and pronounced in the French way, and she thought it was a lovely name. As the train rumbled on through the Dales toward Leeds, Audra's thoughts stayed with the woman she was going to see; she began to review the few things she had gleaned about her from Matron.

It was Audra's understanding that Irène Bell was a successful business-woman who had a strong intellectual bent and was something of a blue stocking. She was devoted to furthering the cause of women's rights and had always been a staunch disciple of the Pankhurst women who had done so much for female emancipation. According to Matron, Mrs. Bell was also a great admirer of Nancy Astor, the American married to Lord Astor, who was the first woman to sit in Parliament. Actively involved in politics herself, Mrs. Bell was seemingly a tireless worker for the Tory Party in Leeds, with many of her own political ambitions—especially regarding Parliament.

There was no doubt in Audra's mind that she was obviously an interesting woman, and one who was quite different to any *she* had ever met. Except for Margaret Lennox, of course, who was a true original, and whom Audra revered, even idealized.

Gazing out of the train window, hardly aware of the fields and hedges speeding by, Audra attempted to visualize Mrs. Bell. Since she had been a friend of Matron's for many years and had grown-up children, Audra reasoned she must be a woman in her middle forties. Instantly she was confronted by the image of a stern and somewhat severe person, perhaps resembling Matron and one who was a model of organization and efficiency.

Audra arrived at this last conclusion because of the tone of the letter she had received from Mrs. Bell earlier in the week. It was detailed and explicit, and her instructions for getting to Calpher House, Upper Armley, left nothing whatsoever to chance. It struck Audra, and for the second time in the last few days, that Mrs. Bell must be an exceptionally thoughtful woman, since she had sent her a First Class rail ticket instead of a cheaper one, as might have been expected under the circumstances. This was a truly considerate gesture, and one which certainly seemed to augur well for the future, at least to Audra's way of thinking. And she suddenly realized how curious she was about Irène Bell, and just how much she was looking forward to meeting her.

Punctuality was one of Audra's strong suits, and she always became agitated if she was late. Throughout the journey, she had glanced at her watch, praying that the train would be on time. Much to her relief it was. It pulled into Leeds City Station at exactly one minute to two, early, in point of fact, by sixty seconds.

Once she had left the bleak and grimy railway station, Audra was plunged into a whirl of traffic and pedestrians hurrying about their business. For a second or two the strident noise and the feverish bustle of the greatest industrial city in the North of England startled and overwhelmed her. The cacophony of sounds was a deafening contrast to the bucolic calm of sleepy, rural Ripon.

But since nothing ever fazed Audra Kenton for very long, she adjusted relatively quickly to her surroundings. After only a brief pause, she sucked in her breath, threw her shoulders back and brought her head up to a proud angle, ready and set to brave anything in this exciting new world awaiting her.

Tucking her handbag tightly under her arm, she walked purposefully across the road to City Square, where the statue of the Black Prince on his charger dominated the scene. She found the tram stop she wanted without any difficulty, and after a ten-minute wait in a small queue she followed the people ahead of her onto a tramcar going to Whingate. This was the terminus in Upper Armley where the tram turned around to go back to the city. Mrs. Bell had told her to stay on the car all the way to the end of the line.

Half an hour later, Audra alighted from the double-decker tram, which she had thoroughly enjoyed riding on, and she stood for a moment, looking around her with burgeoning interest. After all, she might soon be living here.

To her right was the tiny wedge of a park enclosed by spike-topped black iron railings and a neatly clipped privet hedge, which Mrs. Bell had said had the curious name of Charlie Cake Park. To her left was a huge red brick building, sprawling out behind a low brick wall, and she assumed this to be West Leeds Boys' High School.

Audra knew exactly which way she had to go now.

She began to walk ahead at a brisk pace, glancing at the scenery and taking everything in with keenly observing eyes. She saw at once that the village of Upper Armley was picturesque and that it had a quaint Victorian charm. And despite the darkly mottled sky, somber and presaging snow, and a landscape bereft of greenery, it was easy to see how pretty it must be in the summer weather.

Following Mrs. Bell's instructions, which she had committed to her excellent memory days ago, Audra hurried up Greenhill Road in the direction of Hill-Top, the area where the Bell home was located.

It was a nippy afternoon, very blustery, and she had to hold onto her little cloche as she struggled forward, buffeted by the wind that whistled down over the hill with icy ferocity. Audra was shivering when she reached the crest of the hill and drew to a stop in front of a pair of imposing wrought-iron gates upon which hung a large lozenge-shaped plaque. This was made of brass that had been rubbed up to a glittering sheen. It was inscribed with the name *Calpher House* in fancy scroll letters, and it told her she had reached her destination.

Seven

Irène Bell bore no resemblance to the image Audra had conjured up. The woman who walked toward her down the long stretch of luxurious Turkey carpet was tall, lissome, very smart, and she had the brightest, reddest of auburn hair. This had been cut in a sleek and fashionable bob, then shaped into a fringe above penciled brows and velvety brown eyes that shone with great brilliance. High cheekbones and a slender aristocratic nose were peppered with freckles; a rather wide mouth was outlined in scarlet lipstick.

Irène Bell was stunning, and she had an arresting personal style that stopped just short of flamboyance.

She took swift strides through the handsome blue and white living room, filled with antiques, where Audra stood waiting, and there was something reminiscent of the bold tomboy in her manner, the way she moved. In fact, her looks had a marked hoydenish quality; she also appeared to be much younger than her mid-forties. The red wool-jersey dress she wore underscored her intrinsic youthfulness with its long, loose-fitting bodice and pleated skirt, rather short, that swung around her splendid legs.

Audra, sharp-eyed as ever, recognized the dress at once. She had seen a photograph of it only last week in an old summer issue of *Harper's Bazaar*, which she had bought at the second-hand bookstall in Ripon market. It had been designed by a young French *couturière* called Gabrielle Chanel, who was currently all the vogue.

"Hello! Hello!" Mrs. Bell exclaimed, gliding to a stop, thrusting her hand toward her visitor. "So *very* pleased to meet you, Miss Kenton."

Audra took the proffered hand, then found her own being squeezed in the tightest of grips. "Good afternoon, Mrs. Bell. I'm happy to meet you, too."

Giving her a warm and winning smile, continuing to hold her hand, Irène Bell drew Audra forward to the two huge sofas which were positioned opposite each other in front of the fireplace. "So very good of you to travel all this way, Miss Kenton. And in this frightful weather. Yes, so very *good* of you indeed. Do, *do* sit here. Yes, *yes,* next to the fire. Warm yourself after your journey. Cook is preparing hot chocolate. Cora will bring it up shortly. I *do* hope you like hot chocolate. Would you prefer tea? Or coffee, perhaps?"

"The chocolate would be lovely, thank you very much," Audra said, seating herself tentatively on the edge of the blue velvet sofa. Her keen eyes rested on Mrs. Bell, who sat down on the other one.

Now that she was seeing her close up, Audra realized that she had not been wrong about Irène Bell's age after all. She was definitely a woman in her mid-forties, but very well preserved and exquisitely groomed. Although there were tell-tale lines of age around her eyes and her mouth, these were fine, hardly discernible; she had kept her figure and there was no visible gray in her fiery hair, which was natural, not dyed. And her vivacity, her energetic way of moving and speaking with intensity and swiftness somehow added to the impression of youthfulness she projected.

Intuitively, Audra knew that she was going to like this woman, even though she had only been in her presence for a few minutes. There was something open and easy, honest and down to earth about Mrs. Bell, and Audra found herself responding to her on a variety of levels. She sat back, instantly relaxing, feeling suddenly comfortable here at Calpher House. And she, who was usually so shy, so reserved with strangers, was perfectly at ease with Mrs. Bell.

Irène Bell crossed her long and elegant legs, and focused her dark and intelligent eyes on Audra, assessing her, yet without really appearing to do so.

She said in her light, gay voice, "In some ways I do feel rather foolish, Miss Kenton. Asking you to come for an interview like this. Matron Lennox gave you such a wonderful reference, I actually thought of engaging you over the telephone. Without even bothering to meet you personally."

Laughing as though at herself, her velvet eyes glowed with humor as she added, "But then I realized how unfair that would be to you, Miss Kenton. After all, it is important for *you* to like *us.* For you to *want* to live and work here at Calpher House. I knew I must give you the opportunity to come here and look *us* over."

Irène Bell laughed again, leaned back, rested one elbow on the pile of silk cushions, and continued to study Audra discreetly, not wishing to embarrass her. She was intrigued by the young woman who sat before her, who handled herself with such grace and dignity. Margaret Lennox had painted a charming verbal picture of her, and the Matron had obviously not exaggerated. Audra Kenton was smaller than she had expected her to be, even delicate-looking, but she was not terribly concerned about physical stamina. Strength of character, refinement, morality and a pleasant personality were her chief considerations when it came to selecting and engaging a nanny. This girl had every one of these qualities, and more, according to Margaret, whose judgment she trusted.

"Matron Lennox told me that she thought you and I would be compatible, Mrs. Bell, and she felt sure that I could handle the job here easily." Audra leveled her penetrating blue eyes at the other woman, and ventured, "But she *was* vague about it. Perhaps you would be kind enough to give me a few more details, Mrs. Bell."

"Good Lord, of course! I must fill you in, mustn't I? Well now, let me see. As you know from Matron, you would be entirely responsible for our youngest child. Our only son. Our three daughters are grown up. The eldest, Miss Pandora, lives at home. The younger two, Felicity and Antonia, are away at boarding school. Let me explain something, Miss Kenton. I go to business every day. I run the woolen mill I inherited from my father. I also have an exclusive ladies' gown salon in Leeds. *Paris Modes.* I'm quite certain you must know it."

Audra shook her head, looking regretful. "I'm sorry, I'm afraid I don't, Mrs. Bell. The only store I know in Leeds is Harte's Emporium. I went there once with my friend Gwen."

Mrs. Bell said, "My dress shop is not as large as Emma Harte's store. But my imported French gowns *are* beginning to rival those she sells in her Model Room at Harte's. But to continue: Because I am out most of the day, I need a responsible person in charge of the nursery and the baby. A person such as yourself. As to your accommodations here, there is a lovely bedroom, large and comfortable, which overlooks the gardens. It's on the nursery floor, has its own private bathroom. You would have one day off during the week, and every other Sunday. One week's holiday a year. I would provide you with three cotton uniforms for summer, plus a summer coat and hat. The same amount of clothing for winter. Now, regarding the wages—"

Mrs. Bell broke off at the sound of a knock, and glanced toward the door. It opened to admit a plump young maid, who rushed forward rather too quickly, pushing a laden tea cart in front of her.

"Ah Cora, there you are at last!" Mrs. Bell exclaimed. *"Do,* please, be *careful.* Bring the cart over here by the fire. This is Miss Kenton, Cora. Whom I sincerely hope will be joining us at Calpher House. As the new nanny."

Cora and the tea cart came to an abrupt stop with a rattling jolt. She stared at Audra, narrowing her eyes, squinting at her. Then, as if she had decided she liked the look of her, she smiled broadly, bobbed a half-curtsy. "Please ter meet yer, Miss," she said, and proceeded down the long stretch of Turkey carpet, handling the trolley with a kind of dangerous abandon.

Audra inclined her head graciously and returned the maid's smile. "Good afternoon, Cora," she replied, and cringed as she watched Cora's perilous progress toward them. She hoped that nothing would go crashing to the floor, for the maid's sake.

Irène Bell dismissed Cora with a smile and a nod, lifted the silver jug and carefully filled two large breakfast cups, remarking, "We have a wonderful cook, Mrs. Jackson, and the butler is Mr. Agiter. I believe you saw Dodie, the other housemaid, when you arrived? Did she not open the door to you?"

"Yes, she did, Mrs. Bell." Audra rose and went over to the tea cart, took the cup of hot chocolate which was being offered to her.

Irène Bell exclaimed, "Do, but *do,* try one of Cook's hot Cornish pasties, Miss Kenton. They're delicious. And quite renowned hereabouts."

"Thank you." Audra placed the cup of steamy, frothing chocolate on the antique mahogany table next to the sofa, put one of the meat turnovers on a plate and returned to her place.

Taking a sip of chocolate, Mrs. Bell continued, "As I was about to say when Cora came in, your wages would be sixty pounds a year. This is an increase of ten pounds above what I paid the last nanny. Matron Lennox said it would not be fair of me to offer you anything less than sixty pounds. In view of your superior training at the hospital." Irène Bell now leaned forward intently. "Well, Miss Kenton, are you interested in taking the position, do you think?" A perfect, penciled brow lifted eloquently.

Audra was both startled and delighted at the amount of money she would be paid. She said, "I am interested, Mrs. Bell, very much so. However, I would like to meet your little boy before I finally say yes." Audra gave her a forthright look, and her sudden smile was one of sweetness and sincerity. "I'm quite positive I will like him, but I do want to be sure *he* likes *me.*"

"What a lovely sentiment, Miss Kenton. And I'm overjoyed, simply *overjoyed,* that you're going to join our little family." Irène Bell's face, always mobile and expressive, now filled with a mixture of relief and pleasure. Her merry laugh echoed around the room. "I know the baby will take to you. How could he not? He's having his afternoon nap at the moment, but you shall meet him later. And before you leave, I shall show you around Calpher House. And introduce you to the staff."

The motor car slid to a standstill in front of the General Post Office in City Square.

A moment later the uniformed chauffeur was opening the rear door and helping Audra to alight. "Thank you so much, Robertson," she said, giving him an appreciative little smile.

"It's a pleasure, Miss. Good afternoon, Miss." He touched the bill of his peaked cap and hurried back to the driver's seat.

Audra swung around and took a step toward Gwen, who was standing near the steps of the post office where they had arranged to meet.

Gwen's eyes were out on stalks. Instantly recovering herself, she rushed forward to meet Audra. Grasping hold of her hands, she cried in a shrill, excited voice, "Well, aren't *we* posh then! Rolling up in a fancy motor car. Imagine that!"

Audra could not help laughing at Gwen's incredulity. Then she explained, "Mrs. Bell kept me at Calpher House rather longer than I expected. I started to get a little nervous in the end. I didn't want to be late, to have you standing waiting outside in the cold. So she sent me in the car."

"That was nice of her!" Gwen exclaimed, obviously impressed not only by the car but by Mrs. Bell as well. She peered into Audra's face and demanded, "Well, did you take the job then?"

"Yes, Gwen, I did."

"Oh, lovey, I *am* glad!" Gwen threw her arms around Audra, hugged her tightly. Audra hugged her back, and the two of them clung to each other, did a happy little jig and then began to laugh uproariously.

Their frivolity was interrupted by a masculine voice, which said, "They'll be sending the wagon for you two next, the way you're carrying on like a couple of lunatics, and in the middle of City Square, no less."

"Oh hello, Charlie," Gwen said, looking up at her brother, who stood with his hands in his pockets, towering over them both, surveying them through amused eyes. "You're right on time, I see."

"Aren't I always." Charles Thornton grinned at his sister, then gave Audra a shy smile. "Hello, Audra," he said, unable to keep the look of adoration off his face. He thrust his hand at her.

Audra's heart sank at the sight of Charlie, whom she had not expected to join them for the evening, as he no doubt had. She had wanted to be alone with Gwen. They hadn't seen each other for several weeks, and they had a number of things to talk about, especially now that she had taken the job with the Bells.

"Hello," Audra responded in her quiet way, taking his hand, glad she was wearing her gloves. Charlie always had such clammy hands, even in the cold weather. In fact, he had a tendency to perspire, and whilst she knew he could not help it, Audra found this unfortunate physical trait distasteful. She liked Charlie well enough as a person, but she had no wish to have him as her boyfriend. This was Gwen's hope though, and she was forever pushing Charlie at her. Audra fervently wished she would stop doing it. Charlie Thornton was not her type at all. It was not that he was unattractive. He was tall, well built, with broad shoulders, very masculine really, although Audra suspected he would become flabby as he grew older. He had blond hair, a fair complexion and friendly gray eyes. His face, like his personality, was bland. Audra could not help thinking that he was soppy in certain ways, and most of the time she found him dreadfully dull. She supposed he was worthy in many ways, and yet instinctively she knew he was a weak man, ineffectual somehow.

Gwen volunteered, "Charlie's taking us to the pictures later, Audra. He's treating us. We're going to the Rialto in Briggate to see the new Mary Pickford picture. Isn't that nice of him?"

"Oh yes, it is," Audra was quick to agree and forced a smile.

Taking charge as usual, Gwen rushed on, "Well, don't let's stand here like three sucking ducks gawping at each other. We've an hour to waste before we go to the pictures, so let's toddle along to Betty's and have a nice cup of tea."

Audra and Charlie readily agreed.

It had turned even chillier and the snow that had threatened throughout the day began to fall in small fluttering flakes, settling on the ground. The light was being squeezed out of the lowering sky as dusk descended rapidly. Charlie took hold of the girls' arms and hurried them across City Square in the direction of Commercial Street where the cafe was located. As they turned into the street, they all three stopped abruptly, staring into the windows of Harte's department store, captivated by what they saw. The windows had been dressed for Christmas and they were dazzling in the gathering twilight, filled with twinkling colored lights and glittering scenes depicting various fairy tales. One window was devoted to Cinderella, showed her arriving at the ball in her shimmering glass coach, another to Hansel and Gretel, who stood outside the gingerbread house, and yet a third paid tribute to The Snow Queen in all her icy glory.

"How beautiful they are," Audra murmured, lingering a moment longer than the other two, thinking of High Cleugh and the glorious Christmases of her childhood.

"Yes, aren't they just," Gwen said, tugging at her. "Come on, lovey, the snow's really coming down now. We're going to be soaked before we know it."

Gwen tucked her arm through Audra's and kept up a continual stream of conversation as they walked down Commercial Street, living up to her reputation as a chatterbox. Charlie, trudging along on the other side of Audra, interjected a few comments, but Audra remained silent—and reflective.

She was suddenly feeling uncharitable for having had such unkind thoughts about Charlie, who was harmless really and meant well. *All* of the Thorntons meant well, and they had *all* been very good to her. Mrs. Thornton was forever telling her to consider The Meadow her home, and she had even turned the little box room at the end of the second-floor landing into a bedroom for her. Mrs. Thornton had insisted she keep a few clothes there, and when she had visited Gwen in November, she had left behind some toilet articles and a nightgown, which she would be able to use tonight.

Next week she was coming back to Horsforth to spend Christmas with Gwen, and she was well aware that the Thorntons would make her feel like a part of the family, truly one of them, as they always did. They had such a wealth of generosity and kindness in them. And I'm very ungrateful, Audra chastized herself. She knew how much it would please Gwen if she were nice to Charlie, and so she resolved to be pleasant to him, but without leading him on, giving him the wrong impression. *He must not misunderstand*. That would be disastrous. And after the holidays she was going to explain to Gwen, in the gentlest and kindest possible way, that she was not looking for a husband.

Eight

It was a very cold morning. *Icy*.

Perhaps it *would* turn out to be the coldest day of the winter after all, Audra thought, just as the gardener had warned yesterday when she had been returning from her walk. He had put down his wheelbarrow and looked up at the sky, narrowing his eyes and sniffing, as if he had a way of divining such things in this arcane manner.

And then he had made his prediction. "Yer'll be nithered ter death termorra, Miss Audra. T'weather's coming in bad from t'North Sea. Arctic weather, mark my words, lass."

She had never been to the Arctic Circle, but she did not imagine it could be any colder than her bedroom at this moment. It was freezing, and it seemed to Audra that her nose, peeping over the bedcovers, had turned into an icicle. An Arctic icicle.

She slithered farther down in the bed, hunching the covers up over her shoulders, almost obscuring her face entirely, reveling in the warmth of the quilt. It was filled with the down of the eider duck, and Mr. and Mrs. Bell had purchased a baker's dozen of these quilts when they had been on holiday in Munich several years before.

Mrs. Bell had told Audra this when she had come to work at Calpher House, had gone on to explain that the sheet under the quilt was the only other piece of bed linen required. Irène Bell had also cautioned Audra not to wear her thick flannel nightgown, but to discard it in favor of a cotton garment. Although she had nodded her understanding, she had not been absolutely certain that she really understood at all. But later that night, at bedtime, she had done as she had been bidden earlier in the day, and within ten minutes of being in bed she had begun to feel a lovely sensation of warmth permeating her whole body. The heat generated by the quilt was extraordinary, something quite amazing to Audra, and she realized that Mrs. Bell had been correct about the cotton nightie. Anything else would have been far too hot.

She smiled to herself now, remembering her first night here, and then swiveled her eyes to the clock on the mahogany chest as it began to chime. It was only six, but this did not surprise her in the least. She was accustomed to awakening at this hour. It was an old habit left over from her years at the hospital in Ripon. Fortunately the routine was not so rigorous here at Calpher House, and she could stay in bed until seven, even a bit later if she wished.

Audra had truly come to cherish this dawn hour, when all the family were asleep and no one was about except for the servants downstairs. She thought of it as her own special and private time, enjoyed the luxury of lingering in her downy cocoon, without having the need to rush, idly drifting with her diverse thoughts . . . and sometimes daydreaming about the future.

And the future seemed decidedly rosy to Audra on this December morning of 1927.

Certainly the years stretching ahead could not be any worse than the five years which had preceded her arrival at Calpher House, she frequently told herself these days. Naturally optimistic, she always looked at things in the most positive way, anticipating the best. She also expected the best from people, despite her distressing experiences with her Aunt Alicia Drummond. Burying the dreadful hurt she had suffered at the hands of that inhuman woman, she would remind herself that not everyone was cruel, selfish or dishonest, that the world *did* have its ample share of kindly folk. And the Bells and their staff at Calpher House had helped to reinforce this belief in Audra. She had been made to feel welcome from the first day, and she never once forgot how fortunate she had been to find such a congenial place to work.

It was exactly one year ago today that she had started here as the nanny.

From the first moment she had stepped into this house, Audra had felt as if she belonged here. It was as if she had returned after a long journey to a place she had always known. In a way it had been like coming home . . . home to High Cleugh. It was not that Calpher House resembled her beloved former home; as houses they were entirely different in architecture and furnishings. What she had found so familiar, had recognized with such clarity, was the presence of love within these walls.

For the most part, it was the happiest year that Audra had spent since her mother had died and tragedy had struck their little family.

She fitted in well at Calpher House.

Because of her upbringing, her disposition and personality, everyone found her a pleasure to be around, and she was popular upstairs and downstairs. The Bells were kind; the servants treated her with a deference and respect that was marked by friendliness.

After years of frugality and spartan living at the hospital, she was now surrounded by enormous luxury and comfort, the likes of which she had never known even at High Cleugh, where money for anything other than the real essentials had been fairly scarce most of the time. All of their pleasureful little extras had come from Uncle Peter.

The Bells were successful, affluent people and they could afford the best.

And because of Mrs. Bell's giving nature there was an overabundance of everything.

Wonderfully delicious meals emerged from Mrs. Jackson's amazing kitchen, and Audra also got a chance to taste such delicacies as *päté de foie gras,* caviar and smoked salmon. Crystal dishes of bonbons and nuts and Turkish Delight were scattered across small occasional tables in the elegant blue living room, for anyone to nibble on who wished, and even the everyday nursery meals could hardly be called *everyday* because of the way they tasted. Such things as steak-and-kidney pudding, apple dumplings, bacon-and-egg pie, Irish stew, and pork, beef and lamb roasts all had the most distinctive, mouth-watering flavors. As far as Audra was concerned, the cook was the first person to rival her mother in a kitchen; Mrs. Jackson was forever coming up with something extra-special to tempt their palates. Audra's favorites were Little Pigs of Heaven, a warm chocolate dessert that literally melted in the mouth; and Bandit's Joy, a hot potato dish flavored with honey and nutmeg that made a perfect accompaniment to saddle of mutton. She had asked Mrs. Jackson for the recipes for these dishes. On very special occasions, Mr. Agiter, the butler, had been instructed by Mr. Bell to serve her a glass of sparkling, ice-cold champagne. But she was already familiar with this wine, since it had not been out of the ordinary for her Uncle Peter to bring a bottle to celebrate her mother's birthday, or for Christmas Day at High Cleugh. She and Frederick and William had always been allowed one small glass by their mother.

Apart from the delectable food and vintage wines which seemed to flow without cease at Calpher House, there was a plethora of other things which added their distinctive touches to the sense of opulence that prevailed throughout.

Innumerable bowls and vases of flowers and exotic plants punctuated every room downstairs; the latest magazines and newspapers, current novels and other books spilled over large circular tables in the library, in Mrs. Bell's study and most especially in the family parlor where everyone seemed to congregate at night. Sofas and chairs were plump and inviting with piles of soft cushions, or they had their arms draped with fluffy mohair throws from Scotland, to be used on colder evenings wrapped around legs and shoulders.

Startled at first though she had been, and even a bit overwhelmed by all this luxury in one house, Audra had grown accustomed to it. Whilst it would be true to say that she enjoyed the comfort and the cosseting, she nonetheless did not consider it of any great importance in her life. The real reason she was happy at Calpher House was because her employers and the staff were all really good people who cared about others and their well-being.

These aspects of her job aside, it had been a fine year for Audra Kenton in other respects.

The letters which came from her brothers were much more positive these days, and were written in the same optimistic vein that had enhanced their earliest epistles to her. Frederick was growing stronger in health every week, and things had improved immeasurably for them. They both had good jobs in Sydney at long last. William was working in the circulation department of the Sydney *Morning Herald;* Frederick had become private secretary to an industrialist, a Mr. Roland Matheson, and Audra was happy for them, and proud of the way they had coped with their initial bad luck and daunting setbacks. And knowing they were no longer in difficult straits made her own continuing sense of loss and yearning for them that much easier to bear.

Then again, she and Gwen had been able to spend a great deal of their free time together. Mrs. Bell had kindly given her permission to invite Gwen to stay overnight at Calpher House on numerous occasions; she herself frequently traveled across to Horsforth to spend her day off with Gwen. Sometimes they took the tramcar into Leeds to browse in the stores and window-shop, and she was beginning to know the city well. Quite often they went to the picture house, and recently they had seen their first talking picture, *The Jazz Singer,* starring Al Jolson.

June had been a particularly happy month for Audra, mostly because of the attention everyone paid to her twentieth birthday. How different it had been from the previous year, when she had spent that very special day in her life entirely alone. Her brothers' cards had arrived from Australia not only in time but two days early; on the third, a small celebration was held in the nursery, with presents from the Bells and the staff at Calpher House.

And later that week, on Saturday, Mrs. Thornton and Gwen had given a party for her at The Meadow. There had been a splendid summer tea on the lawn. The table, covered in a white cloth, had groaned under the weight of all manner of lovely things—cucumber-and-tomato sandwiches, a Yorkshire pork pie, trifle, strawberries and cream, big pots of hot tea, plus an iced cake with the message *Happy Birthday, Audra* written on it in pink-icing sugar and twenty pink candles encircling the edge. And each member of her friend's family had given her a small but meaningful gift. After tea they had trooped inside for dancing to the latest records which they had played on Gwen's new gramophone. They had done the Charleston to the strains of "Black Bottom," "Ain't She Sweet," and "Yes Sir, That's My Baby," fox-trotted slowly to "Blue Skies" and "Among My Souvenirs," and everyone had enjoyed themselves that night.

Charlie had been present, along with his brothers, Jeremy and Harry, Mike Lesley, his best friend, and a couple of his chums from medical school. He was still attentive to her whenever he got the opportunity, even though she did her best to discourage him.

Once she had moved to Leeds the previous December and settled in with the Bells, Audra had spoken to Gwen about her brother. She had explained to her friend in the sweetest way that, as nice as Charlie was, he was not for her. She had asked Gwen not to encourage Charlie anymore. Gwen had said she understood and agreed at once to stop "fanning the flames." But Audra had seen the hurt in her friend's eyes, and she had quickly added that it had nothing to do with Charlie per se, that men in general did not interest her for the time being. She had then announced, and in a very firm voice, that she had no intention of getting married, of settling down, until she was thirty at least.

Gwen had looked at her askance on hearing this, had eyed Audra with a degree of skepticism, but she had refrained from making any sort of comment. At least until last month—November the fifth to be exact—when she had come to Upper Armley to join in their celebrations on Bonfire Night.

Mrs. Bell had told Audra she could invite Gwen to spend the night at Calpher House, since they were both off duty the following day. After one of the cook's extra-special nursery teas and as soon as it grew dark, they had gone outside for the lighting of the bonfire that Fipps, the gardener, had made in the grounds. They had shared the family's fun, watching the fireworks, waving the sparklers which Mr. Bell had produced and eating piping hot chestnuts and roasted potatoes pulled from the embers of the fire. And then the two of them had gone off to the Guy Fawkes Day party and dance at Christ Church Parish Hall in Ridge Road.

Audra first saw the young man when everyone was crowding around the huge bonfire outside the hall, gathered to watch the burning of the effigy of Guy Fawkes.

He was alone, standing near the porch, leaning against the wall, smoking a cigarette. As he nonchalantly tossed it to the ground, then stubbed his toe on it, he glanced across at the commotion around the bonfire, noticed her, smiled.

Audra looked back at him and experienced a queer sensation, one that was unfamiliar to her. She felt suddenly faint and a little breathless, as if she had been punched.

His face was clearly illuminated in the glow from the fire, and she saw that he was most arresting in appearance.

His dark hair, which came to a widow's peak above a wide brow, was brushed to one side, parted on the left, and he had dark brows, light-colored eyes. His face was well articulated, sensitive, but it was the purity reflected in it that struck her so forcibly, made such a strong and lasting impression.

Their eyes connected. And locked. He gave her a hard, penetrating stare. She flushed to her roots, looked quickly away.

A moment later, when she and Gwen turned around to go into the parochial hall, Audra noticed immediately that he was no longer propping up the wall, and she filled with disappointment.

Once they were inside, her eyes searched for him, but he seemed to have disappeared. She waited for him to come back, but he did not, and the dance fell flat for her after that. As the evening progressed, Audra found it impossible to tear her eyes away from the door for very long, and she silently prayed that he would return. There was something about him that intrigued her.

Although she was asked to dance several times and accepted these invitations, for most of the evening Audra sat it out on the long bench with the other wallflowers. She was quite content to be an observer, watching the dancers, in particular Gwen, who twirled around the floor with various young bucks from the neighborhood, obviously enjoying herself immensely. But Audra thought that none of Gwen's partners looked half as handsome or as fascinating as the dark young man who had so engaged her interest earlier.

Audra had almost given up hope that he would make an appearance again when he came barreling through the door, looking slightly flushed and out of breath, and stood at the far side of the hall, glancing about. At the exact moment that the band leader announced the last waltz, he spotted her. His eyes lit up, and he walked directly across the floor to her and, with a faint smile, asked her if she would care to dance.

Gripped by a sudden internal shaking, unable to speak, Audra nodded and rose.

He was taller than she had realized, at least five feet nine, perhaps even six feet, with long legs, and lean and slender though he was, he had broad shoulders. There was an easy, natural way about him that communicated itself to her instantly, and he moved with great confidence and panache. He led her onto the floor, took her in his arms masterfully, and swept her away as the band struck up *The Blue Danube*.

During the course of the dance he made several casual remarks, but Audra, tongue-tied, remained mute, knowing she was unable to respond coherently. He said, at one moment, "What's up then, cat got your tongue?"

She managed to whisper, "No."

Glancing down at her with curiosity, he frowned, but he did not bother to say anything further, appeared to be lost in his thoughts or concentrating on the dance.

When the music stopped, he thanked her politely, escorted her back to the bench, inclined his head, strolled off.

Her eyes followed him all the way to the front door. And as he walked out into the dark winter night, she wondered who he was and if she would ever see him again. She desperately hoped she would.

Later when she and Gwen were hurrying up Town Street, making their way back to Calpher House, Gwen suddenly blurted out: "Well, I must say, for someone who protests they're not interested in men, you were certainly mesmerized by that chap you had the last dance with. But I can tell you this, Audra, he's bad news. Oh yes, definitely, lovey."

Audra, startled, asked, "How can you say he's bad news? You don't even *know* him."

Gwen took hold of Audra's arm in her usual possessive way, slipped her own through it. She said, "I can tell just by looking at him that he's a real devil. I'm always suspicious of the pretty ones. *Very wary.* They generally end up breaking some poor woman's heart, lovey, maybe even two or three hearts, for that matter. You'd be much better off with somebody like our Charlie. And you know how *he* feels about *you,* lovey. *He hasn't changed.*"

Audra said nothing. Gwen's remarks about the young man irritated and annoyed her. She considered them to be unwarranted and just a shade preposterous under the circumstances. Presumptuous, in fact, and for the first time in their friendship, she was put out with Gwen. The next morning, still rankling somewhat, Audra scrupulously avoided referring to the evening before, and she and Gwen did not discuss the young man again.

But Audra could not help thinking about him.

In the days which immediately followed the encounter, she kept recalling certain things about that night and about him . . . the way he had looked down at her, narrowly, speculatively, through the greenest eyes she had ever seen . . . the turbulent emotions he had aroused in her, feelings she had not believed really existed except in the novels on Mrs. Bell's shelves . . . his ineffable grace as he had moved them around the dance floor . . . the true classical beauty of his face, so unusual in a man.

Now, nearly two months afterward, Audra was still asking herself why she never ran across him in Upper Armley. Ever since the dance she had expected to do so, and she never ceased to look for him when she went out and about with the child who was in her charge. She was convinced the young man came from these parts for she could recognize the local accent when she heard it.

As Audra focused her thoughts on him, an echo of his voice reverberated clearly in her head, and an image of his face leapt before her eyes. And despite the warmth of the quilt, she shivered unexpectedly and gooseflesh speckled her skin. She wrapped her arms around her body, hugging herself. She pictured his face close to hers on the pillow, tried to imagine what it would be like to be kissed by him, touched by him, held by him. Since their brief encounter, the mysterious dark young man had haunted her, intruded on her thoughts at the oddest times.

Presently Audra opened her eyes and endeavored to quench the unfamiliar longings stirring within her. Until she had met *him,* danced with *him,* Audra had never known sexual desire, and of late some of the strange, new feelings she was experiencing confused and frightened her, yet excited her at the same time. She pressed her face into the pillow, wanting to block out the memory of him, and discovered, as she had so often in the past few weeks, that she was unable to expunge the image of his face, his unbelievable eyes. She knew she wanted him.

Turning onto her back, she lay very still, staring up at the ceiling, her eyes wide, unblinking, and she wondered what she would do if she did not run into him again. Dismay gripped her, then instantly dissipated. Audra believed that they *would* meet and that they would come to know each other well. Very well indeed. She felt this in her bones.

A sudden clattering in the corridor outside her bedroom pierced the early morning silence.

Audra started in surprise, then cocked her head, listened. She heard a stifled exclamation, then low unintelligible mutterings, followed by the sound of feet clomping into the adjoining day nursery.

Audra knew that it was Cora going about her morning chores. She suspected that the housemaid had dropped the coal scuttle, which was not an unusual occurrence by any means. Cora, who was perpetually cheerful, had turned out to be a friendly soul, but she was also the clumsiest person Audra had ever met. A day did not go by without a breakage of one kind or another, and the culprit, sadly, was always poor Cora.

There was a loud knock on the door, and Cora's scrubbed and shining face appeared around it. "Mornin', Miss Audra."

"Good morning, Cora," Audra said, pushing herself up on one elbow, smiling in the half light.

"Is it all right if I comes in then, Miss Audra? Ter make t'fire for yer?"

"Yes, of course, Cora."

Cora's plump little body, encased in her pink-striped morning uniform, rotated across the room like a fast-spinning top. She dumped the coal scuttle and the ash pan down on the hearth unceremoniously, then spun over to the huge window. "It's ever so cold out this mornin', Miss. Arctic weather, so Fipps says. Aye, he says it's cold enough ter freeze t'balls off a brass monkey, that he does."

"Really, Cora!"

"That's what he said ter me, Miss."

"But you shouldn't repeat something vulgar like that, Cora," Audra reprimanded softly.

"No, I don't expects I should, least ways not in yer presence, Miss Audra." This was said somewhat apologetically, but, nevertheless, Cora threw her a cheeky grin as she hurried back to the fireplace. She asked, "And what are yer doin' termorra night then, Miss Audra?"

"Nothing special, Cora. My friend Miss Thornton is on night duty at the Infirmary for the next two weeks, so I won't be going to any New Year's Eve parties. I'll be staying here at Calpher House."

"Oh but Mr. Agiter allus has a party for t'staff, yer knows." Cora glanced over her shoulder, smiled with her usual engaging cheerfulness, added, "Yer were ever so shy last December, when yer first started here, and yer wouldn't come downstairs, but I hopes yer'll be with us this year, ooh I *do,* Miss Audra, ever so much.''

"Yes, I will, Cora. Mr. Agiter has already invited me, and I'm looking forward to joining you all for a glass of champagne around midnight . . . to toast in 1928.''

The child's name was Theophilus, Theo for short, and Audra had grown to truly love him in the year she had been taking care of him.

He was an odd-looking little boy, not exactly plain, but then neither was he fancy.

The first time she had set eyes on him, she decided that he was highly individualistic. This turned out to be true—and in many more ways than merely his appearance. Theophilus had a plump, perfectly round little face, not unlike a suet pudding, but his skin was pink and white rather than doughy or pasty in color. His fair hair, soft, silky, straight, had a way of flopping down over two sharply observing black eyes that resembled bright little chips of coal, and he was forever pushing it away with an impatient gesture.

It often struck Audra that these very dark eyes and the pale blond hair didn't quite go together, but then that was Theophilus. He seemed to be made up entirely of spare parts, each bit individually attractive if not specifically designed to go with the others.

Not matched up, are you, my little love? Audra murmured under her breath as she brushed his hair. His appearance usually preoccupied her for a few minutes before they went out, and this morning was no exception. She put the brush down, stepped away, regarded him critically, her head on one side. Reaching out, she straightened his tie, nodded in satisfaction, then bending over, she planted a kiss on his cheek.

"There you are, all ready!'' she exclaimed, taking his hands in hers, helping him to jump down off the table. "And you're as bright as a new penny today, Theo.''

He looked up at her through solemn eyes which were curiously wise and knowing for a six-year-old. "I hope the doctor also thinks that.''

She bit back a smile of amusement, said, "I'm sure he will. Now, run along to see your mother, whilst I get my things together, and then we can be off.''

"Oh yes, I had better do that. Before she leaves for Leeds. My spending money is due today.'' He set his face determinedly, marched toward the door in small but purposeful strides and disappeared into the corridor.

Audra watched him go, turned away, laughing to herself as she crossed the spacious and comfortably furnished day nursery. She had a few minutes to spare before following the boy downstairs, and she stood with her back to the fire, warming herself, thinking of her young charge.

Theophilus Bell never ceased to amaze and amuse Audra. He was a precocious child, although his precocity was not offensive. The cook said he was "old-fashioned'' and this description fitted him perfectly. Audra was not a bit surprised he was the way he was—so serious and self-possessed. He had spent most of his young life with adults; even his sisters were much older than he. Pandora, who had married in the spring and moved out of Calpher House, was twenty-two. Antonia and Felicity, both now attending finishing school in

Switzerland, were nineteen and eighteen respectively, and all three happened to be sophisticated young women who were well educated, well traveled and had been exposed to a variety of people and a great deal of radical thought in this house. And so they also were much older than their years, and, not unnaturally, they had had an influence on their small brother. The girls called Theo "the afterthought," and although Audra disliked this term, considered it to be rather unkind, she realized that there was a degree of truth in it. He had been born to Mrs. Bell when she was forty-two, long after she had expected to bear any more children, and, as she had said to Audra, "Theo just missed being a change-of-life baby, thank heavens."

Audra considered it a small miracle that the Bells had not fallen into the usual trap of pampering and spoiling Theo, which so often happened to an only son who came to his parents later in life and who was their pride and joy. He *was* indulged occasionally, but this seemed to have little or no effect on him, and he was not given to making excessive demands on anyone, nor was he a temperamental child.

In actuality, Theo was a lot like his mother. Certainly he had inherited Irène Bell's quick-wittedness, her intelligence and her studious nature. And if he was sometimes unnerving in his forthrightness, he was, nevertheless, a good child, very obedient, and he had never given Audra one moment's trouble in the past twelve months.

Ten loud chimes, echoing through from the bedroom, suddenly alerted Audra to the hour. Theo had been suffering with a sore throat, and although he was better she was taking him to the doctor this morning for a checkup.

Hurrying through into the other room, she glanced at herself in the glass, smoothed one hand over her hair, newly bobbed that summer, then went to the wardrobe in the corner. She took out her heavy winter coat and hat, and a thick woolen scarf and gloves in anticipation of the Arctic weather which had apparently descended on them, just as the gardener had predicted it would yesterday.

Nine

His name was Vincent Crowther and he was something of a rebel.

He was born in the year 1903, at five minutes to midnight on the twelfth day of June, in the middle of the worst thunderstorm the new century had witnessed.

A lusty, robust nine-pound baby, he came screaming into the world, fists flailing, face red and contorted, and giving vent to such a fierce and angry display of temperament the doctor told the midwife that the baby's tantrums were only outmatched by the violence of the weather outside.

His mother secretly called him her Stormy Petrel thereafter, and she was the least surprised of anyone when her rebellious child grew up to be an equally rebellious man, one who was a maverick to boot and who always stood out in a crowd.

In a sense he was a natural star, one who drew others to him by sheer force of personality, dashing looks and more than his fair share of charm. Further, it did him no harm that he had what his father called "the gift of the gab."

The firstborn of Eliza and Alfred Crowther's eight children, Vincent boasted an almost girlish beauty as a child, but this turned into a masculine type of handsomeness as he matured. And there never was any question about his virility. It was like a gloss on him. In consequence, women fell at his feet swooning, and they had done so since he was sixteen. And he was well versed in their ways, was master of these love and sex games at a tender age. He was twenty-four.

His looks dazzled.

It was his coloring that was so sensational. The gleaming black hair and the black brows were in marked contrast to a light, creamy complexion and cheeks that held a tinge of pink like the bloom on a peach; he had cool green eyes, the color of light, clear tourmalines, fringed with thick black lashes. His eyes and his skin were the envy of his sisters—and most other women.

Matched to the striking coloring and handsome profile was a superb athletic body. He was exactly five feet nine and a half inches tall, well muscled, firm and taut and without one ounce of fat or flab on him.

Immaculate at all times, Vincent considered himself to be a bit of a dandy, loved clothes, wore them with flair and elegance. He cut quite a swathe wherever he went, especially on the dance floor, where his easy grace and good looks showed to such advantage.

He was his mother's favorite.

His siblings were aware of this. They were not jealous. In fact, they shared their mother's feelings about him to some extent. His brothers admired him; his sisters adored him.

Only his father treated him like an ordinary person.

Alfred Crowther loved his firstborn child, but he had no illusions about him. A former sergeant major in the Seaforth Highlanders, Alfred was a veteran of two great wars, having fought the Boers on the African veldt and the Germans on the fields of Flanders. Subsequently, he knew men and their motivations, could read them well, and his own son was no exception. He had a great deal of insight into Vincent.

Alfred recognized there was a lot of devilishness in the boy, not to mention temperament and a good measure of vanity. He thought Vincent was too handsome by far for his own good. But, being a realist, Alfred knew there was not much point in worrying about this eldest child of his, who had been born with the looks of a matinee idol. Fretting would not alter these facts. The elder Crowther believed that what was meant to happen eventually happened. His fatalistic attitude could be ascribed to his Irish mother, Martha, who, when he was growing up, had constantly told him, "What will be, will be, Alf, sure an' it will. 'Tis *preordained,* I am thinkin', this life each one of us poor souls be livin' in this hard and cruel world."

Father and son were good companions. They enjoyed sharing a pint of beer, usually stopped off at the pub together at weekends, and often they went to race meetings in Doncaster and York, especially in the summer weather. However, despite a certain masculine camaraderie, there was not as much intimacy between them as might have been expected. It was his mother who was Vincent's confidante and friend. She always had been. She always would be— until the day she died.

His manifest physical attributes aside, Vincent Crowther was no dunce. In fact, quite the opposite was the truth. He was quick and intelligent; he had powerful analytical ability, which would serve him well later in life, and a retentive memory.

But coming from the working class as he did, he had left Armley Council School when he was fourteen and had found himself a job in one of the tailoring shops in Armley. He had quickly grown bored, mainly because his interests lay elsewhere. He was particularly drawn to building and construction and frequently wished he could have studied architecture.

After leaving the tailoring shop, he had a short spell laboring in the local brickyard, before finally finding an opening with a building firm. He was currently learning his trade; he liked working in the open air, drew pleasure and satisfaction from seeing each building take shape and grow and so fulfill the architect's original vision.

Sometimes Vincent told himself he was going to enroll in night school in Leeds, to learn draftsmanship, but he put this off, was always distracted by other more pleasurable activities. He was partial to dancing, and he had been a voracious reader when a boy, but otherwise he had no hobbies to speak of. For the most part, he spent his free time drinking with his cronies and could usually be found propping up the bar in the tap room of one of the local pubs, quaffing down pints or studying a *tissue,* the pink racing sheet that was published every weekday and was his bible.

He was engrossed in his *tissue* on this cold Saturday morning in late December, wondering which horses to back at today's Doncaster races. In particular he was concentrating on the runners in the one o'clock race, turning the salient facts over in his clever mind, considering the virtues and the weaknesses of the trainers and the jockeys as well as those of the different horses, and carefully weighing the odds.

Vincent was seated at the table in the center of the basement kitchen in the Crowther home at Armley, a tall, Victorian terrace house with two upper floors and huge attics under the eaves. The kitchen, with a big window fronting onto a patch of garden and yard, was a large yet cozy room; eminently inviting, it was comfortably furnished in the manner of a parlor, which was the custom in these parts.

The focal point in the room was the fireplace. This was actually a Yorkshire range, so called because it combined an open fire with an adjoining oven. The range also boasted an arm for supporting a kettle or a stew pot over the fire, and a boiler for heating water. All of these elements were built into the one unit which was about four and a half feet in height and the same in width.

The black iron range was surmounted by a heavy polished wood mantelpiece. On this stood a fancy chiming clock, two brass candlesticks, a tobacco jar, a rack holding Alfred's pipes and a container of spills. The hearth was encircled by a heavy brass fender that was cleaned with Brasso by one of the girls every Friday, and it glittered like gold in the dancing flames of the fire, banked high up the chimney back. Two green-moquette wing chairs flanked the fireplace, faced each other across a large broadloom rug patterned with blood red roses on a deep green background.

In point of fact, roses abounded in this kitchen. They were Eliza's favorite flowers. Pink and white cabbage roses entwined into garlands flowed down the wallpaper to meet scarlet rambler roses scattered all over the green linoleum; rose-patterned white china filled the shelves of a Welsh dresser positioned in a corner; pillows embroidered with yellow rosebuds marched across the dark green leather sofa set against the far wall.

It was a cheerful room with a gay and welcoming ambiance, and it was generally the center of activity, the heart of the family's home life. But this morning it was strangely deserted.

Vincent was alone.

He was glad to have quiet for once, to be able to pursue the serious work of picking out his potential winners in absolute tranquility, without the distracting racket often created by some of his brothers and sisters.

Taking a sip of tea, he continued to peer at the racing newspaper, frowning to himself in his concentration. He had been at this task for almost an hour, and at last he made several selections, wrote down the names of his horses on a scrap of paper, sat staring at the list for a moment. Slowly he nodded his head, satisfied he had made the best choices; then he reached for the packet of Woodbines.

He leaned back in his chair, sat smoking reflectively.

For no reason at all he suddenly thought of the girl. *Again*. She had a way of popping into his head when he least expected. He had met her only once in his life, but when he closed his eyes, he could see her face so clearly, and in such detail, he might have known her forever.

When he had first noticed her standing near the bonfire in the grounds of the Parish Hall, he had instantly and instinctively understood, and without the benefit of knowing her, that she was not the type of young woman whom a man played around with. *She was serious business.*

And since he was not interested in being serious with any girl, or of starting a relationship that would lead to the terrible bondage of marriage, he had fled, rushed to the White Horse for a game of darts and a drink with the lads. But just before ten o'clock he had run all the way back to the hall, hoping to have the last waltz with her.

How shy she had been, so stiff and unbending. Her manner and her attitude had put him off, and he had wandered out of the hall, discouraged and also baffled by her, asking himself why she had bothered to dance with him in the first place. She could have so easily declined his invitation.

But he had been unable to forget her.

Vincent sighed, took a long drag on his cigarette, blew smoke rings up into the air, watched them float away and evaporate as they did. And he decided that thinking about the diminutive Venus de Milo of the bright blue eyes and gorgeous legs was a hopeless waste of time. For one thing, she had apparently evaporated—just like the smoke rings. Ever since bonfire night, he had made a point of popping down to the church dances for a few minutes, looking for her, and he had kept his eyes peeled when he had gone about his business in Armley. He had never once run into her. Furthermore, none of the regulars who attended the church dances every Wednesday and Saturday seemed to know who she was. He had made innumerable inquiries about her for the past two months. The only bit of information he had been able to garner was that her busty blond girlfriend, also nameless it seemed, was a nurse at the Infirmary. Some good that did him. He knew he had about as much chance of ever meeting Blue Eyes again as a snowball in hell.

Perhaps that's just as well, he muttered under his breath. All I need is a *steady* . . . not bloody likely, I don't.

At this moment the front door flew open so unexpectedly and with such force, Vincent sat up with a jerk, looking startled. An icy blast of air blew right through the kitchen, chilling him. It brought with it Laurette and Maggie, two of his three sisters.

They had been to the co-op to do the weekend marketing and each carried two shopping bags filled to overflowing. They were bundled up in navy-blue winter topcoats, green-and-black tartan tam o'shanters and matching long woolen scarves. The cold wind had given them polished-apple cheeks, turned their noses into bright red cherries. Their eyes sparkled and there was such a gaiety and liveliness about them that they brought a delighted smile to his face.

"Hello, Vincent," they chorused, grinning at him.

"Hello, you two beauties," he responded, then exclaimed, "For God's sake, close that door, Maggie."

"Oh, sorry," the twelve-year-old girl said and pushed it with her foot. It banged so hard the frosted-glass panel rattled.

"Watch that glass!" Vincent cautioned and shook his head, mildly exasperated with her.

Maggie mumbled, "Sorry," and followed her elder sister to the counter near the sink, where she deposited her shopping bags of groceries.

Turning to face her brother, starting to unbutton her coat, Laurette said, "It's very quiet in here, Vincent. Where is everybody then?"

"Upstairs. Or out."

"Who's upstairs?" Maggie asked, always inquisitive. Shedding her coat she flung it down on the sofa.

"Hang that up, young lady," Laurette instructed, giving her a sharp look.

Maggie pulled a face but she did as she was told. She pressed, "Who's upstairs then?"

"Our Mam. She's dusting the front rooms. And Jack, who's reading to Danny. Mam says he's got to stay in bed today—because of his bad cold," Vincent explained.

"I knew it! I just knew he wouldn't be any better!" Maggie cried shrilly, rolling her eyes dramatically, showing exaggerated alarm. "I *told* Mam that. He coughed and coughed all night. Poor little Danny, he's always badly. But what can you expect, he's the runt of the litter." She continued to cluck sympathetically like a middle-aged matron of vast experience, then finished in a superior, knowing tone, "Change-of-life babies are often weak in health."

Vincent averted his head, biting down on his laughter. Maggie was a card. None of them ever knew what she would come out with next. His father said she was as old as the hills.

Laurette, however, was not in the least amused, and the look she gave her young sister was stern, disapproving. She thought Maggie was impertinent at times, that the girl saw and heard far too much for her age. But Laurette said nothing. She walked over to the coat closet and put her own things away. Then she took a cup and saucer out of the cupboard above the sink, joined Vincent at the table. She lifted the cozy, felt the pot, poured herself a cup of tea, added milk and sugar.

Vincent watched her all the while, his expression loving. He was concerned about Laurette's well-being at the moment. Just over a year ago she had married their first cousin Jimmy, but it had not worked out. She had come back home to live three months ago, much to his relief. He had believed that particular union to be doomed right from the outset, had never had much time for his cousin, whom he considered to be a bit of a wet rag.

Laurette was a sweet-natured girl, and at twenty-two she was the nearest to Vincent in age. They had always been very close. She was lovely looking with fair, wavy hair, a sensitive face and smokey gray eyes that were enigmatic and soulful. Tall, slender, she had a frame and a build similar to her brother's, but it was young Maggie who truly resembled him with her gypsy-dark hair, widow's peak and large green eyes that were a reflection of his. Olive, the middle sister, was more like Laurette to look at, but she too had dark hair, and she had inherited her mother's pale blue eyes. Olive, who was twenty, had married her childhood sweetheart when she was eighteen, and she and her husband Hal lived near by.

Maggie now joined Vincent and Laurette at the kitchen table.

She stood next to her favorite brother, rested one hand on his shoulder and with the other she slapped a packet of Woodbines down in front of him, along with some loose change.

"Here's your cigs, our Vincent. And don't smoke 'em all at once either. Because I'm not going out again today. Not for nobody, I'm not. Not even you. So there!" Flopping down on the chair next to him, she threw him a challenging look, added, "If you want to know, I'm fed up of being everybody's blinking errand boy!"

He threw back his head and roared. "Aren't you the tough little tiddler this morning. But thanks for getting my cigs, love."

Laurette said, "I can't believe everybody went out . . . on a cruel day like this . . . why, it's blue murder out there, Vincent. Where on earth have they all gone?"

"Dad went to the barber's to get a haircut. Our Frank, the aspiring equestrian, is at Hardcastle's stables, helping to exercise the horses. And the learned Bill took his books back to the library."

"I see." Laurette sipped her tea. There was a short pause. Then she asked, "Olive's not been up this morning, has she?"

"No, not yet."

"Oh, I am glad I haven't missed her. We're supposed to be going to the old-time dancing tonight, and I want to make my arrangements with her." Laurette paused and smiled at her brother as an idea struck her. "Would you like to come with us, Vincent?"

"I would!" Maggie interjected eagerly, swinging her eyes to her sister. "Let me come with you and Olive, Laurette. *Please.*"

"No, you can't, you're too young," Laurette said. "Well, Vincent, what about it?"

He shook his head. "No. Thanks for asking, though."

"But why not?" Laurette demanded. "You'd enjoy it. Come on, say you'll come with us."

He shook his head more vehemently.

Maggie cried, "Oh he doesn't want to go *there,* Laurette! It's too tame. He always goes to the *pub* on Saturday nights. But first he goes down to the Parish Hall and has a look round . . . giving all the girls the once-over, that's what I've heard. I bet that's why he stands in front of that there mirror over there, titivating himself for hours on end. I'm not surprised it drives our dad bats. He's

vain, our Vincent is, and he fancies himself. Anybody would think he's a girl
the way he looks in the glass all the time."

Vincent glared at her. "You're getting to be a right cheeky little bugger,
do you know that, our Maggie?"

Maggie stiffened in her chair, shrieked, "You'd better not let me dad hear
you call me that, our Vincent! Or he'll land you a clout that'll send you right
into the middle of next week!"

"Huh! Fat chance of that!" Vincent shot back.

"Now you two, quieten down," Laurette hushed, scowling at them. She
wagged a finger at Maggie. "You *are* getting too big for your breeches, and so
you'd better watch it from now on. As for you, Vincent, you ought to know
better than to swear at her. Mam doesn't like that either, you know."

"Aye," Vincent muttered, annoyed with himself for permitting the girl to
get his goat in the way that she had.

Maggie, genuinely regretting that she had teased him, leaned across the
table, peered into his handsome face, saw that it was cold and closed. She filled
with chagrin, said softly, "I'm ever so sorry, Vincent, really I am." She reached
out, squeezed his arm. "Let's be friends again. Oh and by the by, you said
you'd give me something, for going for your Woodbines."

"If you're not careful, it'll be a thick ear," he growled.

"Well, I never!" Maggie gasped. "It's the last time I'll do an errand for
you, Vincent Crowther. You don't keep your promises."

For a reason he couldn't explain he began to laugh. His eyes twinkled as
he reached out, rumpled his little sister's hair. Then he pushed a sixpence
toward her. "There you are, love, that's for your money box."

Maggie beamed at him. "Oh no, I'm going to spend it immediately.
Thanks."

Vincent was thoughtful. After lighting a cigarette he murmured in a low
tone, "Don't you think it's about time you settled things with Jimmy, Laurette?
Went to see a solicitor in Leeds . . . about a divorce?"

"Yes, it is, and as a matter of fact, I have an appointment with a solicitor
next Saturday. Jimmy's agreed to everything," Laurette said.

"Dad's going to be ever so pleased to hear *that!*" Maggie announced
before Vincent had a chance to say a word. "He never did think much of that
marriage of yours, Laurette. He says that's how idiots get born . . . first cousins marrying and having babies, I mean."

Laurette gaped at her. She paled and her soft gray eyes suddenly swam. She
stood up unsteadily, rushed over to the door leading to the staircase, yanked it
open. "I think I'll go and help Mam," she whispered in a hoarse voice and flew
up the stairs.

Vincent was furious with Maggie and he turned on her angrily. "Will you
never learn, lass? Your mouth's always open and your foot's always in it, for
Christ's sake!"

"What have I said *wrong* then?" Maggie wailed. "And anyway, our dad
didn't like her marrying Jimmy Wells."

Vincent sprang up, his anger spiraling. He looked down at his youngest
sister in dismay. It took all of his self-control to keep his hands off her. He
wanted to shake her until she rattled. Finally he said, "You know as well as I do
how upset Laurette's been because she didn't get pregnant."

Her defiance fully intact, Maggie declared, "Well, if what Dad says is true, it's a good job she didn't, and that's a fact!"

Vincent lifted his eyes to the ceiling, groaned out loud. "Old wives' tales . . . our Dad's out of date, living in Dick's days." He strode across to the closet, took out his overcoat.

Maggie cried, "Where are you going, Vincent?"

"Anywhere to escape you."

Ten

Vincent saw her through the window of the pet shop.

For a moment he could not believe his eyes.

He stood staring, transfixed. And then he cupped his hands around his face, pressed closer to the glass. Oh yes, it was her all right. As large as life, looking at budgies. Then he noticed the child standing next to her.

Vincent's heart took a dip to his boots.

Was she a married woman? No, that was not possible. She had not been wearing a ring at the dance. And she was certainly too young to have a child as big as the one accompanying her. No, the boy was most likely her brother. And she was probably buying him a budgie, just as he himself had decided to buy his little brother Danny a pet of some sort. That was the reason he had directed his steps toward the shop in the first place.

Well, Vincent thought, standing here isn't going to get me anywhere, so I might as well go inside. His hand went to his tie automatically, and he straightened the knot; then, taking a deep breath, he opened the shop door.

The tinkling of the bell caused the girl to glance over her shoulder. At the sight of him her eyes widened. Seemingly she was as astonished as he had been a moment before.

Vincent smiled at her.

She smiled back, her face dimpling.

He thought her smile was quite the most dazzling he had seen in a long time. Encouraged by her pleasant reaction, he strode across the shop.

She turned around to face him, watched his progress in her direction with quickening interest.

As he drew to a standstill in front of her, Vincent saw the expectant look in her eyes. He took off his hat, stood holding it in his hands. He smiled again, said, "Excuse me . . . I wonder if you remember me?"

"Why yes, of course I do. We had the last waltz at the Parish Hall . . . on Bonfire Night. And I must apologize for not thanking you for asking me to dance that evening. You must have thought me very ungracious."

She was a lady. He stared at her, startled, and momentarily flustered. His voice fled and so did his nerve. Why would a girl of her obvious breeding be interested in the likes of him? he wondered, clutching his hat all that much tighter. A feeling of enormous disappointment trickled through him. *She* was beyond *his* reach. Oh yes, most assuredly she was. And just as she had been tongue-tied at the dance, now it was his turn to be struck dumb, and he felt like a ninny.

There was an awkward silence.

It was the child who broke it. He asked, in a shrill little voice, "What's *your* name?"

The girl exclaimed sharply, but in a low tone, "Now, now, that's most rude of you. Mind your manners, young man."

"It's Vincent Crowther," Vincent said swiftly, grabbing this opportunity. He was surprised that his voice sounded so normal, and this helped to restore his diminished confidence. He glanced down at the boy and grinned at him, thankful for his presence.

The child turned his small bright face up to Vincent's, thrust his hand toward him, announced, "And I'm Theophilus Bell of Calpher House, Upper Armley."

Vincent shook his hand, endeavoring to match the child's enormous solemnity as he said, "I'm very pleased to meet you. And if you don't mind me saying so, that's quite a mouthful of a name you've got, by gum it is, lad."

"It means *beloved of God* in Greek," Theophilus explained, puffing out his little chest importantly. He gave Vincent a shimmering smile and added, "But you can call me Theo for short."

"That's right nice of you. Thanks very much, I will." Raising his head, Vincent now directed his gaze at the young woman. He cleared his throat, and having entirely regained his composure, not to mention his cool cheek, he gave her his most engaging smile, "Well," he said, "you know my name. Can I have the honor of knowing yours?"

"Yes, of course you may, Mr. Crowther. It's Audra Kenton." Her smile was warm, and as friendly as his had been, and she offered him her hand.

Vincent took it in his, was surprised at the firmness of her grip, the strength in her hand as she shook his. Such a small hand it was too, just as she herself was small and delicate. He held onto her hand for longer than was necessary, unable to release it as he gazed into her clear, very bright blue eyes, which reminded him of cornflowers. Unexpectedly, he thought: *I cannot let this woman go. Never. Ever. I want her for the rest of my life.*

He was appalled at his thoughts.

He blinked, finally let go of her hand, glanced away, and he was struck at once by the irrationality of his feelings. The mere idea of marriage was absurd, and to this woman it was positively ludicrous. She was different. Special. A lady. And one who would hardly be interested in *him,* a bricklayer learning his trade. She was obviously a relation of the Bells, who were local gentry, posh folk with pots and pots of brass and lots of clout in the neighborhood. These facts aside, marriage was not part of his present plans; he had a lot of living to do before tying himself to a woman's apron strings. That was a mug's game. Why, he wouldn't even be twenty-five until June.

All of this had flashed through Vincent's head in a matter of seconds, and now he wanted to run out of the shop immediately, to escape before it was too late. But to his own irritation he discovered he could not move. He was rooted to the spot. Suddenly he felt uncomfortable, ill at ease with himself and, therefore, with her, and he began to twist the brim of his trilby in his hands.

Theophilus tugged at Vincent's coat, piped up, *"We're* looking for a budgerigar, Mr. Crowther. What've *you* come to buy?"

Thank God for the boy, Vincent thought. He said, "Well, I don't rightly know, if you want the honest truth." Giving his entire attention to the child, he stooped down, confided, "You see, Theo, I came to get something for my little brother. He's four. But I didn't think to ask him what he'd like before I left the house. So now I'm stuck, sort of. You look like an experienced young man when it comes to pets. Maybe you could make a suggestion or two."

"Mmmm. Let me think a minute." Theo nodded his head sagely, pursed his lips, adopted an expression of great concentration. He swung his observant eyes around the pet shop, leaned into Vincent and said, "It's a bit difficult really, making a proper suggestion, I mean. There's not much to choose from, you see."

Vincent burst out laughing at the boy's blunt words. "You'd better not let Mr. Harrison hear you say that. He thinks he owns the best pet shop in Armley."

"And he does, since it's the only one," Theo replied, grinning, looking inordinately pleased with himself.

"Little boys are meant to be seen and not heard," Audra remarked. But this was the mildest of chastisements. Laughter bubbled up in her throat and her eyes danced. She glanced at Vincent, then shrugged her shoulders. She murmured, "What can you do?"

Vincent said, "He's a right rum 'un, he is that."

Theo's beady black eyes, swiveling between the two of them, settled on Vincent, who obviously fascinated him. He said, "I think you should buy your brother a budgie. At least Mr. Harrison has a big lot of those to choose from. Come on, Mr. Crowther, let me show you." He plucked at Vincent's sleeve. "What's his name? Your brother, I mean."

"Danny." Vincent allowed himself to be led over to the many bird cages which lined one wall of the shop. He and the boy stood regarding them with interest, and after a moment, Vincent said, with some admiration, "I'll say this, Theo, they are beautiful."

Now Audra joined them. Vincent was instantly conscious of her coming to a stop next to him. He was troubled by the emotions she evoked in him, by the strong physical attraction he felt for her. He wanted to take hold of her hand, lead her out of this shop, go with her somewhere so that they could be alone. He wanted to crush her in his arms, to make love to her. His longing stirred within him and he felt the heat rise up into his face and he swallowed hard, tried to concentrate on the birds.

Presently, Audra said, "Theo wants that one over there, on the right, Mr. Crowther. The one in the green cage. What do you think? Do you like it?"

Vincent could only nod.

Theo said, "Audra's buying it for me, Mr. Crowther."

"Aren't you the lucky little lad," he managed to mutter.

"Yes, I am. Go on, Mr. Crowther, pick a budgie for Danny. They're easy to look after. You don't have to walk them like a dog and they don't cost a lot to keep in food. They don't eat much."

"True," Vincent agreed. He was in control again, and he exchanged an amused look with Audra.

Theo pressed on relentlessly, "Now just look at this one! What a pretty bird. I bet Danny would like it. And it's a lovely example of the Australian parakeet . . . greenish yellow body, bright blue on the cheeks and tail feathers, and brown stripes down the wings."

"*Parakeet*," Vincent repeated, sounding baffled. He frowned at Theo. "I thought these were budgies."

"They are. But the budgerigar comes from the parrot family, and there are three hundred and fifteen species of colorful birds in that family," Theo told him proudly, enjoying airing his knowledge. "Lovebirds, lories, cockatoos, cockatiels and macaws, to name a few. I wanted a parrot. I was going to teach it to talk. To say rude words. But you have to be careful when you buy parrots. Because of psittacosis. That's parrot fever, and it's an infectious disease that *people* can catch. It's a bit like pneumonia. Anyway, Mr. Harrison doesn't have any parrots in stock. That's why I'm getting a budgie instead. But one day I *will* own a parrot."

Looking at the child in amazement, shaking his head, Vincent said, "For a little nipper you're certainly a mine of information, Theo. That you are. You sound as if you've swallowed an encyclopedia. *Is* that where you get all of your facts from then?"

"Oh no, I get them from Audra," Theo explained. "She's very clever, you know, and she's taught me a lot since she's been with me. My mother says she's the best nanny I've ever had. If you don't wish to get Danny a budgie, you could buy him one of those canaries over there. *They're* from the finch family." Theo drew Vincent's attention to the other birds, and continued, "They're pretty too, but the best thing about them is that they actually *sing*. I know Danny would like to own a canary. You'd have to teach him to sing, though. The canary, I mean, not Danny."

"Yes, I understand," Vincent said absently. *Nanny,* he repeated to himself. She was the boy's *nanny,* for God's sake, not a posh relative of the Bells after all. She was one of their employees. Of course, that did not alter the facts one iota. Audra Kenton was still a lady. But a lady who worked for a living. Impoverished gentility, he decided.

Perhaps she was not beyond his reach after all. Vincent's hopes soared.

The three of them walked up Town Street together.

Vincent carried the bird cage for Audra. They had bought similar budgerigars in the end, but Vincent had told Joe Harrison to hold his until he returned for it a bit later in the day. And then he had asked Audra if he could escort her and the boy back to Calpher House. She had said yes. Hoisting the bird cage in one hand, he had opened the shop door with the other and ushered her out, grinning from ear to ear, and congratulating himself on his luck this morning.

Now they walked along at a steady pace, side by side and in step, not speaking but comfortable in the silence drifting between them. Theo frisked ahead like a happy little puppy.

Although it was almost noon, the weather was still quite raw, but the wind had died away and it was a shimmering kind of day and crystal clear. The sky, so high and vast above them, was cerulean, cloudless, pristine, and bathed in the silver light of a cold winter sun.

It's turned out to be magnificent, Audra thought, looking about, smiling with pleasure. A tiny burst of joy surged through her, filled her with a lovely inner warmth. A day like this made you realize that anything was possible in life. Anything at all.

Vincent breathed deeply, took a lungful or two of icy air, feeling healthy and robust, as he always did in this type of bright and bracing weather. He stole a surreptitious glance at Audra, thinking how smart she looked in the gray Melton coat and the plum-colored cloche, and then he realized how proud he was to be with her—and to be seen with her in Town Street, the main thoroughfare in Armley and as busy today as it usually was on Saturdays.

Before they reached Calpher House he was going to invite her out, Vincent now decided, even though he was a bit nervous about doing so. If she refused him he would feel like a damned fool; on the other hand, if he didn't ask her he would never know. He wondered where to take her if she did accept. That was a problem. Perhaps he should bring her to their New Year's Eve party tomorrow. No, that wouldn't work. The poor girl would be overwhelmed by his boisterous family. Besides, on their first date he wanted to have her all to himself. He began to wrack his brains for a suitable place to go.

Audra, also lost in her private musings, felt as though she was floating, so buoyed up was she. For two months she had held onto the belief that they would meet again. But when he had walked into the pet shop, she had been completely taken aback. Initially. And then, within minutes, it had all seemed so natural. She knew it was meant to be. The awkwardness she had experienced at the dance was no longer in evidence, and she did not feel in the least shy with him. Quite the contrary, in fact.

He was even more handsome than she remembered and as well dressed as he had been at the dance. He was a charming young man with a pleasant personality, and the way he had behaved with the child had only made her like him all the more. Audra smiled. *Like* was a funny word to use. It hardly described her feelings. She had fallen in love with him in the pet shop.

She looked up at him through the corner of her eye. He was the only man for her. The only man she would ever want.

Vincent glanced down as she was looking up.

Their eyes met and held for a brief moment. He smiled at her lovingly. She smiled back, a little tremulously. A very intimate communication passed between them at this precise moment, and they both caught their breath, staring at each other. And then, fully understanding what had been conveyed without benefit of words, they instantly averted their faces, stared ahead, walked on in silence.

After a short while, Vincent finally spoke. He said, "I hope you don't think I'm being nosy, but how long have you worked for the Bells then?"

"A year," Audra replied. "As a matter of fact, Mr. Crowther, it's exactly one year ago today that I started my job at Calpher House. That's why I bought Theo the bird. As an anniversary gift."

"They should be giving you presents," he said gruffly before he could stop himself. And then for a reason he could not fathom, he experienced a small stab of resentment toward the Bell family.

Audra had caught the odd, disgruntled tone, and she eyed him curiously, for a moment puzzled. But then she smiled at him prettily and said, "They did, Mr. Crowther. At breakfast this morning."

"Well, that's good then, isn't it. I'm glad." He cleared his throat rather loudly and went on, "You don't come from these parts, I can tell that by your voice. You don't speak with a Leeds accent. So where are you from?"

"Ripon's my hometown, and that's where I lived until last year. Have you ever been there, Mr. Crowther?"

"Yes, I have, to the races. It's a lovely spot." His green eyes gleamed with mischief. "And lucky for me, I don't mind telling you. I've always managed to win a bob or two at Ripon races, and there are some nice pubs there too."

Audra nodded. "Yes. And you're from this area, aren't you, Mr. Crowther?"

"Oh aye, I am that. Armley born and bred, that's me. And listen a minute, would you mind calling me Vincent? I keep thinking you're addressing my dad every time you say Mr. Crowther."

Audra laughed. "Of course I will, and you must call me Audra."

"Done," he cried and came to a sudden and abrupt stop. He took hold of her arm and gently broke her stride.

She stared up at him, frowning.

Vincent said, in a rush of words, "Will you go out with me tonight, Audra? I'd like to take you somewhere nice. Maybe into Leeds, to go dancing. Say you will. *Please.*" He flashed her his most winning smile and held her with his eyes.

She said, "I'm afraid I can't. You see I have—"

"You don't have to bother explaining," he cut in sounding huffy and hurt. "I understand." A tinge of pink crept up into his face.

"No, you *don't* understand, Vincent," Audra said firmly. "I was about to say that I'm working tonight. But I would like to go out with you on my next evening off. Really I would."

"Oh," he said, momentarily thrown off balance. He recovered himself instantly, beamed at her. "That's all right then. And when *is* your next night off?"

"This coming Wednesday."

His face fell. "Not till then. Oh dear. Well, never mind. But it'll have to be the church dance that night. How do you feel about going there?"

"I'll enjoy it . . . with you." She offered him a small smile, suddenly feeling shy.

Vincent gave her a long look. "Yes," he said, "So will I, Audra."

They began to walk again.

Within seconds they were at the gates of Calpher House, where Theo stood waiting for them. When they came to a standstill, Vincent turned to Audra and said, "I'll meet you here at the gates on Wednesday, at seven sharp."

"But you don't have to trouble yourself, Vincent. Really. I can find my own way to the Parish Hall."

"*No.* I wouldn't want you walking down there alone."

"Very well then," she said.

He handed her the bird cage.

Theophilus said, "Goodbye, Mr. Crowther. I hope I see you soon. Then you can tell me if Danny liked his budgie."

"I'll do that, Theo. Ta'rar, lad."

Vincent swung to Audra. With a faint smile he raised his hat and was gone.

Audra watched him walk down the hill in long, brisk strides. He turned once, saw her and waved. She waved back. And then she took hold of Theo's hand and led him up the drive, only vaguely listening to the child as he chattered away.

As they drew closer to the house, Audra lifted her eyes and looked at it, thinking of the happy times she had spent here in the past year. And then some deep instinct told her she would not be living at Calpher House for much longer.

Today is the beginning, she thought. The beginning of my life with Vincent Crowther.

He is my destiny. I am his.

They were married five months later.

Some people were astonished; others were not.

The wedding took place at Christ Church in Upper Armley on a sunny June Saturday, a couple of days after Audra's birthday and one week before Vincent would celebrate his.

The bride wore blue. It was a simple yet elegant afternoon dress of crepe de chine, which she had designed herself, cut and sewn with the help of a seamstress from Paris Modes, Mrs. Bell's exclusive gown shop in Leeds. Her cloche was of blue silk swathed in chiffon; her court shoes with Louis heels were of gray suede, as were her elbow-length gloves. She carried a bouquet of pink roses, lily-of-the-valley and stephanotis.

Gwen Thornton was Audra's bridesmaid and Laurette Crowther her matron of honor.

They were dressed in identical frocks of dove-gray crepe georgette overprinted with yellow roses, cloche hats of stitched gray silk, and their posies were of yellow roses.

As they fussed and hovered around her in the entrance hall of Calpher House, Audra thought how truly lovely they looked, both so tall and fair, so young and fresh, and she was proud to have them as her attendants.

Mr. Bell had graciously offered to give her away, and so it was on his arm that Audra walked down the aisle of the beautiful old Anglican church with its Norman architecture and magnificent stained-glass windows.

It was when the organ music swelled and the strains of the hymn "O Perfect Love" reverberated through the high rafters that Audra's throat tightened. Her eyes filled with tears and she ached for her brothers. But knowing she could not permit herself to break down, she took control of herself. She lifted her head higher, looked toward the altar where Vincent was waiting with his brother Frank, who was his best man.

The love illuminating his face, the genuine admiration in his eyes were comforting, reassuring, and she thought how wonderful he looked in his dark blue suit, which was brand-new, the crisp white shirt and silver-gray silk tie.

Within seconds of drawing to a standstill at the altar, Mr. Bell stepped aside. Vincent took his place. His presence and the vicar's kindly expression instantly dispelled the feelings of loneliness she had experienced a second before.

The Reverend Baxter's words seemed to wash over Audra . . . for better or for worse . . . for richer or for poorer . . . in sickness and in health . . . forsaking all others. Of course she forsook all others. How could she ever want anyone but Vincent? The idea was quite unthinkable.

Before she realized it the ceremony was over.

They were married. She was Mrs. Vincent Crowther.

She walked back down the aisle, this time clinging to the arm of her husband as the organist pumped away enthusiastically and Mendelssohn's "Wedding March," joyful, thunderous, filled the church.

She and Vincent lingered on the church steps for only a few minutes, to have their photograph taken, greet his family, friends, the Bells and Matron Lennox, who had traveled over from Ripon for the occasion.

And then, amidst lots of laughter and a deluge of confetti and rice, they dashed to the car waiting at the church gates. Vincent's Uncle Phil drove them to Calpher House, where the champagne wedding breakfast was being given by Mr. and Mrs. Thomas Bell.

Sitting very close to him in the back of the motor car, Audra smiled up at her young husband and then glanced down at the gold band on her finger. She had not thought it possible she could ever be so happy.

Eleven

The moonlight had transformed her into a silver statue.

She stood near the window, motionless, staring out toward the sea, one arm resting on the sill, her body held at an oblique angle, turned inward to the room, her face in profile. It was the white satin nightgown, a mere wisp of a thing, that caught and held the light from the full moon, and in the duskiness of the room it had taken on the sheen and color of pure silver.

There was something ethereal and illusory about her as she stood there unmoving. Unobserved, Vincent regarded her from the doorway, unable to tear his eyes away from her, wanting to prolong this moment, to etch this image of her on his mind and his memory.

She did not seem real to him at all, and it was as if she was part of some dream he had dreamed long ago and was dreaming again. He felt that if he moved or spoke, the scene would shatter and then evaporate, as all dreams did, and that she would be lost to him for all time.

As he gazed at her his longing for her shot through him, and in the same sharp and urgent way that it always did when she was near him. He had never wanted a woman as much as he wanted her. When they had arrived here at the Victoria Hotel in Robin Hood's Bay late on Saturday afternoon, he had been unable to restrain himself. The pent-up emotions, the desire constantly suppressed and held in check for the past five months, had exploded the minute they were alone in the suite. He had taken her to bed at once, before they had even unpacked.

In five days they had hardly left the suite.

He had become the inspired and skillful teacher, enjoying and reveling in this role, she the attentive and ardent pupil, eager, so ready to please. After the first couple of days, she had begun to overcome her modesty and her shyness with him, and now she was very much at ease with him in their lovemaking. She accepted everything and without question, her adoration of him written all over her face. He had been overjoyed to discover that his tender and blushing virgin had a deeply ingrained sensuality, just as he did himself, was thrilled that her ardor was now beginning to match his.

Oh how he loved her, this warm, willing young woman who was his now . . . and forever. His woman. His lover. His wife.

The knowledge that he possessed her in every way was like an aphrodisiac, and just looking at her brought him to searing heat. He fastened his eyes on her slender yet shapely figure, so fully revealed to him through the flimsy texture of the satin that clung to her body in such a provocative way. She was small-boned and finely wrought—but beautifully curvaceous. Her bosom was high, taut under the satin. He could see her nipples standing out sharply.

Heat raged through his loins, and in his groin there was a dull ache. Suddenly he had an enormous erection. He could not remember being as hard as this ever before, not even in the past five days and nights with her, she who charged him up more than any other woman ever had.

He took a step forward. His movement disturbed the air.

She swung her head toward the door, saw him, faintly smiled.

When he reached her side, Vincent took her face in his hands and, tenderly so, looked deeply into her eyes. They were inky black in the dim light. He bent forward, kissed her brow, her eyes, her cheeks and tasted the salt of her tears.

Startled, he drew back, stared at her in bafflement. "Audra, whatever is it, love? Aren't you happy with me?" His erection went down.

"Oh Vincent, yes, I am. Of course I am." She drew closer to him, put her arms around his back, rested her head against his smooth, bare chest. A deep sigh rippled through her.

"Then what is it? Why are you so upset?"

"I'm not upset, truly I'm not." She nestled closer, hoping her body movements would reassure him. She loved this man so very much, with all of her heart and soul and mind. She did not want him to misunderstand her tears.

Slowly, she said, "I was standing here, waiting for you, admiring the beauty of the sea in the moonlight, when all at once I thought of the endless, endless miles of ocean stretching from here to Australia. And quite suddenly I did miss William and Frederick so; it was like a tight pain in my chest, a terrible constriction. I felt very sad, and I longed for them to be here in England. Somewhere. Anywhere. It didn't really matter where, so long as they were under the same sky as me . . . and then I thought of my wedding, and that's when I started to cry. Oh I do wish they'd been there, Vincent, that they had seen us get married." She sighed again, but it was a light sigh and one that was barely audible. "There was a moment in the church, just before the vicar married us, that I felt utterly and completely alone. It was awful."

"Yes, I understand," he murmured gently, stroking her hair, pressing her closer to him. "Of course you missed your brothers, wanted them at your wedding, it's only natural." He kissed the top of her head. "But the instant we were married, you were no longer alone, Audra. And you'll never be alone again. You have me now."

"I know I do, Vincent. And you have me."

"I'll never forget the way you looked on Saturday morning in the church, Audra. Not as long as I live, I won't. You were so bonny in your blue frock. You should always wear blue; it does suit you, love."

He felt her smile against his chest. He knew that her sadness was trickling away, and he was glad of that.

She said, "Vincent . . . tell me again . . . you know, the things you said last night."

He chuckled softly. "I said a lot of things last night. What *things* in particular do you mean?"

"Why you married me."

"Because I love you."

"And why do you love me?"

He laughed, but quietly.

"Tell me," she persisted in a low, whispery voice, and she trailed her fingers across his shoulder blades.

This made him shiver. Instantly he wanted her.

"Because I love the look of you, the sound of you, the touch of your hands. I love the way you feel under my hands. I love every part of you. Oh Audra . . . *love.*" He tilted her head back, kissed her throat, her soft yielding mouth. The blood rushed through him. His desire for her was rampant.

She responded to his kisses ardently. When he moved his lips against hers she opened her mouth slightly so that his warm, loving, probing tongue could enter, rest against hers. His embrace tightened perceptibly, and he kissed her more deeply, passionately, and their teeth grazed.

Audra shifted slightly so that their bodies melded together. Moving closer to him, she felt his hardness against her stomach through the thin fabric of the satin nightgown, and she shivered involuntarily. A fierce and sudden heat began to throb at the core of her, and the shivering intensified as she anticipated what would happen next, thought of the way it felt when he took her to him. The first time they had made love, on their wedding night, she had been apprehensive when she had seen him standing naked before her. But he had loved her with such care and tenderness, and so exquisitely, the pain had only been a few moments of sharp discomfort and now they fitted each other perfectly.

Unexpectedly his kisses ceased.

Stepping back, Vincent slipped the thin straps of her nightgown over her shoulders, pulled it down past her breasts. It slithered to the floor unaided, lay like a gleaming pool at her feet.

Again Vincent gazed deeply into Audra's eyes, his love for her spilling out. He lifted his hand, stroked her cheek. After a long moment he dropped his eyes and kneeling down in front of her, he rested his head against her stomach and his arms went around her. Pressing his hands into the small of her back, he slowly smoothed them over her buttocks, moved her body slightly, adjusted her stance to suit him.

She trembled under his touch, and her desire for him swept through her. Her blood raced, her heart beat rapidly and her skin tingled in anticipation. Reaching out, she stroked his hair, then let her hands fall onto his shoulders, where they rested.

Covering her stomach with light, fluttering kisses, he continued to stroke her back, her buttocks and her thighs. Then he leaned away from her ever so slightly, rested on his heels, brought his hands around onto her stomach, still smoothing and stroking her skin. Finally, his hands came to a stop in the soft silky coils of fair hair that covered the mound between her legs. Slowly, with infinite care, he parted the tender petals, touched the tiny folds of warm, moist skin that protected her womanhood.

He kissed her navel and her stomach. They were long, slow, lingering kisses, and all the while his hands played amongst the musky folds, touching and seeking. At last he brought his tongue to join the quest. He began to nuzzle her, kiss her, and as he did he heard the soft moans in her throat. She gripped his shoulders, straining toward him, and he brought her to the edge of ecstacy.

He stopped abruptly, pulled away from her.

She caught her breath. Her eyes flew open. She gaped at him.

He took hold of her wrist quickly, firmly, pulled her down onto the floor with him. Impatiently, he kicked off his pajama bottoms, stretched out next to her on the carpet, wrapped his body around hers, held her close to him. Wanting to possess her though he was, he wished to prolong their loving for a short while.

Lifting himself up on one elbow, he glanced down. Their eyes locked in a gaze so filled with passion, so intense, so searching in its depth of feeling it seemed to sear them both. Vincent thought he was seeing into her very soul. Her face overflowed with her abiding love for him and her yearning. And looking into those clear green eyes, Audra saw the burning desire in them and the wonderment and the glitter of bright tears, and her heart clenched and she reached up to touch his face.

It was Vincent who finally broke the contact. He found it unbearable, suddenly, to look at her in this manner, so moved was he by her and so choked up with feeling.

Now his glance swept over her body stretched out before him.

How translucent she looked in the moonlight streaming in through the open window. She resembled a piece of perfectly sculpted marble, except that no cold stone was she. She was warm and desirable flesh and blood. How lovely her breasts were, pearly tinted, rounded and smooth, and her nipples were upright and hard like little bursting May buds, deep rose in color.

"Oh Audra," he breathed. "My Audra. You're so beautiful."

She half smiled, lifted her hand, smoothed one finger along his lips, then traced an outline around his mouth in the shape of a bow.

He caught hold of her hand, kissed the palm, then bent over her, brought his mouth to the cleft between her breasts and kissed her, enjoying the fragrant smell of her young sweet skin. Presently, he cupped his hand around her breast, began to fondle the nipple. It sprang up, grew more taut and erect than ever under his caressing fingers. Audra let out a little gasp of joy as his mouth came down on her other breast.

She cleaved to him, ran her hands over his back, then up onto his neck, and she twined her fingers in his crisp dark hair.

"Oh Vincent, Vincent, I love you so much," she whispered hoarsely.

On hearing his name, this endearment, he pulled away from her, moved rapidly. He braced himself above her on his hands.

There was no reason to wait now. He could not wait.

He took her urgently, needing to be joined to her, needing to make them as one. He shafted deeper and deeper, luxuriating in her total embrace, one that enfolded him in warmth and love and made him feel complete in a way that he had never felt except with her.

Oh yes, how he did love her . . . this lovely girl he held in his arms . . . his beautiful wife. She was his. They were made for each other, belonged together. And oh how he fitted into her so well.

Slipping his hands under her body, he lifted her closer to him, clasping her tightly, plunging in and out. And she thrust herself up to meet his long and thrusting strokes. Her arms clung to him, and she matched his fervent loving with an urgency of her own.

He cried out in his rapture, called her name over and over, all the time clutching her to him as though never to let her go. He knew he could not control himself much longer, that he was on the verge of exploding. He thought he might be blacking out. He seemed to be pitching forward from a great height . . . falling, falling, falling.

"Oh, I'm ready," he gasped against her burning cheek. "Oh Audra. Take all of me. *Now.*"

"Oh Vincent!"

She arched her body toward his in the way he liked, meeting his passion, accepting it with love, offering him her passion in return, showing no restraint.

Wave upon wave of pure joy washed over her, and she thought she was drowning in her pleasure and his. Suddenly she was gripped by an uncontrollable trembling, and she crested upon the soaring waves, and as she did she felt an immense shuddering pass through him, and they were united in their shattering release. And then he fell against her, lay exhausted in her arms, and she stroked his hair, rested her head on his, feeling exhausted too and overwhelmed by her emotions.

Eventually Vincent roused himself. "I'm too heavy," he murmured against her throat.

"No, it's all right. Anyway, I like to feel the weight of you on me," she whispered. Then she shook her head. "Why on earth am I whispering?" she wondered out loud, speaking in her normal voice.

"I've no idea. And God knows why we're lying here on the floor." He began to chuckle.

"What's so amusing?"

"I am, love. For months and months all I could think about was making love to you in a nice comfy bed, and now that we have one in the very next room I ignore it, choose the floor instead. Can you beat that!" He pushed himself up on one elbow, moved a strand of hair away from her face. "Anyway, it's all your fault."

"Why?"

"Because you're a little temptress, that's why. There you were, standing by the window in the moonlight and my heart did somersaults. I couldn't resist you. I had to have you. Right here on the floor, no less." He chuckled again. "There's no two ways about it, you do get me going, make me feel hot, love."

Audra made no response, glanced away.

Vincent sensed her sudden shyness, her embarrassment.

That was the curious thing about her . . . she was a mass of contradictions, he had discovered. From the moment he had made her his on the first night of their honeymoon, she had been a generous and giving partner, questioning nothing, doing as he wished. Yet in the aftermath of their lovemaking, she never wanted to discuss the pleasure they had just shared; nor did she like it when he made mention of it. He had noticed that she invariably fell into an extraordinary reticence. A veil went down, shutting him out. He supposed her attitude sprang from her upbringing, her breeding. It was all right to do it, but not to talk about doing it, when you were a lady. Well, no matter. Such things were not really very important in the long run. She was his and he did love her so.

Pushing himself up off the floor, Vincent gave Audra his hand, hoisted her to her feet. After smothering her in a huge bear hug, he found her nightgown for her, slipped it on over her head, then pulled on his pajamas.

"I don't know about you, but I'm famished all of a sudden. Let's have a picnic on that bowl of fruit." As he spoke, he went over to the table and picked it up.

"What a good idea," Audra agreed. "I'm a bit hungry myself."

Wrapping his other arm around her, Vincent walked her into the bedroom. They installed themselves in the middle of the large double bed, where they sat cross-legged, munching on big red juicy apples. A minute or two later, Vincent returned to the adjoining sitting room and retrieved the half-finished bottle of wine he had ordered from room service with their dinner. He carried it back to the bedroom with two glasses, which he filled. Handing one to Audra, he joined her on the bed once more.

After propping a pillow behind his back, making himself comfortable, he lit a cigarette, said, "Tell me some more about High Cleugh, about when you were little."

"Goodness, you are insatiable, and my past is not especially interesting," she replied with a light laugh. "Besides, it's your turn."

He made a face. "There's not much left to tell . . . you know all about my boyish adventures with my friend Redvers Buller." He winked at her. "I can't believe you want to hear about them again, and the scrapes we got into, the canings we got from the headmaster. It's boring stuff."

"But you're such a good raconteur, Vincent."

"Well, I don't know about that, love." He drew on his Woodbine, blew a smoke ring, flashed her one of his cheeky boyish grins. His dancing green eyes glistened as he leaned forward, pinned them on her. He cajoled, "Go on, Audra, let's hear about your mother and your Uncle Peter . . . the Beautiful Edith Kenton and the dashing army captain. I must admit, the two of them intrigue me."

"Aha, you're a true romantic, Vincent Crowther."

"I am?" He sounded doubtful.

"Yes." Audra smiled. "I could tell you about the mystery of my mother's vanishing sapphires, if you like?"

"Your eyes are like sapphires, do you know that?" He gave her a soulful look and blew her a kiss.

"Do you want to hear this story or not?"

"Yes."

As she began to speak he settled back, sipped his wine, listening to her attentively. Vincent was as fascinated and as impressed by Audra's background and family as he was enamored of her. And so not unnaturally he loved hearing about her childhood, and in particular he loved the sound of her melodious voice as she spoke of those days with such love.

Twelve

"Close your eyes," Audra said, "and keep them closed until I tell you to open them."

"Okay," Vincent said, promptly doing as he was told.

Audra looked up at him adoringly. Her happiness knew no bounds today. She reached for her husband's hand, drew him across the grass, saying, "It's all right, there's nothing in your way, just step out as you normally would."

"That's what I *am* doing."

Audra smiled. "It's just a few more steps," she said, guiding him forward. She gripped his hand a little tighter as she told him, "Turn your head toward me, to the left a bit more."

Vincent did as she instructed.

"Now!" Audra exclaimed.

He lifted his lids, blinked for a second or two in the bright morning sunlight, then brought his hand up to shade his eyes. He squinted slightly against the brilliance, trying to focus.

"Look, over there, near the trees . . . in that dell," Audra was saying.

He followed the direction of her outstretched arm. His breath caught in his throat. *"That's* High Cleugh," he said in the strangest of voices, and stared in astonishment at the old manor house.

"Yes." Audra glanced up at him, frowning in concern. "You sound so surprised. Are you disappointed? Don't you think it's as beautiful as I made it sound, as I described it?"

"Oh, I do, I do," he was quick to reassure her. "But it's so big, Audra, and it looks ever so grand. I'd no idea. I mean I just never imagined it was that kind of house, you know, a *mansion.*" He was unable to disguise the awe in his voice. It was obvious he was impressed.

Audra squeezed his fingers. "It looks a lot larger than it actually is, Vincent."

"Maybe so, but it's bigger than anything I've ever been used to, lass. And those gardens, Audra. Why they fair take my breath away, they do that."

Audra beamed at him. "My mother planned and planted them, and those are her delphiniums down near the edge of the river. Whenever I see delphiniums, I always think of her and of High Cleugh."

"I can certainly understand why, love."

"If you look down the river a little bit, over there to your right, you'll see the stepping stones I told you about. That's where we used to cross the river to come up here for our picnics . . . to the Memory Place. Of course, it wasn't called that then. I only gave it that name afterward—" She broke off, glanced away, and there was a hint of sadness in her voice as she finished, "You know, after *they* died, and after my brothers were sent away from me."

"Yes," he said, putting his arm around her shoulder comfortingly.

She looked up into his face, gave him a small smile.

He smiled back, all the while scrutinizing her closely, hoping that coming here had not upset her unduly. Days ago, when he had asked her to show him High Cleugh on their way back to Leeds from Robin Hood's Bay, he had not stopped to think that this might stir up memories that would make her sorrowful. After all, she had agreed so readily, even eagerly. But now Vincent could not help wondering if his forcefulness had been misplaced; perhaps he had been thoughtless. Her vivid cornflower eyes looked suspiciously moist to him.

Vincent cleared his throat. "Are you sure you want to have our picnic here, Audra love?"

"That's what I'd thought. It's so pretty, and there's such a lovely view for miles around. Don't you want to stay?" she asked, sounding worried, as always wishing to please him.

"Yes. Anything you say is all right by me."

Leaning forward, he kissed her cheek, then strode over to the sycamore tree. A few minutes before, he had deposited two brown-paper shopping bags under the spreading branches; he carried these back to the top of the slope above the River Ure, where Audra had remained standing. Taking a large tartan blanket out of one of them, he shook it out, spread it at her feet.

And then, with a great flourish, he did a sweeping bow in front of her, bending low in the manner of an old-fashioned cavalier.

"My cloak for your comfort, m'lady, and pray do be seated so that we can partake of our repast," he said, adopting an exaggerated upper-class accent.

Laughing vivaciously, her eyes sparkling with delight, Audra offered him a small curtsy in return, "Why, Sir Galahad, my grateful thanks indeed." She lowered herself onto the car rug with her usual grace of movement.

Joining in her laughter, Vincent flopped down next to her and remarked, "I must say, it was nice of the hall porter at the Victoria Hotel to arrange this food for us, wasn't it?" As he spoke, he began to take small packages out of the other shopping bag.

"Yes, most kind," Audra agreed, helping him in his task. "Oh look, the hotel chef put in some lovely Scotch eggs," she exclaimed, unwrapping the grease-proof paper, showing him the hard-boiled eggs encased in sausage meat.

Vincent eyed them. "Well, they look as tasty as anything me mam could make," he said, his mouth watering. "And I've just come across a little bag of pickled onions and a slab of fine Wensleydale cheese." He flashed her a huge grin. "We might as well dig in, Audra. Oh and here's your bottle of milk, pet."

"Thank you, Vincent."

They were both hungry after their long drive from Robin Hood's Bay on the East Coast, across the sprawling North Yorkshire Moors and down to Ripon. And so they said very little as they munched on the delicious tidbits in the picnic lunch which had been provided by the hotel.

It was an exceptional June day.

The sky was bright blue and filled with sunshine. The lightest of balmy breezes rustled through the trees, but there were no other sounds except for the faint gurgle of running water, the occasional trilling of the wild birds and the rushing and fluttering of their wings as they flew up into the sparkling summer air.

Neither Audra nor Vincent ever minded these silences which frequently fell between them. In fact, they found them companionable, enjoyed them as much as everything else they did together. They were content to simply be in each other's company, knowing that they did not always have the need to make forced conversation. There was an ease between them; it had been thus since the beginning of their relationship in January.

Audra studied him surreptitiously.

It was the twelfth of June, and he was twenty-five today. But he looked much younger to her. Perhaps this was because of his fresh complexion, the tan he had acquired in the last few days. Although they had been ensconced in the hotel suite for a good part of their honeymoon, the time they had spent out-doors had been put to good use. They had walked a lot, and when she had ventured up onto the precipitous cliffs to paint watercolors of Robin Hood's Bay from that vantage point, he had insisted on accompanying her. He had read his newspaper, studied his racing form and then stretched out next to her, sunning himself.

Suddenly Audra wondered what Vincent would say if she told him that she had not enjoyed her wedding day very much. In point of fact, she would not have enjoyed it at all if he had not been present. Audra laughed under her breath at the ridiculousness of this thought. Obviously, without Vincent Crowther there would have been no marriage in the first place.

He had enjoyed his wedding, though. All aspects of it, too. Smiling, laughing, shaking hands, he had been comfortable with everyone. So much so, she had been struck quite strongly by his carefree manner. He was positively nonchalant; he might have been the lord of the manor at Calpher House. Not that his behavior had been offensive to the Bells or anyone else—only enviable, as far as she was concerned. For she had experienced great unease most of the time, although she had endeavored to hide this behind a gracious demeanor, a bright smile carefully glued into place.

From the outset, she had sensed strange undercurrents at the reception. Vincent had been unaware of them.

To begin with, there had been a certain awkwardness between the Thorntons and the Crowthers, and she had watched this develop into veiled antipathy within the first hour. Her internal discomfort had spiraled into distress, and she had found herself growing quieter and quieter with everyone; Vincent, full of bonhomie, had simply grown more expansive.

At one moment, she had gone into the Bells' elegant dining room looking for Vincent. Here Mr. Agiter, Cora and Dodie had been serving the breakfast buffet, a wonderful selection of good Yorkshire fare and other tempting delicacies from Mrs. Jackson's well-stocked larder. Instantly, she had noticed Gwen and Charlie huddled in one corner, heads together, looking conspiratorial. Just as she was about to turn away, she had observed them fasten their eyes on Vincent, who was on the far side of the room talking to Irène Bell. They had stared at him, daggers drawn.

If looks could kill, he'd drop dead this very minute, Audra had thought, and gooseflesh had sprung up on her arms. Averting her face, she had hurried over to join her husband, had taken hold of his arm almost protectively.

After chatting with Mrs. Bell for a moment or two, she had then excused them both to her former employer, explaining that she wanted Vincent to become better acquainted with Matron Lennox. Still holding onto his arm, she had led him out into the hall. She had felt sick inside. And dreadfully hurt.

She had been relieved, even glad, to leave for their honeymoon as soon as it was possible to do so politely, without giving offense to the Bells. They had been exceedingly generous, and she did not wish them to think she was unappreciative. Naturally, Vincent had wanted to stay longer, he being the social animal that he was.

Audra shifted slightly on the tartan rug, stretched out her legs in front of her and reached for a piece of the Wensleydale cheese, nibbling on it absently, trying to dismiss thoughts of Gwen. She found she could not.

Her best friend disliked her husband.

That was the sad truth, and it troubled Audra a great deal. Unfortunately, Gwen had taken a dislike to Vincent months before she had actually met him— her words on Bonfire Night still echoed in Audra's ears. It was all because of Charlie, of course. Gwen had condemned Vincent without bothering to get to know him, simply because he had been chosen instead of her brother.

How immature Gwen is being, Audra thought. She was disappointed in Gwen; she had certainly expected better of her friend. Having cherished their friendship from the day it had commenced, she was upset that it was threatened. But it was Gwen, not she, who was putting it in jeopardy. She loved Gwen; she did not want to lose her. But she also loved her husband. If she and Gwen were going to continue to see each other, Gwen would have to be more amiable with Vincent. He came first now. And Vincent, being oblivious to the girl's dislike, was always friendly and cordial to her. In Audra's opinion, he should have received better treatment from her old friend.

Swallowing a sigh, Audra leaned back on her elbows, thinking hard. She must find a way to show her how unfair she was being. Audra did not want Gwen to be a casualty of her marriage. She was going to talk to her about this as soon as possible. I shall have to be diplomatic, Audra thought, and immediately began to rehearse what she would say.

For his part, Vincent was ruminating on High Cleugh.

Ever since they had arrived on the slope, he had been stealing glances at it. The old house was now in his direct line of vision across the river, and he felt a compulsion to bring his gaze back to it time and again. And as he did, he could not help thinking of the little cottage he and Audra had found in Upper Armley and which they had rented a month ago.

When they had stumbled on it, quite by accident one day, he had considered them most fortunate. The cottage was sturdy, in good repair, and in a location convenient to his work. But suddenly it had lost its appeal. How small and insignificant it was in comparison to High Cleugh, where his wife had been born and brought up. What he was offering her was so much less.

Swiveling his head, he gazed at her appraisingly and with a flash of unprecedented objectivity. How pretty she was in her buttercup-yellow dress, fresh and desirable in every conceivable way. And she had so many laudable attributes. He was convinced she was going to make him the very best wife. Although he was never given to much introspection, Vincent sank down into his thoughts, contemplating Audra.

If the circumstances of her life had been different, she would never have been permitted to marry him.

This unanticipated thought shook Vincent to the core. The fact that *her* family would have objected to her marrying *him* had never occurred to him before, but now that it had, he knew he was absolutely correct in this assumption, and this knowledge depressed him. He suddenly remembered his mother's dire words. "Asking for trouble, that's what you are, my lad," she had said. "If you marry her, you'll rue the day." Laurette had been against their marriage too, even though she liked Audra a lot. "You're from two different worlds," his sister had said when he had challenged her about her views. "It's not going to work. She's a lady born and bred."

In an effort to convince Laurette that this did not matter, he had told her about Audra's hard life as a ward maid, the drudgery of her demanding work as a nurse at the Fever Hospital. She had gaped at him, incredulous. "Don't be such a fool, Vincent. What's that got to do with anything! Her breeding and her gentility will always be part of her. She's different from you and me, from *us,* and believe me, that *difference* makes a big difference."

Always quick to flare up at the slightest thing, he had flown into a temper and stormed out, bristling with anger. And he had been put out with his favorite sister for weeks. Vincent had a strong mind of his own, and so he had gone about his business, done as he had seen fit. And he had seen fit to marry Audra despite the opposition from his family, which she knew nothing about.

Vincent was still convinced that his mother and his sister were wrong. Surely it was of no great consequence that he and Audra were from different backgrounds. They loved each other. That was all that counted, wasn't it?

Audra, her eyes on Vincent, sensed a change in him. She said, "Are you all right? You look a bit funny."

"Oh I'm fine, love," he said, then laughed somewhat shakily.

"You looked quite troubled a moment ago. Are you sure nothing's bothering you, Vincent?"

He forced a bright smile. "Never felt better," he exclaimed and thought to add, "I'm sorry that this is the last day of our honeymoon, that it's over."

"Not quite." She kissed his cheek, gazed into his face, loving him with her eyes. "We've still got the whole of today and this evening in Harrogate. We'll have a lovely dinner for your birthday at the White Swan. It's a pretty hotel; you'll enjoy staying there."

Audra sat back, tipped her head to one side, went on, "Even though our honeymoon will come to an end tomorrow, our life together is only just beginning, Vincent. Think about that . . . and I know we're going to have a wonderful life, you and I."

"Yes," he said, relaxing.

Audra suddenly grew animated and talkative, and there was a new vivacity about her as they finished their picnic. She spoke to Vincent at length about their future and was full of enthusiasm for all the good things she believed it held in store for them.

Thirteen

"Do you see anything that belongs to you, Audra?" Vincent asked, swinging his alert green gaze around the drawing room of The Grange.

"Those two oil paintings on either side of the French windows and the watercolor on that side wall," she said, "they're by my father. If you look at them closely, you'll find they're signed 'Adrian Kenton.'"

Vincent strode across the floor, peered at the two beautiful landscapes and then at the still life, and nodded his head. He pivoted to face Audra, who hovered near the fireplace. "What else is yours?"

"Most of the wood pieces in here . . . the inlaid chest next to the door, these two small Sheraton tables, and the console over there—oh, and the Meissen clock on it. There are two Chippendale-style chairs, but those must be in another room. She also has my mother's Georgian silver tea service, some smaller pieces of silver and three more paintings, but only one of those is by my father." A confident smile struck Audra's mouth and she patted her handbag. "I have my inventory in here, and the one for the jewelry, so I'm well armed—" Audra stopped, focused on the door as it opened.

Vincent did the same. He was riddled with curiosity about the woman he was going to meet. He had heard a few things about her from Audra, and he did not like what he had heard.

Alicia Drummond paused on the threshold.

Vincent, observing the middle-aged woman with quickening interest, thought: *Narrow*. Everything about her is narrow. Eyes, nose, mouth, face and body. He did not even question that she was narrow-minded as well; he had already surmised *that* from Audra's comments about her.

Audra, who had not seen her relative for almost six years, was startled. She decided that Alicia Drummond had not only aged considerably in this time, but looked as if she were ill. The woman was drawn, haggard even, and excessively thin, and her stony black eyes were sunken into their sockets. Wispy gray hair was pulled back into a bun, and she wore a drab brown silk dress that was unbecoming.

Closing the door behind her, Alicia walked into the room with her usual sedate stiffness. She said fretfully, in her high-pitched voice, "Hello, Audra. When you wrote to me two weeks ago, you didn't say you'd be bringing someone with you. I expected you to be alone. I was surprised when the maid told me you were accompanied by—" She surveyed Vincent, her eyes filling with curiosity and speculation, and finished, "Your young man." It came out sounding more like a question than a statement of fact.

Audra said briskly, "Good afternoon, Aunt Alicia. I would like to introduce my husband to you. This is Vincent Crowther. Vincent, this is my mother's first cousin, Alicia Drummond."

Alicia, rarely at a loss for words, was momentarily speechless. *Husband,* she thought, utterly amazed. This smartly dressed, good-looking young man was married to plain, little Audra. It hardly seemed possible.

Stepping forward, Vincent thrust out his hand. "Pleased to meet you, Mrs. Drummond."

"How do you do," Alicia responded, her cold eyes weighing him up. Vincent spoke nicely, and there was only the merest trace of the broad Yorkshire accent in his vowels, but Alicia caught it. Working class, more than likely, she commented to herself. Well, that explained everything.

Waving a hand airily, in the direction of the sofa, Alicia murmured, "Do sit down, both of you." She herself perched on the edge of a chair and gave her attention to Audra. "Why didn't you let us know you were getting married?"

Ignoring the question, which she considered to be ridiculous under the circumstances, Audra said, "We spent our honeymoon at Robin Hood's Bay, and as I knew we'd be passing close by on our return to Leeds, I thought it would be a good idea to come and see you. I wanted Vincent to meet you, since—"

"I'm glad you did."

"Since he'll be coming back next Saturday. With a van, to—"

"*A van.*" Alicia sounded perplexed.

"Yes. He'll be coming to collect my things."

"*Things?*"

"Yes, my things, Aunt Alicia. Or perhaps I should say my mother's things, which have belonged to me since her death and which you have been . . . *storing* here."

"Gracious me, Audra, don't tell me you're planning to go to the expense of hiring a van to come all this way—from Leeds, you say?—to pick up a few odd bits of valueless furniture."

"Valueless," Audra echoed, giving her a sharp stare. "I wouldn't say that."

"Oh I would. They're not worth much."

"Whatever they're worth I want them. I wish to have my mother's things around me. Besides, they belong to me—and have for a long time."

"It seems to me that a couple of old tables hardly merit such enormous effort," Alicia scoffed. Adopting a scornful expression, she swung to Vincent. "Imagine hiring a van to come and pick up a few sticks of furniture. Audra is being ridiculous, in my opinion. What a waste of money. I'm sure you agree."

"Audra wants her things," Vincent said quietly but with great firmness. "And anything Audra wants I'm going to make sure she gets."

"Quite," Alicia sniffed, looking down her nose at him.

"There's the matter of the jewelry, Aunt Alicia. I will take that with me today," Audra announced.

Alicia opened her mouth, immediately closed it, conscious of the grim determination glittering in Audra's eyes, the implacable curve of her mouth. "I'm not sure the jewelry is here," she improvised. "If I remember correctly, my mother took it to her house for safekeeping."

"You're not *sure,*" Audra repeated. Her expression hardened. "I would think you'd be scrupulously careful with other people's possessions. I'm also rather surprised you didn't get in touch with me yourself weeks ago. You knew I'd be twenty-one at the beginning of this month, that I was coming of age and was therefore legally entitled to what's mine." Audra's laugh was soft but knowing. "Actually, there was no good reason why I shouldn't have had my mother's things years ago. My—"

"You weren't married years ago," Alicia cut in, sounding defensive. "What would you have done with the furniture? Where would you have put it?"

"I'm talking about my mother's jewelry," Audra exclaimed. "And I was about to say that my former employer, Mrs. Irène Bell, said exactly the same thing only a couple of weeks ago. Both she and Mr. Bell were amazed you hadn't been in touch with me early in May, to find out what I wanted to do about my possessions. Mr. Bell's a solicitor, extremely well known in Leeds, and he's very conscious of legalities, all that sort of thing." Audra let her narrowed blue gaze linger on the other woman pointedly.

Alicia flushed, grew uncomfortable under this fixed and probing scrutiny. Ever since she had received Audra's letter, she had been put out. She was reluctant to relinquish the girl's valuables and had been scheming to keep them. But now Alicia was reconsidering her moves. She had no desire to become entangled with a solicitor, or with this husband, who looked as if he could turn difficult at the slightest provocation. Striving to hide her irritation, Alicia stood up. Clearing her throat, she muttered, "There is the possibility that my mother spoke about removing the jewelry to her house, to look after it for you, but that she never got around to doing so. My memory's not what it used to be, I'm afraid. It could still be here. Perhaps I had better go upstairs and check."

"Yes, that would be wise," Audra said.

Alicia hurried out, cursing Audra under her breath. She had not bargained for solicitors and husbands. The girl had caught her off guard.

The minute they were alone, Vincent said in a quiet voice, "She's a right crafty devil, that one."

"I know, and she's trying to steal my things," Audra murmured, also keeping her voice low.

"Don't worry, I won't let her. Anyway, I bet she's afraid you'll bring Mr.

Bell down on her if she does anything wrong. I noticed the way her face changed when you mentioned he was a noted Leeds solicitor."

Audra sat back on the sofa, glanced around, disliking this room as much as she disliked the entire house and those who lived in it. She thought of the cruel things Alicia Drummond had done to her in the past, and a coldness settled over her heart like a hoarfrost. Unexpectedly, an image of her brothers saying goodbye to her as they set out for Australia leapt into her mind and with such vividness she stiffened. Then that awful sense of loss gripped her. She snapped her eyes shut, wondering if she would ever be free of this distressing feeling. Surely she would. After all, she was no longer alone. She had Vincent. He was her family now. Opening her eyes, she swung her head to look at him.

He met her gaze, noticed the bright blueness of her eyes dulling as a sadness crept into them. He squeezed her hand, said, "This place upsets you and it gives me the willies. Let's scram as soon as you've finished your business with the old battle-ax."

Audra nodded.

The two of them sat together on the sofa in silence, holding hands, waiting.

It was not very long before Alicia Drummond returned, carrying the wooden jewelry box. She brought it straight to Audra, thrust it at her with forcefulness and in rather a rude manner. "Here it is," she snapped. "No doubt you want to check, to make sure nothing is missing. And quite frankly, I would prefer you to do so. I don't want to be accused of misappropriating your property—at a later date."

There was no response from Audra.

She sat staring down at the box on her lap. How familiar it was. It had always stood on the dresser in her mother's bedroom at High Cleugh. Sometimes, when she had been a child and playing at dressing up in her mother's clothes, she had been allowed to dip into it, to take out a pin or a brooch or a pendant to wear for a while.

After a moment, she raised the lid, filling with relief now that she had these most personal things of her mother's in her hands at last. She began to sort through the items in the box, fingering each one lovingly. She thought of her mother's elegance and grace, smiled to herself as innumerable memories flooded her, touched off as they were by the different pieces.

She picked up her mother's engagement ring set with three tiny diamonds and gazed at it. My mother wore this for most of her life, Audra thought, and now I shall wear it. She slipped it on the third finger of her right hand, and as she did she experienced a sense of deep satisfaction. She felt as though the ring brought her mother closer; it was like a link to the past. And this pleased her.

Audra had no need to refer to the inventory, since she knew it by heart. The jewelry was intact. Nothing had been taken. And whether or not Alicia Drummond had been wearing it all these years was suddenly beside the point. The box and its contents were now hers, and rightfully so, and this was the only thing of any importance.

Placing the box on the sofa between her and Vincent, Audra opened her handbag and took out the other inventory. Directing her gaze at Alicia, she said, "This is the list of my mother's furniture and silver and paintings which are in this house. I'll leave it for you to look over later. Vincent will come back with two of his brothers next Saturday morning to collect everything. At about ten o'clock. I hope that's convenient?"

Mortified, Alicia could only nod.

Audra placed the piece of paper on one of the Sheraton occasional tables, and went on, "In the meantime, I thought we could take my father's paintings with us today. We have the motor car and they'll fit nicely in the back."

Wanting to be finished with the business and to get Audra away from this depressing house, Vincent sprang up, interjected, "I'd better start taking them off the walls." He glanced at Alicia, explained, "I know which pictures were painted by Audra's father; she already pointed them out to me."

Alicia Drummond thought she had turned to stone.

She could neither speak nor move. She simply gaped at Vincent, watched transfixed as he removed one of the oils, leaned it against a chair, then walked over to the other one, reached his hands up for it.

It was then that something cracked in Alicia Drummond. Years of rigid self-control fell away. "Don't touch my painting! Don't you dare touch it!" she cried, leaping up, rushing across the room, all semblance of dignity evaporating. She grabbed Vincent's arm roughly, peered into his face, shouted with mounting rage, "Don't you dare touch any of my paintings!"

He was flabbergasted at her words and her behavior. He shrugged off her hand, stepped back, swiveled his eyes to Audra on the sofa. They exchanged looks of astonishment.

Audra was on her feet swiftly and hurried across the floor. "They're not your paintings, Aunt Alicia. They're mine," she said in a firm but reasonable voice. She wondered if the woman had lost her senses. "Unless you've forgotten, my father painted them. And they always hung at High Cleugh. They are part of my legacy from my father, and my mother, and I—"

"Your mother!" Alicia screamed, whirling on her. "Don't you mention your mother to me. She was nothing but a whore!"

Audra gasped, recoiled.

Vincent could not believe he had heard correctly.

"Here, watch it," he exclaimed. "Don't you talk like that to my wife. I won't stand for it." He drew closer to Audra, slipped his arm around her and glared at Alicia. "Where do you get off, calling Audra's mother such a terrible thing?"

"Don't you like the word *whore?* Then pick any name you prefer . . . trollop, slut, harlot, strumpet! They all fit her. Because that's what she *was*. She took him away from me, she stole my darling Adrian." Alicia's shrill voice now turned into a wail. Near tears, she rushed on, "He belonged to me. We had an understanding. We were to be married. Until she set her cap at him, turned his head, inveigled him into her bed with her wiles and her fancy ways." The words choked in her throat. Alicia began to take gasping breaths, holding her hand to her chest as if in pain.

Audra was so appalled, so sickened by what she had heard, she could only stare at her relative in horror. "So that's what it's been about all these years," she said finally, shaking her head in disbelief. *"Oh my God!* My brothers and I were punished merely because you were *jealous*. How despicable, to tear us apart when we were children just because of something as futile as that. And when my parents were already dead, when the past no longer mattered. You are a foul woman, Alicia Drummond, foul. As for you and my father—" Audra paused, took a deep breath. "I hardly knew my father, but from what I've heard about him, Adrian Kenton was a fine and sensitive man. I don't believe for one minute that he could have ever been interested in the likes of *you*."

Filling with disgust, Audra turned away from the woman. She said to Vincent, "Please take down the other paintings by my father and then we can go."

Vincent did as she asked.

Audra walked over to the sofa, picked up her handbag and the jewelry box.

Additional restraints, self-imposed over the years, began to snap inside Alicia Drummond. And all of the ancient hatred she had harbored for Edith Kenton, and which had not abated even in death, rose up in her. It seemed to congeal in her face, which was contorted into an ugly mask.

She scurried across the carpet to Audra, leaned close to her face and cried, "Adrian Kenton was not your father! Not your father, do you hear? You're a bastard. *Peter Lacey's bastard*. She was carrying on with him when Adrian was still alive. My poor darling Adrian, having to bear witness to that."

Audra took a rapid step back, shaking her head from side to side frantically, denying the woman's words. "It's not true! It's not true!" she cried.

"Yes, it is," Alicia hissed. "Your mother was an adulteress and you are a bastard!"

"And you are a liar, Alicia Drummond!"

Vincent knew he must act immediately.

He seized hold of Audra's arm and almost dragged her into the entrance hall. Pivoting on his heels, he sped back to the drawing room, grabbed the three paintings he had taken off the walls, then swung to Alicia Drummond.

She stood in the middle of the room, twisting her hands together in agitation. There was a febrile look on her face and a wildness in her eyes. He thought she had gone quite mad.

He said, "I'll be back next Saturday for the rest of Audra's stuff, and everything had better be in good condition—*or else*."

"How dare you threaten me!"

"I'm not threatening you; I just want you to know that I mean business. And the law is on our side; think on it, Mrs. Drummond."

Audra was standing where he had left her in the hall, clutching the jewelry box to her chest. Her face was white and she trembled.

"Come on," he cried, "and get the door please, love, my hands are full."

"Yes," she said, trying to throw off the sense of shock she was feeling, hurrying after him to open the front door.

Once they were inside his Uncle Phil's motor car and driving away from the house, Vincent breathed a lot easier. As he came to the gates at the end of the long driveway, he slowed, eased the car out onto the main road to Ripon. He drove in this direction for a few minutes, wanting to put a bit of distance between themselves and The Grange; soon he brought the car to a standstill, parked under a tall hedge.

Audra and he turned to face each other at precisely the same moment.

Vincent had never seen her looking so pale, and she hugged the wooden box as if she was afraid someone was going to wrest it from her. But at least she had stopped shaking. His heart went out to her as he stared into her eyes. They were awash with hurt. He wanted to make her feel better but was not sure how to do so.

He said softly, "It's all right now, love. And you don't have to set foot in that bloody awful house ever again."

Audra nodded. "Yes," she said.

There was a small silence as they continued to look at each other.

Eventually, she asked in a low voice, "You don't think it's true, do you, Vincent? You don't think that I'm . . . illegitimate, do you?" Her lip began to quiver and her eyes brimmed.

"Oh I don't! I don't!" he exclaimed, his vehemence echoing loudly in the confines of the small car, "you said it yourself and right to her face . . . she's a liar."

"But why would she make up something so awful, something as despicable as that?"

Startled by these questions, Vincent now looked askance at his young wife and said, "Audra . . . *love* . . . you're not daft, you *know* why. She spelled it out to you." His voice changed, grew much harder and sharper. "She's a bloody old cow, bitter and spiteful. Not only that, she's crackers, if you ask me. Off her rocker, that one. I wouldn't be surprised if they cart her off one day, put her away in a padded cell."

"Yes, perhaps you're right," Audra said slowly, wondering if he really was. Her eyes turned reflective as she ruminated on Alicia Drummond. The woman was wicked, wasn't she? *Evil.* Madness might not be involved at all. Audra's mind automatically swung to her brothers, and she sighed as she thought of them, remembering their years of hardship and worry in Australia, and her own problems and loneliness after they had been sent away. The shocking thing was that none of it need ever have happened. It had all been so unnecessary.

"Are you all right?" Vincent asked.

"Oh yes," she murmured, "I was just thinking . . . people can be rotten, can't they?"

"Aye, lass, they can," he agreed, then reached out, touched her arm lightly. "Try and relax . . . nobody's going to steal the jewelry box."

Audra half smiled. She loosened her grip on it, let it rest on her knee, and after a moment or two she remarked, "Well, I suppose we'd better be getting along. We can't sit here all day."

"Okay . . . but where to, Audra? Do you still want to go and see your great-aunt? Or shall we forget it and make tracks for Harrogate instead?"

There was a fractional hesitation on Audra's part; then she said, "I think we should go and see her. She *is* expecting me, and I want you to meet her." Audra gave him a reassuring look. "She's nicer than her dreadful daughter, I promise you."

"Just point me in the right direction."

"We're not very far away, as a matter of fact. Drive down this road, for about ten minutes, until we come to Cobbler's Green on the right-hand side. That's where we turn off. Bedelia Cottage is at the bottom."

Neither of them spoke as Vincent drove along at a steady speed, and it was only after they had turned into Cobbler's Green that Audra said, "It *could* be true, you know."

Instantly understanding what she meant, he answered quickly, "Maybe it could, but I wouldn't spend any time worrying over it, if I were you."

"Why not?"

"Because you'll never know the answer. Your mother is the only person who could have told you the truth, and she's dead."

"She might have confided in Great-Aunt Frances; I told you before, they were close."

"You're not going to ask the old lady, are you?"

"Well . . . well, yes, I may."

But in the end, Audra did not ask her great-aunt anything at all.

From the moment they arrived at Bedelia Cottage, it was easy to see that the old lady was very frail indeed. Even though it was late afternoon, it was still a lovely day, sunny and warm. Nevertheless, the windows were tightly closed and she sat in front of a huge fire in her cluttered parlor, a silk shawl draped around her withered shoulders, her hands outstretched to the warming flames.

Audra led Vincent through the maze of Victorian furniture and bric-a-brac, the long-forgotten smell of the room immediately assailing her. The dry, dusty air held a hint of overripe apples, furniture polish and potpourri, as it had for all the years Audra had been coming here as a child. And when she bent to kiss the wrinkled cheek, she caught a faint whiff of moth balls mingled with lavender water and peppermints and she felt a rush of affection for Frances Reynolds. Sudden nostalgia took a grip on her, held her in its spell for a few moments.

Her great-aunt was overjoyed to see Audra after such a long time, and to meet Vincent. Surprised though she was that Audra had appeared with a husband, she took to him at once, or so it seemed to Audra. She chirped away like a small bright bird, smiling at them benevolently. From time to time she nodded her head and patted Audra's hand, and as she did she plied her with innumerable questions about her life.

Audra, equally glad to see her great-aunt, answered her as best she could, all the while observing the octogenarian closely. She looked as delicate and as translucent as the paper-thin china cups they were drinking tea from, and Audra thought that if she breathed too heavily on her the old woman would shatter. Silver-haired and slight of build for as long as Audra could remember, there was a new fragility, a brittleness about her, and Audra wanted to wrap her in cotton wool.

Old bones, old flesh, soon to turn to dust, Audra reflected silently, and a little shiver ran down her arms despite the warmth of the room. Audra's intuitiveness told her that she was probably seeing her aunt for the last time. Frances Reynolds was very, very old now; her life on this earth was coming to an end. It was then that Audra also knew that it would be quite wrong to start probing into her mother's past. That would be too upsetting to this gentle old lady, who had so adored her mother, who was always so affectionate toward her and who had made Vincent feel so welcome.

And Vincent is correct in what he said, Audra now thought. Only my mother knew the truth and she has taken it to the grave. It suddenly struck Audra that it would besmirch her mother's memory to start talking about adultery and questioning her own legitimacy.

And so she remained silent.

They spent almost two hours at Bedelia Cottage, and it was only when they made motions to leave that her great-aunt mentioned Edith Kenton.

Peering at Audra through ancient eyes, she said in her whispery voice, "When my darling Edith died, Alicia removed all of her papers from High Cleugh. But I took them away from her, because I wanted to keep them for you, Audra, until you were grown up."

Frances Reynolds paused, smiled slightly and shook her silvered head. "Ah, dear child, you are looking so eager, but I'm afraid there is nothing of great importance amongst your mother's papers. Some old letters, her birth certificate, her marriage lines, a few old photographs, nothing much else."

Audra's face fell; then she said, "But I want them anyway."

"Of course you do, my dear, and that is why I kept them safe for you all these years." She glanced at Vincent. "The papers are in that attaché case over there on the floor. Could you bring it here, please?"

"Right away," he said, leaping to his feet. He was back in a moment, offered it to the old lady.

"No, no, give it to Audra; the papers belong to her, Vincent."

"Thanks," Audra said, taking the attaché case from him. She noticed that her mother's initials, "EWK," were stamped in gold on the front between the locks. She snapped these open, peeped inside, touched the papers on the top, then decided to examine everything later, in the privacy of their room, after they arrived at the White Swan Hotel in Harrogate.

"Thank you very much for keeping the papers for me, Great-Aunt Frances, I'm most appreciative."

The old lady smiled and nodded. "I know you were going to see Alicia," she said in her weak voice that slightly quavered. "I presume that you did so and that you collected your mother's jewelry."

"Yes," Audra said and paused awkwardly, afraid to say anything more than this. She glanced across at her husband.

Vincent came to her rescue. "Everything was fine, and I'll be driving over with my brothers and a van next week, to get the furniture and the rest of Audra's things."

The old lady beamed at him and a satisfied, almost triumphant look entered her eyes. She reached for her cane. "Come along, the two of you, let us go into the dining room. I want you to choose a piece of silver for your first home."

Fourteen

"Please, Vincent, you have to get up," Audra said, shaking his shoulder.

He shifted his position in the bed, turned on his back and opened his eyes, blinking in the filtered light coming in through the filmy curtains. "Why?"

"Vincent, you know very well why," Audra exclaimed as lightly as possible, trying to sheathe her annoyance with him. "Gwen's coming to supper."

"*If* she shows up."

"It was my fault last Sunday," Audra said hastily, "I got the dates mixed up."

He threw her a skeptical look, said nothing.

"*Please,* Vincent," she begged, her voice rising, "please get up."

His answer was to reach out and catch hold of her wrist. He pulled her down next to him, wrapped his arms around her and hugged her. He whispered against her cheek, "Come to bed with me for half an hour."

Audra struggled against him. "I can't, you know very well I can't. There isn't time."

"You mean you don't want to," he said and let go of her at once.

Rising quickly, Audra stepped away from the bed and looked down at him, pursing her lips. "You're being terribly unfair."

"Oh no I'm not. You've turned cold on me lately."

She flushed. "I haven't. You always pick the wrong time!"

He swiveled his eyes to the alarm clock on the bamboo night stand. "What's wrong with four-thirty on a Sunday afternoon. It strikes me it's the perfect time."

"We're expecting a guest."

"Ah yes. La-di-da Miss Gwen Thornton." He pronounced the name with acerbity, added, "I don't know what you see in her, why you run after her."

"I don't run after her!"

"Yes, you do. I'm beginning to think you prefer her to me."

"Don't be so ridiculous," Audra exclaimed, staring at him in total astonishment. "You know that's not true." She felt a sudden surge of anger toward him and went on crossly, "Anyway, I'm not in the mood to . . . come to bed, to make love, not after your behavior these past few weeks."

"My behavior! What the bloody hell are you talking about?" He sat bolt upright in the bed and glared at her, his brilliant green eyes flashing as his temper flared.

Audra shook her head, very slowly, swallowing her exasperation with him, suddenly comprehending. "You just don't *know* what you *do,* Vincent, do you?"

"What do you mean?"

"Oh Vincent, *Vincent,* you're impossible. And you make me so mad at times. For one thing, I'm getting impatient with your performance every Sunday at lunchtime. You go off to the pub with your brothers, think nothing about strolling in well after two o'clock, having promised to be back by one at the latest, and then you turn nasty on me because lunch is spoiled . . . as if that were my fault."

"I didn't turn nasty today."

"Yes, you did. Actually, alcohol doesn't agree with you at all; it brings the worst out in you, makes you belligerent and touchy."

He was about to ignore these criticisms, since she had lately developed a habit of carping, but changed his mind. "Don't start giving *me* a lecture," he snapped. "I don't like it. I'm a man, not a kid. I've always gone to the pub on Sundays, ever since I was eighteen, and I'm not going to stop now. Not for you or anybody else. And anyway, everybody goes to the pub on Sundays; it's an old English tradition."

Only with the working class, she thought and instantly hated herself for even thinking this; she despised any kind of prejudice in others. She said, "There's something else . . . you left me alone to mark time at your mother's *again* last night, whilst you went off carousing in the pubs with your brothers—"

"It was our Bill's birthday," he cut in indignantly, all of his defenses going up.

"That's true, and I don't begrudge it when you celebrate a special occasion of that kind. But it wasn't Bill's birthday last Saturday, or the Saturday before, *or* the one before that, when you also went off on your own."

"You didn't have to stay at my mother's last night. You could have gone to the old-time dancing with Laurette. After all, she invited you."

"I'm not married to Laurette, I'm married to you."

He sighed heavily and his mouth tightened in aggravation. "I hope that doesn't mean that I've got to be tied to your apron strings twenty-four hours a day for the rest of my life, because believe you me, I won't be."

Audra bit back the retort on the tip of her tongue, asking herself why she was bothering to argue with him at this particular time. Gwen was due to arrive within the hour and she wanted the atmosphere in the house to be tranquil. All she needed was for Gwen to think there was some sort of trouble between them.

And so she walked to the bedroom door, said softly, "I still have a few chores," and ran downstairs before he could say another word.

Pushing aside her worries about the recent changes in their relationship, she busied herself in the parlor-kitchen of their four-room cottage in Pot Lane. After covering the deal table in the center of the floor with her best lace cloth, she took out several pieces of the beautiful china dinner service the Bells had given them as a wedding present, and went about setting the table for supper.

Once she had finished she glanced at the grate in the center of the Yorkshire range, wondering whether or not to light the fire yet; these September nights soon turned cool. On the other hand, it was still sunny. Thinking of the weather reminded Audra that she needed fresh flowers for the center of the table and for the console in the tiny sitting room next door. She hurried across to the work table next to the sink under the window, found the scissors in the drawer, took the flower basket off the set-pot and went outside.

The cottage did not have a name, only the number thirty-eight painted in white on its green door, and it was one of three in a cul-de-sac behind The Towers in Upper Armley. Each house had a small garden, but Audra's was the most flourishing and resplendent because the previous tenants had cultivated it well over the years. Also, she had tended it diligently herself since they had moved into the cottage in June, and had made some new plantings and other improvements.

The last of the summer roses were full blown, tipped heavy and luxuriant heads down to the dark earth, and as Audra bent over the bushes, she breathed deeply of their scent. It was rich and sweet, and just a little heady, and it made her feel slightly dizzy. She began to cut the roses with great care, not wanting to destroy the fragile blossoms by knocking any of the petals off. She selected mostly from the pale yellow and pink blooms, since these seemed to be fading faster than the others.

"You've no idea how bonny you look, love," Vincent said from the doorway of the cottage.

She glanced up.

He flashed her one of his most beautiful and winning smiles.

She smiled back, understanding that he now wished to make amends. "Thank you," she murmured. Rising, she picked up the flower basket, walked toward him down the flagged garden path.

His eyes did not leave her face. When she came to a standstill in front of him, he put his arm around her affectionately and led her inside. After closing the door and taking the basket out of her hands, he drew her into his arms, kissed her deeply and with growing passion.

Audra responded, held onto him tightly, returned his kisses. And she did so willingly now, all of the resentment which had been building up falling away from her suddenly, unexpectedly. She thought: I love him, he loves me, and that's all that matters really. We'll work out our differences. Somehow we will.

After a moment he stopped kissing her, tilted her face up to his, looked down into her startling eyes. It seemed to him that their bright cornflower blue had turned to the deeper hue of the violet, and as always they reflected her innermost emotions. His own gaze was intense, searching. "Do you have any idea how much I want you at times?" he asked finally, in a hoarse voice.

"Yes." She hesitated, then whispered, "I feel the same way."

Vincent smiled to himself, knowing how difficult it was for her to articulate such things. Trailing a finger down her cheek, he said, "Perhaps Gwen won't stay too late?"

"No, I don't think she will. It's Monday tomorrow."

Vincent leaned closer, murmured in her ear, "Let's make a date to have an early night, Mrs. Crowther."

"Yes, let's."

He hugged her to him, then released her. Swinging away, Vincent walked over to the front door. "I'll be back in time for supper."

Surprised, she asked, "Where are you going?"

"To my mother's."

"But why?"

"I promised Frank I would help him to fill in his military papers . . . Dad's finally given him permission to join the army, and he's very excited, our Frank is. You know how badly he wants to get into a cavalry regiment and go out to India. Can't say I blame him, either. Not the way things are in this bloody country right now." He made a face. "So many men on the dole and more being laid off work every day."

Audra held herself very still. "You're all right at Varley's, aren't you? They're not having problems too, are they, Vincent?"

"No, no, of course not." He smiled reassuringly. "We're in the middle of building that ruddy great house for old man Pinfold and his missis. Anyway, don't *you* worry your little head about such things; that's my job, as the man of the house." He blew her a kiss, flashed his cheeky grin. "Ta'rar, love, I'll see you a bit later."

Fifteen

"So you did get a sofa. *Finally,*" Gwen said, stepping into the little sitting room from the parlor-kitchen.

"Yes," Audra replied, following sharply on her heels, frowning at her friend's back.

Gwen marched up to this piece of furniture, which stood in the center of the room facing the fireplace, and promptly sat down on it. She crossed her legs, settled against the cushions and made herself comfortable.

Audra hovered in front of her, studying her face intently. It was bland, as always, and innocent enough. And Audra knew at once that Gwen had not meant anything mean or unkind by the remark, even though the way she had said *finally* had sounded a trifle catty, as if she thought they hadn't been able to afford one before.

"We bought the sofa two weeks ago," Audra volunteered in her usual quiet way. "We'd been looking for that particular style for quite a while, since before we were married, actually."

"Oh, had you," Gwen said and swung around, brought her face closer to the back of the sofa, the three strands of cheap beads rattling as she moved. She sniffed the material. "Mmmm. *Leather.* Very nice too, Audra. I must admit, I do like the genuine thing. Nothing imitation for me, either."

Audra bit back a smile, walked over to the fireplace. She was amused by the incongruity of this last remark, in view of Gwen's penchant for fake jewelry. Always dripping in it, and a walking advertisement for Woolworth's, she had really outdone herself today. She was bedecked in a curious assortment of colored rhinestones and paste; none of it matched, and she glittered like an out-of-season Christmas tree. But that's my Gwenny, Audra thought with a rush of real warmth, her deep affection for her friend surfacing. She just wouldn't be the same without her beads and bracelets and dangling earrings; they're her trademark, and I don't suppose I would change her, even if I could.

Still smiling, Audra reached for the Swan Vestas on the mantelpiece. "It seems to have turned a little chilly," she said, crouching in front of the grate, striking a match. She brought the flame to the paper and wood chips and went on, "Are you sure I can't get you a cardigan, Gwen?"

"No, thanks very much, lovey, I'm all right. At least I will be now that you're getting the fire going." Gwen smoothed her hand over the skirt of her brilliant red silk dress, explained, "I should have worn something warmer than this, I suppose, but it's brand-new and I wanted you to see it. Do you like it, Audra?"

"It's a lovely frock and it really does suit you," Audra answered truthfully. She stood up, glanced approvingly at her friend.

Gwen preened; she patted her blond hair. "And what do you think of my new marcel wave?"

"I like it, and as a matter of fact I'm considering having one myself next week. Now, shall I make us a cup of tea? Or would you prefer a drink perhaps?"

"I wouldn't say no to a glass of sherry."

"I think I'll join you." Audra went to the hutch cupboard in the corner of the room, took out a bottle of Amontillado and two glasses, carried them to the mahogany console table which stood against the back wall.

Swinging her head, looking over the back of the sofa at Audra, Gwen remarked, "And while we're handing out compliments, let me pay you one. You've made this room look really nice, you have that, Audra. Your father's paintings are beautiful, especially that one over the fireplace, and this furniture of your mother's—well, it looks ever so handsome in here. The place does you proud, lovey."

Audra beamed at her. "Thanks, Gwen, and I am glad you like it. The room's small, of course, but that makes it cozy and comfortable, don't you think?"

Gwen nodded, then let her eyes roam around. "And what did you say the name of this funny green on the walls is?"

Audra laughed. *"Eau-de-Nil."*

"What a strange name." Gwen made a face.

"It means water of the Nile in French, and it's a very popular color at the moment . . . in fashion, I mean."

"Oh is it. Fancy that. Well, you always did keep up with the latest trends in clothes, lovey, didn't you? I keep telling Mum that you're *the* expert on fashion and styles and fabrics and all that kind of thing. I hope you realize how much I value your advice. Yes, you've got the best taste of anybody I know." Gwen accepted the drink from Audra. "Thanks, lovey," she said.

The two women clinked glasses, and Audra stepped up to the fireside, sat down in one of the Chippendale-style chairs which had belonged to her mother. "I'm glad you think so—that I have taste, I mean."

Gwen smiled at her. "And where's Vincent then?"

"He went to his mother's, to help his brother fill out some papers. But he'll be back in time to have supper with us."

Gwen took a sip of sherry, not trusting herself to speak.

It seemed to her that Vincent was always rushing off to his mother's house, on some pretext or another, but she did not dare say this to Audra. Ever since their tense discussion on the subject of Vincent in July, Gwen had been scrupulously careful not to make any critical remarks about him. She had soon realized, on that hot summer day when they went to tea at Betty's Cafe in Leeds, that she was perilously close to losing Audra's friendship, and this had both distressed and alarmed her.

Audra was extremely important to Gwen, and so nowadays she kept a tight rein on her tongue at all times. But privately she believed that Vincent Crowther was not good enough for her friend, and nothing would make her change her mind. There was something about him that did not sit right with Gwen Thornton, although she would have been hard-pressed to pinpoint what this was, if asked. She thought of him as being emotionally dangerous, and her instinct told her he would make Audra extremely unhappy one day.

She wondered, yet again, why he was constantly trotting off to his mother's, if that was where he really had gone, and then dropped this thought. She was delighted he was not at home. This afternoon she wanted Audra to herself for a while. She had something important to tell her and she preferred to do so without Vincent being present. He could be very opinionated. And he expressed those opinions without being asked.

Conscious of the growing silence, Audra leaned forward, peered across the dusky room. The twilight had come down early today, and the only light emanated from the fire. "You're very quiet, Gwen," she remarked. "Are you troubled about something?"

"No, no, nothing's wrong," Gwen was quick to say. She too drew closer, and let her voice sink low as she added, "I don't want you to tell anyone, not even Vincent, but I'm thinking of getting married."

"How wonderful, Gwen dear!" Audra cried, and then her brow furrowed in puzzlement. "But I thought Mike had another two years of medical school? You told me in the spring that he wouldn't be able to afford a wife for a few years."

"Oh but it's not Mike I'm thinking of marrying."

In the dimming light Audra could see that Gwen looked very pleased with herself, and this further perplexed her. "But you told me you were in love with Mike Lesley, and certainly the two of you have behaved as if you were in the past year . . . you've been like a couple of love birds in fact," Audra said, "so what's suddenly happened to change all that?"

"Don't be so dense, Audra," Gwen said with a light laugh. "Obviously I've met someone else."

"Who?"

"It's someone you know—well, sort of—but you'll never guess in a million years," Gwen declared, her voice echoing with glee.

"No, I'm sure I won't, so you'd better tell me."

"Geoffrey Freemantle."

Audra was flabbergasted.

She opened her mouth, then closed it without uttering one single word. She simply gaped at Gwen in disbelief. Taking a deep breath, she said at last, "You don't mean *Doctor* Freemantle? The one who was at the Fever Hospital for a while . . . you couldn't possibly mean *him."*

"Why couldn't I?" Gwen asked with sudden huffiness. "Of course I mean him."

"Oh." Audra put her glass down on the Sheraton table a little unsteadily. She was staggered. If ever a man was wrong for Gwen Thornton, it was Geoffrey Freemantle. He was cold, arrogant, sarcastic and a snob. Good-looking, yes, in a stiff, formal sort of way, and from a wealthy family, too, but he was a pompous and disdainful man, older than Gwen by about fourteen years. Audra found herself filling with genuine dismay and concern. It was hard for her to visualize the gay, laughing, fun-loving Gwen with such a stuffed shirt, who believed himself to be superior to the rest of the human race.

"Is that all you're going to say? Just *oh* and nothing else?" Gwen's voice held a new tremulous quality and her feelings were obviously hurt.

"No, of course it isn't," Audra said, reaching out, squeezing Gwen's arm. Pushing an enthusiasm into her voice which she did not feel, she added, "I'm very, very happy for you, Gwen, really and truly I am. But I must admit to being a bit taken aback, since this was the last thing I expected to hear today. How did it all happen? Do tell, Gwen."

Mollified to a certain extent, Gwen said in a cheerier voice, "Well, after Geoffrey left Ripon, he went up to Northallerton, but he wasn't particularly happy there, so he transferred back to the General Infirmary in Leeds this past spring. Anyway, we kept running into each other in the corridors, and we remembered each other from Ripon. He was always very friendly with me—" Gwen broke off and giggled. "He finally asked me out at the beginning of July. And after one date it happened—just like that!" She snapped her thumb and fingers together, and the glass rings flashed in the firelight.

"It's been a bit fast," Audra commented, very softly.

"Yes, it has . . . just like you and Vincent."

Well, she's had the last word there, Audra thought and said, "How do your parents feel about it?"

Gwen's face immediately underwent a radical change and she bit her lip, looking worried and troubled. "To tell you the truth, Audra, I'm ever so upset with Mum and Dad. They don't seem to have taken to Geoffrey one little bit, and they're not pleased. Course, I think that's because Mike has been such a close chum of our Charlie's for years, and they always hoped I'd marry him. But what can I do? Geoffrey's the one for me, oh yes, he *is,* lovey."

"So you've made up your mind, Gwen?"

"Oh yes, I think so . . . no, I *know* so. And he's quite a catch for me, really he is." Her face began to glow again, reflecting the imitation jewels around her neck, and she appeared to swell with pride. "We've been looking at houses in Headingley, and I think we've found just the right one. It has a dining room, a lounge, a study, and five bedrooms, perfect for when we start a family. Next week, Geoffrey's taking me to Greenwood's in Leeds, to pick out an engagement ring, a *diamond* engagement ring, and the announcement will be in the Yorkshire *Post.*"

"Have you fixed a definite date?" Audra asked next. She forced a bright smile.

"Not exactly, but Geoffrey wants us to be married in the spring, because he's taking me to Paris for our honeymoon, and he says you should only ever see Paris in the spring—for the first time, that is. He's going to fit me out with lots of new clothes too, in Paris, and we're to stay at the Ritz. Can you imagine *that!* And then we'll go down to the Riviera. Geoffrey says mimosa time in the south of France is very beautiful and not to be missed, and we'll be spending a whole week at the Negresco in Nice. It's a very posh place, you know, but then, so is the Ritz."

Gwen finally paused, leaned forward eagerly, fixing her eyes on Audra's face, seeking a reaction.

Audra simply smiled.

Clasping her hands together tightly, Gwen's expression of excitement now changed to one of awe at the glamorous prospects facing her in the future.

"Once we've settled in the house in Headingley, which I'm *certain* we'll buy, Geoffrey is going to leave the Infirmary and set up in private practice. He's going to take consulting rooms on Park Place in Leeds. He aims to be a fashionable doctor, treating the local gentry and society women, and he'll be very successful and rich and I'm going to help him all I can. We'll entertain a lot, for one thing, give elegant dinner parties and luncheons, and that's why I need lots of new clothes. Geoffrey wants me to look very smart."

Audra could only nod, since her dismay was increasing and she did not know what to say. The fake stones Gwen was wearing, glittering so brilliantly in the lambent flames of the fire, held her attention. For a split-second they seemed real, looked like emeralds and rubies and sapphires and not bits of Woolworth's glass. The jewelry will be the first to go, she suddenly thought. He'll make her get rid of it the minute they're married. Audra felt a stab of sadness as she pictured Gwen stripped of all her silly garish baubles which were worthless, yet had always meant so much to her.

Poor little Gwenny, Audra thought, now endeavoring to visualize her friend after *he* had worked his transformation on her, after *he* had dressed her and groomed her and turned her into the kind of Mrs. Geoffrey Freemantle *he* wanted. In her mind's eye she saw a curiously stiff, cold woman, that had nothing to do with Gwen Thornton. But then none of the things Gwen had been saying had much to do with the girl she knew so well and cared so much about.

Getting to her feet, Audra went and snapped on the small lamps standing on the Sheraton side tables flanking the fireplace. Then she hurried over to the console, brought back the bottle of sherry and refilled their glasses.

Knowing Gwen was waiting for some sort of comment after her graphic recital, Audra murmured, "Well, it all sounds wonderful, very wonderful indeed."

After this statement there was no holding Gwen.

Audra realized this when she returned to her chair and offered her friend the warmest of smiles—and her undivided attention.

Always a chatterbox, Gwen talked nonstop for the next half hour about her impending wedding, Geoffrey, his parents, the honeymoon and the life they would lead afterward, and without drawing breath.

Leaning back, sipping her sherry, Audra merely nodded occasionally, aware that she would not be allowed to get a word in edgewise. But she did not really want to; neither was she listening very closely.

Her thoughts were centered on Geoffrey Freemantle. It was patently obvious to Audra why he wished to marry Gwen Thornton. She was much younger than he and was a beautiful blond with a curvaceous figure, who had a vivacious, outgoing personality plus a loving nature. So all in all she was most desirable in every way; she would be to any man. Also, since she was a nurse and the daughter of a doctor, her background was ideal for an ambitious physician, and unquestionably Geoffrey Freemantle was that. Yes, Gwen could not be anything but an asset to him.

What truly bothered Audra was Gwen herself. Why on earth would she want to become *his* wife? He was the antithesis of Mike Lesley, and whatever Gwen now thought about Mike, Audra was aware that she had been genuinely smitten with Charlie's closest chum. There was only one answer: Gwen wanted Geoffrey Freemantle for everything he represented and all the things he could give her—prestige, position, money.

Instantly, Audra tried to dismiss these uncharitable thoughts and yet deep down inside herself she was convinced she was right. Not once in the entire time Gwen had been speaking about Geoffrey Freemantle had she mentioned that most crucial word, *love.* How can a marriage work without love, Audra wondered. Perhaps she ought to talk to Gwen about that. Immediately she decided against doing so, remembering how much *she* had resented Gwen's gratuitous comments about her own marriage.

Anyway, perhaps I'm wrong, Audra told herself. Maybe she does love him. And then, much to her astonishment she thought: But loving a man doesn't necessarily make for happiness, does it?

──────── *Sixteen* ────────

Later that evening, toward the end of supper, Gwen flashed Audra a conspiratorial look. "Shall I tell Vincent my news?"

"Why not?" Audra said, laughing, aware that her friend had been bursting to let him in on her secret all night.

"What news?" Vincent asked, glancing from one to the other.

"I'm getting engaged next week," Gwen announced, then sat back in the chair, beaming and looking pleased with herself.

"Well I can't say I'm surprised." Vincent leaned over and kissed her cheek. "Congratulations, Gwen, and you ought to have brought Mike with you to supper. I like him, he's a straight bloke, and you've made a good choice for yourself."

There was a small silence.

Gwen said quickly, "Oh but it's not Mike I'm marrying."

"Not Mike," Vincent echoed, sounding startled. "Well, I'm blowed! And I thought you two were as thick as thieves. So you've found somebody else then."

"Yes."

"Cut up, Mike is, I'll bet."

Gwen's throat tightened and she discovered she could not speak. She simply nodded.

"Yes, I can well imagine how he's feeling." Vincent gave Gwen a very hard stare. "Mike thought a lot about you, Gwen, he did that."

Gwen said, "I know he did and I cared for him too, but obviously not enough, if I could fall for another man."

"And who's the lucky chap then?" Vincent asked, wondering how she could pass Mike Lesley up for someone else. Mike was very special and, now that he thought about it, the kind of man he would like for his sister Laurette.

"His name's Geoffrey Freemantle," Gwen was saying, giving him a bright, confident smile, "and he's a doctor at Leeds Infirmary. But he's originally from Harrogate and that's where his parents live."

"And when did all this happen? I mean we were all together with Mike at the end of June, so it must've been in the last couple of months, right?"

"Yes, Geoffrey first asked me out at the beginning of July, but I've—"

"All a bit *quick,* Gwen, isn't it?" Vincent broke in peremptorily, and not giving her a chance to respond, he hurried on, "Marriage is a tricky business, you know, so I hope you're really sure about this chap. What I mean is that I *know* for a fact that Mike is the genuine thing, a really fine upstanding man, so I hope this new bloke is just as . . . *okay.* I wouldn't want you to be making a big mistake—a *terrible* mistake, Gwen."

Gwen's mouth tightened in annoyance and she glared at Vincent, bristling. How like him to express his unwanted and unasked-for opinions. She exclaimed coldly, "It just so happens that I've known Geoffrey for a long time —since I worked in Ripon. And as I pointed out to Audra earlier, you and she hardly had what I would call a lengthy courtship. Besides, it's none of your business, so there!" She sat back in a huff, still glaring at him.

"Oh excuse me, I'm sorry I spoke," he muttered and puffed hard on his cigarette, looking annoyed.

Audra could see they were heading for one of their little tiffs, and she exclaimed, "Now you two, stop this, don't spoil a lovely evening. Anyway, I have something to tell you both—a little news of my own."

Vincent swung to her, his brow lifting quizzically. "What news, love?"

"I've taken a job and I start in two weeks."

Vincent's jaw dropped and he stared at her in astonishment.

Gwen, equally surprised, cried, "What *kind* of job? *Where?*"

"At St. Mary's Hospital, here in Armley," Audra explained. It was her turn to look pleased with herself, and she rushed on enthusiastically. "And as a nurse, of course. Mrs. Bell introduced me to the matron there, and I'm looking forward to it immensely. It's a challenge, since I'm going to be on the Maternity Ward."

"Whatever made you *do* such a *stupid* thing?" Vincent demanded furiously, his green eyes blazing, an angry flush spreading up from his neck into his face. "I don't believe I'm hearing you right!"

Audra was so taken aback at his extraordinary outburst, she was momentarily thrown off balance. And then she sat up straighter and retorted, "I don't think it's stupid! I think it's very *smart* of me! After all, I've had a very good training and it's a pity to waste it. Matron Lennox has always said that nursing is a real gift with me, so why shouldn't I put it to good use? Not only that, I *want* to work."

"Well, you can forget it! No wife of mine is going out to work and that's that!"

His temper was boiling very near to the surface, and he shook his head with vehemence. "My God, Audra, what are you thinking about? How could you do such a thing? I can just hear my mates talking, sniggering behind my back because my wife has to work to help support the household."

"But that's not the reason I want to work!" Audra exclaimed.

"Maybe not, but that's what they'll think. Just you remember that I'm the man in this house and the breadwinner and that *I* wear the pants and make the decisions, not you." Glancing at Gwen, he appealed to her by saying, "I bet *you're* not going to work after you're married, are you? Will *you* continue to be a nurse at the Infirmary?"

"No, I won't," Gwen answered softly. She looked at Audra apologetically, reached out, touched her arm. "I'm sorry, lovey, but I'm afraid I *have* to agree with Vincent. He's right, really he is. Anyway, why would you want to go back to nursing in a hospital? It's such demanding work and the money's not much."

"Look, I want to use my skills and be *useful.*" Determined to stand her ground with Vincent, Audra threw him a fierce look. "And why does it matter what people think? You're being absurd—"

"I refuse to discuss this any further, Audra!" he interjected. "The matter's closed!" He brought his fist down on the table much harder than he had intended, and the dishes rattled.

"Vincent, don't be so stubborn!" Audra was so infuriated by his attitude and his behavior that she could barely contain herself. "Being married to you doesn't mean that you can control me, make me do as you say. I would like to have a career in nursing, and it's my right to—"

"There you go again, Audra," Vincent laughed sarcastically. "It's Mrs. Irène bloody Bell talking, not you. I don't want any of her women's rights and suffragette nonsense in my house, lass, and you'd better not forget that!"

Audra sucked in her breath, took a hold of herself. "Oh Vincent, you're being so very unfair," she murmured, softening both her voice and her manner. She took hold of his hand, hoping to placate him, wanting to get her own way ultimately. "You're misunderstanding everything I've said."

He gave her a cold sulky little glance, made no response.

Laughing somewhat self-consciously, Gwen looked from Audra to Vincent, then said, "I don't like to see the two of you quarreling in this way. Come along, kiss and make up."

Knowing that Vincent would do no such thing, and wishing to curtail the quarrel because of Gwen's presence, Audra pushed back her chair and rose. Putting her arm around his shoulder, she brought her face down to his and kissed him on the cheek.

"All right, you win," she said softly. "I'll go to the hospital next week and tell them that I can't take the job." But she was merely making a gesture for the sake of peace and quiet. She did not mean one word she said, and she had no intention of giving in to him.

——————— *Seventeen* ———————

The marriage that had begun with an intense physical passion in the heat of the summer had a winter frost on it by December. And the passion had cooled considerably.

Vincent and Audra were frequently at loggerheads in the latter part of 1928, and certainly the tranquility that had initially reigned in the little cottage in Pot Lane had given way to constant bickering and stormy quarrels.

The odd thing was that they were very alike in many respects, and this was actually part of the problem. Both were stubborn, strong-willed and independent-minded. In consequence, they were forever locking horns. Then again, each believed the other was wrong and therefore at fault. They were young and unable to make allowances for normal human frailties; neither could they compromise, which might have helped to lessen the tension between them.

Vincent, who was too self-involved at this time in his life to see much beyond his own desires and interests, had very little real understanding of Audra.

And surprisingly, she, who usually had so much insight into others, was rarely able to read him accurately because she was so subjective. In fact, Audra's view of Vincent Crowther would always be blurred and off-center, influenced as she was by emotions of the most powerful kind.

Audra was generally in a turmoil about him and filled with conflicting feelings. There were times when she believed she loved him to distraction, others when she was convinced she had nothing but hatred for him. Vincent, as it happened, felt exactly the same way, and he was often as confused about Audra as she was about him.

Another stumbling block in their relationship was their newly acquired habit of arguing violently about almost everything. They were suddenly incapable of discussing any subjects in a quiet and rational way, so that neither of them ever really knew what the other *truly* thought or felt. And their mutual ambivalence about their marriage, and their dissatisfaction with each other, simply grew.

Sometimes they were able to make up in the darkness of their bedroom, drawn to each other—almost against their own volition—by the strong physical attraction they shared. But these occasions were growing rarer because their problems intruded more and more, and also because Audra, in particular, brought her anger to bed with her.

She had been holding a number of grudges against Vincent since September, and the one thing which rankled the most was his adamant refusal to let her return to nursing. She had reasoned, cajoled, argued and pleaded, in an effort to bring him around to her way of thinking. But Vincent had remained as unbending as he had been on the night of the supper with Gwen.

In the end, Audra had been the one to give in, suddenly understanding that if she defied him and took the job at the hospital, he would leave her. And very simply put, life without Vincent Crowther was quite inconceivable to her, whatever their difficulties might be. Therefore, she had allowed his wishes to come before her own, telling herself that her marriage was far more important to her than a job. Somehow she had managed to wear a cheerful expression most of the time, one that did nothing to betray her feelings of disappointment and frustration at his obstinacy.

But when Audra had gone to Calpher House to tell Mrs. Bell what had happened, her eyes had filled with tears and her unhappiness had tumbled out unexpectedly.

Irène Bell had been sympathetic, as she always was toward Audra, and she had done her best to comfort her. And whatever Mrs. Bell had thought privately about Vincent's attitudes, she had wisely kept her opinions to herself. "Perhaps he'll come around," Mrs. Bell had said encouragingly, giving her a hopeful smile.

But Audra knew he would not do so. It was not in Vincent's nature to reverse himself. Or to admit that he was wrong. Similar though they were in some ways, Audra did not share these particular characteristics with him. She was always able to recognize when her judgment was flawed or when she had made an error.

As she hurried down Pot Lane, on this raw afternoon early in December, she was telling herself just how wrong she had been. Wrong to marry him in the first place, and certainly wrong to stay with him as she had, forever wavering about what to do, forever indecisive. She should have packed and left the minute everything had started to go askew in August.

Well, she had done that now. There was no turning back.

She tightened her grip on the small suitcase she was carrying and clenched her teeth, thrusting out her determined chin. The decision had been made. *Finally*. She had walked out on Vincent Crowther and she had no intention of returning.

Deep down inside herself Audra knew that she still loved Vincent. She supposed she would always love him. But she had come to the realization that love was not necessarily enough to sustain a relationship. A couple had to be able to live together in harmony if a marriage was going to be successful. Seemingly she and Vincent could not do that. They were tearing each other apart with angry, hurtful words that were sometimes hard to retract later.

Last night they had had a particularly violent quarrel, their worst yet and one that had left her shaken and despairing.

An hour earlier she had been ironing the last of his shirts in the kitchen-parlor when suddenly she had put the flatiron down on the trivet with a bang, instantly understanding what she must do. She had quickly tidied away the ironing things, changed her clothes, packed a suitcase, then taken her meager savings and left the cottage.

As she had turned the key in the lock, her eye had caught the number thirty-eight painted on the green door and she had stared at it, had felt a strange pain in her chest. And then an immense sadness had fallen over her and she had leaned her head against the stone reveal of the door, closing her eyes, thinking of the past few months here. Simple and ordinary though it was, this humble little house was a palace to her. It was her first home of her own, and it contained not only all of the things she owned in life but in a way her very life itself. Certainly her dreams and expectations for the future were sheltered within its walls. She had believed that these would come to flower here with Vincent, that they would start a family of their own, build a good life together. But that was not meant to be—or so it seemed to her.

Audra had cut off these thoughts, not daring to let her mind run on in this manner. After slipping the key under the doormat, she had picked up her suitcase and almost run out of the cul-de-sac and into the lane.

And now as she headed in the direction of Whingate tram terminal, she was still trying to push aside that sadness, as well as the awful depression that had descended on her. But the feelings lingered. Her dreams were shattered, her hopes were flattened and the sense of loss she had lived with for years loomed, enormous. She had lost again. Lost her husband, lost their life together, lost her future.

Audra's step faltered, and for a split-second, as she hesitated, she almost changed her mind and went back to the cottage. But something inside her said *no;* she plunged ahead determinedly.

The weather, which had been nasty all through the day, had turned ominous.

There was a pewter-colored glaze on the sky and the surrounding landscape was bleak and bereft of color. It was like a painting in *grisaille* with its many tints of gray, and the stark and blackened trees stood out in relief, were like pieces of metal sculpture silhouetted against the lowering sky.

It had begun to drizzle. There was the low boom of distant thunder echoing like cannon across the nearby fields, which stretched in a long, flowing line down to Old Farnley. A storm threatened and the wind was gusting over Hill-Top.

Audra huddled against the railings of Charlie Cake Park, sheltering as best she could as she waited for the tramcar from Leeds to arrive at the terminal. It was long overdue.

Shivering, she tightened the thick woolen scarf around her neck and stamped her feet in an effort to keep them warm. The kitchen of the cottage, with its fire banked up the chimney back, had been so cozy and comfortable she had not realized earlier just how bad it was outside. She stepped forward, glanced down Town Street. This main thoroughfare was strangely deserted; the few pedestrians who were out and about were obviously in a hurry to get home before the storm broke.

What miserable weather it is, Audra thought, and it matches my mood exactly. She drew back into the niche between the park's railings and the policeman's booth, sighing. She had chosen to leave Vincent and yet she was already missing him. How perverse I am, she muttered, not understanding herself. And then she thought: And I'm stupidly of two minds about him still. But I'm doing the right thing. I know I am. *Oh am I? Am I?*

Wrapping her arms around her body, Audra tried not to think about him or to envision his face when he walked in tonight and found that she had gone, found her note. She pushed her hands under her armpits for additional warmth and went on stamping her feet. She was chilled to the bone now, and she could feel the dampness seeping through her Melton coat and the plum-colored cloche.

About twenty minutes later she heard the tram rumbling to a stop at the other side of the tiny wedge-shaped park and then the sound of voices and footsteps as people alighted. Filling with relief, she hoisted her suitcase and hurried forward, and collided bodily with a young woman who came hurtling around the corner at breakneck speed.

They both recovered their balance, started to apologize, stopped in mid-sentence as they recognized each other in the murky, late afternoon light. Audra found herself staring into the pretty face of the sister-in-law who was her closest friend in the Crowther clan. Her heart dropped.

"Audra! For heaven's sake, what are you doing here?" Laurette demanded and broke into warm and affectionate smiles.

"Catching a tram," Audra mumbled and began to edge away.

Spotting the suitcase, Laurette frowned. "Where are you going?"

"I don't know," Audra responded in all truthfulness, then found herself saying, "anywhere, I suppose, as long as it's far away from Vincent."

"What do you mean?" Laurette looked at her intently, her eyes filling with alarm.

"I'm leaving him."

Sucking in her breath, Laurette exclaimed, "Audra, *no,* don't say that. You *can't* leave him."

"Oh yes, I can."

"But where will you *go?* You know you have *nowhere* to go. We're the only family you have."

Ignoring this remark, Audra improvised swiftly, saying, "I can always go to the Fever Hospital in Ripon." She nodded to herself, realizing that this was quite true. "Matron Lennox will find a place for me. I just know she will."

"Audra, listen to me! Please don't do something that you may regret. Reconsider . . . at least about leaving today; it's almost four and the weather's worse. Anyway, by the time you reach Leeds you'll have missed the last train to Ripon. Come on, love, let's go back to the cottage and talk about this," Laurette pleaded, taking hold of Audra's arm.

"Please let go of me, Laurette." Audra tried to shake off her sister-in-law's hand, but Laurette's grip was firm. "Laurette, *please!* This is ridiculous. And I certainly don't want to go back to the cottage."

"Then let's go to my mother's . . . we're only five minutes away, come on, Audra, don't be stubborn. You're shivering, your face is blue with cold and you're going to catch your death of cold out here."

"What's the point of going to your mother's house? I've made up my mind and I won't change it. *I'm leaving Vincent.*"

Laurette drew closer and put her arm around Audra's shoulders, lovingly, almost protectively. She confided softly, "Look, I'm the first to admit I was against your marriage initially, but now that you are married I do think you and our Vincent should attempt to solve your problems and—"

"How can *you* of all people say that to me!" Audra exploded in amazement, looking askance at Laurette. "Let's not forget that *you* are in the middle of a divorce."

"Yes, I know, but that's different. You and Vincent love each other. Jimmy and I didn't, not really."

"Love is not always enough."

"But it's a foundation to build a life on, Audra, really it is."

"I've thought about this for weeks and I'm not going to be persuaded to do something against my will—" Audra broke off as a bell clanged and the tramcar rolled away down the tracks to Leeds.

Audra stared after it in dismay; then she swung toward Laurette angrily. "Now look what you've done! You've made me miss my tramcar! And there won't be another one for half an hour at least," she wailed, then burst into tears of aggravation and frustration.

The profusion of roses on the walls and underfoot and patterning the china on the Welsh dresser looked more glorious than ever on this cold winter's afternoon. They seemed to glow with the vividness of real flowers in the blaze from the fire that roared in the hearth like a furnace, and threw off tremendous heat.

All was welcoming warmth and cheeriness in Eliza Crowther's kitchen. The air was fragrant with the smell of freshly baked bread and mince pies and tea cakes cooling on the set-pot, the sharper aromas of cloves, cinnamon, nutmeg and other spices from the Indies mingling with the fruity tang of candied peel, sultanas and Egyptian dates.

Eliza Crowther had been baking, which she usually did on Friday afternoons, come winter or summer. But today she had been busier than usual. Christmas was only three weeks away and she had been making holiday fare for her large family. She moved with agility between the table under the window and the sink, where she was now placing her dirty mixing bowls and spoons, cleaning up after herself. In a short while she would have to start preparing tea for those members of her family who still lived at home, and she always preferred everything to be spic and span in her kitchen before she commenced a new task.

A woman of medium height and build, Eliza looked all of her forty-nine years. This was mainly because of her plain way of dressing, her severe hairdo pulled straight back in a bun, and her stocky body, which had thickened since the birth of her last child, Danny. But she had an attractive, pleasant face, and good bones, and her pale blue eyes were bright, lively—and coolly appraising.

And just as there was no artifice in her appearance, neither was there a jot of it in her manner. She stood no nonsense from anyone and prided herself on being a hard-working Yorkshirewoman who had her feet firmly planted on the ground. She spoke plainly and to the point, was even a little blunt at times, and she had a saying or an adage for almost everything in life and liberally peppered her speech with them.

After washing and drying all of her cooking utensils, Eliza went to the oven to check her Christmas cakes, date loaves and the huge bacon-and-egg pie she was baking for tea. Satisfied that they were coming along nicely, she returned to the table under the window; she stood screwing down the lids on the jars of the dried fruits she had just used in her cakes.

Since she was not expecting anyone at this hour, she glanced up in surprise when the front door suddenly opened.

Laurette walked in, followed by Audra. They looked pinched and cold and they were shivering.

"You're home early, love," Eliza said to Laurette. "Nothing wrong at work, I hope?"

"No, Mam, it's my early Friday. Have you forgotten?"

"Oh, I had that." Eliza looked at her daughter-in-law. "Hello, Audra."

"Hello, Mrs. Crowther."

Eliza turned back to her jars, finished replacing the last few lids. She had noticed the suitcase Audra was carrying, but she decided not to make any comment. Laurette was now pushing it into the coat closet quickly, as if to hide it. There's trouble brewing for Vincent, Eliza thought, but she said, "When you've taken your coat off, Laurette, you can mash a pot of tea, please, and you, Audra, come over to the fire and get yourself warm. You look nithered to death."

Both young women did as she said in silence.

Laurette was pleased that she had succeeded in persuading Audra to come home with her. Although she had not intended to make her miss the tram, this had served a good purpose in the end. A tender-hearted girl, Laurette had grown to care deeply for Audra. The idea of her sister-in-law wandering the streets of Leeds in this bitter weather had been more than she could stomach. If she won't go home to Pot Lane tonight, she can share my bedroom, Laurette thought, busying herself with the tea caddy. And I'm going to have a few strong words with that brother of mine at the first opportunity I get. We've spoiled him, Mam and Olive and I. And even little Maggie has always done his bidding. I bet he's not easy as a husband, or easy to live with, for that matter.

Audra, for her part, sat hunched in one of the green-moquette wing chairs, staring gloomily into the fire. She had been furious with herself for giving in to Laurette, but now she had to admit that she was glad to be inside in the warmth. The dampness had penetrated her bones and she still felt terribly cold despite the huge fire.

The kettle was hissing and steaming on the hob, as it always was in winter, and Laurette filled the large brown teapot with boiling water, then turned and put it on the table in the center of the room.

Seating herself at the table, she looked across at her mother and said, "Where're Maggie and Danny? It's well turned four and they should be home from school by now, shouldn't they?"

"No, not today. They've gone to the Parish Hall to see about the Sunday school pantomime. They both want to be in it so badly, I said they could go to try out for the parts. It's *Cinderella* they're doing this year."

"Knowing Maggie, she'll want to play the leading role and nothing else," Laurette said with a laugh. "Come on, Mam, have this cup of tea before it gets cold."

Eliza joined the two of them in front of the fire.

She took the other wing chair and, after a sip of tea, focused her attention on her daughter-in-law. "Now then, Audra lass, what's all this about? I saw the suitcase, you know. Are you running off somewhere, or moving in here?"

Audra flushed and bit her lip. But she did not reply, since she had no wish to confide in Vincent's mother.

Laurette volunteered, "I met Audra at the tram stop, Mam. She looked ever so upset and she said she was leaving Vincent, going back to work at the hospital in Ripon. But she missed her tram to Leeds when we were talking, so I made her come home with me."

"I see." Eliza sat up straighter and stared hard at Audra, frowning to herself. "What kind of silliness is this then, lass?"

"It's not *silliness!*" Audra protested indignantly, and before she could stop herself she rushed on with some fierceness, "Vincent's been behaving very *badly* in the past few months! He's not treating me properly, and there's no good reason why I should stay with him any longer!"

"He can't have been hitting you!" Eliza asserted, secure in the knowledge that her son would never strike a woman, even if severely provoked. "So what *do* you mean? Explain yourself, lass."

Knowing that she was trapped, Audra took a deep breath, said in a more even tone, "He leaves me alone a great deal these days, and you *know* he does, Mrs. Crowther. In fact, he's always out at the pub with his brothers and his friends, or at the bookie's office betting, and I don't think that's very fair of him. We might as well not be married, for all we see of each other, the little time we spend together."

Eliza sighed heavily and shook her head. "But that's the way it *is* with us, the way it *is* in our working class world, Audra. Our men toil hard, usually at manual labor, and their way of relaxing, of enjoying themselves, is to go to the pub for a pint, a game of darts, a few laughs with their mates. And what's the harm if they put a few coppers on a horse, have a bit of a flutter once in a while? Surely you don't begrudge Vincent harmless pleasures?"

"No, of course I don't. It's just that I would like to share his leisure hours; after all, I am his wife. But he goes out alone to the White Horse several nights a week, and he always disappears at weekends. He leaves me to my own devices and I'm lonely."

"Aye, I know, but as I said, that's the way it is and the way it'll always be, now that the two of you are married, settled down. It's different when you're courting, it's all sweetness and light like. But once he's got the wedding band on your finger, a man's attitude changes, Audra, and you'd better accept that. Oh aye, you had, lass. All marriages are the same, and you won't notice things so much when you have a few bairns tugging at your skirts. *They'll* occupy your time, mark my words, and you'll be glad to have Vincent out from under your feet, you'll see."

Audra's mouth tightened in annoyance. "I'm not planning on having children just *yet,* Mrs. Crowther. What I would like to do is to return to nursing, but that's another problem between us, because Vincent won't hear of me working."

Eliza was aghast. "I should think he won't!" she exclaimed in a horrified voice. "How could you ever suggest such a thing to him! It would make him feel *small,* much *less* of a man, if his wife went out to work. Whatever would people think? And what would his mates say?"

"I don't know and I don't care! Furthermore, we could really use the money I'd be earning as a nurse," Audra shot back, unable to suppress her irritation any longer. "Vincent and I had the worst quarrel we've ever had last night. It was very nasty really, almost violent. And it was about *money.* I've discovered that we're in serious debt, yes, *deeply* in debt, Mrs. Crowther, and it's Vincent's fault, not *mine,* so don't look so disapprovingly at *me.* He went off and bought things on hire purchase at Wigfalls in Leeds without telling me. He had no right to do that."

"What things?"

"The leather sofa, the wardrobe and the bed."

"And why are you acting so surprised? You knew you had those things; they're in your home, lass, aren't they?"

"Yes, but I didn't know he'd bought them on hire purchase; I thought he'd paid for them outright, paid cash. And the reason I know he didn't do so is because Vincent has missed some payments, and Wigfalls have written a nasty letter, which I opened when it came in the post yesterday. And apparently it's not the first letter they've sent him either." Audra shook her head, her expression baffled. "We need the money so badly, and yet Vincent goes out drinking and gambling as if he doesn't have a care in the world. And he refuses to let me go back to nursing. It doesn't make sense . . . his pride gets in the way of everything, and that's very stupid of him, actually."

"I'm sure there's a right good explanation why he missed a payment," Eliza replied, instantly defending her favorite child, her Stormy Petrel. "Vincent has money in the bank, I know that for a fact."

"No, he doesn't, Mrs. Crowther. He spent his savings on new clothes for the wedding, our honeymoon in Robin Hood's Bay and on other things for the cottage. I offered him my savings, and I said I would willingly sell a piece of my mother's jewelry to help clear up our debts, but he won't let me do anything to help."

"That's because he doesn't need your help," Eliza exclaimed huffily. "He probably has a nest egg tucked away somewhere, and knowing my son he'll only get angrier if you try to cut the legs out from under him. Let *him* deal with these matters, Audra, in his own way, and don't interfere. He *is* the man of the house, after all." Eliza's eyes narrowed slightly, and she went on in a sterner voice, "Anyway, I'm sure you're making a mountain out of a molehill; it's usually six of one and half a dozen of another in any marriage, and yours can't be much different from anybody else's. At least he's not chasing after other women, and you ought to be grateful for *that*. Take my advice, try a bit harder, try to understand Vincent better."

Audra stared at her mother-in-law in utter astonishment. The woman was apparently blaming her for all of their troubles and exonerating Vincent completely. She felt suddenly defeated and misunderstood. "I *have* tried . . . I know you don't like me, but I'm not a bad person—" Audra's mouth trembled, and she turned her head to one side as scalding tears stung the back of her eyes.

Eliza, startled by this statement, exclaimed, "Nay, Audra lass, don't say a thing like that! I *do* like you, I always have, and I think you're a fine young woman."

"Do you?" Audra swallowed down the incipient tears. "But you haven't acted as if you like me, really you haven't, Mrs. Crowther. And you didn't want us to get married, did you?"

"No, that's true, I didn't," Eliza admitted quietly. "But only because you're from a different world to us. I was convinced you and our Vincent would end up wanting different things in life, and I wasn't so far wrong, was I?"

Audra bit her lip. "I don't know; I'm a little confused."

Eliza nodded. "Aye, you are, and that's why you shouldn't be doing owt hasty, like leaving Vincent."

"But if you feel our marriage won't work, why do you want me to stay with him?"

"We're respectable people, and one divorce in this family is enough," Eliza muttered and looked through the corner of her eye at Laurette. She cleared her throat. "Marry in haste, repent at leisure—that's what I told our Vincent. But he wouldn't listen, and I don't suppose you did either, to your friends, I mean. Well, there we are. The two of you have made your bed, so you must lie in it, regardless of whether the mattress is lumpy or not." Leaning forward, giving Audra a sharper look, she finished, "It's always the woman who makes a marriage work, never the man. Just you be remembering that, lass."

"But that's not fair!" Audra cried, her indignation surfacing.

Eliza laughed hollowly. "Whoever said a woman's life was fair? Certainly not women from my walk of life, at any rate." She laughed again, shaking her head. "Anyway, Audra, I expect things'll get better between you and Vincent once the babies start coming along and you have the little ones to love and look after."

"But I want to do something more with my life, to achieve things, and I want to be happy—"

"Happy," Eliza spluttered, looking at Audra as if she had uttered an obscenity. "That's a word you'd better erase from your vocabulary, my girl, and right sharpish. Just you be thankful you've got a roof over your head, food in your stomach and a good husband to provide for you. Happiness is not for the likes of us, Audra, it's for the gentry, for the rich, them as have time for happiness and can afford it. We can't."

What a bleak outlook she has, Audra thought and turned to Laurette. They exchanged knowing glances and Laurette shrugged her shoulders. Then she stiffened slightly and sniffed. "Mam, is there something burning?"

"Oh my God, the Christmas cakes and the pie for your dad's tea!" Eliza leapt to her feet, grabbed the oven towel and yanked open the oven door. She began pulling out her baking tins, exclaiming to Laurette over her shoulder, "Well, don't sit there gawping, lass, get another towel and help me. And Audra, make a bit of space on the set-pot, please."

Laurette and Audra sprang to her assistance and within seconds the Christmas cakes, the date loaves and the bacon-and-egg pie had been spread out to cool. Eliza's critical eyes roved over them, and she nodded happily when she saw none of them had been ruined.

"It's only me, Mam!" The door burst open and Vincent came barging in, pulling off his cap as he did. When he saw Audra, his brows shot up in surprise. "What are you doing here, love?" he asked in the pleasantest of voices, smiling at her warmly.

Last night might never have happened, Audra thought, staring back at him mutely, marveling at his ability to shrug everything off. His nonchalance at this moment was quite remarkable. It annoyed her.

"She's having a cup of tea," Laurette said quickly. "We ran into each other in Town Street, and I invited her back to visit for a little bit."

"Oh, I see." He started to shrug out of his coat, swung to the closet.

Laurette hurried over to him. "Here, let me hang this up for you, Vincent," she said, taking his overcoat. "You get over to the fire and warm yourself up. You look frozen."

She doesn't want him to see the suitcase, Eliza thought, watching her children closely. But he's bound to see it sooner or later. She sighed and turned back to her cakes.

"Thanks, Laurette," Vincent said, rubbing his cold hands together, striding across the room. "I wouldn't mind a spot of tea meself."

"Coming right up," his sister said and went to the Welsh dresser. Bringing a cup and saucer to the table, she lifted the teapot and poured for him.

A moment later the door again flew open and Danny ran into the kitchen, followed more sedately by Maggie, who was feeling very grown-up and important this afternoon.

"We got the parts! We got the parts!" Danny cried to the room at large, throwing his cap and scarf onto the sofa. His overcoat followed, and then he scurried over to the bird cage in the corner. "I'm home, Flyaway," he cooed. He gazed lovingly at the little bird, which Vincent had bought for him and also named.

"Danny, hang up your things at once," Eliza called to her youngest.

"I will, Mam, in a tick."

Maggie, who was taking off her own coat, said, "Oh, I'll do it, Mother."

"And what part have you got, Tiddler?" Vincent asked when the little boy came and stood at his knee a moment later.

Danny looked up at his handsome eldest brother and smiled sweetly. "I'm going to be a page boy. I don't get to say owt, but I do get to carry a luvely red velvet cushion with the glass slipper on it."

Vincent rumpled his hair. "That's grand, lad."

Maggie joined Laurette and Vincent at the table, sat down between them and grinned. "*I* have a speaking part though, a big part too. I'm going to be one of the Ugly Sisters."

"What perfect casting!" Vincent cried and laughed uproariously.

"You are awful, our Vincent!" Maggie screeched, punching him hard on the arm. "And if I'm ugly, then so are you, 'cos everybody says we look exactly alike." She punched him again.

He grabbed hold of her wrist, held her tightly.

"Now then, you two, stop all this roughhousing!" Eliza cried, "your dad'll be home any minute, and he'll be wanting a bit of peace and quiet after his hard day at work."

Eliza walked over to the Welsh dresser and took down two of the largest serving platters. "And you'd better stop to your teas, Audra and Vincent. There's plenty for all of us. There's the bacon-and-egg pie, and I made a lovely jellied tongue yesterday." She peered at Audra over her shoulder. "You will stay?"

"That's up to Vincent," Audra murmured.

"Yes, of course we'll stay, Mam, why not?" He pulled out his Woodbines and lit one.

Audra sank back into the wing chair gratefully and gazed into the fire, her face abstracted.

She preferred to be here rather than alone with him at the cottage, where they were bound to quarrel. In a few minutes his brothers Jack and Bill would return from work and the atmosphere would probably turn boisterous, as it usually did when they were all together. But as rough and ready as the Crowther clan sometimes were, she knew they were good-hearted.

Often Audra did feel overwhelmed by them, and occasionally she saw them looking at her oddly. She sensed that they thought she was standoffish, and frequently they seemed wary with her. But not Laurette and Mr. Crowther. *They* were her real friends in this family, and she was quite certain they truly cared about her, just as she cared about them. They were the ones she would miss when she was back in Ripon. Despite what his mother had said, Audra was still planning to leave Vincent. She would go tomorrow.

"How could you do it? How could you go blabbing to our Laurette and me Mam?" Vincent demanded furiously, the minute they arrived at the cottage in Pot Lane.

Glaring at Audra, he went on heatedly, "I couldn't believe it when Laurette took me up to the sitting room after tea, and told me how she'd stopped you from running off and leaving me. It's bloody *embarrassing,* that's what it is!"

"I didn't go blabbing to them," Audra said evenly, holding herself very still. She was determined not to let him goad her into losing her temper as he had last night. "Laurette told you what happened. If I hadn't run into her at the tram terminal, and quite by accident, neither she nor your mother would know anything."

"Well, they *do* know, and you've gone and humiliated me again!"

"What on earth do you mean?" she demanded, drawing herself up and glaring back at him.

"First you diminish me in front of Gwen, what with all your talk of getting a job, going out to work and behaving as if I can't support you, and now you've been complaining about me to my mother and sister. Anybody would think that I'm the devil incarnate the way *you* bloody well carry on." His sudden laughter was harsh, and there was a sarcastic edge to his voice as he added, "And I thought *I'd* be the one to embarrass *you,* seeing as how you're so very much the lady. But the boot's on t'other foot, it seems to me."

"Please don't worry, Vincent, I won't embarrass you anymore. I won't be around to do so. I'm leaving you tomorrow. For good."

"Suit yourself." He marched across the little parlor-kitchen to the front door and picked up his cloth cap.

"Where are you going?" Audra demanded.

"To the pub," he replied and slammed out of the cottage without uttering another word. The door crashed behind him.

But Audra did not leave the following morning as she had threatened to do. She could not even leave their bed. Her throat was sore, her eyes were watering and she had a raging fever.

By eleven o'clock Vincent was so worried about her he sent for Doctor Stalkley, the local physician who had brought him into the world.

"Influenza, I'm afraid, Vincent," the old doctor pronounced, after he had examined Audra. "There's a lot of it going around in Armley just now. See that she stays in bed and give her plenty of liquids. Not much else you can do, my boy, it has to take its course."

Eighteen

Irène Bell paused on the threshold of the dining room at Calpher House, catching her breath in surprise.

Always a handsome room, with its cranberry-colored wallpaper of flocked velvet and English Regency antiques, it had a special kind of beauty this afternoon. This was due in no small measure to the Christmas decorations which were now in place and which had been created by Audra in her absence.

Mrs. Bell had just returned from a two-day business trip to London, and she stood for a moment longer, taking in the details of the seasonal decor.

She saw that Audra had eschewed tinsel and glitter, instead had turned to nature for her decorative theme. Garlands and branches of evergreens and mistletoe and the traditional hawthorn were much in evidence, tied and swagged with burgundy velvet or gold lamé ribbons. Crystal compotes held miniature pyramids of fruit and fir cones and nuts, and had been trimmed with brightly colored bows; there were masses of white candles everywhere, and two small fir trees stood guard on either side of the fireplace. These were covered with bows and ribbon streamers in rainbow hues, and the tubs were wrapped with gold lamé fabric in the Victorian manner.

In fact, the entire theme had an old-fashioned, Victorian air about it, and it was one which Irène found charming. And as always she was impressed and admiring of Audra's artistic talents, which she believed to be extraordinary.

I wonder how best to compensate her for this marvelous work? Irène asked herself, giving the room a final glance before turning away. *I cannot offer her money; she'll be insulted. She's such a proud young woman. I must find her a very special gift tomorrow, quite aside from her Christmas present from us.*

Crossing the hall in her usual energetic way, Irène Bell mounted the stairs, knowing that her child's former nanny would be in the day nursery with him, unless she had already gone home to Pot Lane.

They were sitting at the table near the fire, with a paintbox and sketching pad spread out in front of them, and they both looked up as Irène walked in saying, *"Hello, hello,"* to them.

Theophilus cried, "Mummy! Mummy! You're home!"

He ran across the floor and flung himself at her joyously. Irène bent down and kissed the top of his head and hugged him to her; then she raised her face and smiled across at Audra.

"Good afternoon, Mrs. Bell," Audra said, smiling back.

"I'm so glad you're still here, Audra. I just saw the dining room and I must thank you for the wonderful decorations; the room looks beautiful, just *beautiful.* You're to be congratulated."

A look of gratification flitted across Audra's pale face. "Thank you, but I did have a few willing helpers, you know."

Irène's brow puckered. "You did?"

"Oh yes, Mrs. Bell. Theo and Dodie, not to mention Cora."

"Cora. Gracious me, you are brave." Irène shook her bright-auburn head. "I don't mean to be unkind, but oh dear, that poor girl does seem to get

clumsier every day. And how kind of you to include her, yes, so *very* kind of you, Audra."

Irène walked over to the table with Theo, where they both sat down.

Audra explained, "Cora's enthusiasm is worth a lot, Mrs. Bell, and she would have been heartbroken if I hadn't asked her to do something. She helped Theo to make the garlands, actually."

"That was a safe job, Mummy," Theo volunteered, earnestly gazing up at his mother. "Audra said there was no risk involved, since all Cora could break was a twig or a bit of wire. Anyway, I kept an eye on her."

"I'm sure you did, darling," Irène murmured, biting back a smile of amusement. She turned to Audra, remarked, "I just can't begin to tell you how much I appreciate your efforts. What with the cook under the weather, Mr. Agiter coming down with influenza, and the unexpected trip to London, I was quite at my wits' end earlier this week. I don't know what I would have done, if you hadn't been able to help me out with the dining room decor, Audra. We have so many dinners planned, and I must admit, I can't help wondering how on earth we'll manage without a butler at Christmas. *Oh dear.*" Irène's gay, freckled face clouded. Instantly, it cleared. "Well, never mind, *never mind.* One can't worry about such things. I shall cope somehow." Irène peered at Audra in the firelight. "How inconsiderate of me, I haven't even asked you about your health, my dear. Are you feeling better?"

"Oh yes, thank you, Mrs. Bell."

"But you look as peaked as you did on Monday, when I came down to the cottage to see you."

"I'm perfectly fine, honestly I am, Mrs. Bell."

Theo said, "Look, Mummy, Audra's been showing me how to paint a scene." He pushed the sketching pad toward her.

Glancing down at it, Irène nodded. "Very good, darling, very good indeed." Her eyes strayed to the left-hand page where Audra had painted a simple landscape for him to copy. But in its very simplicity it was absolute perfection. Irène looked at it for the longest moment, struck by its delicate beauty, the reflection of light she had captured on paper. Finally lifting her eyes to Audra's, Irène said, "This is *lovely* . . . haven't I seen something similar before?"

"Yes, I did a larger version several years ago, and it was hanging in my room when I worked here."

"Of course. And you had given it an unusual name, as I recall."

"The Memory Place," Audra said very softly, "and the painting is of the sycamore tree on the slope opposite High Cleugh . . . where my family and I used to picnic."

"Yes, I remember now." Leaning forward, Irène said in her vibrant and emphatic voice, "You are a remarkably talented artist, Audra, and I can't understand why you don't pursue your painting."

"Oh but I'm not very good, Mrs. Bell, really I'm not," Audra replied with an odd laugh that was at once both dismissive and self-deprecating. "It's just a hobby, after all."

"It could be your profession."

"Oh no, Mrs. Bell, *nursing* is my forte. You know that Matron Lennox said I was truly gifted as a nurse, a real healer."

"Yes," Irène said, very slowly. Her eyes grew thoughtful and, after a short pause, one of her perfectly penciled brows lifted inquiringly. "I presume Vincent did not change his mind and that he is still against your going back to nursing?"

"Yes, he's adamant, I'm afraid." Audra lowered her eyes, then glanced away.

"I see." Irène decided to let the subject drop immediately, understanding that she was treading on dangerous ground. She wondered if there was some sort of trouble between Audra and Vincent, other than their differences about her nursing career. The girl had seemed strangely quiet and withdrawn at the beginning of the week. But then perhaps that was due to her recent bout with flu. Perhaps she was merely a little rundown.

Audra was saying, "And speaking of my husband, I really ought to be going in a few minutes, if you'll excuse me, Mrs. Bell." She took a peek at the nursery clock. "Oh goodness, it's already five-thirty. Vincent will be home from York at seven."

"*Why* has he been to York? What's he been *doing* there?" Theo demanded, as always insatiably curious about Vincent, who fascinated him.

"Really, Theophilus," his mother chastized, "you know it's rude to ask such personal questions."

"Oh that's perfectly all right, Mrs. Bell," Audra said; then explained to the child, "He went with Mr. Varley—you know, the man who owns the building firm—and they were going to have a meeting with Mr. Rowntree . . . something about building an extension onto one of the chocolate factories."

"Ooooh! How *scrumptious!* I wish I could go to a chocolate factory. Do you think Vincent will bring you back a box of Black Magic? They're my favorite, Audra." Theo looked at her hopefully.

"I know they are, but I don't think Mr. Rowntree gives his chocolates away, Theophilus," she responded with a small smile and stood up.

"Oh Audra, please don't go," Theo pleaded, "I hardly ever get to see you these days."

Audra reached out, stroked his fair head with tenderness, filling with love for him. "That's not strictly true," she said gently, "and besides, now that you're a big boy and going to preparatory school, you don't need a nanny. After all, you are seven years old."

"I know—but you *promised* we'd be extra-special chums."

"And so we are." Audra bent forward, kissed his cheek. Theo put his arms around her neck, clung to her for a moment.

Irène Bell said, "Don't behave like a *baby,* Theophilus. You know very well Audra has other responsibilities now that she's married."

"Yes," he mumbled and let go of Audra, although he did so somewhat reluctantly.

"Shouldn't you be getting ready for the pantomime at the Grand Theatre in Leeds?" Irène now suggested, her eyes sparkling with merriment.

"Oh Mummy! *That's* my surprise! And I've been wracking my brains for days!" the child shouted excitedly, jumping down off the chair. "I've been longing to see *Jack and the Beanstalk.*"

"Then run along and wash your hands and face. And Theo, please change your shirt. The one you're wearing is splattered with paint," his mother pointed out.

"Goodbye, Theo," Audra said, blowing a kiss from the doorway.

"Bye, Audra. Don't forget my party tomorrow and please, *please* make Vincent come with you. You will, won't you?"

"I'll do my very best."

As they went down the staircase together, Irène said to Audra, "Theo does have a soft spot for Vincent, doesn't he?"

"Yes, and the feeling is mutual, I believe."

"He seems to be doing awfully well at Varley's, and that must please you."

"Oh yes, it does. Mr. Varley likes him and, of course, Vincent does have a great eye and a marvelous sense of perspective when it comes to architecture. I've told him many times that he's a born builder."

"I think it's most commendable that he's started going to night school," Irène said, turning to face Audra as they drew to a standstill in the hall. "Is he enjoying studying draughtsmanship?"

"Yes," Audra murmured, not wishing to admit that Vincent had only *talked* about enrolling in the course, had never actually done so.

Studying her face closely, Irène Bell saw a flicker of something at the back of Audra's startlingly blue eyes. It was a peculiar look and it alarmed her. She's a very troubled young woman, Irène thought with a flash of intuition. Reaching out, she touched Audra's arm lightly. Her voice was low and warm as she asked, "Is everything all right with you, my dear?"

Audra hesitated.

For a fraction of a second she was on the verge of confiding in Irène Bell, and then she changed her mind. Aside from the fact that her pride and her strong sense of privacy got in the way, her intelligence told her that Mrs. Bell could not help her. Nobody could help her now.

Audra forced a bright smile onto her face. "Oh no, nothing's wrong, Mrs. Bell. Thank you for asking, but everything is fine."

"And your health *really* is all right?" Irène pressed, still not convinced.

There was a small silence before Audra nodded, almost too emphatically.

"You do look *awfully* pale suddenly," Irène insisted, frowning at her.

"It's just the aftermath of the flu, and I am also feeling a little tired now." Audra gently extricated her arm, hurried over to the coat closet. She took out her gray Melton coat and the plum-colored cloche, put them on, glancing in the hall mirror at herself as she adjusted the hat.

A moment later, as she wrapped her woolen scarf around her neck and pulled on her gloves, she asked, "Would you like me to come a little earlier on Christmas Eve? Perhaps there's something I could do to help at Theo's party, Mrs. Bell."

Irène chuckled softly. "Indeed there is, Audra. I'd be most grateful if you would keep an eye on Theophilus and nine other little terrors, at least until the Punch and Judy show starts."

No sooner had the door closed behind Audra, than it sprang open again within the space of minutes.

Irène was halfway up the staircase.

She turned and her face lit up at the sight of her husband.

"Thomas darling!" she cried, "you're home early, how lovely." She sped swiftly down the stairs, across the marble hall and into his welcoming arms.

After hugging her tightly, kissing her cheek, he looked down into her face. His own filled with pleasure. "Did you have a pleasant journey back?"

"Oh yes, thank you, Thomas, and all of my news over a nice cozy drink shortly, before we go to the Grand. But first, take off your coat, and then I'll show you the decorations Audra has created in the dining room."

"I saw her leaving the house as we turned into the drive," Thomas remarked, removing his scarf. "I had Robertson stop the motorcar, and I told her he would run her home if she waited a moment for me to alight, but she wouldn't hear of it. She's always been an independent little thing, though, hasn't she?"

"Yes," Irène agreed.

She linked her arm through her husband's and led him across the floor in the direction of the dining room. "Audra doesn't look terribly well to me, and I have a feeling she and Vincent are not as happy as she would like to have me believe."

"Mmmmm. Handsome chap, Vincent Crowther. Probably ruined too, by his mother and those doting sisters of his, not to mention women—women in the past tense, of course. No, Irène, I don't imagine that that young whipper-snapper is easy to live with. And then of course, he is from a different class."

"Thomas!" Irène exclaimed, drawing away, looking up at him sharply. Her eyes were dismayed. "You know I detest that sort of thing—class prejudice absolutely *incenses* me."

"Yes, but you're not going to change the nature of the English . . . it's endemic. Besides, the lower classes are just as bad as the aristocracy when it comes to that sort of thing. Snobs too, in their own way." He smiled at her somewhat wryly. "And whatever you say, background *does* make a devil of a difference, darling. Audra is a lady, and breeding will out—why it's obvious in everything she does. And unfortunately Vincent will always hold her back, hold her down, you'll see."

Thomas Bell shrugged. "But they are married, and it isn't actually any of our business."

"No, but I'm so fond of her, Thomas."

"Yes," he said.

The Bells paused on the threshold of the dining room. *"Voilà!"* Irène exclaimed, waving her hand toward the room.

For a moment Thomas Bell was startled. "Why it looks exquisite," he managed at last, obviously as impressed as his wife had been earlier.

"Very original, and quite breathtaking," Irène said and then sighed so heavily, Thomas eyed her curiously.

Irène met his direct gaze. She shook her head, and a look of perplexity washed over her expressive face. "Audra thinks she's especially gifted as a nurse, but she's not, she's simply very good and that's all. Of course, she would never believe me if I told her this, since Margaret Lennox has expressed entirely different views to her."

Swinging her eyes toward the dining room, Irène waved her hand at it again. "No, this is where her gift truly lies—in her artistic endeavors. She is an extraordinary painter, Thomas, but she can't see it, and I don't understand why she's so blind." Once again Irène sighed. "Oh Thomas, what a *waste* of talent. That's the saddest part of all."

"Perhaps it is. Poor Audra, she never had much of a chance, really. Life sort of came charging at her full tilt, and when she was so young . . ."

———— *Nineteen* ————

Why ever did I tell Mrs. Bell that I'm fine? I'm not fine at all. And I'm trapped. Whatever am I going to do?

These thoughts pushed all others to the back of Audra's mind as she busied herself in the kitchen-parlor of the cottage in Pot Lane, not long after she had left Calpher House.

I *should* have confided in Irène Bell, she told herself, unexpectedly regretful that she had kept her worries bottled up inside. It helped to air problems, especially if the listener was a sympathetic and understanding person like Mrs. Bell. But she had remained silent when the opportunity had presented itself, and now it was too late.

I really am on my own, Audra thought, just as I've always been on my own since I was fourteen. I have nowhere to go. No one to turn to . . . I only ever did have Matron Lennox, but even she can't help me. She can't possibly give me a job as a nurse now that I'm pregnant.

The despair that Audra had been carrying around with her for days spiraled into sudden panic, and as she put the cups and saucers on the table she saw that her hands shook slightly. Standing absolutely still in the middle of the kitchen, she took rigid control of herself. *Be calm, be calm,* she kept repeating, breathing deeply, reminding herself that panic never accomplished anything.

When Audra felt more composed, she went to look at the lamb stew for Vincent's dinner, which had been simmering in the oven of the Yorkshire range all afternoon. Satisfied that it was slowly cooking to perfection, she made a cup of tea and carried it to the fire, where she sat for a while, mulling over her predicament.

During the two weeks she had been ill with influenza, she had begun to suspect that she was pregnant. For the last few days she had been absolutely certain; a variety of changes in her body could no longer be ignored. When the cold facts had sunk in at the beginning of the week, her first thought had been of flight. She had intended to stick to her plans to leave Vincent.

But this evening, walking home from Calpher House, she had come to realize that this would be a foolish move to make when she was with child. She had no money, no job—and nowhere to run, anyway. Laurette had put it most succinctly when she had said, "We're the only family you have." *It was true.*

But to stay with Vincent? How could she? They only ever argued and bickered. Well, that was not strictly true. At least, not at the moment. He had been solicitous of her well-being whilst she had been in bed with the flu, and exceptionally kind to her, and there hadn't been a cross word between them since she had recovered.

A few days ago, he had asked her, unexpectedly and in a subdued voice, if she still intended to leave him. And she had said *yes,* and as soon as she was well enough to do so. There had been such an odd look on his face when he had turned away, and thinking about it now, she realized, suddenly, that it had been a look of genuine sadness. And she was certain there had been a hint of regret in his eyes, and that he was sorry for all of their angry words, their virulent rows that served no purpose. After all, they had started out with so much. *Oh why can't it be the way it was in the beginning?* she asked herself, and leaning back in the chair, she closed her eyes, thinking of the happy days of their courtship, fervently wishing they would come back.

A little while later, Audra sat up with a jerk, roused from her ruminations by the sound of footsteps on the flagstone path outside. The door flew open and Vincent hurried in, carrying a large bunch of holly dangling from a string.

His face brightened. He was relieved to see her sitting by the fire. These days he never knew for certain whether he was coming home to an empty house or not.

"Hello, love," he said, putting the holly on the floor, taking off his scarf and trilby hat.

"Hello," Audra responded, and she could not help thinking how handsome he looked tonight. The cold wind had brought fresh color to his cheeks, and his green eyes were alive and sparkling under the black brows. She asked, in her usual quiet way, "How was your trip to York?"

"Oh it was grand, and ever so successful, I'm happy to report. It looks as if we'll get the contract, oh yes, very definitely. Mr. Varley is right chuffed and so am I . . . it means all of our jobs are safe, well, for a bit, at least. Which is saying a lot when you look around and see what's going on in the country. Mr. Varley says we're heading for an economic crisis . . ." He let his sentence trail off, but as he struggled out of his coat and hung it up, he added, "Oh and by the by, you can congratulate me."

Audra's brow lifted. "Why? What's happened?"

"I've been promoted. Mr. Varley made me the new foreman this afternoon. There hasn't been one, you know, since old Harry Watkins retired."

"Congratulations *are* in order, Vincent, and I am pleased for you," Audra said enthusiastically, meaning her words. "You certainly deserve it; you've worked hard enough."

"Thanks for that, love." He cleared his throat, picked up the holly and walked across the floor. "I bought this from a farm cart on one of the country roads on the way back. What shall I do with it? Shouldn't it be in water?"

"It'll be all right for a while. Put it on the set-pot. Would you like a cup of tea?"

"Er, no thanks, love." He hesitated, as if uncertain of his next move, and then he walked over to her chair, bent down and kissed her cheek. But he quickly moved away, stood with his back to the fire, warming himself.

"Thank you for the holly, Vincent," Audra murmured, looking up at him with a half smile. "It was nice of you . . ."

"Oh it was nothing . . . do we have any beer left?"

"Yes, there are several bottles in the pantry."

He went to get one, asking, as he strode across the floor, "How's the lad, then?"

"Excited about his Christmas party, and the last thing he said to me, as I was leaving, was to be sure to make you come with me tomorrow."

"Oh, I don't know about that . . ." Returning to the fireside, Vincent sat down in the chair opposite her, his expression reflective.

"Theophilus will be disappointed if you don't go."

Vincent stared at her in surprise, frowning, and there was a hint of bafflement in his voice as he asked, "Would you *mind* if I went? I mean, do you *want* me to go with you."

"Yes, and anyway, Theo has his heart set on it. You know the boy hero-worships you."

He nodded, took a sip of beer, said hesitantly, "Well . . . I do get off work early. Mr. Varley always shuts down at twelve on Christmas Eve."

"Yes." Audra glanced away, sat looking into the fire.

Vincent fumbled in his jacket pocket, searching for his cigarettes.

A silence fell between them.

It was the kind of companionable silence they had so often shared in the early days, and tonight they seemed to be at ease with each other in a way that they had not been for months. Quite suddenly Audra felt his eyes on her, and she brought her gaze to meet his. She held her breath. There was a look of such tenderness and love on his face it was heart-stopping.

She opened her mouth to speak and then closed it without uttering a word, incapable of saying anything at this moment, filled with a bewildering array of emotions. She glanced down at her hands. Her wedding band glinted in the firelight, so burnished, so bright, a symbol of her dreams—and hope for the future. She thought of the baby she was carrying. The child *was* the future . . . just as it was part of the past, their *past,* created out of their love and their passionate feelings and their need for each other. Deep in the inner recesses of her heart Audra understood that in spite of everything her love for Vincent remained intact and unchanged; that was an inescapable fact.

Almost as if he was reading her mind, Vincent threw his cigarette into the fire and rose. He went and knelt next to her chair, and taking her hands in his, he looked deeply into her eyes, which were huge tonight and vividly blue in her wan face.

He swallowed, said tremulously, "Don't leave me, Audra, please don't leave me. On my way home tonight I didn't know whether you'd be here or not, and my heart was in my mouth. It's always in my mouth these days . . . not knowing what to expect. And I thought, what will I do if she's not there? How can I live without her?" He paused, attempted a smile, but it faltered. "The truth is, I can't live without you, and I don't want to anyway. You see, Audra, I love you, I really do."

She knew he meant every word. There was not only a ring of sincerity in his voice, but a desperateness too, and as she returned his penetrating gaze steadily she saw the glitter of tears at the back of his green eyes.

For a moment she could not speak.

"Please don't leave me," he begged again, his voice low and emotional.

Audra touched his face gently, and then to her own surprise she blurted out, "I'm going to have a baby."

Vincent drew back, his eyes widening as he stared at her, and then grabbed her in his arms and hugged her to him. "Oh Audra, what wonderful news!" Immediately he pulled away from her. All the anxiety had been wiped off his face and he was grinning boyishly. "You can't leave me now, you know you can't! Besides, I won't *let* you. You need me to look after you, to take care of you and the baby."

"Yes," she acknowledged, knowing this was the truth.

"We'll have a better life together, I promise," he said with genuine feeling. "And I promise I'll be a better husband, I really will, Audra."

• • •

At first he was true to his word.

The kindness he had shown during her bout with influenza continued, and he was more considerate than he had ever been to her, or anyone else, for that matter. At night he rushed home from work to be with her, and he never left her side in his free time, not even on weekends, when he was accustomed to going off on his own with his friends. He fussed over her, cosseted her, and was a model husband and expectant father.

Tranquility descended on the little house in Pot Lane.

Audra was content in a way she had never been in her entire life, and grateful to have peace and quiet—and also rest. Her pregnancy was turning out to be a difficult one. The morning sickness was unusually severe, and the nausea often continued during the day; she felt out of sorts in her general health and was constantly debilitated.

In the beginning, Vincent was concerned for her and sympathetic about her condition. But it was not very long before his patience gave way to irritability and, worst of all, boredom.

Just before Christmas, when they had reconciled, they had done so lovingly and had assumed their marital relationship. But once again this had ceased. Vincent more or less understood Audra's physical withdrawal from him, since he thought that an expectant woman might not be overcome by sexual desire for her husband. What truly troubled him was her lack of real interest in him and his daily life. He found her attitude strange and hurtful.

And so not unnaturally, given his nature, he soon began to find domesticity stifling. He did love Audra, and he did want to be married to her, but he also craved the life of a bachelor. This was not because he needed to chase after other women, for indeed he did not, but rather because he missed the camaraderie of masculine company, of roistering around with his friends in the pubs and betting at the bookie's office and the race track. He had done all of these things all of his adult life and he saw no reason to change his habits.

He also resumed his constant visits to his mother's house and, very simply, he did so because he missed the hurly-burly atmosphere and the joviality of being part of a big family, particularly one filled with affection and warmth for each other as the Crowthers were.

And he did not feel guilty about his behavior in any way, mainly because Audra had become completely absorbed in the baby. It seemed to Vincent that her entire being was concentrated on the child she was carrying, and to the exclusion of all else.

He was not mistaken in this belief.

The baby represented so much to her, perhaps more than he could truly conceive or understand. To Audra, the baby was not only the fruit of their love and their first child, but the beginning of that family of her very own which she had so craved for so many years.

Terrified of endangering the baby in any way, she took care of her health so scrupulously and so obsessively that even Laurette grew impatient with her on occasions; and when she was not fussing over herself, her health and her diet, she was preparing for the great event as if this was the first child that had ever been born.

The second bedroom at number thirty-eight was turned into a nursery, with great attention paid to the smallest detail, both decoratively and hygienically. She involved almost every member of the Crowther clan, insisting that they help with the scrubbing, cleaning, wallpapering and painting of the room. And then, after she had sold a small, diamond bar pin of her mother's, she went to Harte's in Leeds, where she purchased a set of charming nursery furniture that was also beautifully made.

Vincent's sister Olive was renowned in the family and amongst her friends for the exquisite garments she knitted, and in the past year she had been teaching this practical hobby to Laurette. Audra asked Olive to help her with her own knitting, and within a short space of time she had cunningly pressed both Olive and Laurette into making clothes for the baby. The three young women knitted as if their lives depended on it, and they were a comical sight when they were together, their needles clicking, their eyes glazed in concentration on their patterns, oblivious to everything. Bonnets, bootees, leggings, cardigans, jackets, and blankets for the cot and the pram were the result of their efforts. Later Audra sewed and embroidered a variety of other baby clothes, and she crocheted two beautiful lacey shawls; it was not long before a superb layette had been created. As Audra put the tiny garments away in the bedroom chest, she carefully placed tissue paper between the layers of finely worked items, feeling very proud of this exquisite wardrobe of clothes for her unborn child.

Yet with all of her domestic activities and despite being surrounded by innumerable and often boisterous Crowthers, there were times when Audra felt more isolated and alone than ever. This was due, in part, to Vincent's defection, and because she had no real kin of her own. Try though she had to become closer to Eliza, she had been unable to do so. She was still wary of her mother-in-law and cautious in her presence. She believed that Eliza had blamed her for all of their problems months before and continued to hold her responsible, whilst exonerating Vincent. Although this was not true, nothing would have convinced her to the contrary.

On the other hand, Laurette and Audra were warm and loving with each other, and Audra enjoyed a good relationship with Alfred Crowther, who considered his son extremely fortunate to have such a fine young woman for a wife. In fact, Alfred was disapproving of Vincent's behavior and minced no words when telling him so, which he did with increasing frequency. It was Vincent's father and his favorite sister who helped Audra through some difficult moments and trying situations at this time in her life.

Oddly enough, there were no rancorous feelings between Audra and Vincent during her pregnancy, even though they were in a sense leading quite separate lives. They no longer quarreled bitterly, and even their bickering had ceased. It was as if a truce had been declared between them. They were civil, even cordial with each other—and totally preoccupied with their own problems and with themselves.

The harsh winter gave way to the most glorious spring anyone had seen in years. Blue skies and bright sunshine lifted everybody's spirits. So did the trees bursting with green buds and the appearance of the first daffodils and crocuses, shooting up early to sprinkle the dark earth with brilliant yellow and purple.

And then suddenly it was the occasion of Gwen's marriage to Geoffrey Freemantle. Audra had had to decline Gwen's request to be matron of honor, because she felt she would look ungainly in her condition.

But she and Vincent did attend the wedding at St. Margaret's Church in

Horsforth on a sunny, breezy Saturday afternoon in the first week of April in 1929.

Audra had made herself a new maternity dress and matching loose coat of navy blue bouclé wool, and had bought herself a gay little hat made of straw and trimmed with midnight lace and deep blue roses. When Vincent saw her in the stunning outfit, he exclaimed at her prettiness, but Audra looked at him skeptically as she followed him out of the cottage. She felt like a small whale, and there was no question in her mind that she looked it.

As they drove over to Horsforth in his Uncle Phil's car, borrowed for the occasion, Audra thought of Gwen and of the way their friendship had begun to drift during the winter months. Between her work at the Infirmary, furnishing and decorating the house in Headingley and planning her wedding, Gwen had had little time for her, for anyone else, it seemed. Also, the circumstances of their very different lives these days were slowly coming between them.

There was another problem too, in that Vincent had become even friendlier than ever with Mike Lesley, Gwen's former boyfriend. In consequence, Vincent did not want to make friends with Geoffrey Freemantle, whom he persisted in referring to as "the usurper," and even if he had, Audra knew that the snobbish doctor would have looked down on Vincent.

I'm going to lose Gwen eventually and all because of Geoffrey Freemantle, Audra thought as she sat staring out of the car window, and she filled with sadness.

Later, as she stood in the pew with Vincent, watching Gwen walk slowly down the aisle on the arm of her father, the sadness seemed to intensify, as did a peculiar sense of distance. Gwen looked so beautiful, more beautiful than she had ever been, and Audra was momentarily stunned. This was a different Gwen than the one she had known.

She wore a crinoline gown of cream lace over cream satin, a veil and a long train of Alencon lace; the veil was held in place by a coronet of waxy orange blossoms. She carried a bouquet of white roses whose petals were tinged with the palest of pinks. A diamond heart on a strand of pearls glittered at her throat and there were diamonds in her ears. Gwen was a radiant bride, blond and blue-eyed and everybody's idea of the typical English rose, and there was no question that on this very special day in her life she was absolutely breathtaking.

And I've already lost her, Audra thought wistfully. She's gone from me. Gwen's entered a new world, one *I* shall never know. Suddenly she was choked with tears and there was an odd ache in the region of her heart.

There was a time in my life when I had absolutely nothing and no one. All I had was Gwen, Audra thought. *And she was so good to me. I'll never forget her for that. I'll always love her and she'll always be my best friend. Not even Laurette can take her place, dear though she is and so loving and loyal.*

Gwen drew level with Audra and smiled with warmth and radiance.

Audra smiled back, looked fleetingly but deeply into that pretty face, and she said goodbye to her friend in the silence of her heart. And she wished Gwen nothing but happiness and joy all the days of her life.

Even though her sense of loss enveloped her, Audra did manage to seem carefree at the reception. This was held at The Meadow, and Audra experienced a little spurt of pleasure to be back in that house where she had spent so many happy hours. But whereas she was able to put up a good front, she noticed that the Thorntons were not so successful at this bit of deception. Audra decided she had rarely seen a family looking so glum.

She had not been in the drawing room long before Mrs. Thornton led her into a quiet corner, to speak to her alone. Phyllis Thornton immediately confided, without any preamble, that none of the family cared very much for Doctor Freemantle. Audra tried to cheer her up by saying positive things, but Mrs. Thornton was not deceived. She shook her head mournfully. "We think he's an odious man, and you don't like him either, Audra, whatever you say . . . poor Gwenny, whatever has she done?" Mrs. Thornton sighed heavily before gliding off to greet some wedding guests who had just arrived.

Audra's eyes followed her. She was filled with sympathy for Mrs. Thornton, who had always been kind to her. Vincent joined her and they went over to the buffet, where they took a selection of tea sandwiches, then moved away. Charlie found them a few minutes later, and he brought over his fiancée to meet them. She was a petite girl called Rowena, who, Audra immediately noticed, was molded from the same clay as she was. She smiled. Perhaps it was true that men always fell for the same type of woman. But she was glad that Charlie had found someone he so obviously cared about. That he was indeed smitten with Rowena was written all over his face.

After the introductions had been made, Charlie lowered his voice and pronounced Gwen's marriage to be a horrible mistake. "My parents are heartbroken, and so am I," he confided. He and Vincent were soon picking the doctor apart, and agreeing that Gwenny should have married the devoted and desirable Mike Lesley.

Why are people always so dreadful at weddings, Audra wondered at one moment. She had no ready answers for herself.

Gwen's marriage was the highlight of the spring and the early months of summer. Audra and Vincent plodded along in much the same way, absorbed and preoccupied with themselves.

Audra was on her own a lot more than ever, since Vincent was now spending two and three days a week in York. Varley's was building the small extension onto Rowntree's chocolate factory, and Mr. Varley had put him in charge of the project. But neither Audra nor Vincent minded too much about these absences; they were both far too relieved that he still had a job.

More and more men were on the dole, and when Audra went to Calpher House she would see them standing outside the Labor Exchange at Hill-Top and her heart went out to them. They looked so without hope. And she thanked God that Vincent was not one of them.

By the end of June the building job in York was completed, and Vincent was again working locally and living at home all the time. It was a scorching Saturday morning at the beginning of July that Audra experienced her first contractions. Vincent rushed her to St. Mary's Hospital in his Uncle Phil's car, and several hours later their first child was born. It was a boy.

They had chosen his names weeks before. He was to be baptized Adrian Alfred, after their respective fathers. But right from the beginning Vincent called him Alfie and the name stuck.

Everybody loved Alfie.

He was a happy, laughing, easy-going baby with bright green eyes, dark silky hair, and a cherubic face. He hardly ever cried, and his disposition was so sweet that Vincent and Audra considered themselves to be the most fortunate of parents. All of the Crowthers petted and spoiled Alfie, most especially Eliza and Alfred, who doted on their first grandchild. But his aunts adored him too, and Audra knew there would never be a shortage of baby-sitters, whenever they were required.

As the months passed, Alfie only became sweeter and happier. He gurgled and laughed and kicked his legs a lot, whether lying in his cot or his pram, and when Audra wheeled him out on Town Street, total strangers would stop her to go into raptures over "the beautiful child." He was the kind of cuddly baby that everyone wanted to pick up and squeeze and kiss. Audra soon learned to be on guard about this, forever trying to prevent it, afraid as she was of Alfie being exposed to germs.

She loved her child to distraction. Sometimes she would stop her work and go out into the little garden to look at him. As she peered down into the pram, she was certain his face lit up at the sight of her, that there was recognition in his dancing green eyes, and this made her heart leap. She had never known such happiness as this tiny person gave her.

It was obvious to Audra and everyone else that Alfie was going to favor Vincent in his looks; certainly his vivid coloring echoed his father's perfectly. Vincent loved his son as much as Audra did, and both parents were aware that their infant boy was unusually alert and bright. He was already showing signs of exceptional intelligence by the time he was six months old, and they took great delight in little Alfie and were proud of him.

In a way, the child had brought them together again.

Their relationship had improved, and there was a peaceful atmosphere in the cottage in Pot Lane. Vincent stayed home more during the week now, and when he went out on Saturday nights, Audra accompanied him more often than not. This latter development was due in no small measure to Laurette, whose own circumstances had changed—and for the better.

Vincent had played matchmaker successfully.

His favorite sister and Mike Lesley were courting. Laurette was constantly issuing invitations to Audra, and these were readily accepted. The two men enjoyed each other's company, and Vincent was quite happy to forego his Saturday nights at the pub to take his wife out with the other couple.

These four shared a love of music, in particular the popular operettas of Sigmund Romberg and Victor Herbert. Since these were currently all the rage, touring companies from London came regularly to the Grand Theatre in Leeds, and Mike was the first to buy tickets for such hit shows as *Naughty Marietta, The Desert Song,* and *The Student Prince.* Sometimes they went dancing to the Mecca, or to see the latest talking pictures, but whatever they did, they generally had fun together.

The foursome became a regular thing during the summer and autumn of 1929, and they were all looking forward to spending Christmas together. Audra, for one, was especially happy this year. Her marriage was suddenly steady, she had a family of her own, and there was harmony in her home.

──────── *Twenty* ────────

Audra and Laurette walked slowly up Pot Lane in the gathering twilight of the January day.

It was the first week of 1930. The beginning of a new year and of a new decade.

Both young women were full of good spirits and happier than they had been in years. Despite the worsening conditions in England and the world economic crisis, their own futures seemed rosy—and secure at last.

Audra was content with her life and with Vincent. And, of course, there was Alfie, her darling little baby, who grew more beautiful by the day, who was the joy of her life. Vincent continued to do well at Varley's; he had had an increase in pay and they were finally out of debt. Things had never looked better.

As for Laurette, she was filled with a marvelous sense of euphoria. She was deeply in love with Mike Lesley, and he with her, and last night they had become engaged; they planned to be married in the summer.

Although Mike was still studying medicine at Leeds University, his bachelor uncle had recently died and left him a small inheritance. This welcome little windfall had enabled them to speed up their marital plans, since it would enable Mike to support a wife until he qualified as a doctor at the end of the year. And so her head was teeming with thoughts of her wedding, her trousseau, finding a house in Upper Armley, where they wanted to live, and making a comfortable home for this man whom she so adored.

Earlier in the day, the two young women had celebrated Laurette's engagement.

Audra had insisted on treating her sister-in-law to lunch on this very special occasion. Since they only ever went to Betty's Cafe in Leeds, she had decided that a change was definitely in order, and she had been happy to splurge. It had been worth it just to see the look of surprise and delight on Laurette's face when she had led her into Turkish Delight, the charming cafe with an oriental theme in Harte's.

After lunch they had wandered around the elegant department store for a while, playing their favorite game of pretend shopping. They had looked at the exquisite couture dresses and evening gowns in the Model Room; exclaimed over fox and beaver and ermine coats in the Fur Salon; tried on chic hats in the Millinery Box; doused themselves with a variety of expensive French scents at the perfumery counter. And, all in all, they had enjoyed this harmless bit of fantasy, this brief escape from their everyday lives.

Later they had gone to Leeds Market in Kirkgate, as they usually did every Saturday afternoon. "Down to earth with a bang," Laurette had said with a wry laugh, as they had trudged around the produce stalls, looking for good buys.

Audra had also laughed as she had picked up a cauliflower and examined it. She had murmured, "Everyone's looking at us, or I should say *sniffing* us. We must really and truly *pong* after all that perfume we sprayed on ourselves."

"We probably smell like a Chinese whorehouse, as our Vincent would say."

Giggling and laughing like a couple of giddy, carefree school girls, they had plunged through the throngs of shoppers, found their bargains and left the huge market with laden shopping bags, making their way to Upper Armley on the tram.

Now, as they headed along the darkening lane in the direction of the cottage, they were both shivering in the chill wind that had blown up. During the week it had rained a lot, and the wind carried with it the pungent odor of dripping foliage, wet earth and moldering leaves. There was a dampness on the air and a mist was coming down, and both presaged more rain.

"These wet leaves are treacherous on the path," Audra exclaimed, "so do watch your step, Laurette."

"Yes, I will, and listen, Audra, thank you for a lovely day. I've really enjoyed myself, especially our lunch and browsing in Harte's. Now I'm looking forward to a nice cup of tea. I suddenly feel jiggered."

"I'm a little tired myself," Audra confessed. "All those people in the Market, I've never seen it so busy."

"I've had enough of crowds for one day . . . I'm certainly relieved we're not going dancing tonight, I don't think I'd last very long."

"My feet are killing me too," Audra said, as they went down the steps into the cul-de-sac.

Before they reached the end of the flagstone path, the door of number thirty-eight flew open and Maggie stood in a circle of light, peering out into the gloomy night. *"Audra? Laurette?"*

"Yes, it's us," Audra responded, hurrying forward. She had caught an odd note in the fourteen-year-old's voice, and a warning signal went off in her head. "Is everything all right?"

"It's our Alfie," Maggie said tensely, opening the door wider, stepping aside to let them enter. "I think he's right badly, Audra."

Audra dumped her shopping bags on the floor and flew across the room without bothering to remove her coat. She bent over the bassinet in the corner of the kitchen, staring anxiously at Alfie.

She saw at once that her baby was indeed not well. His eyes were glazed and he was obviously feverish. Pulling off her gloves, she reached out, touched his flushed cheek lightly with the tip of one finger. His little face was burning. Instantly she became alarmed. But it was not in Audra's nature to panic; also, because of her training as a nurse, plus Matron Lennox's belief that she was a gifted healer, she felt confident and certainly capable of looking after her own child when he was ill.

Straightening up, she struggled out of her gray Melton coat, tossed it on a chair, hurried to the kitchen sink to wash her hands.

She said to Laurette, "Please get me the thermometer out of the medicine chest in the cupboard near the pantry. Then clear the tea things away and put a clean towel on the table, please. I want to examine Alfie under the light and sponge him down, to cool him. Could you also bring his toilet basket, oh, and dampen his flannel for me, would you please, whilst you're at it?"

"Right away." Laurette bustled around the kitchen, doing as Audra requested.

After Audra had washed and dried her hands, she rinsed the thermometer in cold water, placed it on the kitchen table, then went to get her child. She lifted him out of his bassinet carefully and carried him to the table, where she slipped off his cardigan and romper suit, and removed his vest and his nappy. And there was gentleness and tenderness in her every movement as she handled the infant.

She took Alfie's temperature, looked up at Laurette and shook her head. "It's a hundred and four, but I'm not really surprised, he's awfully feverish. Give me the flannel, would you please, Laurette?"

"What do you think he's got?" Laurette asked, sounding worried as she brought the face cloth to Audra.

"I don't know. It could be any one of a number of children's ailments—measles, chicken pox, scarlet fever. On the other hand, I don't see any sign of a rash or spots . . ." She let her sentence trail off, finished sponging his fat little legs, his plump little feet, then dusted him down with Fuller's Earth Powder. As she began to dress him again, she said to Laurette, without looking up, "But he does have such a *high* temperature. I wonder if I ought to give him a Fenning's Fever Powder? Or some gripe water? No, I'd better not. I think I have to send for the doctor."

Laurette nodded. "Yes, perhaps you should." She glanced at the clock. "If only Mike were here, he could examine Alfie. I can't imagine what's keeping him and Vincent."

"I can run down for Doctor Stalkley," Maggie volunteered, her voice shrill and anxious.

"Yes, I think you'd better," Audra murmured, lifting Alfie in her arms, taking him back to his bassinet. Turning to face Maggie, she said, "But before you do, tell me everything you can about the way Alfie acted this afternoon, what time you realized he wasn't well, and any symptoms you noticed—anything odd about him."

Maggie had been worried out of her wits for hours. She had been afraid to take Alfie to the doctor's office, for fear of endangering him further; for the same reason, she had not dared to leave him alone whilst she went to fetch the doctor. Now she was not only nervous but on the verge of tears.

She said with a tremor, "Vincent and Mike went off to the football match at about one. Just after that, our Alfie started to cry, and he kept crying off and on for ages, and he was ever so fratchy and that's not like him, he's always so good. I kept going to check on him, Audra, honest I did, to see if he was all right, to see if he was wet. But his nappy was dry, and there were no pins sticking in him. Then a bit later, it must've been three or so, I saw how red he was getting. It was ever so hot in here, and I took him into the sitting room to cool him down. We sat there a bit. I was nursing him on my lap, singing to him, and he started to vomit, and in ever such a funny way, Aud—"

"Describe the vomiting," Audra interjected, stiffening.

"I don't know how to, it's difficult to describe," Maggie wailed and looked at Audra, conscious of the sudden change in her sister-in-law. Audra's acute anxiety had instantly transmitted itself to Maggie.

"*Try.*"

Maggie gulped, wracking her brains for the right words.

She took a deep breath, said, "The vomit sort of came straight out of him. It was like somebody gave him a *thump* on his back and knocked it out. What was funny was that Alfie didn't heave, or do anything like that."

Projectile vomiting, Audra thought, with a stab of dread. That is what Maggie has tried so hard to describe. Oh my God. *Meningitis.* It simply can't be. Audra stood very still, knowing that it was imperative she keep a firm hold on herself, that she stay absolutely calm and clear-headed. For her baby's sake she must not permit emotion to cloud intelligence and judgment.

Swallowing her apprehension, Audra turned to the crib and peered down at Alfie. He looked so listless, and he was as flushed as before.

"Hurry to the doctor's, Maggie," Audra instructed. "Tell Doctor Stalkley that Alfie is ill, and that he must come immediately."

Maggie shot across the kitchen and snatched her coat from the closet. "What do you think's wrong with our little Alfie then, Audra? It's not serious, is it?"

"I can't be certain, but the vomiting and the high fever do worry me."

"I'll tell t'doctor about both things," Maggie said, pivoting at the front door. "And I'll run all the way there, and as fast as me legs'll carry me."

The moment they were alone, Laurette asked anxiously, "Audra, whatever is it? You've turned as white as a sheet. What on earth *is* wrong with Alfie? You must have some idea."

"I'm not sure, really I'm not," Audra replied, striving to keep her voice steady, not daring to say the name of that most ghastly illness. She had seen two children die of it when she had been a nurse at the Fever Hospital, and their suffering had been pitiful to witness.

Laurette stood up. "Well, you look awful, and I'm going to make us a pot of tea." She hurried to the sink to fill the kettle, glad to keep busy. She wished Mike were here. His presence was always comforting, and Audra had faith in his judgment.

Audra sat up slightly in the easy chair, thinking hard. She had committed a great deal of medical information to memory in the past. Suddenly, in her mind's eye, she pictured the page of her hospital textbook which dealt with meningitis. She sat staring into space, saw every word on that page quite clearly, as though someone held the book in front of her. *Meningitis: Acute inflammation of the membranes of the brain and spinal cord, or both. Also called "spotted fever," due to extensive spotting of the skin in severe cases. Symptoms: Severe headache, high fever, frequently neck and back rigidity; also twitching or convulsions. Severe vomiting is common, known as projectile vomiting due to sudden ejection of vomit to some distance; spotting of skin in severe cases; delirium, coma.*

Once more, Audra leapt to her feet and rushed over to the bassinet. Her eyes flicked over Alfie seeking signs of the symptoms she now so clearly recalled. But she saw nothing unusual. The child remained flushed, but there was no evidence of twitching or convulsions, or neck rigidity, and certainly there had been no rash on his body when she had examined him a few minutes earlier.

She let out a sigh of relief. Of course it's not meningitis, she told herself. How could it be? Anyway, Alfie's probably coming down with a winter cold, or influenza at the worst. *But his high fever, what about his high fever?* a small voice nagged at the back of her mind.

Alfie began to cry, wiping this thought right out of her head. She bent over the bassinet, reached for him.

"Hush, sweetheart, hush, my little darling," she murmured, holding him tenderly against her breast. She smoothed her hand over his dark head and across his small back, hushing him softly. Immediately, Alfie stopped crying and nestled into her. Audra walked up and down, soothing him, murmuring to him gently, and she was filled with such love for her child she thought her heart was going to burst.

And as she continued to pace back and forth in front of the fire, desperately trying to give comfort to her tiny son, she began to pray. *Oh please, God, don't let anything happen to my baby. Protect my little Alfie, please keep him safe and make him well again,* she entreated silently. And she kept repeating the words over and over again as she waited for the doctor to come.

——— *Twenty-One* ———

Alfie died.

His death was so unexpected, so swift, everyone was stunned and disbelieving. One minute he was a healthy, robust baby, laughing and gurgling in his crib, the next he was gone from them.

On that fateful Saturday evening, Doctor Stalkley had come to the cottage at once, following sharply on the heels of Vincent and Mike, who had walked in from the football match a few minutes before.

After examining Alfie, neither the doctor nor Mike believed that he had meningitis. Despite the peculiar vomiting in the afternoon, which had not recurred, his only symptom was the high temperature. "Not enough to go on," Doctor Stalkley had said. "I'll come back tomorrow morning, but meanwhile keep a close eye on him, Audra." Picking up his Gladstone bag, striding to the coat closet, he had motioned to Maggie. "Now, lassie," the old Scotsman had said, "you'd best be coming back to my office with me, and I'll give you a drop of medicine for the wee bairn."

Because the doctor and Mike had been so hopeful for Alfie's recovery from whatever it was that ailed him, Audra and Vincent had taken heart. Following the doctor's instructions explicitly, they had watched over Alfie all weekend, had not left him alone for one moment.

Audra had sponged him down frequently, to keep him cool and refreshed; she had given him the fever medicine at the prescribed times and had generally tended to him with all the skills of the professional nurse that she was. And she had hardly closed her eyes during that time.

But Audra did not care about sleep. Alfie's health was the only thing that mattered to her and Vincent. By Sunday night the entire Crowther family believed that Alfie was over the worst of his mysterious ailment. The febrile look had vanished from his eyes, and the scarlet flush had disappeared from his plump cheeks.

But on Monday morning, just before noon, the child had had a relapse.

Audra's worst fears had been confirmed.

Alfie had started to have convulsions, and the tiny spots, which looked like bright red pin pricks, had begun to appear on his milky skin. Endeavoring to control her terrible fear for her child, Audra had wrapped him in several woolen shawls and rushed to the doctor's office.

Doctor Stalkley had taken one look at Alfie and shaken his head. After a rapid examination, he had dispatched Audra to St. Mary's Hospital, just a short distance away. He promised to visit Alfie as soon as his morning office hours were over, when he started his daily rounds in the district.

Whilst she had waited for Alfie to be admitted to the children's ward, Audra had cradled him in her arms, cooing to him softly, fighting back her tears. It had been wrenching to leave him. And she had fervently wished that she was a nurse at St. Mary's, so that she could care for her beloved child herself.

Four days later Alfie came home to them in a small pine coffin.

Burdened with sorrow, Vincent dragged himself to every window in the cottage, closing the curtains to shut out the light until after the funeral, as was the custom in the North.

And then he went to comfort his wife.

Audra was inconsolable.

"Why couldn't I make him better?" she kept asking Vincent as she stood by the side of the open coffin, blinded by her scalding tears. "Matron Lennox says I'm an exceptional nurse," she sobbed, "so why couldn't I make our baby get well?"

"Audra . . . *Audra love,* nobody could have helped our poor little Alfie. It's not your fault; it's nobody's fault. Meningitis is generally fatal in small babies. Mike told me so," Vincent said quietly, "and you know that yourself, lovey."

"I should have kept him at home, nursed him myself, not left him to strangers," she cried, clutching Vincent's arm, staring at him wildly. "If I hadn't let Alfie go into the hospital, he'd be alive. He would, I just know he would!"

"No, love, that's not true," Vincent said gently, drawing her to him, smoothing her hair away from her ravaged face. "They did their very best up at St. Mary's, and they fought hard for Alfie's life. It just wasn't meant to be, Audra love."

Vincent led her out of the sitting room where the coffin stood, and took her back to the kitchen. He held her in his arms and tried to give her solace, and her tears drenched the front of his shirt, and they wept together for their child.

Eliza and Alfred came to see their dead grandchild, to share the grief of their son and daughter-in-law and do what they could to help.

Alfred, the ex–sergeant major of the Seaforth Highlanders, a tough and stalwart soldier, broke down and sobbed openly at the coffin. He was profoundly moved at the sight of Alfie, his namesake. In death, the child's beauty seemed more potent than ever and perfect in its waxlike state. Alfie looked as if he was merely sleeping. But when Alfred bent over and kissed the delicate cheek, its immense coldness struck him like a knife in the chest, and he clutched at Eliza's arm. She endeavored to comfort him, though her own sorrow was enormous.

When they joined Vincent and Audra in the kitchen a while later, Alfred looked around him, as if dazed, and asked in a shaken voice, *"Why?* Why has our little Alfie's life been snuffed out? He was only a baby, and nothing but pure joy . . . tell me why he has been taken from us so cruelly?"

No one had an answer for Alfred.

──── *Twenty-Two* ────

It was a golden day in late October, one of those especially glorious Indian summer days that so often occur in the autumn, just before the harsh winter sets in. The sky was the color of speedwells and luminous in the sunlight and the breeze was light, almost warm.

What a grand afternoon it is, Vincent thought, lifting his eyes, enjoying the radiance of the day. I hope this weather lasts till the weekend. Turning off Town Street, he increased his pace as he heard the church clock strike three. He was heading down Ridge Road in the direction of H. E. Varley and Son, Builders, and he did not want to be late for his appointment with Mr. Fred Varley.

It was a Thursday, almost the end of a week that had been exceptionally hard. He had pushed his men relentlessly to finish the warehouse they were building onto Pinfold's woolen mill, and by noon tomorrow the job would be completed. No doubt that was why Mr. Varley wanted to see him, to congratulate him, and there was bound to be a nice bonus for himself and his crew.

At the thought of a little extra money, Vincent began to whistle and he stepped out jauntily. He touched his cap, smiled and nodded as he passed the vicar's wife near Christ Church Vicarage, and then crossed the road. A few seconds later he was entering the builder's office and greeting Maureen, Mr. Varley's secretary.

"Hello, love," he said, taking off his cap, giving her a broad smile. "Mr. Varley sent for me."

"Good afternoon, Vincent," Maureen replied and nodded her head toward the door. "You can go in; he's waiting for you."

Mr. Varley was speaking on the telephone, but as Vincent hove in view in the doorway, he immediately said goodbye, hung up and beckoned for Vincent to enter.

"There you are, lad, come in, come in, and sit yourself down."

"Thanks, Mr. Varley." Vincent lowered himself into the chair facing the desk. "The Pinfold job will be finished tomorrow at noon," he went on, "the lads have done right well, Mr. Varley, and I know you'll be pleased when you see the warehouse. It's a bit of good building work, even though I do say so myself."

"Aye, I'm sure it is, lad, you're a good worker, and a good foreman, the best I've ever had, in fact." Fred Varley cleared his throat. "That's why it's so hard for me to tell you this . . . I've got some right bad news for you, I'm afraid, Vincent, I do that. I'm going to have to shut up shop."

Vincent stared at him, for a moment uncomprehending. "Close down?" he said swiftly, raising his brows. *"Close Varley's?"*

"Aye, lad—as of tomorrow."

"Oh my God!" Vincent was shocked. "I don't understand," he began, and then faltered as all of the implications sank in.

"I'm going to have to go into bankruptcy, I've no alternative," Varley said.

"But why? We've had a lot of jobs in the last few months—"

"Aye, I knows we have, lad," Mr. Varley cut in. "But some of the buggers haven't paid up yet, and I've no bloody idea when they will. I've been operating on credit for a hell of a long time, Vincent, and I'm so heavily into the bank, I don't dare borrow more, and I doubt that they'd lend it to me now, anyway. I'm mortgaged up to the hilt." Shaking his head sadly, he finished, "There's no two ways about it, I've got to cut my losses. Only one way to do that . . . *close down.*"

"I can see what you mean," Vincent mumbled, his eyes troubled as he looked across the desk at his employer. He was thinking not only of himself but of the other men who would be thrown out of work tomorrow. They were all married men, too, except for Billie Johnson, the plumber's mate.

Varley said, "Naturally, I'll tell the lads meself. Tomorrow. I wouldn't be leaving owt like that to you, shirking me duty, so to speak. I shall be able to meet this week's payroll, but that's about it. No severance pay, no bonuses, nowt like that, I'm sorry to say." Fred Varley added, "When you get your cards tomorrow, Vincent, I should go up and sign on at once at the Public Assistance Board, if I was you. Better start drawing the dole as soon as you can."

Vincent nodded grimly.

"I'm hoping I'll be able to sort out this mess," Mr. Varley remarked, rising, obviously wanting to terminate this difficult conversation. "And things are bound to turn around in the country right soon. The Depression can't last forever. I intend to start afresh, you knows, and in the not too distant future, and what I want to say is this—when I do open up again, there'll be a job for you, Vincent. I do hope you'd come back to me."

Vincent also stood up. "Thanks, Mr. Varley, and yes, I would. You've always been very decent with me, very fair indeed. And I'm sorry your business has gone down the drain, really sorry."

"Aye, lad, so am I. And I'm doubly sorry for you and the rest of the men. I know how rough it's going to be on all of you."

"I'll see you tomorrow then, Mr. Varley. Ta'rar."

"Ta'rar, lad."

—— *Twenty-Three* ——

Vincent Crowther sat in the recreation grounds, behind the park in Moorfield Road, smoking a Woodbine.

He was no longer aware of the beautiful Indian summer afternoon, and all of his earlier jauntiness had dissipated. He was engulfed in his worries about earning a living in order to support himself and Audra.

Only the other day he had read in the Yorkshire *Post* that there were one million, nine hundred thousand men out of work in England. Plus one, he muttered under his breath, now that I'm about to join them. The idea of going on the dole appalled him. But he would have to do so, since there was nothing else he *could* do until he found another job.

When he had left Varley's office he had felt as if he had been kicked in the stomach and the feeling persisted. He had wandered into the little park twenty minutes ago, hoping to clear his befuddled head, marshall his swimming senses before he went home. But he was still stunned, and just a bit bewildered. He had believed Fred Varley to be shrewd and successful, had never once imagined that the firm could go out of business, that Fred Varley, of all people, would go down. Just goes to show, he thought, you never really know about anybody.

Vincent had no idea where to begin to find work, for the simple reason that there weren't any jobs to be had. Nor did he have any idea how he was going to break this terrible news to Audra.

What a blow it'll be for her, he thought, and just when she was on her feet again after little Alfie's death. He groaned out loud, then took a long, satisfying drag on his cigarette. He suddenly held it away, looked at it with a frown, asking himself how long he would be able to afford his Woodbines. And his pint of bitter. And a bet on the ponies on Saturday afternoons. A grimness settled over him. The prospects looked bleak. Bloody bleak indeed.

Rubbing his hand over his forehead, he closed his eyes, thinking about the money he had in the Yorkshire Penny Bank. Not much really. His savings would only tide them over for a month, at the most. And all he could expect to get on the dole was something like a pound a week for the two of them, perhaps a shilling or two more. Obviously he was going to have to do his damnedest to get a job, no matter what it was, or where it was, for that matter. He might well have to try other areas of Leeds, such as Bramley, Stanningley or Wortley, or go ever farther afield to Pudsey and Farsley.

"Well, well, well, if it's not the gentleman of leisure! I wish I had time to sit on a park bench in the *rec* and idly fritter away the afternoon—*and* in the middle of the week no less!"

Vincent recognized the deep, masculine voice of his friend and brother-in-law, and he opened his eyes, stared into Mike Lesley's warm and friendly face peering down into his. "Yes, that's what I am, Mike," he said with a weak laugh, "a gentleman of leisure . . . as of about half an hour ago. Yes, I've joined the ranks of the unemployed, like the rest of me mates, and half the bleeding country."

Mike sat down heavily and frowned at his friend. "I know you're not joking, Vince. I know you *wouldn't* joke about anything as serious as this, but what happened? I thought Varley's was the one building firm in these parts that was doing well."

"So did *I;* so did *everybody*. But old man Varley just broke the news to me himself, about half an hour ago. He's going into bankruptcy."

Mike shook his sandy head slowly, his expression immediately turning dismal. "The situation's dreadful. I heard of three other companies that have gone down in the last month, and God knows where it's all going to end. But look here, Vincent, you're a skilled man, surely you'll be able to find something fairly soon—"

"Not bloody likely!" Vincent interrupted. "Even Mr. Varley has seen the writing on the wall, as far as I'm concerned, that is. He suggested that I sign on at the Labor Exchange at once."

Mike was silent. He shrugged further into his tweed overcoat, and his compassionate hazel eyes filled with concern for his best friend. He wondered if there was anything he could do to help Vincent find a job. He doubted it.

There was a momentary silence between these two young men who had gravitated to each other from the first moment they had met. They had grown even closer in the last couple of years. He was younger than Vincent, but he was blessed with great insight. If anyone understood the unusually complex man who was Vincent Crowther, then it was Mike Lesley.

Suddenly Vincent said, "How ever will I tell Audra that I've lost my job?"

"You'll tell her in the same way that you've told me, very directly," Mike said.

"She's going to be upset, to put it mildly . . . I couldn't stand it if she fell back into that awful depression. When I think of this spring, when she was so ill after Alfie died, I tremble in me boots, I do that, Mike. Audra was so odd, she was like a stranger to me."

"Yes, she *was* in a bad way," Mike conceded, "but a lot of women react as she did when they lose a child, especially when it's the first baby. They're demented for a while. And her loss was a terrible one, in that she's had so many other losses in her life already."

"Yes, she has. Poor Audra."

"Look here, Vince, my money is on your wife. Why she's got more character in her little finger than most people have in their entire bodies. She's a fighter, and she's full of Yorkshire grit and determination. I have a strong feeling that that wife of yours will take this news without flinching."

"I hope to God you're right, Mike, I do that." Vincent pushed himself up off the park bench. "Well, there's no point putting it off. I'd better get on home and tell her."

"I think you should." Mike rose and the two of them walked across the recreation grounds together.

"Do you still want to go to the City Varieties on Saturday night?"

"Of course I do!" Vincent exclaimed. "I can see no reason to change our plans. Anyway, Audra and Laurette have been looking forward to going. I wouldn't want them to be disappointed."

"Neither would I," Mike agreed.

The moment he strode into the cottage in Pot Lane, Vincent knew that something had happened—something special.

There was a record playing on the gramophone in the sitting room, filling the house with the strains of a Gilbert and Sullivan song from *The Mikado*. A vase of bronze and yellow autumnal chrysanthemums stood in the center of the table, which had been covered with a lace cloth and laid for supper with their best china. He surveyed the table, wondering if someone had been invited, but saw at once that it was set only for two. Glancing around the kitchen-parlor with quickening interest, Vincent next noticed the bottle of red wine on the set-pot; then he sniffed. His mouth began to water as he recognized the faint aroma of his favorite lamb stew coming through the oven door, which was slightly ajar. Pursing his lips, he wondered what was afoot, his curiosity truly fired now.

He had just taken off his coat and cap and hung them in the closet when the staircase door opened and Audra stepped into the kitchen. She wore a pretty, delphinium-blue blouse that matched her eyes and a dark skirt—plus the biggest smile he had seen on her face in ages.

"You look nice, love," he said, observing her appreciatively through his narrowed green gaze, half smiling as he spoke. He waved his hand around the room. "What are we celebrating then? Have you come into some sort of windfall?"

"You might say we've had two windfalls, in a sense . . ." She left her sentence dangling and ran to kiss his cheek. Then she stood away from him, gave him a queer, almost smug smile and led him by the arm to the fireside. She took an envelope off the mantelpiece, waved it in front of his eyes. "First, there is this! It's a letter from that firm of solicitors in Ripon—you know, the ones who wrote to me in June to tell me that Great-Aunt Frances Reynolds had died and that she had left me something in her will. You thought it was going to be another piece of silver, or that china teapot I admired, but it isn't either thing. It's *fifty pounds,* Vincent! Wasn't that lovely of her?"

"Aye, lass, it certainly was," he said with a grin, thinking that Audra's little legacy could not have come at a more propitious time. He was about to say so, wanting to tell her that he had lost his job, get the unpleasant task over with, when she prevented this. She flung herself at him and hugged him so tightly he was taken aback.

But he hugged her in return, stared down into her face.

He saw that it was filled with laughter and her bright eyes were more brilliantly blue than ever and there was a radiance about her. "What is it, Audra? You look like the cat that's swallowed the canary. Right chuff with yourself, my girl, that's what you are!"

"Yes, I am, Vincent. I went to see Doctor Stalkley this morning and he's confirmed it to me. I'm two months pregnant; we're going to have a baby . . . next May."

It seemed to Vincent that his heart did a tiny somersault of joy. He had been praying that she would get pregnant. Another child would fill the terrible void Alfie had left, and for both of them, not just her. His grief had been as acute as hers, and he still thought about his dead son with sorrow.

Vincent drew her closer, pressed her head against his chest, stroked the crown of her burnished head. "You couldn't have told me anything better, love," he said. "I've been hoping to hear this for months, I really have. No wonder you're chuffed . . . so am I."

"I thought you would be, Vincent."

His response was to tighten his arms around her. And he decided not to spoil the special evening she had planned for them by giving her his bad news. He would tell her about Varley's going bankrupt tomorrow. That was soon enough.

Unexpectedly, and much to his astonishment, he suddenly felt optimistic about finding a job. The baby was a lucky omen.

Twenty-Four

"Oh, Audra, what a bonny little girl!" Gwen cried, her face lighting up as she bent over the hospital bed to look at the new-born infant in Audra's arms. "She's just perfect."

"Thank you, Gwen. I think so, too, but then I'm her mother, so I suppose that's natural." Audra smiled up at her friend, who had dropped in unexpectedly to visit her at St. Mary's Hospital, then turned her eyes to the bedside table. She let them rest on the lavish bouquet Gwen had placed there a moment before. "And thank you for the flowers, they're lovely."

"Well, you always did like yellow roses, lovey. There's also this . . ."

Gwen placed a package on the bed. "It's for—" She stopped, glanced at the baby and laughed. "You haven't told me her name."

"Goodness, how stupid I am. We're going to call her Christina. Do you like it?"

"Oh I do, it's ever such a pretty name." Seating herself on the chair next to the bed, Gwen leaned forward and touched the gift. "Shall I open this for you . . . and Christina?"

Audra laughed. "Please."

"I hope you like it," Gwen murmured as she untied the ribbon around the fancy box and took off the lid. She lifted out a shell-pink dress with deeper, rose-pink smocking across the front, and held it up for Audra to see. "It's silk and it's handmade." She looked at Audra expectantly.

"Oh Gwen, it's exquisite and I love it! Christina will look so pretty in it, but you *are* extravagant." Audra reached out and squeezed Gwen's hand.

Gwen beamed with pleasure. She leaned back in her chair and regarded Audra thoughtfully. "I must say, you do look well. Certainly a lot better than you did after you'd had Alfie—" Her voice quavered as she said his name, and she stopped, her expression chagrined. "Oh, I'm sorry . . ."

"Don't be so silly, Gwenny, we can't avoid mentioning Alfie's name occasionally, and it doesn't upset me, truly it doesn't." Audra smiled at her reassuringly. "I've recovered from his death now, in the sense that my grief *has* lessened. It's not too painful anymore. Of course, I shall never forget Alfie and I shall always love him, but there's Christina now."

Audra dropped her eyes to the child in her arms and smiled down at her, then glanced at Gwen. "I feel quite wonderful, really. It was an easy birth, just as it was an easy pregnancy. It's odd, isn't it, that I had such a bad time with Alfie. But I hardly knew I was carrying Christina, and the delivery was over before I could blink—well, almost."

Gwen nodded her stylishly bobbed blond head. "Yes, it often happens that way." She gazed out of the window almost absently, and a wistful expression flitted across her face. "You are lucky . . . I wish I could get pregnant."

"Oh you will, just give it time."

"*Time!*" Gwen laughed softly. "It's May of 1931. I've been married exactly two years and one month." She gave a little shrug of her shoulders, added, "But then again, Geoffrey says I'm too anxious, too tense, and that I must relax about having a baby."

"Perhaps he's correct. After all, he is a doctor. And how is Geoffrey?"

"Oh he's all right." Gwen jumped up abruptly. "The nurses on this ward seem to be very careless in the execution of their duties. These roses will be half dead by the time one of them decides to bring a vase." She reached for the bunch of flowers. "I'll put them in water . . . be back in a jiffy."

Audra's eyes followed Gwen as she walked up the ward. She had changed a lot in the last two years, as Audra had known she would. *He* had changed her . . . changed the way she dressed and spoke and walked, and perhaps even the way she thought. And she had changed yet again since the last time they had met. There was definitely something odd about Gwen today, something that Audra could not quite put her finger on. They saw each other infrequently these days, since their friendship had continued to drift after their marriages. And so the slightest difference in Gwen was most apparent to Audra, the shrewd observer, when they did meet. It has to do with her appearance, Audra now thought, frowning. Was it her outfit? Certainly the black linen dress and jacket were rather stark with their lack of adornment. Also, the somber color drained the life from her face. But no, it was not her clothes.

Puzzled, Audra let her eyes rest on Gwen as she marched back to the bed, carrying the vase of roses. And as she drew nearer, Audra knew, suddenly, what it was that was so different about her friend today. *All of the light in her eyes had died.* She's no longer happy with him, Audra thought, if she ever was. That's why she doesn't want to talk about him, the reason she leapt up and rushed to put the roses in water. Oh poor Gwenny, she expected so much from this marriage, envisioned such a wonderful life for herself with Geoffrey, and I bet it's pure hell.

"Thank you," Audra murmured when Gwen placed the vase on the nightstand. She scrutinized her surreptitiously. Yes, there *was* a sadness behind those pretty pale blue eyes and a funny little droop to Gwen's mouth which had not been there before.

Gwen interrupted her thoughts when she announced, "I just want you to know that I gave that young nurse a good ticking off."

"I bet you did . . . you see how it is, Gwen; when you're back on a ward you want to take charge . . . old habits die hard, don't they?"

"Yes, perhaps they do." Gwen sat down, went on, "Whilst we're on the subject of nursing, are you going back to work for that woman in The Towers when you get out of hospital?"

"You mean Mrs. Jarvis . . . oh yes, I *promised* her, and I can't let her down. She's not at all well, and besides, we need the money."

A sympathetic look flashed across Gwen's face as she remarked, "It must be awful for you, lovey, Vincent *still* being out of work."

"Well, it's worse for him, really," Audra said softly, eyeing Gwen carefully, detecting criticism in her tone. "The frustration of not being able to find a job is dreadful for him, as I'm sure you can appreciate. Vincent's not a layabout, or a lazy man, you know, and—"

"I wasn't suggesting anything like that!" Gwen cried, flushing slightly.

Ignoring this comment, Audra continued speaking in an even voice, "He's out again this afternoon, doing the rounds. He's very responsible, and he follows up on every lead."

"It must rankle with him a bit," Gwen murmured. "I mean he was always dead set against you going out to work."

"Yes, he was, and don't think he's changed his mind, because he hasn't. However, that's the way it has to be just now."

"Yes, I realize that, lovey. The last time we saw each other, in March I think it was, you told me that your William had written to suggest that you and Vincent join him in Australia. Didn't that idea come to anything, then?"

"No, it didn't, and I never expected it would. Vincent might give lip service to the idea of emigrating, Gwen, but he wouldn't leave England. He grumbles, of course, about the Depression, the present conditions, and he calls the government and the politicians every nasty name he can think of, but he loves this country."

Audra shook her head slowly. "No, he wouldn't leave his mother and father and the rest of the family—they're very close-knit, you know, the Crowthers. And there was another reason—I didn't really want to go myself. Of course, I'd love to see William and Frederick again, but I don't think I'd want to live in Australia. Not anymore. It's *so* far away."

Gwen grimaced. "Yes, I know what you mean; it does seem like the back of the beyond." Waving her hand up and down in front of her face, Gwen now exclaimed, "Phew! It has grown hot in here all of a sudden, but then it's very warm for May, isn't it?" She slipped off her jacket and hung it on the back of the chair. "Didn't you tell me that your Frederick got engaged? Is he married yet?"

Audra did not respond.

Gwen looked at her curiously. "What's the matter? Why are you staring at me like that?"

"What on earth have you done to your arm?" Audra asked, unable to take her eyes off Gwen. The dress she was wearing was sleeveless, revealing an arm that was badly swollen and dark brown with fading bruises.

With a small, embarrassed laugh, Gwen said, "Doesn't it look awful! I fell down the cellar steps the other day. Geoffrey was furious with me for being such a clumsy thing. We were going to a dance that night, and I wasn't able to wear my new dress with cap sleeves, and I paid such a lot for it in the Model Room at Harte's. Geoffrey said I could have killed myself, and he was ever so cross that I was anywhere near the cellar steps to begin with." She laughed a little nervously.

"I'm not surprised that he was angry, and you *could* have killed yourself. I remember thinking how steep the cellar steps were, when I first came to see the house. You must be more careful," Audra cautioned.

"Yes, I know." Gwen stood up, appeared restless all of a sudden and strolled over to the window. She peered through the glass, stiffened, then swung to Audra. "Mike and Laurette are coming through the hospital gates with Vincent. I'd better be going."

"But they'd all love to see you and say hello to you."

Gwen laughed awkwardly, then remarked, "I don't really want to see Mike, to tell you the truth."

"Oh you are being silly. Now that you're both married there's no reason for you to feel self-conscious."

"I know, but they're your family and I'd only be in the way. And I really should be getting back to Headingley. I've things to do . . . we're having another dinner party tonight, and that maid of mine bears watching."

"I wish you'd stay."

Gwen shook her head with a faint smile. "No, I must be off." She lightly touched the top of Christina's head, bent to kiss Audra's cheek. "Bye-bye, lovey, I'll see you again soon."

"Goodbye, Gwenny," Audra said, very quietly, knowing it would be a long time before she set eyes on her again. "Thanks for coming to see me."

Audra watched her dear old friend hurrying off down the ward and she thought: Oh Gwenny, you'll run right into Mike on the front steps of the hospital.

"How're my girls?" Vincent asked, bending over, kissing Audra on the cheek, then peeping at his daughter in her arms.

"We're both blooming," Audra said, smiling, glancing up at him quickly. She knew from his expression that he had not found any work.

Laurette came forward to greet her with great affection and warmth, then said, "Mam's sent this small fruit pie; she thought you'd enjoy it."

"I shall, and please thank her for me, Laurette."

Vincent perched on the edge of the bed, said, "We just ran into Gwen, and she skittered off down the path as if we were carrying the Black Death."

"She had to get home," Audra told him. "She said something about a dinner party."

"I had a feeling she didn't want to engage in a conversation with Mike," Laurette volunteered, looking from one to the other.

"Aye, maybe you're right," Vincent said, nodding his head. "And I'm sure the feeling's mutual. What could he possibly have to say to *her?*"

Audra asked, "Where is he, anyway?"

"He stopped in to see a patient in another ward. He'll be here in a second," Laurette told her, then asked, "Can I hold Christina for a few minutes, Audra?"

"Of course you may. Here, come along, take her from me, dear."

Audra was glad to change her position in the bed, stretch a little. For a few seconds there was a quietness among the three of them, and Audra watched Laurette rocking the baby, cooing to her softly, holding her so tenderly. She suddenly said, "Vincent and I wondered—hoped actually—that you would be her godmother, Laurette, and that Mike would be her godfather."

"Oh I'd love to be!" Laurette exclaimed excitedly, "and I know Mike would too." She hesitated, then asked, "But who's the other godmother going to be? Gwen, I suppose."

"No, I have a feeling that wouldn't work somehow," Audra replied, looking at Vincent. "Do you?"

"I never did, and I'm certainly glad you've changed your mind." He grinned, glanced along the ward and added, "And here comes Mike now."

Mike made a beeline for Audra.

After kissing her cheek and squeezing her shoulder gently, he said, "No need to ask how you're feeling. For a woman who had a baby only two days ago, you look marvelous . . . I presume everything's all right, no problems of any sort?"

"No, none." Audra returned his smile, thinking yet again that he was the kindest man she had ever met. The compassion in his soul was reflected in those clear, caring eyes of his, and she knew he would become a successful doctor. His presence, his deep, warm voice, his concern engendered confidence; all were comforting. It's a gift, she thought, that sweetness of his. No wonder all of his patients love him.

Realizing that Mike was still hovering over her, looking down at her as if waiting for her to say something further, Audra remarked, "Doctor Stalkley was here earlier, and he says I can go home in a few days."

"He knows best, of course—just don't rush it," Mike warned and strode over to his wife. Resting his hand on Laurette's shoulder, he looked down at the baby in her arms and said, "She's going to be a bonny child."

"We'd like you to be Christina's godfather, Mike," Vincent announced. "Laurette's already agreed to be her godmother. So, what do you say?"

"I say yes." Mike grinned at them all. "You've just got yourself a godfather, and who's the other godmother?"

Vincent and Audra exchanged glances, and Vincent said, "I was thinking about our Olive. Audra, how do you feel about her?"

"She'd be perfect . . . yes, do let's keep it in the family."

Laurette said, "Olive will take her responsibilities as a godparent very seriously, as we will, naturally."

"Yes," Vincent agreed, "I know you'll all do your duty." He rose, went to his sister, stretched out his arms. "Can I borrow my little girl from you for a minute or two, Laurette? I haven't held her today."

Laurette gave the child to him and he stood looking down at her as he settled her comfortably in the crook of his arm, adjusted her shawl. Her skin was smooth and clear, and her features seemed quite well defined to him. Her face was not red and crumpled as Alfie's had been at birth. A feeling of awe crept over him as he continued to gaze at Christina and his heart twisted with love for her. He said, at last, "From the minute I heard from Audra that she was expecting, I felt this baby was a lucky omen. And she is, and she's going to turn out to be special."

"Very, very special," Audra added, "and I am going to give her the world."

They all looked at her in surprise.

There was a curious silence. Her words seemed to hang there in the air.

Laurette smiled, then bit her lip, not sure how to properly respond to this extraordinary statement.

Vincent walked toward the window with the baby, stood looking out, his silence pointed.

Mike's worried eyes followed him. From the tense set of his shoulders, he knew that Vincent was angered by Audra's comment. Well, it *had* sounded . . . possessive, to say the least. Couldn't she have said *we?* he thought.

Clearing his throat, wanting to bridge the awkward moment, Mike said, "That's a lovely sentiment to express, Audra."

"Oh but I mean it very seriously!" she shot back, in the strongest of voices, and pinned him with her eyes.

He had always known she had determination and guts, but now Mike saw something he had never seen before. There was a cold implacability in the set of the mouth and the thrust of the jaw, a terrible relentlessness in those extraordinary cornflower blue eyes. She not only *means* it, by God, he thought, but she's going to make it a crusade. And God help anyone who gets in her way, and that includes Vincent.

Twenty-Five

And so it became a driving force in Audra Crowther's life—the desire to give Christina the world.

It was all she thought about from this moment on, and the struggle toward this goal, one which would last for over twenty years, began that summer of 1931.

The moment she came out of the hospital, Audra went back to work for Mrs. Jarvis, whom she had nursed for four months before Christina's birth. She had promised the old lady she would resume her duties after the confinement;

this aside, they desperately needed the money. Vincent only received twenty-five shillings on the dole, a two-shilling increase per week now that they had a child. It was hardly enough to support the three of them.

The job with Mrs. Jarvis was neither difficult nor complex; it was convenient, in that the invalid lived in The Towers, only a few minutes away from the cottage on Pot Lane.

But Audra preferred hospital work to private nursing. After only a month of looking after Mrs. Jarvis, again she made it clear to the old lady that she was going to apply for work at St. Mary's. She did so at the beginning of July.

There was a vacancy at the hospital in November and Audra got the job. To her enormous delight she was assigned to the children's ward.

Audra knew that she had been given this most coveted position because of the strings Matron Lennox had pulled, the influence Mrs. Bell had exerted on Matron Fox. But this did not trouble her in the least. She had the job and that was all that mattered.

By the spring of 1932, Audra was settled at the hospital and enjoying it. Matron Fox had taken a liking to her, she was popular with the doctors, and she envisioned promotions coming her way soon. She never thought of these promotions, which she *knew* would be forthcoming, in terms of self-aggrandizement; very simply they would bring her more money, and that was why she wanted them. Money for Christina . . . for her clothes, her education, her future.

Although she could not save a single penny for Christina at the moment, she had every intention of doing so within the next couple of years. Audra had made long-term plans, since she believed this was the only way she would succeed, given her resources. She already had an idea for earning extra money, and she was going to put it into operation once she felt she was truly entrenched at the hospital. She was going to become a dressmaker in her free time.

Nursing gave Audra a sense of gratification, and she threw herself into it with her usual enthusiasm and energy, and as she went about the wards there was a new spring in her step, a smile on her face.

But things were not happy at home.

There was trouble between Audra and Vincent yet again, and their curious marriage was once more on a rocky footing.

In a way, the rift that had recently developed between them was mostly Audra's fault this time. Her entire attention was focused on Christina, whom she loved with an almost abnormal ferocity, perhaps because she had already lost one child in death.

Vincent also loved his little girl, but he had overwhelming problems of his own to contend with and, being a young and virile man, he had urgent needs as well. He wanted a relationship with his wife that was normal on every level. Sadly, Audra was not merely preoccupied with Christina and her work, she now had no interest whatsoever in Vincent sexually.

She had stopped sleeping with him some months earlier, and this rankled. He was filled with frustration at being jobless and relegated to looking after the child. Audra's physical coldness and rejection were beginning to aggravate his growing bitterness in general.

One Saturday evening in April, after Christina had been put to bed in her room upstairs, he decided to have it out with Audra.

He bided his time until she had cleared the table and washed the dishes. But once she had settled herself in front of the fire and picked up her darning, he switched off the wireless and took the chair opposite her.

"Why did you do that?" she asked without looking up, intent on mending the hole in his sock.

"I want to talk to you, Audra, and very seriously," Vincent said, leaning forward urgently, fastening his eyes on hers.

"Oh," she said, and dropped the darning into her lap, instantly aware of his stern tone. She sat back, gave him her undivided attention.

This is exactly what he had intended. He said, "We have *very* serious problems, you and I, Audra, and it's about time we got them out in the open. No more shoving them under the rug because you—"

"Problems?" she cut in, looking at him oddly. "What do you mean, Vincent?"

"Come on, Audra, don't play daft with me. You know very well what I'm talking about. Our problems in bed, that's what. You forever turn away from me. Don't you love me anymore?"

As usual when he spoke about sex, a faint blush touched her cheeks. She exclaimed, with some indignation, "Of course I love you."

"Strange way you have of showing it. An iceberg has nothing on you."

"Oh Vincent, how unfair you are! Please don't be like this. I do care for you, I do love you. But . . . well . . . I'm fearful of getting pregnant again. Look, you know as well as I do that another child would stretch our resources to the limit. We hardly have enough money as it is—"

"It's not my fault that the bloody country is in such a mess!" he hissed, interrupting her, throwing her an irate look. "You can blame Ramsey Macdonald and his blasted government for that! I'm not the only man out of work. There are two million eight hundred thousand of us now. And we're not simply jobless but desperate, and diminished as men because we're reduced to being on the dole—"

"You're misunderstanding me! I *wasn't* pointing a finger, Vincent. I would never do that. I *know* it's not your fault, and I also know how hard you try every day to find something. However, if we had another child it would jeopardize Christina's chances . . . don't you agree? Don't you *see* that?"

"Oh yes, I bloody well see it all right. You're planning this glittering future for her and she's not yet one year old. I sometimes wonder about you, Audra, wonder about your sanity."

He jumped up, his anger getting the better of him, and strode to the coat cupboard, grabbed his sports jacket off the hook and threw it on.

"Where are you going?" she asked, surprised that he was suddenly curtailing their important discussion, yet relieved at the same time.

"To my mother's."

"*Naturally*. And after she's sympathized with you, fussed over you, she'll give you more money to go to the pub, as she always does."

"What goes on between my mother and me is none of your bloody business," he exclaimed, glaring. "I've never asked you for a single penny and I never will."

She made no response.

He flung himself out of the house but resisted slamming the door behind him. He did not want to awaken his child.

• • •

As he walked down Town Street ten minutes later, Vincent's temper began to cool. Nonetheless, he did not excuse Audra's attitude; nor did he forgive her in his heart. If anything, he held a bigger grudge against her than before. He was not sure why, although she *had* managed to really get his goat tonight.

If I were a rich man, he mused, married to a cold, indifferent woman like Audra, I would take myself a mistress. She would be beautiful, accessible and very loving, and I would keep her in great style. Unfortunately I'm not rich, so I can't afford a mistress.

A thought struck him. He *could* afford Millicent Arnold, who would not cost him anything except a few good manners, some sweet talking and a little of his persuasive charm. Millie was not especially beautiful, but she had a pleasant face and a gentle nature. Most importantly, she had always had a soft spot for him, and for a number of years, now that he thought about it.

There's nothing like a woman who truly yearns after you, he thought. And instantly Vincent changed his plans.

He did not go to his mother's house. Nor did he stop off at the White Horse, where he knew his brothers Jack and Bill would be playing darts and waiting for him.

Instead he went to visit Millicent Arnold, a widow woman at only thirty-five and childless, who, he was quite certain, would give him a very warm welcome indeed.

Hurrying up Moorfield Road, he almost ran across the recreation grounds and through the gate at the far side, then sped up the ginnel that led to Rose Cottage. This was where Millie lived alone, now that Ted was dead these past two years. The house was in a tucked-away corner of Armley, and this pleased him. If he was lucky enough to become a frequent visitor, it was better that no one saw him coming and going.

After knocking several times and getting no answer, he turned away, disappointment filling him.

Then the door sprang open and Millie was exclaiming, "Why, Vincent, whatever brings you to *my* doorstep on a Saturday evening?"

"Well, it's like this," he said, pivoting, smiling down into the warm velvet-brown eyes upturned to his, "I was walking across the *rec* when I remembered what you said to me last week, you know, when we ran into each other near the library. You told me you were getting more lonesome and blue by the day. Know something strange, Millie? So am I . . . so am I . . ."

"Are you really, Vincent?"

He nodded, smiled his most engaging smile and leaned against the door jamb, let his eyes roam over her provocatively. He had not realized what a voluptuous figure she had. Suddenly he began to chuckle in a way he had not chuckled for years and his vivid green eyes danced.

"I was heading for the pub to meet my brothers, when I thought of you, Millicent, thought of how lonely you are, of how lonely I am." He paused. "It struck me that you might like a bit of company, and that you might be kind enough to offer a very thirsty man a beer."

Millicent swallowed, hardly daring to believe her good fortune that he had stopped by to see her. She had wanted him for years, for as long as she could remember, even when Ted was alive. She parted her moist lips, but said nothing. She simply took him by the arm and gently pulled him inside.

"Several beers, if you can drink them," she said at last, allowing her breast to brush against him, propelling him across the entrance hall.

Millie stopped abruptly, squeezed his arm and peered up into the handsome face which was now staring down at hers. A slow and languorous smile touched her lips. "And perhaps a spot of supper, too? You *can* stay to supper, can't you, Vincent?"

"I can indeed," he said, throwing his shoulders back, standing up straighter, feeling like a man again.

With great confidence, he put his arm around her slender waist and escorted her into the sitting room. And as she nestled closer to him he knew he had nothing to worry about tonight.

Vincent's daily routine did not change, even though he had plunged into an affair with Millicent Arnold.

He was discreet.

He liked Millie, enjoyed her company, basked in her affection for him, enjoyed the way she catered to his every need. And they found a great deal of pleasure and release in their long hours of lovemaking in her large and comfortable bed at Rose Cottage.

But it was a physical liaison, nothing more than that.

Vincent knew it would not last very long, as did Millie herself, and they agreed to simply let it run its course. They had also agreed there would be no recriminations on either side when one of them ended it.

All of this apart, Vincent was too responsible a man to neglect the child he adored, or to curtail his search for work simply because of a dalliance. He only visited Millie once a week, wanting to be disciplined about seeing her, and he was circumspect. He went to Rose Cottage only at night.

He continued to plod along as he had these many months.

He looked after Christina in the morning, wheeled her down to his mother's house around noon, where he had a lunchtime snack with her and Danny. And usually he left Christina in his mother's care for the remainder of the day, returning for her around four o'clock.

Almost every afternoon, and without fail, Vincent scoured the city and the outlying districts, looking for work. Sometimes he was fortunate enough to stumble on an odd job, but it was never for more than a day or two. Nothing permanent came his way.

And as the spring and summer slipped by, and autumn gave way to the winter months, Vincent Crowther began to acknowledge that nothing *was* going to turn up. The government was in the deepest and most prolonged depression ever known. England was truly on the edge of disaster, as was the entire world, since by now the economic crisis was global. In his bones, Vincent felt they were in for a long siege, and certainly there was trouble brewing everywhere; riots and hunger marches were becoming the norm.

Leeds, like the other great industrial cities, was acutely hit. The Salvation Army opened soup kitchens; other charitable organizations provided clothing and boots for the children who needed them, and also helped those who wished to leave the depressed areas to do so.

Vincent had never seen so many men on the streets—queuing up at the Labor Exchanges, loitering outside the bookies' offices and the pubs, or simply standing about in groups on street corners, looking glum and disgruntled, commiserating with each other. And there was an air of doom hanging over them all. As he looked around him, Vincent shoved aside the feelings of hopelessness that frequently invaded him these days, and dug deeper into himself for inner strength. He knew he had to keep going no matter what, and that he must keep his spirits up as best he could.

Although Vincent had never wanted Audra to go to work, he now thanked God that she was a nurse at St. Mary's. He was also grateful that other members of the Crowther clan were still working; it was a consolation to know that his parents were better off than most.

His father was with the transportation department of Leeds Industrial Cooperative Society, where he had worked for a number of years, and his job appeared to be secure. Bill was a librarian at one of the public libraries, and Jack, who was studying landscape gardening at night, had a job with the Leeds City Parks Department. Even Maggie had managed to find work in a tailoring shop in Armley, doing button holes on men's jackets.

These three did not earn as much as their father by any means, but their combined wages added up to more than most people had to live on. And so there was always plenty of good nourishing food on his mother's table and coal in her cellar, and Vincent knew that whatever happened, Audra and Christina would never go cold or hungry as many folk did in these terrible days.

As Christmas of 1932 approached, Vincent doubled his efforts to find employment, desperately wanting—and needing—to provide something for his little family over the holidays. He wanted to be able to buy a gift, however small, for Audra, a toy for Christina, and put a few luxuries on their table.

There were several big snowstorms in the early part of December and the snow settled. Many of the driveways were blocked, and late one Friday afternoon Vincent finally hit it lucky and got himself a job shoveling snow at one of the big houses nearby. Since it was already growing dark, the housekeeper told him to come back the following day at nine o'clock.

Saturday morning dawned bright but bitterly cold, and there was a biting wind. But Vincent did not care. He was so excited about earning a bit of money, nothing was going to deter him. Audra, who had the weekend off from the hospital, insisted he wrap up well. She made him put on two pullovers under his sport jacket, and, as he buttoned his overcoat, she tied a thick woolen scarf around his neck, handed him his woolen gloves.

He kissed her cheek, then said, "It shouldn't take me more than three hours at the most to clear the drive at Fell House, so I'll be back in time for lunch, love."

"I think I'll make a large pot of soup today; you'll be needing something like that after being outside in this weather," she remarked, walking with him to the door. The icy blast hit her in the face as he stepped out, and she shivered. "I'm not going to take Christina for a walk this morning; it's far too cold."

"No, I wouldn't if I were you. Ta'rar, love, see you later." He strode off down the path, turned and waved. His mood was jubilant.

Audra was very busy all that morning, looking after Christina, making the vegetable soup, doing her household chores. The time sped by.

Before she knew it, the clock was striking twelve. After setting the table for lunch, she turned on the wireless, took Christina in her arms and sat down by the fire to feed her.

When Vincent had not returned by one o'clock, Audra began to wonder what had happened to him; by two she was truly concerned. He could be tardy when he went to the pub with his brothers and friends, but never when he was working. He always came straight home from work for a cup of tea or a snack, and to change his clothes if he was going out later.

After putting Christina back in the small cot she kept in the kitchen-parlor, Audra poured herself a cup of soup but discovered she was not very hungry.

From time to time, she went to the window, parted the curtains and peered out, but there was no sign of him.

It was almost three o'clock when she heard the sharp, metallic ring of his boots on the path outside.

"I was getting dreadfully worried," she said, as he walked in and closed the door behind him. "I couldn't imagine what had happened to you."

"There was a lot of snow to shovel," he said, pulling off his cap, unwinding his scarf, slowly removing his gloves, which were hard with frozen snow. "More than I'd bargained for . . . the front driveway, two long terraces, the path down between the lawns, and the back yard."

"All those areas to clear! You must be exhausted, Vincent, and you're blue with cold. Come to the fire and get warm."

"They didn't even offer me a cup of tea at twelve—"

"My God, what kind of people are they!" She stared at him aghast.

He did not answer her.

As he came toward the fire, Audra saw something in his face that alarmed her. "Vincent," she began and hesitated. "Are you all right?" she asked, watching him carefully.

He remained silent, stood with his back to the fire, warming himself. After a moment he put his hand in his pocket, brought something out. He turned a pinched and tired face toward her and opened his trembling hand.

"This is what they paid me," he said in a voice that rang with bitterness, showing her the coin in his palm.

For a moment Audra could not believe her eyes. "Sixpence!" She was horrified. "They paid you *sixpence* for *six hours work*. But that's outrageous . . . those people—"

She could not go on; her anger choked her.

"Yes . . ."

Audra took a deep breath, steadying herself. "Oh, Vincent, Vincent dear . . ." She leapt to her feet and hurried to him, her face grave with concern. She took hold of his arm in the most loving way. "I'm never going to let you do anything like this again. Never."

He shook his head, glanced away. After a minute or two, he turned to her. His eyes were bleak.

"There's a blight on this land," he said.

——— *Twenty-Six* ———

"*Happy birthday to you, happy birthday to you, happy birthday dear Mam, happy birthday to you.*"

The second she had finished singing, Christina flew across the room, hurled herself bodily against Audra, almost knocking her over, and hugged her tightly.

Then she looked up at her mother, said, "We're giving you a birthday party, Mam. We planned it all by ourselves, and it's just for the three of us. It's a surprise."

Audra smiled down into the small, eager face lifted up to hers. "Why, how lovely, darling," she said, brushing a strand of hair away from the six-year-old's forehead, thinking how much she looked like her father today.

Although Christina had her hair and her coloring in general, she had inherited Vincent's finely chiseled features, Laurette's smokey gray eyes. She's certainly more of a Crowther than a Kenton, at least in her appearance, Audra thought yet again. This resemblance had always been marked, but it seemed more pronounced than ever lately. Christina had recently shot up, and she was going to be tall; this was another Crowther characteristic.

"Happy birthday, love," Vincent said, walking over to her, kissing her on the cheek.

Audra said with a faint laugh, "And I thought you'd forgotten it."

He grinned, took a puff on his Woodbine. "How could we? You've dropped enough hints lately," he teased.

"*Mam, please* . . . come on, come *on!* In here!" Christina cried, catching hold of her hand, pulling her away from the front door of the cottage in Pot Lane. "You've got to come in here, into the sitting room—you too, Daddy. Oh please come *on!*"

Laughing, Audra placed her handbag on the small table near the door, allowed herself to be dragged across the floor and into the next room by the surprisingly strong and determined little girl.

"There," Christina said, giving her a tiny, gentle push, "sit there, Mam, on the sofa, and you, Dad—" She glanced over her shoulder at Vincent, added "—can sit in that chair."

"Right you are." As an aside to Audra, he said, "I think we've got the makings of an army general in this one."

Audra nodded, amused. She sat back, smoothed the skirt of her summer cotton frock and looked across at Vincent expectantly.

He gazed back at her, poker-faced; his expression revealed nothing.

Christina darted to the antique chest in the corner and returned with a number of envelopes. "Here are your birthday cards, Mam; the postman brought them just after you'd gone to the hospital this morning. I'll give them to you one by one." She handed Audra a card, then leaned forward slightly, peering at her mother, trying to see the card she held. Unable to conceal her curiosity any further, Christina asked, "Who's it from?"

"Auntie Laurette and Uncle Mike." Audra showed her the card. "Bluebirds sitting on a branch, isn't it pretty?"

Christina nodded. "If you give it to me, I'll put it on the mantelshelf . . . oh thank you, Mam." She offered Audra another envelope. "Open this *next* . . .''

Audra noted the Australian postmark, recognized William's handwriting. "Well, we *all* know exactly *who* it's from, don't we?" she exclaimed with a little laugh.

"May I see it?" Christina came to Audra, stood with one small hand resting on her mother's shoulder, looking at the card with her. "This one's pretty too, Mam, but there's lots more yet."

The cards were slowly handed over, opened, exclaimed about and lined up with care on the mantelpiece. There was another one from Sydney, from her brother Frederick and his wife Marion; others from various members of the Crowther clan; and one from Gwen, who still remembered her birthday.

The last of the pile was presented with something of a flourish by the solemn child, who was so intent on making this a special day for her mother. "It's from us," she whispered, leaning closer to Audra, touching her cheek lovingly. "Dad picked it really, but he took me to the shop with him and I helped."

Audra ripped open the envelope and pulled out the birthday card. It was the most expensive of the lot, made of glossy paper, with a yellow silk cord slotted through it and tied around the spine. The picture on the front was of a bowl of yellow roses standing on a table near an open window, and fluttering above the bowl was a red butterfly.

"It's just beautiful," Audra said, before looking inside the card and reading the short, printed verse. Vincent had written underneath this: *Wishing you many happy returns of the day, with lots of love from your dearest husband and daughter,* and he had signed his name, and Christina had added her own signature. "Thank you, it's the loveliest birthday card I've *ever* had in my whole life," she told them, looking up, smiling first at Christina, then at Vincent.

They beamed back at her.

Christina said, "I'll get your present, Mam."

She flew to the chest, took a package from a drawer and carried it back to her mother. "This is from Dad and me," she said, smiling gravely, handing Audra the gift.

Audra slipped off the ribbon and paper, wondering what they had bought for her, filled with swelling happiness that they were making such a fuss over her birthday. She was so very touched she could hardly speak for a moment.

She found herself holding a framed watercolor. As she turned it slightly, the better to see it, her eyes widened and she caught her breath in surprise and delight. The painting was of a summer garden at sunset, and the scene was filled with golden light. There were raindrops caught on a cluster of leaves, as if there had been a brief shower before the artist had picked up the paintbrush.

The watercolor was small but quite lovely, even though it was flawed in parts and needed much more work; one side of it was unfinished and amateurish, and yet there was something distinctive about the scene, something that caught and held the attention. How fascinating, Audra thought, her eyes narrowing as they lingered on the painting. It looks curiously like my father's work.

But Audra knew that Vincent had not managed to find a very early watercolor by Adrian Kenton.

Christina's name was boldly and clearly written in one corner, but even if it had not been, she would have recognized this as her daughter's creation. As awkward and childlike as certain aspects of the painting were, Christina had managed to do one thing—capture light on paper. She had sometimes shown this ability in the past, and it was no mean feat. With this new piece of work, she had demonstrated just how much she had developed lately. The girl had displayed a remarkable talent for drawing and painting since she was four years old, but her latest endeavor proved that she was more than merely talented. She was extraordinarily gifted. Audra felt a sudden tingle of excitement at this discovery, and she filled with immense pride in her child.

Lifting her head, she found herself staring into a pair of large gray eyes worriedly fixed on her face.

"Don't you like it, Mam?" The child's lip quivered.

"Oh Christie, I do! I really do! It's simply beautiful, darling. Thank you so much." Audra brought the little girl into her arms and held her close. "I'm sorry I didn't say so immediately, I was far too busy admiring it, I'm afraid."

Christina looked into her mother's eyes, her own shining with joy. "I painted it specially for your birthday, Mam, and Dad took it to Mr. Cox's shop in Town Street and had it framed. That's why it's from the two of us . . . 'cos Daddy paid for the frame."

Giving her husband a radiant smile, Audra said, "Thank you . . . it's the best present you could have given me, really it is. I shall treasure it always." Her bright blue eyes held his with keenness. "And it *was* worth framing, Vincent, wasn't it?"

"Aye, it was that. I recognized the beauty of it the minute our Christina showed it to me." There was a proud expression on his face as he added, "You're a right clever little lass, love."

Christina looked pleased, then turned to her mother, asked, "Where shall you put it, Mammy?"

"Well, let's see . . . I know *one* thing, it's going to take pride of place in *this* house," Audra declared. "What about here, on the mantelpiece? For the moment, anyway."

Audra rose as she spoke, crossed to the fireplace and propped the painting on the shelf in the midst of the birthday cards.

Turning, she asked her daughter, "And whose garden is it? Where did you go to paint it?"

"Calpher House . . . I went up to see Mrs. Bell to ask her if I could . . . and I went all by myself. And she said yes, I could paint her garden for you, and so I picked that sweet little corner near her roses . . . she kept coming out to see how I was doing. She was ever so interested. It was last week that I did it, Mam, and she made me come inside when it rained and she gave me a glass of milk and a Cadbury's chocolate finger, no *two,* and after it stopped raining, I went out and I started all over again. I liked the garden better then . . . it sort of glistened after the rain."

Audra nodded. "You certainly captured that feeling beautifully, Christina, and it's the best work you've done so far . . . you've made leaps and bounds."

The child glowed.

Vincent said to his daughter, "Now, Christie love, what about the tea party then? Isn't it about time?"

"Oh yes! Mam, come on, and you too, Dad!"

——— *Twenty-Seven* ———

It was the most splendid tea party.

Audra was not permitted to do anything.

And so she sat at the table in the kitchen-parlor, watching her husband and her child bustle around, getting everything ready. She had noticed earlier how they had both dressed up; they had turned her birthday into a truly special occasion, and she could not help but feel happy and flattered. She just wished she had had time to change out of the cotton frock she had worn to work that day, to put on something more attractive herself, but Christina had not given her the chance.

How handsome Vincent looks, Audra thought, watching her husband as he moved around the kitchen-parlor. He wore a dazzling white shirt, a burgundy tie and dark gray slacks, and he had obviously rushed home from work to shave again and to change his clothes for the tea party. She could see that he was also freshly barbered, and his black hair, brushed sleekly back to reveal his widow's peak, was still damp with water.

As for Christina, she looks adorable, Audra thought. Yes, she's the prettiest thing imaginable today.

Her little daughter had donned her best party frock of pale-blue silk trimmed with narrow bands of white lace down the bodice and on the skirt. She had put on clean white ankle socks and her Sunday-best shoes with ankle straps, made of shiny black patent leather. A blue silk ribbon was tied around her head and finished in a bow on her crown. Audra smiled to herself. Vincent had done quite a decent job of fixing the bow.

Audra sat back in her chair, now eyeing the table with interest. It was covered with their good linen cloth and set with their best china, which only came out for visitors. She saw that a linen serviette had been placed on each plate and there was a posy of yellow roses from the garden in a glass vase in the center. Again she smiled. She fancied these were her daughter's touches.

Vincent went to the set-pot and turned off the kettle, which was whistling on the gas ring. He made a big pot of tea in the silver pot from High Cleugh; Christina brought out plates of food from the pantry.

She explained, in her piping child's voice, "The teeny-weeny sandwiches are made the way you like them, Mam, and they're all your favorites . . . potted-meat spread, tomato and cucumber, and Dad bought a tin of salmon at the co-op, and we made lots of sandwiches with it."

"They all look delicious," Audra said. "You have been working hard, haven't you?"

"Dad helped," Christina said and made several more trips to the pantry, returning with chocolate biscuits, currant buns with white, sugar-icing tops, scones and raspberry jam. "Grandma made the buns and the scones for me," she explained to Audra, and ran back to the pantry one more time. "Strawberries, Mam!" she announced, depositing the dish in front of her mother. "Oh and the cream! I forgot the cream!"

"Come on, Christina love, sit yourself down now," Vincent called, bringing the teapot to the table, pouring for the three of them. "I don't know about my two girls, but I'm famished."

During tea, Audra and Vincent chatted amiably.

She spoke of her busy day at St. Mary's Hospital, where she was now a sister and in charge of the two children's wards as well as the maternity ward.

He spoke about the temporary job he and Fred Varley had, building stables onto the Pinfold mansion in Old Farnley. They were doing it together, working side by side, since Fred Varley had not been able to open up again after his bankruptcy, at least not in a big way. Varley took on small building jobs, when he could get them, and usually it was Vincent he employed to help him.

"But he'll open up shop again soon, and permanently," Vincent said. "He will that, never fear." And Audra nodded her head and crossed her fingers under the table, praying that this was true. Vincent loved his work, and things were a lot easier between them when he had a job and was earning money and supporting them himself. She had slowly come to understand that it was his frustration when he was out of work that caused some of their greatest problems.

Vincent started to talk about his brother Frank, who was in the Ninth Lancers—a cavalry regiment—and with the British Army in India. He was coming home on leave, and Vincent had decided that the entire Crowther clan should give a party for Frank's homecoming.

Christina kept her ears cocked as she always did when she was with her parents, looking from one to the other, her large gray eyes wide and missing nothing.

She was attentive to their every word as she munched on her sandwiches. Occasionally she made a remark of her own, but mostly she listened. They were both so clever, her mam and her dad. She loved to hear them talk. Her mam had such a lovely voice, so soft and musical.

She always enjoyed times like this when they were so friendly with each other, and her mother smiled a lot and her eyes got very, very blue and very bright; she didn't like it when they squabbled. Then her father went out, banging the door behind him with a crash and didn't come home until ever so late at night when *they* were fast asleep. Her mother was always cross with him for days after and looked at him in a queer way through the corner of her eye and tightened her lips.

Once, last year when she had been little and not grown up like now, her mam had waited up for her dad to come home after a row. They had shouted at each other, and her mam had screamed, "If that's the way you feel about it, then go back to your fancy woman." She had heard it all, because she had been so surprised to hear her mam shouting that she had crept out of her room, had hung over the bannisters to listen.

And for days afterward she had worried that her dad was going to go away and live with the woman who was fancy. She had wondered if *they* weren't fancy enough for him. Perhaps if they made themselves fancy, he would stay, she had thought, but she hadn't been sure how to do this.

Finally she had asked her grandma what a fancy woman looked like. Her grandma had sucked in her breath, had stared hard at her, had asked where she had heard something like that, and she had fibbed, had said, "At school." She didn't know, even now, why she had fibbed to Grandma, except that somehow she knew she should not talk about things that happened at home. Her mam never did when *she* went to Grandma's. She hardly said anything at all, and she wasn't a bit like *her mam* when she was at Grandma's house. She was different, somehow.

But in the end they hadn't had to get themselves all fancy, because her dad had not gone away. A short while after each terrible quarrel her mam and her dad were all smiles again, and loving, and forever kissing each other on the cheek and hugging. It was always like that with them.

Her father's sudden laughter brought Christina out of her reverie.

She looked at him alertly.

His expression was merry and his green eyes were all sparkly like the necklace Auntie Gwen wore when they went to tea at her house in Headingley, except that they didn't go to Auntie Gwen's anymore. And her mother was laughing too, and her eyes danced and danced with blue lights and she knew her mother was happy today.

Christina did not understand why her parents were laughing in this way; she had missed what her mother had just said. But she began to laugh too, wanting to be part of it, part of them, part of their happiness and gaiety.

Vincent, still chuckling, said, "Oh and by the way, Audra, Mike's bought tickets for the Grand Theatre on Saturday . . . it's Noël Coward's *Cavalcade.* He's invited us, so that's another nice birthday treat for you, love."

"How sweet he is, and so thoughtful."

Christina asked, "Will Auntie Maggie be looking after me when you go out on Saturday night?"

"She will that, love."

"Oh goody, Dad. We have such fun and she always lets me stay up late."

"She does!" Audra exclaimed.

"It's time for the strawberries, Mam, I'll serve," Christina cried, jumping down off her chair. "And you get to get the most, 'cos it's your birthday."

"Don't be so silly," Audra demurred. "We'll all have exactly the same amount; it's share and share alike in this family."

"No, *you* have to have the most," Christina insisted as she carefully spooned the fruit into the small glass dishes she had brought from the sideboard.

They had not had strawberries for a long time, because they were so expensive and such a special treat. And so none of them spoke as they ate them slowly, savoring every bite, but their eyes shone and they smiled at each other with their eyes. And when they had finished, they all three agreed that these were the *best* strawberries they had ever eaten . . . sweet and succulent.

But the highlight of the tea party was the birthday cake.

Christina and Vincent fussed over it in the pantry, before the child walked out, sedately, carrying it high in front of her.

And father and daughter cried in unison, "Happy birthday! Happy birthday!"

Drawing to a standstill in front of her mother, Christina said, "I'm sorry there's only one candle, Mam, but that's all that was left from my birthday cake. The others were ever so burned down."

"I don't mind, Christie. One candle is certainly better than none."

"That's what I told her," Vincent remarked, sitting down opposite Audra. "And I also said you'd probably prefer one candle to thirty."

Audra gave him a small, rueful smile. "I can't believe that I'm actually thirty years old today. Vincent . . . where have all the years gone?"

Vincent shook his head, smiled faintly. "Don't ask me, lass. I've no idea. And I'll be thirty-four in nine days . . . or had you forgotten?"

Before Audra had a chance to answer, Christina cried, "We have to have a party for you too, Dad!"

Christina knelt to say her prayers.

Audra sat in the rocking chair and listened.

Once she had finished the long ritual of blessing her uncles in Australia and every member of the Crowther clan, Christina clambered up onto her bed and slid down between the sheets.

Rising, Audra went over to her, tucked in the covers and straightened the quilt, then sat on the edge of the bed. She smoothed her hand along her child's innocent cheek and smiled at her. "It was a lovely birthday party, Christie, thank you."

Christina smiled back. Then she asked anxiously, "We can have a party for Daddy, can't we?"

"Of course we can. It wouldn't be fair if we didn't . . . you had yours last month and there was mine today—so it's his turn next." Audra leaned forward, kissed her daughter.

Plump little arms reached out and went around Audra's neck. Christina nuzzled against her mother, filling with pleasure at the familiar smell of her cool fresh skin and the scent of gardenia flower essence behind her ears. She whispered, "I love you, Mam."

"Oh darling, I love you, too. So very much. Come on, curl up and go to sleep. It's very late now. Sweet dreams, honeybunch."

"Yes, Mam. 'Night, Mam."

Christina did not fall asleep immediately.

She lay in bed watching the sky through the window. They had let her stay up way past her bedtime tonight, since it was a special occasion and now it was very dark outside.

The sky was inky black and filled with glittering stars, oh so far away, and the moon was as round as a silver half crown and just as shiny. A full moon, her father had said, just before she had been packed off to bed.

Oh how she loved her dad. And her mam. She liked it the best when it was just the three of them . . . her mam and her dad and her. Her dad had invited Auntie Laurette and Uncle Mike to the tea party. She was ever so glad they hadn't been able to come. It wasn't that she didn't love them. She did. She loved all of her aunts and uncles and her grandma. And Grandpa. Especially Grandpa. She liked the way he smelled of leather and Gentleman's Hair Pommade and eucalyptus pastilles that he sometimes gave to her secretly, when no one was looking, and he took her upon his knee and told her stories of many wondrous things. She didn't mind that his big white curly moustache tickled her when he kissed her, or that he puffed away on a pipe that filled Grandma's kitchen-parlor with smoke and made her eyes water. He called it, "My fine Calabash," and he wouldn't let anybody touch that pipe of his, not even Auntie Maggie, whom he thought the world of, so her dad said.

But she loved her mam and her dad the most. More than the whole world put together. They belonged to her. And she belonged to them. She wouldn't want any other mam and dad. Hers were special. She just knew they were.

She snuggled down in the bed and closed her eyes, slowly drifting off to sleep. She could hear the murmur of their voices floating up the staircase . . . soft, warm, loving voices . . . she always felt so safe when she heard their voices . . .

"She's a very special child, Vincent," Audra said, settling back against the sofa in the sitting room.

"Yes, she's clever."

"What she has is more than cleverness, more than talent even . . . she's exceptionally gifted, Vincent." Audra let her eyes rest on the mantelpiece where the painting stood, propped up in the middle of the birthday cards. "Before tea, you said you were struck by the watercolor, so much so you decided to have it framed."

"Aye, no two ways about it, I was impressed." Vincent glanced at the painting Audra had done years before of the Memory Place, then let his eyes wander to the back wall where a landscape by Adrian Kenton hung. "Our Christina gets it from you and your father, Audra—her artistic talent, I mean."

"Yes, she does. But she's going to be a much better artist than I am when she grows up . . . and she'll probably be better than my father too. The indications are already there."

"There shouldn't be any doubt in your mind anymore about who your father really was, Audra." He gave her a slow smile.

"Oh, there isn't, and I don't suppose there ever was actually. I knew my mother would never do anything to hurt my father whilst he was alive. It was not in her nature to do anything shoddy. I think I've always known that she and Uncle Peter only ever became involved much later, after she was widowed."

Vincent nodded and reached for his glass of beer. He was glad that they had laid that old ghost finally.

They were both silent for a while, each lost in diverse thoughts.

The June evening had turned coolish, and Vincent had put a match to the fire whilst Audra had been putting Christina to bed. Now she sat staring into the flames, thinking of the child who lay asleep upstairs: the very gifted child, the child she had always known was going to have a glittering future.

Suddenly, Audra leaned forward, startling Vincent as she exclaimed, "Yes, we must do it!"

"Do what?" he asked, looking at her curiously.

She did not answer this question directly; instead she said, "I've been helping her the best I can for the last couple of years, and I'll continue to do so, but there's only so much knowledge *I* can impart, since I'm self-taught."

"Yes," he said.

"She'll have to go to art school when she's sixteen. They won't accept her at Leeds College of Art before then. Later she'll have to go to London. To study at the Slade—no, better still, at the Royal College of Art."

"How are we going to pay for all this?" he demanded, his voice rising sharply. "We'll never be able to afford an education like that for her, not even if the Depression ends and I get a permanent job. It'll cost *thousands.*"

"Yes, I know, but we'll do it," she replied, very firmly. "We must, Vincent, we must!" There was an eagerness in her voice, an excitement he had not heard for a long time. "Christina must be given every chance," Audra rushed on. "I won't have her cheated just because of a lack of money. She has a gift

. . . it must be trained. She is going to be a brilliant painter, a great artist, Vincent."

"Well," he said slowly, his voice sinking, "I just don't know . . ."

Audra sat up straighter and gave him one of her penetrating stares. "There can be no hesitation on our parts, Vincent, none whatsoever. We must strive toward this goal, whatever the sacrifice. Christina must have that chance. And I, for one, am going to make sure she gets it!"

———— *Twenty-Eight* ————

"I don't know what to do about Audra anymore, Mike, I don't really. I'm at the end of my tether," Vincent said in a shaky voice.

He jumped up and strode over to the window, where he stood looking out, narrowing his eyes against the bright April sunlight.

Mike said, "Yes, I'm aware how worried you've been." The young doctor frowned, conscious of his friend's anxiety, as well as his frustration at being jobless. Vincent's emotions were close to the surface these days, and the set of his shoulders indicated to Mike just how tense and distressed he was this morning.

"What can I do to help—" Mike began, but broke off as the sitting room door swung open.

Laurette backed herself into the room, carrying a tray. She turned and marched over to the fireplace. "Sorry I took so long with the coffee," she said brightly, "but I had to check on the Sunday joint and the roast potatoes . . ." Laurette paused in midsentence, suddenly noticing Mike's troubled face, Vincent's rigid stance.

"Oh," she said quickly, "am I interrupting something? I'd better take my cup of coffee back to the kitchen and leave you both in peace."

"No," Vincent said, spinning around, coming back to the seating arrangement near the fireplace. "It's not anything you can't hear." Lowering himself into a chair, he took out his cigarettes, lit one.

Laurette passed around the cups of coffee, then sat down, looking at Vincent expectantly, waiting for him to continue. For a moment Laurette observed her brother.

Vincent sat staring into the fire morosely, his face brooding as he smoked his cigarette.

Finally, hoping to draw him out, she asked, "Where did you say Audra and Christina have gone today?"

"To Fountains Abbey," he said without looking up. "Another painting lesson in the country, a field trip, as Audra calls it." At last he turned his face to Laurette, and added, "But you know she always takes Christie out to paint, on her Sundays off from the hospital."

"Yes, and I think it's admirable the way she's exposing her to paintings in the big houses like Temple Newsam and Harewood. Audra's giving Christie a good grounding, Vincent, and she'll be well prepared for art school."

Vincent nodded but made no comment.

Mike remarked, "You said you didn't know what to do about Audra anymore. Let's talk about it . . . it does help to get it off your chest, and that's really why you came to see us this morning, isn't it?"

"Yes, that's true, Mike." Vincent cleared his throat. "It's Audra's health that I'm worried about. She's pushing herself harder than ever these days, stretching her strength to the limit. You both know what her schedule's like . . . she's working damned hard at the hospital and taking on additional duty, whenever she gets the chance, for the extra money. Then, when she comes home, she's looking after us, cooking, cleaning, washing and ironing. *And* she's tutoring Christie in art. And when she's not doing that, she's toiling at that bloody sewing machine Mrs. Bell gave her, doing alterations and making clothes for people. The work aside, she scrimps and scrapes, does without herself, in order to save every penny she can for Christina's education."

They both looked at him attentively, their faces sympathetic.

Vincent shook his head slowly. "It's this relentless pursuit of money that troubles me, and I'm powerless to stop it. Helpless, really." Unexpectedly, Vincent's voice shook again. "I daren't interfere, daren't say a word . . . when I have in the past, she's bitten my head off . . . I was hoping *you'd* talk to her, Mike, you know, as a doctor. She'd listen to you."

"I doubt that, Vince," Mike answered, his tone gloomy. "Of course, I'd be willing to try, but I'd be wasting my breath. And so would Laurette, as close as she is to Audra. No one, nothing is going to stop Audra. She's single-minded and she's stubborn."

"Aye, I know that only too well," Vincent muttered. "All this started years ago when Christina was first born. I told Audra at the time that she was propelled by a terrible driving force within herself, and I was right." He ran his hand over his weary face. "There's nothing wrong with being ambitious, wanting the best for a child, I realize that. But what Audra's been doing these past few years—well, it's bloody abnormal if you ask me."

Laurette said, "I'm not sure if abnormal is quite the right word, Vincent—" She hesitated, searching for the correct expression to convey the sudden thought that had struck her. Then she said, slowly, carefully, "What we're witnessing is an act of will, and one so selfless, so powerfully motivated it's . . . well, it's just *awesome* to watch."

"Bloody frightening, you mean," Vincent said harshly. He took a deep breath, tried to soften his voice. "Look, Laurette, I want the best for our Christie, I really do. But there's a limit to what people in our circumstances can do. Audra's reaching for far too much for the lass. And anyway, it's not fair to the child; she has no little friends, no fun. I love Audra . . ." He paused, cleared his throat. "I don't want her to collapse, to get sick. I'm only trying to protect her."

"I don't think she'll pay any attention to any of us, as I said, but I *will* have a talk with her tomorrow, Vince," Mike promised. "I'll be up at the hospital to see patients, and I'll find an opportunity to say something to her. I'll insist she has a general checkup, just as a matter of routine. At least that might ease your mind."

"Oh it will, Mike, it will. Thanks ever so much."

Laurette smiled at her brother, patted his arm. "Try and relax a bit, love; it'll be all right."

Vincent nodded, put another cigarette in his mouth, struck a match.

"Will you stay for Sunday lunch?" Laurette asked. "It's roast lamb, new potatoes and spring cabbage—all the things you like."

"No, thanks though. I said I'd meet our Bill and Jack for a drink at the Traveler's Rest at Hill-Top; then I'll probably walk back to our mam's with them, have a spot of lunch there." Vincent eyed his sister, said in a careful tone, "I don't want you to say anything to Mam, but our Bill is thinking of going into the Merchant Navy."

Staring at him, her eyes widening, Laurette said, "She's not going to like that! Not with our Frank already in the army."

"I know she won't." Vincent turned to his brother-in-law. "There's going to be a war, Mike. The writing's on the wall, what with Hitler on the march, invading parts of Czechoslovakia in March and now, just last week, the man was making impossible demands on Poland—"

"I was reading about that in the *Sunday Express* before you came in," Mike interrupted. "The man's getting greedier than ever, territorially speaking, demanding that the Free City of Danzig be ceded to Germany. It seems we've pledged to support Poland in this new crisis; so has France."

Their troubled eyes locked.

"It's an uneasy peace we have at the moment, Mike, and it won't last long . . . we'll be at war with Germany before the end of the year, mark my words."

"Don't say that!" Laurette exclaimed, looking from her brother to her husband. "Will you . . . will you both have to go if there's a war?"

"Yes," Mike said.

—— *Twenty-Nine* ——

"What a lovely morning it is," Audra said, walking to the open door of the cottage in Pot Lane, standing on the doorstep, looking out. She lifted her eyes. "And the sky's so cloudless, Vincent."

"Yes, it *is* a bonny day," Vincent agreed, joining her in the doorway. He followed her gaze. It was directed to the bottom of the small garden where Christina sat sketching, and he smiled with pleasure at the sight of his child. "And much too nice to stay inside . . . I think I'll come with you this afternoon—if you'll have me, that is."

Audra looked at him in astonishment. "But you always go to the White Horse on Sunday at lunchtime—" She broke off as her laughter bubbled up and her eyes grew bright with happiness. "But we'd love it if you came with us. We're not going far, only to Temple Newsam. I want Christie to study some of the paintings there, in particular the Old Masters."

Vincent put his arm around her, squeezed her shoulder, stared down into her face. He saw the tiredness behind the sudden radiance filling her face at this moment, and his heart tightened. She was still pushing herself too hard, despite Mike's friendly lecture in the spring, and she worried him a lot. But she would not listen to him; his words seemed to make no impression on her. She continued to toil as she always had.

Vincent said in a rush, "Listen, love, I've got an idea, a wonderful idea. Let's get ready and go to Temple Newsam *now*. Well, in about half an hour or so. You know, make a day of it, Audra. We could take a picnic with us . . . that'd save you struggling over a hot stove, cooking Sunday lunch before we go. Come on, what do you say?"

Audra nodded her head, smiling. It was not often that he ventured out with them on these Sunday art excursions, and she was delighted. She looked over her shoulder at the clock on the mantelshelf. "It's ten past eleven already . . . but oh *yes,* why not!" Swinging to face the garden, shading her eyes against the sunlight, she called, "Christie, Christie, come inside, please. Your daddy's coming with us to Temple Newsam, and we're taking a picnic lunch with us and I need you to help me."

"Oh!" Christina cried and leapt to her feet, excited that her father was going too.

"Let's start making the sandwiches first," Audra said, bustling over to the pantry.

"Can I do anything to help?" Vincent asked.

"Not really, but you might put the wireless on. It would be nice to have a bit of music this morning."

"Done," he said, striding to the set, twiddling the nob. "Ah, here's a nice bit of music . . . why it's the *Blue Danube,* Audra. Fancy that—the first dance we had together at the Parish Hall, all those years ago."

Turning her head, she gave him the sweetest of smiles; then she frowned as the music stopped abruptly. "Oh dear, don't tell me that the wireless is broken again."

"We interrupt this program to bring you an important message from the Prime Minister," a BBC announcer was saying.

Vincent and Audra stared at each other, neither of them moving as the voice of Neville Chamberlain flowed out of the set, telling them and the rest of the country that Hitler had invaded Poland and England was now at war with Germany.

"Now may God bless you all and may He defend the right." The Prime Minister's voice, so grave and somber, was replaced by the national anthem, and the familiar strains of "God Save the King" reverberated around the kitchen.

"It's September the third today," Vincent muttered, glancing at Audra through troubled eyes. "I've been expecting a war, but it's come sooner than I thought it would."

"Yes." Audra lowered herself into the nearest chair, feeling weak in the legs as the implications of the Prime Minister's message sank in.

Christina looked from her mother to her father, her eyes puzzled. "What does it mean? What's going to happen, Dad?"

"We're going to be fighting the Germans, but don't you worry, pet, everything's going to turn out all right in the end."

"What shall we do about Temple Newsam?" Audra suddenly said. "Perhaps we'd better not go today, after all."

"Oh Mam, don't say that," Christina cried, "not when Daddy said he'd come with us."

Christina's face was so crestfallen and she sounded so let down, Vincent could not help exclaiming, "Oh what the hell, let's go, Audra. It'll probably be the last chance we get to do something together like this for a long time."

"That's true," Audra said hesitantly.

Eagerly, Christina asked, "Can we go then, Mam?"

"Yes—run upstairs and change your frock. Your daddy will help me to finish preparing the picnic."

"Shall I wear my yellow cotton frock with the primrose pattern?"

"If you like, dear."

When they were alone, Vincent said, "I don't know when the recruiting offices will open—tomorrow or Tuesday, I expect." He paused. "But I'm going to volunteer as soon as they *are* open for business."

"Yes," she said, "yes, I knew you would, if war came."

"Aye, like every Englishman worth his salt. God knows, I don't wish war on any of us; it's going to be hell on earth, but maybe I can now stand up and be a man."

She stared at him in amazement. "You've always been a man to me, Vincent."

Vincent Crowther joined the Royal Navy on Tuesday, and by the end of the week he had been sent to the big naval barracks at Harwich to start his basic training.

The cottage in Pot Lane seemed quiet and empty without him. It was the first time they had been separated since their marriage, and Audra soon began to realize just how much she missed him.

They had an odd marriage in some ways, she was the first to admit that, but in spite of their quarrels and differences, they loved each other. And they had this glittering prize who was their daughter Christina, and it was she who bound them together irrevocably.

And so as she went about her work at the hospital and at home, Audra thought about Vincent and worried about him and wondered how he was getting on in the Royal Navy.

Soon his letters started to come on a regular weekly basis, and she and Christina sat and pored over them and talked about him lovingly, and they could not wait for his first leave.

Because of his absence, Christina had to look after herself during the day when Audra was working at St. Mary's. "I don't mind, Mam. I can manage, honestly I can," the girl kept telling her, and this was the truth. Christina was exceptionally grown-up for an eight-year-old, mostly because of her intelligence and the practical domestic training she had been given by her mother, but also because she had been surrounded by adults all of her life.

In particular, she was close to her Auntie Laurette, and when Audra was on night duty, Christina now slept at her aunt's house. Mike Lesley had enlisted in the Medical Corps, and since she was alone, Laurette was happy to have her niece for company. With Mike's departure, Laurette had gone back to work. Wanting to do her bit for the war effort, she had taken a job as secretary to the managing director of an engineering firm in Armley which was now making bombs.

Every day, when her mother was at work, Christina went to her grandmother's for lunch, as she had done since she was a baby and had been taken there by her father in her pram. Eliza's cheerful kitchen with its plethora of roses had always rung with laughter and the jollity of her boisterous family. But now it was deathly quiet.

Bill had joined the Merchant Navy, Jack had gone into the army, and Maggie had enlisted in the ATS—the Auxiliary Territorial Service. She had first gone to a training center near Reading for a month's basic army training, then on to a huge camp in Shropshire, where she was learning to use antiaircraft instruments. Hal, Olive's husband, was in the Royal Air Force, and only Alfred and Danny, who was just sixteen, remained at home.

The Crowthers were suddenly a family of women, except of course for Alf and his youngest son, whom they all knew would go when he was old enough, and they drew closer as England mobilized for war.

Barrage balloons and searchlights, air raid sirens and the "all clear" signal, blackout curtains at every window, identity cards, air raid shelters and gas masks —all became quite commonplace. So did food rationing, clothing coupons, petrol rationing and shortages of every kind, and air raid drills conducted by members of the Civil Defense. Mr. Trotter, the local air raid warden for Pot Lane became a familiar and friendly face to Audra and Christina.

As trying and as difficult as these times were, Audra kept to her regular routine of years standing, and she insisted that Christina do the same. Aside from her school work, the tutoring in art continued, and Christina was expected to work at it with dedication every day.

But they had their little pleasures too, and in particular they loved going to the pictures to see the latest films from America, as well as those made at home. They were also rabid fans of the radio and listened to everything from the news to comedy and musical programs. It was the cinema that always won out, though, and they went once a week, sometimes twice, usually accompanied by Laurette.

One Saturday afternoon in late October of 1939, Audra, Laurette and Christina were having tea in the kitchen of the cottage, before going to the Picturedrome to see the latest Robert Donat picture, *Goodbye, Mr. Chips*.

Laurette, who was a real fan and read a lot about films and film stars, had been telling them about the movie, relating something of the story.

"Don't tell us any more," Audra exclaimed. "Otherwise you'll spoil it for us."

"Oh sorry," Laurette apologized, and, changing the subject, she went on, "What *I* can't wait to see is *Gone with the Wind*. I've been reading about it in *Picturegoer Magazine* and it sounds wonderful. Vivien Leigh looked so beautiful in last week's issue, and Clark Gable! *He's* just gorgeous."

Audra grinned. "If Mike heard you, he'd be jealous—" She glanced over her shoulder at the sound of knocking on the front door.

"I'll go," Christina cried, slipping off the chair, excusing herself from the table, running to open the door. "Oh hello, Mr. Trotter," she said, staring up at the air raid warden.

"Hello, love, is your mam in?"

"Yes, Mr. Trotter." Christina opened the door wider. "Please come in."

Jim Trotter took off his metal helmet, stepped into the house. "Good evening, Mrs. Crowther," he said, smiling warmly at Audra. "I'm ever so sorry to trouble you, just when you're having your teas, but I stopped by to have a word with you about Miss Dobbs in the corner cottage."

"What about Miss Dobbs?" Audra asked, regarding the older man curiously.

"Well, you see, it's like this, Mrs. Crowther, she never comes to the air raid drills, and I don't know what's going to happen to her when there's a real air raid, I don't really."

Audra frowned. "She'll join us in the bomb shelter at the bottom of the garden, Mr. Trotter. My father-in-law built it for us and Christina and I have made it relatively comfortable and—"

"Oh but she won't *go* into the air raid shelter, Mrs. Crowther," Jim Trotter exclaimed, interrupting her. "I've just had a word with Miss Dobbs about that and I got a real flea in me ear for me trouble, I can tell you."

"Oh," Audra said, giving him a baffled look.

"You'll never believe what she said to me," Mr. Trotter went on.

"No, I don't suppose I will," she said. "What did Miss Dobbs say?"

"Well, she sort of looked at me funny like, as if I'd landed from another planet, and shouted, 'Go and sit in that hole, yonder down the garden, sit *under* the ground. Not likely, lad. I'm going to be in the ground a long time when I'm dead, so I'll be staying up here as long as I'm alive, and if I get hit by a bomb, I get hit by a bomb.' Them's her exact words, Mrs. Crowther."

Audra tried hard, but there was no way she could keep her face straight. Christina and Laurette also began to laugh.

Jim Trotter looked at them all askance, then addressed Audra. "It's no laughing matter, Mrs. Crowther," he said indignantly.

"No, I know it's not," Audra gasped, "but I sort of share her sentiments about sitting in a hole under the ground."

"I sincerely hope you don't, Mrs. Crowther!" There was sudden alarm on Jim Trotter's face. "I'd be very upset indeed if I had two of you in this yard being *difficult*."

Audra nodded, biting her lip, unable to speak. She was finding it difficult to suppress her laughter.

Trotter went on, "What am I going to do about Miss Dobbs? I mean, I'm responsible for everyone in these houses on Pot Lane."

Understanding, all of a sudden, why he had come, Audra said as soberly as she could, "I'll do my best to get Miss Dobbs to come into the shelter with us when there's a raid, Mr. Trotter. But I can only try; I can't force someone against their will."

"Thank you very much, Mrs. Crowther, I'm grateful for your cooperation. Good evening." The warden took his leave quickly.

As his footsteps faded away down the path, Audra managed to compose herself. "Poor Mr. Trotter . . . he always seemed to like me, but I don't think he's going to feel quite the same way about me ever again. Oh dear . . ."

"Don't be silly," Laurette said. "You were right when you said we had to keep a sense of humor in these awful times. If we didn't, I think we'd all go mad."

The English had mobilized for war, and then nothing very much had happened on the home front.

In fact there was such inactivity in the air and on the land that this period soon became known as the "phony war."

At sea, though, war had started almost at once in September; in October the battleship *Royal Oak* was torpedoed as she lay in Scapa Flow, supposedly in safe harbor and secure from German attack. And by the middle of November something like 60,000 tons of British shipping had been sunk by the dreaded and deadly magnetic mines.

Every time Audra picked up a paper or listened to the wireless, her heart filled with fear. The news of the war at sea was never anything but disastrous, and she worried about Vincent all the time now that he had been assigned to a destroyer and was somewhere out there at sea. Every letter she received from him brought a sigh of relief, as did his letters to his mother.

Although he did not get leave for Christmas of 1939, he did come home in January of 1940 on a seventy-two-hour pass from Hull, where his ship was docked after a stretch patrolling the North Sea.

Audra had asked for time off from the hospital, so that she could be with him for his entire stay, and Matron Fox had been happy to give it to her. And so she was waiting for him at the cottage on that cold and drizzly Thursday afternoon, wearing the delphinium-blue blouse he liked so much and a dark gray skirt.

The moment he walked through the door, she saw how proud he was to be in the Royal Navy, to be wearing the uniform. He held himself very straight, with his shoulders thrown back, and looked taller than ever, and there was a new air of assurance about him, a confident look in his bright green eyes.

Audra flew across the floor to him, and he hugged her tightly, held her away, looked deeply into her eyes and then gave her a long and loving kiss on the mouth.

"It's nice to be home, love," he said, finally releasing her.

"And it's nice to have you back! I've missed you; *we've* missed you."

"Yes, it's been the same for me."

A few minutes later, as they sat drinking their cups of tea, Audra gave him all the news about the Crowther clan and his brothers and Maggie, who were away in the service. Then in a soft voice she told him how worried she had been for months on end.

"All I read about are naval disasters, Vincent. Aren't we ever going to have a victory?"

"We did have one, in December, Audra!" he exclaimed, looking at her fiercely. "Don't tell me you've already forgotten that three British cruisers scuttled the German battleship *Graf Spee* during the Battle of the River Plate?"

"No, I haven't, but I was thinking of something closer to home—"

"The *Graf Spee* had eluded the British Navy for months, and sinking her was a tremendous feather in our caps . . . don't think it hasn't had a demoralizing effect on the Jerries, because it has." Vincent's face glowed. "Winston's right pleased, I can tell you that."

Audra smiled indulgently. "Don't tell me you're on a first-name basis with the First Lord of the Admiralty," she teased. "Does Mr. Churchill *know* that you are?"

Vincent grinned. "We all call him Winston, behind his back, of course. We all love him—that's why." He leaned forward with a certain eagerness. "Do you know how the Admiralty announced his return last September? I mean, announced it to the entire British Fleet."

Audra shook her head. "How could I?"

After taking a long draw on his cigarette, he said, "Just the words *Winston is back!* But it was a hell of a bloody compliment to him . . . a joyful salute. Aye, he's a great man, Churchill is, lass. He ought to be Prime Minister. He probably will be too; *everybody's* dissatisfied with Chamberlain."

"Wouldn't you be upset to lose . . . *Winston* as First Sea Lord?"

"Yes, but I'd rather have him at the helm of this country than anybody else, I bloody would—" Vincent broke off, glanced around as he heard the door open.

"Daddy!" Christina dropped her satchel and sped across to him without taking off her coat and hat. She flung herself into his outstretched arms. They hugged and hugged each other, and then Vincent pulled away and asked, "How's my little poppet?"

Christina stared up into his familiar, much-loved face, and burst into tears.

"Now then, what's all this, love?" Vincent asked, pulling her back into his enfolding arms, smoothing his hand over her hair gently.

Christina's shoulders shook and she gasped for breath as she clung to him. "I—I—thought I'd never—never—see you again," she sobbed. "I've been so worried, Daddy. I thought your ship would get sunk."

"Aren't you the silly duck egg!" Vincent laughed and chucked her under the chin. "Nothing's ever going to happen to me, little Miss Muffet. Come on, take your coat off and let's go to the table and have the nice tea your mam's made. Then later we'll walk down to see your grandma." He leaned into her, his eyes twinkling and said in a half whisper, "And tomorrow I'm taking you and Mam to the pictures in Leeds. You'll like that, won't you?"

Christina nodded her head, her eyes shining.

Audra smiled as she watched the two of them together. He had always been a loving father to Christina; she could never take that away from him.

Vincent's leave came to an end all too quickly.

Audra got up at five o'clock on Sunday morning, to make breakfast for him whilst he shaved and dressed.

Eggs were a precious commodity, very scarce, but Audra had managed to get hold of two. She had cooked one for Christina's tea the day before, and now she fried the second for Vincent, along with a tomato and a small piece of bacon which Eliza had given her.

When Vincent saw the egg on his plate, he was upset. "Oh you shouldn't have," he said, frowning at her. "You should have kept it for yourself. Come on, take half of it to eat with your toast."

Audra prevented him from dividing the egg. "Thanks, but I'm not very hungry. Please eat it, Vincent; you won't get anything else for hours and hours. You told me the troop trains are running slowly, and you've no idea what time you'll get back to Hull today."

"That's true." Nevertheless, he ate the egg reluctantly, and he wished she had kept it for Christina, if she did not want it for herself.

Neither of them said much during breakfast. They were both aware that he was going back to fight a war, and they had no idea when they would see each other again. It could be months on end, maybe even years.

As the clock struck six, Vincent stood up. "I'd better be going. My train's at seven."

"Yes."

As he put on his regulation navy topcoat, picked up his sailor hat and brought his kit bag to the door, he said, "I kissed Christie before I came down for breakfast . . . I don't want to go upstairs again; I might wake her. Say goodbye to her for me."

Audra nodded, too choked to speak. She came to him in the doorway, stood on tiptoe to kiss him. He kissed her in return, held her tightly for a moment longer.

"Please be careful, Vincent," she managed to say in a tight voice.

"I will, don't fret, love. I'll write . . ."

A second later he was gone.

Suddenly she was standing alone in the kitchen.

She ran to the window, parted the curtains, watched him hurrying down the path in the remote light of the January dawn.

Instinctively her hand came up to her heart, fearing for him, fearing for his safety. Come back to me, she whispered in the silence of the empty room. And Audra stood there for a long time after he had disappeared from sight, facing an irrefutable fact. Her love for Vincent Crowther was undiminished, despite all of their troubles and problems over the years.

Thirty

Spring came, bringing with it an end to the "phony war."

Audra sat glued to her wireless in the evening, whilst Christina did her homework or sketched and painted. And the more Audra heard, the more she became alarmed for her husband and the rest of the family and friends who were fighting the enemy.

Events were moving so rapidly she could scarcely keep track of them. On April 9 Hitler invaded Denmark and Norway. Denmark fell at once, but the valiant Norwegians fought back heroically and appealed to Britain for help. Immediately naval and military forces were dispatched.

For the next three weeks Audra behaved like a sleepwalker, doing everything automatically, as if by rote. She knew from the news on the radio that Vincent's destroyer was amongst those ships which had sailed to assist the Norwegians. She was frozen with fear and for once her optimistic nature seemed to desert her completely.

The news grew more grim by the day; and every time she picked up a newspaper her heart lurched.

The Luftwaffe all but demolished the British forces as they tried in vain to help the Norwegians, but by the end of the month most of the British had been evacuated. Vincent's ship finally limped back into British territorial waters; miraculously he was safe. The losses to the forces were enormous, and it soon became clear to Audra and the rest of the country that the failure to heed Winston Churchill's warnings in the past had been disastrous.

"Thank God he's finally been made Prime Minister," Audra said to Laurette as they sat close to the wireless on the evening of May 13. That morning Churchill had given his first speech as Prime Minister to the House of Commons. In a few minutes he was to address the nation.

. "Vincent has always said that Churchill is the only man to lead us out of this mess, and I know he's right," Audra said.

Laurette nodded. "I agree, but even so, I think we're in for a long siege."

"Still, we have a *real* leader now—" Audra stopped, tapped Christina on her shoulder and motioned to the radio, then brought her finger to her lips.

The three of them sat perfectly still, straining to hear every word, mesmerized by the extraordinary voice and rhetoric of Winston Churchill bringing hope and courage and inspiration to the English people.

Audra and Laurette were buoyed up that evening, but as the days passed Audra knew that her sister-in-law had been correct. They *were* in for a siege, and it would be both long and deadly.

First there was the hell of Dunkirk.

Thousands upon thousands of British and Allied troops were stranded on the beaches of France, cruelly caught between the sea and the advancing German army. England held its breath. And then only through acts of desperate heroism were they rescued by a motley armada of British destroyers and cruisers, pleasure launches, rowboats, trawlers, yachts and even barges. Civilians had answered Winston Churchill's plea for everyone who had a vessel to pitch in and help the Royal Navy get the boys off the beaches. In doing so they saved lives by the hundreds of thousands—and gripped the imagination of the whole of England and her allies with their extraordinary valor.

The great epic of Dunkirk was an inspiration to everyone, and when Audra went around the general adult wards in the hospital, which she was now supervising, she saw how high morale was amongst her patients. Men and women alike took hold of her hand, and with tears in their eyes they spoke of their pride and their patriotism, and mentioned Churchill with reverence and love.

Audra herself had immense faith in Winston Churchill, this man who had said to them only a few weeks before: *"I have nothing to offer but blood, toil, tears and sweat."* She understood words like that only too well, and she also understood that Dunkirk was only the beginning . . . Churchill had warned the British people on June 4 that a terrible storm would soon break over them to test them all. And it did.

France fell.

Suddenly England stood alone.

And in August the might of the German Luftwaffe was flung against the country in bombardments that were to continue for months to come.

The Battle of Britain had begun.

At first the bombings were centered on London and the southern counties, but they soon became more widespread, and many of the industrial cities and airfields in the midlands and the north became prime targets.

Audra was cutting roses in her garden one Saturday afternoon when the drone of planes and the harsh and relentless rattle of machine-gun fire broke the silence of the sultry day.

Her head flew up with a jerk. As she squinted against the sun, she saw desperate aerial combat raging in the blue summer sky immediately above her house and her precious little world.

To Audra it was a horrifying and shocking sight, this dog fight between the Royal Air Force and the Luftwaffe. That it could happen over England in the middle of the day stunned her. She was momentarily rooted to the spot as she continued to stare up into the sky. Then one of the planes exploded in a great burst of flames and began to fall.

"Mam! Mam!" Christina cried, flinging down her brush and palette, running up the flagstone path.

The girl's voice roused Audra, galvanized her into action. Grasping Christina's hand she raced her child back along the path and into the air raid shelter.

"I thought we'd better come in here for a few minutes, just in case of falling debris," Audra said, giving her nine-year-old child a reassuring look. She forced a bright smile. "I suppose we could have gone into the house, but I seem to run for the shelter these days."

"It was such a lovely afternoon, and it happened so suddenly, Mam, didn't it?"

"Yes." Audra stared at the corrugated-iron wall of the shelter, an abstracted look crossing her face as she murmured in a saddened voice, *"Hearts at peace, under an English heaven."*

"That's Rupert Brooke, from the book your mother gave you long ago, isn't it, Mam?"

Audra nodded. "Yes, it is, and as I looked up into our lovely English sky a few minutes ago, Christina, and saw those planes going at each other hammer and tongs, that line of verse flashed through my mind, and I couldn't help wondering just when our hearts *would* be at peace again."

A flicker of fear touched Audra's blue eyes, and she added, "It might easily have been Theo up there . . . he is so young, only nineteen. But then, all of our Air Force boys are young. Oh, I pray that Theo is safe, Christie, I pray for him every day."

"Yes, Mam, so do I, when I pray for Daddy and Auntie Maggie and Uncle Mike, and all of my uncles and everybody who's fighting for us."

It was not long after this incident that the Germans stepped up their bombing raids on England, and although London was the chief target, Leeds was one of the northern cities that came in for heavy pummeling.

Audra and Christina now found themselves living in the air raid shelter almost every night. But they were the only occupants. Audra had been unable to persuade old Miss Dobbs to join them; the family in the third cottage in the cul-de-sac had closed it up for the duration and moved to the country to stay with friends.

If Laurette was visiting them when the banshee wailing of the sirens started, Audra insisted that she spend the night with them in the shelter. She would not allow Laurette to walk home to Moorfield Road during a raid, even though the sky was brilliant with searchlights. Audra believed in following regulations, and they had been warned by the Civil Defense to stay inside.

The shelter was now well equipped with cots, blankets and pillows, candles, paraffin lamps, a kerosene stove for heat, and a first-aid kit. Audra had stacked up tins of food, and every day she and Christina carried bottles of fresh water down to the shelter in case of emergency.

But in spite of the bombings, the perpetual fear, the worry about Vincent and the rest of their family and friends, and the hardships in general, life somehow went on.

The newspapers were full of talk about the German invasion of England in late August, but the English seemed to take this with their usual imperturbability.

Audra's attitude seemed to sum up the universal feeling when she said to Christina one day in late August, "Invasion or no invasion, you're starting at Miss Mellor's Private School for Girls when the winter term begins in September. You've got to have an education, whether the Germans land here or not.

Besides, as Winston Churchill said, we'll fight them in the hedges, if we have to, and demolish them to a man."

"You mean I *am* going to Miss Mellor's School after all!" Christina cried excitedly, breaking into smiles.

The two of them sat on the upper deck of the tram car going into Leeds, and Audra turned to look at her. "Of course you are. Why do you sound so surprised?"

"Well, you haven't mentioned it lately, even though I passed the entrance exam. I thought you'd changed your mind."

"Now why on earth would I change my mind, dear?"

"I thought Grandma might have said something to you, Mam."

"Grandma?"

"Yes. I heard her telling Grandpa that you oughtn't to be sending me to a private school, that Christ Church was good enough. She said you had big ideas for me and that they'd only lead to trouble. I thought she'd said the same to you and that you'd listened to her."

"That'll be the day," Audra replied with a hint of acerbity. "And just as a matter of interest, what did Grandpa say in response to Grandma's comments?"

"He said you were wise to reach for the stars, that he admired you for it, and then he told her I was going to be a great artist one day."

Audra smiled to herself. "Your grandfather is quite right, Christie."

Christina tucked her arm through her mother's companionably. "Is that why we're going to town, Mam? To buy my school uniform?"

"Yes, it is, and I'm thrilled you're going to start at Miss Mellor's, Christie. They have an excellent fine arts program, and I've had several long chats with the art teacher. She knows all about our plans, and she'll prepare you well for Leeds College of Art."

"And then after that I'll go to the Royal College of Art in London, won't I, Mother?" Christina looked into Audra's face, her gray eyes bright with anticipation.

Audra could not help laughing. "Of course, I promised, didn't I? But they won't accept you until you're twenty, you know. We've a long way to go yet."

Christina and Audra had always been close, but they drew closer than ever during the war years. With Vincent away at sea it was just the two of them, and although they saw Laurette at least once a week, they were mostly on their own.

The glittering future she had planned for her child occupied Audra most of the time. When she wasn't scrimping and scraping to pay for Christina's education, she was finding ways to expand the child's mind in other areas as well as in art.

Wartime conditions being what they were, there were not many plays coming to the theater in Leeds. But when something new did open, Audra always tried to get tickets for them; she took Christina to classical music concerts and to the opera whenever a company came to the Leeds. But these pleasures aside, books and especially the English classics were also part of Audra's cultural program for her daughter, and Christina acquired a love of reading early in her life.

As always, films were the mainstay of their entertainment during the forties, and they both derived a great deal of pleasure from their Saturday night jaunts to the local cinema. Usually Laurette accompanied them, for she and Audra had become dearer friends than ever, bound by so many common bonds and family ties, but mostly because of their love for each other.

As the war years dragged on, leaves were few and far between, and neither Vincent nor Mike came home more than once between the summer of 1941 and the winter of 1942.

Both women worried a lot about their husbands and about the rest of the Crowther family who were in the services. But they were women of strong character, and they learned to live with constant air raids, life in the shelters, rationing, shortages and hardships, and the terrible fear of losing loved ones. And they did so without complaint, always endeavoring to look to the future, to the day when Britain would win the war and life would return to normal.

In October of 1944 Audra had a wonderful piece of good luck. Margaret Lennox, whom she had always idolized since her days in Ripon, was appointed matron of Leeds Infirmary. And almost immediately she telephoned Audra at St. Mary's to offer her the position of sister in charge of the main surgical ward. Audra accepted the job over the telephone, and without having to think twice. The money was more than she was presently earning, the job a challenge. Also, Audra had always dreamed of working with Matron Lennox again.

It did not take Audra long to settle into life at Leeds General Infirmary, even though it was a vast and hectic hospital and not as cozy and intimate as St. Mary's had been. But she found the work stimulating, and satisfying, and as she plunged into it with her usual energy and concentration, she realized that it was helping to keep fear at bay.

To Audra's vast relief the beginning of 1945 brought good news of allied breakthroughs all over Europe. The tide was turning, and there was no longer any question who was going to win the war. It was only a matter of time.

Soon Audra was reaching for the newspapers and switching on the radio with eagerness rather than dread. By the spring she had started to take heart, as had the whole of Britain, and on May 7 the Germans surrendered unconditionally at Reims in France.

Suddenly the war in Europe was over.

Audra and Christina could hardly believe it. They laughed and they wept as they embraced each other fiercely in the cottage in Pot Lane.

Two days earlier, Christina had celebrated her fourteenth birthday, and now she said to Audra, "But this is my best birthday present, Mam, knowing that it's over and that Daddy's safe."

"Yes, it is, darling," Audra replied. She glanced at the collection of framed photographs lined up on the sideboard: Vincent, her brother William in the Australian Forces, Mike, Theo Bell, Maggie and Vincent's brothers Frank, Jack, Bill and Danny, and Olive's husband Hal. How smart they looked and so proud in their various uniforms.

She turned to Christina and said, softly, "They're all safe, thank God! How lucky we've been . . . luckier than most."

———— Thirty-One ————

Audra Crowther was so concentrated on what she was doing in the next few years she hardly ever had time to pause, except to look at her lovely and gifted daughter.

But one day she found herself staring into the mirror on her dressing table —and taking stock.

It was a warm day in July of 1951, and later that afternoon Christina was graduating with honors from Leeds College of Art. It was a most important occasion in her daughter's life as well as her own and Vincent's, and so not unnaturally she wanted to look her best.

Audra leaned closer to the glass, inspecting her face.

There were a few faint tell-tale lines around her eyes, and the stubbornness and resoluteness that had always marked her face seemed more pronounced than ever. But aside from these little flaws, if they could be called that, and a hint of gray at her temples, she decided she did not look too bad for forty-four.

Her light brown hair, cut short and framing her face in a flattering style, was still thick and luxuriant; her creamy complexion was as flawless as it had always been, and the blueness of her eyes had not dimmed over the years.

And I've kept my slim figure, she added, reaching for the bottle of foundation lotion. Usually she only had time to dab a powder puff on her nose and put on a trace of lipstick, before dashing off to Leeds Infirmary, where she still worked and was now a senior member of the staff. But today she was going to take her time and do a proper job of making herself up, and to this end she had borrowed some of Christina's cosmetics.

After smoothing on the foundation, she powdered her face, dusted off the excess, added rouge to emphasize her high cheekbones, then used brown mascara on her lashes, before outlining her mouth with pink lipstick.

Satisfied that she had done the best she could, Audra sat back and regarded herself. She was momentarily startled by her own reflection. The makeup had brought out her best features and highlighted her eyes and her skin. Her face had taken on a fresh look, seemed more vibrant and alive. Pleased with the effect she had created, she brushed her hair, smoothed it into place with the comb and then, as a final touch, she added a dab of her favorite gardenia perfume behind her ears.

Standing up, Audra walked across the bedroom to the wardrobe and took out the tailored navy-blue silk dress she had made for herself last week. It was a perfect copy of a Christian Dior afternoon dress she had seen in *Vogue* magazine earlier in the year, and she had clipped out the photograph, as she always did when she saw a style she liked, whether it was for herself or for Christina.

After placing the dress on the bed, she took out her navy bag, white fabric gloves, the small navy straw hat trimmed with a single white rose and the pair of navy court shoes she had bought yesterday.

Once she had slipped on the dress and shoes, Audra returned to the dressing table and sat down again. She put on her hat, added the marquisite earrings Vincent had given her for Christmas, her mother's engagement ring, and her watch, and then she slid open the drawer and took out the box containing Laurette's pearls.

Lifting the lid, Audra stared at them, admiring them. There was only a single strand, but the pearls were of good quality. Mike had bought them for Laurette at Greenwood's, the finest jewelers in Leeds, not long after the end of the war, and her sister-in-law had so loved them.

Audra sighed, touched by a sudden fleeting sadness for her darling Laurette, who had died three years ago. It had been sudden; she still hadn't quite recovered from the shock. None of them had. Laurette had looked so well in the spring of 1948, but she had fallen sick that summer and by November they were burying her. It had been cancer. She was thankful that Laurette had gone quickly, that her suffering had not been prolonged. She missed her so very much. There would always be a void without Laurette—and for all of them.

Remembering the time, Audra sat up straighter in her chair. She took the pearls from the box and fastened them around her neck, looking in the mirror again, touching the necklace, smiling softly to herself. And she let go of the sadness, let go of the painful memories of Laurette's passing. The last thing *she* would have wanted was for her to be sorrowful on a day like this. Laurette had always been so terribly proud of Christina.

Rising, Audra went to the bed, picked up her gloves and bag and hurried down the stairs. She dropped her things on the hall table next to the telephone and paused, glanced at the grandfather clock, wondering what had happened to Vincent. He had said he would be home by one-thirty and it was already one forty-five.

Aside from the shock and anguish they had suffered with Laurette's death, the last few years had been good to the Crowthers. They no longer lived in the cottage in Pot Lane. They had moved into this much larger house in Upper Armley in 1949. It was not far from Charlie Cake Park, and it had three bedrooms, a dining room, a sitting room, and a big, family-style kitchen–parlor, where, as usual, everyone seemed to congregate. The rooms were spacious and there was a light, airy feeling about the house in general.

In particular, Audra loved the long back garden. She had planted it with rose bushes and delphiniums and a variety of other flowers, and with its smooth green lawn stretching down to two shady trees at the bottom, it was a paradise in the summer weather. Audra derived much enjoyment from it, and from her flowers and the small vegetable plot she had started near the high back fence beyond the trees.

Vincent was more prosperous. Immediately after he was demobilized, at the end of the war, he had gone into partnership with Fred Varley and his son, Harry. And finally, after talking about it for so many years, he had enrolled in night school in Leeds, to study architecture and draughtsmanship. He no longer worked outdoors on the building sites, but ran the business with Fred; he did most of the planning, drawing and paperwork. Varley and Crowther was a small company, but they were kept busy with local building projects and Vincent was earning a decent living, and he was able to support his family himself. The money Audra earned at the Infirmary went into the bank for Christina's education and her clothes.

The war had changed Vincent Crowther.

His turbulent character and restless ways had been tempered by the death and destruction he had witnessed in the navy. He still liked to go to the pub on weekends, and he continued to bet on the horses, but he no longer indulged himself in romantic flings with other women.

Not that his relationship with Audra had changed. But after twenty-three years together they were used to each other. It was an enduring marriage, it seemed, and they shared a bond, one that truly welded them together: their immense pride in their daughter, who had turned out to be very special indeed.

Audra was thinking about Christina and the clothes she still had to make for her as she filled the teapot and carried it over to the table. There were only ten days left before they went to London to get Christie settled in the little studio flat. Well, she would have time to cut and sew at least one more dress in that time, and the remainder of her clothes for college would have to be sent by parcel post.

"Sorry I'm late," Vincent said, barging in through the back door in a great rush. "There was such a lot of traffic between here and Pudsey, I thought I'd never get here—" He cut himself short, stared at her through narrowed eyes. "What have you done to yourself, Audra?"

"I haven't done anything," she exclaimed, stiffening, giving him a defensive look. His tone had sounded critical.

He held his head on one side and studied her thoughtfully. "It must be the hat, or maybe it's the new dress—"

"Oh for heaven's sake it's the makeup," she muttered. "I'm wearing some of Christie's foundation lotion and rouge."

"I like it," he said, grinning at her. "You look nice. Ever so nice, love. You should wear makeup more often."

Audra half smiled and then glanced away quickly. She felt suddenly self-conscious under his unexpected scrutiny. Vincent had not looked at her like that in years. She said, "Do you want a cup of tea now? Or later, after you've changed your shirt and suit?"

"Later. I won't be but a few minutes." He hurried out.

Audra remained standing near the kitchen table, staring after him, thinking how well he looked.

Vincent had hardly changed over the years, hardly aged at all. Last month he had celebrated his forty-eighth birthday, but he appeared to be much younger. There wasn't a gray hair on his head and his face had retained a certain boyishness, and the smoothness of his cheeks and brow, along with his fresh complexion, only underscored his youthfulness.

She took a chair, sat waiting for him to return, thinking about him, wondering if he ever had love affairs these days. Years ago she had suspected that he saw other women, even though there had never been gossip, nor had she had any proof. But their relationship had been so bad at times she had supposed he found solace for his woes in more welcoming arms than hers.

A deep sigh escaped her, and she shook her head, mildly irritated with herself. She was having such strange thoughts today. First she had been on the verge of tears, dwelling on Laurette, missing her, and now here she was brooding over all sorts of imponderables about Vincent. And as if it made any difference now.

"Let's have that cup of tea, Audra," Vincent exclaimed, coming back into the kitchen. "We haven't got much time to waste."

He sat down opposite her and reached for the teapot. "Did our Christie get off all right?"

"Yes," Audra said. "She left at noon. She said she had several things to check in the college gallery—the exhibition, I expect. She always fusses about having the proper kind of light on her paintings—you know what a perfectionist she is; everything has to be exactly right."

"Just like her mother," he said with a laugh. "Come on, love, get your bits and pieces together and let's be off. We don't want to miss the ceremony; it's something you've been looking forward to for the last twenty years."

Audra smiled. "That's absolutely true. And so have you."

Later, as they were driving into town, Audra suddenly put her hand on Vincent's knee and squeezed it.

He glanced at her through the corner of his eye. "What?"

"I *know* that one day Christina will be as famous as those other two great Leeds College Art students, Barbara Hepworth and Henry Moore."

Vincent nodded. Who was he to argue with her? She had always been right about their daughter thus far.

Christina
1951 to 1965

Thirty-Two

Christina loved the little flat in London.

It was in a tall, narrow house in Chester Street, not far from Belgrave Square. The house belonged to Irène Bell, and Christina and her mother had stayed at the flat several times in the past when they had come to London on their educational trips, to visit the many galleries and museums. And so she already knew it well.

Irène Bell was renting the flat to Audra for four guineas a week. Audra thought it was a bargain at the price, and indeed it was, but Christina knew that Mrs. Bell hated charging her mother rent. She would have much preferred to let her have it for nothing. But as she had explained privately to Christina, that was not Audra's way of doing things. "Your mother's too shrewd," Irène Bell had said. "If the rent doesn't seem right to her, she'll be suspicious." Christina had agreed, and together they had arrived at a suitable figure.

The flat was on the top floor of the house, was in fact converted attics with a living room, bedroom, bathroom and kitchen. It had its own front door and was a self-contained little dwelling within the house.

Originally, Irène Bell had created the studio flat at the top of her house for her daughters to live in at different stages of their lives. It had been a *pied-à-terre* for them and later for Theo, when he had been studying law at Cambridge and came to London on weekends occasionally. Theo, who was thirty and a barrister with chambers in the Temple, had recently married, and he and his wife Angela occupied the town house. Sometimes Irène Bell came to stay with her son and daughter-in-law, but only rarely. She was in her seventies now, and since Thomas Bell's death three years before, she rarely ventured far afield. She liked to hold court at Calpher House, and have her children and many grandchildren visit her there.

On the day that Christina and Audra had arrived from Leeds, the Bells' house in Belgravia was deserted. Theo and Angela were away on holiday in France, but Mrs. Bell had given Audra a set of keys and told her they should make themselves at home.

This they had done and now, at the end of the first week in London, Christina was settled in the studio under the eaves. Her easel, spare canvases, paints and brushes had been unpacked and put away, as had her books, her other possessions and her clothes.

These filled the large closet in the bedroom and every time Christina looked inside she was impressed with the spectacular selection of outfits her mother had made for her.

The measuring, cutting, pinning, sewing and pressing had gone on for the last eight months, but it was only when she saw everything hanging there together that she realized what an extraordinary undertaking creating this stylish wardrobe had been for her mother.

"I'm going to be the best-dressed girl at the Royal College of Art," Christina said to Audra late on Friday afternoon as she took a pearl-gray silk dress from the closet, held it against herself, stared in the mirror.

"I should hope so," Audra said with a light laugh, watching her from the doorway of the bedroom. "I certainly worked hard enough."

"Oh Mummy, you did! I *know* you did. Thank you for all of my lovely clothes, for all the time and effort you put into them, and the money you've spent. You're a wonder, Mother, you truly are."

"I don't know about that," Audra said, hastily brushing aside the thanks and the compliment. But nevertheless she looked pleased as she came into the bedroom and sat down on one of the twin beds.

Christina swung around, still holding the silk dress pressed close to her lithe body. "What do you think about this for the theater tonight, Mummy?"

Audra nodded her approval.

Christina flashed her a vivid smile, hung the dress on the top of the closet door and said, "I'd better find the right shoes and bag . . . the black patent, I think. And perhaps I'll take the gray silk Dior shawl Grandma gave me for my birthday, just in case it gets cool later."

"I doubt that's going to happen," Audra said, "it's been awfully hot today. In fact, I think we're in for a heat wave this weekend."

"Don't say that, Mother!" Christina made a face. "Not when we've planned to go to Windsor Castle for the day on Sunday. I don't fancy the idea of sweltering in the scorching August sun all day, as we tramp around the grounds."

Audra smiled as she leaned back against the pillows, watching her daughter take out her accessories for the evening, thinking how striking she was to look at.

Christina's light brown hair of childhood had turned years ago to a deeper, richer chestnut, and in the summer it was always shot through with reddish golden streaks from the sun. Her resemblance to her father was marked, and although she was not strictly beautiful, she had an arresting face with clear, chiselled features and a lovely complexion like Audra. Her huge gray eyes, so soft, so smokey, were Laurette's eyes, and Christina had inherited the Crowther height; she stood five feet seven in her stocking feet. This pleased Audra. She had always hated being short.

Her attractive appearance and her obvious artistic gifts to one side, Christina had turned out to be an exceptional young woman in other ways. Everyone agreed on that. Despite Grandma Crowther's predictions that the private school and Audra's big ideas would lead to trouble, this had not been the case. Christina had not grown up to be difficult, rebellious or a snob; nor had she turned on her parents, preferring her college friends to them. Quite the contrary, in fact. She was a loving daughter, who adored Audra and Vincent in much the same way as they adored her, and, as she had done when she was a child, she enjoyed their company, believed *them* to be special.

Audra Crowther had done her job well.

Apart from providing Christina with the best of everything within her power, she had given the girl the best of herself. She had taught Christina the proper human values, instilled in her a sense of honor, duty and purpose.

Drawing on her own genteel upbringing, Audra had reared her to have consideration for others. But perhaps most importantly of all, Audra had given Christina something else of incalculable value—a feeling of self-worth. And so she was remarkably secure.

Though frequently uncommunicative and undemonstrative with Vincent, which had always been at the root of the trouble between them, Audra had been able to express her love for her child verbally and with a show of physical affection. Yet with this unconditional love had come discipline, and from both her parents. Vincent, in particular, had been very strict with Christina when she had been a teenager and especially about boys.

Yes, she does have a certain kind of grace, Audra commented to herself, continuing to observe her daughter as she moved around the bedroom. But she's not perfect by any means, and of course who is? Christie does have Vincent's quick, rather violent temper, and his expensive tastes, his love of clothes and the finer things of life. And she can be impetuous. But, withal, she's not a spoiled girl. Audra smiled. How many times had Eliza said, 'You're spoiling that girl, Audra, and so is Vincent. You'll both live to regret it . . . oh yes, spare the rod and spoil the child.' An echo of her mother-in-law's voice reverberated in her head.

"You're looking pensive, Mummy. Is something wrong?"

Audra sat up with a start. "No." She laughed wryly. "To tell you the truth, I was thinking of your grandma. She always said my plans for you were far too elaborate and high flown. And la-di-da . . . That was her favorite expression for anything that had to do with me when you were little."

"Don't I know it. She's old-fashioned and so class-bound, poor old thing. But she means well, Mummy, and she's always been very loving with me." Christina grinned. "But then I'm the only child of her darling Stormy Petrel."

"Stormy Petrel?"

"Yes, that's what she called Daddy when he was first born, and when he was a little boy. Didn't she ever tell you that?"

"No. But then your grandma and I have never been close, never seen eye to eye on anything much, and certainly her ideas about a woman's place in the world have always gone against the grain with me."

"What do you mean?"

"Your grandma has always believed that women should . . . well, be subservient to men. Long before you were born, she was horrified when I said I wanted a nursing career. She told me it was my duty to settle down and have babies and toe the line and cater to your father."

"I can understand her saying that, Mother. I don't think she approves of my coming to London and attending the Royal College of Art at all. She seems to think it's a waste of money. When I went to say goodbye to her and Grandpa the other day, she clucked and said something about it being a terrible expense, when I was bound to give up my art to get married and have babies the moment I met the first suitable young man."

Audra smiled faintly. "That sounds like Eliza . . ." She paused reflectively, and then after a moment she fixed her bright blue eyes on Christina. "You know, Christie, I am glad you're ambitious, that you want a career for yourself, as well as those other things in life. You can have them all, you know, you really can. In fact, there's nothing you can't have if you try hard enough, work hard enough and strive toward a goal. And never, never limit yourself—"

Christina interrupted, smiling at Audra, "Just as you've taught me to . . . and I remember very well what Grandpa said that September you sent me to Miss Mellor's, when Grandma was doing her usual bit of grousing. He told her you were right to *reach for the stars*. He's always admired you for that, Mummy." The phone rang and Christina turned to the small desk and reached for it.

"Oh hello, Daddy. How are you?" There was a short pause as she listened carefully; then she looked across at Audra, nodding and smiling. "Yes, Daddy, I understand." There was another pause. "Yes, we went to lunch at Fortnum's, and then we spent the afternoon at the Tate looking at the Turners." Christina laughed at a remark of her father's, then finished, "Let me get Mummy for you now."

Audra rose and went to take the telephone from her daughter. "Hello, Vincent. Is everything all right?" she asked and immediately fell silent as Vincent spoke to her in a rush of words.

Christina slipped out, smiling to herself. She crossed the miniscule hall and went into the kitchen that adjoined the living room; after putting the kettle on the gas, she took endive, lettuce and tomatoes from the refrigerator and began to wash them.

A few minutes later, Audra joined her in the small galley-style kitchen. "Let me help you," she said.

"There's not much to do, really." Christina glanced over her shoulder and remarked, "Honestly, Daddy's getting to be such an old fuss pot. I can't have a conversation with him at the moment without him telling me to watch me step, and he keeps saying, 'Think on, love, think on.' I don't know what's got into him lately."

"Well, you're *still* his little girl, and he's a bit worried about you being out on your own, I suppose."

"Mmmmm," was Christina's only response as she began to peel a tomato. Suddenly she giggled and said, "Gosh, you're going to have a *huge* phone bill, Mum, when you get home. Daddy's hardly been off it this week." She began to giggle, and her eyes were mischievous. "I do believe he's courting you again."

"Don't be ridiculous!" Audra exclaimed.

That evening Christina took Audra to see her favorite actress and actor— Vivien Leigh and Laurence Olivier.

They were starring in the Festival of Britain production of Shaw's *Caesar and Cleopatra* and Shakespeare's *Antony and Cleopatra,* each play being performed on successive nights.

This was Christina's big surprise for her mother.

Audra knew they were going to the theater, but she had no idea what they were going to see, and she was thrilled when Christina told her their destination as they sat on the bus.

"There's no point in seeing one play without the other, so I bought tickets for both nights, Mummy, and we'll be coming back tomorrow."

"Oh darling, how extravagant you are, just like your daddy," Audra said, but her face glowed with happiness.

"This is a theatrical *first,* Mum. I know we're in for a splendid evening in the theater, one we're not likely to forget," Christina remarked, filled with pleasure that she could do something nice for her mother.

Audra could hardly contain her excitement as they took their seats in the theater, and she reached out and squeezed her daughter's hand, whispered, "Thank you, Christie, for thinking of this very special treat for me . . . I know I'll never forget it."

Before either of them realized it, Audra's second week in London came to an end.

It had been a wonderful time for them both. Apart from getting Christina settled in the flat before she started her courses at the Royal College of Art in September, they had been able to share some happy days together. They had been to see other plays and to the pictures, which they always enjoyed; they had visited museums and as many art galleries as they could cram in.

Vincent had given Audra some money before they had left Leeds and told her to take themselves out to dinner on him, and this they had done, booking a table at a little bistro called Chez Jacques. There had been days when they had simply pottered around the little flat and gone for walks through Green Park and down by The Mall, or window-shopped in Bond Street and browsed around Hatchard's, Audra's favorite bookstore. But every minute had been precious to mother and daughter, and Audra would never forget her two weeks with Christina at this time in her daughter's life.

"My stay in London has been so special," Audra said as they sat in the taxi going to King's Cross railway station, on Friday morning at the end of her stay.

"And for me too, Mummy," Christina replied and instantly became silent. She suddenly realized how much she was going to miss her mother, and it also registered, forcibly, that from today onward she was going to be on her own.

They were both a little sad as they walked down the platform toward the train for Leeds, and just before Audra boarded, Christina hugged her, said in a tremulous voice, "I'll never be able to thank you enough, or repay you for everything you've done for me, Mummy. You've been the best, the most wonderful mother in the world."

Audra stared at Christina, a look of surprise crossing her face. "But I only did my duty," she said.

Audra had told Vincent not to meet her at Leeds City station and being as frugal as always she took a tram back home to Upper Armley.

From the moment she let herself into the house she was conscious of the quietness; she was stunned by it, really. As she put her suitcase down in the hall and took off her hat, she felt the tears she had suppressed throughout the day begin to brim in her eyes. All of the sunshine has gone out of my life, she thought, groping in her pocket for her handkerchief.

Vincent also felt Christina's absence when he came home from work that evening. But he did not say anything to Audra, aware of her sadness. Instead he chatted about her trip, endeavored to draw her out about it, believing this would lift her out of herself. And it did for a while.

But after supper, as they sat drinking their coffee in front of the fire, she retreated into herself. So did he, and they were lost in their own thoughts for a short while.

Suddenly, Vincent felt that he had to talk to her about his feelings, and he looked across at her and murmured, "It's odd, isn't it, not having our Christie around? So quiet, Audra."

"Yes."

Vincent sighed softly. "Well, lass, she's gone from us now. I don't suppose she'll ever come back here—to live, I mean."

Audra frowned at him. "I don't want her to, Vincent. If she did that, what would it have all been about?"

"Aye, that's true. You said you'd give her the world when she was a baby in St. Mary's Hospital, and you have, love."

Vincent sipped his coffee, then took out his packet of cigarettes. He toyed with them for a few minutes, before putting them down on the coffee table. He fixed his eyes on her. "We've been through a lot, Audra, you and I."

"Yes, we have." She met his gaze. A curious thought struck her, and before she could stop herself, she said, "We've been tested, I think."

He stared at her intently.

"But we've come through all right. We have, haven't we, Vincent?"

He nodded, then cleared his throat. "I was thinking that you might like to go away with me next weekend . . . now that we're alone there's no reason why we can't do that, is there?"

Audra was flabbergasted. "Where to? Where would we go?"

"Robin Hood's Bay?"

"Why?"

"Because that's where we went on our honeymoon—" Vincent paused, took a deep breath. "It's not too late for us, is it, Audra? Couldn't we start all over again, as if this was the beginning?"

"Perhaps it is," she said.

—— *Thirty-Three* ——

Although she missed her parents and was frequently homesick, Christina soon settled into her new life of independence.

She was exhilarated by the excitement of London and all of the attractions it offered, but because she was aware of the supreme effort which had been expended by Audra to bring her to this point in her life, she was an assiduous student.

Christina had no intention of falling into bad ways, neglecting her studies and so risk disappointing her mother. This aside, she was a hard worker by nature and ambitious.

From the first day she started in September, her classes at the Royal College of Art in Kensington were challenging and stimulating, and she threw herself into her work with enthusiasm and dedication.

It was at this time—the early fifties—that the college was starting to be known as the art mecca of the world, and it was teeming with gifted people; tutors and students alike, and in all departments, from figurative and landscape painting and sculpture to textile, costume and scenic design.

From the day she had applied for entry into the college earlier that year, had submitted her best work, then been interviewed and accepted, the tutors at the college had been aware of her extraordinary gifts as a landscape painter. Since her childhood, Christina had seen everything in terms of light, and her paintings seemed drenched with it, whether it was the golden light of a sunlit summer day, the cold, pewter-colored light of a Yorkshire sea in a winter storm or the brilliant luminous light that suffused the Dales in spring. Because of the quality of her work and her dedication to it, Christina was soon a favorite with her tutor, as well as other members of the staff, who all saw in her the ideal student.

Being an open, outgoing and friendly young woman, Christina was also popular with her contemporaries, and within her first couple of weeks at college she quickly made a number of friends of both sexes. But the one she gravitated to the most, and who was her special favorite, was a girl of her own age called Jane Sedgewick.

Jane was ebullient, good-natured and something of a madcap. Pretty and dashing, with flaxen hair and eyes the color of pansies, she was one of the most engaging girls Christina had ever met.

They were painting together in one of the big studios on a particular afternoon in September when she completely endeared herself to Christina.

Unexpectedly, Jane began to camp it up. Adopting the stance of a tragedienne, she cried dramatically, in a voice of mock despair, "My work looks like the devil's brew compared to yours. Alas, alack, woe is me." She paused, brought her clenched fist up to her chest and rolled her eyes to the ceiling. "I have no alternative but to kill myself. But before I put an end to this sweet young life . . . grant me one last favor."

"Of course, what is it?" Christina asked, playing along with her, laughing at her histrionics.

"Come and have coffee with me after class."

Still laughing, Christina accepted the invitation. A little later they wandered off down by the side of the Victoria and Albert Museum, chatting animatedly on their way to a coffee shop nearby. And neither girl knew that this was the beginning of an extraordinary friendship, one which was to last all of their lives.

Over several cups of *espresso* they learned more about each other. After Christina had told Jane something about herself, it was her turn to listen and she did so attentively. She was startled to discover that Jane was the eldest daughter of Dulcie Manville and Ralph Sedgewick, a husband-and-wife acting team equally as famous as the Oliviers, in their own way. And then she thought: But that explains her theatricality.

The Sedgewicks had appeared in countless films made by Gainsborough Pictures in the forties, and Christina and Audra had seen all of them at the Picturedrome in Armley.

She told Jane, "Gosh, my mother will be *thrilled* to hear that I know you. She's a great fan of your parents, and so am I. In fact, when she was here in August, we went to see them in *Lovers' Quarrel* at the Haymarket. We laughed our heads off; it was simply marvelous, the best comedy we've seen in years."

"How would you like to meet the old folks in person?" Jane asked. "Do come and stay with us this weekend. We'd love to have you."

Christina stared at her in surprise. "But are you sure it's all right? It is a bit last-minute, isn't it? I mean for them. Today's Thursday, Jane."

"Oh that's no problem; we have a jolly old crazy household. Come on, *do* say yes. We'll have some fun, and the grounds are pretty, so you can paint if you want to. Mind you there's only one problem—" Jane made a sour face. "My siblings, the little monsters, are positively *revolting,* but I suppose we don't have to bother with them. So, will you come?"

"Why yes, I will, thank you very much," Christina said smiling. "It's a lovely invitation."

Christina and Jane drove down to Kent the following afternoon in Jane's beaten-up MG sports car painted a vivid yellow.

The Sedgewicks owned an old country house called Hadley Court in the pretty village of Aldington. Not long after they had left the village behind, Jane slowed down and pointed to a beautiful Tudor manor, long and low with leaded windows, set behind large iron gates and just visible from the road.

"That's Goldenhurst, Uncle Noël's house," Jane explained. "He's my godfather and quite a dear. On Sunday morning we'll be going over to his house for drinks and a slap-up Sunday lunch. It'll be quite mad, of course; he always has the most scandalous and outrageous people as house guests. But at least we'll have a giggle and escape the *revolting* monsters for a while."

Christina gave her a puzzled look. "What's wrong with your brothers and sisters?"

"They're little beasts. You'll soon see."

"And when do your parents come down to the country?"

"After the Saturday night performance. They flee the theater still wearing their makeup and race down here at breakneck speed, arrive at midnight. That's when you'll meet them, *if* you can stay awake to have sandwiches and coffee with them at that hour."

Jane swung the MG into a long driveway that twisted and turned up to the house, and Christina fell in love with it the minute she saw it. In a way, the architecture reminded her of High Cleugh, which her mother had often taken her to see when she was a child. They had had picnics on the slope near the Memory Place, and her mother had told her about the house where she had grown up. And later she had gone back to the slope above the River Ure and painted High Cleugh as a gift for Audra.

Hadley Court was a rambling old place with odd-shaped rooms, great fireplaces, flaring windows and lots and lots of character. The grounds were pastoral and romantic-looking, with weeping willows and a lily pond and randomly planted flowers that gave it an Old World air. Later when Christina strolled around the gardens, her fingers itched to put their misty green beauty and the soft southern light of Kent on the canvas she had brought with her.

As Jane had promised her, the weekend was a lot of fun.

But Christina did have a few surprises, and she soon discovered that her new friend had a tendency to exaggerate.

The revolting siblings, as Jane called them, were not revolting at all; nor were they little beasts. Hadley and Lyndon, eleven-year-old twins, were tow-headed, freckle-faced boys who were cherubic and well behaved. Jane insisted that this was because she had terrified them into toeing the line that weekend by making all manner of dire threats against them. Their sister, nine-year-old Poppy Louise, was an enchantress with huge pansy-colored eyes like Jane's and bright red-gold hair. And she captivated Christina with her winning smiles and fanciful child's chatter.

As for Dulcie and Ralph Sedgewick, they were gracious and charming to her and made her feel like a member of the family immediately. They were not a bit as she had expected them to be, not at all theatrical or showy. They were both cultivated and witty. Ralph, in particular, was most amusing. Christina quickly decided that it was Jane who had all the flamboyance in this family.

Uncle Noël turned out to be Noël Coward, and Christina was rendered speechless when she walked into the living room at Goldenhurst on Sunday and found herself being introduced to Laurence Olivier and, shortly thereafter, to Vivien Leigh.

When she finally managed to get Jane into a corner, Christina whispered, "What do you mean outrageous and scandalous house guests! You might have warned me!"

Jane giggled and rolled her eyes. "But it wouldn't have been any fun if you'd known Larry and Viv were coming." Her face sobered, and she took hold of Christina's arm, staring anxiously into her face. "You're not angry with me, are you? I couldn't bear it if you were."

Christina said, "No, of course I'm not, Janey," and gave her a reassuring smile.

After this first weekend, Christina became a regular guest at Hadley Court and a constant visitor to the Sedgewick's flat in Mayfair. Dulcie Manville Sedgewick had taken a great liking to Christina and thought her to be a wonderful influence on her rather scatterbrained daughter.

Being an only child, Christina revelled at being in the midst of the loving and amusing Sedgewick family, and enjoyed meeting the celebrated personalities who populated their parties—show-business folk, writers, journalists and politicians.

Yet this exciting and glittering world, as captivating as it was, did not unduly dazzle Christina, and her feet were always planted firmly on the ground, her dedication to her painting intact.

And as always she was devoted to her parents, most especially Audra. During the next nine months her mother came twice to stay at the little studio flat in Chester Street, and Christina often went up to Yorkshire for weekends, and always during the holidays when the college was in recess.

Christina knew that her mother lived for these times when they were together and that she derived enormous vicarious pleasure as she listened to anecdotes about the Sedgewicks and her other friends, the parties and elegant dinners she attended.

Audra's pride in her daughter knew no bounds. Christina's record at the Royal College of Art was brilliant, and her popularity and success in social circles was gratifying, another reason for Audra to rejoice. She knew, at last, that she had kept the vow she had made to herself years ago. She had given her daughter a far better life than she herself had known. And she was satisfied that her own life, and everything she had done for Christina, had been justified.

Christina's first and second years in London were full of numerous challenges and new experiences, and were productive periods for her. Only one thing marred her happiness—the knowledge that her mother was still working.

Although Vincent was a partner in Varley and Crowther and doing quite well, he was still not earning enough to carry *all* of the family's financial burdens. Audra had continued nursing at the Infirmary essentially to support Christina's life in London. It was she who paid Christina's tuition, rent, and gave her an allowance, bought the fabrics for her clothes, and other clothing.

Christina was acutely aware that without these commitments her mother would be able to cease her endless toil and have a much easier life.

And so at the end of her second year at college, Christina cautiously suggested getting a part-time job to help out. Audra was furious and adamant in her refusal to even consider such a thing, believing it would distract Christina and interfere with her studies. But she had not bargained for her daughter's stubbornness and determination. Christina was as strong-willed as Audra, and she resolutely set out to curtail the flow of money from Leeds to London.

She did not dare get a job, but she did adopt a more frugal way of living, and she cut down on overhead by moving in with Jane. Her best friend had been asking her to share her flat in Walton Street for ages, and since it was owned by Jane's Aunt Elspeth, who had lived in Monte Carlo since her marriage, the rent was nominal. "Oh just give me a pound a week," Jane had said when Christina had asked her what her share would be.

Christina also decided she must start making her own clothes. Whilst this step might not save money exactly, it would take the job off her mother's back. She was egged on by Jane, who knew she had a great flair for designing. In fact, Christina had inherited Audra's cleverness with scissors and a needle; also, she had stood at her mother's knee for years, watching her make beautiful garments for themselves as well as for other people and technique had brushed off. In no time at all she had revamped some of her old dresses and created a couple of new ones, and she was inordinately pleased with herself.

Audra was not. However, she finally came to admit that the sewing was not injuring her daughter's work at the Royal College of Art. Grudgingly, she agreed that the hand-painted dresses and jackets and the starkly tailored suits had elegance and originality.

Christina found time to make a hand-painted blouse for her mother in the autumn of 1953, and she took it with her when she went to Leeds for the winter holidays.

Audra was thrilled when she opened the box on Christmas Day and immediately exclaimed over its beauty and the wonderful mingling of the blue delphiniums on the paler blue silk.

"But you shouldn't have," she chastised mildly. "All this sewing is taking you away from your studies."

"No, it isn't," Christina said with a laugh, hugging her. "I wanted you to have something beautiful, something that I had painted and made for you, Mummy."

That particular December was a happy time for the Crowthers. They had a simple family Christmas and in January Christina returned to London to resume her classes at the Royal College of Art.

She launched herself into her final courses with the immense enthusiasm and the extraordinary dedication she had previously shown, knowing that she would be graduating in August. She wanted to do well not only because of her own sense of pride, but for her mother.

Thirty-Four

Vincent saw Christina before she saw him.

She had alighted from the London train at the far end of the platform and he caught flashes of her as she dodged in and out between the other passengers now hurrying toward the exit turnstile.

How young and lovely she looked in the belted camel coat and the very high-heeled court shoes she always wore. She stepped out briskly, her shoulders thrown back, her head held erect; there was something very confident about her, and this pleased him.

She would be twenty-three next month. He could hardly believe it. It seemed like only yesterday that he had been pushing her around in her pram. She had grown up to be a good girl, with a good head on her shoulders. He trusted her implicitly. When she had first gone to live in London, he had worried about her, been concerned about her judgment of situations and people, and particularly men. And then one day he had wondered why he was fretting. They had brought her up properly; she knew the difference between right and wrong. He had stopped worrying that instant. Yes, their daughter was a credit to them.

Suddenly Christina caught sight of him, waved, increased her pace, her face illuminated by the brightest of smiles.

Vincent hurried forward, smiling and waving himself.

They came to a standstill in front of each other.

"Hello, Daddy," she cried, dropping her suitcase.

"Hello, pet," he said, beaming at her, reaching for her.

They embraced, laughing, then stepped away, staring into each other's faces. It was Good Friday afternoon and they had not met since Christmas and, as they usually did after an absence, they took stock of each other.

He looks a bit tired, older, Christina thought, surprised. Her father rarely showed his age.

She's more radiant than ever, Vincent thought, and his heart tightened imperceptibly. He knew she was going to be upset when he told her about Audra and that her radiance would be diluted somewhat. He wondered when he should tell her. Well, certainly before they got to the house.

"Come on, love," he said, lifting her suitcase, taking her arm, hurrying along the platform with her. "Your mam's waiting for you, and as anxiously as always."

"I can't wait to see her either. Where are you parked, Dad?"

"Just outside the station, and I'll have you home in no time at all."

As Vincent drove them up Stanningley Road in the direction of Upper Armley, Christina chatted to her father about her plans for the Easter holidays. "I thought I'd spend the weekend at home with you and Mummy, and then if it's all right with the two of you, I'd like to go off on one of my field trips to paint for a few days."

"That's fine, Christie. Where were you thinking of going?"

"Originally I had the Lake District in mind, but I want to do a seascape and I was toying with the idea of going to the East Coast . . . Whitby, Scarborough, Flamborough Head, somewhere around there. What do you think?"

"All of your childhood haunts, eh? Well, you could do worse to pick one of them, but what about up near Ravenscar? There are some very dramatic views from the cliffs, and there's a nice hotel nearby. We like you to be comfortable when you're off on these field trips, you know."

"You both spoil me," she said, laughing. "I wish Mummy could get a couple of days off from the Infirmary to come with me. It'd do her good, don't you think, Daddy?"

Vincent was silent. He pulled the car onto the side of the road and braked, turned to face his daughter. "There's something I have to tell you—"

"What is it?" she cried, cutting him off, knowing at once that something was terribly wrong from the tone of his voice, the concern in his vivid green eyes. "It's Mummy, isn't it?"

Vincent nodded. "I'm afraid it is, love."

She reached out, clutched at his arm, stared at him, anxiety filling her face. "What's the matter?" she demanded.

"Your mam's been ill, gravely ill, Christie. She collapsed three weeks ago with viral pneumonia. She was in the Infirmary for over two weeks . . . there were complications at first; the doctors were worried about her lungs. Don't look so frightened, love, she's fine now. She's recuperating at home."

Christina was momentarily stunned.

She sat staring at her father for a few seconds, and then she exclaimed, with a flash of anger, "Why didn't you let me know? How unfair of you, Dad, to keep me in the dark. I should have been with her and certainly last week, once she was at home." Her angry stare intensified, and she added furiously, "You should have told me!"

"I didn't dare go against your mother's wishes, Christie love," Vincent said quietly. "I didn't dare upset her, and I would have if I'd sent for you. She didn't want you to be worried. You know what your mam's like."

"I don't understand you, I don't really," Christina cried, shaking her head in perplexity. "I can't imagine why you listened to Mummy. And anyway, who *has* been looking after her since she's been at home?"

"I have," Vincent said, turning on the ignition, glancing behind him before pulling out. "I took a week off from work. We're not very busy at the moment, and I had some holiday time due me, anyway."

"I could have come up last week," Christina snapped, her annoyance unabated. "I was just marking time in London, waiting to come home. I didn't have any special classes at the college."

Vincent realized that it would be wiser to remain silent. With their similar temperaments they could quarrel very easily, and that was the last thing he wanted today. He put his foot down on the accelerator and concentrated on his driving.

Halfway up Ridge Road, he glanced at her quickly out of the corner of his eye and said in the softest but firmest of voices, "I hope you've calmed down, our Christie. I don't want you barging into the house full of belligerence and upsetting your mother."

"God, Dad, you're impossible at times! How could you even think I would do such a thing?"

• • •

Audra's eyes looked bigger and bluer than ever in her face, which was drawn and chalky in color and reflected her suffering of the last few weeks. It lit up at the sight of Christina standing in the doorway.

"Hello, darling," Audra said in a weak voice, half pushing herself up on her elbows as Christina sped to her bedside.

"Oh Mummy, Mummy darling," Christina whispered, kneeling down, taking Audra in her arms tenderly, embracing her. "You should have let Daddy send for me," she murmured against her mother's hair, "you really should have." Releasing her, she sat back, regarding her carefully, wanting to assess her true condition.

Audra lifted her hand, touched Christina's face. "You have your studies and they're more important than anything else right now."

Although Christina did not agree with this, believing that her mother's health came first, she nodded her head. Rising she went to the bay window, pulled a chair closer to Audra, sat down.

Vincent came in, hovered near the foot of the bed. He said to Audra, "How do you feel, love? Are you all right? Comfortable?"

"Yes, thank you, Vincent."

"I'll go and put the kettle on," he said.

Christina leaned forward after her father had left the room, said in a cheery tone, "Well anyway, I'm here now, Mummy, and for the next week I'm going to look after you. I'm going to pamper and spoil you in the way you deserve."

A frown creased Audra's brow. "At Christmas you told me you were thinking of going off on a field trip to the Lake District. I hope you haven't changed your mind because of me."

"No, no," Christina said quickly. "My tutor doesn't think it's necessary. I have plenty of finished paintings in hand."

"It'll be nice to have you here for the whole week," Audra murmured, settling back against the pillows, her face suffused with sudden contentment. "How's Jane?"

"As sweet as always, Mummy, and she sends you her love."

"I'm glad you have her for a friend and that you're happy sharing the flat in Walton Street with her. It's such a charming, cozy place." Another smile flitted across Audra's thin face. "Tell me everything you've been doing . . . you know how I love to hear about your exciting life in London."

"Yes, I will, but first I'm going downstairs to help Daddy . . . would you like to have something to eat with your cup of tea?"

"No, I'm not hungry, darling, but thank you."

Christina ran downstairs, wanting to alert her father that she had changed her plans before he blurted something out in front of her mother.

She found him in the kitchen unwrapping a slab of butter. He looked up as she came in. "Oh there you are, love. I bought some hot-cross buns at the confectioner's earlier. I thought I'd butter one for your mam."

"She said she's not hungry, Dad."

"Oh but she'll eat this," he said confidently. "She always likes a hot-cross bun at Easter, you know that. It's sort of a tradition with her, from her childhood at High Cleugh . . . having one on Good Friday." He sliced the bun in half and began to spread the butter on it. "You may think your mother looks haggard, but she's a lot better, Christie, she really is, and very much on the mend now."

Christina nodded. "Look, I just wanted to warn you not to say anything to her about my field trip to the East Coast. I'm staying here to look after Mummy for the entire week."

"Oh but she won't like that, it'll upset her—"

"I've already told her, Dad!" Christina interjected firmly. "So *please* don't say anything. I just told her my tutor didn't think it was necessary."

"Very well then." He glanced up and his eyes filled with love for his only child. "You're a good lass, Christie, and it'll be a real tonic for your mother to have you here for a while. Better than any medicine."

It was a busy week for Christina.

She took over the running of the house; she cleaned and shopped and cooked and ironed, and looked after her mother with efficiency and the greatest devotion.

When the Easter weekend was over, she insisted that her father return to work, and he did so, although he protested vociferously about her bossiness to her mother. She heard him say to Audra as she passed their bedroom one morning, "I always warned you we had the makings of an army general in that one, and I knew I was right. She's just proved it to me. And I'll tell you something else, I wouldn't like to work for *her*."

Christina had smiled as she had gone about her chores. She knew very well from whom she had inherited her bossy nature: her father.

Nursing her mother, pampering her and catering to her every need gave Christina a great deal of satisfaction. But as the week progressed it struck her that her mother had been making a stupendous effort to be bright and lively for her benefit.

It was now becoming obvious that this effort had been a terrible strain. Toward the end of the week Audra looked drained of all strength, and Christina's concern grew.

On Friday, her last morning at home, she was upset when she saw that her mother had only picked at the breakfast she had made for her. The scrambled eggs and bacon were untouched, the toast only half eaten, the peach unpeeled.

"Mummy, you've got an appetite like a sparrow! I shall be sick with worry once I've left."

"Don't be so silly, dear. I'm not hungry at the moment, that's all it is; and don't forget, I have been quite ill, Christie. My appetite will improve when I get my energy back, when I'm up and about again."

"I think I'd better stay at home another week."

"Absolutely not, I won't hear of it. There are your studies to think about. You mustn't neglect them, and this *is* your last term."

Christina sighed and lifted the tray, placed it on a nearby chest. She came to the bed and sat down, took hold of her mother's hand. "Can't you try and eat the peach if I peel it for you?"

"No, but thank you." Audra squeezed her hand. "It's been lovely to have you here, darling, but now you must get back to your life in London, the college, your friends," she said, smiling deeply at her daughter.

Christina smiled back; then her smile slipped.

In the bright sunlight of the April morning her mother's face was clearly illuminated, and for the first time in years she saw Audra with stunning objectivity. And as her eyes remained fixed on that wan face that was so very dear to her, Christina was appalled.

She thought: How she's aged in the last three years. She's not quite forty-seven, but she looks like an old woman today.

Her mother's life of sacrifice and struggle flashed through her mind with such breathtaking clarity Christina was suddenly filled with an aching sorrow. And then her heart clenched with feelings of tenderness and compassion for this small, fragile-looking woman who stood ten feet tall in her eyes.

Unexpectedly choking up, Christina leaned forward and embraced her mother, not wishing her to see the emotions unexpectedly overwhelming her.

And as she clung to Audra it became clear to Christina that she could not permit her to continue living her life in this way. I can't, I simply can't, she said to herself. All of this work and sacrifice and struggle for *me* must come to an end.

I myself will end it.

Thirty-Five

Later that day, as she sat on the train going back to London, Christina could not expunge the image of her mother's worn face from her mind.

Furthermore, she knew that it would continue to haunt her for a very long time.

As she sat staring morosely out of the train window, she asked herself what she was going to do. One thing was certain . . . she could not allow her mother to go on supporting her after she had graduated from the Royal College of Art later that summer.

Christina sighed heavily and leaned her head against the window. It would take years to establish herself as a landscape painter, to make a name for herself, to start selling her work and earn a living. She was well aware of that, as every young artist was these days.

And so was Audra. How many times had she said in the last couple of years: "Don't be concerned, Christie. You just continue to paint your beautiful pictures and let me worry about the money and where it's coming from."

Remembering these words sent a wave of coldness through Christina, and she shivered involuntarily. That was the crux of the problem—well, at least part of it—her mother's determination to support *her* until she was famous and her paintings were in great demand.

Christina shivered again and goose bumps speckled her arms. It was as if somebody had walked over her grave. Was her mother going to have to continue working at Leeds Infirmary until she was a very old woman, in order to pay *her* rent, buy *her* clothes, put food on *her* table, pay for everything she needed in *her* life?

No, Christina said under her breath. *No.* I won't let her be a drudge anymore, to earn money for *me.* I won't. I will end it, just as I vowed I would this morning. But how? And what am I going to do? She huddled in the corner of the seat and closed her eyes. Whatever am I going to do? How will I solve this dilemma? she asked herself.

The wheels of the train turned and turned and turned relentlessly, and they seemed to pound this question into her brain. By the time the coach was pulling into King's Cross Station, she had a splitting headache and felt slightly faint. She wondered if she was coming down with the flu.

And it would be raining, Christina thought miserably as she glanced out of the window and then pulled her suitcase down off the rack above her head when the train came to a final shuddering halt.

A few seconds later, as she hurried along the platform, she decided to take a taxi home to Walton Street, even though being careful with money was now uppermost in her mind. It was absolutely imperative to Christina that she get back to the flat quickly. She needed to be enveloped in its peacefulness and solitude. She had some hard thinking to do tonight, some hard choices to make.

In the past when she had come back from Yorkshire after the holidays, Christina had been disappointed if Jane was not already ensconced in Walton Street and waiting for her. But as she let herself in tonight she was pleased that her friend was not returning from Hadley Court until Sunday evening.

Christina had to wrestle with her problems, to find a solution to each one of them. Before she settled down to do this, she rang her father in Leeds to tell him she had arrived safely. "Don't disturb Mummy," she said, after a brief chat with him. "Just give her a big hug and a kiss from me." After hanging up the phone, she unpacked her suitcase, then ran a bath.

She soaked in a hot tub for a good fifteen minutes, emptying her head of everything, endeavoring to relax, and as soon as she felt a little of the tension easing out of her aching muscles, she stepped out of the bath and dried herself hard.

Later, wrapped in a toweling robe, she sat curled up on her bed, drinking a cup of Nescafé with cream and sugar. Slowly her eyes began to roam around her room . . . there was one of her paintings on each wall, and her gaze finally settled on her latest, which she had called *Lily at Hadley*. It was an oil of the lily pond at Hadley Court, and it abounded with many shades of green . . . the murky green-blue of the pond water, the lighter, softer green of the spongy moss trailing over the edge of the pond, the polished, glossy green of the floating lily pads. The only other colors were the sharp, pure white of the single lily, its petals beautifully defined and glistening with drops of crystal dew, and the color of the light, a narrow corridor of radiance that filtered through the junglelike foliage in the background of the painting. This light held a hint of yellow, appeared to shimmer with sunlight as it touched the water, then spread out in a spraylike effect, became diffused over the lily itself.

Christina put down the cup of coffee on the bedside table and turned on her side, pressed her face into the pillow. She found it unbearable to look upon that painting, or on any of her paintings for that matter. All of her joy in her art had been suddenly snuffed out, extinguished by her immense pain.

Too high a price had been paid for it.

Audra's years of punishing, brutal toil . . . her health . . . all the little luxuries and comforts she might have bought for herself . . . a holiday occasionally . . . a new outfit.

A lump formed in Christina's throat. How long had she seen her mother wearing the same navy blue reefer coat? Winter after winter, for years and years. The tears came then, pouring out of her eyes, and she wept for her mother and for all of those lost years in Audra's life when she had been slaving away in order to give *her* a future. And she cried until there seemed to be no tears left inside her, and finally she dozed.

Christina felt as if she was falling . . . falling through dark space, and she snapped her eyes open, half sat up with a start, coming awake. She wondered where she was for a moment, feeling disoriented, and then she realized she was lying on her bed in the Walton Street flat. She glanced at the alarm clock. It was almost one in the morning. She had slept for hours, an exhausted sleep.

She turned out the light, fell back against the pillows and closed her eyes. Her mind turned on her dilemma yet again. It struck her that getting a job to support herself whilst she painted would be easy enough, but that was not the real issue. *What was crucial was the debt she owed her mother.*

This sudden revelation was so enlightening it brought her upright in bed again. And as she stared out into the darkness of the room she understood then what had been troubling her for hours: *the debt she owed her mother.* That was it. And she must repay it.

If I do not, it will weigh heavy on my conscience all the days of my life, she thought. And that I could not bear.

Thirty-Six

"Listen, Crowther, I know something's been troubling you for weeks, and tonight we're going to talk," Jane announced aggressively, pouncing on Christina the moment she walked into the flat.

Christina stared at her, closed the door, then allowed Jane to take her arm, to propel her into their living room.

After gently pushing her dearest friend down onto the sofa, Jane took the chair opposite. "I am right, aren't I, Christie?" Jane pressed. "Something *is* terribly wrong, isn't it?"

"Yes," Christina admitted. "I *have* been wrestling with a problem, a number of problems really, and I've wanted to talk to you, to unburden myself, but . . ." Christina paused, shook her head slowly, looked out the window, a faraway expression touching her lovely eyes.

Jane sat watching her, waiting patiently now, understanding that Christina was finally going to confide in her. She was filled with relief. Her friend had not been at all like herself for the past two months, ever since she had returned from Yorkshire after the Easter holidays. She had been subdued, distracted, irritable and gloomy by turn, and every time Jane had approached her she had denied there was anything amiss.

Finally, Christina spoke. "First, I must apologize, Jane," she said, giving her a loving look. "I know I haven't been easy to live with and that I've been snippy at times. I'm sorry . . . forgive me?"

"Don't be so silly, there's nothing to forgive. But if it makes you feel any better, yes, I do forgive you."

A fleeting smile crossed Christina's face. She went on, "I've been struggling to make some decisions, and I didn't want to talk to you until I had."

Jane returned Christina's long thoughtful look but made no comment.

"I've decided to give up my art," Christina said softly.

"You can't be serious!" Jane shouted, sitting bolt upright.

"Yes, I am."

"I won't let you!" Jane bellowed.

Christina shook her head vehemently. "You can't stop me. And anyway, listen who's talking. *You* told me six months ago that *you* were going to give up *your* art to become a scenic designer. I distinctly remember you telling me that you had no intention of starving in a garret in the faint hope that somebody would buy one of your paintings one day. In fact, you went on to add that art lovers who had money to spend bought only big-name artists, such as Renoir, Van Gogh, Monet, Picasso, et cetera, et cetera, et cetera."

"But you're better than I am!"

Christina ignored this remark. She said, "Several classmates—Jamie Angers, Danielle Forbes and Patricia Smith—are going into other areas of art— textile design, interior design, costume and scenic design, like you are."

Jane repeated, "But *you* are better than *we* are." Her deep-violet eyes swept the room, and she waved her hand at two of Christina's paintings hanging on the walls. "Look! Just look! How can you give *that* up?"

"Very easily," Christina said, her voice so low it was hardly audible. "Since it's costing a woman's life."

"Whose life?" Jane cried.

"My mother's."

Christina did not give Jane a chance to respond to this. She began to speak slowly and carefully, and she explained everything to Jane, recounting the history of Audra's background, the years of hard work and sacrifice on her behalf. And when Christina had finally finished, Jane had tears in her eyes.

And Christina continued, "You see, Jane, I don't believe I could convince her to stop working, even after I graduate later in the summer. She'll insist on supporting me until my paintings start selling. She's stubborn, implacable really. I could get a job, earn a living whilst I paint, and send the money she sends me back to her. And I suppose I could eventually convince her that I can stand on my own two feet, and so put an end to her toiling. But none of that is quite good enough for me, Janey."

"I don't think I'm following you, Christie."

"It's simply not enough for me to just say to her: *Thank you, I can look after myself now, Mother.*" Christina shook her head. "No. I have a terrible need, a compelling need, to bring ease and comfort to her life. I want to give her the kind of luxuries she's never known. And the kind of luxuries I'm thinking about cost money . . . oodles and oodles of money. As a struggling artist it would take me years and years to earn enough to give her those things. I don't have time; I want her to have them as quickly as possible, whilst she's still young enough to enjoy them."

"But how are you going to make your pots and pots of money?" Jane asked, looking at her in bafflement.

"I'm going into business—that's where the money is . . . and I mean *business* with a capital B. I'm going to become a fashion designer, but I aim to be a rich and famous fashion designer—and very very quickly."

"But how are you going to get started?"

"Actually with your help."

"My help."

"Your mother's really, if you'll give me your permission to talk to her about this project."

"Of course you can talk to her. But how can Mummy help?"

Christina leaned forward, sudden enthusiasm filling her eyes, extinguishing the worry of earlier. "She's constantly after me to make her one of my hand-painted silk dresses, and she told me only a few weeks ago that she could sell them like hot cakes to her friends, if only I had a secret hoard of them tucked away somewhere. She was laughing when she said that—about her friends, I mean—but I bet some of them would be interested in buying from me. You know, at that party your mother gave for her American agent, both Polly Lamb and Lady Buckley were admiring of my hand-painted silk jacket. They both wanted to know where I'd bought it. Don't you see, Janey, my hand-painted evening clothes are very original, my *exclusive* design, and they *would* be a beginning. Later on, I could make my tailored suits . . . everyone so admires those."

"You're right!" Jane exclaimed. "You *must* talk to Mummy, get her measurements, and then design the dress for her. And I'm sure she won't mind if you approach her friends, especially those who were so interested at the cocktail party."

"Oh, I am glad you agree! However, there's a slight problem." Christina threw Jane a worried glance. "Do you think your mother would give me half the money in advance? You know, pay half the price of the dress before I deliver it? And get her friends who order dresses to do the same? If they did, it would help me immensely. I could use the money to buy the fabrics and the special paint I need."

"Of course Mummy will pay up front, and she'll jolly well make sure her friends do too." Jane sat back, looking confident, then screwed up her mouth in a thoughtful way. "But that's not the real solution, Christie. If you're going into the fashion business and want it to become *big* business, then you must have working capital."

Christina laughed hollowly. "Don't I know it . . . however, I'm afraid I don't have a bean to my name."

"Oh but I do!" Jane announced gleefully. "I have the five thousand pounds that Granny Manville left me, and the money's just sitting there in Lloyds Bank earning a bit of interest that's worth tiddlywinks. I'm going to lend you my five thousand pounds!"

"Jane, that's truly a wonderful gesture, but I couldn't possibly borrow money from you," Christina protested.

"You're going to take it . . . I shall *force* you to take it. If you have a bit of decent capital behind you, the business will grow much faster, and things will run better. You could take on a seamstress, maybe even two, and also find small premises."

"Yes, you're right. As a matter of fact, I had made those sorts of plans," Christina remarked standing up, walking over to the fireplace. She ran her hand over her mouth, pondering for a moment. "Of course, I hadn't intended to branch out like that until next year, when I'd already made a little money." Christina directed her steady, smokey gaze at Jane. "If you lend me your five thousand pounds, I could do it sooner, that's true. So—thank you, I accept your offer, and I'm very grateful, Janey darling." She went over to Jane's chair, bent down and hugged her.

Jane immediately sprang to her feet, hugged Christina in return, her face wreathed in smiles. Then she thrust out her hand. "Shake, partner. I'll draw the money out of my savings account tomorrow morning first thing, and *voilà,* you'll be in business!"

They stood in the center of the floor, shaking hands and grinning broadly at each other.

Jane said, "And I'll help you any other way I can, rustle up business—" Jane broke off and her face fell.

"What's the matter?" Christina asked.

"How on earth will you break this news to your mother? She'll be devastated when you tell her that you're giving up painting. Oh my God, Christie, she'll be dreadfully upset."

"Yes, I know," Christina agreed, sounding suddenly gloomy. "Don't think I haven't wrestled with that problem for weeks, because I have. And I've come to the conclusion that it's better I don't tell her anything at all right now. Once I've graduated in August, I shall let her think that I'm painting away, and about four or five months after that, let's say around Christmas, I'll tell her I've sold some of my work and that I can start supporting myself."

"Do you think she'll believe you?" Jane asked.

"I hope so, Janey, I sincerely hope so."

——— *Thirty-Seven* ———

Artistic talent was not the only thing that Christina had inherited from Audra.

She had her mother's penchant for hard work, her physical stamina and energy, her stubbornness and her determination to succeed at whatever she did.

And all of these characteristics came into play in the first six months she was in business, and they were fundamental to her extraordinary success in this relatively short period of time.

Christina also discovered that she had a good head for business, something she had not realized she possessed, and this too played a large role in her rise to stardom in the world of haute couture.

Even so, perhaps her greatest strength was her gift for translating art into fashion, in the form of the exquisite, elaborately painted evening gowns and coats and jackets which were to become her lasting trademark and which would always be in demand throughout her career.

Jane said to her one afternoon, "Fortuny became renowned for his pleated-silk Delphos gowns, Chanel for her cardigan suits, Dior for his New Look and Balenciaga for his perfect cutting. *You* are going to be known for your translation of art into couture, for your incredible paintings on silk. Those gowns will soon become classics, just like Poiret's beaded evening gowns. People are going to keep your dresses for years and years to come, Christie, my pet."

Christina accepted this compliment from her friend and partner, knowing that she was speaking from the heart. Then she suddenly broke into laughter and exclaimed, "I shall also be remembered for my ability to work eighteen hours a day, seven days a week, for weeks and weeks and weeks on end."

"Yes, that's true," Jane admitted, grinning at her. "You *have* worked like a galley slave these last few months, but let's face it, the effort was worth it. We're inundated with orders—" Jane gave Christina an amused look. "When I told Mummy you were toiling in the salt mines these days, she said that surely I must mean the gold mines! And listen, talking of the orders piling up, shouldn't we try to find another seamstress?"

Christina nodded. "Yes, and the word is already out. Elise and Germaine are asking around amongst their friends in the French community, and I'm sure they'll dig somebody up pretty quickly."

"I hope they do; otherwise *we'll* be the ones sitting at the sewing machines, not to mention the handwork. Which would be all we need after painting the damn things!"

Christina said, "Listen, I'm very grateful to you for helping with those mandarin sleeves on the two chiffons for Mrs. Bolton." She eyed her friend with amusement. "You've got pink paint all over your nose . . . still, you really do do the best butterflies in town."

Jane giggled, felt her nose. "I'm glad to help. I just wish I could do more in the business for you. I feel sort of useless to you most of the time . . ."

"Don't be silly; you're invaluable, Jane! You work on the accounts, do a bit of everything really, and furthermore, without you there would be no business. Don't let's forget your five thousand pounds."

"It's a good investment, Crowther. Aren't I the shrewd one, backing *you*." Jane rolled her eyes villainously, then went to empty the coffee pot in the small kitchen adjoining the office.

Christina leapt to her feet, stretched and walked over to the window, stood looking out into the backyard behind "the factory," as she called their premises. She had found these in August, not long after graduating from the Painting School of the Royal College of Art. Previously a greengrocer's shop and living quarters, the building was located at the far end of the King's Road; and aside from its reasonable rent, she considered it to be perfect for her needs for several reasons.

There was a great deal of natural light coming in through the windows, which was essential for the painting of the fabrics and the sewing of the garments; then again, the space was more than adequate, even allowed for growth, since the living quarters attached offered plenty of room for additional staff if and when they were required.

The shop part, where vegetables had been sold until very recently, had been transformed into a small reception area. Here clients could wait to be measured and fitted. Christina and Jane had painted all of the interiors white, except that for the reception room they had used soft pearl-gray paint on the walls here and had hung a cafe curtain of gray watered silk across the window fronting onto the street. It prevented pedestrians from looking inside, offered a degree of privacy to the waiting clients. Dulcie had given them an oriental rug, several chairs, a table and a lamp, all castoffs from Hadley Court, and with the addition of a couple of potted plants and some of their own drawings on the walls, the girls had created a cheerful effect.

The living room behind the shop had been turned into a general office; upstairs, one bedroom had become the sewing room, a second smaller bedroom was the fitting room, while the third and largest bedroom was the studio where Christina worked. It was here that she painted the fabrics for the evening clothes, and where Jane and a couple of their former classmates helped her out at times by painting sleeves. Since the major artwork on the gowns and coats was signed by Christina, she would permit no one else to do this.

Now, as she stood staring out of the window on this gray March afternoon in 1955, the hand-painted fabrics were very much on her mind. She swung to face Jane and said, "Listen, I know we're making a great deal of money with the evening clothes, but I do think I have to start designing other garments and expand the line."

"I've been expecting you to say that . . . the painting is very time-consuming, Christie. I think you *must* always make the hand-painted clothes, they are your trademark after all, but perhaps you can cut down on them a little."

"Yes, and I'll start designing the tailored suits and dresses your mother admires so much . . . she's a good judge of what will sell, Janey."

"That's true, and talking of my mama, I had better love you and leave you," Jane murmured, rising to her feet. "She'll be mad if I'm late for my appointment with her and Gregory Joynson, and I do have to dash home and change first. So, Crowther, aren't you going to wish me luck?"

"Of course I am, and I know he'll like your preliminary costume designs . . . they are out of this world."

Jane gave her a sly wink as she picked up her handbag and coat. "It's a good job the star likes them, isn't it? Thank God for my mother, the actress, who is such an advocate of nepotism." Pausing at the door, Jane added, "And don't stay here burning the midnight oil, Crowther, you're starting to look tired."

"No, I won't. See you back at Walton Street later."

Once she was alone, Christina went upstairs and turned on all of the powerful overhead lights which she had had installed in the big studio so she could work at night. She looked at the fabric she had finished painting that morning and nodded her head in satisfaction.

The painting was of white calla lilies on black chiffon, and she had worked on the large piece of fabric before she had started to design the actual dress. This she planned to do tomorrow, and she would design and cut the dress to fit the painted motif. She often adopted this method; other times, she would create the style of the dress or gown or coat, make the *toile,* cut the front and back panels and then paint her flowers within the framework of the garment. She never limited herself, always left herself open to her art, and in a sense she let the art dictate the style of the piece of clothing. For this reason none of her hand-painted clothes were ever alike.

Christina checked several other fabrics, then returned to her office downstairs, where she sat down at her desk. Pulling a piece of writing paper toward her, she started a letter to her parents. She always wrote to them once a week and phoned every Sunday without fail, and her weekly letter was due today.

She sighed to herself as she filled the pages with lies . . . lies about the paintings she was selling . . . lies about her social activities . . . lies about her life in general. She had to invent because she had no personal life at all at the moment, and no boyfriend either, since her last rather lame romance with a fellow student had fizzled out, like the others in the last few years.

Putting her elbow on the desk, resting her head on her hand, Christina racked her brains for something exciting to make up, to recount to her mother. Audra so loved hearing about her dazzling social life with Jane and the Sedgewicks and the other celebrated people she met at their parties.

Leaning back in the chair, she put down the pen, thinking suddenly of Dulcie Manville. What a good friend she had been, and how sweet she had been to her parents when they had come to London for her graduation. Jane had moved out of the Walton Street flat, had gone back to her parents' Mayfair home for a few days, so that Vincent and Audra could stay with her. They had enjoyed being with her, and their trip had been an enormous success all around.

The Sedgewicks had given a party for Jane and her to celebrate their graduation. Dulcie had seemed taken aback when she had met her father, and now Christina smiled to herself as she remembered Dulcie's reaction. She had taken her to one side and remarked, "You might have told me your father looked like Robert Taylor, Christie. My goodness, if he were an actor, his face would be his fortune, my dear." Later that evening, when she had repeated the comment to her parents, her father had looked tickled to death, but her mother had seemed put out, even irritated, and she had known then that her mother was terribly jealous of Vincent.

Those two, Christina muttered under her breath, reaching for the pen again. I'm always on a roller coaster ride with them, and they're either at each other's throats or in each other's arms. She thought of her parents with a sudden rush of warmth and affection. She loved them both very much, and she had always tried to walk a line between them, doing a balancing act in a sense, endeavoring not to take sides, not wishing to hurt either one. And I think I've succeeded, she added to herself as she attempted to finish her letter of lies. But they're only white lies, she thought.

It was nine o'clock when Christina finally left "the factory" and headed down the King's Road in the direction of Sloane Square. Her thoughts still lingered on her mother as she walked along at a brisk pace. She had managed to convince Audra not to send any more money, by vehemently insisting that her work was now selling well. But what troubled Christina was that Audra was still working at Leeds Infirmary. "She won't listen to me, lass," her father had said when she had tackled him about it during the Christmas holidays. "Your mother's always had a mind of her own, and I'd be the last one to make her change it." Audra had not listened to her either, and she had eventually let the matter drop.

Well, at least I have the satisfaction of knowing she is keeping the money she earns for herself, Christina thought, dropping the letter in the box at the post office in Sloane Square. It's a huge relief to know she's no longer working simply to support me.

Ever since she had given up her landscapes, Christina had not thought too much about this move. As far as she was concerned, her decision was irrevocable, and she did not harbor any regrets. Carving a niche for herself in the world of high fashion, and in a big, big way, had now become the most powerful motivating force in her life. Christina believed that only by making money, vast amounts of it, could she repay her immense debt to her mother by surrounding her with comfort and every luxury imaginable. And she hoped soon to be able to do this.

Now, as she hurried along Sloane Street, tightening her headscarf against the March wind, Christina thought of the large order for clothes she had received from the actress Miranda Fowler. The star was leaving in three months for New York, where she was to appear in a Broadway play, and had asked Christina to make as many evening clothes as she could for her.

How ever will I get them finished in time, Christina wondered, as she let herself into the flat on Walton Street. And over a sandwich and a glass of milk she started to make notes that night, focusing on the designs with her usual concentration.

In the next few days it seemed to Christina that inspiration dwelt in her fingertips.

Her sketching pad was soon filled with the first early drawings for the Miranda Fowler wardrobe, and ideas flowed out of her without cease as she visualized the clothes in her fertile imagination. Forms, shapes, styles, colors, flower formations, fabrics, embroideries . . . all jostled for prominence in her head. Within ten days she had edited her initial ideas and sketches, selected her favorites, completed the drawings and started to pick the materials she would use.

For several days chiffons, silks, satins, brocades, crepes and georgettes swirled around her in a dizzying array of colors. Slowly these, too, were edited down until she had settled on silk, chiffon and georgette for the evening dresses, heavy satin for evening pajamas and a long evening coat, brocade for two jackets to wear with silk pants.

When the actress came to have her measurements taken, she was delighted with the drawings and fabrics; Christina explained that if she was to create a full wardrobe of evening clothes for her, not all of them could be hand-painted. The new client said this was acceptable.

Christina worked around the clock, whilst the two French seamstresses sewed like demons to finish the wardrobe for the celebrated musical comedy star. Several weeks after she had commenced work on the clothes, Christina hired another Frenchwoman, a friend of Germaine's, called Lucie James. Lucie came highly recommended, and aside from being an excellent needlewoman, she had a fine reputation as a cutter and had worked at the Balenciaga salon before the war and her marriage to an Englishman in 1938. Lucie had previously worked for Mr. Michael, the couturier with a salon in Carlos Place. It did not take Christina long to realize that she had a real find in Lucie. She knew Lucie would take some of the burdens of cutting the garments away from her, which meant she could devote herself to the painting.

It had been a supreme effort on all of their parts, and a monumental achievement, to have the clothes ready by the date Miranda Fowler had specified. In point of fact, Christina was a little ahead of time, and early one warm evening toward the end of May, she took Jane upstairs to see the rack of clothes in the studio.

Flipping the switch, flooding the studio with light, she pulled the sheet off the rack and cried, "The unveiling . . . ta-da ta-da! And before I show you each elegant and exquisite creation, let me just say this . . . once Miranda Fowler has paid me, I'll be able to finally repay you your five thousand pounds. Isn't that wonderful news, Janey?"

"Yes, it is, but there's no real hurry," Jane said, and then she went into raptures over the stunningly beautiful outfits.

When the two girls had returned to the office, Christina said, "Look, I'm taking my three lovely women to dinner tonight, a special treat for them, for all the hard work they've put in. Why don't you come with us, Janey? After all, you're part of the family."

"Oh that's lovely of you, but I really am whacked," Jane said. "I've been pushing myself hard on those costumes for the play, and I've got to solve the problem with those blasted ruffs tonight. They won't stay stiff, and starch is so scratchy against the actors' necks. Oh God, why does my mother have the urge to play Elizabeth Tudor?"

Christina laughed at the look on her face, and pointed out, "It might do you good to come with us . . . it would take your mind off those ruffs."

Jane shook her head. "Thanks, but no thanks. I shall do some work, make a fried-egg sandwich and go to bed early." She eyed Christina dourly and her pretty young mouth twisted in a grimace. "Romantic life we both lead these days, isn't it?"

"We'll make up for it when we're both rich and famous."

"You bet we will," Jane said with a leer. "And listen, Crowther, don't come banging and clattering into the flat tonight. I really meant it when I said I intend to go to bed early."

"You can sleep late tomorrow—it's Saturday."

"Fat chance of that." Jane picked up her briefcase. "Have a lovely meal, darling."

It was a few minutes after eleven when Christina walked down Walton Street that night, after taking her three employees to dinner.

She was suddenly feeling weary.

It had been a hard few months and for the first time in ages she had relaxed during the evening, had finally let go; the rich meal at Ox on the Roof restaurant and the red wine had also had an enervating effect on her. She could not wait to get undressed and climb into bed.

Remembering that Jane had said she was going to sleep early, Christina could not help wondering why all of their living room lights were blazing. As she drew to a stop in front of the house where they lived on the top floor, she looked up at the windows, frowning to herself.

I expect she's forgotten to turn them off, she muttered, unlocking the street door, climbing the steep flight of stairs to their landing.

Christina was fumbling with her key chain, standing outside the door of the flat when it suddenly flew open.

Surprised, she jumped and glared at Jane. "Honestly, you scared me—" she began and stopped when Jane grabbed her arm.

Jane hissed, "Your parents are here. And your mother is absolutely *furious* . . . she can't take her eyes off your paintings hanging on our walls."

"Oh my God," Christina whispered back, blanching. "How stupid I am."

——— *Thirty-Eight* ———

The coldness in her mother's startling blue eyes blinded her.

She hesitated in the doorway. All of her strength ebbed out of her and she was gripped by a terrible internal shaking.

Her parents sat together on the sofa. They both looked as if they had turned to granite.

No one spoke.

Somewhere behind her in the hall, Jane hovered nervously.

She could move neither forward nor backward. She had turned to stone like her parents.

At last she found her voice. "Hello, Mummy, Daddy . . . this is a surprise."

"Apparently so," Audra responded in an icy tone that matched her eyes.

Christina swallowed.

Vincent glared.

Audra suddenly sprang up, startling them.

She began to move around the room rapidly, pausing briefly at each one of Christina's paintings, saying their names in a clipped, cold voice, *"Elms in Winter . . . Sky at Gunnerside . . . Houghley Beck . . . Edith's Delphiniums,* and through the open door of your bedroom—" She snapped off the end of her sentence, pivoted to face Christina, and glaring at her, she finished, "I can see *Lily at Hadley.* You told me you had *sold* all of these paintings. You lied to me, Christina. *Why?* And how are you managing to live? How are you paying your bills? Something is wrong, very, very wrong here. I demand to know what's going on at once! *At once, do you hear me!"*

Christina moved forward, galvanized by her mother's angry words, knowing she had to get this over with once and for all.

She drew to a stop next to Audra. She took a deep breath. "Mummy, I have something to tell you, something I've been wanting to tell you for ages . . ." She looked down at her mother, so fragile, and she was instantly intimidated by the force of Audra's personality, the indomitability reflected in her face. She could not go on. Her nerve failed her.

Audra's bright blue eyes impaled hers. "I'm waiting, Christina."

In a great rush of words, Christina blurted out, "I've given up my painting. I've become a fashion designer. I decided it wasn't worth it, being a struggling artist. You see, I wanted to make money. My clothes are lovely, beautiful really; I know you'll like them—"

"You gave up your art to become a *dressmaker!"* Audra gasped, stunned, stupefied. She gaped at Christina. All of the color drained out of her face and her eyes were stark with incredulity. "You gave up your art!" she repeated. "You threw away your great gift for creating beauty for . . . a *commercial* venture. I can't believe it! I just can't believe it!"

Audra shook her head from side to side as if denying this awful knowledge.

She suddenly cried, "And after all I did for you! After all I did to give you your art! Oh my God, when I think of all my years of gruelling work and sacrifice and scrimping and scraping, and going without to give to you, and giving and giving of myself until I had nothing left to give, and always putting you first, always putting you before your father, neglecting him—"

Audra was unable to continue.

She turned to Vincent. A look of excruciating pain mingled with overwhelming sorrow settled on her face, and her eyes, dark with hurt now, filled with sudden tears. "Oh Vincent—" She reached out for him blindly, the tears falling unchecked, blurring her vision.

He was by her side in a flash.

His arms went around her, and he held her protectively against his body, one hand patting her shoulder, comforting. He looked down at her and he sighed, ever so lightly, and then he lifted his head.

Vincent leveled his gaze at his daughter. He stared as if seeing her for the first time.

Christina flinched under his hard, cold scrutiny. Her mouth began to tremble.

Disdain flashed onto Vincent's handsome face, and his eyes were steely green and uncompromising. "You've just broken your mother's heart," he said in a voice that shook.

Without another word he turned his back on Christina and led the weeping Audra from the room.

Christina stared after her parents speechlessly. And then she ran forward, caught up with them in the hall. "Daddy . . . wait," she cried, reaching out, grasping his sleeve.

He shook her hand off, a certain harshness in his movements, and glanced over his shoulder. "Don't *you* Daddy me," he snapped. "I've had enough of *you* for one night, Christina. I never thought I'd live to see you hurt your mother so cruelly."

Christina recoiled at his words, and she remained rooted in the doorway of the flat as her mother and father crossed the landing and went down the stairs together.

From behind her, Jane whispered, "Oh God, Christie, that was simply ghastly. Are you all right?"

When Christina did not respond, Jane put her arm around her dearest friend and drew her inside. She pushed the front door closed with her other hand, walked Christina through the hall and into the living room, pressed her down onto the sofa.

Christina began to shake uncontrollably, and she looked at Jane helplessly. "I must go after them," she began and immediately burst into tears.

"Oh darling, don't, don't," Jane murmured, her voice consoling as she lowered herself onto the sofa and took Christina's hand in hers. "You can't go after them, and it wouldn't do any good, not tonight." Jane gave her a quick hug and rose, hurried out.

She returned a moment later with a large handkerchief. "Here, wipe your eyes," she said, giving it to Christina, "and I'll get us a drink. I think we could both use a brandy."

After mopping her eyes and blowing her nose, Christina accepted the cognac from Jane, took a long swallow. She said, "Perhaps I'd better ring them in a little while. They must be staying in the studio flat at Theo's; they have *carte blanche* to stay there any time they—"

"Oh no, they're at a hotel," Jane interjected and grimaced. "Oh botheration, what an idiot *I* am! I should have asked your father which hotel, when he mentioned it."

"Oh Jane . . ." She fell back against the sofa, her misery growing more acute by the moment. "I simply assumed they were at the house in Chester Street; now I'll *never* find them this weekend."

"Perhaps they'll phone you tomorrow," Jane said, her face brightening at this thought. "Oh yes, I'm sure they will."

"I doubt it very much. Mummy is devastated and my father's furious with me." Christina rubbed her hand over her weary eyes and asked, "Tell me what happened this evening?"

"They arrived at about ten-fifteen. I'd gone to bed earlier, but the phone kept ringing. The calls were stupid too . . . first Gregory Joynson called to complain that one of my costumes for Mummy clashed with a pillow on the stage—he's such a nit. Then she rang up, worrying about those damned Elizabethan ruffs. I'd no sooner hung up on her, when Harry Manderville phoned to invite us to some stupid arts ball next month. In sheer desperation I finally took the phone off the hook. I promptly fell asleep. The next thing I knew, the intercom was buzzing for all it was worth. It was your father, telling me they were downstairs. Naturally, I asked them to come up—what else *could* I do? Besides, I was half asleep, and I didn't even think of the paintings."

"Oh Jane, I don't blame *you* for anything!" Christina exclaimed. "Of course you had to ask them upstairs. But did they say why they were in London? They don't usually take it into their heads to come up to town, not just like that."

"Your father apparently had the brilliant idea of bringing your mother to London to see you—as a special treat. They wanted to surprise you; that's why they didn't let you know they were coming."

"If only they had . . . we could have taken the paintings down, stored them at the factory, and they would never have been any the wiser."

"Only too true," Jane agreed and threw Christina an apologetic look. "I must admit, I do feel a bit responsible. If I hadn't had the phone off the hook, they would have got through to me . . . you see, they had been trying earlier. When it was constantly busy, they went to have supper somewhere, tried to ring us again later. They were worried and decided to come over when the operator told them the line was out of order. Oh hell, if only I'd spoken to them, I could have reassured them that everything was all right, prevented them from coming here until tomorrow, and certainly I could have done the necessary and removed the paintings."

"Oh Jane, please don't feel responsible. *Please.* If I hadn't taken the women out to dinner, I would have been here myself. Life is always full of *if onlys* and *buts* and *maybes*. You know that as well as I do."

Christina's eyes roamed around the living room, and she remarked quietly, "I suppose my mother spotted the paintings right away."

"Do you have to ask! Of course she did; you know she doesn't miss a trick, and who *could* miss these? They're larger than life. I realized immediately what a couple of fools *we'd* been, and I rushed to the kitchen, put the kettle on . . . I felt violently sick, and the only thing I could think of doing was making them a cup of tea. It was a jolly strained hour too, being here with them, waiting for you to return."

"Did she ask you a lot of questions—about what I was doing?"

"Not one, and neither did your father."

Christina looked at her watch. "I keep telling myself they'll ring, but that's just wishful thinking on my part. I know they won't."

"They will tomorrow, you'll see."

Christina nodded, knowing Jane was only trying to make her feel better. She also knew her friend was wrong.

• • •

Christina could not sleep.

She did not even try. She lay in bed thinking about her mother and waited for the morning to come.

At seven o'clock she snapped on the bedside lamp, drew her telephone book toward her and found Mike Lesley's number. During the dawn hours it had struck her that if anyone knew where her parents were staying, it would be Uncle Mike. She dialed the Leeds number quickly, now that it was a reasonable hour to telephone him.

"Doctor Lesley here," he said, answering immediately, sounding wide awake.

"Hello, Uncle Mike. It's Christie."

"Yes, I know. Good morning, dear."

"I'm sorry to disturb you so early, but I thought you might know which hotel Mummy and Daddy are staying at. We had a bit of an upset last night and—"

"Yes, your father told me all about it a short while ago."

"Oh. So you must know where they are."

"Yes, they were staying at Brown's, Christie. But your father called me about half an hour ago, and they were just checking out to drive back to Yorkshire. You won't reach them now."

"Oh damn," she exclaimed, "and I was hoping to see them this morning, to explain . . ." Her disappointment choked her, and she left her sentence dangling.

Mike said, "Perhaps it's just as well they've left, Christie dear. I think you'll be far better off talking to your mother later. In a few weeks, when she has calmed down."

"Oh no, I don't think so, Uncle Mike. I have to talk to her in the next *day* or two. She was so distressed last night and terribly hurt. Didn't Daddy explain everything to you?"

"Yes, he did, Christie."

"So you know that I've given up my painting, that I've become a designer?"

"Yes."

"And you don't approve either?"

"It's your life, Christina, and you must live it as you see fit . . . and I'm sure you have your reasons for doing what you've done, good reasons."

"Oh Uncle Mike, I do, I do. And I must make Mummy understand them. You see, I couldn't let her go on supporting me, I really couldn't. I have to take care of myself from now on. The fact that she was still slaving at the Infirmary to give me financial help was just intolerable to me. I have a real talent for fashion designing, and I saw a chance to make a success out of it, to make money. Not only money for me, but money for my mother. I do want to repay my great debt to her."

"Oh Christie . . ." There was a silence at the other end of the telephone and Mike sighed heavily. He said softly, "Your mother didn't do what she did looking for a reward, Christie. Her reward is her pride in you."

"That may be enough for Mummy, but it certainly isn't enough for me, not by a long shot. I want her to have so much more—I want her to have the best of everything money can buy actually, and I won't rest until she has it!"

"No, I don't suppose you will," he said with dawning comprehension.

"There's too much of Audra in you. But I wonder if *she* will ever understand that you are repeating the pattern."

"What do you mean?" Christina asked, tightening her grip on the receiver. "I'm not following you, Uncle Mike."

Mike Lesley did not answer this in a direct way. Instead he said, "Years ago your father came to talk to me about your mother; he was worried about her health, you see, worried about the way she was working, pushing herself to the limit. It was the spring of 1939. I remember the year very well, because war broke out that September. Anyway, your father said that what your mother was doing to ensure that you had a glittering future was abnormal. Laurette said she didn't think that abnormal was quite the right word. And then she told your father and me that we were witnessing an act of will. Yes, an act of will so powerfully motivated and so selfless it was awesome to witness."

Tears sprang into Christina's eyes and she blinked, brushed them away with her fingertips. She said, "And it was exactly that, wasn't it?"

"Yes, my dear. And now you are committing your own act of will, and your mother won't be able to stop you, just as your father was never able to stop her."

"But why do you say she won't understand, Uncle Mike?"

"Because she'll never accept the fact that you've given up your art in order to pay your debt to her. She would find that absolutely preposterous. And if you tell her that this is the reason why you have gone into business, her answer will be very simple, Christie. She'll insist you go back to painting pictures because she doesn't want the best that money can buy."

Christina was silent. "Yes," she said after a short pause, "perhaps you're right. But I have to do what I believe I have to do."

It was his turn to be silent.

Waiting, Christina heard him sigh deeply at the other end of the phone. "So be it," he said at last. "And God bless you, Christie."

Thirty-Nine

"I want to go big, and I really mean *big*," Christina said. "And I want to do it at once. *Now!*"

Startled, Jane stared at her, removed a couple of pins from her mouth and waved them at Christina. "I do wish you wouldn't make your important announcements when I have these between my teeth. I almost swallowed them."

"Oh sorry."

Jane grinned. "Okay, so you want to go big. I'm all ears; tell me more, Crowther."

"I fully intend to in a minute," Christina replied, walking across the studio to the corner where Jane was working on a costume for Dulcie.

It was a scorching hot July afternoon, and in an effort to beat the heat Jane had tied her pink cotton shirt under her bust to reveal a bare midriff, exchanged her skirt for a pair of white cotton shorts, discarded her shoes and stockings, and swept her long, wheat-colored hair on top of her head.

Christina could not help thinking how pretty her friend looked, despite the somewhat messy hairdo, makeup that had streaked and lipstick that had been chewed off. Her admiration and deep affection for Jane Sedgewick welled up in her. How lucky she was to have her friendship.

"How about a glass of lemonade?" Christina asked, putting the tray she was carrying down on the table, unscrewing the cap of the bottle. "You must be parched, Jane; it's sweltering in here."

"I know, I think we have to buy another fan. And thanks, I will have some of that stuff." Jane stepped away from the dressmaker's dummy, eyed the Tudor-style theatrical costume she was working on, then swung around, sat down on a stool nearby and took the glass of lemonade from Christina. "So go on," she said, "tell me about your plans. Knowing you, I bet you've got them all worked out."

"Sort of," Christina admitted and perched on the end of the table. "We've been in business for ten months and we've done extremely well. But we could sell twice as many clothes if we could produce them. I think we should expand, go big, as I just said."

"How?"

"Hire more cutters and seamstresses, as well as office staff, and take show-rooms in the West End."

"That'll cost money. Even if you keep my five thousand pounds in the business, that won't be enough, Christie."

"I know. I need about fifty thousand actually."

Jane whistled. "As much as that! *Gosh!* But yes, I think you're right."

"I know I am," Christina asserted. "I've worked it all out on paper. Aside from the salaries, we'd have to carry plenty of stock—fabrics, other supplies, and then of course there would be the rent of the showroom. I've looked at several in the last week, and they're expensive, especially those in Mayfair, which is where I feel we should be."

"You do mean *big* when you say big, don't you?"

"Yes, and *fancy*. About the fifty thousand, Jane, I think we could borrow it from the bank, even though neither of us has any collateral, if your mother would be our guarantor—you know, guarantee the loan or the overdraft, if that's what it's going to be."

Jane shook her head, frowned hard, and bit her lip. "No, I don't think that's a good idea—going to the bank, I mean. I'd rather borrow the money from Mummy, and I think she'd give us at least half. I know Aunt Elspeth would cough up the rest, because she once asked me if you needed money for the business. So I know she'd go for it, and she is a great fan of you and your clothes."

"Jane, that would be wonderful if they would do it . . . do you honestly think they'd take a gamble on me?"

"Yes, I do. Besides, backing you is hardly a gamble, and we all know that."

"I'd prefer to make it a loan, repayable with interest, of course, if that'd be all right with them. We don't need too many partners, do we?"

"No, you're right there. Not that Mummy or Aunt Elspeth would inter-fere, but still, I agree with you, I prefer they lend us the money." Jane jumped off the stool.

"Let's go down to the office and phone Mummy now," she cried, full of tremendous enthusiasm for Christina's latest scheme. "I know she's at home learning her lines, and once we've spoken to her, I'll call Aunt Elspeth in Monte Carlo. Oh this *is* exciting, Christie, and I know they'll jump at it. You'll see . . . by next week we'll really be rolling. Rolling in a *big* way, just like you want, heading for the *big* time."

Jane skipped and danced across the studio, did a Highland Fling when she reached the doorway, and then tripped down the stairs singing, "We're heading for the big time, the big time, the big time."

Christina followed more sedately, laughing at her friend's exuberance and keeping her fingers crossed, praying that Jane was right.

She was.

Dulcie Manville and her sister Elspeth D'Langer provided the extra working capital Christina Crowther needed to expand her haute couture business and move to the West End.

Elspeth flew from France four days after receiving Jane's phone call. She and her sister and the girls had several meetings with Dulcie's solicitors. It was during these meetings that Dulcie and Elspeth decided that Christina needed more cushioning in case of unforeseen emergencies. And so they increased their loan to one hundred thousand pounds, by putting up fifty thousand each.

This was the amount Christina finally deposited in her business account at the bank before the month of July was out, after the necessary papers had been drawn and duly signed by everyone.

In a sense the hard part started *after* this.

Christina found she had to split herself in two.

By day she was the businesswoman. She interviewed office staff; she saw seamstresses, cutters, needlewomen who did only hand sewing and embroidery work, and hand pressers, and as always she hired on the very best in every area. Lucie James, whom she had promoted to head of the workrooms, had good advice and suggestions to make. Lucie had a great many friends in the French community in London, and it was she who introduced Giselle Roux to Christina, suggested she be taken on as head *vendeuse* in charge of the showroom. Giselle, like Lucie, was married to an Englishman, and had lived in London since 1952. An elegant and sophisticated woman in her thirties, she had been a *vendeuse* at the Pierre Balmain salon in Paris, and was experienced and responsible. Christina left the hiring of the other saleswomen to Giselle, trusting her judgment completely. And when she wasn't interviewing, and hiring staff, Christina was looking at possible showrooms, tramping through buildings throughout the West End of London, and growing more and more discouraged.

Just when she had given up hope of ever finding the right building, she stumbled on a small but elegant town house on Bruton Street in Mayfair.

The real estate agent showed her around the house on a muggy, drizzly Saturday morning late in August, but despite the weather, Christina saw at once how airy the rooms were, especially on the upper floors.

She rented it immediately, knowing it was ideal. The house was in good condition, needed little work.

There was plenty of space, on six floors, for offices, workrooms and a studio for herself, plus two large reception rooms which opened off a central hall and would be perfect for the showrooms.

These were on the second floor of the house, had high ceilings, fireplaces, tall French windows opening onto little balconies, and their dimensions were spacious. As she walked between the two light-filled rooms, Christina visualized how charming and elegant they would look, decorated entirely in her favorite soft shades of gray and white, with thick carpeting and shimmering crystal chandeliers dropping from the ceilings.

By night she shed the role of businesswoman, became the creative artist.

Long after everyone had left the factory on the King's Road, Christina worked on her designs for her first collection under the Christina label. It was a summer collection and she planned to present it to the public and the press at the beginning of 1956. She had only five months to create the sixty-five outfits she wanted to show, and so she knew she had her work cut out for her. This was her first collection proper, since in the past ten months she had simply shown clients sketches and fabrics, and then made the garments to measure for them.

Designing an entire line of clothes with a distinctive underlying theme was tremendously challenging to Christina, and it was the excitement, the sheer exhilaration of such a huge creative effort that fed her natural energy, kept her going at an extraordinary pace. For aside from designing the outfits themselves, she had to design or select the accessories to go with them. To her, each dress or suit or coat was not finished until it had been properly accessorized down to the last detail. She saw it as an entity.

Although Christina was thrilled that she was now being launched in the way she wanted and was deriving a great deal of artistic satisfaction from her work, one thing marred her happiness. This was her estrangement from her mother and father.

After their terrible upset in May, she had telephoned them often and had been up to Yorkshire to see them, and she had written regularly. Her father had warmed up a little, but her mother was still cold and so distant that Christina had decided to take Mike Lesley's advice. In consequence, she did not divulge her real reason for giving up her life as an artist—her overwhelming desire, her genuine need, to give her mother a life of total comfort and ease as a way of repaying her debt to her.

Christina harbored the belief that she and her mother would be reconciled one day soon. She knew Audra loved her far too much to remain angry with her for very long. She also hoped that her father was already exerting some influence.

In the meantime, she was going to do her damnedest to make them proud of her.

Forty

Christina stood in the hallway that linked the two reception rooms, looked first to her right and then to her left.

Each room was a replica of the other: pearl-gray walls and matching carpet, white-painted fireplaces, French crystal chandeliers and wall sconces, and antique Venetian mirrors.

The two rooms flowed into each other beautifully, just the way she had planned. She nodded in approval, appreciating the cool, calm feeling produced by the pearl gray and the hint of white. This essentially monochromatic scheme was unrelieved by any other color—and purposely so. Christina did not want anything to distract from her clothes or compete with them. Even flowers were barred from these two rooms, appeared only in hallways of the Bruton Street house.

Turning, Christina glanced at the floral arrangement on the Louis XVI console in the hall. It was composed entirely of white flowers and once again she nodded, knowing it was exactly right, perfect in this particular spot.

Moving forward, she hurried into the larger of the two rooms and looked around for the umpteenth time on this cold January day, checking every detail.

A runway now divided the room in half, and on either side of it stood rows of little gilt chairs. Christina experienced a tingle of excitement, feeling the thrill of it all. In less than an hour her first couture collection was going to be presented to the world. She took a deep breath and clasped her hands together, sudden apprehension tugging at her as she thought of the clothes she had designed.

"Mademoiselle—"

She swung around to see her head *vendeuse* hovering in the doorway that led out to the dressing rooms in the back, where the models were getting ready for the show which was due to commence at three.

"Giselle!"

"I came to wish you *bonne chance,* Mademoiselle, good luck," the French-woman said, smiling at her warmly.

"Thank you, Giselle," Christina replied, also smiling, then she gave her a hard stare. "The collection *is* all right, isn't it?"

The head *vendeuse* brought her fingertips to her lips and kissed them, then blew the kiss into the air. "Not all right, Mademoiselle, superb, simply *superb*. When I was at the House of Balmain, I always told Monsieur that when there was the great excitement in the workrooms there would be the thunder in the chairs—" She paused, waved her hand at the golden rows and added confidently, "And at the House of Christina we have the excitement in the work-rooms—so be assured there *will* be the great applause out here."

A young assistant dresser poked her head around the door at the far end of the room. "Sorry to interrupt, Miss Christina, but Madame Roux is needed."

"Excuse me, Mademoiselle," the head *vendeuse* said and hurried out.

Christina walked over to the fireplace and stood with her back to it. She looked down the entire room, through the hallway and into the adjoining room, her eyes following the first runway and then the second. And in her imagination she visualized the models walking, turning, swirling, halting, pos-ing, showing off her clothes to their best advantage. She loved each garment she had designed and she could only pray that everyone else would. She asked herself how she had done it, how she had finished this collection in so short a time, and she had absolutely no idea whatsoever. Blood, toil, sweat and tears, she said under her breath, thinking of Winston Churchill's memorable line from the war years when she had been a child.

Turning around, she stared at herself in the Venetian mirror above the fireplace. She had thought she looked tired and pinched earlier, and she had put on more rouge than she normally wore. But it seemed to have been absorbed into her skin. She was pale again. Perhaps it was the black suit that was pulling the color from her face. She always needed more makeup when she wore black.

Christina stepped back, regarded herself, holding her head slightly on one side, studying the suit. Beautifully cut and tailored, it was a masterpiece of engineering. Its only adornment was a white gardenia pinned on one shoulder

—the white gardenia that she had chosen to become her own special motif, her trademark.

Lifting her hand, Christina smoothed her hair.

It was then that she saw them reflected in the mirror, standing in the doorway, looking uncertain, hesitant.

For a split second she thought it was her imagination playing tricks. But of course it was not. She turned slowly, opened her mouth to say something. No words came out. She simply stood there, staring, unable to move.

Her mother took a few steps forward and then stopped abruptly. Audra said, "We had to come . . . we couldn't stay away. Not today."

"Oh Mummy—"

"Christie darling—"

Both women moved at the same time. They met in the middle of the floor.

Audra looked up at Christina and her bright blue eyes filled with tears. "I've missed you so much . . ."

Christina reached out, put her arms around Audra, hugged her mother to her as if never to let her go. "Oh Mam, I've missed you too; you'll never know how much."

Suddenly Vincent joined them, and he put his arms around them both, and they all three cried a little, then laughed. And finally Christina stepped away and looked at her parents, and her happiness was reflected in her shining eyes, her joyous smile.

"I'm so glad you came, so very, *very* glad. It means so much to have you here." She broke off, then looked deeply into Audra's face and asked, almost in a whisper, "Have you forgiven me, Mother?"

"There's nothing to forgive, Christie," Audra answered, her voice gentle, loving. "I was angry and upset with you, and dreadfully, dreadfully hurt. But I realize now that I was wrong to cut you off in the way that I did. As your Uncle Mike said to your Daddy and me quite recently, you had to do what you had to do." A lovely smile touched Audra's mouth. "I may have given you the chance to have a better life, but I cannot live that life for you. I came to realize this, and I knew that I had to make my peace with you, darling."

Christina bent forward and kissed Audra's cheek. "Today is going to be the best day for me, now that you and Daddy are here."

Turning to Vincent, she took his arm, squeezed it affectionately, reached up and kissed his cheek. "Thank you for bringing her, Daddy, and for being here yourself. I love you both very much."

Vincent put his arm around Christina's shoulders. He said, "We love you too, Christie, and when your invitation came with your little note, I told your mother we couldn't miss this important day in your life."

Forty-One

Christina Crowther became a superstar in the international fashion firmament overnight.

Success was so instantaneous, orders so overwhelming, she knew within the first twenty-four hours that additional space had to be found, extra help hired, more fabric ordered—and at once. There was no time to waste.

Elise, Germaine and Lucie handled all of these details, with speed and efficiency, whilst Giselle Roux and her small showroom staff coped with clients who came flooding in through the doors of the Bruton Street house.

Christina's private clientele bought extensively from the collection, as did innumerable new customers, but there were some gigantic orders from stores which not only staggered Christina but also the more experienced Giselle.

The buyer from Bergdorf Goodman in New York was so dazzled by the clothes she took almost the entire collection, as did the buyer from the Haute Couture Salon at Harte's in Knightsbridge. It was she who announced to everyone that Christina was the fashion discovery of the decade, and pointed out that there hadn't been such a sensational success and a stampede like this since Christian Dior opened his own salon in 1947 and introduced his now-famous New Look. Giselle concurred, said, "It *is* the same, *vraiment*, Mademoiselle, truly, it is." Christina believed her.

These orders represented hundreds and hundreds of thousands of pounds. Christina had become very big business in one leap from the former greengrocer's shop on the King's Road to the elegant town house in Mayfair. It was a gigantic leap.

The cause of all the excitement and furor was the collection Christina had called the Flower Line. And indeed it was exactly that, with the theme of the flower running throughout.

The evening clothes were exquisite and extraordinary, featuring all manner of flowers from the exotic orchid to the simplest kind of blooms. When her first big collection had been conceived months before, Christina had realized she could not paint every evening garment personally. It was far too time-consuming. And so she had hired several clever artists to copy her paintings, insisting on perfect duplication.

But she had also had some of her own flower paintings handscreened onto fabrics, and these prints on romantic, floating chiffons and georgettes were as much of a sensation as the hand-painted garments. Evening and cocktail dresses made from these prints would become huge sellers and remain popular forever, earning her millions of pounds and millions of dollars over the years.

Other evening gowns of heavier-weight silk had a single but dominant flower motif. This might be on the skirt at the back and front, on the bodice and the one shoulder; sometimes it was repeated on the skirt and the bodice. But this single flower was always heavily encrusted with jewelled embroidery and was like an enormous piece of jewelry, in point of fact. These evening gowns were also snapped up instantly, with no questions asked about the price.

All of Christina's evening clothes in the Flower Line were lavish and very feminine, and they caused most people to gasp in delight when they first set eyes on them. Colors ranged from white and delicate pastels to vivid red, yellow, sapphire and summer black, which Christina had always advocated.

The flower theme was preserved all the way and reappeared in the day wear, this time in the actual contour of the clothes.

Suits, coats and dresses boasted a slender skirt, but from the waist up, the tops were slightly oversized, as were the shoulders, but these were softly rounded, not squared off. The shape of all these garments suggested a flower on a delicate stem.

The day wear was austere in some instances, immaculately cut and tailored, often with an architectural feeling, and it was undeniably chic.

Fabrics were light and included silks, cottons, linens and light wool crepes. Colors were clear, often sharp, with many pinks and mauves and lovely English blues, and greens that ran from bright emerald to the softer lime. And each garment, whether for day or evening, was perfectly accessorized for the total look Christina insisted on presenting.

Apart from her acceptance by the public, Christina had become the darling of the press. They loved her. The fashion editors from *Vogue, Harper's Bazaar* and *Queen* were sophisticated women who had seen it all. None of them was readily fooled and they could as easily spot a phony as they could recognize and applaud genuine talent. They knew at once that Christina was no flash in the pan, that she would go from strength to strength.

As for the popular newspapers, they adored her too.

She was wonderful copy for them. A new discovery who was all the rage, young, immensely talented, good-looking—and from an ordinary background, a girl from the provinces. This made her specially attractive to them, since their readers could identify with her, and certainly with Vincent and Audra, who had been much photographed with her at the unveiling of her collection in January.

Christina enjoyed her success, basked in it a bit. But her feet continued to be firmly planted on the ground, and she understood deep in her heart that the best part of it all was the pride her parents had in her. She would never forget the expressions on their faces as *she* had watched *them* watching the gorgeous models parading down the runway, to the sound of the thunderous applause, under the glittering lights.

And as Jane said later that evening, after the three Crowthers had been to dinner with the three Sedgewicks, "They were beside themselves with happiness and pride, Christie. I thought they were going to burst at the seams during the show, and I do believe your father had tears in his eyes at one moment." Christina had smiled and nodded, and then she had repeated her mother's lovely words to Jane.

The words continued to echo in Christina's head weeks later. Audra had come up to her at the champagne reception after the show, had given her a half apologetic smile, and said, "This is a lot more than dressmaking, Christie. *This is art.*"

Although Christina had promised to go with Jane to the French Alps for a winter vacation in February, in the end she was only able to have a long weekend with her at the ski resort. There was too much activity at the fashion house and she could not neglect her flourishing business.

But the four days she did spend in Alpes d'Huez with Jane were relaxing and the two girls had great fun. There were plenty of attractive admirers around to take them for cocktails in the evening or fondue suppers and sometimes dancing afterward at one of the rustic Alpine bars.

Christina did not ski and she had no intention of even trying, but she enjoyed watching the athletic Jane whiz down the slopes. Her friend was a crack skier and an expert skater. And on Sunday afternoon, as Christina sat at the open-air rink, her eyes were glued to Jane in admiration as she floated and pirouetted across the ice.

It was then that a thought struck Christina . . . the thought that women needed clothes which were relaxed and loose, to allow for ease of movement and comfort. And several new ideas for her winter collection began to germinate. This prescience, this ability to forecast coming trends, would prove to be another secret of her success. For it was her vision that lifted Christina Crowther from the ranks of the merely talented designers into the stratosphere of the truly brilliant.

The ideas which had come to her at the ice rink in the Alps immediately went onto the drawing boards in her studio at the top of the Bruton Street house, when she returned to London. Christina was aware that her winter collection had to be in production by May if it was to be ready for showing in September of that year. And so she kept her head down working hard all through the remainder of February and into March, as did Jane.

Jane's career as a costume designer was flourishing.

The clothes she had designed for her mother and the rest of the cast in *Elizabeth Regina* had been highly acclaimed, and she had gone on to do the costumes for another West End production. During the spring of 1956 she was busy at work on the entire wardrobe for a film soon to be shot at Elstree Studios, and once this was completed she was planning to go to New York for several months. She had recently signed a contract to design the costumes for a Broadway show, a musical that was apparently going to be spectacular. Not unnaturally, she considered this to be a great challenge and was looking forward to her sojourn on the other side of the Atlantic.

But in spite of all their work, the two friends managed to have a busy social life, and in many ways this was the most hectic spring and summer either of them had ever experienced.

At the beginning of May, Ralph Sedgewick invited them to come and stay at the villa he and Dulcie had rented in the South of France for the month of June.

"Do let's go," Jane said. "We both need a holiday, but especially you, and Beaulieu-Sur-Mer is such a pretty place. And listen, Crowther, after we've had a few days of rest and recuperation, we can take a car and drive up to Grasse, so you can investigate that perfume idea."

"Of course!" Christina exclaimed. "What a wonderful suggestion that is, Janey. And I'd love to come. I'll ring your father tomorrow, to thank him and accept."

For the next few weeks Christina turned her attention to the perfume she wished to market under the Christina label. Her name had already acquired cachet on both sides of the Atlantic, and she knew that a perfume was an inspired idea.

This had actually been the brainstorm of Giselle Roux, immediately after the immense success in January. "You must have the *parfum*, Mademoiselle," the head *vendeuse* had told Christina. "That has always been the tradition with the grand *couturiers* . . . Dior, Chanel, Balmain, Balenciaga, Givenchy. Yes, yes, you must do it, you must; it is *important,* Mademoiselle."

"But how would I go about it?" Christina had asked. She had seized on the idea at once, seeing its tremendous possibilities.

"First, Mademoiselle, you must consider the fragrances . . . the ones that give you pleasure . . . the special scent of *les fleurs,* your favorite flowers. Perhaps the rose . . . the lily of the valley . . . the jasmine. Then you must go to Grasse, Mademoiselle. Here is the center of the French *parfumerie* industry, and here they will create for you the special Christina *parfum,* Mademoiselle."

Christina had thanked her head *vendeuse,* and had promised to look into it. She had been far too busy designing her winter collection to follow through immediately, although she had mentioned it in passing to Jane. But she had put it at the top of her list of important future projects.

Now with the trip to the South of France coming up in June, Christina asked Giselle to make arrangements for her to visit some of the men who created the scents, who were working in Grasse. The head *vendeuse* had written off at once to a contact in Paris.

"Gardenia!" Christina said to Jane as they sat in the rented car driving to Grasse, during the latter part of June. "It must be gardenia. That's the one fragrance that I keep coming back to . . . it's very evocative . . . perhaps because my mother always wore gardenia scent when I was a child. It was called Gardenia Flower Essence and Mrs. Bell used to buy it for her at Harrods as a gift."

"I like the smell of gardenias too," Jane replied, "but you've got to come up with a better name. You can't call it just *gardenia.* That's far too mundane. You must find a fancier name."

"Blue Gardenia," Christina suggested.

"No, there was a movie with Alan Ladd called—"

"That was *The Blue Dahlia,"* Christina shot back, grinning. "Listen, Janey, I *do* like Blue Gardenia. It has a nice ring to it, and my mother does have the bluest of eyes . . ."

Jane smiled. "Then Blue Gardenia it must be. Actually, I like it, too, especially since you're naming it for your lovely mum." Jane suddenly began to sniff the air blowing in through the car windows. "Gosh, I can smell the flowers already. We must be nearly there," she said, slowing the car.

"Yes, we are," Christina exclaimed. "Look, there's Grasse in the distance. I'd better keep my eyes open for the hotel when we get into the town . . . we're staying at a place Giselle recommended—Le Regent."

Christina and Jane spent three days in the lovely little town of Grasse, which was situated in the Alpes Maritimes high above Cannes. It was a charming spot, ancient and totally surrounded by field upon glorious field of flowers and magnificent rose gardens. Fragonard, the great French painter, had been born here, and there was a Fragonard Museum, which of course the girls gravitated to the first chance they had. They also spent time going around the splendid Gothic cathedral, and visiting the many famous gardens.

But mostly they visited the various perfumeries, sniffing scents and talking to the chemists. In the end, Christina settled on two fragrances which would be created specially for her, to be marketed the following year. One would have gardenia as its base, the other roses, and their names would be Blue Gardenia and Christina, respectively.

Forty-Two

"I don't think I've seen Hadley Court ever looking quite as beautiful as it does tonight," Christina said, turning to Jane's father, smiling at him. "The flowers and candlelight inside the house create such a magical effect, and the gardens out here . . . why, they are *ethereal* in the reflected light from the house."

The famous actor, tall, rangy, with the look of a professor about him, followed her gaze across the lawns of his country manor house in Aldington in Kent.

"Yes, the gardens do have a special quality, especially when viewed from this terrace . . . they're like a backcloth on the stage tonight, almost too perfect to be real. But I don't suppose there is anything quite as lovely as an English summer evening, after a day of truly glorious weather," Ralph said, his mellifluous voice echoing on the warm air.

His was one of the most celebrated voices on the English stage, and Christina never tired of listening to it.

Ralph continued, "You said *magical,* Christie, and I do believe the entire evening has had a touch of magic to it, everything has gone so beautifully. And out here, now, it's so balmy, and there's not a whisper of that frightful wind we often get down here. Yes, we've been lucky; it's been perfect July weather for Janey's party."

Turning to look at Christina directly, Ralph Sedgewick adopted a fatherly manner toward her, asked, "Have you enjoyed yourself, my dear?"

"Oh yes, I have, Ralph, thank you very much. It's been a simply gorgeous evening, but I am a little sad that Jane's going off to New York for four or five months—I'm going to miss her terribly. Oh gosh, that sounded so selfish! I know you and Dulcie are going to feel it too, when she's gone."

"Yes, we are," he admitted, "but I'm hoping we might be lucky enough to do a play on Broadway whilst she's there. David Merrick wants us for a new comedy, so our American agent tells us. Anyway, Christie, aren't you planning to go over to the States for a visit in October? At least I think that's what Dulcie said to me?" He made this sound like a question. "Or am I mistaken?"

Christina suppressed a smile of amusement. Ralph's absentmindedness was an old joke within the Sedgewick family, and Jane was forever saying the only thing her father could remember was his part in a play.

"No, no, you're not wrong, Ralph. I do hope to be going over to America then," Christie told him. "My clothes have done well in New York, and Bergdorf Goodman have invited me to show my winter collection, after it's opened here in London, of course."

"Congratulations, Christie, that's wonderful." He squeezed her arm, smiled at her through warm hazel eyes. "I must admit, I am extraordinarily proud of you and my little Janey . . . you've both done wonderfully well since you graduated from the Royal College and—"

"There you are!" Jane cried.

Christina and Ralph swung to face her.

She glided through the French doors and out onto the terrace, her feet barely touching the ground. She was exceptionally happy tonight and she looked ravishing. Her Christina gown was made of tulle and lace, and it had a bouffant skirt decorated with lover's knots picked out in silver and pearl sequins, and it floated around her like a soft hazy pink cloud shot through with iridescent lights.

"I've been looking all over for the two of you. What a couple of fuddy-duddys you are, standing there, nursing your drinks . . . and *gossiping,* I've no doubt," Jane said. "What am I missing? No, don't bother to tell me. You should both be inside, dancing and whirling around the floor."

She grinned at them, tucked her arm through her father's. "I must say, Daddy, that's a really super band you found. They've got a fabulous beat, and they've got everybody really going at it, jiving it up. Come on, let's go inside and shake a leg," she finished gaily, her voice and her face filled with her infectious girlish laughter.

Ralph gave her an indulgent look. "I'm afraid I'm a little too old for that sort of thing," he announced. "And it's jolly warm indoors; that's why Christina and I came out here in the first place, to get a breath of fresh air."

He swung to face the gardens again, put his brandy balloon down on the stone wall of the terrace, reached into the pocket of his dinner jacket and took out a gold cigarette case.

After lighting a cigarette, he asked, "Where's your mother, by the way? Don't tell me she's jumping up and down like a mad thing . . . not in this heat, I hope, and at her age."

Jane giggled. "Honestly, father of mine, you do make Mummy sound old. She's only fifty-one, for God's sake. But no, she's not dancing, she's talking to Miles, who arrived a little while ago. And all on his little *own* too—" Jane paused dramatically, rolled her eyes and made an ugly face.

"Miles is here!" Ralph sounded and looked extremely pleased.

"He certainly is," a light, amused, masculine voice said from the direction of the French doors.

"Miles, old chap! How wonderful that you could make it after all!" Ralph hurried forward, his hand outstretched.

The two men clasped hands, beamed at each other. They had only recently become friends, but they had liked each other immediately.

Miles said, "So sorry I wasn't able to get here in time for supper, Ralph, but I got caught up in town . . . nothing I could do about it really . . . *you* know how it is . . . in *my position* . . ." He allowed his voice to trail off, as if suggesting he had been detained by important government business that could not be discussed. Top secret sort of stuff. Miles knew he had no need to explain his tardiness. Politicians were generally excused for this little social sin, if not for anything else they did.

Now he glanced at Jane, whom he had already greeted inside the house, and acknowledged her again with a slight nod.

Ralph asked, "Are you quite positive you don't want something to eat? I know the buffet is still being served, Miles. Certainly I must get you a drink. What would you like?" Ralph came to a stop as he realized that Miles's attention was focused behind him.

Ralph swung around, apologetic. "How frightfully rude of me, Christina, my dear. Don't hang back there. Do come and meet Miles."

"Yes, you must meet Miles," Miles said, stepping out into the middle of the terrace.

Jane said, "Excuse me, I'm going to get myself a glass of the old bubbly."

Christina moved forward slowly, conscious of the blue radiance of the eyes fixed so intently on her. There was a sudden constriction in her chest.

As he watched her approach, Miles Sutherland thought he had never seen such a lovely young woman. Her chestnut hair was swept up on top of her head to form a crown of curls. It was an odd style, reminiscent of the 1940s, and yet it suited her. She was dressed in a simple gown. Chiffon. Pale gray, Grecian in style. One shoulder bare. She wore a choker of beads and earrings that matched. Gray stones, resembling those huge gray luminous eyes that seemed to swamp her face. Opals? Moonstones? He wasn't sure.

He smiled, sensing a certain shyness in her, wanting to put her at ease.

Ralph cleared his throat, "Christina, may I present Miles Sutherland, one of our most brilliant politicians, as I'm sure you're aware. And Miles, this is Christina Crowther, Jane's dearest friend and flat mate, whom we consider to be a member of the family, actually."

"How do you do," Christina said.

Miles took the cool, tapering hand in his and held it tightly. Slowly he increased the pressure of his fingers, not wishing to let go of it. He knew at once that he wanted her. He aimed to have her.

"I'm very pleased to meet you," Miles said finally, and reluctantly released her hand, adding, "I've heard a great deal about you—from my sister. She wears your clothes."

"Your sister?" she repeated, feeling like an imbecile for not knowing who his sister was.

He said, "Yes, Susan Radley."

"Lady Radley?" she asked and felt even more foolish.

He smiled, as if amused. "Yes." He glanced at Ralph, said, "I wouldn't mind that drink, old chap. If you would show me where the bar is, I'll—"

"No, no, stay where you are, Miles," Ralph insisted. "What would you like to have?"

"Scotch, I think, with a splash of soda. Thanks, Ralph."

Ralph Sedgewick looked at Christina. "You haven't touched your cognac, my dear. Would you prefer something else perhaps?"

"Please . . . a glass of champagne would be nice." She suddenly wished Ralph would not go away and leave her with this man who continued to stare at her with his curiously hypnotic eyes.

They were alone on the terrace.

Miles smiled a lazy sort of smile, gave her a searching look, as if answering a question in his own mind, then took out a packet of cigarettes. He offered her one silently. She shook her head.

After striking a match, drawing on the cigarette, he said in that same amused, superior voice, "Your newspaper photographs don't do you justice, don't you know . . . they make you look much older too . . . and tell me, how do you manage to cope with our national press? I find them a bit pesky myself, at times."

Christina ignored the backhanded compliment he had paid her, said carefully. *"I* find the press—wonderfully well, thank you very much. They're certainly decent to me, but then I'm not a brilliant politician who's always making national news."

"Touché." He laughed, moved closer to her and leaned against the stone balustrade, his posture nonchalant. He said, "That choker you're wearing . . . are those moonstones?"

"No, they're just gray glass beads, but I liked the milky effect they have, that's why I bought them."

"Do you ever wear opals?"

She shook her head.

He stared at her, his gaze speculative, appraising, bold.

She found herself returning his stare unblinkingly.

He said at last in a low, quick voice, "You should, you know. Opals would look lovely against that extraordinary skin . . . with those extraordinary eyes . . ."

Christina was startled. She could not answer him. Her legs needed support. She sat down on the balustrade.

Miles Sutherland could not tear his eyes away from her. She touched him in a way that he had not been touched in years and he felt curious stirrings within himself. And his physical desire for her was hot and urgent.

To Christina's immense relief Ralph walked out onto the terrace carrying their drinks.

She sat sipping her champagne, listening to the murmur of their voices as they spoke at length about British politics. But she was not really hearing anything at all. She was studying Miles Sutherland, wondering what it was about the man that so unnerved her. Was it his great presence? Force of personality? Charisma? She was not certain. He was not the most handsome man she had ever met, but he did have an attractive face, lean, intelligent, composed of uneven planes and angles. His hair was a dark blondish brown that had a hint of gray at the sides. Slim in build, he was not much taller than she was, only about an inch or so in fact.

It was his eyes, of course, that so mesmerized. They were a lovely clear blue that reminded her of English sky on a summer day.

The two men continued to talk for a while, and she listened, let his voice roll over her, absorbing it, committing it to memory. It was full of nuances and inflections. She pictured him speaking in the Commons.

And suddenly Miles was standing in front of her, saying goodnight.

"It was so nice to meet you," he said in an indifferent voice.

Christina slid off the balustrade, took his hand, shook it briskly. "I enjoyed meeting you," she said, forcing cheerfulness.

Later, when she was in bed, she wondered why she was feeling so disappointed and let down.

——— *Forty-Three* ———

Jane exclaimed, "What a nerve he's got, strolling in here, trying to seduce you!"

"He didn't stroll in," Christina corrected. "He phoned me at Bruton Street. And he's not trying to seduce me."

"Oh yes he is."

"Don't be so silly, Janey . . . over lunch?" Christina began to laugh.

"*After* lunch," Jane cried fiercely. "The French call it a *matinée.*"

"This is London, not Paris, remember?"

Jane chewed her inner lip nervously. "My God, Mummy would have a fit —she'd be absolutely furious if she knew; after all, you met him through us down at Hadley."

"You're not going to tell her?" Christina sounded horrified.

"Of course, I'm not." Jane looked at her askance. "God, you can be stupid at times, Crowther . . . and you'll certainly be *bloody* stupid if you go out with Miles Sutherland."

"*Why?*"

"Because he's dangerous. Emotionally dangerous. I just know it in my bones."

"You're the one who's being stupid now, and far-fetched. How can he possibly be dangerous to me?" Christina demanded.

"He's married, for one thing."

"Estranged, separated. Everybody knows that. It was all over the newspapers ages ago."

"But he's not divorced, Christie."

"I don't know why you're acting this way, Jane, I really don't. Miles seems to be a nice man, and I'm sure he's decent and honorable too."

Jane let out a guffaw. "I bet he's a cad."

Christina gaped at her. "I don't know what's got into you today, making such sweeping statements."

Jane stared at her dearest friend. "Okay, let's go over a few facts. Miles Sutherland is good-looking and charming and he cuts quite a swathe at parties, I'll grant you that. But let's not forget that he also cuts quite a swathe in the House of Commons and that he is a brilliant and ambitious politician."

"I'm not sure I understand what you're getting at, Janey."

"Oh for God's sake, Christina, don't be so bloody dense! There happens to be a woman in his life already, a woman called Candida Sutherland, who is his wife and the mother of his three brats. Who just happens to be the daughter —actually the only child—of one of Britain's foremost industrialists. She's got pots and pots and *pots* of money, and if—"

"I *know* all that."

"And you can be damned sure that Miles Sutherland *knows* which side *his* bread is buttered on, my darling. Oh yes. When a man's a Member of Parliament and a leading light in the Labor Party, with a spectacular career unfolding, his wife's money comes in very useful indeed. Do you think he's going to jeopardize all that—"

"Jane, stop this!" Christina spluttered. "You're being absolutely preposterous." She let out a funny little laugh and eyed Jane curiously. "The way *you're* talking, anybody would think we're having a wild affair when—"

"I bet he'd love that! Miles Sutherland looks very randy to me."

"—when I hardly know the man. Besides, he's only invited me to lunch."

Jane looked at her through narrowed violet eyes. "When a man like Miles Sutherland invites a woman like you to lunch, he has only *one thing* on his mind and it's certainly not buying you a decent meal."

"I am going to have lunch with him, Jane, no matter what you say," Christina asserted in a firm tone.

"I wish you wouldn't . . . you just won't be able to cope with it."

"With *what?*"

"His bloody fatal charm and smooth talk and all that sort of codswallop. Don't forget, he's a politician and they've got the gift of gab, Mummy says."

"I can take care of myself, Jane."

"No, you can't."

Christina said slowly, almost reflectively. "My mother had a friend once— Gwen. *Auntie* Gwen I used to call her when I was little. They were very close when they were young women, nurses at Ripon Fever Hospital. But Gwen never did like Daddy much, which naturally made Mummy furious, and then Gwen married some twerp called Geoffrey Freemantle. Geoffrey sort of came between them too, as my father had, in a way."

Christina paused, took a deep breath. "And I just don't want that to happen to *us*, Janey, I really don't. So let's make a pact right now. Let's agree that men will *never* come between us. Let's try and be above all that sort of thing. What do you think?"

"Oh Christie darling, of course I agree with you completely! We mustn't let the men we get involved with make one single ripple between us."

Later that evening Christina and Jane went to Le Matelot in Belgravia for dinner.

They both liked the little bistro with a nautical theme and casual ambiance. It reminded them of their trip to the South of France the month before.

As they sipped their glasses of white wine, waiting for the first course, Jane asked, "What happened to her?"

"Who?" Christina looked puzzled.

"Your mother's friend—Gwen."

"Oh gosh, Janey, that's quite a sad story really. Her life wasn't very happy with the Geoffrey person. He turned out to be a wife beater, for one thing."

"My God, how awful!" Jane exclaimed, looking horror-struck.

"Yes, it was." Christina leaned her elbows on the table, said, "When I was small Mummy began to suspect there was something odd going on there, at least that's what she told me when I was grown up. You see, poor Auntie Gwen was always having these terrible accidents . . . falling down the cellar steps, or some such thing, and it began to worry my mother. At first she thought Gwen had an illness—you know, a brain tumor or something like that—and then it finally dawned on her. And she tackled Gwen about it, but of course Gwen denied it, and that's when we stopped going to see her."

"And what happened to Gwen in the end?" Janey asked.

"During the war she came to see us. Unexpectedly. I remember it very well because she brought me some pretty glass beads. I must have been about ten or eleven at the time. Anyway, she came for tea and stayed the evening, and after I'd gone to bed she apparently told my mother everything. I think she must have been at the end of her rope by then. Eventually Mummy persuaded her to move back to live with her parents, although I believe *that* took a lot of doing." Christina sat back, took a sip of wine.

Jane said, "Go on . . . I'll kill you if you don't finish the story."

"My mother talked to Gwen's brother, Charlie," Christina explained, "and he told the husband that he'd better not come near Gwen again. And he didn't."

"And she got a divorce."

"No, but the Geoffrey fellow was killed during the war. He wasn't in the forces, but he was here in London on some business, in 1944 I think it was, and he was killed during a bombing raid."

"And where's Gwen now? What happened to her in the end?"

Christina smiled, and her eyes lit up. "Her story had a happy ending really, Janey. She married my Uncle Mike in 1952. He was a widower by then and very lonely. It was my mother who persuaded him to join them for dinner with Gwen. You see, years before *they'd* gone out together. I suppose you could say they picked up where they left off."

"Hardly that," Jane said with a laugh. "But I *am* glad her life finally turned around . . . poor woman." After a short pause, she said, "Christie, about Miles—"

"What about him?"

"When are you having lunch with him?"

"Friday—the day after tomorrow," Christina said.

Jane sat back and grimaced, eyeing her friend with concern. "That's the day I leave for New York, and since I'm booked on the ten o'clock flight, you'd better call me later in the day and tell me what happens. I shall be all ears!"

Christina burst out laughing. "Oh Jane, you are impossible. Nothing's going to happen . . . but I'll phone you anyway to make sure *you're* all right, that you've arrived safely in little old Manhattan."

"Do you find Miles so irresistible, Christie? I mean, are you madly attracted to him?" Jane probed.

"He's quite attractive," Christina murmured, wanting to sound as non-committal as possible, not daring to confide her true feelings to Jane.

He canceled the lunch at the last minute.

"I'm so frightfully sorry to do this," he said in an apologetic voice when he telephoned her on Friday morning, "but I can't meet you today as we arranged. Something's come up . . . it's all become *rather* complicated. Do forgive me, Christina. Another time perhaps?"

"Oh," Christina said, gripping the receiver much tighter, sitting down behind the desk in her studio at the Bruton Street house.

"I say, I have a much better idea!" Miles exclaimed, as if something brilliant had just struck him. "Why don't we have *dinner* next week? I see from my calendar that I'm awfully jammed with luncheon engagements . . . what about having dinner with me on Tuesday evening?"

"I'd love to, Miles, but I can't," Christina said, genuinely regretful. "I'm going to Paris on Monday."

Disbelief echoed in his laughter. "Paris in July. You're going to find that all the Parisians have fled. There'll be no one there but American tourists."

"I'm going on business," she explained softly, feeling her disappointment about the canceled lunch so acutely her throat was tight.

"Business or pleasure, it's still one of my favorite cities. When do you plan to return?"

"In about ten days."

"Then I shall give you a ring in . . . let's say two weeks? Is that all right, Christina?"

"Yes, that'll be lovely, Miles."

After she had hung up, she stared at the phone for a long time. It troubled her that he aroused such strong feelings in her.

———— *Forty-Four* ————

Although she no longer painted landscapes, Christina still saw everything in terms of light.

And the first week she was in Paris, it seemed to her that every single day was filled with a luminous light that was glorious. As she went from the Ritz Hotel, where she was staying, to her various appointments, she would look up and marvel at the shining sky flung high like a canopy of pale blue silk above this most beautiful of cities.

The weather was perfect, mild, sunny and without the mugginess that had made London so unbearable before she had left. Yet despite her appreciation of the radiant skies, the sunlight shimmering on the river Seine and leaking through the leafy green cupolas of the trees, and casting its soft golden glow on the wide boulevards and ancient buildings, Christina had no desire to put what she saw on canvas.

The day she had given up her painting she had vowed she would not hanker after it, or have regrets, and she had not.

In some ways, it was a relief for her not to have to strive to top the world's most renowned painters, which was something her mother had somehow always believed she could do. It would be impossible for anyone to better J. M. W. Turner, that greatest of all the nineteenth-century English landscape artists, who had captured light on canvas with such brilliance. Or Van Gogh or Renoir or Monet, who had done something of the same.

And in all truth, Christina enjoyed her work as a fashion designer. It was a constant challenge, and she was savoring the business side as well as the creative endeavor it involved.

And not unnaturally, the extraordinary acclaim she was receiving gave her great pleasure, whilst the money she was earning was more than gratifying—it was positively thrilling. She knew that by the end of the year she would be able to repay her loans to Dulcie and Elspeth. But most important of all, her mother had finally retired from Leeds General Infirmary and had agreed to accept a check every month from her. It had been a battle, but *she* had won in the end, thanks in no small measure to her father, who had run interference for her. He had understood how much it meant to her.

This week, as she had gone from her appointments with the perfume manufacturer to meetings at the fabric houses, and generally attended to her business, she had managed to find time to go shopping for gifts for her parents. For her mother she had found butter-soft kid gloves and a silk scarf and several blouses; for her father, silk ties and voile shirts and an elegant cigarette lighter. Jane had not been left out, and she had bought her dearest friend a glamorous silk evening shawl from Hermès in a mixture of the pretty pinks Jane loved.

Christina thought of Jane now, as she walked slowly across the Place Vendôme toward the Ritz Hotel early on Friday evening at the end of her first week in Paris. It didn't seem possible that Jane had left for New York only last Friday. It felt so much longer.

She missed her a lot, but then they had been inseparable for the last five years, so that was only natural, she supposed. Jane was the best friend she had ever had, and the only close friend really. Her mother had kept her so busy with her painting when she was growing up there hadn't been much time for playmates when she was little, or chums when she was a teenager. It had always been painting lessons and field trips and museums and galleries and being force-fed art, art, art. Now that she looked back, she realized that she had spent most of her growing-up years with Audra, until she had left for the Royal College of Art in London.

Christina smiled to herself as she went through the doors of the Ritz, remembering with some affection the little Hôtel des Deux Continents where she and Jane had stayed on several trips to Paris in their college days. It had been a far cry from this elegant edifice where Hemingway had once hung out and movie stars and princes stayed. She wished Jane were here with her on *this* trip, staying *here* . . . what fun they would have together.

Her suite was in the other wing of the Ritz, at the Rue Cambon side of the hotel, and she had to traverse a long gallery of shops to reach the smaller of the two lobbies. But she did not stop to browse as she usually did; she was far too anxious to get up to her suite, take off her shoes and order a pot of tea. It had been a hectic day and she had walked a lot, since most of her appointments had been close to each other.

The *concierge* smiled pleasantly as he handed her the key to her suite, and told her no, there were no messages, in answer to her question. Smiling back, murmuring her thanks, she swung around, took a step toward the elevator.

It was then that she saw him.

She stopped dead in her tracks, staring.

His eyes were riveted on her. He rose from the chair, walked toward her in easy, graceful strides.

She was dazzled by the blue radiance of his eyes.

As he drew level with her, he said, *"Hello."*

"Miles." After a pause, finally finding her voice, she managed, "What are *you* doing here?"

The small, amused smile she remembered so well tugged at one corner of his mouth. "I'm staying here," he said. "I always stay at the Ritz when I'm in Paris."

"Oh."

He put his hand under her elbow purposefully and escorted her to the elevator. They did not speak riding up, and he followed her out at her floor; when they reached the door of her suite, she fumbled with the key and, in her nervousness, dropped it.

He picked it up, put it in the lock, turned it, held the door open for her, then stepped inside after her. He leaned against the door watching her move ahead of him, so willowy and lithe. She had the most gorgeous legs. Why hadn't he noticed that before now? But how could he have known it? She had been wearing the long gray Grecian gown at Hadley. He knew one thing, though. The heat was in him again, as it had been the night he had first set eyes on her at the beginning of the month. That was why he was here, wasn't it?

Strolling across the foyer toward the sitting room, Miles leaned against the door jamb, still watching her, fascinated by her. He couldn't wait to take her in his arms, to make love to her. He would like to do that right now, at this very moment. Yet he knew he could never make a move like that. He was a gentleman, and he did not want to frighten her by pouncing on her in a predatory manner. She struck him as being naive and inexperienced, at least where men were concerned. Beyond all of these things, though, he wanted to get to know her a little better, to savor her and enjoy the anticipation of his ultimate possession of her.

Christina placed her handbag and document case on a chair and pivoted so suddenly she startled him.

She said, "It's not a coincidence, is it?"

"Of course it isn't, Christina."

He moved into the room, came to a stop next to her and took her hand in his, held onto it tightly, crushing it between his fingers. He looked at her deeply, his face close to hers, their eyes on a level. He said, "I decided I didn't want to wait two weeks to take you out to dinner. That's why I'm here . . . to have dinner with you. Tonight—I hope? You are free?"

"Yes." She searched his face, her brows drawing together in a pucker. "Don't you have business here too? I mean, you didn't fly from London to Paris simply to have dinner with me . . . surely not?"

"I most certainly did."

"Oh." She felt the sudden rush of heat to her face and there was that tight feeling in her chest again. She wanted to look away but she found she could not. His eyes held hers in the same mesmerizing way they had at Hadley Court.

Miles smiled an odd little smile and let go of her hand, walked over to the window and parted the curtain, looked down into the gardens below. Swinging to face her, he said lightly, "If it weren't July and the tourist season, I'd take you to Maxim's tonight, but since it is, and since I didn't bring a dinner jacket, which is obligatory masculine dress on Fridays, shall we dine in the gardens here at the hotel?"

"Anywhere you wish. Yes, here would be lovely, Miles."

"Then I'll meet you downstairs in the American Bar at—" He pushed up his cuff, glanced at his watch. "Eight o'clock? Is that all right with you? It does give you an hour to change and dress."

"That's plenty of time, thank you."

He came across the room, paused as he drew alongside her and looked deeply into her face for the second time in a few minutes. He took her hand, kissed her finger tips, then said, "Of course I came to Paris because of you. Believe it—it's true. You see, I haven't been able to get you off my mind since we met at Hadley."

He was gone before she could say a word in response, striding across the sitting room, through the foyer and out of the suite. He did not look back as she somehow thought he might.

The door clicked softly behind him.

She was standing alone in the middle of the floor.

She blinked, for a moment unable to absorb everything that had happened in the space of . . . what? Fifteen minutes, at the most? He had followed her to Paris as soon as he could get away . . . he had been in the lobby waiting for her to return this evening . . . and of course he had more on his mind than buying her a decent meal, as Jane had so succinctly put it. But then so did she.

She had not been able to stop thinking about Miles Sutherland for the past two weeks, and her disappointment over the canceled lunch had been so acute it had lingered for days. Walking through into the bedroom, unbuttoning her black linen dress, Christina let her mind rest on Miles.

He was unlike any man she had ever met. And he *was* a man. Not like the students she had gone out with, or the young fellows she had dated in the last couple of years.

Miles Sutherland was, after all, a man of the world. A little shiver ran through her as she slipped out of her dress and went to the armoire, thinking about Miles. She shivered again, remembering how intensely and passionately he had looked at her as he had held her hand, then kissed her fingers. She had thought, for a moment, that he was going to take her in his arms, and she had felt weak with desire for him. Her excitement and anticipation about the evening accelerated. And as she gave her attention to the clothes hanging in front of her, she could not help wondering what sort of evening it would turn out to be.

Her hand settled on a cocktail dress made of a chiffon that was striated in a melange of lilacs and mauves that bled into each other and faded to the softest of grays. Sleeveless, it had a ruched bodice and a very low vee neckline at the front and the back, and a full gathered skirt.

She knew how alluring she looked in it. She wanted to be as irresistible to Miles Sutherland as he was to her.

A few minutes later, as she pinned up her hair before taking a bath, she peered at herself in the bathroom mirror. She saw his face in her mind's eye so vividly and felt his presence so strongly he might have been standing behind her looking at her in the glass.

"Oh Miles," she said out loud. "I haven't been able to get you out of my mind either."

——— *Forty-Five* ———

His heart quickened at the sight of her.

She stood poised at the entrance to the bar, wearing a dress the color of lilacs in the spring, and the choker of milky-gray glass beads encircled her throat and her hair was upswept in a coronet of curls as it had been on the night he had first met her in Kent.

He was on his feet at once and halfway across the small bar before she saw him, and when she did a smile struck her face and she came forward in a rush, and as they met he caught a faint whiff of her perfume, something light and fresh and green-smelling, which evoked sunny summer meadows.

Neither of them spoke. They looked at each other, their eyes locking for a split second.

And then he took hold of her arm and drew her toward the table in the far corner, where the bottle of Dom Perignon sat in a bucket of ice and his cigarette was smoldering in an ashtray next to the glass of good Scotch whisky he had been fortifying himself with before she arrived.

They sat down opposite each other, and he stubbed out the cigarette and lifted his head and smiled at her, very deeply, and she smiled back at him in the same way.

In one sense, he was glad to have the table between them. It was a welcome barrier since it prevented him from doing something foolish, like taking her in his arms and kissing her and so making a spectacle of himself in public. And anyway, he wanted to look at her, study her face, reinforce the image of her that had been etched in his mind for several weeks.

"You were drinking champagne at Hadley, so I ordered a bottle," he said. As he spoke he heard the tightness in his voice and he was amazed. The tension had been building up in him since he had decided to come here to Paris, and the last hour of waiting for her to change and join him had become unbearable. "Is that all right with you?" he went on, trying to relax, motioning to the waiter to come and open the bottle.

"Why yes, thank you, Miles, it's lovely," she said, "and I only ever drink white wine or champagne, never hard liquor. Anyway, champagne *is* so festive and this *is* a special occasion, after all."

"It is?" He looked at her alertly.

"Absolutely."

"Why?" he asked, fishing. He leaned over the table ever so slightly.

"Because it's not often that I get taken out to dinner by a celebrated English politician . . . and one who flies across the English Channel, no less, in order to do so."

He saw the merriment in her eyes, the laughter bubbling under the surface, and he felt the sudden, unexpected laughter in himself, realizing that she was teasing him, and he thought: Thank God she has a sense of humor.

"The flight was well worth it," Miles replied, letting his eyes rest on her appreciatively, "just to have the view from where I'm sitting—it's quite lovely."

"Thank you."

The waiter poured the champagne. Miles tasted it and nodded, and the waiter filled their flutes. Miles raised his glass. Clinking it against hers, he said, "To our first evening together."

"Yes—and to our dinner. It's probably the most expensive you've ever had to buy, if you include your airfare and the hotel room here. Unless, of course, you do this kind of thing frequently, then I realize it must be nothing exceptional at all."

He stared at her intently, wondering if she was insinuating something about other women, but he saw at once there was no innuendo behind her words. Her expression was guileless.

Then her laughter rippled on the air between them, light, amused.

Miles took in her merry face and dancing gray eyes and he burst out laughing too. The laughter helped to ease his tension, though not much. He had wanted her for two weeks, had fantasized about making love to her so many times he had worked himself up into a terrible state. Now that he was finally with her, he was focused entirely on her, and his whole body was taut with his desire to possess her. He knew he would explode before the night was out if he did not make love to her.

Christina sipped her champagne, eyed him quizzically, asked, "Miles, what would you have done if I'd had another date tonight?"

He sat back, took a cigarette, struck a match, the bright blue eyes still crinkling at the corners with laughter. "That possibility had occurred to me, I must confess."

He leaned across the table in an intimate manner, explained, "I would have invited you to dine tomorrow or Sunday, and if you'd had engagements for those evenings, I would have asked you out to lunch or suggested that we have drinks on one of those days. And in the end, I would have probably settled for a cup of tea, or breakfast, or a walk in the *bois* or whatever you'd agreed to do with me. You see, I did want to get better acquainted with you, Christina, and I can be very, very persistent."

"Yes, I know."

"You do?" He raised an eyebrow. *"How?"*

"From what I've read about you in the newspapers over the past few years. You seem to have a reputation for stubbornness and determination . . . you certainly keep going after the Tories, keep *them* on their toes in the House of Commons, don't you?"

He grinned, drew on his cigarette. "That's the duty of members of the shadow cabinet . . . to keep the opposition off balance, you know."

Miles leaned back in the chair, studied her face thoughtfully. "I meant what I said at Hadley—those photographs I've seen of you in the papers and magazines definitely do *not* do you justice. Far too grainy in the papers particularly, and they make you look older." He paused, then asked, "How old *are* you, Christina?"

"I was twenty-five in May."

He was surprised. He had thought she was about twenty-seven or even twenty-eight. Not that she looked it, but there was her enormous success as a *couturière* to consider; also, she had a certain reserve in her manner, a caution, a prudence almost, and these things suggested maturity to him somehow. *Twenty-five.* She was so young really, just a girl.

Miles said, "I'm much older than you—I'm thirty-eight."

"Forty."

He threw back his head and roared.

Christina sat back, gazing at him, her eyes filling with mischief.

"Well, well, well, how's that for a small display of male vanity? And how did you know my real age? I don't think I've ever seen it mentioned in the newspapers, at least not lately."

She had gone to the library and looked him up in one of the political reference books, but she had no intention of admitting this. So she lied, "I think Jane must have told me."

"Oh yes, of course, my sister is very friendly with Dulcie. But then you know that, since it was Dulcie who introduced Susan to you—and your gorgeous clothes." He poured more champagne into their glasses. "You've done awfully well in your career as a fashion designer and become quite a celebrity too—and all in a very short few years. I admire women of accomplishment and brains . . . I want to know all about you and how you did it, Christina. Will you tell me?"

"Yes, if you really want to hear."

"I most certainly do."

She kept her recital succinct, recounting her years of growing up in Yorkshire, meeting Jane at the Royal College of Art, and then she told him about her decision to become a *couturière*. But she did not reveal her real reason for giving up painting, preferred to let him think that she had done so because fashion designing was her first love.

Fifteen minutes later she finished. "There, you have it all in a nutshell." She reached for her glass, took a long swallow of champagne.

"It's been a meteoric rise. I salute you," he said, giving her a look of sincere admiration. He had enjoyed listening to her. She had a pleasant, well-modulated voice, and suddenly he was feeling curiously soothed. Perhaps this was because he knew she was his captive for the next few hours, and a lot could happen in that time.

Christina smiled at him, said, "Now it's *your* turn to tell me all about *you*, Miles." What she had read in the reference book had been scanty, and she wanted to know as much as possible about him.

"There's nothing very exciting to tell," Miles said, with a shrug, a small smile. "I was born in London. Grew up there and in Suffolk. Went to Eton, Oxford, studied law, practiced as a barrister for a short while. Preferred politics, you know. Won my first election when I was twenty-seven. Became a Member of Parliament and have managed to keep my constituency in Manchester over the years. Very loyal voters, fortunately. My parents are still alive, thank God, and I have just the one sister. No hobbies, no interests really, other than politics. I do love them, they're my life, actually." He stubbed out his cigarette, lifted his glass. "That's *my* potted biography. Rather a dull chap, wouldn't you say?"

She shook her head. "Quite the contrary," Christina answered and thought: But he didn't mention his wife.

As if he had read her mind, Miles brought his head closer to hers, fixed her with a hard stare and his voice was low, suddenly intense, when he said, "Oh and by the way, I'm separated from my wife."

"I know you are."

"Jane told you?"

"No, I saw an item in William Hickey's column in the *Daily Express*—when you became estranged."

"But that was two years ago." He gave her an astonished look. "Isn't that odd—we've both read so much about each other and remembered it." He stopped; his mouth twitched with hidden amusement. "Do you think it signifies something special?" he asked in a teasing tone.

"Yes, that we both have excellent memories for the rubbish we read in the gossip columns."

Miles grinned, enjoying her more than ever, then reached out, took her hand in both of his. "Oh I think it's more than that," he said.

"What do you mean?"

"I'll tell you later." He motioned to the waiter, reached inside his jacket for his wallet. "I think perhaps we ought to go out to the gardens for dinner. I don't want to lose the table."

Forty-Six

The tension that had eased out of him in the bar took hold of him again during dinner.

It happened so unexpectedly he was startled, and to his amazement he thought his hand was going to shake and so he put down his fork, sat back, looked across at her.

There was a hurricane lamp on the table between them, and in the flickering light of the candle her face had taken on a mysterious cast, and as she moved slightly a shadow obscured her mouth. He wanted to kiss that mouth, crush it under his own, take her to him, love her with all the strength of his body. He wondered why they were squandering their time here in the restaurant.

Christina reached for her glass of Montrachet, took a sip, regarded Miles over the rim, feeling the potency of his presence more than ever. Aside from being charismatic, he was an elegantly dressed man and this pleased her. She studied him surreptitiously, thinking how well he looked in the chalk-stripe gray suit and the pale blue shirt that emphasized the color of his eyes.

Suddenly she saw those mesmeric eyes change, darken, as if he was troubled, and a fretful expression flicked onto his narrow, intelligent face and his mouth tightened noticeably.

What was wrong? Did he now regret his actions? Was he sorry he had flown to Paris after all? Dismay lodged in the pit of her stomach. What if he said a polite goodnight to her at the end of the evening and left it at that? Perhaps she had imagined that look in his eyes at Hadley Court and earlier this evening in the bar. Perhaps it was all wishful thinking on her part. She didn't want him to leave her alone after dinner. She wanted to be with him. *She wanted him.*

Before she could stop herself, she leaned forward, asked, "Is there something wrong, Miles?"

"No, of course not," he exclaimed, rousing himself, pushing aside his erotic thoughts of her. He picked up his glass, drank, then asked, "Whatever made you think there was?"

"You look distressed—" she blurted out and stopped, stared at him, saw the amusement crossing his face.

"Did I?" He put his glass down, took a packet of cigarettes out of his pocket. "Do you mind if I smoke?" He looked at her inquiringly. She shook her head. Then he went on, "I'm afraid I'm not very hungry."

"Neither am I."

"So I notice," he murmured as he glanced at her plate. She had merely toyed with the veal medallions as he had himself; she had barely eaten a mouthful.

Now Miles lifted his head. His eyes settled on her eyes. And he saw something in them that brought him up with a start. There was a new awareness of him in them and a sexuality reflected there as well. He had always known she was interested in him. He had seen that quickening curiosity mixed with speculation illuminate her face at Hadley Court. But was she feeling *exactly* what he was feeling? Could it be that she desired him as much as he desired her?

Miles bent forward and said in the quietest of voices, without preamble, "When you get to know me better, you'll soon discover that I can be brutally frank, but at least you'll always know exactly where you stand with me. I want to be frank now, to say this to you . . . let's not be juvenile about tonight. We're both adults and you know as well as I do why I came to see you in Paris." He reached across the table, gripped her hand tightly. "I want to be with you, Christie, to hold you in my arms, to make love *to* you and *with* you. Do you want me in that way?"

"Yes, Miles, I do," she whispered.

"Then I don't think we should torture ourselves any longer. Let me get the bill and we'll get out of here."

He took her in his arms the moment they entered her suite, pushing the door closed with his foot.

Drawing her to him roughly, he brought his mouth down hard on hers and kissed her passionately, parted her lips, pushed his tongue in her mouth, began to savor hers. Then he tightened his hold so that she was welded against the hardness of his growing erection and ran his hand over her shoulders and her back and onto her buttocks.

Her arms were around his neck and she was returning his kisses with an ardor that was as fervent as his, and she let her tongue slip under and over his, and she felt a shiver run through him.

Christina thought she was dissolving into Miles, becoming part of him, and she held onto him tightly, afraid that her legs were going to buckle. And then unexpectedly he broke away from her and lifted her up in his arms and carried her into the bedroom.

The bed was huge and the sheets gleamed whitely in the corridor of light streaming in from the sitting room. He laid her on it, took off his jacket, flung it on a chair, kicked off his shoes.

As he took a step toward the bed she opened her arms to him, and he saw the intensity and longing on her face and his heart leapt with anticipation and excitement. He slipped off her sandals, tossed them on the floor, lay down on the bed next to her. Again she opened her arms to him and he came into them, embracing her, pressing her tightly to his chest.

"Christie, oh Christie," he said against her neck. "I want you so much. I've ached for you since the night I saw you on Ralph's terrace."

"Oh Miles, I know. I want *you*, I've longed for *you* . . ."

He raised himself on one elbow, looked down into her face, touched her cheek gently. He gave her a searching look, murmured, "Oh darling, if only you knew how much you've haunted me." He kissed her. It was a long, slow, melting kiss. She yielded her mouth up to his demands. He sucked her tongue into his mouth, and he felt the ecstasy of their prolonged kiss shoot down to the pit of his stomach. Every one of his senses strained toward her. Possession of her was the only thing that mattered to him at this moment.

With one hand, he caressed her face and her throat, then slid his fingers down the vee of her dress to touch her breast, and he experienced a thrilling sensation as he realized she was not wearing a bra.

He bent his head over her, parted the neckline, slipped his hand under her breast, lifted it out of the dress, took the hardening nipple in his mouth. He drew up her chiffon skirt, trailing one hand along her leg, finding the silky feel of her stocking erotic, and when his hand came to rest on the bare flesh of her thigh, he raised his head, sighed deeply, then put his mouth gently on hers. His fingers came to their final resting place between her legs, and as they crept inside the silken panties he felt the moistness of her, knew that she truly yearned for him as passionately and as anxiously as he yearned for her.

Against her ear, he whispered, "Take your dress off, darling," and immediately he stood, began to shed his clothes.

Christina did the same, feeling quite unself-conscious in front of him. She was undressed first. She lay down on the bed, let her eyes rest on him as he came toward her. Miles had a lean, taut body, without an extra ounce of flesh on it, and she felt that athletic hardness, the strength of it, as he took her firmly in his arms and wrapped his long legs around her.

His hands went up into her hair, pulling out the pins, and once her hair was flowing freely around her face, he slipped both his hands up into it once more, held her head very tightly between them, started to kiss her face and her neck and her mouth.

But he stopped abruptly, said in an urgent voice that was low and thick with desire, "I've got to have you now, I can't help it. I'm sorry. I've got to be inside you, Christie."

"Yes, yes, I know."

He braced himself above her on his hands, looked down into her face, experiencing the most overwhelming feelings for her. And instantly he saw the radiance that filled her face, saw the joy and desire for him in her marvelous eyes, and he knew everything he needed or ever wanted to know.

Christina reached up to touch his hair, then smoothed her hand along his tense cheek, looked up into his eyes, her gaze penetrating. "Oh Miles," she sighed, "oh Miles."

He lowered himself on top of her, pushing his hands under her buttocks and drew her closer to him. And as he entered her he felt a rush of intense heat searing through his whole body, reaching up to touch his heart and then his mind. He plunged deeper into her, quickly, expertly, and she moved against him and they found their own rhythm immediately, their entwined bodies rising and falling together. And he thought triumphantly: *I knew it. I knew it would be perfect with her, that we were meant for each other, that we would be as one.*

And Christina, clinging to him, thought: *I never realized it could be like this. I want all of him, every part of him. I want to be bound to him always, to be in his arms always. I belong to him now. He has made me his tonight. Irrevocably and completely his.*

Suddenly Miles felt a great wave of strength and passion surging through him unchecked, and he could no longer restrain himself, and unable to hold back he cried against her tumbled hair, "Oh my darling my darling, I'm so sorry I can't help it I'm coming oh please come to me my darling."

"I will, I will, Miles! Oh Miles!"

"Christie, *now*. Oh my Christie! Oh my God!"

• • •

The match flared in the semidarkness of the room as he lit a cigarette, inhaled deeply, then turned to her and said softly, "I'm sorry, that was too quick. It'll be better next time."

"Don't be so silly, Miles . . . it was wonderful, you're wonderful."

"Ah, but you're prejudiced, my love."

"Well yes, I am, but nevertheless what I just said *is* true." She smiled at him.

Miles smiled back. It was a tender smile, and he put his arm around her, pulled her closer, so that her head rested against his chest.

"May I ask you a question, Miles?"

"Of course."

"What did you mean when you said that our reading things about each other in the newspapers and remembering them signified something special?"

"It suddenly struck me in the bar earlier that perhaps we'd been unconsciously drawn to each other before we actually met at Jane's party."

She smiled against his chest. "I think I was."

"So was I . . . I do believe," he admitted.

Christina confessed, "When I saw you come out onto the terrace at Hadley, I got a terrible pain in my chest, a tightness that was really quite awful, and I felt very wobbly all of a sudden."

Miles smiled. She was so open and ingenious. Relatively few women would have told him something so revealing at this stage in the relationship. But he was glad she had. It confirmed his opinion that she was straightforward and an innocent despite her sophisticated circle of friends. He liked this about her. He was pleased she was untarnished by other men.

"If it makes you feel any better, Christie, I had a strong reaction to you, too. I knew I had to see you again." He drew on his cigarette. "And I really was most frightfully annoyed when I had to cancel lunch at the last minute."

"So was I . . . well, disappointed really, Miles . . . when did you decide to come to Paris?"

"Earlier in the week. Fridays are generally quiet in the Commons, are usually devoted to uncontroversial issues and private bills, and I knew I could get away early, so I booked a flight—"

"And obviously rang up Bruton Street to ask where I was staying."

"I did."

"I'm surprised my secretary didn't tell me."

Miles chuckled. "I said I was calling for Susan Radley, that she wished to send you flowers and needed the name of your hotel in Paris. I explained you weren't to be told, since the flowers were meant to be a surprise. And I thought to add that I was the florist."

Christina laughed. "Aren't you the crafty one," she teased. "And why didn't you want me to know you were coming to Paris? Obviously you *didn't*, from what you've just said."

"I wanted to surprise you."

"How did you know I wasn't meeting someone here? A special man? A lover?"

"I hoped and prayed you weren't." Stubbing out the cigarette, Miles bent over her, kissed her brow, whispered, "Are you glad I decided to hop over?"

"Yes, Miles, very glad." Her arms went around him and they kissed quietly, and then Christina placed her hands on his bare chest and gently pushed him away, looked up at him. "Are you going to stay through tomorrow too?"

"Oh yes, indeed I am. In fact, I'm going to stay all weekend. I'm not leaving until early on Monday morning, my sweet." The lazy smile touched his mouth and he took hold of her shoulders, forced her down onto the pillows. Kneeling over her he began to stroke her breasts and then her stomach, murmuring, "Now lie still, don't say a word, I want to make love to you in a very special way . . ."

They got up at midnight and went out.

Miles loved jazz and he took her to one of his favorite old haunts, the Mars Club, just off the Champs-Elysées. It was dark and smokey and intimate, and they sat squashed close together on a red plush banquette, holding hands, and he drank warm Scotch and she sipped icy white wine. And between sets he talked jazz, told her about Bix Beiderbecke and Charlie Parker and Fats Waller and Django Reinhardt and Louis Armstrong. And from time to time he would kiss her cheek unexpectedly, or squeeze her knee and smile into her eyes, and as the minutes ticked by, Christina fell more and more in love with Miles Sutherland.

Later they went off to Les Halles, the old produce markets, to have the famous onion soup at one of the little cafes, and as they spooned it up hungrily and ate the toasted French bread and runny cheese that floated on top, he spoke of his childhood, of growing up in the rambling old country house in Suffolk that had been his family's home for centuries. And she listened attentively, relishing every word, enjoying hearing about his youth and his father and mother, and it was almost six in the morning when they returned to the Ritz, holding hands and laughing, still wide awake and excited about discovering each other.

Miles opened the door of her suite and followed her inside.

"You're not going to throw me out?" he asked, removing his jacket, loosening his tie, slipping off his shoes. "I *can* sleep here with you, can't I? Please don't banish me . . ."

Her answer was to smile at him, a long, slow smile, and to offer him her hand. He took it in his and together they walked into the bedroom.

Miles closed the door and locked it, and he took her in his arms, whispering her name over and over again as he lifted her in his arms and carried her to the bed. And they made love once more and slept and made love, and that's the way it was for the rest of the weekend.

Forty-Seven

"No two ways about it," Miles said to Christina on Sunday night, "I've got a really horrendous week ahead of me."

They were having dinner at La Coupole on the Left Bank and she looked at him, put her fork down on her plate. He hadn't sounded serious at all during the weekend. Now he did. "What do you mean?" she asked, reaching for her glass of wine.

Miles leaned closer. "Hugh Gaitskell is going to be coming down hard on

Anthony Eden because of the trouble with Nasser and the Suez Canal. I'm going to be really slogging it out with my opposition, especially as one of Hugh's protégés. But then I suppose the entire shadow cabinet is going to be on the attack. It's such a terrible mess."

"You don't really think there's going to be a war in the Middle East, do you?"

Miles nodded and his face became instantly grave. "I'm afraid so—Egypt —because of the Canal problems. But let's not discuss it tonight. When will you be coming back to London, Christie?"

"Not until Saturday. My lawyer Maître Bitoun needs me here to conclude everything with the perfume manufacturer."

Miles took hold of her hand and he gave her a mischievous look. "Shall I come back next weekend . . . to be with you here?"

"Oh Miles, could you?" Her face flushed up and her eyes sparkled. "That would be wonderful, wouldn't it?"

"That's what I think," he said and grinned.

After dinner they walked for a while, and then they took a rackety old cab, the only one they could find, back to the hotel. "I swear to God he's three sheets to the wind," Miles muttered in her ear as they sat on the back seat holding hands while the driver weaved his way across Paris.

Later that night in bed, as he held her in his arms, Miles said in that low, intense voice of his, "I'm afraid I'm getting rather entangled with you, Christie."

"And I with you, Miles."

"I know I shouldn't, that we shouldn't, but I just can't seem to stop myself, or *you,* I suppose."

"Why shouldn't we get involved?" Christie asked, drawing closer, wrapping one leg over his body, tightening her arms around him.

A deep sigh rippled through Miles and for a moment he did not respond; then he said, very quietly, "I've nothing to offer . . . she'll never divorce me . . ."

"I don't care."

"You might one day, Christina."

"Why won't she? Divorce you, I mean?"

"I've not been able to fathom it, actually. You see, she doesn't want me, but she doesn't want anyone else to have me either."

"Do I? Have you, I mean? Do I have just a tiny little half inch of you?"

He smiled. Now it was her turn to fish. He had been doing that almost the entire weekend in a variety of different ways, at times feeling as foolish as a lovesick schoolboy.

Miles said, "Yes, you do . . . just a tiny little half inch of me, as you said." He bent over her, kissed her hair. "However, I think too much of you to play games with you, darling. I want this, want us, want you. Yes, I *damn well* do want what we've started this weekend to continue . . . selfishly I want it. But if we do continue, it would have to be clandestine. That's not fair to you. If Candida ever found out, she would create a frightful scandal. I couldn't afford that . . . there's my political career—don't you see?"

"I do. But *I* want *us* too, Miles. *I want you.* Look, we can be careful. We don't have to go out . . . be in public. I don't mind it being secret."

"You'll mind one day, Christie."

"Oh no, I won't, Miles."

He made no response. He held her close in his arms and eventually they both fell into an exhausted sleep.

Miles left for London the following morning.

He thought about this last conversation a lot in the ensuing week, as he went from his flat in Knightsbridge to the House of Commons, and about his other business. And over and over again he asked himself if he ought not to take matters into his own hands and simply terminate their relationship. Miles Sutherland was a responsible man and bore no resemblance to the cad Jane Sedgewick had conjured up in her girlish imagination. In point of fact, he was just the opposite. He was a man of honor, a man of commitment. He longed to be free of his neurotic wife; he had no interest in her money or her father's money, since he was a man of private wealth himself.

End it now, before it gets out of hand, he kept saying to himself, but then he would telephone Christie at the Ritz in the evening, as he had said he would, and the sound of her voice drove any thoughts of rational action right out of his head. He wanted this woman in a way he had never wanted a woman before. He was hopelessly involved with her whether he wanted to be or not. *He could not change the way he felt.*

And so on Friday afternoon he flew back to Paris.

The minute Miles walked into her suite and saw Christina, he felt his heart skip a beat and his spirits lift, and he knew that *he* would never be the one to put an end to their love affair. She was like air and light and sun to him.

Christina had second-guessed him. Before he even got a chance to say he did not wish to go out to a restaurant to dine, she informed him that she had ordered smoked salmon, Brie cheese, French bread and fresh fruit, and that they were about to have a picnic. "In bed," she said gaily, laughing as she brought him a glass of Scotch with ice and a splash of soda, mixed exactly the way he liked it.

After they had sipped their drinks, Miles put his hand in his pocket and brought out a small red leather jewel case. "These are for you, Christie. Opals . . . remember how I said you should always wear opals the night we met?"

"Oh Miles, they're so beautiful!" she exclaimed, "exquisite." She glanced up at him, her eyes shining. "I've never seen anything with such fire . . ."

"Yes, and they're going to look superb on you. Come, let's see."

He led her to the mirror and she fastened the earrings on, and admired them, and he admired her wearing them and they laughed, enjoying being together again. And then she ran into the bedroom and returned with a package.

"This is for you," she said.

He was grinning with pleasure as he tore off the paper. "Oh my God, you *really* shouldn't have!" He shook his head, looking down at the Cartier gold cigarette case in his hand. "Now, my girl—"

She silenced him with a kiss.

Much, much later when they made love, it seemed to Miles that he had never touched her before. Every part of her body seemed fresh and new to him, and more beautiful than ever. And at one moment, at the height of his passion, as he soared above her in ecstasy, he cried out, "I love you, Christie! I've fallen in love with you!"

"And I love you, Miles! Oh my darling, I love you so much!"

It was a rapturous affair.

They were obsessed with each other. This was not a question of one loving the other more. They were crazy about each other. They were deeply and intensely involved on every level. It was her first real love affair; although Miles was worldly and had had other affairs, he realized that this was the first time he had ever been truly in love.

At one point that weekend, Miles had the brilliant idea of coming to Paris every Friday. He felt safer here, free from prying eyes. And so they made their regular weekend trips through August. "But we must start going to another hotel," Christie said at the end of the month. "We can't continue to stay at the Ritz . . . we're becoming a couple, in quotes, and people are beginning to notice us."

And so they stayed at the George V and the Prince des Galles and the Lancaster and the Raphael. It became a joke for a while, but then Miles decided they had better stop flying in and out of Paris anyway, because that was becoming noticeable too.

"We're going to have to find a little hideaway somewhere in England," he said to Christie on their last trip to Paris. "Why don't you get onto it next week, my sweet?"

───── *Forty-Eight* ─────

It was pouring.

There was a high wind that blew the rain against the windows, and the sound was like hundreds of nail heads striking the glass.

But in the library of the small country house in the Cotswolds all was warmth and muted light and tranquility on this cold day in early November.

Christina was stretched out on the sofa, listening to the rain. It was oddly soothing, and she felt herself drifting with her thoughts, enjoying the aimlessness of this lazy Sunday afternoon.

She stole a secret look at Miles, as she constantly found herself doing. She loved him so much, more than she had ever believed it was possible to love a man. Her career mattered to her and she worked hard. But he was her whole reason for being now.

She existed for the weekends. These were the best times . . . being alone together in this charming and secluded house just outside Cirencester, which she had found quite by accident at the beginning of October. It was available for six months, and since it was furnished they had had nothing to do but buy groceries and move in.

They were involved in an extremely secretive affair. But she didn't care. She didn't need other people, only Miles. They were together whenever he was free during the week; they couldn't go out, so they usually stayed in at the Walton Street flat. And also, since he was often preoccupied with the goings-on in the Commons, the weekends were the most relaxed. They did very little . . . read and talked . . . and went for walks . . . she loved cooking for him, taking care of him, sharing his thoughts, his feelings, his extraordinary passion and his vibrant sexuality. And his tenderness. He was such a mixture.

He sat opposite her in a chair by the fire, engrossed in *The Observer*. The rest of the Sunday papers were scattered at his feet, discarded after he had plowed through them doggedly, muttering and cursing under his breath, sometimes laughing out loud, or exclaiming *"Damnation!"* and then grinning at her sheepishly, and explaining and sharing. Always sharing everything.

His face was tense at this moment. She knew he was worried about the situation in the Middle East. They were engaged in hostilities with Egypt because President Nasser had nationalized the Suez Canal. Britain and France and Israel had bombed Cairo, and Miles was still fuming in private, and driving points home in the Commons.

As if he suddenly became aware of her eyes on him, he looked across at her over the top of the paper, asked, "What is it, Christie?"

"Nothing, darling," she replied, sitting up, swinging her legs to the floor. "Just admiring you."

"Aha!" he exclaimed and eyed her wickedly. "In that case, if you so admire me, shall we climb the stairs together for a little sweet dalliance on this quiet Sunday afternoon? What better thing is there to do than make love on a wet day?"

"Honestly, Miles, you are impossible!"

"That's not what you said to me last night . . . you were full of compliments last night."

Her response was to walk over to him, take the paper out of his hands and sit down on his knee. She leaned into him, kissed him on the cheek. "Well, you were terrific last night."

He smiled his faintly amused little smile, took off his horn-rimmed glasses and rubbed his eyes. "I think I've had it with the papers . . . I wouldn't mind some air. Shall we go for a walk? You're the only person I know, other than myself, and apparently the Queen, who likes to walk in the country in the rain."

"Yes, come on, let's go, Miles." Christina jumped up, then offered him her hand.

Miles held her in his arms, looking down at her, watching the play of light on her face. He loved her far too much, he sometimes thought.

Christina opened her eyes and stared up at him. Then she smiled. "You're spoiling me . . . you're always making love to *me*, Miles . . ." She touched his cheek lingeringly.

"Mmmm, that's quite true," he said, and pushed her farther down in the bed, and wrapped his legs around her. "I *am* turning into an unselfish sort of bloke, aren't I? But we can always correct that, or rather, you can, you know. I'm very available right now."

He brought his mouth to hers, kissed her slowly, sweetly until the heat began to flow through him, charging him up, making his heart race, his passion soar. He felt her hands in his hair, on the back of his neck, smoothing down over his shoulders. He wanted her. He seemed to want her more and more every day. He could never get enough of her.

His voice was low and thick with emotion as he said, "Kiss me, Christie, oh please kiss me, my darling."

She sat up and knelt over him and stared into his face intently. She had grown to so love that face. It could block out everything, the image of it filling her mind absolutely until she was overwhelmed by it.

She ran her hands over his chest and down onto his flat hard stomach. His skin was as smooth and as dry as polished marble, glistening pale gold here and there where the half light shone on the fine blond hair on his lithe body. She moved to kneel between his legs and felt an involuntary quiver run through him as she put her hands on his thighs.

Christina looked up at Miles and saw that he was gazing down at her, his eyes a reflection of her own, awash with desire and love. Her throat tightened and her heart was clattering as she bent toward him, her mouth anxiously searching out the center of his passion just as his own had searched for hers a short while before.

He groaned as her mouth made contact with his body. "Oh God, Christie, what do you do to me?"

She filled her mouth with his sex, her lips lingering lovingly on him.

Now Miles was truly hers, spread out before her, immobile and breathless, offering himself up to her, a gift of love. And she was possessing the very core of him, his life's essence, his soul, and at that moment he belonged entirely to her.

He ran his fingers through her thick and tumbled hair, and caressed her shoulders, then brought his hands down to clasp hers gently resting on his stomach. He clenched his fingers around hers in a tenacious hold. An aching moan trickled from his throat.

She lifted her eyes and saw a fleeting flash of anguish smudge out the bright blue of his eyes, so that they became dark and flaring.

Suddenly Miles moved, put his hands around her face, lifted it up. He leaned down to her, kissed her sweetly, and then gently pulled her up the bed to him. He said, "I want you, Christie, want to be inside you. I must be enveloped in that lovely warmth that is you, my darling."

Suddenly he was on top of her, floating over her, and she was drowning in the midnight blueness of his eyes. He entered her almost roughly, and she began to quiver as she felt the rock-hard thrust of him. It was as if they ignited each other, moving in a rhythm that soon began to attain greater intensity. His passion seemed to spiral up and up, and she met its flight, rising higher and higher with him, at one with him. There was no separation any more.

Miles opened his eyes and looked at her and cried harshly, "Oh God! Oh you! Oh I—" He crushed his mouth on her, devoured her lips, her tongue.

"I want all of you," he whispered against the hollow of her neck. "All of your essence, all of your breath, all of you!"

Christina felt as if he had reached up and touched her heart. And then, as if from a long distance, she heard his name being called. But it was she who was shouting, "Miles! Miles! I love you!"

They clung to each other with a kind of desperateness, were welded together in an embrace that was primal and full of need. His mouth sought hers briefly, and as he drew all of her strength into him, he rushed headlong into the core of her.

And she heard him cry, "Christie! Christie! I love you I love you I can't live without you don't ever leave oh my God I'm coming come to me my love."

•••

He lay motionless with his head on her shoulder.

Christina felt dazed. She looked down at his translucent face and her tears welled up. What was it about his face? This face that so moved her, touched some inner spring of memory so poignant it made her want to cry at times.

Miles opened his eyes. "What happens to us when we're together like this?"

"I don't know. I think we float off somewhere. At least I do. Haven't you noticed that in me, Miles?"

"No, but then I'm wherever it is you are, Christie."

"Have you ever been there before? With anyone else?"

"No." He cleared his throat, said softly. "I think I know what happens to *us,* darling . . . when the sex act is so perfect, as it is with us, then that combination of the most intense physical pleasure and ecstasy, along with complete mental and emotional connection, makes the experience transcendental. We're transported to a higher level of consciousness."

"Yes, Miles, I think we are."

He stroked her hair, turned her face to his, murmured, "Set me as a seal upon thine heart, as a seal upon thine arm, for love is strong as death—" He paused and frowned. "Now I've gone and ruined it because I can't remember any more."

"Jealousy is cruel as the grave," Christina supplied.

"Yes, that's it. What comes next?"

"I can't remember either, but I know a bit of the next verse. Many waters cannot quench love, neither can the floods drown it. You see, I know my Bible too."

"Yes . . ." Miles was hesitant and then he said, "Christie, there's something I haven't told you . . . I did something when you were in New York for your show a couple of weeks ago . . ."

When he did not finish his sentence and because he sounded so serious, grave even, she sat up swiftly, stared at him. "What did you do?"

Miles also sat, reached for a cigarette on the bedside table, and lit it. He took a long draw, and then looked at her, said slowly, carefully, "I did something I vowed I would never do ever again. I went to see Candida. To ask for a divorce."

"And?"

"The answer was *no.* Many *no's* were flung at me, along with a variety of threats about creating a scandal if I broach it again." He exhaled. "I went to see her because I want to marry you, Christie. I don't want this creeping around corners, being unable to take you out with me. I want you as my wife." He shook his head sadly. "But it seems that's not to be."

"I don't care," she exclaimed, coming into his arms. "It doesn't matter. Nothing matters, Miles, as long as we can be together."

Forty-Nine

"What's the matter, darling?" Miles asked, walking across the living room of the Walton Street flat. "Don't you like the necklace?" He looked down at her, narrowing his eyes, trying to ascertain why she appeared to be so upset.

Christina's hand went up to her neck and she touched the lacey cobweb of delicate gold chains set with diamonds and opals, then lowered her eyes to look at it. "Miles, it's the most beautiful gift I've ever had. I love it."

"Then why such a long face, Christie?" He lowered himself onto the sofa next to her and took her slender, tapering hand in his. "Is it because I can't spend Christmas with you? Because if it is, I'll try to do something about cutting the holiday short. Look, I have an idea, I'll spend the day with you on Christmas Eve," he said, improvising rapidly. "Then that evening I'll drive down to Suffolk in order to have dinner with the boys and my parents. I'll spend Christmas Day with them, come back to town for Boxing Day with you, and—"

"Miles, no, I won't permit you to split yourself in two like that, or change your plans at this late date. Besides, it would be impossible for me to change mine. My parents would be so unhappy if I didn't go to Yorkshire. They've been looking forward to it, and I haven't seen much of them lately, you know that."

"Candida isn't going to be there, if that's what you're thinking. She really is going to take Monica up to Scotland. They're to stay at her father's shooting lodge with him." Miles shook his head in puzzlement. "I'll never know why she suddenly said I could have the boys, I really won't."

Christina sat staring ahead at the fireplace.

Miles lifted his hand, turned her face to his. "That is the God's honest truth, darling. Candida won't be at Broxley Hall." When she remained silent, he exclaimed, "You do believe me, don't you, Christina?"

She heard the anxiety in his voice and saw the alarm on his face, and she squeezed his hand. "Oh Miles, I know very well you'd never lie to me, it's not in your nature."

Miles looked deeply into her face. Her emotions were always explicit in her eyes. They usually told him everything. He saw that she was still perturbed but decided not to press her for the moment. They would not be seeing each other for a week, the longest they had been apart in the last six months. He had wanted it to be a very special night and he had no intention of spoiling it.

Almost as if he had telegraphed this thought to her, Christina pushed a bright smile onto her face and jumped to her feet. "Darling, fling a couple of logs on the fire and open the champagne, and let's settle in for a really gorgeous evening. I'm going to get your presents . . . after all, this *is* our Christmas tonight."

"Righto," he said, standing, smiling at her. He pulled her to him, kissed the hollow in her neck. "I do love you so much."

She extricated herself gently and ran to the bedroom, turned in the doorway. He was standing watching her intently. She blew him a kiss.

Miles was fiddling with the cork in the champagne bottle when she came floating back into the room, her arms full of packages. "Those are not all for me, are they?"

She grinned at him and carried them over to the fireplace. "One more trip, and that's it."

He shook his head, laughing with her, and his heart was full of love. There was no woman in this world quite like his Christie.

"You've always hankered after this," she said, walking toward him, carrying a large parcel wrapped in brown paper. "And I especially want you to have it. And it's with all of my love, my darling."

He took the parcel, knowing it was one of her paintings. Since he had admired them all, he did not know which one this was. He smiled at her. "Thank you, Christie. I know it's one of your paintings from the shape . . . which one is it?"

"Open it and see for yourself." She stood with her back to the fire, watching him as he carried the package to the sofa and tore off the paper. When he had the painting in his hands, he held it up and exclaimed, "Oh Christie, *Lily at Hadley* . . . oh Christie, how generous of you to give me this particular one. I know it's your favorite. Thank you." He put the painting against the sofa, came over and hugged her tightly.

Christina saw he was pleased, and this pleased her. She said, "It only became my favorite *after* we met at Hadley Court . . . and that's why I want you to have it, because it will always remind you of me."

His smile slipped, and he frowned at her. "Are you going away?"

"No, silly. Why do you ask that?"

"It was the way you said *remind me of you* . . . as if I'd need reminding of you when you're always going to be with me."

"Of course I am, Miles. Now, how about a glass of champagne before you open the rest of your presents."

He went to pour the drinks. "I had a Christmas card and a scribbled note from Ralph and Dulcie. I understand they're going to stay in New York for a while, what with that picture coming up in Hollywood and the possibility of a Broadway play. And what have you heard from Jane lately?"

"She was grumbling about the little monsters going over to New York for Christmas when she called me yesterday at the office. But otherwise she doesn't have much news. She is going to do the costumes for the new Hal Prince play on Broadway and she said she'd be staying on for another six months."

"Good for her. Jane's a talented girl." Miles brought their drinks and they clinked glasses. "Happy Christmas, my sweet."

"Happy Christmas, Miles."

They sat in front of the fire, slowly demolishing the bottle of Dom Perignon whilst Miles opened his gifts one by one, thanking her profusely, exclaiming over the books and jazz records, the ties and the silk dressing gown.

But it was the pair of sapphire cuff links that stunned him. "They're quite extraordinary," he exclaimed at last, holding them in his hand, admiring them. "You're far too extravagant."

"Listen who's talking," she said, coming to kneel next to his chair, looking up at him adoringly. "Do you really like them?"

"You know I do."

"So do I . . . they match your eyes."

He smiled and put his hand in his pocket, brought out a small box. "And this is another Christmas present from me."

It was a ring, a large opal ring surrounded by diamonds. It matched the necklace he had given her earlier, and the ring was equally exquisite.

"Thank you so much, Miles. How lovely it is." She slipped it on her right ring finger, held her hand out, looking at it.

Miles said, "Wrong hand, darling." He pulled the ring off and put it on her left hand. "Let's just say I prefer to see it there—" He broke off, staring at

her. Tears swam in her lovely gray eyes and her lip trembled. "Christie, whatever is it?"

She shook her head, brushed her eyes with her hand, swallowed.
"Miles . . ."

"Yes, darling, what is it? Whatever's wrong?"

Christina looked at him carefully. Her eyes held his. "I'm pregnant."

She saw the instant flash of happiness and pride in his eyes, the sudden
delighted smile he couldn't suppress and which revealed so much. And then his
face was wiped clean like an empty slate. "Oh Christie," he said and shook his
head slowly. "Oh Christie . . ."

And she could not fail to miss the dismal tone, the misery in his eyes, the
worry which was now enveloping him. She knew him far too well. "But you
were pleased a second ago!" she cried, taking his hand. "I know you were!"

"Of course I was, but—" He was unable to continue. Miles swallowed,
and deep within himself he knew that he had never loved her so much as he did
at this moment.

She said, "I wasn't going to tell you tonight. If you hadn't taken the ring
off my right hand and put it on the other, I wouldn't have."

"I'm glad you did . . . we're in this together. You can't carry such a
burden all alone, Christie."

"I didn't want to worry you, not with Christmas just around the corner. I
didn't want to spoil it for you . . . you don't get to see the boys enough as it
is."

He touched her cheek. "You're always so thoughtful, my lovely Christie."
He sat back in the chair, then said, "Well, this does present us with a problem,
doesn't it, darling?"

She nodded. "Miles, I don't want to have . . . an abortion, I just don't. I
realize a baby would be difficult for you to handle, but I was thinking—"

"Christie, a baby wouldn't be difficult, it would be *impossible*. I don't want
you to have an abortion either." His brow furrowed. "I just don't know what
the solution is right at this minute."

"Why couldn't I have the baby, Miles? Who would know it was yours.
Only you and I . . . I'm healthy financially, I can take care of everything,
and—"

"I'm not sure that would work," he interrupted swiftly. "What if something leaked out . . . my political career . . ."

"Yes, I know, there are so many things to consider, aren't there?"

"When did you find out?"

"Four days ago."

"You should have told me before. I can't bear to think how dreadfully
worried you must have been, Christie. It was wrong of you not to confide in
me."

"I didn't want to upset you before Christmas."

"How pregnant are you?"

"Six weeks."

He brought her into his arms and held her close, stroked her head. "We'll
think of the proper solution," Miles murmured. "Try not to worry, darling.
We'll cope with everything after the holidays."

────── *Fifty* ──────

Although Miles had told her not to worry, Christina did little else for the next twenty-four hours as she prepared to go to Yorkshire to spend Christmas with her parents.

She worried about Miles. She worried about herself. She worried about the baby. Or more precisely, she worried about what to do about the baby.

Christina knew Miles Sutherland loved her with all of his heart and that he did not want her to have an abortion. She also knew deep within herself that he wanted the baby, wanted *their* child. Yet she was too pragmatical a woman not to understand that there was his political career looming over their heads.

He had once said to her, not in the heat of passion, but quietly on one of their long walks in the country, "You're my life, Christie." But this was not strictly true. His political career was his life. And she could never ask him to give it up for her. To live openly with her. To have their baby.

If she did ask him, he would consider it, might even do it. But one day he would regret it, and she would regret it even more. To ask this man whom she loved so desperately to sacrifice his career would mean that she did not love him at all.

Politics and Miles Sutherland were too intertwined ever to be separated the one from the other. Miles would wither away without his constituency, his political cronies, the House of Commons and his life in that combative and exciting arena. Winston Churchill had once said he was a child of the House of Commons. So was Miles Sutherland.

And I am on the horns of a dilemma, I really am, Christina thought the following evening as she walked in from the Bruton Street fashion house at eight o'clock. Miles had left for Broxley Hall in Suffolk that morning, as loving and as concerned as he had been when she had broken the news. She had finished her Christmas shopping and then gone to her office to sign checks, give out Christmas gifts, and to attend the Christmas party Giselle had given for the staff.

Now here she was with nothing to do but worry until tomorrow morning, when she was taking the Pullman to Leeds. After hanging up her coat, she put a match to the fire that Mrs. Green, the char, had laid earlier, then hurried into the kitchen. She was not particularly hungry but knew she ought to eat something, so she opened a can of tomato soup. As she waited for it to heat on the gas ring, she made herself a sandwich from the smoked salmon left over from last night's dinner.

Ten minutes later Christina took her light supper into the living room, and ate it in front of the now blazing fire. Her mind turned over various possibilities. She could have the baby and perhaps risk losing Miles. She could have an abortion. She could disappear, move to a foreign country, have the baby and live abroad for the rest of her life. Miles could visit her from time to time.

She jumped up and began to walk up and down the room. How stupid I am, she thought. None of those possibilities would work. There is only *one* solution: Miles has to force Candida to give him a divorce so that we can be married. Of course! Why hadn't she and Miles thought of it last night. Only because they were now both browbeaten into believing there never would be a divorce. But perhaps something could be worked out after all. Christina returned to the chair by the fireside and relaxed for the first time in several days.

Resting her hands on her stomach, she thought about the baby. *Their* baby. *His* baby. It thrilled her to think that part of Miles was now growing inside her. She was going to have the baby. She was going to marry Miles. It was going to work out.

The shrilling telephone made her jump in surprise. She went to answer it. He said, "Hello, my love, how are you?"

"Miles, I'm wonderful. I've just had a brilliant idea."

He laughed into the telephone. "So have I. But tell me yours first."

"You've got to go to *you know who* again and make her give you your freedom."

"Well, I always knew I loved you for a reason, and it's obviously your brains! And great minds do think alike, it seems. I thought of the same thing this evening, and I couldn't wait to get through dinner to ring you. I *will* see Candida again, Christie, as soon as she's back from Scotland. We'll sort this out, you'll see. Everything's going to be all right."

"I feel so much better suddenly. Christmas isn't going to be so difficult after all."

"No, and we'll be together next week. Listen, darling, are you sure you don't want me to ring you in Leeds?"

"Perhaps you'd better not. I don't want to have to start explaining who you are. You know what parents are like."

"I do, my sweet. I love you, Christie."

"I love you, Miles."

"Where to, miss?" the cabbie asked, after he had stowed her suitcase in the cab.

"King's Cross, please."

"Right you are, miss."

Christina sat back, smoothed the skirt of her coat and glanced out of the window. It had started to snow. Just small flurries, but it seemed to be settling. She wondered if it would be a white Christmas, whether it was snowing in Yorkshire.

She looked at her watch. She had plenty of time to catch the ten-thirty restaurant car going to Doncaster, Leeds and Harrogate. The best morning train on the Northern run, it went on up to Edinburgh. Scotland, she thought, her mind turning to Candida. Miles would get his freedom. They would marry. She would have their baby. She let her hand stray onto her stomach. It was flat. Nothing showed yet. But in a few months she would look pregnant. She would have to start thinking about designing herself a wardrobe of maternity clothes . . .

Neither the cab driver nor Christina saw the huge truck go into a skid on the slippery road which was wet with snow and drizzle. The truck slammed hard into the passenger door of the cab and sent the vehicle spinning across the road and into a lamp post.

Christina was flung off the seat. She hit her head on the glass partition in front of her and landed on the floor in a crumpled heap. She was unconscious when they got her out of the mangled cab and put her in an ambulance bound for Middlesex Hospital. Miraculously her injuries were minor, mostly a light concussion and bruises. But an hour after being admitted to the emergency room she lost the baby.

Fifty-One

Christina felt empty and desolated for weeks after she lost the baby. Miles was devastated too, and he was kind and loving to her, but it took her a long time to heal.

Slowly she began to pick up the threads of her life, put aside her sadness about the miscarriage. Her work was demanding and it helped to keep her going. It wasn't just the loss of the baby which troubled Christina in the early part of 1957. She had also come to believe that she and Miles would always be hampered by a wife who refused to divorce him. Under normal circumstances they could have lived openly together, but a politician was far too vulnerable, especially a man like Miles, and they would never be able to take that step.

He had gone to Candida again in February and asked for a divorce. Once more he had been refused. And he had come back to Walton Street looking defeated and humiliated. Christina's heart had gone out to him that night.

As he had sipped the Scotch and soda she had handed him, he had said, "I literally went down on my bending knees and begged. That woman's made of stone."

And then at the end of the month the bombshell had dropped. His sister had told him that they had been seen together in the Cotswolds. Even their weekend house, always so comforting and reinforcing for them both, suddenly became a prison. Their relationship seemed to grow more secretive and restrictive than ever.

For the first time since they had fallen in love, she and Miles began to quarrel. Small, insignificant quarrels admittedly, but nevertheless the harmony, the tranquility they had always enjoyed together had gone slightly askew.

In April Christina was sure of only three things: Miles would never be able to rid himself of Candida, except perhaps through death; his political career came first; and she could no longer support the way she herself was living. Her life was built around him, his needs, and the circumstances of his work and the life he had had before they had met. It was impossible for her to continue.

It became clear to Christina in July of that year that there was only one solution to her predicament. She had to leave England for an extended stay in the United States. Only by putting distance between herself and Miles could she ever hope to break off the relationship. She loved him so much she knew that if she stayed in London she would never have the strength or the will to give him up. And she had to give him up to save her own life. The pain she was experiencing was now too great a price to pay for stolen moments. Also she wanted all of the things he had always said she would want one day: a normal life, a husband, children . . . and dignity. She could no longer bear to crawl around corners with Miles. And having to hide in the country had become the last straw.

She did not consult with him about her plans, nor did she confide in him. She knew he would never let her go. It would have to be a *fait accompli* when she told him. Her first step was to make Giselle Roux head of the House of Christina on a temporary basis for the next year. She gave her parents the keys to the Walton Street flat and told them to use it once a month. Her secretary Liz was given another set of keys to deal with the post and other day to day matters, since Christina did not want to give up the flat and neither did Jane. And she put plans in operation to start up a New York branch of the House of Christina. She had plenty of money to finance this project and a long list of loyal American clients. And finally, she had her dearest friend Jane, who was waiting impatiently for her to come. Christina had confided in Jane long ago, and when she had decided to break with Miles she had taken her close friend into her confidence again.

The last person she told was Miles.

"You looked so beautiful tonight, Christie," Miles said, as he sat down in the Walton Street flat and took the glass of white wine from her. "Cool as the proverbial cucumber," he said, giving her a glance that was both loving and appraising.

She hurried into the kitchen on the pretense of getting ice, suddenly overcome by her love for him. He looked good tonight, dressed in a light beige summer suit. Pale colors always sat well on him. She understood, as she filled the ice bucket, that she could not spend the evening with him as she had planned. She had to tell him at once. Immediately. It was too unnerving for her to be with him.

He said, as she went back into the sitting room, "I've always liked you in lime green, Christie, but you should be wearing my opals with that dress." He frowned. "I haven't seen them on you lately. Don't you like them any more?"

"Yes, I do, Miles, I love them. But they are so valuable, I keep them locked away." She cleared her throat, sat down on the edge of the chair and looked across at him. She said as steadily as she could, "Miles, there's something that I have to tell you."

He was instantly aware of her grave tone and knew at once that something was dreadfully amiss.

"I'm going away, Miles. I can't live here in England any longer," Christina said. He tried to interrupt her, but she held up her hand. "No, Miles, you must let me finish, you really must. *You* can't go away, you're a Member of Parliament, but *I* can and I'm going to New York. Tomorrow. For at least a year."

"But darling, why, for God's sake, *why?*" he demanded furiously, his face white, his eyes stark with shock.

"Because our life together is insupportable, Miles. I love you, I love you so very, very much, my darling, but I can't continue. I must put distance between us in order to start a new life for myself, don't you see?"

"I'll go and ask Candida again!"

"It won't work, Miles. You know that as well as I do. She'll never divorce you. I must go to save my own life."

He was on his feet and across the room, pulling her up and off the chair and into his arms. "I love you, Christie. You're my life. For God's sake, please don't leave me."

"I'm not your *whole* life, Miles . . . only a part of it. You have your political career and you have your children, but mostly you have your career. It won't be easy for you, but you'll be all right—" She could not continue. She slipped out of his arms, moved toward the fireplace.

He stared at her. He thought the world had just come to an end. *His* world had.

Christie said, "Miles, if you love me, you'll let me go, you'll set me free . . ." Tears spurted from her eyes. She couldn't control them. "If you love me as much as you say you do, you'll give me this chance, never get in touch with me, never see me again. You'll let me be in peace."

"Christie," he cried desperately, "please, my darling, we'll find a way, we'll find a solution."

She shook her head. "There is only one way for us now, Miles. *You must let me go.*"

A million thoughts rushed through his head. So many things he had never told her, never shared, so many loving words he had never spoken, so much he still had to give her. He loved her with every fiber of his being. And because he did, he had to give her this chance she asked for. Too late now to do it all differently. Too late now with her.

Miles took a shaky step toward her and then stopped. He could not go and kiss her. He did not dare.

"Goodbye, my darling," he said, and stumbled out of the room. And as he ran down the stairs, he was blinded by his tears and he knew he would never love like this again.

She wept all the way across the Atlantic.

Jane met her at the airport, took one look at her and bundled her into the waiting limousine.

"Thank God they invented dark glasses," Christie said, trying to be light and normal with Jane, and then promptly burst into tears again.

Jane took her in her arms, patted her back and told her to cry it all out, and Christina sobbed all the way into Manhattan as Jane made sympathetic and loving noises.

The tears were endless. But somehow she managed to go about her business, to lose herself in her work. It was work she loved and it helped to keep grief at bay. And she *was* grieving for Miles, she knew that. She also understood somewhere in the hidden regions of her heart that she would always grieve for him. He had been her first real love and they had loved each other so very much.

But as the weeks turned into months she became more controlled, and one night she actually fell asleep without shedding a single tear.

The next morning at breakfast, she said to Jane, "I think I'm on the mend. I didn't cry myself to sleep last night."

"I'm glad, Christie," Jane said quietly. She had understood from the beginning that Christie was truly suffering, and that she was broken-hearted, and so she had been kind, supportive, and continued to be so. Nor had she ever said one mean thing about Miles. Now she murmured, "But it *has* been a long time, you know."

"What do you mean?" Christie asked, stirring her cup of tea, giving Jane an inquiring look.

"It is the first week of December, and you arrived here in July. Six months of tears! My God! That must be some record."

Christina began to laugh.

So did Jane, and she said, "Now I know you're really on the mend, Crowther. And perhaps you'll help me plan my Christmas party . . . our Christmas party."

"Are we having one?"

"We are . . . I want you to meet this actor chap, Simon; you'll approve I hope, because I'm actually thinking of marrying him."

"How long has *that* been going on?" Christina cried. "Haven't I noticed the actor chap around here, or what?"

"Oh no, he's new . . . and adorable."

"Actors make lousy husbands, Janey."

"Are you throwing aspersions on my father?" Jane demanded a little indignantly. "Mummy wouldn't like that."

"Ralph is different," Christina said.

"So is Alex Newman."

"I thought you said his name was Simon."

"It is, Christie. Alex Newman is for you."

Christina held up her hand. "Oh no . . . I'm not ready for men yet!"

But she had not bargained for Alex Newman.

She realized that he *was* different from the moment she met him. He had a distinction that set him apart, and that had nothing to do with his dark good looks or his charm.

Jane brought him over to be introduced and Christina had no idea as she shook his hand that he had already decided to marry her as he had looked at her from across the room.

He was charming to her all evening, and attentive to her needs throughout the party. He made her laugh a lot and she enjoyed his dry wit and found herself taking to him. But when he asked her out the following evening, she shook her head. "Thank you so much, but I don't think so."

"Aren't you ready yet?" he asked quietly.

She drew back slightly. "What do you mean?" She wondered if Jane had told him something about her problems, her unhappiness, and then realized her friend would not have done a mean thing like that.

"Don't look so affronted," Alex said, smiling. "Instinctively, I feel that you've been hurt recently. By a man. And I thought that perhaps explained your reluctance to accept my invitation to dinner." He grinned at her rather boyishly. "Obviously it's me you don't like."

"Oh but I do like you, Alex, a lot," Christina said. "And yes, I will come out with you tomorrow night."

He smiled and went to fetch them both an afterdinner drink, and they sat by the fire for a long time, chatting about innumerable things, and found they had common interests.

Alex said, "I understand from Jane that the House of Christina is ready to be launched early next year, so I guess that means you'll be living here permanently?"

"Oh no, I don't suppose so," Christina said quickly. "The London house needs me, and so I imagine I'll commute back and forth across the Atlantic. I gave myself a year to get everything rolling properly here."

"I see. But your business will be bigger here, won't it? Eventually. I would have thought that you could sell twice as much in New York as you do in London."

Christina looked at him with interest, knowing that he was a banker, and for the rest of the evening they talked about business. And later, after everyone had left and she was helping Jane to clear away the glasses and plates, she found herself thinking about Alex Newman and his fascinating marketing ideas.

As she and Jane washed the crystal glasses, Christina suddenly said, "I did like Alex. You were right, he is a lovely man and different."

"And rich," Jane said, grinning at her. "Not that that makes any difference to you."

"No, it doesn't. And don't get any ideas, Janey Sedgewick, I'm only interested in him as a friend. I liked his ideas about business, and he says he'll be happy to help me any time."

"I'll bet he will," Jane cried, rolling her eyes and laughing. "And apart from being charming, good-looking, rich and intelligent, he's also single."

"He sounds like Mr. Perfect," Christina remarked. "So why isn't he married?"

"I believe he's divorced."

Christina shook her head and seemed to shrink into the wall, and she turned away, walked back into the living room.

Jane ran after her at once. "Oh Christie, darling, I'm so sorry. I didn't mean to upset you."

"You didn't, Janey, really. I don't think I'm ready for other men yet."

"But go out with Alex tomorrow. He's so nice, and I know he's taken to you. Please, for me."

And so Christina met Alex Newman for dinner at Le Pavillon the following evening. She did not know then that he would be the one to heal her wounds and make her whole again.

Fifty-Two

"Mommy, why won't you tell me what we've bought Grandma for her birthday? I want to know!"

Christina looked down at her six-year-old daughter and said, "Ssshhh, Kyle, don't shout in the middle of the street."

"But why won't you tell me?" Kyle wailed.

"Because you can't keep a secret, and Daddy and I daren't risk confiding in you, since it is such a special gift. We're afraid you'll blurt it out, and then it won't be a lovely surprise for Gran."

"Oh Mommy, I won't," Kyle protested indignantly. "I'm not a baby like Auntie Janey's Clarissa."

Taking hold of the child's hand firmly, Christina walked her across Grosvenor Square in the direction of South Audley Street. It was a bright June day in 1965 and Audra would be fifty-eight years old this week. She and Alex were giving a small dinner for her tonight at their flat in Eaton Square, and Kyle had been a pest for days, badgering her about the gift.

"Please tell me, Mommy!"

"I'll make a deal with you, Kyle," Christina murmured, curbing her exasperation. "If you don't mention it again in the street, I'll tell you when we get home—is that agreed?"

"Oh yes, it is."

They walked on in silence, much to Christina's relief. She was preoccupied with her business and wondered whether to stop in at Bruton Street for a few minutes to talk to Alex and Giselle about the winter collection now being produced. She decided against it. Her parents, Janey and her husband Simon, and the Sedgewicks would be arriving around six-thirty, and it was already four. Better perhaps to get back to Eaton Square.

She was thinking about her dress for the evening when she saw him getting out of a chauffeur-driven car ahead.

Her step faltered for a split second, but she went on walking at the snail's pace Kyle always adopted.

He swung away from the car, turned his head, looked down the street in her direction. He saw her immediately. He stopped in the middle of the pavement, stood stock still, as if immobilized by shock, and she realized he was waiting for her.

And then he began to walk, very slowly, toward her, his eyes riveted on her face.

How extraordinary, he hasn't changed at all in eight years, Christina thought. A little grayer at the temples, but he looks exactly the same as he always did. He was famous now. The Labor Party had won the last general election in 1964 and he was a minister and very important in the British Government. Some said he would rise to be Prime Minister one day. Candida had divorced him six years ago to marry some impoverished Frenchman with a grand title, a duke or a count, she wasn't sure. Occasionally she saw his name linked to various women in the columns, but he had never remarried.

As they drew closer Christina's heart began to thunder in her chest and her mouth went dry.

"Hello, Christina," he said softly when they finally stood in front of each other.

"Miles—" She could not say anything else for a moment. She was blinded by the blue radiance of his eyes, deafened by the noise in her chest. At last she managed, "It's lovely to see you after all these years."

"Yes . . . eight years, Christie, a long time."

"Yes. Congratulations, Miles . . . on all of your wonderful successes, becoming a cabinet minister."

"And yours, Christina. I see your name wherever I look—perfume, clothes, sunglasses, lingerie, hats—" Miles was overcome. He held himself still, afraid that he would grasp her arm, drag her with him to some place, any place, where they could be alone, where he could take her in his arms and tell her how much he still loved her.

Neither of them could move on, or tear their eyes from each other. Time stood still for them both.

A thousand memories flooded her mind, and as she looked at him she knew he was remembering so many things himself.

"Mommy."

The child's voice broke the spell.

Miles looked down. He cleared his throat. "I'm Miles. What's your name?" he asked in his resonant voice, offering her his hand.

She took it, smiled up at him, her little cheeks dimpling. "I'm Kyle."

"How old are you, Kyle?"

"I'm six."

He lifted his head. "Oh Christie—"

She saw the pain in his eyes and the sudden glitter of tears. And there was such yearning on his lean, intelligent face, she knew then that he had never stopped loving her and that he was thinking of their child, the one she had lost. And she knew too that he had never remarried because of her.

Christina's eyes brimmed. "Miles, oh Miles," she said and her voice trembled.

"Don't," he said, sounding as shaky as she, putting his hand on her arm. "Oh please don't, my dear, it's hard enough for me to bear. Take care of yourself, Christie . . . goodbye, Kyle."

He pivoted and walked back to the house where his car was parked, and sprang up the steps. And she waited until the door had closed behind him before she started to walk again.

"Why are you crying, Mommy?"

"I'm not."

"Yes, you are."

"It's the wind in my eyes."

"There isn't a wind, Mommy."

"I'm taller than you, and up here there's a wind."

"Oh."

"Let's find a taxi," Christina exclaimed, brushing her wet cheeks with her fingertips, hurrying her daughter forward.

"You promised to tell me about Grandma's present when we got home," Kyle said immediately as they entered the flat in Eaton Square.

Christina looked down at her, nodded. "Yes, Kyle, that's quite true, I did. However, I didn't say what *time* I would tell you. You'll know when Grandma knows—later this evening."

"That's not fair!"

At this moment, Nanny Fraser, the lovely Scotswoman who looked after Kyle, appeared in the entrance foyer and scooped Kyle up and off to the nursery.

Christina went down the hall and into her bedroom, dropped her handbag on the bed, and crossed to the adjoining bathroom. She locked the door, turned on the taps in the washbasin, found a hand towel and buried her face in it. And then she leaned against the wall and sobbed and sobbed until there were no tears left inside her. She wept for the child she had lost, the love she had lost. And she wept for Miles, and for his loneliness and for the tragic circumstances of his life and for all that he had missed with her.

And when she was finally calm, she washed her face and went out to the bedroom to redo her makeup and dress for her mother's birthday dinner. Earlier that day she had selected a mauve silk dress and matching mauve silk shoes, and all of the opals that Miles had given her. They went so well with the lilac colors. And now as she held them in her hands, she thought how odd it was that she had chosen to wear them tonight, had taken them out of the safe that very morning. She never before had bumped into Miles in all the years she had been traveling back and forth between London and New York.

Once she was dressed, Christina left the bedroom, hurried in the direction of the living room to inspect it before their guests arrived. In the entrance hall she heard Kyle's shrill voice echoing from Alex's study and she walked across to it, stood in the doorway. And Kyle was saying, "And after he left us, Mommy started to cry."

Alex looked up, smiled. But his eyes were momentarily perplexed as he came toward her. "Hello, my Chris-Chris," he said. "You're looking beautiful tonight. Very beautiful."

She met him halfway, stretched out her hands to his, looked up into his face, loving him with her eyes. She was so glad she was married to this man.

He kissed her cheek, turned to his child. "Hey, little poppet, shouldn't you run along and get changed? Grandpa and Grandma will be here any minute."

Once they were alone, Alex took her in his arms and held her very tightly. He said against her luxuriant hair, "So you finally ran into Miles Sutherland, and after all these years."

"Yes." There was a small silence. She said, "I felt so sad for him, Alex. That's why I cried after he left; it was for no other reason."

"I realize that, Christie. I suspect he's a lonely man, in spite of all the glory and the power."

"Yes." And then she murmured, "It really is the only reason, you know."

Alex held her away from him, smiled and shook his head. "Do you think I don't know where I stand with you after seven years of marriage?"

"Was it Miles?" Jane asked, looking at her intently. "The man whom you ran into this afternoon?"

Christina nodded and pursed her lips. "So she's told you as well, the little monkey . . . she's told your parents too, I think."

Jane squeezed her arm. "Don't be annoyed with her, Christie darling. You know what children are like, and anyway, no one's paid any attention."

Christina laughed hollowly. "Want to bet?" She drew Jane closer to the window and edged her out onto the terrace of the penthouse. "My mother came up to me a little while ago, and asked me who we ran into this afternoon, who the man was. Then she had the nerve to ask me if I was happy with Alex."

"You are, aren't you?" Jane suddenly looked worried. "You don't still hanker after Miles, do you?"

"Oh Christ, Janey, how can you of all people ask a question like that? You know how much I adore Alex. I have the best marriage in the world, the best of everything." Christina took a sip of champagne, eyed Jane carefully and said, "Now it's my turn to ask you a question, one that's been on the tip of my tongue for years . . . what did you ever have against poor Miles? You were always so down on him."

Jane gave her a small shamefaced smile. "I think I was rather attracted to him and furious because he never paid me a blind bit of notice. And then when he started chasing after you I was worried, Christie. I really thought you were going to be hurt." Jane dropped her voice. "And you were."

"Not irreparably, I wasn't."

"Thank God." Jane walked to the edge of the terrace, looked down at the leafy gardens in the center of Eaton Square, then turned. "Everything's all right

with Simon and me again, Christie. It was all a storm in a teacup last week
. . . well, you were forever cautioning me about marrying an actor."

Christina smiled, took hold of her arm, drew her back toward the French
windows. "I knew it would be fine. Now I think we'd better go inside. I know
Alex wants me to say my little piece to Mummy, and then we'll give her our
present, so that we can pack Miss Tattle Tale off to bedibyes."

Alex cleared his throat and said, "Could we possibly have a little quiet,
please? Christie has something to say."

Everyone stopped talking and Christina walked into the center of the
room, leading Kyle by the hand. The child, wearing one of her best party
frocks, was carrying a gift-wrapped box.

Christina smiled at her guests and then her eyes settled on Audra. She said,
"I had an idea last year, Mummy, and I confided it to Alex. He loved it as much
as I did . . . it was an idea for this year's birthday present for you . . . from
the three of us. It comes with all of our love, and we hope you're going to
enjoy it as much as we believed you would when we bought it for you a few
months ago."

Kyle looked up at her mother and Christina nodded. "Yes, go along, Kyle,
give our gift to Grandma."

"Here you are, Gran," the child said, offering her the box, and then she
put her arms around Audra's neck and kissed her cheek. She leaned against her
grandmother, said, "Please hurry up and open it, Gran, 'cos they didn't tell me
what it is . . . Mommy says I can't keep secrets."

Everyone laughed.

Audra, her face flushed with happiness, untied the blue ribbon, pulled off
the crinkly silver paper and lifted the lid. She stared inside the box and then
frowned. "What is it?" she asked, throwing Alex and her daughter a puzzled
stare as she took out the old iron key. She glanced at Vincent sitting next to
her. "Do you know what this key's for?" she asked her husband.

Vincent shook his head, although he knew very well. He had been in on
the secret right from the outset and was very much a part of it all.

Christina said, "It's the key to your new house, Mummy . . . yours and
Daddy's. Alex and I have bought High Cleugh for you. That's your birthday
present . . . your childhood home."

Audra opened her mouth. No sound came out. She looked at the key in
her hand, then at Vincent, and she pushed herself up off the sofa unsteadily.
She had paled and her eyes were exceptionally bright as she went to her daughter and son-in-law. She shook her head, glanced once more at the key.

"I never thought I would ever hold this key in my hand again . . . thank
you, Christie and Alex, thank you so much for giving me back that house."
She reached out and took hold of Christina's arm, afraid that her legs were
about to give way under her. The tears welled up and she leaned into her
daughter and whispered, "Oh darling, thank you, thank you." And then Audra
smiled and she went on smiling all night.

Christina rested her head against Alex's bare chest and listened to him
breathing lightly, smoothing her hand along his arm.

"Do you think Mummy enjoyed her birthday dinner, and that she's excited about owning High Cleugh?"

Alex smiled. "Yes, to both of those questions. In fact, I think excited is far too mild a word . . . how about ecstatic or overwhelmed?"

Christina laughed, wrapped her legs around him. "Oh Alex, it was a lovely evening, thanks for helping to make it possible."

He said nothing, stroked her hair, held her head against him tenderly. He loved his wife so very much. He had from the first moment he had set eyes on her in New York, at that party of Janey's. He had looked across the room at her and his heart had jumped and he had known he was going to marry her. Suddenly he wished his child had not carried home tales about this afternoon's encounter. He would have preferred not to know that Christina had run into Miles Sutherland. All that had been over so long ago, but he hated the thought that she had seen him again. Miles had caused her so much pain in the past. Then he chastised himself for being so selfish. It was better he knew, just in case Christie wanted to spill out her thoughts. She had never told him much about Miles, but he had known in Paris on their honeymoon that the man had had a deep effect on her and that she had loved Miles. But then he had loved another woman before Christie. Everyone came with a history and a past. But he didn't suppose Christie would say much to him about the British politician. She was secretive about Miles, and yet she told him her thoughts and feelings on everything else. They *shared*—that was one of the reasons they had such a good marriage; it was also the reason why they worked so well in business together. They were the best team. He had taken the House of Christina and made it into an international business worth billions. She had the artistic talent, he had the business acumen and by licensing her name she had become bigger than ever.

"Are you happy with me?" she asked suddenly.

"You know I am, my Chris-Chris."

"Are you sorry I can't have any more children? Would you have liked another child, Alex?"

"No, Kyle is quite enough," he said, and then groaned in mock horror. "Imagine two like her."

"Be serious."

"I am . . . it's fine the way it is, darling. As long as you're happy, Christie. You are, aren't you?"

"Yes, I am. Are you sorry we never had a son? You know, a son as in son and heir . . ."

"No, and anyway, we have a daughter and heir, and that's sufficient for me." He sensed her smile and he bent over her, moved her head slightly, brought his face down to hers.

He found her mouth with his and kissed her softly, slid his tongue alongside hers. And slowly and gently he began to make love to her, touching her breasts and stroking her body, letting her know how much he loved her and telling her in a thousand different silent ways that *he* would never hurt her.

And with delicacy and expertise he brought her to new heights of passion, and as she stiffened and began to spasm he took her to him, entered her swiftly, and made her his. Not only for tonight, but for always.

EPILOGUE

Kyle, Audra and Christina 1978

Epilogue

"I don't want to paint dresses like she does, I want to paint pictures," Kyle said to her grandmother.

Audra flinched at these words. There's nothing like getting to the heart of the matter, she thought, but oh the brutality of the young. She said, "I know you've wanted to paint, to be an artist, for the last couple of years, Kyle dear, but I'm not sure you've gone about this in *exactly* the right way—with your parents, I mean."

"It's not Daddy, he doesn't care whether I go into the stupid business or not. It's *her!*"

"Now look here, Kyle, I won't allow you to speak about your mother in that tone of voice. You *are* being unfair, you know."

Kyle threw Audra a half apologetic look, but her mouth settled into sulky lines. "Anyway, I can't imagine why I'm defending Daddy, he's always on her side. He always has been. For as long as I can remember it's been the two of them against me . . . even when I was little I felt left out. They were the best team. That's what they always said, and it *was* just the two of them, Gran. I wasn't included."

Audra looked at Kyle in astonishment and sighed heavily. She wanted to shake her granddaughter, and if they hadn't been in the restaurant of the Carlyle Hotel, having coffee after lunch, she would have done so. "You're quite wrong, Kyle, in that assumption. I can distinctly remember when you came to England in 1965 . . . you were walking around, singing, 'We're the best team, the best team, Mummy and Daddy and me.' I remember it so well because it was the year your parents bought High Cleugh for me. You were six. And your parents have never shut you out. *Never.* You've been included in everything. They've been wonderful parents and they love you very much."

"They love each other more than they love me."

"Don't be so ridiculous," Audra snapped, genuine anger surfacing. "Of course they love each other—they've never been anything *else* but very much *in* love, as a matter of fact. And you should thank your lucky stars they have, Kyle. What do you want to be? A child of a broken marriage?"

"I didn't mean it that way," Kyle answered swiftly, a chagrined expression flickering on her face. "It's just that I'm so upset, Grandma. I hate the fashion business and everything about it. I don't want to design clothes and sit behind a desk and do trunk shows and cope with imbecilic models who starve themselves to anorexic death and primp and pile ten pounds of icky goo on their faces every day. I want to paint what I see."

Her young face suddenly lost its petulant look, became gloriously alive, and all of her rebelliousness seemed to fall away from her. Kyle sat forward eagerly, and her dark eyes shone. "I want to paint landscapes and seascapes, like

I did last summer when I was in Yorkshire with you, Gran. Oh it was lovely, being there at High Cleugh, going to Robin Hood's Bay and the Dales, and sitting with my easel and being quiet and putting beauty down on canvas, as I saw it my particular way . . . through my own special angle of vision. I was so happy last summer with you, Grandma. Happier than I've ever been. And then I had to come back here to New York and go out with Mom on the road. Stupid trunk shows! I detest them. And I detest the Fashion Institute."

Audra reached out and took the girl's hand. "I know things have been difficult lately, dear."

"I'm getting so that I can't function properly anymore, I'm so frustrated and unhappy." Kyle took a deep breath. "All it would take to make me happy is to be allowed to go to the Royal College of Art in London for a couple of years and then become a landscape painter. But she'll never understand *that*. All she's interested in is making money."

Audra's eyes welled with tears. "Oh Kyle, that's not true," she said and stopped, found her bag on the banquette, opened it, groped for her handkerchief.

Kyle was distressed and she squeezed her grandmother's arm. "I'm sorry, Gran, I didn't mean to sound nasty. I'm sorry too if I've hurt your feelings; after all she is your daughter."

"And she's your mother, Kyle, and the best mother in the world," Audra exclaimed. "Take my word for it. She only wants the best for you. Why, she'd give her life for you. I've been on your side all along, but I'm not going to be much longer if you play the spoiled child, and speak of your mother in this unkind and disrespectful way." Audra fixed her piercing blue eyes on Kyle. "Do I make myself clear?" she asked in a stern and reprimanding voice.

"Yes, Gran," Kyle replied meekly. She had always been a bit afraid of Audra.

"Very well. Now listen to me, and you'd better listen very carefully . . . and perhaps when I've finished you'll understand your mother's motivations, understand *her*, understand why she loves her business so much. All right?"

Kyle nodded.

"Your mother was a landscape painter, and she sacrificed her art for the business. She once had what you want so badly right in the palm of her hand. And she was brilliant, Kyle. But she gave it all up for *me* . . . to make money for *me* . . . to give *me* the comforts and luxuries she thought I was entitled to have." Audra grasped Kyle's hand, held onto it tightly. "I'll tell you about it . . . Christie should have told you, but she hasn't . . . so I shall tell you now."

Kyle gave her grandmother her entire attention, and as Audra continued to speak much of the anger and irritation with her mother which had been building for the past year dissolved. And when Audra had finished, Kyle's eyes were moist too. "What an extraordinary thing Mom did for you, Gran. I wish she'd told me." Kyle bit her lip. "Do you think she misses painting? Do you think that's why she doesn't have much of her own work around in the New York apartment and the house in Connecticut? I mean, you have most of it at High Cleugh, and Aunt Janey has some. Perhaps she doesn't want to be reminded too much about what she gave up."

Audra winced. Kyle's excruciating honesty was unnerving at times. "Perhaps she misses it . . . I don't really know. We never speak of it. We never have actually, not even in the beginning. But I've been wrong, Kyle. We should have talked, she and I." Audra settled back against the banquette, looking reflective. I was always afraid of saying the wrong thing, of upsetting her, Audra thought. Yes, I was wrong and in so many ways.

"I don't know what to do, Grandmother," Kyle muttered. "I feel awful. I've been mean to Mom for months and months. I must have hurt her dreadfully."

Audra patted her hand. "You won't have any problems with your mother . . . I know my daughter very well. She loves you so much. She'll accept your apology and forgive you at once."

"Do you think so, Gran?"

"I *know* so." Leaning closer, Audra smiled for the first time in days. "I think I've come up with a compromise for the two of you. I've been wracking my brains all week, and I think I have the solution, Kyle darling."

"Oh God I hope so, Grandma. What is it?"

"I'm going to talk to your mother again when we get back to the apartment. If she's still insistent that you go into the business, I'm going to ask her to give you a sabbatical. Mind you, Kyle, you've got to promise to give her three years in the business later, if she gives you three years now, allows you to come back to London with me next week. We'll apply at once to the Royal College, and in the meantime, until you're accepted, you can live with me at High Cleugh and paint to your heart's content. So . . . what do you think?"

"Gran, it's brilliant! Brilliant!"

"Do you agree to keep your end of the bargain?"

"Yep. I do! I do!" Kyle's face glowed.

When they left the Carlyle Hotel, they walked down Madison Avenue a short way.

It was a pretty Saturday afternoon at the end of May and the lovely weather had brought many people out to gaze in the windows of the elegant boutiques and browse in the art galleries.

"I think I'd like to go up to Park Avenue and take a cab back to the apartment," Audra said, reaching for Kyle's arm. "There are too many people about now."

"Are you all right?" Kyle looked at her grandmother worriedly.

"I feel a bit tired suddenly."

Kyle hailed a taxi on Park Avenue and helped Audra inside, and within ten minutes they were alighting in front of the apartment building on Sutton Place where the Newmans lived.

"Now let me do the talking," Audra insisted firmly as they went up in the elevator. "Keep that busy tongue of yours still for once. And when I've said my piece, you can apologize to your mother for your recent behavior. And you must do that, Kyle, whatever happens. Understand?"

"Yes."

Audra was disappointed when they let themselves into the hall.

The huge apartment was deathly quiet and seemed deserted. She knew Alex had had a luncheon engagement to keep, but she had expected her daughter to be home. Then Audra heard footsteps echoing in the marble gallery adjoining the foyer.

Suddenly Christina was standing there, smiling at them, looking impossibly young in a pair of blue jeans and a white silk shirt and lots of heavy gold jewelry. And she was positively radiant. The worry and anxiety and rage which had been etched on her face for the past week had completely washed away. She was like a new person. Or rather, like her old self.

"Hello, you two," Christina said brightly, coming forward eagerly, smiling. "Did you have a nice lunch? A good talk?"

"Yes, thank you, we did, Christie." Audra narrowed her eyes, wondering what had wrought the change in her daughter.

"I am glad, Mummy," Christina said.

"I'd like to talk to you," Audra announced rather abruptly.

"Then let's go into my study." Christina spun around and walked down the long gallery in the direction of her den.

Kyle looked at her grandmother inquiringly. Audra shrugged in answer to the unasked but obvious question. They were both puzzled by the marked difference in Christina and hurried after her, riddled with curiosity.

She stood in the center of the study, waiting for them. "What do you want to talk to me about, Mother?" she asked.

Kyle went and perched on the arm of the sofa, and Audra sat down in a chair. She said, "Christie, I think I've come up with a solution to Kyle's—"

"Just a minute," Christina exclaimed, holding up her hand. "Before we get into that, I want to tell you about the plans I've made for your birthday next week, Mummy. Your seventy-first birthday—"

"Really, Christie," Audra interjected crossly. "I'm not interested in my birthday. I've better fish to fry this afternoon. Kyle is much more important than—"

"I *insist* on discussing this first, Mother," Christina cut in, her voice strong and firm. "And I also want to give you two of your gifts today."

Audra was furious and her mouth tightened. But she knew better than to interrupt.

Kyle was also annoyed but controlled her own flaring temper. Whatever her grandma said to the contrary, her mother *was* impossible.

Christina walked to the fireplace and stood next to it, resting one hand on the mantel. She said slowly, carefully, "My first gift to you, Mummy, is the thing I know you truly want the most in your deepest heart . . . a granddaughter living in England and studying at the Royal College."

Audra and Kyle stared at Christina and then at each other. They were stunned.

"I've done a lot of soul searching in the last few days, and I know how wrong I've been about Kyle—" Christina glanced at her daughter, smiled warmly. "Kyle must have her chance to follow her own lodestar. As you put it to me years ago, and then again the other day, a child is only ever lent to you. And so I want her to do whatever she wants with her life . . . it *is* hers, after all."

Audra stared speechlessly at her daughter.

"Mom! Mom! Do you really mean it?" Kyle shrieked, jumping off the sofa, running to Christina, grasping her arm.

"Yes, darling, I do. I shouldn't have tried to push you into the business against your will."

"Oh Mom, I've been rude and cruel and impossible. I'm so very *sorry*. Can you ever forgive me, Mom?"

"There's nothing to forgive, Kyle. I simply want us to be friends again and I want you to have what makes you happy."

"Mom!" Kyle flung her arms around Christina and kissed her, and they pulled away and looked at each other and laughed and hugged again.

Audra watching them both, thought: Thank God, thank God. Everything's going to be all right after all.

Christina exclaimed, "And now for your second birthday present, Mother. I'll just go and get it for you." She hurried across the floor.

"Why do *you* think she changed her mind, Gran?" Kyle asked the minute they were alone. She was flushed and excited, could hardly contain herself.

"I've no idea. But your mother's always had her feet on the ground, had a lot of common sense, and perhaps she finally realized as I once did, that you can't live somebody else's life for—"

"Hello, Audra love."

Audra turned her head sharply at the sound of the familiar voice, and surprise widened her eyes. She pushed herself to her feet and went to him, saying, "Vincent, my goodness! However did you get here?"

"By Concorde," he said and swung his handsome silver head to Alex, who stood behind him beaming. "This son-in-law of ours arranged everything. He came to meet me at the airport early this morning, sneaked me in here while you were asleep, then took me out to lunch after you'd gone off with Kyle." Vincent smiled at her, "Alex and Christie wanted to surprise you. I've come for your birthday, love."

"And it *is* a surprise," Audra exclaimed, standing on her tiptoes, kissing his cheek. He smiled at her and as he put his arm around her, drew her closer, Audra murmured, "Oh it's so good to see you. I've missed you this past week, Vincent, I really have."

"And I've missed you, Audra." Vincent glanced across at Kyle. "Now, love, what about a kiss for your grandfather?"

She flew to him. They embraced in the middle of the floor and then, arms linked, they walked over to the sofa and sat down. They had always been the best of friends, and had spent a lot of time together when she had come to England as a child.

Audra turned to Alex. "Thank you for bringing Vincent here, Alex, it was such a lovely gesture. And now that I think about it, my birthday wouldn't have been the same without him, it really wouldn't . . . we've always spent it together for exactly fifty years."

Alex put his arm around his mother-in-law, the other around his wife. "It was Christie's idea," he said.

"No, it wasn't, it was yours," Christina contradicted, smiling up at him, her luminous gray eyes shining with love.

Alex bent down, kissed Christina's brow, said, "It doesn't matter who thought about it—as long as it makes everyone happy."

"Yes, that's true," Audra agreed.

She looked across at Vincent and Kyle sitting on the sofa, allowed her eyes to rest on her granddaughter. Then she turned to Christina. "Kyle is the fulfillment of life's purpose . . . my life and yours. *She* reaps the benefit of all that we sacrificed for each other, and that's not such a bad thing, is it?"

Christina looked down at Audra. "No, it's not, Mother, it's really quite wonderful."

Reaching out, Audra took Christina's hand in hers, and her bright blue eyes were radiant with happiness as she added, "And in letting her go you have kept her for always."

BARBARA TAYLOR BRADFORD gained international fame with the publication of her first novel, *A Woman of Substance*. The sequel, *Hold the Dream*, also rose to the top of the bestseller lists around the world, as did the third book in this phenomenal trilogy, *To Be the Best*. Her other books, *Voice of the Heart* and *Act of Will*, were also bestsellers. Born in the town of Leeds in Yorkshire, England, Mrs. Bradford lives with her husband, movie producer Robert Bradford, in New York City.